The Year's Best Fantasy and Horror

ALSO EDITED BY ELLEN DATLOW AND TERRI WINDLING

The Year's Best Fantasy: First Annual Collection
The Year's Best Fantasy: Second Annual Collection
The Year's Best Fantasy and Horror: Third Annual Collection
The Year's Best Fantasy and Horror: Fourth Annual Collection
The Year's Best Fantasy and Horror: Fifth Annual Collection
The Year's Best Fantasy and Horror: Sixth Annual Collection
The Year's Best Fantasy and Horror: Seventh Annual Collection
Snow White, Blood Red
Black Thorn, White Rose

The Year's Best Fantasy and Horror

EIGHTH ANNUAL COLLECTION

Edited by Ellen Datlow
and Terri Windling

ST. MARTIN'S GRIFFIN ≈ NEW YORK

to
Doris Liebowitz Datlow
and
Nathan Datlow

Library of Congress Catalog Card Number: 91-659320

Paperback ISBN 0-312-13219-0
Hardcover ISBN 0-312-13220-4

First Edition: August 1995

A Blue Cows–Mad City production.

"A Friend Indeed" by David Garnett. Copyright © 1994 by David Garnett. First published in *Interzone*, November 1994. Reprinted by permission of the author.

"Sometimes, in the Rain" by Charles Grant. Copyright © 1994 by Charles Grant. First published in *Northern Frights 2* edited by Don Hutchison; Mosaic Press. Reprinted by permission of the author.

"Rain Falls" by Michael Marshall Smith. Copyright © 1994 by Michael Marshall Smith. First published in *The Mammoth Book of Werewolves* edited by Stephen Jones; Robinson Publishing (U.K.), Carroll & Graf Publishers, Inc. (U.S.). Reprinted by permission of the author.

"That Old School Tie" by Jack Womack. Copyright © 1994 by Jack Womack. First published in *Little Deaths* edited by Ellen Datlow; Millennium, an imprint of Orion Books Ltd. Reprinted by permission of the author.

"Animals Behind Bars!" by Scott Bradfield. Copyright © 1993 by Scott Bradfield. First published in *Conjunctions 21*, Bard College Literary Magazine. Reprinted by permission of the author.

"Monuments to the Dead" by Kristine Kathryn Rusch. Copyright © 1994 by Kristine Kathryn Rusch. First published in *Tales from the Great Turtle* edited by Piers Anthony and Richard Gilliam; Tor Books. Reprinted by permission of the author.

"Unterseeboot Doktor" by Ray Bradbury. Reprinted by permission of Don Congdon Associates, Inc. Copyright © 1993 by Ray Bradbury. First published in *Playboy*, January 1994.

"Young Woman in a Garden" by Delia Sherman. Copyright © 1994 by Delia Sherman. First published in *Xanadu 2* edited by Jane Yolen; Tor Books. Reprinted by permission of the author.

"The Man in the Black Suit" by Stephen King. Copyright © 1994 by Stephen King. First published in *The New Yorker*, October 31, 1994. Reprinted by permission of the author.

"In the Tradition . . ." by Michael Swanwick. Copyright © 1994 by Michael Swanwick. First published in *Asimov's Science Fiction*, November 1994. Reprinted by permission of the author.

"Words Like Pale Stones" by Nancy Kress. Copyright © 1994 by Nancy Kress. First published in *Black Thorn, White Rose* edited by Ellen Datlow and Terri Windling; Avon Books. Reprinted by permission of the author.

"Märchen" by Jane Yolen. Copyright © 1994 by Jane Yolen. First published in *Merveilles*, May 1994. Reprinted by permission of the author, and the author's agent, Curtis Brown, Ltd.

"Giants in the Earth" by Dale Bailey. Copyright © 1994 by Mercury Press, Inc. First published in *The Magazine of Fantasy & Science Fiction*, August 1994. Reprinted by permission of the author.

"A Conflagration Artist" by Bradley Denton. Copyright © 1994 by Bradley Denton. First published in *A Conflagration Artist* by Bradley Denton; Wildside Press. Reprinted by permission of the author.

"Report" by Carme Riera. Copyright © 1993 by Carme Riera. From *The Origins of Desire: Modern Spanish Stories* edited by Juan Antonio Masoliver, published by Serpent's Tail, London (1993). Reprinted by permission of Serpent's Tail Books.

"The Village of the Mermaids" by John Bradley. Copyright © 1994 by John Bradley. First published in *Asylum Annual, 1994* edited by Greg Boyd; Asylum Arts. Reprinted by permission of the author.

"—And the Horses Hiss at Midnight" by A. R. Morlan. Copyright © 1994 by A. R. Morlan. First published in *Love in Vein* edited by Poppy Z. Brite and Martin H. Greenberg; HarperCollins Publishers. Reprinted by permission of the author.

"The Entreaty of the Wiideema" by Barry Lopez. From *Field Notes* by Barry Lopez. Copyright © 1994 by Barry Lopez. Reprinted by permission of Alfred A. Knopf, Inc.

"White Chapel" by Douglas Clegg. Copyright © 1994 by Douglas Clegg. First published in *Love in Vein* edited by Poppy Z. Brite and Martin H. Greenberg; HarperCollins Publishers. Reprinted by permission of the author.

"The Stone Woman" by Linda Weasel Head. Copyright © 1989 by Linda Weasel Head. First published in *Cutbank #25*; University of Montana. Reprinted by permission of the author.

"Coyote Stories" by Charles de Lint. Copyright © 1994 by Charles de Lint. First published as a Triskell Press chapbook. Reprinted by permission of the author.

"The Box" by Jack Ketchum. Copyright © 1994 by Dallas Mayr. First published in *Cemetery Dance*, Spring 1994. Reprinted by permission of the author.

"A Fear of Dead Things" by Andrew Klavan. Copyright © 1994 by Andrew Klavan. First published in *Phobias* edited by Martin H. Greenberg, Richard Gilliam, Edward Kramer, and Wendy Webb; Pocket Books, a division of Simon and Schuster, Inc. Reprinted by permission of the author and the author's agent, The Karpfinger Agency.

"He Unwraps Himself" by Darrell Schweitzer. Copyright © 1994 by Darrell Schweitzer. First published in *Weird Tales* #308. Reprinted by permission of the author.

"Chandira" by Brian Mooney. Copyright © 1994 by Brian Mooney. First published in *The Mammoth Book of Frankenstein* edited by Stephen Jones; Robinson Publishing (U.K.), Carroll & Graf, Inc. (U.S.). Reprinted by permission of the author.

"Fever" by Harlan Ellison. Copyright © 1993 by The Kilimanjaro Corporation. Reprinted by arrangement with, and permission of, the Author and the Author's agent, Richard Curtis Associates, Inc., New York. All rights reserved. First published in *Mind Fields: The Art of Jacek Yerka, The Fiction of Harlan Ellison*; Morpheus International.

"The Best Things in Life" by Lenora Champagne. Copyright © 1994 by Lenora Champagne. First published in *The Iowa Review*, Spring/Summer 1994. Reprinted by permission of the author.

"Mending Souls" by Judith Tarr. Copyright © 1994 by Judith Tarr. First published in *Deals with the Devil* edited by Mike Resnick, Martin H. Greenberg, and Loren D. Estleman; DAW Books. Reprinted by permission of the author.

"The Ocean and All Its Devices" by William Browning Spencer. Copyright © 1994 by William Browning Spencer. First published in *Borderlands 4* edited by Elizabeth E. and Thomas F. Monteleone; Borderlands Press. Reprinted by permission of the author.

"Strings" by Kelley Eskridge. Copyright © 1994 by Kelley Eskridge. First published in *The Magazine of Fantasy & Science Fiction*, August 1994. Reprinted by permission of the author.

"Superman's Diary" by B. Brandon Barker. Copyright © 1994 by B. Brandon Barker. First published in *Global City Review: Dr. Jekyll and Mr. Hyde*, Spring 1994. Reprinted by permission of the author.

"Isobel Avens Returns to Stepney in the Spring" by M. John Harrison. Copyright © 1994 by M. John Harrison. First published in the U.K. in *Little Deaths* edited by Ellen Datlow; Millennium, an imprint of Orion Books Ltd.; first published in the U.S. in *Omni* magazine, November 1994. Reprinted by permission of the author.

Contents

Acknowledgments xi
Summation 1994: Fantasy Terri Windling xiii
Summation 1994: Horror Ellen Datlow xxxiv
Horror and Fantasy in the Media: 1994 Edward Bryant lxxvi
Comics 1994 Will Shetterly and Emma Bull xc
Obituaries xciv

TRANSMUTATIONS Patricia A. McKillip 1
BOTTOM'S DREAM (poem) Rachel Wetzsteon 8
LA PROMESA Leroy Quintana 10
AWEARY OF THE SUN Gregory Feeley 15
A WHEEL IN THE DESERT, THE MOON ON SOME SWINGS Jonathan Carroll 45
WHO WILL LOVE THE RIVER GOD? Emily Newland 53
BROTHERS Joyce Carol Oates 57
SUBSOIL Nicholson Baker 71
ELVIS'S BATHROOM Pagan Kennedy 80
YET ANOTHER POISONED APPLE FOR THE FAIRY PRINCESS A. R. Morlan 91
THE BIG GAME Nicholas Royle 99
BUENAVENTURA AND THE FIFTEEN SISTERS Margarita Engle 109
DE NATURA UNICORNI Jane Yolen 115
BLUE MOTEL Ian McDonald 124
A FRIEND INDEED David Garnett 145
SOMETIMES, IN THE RAIN Charles Grant 151
RAIN FALLS Michael Marshall Smith 160
THAT OLD SCHOOL TIE Jack Womack 168
ANIMALS BEHIND BARS! Scott Bradfield 190
MONUMENTS TO THE DEAD Kristine Kathryn Rusch 207
UNTERSEEBOOT DOKTOR Ray Bradbury 219
YOUNG WOMAN IN A GARDEN Delia Sherman 227
THE MAN IN THE BLACK SUIT Stephen King 246
"IN THE TRADITION . . ." (essay) Michael Swanwick 262
WORDS LIKE PALE STONES Nancy Kress 284
MÄRCHEN (poem) Jane Yolen 295
GIANTS IN THE EARTH Dale Bailey 296
A CONFLAGRATION ARTIST Bradley Denton 305
REPORT Carme Riera 310
THE VILLAGE OF THE MERMAIDS (poem) John Bradley 316
—AND THE HORSES HISS AT MIDNIGHT A. R. Morlan 320
THE ENTREATY OF THE WIIDEEMA Barry Lopez 325
WHITE CHAPEL Douglas Clegg 331
THE STONE WOMAN (poem) Linda Weasel Head 350
COYOTE STORIES Charles de Lint 351

THE BOX Jack Ketchum 356
A FEAR OF DEAD THINGS Andrew Klavan 364
HE UNWRAPS HIMSELF (poem) Darrell Schweitzer 374
CHANDIRA Brian Mooney 376
FEVER Harlan Ellison 390
THE BEST THINGS IN LIFE Lenora Champagne 392
MENDING SOULS Judith Tarr 399
THE OCEAN AND ALL ITS DEVICES William Browning Spencer 408
STRINGS Kelley Eskridge 423
SUPERMAN'S DIARY B. Brandon Barker 436
ISOBEL AVENS RETURNS TO STEPNEY IN THE SPRING M. John Harrison 444
THE SISTERHOOD OF NIGHT Steven Millhauser 463
WINTER BODIES Noy Holland 471
THE SLOAN MEN David Nickle 473
IS THAT THEM? Kevin Roice 486
THE KINGDOM OF CATS AND BIRDS Geoffrey A. Landis 498
ANGEL COMBS Steve Rasnic Tem 509
SNOW, GLASS, APPLES. Neil Gaiman 517

Honorable Mentions: 1994 526

Acknowledgments

I would like to thank Kathe Koja, Merrilee Heifetz, William Meikle, William Congreve, Linda Marotta, Jessica Amanda Salmonson, Stephen Jones, Lawrence Schimel, George Gabriel, Amy Grech, Eleanor Lang, and Gardner Dozois for their encouragement, help, and/or suggestions. Thanks to all the writers, editors, and publishers who sent me material for this volume.

A special thanks to Gordon Van Gelder, Jim Minz, and Jim Frenkel for continued support, and to Tom Canty for his wonderful art and design. And of course, thanks to Terri Windling, who helps keep it fun.

(Please note: It's difficult to cover all nongenre sources of short horror, so should readers see a story or poem from such a source, I would appreciate it being brought to my attention. Drop me a line c/o OMNI Magazine, General Media, 277 Park Avenue, 4th floor, New York NY 10172-0003.)

I'd like to acknowledge Charles N. Brown's *Locus* magazine (Locus Publications, P.O. Box 13305, Oakland CA 94661; $50 for a one-year first-class subscription [12 issues] $40 for a second-class subscription. Credit-card orders [510] 339-9198); and Andrew I. Porter's *Science Fiction Chronicle* (S.F.C., P.O. Box 022730, Brooklyn NY 11202-0056; $36 for a first-class subscription [12 issues] $30 for a second-class subscription). Both were invaluable reference sources throughout the Summation.

I would also like to acknowledge the following catalogs, all of which provide excellent sources for ordering genre material by mail: The Overlook Connection, P.O. Box 526, Woodstock GA 30188; Mark V. Ziesing, P.O. Box 76, Shingletown CA 96088; and DreamHaven Books and Comics, 1309 4th Street SE, Minneapolis MN 55414.

—Ellen Datlow

It takes a lot of people to put together a book like this one. I am grateful to all those who sent material and shared their thoughts with me. *Locus, PW, The Hungry Mind Review*, and *Folk Roots* magazines have been invaluable reference sources.

I am most grateful to Bill Murphy, the hard-working editorial assistant on the fantasy half of this volume; and to Ellen Kushner and Charles de Lint for music recommendations. Thanks also to Ellen Steiber, Beth Meacham and Tappan King, Munro and Robin Sickafoose, Elisabeth Roberts, Patrick Nielsen Hayden, Don Keller, Delia Sherman, and Jane Yolen. Special thanks go to our St. Martin's editor Gordon Van Gelder; to series packager Jim Frenkel and his assistant Jim Minz; to our artist Thomas Canty; and to my editorial partner Ellen Datlow.

—Terri Windling

I'd like to thank the editors for a superb book, our columnists, Ed Bryant, Emma Bull, and Will Shetterly, our St. Martin's editor, the ever-ready Gordon Van Gelder, and my assistant, Jim Minz. Also, thanks to our hard-working interns, Jim Feken, Amy Fuchs, Mark Mager, Melanie Orpen, Andy Scott, and Paul Wiesner. Lastly, big thanks to my wife, Joan D. Vinge, who understood that this year was a little crazy.

—James Frenkel

Summation 1994: Fantasy
by Terri Windling

In this anthology, we have once again collected a representative sampling of the very best fantasy fiction published in the English language in the past year. (To publish a *complete* edition of the year's best would take a volume twice this size, for there is, happily, a great deal of magical short fiction being published today.) Some of this fiction comes from fantasy genre magazines and anthologies; the rest of it comes from many other sources: mainstream anthologies, literary quarterlies, small press publications, children's collections, and compilations of foreign works in translation. For the purposes of this volume, our definition of *fantasy fiction* is a generous one, embracing many diverse forms of storytelling, from fairy tales to magical realism, from swords-and-sorcery to surrealism; in other words, any fiction and poetry rooted in the fecund soil of myth, magic, and dream.

This broad definition of fantasy fiction has sparked some debate within the fantasy field. Some critics have expressed concern that genre fiction is becoming too diffused by books such as this, which ignore category boundaries between genre and mainstream literature. At the other end of the spectrum, there are critics worried that the inclusion of genre and fairy tales mars an otherwise "serious" volume of contemporary horror and magical realism. In my opinion, there is ample room in our field for a "best of" genre fantasy annual (such as those previously edited by Lin Carter and Arthur Saha), or a "best of" horror annual (such as that previously edited by Karl Edward Wagner), or a "best of" swords-and-sorcery annual, or even a "best of" magical realism annual . . . but this particular volume is meant to be none of those things. This volume is dedicated to presenting the best fantasy fiction published each year in all its rich diversity of form.

Our task is twofold: first, to collect the best stories published in-genre in one accessible edition, and second, to seek out magical stories published in more out-of-the-way venues in order to make them available to lovers of fantastic fiction. The second of these tasks is a challenging one—and, to my mind, as important as the first. Few fantasy readers can take the time, as we do, to scour publishers' catalogs, review magazines, library shelves, literary quarterlies published from Alaska to Texas and filled with primarily realist works, books translated from foreign languages, and the offerings from small regional presses to track down those stories and poems that have mythic, folkloric, or magical contents. Long before packager Jim Frenkel started the ball rolling that was to become *The Year's Best Fantasy and Horror* series, I often wished that someone out there would publish an annual guide to such stories—little dreaming that one day it would become my own pleasant job to do so. Our "critical agenda" in printing these stories here is actually a simple one: these are stories we believe fantasy readers will enjoy, and therefore they should not be missed.

In the introduction to the new SF/fantasy magazine *Century*, editor Robert K. J. Killheffer compares the division of modern fiction into distinct, separate genres to modern urban planning where cities are artificially divided into separate residential, commercial, cultural, and industrial districts. Killheffer cites studies indicating that the healthiest urban neighborhoods are the more chaotic and organic ones, where all these elements coexist side-by-side; he then goes on to use this as a metaphor for the city of literature, promising, in the pages of his magazine, a literary neighborhood in which "in one house [there is] a tale of magic realism; in another, one of alien invasion; across the street, a psychological horror story living upstairs from a tale of small-town sorcery or a young woman's coming of age."

This interesting metaphor applies to the kind of inclusive volume we've created here, where contemporary stories sit side-by-side with historic fabrications, fables and fairy tales—

dark, bright, and all the colors of the spectrum that lie in-between. It is difficult to come up with a hard-and-fast definition of what precisely a fantasy story is. I have yet to hear a truly satisfying one; it is the nature of faery, after all (as J. R. R. Tolkien once pointed out) to be elusive and resist definition. How are stories chosen for this collection then? Generally by asking the following questions: "Was it magical, mythical, memorable? Was it moving, provoking, evocative of that most mysterious of feelings: a sense of wonder?"

There are stories in the pages that follow that quietly stretch the boundaries of what we usually think of as fantasy fiction: Barry Lopez's unusual exploration of the nature of aboriginal Myth and Truth; Steven Millhauser's meditation on Mystery; Margarita Engle's paean to the power of Storytelling; and several others. You'll also find traditional fantasy material well represented herein: unicorns, mermaids, princesses, witches, ghosts, Celtic fairies, and more. There are stories set in cities, suburbs, castles, and Elvis's bathroom; in Cuba, France, Mallorca, on the Mexican border, and Once Upon a Time.

For those who prefer to stick more closely to traditional genre fare, I highly recommend *The Oxford Book of Fantasy Stories*, a recent collection skillfully edited by Tom Shippey (Oxford University Press). For those willing to strike off into the uncharted territory that lies beyond the fields we know (to borrow a phrase from that master fantasist, Lord Dunsany), we offer this volume of treasures we culled from the 1994 publishing year.

The big news in the fantasy field in the last year has been in short fiction. Two new magazines appeared on newsstands: *Realms of Fantasy* and *Century*. *Realms of Fantasy*, which debuted in the fall of 1994, is put out by the Sovereign Media Company, the publishers of *SF Age*. Shawna McCarthy (formerly of *Isaac Asimov's SF Magazine*, then a book editor at Bantam Spectra) was chosen to edit *Realms of Fantasy*. It contains fiction, art, and nonfiction columns on books, media, games, and mythology. This is fairly standard genre fare, aimed at the large traditional fantasy/swords-and-sorcery audience, published in a slick, professional newsstand format and lavishly illustrated with four-color art. Fiction contributors have included Charles de Lint, Neil Gaiman, Tanith Lee, and Louise Cooper, as well as a rather high percentage of lesser known writers. The art of Michael Whelan, Brian Froud, James Gurney, Thomas Canty, and others has been featured on the cover and in the magazine's "Gallery" section, which is, I am told, one of their most popular features. (Subscription information: PO Box 736, Mt. Morris, IL 61054.)

Century is another kettle of fish altogether, taking the literary high road with a blend of thought-provoking fantasy, science fiction, horror, and magical realism packaged in an elegant "little magazine" format. Published by Meg Hamel and edited by Robert K. J. Killheffer (formerly of *Omni* magazine), it is an excellent, stylish magazine and a very exciting addition to the field. Contributors to the first issue (which debuted in the winter of 1994/95) included William Browning Spencer, Jonathan Lethem, Kelley Eskridge, and J. R. Dunn. I hope this gets the reader support it deserves; I would hate to see such a quality endeavor disappear. (Subscriptions: PO Box 9270, Madison, WI 53715-0270.)

As for novels, there was nothing startlingly new or wildly innovative published in-genre in 1994 (such as last year's *The Iron Dragon's Daughter* by Michael Swanwick); no sudden new trends or directions. Still, there were solid, worthy additions to the field by the likes of Lisa Goldstein, Nancy Springer, and Robert Holdstock, as well as a few strong first-novel debuts, all of which will be discussed further below. Elizabeth Hand, Caroline Stevermer, and Charles de Lint have each written novels about mysterious happenings during their protagonists' college years. I wouldn't exactly call this a new trend (Pamela Dean's *Tam Lin* and other fantasy books have been set on college campuses before), but it is interesting to see three such novels in one year, and to compare the completely different ways each author has handled the theme.

In the mainstream, it was once again a good year for magical and mythic fiction. This was particularly true in North America, where the recent renaissance in Native American and Latino fiction has caused the wider publication of many wonderful works. Writers like Thomas King, Greg Sarris, Susan Power, N. Scott Momaday, Leslie Marmon Silko, Linda Hogan, Susanna Moore, and Sherman Alexie draw upon the ancient stories of tribal peoples in modern fiction and poetry poised between realism and magical realism. Sandra Cisneros, Leroy Quintana, Laura Esquivel, Isabel Allende, Rosario Ferré, and other Latino writers have become popular with mainstream readers and critics despite stories that often eschew the modern North American bias for strict realism in contemporary fiction. These are the areas to watch at the moment for the most innovative use of magical narrative.

Two of the most exciting fantasy book publications of the year, however, were in neither genre nor mainstream fiction. They were nonfiction works about the roots of the field: mythology and fairy tales. *From the Beast to the Blonde* by Marina Warner (Chatto & Windus-UK) is one of the most extraordinary explorations of the history and nature of fairy tales, myth, and symbolism that I have yet come across; no serious fantasy lover's bookshelf should be without it. Warner is a British novelist, historian, and critic, who was chosen to deliver the prestigious Reith Lectures on BBC Radio in 1994. Those six lectures—a cultural critique blending mythology, classic literature, pop culture, and politics—were also recently published in an edition titled *Six Myths of Our Time: Little Angels, Little Monsters, Beautiful Beasts and More* (Vintage). I cannot praise Warner's work highly enough. I also recommend Jack Zipes's *Fairy Tale as Myth* (University of Kentucky Press), lively new work by one of America's most important fairy-tale scholars; particularly interesting were his chapter on "Oz as American Myth" and his wry look at Robert Bly's *Iron John*.

Another highlight of 1994 was the debut of *Spectrum: The First Annual Collection of the Best in Contemporary Fantastic Art*, edited by Cathy Burnett and Arnie Fenner (Underwood Books, PO Box 253, Penn Valley, CA 95946), a collection of 195 images that presents a "Who's Who" of the fantasy illustration field. Illustrators Michael Whelan, Don Punchatz, Dave Stevens, and Rick Berry, along with Arnie Fenner (art director, Mark Ziesing Books), Tim Kirk (art director, Walt Disney Studios) and Lisa Tallarico-Robertson (art director, Andrews & McMeel) were the jury for the 1994 edition, which also features the winners of the Chesley Awards presented by the Association of SF/Fantasy Artists.

Magical art was also showcased in the Dream Weavers traveling art exhibition that opened in Virginia in 1994. Curated by artist Charles Vess and Cindi diMazo (of Philomel Books), this beautiful exhibit featured the works of internationally known artists (primarily from the children's book field), such as Brian Froud, Alan Lee, Gennady Spirin, Ruth Sanderson, James Gurney, Dennis Nolan, David Christiana, and others who are (as the exhibition catalog notes) the modern heirs of the Golden Age illustrators like Rackham, Nielsen, and Dulac. The exhibition is traveling to museums and galleries around the country through October 15, 1995. Copies of the catalog, which features text by Cindi diMazo and Charles de Lint, along with a sampling of works from the show, is available from: William King Regional Arts Center, PO Box 2256, Abingdon, VA 24212.

In music, the bright spots of the year were magical releases by two accomplished singers: Canada's Loreena McKennitt, with a new CD titled *The Mask and the Mirror*, featuring original songs by McKennitt including "The Mystic's Dream" and "Prospero's Speech" (with lyrics adapted from Shakespeare); and England's June Tabor, with *Against the Streams*, a CD of both new and traditional tunes, as well as Tabor's beautiful rendition of Jane Yolen's haunting poem, "Beauty and the Beast."

These were the highlights of the 1994 year in fantasy; now on to the fiction itself. Once again, I won't claim that I have managed to read every work of fantasy, magical realism, and surrealism published in this country and abroad—but I certainly made a good stab at it. I also culled opinions and recommendations from the community of fantasy writers, editors, and publishers in the U.S. and U.K. in order to put together the following list of novels published in 1994 that no fantasy lover should overlook:

In alphabetical order . . .

Night Relics by James P. Blaylock (Ace). Blaylock is one of the finest writers to grace the field, and this dark fantasy tale of murder and ghosts is no exception to the general high quality of his work. A haunting, chilling novel set in the dry wildlands of Southern California, deftly evoking the singular, mysterious beauty of such environments, it is also a powerful character study that ranks with the best in contemporary realist fiction. Blaylock walks a careful line between fantasy and horror in this splendid new book, his best to date.

The Marriage of Cadmus and Harmony by Roberto Calasso (Knopf-h/c); (Vintage-trade paper). This amazing work of fiction is without doubt the top book of mythic fantasy to be published in the last several years. Calasso has created a complex and intellectually dazzling novel using ancient Greek mythology to explore the origins of Western thought. First published in Italy in 1988, the novel has been translated from the Italian by Tim Parks.

From the Teeth of Angels by Jonathan Carroll (Doubleday). Carroll continues to be one of the most talented and original writers of our day, with works that fall on the boundary line between dark fantasy and mainstream fiction. Set in contemporary Europe and Los Angeles, involving characters who will be familiar from previous Carroll tales, this brilliant page-turner is his best one yet: probing the nature of death, revenge, love, and the power of redemption. Carroll has a gift for creating characters so real you'd swear you just had dinner with them the night before—which makes the supernatural events that unfold in their lives all the more harrowing.

Love and Sleep by John Crowley (Bantam). We've waited seven years for this one, the second book in the quartet that began with Crowley's *Egypt*. Was it worth the wait? Absolutely. No one writes prose finer than Crowley, and his growing story is a masterpiece. These books tell two parallel stories at once: one is an exploration of Renaissance magic and gnosticism, the other is a contemporary story about a historian of the esoteric living in a village in upstate New York . . . along with werewolves and witches, astrologers and angels, alchemy and the secret history of the world. Crowley is creating a master work of fantasy here; let's just hope we don't have to wait another seven years for volume three.

Memory and Dream by Charles de Lint (Tor). Set in the author's fictional city of Newford, this 400-page "urban fantasy" novel is stocked with his usual assortment of punky, artistic, streetwise characters. Half of the novel follows, in alternating sequences, de Lint's three protagonists (a writer, a painter, and a small press publisher) during their college years in Newford. What makes this book stand out from the rest of de Lint's work, however, are the chapters set years later, when two of the three have reached middle age and must confront the ghosts of their past. This is the author's most mature work to date, and bodes well for the stories to come.

Summer King, Winter Fool by Lisa Goldstein (Tor). Goldstein is an American Book Award–winning author with a magic touch: she seems to handle well every subject she tackles. Her novels have varied greatly in subject and style, from the Marquezian magical realism of *Tourists* and the French surrealism of *The Dream Years*, to an alternate history of England in last year's *Strange Devices of the Sun and Moon*. Her latest is pure "high fantasy"—and provides an excellent example of what an intelligent writer can do with the form. The novel is set in an imaginary world with both Renaissance and Elizabethan flavors, and ghosts who wander the cobbled streets, and magic intermingled with poetry. It is a deliciously enchanted work.

Waking the Moon by Elizabeth Hand (HarperCollins). Another one of the college novels published this year (although the U.S. edition has only just come out in 1995), Hand's latest is a terrific contemporary fantasy set on a fictional college campus, vividly rendered, as one reviewer aptly expressed it, with a skill worthy of Evelyn Waugh. Hand has created a suspenseful, panoramic story of murder, conspiracy, and ancient secret societies, with ample doses of Pre-Minoan goddess mythology thrown in for good measure. Like the de Lint book above, Part I of Hand's novel follows her three protagonists during their school years; Part II takes place many years later, when only two of the three are still alive.

Stranger at the Wedding by Barbara Hambly (Del Rey). A very skillfully rendered magical comedy of manners set in an imaginary world reminiscent of eighteenth-century London, this book is richly detailed and goes from frothy to dark before the tale is done. Ostensibly the tale of a wealthy man's daughter who returns home from college (yes, another magical college) to thwart her sister's arranged marriage, the novel is also a rumination on the politics of families, and of the marriage bed. In culmination, the novel packs a punch—and is among the best works by this author to date. Hambly is a prolific writer, yet maintains a consistency of quality that is astonishing. Her latest is a highly entertaining fantasy, but a thoughtful one as well.

Merlin's Wood by Robert Holdstock (HarperCollins). This hauntingly beautiful short novel is set in the forest of Broceliande on the coast of France, in the Celtic region of Brittany. It contains the rich mix of myth, history, and anthropological lore we have come to expect of Holdstock, the author of the "Mythago" sequence of novels set in primeval English woodland. The author blends the ancient legends of the forest, such as that of Vivian and Merlin, with a modern story of love, loss, and ghosts . . . the result is compelling and utterly magical. The book also contains two unrelated short stories, both of them reprints.

The Following Story by Cees Nooteboom (Harcourt Brace). Don't overlook this European fantasy, which you'll find tucked away on the mainstream shelves. It is a magical and sardonic tale about a funny-looking man who adores beauty above all things. Nooteboom's highly unusual little love story won the European Literary Prize for Best Novel in 1993. *The Following Story* is an absolute treasure, and well worth seeking out.

Towing Jehovah by James Morrow (Harcourt Brace). James Morrow could be called the Salman Rushdie of America, for he uses religious myths as the inspiration for his serio-comic, magical realist fiction. In Morrow's case, Biblical stories have provided the material for his unique work: his previous novel, *Only Begotten Daughter*; the hilarious "Bible Stories for Adults"; and his latest novel, *Towing Jehovah*, a brilliant satiric work in which the corpse of God is found floating in the South Atlantic.

The Grass Dancer by Susan Power (Putnam). Power's ambitious novel is a fine work of American magical realism set on a Dakota Sioux reservation from the mid-1800s to the present. This multigenerational saga is anchored by its central story of two extraordinary ghosts: a murdered warrior woman, and the man who marries her spirit after her death. Their spirits remain a vital force in the lives, dreams, and visions of their descendants for generations to follow. The result is a richly mythical novel—which is, amazingly, the author's first. It is a strong debut, and Power is clearly a writer to watch in the future.

One Dark Body by Charlotte Watson Sherman (Harper Perennial). You might remember Sherman as the author of *Killing Color,* a lively collection of both magical realist and realistic stories which drew, in part, on African-American oral traditions. Now Sherman has written an enchanting, heartrending contemporary novel about an abandoned young girl, a fatherless boy, and an elderly folk healer. This one is a delight.

Larque on the Wing by Nancy Springer (Morrow/AvoNova). Springer's latest is best described as a fantasy version of a women's midlife crisis novel—and yet I hesitate to call it that for fear of turning off male and younger readers. Don't be dissuaded! The book is an offbeat, entertaining work of contemporary fantasy. The protagonist of the novel is a woman who has spent her life coping with the bizarre paranormal phenomena that constantly manifest around her. As a result, *her* version of midlife crisis is rather extreme . . . to say the least.

A *College of Magics* by Caroline Stevermer (Tor). This is the third of our "college novels," and a charmingly distinctive one at that. The world of Stevermer's Greenlaw College is close to that of Europe in the nineteenth century—but it is a magical world where imaginary dukedoms coexist with Paris and the Orient Express. Stevermer has created an ancient women's college where witchcraft is an academic specialty—and she does so with the sly wit and sparkling prose that have earned her a cult following among aficionados of the field.

First Novels:

The best first novel of the year is the Susan Power book mentioned above; however, there were several other notable debuts in 1994:

Rhinegold by Stephen Grundy (Bantam). This formidable, 700-odd-page volume works with the Germanic material that inspired Wagner's Ring Cycle, and does so in a manner that manages to be both scholarly and entertaining.

Among the Immortals by Paul Lake (Story Line Press). Written by a poet, this is a strange, literate, and enjoyable dark fantasy about vampires, Percy Bysshe Shelley, and the politics of modern academia, set in Berkeley, California.

Aurian by Maggie Furey (Legend). This first volume of yet another "medieval quest" trilogy is made distinctive by the fact that it is quite well written. Definitely a writer to keep an eye on.

Witch and Wombat by Carolyn Cushman (Warner Questar). A charming and intelligent work of humorous fantasy by an author with a good grounding in folklore and fairy tales.

Wizard's First Rule by Terry Goodkind (Tor). This one made news long before the book's actual publication, due to the fact that the young first novelist received an advance far in excess of those earned by many established authors. The publisher is clearly betting that Goodkind's rather Tolkienesque series will reach the same large audience as Terry Brooks's *Sword of Shannara.* So is the book merely crass commercial hackwork? Well, it's derivative, to be sure, and I can't recommend it to serious literary readers, but it does have a certain charm and earnestness about it. It will be interesting to see what this author does in the future (aside from hit the best-seller lists, that is).

Oddities:

The "Best Peculiar Book" distinction for 1994 goes to *The Lost Book of Paradise: Adam and Eve in the Garden of Eden* by David Rosenberg (Hyperion). Rosenberg creates a literary whodunit as he tracks down a female poet-scholar, from the ninth century B.C., who is herself seeking the lost book of the title. Told primarily in verse and fragments of song, it is a strange and endearing little volume of love, desire, and imaginary scholarship.

The runner-up is: *The Circus of the Earth and the Air* by Brooke Stevens (Harcourt Brace). An odd, engaging book that hovers on the edge between realism and surrealism; a contemporary man's search for his missing wife among conjurers and circus folks—complete with old photographs of circus performers in the text.

Other recommended fantasy novels published in 1994:

Imaginary World Fantasy:

500 Years After by Steven Brust (Tor). The long-lived hero of *The Phoenix Guards* reunites with his friends and comrades after five centuries. This is a splendid magical swashbuckler in the rousing tradition of Dumas and Sabatini. I recommend it highly, but a familiarity with Brust's other work is advisable for full enjoyment of the author's unique wit.

The Dubious Hills by Pamela Dean (Tor). Dean is quietly becoming one of the best writers around for fantasies that, like Le Guin's, McKinley's, or Wynne Jones's, can be enjoyed by young and old alike. Her latest is an exploration of magic and human nature.

Riding the Unicorn by Paul Kearney (Gollancz). The basic plot is fairly predictable: a man is pulled from our own world into a magical fantasy realm by mysterious forces who intend to use him as a tool in their political machinations. However, the book is well written and intelligent, and Kearney manages to breathe new life into such familiar material, which is no mean feat.

The Wolf in Winter by Paula Volsky (Bantam). Volsky is a reliably entertaining storyteller, as her latest Imaginary World fantasy demonstrates. This one has a Slavic flavor, set in a colorful magical world roughly equivalent to eighteenth-century Russia, involving necromancy and the intrigues in an eccentric aristocratic family.

The Grail and the Ring by Teresa Edgerton (Ace). Edgerton's latest is standard medieval fantasy, but she handles the form well and breathes freshness into plots that could all too easily become generic in less capable hands. It is the fifth book in her "Celydonn" series, although it can be read alone.

The Legend of Nightfall by Mickey Zucker Reichert (DAW). This is standard but enjoyable quest fantasy, from a publishing company that excels at putting out entertaining fantasy adventure series. Although not as well known as some other writers, Reichert's solid storytelling skills make her one of the best on the DAW list.

Keeper of Cats by Elizabeth H. Boyer (Del Rey). Here's another underrated writer, with a thoroughly enjoyable mystery novel set in an imaginary land. The novel is connected to Boyer's other books, but is easily read alone.

The Seeker's Mask by P. C. Hodgell (Hypatia Press). This is the long-awaited third book in Hodgell's quirky and wonderful "Godstalk" dark fantasy series, published in a signed limited edition with an introduction by Charles de Lint.

Witch Queen of Vixania by Morgana Baron (Nexus). Swords-and-sorcery erotica anyone? The book is reportedly the first in a series.

The following Imaginary World fantasy novels were best-sellers in 1994, beloved by large numbers of readers in this country and abroad: *The Tangle Box* by Terry Brooks (Del Rey); *The Hidden City* by David Eddings (Del Rey); *Shadows of a Dark Queen* by Raymond E. Feist (Morrow); *Wizard's First Rule* by Terry Goodkind (Tor); *Lord of Chaos* by Robert Jordan (Tor); *Storm Warning* by Mercedes Lackey (DAW); *The Seventh Gate* by Margaret Weis and Tracy Hickman (Bantam).

Mythic and Historical Fantasy:

The Secrets of the Camera Obscura by David Knowles (Chronicle). A dark, disturbing, fascinating murder mystery with fantastical elements, about the dark spell caused by a room-sized camera—and the history of the camera itself (created by two Chinese inventors, used by da Vinci and Vermeer . . .). This is a complex and dazzling work.

A Dangerous Energy by John Whitbourn (Gollancz). Although the book didn't completely hang together by the end, it got off to such a rousing good start that I still consider it one of the most interesting of the year. It is an alternate history fantasy, with decidedly Dickensian overtones, set in the present day of a magical version of England. Check this one out.

The Flight of Michael McBride by Midori Snyder (Tor). One of my favorite books of the year, this is a fantasy novel set in the American West of the 1870s, following the flight of a young New York City Irishman to the wilds of the Texas frontier. Snyder has done a beautiful job of mixing the immigrant and indigenous myths of North America (Irish, Spanish, Native American, and others) into a uniquely American fantasy.

Lord of the Middle Air by Michael Scott Rohan (Gollancz). This terrific fantasy page-turner, set in the thirteenth century, makes deft use of the history and magical legends to be found in the Scots border country. Rohan is one of the best at this kind of work, and he's got rich source material to work with here.

Finn MacCool by Morgan Llywelyn (Forge). Llywelyn's skillfully crafted Irish novel walks in the shadowy realm between history and mythology. Llywelyn is at her best when working with the ancient Celtic legends she loves, and this entertaining story of the hero Finn MacCool is no exception.

The New Moon with the Old Moon in Her Arms by Ursule Molinaro (McPherson & Co.). This is a surprisingly suspenseful feminist reinterpretation of classical Greek history and myth. Written in a fragmented postmodernist style, it won't be to everyone's taste, but it's definitely an interesting read.

Throne of Isis by Judith Tarr (Tor). Like her previous historical fantasy, *Lord of the Two Lands,* this one is set in Egypt and is written with the intellectual and historical rigor that is Tarr's trademark. It is the story of Antony and Cleopatra set against a background of politics and Egyptian mysticism.

Arabian Nights and Days by Naguib Mahfouz (Doubleday). A fascinating reworking of the Arabian tales of "The Thousand and One Nights," by one of the best writers from that part of the world. This book was first published in Arabic in 1982 and only recently translated into English.

Bless Me, Ultima by Rudolfo A. Anaya (Warner). A new reissue of this important Mexican-American novel, which beautifully melds Old World and New World folklore into a contemporary story, set in a New Mexican village near the end of World War II.

The Corn King and the Spring Queen by Naomi Mitchison (Soho Press). It's great to see this back in print at last. Drawing upon the material of Frazier's massive mythological study, *The Golden Bough,* Mitchison created a mythic fantasy that is a "lost classic" of the field. Now, thanks to Soho Press, it is lost no longer. They've even put it in a nice new package with a Gustav Klimt cover.

Contemporary and Urban Fantasy:

Brittle Innings by Michael Bishop (Bantam) is a wonderful novel best described as a Southern gothic World War II coming-of-age baseball story featuring Frankenstein's monster. I'm not sure whether this should be classified as fantasy or SF, but whichever it is, it's terrifically entertaining.

Brother to Dragons, Companion to Owls by Jane Lindskold (AvoNova). Lindskold's book is a hard one to classify, falling somewhere between dark urban fantasy and science fiction. Whatever you want to call it, it's a terrific read. The book is about an (ostensibly) autistic heroine, who can speak only in literary quotations, wandering the mad and dangerous streets of an unnamed, East Coast American city. It is a complex, utterly original work of speculative fiction.

Primavera by Francesca Lia Block (Roc). The terrific sequel to last year's *Ecstasia* is by an author whose work is also far too original to classify easily. *Primavera* follows the wanderings of the daughter of two of the rock musicians from the previous book, in a world much like our own, seen through a surrealistic and mythic lens.

Something Rich and Strange by Patricia A. McKillip (Bantam). McKillip's short novel about the magic of the sea is lyrical, romantic, and beautifully penned in the distinctive and poetic prose that we have come to expect from this master fantasist. Set in the present day on the north Pacific coast of America, McKillip's latest is a tale of mermaids and mermen, and their encounters with mortal beings (echoing and updating Irish legends on the same theme). Beneath the language of a modern fairy tale, the author speaks with eloquence about the magic created by art, sensuality, and tenacious love.

Finder by Emma Bull (Tor). Bull uses the rock-and-roll flash and dazzle of the "Borderland" urban fantasy series as the background for this mature and emotionally rich mystery novel. This is Bull's first fantasy since her ground-breaking debut novel, *War for the Oaks*. Like that novel, *Finder* is witty, stylish, and ultimately moving.

Resurrection Man by Sean Stewart (Ace). This is another difficult-to-classify book, weaving elements of fantasy, horror, mystery, alternate history SF, and mainstream fiction into one unusual package, set in the 1990s in a magically altered America. It is a dark, complex and well-realized story, using fantasy as a backdrop to Stewart's insightful character explorations and the intricacies of family relationships.

Temporary Agency by Rachel Pollack (St. Martin's). This New Age fantasy is set in the same world as Pollack's award-winning novel *Unquenchable Fire*.

Bride of the Rat God by Barbara Hambly (Del Rey). This strange and wonderful novel is set on the streets of Hollywood in the Roaring Twenties. Hambly skillfully evokes a haunted California in a book that is funny and surprisingly dark by turns. Combining Chinese magic with the behind-the-scenes madness of the silent film industry, the author has created a memorable and extremely original magical mystery novel.

Wizard of the Pigeons by Megan Lindholm (Hypatia Press). This reprint of a now classic work of urban fantasy is published in a signed, limited edition, with an introduction by Elizabeth Ann Scarborough.

Fantasy in the Mainstream:

The Zoo Where You're Fed to God by Michael Ventura (Simon & Schuster). A terrific novel about a man on the verge of a nervous breakdown who begins to "see into the souls" of animals. Work by this poet and essayist is always luminous and inspiring.

Away by Jane Urquhart (Viking). A gorgeous and subtly mystical novel (that comes in a beautiful Pre-Raphaelite package) about four generations of Irish women, set in the Old World and the New. Highly recommended.

How the Night Is Divided by David Matlin (McPherson & Co.). A powerful first novel set among the clashing cultures and myths of the Mojave Desert of California in the 1940s and 1950s. Recommended.

Inagehi by Jack Cady (Broken Moon Press). A haunting murder mystery (with mystical overtones) about a contemporary Cherokee woman; lyrical and memorable.

The Magic Touch by Rachel Simon (Viking). This lovely first novel, from the accomplished short-story writer, is about the supernatural power of human sexuality.

The Serpent's Gift by Helen Elaine Lee (Atheneum). A wonderful, ambitious first novel rooted in African-American folklore, this is about the transcendent power of storytelling and dreams.

The Myth Man by Elizabeth Swados (Viking). Written by a well-known composer/performance artist, this novel is about a nine-year-old girl (rendered mute by sexual abuse) who becomes an actor in a "metaphysical vaudeville" show, traveling from New York to the Amazon. It is an intriguing book, skillfully evoking the "magic" of traveling theater.

The Feast of Fools by John David Morley (St. Martin's). A rich tapestry of a book; contemporary fiction infused with classical mythology and art.

Time and Time Again by Dennis Danvers (Simon & Schuster). An intriguing, suspenseful literary love story, linking present-day characters with those from eighteenth- and nineteenth-century America.

The World at Noon by Eugene Mirabelli (Guernica Editions/University of Toronto). A weird and fascinating magical realist novel that moves between contemporary Boston and nineteenth-century Italy. Full of ghosts, centaurs, and goddesses.

White Man's Grave by Richard Dooling (Farrar, Straus & Giroux). A wild, satiric novel about African witchcraft and American politics.

The Assault by Reinaldo Arenas (Viking). A strange, dark, surrealistic allegorical fantasy.

Poor Things by Alasdair Gray (Harcourt Brace). This is the first U.S. paperback publication of this wonderful dark fantasy set in Victorian Scotland. In England, it won the Whitbread Award and the Guardian Fiction Prize.

Young Adult Fantasy:

The best fantasy work published for younger readers this year was *Time and the Clock Mice, Etcetera,* by Peter Dickinson (Delacorte). This splendid young adult fable is reminiscent of Thurber's *Thirteen Clocks.* It is illustrated by Emma Chichester-Clark, and highly recommended. The following were also among the best of the year:

Journeyman Wizard by Mary Frances Zambreno (Harcourt Brace/Jane Yolen Books). This sequel to *A Plague of Sorcerers* is a well-written magical murder mystery about a spellmaker's apprentice.

Time for Andrew: A Ghost Story by Mary Downing Hahn (Clarion). A lovely time travel story in which a young boy goes back to 1910 to trade places with his identical great uncle. Delicious stuff.

Painted Devil by Michael Bedlam (Macmillan/Atheneum). A dark magical realist fantasy about dolls, puppets, and magic; the book is intelligently written and atmospheric.

Gold Unicorn by Tanith Lee (Macmillan/Atheneum). An entertaining and magical YA fantasy. The sequel to *Black Unicorn.*

Salamandastron by Brian Jacques (Ace). Book #5 in the best-selling (and delightful) Redwall series, about sentient rodents.

Fangs of Evil and *Shadow of the Fox* by Ellen Steiber (Random House). These two novellas are part of a series of "Chillers" for very young readers. The first, despite the title, is actually a lyrical, haunted story set on the moors of England, inspired by Lafacadio Hearn's gentle Japanese story, "The Boy Who Drew Cats." The second is set in old Japan and beautifully retells the "fox wife" folk legend.

Despite publishers' complaints that short fiction doesn't sell, there were quite a number of anthologies published in the last year, many of them "theme anthologies" that ran the gamut from magical cat stories to sagas of women warriors to fantasy tales about Elvis. Here are the best of the 1994 crop:

The Oxford Book of Fantasy edited by Tom Shippey (Oxford University Press). The thirty-one stories herein provide an historical overview of the fantasy genre and its roots, reprinting classic stories from the 1880s, through works by present-day writers in the field. Shippey, a respected academic, has done an excellent job in his selection of these tales. I highly recommend this one; it's an extremely readable, balanced look at more than a century of the development of the field.

Fantasy Stories edited by Diana Wynne-Jones (Kingfisher). This is a young adult anthology of eighteen fantasy stories (and excerpts from novels), from C. S. Lewis and L. Frank Baum to Joan Aiken and Jane Yolen. The book provides an excellent introduction to the field for younger readers. The edition also contains an original long story by Jones, who is no slouch as a fantasist herself.

The Outspoken Princess and the Gentle Knight edited by Jack Zipes (Bantam). This is a good reprint anthology of fifteen modern fairy tales by Tanith Lee, Jane Yolen, A. S. Byatt, Lloyd Alexander, John Gardner, and others. The editor is a fairy-tale scholar, and provides a strong introduction to the book. The illustrations are by Stephanie Poulin.

Xanadu 2 edited by Jane Yolen and Martin H. Greenberg (Tor). Yolen has done a great service to the fantasy field by providing a forum for the publication of original fantasy stories. In addition to the tales (by Delia Sherman and Patricia A. McKillip) chosen for this volume of *Year's Best*, the anthology contains good stories from Martha Soukup, Barbara Hambly, Megan Lindholm, and Yolen herself, as well as fine poetry by Carol Edelstein, Susan Solomont, and Bruce Boston. (*Xanadu* 3, which was published at the very beginning of 1995, will be covered in the next *Year's Best.*)

Tales from the Great Turtle: Fantasy in the Native American Tradition edited by Richard Gilliam and Piers Anthony (Tor). The quality of the stories is uneven, but this is a worthy volume overall. I applaud the editors' attempts to mix works by Native American authors with works by better known Anglo fantasists, although it is a pity that most of the best Native American writers (like Momaday, Silko, Sarris, and Alexie) are not represented. Still, there are good stories here, most notably by Steve Rasnic Tem, William Sanders, Jack Dann, Kristine Kathryn Rusch, and Jane Yolen.

Weird Tales from Shakespeare edited by Katharine Kerr and Martin H. Greenberg (DAW). This quirky anthology contains entertaining tales by Brian W. Aldiss, Charles de Lint, and Esther M. Friesner, as well as one superlative story by Gregory Feeley, reprinted herein.

Alien Pregnant by Elvis edited by Esther M. Friesner and Martin H. Greenberg (DAW). An endearing and completely wacky anthology on the theme of tabloid headlines, this cleverly conceived confection has good stories from Barry N. Malzberg, Laura Resnick, Kristine Kathryn Rusch, and others.

Blue Motel: Narrow Houses Volume 3 edited by Peter Crowther (Little, Brown-UK). Though the series is geared more toward horror fiction, this volume also contains strong fantasy stories by Michael Moorcock and Brian W. Aldiss, and an Ursula K. Le Guin science fiction tale that has some fantasy elements.

By the Light of the Silvery Moon edited by Ruth Petrie (Virago). This collection of short stories was put together to celebrate the tenth birthday of Silver Moon Women's Bookshop in London. It contains three good fantasy stories—by Lisa Tuttle, Sara Maitland, and Hanan al-Shaykh.

Am I Blue? edited by Marian Dane Bauer (HarperCollins). A brave young adult anthology with stories about gay and lesbian teenagers. The charming title story by Bruce Coville is a fantasy, and Jane Yolen contributes a moving tale from the world of her *Sister Light, Sister Dark*. Francesca Lia Block has the killer story in the volume though; it, all alone, is worth the price of the book. It is *almost* a ghost story, but not quite (or else we would have had an excuse to reprint it here!).

The Dedalus Book of Polish Fantasy edited and translated by Wiesiek Powaga (Dedalus). A reprint anthology of tales that are more supernatural than magical, with an abundance of tales about the devil. Stories by Bruno Schulz, Stefan Grabinski, and others represent fantastic storytelling that ranges over more than a century, from the early romantics to contemporary writers.

Black Thorn, White Rose edited by Ellen Datlow and Terri Windling (AvoNova). This collection was, naturally, also one of my favorites of the year. You'll have to decide for yourself whether it is one of yours. A sequel to last year's *Snow White, Blood Red*, the volume contains new adult fairy tales from Peter Straub, Roger Zelazny, Howard Waldrop,

Storm Constantine, Patricia C. Wrede, Midori Snyder, and others, as well as poetry by Ellen Steiber and Lawrence Schimel.

As for single-author collections of short fiction, the following two are in a tie for the best of the year:

A Knot in the Grain and Other Stories by Robin McKinley (Greenwillow). This Newbery Award–winning author is acknowledged to be one of the finest prose stylists in our field—particularly when she is handling fairy-tale material, as she does in this excellent collection. *A Knot in the Grain* proves once again that McKinley's reputation is well deserved. The book contains five stories, two that are original to the collection; four of the five are fantasy.

Travellers in Magic by Lisa Goldstein (Tor). This collection of fifteen stories shows the impressive range of a writer who has, over the last ten years, quietly earned a place for herself as one of the most talented writers working in the field today. Despite the award-winning splash of her first novel, *The Red Magician*, Goldstein continues to be somewhat underrated within the fantasy genre. This strong collection may finally win her the rich acclaim that she deserves.

The best children's collection of the year is *Here There Be Unicorns* by Jane Yolen (Harcourt Brace). Yolen remains the undisputed master of the original fairy-tale form. She seems to toss them off almost effortlessly, and yet each tale rings with that same authentic magic to be found in the classic stories of Charles Perrault, Hans Christian Andersen, or Oscar Wilde. Yolen's latest is beautifully illustrated by David Wilgus, and it transcends the potentially saccharine unicorn theme to offer up superb tales and poetry about the mythic beast.

Other recommended short fiction collections from 1994:

Women and Ghosts by Alison Lurie (Doubleday). This entertaining collection is by a mainstream writer with a penchant for fantasy and fairy tales. The volume contains nine contemporary ghost stories, mixing original tales and reprints.

The Grandmother's Tale and Selected Stories by R. K. Narayan (Viking). This volume collects the works of the well-known Indian writer. Many of the stories are magical realist in nature—and quite beautiful.

Grand Avenue by Greg Sarris (Hyperion). These lovely interconnected short stories, with mystical and folkloric resonances, are part of the current Native American literary renaissance.

East West by Salman Rushdie (Viking). A thoroughly enjoyable collection, although not among the author's best work. Several of the tales have fantasy elements—and the one about *Star Trek* is a hoot.

Unconquered Countries by Geoff Ryman (St. Martin's). This collection contains the World Fantasy Award–winning story "The Unconquered Country," a brilliant blend of fantasy, SF, and uncompromising realism.

Shades of Darkness: More of the Ghostly Best of Robert Westall by Robert Westall (Farrar, Straus & Giroux). The second volume in a two-book "best-of" collection by an absolute master of dark fantasy.

A Creepy Company by Joan Aiken (Dell Yearling). Ten young-adult dark fantasy stories from another British master of the ghostly tale.

Double Feature by Emma Bull and Will Shetterly (NESFA Press, PO Box 809, Framingham, MA 01701). This limited edition contains ten stories by fantasists Bull and Shetterly, two essays by Bull, and an introduction by Patrick and Teresa Nielsen Hayden.

Sports & Music by Lucius Shepard (Mark V. Ziesing). This is a signed, limited edition of two stories, one of which is fantasy, by this iconoclastic and skillful writer.

Silver Lady and the Fortyish Man by Megan Lindholm (Hypatia Press, c/o Full Moon

Books, 360 West First, Eugene, OR 97401). This is a signed, limited edition of a single fantasy story by this talented fantasist.

Doughnuts by James P. Blaylock (A.S.A.P., 23852 Via Navarra, Mission Viejo, CA 92691). This is a contemporary realist story, mentioned here because it is by an author well known to the fantasy field—and because it is so damned good! This stylish limited edition publication also contains an introduction by Lewis Shiner, an appreciation by Lucius Shepard, an afterword by Tim Powers, and photographs by Viki Blaylock. The edition is signed by all of the above.

For those who like literary surrealism:

Queen of Terrors by Robert Kelly (McPherson & Co.). New stories and prose poems by this consummate literary stylist, many of them quite magical in flavor and language.

A Music Behind the Wall by Anna Maria Ortese (McPherson & Co.). The collected tales of this celebrated Italian author.

Incidences by Daniil Kharms (Serpent's Tail). Kafkaesque absurdist short-shorts from a Russian writer (1905–42) whose works were banned until the 1980s.

The Complete Butcher's Tales by Rikki Ducornet (Dalkey Archive Press). Surrealistic short-shorts—somewhat dark and disturbing.

Genuinely Inspired Primitive: Short Forms and Ruminations by Cliff Burns (chapbook, available from: Box 478, Iqaluit, NWT, X09 0H0, Canada). Surrealistic short-shorts from this Canadian writer.

For poetry lovers, I recommend:

Going Out with Peacocks by Ursula K. Le Guin (HarperPerennial). Fifty-four dazzling poems from this exceptional writer.

The Hand of Poetry: Five Mystic Poets of Persia (Omega Publications). The poems of Sanai, Attar, Rumi, Saadi, and Hafiz, translated by Coleman Barks, with essays by Inayat Khan.

Loose Women by Sandra Cisneros (Knopf). These are wonderful poems on the theme of women in love, woven with nursery rhymes and Greek myths.

Songs by Brigit Pegeen Kelly (BOA Editions). Poetry by an American prize-winning writer, some of it beautifully mythic in content.

As for short fiction in the magazines:

The most notable magazines in the fantasy field this year were the brand-new ones listed above: *Realms of Fantasy* and *Century*. That said, *The Magazine of Fantasy & Science Fiction*, edited by Kristine Kathryn Rusch, continues to be the best source for good fantasy tales on the newsstands; our Honorable Mentions list contains more fantasy stories from *F & SF* than from any other magazine. *Omni*, edited by Ellen Datlow, remains a dependable source for high-quality, highly literate tales. The English speculative fiction magazine *Interzone*, edited by David Pringle, continues to maintain a commendably high standard in its selection of tales. *Asimov's Science Fiction*, edited by Gardner Dozois, also publishes some good fantasy material although its emphasis is on science fiction; so does *Worlds of Fantasy & Horror* (formerly published as *Weird Tales*), edited by Darrell Schweitzer and George Scithers, although its emphasis is on dark fantasy/horror. In addition, fantasy and magical realism has popped up in *The New Yorker*, *Esquire*, *Harper's*, and *Playboy* (as well as in a number of the American literary quarterlies) in 1994.

These are all magazines you can find on the newsstands. If you want to look a little farther afield for fantasy stories, they can be found in a number of smaller magazines as well. The best of them are:

The Printer's Devil: A Magazine of New Writing edited by Sean O'Brian and Stephen Plaice, Top Offices, 13a Western Road, Hove BN3 1AE, U K (a terrific, quirky British literary magazine, mixing magical realism in with other strictly realist fare).

Crank! edited by Bryan Cholfin, Broken Mirrors Press, PO Box 380473, Cambridge, MA 02238 (an excellent quarterly speculative fiction magazine).

The Third Alternative edited by Andy Cox, 5 Martins Lane, Witcham, Ely, Cambs, CB6 2LB, UK (a good eclectic, cross-genre small British 'zine).

The Urbanite edited by Marc McLaughlin, PO Box 4737, Davenport, IA 52808 (a literate, quirky, "urban fiction" 'zine, published in a clean, readable format).

Strange Plasma edited by Steve Pasechnick, Edgewood Press, Box 380264, Cambridge, MA 02238 (published its final edition in 1994, which is too bad—this was a good one).

Other small magazines you may be interested in:

Pulphouse, published quarterly, edited by Dean Wesley Smith, Box 1227, Eugene, OR 97440 (SF, fantasy, and horror).

Marion Zimmer Bradley's Fantasy Magazine edited by M. Z. Bradley, PO Box 249, Berkeley, CA 94701 (primarily swords-and-sorcery–type fantasy).

The Silver Web edited by Ann Kennedy, Buzzcity Press, PO Box 38190, Tallahassee, FL 32315 (specializes in surreal fantasy, in an attractive format).

Magic Realism edited by C. Darren Butler and Julie Thomas, Pyx Press, Box 620, Orem UT 84059-0620 (this nice little 'zine of surrealist and magical realist works has cut back from three issues to two a year).

Pirate Writings edited by Edward J. McFadden, 53 Whitman Avenue, Islip, NY 11751 (SF, fantasy, mystery).

After Hours edited by William G. Raley, PO Box 538, Sunset Beach, CA 90742-0538 (dark fantasy and horror).

Sirius Visions edited by Marybeth O'Halloran, Claddagh Press, 1075 NW Murray Road, Suite 161, Portland, OR 97229 (a tabloid-format speculative fiction magazines that publishes what it bills as "the literature of hope").

The Thirteenth Moon edited by Jacob Weisman, 1459 18th Street, San Francisco, CA 94107 (a small fantasy 'zine).

Year 2000 edited by Blythe Ayne, PO Box 84184, Vancouver, WA 98684 (a small speculative fiction 'zine).

TransVersions edited by Dale L. Sproule and Sally McBride, Specialty Reports, 1019 Colville Road, Victoria, BC V9A 4P5 Canada (a new small speculative fiction 'zine).

1994 was a good year for nonfiction and folklore works of interest to fantasy readers. A selection of recommended books published this past year:

From the Beast to the Blonde by Marina Warner (Chatto & Windus). See description on page xv. Highly recommended.

Six Myths of Our Time by Marina Warner (Vintage). See description on page xv. Highly recommended.

Fairy Tale as Myth by Jack Zipes (University of Kentucky Press). See description on page xv. Highly recommended.

The Trials and Tribulations of Little Red Riding Hood by Jack Zipes (Routledge). A revised and expanded edition of this interesting analysis, including thirty-five versions of the tale (from the Brothers Grimm to Angela Carter).

The Arabian Nights: A Companion by Robert Irwin (Viking). Irwin explores these legends in folkloric and cultural context as the adult tales they were (not as children's stories, as they are known now). He also analyzes their influence on Voltaire, Dickens, Borges, and the modern science fiction field.

Flesh and the Mirror: Essays on the Art of Angela Carter edited by Lorna Sage (Virago). This collection of thirteen essays explores the works of the late Angela Carter, one of the most important and influential fantasists of the late twentieth century.

Signs of Borges by Sylvia Molloy (Duke University Press). An insightful critical analysis of the work of the Nobel Prize–winning magical realist writer, translated from the Spanish by Oscar Montero.

C. S. Lewis in Context by Doris T. Myers (Kent State University Press). A strong analysis of Lewis's work, including his fantasy novels.

Classic Fantasy Writers edited by Harold Bloom (Chelsea House). This is a fascinating guide to the fourteen writers considered by Bloom to have most strongly influenced the adult and children's fantasy literature fields, marred only by the fact that it is oddly restricted (with a single exception) to male authors: L. Frank Baum, William Beckford, James Branch Cabell, Lewis Carroll, Lord Dunsany, Kenneth Grahame, H. Rider Haggard, Lafacadio Hearn, Rudyard Kipling, Andrew Lang, George MacDonald, Beatrix Potter, and Oscar Wilde.

Wordsmiths of Wonder by Stan Nicholls (Orbit). This book contains interviews with fifty writers of science fiction, horror, and fantasy. The latter include Michael Moorcock, Robert Holdstock, Stephen R. Donaldson, and Tanith Lee.

Storytellers: Folktales and Legends from the South edited by John A. Burrison (University of Georgia Press). A lovely collection of 260 short tales from 112 traditional storytellers.

Quests and Spells edited by Judy Sierra (Kaminski Media Arts, Ashland, Oregon). This small collection of European fairy tales is particularly geared for oral storytellers.

Creole Folktales by Patrick Chamoiseau (The New Press). Chamoiseau's book wonderfully evokes his childhood in Martinique—its tales, its history, its spicy foods. . . . Highly recommended.

Daughters of the Moon edited by Shahrukh Husain (Faber and Faber). Now a psychotherapist in London, Husain was born and brought up in Pakistan. She has put together a terrific book (beautifully packaged by the publisher), which contains intense, magical women's stories from all over the world. Highly recommended.

Power of Raven, Wisdom of Serpent by Boragh Jones (Lindisfarne Press). Jones's book is an interesting exploration of spirituality and ritual in the life of early Celtic women.

The Short, Swift Time of Gods on Earth: The Hohokam Chronicles by Julian Hayden, Donald Bahr, William Smith Allison, and Juan Smith (University of California Press). The first publication of this fascinating text of creation myths recorded from Pima Indians in 1935.

A *Fairy Tale Reader* by John and Caitlin Matthews (Aquarian). This lovely edition contains fairy tales, lore, and commentary by this expert team of British folklorists (best known for their work with Arthurian myths). Recommended.

Children's picture books are an excellent source for magical tales and magical artwork. The following recommendations are not only for children, but for adult collectors of fine fantasy as well:

Black Ships Before Troy written by Rosemary Sutcliff, illustrated by Alan Lee (Frances Lincoln Ltd.). This is one of the most gorgeous books to come along in many a year. The text, a retelling of *The Iliad*, is one of the last things the great British writer Rosemary Sutcliff finished before her death. The power of the text is fully complemented by the art of master watercolorist Alan Lee. It's a stunning book and won Britain's highest honor for children's illustration, the Kate Greenaway Medal.

A *Tooth Fairy's Tale* written and illustrated by David Christiana (Farrar, Straus & Giroux). Christiana is rapidly becoming one of my very favorite contemporary illustrators with charming, utterly magical books like this one. He's got a take on fairies that is quirky, modern, and distinctly his own.

The Girl in the Golden Bower written by Jane Yolen, with illustrations by Jane Dyer (Little, Brown). The story, an original fairy tale by the master fantasist, is worth the price of the book alone. Add Jane Dyer's lovely paintings and the edition is a real treasure.

Good Griselle written by Jane Yolen, illustrated by David Christiana (Harcourt Brace).

Here we get Yolen and Christiana *together in one volume*. What heaven. Thank you, Harcourt Brace.

The Three Golden Keys written and illustrated by Peter Sis (Doubleday). This moving reworking of three Czechoslovakian fairy tales becomes a fable of the author/illustrator's own lost childhood in Prague. Highly recommended for the splendid text and art alike.

Night of the Gargoyles written by Eve Bunting, illustrated by David Wiesner (Clarion). This is an enchanting story about what happens to gargoyles by night. Wiesner's illustrations are terrifically mysterious.

The Book That Jack Wrote, written by Jon Scieszka, illustrated by Daniel Adele (Viking). This hilarious book is by the author of the notorious *Stinky Cheese Man*. Adele's illustrations are weird, wild, and toothy.

Under the Moon written by Dyan Sheldon, illustrated by Gary Blythe (Dial). Blythe is an amazing painter, working with oil paint on canvas. His illustrations for this modern Native American tale are exceptionally fine.

The Princess and the Lord of Night written by Emma Bull, illustrated by Susan Garber (Harcourt Brace). Bull turns out to be as fine a storyteller in children's fiction as she is in the adult fantasy field—which comes as no real surprise. This is a lovely fairy tale.

Ship of Dreams written and illustrated by Dean Morrissey (Mill Pond Press). Morrissey is one of the best illustrators now working in the tradition of such American painters as Norman Rockwell and Howard Pyle. He is best known among adult readers for his many fantasy bookcovers, but his talents are well suited to the children's picture-book form. This is a sumptuous book, a magical fantasy journey reminiscent of Winsor McCay; it should not be missed.

Other picture books of note, briefly mentioned:

The Fairy Tales of Oscar Wilde illustrated by Isabelle Brent (Viking), with an introduction by folklorist Neil Philip.

Jaguarundi written by Virginia Hamilton, illustrated by Floyd Cooper (Blue Sky Press/ Scholastic), a dreamlike, magical animal tale set deep in the rain forest.

William Shakespeare's The Tempest retold by Bruce Coville, illustrated by Ruth Sanderson (Doubleday). A nice edition for children.

The Ice Palace written by Angela McAllister, illustrated by Angela Barrett (Putnam). The illustrator has created beautiful dreamscapes here.

Pablo and Pimienta written by Ruth M. Covault, illustrated by Francisco Mora (Northland). A sweet tale about a boy's friendship with a coyote, set on the Arizona/Mexico border. The text is in both English and Spanish.

The Sleeping Lady written by Ann Dixon, illustrated by Elizabeth Johns (Alaska Northwest). A nice retelling of this folktale from Alaska.

The Rough-faced Girl written by Rafe Martin, illustrated by David Shannon (Putnam). A fascinating Algonquin Indian version of Cinderella, published last year but not seen until now.

Non-sense written by Edward Lear, illustrated by James Wines (Rizzoli). A quirky little edition of Lear's nonsense poems.

King Kong written and illustrated by Anthony Browne (Turner). An odd cross between a picture book and a graphic novel, based on the old film.

Other art publications of note:

Lady Cottington's Pressed Fairy Book by Terry Jones and Brian Froud (Turner). Monty Python's Terry Jones wrote the text for this wild book conceived and created by Brian Froud (illustrator of *Faeries*, designer of the movies *The Dark Crystal* and *Labyrinth*). This is a hilarious, rude, and very British treatment of fairies and has to be seen to be believed.

(The promotion video produced by Jones and Froud is hilarious, too, if you ever get the opportunity to see it. Jones, in drag, is the elderly Lady Cottington. And, a bit of trivia here: the young Lady Cottington is played by the daughter of illustrator Alan Lee.) The production values of the book are gorgeous, and altogether it is an utter delight. Highly recommended.

Brian Froud's Faerielands (Bantam). Froud's distinctive faery art is also the inspiration behind this series, packaged by Byron Preiss. Froud created fifty drawings and paintings of faery creatures, which were then divided among four authors who were each to write a novella inspired by the work. The first two novellas were published by Bantam in 1994: Charles de Lint's *The Wild Wood*, and Patricia A. McKillip's *Something Rich and Strange*. The series was then cancelled when Bantam downsized its SF/fantasy list. (The authors of the final two novellas are revamping their stories for another publisher, but there is sadly, at this time, no immediate plan for publication of the rest of Froud's beautiful *Faerielands* art.)

Mind Fields: Art by Jacek Yerka, Fiction by Harlan Ellison (Morpheus International). This beautifully produced volume contains the haunting, surrealistic paintings of a Polish artist influenced by Hieronymus Bosch and Peter Brueghel. The pictures are complemented by thirty-three equally haunting short-short stories and prose poems by Ellison. A fascinating collaboration.

Pastures in the Sky by Patrick Woodruffe (Pomegranate). Woodruffe is another artist whose debt to Bosch is evident in his richly detailed paintings and constructions. The best of his art is the visual equivalent to literary magical realism. *Pastures in the Sky* is, in essence, the catalog of a touring exhibition of this British artist's work.

The Age of Innocence: The Romantic Art of Jeffrey Jones edited by Arnie Fenner and Cathy Burnett (Underwood). This is a lovely book, collecting the fine art of a master painter who has not only graced the fantasy field with his impressionistic and highly romantic work, but also strongly influenced a whole generation of artists including Thomas Canty and Jon J. Muth. Highly recommended.

Michael Parkes with text by Hans Redeker, translated by Michael O'Loughlin (Steltman). This is one of the most beautiful art books I've seen in a long time, collecting the sensual, magical work of an artist better known in Europe than in this country. Although occasionally Michael Parkes's art has a commercially slick, overly airbrushed feel to it, at his best he is one of the very top artists in the fantasy field. Definitely check this one out.

The Goddess Paintings of Susan Seddon Boulet with text by Michael Babcock (Pomegranate). Boulet is an English artist who was raised in Brazil and now makes her home in the American Southwest. Her shamanistic, mystical paintings have been popularized by their use on greeting cards and calendars and published in one previous collection, *Shaman*. Her new collection concentrates more on classical and Celtic mythology than on the Native American myths evident in previous work. At her best, her work is luminous. Also keep an eye out for *Buffalo Gals, Won't You Come Out Tonight* by Ursula K. Le Guin (Pomegranate), an edition of Le Guin's fine short story beautifully published in picture book form with paintings by Boulet.

Return of the Great Goddess edited by Burleigh Muten (Shambala). A rich collection of paintings, sculpture, and photography (mixed with literary excerpts and poetry) on the theme of the goddess. A handsome little treasury edition.

The Surrealists Look at Art edited by Pontus Hulten (Lapis). This is a new collection of eight essential surrealist texts (translated from the French) by Breton, Eluard, Tzara, Aragon, and Soupault, along with lavish illustrations—some of them quite rare. It is a beautiful book that has won several prizes for its design.

The Paper Cuttings of Hans Christian Andersen by Beth Wagner (Ticknor and Fields). Few people realize that in addition to being famous as writer of fairy tales, Andersen was also known as an artist in his time. He was particularly fond of making intricate paper cuttings, deftly working with a huge pair of scissors while he was telling his classic stories. This edition collects many magical examples of his work.

Mermaids and Magic Shows: The Paintings of David Delamare with text by Nigel Suckling (Paper Tiger). A lavish edition of the magical paintings of Delamare.

Dragon Moon, text by Chris Claremont and Beth Fleisher, art by John Bolton (Bantam Spectra). An entertaining graphic novel in which ancient Celtic legends are played out in the modern world.

The 1994 J. R. R. Tolkien Calendar, art by Michael William Kaluta (Ballantine). A labor of love, this project has been years in the making for Kaluta. The artist is a talented comics and book illustrator (as well as a former member of the Studio with Barry Windsor-Smith, Jeff Jones, and Berni Wrightson). It's a beautiful publication.

Despite commercial constraints that severely limit artists working in the area of book jacket and cover design and illustration, there were still some exceptional works that stood out from the rest on the fantasy bookshelves in 1994. To mention just a few of the notable cover treatments last year, for which the illustrators and their art directors deserve special commendation: Dave McKean's flashy modernistic treatment of Geoff Ryman's *Unconquered Countries* (St. Martin's); Mel Odom's distinctively stylized work for Francesca Lia Block's *Primavera* (Roc); John Jude Palencar's mystical treatment of Marion Zimmer Bradley's *The Forest House* (Viking); Bryan Leister's Pre-Raphaelite painting for Robin McKinley's *A Knot in the Grain* (Greenwillow); Thomas Canty's subtle sepia-toned drawing for Lisa Goldstein's *Travellers in Magic* (Tor); John Howe's ghostly imagery for Charles de Lint's *Memory and Dream* (Tor); Brian Froud's mysterious masked woman for Charles de Lint's *The Wild Wood* (Bantam); and Gervasio Gallardo's surrealistic imagery for *Omni Visions Two* (Omni Books). A sampling of the best cover illustrations and other commercial artwork published in 1994 will be published in the forthcoming Second Annual edition of *Spectrum*, edited by Cathy Burnett and Arnie Fenner (Underwood).

Traditional folk music is of interest to many fantasy readers because the old ballads (particularly in the Celtic folk tradition) are often based on the same folk- or fairy-tale roots as fantasy stories. Contemporary "world beat" can be considered the musical equivalent to contemporary mythic fantasy: these musicians are taking ancient folkloric themes and rhythms and updating them for our time.

The two most magical releases of the year were those mentioned above (June Tabor's *Against the Streams* and Loreena McKennitt's *The Mask and the Mirror*); however, there was also plenty of other good material to choose from in 1994. Charles de Lint (a fantasy writer and member of the Celtic band Jump at the Sun), Ellen Kushner (a fantasy writer and host of "Sound and Spirit," a weekly musical exploration of the human spirit, on Public Radio International), and I have come up with the following list of recommended releases:

Ready for the Storm is the second release from a young Northern Irish band who debuted to raves in 1990. Charles has come up with the best description of their music I've heard yet: "Imagine the next generation of the Bothy Band or De Dannan, while Mary Dillon [vocalist with Deanta] sounds as though she stopped by from Faeryland to record her tracks." Members of the band, as well as their families and friends, also participate in two other traditional Irish bands: Dervish (most recent release, *Harmony Hill*) and Óige (most recent release, *Live*).

Ireland's The House Band has been around since 1985, making their reputation with an extraordinary acoustic range of Irish, Scots, English, Welsh, Scandinavian, Balkan, and African music. Their latest, *Another Setting*, is terrific. The Bucks is made up of

Terry Woods (from the Pogues, as well as a founding member of Steeleye Span) and Ron Kavana (one of Ireland's best singer-songwriters). Their lively latest release is *Dancin' to the Ceilí Band*. Eileen Ivers is a native New Yorker who is the most successful American-born competitor in the history of the All-Ireland traditional music championships. Best known as the fiddle player for Cherish the Ladies (an all-women band), Chanting the House, and Hall and Oates, she now has her own wonderfully eclectic release, *Eileen Ivers*, on which she is accompanied by seventeen accomplished musicians drawn from traditional music, jazz, and rock. Her Irished-up version of "Pachelbel's Canon" (retitled "Pachelbel's Frolics") alone is worth the price of the CD.

The release that Charles calls "probably my favorite of the year" is *The Golden Dawn* by Loretto Reid (flute, concertina) and Brian Taheny (fiddle, guitar). "Besides being a brilliant musician," Charles says, "Reid writes some of the most beautiful music in a traditional style. Most of the tunes on this short album are her own, and you'd never know they weren't traditional. Originally from County Sligo, the pair now live in Ontario (Reta Ceol, 1561 Williamsport Drive, Mississauga, Ontario, Canada, L4X 1T7). This album is just great. There's not a bad cut on it, and when I play it I tend to stick it on repeat and let it go through a half-dozen times."

Ellen Kushner's favorite of the year is *The Sweet Sunny North*. "You could get the entire soundtrack for the world's greatest postmodern fantasy trilogy from this album," she says. "It was compiled in Norway by the great musicians/collectors Henry Kaiser and David Lindley, whose Malagasy album, *A World Out of Time*, turned everyone's head around in 1992. It opens with the chanting of a reindeer shaman, and includes teasing women's vocals, hardanger fiddle duets with Hawaiian guitar . . . and even a Pakistani/Norwegian jazz singer. I'd also like to call people's attention to the recent rash of recordings of the music of the eleventh-century scholar, composer, and visionary, Abbess Hildegard of Bingen. My favorite so far is from the women's group Sequentia. The single song that refuses to leave me this year is a cover of Robin Batteau's "Guinevere," recorded by Lucy Kaplansky on her altogether delicious album *The Tide*. If you're someone who chooses albums for their lyrics, this is my pick for you: there's not a bad song on here."

My own favorite of the year (aside from the McKennitt and Tabor CDs) is *Turf* by Luka Bloom. This is the one I find myself playing over and over again, and it is fortunate that my housemate loves it too or we would have come to blows by now. Bloom's real name is Barry Moore, and he's the brother of Ireland's famous Christy Moore (formerly of Planxty). Bloom's music owes a debt to traditional music but goes beyond it into original tunes that are sensual, romantic, political, powerful. His song "On Diamond Mountain" is an absolute killer; he has also recorded a mermaid ballad written by Mike Scott of the Waterboys.

I've also fallen in love with the Poozies, four women musicians from England and Scotland: Karen Tweed, Sally Barker, and (from Beating Harps) Patsy Seddon and Mary Macmaster. They have two infectious releases out: *Chantoozies* and *Dansoozies* (PO Box 8, Lutterworth, Leicestershire, LE17 45N, UK). For an absolutely *gorgeous* CD of traditional tunes from both England and India, try Sheila Chandra's *Zen Kiss*, another best of the year. Her voice is nothing short of stunning. Ingrid Karklins is another powerful singer; she's a Texan/Latvian singer-songwriter whose work manages to be traditional and avant-garde at once. Her latest release is *Anima Mundi*. Mili Bermejo mixes the music of her Mexican and Argentinian roots with jazz on the Mili Bermejo Quartet's *Casa Corazón*. She has a lovely deep, rich voice, and the range of her music is impressive.

Varttina is a band that backs up extraordinary female vocal harmonies with music played on both traditional and exotic instruments. This unique Finnish band has been in the top ten on the World Music charts with their new release, *Oi Dai*.

The Ukrainians are a wild band, mixing traditional tunes with covers of Lou Reed and

The Smiths songs on *Vorony*. Ad Vieille Que Pourra is a marvelous cutting-edge world beat band from France, and their latest, *Musaique*, is highly recommended. Tarika (formerly called Tarika Sammy) is another cutting edge band that mixes traditional music from Madagascar with punk and rock rhythms. Their new release is *Bibiango*. Haiti's hot young roots band Boukan Ginen ("Fire from Africa") debuted with an American release in 1994: *Jou a Rive*. Cuba's folkloric ensemble Clave y Guaguanco mixes secular music with sacred Afro-Cuban styles from the Yoruba and Palo traditions on their latest, *Songs and Dances*.

On our own native shores, I recommend the latest exquisitely beautiful CD of Native American flute music from Navajo-Ute musician R. Carlos Nakai: *Feather, Stone and Light*. Naikai is accompanied by William Eaton on lyraharp guitar and Will Clipman on percussion; the result is utter magic. Nakai has also released *Island of Bows*, another hauntingly lovely CD mixing Native American flute with traditional Japanese instruments, played by the Wind Traveling Band. Peter Kater has teamed up with Iroquois singer Joanne Shenandoah on *Life Blood*, a beautiful CD of mythic chants drawn from ancient Iroquois tradition. And Robbie Robertson (from The Band), along with the Red Road Ensemble, has put out a terrific CD called *Music for Native Americans*, which mixes rock and traditional tribal music and is another favorite of the year.

If all this world beat music is new to you, I recommend three compilation CDs: Green Linnet's *Heart of the Gaels*, Narada's *Celtic Odyssey*, and Rhino's *The Best of World Music*.

The World Fantasy Convention (an annual professional gathering of writers, illustrators, publishers, and readers of both fantasy and horror fiction) was held in New Orleans, Louisiana, in 1994 (October 27–30). The Guests of Honor were: Ramsey Campbell, George Alec Effinger, Damon Knight, and Kate Wilhelm, writers; Jill Bauman, artist; aided and abetted by toastmasters George R. R. Martin and Tim Powers. The World Fantasy Awards were presented at the convention. Winners (for work published in 1993) were as follows: *Glimpses* by Lewis Shiner for Best Novel; "Under the Crust" by Terry Lamsley for Best Novella; "The Lodger" by Fred Chappell for Best Short Fiction; *Full Spectrum 4* edited by Lou Aronica, Amy Stout, and Betsy Mitchell for Best Anthology; *Alone with the Horrors* by Ramsey Campbell for Best Collection; Alan Clarke and J. K. Potter for Best Artist; Underwood-Miller, for publishing, Special Award/Professional; Marc Michaud, for Necromicron Press, Special Award/Non-Professional. The Life Achievement Award was given to Jack Williamson. Judges for the award were Stefan Dziemianowicz, James Frenkel, Mary Gentle, Lisa Tuttle, and Chet Williamson. For information on the next World Fantasy Convention, to be held in Baltimore, MD, write: World Fantasy Convention, Baltimore Gun Club, PO Box 19909, Baltimore, MD 21211-0909.

The Fourth Street Fantasy Convention (an annual literary convention devoted specifically to fantasy) was held, as always, in Minneapolis (July 1–3). For information on the 1996 convention, write David Dyer-Bennet, 4242 Minnehaha Avenue South, Minneapolis, MN 55406.

Mythcon (a scholarly convention sponsored by the Mythopoeic Society and devoted to fantasy) was held in Washington, DC (August 5–8). Guests of Honor were: Madeleine L'Engle, Verlyn Flieger, and Judith Mitchell.

The International Conference on the Fantastic in the Arts (a scholarly convention embracing fantasy, horror, and science fiction) was held, as always, in Ft. Lauderdale, Florida (March 16–20). The Guests of Honor were: Roger Zelazny, Ben Bova, and Brian W. Aldiss. The 1996 convention will be held March 20–24. For information write IAFA, College of Humanities, 500 NW 20th HU-50 BA, Florida Atlantic University, Boca Raton, FL 33431.

That's a brief summation of the year in fantasy; now on to the stories themselves.

As usual, there are some stories (particularly the lengthy ones) that we do not have room to print even in an anthology as fat as this one. I consider the following ten tales to be among the year's best along with the stories and poems collected in this volume. I strongly recommend seeking them out if you haven't come across them already:

In alphabetical order . . .

"I Died, Sir, in Flames, Sir," by Richard Bowes, from the June issue of *F & SF*.

"Fugue and Variation," by Stuart Falconer, from the July issue of *Interzone*.

"Last Summer at Mars Hill," by Elizabeth Hand, from the August issue of *F & SF*.

"Bible Stories for Adults #20: The Tower," by James Morrow, from the June issue of *F & SF*.

"Coyote Ugly," Pati Nagle, from the April issue of *F & SF*.

"A Man on Crutches," by Paul Park, from the January issue of *Omni*.

"Last Rites and Resurrections," by Martin Simpson from the Spring/Summer issue of *The Silver Web*.

"The Spinner," Martha Soukup, from *Xanadu 2*.

"I Know What You're Thinking," by Kate Wilhelm, from the November issue of *Asimov's*.

"Don Chico Who Flies," by Eraclio Zepeda, from the Fall issue of *TriQuarterly*.

I hope you will enjoy the stories and poems that follow. Many thanks to the authors and publishers who allowed us to reprint them here.

Summation 1994: Horror
by Ellen Datlow

News of the Year:

The Hearst Trade Book Group was taken off the market late February after two years of dithering, but the damage caused by media speculation and the on-again off-again sale has taken its toll, despite the hiring of several new senior editors for Morrow. Adrian Zackheim, Morrow's editorial director for adult trade books, left the company, as did Howard Kaminsky, president of the Trade Book Group, the latter citing personal reasons. However, top publishing executives said that they believe Hearst had put pressure on Mr. Kaminsky to quit his post because of the company's poor performance. In mid-May, William Schwalbe was named editorial director of Morrow and was given the mandate from Hearst to spend more money on high-profile acquisitions as well as on advertising and marketing. In August, Elizabeth Perle McKenna was appointed to the new position of vice-president and publisher of the Hearst Book Group, where she is responsible for coordinating the adult publishing programs for William Morrow and Avon Books. But vacancies in several high-level positions have still not been filled.

Viacom Inc., owner of Paramount Publishing—formerly known as Simon & Schuster—went back to that more identifiable name, Simon & Schuster. Speculation remained that Viacom would sell the publishing operations to help repay its debt. The abrupt dismissal of chairman and chief executive Richard E. Snyder in mid-June did nothing to allay those rumors. For more than thirty years, Mr. Snyder helped build Simon & Schuster from its core trade divisions into a huge publishing conglomerate. According to Viacom president and CEO Frank J. Biondi, Jr., the reason for Snyder's dismissal was "essentially a difference of philosophy and style, not a single event. . . . It had become evident over the period of time we'd been dealing with him that there were strong differences of opinions to how the businesses should be run." Snyder has been at the center of various controversies over the past several years, including the uproar over the signing, then cancellation, of Bret Easton Ellis's ultra-violent *American Psycho* and the firings of Summit head Jim Silberman, literary editor Allen Peacock, and Poseidon head Ann Patty. Jonathan Newcomb, S & S president and COO, is the new CEO.

Susan Moldow left HarperCollins in mid-May to become publisher at a revamped Scribner's.

Random House, Inc., laid off nearly 10 percent of two hundred employees in its juvenile and merchandise group, which publishes the company's children's books. In addition, two senior editors at Alfred A. Knopf, Gordon Lish and Corona Machember, left at the end of the year. Lish declined to call his departure amicable, although Machember says she will become an independent editor and did call her departure amicable.

Dell Books started a new trade paperback imprint of literary dark fiction called Cutting Edge. The line, founded by Jeanne Cavelos, editor of the Abyss horror line, debuted in September with Patrick McCabe's award-winning novel *The Butcher Boy* and will publish about three titles a year. A month before the first book's release, Cavelos unexpectedly resigned to take a teaching job in New Hampshire. Cavelos was an editor at Doubleday for a year before going to Dell where she edited for six years. She started the Abyss line in 1990 when most publishers were cutting back on horror, emphasizing literary horror, and launched new writers Kathe Koja, Poppy Z. Brite, Nancy Holder, Brian Hodge, and Melanie Tem. The cover art and designs were sophisticated, impressionistic, and sexy in a way that was worlds apart from the usual horror cover art. Cavelos won the World

Fantasy Award in 1993 for her editing of Abyss. It has since been decided that some of the books, which have been given over to various editors within Dell, along with new acquisitions, will be published in the line, but not necessarily on a monthly schedule. The Cutting Edge line is to be continued with Betsy Bundschuh as editor.

The new HarperCollins SF/fantasy imprint, HarperPrism, launched its new line in November, headed by Editor in Chief John Silbersack. The first list included an erotic vampire anthology edited by Poppy Z. Brite (and an uncredited Martin H. Greenberg) in trade paperback. Silbersack has hired Christopher Schelling, formerly of Roc, as executive editor.

St. Martin's CEO Thomas McCormack announced that the company would be launching an American counterpart to Picador, the U.K. literary line of trade paperback and hardcover books. Picador, founded in 1972, has published works by Toni Morrison, Cormac McCarthy, Doris Lessing, Don DeLillo, and Salman Rushdie, Scott Bradfield, J. G. Ballard, Eric Kraft, and Jewell Parker Rhodes. The line, under George Witte, will be publishing thirty-six to forty fiction and nonfiction titles in its second year, beginning January 1995.

Chronicle Books, which successfully published *Griffin and Sabine*, is expanding its fiction program of classic reprints and paperback short-story collections with a series of hardcover novellas launched in June. The first releases were David Knowles's *The Secrets of the Camera Obscura* and *The Forty Fathom Bank* by Les Galloway. The Knowles is dark and strange. In the fall, Chronicle reprinted William Kotzwinkle's *Swimmer in the Secret Sea*.

Masquerade Books, the publisher known for its erotic fiction and nonfiction, has started two new imprints to accommodate science fiction and horror. The Rhinoceros adult fiction line brought out *Equinox*, the retitled reprint of Samuel R. Delany's classic *The Tides of Lust*, and the complete version of Delany's lauded autobiography, *The Motion of Light in Water*, and Philip José Farmer's SF/horror novel *The Image of the Beast*. The Richard Kasak Books imprint published *Unnatural Acts and Other Stories* by Lucy Taylor, an expansion of last year's collection of the same title, published by Tal. The imprint also published Delany's new mainstream erotic novel *The Mad Man*.

Carroll & Graf quietly and without fanfare has built up an important program of science fiction, fantasy, and horror/suspense over the past few years. With a carefully coordinated publishing alliance with the United Kingdom's Robinson Publishers, C & G is the American publisher of Thomas Ligotti and Brian Stableford, Brian Aldiss, Elizabeth Massie, and Kim Newman, the *Mammoth Book* series of various horror anthologies and novels, and reprints of such classics as Theodore Sturgeon's *Some of Your Blood*, Philip K. Dick's *Time Out of Joint*, and H. P. Lovecraft's *The Watchers Out of Time*.

White Wolf, a publisher of role-playing games since 1986, launched a separate but related fiction line of novels and anthologies beginning with four anthologies set in their "World of Darkness." The press is reprinting, in an attractive, mass-market format, the *Borderlands* anthology series, edited by Thomas F. Monteleone, and will reprint the Sonja Blue novels by Nancy A. Collins. Stephen Pagel, formerly national SF, fantasy, and role-playing buyer for Barnes & Noble, recently joined the company to head sales.

Specialist press Underwood-Miller has split into two separate entities after eighteen years. Tim Underwood will publish Underwood Books out of California. Chuck Miller will publish as Charles F. Miller, Publisher, out of the former Underwood-Miller address in Pennsylvania. Started in 1976, Underwood-Miller has, over the years, published a wide range of reprint and original material in and out of the genre, including works by Jack Vance, Bernie Wrightson, *The Masters of Darkness* series edited by Dennis Etchison, and *Horrorstory* volumes three, four and five—the collected hardcover editions of Karl Edward Wagner's *The Year's Best Horror*. The first titles published by Underwood Books were *Age of Innocence*, a collection of Jeffrey Jones's artwork, and *Spectrum*, an anthology of fantastic artwork selected from the recent art contest, edited by Cathy Burnett and Arnie Fenner. Charles F. Miller's first releases were *Virgil Finlay's Far Beyond*, a collection of artwork, and a reissue of *Bernie Wrightson's Frankenstein*, an illustrated book.

Weird Tales changed its name to *Worlds of Fantasy & Horror* effective with the summer 1994 issue. The numbering started over with Volume 1, Number 1. The oldest of the specialty magazines, *Weird Tales*'s first issue appeared in 1923, but the original magazine folded in the early 1950s and since then has been revived several times. The current incarnation started in 1988 with issue #290. It is published by George Scithers. The magazine has been mostly quarterly, but has only managed two issues in each of the last two years. The title, licensed to Terminal Publishing, expired and the renewal ran into legal and financial problems. The agreement to revert the title has been "amicable" according to the principals. *Aberations* magazine was sold by Jon Herron to a partnership comprised of the former senior editors of the magazine—M. Andre-Driussi, R. Blair, and E. Turowski. The new company is called Sirius Fiction and debuted with issue #15 (December 1993), with the title changed to *Aberrations*. The magazine is a monthly. Jonathan Bond relinquished the editorship of *Pulphouse* to concentrate on his fiction writing. Dean Wesley Smith, the publisher, is taking over editing duties. *Amazing* reappeared in its new digest-size format with the spring issue. Late in the year it was announced that the magazine was for sale; *Aboriginal SF*, edited by Charles Ryan, is for sale. *Midnight Zoo*, edited by Jon Herron, folded. *Cemetery Dance*, edited by Richard Chizmar, canceled its fall issue because of illness but should be back on schedule in 1995. *Strange Plasma*, edited by Steve Pasechnick, ceased publishing with its eighth issue. *Century*, a bimonthly magazine of speculative fiction, debuts with its spring 1995 issue. The trade paperback magazine, edited by Robert K. J. Killheffer, the former assistant fiction editor of *Omni*, aims at publishing literate science fiction and fantasy. *Phantasm*, the new incarnation of the short-lived horror magazine *Iniquities*, is edited by J. F. Gonzalez and scheduled to publish quarterly. The editor intends to concentrate on fiction; the only nonfiction will be a review column focused on more obscure genre titles and a film column focusing on "little known, classics, and low-budget genre films." *Skull* was launched by Mike Baker, who has suspended publication of his nonfiction magazine *Afraid* to focus on fiction. *Deathrealm*, edited by Mark Stephen Rainey, suspended publication for a few months as it went through a change in publisher. Stanislaus Tal is no longer connected with the magazine and Rainey, owner of *Deathrealm*, announced that the magazine will be back on a quarterly schedule with #23 in March 1995. A partnership consisting of Lawrence Watt-Evans and Terry Rossio, under the name Malicious Press, has been formed to publish the magazine.

With the death of Karl Edward Wagner, DAW Books has decided to discontinue *The Year's Best Horror* series. The series was doing only marginally well for the past few years, with DAW continuing to publish it out of respect for the outstanding and very personal job that Wagner was doing and his great dedication to that job.

Eclipse Comics, publisher of graphic works based on stories by Clive Barker and Dean Koontz and the artbook *Clive Barker: Illustrator*, is in serious financial trouble. A lawsuit is pending over nonpayment of artists, and the copublishing deal with HarperCollins (US) has been abandoned because of money Eclipse claims is due them from HarperCollins (US). Complicating the problems is the ongoing divorce between two of the company principals.

Censorship continues as a Largo, Florida, jury found a comic book produced by artist Michael Diana to be obscene. The twenty-four-year-old author, jailed briefly following the trial, was sentenced to three years probation and a $3,000 fine. As conditions of Diana's probation, the county-court judge ordered him to undergo a psychiatric evaluation, avoid contact with anyone under eighteen, and to take a college course in journalism. The judge also authorized periodic searches of his home to prevent him from producing any obscene drawings, even for personal use. Diana's 'zine, only available through the mail, purportedly included stories dealing with rape, murder, drugs, child abuse, and dismemberment. *Gauntlet* magazine goes into this in more detail.

Nan A. Talese/Doubleday held the "Alison Lurie Write an Original Ghost Story Contest," established to celebrate Lurie's 1994 collection *Women and Ghosts*. The winner, awarded $500 for the best unpublished and unsold ghost story by a U.S. or Canadian writer (outside of Quebec), was announced in December to be James Sarafin, for his story, "The Word for Breaking August Sky." The story will be published in *Alfred Hitchcock Mystery Magazine* in the July 1995 issue.

News from England:

Stephen Jones was named editorial director of the new Robinson imprint, Raven, specializing in mass-market horror and fantasy. The line debuted in August with the publication of *Knights of Blood* by Scott MacMillan and Katherine Kurtz, and is initially publishing one title a month; Penguin U.K. announced the launch of a new mass-market horror/dark fantasy line, Creed, with an April 1995 premiere. The line is being run by Signet U.K. executive editor Luigi Bonomi, who is also in charge of Roc U.K. Jo Fletcher will be working on books for all three imprints as well. Writers signed up include Storm Constantine, Graham Joyce, Freda Warrington, and Nancy Baker. *Snow White, Blood Red* and *Black Thorn, White Rose*, edited by Ellen Datlow and Terri Windling, have also been bought by the new imprint. The emphasis will be on supernatural horror "rather than mere gore and grue"; Jo Fletcher is now working for Victor Gollancz; Ramsey Campbell has dropped out of the co-editorship (with Stephen Jones) of the *Best New Horror* series; Ringpull captured the attention of the media when the first novel they published, Jeff Noon's *Vurt*, won the Arthur C. Clarke Award and then was sold in the United States for a large amount to Crown Publishers; Ringpull also reprinted Harvey Jacobs's novel *Beautiful Soup* and planned to launch a new list, but sadly they went out of business in 1995; Barrington Press, published by Chris Kenworthy, shut down. The small publisher distinguished itself by publishing three quite good crossover anthologies as well as Nicholas Royle's first novel *Counterparts*.

The British Fantasy Awards were given out in Birmingham, England, at the British Fantasy Convention, which was held during the first weekend of October. The winners: *The Long Lost* by Ramsey Campbell (Headline) won the August Derleth Award for Best Novel; "The Dog Park," by Dennis Etchison (*Dark Voices* 5-Pan), won for Short Story; *Dark Voices 5* edited by David Sutton and Stephen Jones (Pan) won for Best Anthology/Collection; *Dementia 13* edited by Pam Creais won for Best Small Press; Les Edwards won for Best Artist; Poppy Z. Brite won for Best Newcomer; and David Sutton won the Special Committee Award.

A note from even farther away: Thai author Mom Rajawongse Kukrit Pramoj, former prime minister of Thailand, has been accused of plagiarizing John Wyndham's *The Midwich Cuckoos*. Kukrit's novel, published several years ago in Thai, is called *Kawao Ti Bangphleng* (translated by S. P. Somtow as *The Cuckoos of Bangphleng*). The plagiarism was revealed in a detailed article published by Somtow in a Thai English-language magazine.

And the first issue of the new Australian horror magazine *Bloodsongs*, from Melbourne's Bambada Press, received a category 1 rating from the Australian Office of Film and Literature classification, meaning shops must display it in a sealed bag and that the magazine can not be sold to anyone under eighteen. *Bloodsongs* is the first horror magazine to get newsstand distribution in Australia.

The Horror Writers Association held its annual meeting and Bram Stoker Award banquet June 3–5 at the Sahara Hotel in Las Vegas. Winners were: Novel: *The Throat* by Peter Straub (Dutton); First Novel: *The Thread That Binds the Bones* by Nina Kiriki Hoffman

(AvoNova); Novella: "The Night We Buried Road Dog" by Jack Cady (*F & SF*) tied with "Mefisto in Onyx" by Harlan Ellison (*Omni*/Mark Ziesing); Novelette: "Death in Bangkok" by Dan Simmons (*Playboy*/*LoveDeath*-Warner); Short Story: "I Hear the Mermaids Singing," by Nancy Holder (*Hottest Blood*); Collection: *Alone With the Horrors* by Ramsey Campbell (Arkham House); Non-Fiction: *Once Around the Bloch* by Robert Bloch (Tor); Other Media: *Jonah Hex: Two Gun Mojo* by Joe R. Lansdale (DC/Vertigo); Special Trustees Award: Vincent Price; and Life Achievement: Joyce Carol Oates. Initially, Ellison's novella was not announced as one of the winners. But after discovering that some of the rules were changed without approval of the board or the membership, HWA secretary James A. Moore and HWA president Dennis Etchison made a decision to give the award to Ellison as well as Cady.

Novels:

Although horror was being declared dead as a marketing category, and fewer novels were labeled "horror" in 1994, the major publishers continued to publish what I and most other readers would call horror. In addition, many fine dark novels were published by mainstream publishers *as* mainstream. Here is my completely biased reading list for 1994.

Wireless by Jack O'Connell (Mysterious) is set in the same fictional town of Quinsigamond as O'Connell's previous novel, *Box 9*. *Box 9* verged into SF/horror territory by introducing a new street drug that works on the language center of the brain, causing the user to process thoughts hundreds of times quicker than normal, and in the case of an overdose, pushing the user into violence and insanity. The *Wireless* of the new novel's title is a retro hangout for jammers—the radio wave equivalent of computer hackers—who evade the law while wreaking chaos on the airwaves. The two main groups of jammers—of different generations—are rapidly diverging in philosophy and method. Meantime, a crazed ex-FBI agent hates them all and torches those he can in the interest of tracking down the leaders. Antic, volatile, clever, and entertaining.

The Horses of the Night by Michael Cadnum (Carroll & Graf) is on the surface about a deal with dark powers, but Cadnum's luminous writing and imagination create a far more complex piece of horror. The protagonist is a visionary but unappreciated architect, a humanitarian, born into a formerly wealthy San Francisco family—a family respected despite the madness, murder, and recklessness that plague it. He is approached by a mysterious being and finds himself making decisions that appear to have negative consequences for others while helping him realize his own ambitions. This novel is an incredibly beautiful journey from supernatural thriller through psychological horror to a meditation on ambition, dreams, and the price paid to achieve them. Highly recommended. Cadnum also published *Skyscape* last year, but I haven't read it.

Sineater by Elizabeth Massie (Pan/Carroll & Graf) was first published in 1993 in the United Kingdom, and won the Bram Stoker Award for First Novel. Massie has honed her writing skills and made her reputation writing short stories so the richness of characterization in this novel should come as no surprise to her fans. In the Blue Ridge Mountains of Virginia, the Barker family live as pariahs because the father is the community's sineater; he who bears the sins of the community's dead. No one is allowed to look upon him, not even his children, and he lives in isolation in the woods. The younger son is befriended by another outsider, who is the nephew of the local religious sect's leader. When bad things start to happen to those who associate with the Barker family, the religionists launch a campaign against the family for not keeping to the old ways. This is a well-written and engaging Southern gothic.

Something very interesting is happening to the "serial killer" novel. Thomas Harris's *Red Dragon* and *The Silence of the Lambs* knocked readers out with their freshness. Since then the imitations have been churned out by the dozen—but there are still some fresh and interesting turns on the theme, like David Lindsay's *Mercy*, Bradley Denton's *Blackburn*, Paul Theroux's *Chicago Loop*, and David Martin's *Lie to Me*. Now, we're seeing a rash of "literary" serial killer novels, some more artistically and commercially successful than others.

Going Native by Stephen Wright (Farrar, Straus & Giroux) is a nightmarish journey across early 1990s America, introducing a variety of hustlers, yuppies, and other assorted characters bound by the thread of the "shapeshifting" serial killer who touches their lives. The brilliance of this by turns hilarious, depressing, shocking, and ultimately haunting novel is in the writing—the author writes with a clarity and vision that will make this a classic. Highly recommended.

The Alienist by Caleb Carr (Random House) is a fine novel of detection in addition to being a fascinating social history of New York City. In 1896, young transvestite male prostitutes are being murdered and a psychologist (the "alienist" of the title) uses his revolutionary ideas to track down their killer. The unorthodox psychologist enlists his former college classmate and longtime friend, a crime reporter for the *New York Times* (the narrator of the novel), and Sara Howard, one of the first women with the distinction of working for the police department (as secretary), at the behest of the new reformer, police commissioner Theodore Roosevelt. By analyzing forensic evidence, the three build a psychological profile of the killer, which helps greatly in identifying him. Carr has obviously done his homework researching the history of police detection and the development of forensics, and his use of this material gives *The Alienist* a lovely quirkiness and verisimilitude. My only quibble is that the narrator occasionally has a too contemporary a sensibility and sensitivity about the societal ills of his era. Despite this auctorial intrusion, the book is highly recommended. In contrast, E. L. Doctorow's newest, *The Waterworks* (Random House), is pallid, with a bare minimum of mystery, local color, or characterization. The Doctorow takes place in New York, too, though a bit earlier than *The Alienist*—in the 1870s—and the narrator is also a journalist.

Nevermore by William Hjortsberg (Atlantic Monthly Press) also mines historical New York City for its mystery plot. In this entertaining fantasy, Harry Houdini and Arthur Conan Doyle, uneasy friends (uneasy because of their wildly diverse views on the cult of spiritualism prominent in the 1920s), join forces to track down a killer who is using Edgar Allan Poe's fictions as inspiration. Poe himself makes an occasional appearance in the book. Houdini is portrayed as vain and egotistical and deeply sentimental about his dead mother. *Nevermore* suffers in comparision to *The Alienist*, as Hjortsberg never completely succeeds in bringing the New York of that era to life. Lovers of the hard-boiled horror novel, such as Hjortsberg's *Fallen Angel*, might be disappointed by this light romp.

Headhunter by Timothy Findley (Crown) is a modern and self-aware retelling of Conrad's *The Heart of Darkness*. According to schizophrenic Lilah Kemp, Kurtz has escaped from page 92 of Conrad's novel and is now a thoroughly modern man, a psychiatrist who indeed uses his power in evil ways. The story takes place in a futuristic Toronto during a plague allegedly carried by birds, and a government campaign to rid the city of them. (Where is PETA [People for the Ethical Treatment of Animals] in all this and why aren't there signs of demonstrators protesting these massacres? Something feels askew without at least a nod to this.) Peopled by extraordinary characters, including a woman convinced that birds are flocking to her for safety, a grotesque men's club for the rich and powerful, and an unhappy wife whose plastic surgeon husband has remade her into a beauty she cannot recognize. The literary games don't hurt the novel's flow; this book is suspenseful, dark, twisted, and complex. Findley is utterly in control of the material. Highly recommended.

The Game of Thirty by William Kotzwinkle (Houghton Mifflin/Seymour Lawrence) is a deftly written mystery by the author of the World Fantasy Award–winning novel *Doctor Rat*. A dealer in antiquities is found murdered in New York City, his internal organs missing. His grieving daughter hires an unusually compassionate private eye to catch the killer. A missing solid-gold scepter that belonged to Egyptian royalty may be the motive . . . or might the motive be something uglier than mere greed? The game of thirty is an ancient Egyptian board game that behaves as oracle and occasional commentator on the action. Kotzwinkle's light touch makes a striking counterpoint to the dark undercurrents. Entertaining.

In the Lake of the Woods by Tim O'Brien (Houghton Mifflin/Seymour Lawrence) is by the author of the National Book Award–winning novel *Going After Cacciato* and *The Things They Carried*. An unhappy boy-turned-magician-turned-soldier and later politician is ruined by the disclosure of a secret he has kept for twenty years. He and his wife leave civilization after the electoral disaster to figure out what to do with the rest of their lives. She disappears. The whole story is told as material gathered by a journalist intrigued by this man who magicked a life for himself by his deft sleight of hand. O'Brien continues to mine the Vietnam War and U.S. involvement in it for riches that he transmutes into art with his beautiful writing and interesting plot structure. Compulsively readable.

Curfew by Phil Rickman (Berkley), published as *Crybbe* in the U.K. (Headline), is an excellent example of how supernatural horror can be made fresh by a talented, creative writer. The difference here is the quality of characterizations. A rich, arrogant pop promotor/entrepreneur wants to make the dour and dull Welsh bordertown of Crybbe into a New Age center, against the wishes of the townspeople. Crybbe is a "bad" place; the standing stones that have been removed were taken away for good reason. The townspeople won't talk but the Preece family continues to ring the curfew bell one hundred times nightly at 10 P.M. An heroic dog, several intelligent skeptics, New Agers, ex-husbands, and impressionable adolescents all contribute to a nice mix, as historical evils reassert themselves in the present. It's not a first novel as Berkley declares it to be (Rickman's first was published in the U.K. only), but this is an excellent second novel.

They Whisper by Robert Olen Butler (Henry Holt) is a mesmerizing novel about a man who loves women and the woman who unwittingly destroys him emotionally when she slides into insanity. Fiona—abused as a child and emotionally damaged beyond repair—hates herself and cannot fathom that she is loved or deserves to be loved. Constantly challenging her husband to prove his love, she becomes increasingly irrational and destructive both physically and emotionally. This erotic novel is beautifully written and painstakingly structured to reveal bits and pieces, a little at a time. It's reminiscent, both in tone and in its oblique depiction of the manifestations of madness, of William Goldman's *The Color of Light*. Literary with horrific elements, an air of menace bears down on the entire novel.

Throat Sprockets by Tim Lucas (Dell/Cutting Edge), though flawed, is the best first novel of the year, a postmodern journey into sexual obsession and perversion—Kathe Koja territory. A man wanders into a porn theater and watches a movie that eroticizes women's throats. He is drawn into the obsession, breaking up his marriage but unleashing his latent creativity. For him, the throat, a bridge between mind and body, "exists to put distance between the head—the house of our higher soul, of our spiritual nature—and the body of our animal passions and appetites. . . . In the drama of our minds and bodies, our throats . . . the *throat* is a Disaster Area." The novel presents film as narcotic, as dangerous device. Light on plot and with a weak last third, the book nonetheless possesses a pervasive sense of dread; this is an unnerving, sophisticated, and passionate novel. Lucas's film expertise (he's publisher of *Video Watchdog*) comes in handy. Suspenseful and terrifying, with some beautiful writing, it's highly recommended.

From the Teeth of Angels by Jonathan Carroll (Doubleday) is an exuberant novel about facing death, in a reality where Death can be seen as an entity with more power and more substance than is implied by the notion of God and the Devil contending for human souls.

The characters in Carroll's novels face real tragedy—AIDS, rape, the horror of Yugoslavia's self-dismemberment. His characters talk cool but the writing is full of emotion. Using letters, tapes, and stories-within-stories to tell his tale, Carroll writes diamond-sharp prose about characters whom the reader longs to meet off the printed page. Satisfying. Highly recommended.

Strange Angels by Kathe Koja (Delacorte Press) starts off with a difficult problem to overcome—its unlikable protagonist, a photographer with no imagination, is a loser and a user. His girlfriend, an art therapist, has been supporting him. One day she brings home drawings by one of her patients, a young man. He becomes obsessed with the art and artist and comes to believe he must save the schizophrenic patient from the psychiatric establishment. Driven by selfishness, he wants to possess the young man's brilliance. But when he brings the patient home to live with him, and with the arrival of another who's a "strange angel"—a mentally ill woman who loves the patient—he becomes the observer/caretaker of them both, giving the reader a harrowing view of mental illness taking control of the lives of those around the afflicted. It's fascinating watching these three characters crash and burn; by the end the reader comes to sympathize somewhat with the photographer.

The Nihilesthete by Richard Kalich (The Permanent Press) makes an interesting companion to *Strange Angels* because it too is about a talentless person reacting to someone who is creative. This novel was published several years ago; I was only recently able to track down a copy. A misanthropic social worker who despises and claims not to understand beauty, develops a "relationship" with one of his clients—a limbless, mentally diagnosed idiot, who cannot speak except in cat meows. But the idiot is a lover of beauty and an artist. The caseworker begins a cruel game of power that is suspenseful and painful to read. Highly recommended.

The Totem by David Morrell (Donald M. Grant) is the expanded hardcover edition of this entertaining 1979 novel about a former city cop who thinks he's escaped the violence of the city by becoming police chief in a largish town near the Rockies. Fat chance. (This is a horror novel after all.) A rabies-type-virus outbreak spreads like wildfire, dovetailing with the town's guilt over a murderous incident with some hippies years before. According to Morrell's interesting introduction, this edition is quite different from the earlier, truncated version. The book is beautifully designed and illustrated by Tom Canty. A trade edition is available for $24.95 plus $2 p&h. The deluxe edition, limited to 1,000 numbered copies, costs $100 plus $5 p&h, and is signed by Morrell and Canty. The seven-by-ten-inch book is enclosed in a stamped traycase. It contains nine full-color tipped-in plates and nine duotone panels. Payable to Donald M. Grant, Publisher, Inc., PO Box 187, Hampton Falls, NH 03844.

Mallory's Oracle by Carol O'Connell (Putnam) is an important suspense debut with a fascinating protagonist—another woman outsider (as in last year's runaway success, *Smilla's Sense of Snow*). The story is about a hard case, adopted off the street as a child by a policeman and his wife after she is caught stealing a car. Now twenty-five, she's only partly civilized, and works as a computer whiz for the police. With an invisible serial killer, occultism, magic, and inside trading, and a host of interesting characters, *Mallory's Oracle* is not surprisingly an Edgar nominee for Best First Novel of 1994. Highly recommended.

Dogs of God by Pinckney Benedict (Nan A. Talese/Doubleday) is a beautifully written literary novel about ugly, violent misfits and violent menace. There are scenes of surreal moment, such as the one where wild pigs rampage through a rundown shack, ripping each other apart, and an owl swooping down on its prey, watched by a starving young man who sees his prey stolen by the quicker predator. A vicious wannabe drug lord is so amoral that he can't understand why anyone would prefer eating grubs for subsistence to cannibalism. The novel ends with hallucinatory transcendence.

Complicity by Iain Banks (Little, Brown-UK/Nan A. Talese/Doubleday) is a mainstream mystery about politics, morality, and violence, but should hold the interest of the horror reader. A burnt-out Scottish journalist is involved in a highly sexual relationship with a friend's wife, while lackadaisically following up dubious leads on various political goings-on. Despite, or perhaps because of, his inability to take responsibility for his actions or inaction, he is implicated in a series of violent attacks on greedy, unethical politicians and businessmen. After a long interrogation, the police are convinced that even if he didn't do it he knows who did. He's forced to dig deep into a past he has almost forgotten to find the perpetrator. A good read.

Novel Listings:

The following are some of the noteworthy novels published in 1994:

Merlin's Wood by Robert Holdstock (HarperCollins-UK); *Panic* by Chris Curry (Pocket); *The Select* by F. Paul Wilson (Morrow); *Taltos* by Anne Rice (Knopf); *Frankenstein's Children—The Creation* by Richard Pierce (Berkley); *The Orchid Eater* by Marc Laidlaw (St. Martin's); *65mm* by Dale Hoover (Dell/Abyss); *When First We Deceive* by Charles Wilson (Carroll & Graf); *Love Bite* by Sherry Gottlieb (Warner); *Passion* by I. U. Tarchetti, translated by Lawrence Venuti (Mercury House); *Spanky* by Christopher Fowler (Warner-UK); *The Vanishment* by Jonathan Aycliffe (HarperPaperbacks); *Deadweight* by Robert Devereaux (Dell/Abyss); *Radon Daughters* by Iain Sinclair (Jonathan Cape-UK); *The Listeners* by Christopher Pike (NEL); *The Wise Woman* by Philippa Gregory (Pocket); *Shelter* by Jayne Anne Phillips (Houghton Mifflin); *The Night Inside* by Nancy Baker (Fawcett Columbine); *Brian Froud's Faerielands: The Wild Wood* by Charles de Lint (Bantam Spectra); *Brian Froud's Faerielands: Something Rich and Strange* by Patricia A. McKillip (Bantam Spectra); *Profile* by C. J. Koehler (Carroll & Graf); *Corruption* by Andrew Klavan (Morrow); *Personal Darkness* by Tanith Lee (Dell/Abyss); *The Dark Room* by Junnosuke Yoshiyuki translated by John Bester (Kodansha International); *Fires of Eden* by Dan Simmons (Putnam); *The Mad Man* by Samuel R. Delany (Richard Kasak Books); *Pandora* by Alan Rodgers (Bantam); *Archangel* by Garry Kilworth (Gollancz-UK); *One Rainy Night* by Richard Laymon (Headline); *The Carnival of Destruction* by Brian Stableford (Carroll & Graf); *Revenant* by Melanie Tem (Dell/Abyss); *Grave Markings* by Michael A. Arnzen (Dell/Abyss); *Near Death* by Nancy Kilpatrick (Pocket); *Sins of the Blood* by Kristine Kathryn Rusch (Dell/Abyss); *The Unusual Life of Tristan Smith* by Peter Carey (Faber & Faber); *The Long Lost* by Ramsey Campbell (Tor); *An Absence of Light* by David Lindsey (Doubleday); *The Secret of Anatomy* by Mark Morris (Piatkus); *The Blood of Angels* by Stephen Gregory (Piatkus); *Fine Lines* by Simon Beckett (Simon & Schuster); *Robinson* by Christopher Petit (Viking); *Sideshow* by Anne D. LeClaire (Viking); *Millroy the Magician* by Paul Theroux (Random House); *The Quorum* by Kim Newman (Carroll & Graf); *Poor Things* by Alasdair Gray (Harcourt, Brace); *The Golem Triptych* by Eric Basso (Asylum Arts); *Dream Palace* by Amanda Moore (Carroll & Graf); *The Museum of Love* by Steve Weiner (Overlook Press); *The Hollowing* by Robert Holdstock (Roc); *Desert Kill* by Philip Gerard (Morrow); *Prophecy* by Peter James (St. Martin's); *Perfectly Pure and Good* by Frances Fyfield (Pantheon); *Gloria* by Mark Coovelis (Pocket); *Dissociated States* by Leonard Simon (Bantam); *The Woman Between the Worlds* by F. Gwynplaine MacIntyre (Dell); *My Idea of Fun* by Will Self (Grove Atlantic); *The Circus of the Earth and the Air* by Brooke Stevens (Harcourt, Brace); *Marble Skin* by Slavenka Drakulic (Norton); *Night Relics* by James P. Blaylock (Ace); *The Scold's Bridle* by Minette Walters (St. Martin's); *Hula* by Lisa Shea (Norton); *Amnesia* by Douglas Cooper (Hyperion); *Everville* by Clive Barker (HarperCollins); *Caliban's Hour* by Tad Williams (HarperPrism); *Dark Rivers of the Heart* by Dean Koontz (Knopf); *The Devil's Own Work* by Alan Judd (Knopf); *The Dissolution of Nicholas Dee* by Matthew Stadler (HarperPerennial); *Snow Angels* by Stewart O'Nan (Doubleday); *The Secret Life of Laszlo Count Dracula* by Roderick Anscombe (Hyperion); *The Informers* by Bret Easton Ellis (Knopf); *Insomnia* by Stephen King (Viking); *The Medusa Child* by

Sylvie Germain (Dedalus); *Lunch* by Karen Moline (William Morrow); *Trash* by Amy Yamada (Kodansha); *Elephantasm* by Tanith Lee (Headline); *A Son of the Circus* by John Irving (Random House); *Mr. Vertigo* by Paul Auster (Viking); *The Caveman's Valentine* by George Dawes Green (Warner); *The Witch's Hammer* by Jane Stanton Hitchcock (Dutton); *The Mysterium* by Eric McCormack (St. Martin's); *Dead in the Water* by Nancy Holder (Dell/Abyss); *Dark of the Eye* by Douglas Clegg (Pocket); *The Fury* by John Farris (Severn House-first hc); *The Minotaur* by John Farris (Severn House-first hc); *The Man in the Moss* by Phil Rickman (Macmillan-UK); *Plato, Animal Lover* by Laren Stover (HarperCollins); *The Secrets of the Camera Obscura* by David Knowles (Chronicle Books); *Brittle Innings* by Michael Bishop (Bantam); *Rat* by Andrzej Zaniewski (Arcade); and *Borderliners* by Peter Høeg (Farrar, Straus & Giroux).

Anthologies:

In order to save space and avoid repetition, authors of notable stories in each anthology are no longer listed here but will be on the recommended list at the back of the book.

There is no sign that the horror anthology market is contracting; a good thing, since there are few regularly published professional horror magazines.

Young Blood edited by Mike Baker (Zebra) is a noteworthy attempt to bring younger (and theoretically newer) horror writers to the attention of readers. The cut-off age is thirty. The results are mixed. The first third (over 120 pages) of the book is filled with stories written by BIG names, such as Edgar Allan Poe, Stephen King, and Robert E. Howard before they were thirty. The rest of the fictions are vivid, interesting, and varied, but barely a handful are *stories*; most are vignettes aiming at effect, a criticism I've leveled against horror writing before (age doesn't seem to be a factor). But some of the work in *Young Blood* is promising.

Surprisingly, 1994 seems to have turned out to be the year of a mini Lovecraft revival. Fans of H. P. Lovecraft will be delighted to know that there were several good anthologies out in 1994 using his mythos. *Cthulhu's Heirs: New Cthulhu Mythos Fiction* edited by Thomas M. K. Stratman (Chaosium) is an original anthology (with two reprints) based on the *Call of Cthulhu* role-playing games, and I admit to being pleasantly surprised by the quality of the stories. Most are well written and a few are quite good. *Shub Niggurath Cycle: She Who Is to Come* edited by Robert M. Price (Chaosium) is half reprints, half original stories. The general quality is high and the reader needs no knowledge of the role-playing game to comprehend and enjoy the stories. $9.95 each, payable to Chaosium Books and Games, 950-A 56th Street, Oakland, CA 94608-3129.

Shadows Over Innsmouth edited by Stephen Jones (Fedogan & Bremer) is a terrific anthology spawned by Lovecraft's "big fish story." Included is the novella that inspired it all—and sixteen originals and reprints from some of the best British writers in the field today. Illustrations by Dave Carson, Martin McKenna, and Jim Pitts are excellent and help make this book collectible. Highly recommended. Trade edition costs $27. The limited edition of 100 copies costs $95 apiece, payable to Fedogan & Bremer, 700 Washington Avenue SE, Suite 50, Minneapolis, MN 55417.

The Starry Wisdom: A Tribute to H. P. Lovecraft edited by D. M. Mitchell (Creation Press-UK) has some experimental fiction as well as more traditional stories. Generally, the latter are more successful and I'd guess would be preferred by Lovecraft fans. Excellent art and design, although the binding began to separate after several readings. $15.95 payable to Creation Books, 83 Clerkenwell Road, London EC1, United Kingdom.

The King Is Dead: Tales of Elvis Postmortem edited by Paul M. Sammon (Delta) has a fun mixture of stories and essays about the great one. Some of the fiction only mentions in Elvis in passing (no pun intended), which is fine and dandy. Some excellent fantasy and dark fantasy.

Shock Rock II edited by Jeff Gelb (Pocket). Yup, it's the follow-up, with sleazoid, drugged out, talentless rock 'n' roll boys banging their guitars and multitudes of dumb, boozy or drugged-out, sex-starved groupies. A sociological nightmare. This one-note depiction of the boys in the bands is distressing and depressing, a violent yawn. Only a few stories stand above the morass.

The Mammoth Book of Werewolves edited by Stephen Jones (Carroll & Graf) is, like 1993's *The Mammoth Book of Zombies*, a large anthology of mostly reprints with some excellent original stories, a poem, and a terrific novella by Kim Newman. The Michael Marshall Smith story is reprinted herein.

Phobias edited by Wendy Webb, Richard Gilliam, Edward Kramer, and Martin H. Greenberg (Pocket) is a solid horror anthology with some very interesting stories from a wide range of contributors. The editors have succeeded in avoiding repetition. The Andrew Klavan short story is reprinted here.

The Science of Sadness edited by Chris Kenworthy (Barrington) is the third in this small-press anthology series from the United Kingdom. Each perfect-bound trade paperback has looked attractive, providing a worthy showcase for newer British writers and the cross-pollination of fiction between genres. Highly recommended, but unfortunately, it's out of print.

Northern Frights 2 edited by Don Hutchison (Mosaic Press-Canada) is the worthy follow-up to the World Fantasy Award–nominated anthology *Northern Frights*. There is some excellent fiction here from north of the border, including two, by Charles Grant and David Nickle, that are reprinted in this anthology. The book can be ordered for $13.95 from Mosaic Press, 85 River Rock Drive, Ste. 202, Buffalo, NY 14207.

Blue Motel: Narrow Houses Volume 3 edited by Peter Crowther (Little, Brown-UK) has the most consistently *interesting* stories of the series (which included *Narrow Houses* and *Touch Wood*). As the theme of "superstition" broadens, the stories have gone farther afield. This volume includes horror, fantasy, and, surprisingly but happily, science fiction. Indeed, some of the best stories—Kathleen Ann Goonan's, for example—are most definitely SF. The Ian McDonald is reprinted here. One of the best anthologies of the year—highly recommended.

Voices From the Night: twenty-seven stories of horror and suspense edited by John Maclay (Maclay Associates) has some ugly and gross stories by familiar names, but too few chills and too little depth. The unenlightening introductory notes are occasionally incoherent. Nice production, bad proofreading. $60 plus $1 shipping for one of 750 numbered and signed slipcased edition. Maclay & Associates, PO Box 16253, Baltimore, MD 21210.

Borderlands 4 edited by Elizabeth E. Monteleone and Thomas F. Monteleone (Borderlands Press), in contrast, provides mostly excellent introductions—although it seems unnecessary to announce that there are no vampires, werewolves, serial killers, ghosts, zombies, mummies, or devil children in the stories, as if their omission influences quality. (And in fact, there *is* a story with several serial killers.) It's what the writer does with these archetypes that counts. Despite this, *Borderlands* 4 is an all-around very good anthology. The William Browning Spencer story is reprinted here. Limited to 500 numbered and slipcased books, signed by the contributors. The attractive cover is by Thomas F. Monteleone and Nelson Ignacio. $65 payable to Borderlands Press, PO Box 146, Brooklandville, MD 21022. 800-528-3310.

Love in Vein edited by Poppy Z. Brite (and Martin H. Greenberg, uncredited except on copyright page) (HarperPrism) is a refreshingly strong anthology on a theme one might think pretty played out. But vampires and vampirism of all sorts seem to have maintained as persistent a hold on writers' imaginations as on readers'; the theme continuing to inspire fascinating and occasionally original material. One of the best anthologies of the year, *Love in Vein* has only a few disappointing contributions. The A. R. Morlan and Douglas Clegg stories are reprinted here. Highly recommended.

Asylum Annual, 1994 edited by Greg Boyd is a perfect-bound magazine/anthology with a nice literary mix of surreal prose and poetry with occasional darker touches. Don Webb and Thomas Wiloch are represented. Recommended for adventurous readers. Can be bought directly from the publisher for $10 an issue, payable to Asylum Arts, PO Box 6203, Santa Maria, CA 93456.

White Wolf's new program, publishing novels and anthologies based on their role-playing, has had varying results. The first two anthologies, published in paperback, *The Beast Within: A Vampire: The Masquerade*™ Anthology and *When Will You Rage?: A Werewolf: The Apocalypse*™ Anthology, both edited by Stewart Wieck, are closely tied into the games and are dull, even occasionally incomprehensible without knowledge of the games from which they derive. Of the other two (both hardcovers), one, *Elric: Tales of the White Wolf* edited by Edward E. Kramer, is an anthology of original stories about the character and world that Michael Moorcock created (White Wolf is reissuing Moorcock's fifteen-book "Eternal Champion" series). Few of the stories stand alone. The writing is uniformly good, but because the contributors are bound by stringent rules, there isn't as much variety as readers might like. Elric fans should enjoy it nonetheless. The beautiful jacket art is by Brom. In contrast, the fourth anthology, *Dark Destiny* edited by Kramer and Richard Gilliam, is quite good, despite depending on the *World of Darkness* template. It contains a more varied and therefore more interesting group of stories, most not dependent on familiarity with the gaming material. *Dark Destiny* has a nice-looking jacket designed by Michelle Prahler, beautifully rendered line drawings throughout by John Cobb, and good production values.

Cold Cuts II: More Tales of Terror edited by Paul Lewis and Steve Lockley (Alun Books) is a second volume of short horror stories from Wales. The emphasis is on psychological horror and the editors have come up with a fine collection of material from some of the best British writers around. Not a clinker in the bunch. Highly recommended.

London Noir edited by Maxim Jakubowski (Serpent's Tail-UK) is an excellent anthology of dark suspense with some very disturbing and powerful stories by horror and suspense authors including Christopher Fowler and Andrew Klavan.

Dark Voices 6 edited by David Sutton and Stephen Jones (Pan) has drifted back to the mixed blessings of its predecessor—the annual *Pan Book of Horror*. An awful lot of misfires and very predictable stories, but as usual, a few standouts.

Deadly After Dark: The Hot Blood Series edited by Jeff Gelb and Michael Garrett (Pocket) has a good mix of sexual horror stories although there are still too many clinkers. A second A. R. Morlan story is reprinted here.

Black Thorn, White Rose edited by Ellen Datlow and Terri Windling (AvoNova) is the second in a series of anthologies containing original stories based on traditional fairy tales. Most of the stories are dark in tone.

Little Deaths edited by Ellen Datlow (Millennium-UK/Dell) is an anthology of mostly original stories of sexual horror. Contributors hail from horror, science fiction, fantasy, and the mainstream. Stories by Jack Womack and M. John Harrison are reprinted here.

The Earth Strikes Back edited by Richard Chizmar (Mark V. Ziesing) has a strong author line-up and an important theme but, for the most part, disappointing, heavy-handed stories. There's an awful lot of mutated sludge and only a few stories stand out. Dust jacket designed by Arnie Fenner, interiors by Robert Frazier. Published only in a trade paperback edition, which can be ordered from Mark V. Ziesing for $18.95 plus $2 p&h. Address on acknowledgments page.

South from Midnight edited by Richard Gilliam, Martin H. Greenberg, and Thomas R. Hanlon (Southern Fried Press) is the limited-edition hardcover anthology put out by the 1994 World Fantasy Convention committee. The stories here all have a Southern flavor, with New Orleans (the site of the convention) occasionally taking a starring role.

A good mix of fiction in a beautiful hardcover designed by Peggy Ranson, with photographs by the late, great photographer of New Orleans, Clarence John Laughlin. But no author bios, no running heads for individual stories, and no accents for all the French words. $25 payable to Southern Fried Press, PO Box 791302, New Orleans, LA 70179-1302.

The Mammoth Book of Frankenstein edited by Stephen Jones (Robinson-UK/Carroll & Graf-US) is an effective combination of original and reprints on the Frankenstein theme. The 570-plus-page volume also includes the entire original novel by Mary Shelley, and novels on the theme by Peter Tremayne and David Case.

The Best of Whispers edited by Stuart David Schiff (Borderlands Press-Whispers Press) is a lovely eulogy for one of the major venues for horror during the 1970s and early 1980s, *Whispers* magazine. In addition to such award-winning classics as "The Chimney," by Ramsey Campbell, "The Dead Line," by Dennis Etchison, "Leaks," by Steve Rasnic Tem, and "Beyond Any Measure," by Karl Edward Wagner, there are six originals here. Jacket and frontispiece by Lee Brown Coye. Highly recommended. $65 limited edition. Order from Borderlands Press.

Weird Menace edited by Fred Olen Ray (American Independent Press) is an anthology that takes readers back to the past, when women were big-boobed, helpless victims and hunky men were heroes. Too graphically sexual for the younger crowd, too silly for the older, this book might be a fun collector's item. It's self-described as "a tasteless tailspin into terror." Fans of B-movies will recognize Fred Olen Ray as the director of many videos. I won't embarrass the contributors by giving their names but if you want to order this trade paperback (first of a projected series) it's $12 plus $2 p&h, payable to American Independent Productions, Inc., PO Box 1901, Hollywood, CA 90078.

Point Horror: Thirteen More Tales of Horror edited by A. Finnis (Scholastic-UK) is a young adult collection with good writers and nicely set-up stories with mostly pat twist endings. Considering some of the usually reliable contributors, though, this is a disappointment.

Return to the Twilight Zone edited by Carol Serling (and Martin H. Greenberg, credited only on the copyright page) (DAW) is a second volume of TZ-type stories. Inconsistent in quality, the stories rarely go beyond the twist ending and a few telegraph that ending two pages in. Included is a reprint by Rod Serling.

The Anthology of Fantasy and the Supernatural edited by Stephen Jones and David Sutton (Tiger Books-UK) is an excellent, mostly original anthology in the tradition of *Fantasy Tales*, the magazine that Jones and Sutton edited 1977–92. Stories by Nicholas Royle and Steve Rasnic Tem are reprinted here.

Ten Tales (no editor listed) published by James Cahill, was issued in a limited slipcased edition of 250 copies signed by all the authors, including Harlan Ellison, Joe R. Lansdale, Richard Laymon, Lucius Shepard, and others. Foreword by Lawrence Block and introduction by Poppy Z. Brite. Originally scheduled for 1993. I believe that these stories are nongenre and some have been published previously. $125, payable to James Cahill Publishing, 9932 Constitution Drive, Huntington Beach, CA 92646.

Other anthologies with minimal horror:

Deadly Allies II: Private Eye Writers of America and Sisters in Crime Collaborative Anthology edited by Robert J. Randisi and Susan Dunlop (Doubleday) is a solid mystery anthology, but has only a couple of stories dark enough to interest horror readers; *Xanadu 2* edited by Jane Yolen (Tor) has very little dark material this time around; *Meltdown: An Anthology of Erotic Science Fiction and Dark Fantasy for Gay Men* edited by Caro Soles (A Richard Kasak Book) is basically gay porn with some fantasy and SF thrown in for respectability—kind of ironic, considering how most genre fiction is treated; *Bruce Coville's Book of Ghosts: Tales to Haunt You* (Apple/Scholastic) is more depressing than frightening but has some excellent stories; *2nd Culprit: A Crime Writers' Association Annual* edited by Liza Cody and Michael Z. Lewin (St. Martin's); *Deals With the Devil* edited by Mike Resnick, Martin H. Greenberg, and Loren D. Estleman (DAW) has a few very strong dark stories; *Tales From the Great Turtle* edited by Piers Anthony and Richard Gilliam (Tor); *Crime Yellow: New Crimes 1* edited by Maxim Jakubowski (Gollancz-UK) is the *New Crimes* Series that started with Robinson, moved to Constable, and is now with Gollancz; *3rd Culprit: A Crime Writers' Annual* edited by Liza Cody, Michael Z. Lewin, and Peter Lovesey (Chatto & Windus-UK/St. Martin's) has some good dark fiction; *Famous Irish Ghost Stories* edited by Mairtin O'Griofa (Sterling/Main Street) gives an Irish flavor to the traditional tale; *The Ghost of Elvis and Other Celebrity Spirits* by Daniel Cohen (G.P. Putnam & Sons) recounts various sightings of Elvis, Abraham Lincoln, Queen Victoria, and others; *The Origins of Desire: Modern Spanish Short Stories* edited by Juan Antonio Masoliver (Serpent's Tail) collects Spanish short stories from the past two decades. From the introduction: "Practically all current fiction is imbued with fantastical elements in the shape of dreams, terror, mystery, omens, or supernatural phenomena, erasing the boundaries between everyday reality and imagination." Disappointingly, the resulting book is twenty-nine very short stories going nowhere, providing little disquiet and straining for effect. *Prairie Fire, a Conadian Magazine of New Writing* was given out at the World SF Convention in Winnipeg. Volume 15 No. 2 concerned itself with "Conadian Speculative Fiction" and was edited by Candas Jane Dorsey. Some very good dark SF; *Bizarre Dreams* edited by Caro Soles and Stan Tal (Bad Boy) is supposed to explore "the dark side of human fantasy," but most of the stories concentrate more on graphic gay erotica rather than horror and dark material. Only a few authors in this anthology successfully combine the two elements, transcending dull writing about the pounding of sex organs with style, heat, and horror; *Blood Kiss: Vampire Erotica* edited by Cecilia Tan (Circlet Press, Inc.); *Mysterious Christmas Tales* with illustrations by David Wyatt (no editor credited) (Point/Scholastic Children's Books) has a few good darker stories; *The Junky's Christmas and Other Yuletide Stories* edited by Elisa Segrave (Serpent's Tail) has dark stories by William S. Burroughs, Frank Tuohy, William Trevor, and other writers.

Reprint Anthologies:

(I have not seen some of the following.)

Death on the Veranda: Mystery Stories of the South edited by Cynthia Manson (Carroll & Graf) collects sixteen stories that originally appeared in *Ellery Queen's Mystery Magazine* and *Alfred Hitchcock Mystery Magazine*. Spanning the 1920s up to 1993, it includes stories by Flannery O'Connor, Raymond Carver, MacKinley Cantor, and Eudora Welty; *The Oxford Book of Fantasy Stories* selected by Tom Shippey (Oxford University Press) is the companion volume to Shippey's 1993 anthology *The Oxford Book of Science Fiction*. A collection of varied stories by H. P. Lovecraft, Clark Ashton Smith, C. L. Moore, Fritz Leiber, Manley Wade Wellman, Avram Davidson, Angela Carter, Tanith Lee, Lucius Shepard, and Robert Holdstock; *H. P. Lovecraft's Book of Horror* edited by Stephen Jones and Dave Carson (Robinson-UK) collects twenty-one stories recommended by Lovecraft in his groundbreaking essay *Supernatural Horror in Literature*. The essay is reprinted here as well; *Playboy Stories: The Best of Forty Years of Short Fiction* edited by Alice K. Turner (E. P. Dutton) collects a piece of fiction from each year in which *Playboy* has published original stories. Included are many writers who veer into the macabre and the fantastic, such as Charles Beaumont, Ray Bradbury, Shirley Jackson, Roald Dahl, John Collier, Jorge Luis Borges, T. Coraghessan Boyle, Ursula K. Le Guin, Isaac Bashevis Singer, Joyce Carol Oates, and Haruki Murakami; *Holy Terror* edited by Carol Anthony (Carroll & Graf) collects twenty-six stories in which crime meets religion, with contributions by Ruth Rendell, Tony Hillerman, Frederick Forsyth, P. D. James, Isaac Bashevis Singer, and others; *Women of Mystery* and *Women of Mystery II*, both edited by Cynthia Manson (Carroll & Graf), collects stories by Sharyn McCrumb, Marcia Muller, Joan Hess, Ruth Rendell, and others from *Ellery Queen's* and *Hitchcock*; *Seacursed: Thirty Terrifying Tales of the Deep* edited by T. Liam McDonald, Stefan Dziemianowicz, and Martin H. Greenberg (Barnes & Noble Books) is exactly what the title and subtitle suggest, with contributions by among others, Roald Dahl, Jack Cady, Roger Zelazny, Nancy Holder, Robert Aickman, Joseph Conrad, Jack Dann, and a short novel by William Hope Hodgson. Also, *100 Creepy Little Creature Stories* selected by Robert Weinberg, Stefan Dziemianowicz, and Martin H. Greenberg (Barnes & Noble Books) reprints very short stories by M. R. James, August Derleth, Ramsey Campbell, Ambrose Bierce, Joe R. Lansdale, Horacio Quiroga, Lafcadio Hearn, Donald A. Wollheim, Carl Jacobi, Thomas Ligotti, Steve Rasnic Tem, among others, with seven originals; and *100 Wild Little Weird Tales* edited by Weinberg, Dziemianowicz, and Greenberg (B&N) uses stories from the first incarnation of *Weird Tales* (all available only at Barnes & Noble bookstores); *Grails: Visitations of the Night* and *Grails: Quests of the Dawn* edited by Richard Gilliam, Martin H. Greenberg, and Edward E. Kramer (Roc) are a slightly expanded two-volume trade paperback set of the 1992 World Fantasy Convention special giveaway hardcover, *Grails: Quests, Visitations and Other Occurrences*. Each volume has several original stories, few as good as those in the earlier, already massive tome; *The Year's 25 Finest Crime and Mystery Stories: Third Annual Edition* edited by the Staff of *Mystery Scene* (Carroll & Graf) has a crop of the best of 1993 including the Edgar Award—winning "Keller's Therapy," by Lawrence Block, and stories by Ruth Rendell, George Alec Effinger, Tony Hillerman, Robert Bloch, and F. Paul Wilson. The venues for original publication are more limited than last year's choices; *The Year's Best Mystery and Suspense Stories 1994* edited by Edward D. Hoch (Walker) also contains Block's award winner in addition to stories by Kate Wilhelm, Donald E. Westlake, David Ely, and Miriam Grace Monfredo. There is some overlap with the Carroll & Graf book; *The Best From Fantasy & Science Fiction* edited by Edward L. Ferman and Kristine Kathryn Rusch is an odd "45th anniversary anthology"—there's nothing in it prior to 1988. A *Modern Treasury of Great Detective and Murder Mysteries* edited by Ed Gorman (Carroll & Graf) and introduced by Jon L. Breen's concise overview of changes in the mystery field during the past twenty years—stories by Margaret Millar, Robert Bloch, Lawrence Block, Sharyn McCrumb, Edward Bryant, F. Paul Wilson, and others; *Fun and Games at the Whacks Museum and Other Horror Stories* edited by Cathleen Jordan (Simon & Schuster Books for Young Readers); *Tomorrow Sucks* edited by Greg Cox and T. K. F. Weisskopf (Baen) contains eleven stories of scientific vampirism by writers such as Ray Bradbury, Roger Zelazny, Brian Stableford, Keith Roberts, Spider Robinson, Susan Petrey, and S. N. Dyer (but must "Shambleau," by Moore, be reprinted yet again?); *The Norton Book of Ghost Stories* edited by Brad Leithauser (Norton) collects twenty-eight stories, five from Henry James, five from M. R. James, the rest by authors such as Saki, Oliver Onions, Shirley Jackson, John Cheever, and A. S. Byatt. The narrow selection may indicate a lack of familiarity with much of the field; *Great Irish Tales of the Unimaginable: Stories of Fantasy and Myth* edited and introduced by Peter Haining (Souvenir) has twenty-four stories inspired by Celtic legends and folklore by W. B. Yeats, James Joyce, and lesser-known names; *Tales from the Rogues' Gallery* edited by Peter Haining (Little Brown-UK) has fictions, fantasies, and documentary studies of murderers from history; *Mystery For Christmas* edited by Richard Dalby (St. Martin's/A Thomas Dunne Book—1st US pub.) anthologizes twenty-three tales of murder, ghosts, and bizarre disappearances; *Fantasy Stories* edited by Diana Wynne-Jones (Kingfisher-UK, YA) has one original novelette by the editor and reprints by Charles Dickens, Thomas Hardy, Muriel Spark, and H. R. F. Keating; *The Best New Horror* edited by Stephen Jones and Ramsey Campbell (Robinson-UK/Carroll & Graf-US) collects stories by Kathe Koja, Edward Bryant, Poppy

Z. Brite, Thomas Ligotti, Elizabeth Hand, Dennis Etchison, and others. Two stories overlap with *The Year's Best Fantasy and Horror: Seventh Annual Collection* and three (two different ones) overlap with Karl Edward Wagner's *The Year's Best Horror Stories XII* (DAW). The only story in all three volumes is the British Fantasy Award–winning "The Dog Park," by Dennis Etchison; *The Mammoth Book of Erotica* edited by Maxim Jakubowski (Carroll & Graf) has horror reprints by Kathy Acker, Lucy Taylor, Clive Barker, Adam-Troy Castro, and an excerpt from Anne Rice; *The Young Oxford Book of Ghost Stories* edited by Dennis Pepper (Oxford University Press) reprints ghost stories by E. F. Benson, Vivian Alcock, M. R. James, Gerald Kersh, E. Nesbit, and Robert Westall, with three originals; *Deadly Sins* by Thomas Pynchon, Mary Gordon, John Updike, William Trevor, Gore Vidal, Richard Howard, A. S. Byatt, and Joyce Carol Oates with illustrations by Etienne Delessert (Morrow) collects essays originally commissioned and published in *The New York Times Book Review*; *Lust, Violence, Sin, Magic: 60 Years of Esquire Fiction* edited by Rust Hills, Will Blythe, and Erika Mansourian includes stories by fantasists T. Coraghessan Boyle, Flannery O'Connor, William Kotzwinkle (a piece that eventually went into his novel *The Fan Man*), Ray Bradbury's classic, "The Illustrated Man," and Gabriel García Márquez; *Wolf's Complete Book of Terror* edited by Leonard Wolf (Newmarket Press) collects forty-one tales of terror, many familiar, but a few refreshingly new, such as those by Joyce Carol Oates, Kathe Koja, and others, like the Le Guin, not often found in horror anthologies; *The Chatto Book of Ghosts* edited by Jenny Uglow (Chatto & Windus-UK); *Ghostly Haunts* edited by Michael Morpurgo and illustrated by Nilesh Mistry (Pavilion Books-UK); *The Penguin Book of Indian Ghost Stories* edited by Ruskin Bond (Penguin Books India, Ltd., 1993); *The Frankenstein Omnibus* edited by Peter Haining (Orion-UK) is a huge historical overview of short fiction (many early tales forgotten or by writers unknown today) related to the Frankenstein archetype. Includes movie and television scripts, and short stories by Herman Melville, H. P. Lovecraft, Fritz Leiber, Brian Aldiss, William Tenn, Kurt Vonnegut, Jr., Arthur C. Clarke, and Theodore Sturgeon; *The Penguin Book of Scottish Folktales* edited by Neil Philip (Penguin-UK); *Wild Women: Contemporary Short Stories for Women Who Run with the Wolves* edited by Sue Thomas (Penguin-UK) includes stories by Angela Carter, Tanith Lee, and Lisa Tuttle; *Murder For Halloween* edited by Michele Slung and Roland Hartman (Mysterious Press) is an entertaining, mostly reprint anthology of such classics as "The Cloak," by Robert Bloch, "The Black Cat," by Edgar Allan Poe, and "Walpurgis Night," by Bram Stoker, with a few good originals, including one by Ed McBain and a brilliant mystery novella by Peter Straub; *Masterpieces of Terror and the Unknown* edited by Marvin Kaye (St. Martin's) collects some rarely anthologized stories by writers such as Joyce Carol Oates, Richard Matheson, Winston Churchill, and Jack Vance, and several original stories; the stories in *The Outspoken Princess and the Gentle Knight: A Treasury of Modern Fairy Tales* edited by Jack Zipes, illustrated by Stéphane Poulin (Bantam) are like no fairy tales you read as a child. Here, Little Red Riding Hood knows the score, a brave but monogamous bull bites the dust, and there are no shrinking violets. Stories by Jane Yolen, Tanith Lee, A. S. Byatt, and Ernest Hemingway.

Short Story Collections:

The Early Years (Fedogan and Bremer) collects all of Robert Bloch's stories from his out-of-print collections, *The Opener of the Way* and *Pleasant Dreams*, plus three previously uncollected stories. This important 500-plus-page hardcover contains thirty-nine stories in all, by the writer who created the character of Norman Bates. None of these stories appeared in the erroneously titled *Complete Short Stories of Robert Bloch*. Jacket art by Jon Arfstrom. $29 for a trade edition and $60 for a 100-copy limited edition, plus $1.50 p&h per book. Also, Carl Jacobi's collection of fifteen stories, *Smoke of the Snake*, with jacket art by Jon

Arfstrom and interior illustrations by Roger Gerberding. $28 + $1.50 payable to Fedogan and Bremer. See address under Anthologies page xliii.

Noctuary (Carroll & Graf) is Thomas Ligotti's third collection. All but one story have appeared in various magazines and anthologies (although first publication credits are omitted). The normally reticent Ligotti graces the collection with an intelligent meditation on "weird fiction."

Oddly Enough by Bruce Coville from Harcourt Brace's Jane Yolen imprint is an excellent collection from this YA author. Beautiful, clever, moving, and funny stories, three of which are original to the collection. "Blaze of Glory" is particularly good (fantasy).

St. Martin's Press collects four novellas by Geoff Ryman in *Unconquered Countries*: the World Fantasy Award–winning "The Unconquered Country," "O Happy Day!" and two originals, one of which, "Fan," was nominated for the Nebula Award.

Irrational Numbers by David Langford (Necronomicon Press) is a collection of one excellent reprint (from *The Weerde: Book 2*) and two excellent new Lovecraftian tales with illustrations by Jason C. Eckardt. $5.95 payable to Necronomicon Press, PO Box 1304, West Warwick, RI 02893.

The Flesh Artist by Lucy Taylor (Silver Salamander Press) has a bit more torture and mutilation than I feel comfortable reading about, but Taylor is doing some interesting experimenting in voice and tone. Introduction by Norman Partridge. Published in three formats: 50 copies, bound in leather, numbered 1–50 for $65; 300 copies, bound in cloth numbered 1–300 for $30, and 500 copies, perfect-bound, unnumbered for $12. Also from Silver Salamander comes Kim Antieau's first collection of science fiction, fantasy, and horror, *Trudging to Eden*. It includes six new stories in addition to the reprints. Introduction by Charles de Lint. Same prices and formats as above. $2.00 p&h per book. Can be ordered through Blue Moon Books, 360 West First, Eugene, OR 97401.

Unnatural Acts and Other Stories (Richard Kasak) by Lucy Taylor is an expansion of her three-story chapbook published two years ago. The nine stories are an effective mix with five originals. Some of Taylor's work is brilliant, such as "The Safety of Unknown Cities," which has since been expanded into a novel. All of her work is intense, some is grotesque, and occasionally she veers into the repellant. There's a fine line between inspiring terror/horror and repugnance, and Taylor still crosses that line far too often. Yet she is capable of writing with great subtlety.

Black Leather Required by David J. Schow (Mark V. Ziesing) collects twelve stories and a playlet in a hardcover attractively produced and designed by Arnie Fenner and Robert Frazier. Raunchy and raucous, sometimes simply gross, the stories at the very least sing with energy and sparkling prose even if on occasion they don't quite satisfy. Included is a beautiful, melancholy sort of ghost story, "Sand Sculpture." $29.95 for the trade hardcover; $65 for the limited edition. No first publication credits are given.

The Calvin Coolidge Home for Dead Comedians and *A Conflagration Artist*, both by Bradley Denton, are published in three editions by The Wildside Press. The premier edition consists of 26 lettered copies, bound in elephant-hide paper and imported French snakeskin cloth, signed and slipcased in mahogany. $250 per set; a deluxe edition of 100 signed and numbered copies bound in leather and imported French snakeskin cloth. Without slipcase: $125 per set; trade edition of 300 copies bound in elephant-hide paper and snakeskin cloth without slipcase is $35 per volume. Introductions by Steve Gould and Howard Waldrop, respectively. Both books are illustrated by Doug Potter. $4 p&h, payable to The Wildside Press, 37 Fillmore Street, Newark, NJ 07105. "A Conflagration Artist," original to the collection, is reprinted here.

Travellers in Magic by Lisa Goldstein (Tor) is this American Book Award winner's first collection. Goldstein writes literate contemporary fantasy (with a touch of magical realism), making occasional forays into the past. Darkness lurks around the edges. Two of the stories are originals.

Hostilities: Nine Bizarre Stories by Caroline McDonald (Scholastic) is an excellent collection of ghostly tales for young adults.

People of the Night by s. darnbrook colson (Three-Stones Publications) is part of the Detours chapbook series. It contains three tales of post-apocalyptic sleaze, ugliness, and savagery. The title story is all build-up leading to very little. This 1,000-copy limited paperback has an introduction by Wayne Allen Sallee and cover art by B. E. Bothell. $5.95 payable to Three-Stones Publications, PO Box 69917, Seattle, WA 98168-0817.

Haunted: Tales of the Grotesque (E.P. Dutton/A William Abrahams Book) is by the multitalented Joyce Carol Oates, who writes stories ranging from mainstream to SF, fantasy, and horror. This is her second collection of dark stories (*Night-Side* was the first). The stories are from a variety of publications: mainstream, literary press, science fiction magazines, and horror anthologies. Oates's short essay defines the grotesque as a more visceral horror than that of, say, Victorian ghost stories, which are usually too genteel to be considered horror. Grotesque horror is the antithesis of "nice."

The Earth Wire and other stories by Joel Lane (Egerton) is a wonderful collection by one of several talented young British male writers. The stories portray a desolute, postindustrial, post-Thatcherite, very gray Great Britain, with personal relationships the only thing that can ever bring life to the cities and their inhabitants. Lane depicts an almost devolutionary process of urban decay and depression. This peculiarly horrific science fiction uses a running motif of relationships with actual physical bonds. A few of the stories don't pay off but the talent is evident even in the few missteps. Beautiful production in classy paperback. Egerton Press, 5 Windsor Court, London N15 5JQ, England, 6.99 pounds—$20 in the United States. It may be sold out by the time this appears, so query first.

Altmann's Tongue by Brian Evenson (Alfred A. Knopf) marks the auspicious debut of an author of strange, unsettling, and ultimately frightening vignettes and tales of horror. The stories, mostly contemporary and psychological rather than supernatural, occasionally remind one of Mary Gaitskill's collection *Bad Behavior*. Some of the stories have appeared in genre venues like *Air Fish* and *Magical Realism*. Others are from literary magazines.

Haunted Bayou and other cajun ghost stories by J. J. Eneaux (August House) are "life affirming" (read moralistic) folktales. Similar in feel to urban legends but with a cajun flavor.

Shades of Darkness: More of the Ghostly Best Stories is the second volume of collected short fiction by the late Robert Westall (Farrar, Straus & Giroux). Westall, a master of the subtle ghost story, was usually marketed in the young-adult category (as is this collection), which may have prevented him from developing a larger audience. Contains one excellent original.

Brian Lumley's second collection of short stories, *Dagon's Bell and Other Discords*, was published in the United Kingdom by New English Library. Lumley often delves into Lovecraftian territory with notable results. Included is one of my favorites, the chilling "The Picknickers."

Terminal Weird by Jack Remick (Black Heron Press) has interesting cross-genre material: most of the stories are surreal, reminiscent of Tim Ferret's fiction. Not for everyone but of interest to those who enjoyed the (unfortunately now defunct) magazines *Strange Plasma* and *New Pathways*. Some of the stories first appeared in *Pig Iron Magazine*, *Carolina Quarterly*, and *The Anchovy Review*. Black Heron Press, PO Box 95676, Seattle, WA 98145.

Nightshades by Tanith Lee (Headline) was mentioned last year but not seen until 1994. A wonderful collection of twelve varied stories and one novella, all originally published in the late-1970s and 1980s.

Under the Crust: Supernatural Tales of Buxton by Terry Lamsley (Wendigo), with photographs of Michael Patey-Ford, took the field by storm last year when the self-published collection and two of the stories were nominated for the World Fantasy Award (the title novella won). I'm afraid this was one book I missed in 1993. It was self-published by

Lamsley in Great Britain and Karl Edward Wagner told me about it this past September. Karl was the one who brought it to the attention of the World Fantasy judges as well. All that aside, the book is a very nicely produced trade paperback, with some wonderfully creepy stories in it.

Hollywood Nocturnes (Otto Penzler/Scribner's) collects five previously published stories and an original novella by crime writer James Ellroy, along with an introduction by Ellroy explaining how he came to write "Dick Contino's Blues." Ellroy's métier is dark, edgy suspense, usually quite good.

Those Whom the Old Gods Love by Harvey Peter Sucksmith launches The Ghost Story Press's series of new, previously unpublished collections, each to be signed by the author. These will alternate with reprints of older rare collections. *Those Whom the Old Gods Love* is a determinedly old-fashioned collection of nine ghost stories that vary in effectiveness. Most are deadly serious and not much fun. Only one is previously published. An insufferably smug introduction defines how a ghost story *must* be written. This book is especially disappointing because the volume is a nicely produced hardcover with excellent jacket and interior illustrations by Andrew King. The edition, now out of print, was limited to 200 numbered copies signed by the author; *Tales of the Grotesque* by L. A. Lewis, with stories originally published in the 1930s "Creeps" series, is also limited to 200 copies at £16.50 plus £4.50 for airmail postage; *Story of a Troll-Hunt* written and drawn by James McBryde is a hardback facsimile of a privately printed edition published in 1899 with an introduction by M. R. James. Limited to 300 copies at £16.50 plus £5.75 airmail postage; and *Tales of the Supernatural* by James Platt, originally published in 1894 as an extremely fragile ephemeral shilling paperback. Limited to 300 numbered copies with an introduction by Richard Dalby and a posthumous memoir by Platt's brother William. £20 plus £4.45, payable by international money order or British £-check to Ghost Story Press, BM Wound, London WC1N 3XX, United Kingdom.

The Ghost Story Society and Ash-Tree Press have collaborated on another interesting little item, *Lady Stanhope's Manuscript and Other Supernatural Tales*, an anthology of five original stories edited and with an introduction by Barbara Roden. A few of the stories are excellent. This paperback is illustrated by Pat Walsh, Dallas Goffin, Nick Maloret, and Alan Hunter; *Two Ghost Stories* by L. T. C. Rolt, both reprints, edited by Christopher Roden and Barbara Roden with an introduction by the former, illustrated by Dallas Goffin. The cost is $9 for nonmembers of the Society. One can join the Society for $30, airmail membership, or $24 for surface mail. Members receive *All Hallows*, the thrice-yearly journal of the Ghost Story Society. Members can exchange thoughts and ideas via the Journal, and at occasional meetings. The Ghost Story Society, Ashcroft, 2 Abbotsford Drive, Penyffordd, Chester, CH4 OJG, United Kingdom.

Doorway to Eternity by Sean Williams (MirrorDanse Books) collects three novelettes by this young Australian writer. Two are science fiction and one is a ghost story, but there are horrific aspects to all three. Foreword by Bill Congreve, illustrations by Antoinette Rydyr and Steve Carter. This small trade paperback is limited to 400 copies; the first fifty are signed. Prices are $15 A on an Australian bank or $11 U.S. cash, payable to MirrorDanse Books. 1/26 Central Avenue, Westmead, NSW 2145 Australia.

Wordcraft of Oregon published Misha's cross-genre collection of twenty-three stories, *Ke-Qua-Hawk-As*. About half the stories are originals. Cover and interior art is by Ferret. This 96-page, perfect-bound limited edition of 250 is signed and numbered and costs $8.95. Lance Olsen's surreal collection of twenty-one short stories, *Scherzi, I Believe*, was published under the Jazz Police Books imprint. Suitably surreal cover art is by Andi Olsen. Also limited to 250 signed and numbered copies. 130 pages, perfect-bound, this one costs $9.95. Both payable to Wordcraft of Oregon, PO Box 3235, La Grande, OR 97850.

The Small Dark Room of the Soul and other stories by Matthew J. Pallarmy (San Diego

Writers' Monthly Press) is available for $9.95 plus $2 postage as a trade paperback and a limited edition for $14.95 plus $2 postage from San Diego Writers' Monthly Press, 3910 Chapman Street, San Diego, CA 92110.

CD Publications published Joe R. Lansdale's newest collection, *Writer of the Purple Rage*, with an introduction and story notes by Lansdale. The book has a suitably grotesque jacket art by Mark Nelson. The limited edition of 500 copies features a comic adaptation called "The Grease Trap," illustrated by Ted Naifeh (and which originally appeared in *Under Ground*), the comic script, and an essay that Lansdale wrote about Ray Bradbury's *The October Country* for *Horror's 100 Best Books*. The collection reprints such Lansdale classics as "The Phone Woman," "Incident on and off a Mountain Road," and "Drive-in Date" and includes some good new material. A trade edition is also available for $25 payable to CD Publications, PO Box 18433, Baltimore, MD 21237.

Barry Hoffman, publisher of *Gauntlet* magazine, has started a hardcover imprint and intends to publish two books a year. The debut title, published in September, was Nancy A. Collins's first collection, *Nameless Sins*, with an introduction by Joe R. Lansdale and an afterword by Neil Gaiman. It features twenty-four stories spanning Collins's career from the early eighties through 1994, including the classics "Freaktent," "The Two-Headed Man," and "The Sunday-Go-to-Meeting Jaw." I personally prefer Collins's "Southern" stories—her distinctive voice is used best in these. The striking jacket collage is by Joe Christ. Limited to 500 signed, numbered, slipcased copies at $60. Payable to *Gauntlet*, 309 Powell Road, Springfield, PA 19064.

Borderlands Press published a new edition of Harlan Ellison's classic collection, *The Beast that Shouted Love at the Heart of the World*, which includes Ellison's original introduction and a lovely appreciation of Ellison by Neil Gaiman. Overton Lloyd produced the excellent cover art; the book is nicely designed by Ellison and Borderlands publisher Thomas F. Monteleone. The signed, numbered, slipcased 500-copy limited edition is $65. A lettered deluxe edition was announced for $450. Pay Borderland Press. See address under Anthologies on page xliv.

Earth Prime Productions published Cliff Burns's *Genuinely Inspired Primitive*, a collection of his vignettes and prose poems with cover and interior graphics by Sherron Harman Burns. $4.95, payable to the author, Box 478, Iqaluit, NWT XOA OHO, Canada.

P. H. Cannon is the author of three stories that place P. G. Wodehouse's Jeeves and Bertie Wooster into the middle of Lovecraft stories in Wodecraft Press's *Scream for Jeeves: A Parody*. The book includes an essay on Wodehouse, Lovecraft, and Arthur Conan Doyle and illustrations by J. C. Eckhardt for $7.50 in paperback and $20 for a hardcover edition plus $1.50, payable to Necronomicon Press, See address under Collections on page l.

Graham Masterton's *Fortnight of Fear* (Severn House) collects fourteen recent stories (no publication credits given) including "Hurry Monster," which appeared as a chapbook a few years ago, "Eric the Pie," which was censored in the U.K., and other stories from various anthologies.

Transylvania Press is Canadian Robert Eighteen-Bisang's new press devoted to vampire fiction. In its first year it brought out *The Vampire Stories of Chelsea Quinn Yarbro*, seven stories about the Count Saint-Germain, plus two others, one original. Introduction by Gahan Wilson, appendices by Yarbro, and bibliography by publisher Robert Eighteen-Bisang. The 500-copy signed, numbered, slipcased hardcover edition features jacket art by Donna Baspaly and Patricia Peacock. $65 payable to Transylvania Press, Box 154, 106-1656 Martin Drive, White Rock, BC V4A 6E7, Canada.

Other Collections:

The Supernatural Tales of Sir Arthur Conan Doyle edited by Peter Haining (Foulsham); *Ghosties and Ghoulies* by Stanley Robertson (Balnain Books-UK); *Fine Feathers and Other*

Stories by E. F. Benson, edited by Jack Adrian (Oxford University Press-UK); *Mad Monkton and Other Stories by Wilkie Collins* (Oxford University Press-UK); *Shadows & Whispers: Tales from the Other Side* by Colin McDonald (Penguin/Cobblehill), a YA collection of eight horror stories; *Women and Ghosts* by Alison Lurie (Nan A. Talese/Doubleday) is more fantasy than horror—not very spooky; Rikki Ducornet's *The Complete Butcher's Tales* (Dalkey Archive Press) takes stories from this fantasist's earlier literary-press collections and uncollected magazine stories; Damian Sharp's debut, *When A Monkey Speaks: and Other Stories From Australia* (HarperCollins West), is a varied collection of eleven stories. Sharp writes adroitly of the relationships of his characters to the wildness and beauty of the land. There's no outright horror here, but it's still worth a look; *The Stories of Stephen Dixon* (Henry Holt) collects sixty stories culled from thirty years by an author compared to Kafka, Beckett, and Lewis Carroll. Snappy, sharp dialogue and matter-of-fact absurdity are his hallmarks; *A Tupolev Too Far* (St. Martin's) collects mostly recent stories by Brian Aldiss from such varied sources as the magazines *Interzone*, *Fantasy & Science Fiction*, and *Punch* and the anthologies *The Ultimate Frankenstein*, *Other Edens 1* and 2, and *Dark Fantasies*; *Without A Hero and other stories* by T. Coraghessan Boyle (Viking) is Boyle's fourth collection of witty and often nasty satire that crosses over into fantasy and the horrific more times than not; *Good Bones and Simple Murders* by Margaret Atwood (Doubleday) collects stories from two earlier volumes, *Murder in the Dark* and *Good Bones*; a trio of mainstream collections: *Dear Dead Person* (High Risk) is an interesting debut collection by Benjamin Weissman. The best of these highly stylized stories are those about surreal psychokillers. Some are mere vignettes that try too hard to be cool; *The Other World* by John Wynne is a so-so collection. Serial killers and maimers and rapists have jumped into the mainstream short story—there are the same domestic squabbles but now there's the added oomph of danger and a whiff of violence. The dull, placid mainstream short story of the eighties has given way to the dull, violent mainstream short story of the nineties; in contrast, *A Stranger in This World* by Keven Canty (Doubleday) is a nicely twisted group of dark and ugly stories in which people invariably do the wrong thing. It's worth looking for. Strangely, the typeface used has no question mark and uses instead what looks like a foreign letter. What happened to readable type and intelligent book design? *Human Nature* by Alice Anderson (NYU Press) is utterly horrifying and graceful nongenre poetry about incest and its legacy of pain, guilt and violence; *Mysteries of the Worm* by Robert Bloch (Chaosium) is a revised and expanded collection of Bloch's Cthulhu Mythos stories which includes three additional stories, a new introduction by Robert M. Price, the original introduction by Lin Carter, and the author's afterword; *A Darker Side of Pale* by Sabine Bussin (The Book Guild-UK) is a collection of macabre tales based on traditional horror motifs; *Irish Ghost and Hauntings* by Michael Scott (Warner-UK); *Don't Open the Door After the Sun Goes Down: Tales of the Real and Unreal* by Al Carusone (Clarion-YA); *Scared to Death and Other Ghostly Stories* by Josephine Poole (Hutchinson-UK-YA); *The Real Opera Ghost and Other Tales* by Gaston Leroux (Alan Sutton-UK) collects ten macabre stories by the author of *The Phantom of the Opera*. Edited and with an introduction by Peter Haining.

Nonfiction Magazines:

Afraid: The Newsletter for the Horror Professional, edited by Mike Baker, is in its third year of publication. It missed the February issue because of the L.A. earthquake but was back on schedule with March. There are some useful regular columns such as "The Good News," market reports, and book reviews and there's usually at least one provocative, or at least annoying, article by one of the regulars. Number 25 had a good article by J. F. Gonzales about starting a magazine and what to expect. Baker announced the magazine would experience a hiatus in early 1995. *Afraid*, 857 N. Oxford Avenue #4, Los Angeles, CA 90029.

The Gila Queen's Guide to Markets, edited by Kathryn Ptacek, is jam-packed with publishing news and market information. It regularly publishes special issues with mini market reports on topics such as contests, New Age publications, romance markets, health/medical/fitness markets and useful articles on surviving a convention, being on a panel, pros and cons of writers workshops. Attractively laid out and easily read, this is a must for writers looking to expand their markets. A one-year subscription (12 issues) is $30 (U.S.), $34 (Canada), $48 (overseas). Single issues available for $5. All funds in U.S. dollars: checks and money orders payable to Kathryn Ptacek, *The Gila Queen's Guide to Markets*, PO Box 97, Newton, NJ 07860-0097.

Necrofile, edited by Stefan Dziemianowicz, S. T. Joshi, and Michael A. Morrison, covers a variety of horror material in its reviews and essays and is the major critical journal of the horror field. In #11, Rob Latham reviews novels by Richard Christian Matheson, Philip Nutman, and John Skipp and Craig Spector. His sometimes insightful critique of the splatterpunk movement and its relationship to science fiction's cyberpunk movement of the early 1980s is weakened once he starts naming names. First praising the only writers from the cyberpunk movement he respects, he then calls others "affiliates," "coattail-riders or shrewd hacks" or "cynical copycats strip-mining a profitable subgeneric niche . . ." He does the same with the splatterpunks. While readers might agree that there are a lot of people out there writing generic cyber- or splatterpunk, his judgment of *motivation* in writers he doesn't know personally is pretty harsh, not to mention unfair. Number 12 hasn't got anything as controversial as the Latham review. All the issues have thoughtful in-depth reviews of novels, anthologies, collections, and nonfiction; mini book reviews; and Ramsey Campbell's regular column. A one-year (four-issue) subscription is $12, payable to Necronomicon Press and well worth the while of any serious horror reader. Other regular journals from Necronomicon Press are: *Other Dimensions*, edited by Stefan Dziemianowicz. The second issue has an in-depth critique of the movie version of Clive Barker's "The Forbidden," (*Candyman*) by Douglas E. Winter, an article by Brian Stableford on the ongoing censorhship problems of David Britton's *Lord Horror*, and a piece on the demise of the horror anthology in comic book form by Jack Skrip, plus some reviews. $5. *Lovecraft Studies* edited by S. T. Joshi, $5; *Studies in Weird Fiction*, also edited by Joshi, purports to "promote the criticism of fantasy, horror, and supernatural fiction subsequent to Poe; particular emphasis will be given to such writers as Arthur Machen, Lord Dunsany, Algernon Blackwood, Clark Ashton Smith, William Hope Hodgson, Robert E. Howard, M. R. James, Ramsey Campbell, T. E. D. Klein, and others." Why them, and what others? It's clear that this magazine represents the editor's odd literary enthusiasms, yet there are critical pieces on Shirley Jackson, Poppy Z. Brite, and Dennis Etchison. Joshi himself has been developing a reputation in the past year as one of the *nastiest* reviewers in the horror field. Both journals are $5 per year. Number 14 has an essay on Edgar Allan Poe that Karel Čapek wrote when he was eighteen, published here in English for the first time. See address under Collections on page l.

Fangoria, edited by Anthony Timpone, is the gorefest of the horror movie magazines, big on special effects, the ickier the better. *Fango* has the best photo previews of splatter movies and seems to be aimed at the teens who flock to them. Unfortunately, most coverage of the more commercial films seems dictated by the studios' publicity. But the rest, the book reviews, David J. Schow's entertaining "raving and drooling" column, and the Louapre and Sweetman *Wasteland* cartoon are the best things about the magazine (not to mention the joy of reading it on the subway, with the always-disgusting cover prominently displayed). There was extensive coverage of *The Crow* in the June issue, with a personal point of view, by Schow, who co-wrote the screenplay with John Shirley. The October issue had an important article by Mark Kermode on the increase of censorship in the United Kingdom. Finally, a *Gorezone* special Frankenstein collector's issue with excellent pieces by David

J. Skal and Linda Marotta coincided with the opening of Kenneth Branagh's *Mary Shelley's Frankenstein*.

Gauntlet: Exploring the Limits of Free Expression edited by Barry Hoffman. The theme of #7 is "In Defense of Prostitution." It's the best issue yet, marred only by an exploitative cover. Activist and artist Carol Leigh guest edited this issue, which explores many different points of view on this provocative subject, ranging from those involved in the sex industry to those offended by it. Number 8 focuses on cults, with an article about Scientology's supposed litigation against negative media and part 1 of an exposé of Alcoholics Anonymous and other twelve-step programs. Also discussed is the Mike Diana controversy in Florida's Pinellas County, extensively quoting Diana himself. A one-year (two-issue) subscription is $22, payable to *Gauntlet*, Inc., Dept. SUB94A, 309 Powell Road, Springfield, PA 19064.

Scarlet Street, edited by Richard Valley, concentrates on (mostly Sherlockian) mystery movies and sometimes covers horror. Number 13 has a profile of noir actress and director Ida Lupino, with a few quotes masquerading as an "exclusive interview." Numbers 14 and 15 are markedly better than the last several issues. There are excellent articles about Joan Crawford and Ann Blyth in *Mildred Pierce*, the movies *Village of the Damned* and *Children of the Damned*, an interview with Robert Bloch and one with Barbara Shelley. Covers some of the more obscure filmmakers of old fantasy/mystery films. Subscriptions are $20 a year (four issues), payable to *Scarlet Street*, Inc., 271 Farrant Terrace, Teaneck, NJ 07666.

Mystery Scene, edited by Joe Gorman, covers a minimum of horror, mostly in reviews by Charles de Lint. Number 42 had an article on the decision by Hyperion's Bob Miller to publish *The Diary of Jack the Ripper* despite the question of its authenticity. $35 for six issues, payable to Mystery Enterprises, PO Box 669, Cedar Rapids, IA 52406-0669.

The Scream Factory #13 is dedicated to the theme of science fiction/horror. This issue, edited by Bob Morrish, Peter Enfantino, and John Scoleri, boasts its first four-color cover. Stacy Drum's cover art is excellent, as are his interior illustrations. Other good interior illustrations are by Carlos Batts, Lari Davidson, Alfred Klosterman, Allen Koszowski, Keith Minnion, Scot D. Ryersson, Deryck T. Santiago, and David Transue. The issue concentrates on the crossover between horror and science fiction in books and movies. My only complaint is that while the issue does a marvelous job covering the historical perspective, it shortchanges the reader on coverage of contemporary crossover within the two fields. Issue #14 has an excellent in-depth review by Tom Deja of the first year of DC's Vertigo line, and quite a few articles on "mummies," not a subject that interests me all that much, and on horror and westerns. *The Scream Factory* continues to be an interesting and important critical magazine specializing in horror and dark suspense. The theme issues are especially rich for the connoisseur. Subscriptions are $21 for four issues, payable to Deadline Press, PO Box 2808, Apache Junction, AZ 85220.

Video Watchdog: The Perfectionist's Guide to Fantastic Video edited by Tim Lucas. Yeah! It's all in the details and that's what this mag is best on. The altered states of your favorite videos. Number 23, an Orson Welles issue, discussed in detail the master's original intentions for *The Lady From Shanghai*. $24 for a one-year (six-issue) subscription, payable to *Video Watchdog*, PO Box 5283, Cincinnati, OH 45105-0283. The new annual *Video Watchdog Special Edition #1* is, at 176 pages, more than double the size of the regular issues and jam-packed with more of the usual, including a profile of panther woman Kathleen Burke from *The Island of Lost Souls*. The theme for the issue is Beauty and the Beast. $7.95 (bulk mail), $9 (first class) for the special issue. Same address as above.

Psychotronic Video® edited by Michael J. Weldon. Number 18 has a profile/interview with Dario Argento. The extensive obituaries column, book reviews and video reviews are very useful. This is a great magazine for obscure movies and videos. $22 for a six-issue subscription, payable to *Psychotronic Video,* 3309 Route 97, Narrowsburg, NY 12764-6126.

Carnage Hall issue 5, edited by David Griffin, is the best one yet with an interview with John Clute, critic extraordinaire; an erudite essay by the editor on Wilderstein, the estate on which Barry Moser modeled his illustrations for Nancy Willard's retelling of Beauty and the Beast; essays by Jessica Amanda Salmonson and Jeff VanderMeer; and criticism by Melli Morrison that succinctly and ascerbically argues that "publisher" and "editor" are two functions that usually should be kept separate in magazines. The magazine is generally less nasty and more useful as criticism this time around. Irregularly published, $5 per issue, payable to David Griffin, PO Box 7, Esopus NY 12429.

Magazines:

The reader should be aware that most small-press magazines are published out of love, and that most small-press editor/publishers have full-time jobs in addition to their magazine obsessions. So, few of these magazines are able to keep to their stated schedules and many fail after a few issues.

That said, 1994 was a good year for the small-press magazine watcher. I couldn't pick a top ten because of the influx of promising new magazines from within the United States, from the United Kingdom, and from Australia.

Bloodsongs, edited by Chris A. Masters and Steve Proposch, is a new horror magazine from Australia. The first issue has a striking full-color cover by Louise Beach and excellent layouts. The tiny type needs to be enlarged and some of the fiction headings are so highly designed that they're hard to read, but on the whole the magazine is quite promising. There's an interesting article about the growth of horror as a distinct market in Australia (reprising Leigh Blackmore's introduction to the anthology *Terror Australis* last year), interviews with editor Leigh Blackmore and Ramsey Campbell, reviews of videos, movies, books, and magazines, and some good fiction and poetry. The second issue has a good slick cover, imaginative layouts, and good art. The editors have taken the type size up a point, which helps. The third issue's fiction was disappointing but there was some good poetry and good review columns, interviews with Poppy Z. Brite, Ed Lee, and Lydia Lunch. A six-issue subscription can be ordered for $50 airmail, $40 seamail, with an international money order or bank draft (no personal checks), payable to Bambada Press, PO Box 7530. St. Kilda Road, Melbourne VIC 3004, Australia. Or if you're unsure, try a single issue at $8 airmail, $7 seamail.

Weird Tales, edited by Darrell Schweitzer, published an excellent Tanith Lee issue illustrated throughout by Phil Parks. The fiction, including three very good stories by Lee and, in general, an excellent mix of weird and horrific stories and poetry by the other contributors. One poem, by Schweitzer, is reprinted herein.

Worlds of Fantasy and Horror #1 is the renamed *Weird Tales.* It has an excellent opening essay by Douglas E. Winter discussing the place of "horror" in literature, the decreasing use (thank god) of the genre label, and horror's return to the mainstream where it belongs. There's also an interview with Fred Chappell. The fiction was a little disappointing the last issue, but still very good. I'm a great fan of the art of Ian Miller, but this cover is not one of his best. There were good interior illustrations by Stephen E. Fabian, Jason van Hollander, Janet Aulisio, Denis Tiani, Allen Koszowski, Vincent di Fate, and Rodger Gerberding. A four-issue subscription costs $16, payable to Terminus Publishing Co., Inc., 123 Crooked Lane, King of Prussia, PA 19506-2570.

Cemetery Dance, edited by Richard Chizmar, remains the best horror magazine available in the United States. The winter issue ran a very good mix of fiction, an account of an appalling business dinner told by Thomas F. Monteleone in his column, and a good cover by Alan M. Clark. In the spring issue, the fiction was disappointing, except for Jack

Ketchum's "The Box," reprinted here. Also, there was an article by Douglas E. Winter about censorship, and an interview with Joe R. Lansdale. The fall issue was cancelled because of illness, but Chizmar's CD Publications' book schedule was maintained. For a one-year (four-issue) subscription send $15, payable to CD Publications. See address under Collections on page liii.

Not One of Us, edited by John Benson, produced only one issue during 1994. There was some good fiction in issue #12 but the interior art reproduction was poor. The magazine will be changing schedule and format in 1995, moving to 52 pages and coming out March and September. Single copies are $4.50, payable to John Benson, *Not One of Us*, 44 Shady Lane, Storrs, CT 06268.

Phantasm is a new horror magazine started by J. F. Gonzales, one of the editors of *Iniquities*, which stopped publishing after three issues. Some of the fiction in the new magazine was intended for issue #4 of *Iniquities*. The fiction in this debut issue is very good, mostly horror and a bit of fantasy thrown into the mix. Subscriptions are $14 (four issues) or $4 for a single issue, payable to Iniquities Publishing, *Phantasm*, 235 E. Colorado Boulevard, Suite 1346 Dept. S, Pasadena, CA 91101.

Bizarre Bazaar edited by Stanislaus Tal, Volume Three. This annual anthology series is improving in quality. As usual, it's a mixed bag. Excellent illustrative work by David Modler, Roger Gerberding, t. Winter-Damon, Augie Weidemann, Marge Simon, Harry Fassl, and Harry O. Morris. $8.50, payable to Tal Publications, PO Box 1837, Leesburg, VA 22075.

Deathrealm, edited by Mark Rainey, was disappointing in 1994, with inconsistent fiction but good art and covers by Michael Thom and Phillip Reynolds. Number 22 had an interesting article about John Wayne Gacy by Wayne Allen Sallee. A one-year (four-issue) subscription can be ordered for $15.95, payable to *Deathrealm*, 2210 Wilcoz Drive, Greensboro, NC 27405. The magazine missed its winter issue while undergoing a change in publishers.

Expressions of Dread: Third Annual, edited by Spencer Lamm, has an excellent interview with and portfolio of artist Marshall Arisman's work plus interviews and art by Harry O. Morris and J. K. Potter. Also, the magazine showcases art of the criminally insane and ran interviews with John Wayne Gacy, Richard Christian Matheson, Bruce Campbell (of *Evil Dead* fame), and Poppy Z. Brite. There's good original fiction, some excellent reprint fiction, and a step-by-step article on embalming. This perfect-bound magazine boasts good production values and readable layouts. The 102-page issue is $9, payable to Spencer Lamm, 23 N. Henry Street, Apt. 1, Brooklyn, NY 11222. The 52-page second issue is still available for $5.

Grue #16, edited by Peggy Nadramia, is a well-designed digest-sized magazine that looks terrific, with appropriate, good-looking, and for the most part, classy art by Timothy Patrick Butler, H. E. Fassl, Peter H. Gilmore, Harry O. Morris, and Phil Reynolds. There's some excellent fiction and poetry, including stories by Emily Newland and Kevin Roice, reprinted here. A three-issue subscription is $13, payable to Hell's Kitchen Productions, Inc., PO Box 370, Times Square Station, New York, NY 10108-0370. Although advertised as coming out three times a year, it often misses its schedule. However, because of its high literary and visual quality, it's a good magazine to support.

Terminal Fright, edited by Ken Abner, is a new magazine that is still reworking its layouts issue to issue. Some powerful fiction—odd and subtly disturbing. For a subscription (has been bimonthly but is going quarterly with the fifth issue), send $26 payable to *Terminal Fright*, PO Box 100, Black River, NY 13612.

Dreams From the Stranger's Cafe, edited by John Gaunt, comes from Yorkshire, England, and although it's already in its second year, I only saw issue #4 in 1994. Excellent fiction, good art, clean and readable design. A four-issue subscription is $25. One issue is $7, payable to John Gaunt, 15 Clifton Grove, Clifton, Rotherham, South Yorkshire S65 2AZ, England.

The Silver Web, edited by Ann Kennedy, is a semiannual, and although billed as "a magazine of surreal," it always has a good variety of fiction. 1994 was no exception, with some excellent dark fiction and poetry. In #11, H. E. Fassl's art was showcased and he was interviewed by t. Winter-Damon. Other notable art was by Michael Betancourt, Harry O. Morris, Phil Reynolds, Michael Shores, and Margaret Warren. A two-issue subscription is $10, payable to *The Silver Web*, PO Box 38190, Tallahassee, FL 32315.

Aberrations is now edited by Richard Blair and Michael Andre-Driussi. The fiction on the whole has improved. A subscription is $31 (12 issues) payable to Sirius Fiction, PO Box 460430, San Francisco, CA 94146.

Tales of the Unanticipated, edited by Eric M. Heideman, always contains a good mix of SF, fantasy, and horror. It's published at eight-month intervals by the Minnesota SF Society; #13 came out in 1994. A four-issue subscription is $15, payable to the Minnesota SF Society, PO Box 8036, Lake Street Station, Minneapolis, MN 55408.

Skull: The Magazine of Dark Fiction, which debuted in the fall, is published and edited by Mike Baker, also editor of *Afraid*. The first two issues of this all fiction magazine bode well with a simple, readable design and some very good original fiction by new and established writers. A one-year subscription (six issues) is $25, payable to *Skull*, P.O. Box 1235, Burbank, CA 91507. Sample issue $7.50.

Crypt of Cthulhu, edited by Robert M. Price, is *the* magazine for Lovecraft enthusiasts. It's been around for quite a long time and with the mini Lovecraft revival should gain some more readers. A mixture of new stories and nonfiction on Lovecraftian scholarship. Available from Necronomicron Press for $5.95. See address under Collections on page l.

Palace Corbie #5, edited by Wayne Edwards, has become an annual in trade paperback format with b&w interior illustrations by Stacy Drum. The subtle full-color cover by the same artist is beautiful. A good issue with over thirty-five consistently well-written stories and poems and one excerpt from a forthcoming novel. $10.95, payable to Merrimack Books, PO Box 83514, Lincoln, NE 68501-3514.

Eldritch Tales 29, edited by Crispin Burnham, is copyrighted 1993 but was shipped in 1994. This issue has excellent art and some good fiction. $24 for a four-issue subscription, payable to Crispin Burnham, *Eldritch Tales*, 1051 Wellington Road, Lawrence, KS 66049.

A Theater of Blood issue 5, edited by C. Darren Butler, has been around for more than a year, but this is the first issue I've seen. Blair Wilson's cover art is terrific and makes great use of the light reddish paper. Some of the fiction and poetry is very good. The editor announced a change of format after #6. $2.50 for issue 5, payable to Pyx Press, PO Box 620, Orem, UT 84059-0620.

Transversions, edited by Dale L. Sproule and Sally McBride with poetry editor Phyllis Gotlieb, is a new 5½-by-7-inch magazine with a nice cross-genre mix of fiction and poetry. Excellent b&w interiors by Cathy Buburuz, Randy Nakoneshny, and Charles de Lint and a good color cover by Jeff Kuipers. An impressive debut. $18 for a four-issue subscription (the magazine is scheduled to appear two to three times a year) and single issues are $5, payable to Specialty Reports, 1019 Colville Road, Victoria, BC V9A 4PS, Canada.

Dead of Night, edited by Lin Stein, had excellent front and back covers by Steven B. Gould, good interior illustrations, and some very good fiction. Also an excellent magazine review column by t. Winter-Damon. A four-issue subscription is $15, payable to *Dead of Night* Publications, 916 Shaker Road, Suite 228, Longmeadow, MA 01106-2416.

The Magazine of Fantasy & Science Fiction, edited by Kristine Kathryn Rusch, one of the longest-running genre magazines, publishes some excellent horror. A story by Dale Bailey is reprinted herein.

Fantasy Macabre, edited by Jessica Amanda Salmonson, is always attractive and has an admirable mix of baroque decadence in its fiction and art. Includes some interesting poetry reprinted from the original *Weird Tales*. A good issue. $12 for three issues or $4.50 for a single issue, payable to Richard H. Fawcett, 61 Teecomwas Drive, Uncasville, CT 06832.

Thunder's Shadow, edited by Erik Secker, is an unusual item—a collector's magazine with original fiction by professional writers. In this it is similar to Dave Hinchberger's *The Overlook Connection Newsletter*, which often runs excerpts from new novels. The *Thunder's Shadow* February issue has three original stories. $12 for a four-issue subscription, payable to *Thunder's Shadow*, PO Box 387, Winfield, IL 60190.

The Thirteenth Moon, edited by Jacob Weisman, has a good mix of dark fiction and poetry, nonfiction articles and reviews of books and music. A four-issue subscription is $24, payable to *Thirteenth Moon Magazine*, 1459 18th Street #139, San Francisco, CA 94107.

Grotesque, edited by David Logan, is a horror magazine from Northern Ireland and publishes a good readable mix of stories. $7 per issue or $25 for four issues (surface) payable to *Grotesque* Magazine, David Logan, 39 Brooke Avenue off Barn Road, Carrick-Fergus, Co. Antrim, Northern Ireland BT38 7TE.

Back Brain Recluse #22, edited by Chris Reed of the United Kingdom, has a great cover, excellent layouts and art, but has suddenly become so overdesigned that it's occasionally difficult to read. (e.g. it was necessary to look up the stories by Rymland and Kirby in the Table of Contents to get their titles.) Despite this overenthusiasm, the content is excellent. Particularly good in addition to the fiction and faction by Uncle River is the "Directory" listings with mini-reviews of various small-press magazines. There are ten stories—not much horror but a good darkish piece by Don Webb—and some weird-but-true stories by Uncle River, and excellent review columns. The superb, elegantly simple cover was designed in-house. Single copies $10 airmail; four-issue subscription $26, payable to Anne Marsden, 1052 Calle del Cerro, #708, San Clemente, CA 92672-6068. This is the first issue in fifteen months, but Reed hopes to publish every six months.

Chills Number 8, edited by Peter Coleborn and Simon MacCulloch, is published by the British Fantasy Society. The magazine, free with membership, always has good-to-excellent fiction and poetry. It's a shame it only appears once a year. $32 for membership; members receive a regular newsletter and several magazines (including *Chills*). Monies payable to The British Fantasy Society, The BFS Secretary, c/o 2 Harwood Street, Stockport, SK4 4JJ, United Kingdom.

All Hallows: The Journal of the Ghost Story Society is another excellent magazine for both fiction and nonfiction. Number 6 had a fascinating essay by Jack Adrian tracking down an obscure E. F. Benson collection. A continuing series on ghost-story cover artists profiled Felix Kelly and Michael Ayrton in the two issues that I saw, and there's an excellent article on censorship by Ramsey Campbell. Good art by Pat Walsh, Alan Hunter, Felix Kelly, and Nick Maloret and excellent reviews. For membership information, see under Collections on page lii.

The Third Alternative, edited by Andy Cox, is from England and improved steadily throughout 1994. Good covers by Rik Rawling and Dave Mooring—and some very good horrific stories and poetry. The fourth issue was the best so far, with excellent fiction and art—a magazine to watch. $6 per issue, $22 four-issue subscription, payable to *The Third Alternative*, 5 Martins Lane, Witcham, Ely, Cambs CB6 2LB, England.

Threads: Dark Fantasy summer special #1, edited by Geoff Lynas, has excellent art by Mark Sorensen-Browne, Kerry Earl, Darren Blackburn, Jane Adams, Wayne Peters, and Russell Morgan and some very good fiction. The magazine is a quarterly publishing cross-genre material, but this issue concentrates on dark fantasy. $6 (cash) for a single issue, $20 (cash) for a four-issue subscription. (The editor is trying to make better payment arrangements in 1995.) Payable to G. Lynas, First Rung Publications, 32 Irvin Avenue, Saltburn, Cleveland RS12 1QH, England.

Skeletal Remains is a poetry series featuring one small-press poet per issue. In 1994 the poets were Lisa Lepovetsky, Holly Day, and John Grey. $2 per issue, payable to Richard L. Levesque at 2227 Woodglen Drive, Indianapolis, IN 46260.

The Urbanite, edited by Mark McLaughlin, usually publishes a varied mix of fiction. Issue 4 was "The Strange Pets Issue" and had some good horror. $13.50 for three issues, payable to Urban Legend Press, PO Box 4737, Davenport, IA 52808.

Realms of Fantasy, edited by Shawna McCarthy, is a new glossy bi-monthly published by the same people as *Science Fiction Age*. It aims to cover all types of fantasy but so far has had only one dark story, a reprint by Neil Gaiman in the first issue. The reviews cover fantasy and horror and some of the articles and pictorials are horrific in nature. The second issue has an excerpt from artist J. K. Potter's *Horripilations*, published in the U.K. in 1993, and a piece on the film version of *Interview With the Vampire*. Also, my co-editor Terri Windling has been writing intelligent, thoughtful essays on different aspects of fantasy.

Dreams and Nightmares, edited by David Kopaska-Merkel, is a reliable source for fantasy and dark fantasy poetry. Number 42 is more experimental than usual and also less successful. Number 43 was back up to speed. $10 for a six-issue subscription, payable to David C. Kopaska-Merkel, 1300 Kicker Road, Tuscaloosa, AL 35404.

After Hours edited by William Raley. 1994 was the last full year of this small-press magazine. It had some very good fiction, and one issue had a good cover by H. E. Fassl.

Psychotrope, edited by Mark Beech, is another new magazine from the U.K. The two 1994 issues both had good cover art, interesting interior art, and good, literate fiction. It's a 46-page, digest-sized, saddle-stitched magazine. A four-issue subscription is $20, payable to Mark Beech, Flat 6, 17 Droitwich Road, Barbourne, Worcester WR3 7LG, England.

Other magazines that published notable horror:

Crossroads edited by Pat Nielson; *Pulphouse* edited by Dean Wesley Smith; *Wicked Mystic* edited by Andre Scheluchin; *Amazing Stories* edited by Kim Mohan; *Shadowdance Magazine* edited by Michelle Belanger; *Argonaut* edited by Michael Ambrose; *Tomorrow Speculative Fiction* edited by Algis Budrys; *Space and Time* edited by Gordon Linzner; *Ellery Queen's Mystery Magazine*, edited by Janet Hutchings, publishes an unusually rich mixture of mystery/suspense/dark almost-fantasy in its pages; *Alfred Hitchcock Mystery Magazine*, edited by Cathleen Jordan, occasionally publishes dark material, but generally, is not as edgy as *Ellery Queen's*; *Omni Magazine*, the fiction edited by myself, Ellen Datlow, occasionally publishes dark material; *Asimov's Science Fiction Magazine*, edited by Gardner Dozois, occasionally publishes dark material; *Playboy*, edited by Alice K. Turner, occasionally publishes dark fiction; *Dementia 13*, edited by Pam Creais out of England, was disappointing compared to last year; *Heliocentric Net*, edited by Lisa Jean Bothell, had excellent interior art by Cathy Buburuz, Randy Moore, and Bob Crouch, but needs to watch a tendency to overdesign, particularly the poetry; *Peeping Tom*, edited by Stuart Hughes, had disappointing fiction compared to 1993; *Thin Ice* XV edited by K. Jurgens; *Prisoners of the Night* #8, edited by Alayne Gelfland, specializes in vampire stories; *On Spec: The Canadian Magazine of Speculative Writing*, edited by The Copper Pig Writer's Society, is the premier (possibly the only) such magazine in Canada. It's top-notch in all respects and while there isn't often any horror, it's always interesting. $18 for a year's (four issues) subscription, payable to *On Spec*, PO Box 4727, Edmonton, Alberta T6E 5G6, Canada.

Small Press:

Slippin' Into Darkness by Norman Partridge (CD Publications) is the debut novel by the winner of the 1993 Stoker Award for his collection *Mr. Fox and Other Feral Tales*. 500 signed and numbered copies featuring full-color wraparound dust-jacket artwork and five interior illustrations by Alan M. Clark. $35. CD Publications also brought out Joe R.

Lansdale's dark suspense novel *Mucho Mojo* in a 400-copy signed and numbered limited edition with a full-color dust jacket by Mark Nelson. See address under Collections on page liii.

Less Than Human by Gary Raisor (Overlook Connection Press) is the long-awaited hardcover edition of Raisor's first novel which was published by Diamond in 1992. A trade hardcover edition of 1,000 copies with an introduction by Joe R. Lansdale, a wraparound color dust jacket with art by Guy Aitchison, and illustrated endpapers is available for $29.95 and a 300-copy limited edition signed by Raisor, Lansdale, and Aitchison and slipcased in a natural-finish oak coffin, lined with red crushed velvet—complete with brass hinges and latch—is available for $200. Add $2 per book for postage. Both payable to Overlook Connection Press, PO Box 526, Woodstock, GA 30188.

Dark Rivers of the Heart is a new epic novel by Dean Koontz, illustrated by Stephen Gervais. This Charnel House edition is limited to 500 numbered copies signed by the author and artist (which is sold out) and a 26-copy lettered edition. The book is printed on custom-milled paper in an oversize 6½-by-11-inch format, bound in Japanese fabric with front and back inlays, and housed in a handmade slipcase, with four full-page illustrations and a frontispiece. Joe Stefko, publisher of Charnel House, reports that "Unfortunately, of the edition of five hundred books—two hundred were damaged in production, reducing the edition to three hundred. A correction of a later binding or a rebinding was rejected by the publisher to maintain the integrity of the existing edition and to eschew a dubious 'state' of the book. This has resulted in a lawsuit seeking damages and a court order to have the damaged books destroyed." The lettered edition, $750, is hand-bound in full leather with a leather inlay on the front board. Charnel House, PO Box 633, Lynbrook, NY 11563.

Mark Ziesing took a break from his expensive hardcover editions and put out *Sports and Music* by Lucius Shepard, a chapbook with two short stories: "Sports in America" and "A Little Night Music." The attractive paperback with color cover by Arnie Fenner is limited to 1,000 signed and numbered copies and was designed by Fenner and Robert Frazier. A good collectible at $10. Ziesing's address is on the acknowledgments page.

Black Sun, a chapbook written by Douglas E. Winter (One Eyed Dog), illustrated by Stephen R. Bissette, and designed by Michael Barry, is a moody, Sergei Leone–influenced post-apocalypse story, with excellent production values. Signed and limited paperback edition of 500. $10.95, payable to One Eyed Dog, PO Box 28365, Washington, DC 20038.

Not Broken, Not Belonging by Randy Fox and Alan M. Clark (Roadkill Press) is a collaboration based on a concept by Clark about a woman who has been missing for six months who seems to come back from the dead with weird structural changes in her brain. $6 plus $1 postage. Roadkill also published an odd little transformation tale by Carrie Richerson called *Geckos* with illustrations and decorations by Alan M. Clark. $7 plus $1 postage. Both paperbacks are signed and limited to 300 copies. Order from Little Bookshop of Horrors, 10380 Ralston Road, Arvada, CO 80004.

Mysteries of the Word by Stanley Wiater (Crossroads Press) is a cute but not very scary story done as a 17-page chapbook illustrated by Gahan Wilson and with an introduction by Jack Ketchum. This paperback, limited to 250 signed and numbered copies, looks good and costs $10, payable to Thomas Crouss, Crossroads Press, PO Box 10433, Holyoke, MA 01041.

A revised version of Michael Shea's World Fantasy Award–winning novel *Nifft the Lean* (Darkside Press) with an introduction by Tim Powers and with illustrations by Alan M. Clark was limited to 52 deluxe wooden slipcased editions bound in leather (inquire about availability) and 452 hardcover editions at $65. Both editions are signed.

Silver Salamander brought out a new collection by Thomas Ligotti, *The Agonizing*

Resurrection of Victor Frankenstein, Citizen of Geneva and Other Gothic Tales of Terror. Released in two states: 26 lettered and 125 clothbound, both editions are signed by Ligotti and Michael Shea, who wrote the introduction, and they are both sold out. Also, Nancy Springer's novella, "The Blind God Is Watching" (Silver Salamander), with jacket art by Alan M. Clark; *Blood and Ivory* collection by P. C. Hodgell and *Wizard of the Pigeons* by Megan Lindholm (both Hypatia) and *The Judas Cross* by Charles Sheffield and David Bischoff (Special Editions Press).

In October, *Gauntlet* published a 35th anniversary edition of Robert Bloch's classic novel, *Psycho,* featuring the author's preferred text and a new preface by Bloch (rightly expressing his disgust with Hollywood types—but not Hitchcock, who always credited Bloch—for having appropriated credit for his work once a film was made). Introduction by Richard Matheson, and Afterword by Ray Bradbury, with jacket art by Alan M. Clark. Limited to 500 signed, numbered, and slipcased copies for $60, plus $3 for p&h. See address on page lvi.

Necronomicon Press brought out Donald R. Burleson's *Four Shadowings,* a mini-collection of four original stories illustrated by Robert H. Knox. $5.95 plus $1.50 p&h, and a chapbook collection of two stories written by Robert H. Barlow and extensively revised by H. P. Lovecraft, with a detailed introduction by S. T. Joshi, and facsimile reproductions of the original manuscripts showing Lovecraft's editing. $3.95 plus $1.50 p&h. See address under *Necrofile* on page l.

Paper Moon Press published a double by P. D. Cacek and Ru Emerson, "Mid-Wife Crisis" and "Midwife's Nightcap," respectively, in an attractive signed paperback edition, $5 plus $1.05 p&h.

Transylvania Press, specializing in vampiric material, debuted appropriately enough with its publication of the rare text of Bram Stoker's *Dracula* from 1901. Publisher Robert Eighteen-Bisang and Raymond T. McNally explain in their foreword and introduction that *Dracula* was first published in 1897 at 162,000 words. Stoker abridged and revised the book in 1901, when it was published with 137,000 words. Most scholars consider this version much more readable than the original. This new edition is from one of only six copies of the 1901 version known to exist. The simple red-on-black cloth cover is very effective. The original paperback cover, digitally enhanced, is the frontispiece and also stamped in miniature on the cover. This important book for vampire lovers and scholars is limited to 500 copies in slipcase, available for $65. Transylvania Press also published a harcover edition of Sherry Gottlieb's first novel, *Love Bite,* a sharp and snappy police procedural. Limited to 500 copies signed by the author and the jacket artist, Alan M. Clark, for $65. Both payable to Transylvania Press, Inc. See address under Collections on page liv.

Morrigan Publications/The Dog Factory brought out Tim Ferret's horror short story "We Murder" as a chapbook, with cover and illustrations by Ferret in a signed limited edition of 200 for $11.95, payable to Morrigan, c/o TCI Dept. 64, Box 597004, San Francisco, CA 94159.

Brian Lumley's 1978 novel, *The Clock of Dreams* (W. Paul Ganley), received its first hardcover publication, with jacket and interior artwork by Dave Carson. The book is $42.50 for the deluxe; $26.50 for the trade edition, plus $2 p&h, payable to W. Paul Ganley, Box 149, Buffalo, NY 14226-0149.

The House Next Door by Anne Rivers Siddons (Old New York Book Shop Press) has been published in a limited edition of 450 numbered and signed copies, with a new foreword by Stephen King, bound in Rust Holliston Linen Finish woven cloth and hand-painted morocco paper boards, and enclosed in a cloth box. Each of 26 lettered copies bound in calf costs $250; the remainder are cloth and cost $150, payable to the publisher, at 1069 Juniper Street, Atlanta, GA 30309.

The British Fantasy Society came out with *Clive Barker: Mythmaker for the Millennium* by Suzanne J. Barbieri, with an introduction by Peter Atkins, cover by Les Edwards, and interior illustrations by Pete Queally. Trade paperback, $14, payable to The British Fantasy Society. See *Chills* on page lx for address.

Tal Publications brought out a trio of vampire chapbooks. *Sex and the Single Vampire* by Nancy Kilpatrick, is actually one long novella divided into three parts, rather than three individual stories. The attractive cover art is by the author. The other two volumes (unseen) are *Sex and Blood* by Ron Dee and *Shrines and Desecrations* by Brian Hodge. They can be ordered as a set for $14.95 postpaid, or individually for $6.95 each postpaid, payable to Tal Publications, PO Box 1837, Leesburg, VA 22075.

Edition Phantasia published a hardcover book of Ramsey Campbell's story "The Guide" in a dual-language English/German edition. The English half has original illustrations by J. K. Potter. The German half is illustrated by Herbert Brandmeier. The story was first published in Paul F. Olson's and David B. Silva's anthology, *Post Mortem*. This slipcased edition is limited to 200 numbered copies and is signed by Campbell and both artists. Write to Joachim Korber, Edition Phantasia, Wunschelstr. 18, 76756 Bellheim, Germany. Mark V. Ziesing carries this wonderful collector's item, $68 postage paid.

Borderlands Press and Spiderbaby Grafix jointly published a hardcover edition of Alan Moore's scripts of Book One of *From Hell* illustrated by Eddie Campbell and with an afterword by Stephen R. Bissette. This is Moore's version of Jack the Ripper and also features the author's sidebars. It was published in two limited editions: 1,000 copies signed, numbered, and slipcased, $95; and 26 deluxe lettered copies, $450.

Voices From Shadow edited by David Sutton celebrates the twentieth anniversary of the fantasy literature review, which was published from 1968 to 1974. A selection of articles from the magazine has been revised and collected, including an in-depth examination of Robert Aickman, a tribute to Virgil Finlay illustrated by two of Finlay's pieces of art, and a reassessment by Ramsey Campbell of the comments he made about H. P. Lovecraft in 1969. $11 postpaid, payable to David Sutton, Shadow Publishing, 194 Station Road, Kings Heath, Birmingham, B14 7TE, United Kingdom.

Deus-X by Joseph Citro. This novel was published in an attractive hardcover edition illustrated by Stephen R. Bissette. A limited edition signed by author and artist costs $54; the trade edition is $24.95, payable to Twilight Publishing Co., 18 Oaktree Lane, Sparta, NJ 07871.

Nonfiction:

Midnight in the Garden of Good and Evil by John Berendt (Random House) is a look at the underside of Savannah society with a bit of hoodoo and voodoo thrown in. Starring are a hormonally enhanced drag queen, a nouveau riche antique expert who loves his eccentric, monied life, a talented piano player/drunkard who squats in glorious old houses, and other assorted loons. Underneath the Southern graciousness and backbiting lurks a contemporary classism and racism. Reads like fiction.

The Hot Zone by Richard Preston (Random House) is the scariest, most horrific book of the year. It is the true story about a virus (with several different strains) thought to come from the Central African rain forests that can, at its most virulent, kill nine out of ten of its victims in a few days, with shocking, ugly ferocity. This Ebola virus broke out in the Reston, Virginia, Monkey House, a research laboratory outside of Washington, D.C. Five hundred monkeys were put down and the laboratories sterilized by a top-secret military SWAT team assembled to contain the outbreak. The author writes so well (and suspensefully) that the book reads like a novel with the reader often not knowing who will survive the contagion and who will not. The bottom line is that the virus was contained—this time—but the experts still don't know how it's transmitted to humans or how to cure it. Preston also tells of the origin of such viruses that have lived undetected for centuries in the rain forests that, being depleted, are fertile ground for these diseases, just waiting to "crash" into the human population. Highly recommended.

Beyond Belief: Bizarre Facts and Incredible Stories From All Over the World by Ron Lyon and Jenny Paschall (Villard) is a light, entertaining companion to a television series. The "failures" chapter flops but the "eccentrics" chapter is fresh and fun—with entertaining bits about experts in taxidermy and the cleanliness-obsessed Beau Brummel. "Odd laws" are also interesting but could be more so with more information: e.g. in sixteenth- and seventeenth-century Turkey, anyone caught drinking coffee would be put to death; in Alaska it is illegal to look at a moose from the window of an airplane or any other flying vehicle— Why? one might ask, about both tidbits.

Much better is *The Book of the Weird* by Barbara Ninde Byfield (Main Street Books/ Doubleday), originally published back in 1973 as *The Glass Harmonica*. It's a marvelously inventive, entertaining, and sometimes even informative book illustrated by the author. "Witches lead disorderly lives, hate salt, and cannot weep more than three tears." Byfield covers topics from giants, elves, and ogres, to the various personnel in palaces versus those in castles, the difference among alms, the dole, and vail, and anything you might want to know about damsels.

The Ghost Book of Charles Lindley, Viscount Halifax (Carroll & Graf) was first published as two volumes in the 1930s. The book was comprised of extracts from his journals of eyewitness accounts of supernatural phenomena, related by friends and relatives. Lord Halifax would read these stories aloud to his family on special occasions. The oversized trade paperback combines the two volumes and, according to the publisher, is available for the first time in many years.

The Dean Koontz Companion edited by Martin H. Greenberg, Ed Gorman, and Bill Munster (Berkley) is a marvelous book for Koontz fans, including interviews with him, essays about and by him, his introductions to other writers' books, his first published short story, and even a how-to on writing suspense. Includes an annotated bibliography.

The Fearmakers: The Screen's Directorial Masters of Suspense and Terror by John McCarty (St. Martin's) is actually edited by McCarty, with some pieces written by him and other articles contributed by various writers conversant with horror films. Covers twenty "fearmakers" including a few of the more obscure such as Roland West, Jack Arnold, and Terence Fisher. Entertaining but superficial and facile, it's for the beginner, not the connoisseur.

Vampires: Restless Creatures of the Night by Jean Marigny (Discoveries/Harry N. Abrams, Inc.) is a real treasure for vampire fans. This miniature trade paperback is lavishly illustrated with color and b&w fine art relating to the history of vampires through the ages, beginning with the first references to blood drinkers in ancient Persia, Babylon, and China. Throughout recorded history there are textual examples and artistic renderings of different aspects of vampirism: blood lust and a fascination with blood as a vital force in life, belief in the undead, corpses having the power to cause the death of living persons from a distance, etc. In the fourteenth century, rumor of vampirism became endemic, coinciding with a serious outbreak of bubonic plague. Some of these beliefs may have originated because people were sometimes buried in vaults while still alive. This has better art and more detail than most books of this sort. Highly recommended.

Mary Shelley's Frankenstein: The Classic Tale of Terror Reborn on Film by Kenneth Branagh (Newmarket Press) is a very nice coffee-table trade paperback about the making of the movie. Branagh explains that he intended to stay as close as possible to the original book while fixing various inconsistencies in the plotting. Includes the entire screenplay and many richly colored stills from the movie.

Cannibal Killers: The History of Impossible Murderers by Moira Martingale (Carroll & Graf) is grisly and entertaining reading that sticks to case histories of some of the most infamous killers of history and gleefully describes their crimes. The last two chapters—providing the book with "social value"—attempt to coordinate studies on motivation from many sources on criminology; the result is unfocused, sloppy analysis with alarmingly unreliable information.

A Father's Story by Lionel Dahmer (William Morrow and Company) is a moving and fascinating document of self-discovery and attempted exorcism of guilt by association by the father of the serial killer necrophile/cannibal Jeffrey Dahmer. Lionel Dahmer recounts his son's life (as much as he knew of it) and tries to come to terms with the begetting of a monster. Although Dahmer was a bit strange from early adolescence, his is not the typical case of an escalation of violence that should have been noticeable to everyone around him. Lionel dissects some of his own antisocial impulses as a youth and concludes that genetics might be partly responsible for his son's perversions. A fast read and a good one.

Reading the Vampire by Ken Gelder (Routledge) is occasionally readable but more often mired in academic jargon. Gelder seems barely cognizant of contemporary vampire literature beyond the novels of Anne Rice or Stephen King. He mentions Suzy McKee Charnas and Chelsea Quinn Yarbro in passing, but it's clear from certain remarks that he was only recently made aware of Dan Simmons's *Carrion Comfort* and S. P. Somtow's *Vampire Junction* and *Valentine*. He hasn't done his literary homework on the subject. There is some interesting material here, but the academic blinders hinder what could be a solid critique on vampire literature.

The Complete Guide to Mysterious Beings by John A. Keel (Main Street/Doubleday) is a book updated from 1970. It's a pretty down-to-earth look at various "mysteries" ranging from multiple sightings of giant sea serpents and yeti to UFO abduction and visiting angels.

Stigmata: A Medieval Phenomenon in a Modern Age by Ted Harrison (St. Martin's) is a well-reasoned and fascinating survey of a persistent (albeit rare) phenomenon—in which ordinary people have suffered spontaneous lesions on their hands and feet resembling the marks of Christ's crucifixion. The first official bearer of stigmata was St. Francis of Assisi in the thirteenth century—why none before him? Since then, most stigmatics have been female. Harrison investigates the early cases (which are impossible to check for credibility) as well as contemporary stigmatics. Most of the evidence seems to indicate that sometimes the marks are real, but there seems to be no evidence of divine intervention. They are no less explicable than hypnosis, Indian mystics walking on coals, Native American trance states, etc.; in other words, self-induced and psychosomatic. After a while individual cases start to blur, but it's still a very interesting study for believers and skeptics alike.

The Journal of a Ghosthunter by Simon Marsden (Little, Brown-UK) is a beautiful coffee-table book graced with Marsden's extraordinary b&w photographs taken with infra red. The photographs of various haunted castles from Ireland to Transylvania are beautiful, dreamlike, and eerie. Marsden's text, incorporating ghost stories told to him and histories of the ruins he visits, is detailed and nicely written if a little too credulous. His other books include *Phantoms of the Isles* and *Visions of Poe.*

Ghostmasters: A Look Back at America's Midnight Spook Shows by Mark Walker (Cool Hand Communications) is a rousing history of a part of Americana barely remembered. The midnight ghost shows, developed by stage magicians during the late 1920s and '30s, hit big just as spiritualism was being taken less seriously by the public. The performers used many imaginative methods to fool and entertain audiences: luminescent paint (developed by Alexander Strobl in 1924), totally blacking out the theater, throwing popcorn kernels, rice, and cooked spaghetti into unsuspecting audiences, and shooting audience members with ice water from water pistols. Walker's profiles and descriptions of the individual specialties of the best and most prominent purveyors of the ghost shows gives a real feel for an entertainment that no longer exists. The ghost shows gave way to "monster shows" after

World War II, as audiences got younger, more demanding, and more interested in creatures like Dracula and the Frankenstein monster than in ghosts. By the 1950s, the shows were in decline because of inferior performers cashing in on a good thing, rising operating costs, television's lure, and the demolition of many of the great movie palaces. Also included are numerous b&w publicity stills and handbills advertising the shows. A marvelously entertaining bit of nostalgia. Highly recommended. $29.95 from Cool Hand Communications, Inc., 1098 NW Boca Raton Boulevard, Suite #1, Boca Raton, FL 33432.

Monsters of the Sea by Richard Ellis (Knopf) is a wonderful reading and visual experience for anyone interested in fantastical and real creatures of the sea, such as sea serpents, mermaids and manatees, krakens and giant squid. A gracefully written and lavishly illustrated treasure trove. Beautiful, well researched, and rich in detail. Highly recommended.

Antichrist: Two Thousand Years of the Human Fascination With Evil by Bernard McGinn (HarperSan Francisco) is a readable, accessible "history of the belief in a final human opponent of all goodness, the Antichrist." McGinn goes into the origins of the legend and follows it historically up to the present. He mentions such pop cultural uses of the legend in text and film—including Gaiman and Pratchett's *Good Omens* and Charles Williams's novel *All Hallow's Eve.*

Paul Davies' *The Last Three Minutes: Conjectures About the Ultimate Fate of the Universe* (Basic Books) is the perfect irreverent antidote to the above. Davies, in his smart-assed, fast-paced manner, makes the coming end of the world almost fun. For example, he writes, "In the year 1856, the German physicist Hermann von Heimholtz made what is probably the most depressing prediction in the history of science. The universe, Heimholz claimed, is dying." The book won the Templeton Prize for Progress in Religion.

Shock Xpress 2: The Essential Guide to Exploitation Cinema edited by Stefan Jaworzyn (Titan Books), the follow-up to the first volume, has blood and guts and flesh, lots of flesh in this one. But there's also a good article on the movies of French director Georges Franju, a brief history of Barney Rosset's Grove Press, and a terrific piece by Anne Billson (author of the novel *Suckers*) about "insidious little globs"—unexpected scenes of violence and/or horror in nongenre movies. The book covers some very obscure moviemakers and their movies.

Scent: The Essential and Mysterious Powers of Smell by Annick LeGuérer (Kodansha) introduces a new trade paperback line by this respected publisher, and this fascinating book is the perfect debut. LeGuérer investigates scent and its relationship to myth, psychology, religion, ritual, sex, seduction, magic, social classes, and early pharmacology and healing practices. It discusses everything from odor and seduction to the plague and the belief that "because corrupt men so offend God with the cadaverous stench of their souls that they draw down His wrath among themselves" to its complement, "the odor of sanctity," that holy men and women supposedly emit (alive or dead). A good read, although some of the more provocative "facts" LeGuérer presents could use more critical evaluation than she provides.

Killing For Culture: An Illustrated History of Death Film From Mondo to Snuff by David Kerekes and David Slater (Creation Books) claims that it's about the "marketing of outrage," about actual death on film, and how death interacts with the media. The book is an absorbing read, starting with its description and analysis of *Snuff,* the 1976 movie that made history with its implication of actual death onscreen. In fact, this Manson-inspired exploitation movie was the beneficiary of a brilliant marketing ploy by a distributor stuck with an unsalable product. The authors critique feature films such as *Videodrome* and *52 Pick-Up,* which incorporate snuff elements, and review the history of the "Mondo" movies, from *Mondo Cane* to *Faces of Death.* A good book on an intriguing topic.

The Research Guide to Bodily Fluids by Paul Spinrad (Re/Search). Yes, it's tasteless and disgusting. What do you expect? Unfortunately, this one has no illustrations. There are sections such as "Fart Fact and Fictions," "Scatalogical Lives of the Great," "Bodily Functions in the Cinema." An entertaining book to browse through but it seems a little thin. One wishes for more . . .

Nonfiction Listings:

Arthur Machen & Montgomery Evans: Letters of a Literary Friendship, 1923–1947 edited by Sue Strong Hassler and Donald M. Hassler (Kent University Press) is a collection of almost two hundred letters exchanged by fantasy and horror writer Machen and book collector Evans, with commentaries on many of the cultural, political, and literary issues of the day; *Edgar Allan Poe and Arthur Machen* edited (uncredited) by Ray B. Russell (Tartarus Press) is a chapbook anthology demonstrating similarities between the two writers. Limited to 100 copies; *The Apparition in the Glass: Charles Brockden Brown's American Gothic* by Bill Christophersen (University of Georgia Press) is an examination of Brown's gothic novels and how they reflect the events of their time; *Anne Rice* by Bette B. Roberts (Macmillan/Twayne), a critical appraisal; *Clive Barker's Short Stories: Imagination as Metaphor in the "Books of Blood" and Other Works* by Gary Hoppenstand (McFarland) with a foreword by Barker. $32.50 plus $2 postage, payable to McFarland & Company, Box 611, Jefferson, NC 28640; *From Faust to Strangelove: Representation of the Scientist in Western Literature* by Roslynn D. Haynes (Johns Hopkins University Press); *Science Fiction & Fantasy Book Review Annual 1991* edited by Robert A. Collins and Robert Latham (Greenwood Press); *The Critical Response to Bram Stoker* edited by Carol A. Senf (Greenwood Press); *H. P. Lovecraft in the Argosy: Collected Correspondence from the Munsey Magazines* edited by S. T. Joshi (Necronomicon Press).

The Oxford Book of the Supernatural edited by D. J. Enright (Oxford University Press) is a collection of literary accounts of various manifestations of the supernatural from apparitions to angels, monsters, and dreams. For the casual browser rather than the serious aficionado; *In Search of Dracula: The History of Dracula and Vampires* completely revised by Raymond T. McNally and Radu Florescu (Houghton Mifflin) is a classic, with a jacket illustration by Edward Gorey; *The World of Ghosts and the Supernatural* by Richard Cavendish (Facts on File) is your average coffee-table compendium with lots of illustrations and bits of superficial text; *Witchcraze: A New History of the European Witch Hunts* by Anne Llewellyn Barstow (Pandora/HarperCollins) is a feminist view of the witch hunts as nothing less than an "ethnic cleansing" of independent women in reformation Europe; *The Beast Within: A History of the Werewolf* by Adam Douglas (Avon) looks like a good, solid, informative book on the subject, despite its cover; *Saints: A Visual Almanac of the Virtuous, Pure, Praiseworthy, and Good* by Tom Morgan (Chronicle) is straightforward and far too serious; *Supernatural Britain: A Guide to Britain's Most Haunted Places* by Peter Hough (Piatkus Books) with color and b&w photographs, maps, and illustrations; *The Devil in the New World: The Impact of Diabolism in New Spain* by Fernando Cervantes (Yale University Press); *The Vampire Book: The Encyclopedia of the Undead* by Gordon J. Melton (Visible Ink); *The National Directory of Haunted Places* by Dennis Hauck (Athanor); *Haunted America* by Beth Scott and Michael Norman (Forge); *The Witches' Companion* by Katherine Ramsland (Ballantine).

Whispers: The Voices of Paranoia by Dr. Ronald K. Siegel (Crown) tries to investigate the actual experience of paranoia, as the author studies twelve people with the condition. *Dead Men Do Tell Tales: The Strange and Fascinating Cases of a Forensic Anthropologist* by William R. Maples, Ph.D., and Michael Browning (Doubleday), yet another expert in the scrying from skeleton and skull sweepstakes; *Bag of Toys: Sex, Scandal, and the Death Mask Murder* by David France (Warner) is about the infamous murder of a young Norwegian student by art dealer Andrew Crispo and his bodyguard Bernard LeGeros (who was the only one convicted of the crime); *Autobiography of a Face* by Lucy Grealy (Houghton

Mifflin) is a moving memoir of a young woman who spent a good part of her life dealing with the facial disfigurement caused by cancer surgery when she was a child; *Little Girl Fly Away* by Gene Stone (Simon & Schuster) is a weird true story of a woman who is harassed and tormented by what turns out to be another personality within herself; *Death to Dust: What Happens to Dead Bodies* by Kenneth V. Iverson, M.D. (Galen Press), is a 700-plus-page book with wonderful chapter headings such as "I'm Dead, Now What?" and Iverson tells you about death certificates, "My Body and the Pathologist," "Wayward Bodies," and "Going Out in Style." Despite the headings, the book is quite serious and was written to encourage organ donations; *Women of the Asylum: Voices From Behind the Walls, 1840–1945* by Jeffrey Geller and Maxine Harris (Anchor); *Genocide: The Shocking True Story of America's First Serial Killer* by Harold Schecter (Pocket); *The Bone Garden: The Sacramento Boardinghouse Murders* by William P. Wood (Pocket); *Witness Against the Beast: William Blake and the Moral Law* by E. P. Thompson (The New Press); *Egyptian Mummies: Unraveling the Secrets of an Ancient Art* by Bob Brier (William Morrow); *The Complete History of Jack the Ripper* by Philip Sugden (Carroll & Graf); *The Black Museum: New Scotland Yard* by Bill Waddell (Little, Brown-UK).

Giant Monster Movies by Robert Marrero (Fantasma Books) details the early history of such movies including biographical material on Willis O'Brien, mentor to Ray Harryhausen; *The Overlook Film Encyclopedia: Horror* by Phil Hardy (Overlook) is a massive reference book with lots of nicely reproduced b&w and color stills, which covers foreign as well as American films in chronological order by year; *Japanese Science Fiction, Fantasy and Horror Films* by Stuart Galbraith IV (McFarland); *Christopher Lee, Peter Cushing and Horror Cinema* by Mark A. Miller (McFarland); *Universal Horrors: The Studio's Classic Films 1931–1946* by Michael Brunas, John Brunas, and Tom Weaver (McFarland); *Horror Film Directors 1931–1990* by Dennis Fischer (McFarland); *Songs of Love and Death: The Classic American Horror Film of the 1930s* by Michael Sevastakis (Greenwood Press); *Laughing Screaming: Modern Hollywood Horror and Comedy* by William Paul (Columbia University Press); *Science Fiction, Horror & Fantasy Film and Television Credits Supplement 2: Through 1993* by Harris M. Lentz III (McFarland & Co.); *The Films of Stephen King* by Ann Lloyd (St. Martin's); *More Things Than Are Dreamt Of: Masterpieces of Supernatural Horror From Mary Shelley to Stephen King in Literature and Film* by Alain Silver and James Ursini (Limelight Editions, 118 East 30th Street, New York, NY 10016); *How We Die* by Sherwin B. Nuland (Knopf), winner, 1994 National Book Award.

Graphic Novels:

The Sandman: World's End by Neil Gaiman, illustrated by Michael Allred, Gary Amaro, Mark Buckingham, Dick Giordano, Tony Harris, Steve Leialoha, Vince Locke, Shea Anton Pensa, Alec Stevens, Bryan Talbot, John Watkiss, and Michael Zulli, and with an introduction by Stephen King. A wonderful Chaucerian gathering of people taking cover during a "reality storm" and telling stories to pass the time. Here are stories of fairies, of different worlds, and stories within stories. A beautiful compilation.

Creatures Features (Mojo Press) is what Fred Olen Ray's *Weird Menace* tries to be—gross-out EC comic horror. There are six stories, one written by Joe R. Lansdale; *Underground 1–4* is a shared world created by Andrew Vachss (Dark Horse), in text and art with some excellent writing by Kij Johnson, Andrew Vachss, and John Weeks, and fine artwork by Ray Lago, Ted Neifeh, and Douglas Winter.

The Biologic Show: Number 0 by Al Columbia (Fantagraphics Books) is a graphic novel anthology of nine bizarre stories with mutating body parts, strange and psychotic characters, two-headed girls, and other monstrous creatures. Reminiscent of David Lynch's classic first film, *Eraserhead*. Here are beautiful renderings of ugliness and shocking visions: death, pregnancy, mutilation . . . Highly recommended.

The Mystery Play by Grant Morrison and John J. Muth (Vertigo/DC) is a good match of talents. A small depressed town in England restages medieval religious plays in order to inspire the townspeople in the midst of political scandal. The man playing god is murdered and this violent act unleashes bitterness and fear among the populace. The police investigator is not quite what he seems. A journalist just wants *out*. The story is clever but a bit too oblique. The art is in the gorgeous watercolors typical of Muth's best work. It's a beautifully produced hardcover; another Vertigo title is *The Heart of the Beast: A Love Story*, written by Dean Motter and Judith Dupre and illustrated by Sean Phillips, a clever update of the Frankenstein story set in the New York City art scene. Young aspiring actress meets nice (but mysterious) young man with a past . . .

The City by James Herbert and Ian Miller (Pan) is really Miller's baby—although the world is a post-apocalyptic version of Herbert's rat novels. Humankind is defeated, rats rule, and what's left of the city is ugly and grotesque. Text is minimal but barely needed with Miller's Boschian vision in full glorious gear.

Brief Lives is a Sandman compilation from Vertigo written by Neil Gaiman and illustrated by Jill Thompson and Vince Locke, with an afterword by Peter Straub. Delerium, the goofy punk sprite, is the prime mover of this series when she yearns to see her brother Destruction once more (he disappeared three hundred years earlier). She enlists her other brother Morpheus in tracking him down, bringing excitement and/or death to the various people they encounter on the way.

From Inside by John Bergin (Kitchen Sink) is a beautifully rendered post-apocalyptic tale of a young pregnant woman who awakens on a mysterious train. Bergin's dark vision takes her and her fellow passengers past rivers of blood and scenes of desolation and destruction as she tries to remember her past and come to terms with the imminent birth of her baby. The powerful images of birth and death bombard the reader as they do the protagonist. A dark, unforgettable vision. Highly recommended.

Another one of the best graphic novels of the year is *Mr. Punch*, the collaboration between Neil Gaiman and Dave McKean (A VG Graphic Novel). Here is a perfect combination of art and the written word. It is, like their earlier collaboration, *Violent Cases*, a look at violent and frightening world from a child's point of view, using the traditional Punch and Judy show as a recurring theme. Highly recommended.

Illustrated Books . . . for Children:

ABC by William Wegman (Hyperion) is another fun use of Wegman's famous weimaraners as they pose for the alphabet. The dogs pose for each letter, in and out of costume, in full-color photographs—Battina with a sock on her nose poses as an Elephant, Fay wears a Gown, for example, and in addition, the animals illustrate words in doggy body language in b&w. An entertaining way to teach the alphabet to children.

Diane Goode's Book of Scary Stories and Songs (Dutton Children's Books) is a charming collection of familiar and unfamiliar folk and fairy tales and songs with suitably wacky and creepy color illustrations. Spooky for children, fun for adults.

Night of the Gargoyles by Eve Bunting, illustrated by David Wiesner (Clarion Books) answers the question, "What *do* gargoyles do at night?" According to this charming b&w illustrated book they romp in the museum checking out the armor, hang out with their friends from other corners, and complain about bird doo.

The Boy Who Ate Around by Henrik Drescher (Hyperion Books for Children) goes to a lot of trouble to avoid eating lizard guts and worms (really cheese soufflé and string beans) for dinner. He turns into bigger and bigger monsters, consuming his family, friends, neighborhood, and eventually the world and every one and thing in it. When Mo, the boy, decides he's lonely he brings everything back, and lo and behold, his parents promise not to make him eat the dreaded soufflé and string beans ever again. A bit of wishful thinking here. Colorful and clever with monsters galore.

Edward Lear's Non-sense illustrated by James Wines (Rizzoli) is a new sepia-toned watercolor edition of this classic book of limericks. The artist is an architect by profession, and this beauty is his first illustrated book.

The Frog Princess, a Russian folktale retold by J. Patrick Lewis with sumptuous paintings by Gennady Spirin (Dial), is beautiful to look at with its finely detailed embroidery work. The tale combines several Russian folktales including Koschei the Deathless and Baba Yaga in addition to the frog transformations. The art is more impressive than the text.

Spooky Stories for a Dark and Stormy Night compiled by Alice Low and illustrated by Gahan Wilson (Hyperion Books for Children) is a book of traditional folktales and ghost stories retold for children and enlivened by the charmingly grotesque full-color drawings by Wilson.

The Three Golden Keys by Peter Sis (Doubleday) is a gorgeous love letter to the author/artist's young daughter about Prague, his homeland. Hidden faces, cat images, and some take-offs on Arcimboldo. Plus three folk tales. Scrumptious.

The Book That Jack Wrote by Jon Scieszka, with paintings by Daniel Adel (Viking), is a clever joke on the rhyme with the similar title. Hapless Jack is crushed by various objects. The art makes this one worthwhile—included is a cat with human nose and teeth dressed in a clown/courtier suit, a rat's tail trailing from its mouth like spaghetti. Funny and collectible.

Roald Dahl's Revolting Recipes illustrated by Quentin Blake (Viking Children's Books) is an attractively bizarre collection of recipes taken from various of Dahl's children's books, including Stink bug eggs, Hot frogs, Wormy spaghetti, and the Enormous Crocodile—surprisingly most of them look quite edible. Don't forget, Dahl was the author of the famous *Alfred Hitchcock Presents* "leg of lamb" episode.

The Nose by Nikolai Gogol is retold for children by Catherine Cowan with paintings by Kevin Hawkes (Lothrop, Lee and Shepard). This simple story of a stray nose that appears in the bread of the barber and takes off for a life on its own is sweetly told and vividly illustrated in full color.

. . . and for Adults:

Gahan Wilson's Still Weird (Forge) is a huge selection of b&w cartoons from the career of master artist of the macabre, Gahan Wilson. In the volume are one hundred new cartoons and one hundred appearing in book form for the first time. Several cartoons are poorly reproduced. Still, this is a must for Wilson fans.

Anthony Brown's *King Kong* (Turner Publishing) is the first illustrated version of King Kong in book form. Brown has, for no apparent reason, transformed Fay Wray, the "beauty" of the story, into Marilyn Monroe (no other cast member is changed)—and the adaptation loses something in translation. But it's still entertaining.

Mind Fields: The Art of Jacek Yerka and the Fiction of Harlan Ellison (Morpheus International) is a beautiful and effective melding of art and text by two major talents. Ellison has written thirty-three original stories, vignettes, and essays to match up with thirty-four works of surreal art by this Polish artist. Yerka's art has been compared to that of Magritte, Brueghel, and Dalí. Three of the stories were published in 1993, including "Susan," which appeared in *The Year's Best Fantasy and Horror: Seventh Annual Collection*. Morpheus also brought out *The Fantastic Art of Jacek Yerka: A Portfolio of Twenty-two Paintings*, most of which are not in *Mind Fields*. The text, supplied by the artist, is mostly autobiographical. The color reproduction of this surrealist's acrylics is excellent. Morpheus is currently the most important publisher of fantasy and horror art. They have regularly been publishing H. R. Giger's work in gorgeous hardcover and trade paperback editions. *Giger's Alien*, documenting the production of the film, though originally published in 1979 in hardcover, saw its first trade paperback edition when Morpheus published it in 1994.

Introducing Kafka by David Zane Mairowitz and Robert Crumb (Kitchen Sink) is a wonderful collaboration based on the life and works of Franz Kafka. Mairowitz deftly weaves the facts of Kafka's life in with his fictions while Crumb interprets *The Metamorphosis*, bits from *The Trial, The Castle, In the Penal Colony*, and other works in his own unique manner. Highly recommended.

Michael Parkes (Steltman) is the fourth collection of art by this fine surrealist, much of whose work appeared in *Omni* during the magazine's early years. The oils and stone lithographs here represent a sampling of his oeuvre from 1977–92. He uses classical images in unusual ways, creating dreamlike tableaux with beautiful women, domestic, wild, and grotesque animals, and clowns. Flight is a continuing motif in his work, as are swans and cats. A beautiful book published in The Netherlands (no price listed). Steltman Galerie and Editions, Spuistraat 330, 1012 VX Amsterdam, the Netherlands. Fax: 31-(020)-6207588.

Harm's Way: Lust & Madness Murder & Mayhem edited by Joel-Peter Witkin (Twin Palms Publishers) groups four different sets of photographs with textual commentary. The first group consists of evidentiary shots of murder victims (reprising some of the same material from Luc Sante's excellent book *Evidence*), treating death as artistic still life. The second group are medical photographs from the Burns archives with commentary by Stanley B. Burns, M.D. Here is the smallest woman ever known to have existed. She weighed 5 pounds and was 20 inches tall. She died at age twenty-six in 1890. And a woman who has a hole in her nose from syphilis, an abused baby (some of these photographs were used as social documentary by those trying to improve the lives of the poor), a man in isolation for smallpox. The third section is from Dr. Alfred C. Kinsey's Institute For Sex Research and catalogues various sexual practices. The fourth is English psychiatrist Hugh W. Diamond's collection of photographs taken by him of patients in the Surrey County Asylum where he practiced.

Images by David Lynch (Hyperion) is either 1) an expensive vanity production to make David Lynch happy or 2) a crass attempt by the publisher to make a buck off the Lynch name. Or both. This $40 coffee-table book is in two parts. The first section is comprised of b&w movie stills from Lynch's films, in reverse chronological order. The second part has drawings and photographs of Lynch enthusiasms such as sparkplugs and a trip to the dentist, biological constructions, and reproductions of his paintings. Real fans will see this as a further peek into the man's mind (isn't that what all his movies are about anyway?). No commentary or context provided.

In contrast, Peter Greenaway, director of such movies as *A Zed and Two Noughts, The Draughtman's Contract*, and *The Cook, the Thief, His Wife, and Her Lover* has written *Flying Out of This World* (The University of Chicago Press), a beautiful and illuminating art book. This is the second volume in a series developed by the Louvre and devoted to innovative writing on the visual arts. As guest curator, Greenaway selected from the Louvre's collection of European prints and drawings ninety-one masterpieces that illustrate the human longing for flight. Illustrations by Goya, Brueghel, and Redon, among others.

Soul in the Stone: Cemetery Art From America's Heartland by John Gary Brown (University Press of Kansas) is a beautiful-looking coffee-table book of funerary art but his definition of "heartland" is a bit muddied, covering everywhere from the Nebraska to Illinois to Colorado and New Mexico. The cemetery art in this book is beautiful, but it isn't any different from that in other parts of the country I'm familiar with, from Maine to New York to Louisiana.

Charles Burns' Modern Horror Sketchbook (Kitchen Sink) is for avid Burns collectors—it's a peek inside his head at ideas, characters, monsters, etc., that may or may not have become part of his work.

Odds and Ends:

Ruthenshaw: A Ghost Story by James Lees-Milne (Robinson) is a ghost story in a lovely little package. It's a pity that the story itself is not more original or spritely. It comes across as old-fashioned rather than classic. The book is hardcover with wood engravings and uses "hot type." $15 for thirty-one pages.

The *Loompanics Unlimited* book catalog is always fun to browse. The self-proclaimed "lunatic fringe of the libertarian movement" is an important source for books on subjects ranging from tax evasion and revenge to locks and locksmithing, anarchism, bombs, and explosives, and reality creation—many of which are unavailable through any other outlet. Some of the newest offerings are *The Electronic Sweatshop, Great American Hemp Industry, Jim Rose Circus Sideshow Video, Pills A-Go-Go,* and *Secrets of Methamphetamine Manufacture,* 3rd edition. The catalog is available for $5 from Loompanics Unlimited, PO Box 1197, Port Townsend, WA 98369.

The Overlook Connection, run by Dave and Laurie Hinchberger, is a book catalogue focusing on horror and dark suspense. Articles, updates, excerpts from new novels, and interviews. PO Box 526, Woodstock, GA 30188.

The 1995 Mütter Museum Calendar is the best of this always intersecting calendar, put out by the Mütter Museum of the College of Physicians of Philadelphia. I finally visited the museum itself; it is highly recommended for its two floors of medical oddities: implements used for lobotomies, a cabinet of "ingested objects" sorted by drawers, the world's largest colon. The 1995 calendar is in four color and duotone on high-quality stock. The highlights are "Murderer's Brain," photographed by Olivia Parker—John M. Wilson, who was hanged in Norristown in 1887; "Foetal Pig in Boiler Room," photographed by Max Aguilera-Hellweg—a "severely malformed nose in the form of a tube"; and "Wax Model of the Widow Sunday" by Rosamond Purcell—a woman in the nineteenth century who by the time she was eighty years old had a 10-inch horn on her forehead. Highly recommended. Can be bought in bookstores and through the museum for $14.95.

The Psychotronic Movie Calendar for 1995 by Michael J. Weldon (St. Martin's) is a fun calendar for anyone interested in trash monster movies. Full-page b&w movie posters grace each month and almost every day has *something* notable in filmland, from Johnny Eck's death to *Mothra's* debut in Tokyo. See address under Magazines on page lvii.

The 1995 Lovecraftian Horror Calendar with b&w mythos art by Allen Koszowski, H. E. Fassl, Jason C. Eckhardt, Phil Reynolds, and others—each month depicts a different mythos tale including selections from H. P. Lovecraft, Thomas Ligotti, Ramsey Campbell, Robert Bloch, and others. It also features important dates in the history of the horror genre. $9.95 postpaid payable to Kevin Ross, Artefact Publications, 1210 Greene Street, Suite 4, Boone, IA 50035.

Black Sunday 1995 Calendar signed by Barbara Steele! Mario Bava's classic horror film, banned in Great Britain until 1968 (it was made in 1960) comes in a deluxe limited edition with never-before-seen photos and text by Tim Lucas. $25, payable to *Video Watchdog.* See address under Nonfiction Magazines on page lvi.

The 1995 H. R. Giger Calendar (Morpheus International) is, as in the past, filled with glorious macabre art by the Swiss artist who designed the Alien. This is not a calendar to write on: the background is black, but it shows off the art perfectly. $14.95.

Autoerotic Fatalities by Robert R. Hazelwood, Park Elliot Dietz, and Ann Wolbert Burgess (Lexington Books) is another entry in the annals of things people will do to make themselves feel good, and incidentally, the inspiration for Jack Womack's "That Old School Tie." These are case histories of people (mostly men) who died by accident during autoerotic sex acts. Makes fascinating reading.

Cinderella's Revenge by Samuele Mazza (Chronicle) is an oddity. Pictures of shoes designed *not* to be worn. It was first published in Italy in conjunction with an exhibit for which Mazza, a fashion designer, commissioned the actual shoes. There are essays by five Italians, but the reader is given no information on who these writers are, and so have no context within which to judge their words. The shoes are beautiful, funny, grotesque; an ode to foot fetishism.

Lady Cottington's Pressed Fairy Book by Terry Jones (of Monty Python fame), illustrated by Brian Froud—their names are only on the copyright page, not the cover (Turner Publishing)—is a wicked joke, opening with a disclaimer requested by the Royal Society for the Prevention of Cruelty to Fairies, which asks the publisher to make it clear that no fairies were injured or killed during the manufacture of the book. Angelica Cottington was the child purportedly surrounded by fairies in the famous Victorian photograph. For some reason she is plagued by the creatures her whole life but no one will believe in their existence. Early on she discovers that by sitting very still with a large book on her lap, inquisitive fairies would flutter around her and she could lunge and snap the heavy book, catching them between the pages (like pressed flowers). Over the years she tries to give up the habit but is unable to; in the meantime the fairy and goblin antics become more and more lewd and frenzied. Imaginative and effective design and production—the cover looks like it's partially leather bound. Highly recommended.

The Faber Book of Murder edited by Simon Rae (Faber & Faber-UK) is a massive (500-plus pages), entertaining tome of excellent extracts, excerpts, poems, quotes, and vignettes about murder dividing organized alphabetically under subjects that interest the editor. So you've got pieces concerning cannibalism by Lord Byron and Thomas Harris, dismemberment by Ian McEwan, and murder by guitar by Kinky Friedman. This is a rare compendium that inspires the reader to go back and read or reread the source material. Highly recommended.

Averse to Beasts: 23 Reasonless Rhymes by Nick Bantock (Chronicle) is a charming, nasty, and amusing package including a hardcover book plus a tape of rhymes about turkey vultures and their manners, Llamas in pajamas, a rabbit's revenge for some motorists making roadkill of its brethren, and a city wolf after virgin wool. All illustrated by Bantock, the creator of *Griffin and Sabine*.

Stations: An Imagined Journey by Michael Flanagan (Pantheon) is a beautiful book purported to be the photo-diary of a Baltimore brakeman killed in a train crash in 1982. It has thirty-nine color images of two old railroads and is embellished with commentaries and reminiscences by McKay's cousin and excerpts from old newspapers. A six-generation family history juxtaposed against the horrors of their times. Lovely oddball item.

Blaster: The Blaster Al Ackerman Omnibus (Feh! Press) has sixty-six stories, letters, and intros by an earthy humorist of whom one editor has said "like if Aesop had been locked in a dungeon and tortured for a couple of years before being set loose to write." $12.95, payable to Feh! Press, 200 E. 10th Street #603, New York, NY 10003.

The Wild Party by Joseph Moncure March with drawings by Art Spiegelman (Pantheon) is a beautifully packaged (with red velvet endpapers) jazz-age novel in verse that was originally considered too hot to publish when it was written in 1926. But in 1928 a limited edition of 750 copies was printed and the book became a succès de scandale banned in Boston. Moncure went on to write a bestselling novel, *The Set-Up*, the story of a washed up black boxer, and then to Hollywood to write screenplays. *The Wild Party* was made into a movie in 1975 with Raquel Welch. The story is still pretty sexy and the Spiegelman illustrations enhance the text. This is the poem that William Burroughs has said made him want to be a writer. The impending violence is palpable.

Rituals of Love: Sexual Experiments, Erotic Possibilities by Ted Polhemus and Housk Randall (Picador-UK) is an engaging, personal book about S&M and bondage, with photographs and interviews with monogamous couples hetero and not, involved in other than straight sex.

Only two sets of trading cards this year: *The Ed Wood Players* with drawings by Drew Friedman featuring all the characters, oops I mean actors, you know and love from his movies. Mini-bios of each of the thirty-six; and *RIP: Real Monsters and Demons and Ghosts*, forty-two glossy, coffin-shaped cards of "chilling events." The set was conceived and designed by Eric Nesheim and authored by several writers, with illustrations by Mark Nelson, Richard Sala, and others. Both sets are from Kitchen Sink Press.

Horror and Fantasy in the Media: 1994
by Edward Bryant

In his magnificently detailed cinema wrap-up in *Locus*, the newspaper of the science fiction field, Frank M. Robinson totaled the figures and showed us that in 1994, genre films of the fantastic took in better than one *billion* dollars. That's close to the projected budget of Kevin Costner's summer 1995 adventure epic, *Waterworld*. Just kidding about the Costner project, folks, but still . . . A hundred million here, a hundred million there, and pretty soon you're talking real money.

Disney's animated hit *The Lion King* alone grossed $300 million, and that's before little matters such as the videocassette release. On the other hand, the art-house circuit release *Cronos*, one of the finest fantasy releases of the year, sold a mere $463,000 in tickets. Twelve bucks of that was mine. I saw the film twice. In its own strange way, *Cronos* was the best horror picture of 1994. Never mind that it was a two-year-old Mexican production that finally clawed its way into a U.S. release. Directed by Guillermo Del Toro, *Cronos* told the story of an aging antique dealer (Federico Luppi) who stumbles upon the Cronos Device, a niftily constructed centuries-old biomechanical machine that can bestow the gift of immortality. In form, it's something like an extremely violent Fabergé egg. Trouble is, the immortality process turns the recipient into something of an untraditional, though still blood-drinking, vampire. In the meantime, a dying industrialist (Claudio Brook) dispatches his brutal but not terribly swift nephew (Ron Perlman) to recover the Cronos Device. The virtues of this marvelously constructed picture are many. Production values are high, the script is literate; humor and horror exist side by side, along with a solid, character-driven plot. The style is evident in every frame. Best of all, *Cronos* recaptures and updates some of the warm and dark human feeling that was generated by the Universal horror films of the 1930s. The relationship between the antique dealer and his young niece is believable and affecting—and it's good to see a little-girl role in which the character actually gets to *do* something. I hope director Del Toro gets the opportunity to create much more in this vein.

The best outright-fantasy film of the year? I'd have to pick *The Mask*. Based on the John Arcudi/Doug Mahnke comic book, this was a magnificently manic translation that used state-of-the-art ILM computer graphics to create effects that evoked the feeling of live-action Tex Avery cartoons. I've got to confess something. I hated *Ace Ventura: Pet Detective*. So I was dubious about seeing Jim Carrey in *The Mask*. I shouldn't have worried. Carrey carried off the role of the nebbish converted by an ancient Scandinavian mask into a literally elastic-featured superhero brilliantly. The movie was smart, funny, and included wonderful dance numbers. Even the cute dog handled his role well. Cool.

Finding a best science fiction feature film for the year was hopeless. There simply wasn't one. The best a viewer could do was to compare the problems of all the so-so SF pictures. Okay, so there was *Star Trek: Generations*. We got to see Patrick Stewart and William Shatner in the same movie. Even better, we got to see a convincingly irritable Malcolm McDowell finish off Bill Shatner. That led to a triumph of set designer over writer or director. In the final scene, Stewart stands at the head of Shatner's cairn as the camera pulls back. Judging from the size of the grave, Shatner's only about four feet tall, or else Stewart chain-sawed the deceased Captain Kirk into itty-bitty manageable chunks. But the shot frames nicely. So I'm being picky, you say? More to the point, the movie's yet another *Star Trek* feature in which metaphysical effects crowd out things like more complex characters or an interesting (and original) story.

Ah, but what about Roland Emmerich's *Stargate*? Well, it has neat effects as we travel through an ancient interstellar teleportation device to an alien desert planet that really doesn't at all resemble Yuma, Arizona (where it was shot). Kurt Russell has one piece of character business, and then gets to run glumly around the alien world as the leader of the military mission zapped through the stargate. James Spader, sometimes a quite impressive actor, somnambulates through his thankless role as a crack linguist. Jaye Davidson is wasted as a morphing alien god. While the visuals are nice, many in the audience end up stunned into oblivion by simple but confusing elements such as completely inexplicable alien elevators. . . .

Timecop's another gorgeous production in terms of its special effects. Jean-Claude Van Damme is the officer of the title whose job is to clamp down on time-hopping bad guys who are attempting to manipulate the past in order to profit in the future. Ron Silver's the rogue senator who's the most cunning crook of them all. As with most other time-paradox melodramas, the goddess of logic soon throws up her hands, leans back, and is absorbed by the pretty pictures. Too bad.

Robert A. Heinlein's *The Puppet Masters* finally made it to the screen. Donald Sutherland had a good round as Heinlein's Old Man character. Though set in the present, the film bore a strange and disorienting feeling of juxtaposition, as though it really wanted to be a fifties B-movie. Part of that problem was a reasonable faithfulness to Heinlein's original novel. Once again, U.S. security agents are trying to figure out what's going on with an alien incursion in Iowa. The malevolent ETs are amorphous brain-controllers that hump up your back and rest between your shoulders. But in this contemporary production, and just like in the 40-plus-years-old novel, the young female agent discovers she can use her cleavage to determine who's an alien and who's not, simply by how they respond to her mammalian characteristics. Ah, the battle between the biological imperatives and political sensitivity . . .

So why do another remake of *Body Snatchers*? Well, basically because Jack Finney's story is extremely sound and lends itself well to 1956's Don Siegel, 1978's Philip Kaufman, and 1994's Abel Ferrara. Each generation seems to appreciate getting this paranoid tale of earthly invasion by enforced conformity redressed for its own particular decade. Hard-nosed director Ferrara (*Bad Lieutenant*) helms a version much more like the original than the 1978 version. This is 87 minutes of tight, edged, stylish, no-nonsense attitude. It's a B-movie for the nineties. There should be a lot of genre movies like this one out in the marketplace. There aren't. Warner Bros. kept this one on the shelf for a year or so, apparently because they couldn't quite figure out how to market it. I ended up seeing it in general release at one of Landmark Theatres' art houses. So did it reach the audience who would most have appreciated it? Probably not. At any rate, Ferrara's version is tight and in your face. Gabrielle Anwar's dad is an EPA inspector who takes his wife and two kids to a Southern Army base to check out toxic contaminations. Unlike earlier versions, we get to see just how the alien pods replicate the real humans, and then what happens to the originals. It's all suitably disgusting. Since the script sets the production on a military base, there would seem to be some tongue-in-cheek speculation about whether anybody would notice if all the local populace became a homogeneous, emotionless mass. R. Lee Ermey, a career soldier before Stanley Kubrick seduced him into acting in *Full Metal Jacket*, does a good job as the base commander. Meg Tilly plays Anwar's mother and uses a body double named Jennifer (no last name) for her big nude scene. Forrest Whitaker plays the base medic, but doesn't get to do nearly enough. All in all, *Body Snatchers* does its job economically and well. I think its only real problem is that it does have to compete not just against many viewers' memories of the other two versions, but the whole gestalt image, familiar to a large chunk of pop culture consumers, of the body-snatchers concept, through all manner of pod-people references, myths, and parodies.

* * *

Back over on the darker, supernatural side of things, a lot of viewers were tremendously curious both about Neil Jordan's *Interview With the Vampire* and Kenneth Branagh's *Mary Shelley's Frankenstein*. Irish director Jordan had made his big commercial splash with *The Crying Game*; but those of us who haunt odd screenings were already quite familiar with *The Company of Wolves*, his version of two offbeat takes on "Little Red Riding Hood" by Angela Carter. *Company* was an intriguing and stylish film that was marketed horribly when it was released in the United States. *Interview* didn't monopolize the headlines in the way the O.J. trial has, but it still garnered considerable press attention after Tom Cruise was cast as the vampire Lestat. First, novelist Anne Rice was outraged; then she reversed herself and did her level best to display her approval of the movie.

For the rest of us, the film was a fairly good translation of the novel. The homoerotic content still seemed to be there, though never incredibly obvious. There will be plenty of callow young gothic punkers who probably thought that all the guy vampires were just good friends.

The film's overall approach was lush, but the results were not always involving. There were moments, though. The scene in which vampiric depredations are committed upon toy poodles was perversely hilarious. The scene in which the Parisian vampires, pretending to be faux vampires in their theatrical act, hungrily batten on a helpless human victim was brilliantly cinematic and utterly chilling.

Brad Pitt and Antonio Banderas were competent in their young-blood roles. Kirsten Dunst was a wonderful surprise in her role as the child vampire Claudia. The film version sprang a surprise ending on the book readers. Perhaps the most troubling image in the whole production came as I pondered the aging Lestat. After two centuries, the poor boy looked a little the worse for wear. But when Louis tracks him down in contemporary New Orleans, Tom Cruise-as-Lestat, with his pallid skin, distinctive nose, and stringy hair, looks like nothing so much as the ghost of Tiny Tim (the singer, not the Dickens character). That colored the whole rest of the picture for me.

So *Interview With the Vampire* was a quite creditable production, but certainly not the definitive vampire flick. Footnote: Anne Rice's *other* movie for the summer, the Garry Marshall–directed *Exit to Eden*, augured itself right into the ground. Starring Dana Delany, Dan Aykroyd, and Rosie O'Donnell, this picture may simply have showed that a tremendously broad comedic version of Rice's erotic novel was not really the instrument to sway the American viewing public to react sympathetically to an acceptance of S&M as fluffy escapist fare.

Kenneth Branagh's contribution to the Frankenstein canon was treated horribly by the critics. I got the feeling that *Mary Shelley's Frankenstein* received much the same reaction as did Walter Murch's *Return to Oz* a decade ago. Both directors had the temerity to reinvent a cultural icon, something audiences don't always appreciate. Just as *Return to Oz* was dark and more like L. Frank Baum's original work and less evocative of the MGM classic, so *Mary Shelley's Frankenstein* moved away from many of the fond memories viewers still have of Boris Karloff with bolts in his neck.

Some viewers couldn't figure out what the framing scenes in the frozen Arctic were all about. Others seemed disturbed that the monster (Robert DeNiro) was quite the articulate and intelligent fellow once he got his wits about him.

Publicity aside, the movie was not a strictly faithful translation of Shelley's seminal novel, but it was still one of the most accurate interpretations ever filmed. Splashy and operatic in Branagh's filming (he also played Victor, the good doctor), the film had its moments of repellent horror and genuine compassion. The "creation of life" scene would have done credit to any of Francis Ford Coppola's operatic dramas. Branagh did well, and someday he'll get his proper recognition.

Much more contemporary, but even splashier, was Alex Proyas's *The Crow*. This is the infamous adaptation of J. O'Barr's dark, brooding comic book in which star Brandon Lee was accidentally shot to death shortly before the end of filming. The script by John Shirley and David J. Schow is quick-moving and hip.

The Crow is a modern, street-gritty, urban fantasy about a rock musician, murdered along with his lover, who comes back to life to exact retribution. Shot at music-video pace, mostly at night, the film generated a few audience complaints (at the premiere I attended) that the movie was (literally) too dark and too loud. To paraphrase criticism of alternative rock, maybe the audience in question was just too old.

In any case, *The Crow* is a nice piece of semiotic filmmaking with style and attitude up the wazoo. It blends its comic-book violence with some humane character relationships, poses a few fascinating technical exercises as the filmmakers covered for their star's untimely absence, and is particularly affecting for its medium-is-the-message intersection of fantasy and tragic reality.

For a brave attempt at meta-filmmaking—making a fantasy movie about making fantasy movies—I hope you all gave *Wes Craven's New Nightmare* a try. Now, those of you counting on fingers and toes may just have assumed this was merely *Nightmare on Elm Street, VII*, and given it a pass the way you would most other sequels. That would have been doing this film an injustice. Keep in mind I'm speaking as one who thought Craven's original *Nightmare*, a decade ago, was a firstrate piece of scary storytelling that went far beyond simple-minded slashery. It was an imaginatively mounted production that spookily evoked the treacherous interface between dream fantasy and waking reality.

Long at odds with New Line, director Craven made his peace and agreed to put together the new sequel. It's not as good as his original, but it's certainly more successful than any of the films between. The conceit in the present chapter is that Wes Craven (playing himself) is making a new Freddy Krueger flick with Heather Langenkamp and Robert Englund (both also playing themselves as actors). In Craven's office, we get to see a rack of books that includes both a clutch of Stephen King novels and Dan Simmons's vampire novel, *Children of the Night*. We also get to see some real-life New Line executives, including head honcho Robert Shay.

The filming-within-the-filming turns sinister when Freddy starts making his forays from the dream world to the "real." This time around, Freddy retreats from his Vegas comedy-club persona and takes on a much more malevolent persona. That's all for the good.

The movie (the one *we* all see) eventually mires a bit in melodrama, but most of what has gone before is fascinating and entertaining. One is left wishing that the *process* of scaring an audience through fantasy had been better explicated and left at the heart of the film. But the glass is not really half empty; it is, in fact, more than half full.

The producers of *Brainscan* tried to create a new franchise villain à la Freddy Krueger. As a fantasy/reality border-walker called the Trickster, stage actor T. Ryder Smith did his over-the-top best, but he couldn't help teenagers Edward Furlong and Amy Hargreaves bring off this movie about kids, angst, and fantasies come to unwholesome and dangerous life. John Flynn directed from a script by Andrew Kevin Walker. All tried valiantly, but to little avail.

Rachel Tallalay's *The Ghost in the Machine* opens fantastically when a Cleveland pattern killer (his victims are drawn from stolen address books—how he steals so many address books, and what he would do if he ran into a truly social person with hundreds of friends and acquaintances is something of a mystery in itself) gets possession of one page of Karen Allen's address book. But when he's on his way to do in divorced mom Allen and her young son, he has a car wreck and ends up in a hospital MRI unit. While he's being scanned, an electrical storm and enormous power surge put the killer's brain scan into the mainframe of a huge data service. You can probably see where this one's going. Chris

Mulkey plays the genius onetime computer outlaw who tries to figure out what's really going on and do something about it. The depiction of the terrible things a computer and data bank can do to one's life is nicely depicted (though Gordon R. Dickson and others have done it better in prose) and the vulnerability of a human to her home's electrical system is shown with sufficient paranoid enthusiasm (though, again, there's a superior predecessor in John Varley's "Press Enter □"). The effects are cool, though the filmmakers clearly had a hard time grasping exactly what a particle accelerator is or does. After a smart beginning, this one dumbs down all too quickly.

Wolf is pretty darn good. This is a big summer film based on the novel by Jim Harrison. Who, you ask? Jim Harrison, the Michigan upstate mainstream writer. You maybe saw the rather dumbed-down version of his novella, *Revenge*. Kevin Costner and Tony Scott couldn't quite carry the thing off.

Anyhow, *Wolf* is a class act all the way. Admittedly it took a good many years and quite an adventure in combatting studio politics to get it made at all. Fortunately, Harrison's friendship with Jack Nicholson helped quite a lot. History seems to have it that Harrison wrote somewhere from three to five versions of the script before giving up in frustration. Wesley Strick was brought in to do another rewrite. Finally director Mike Nichols got Elaine May to do a final uncredited rewrite, beefing up the female lead.

And so it came to be, this fast, literate, funny, violent tale of lycanthropy in the contemporary New York publishing world. Jack Nicholson plays a famous book editor about to be canned by the international tycoon (Christopher Plummer) who's just bought the publishing house and plans to turn it into a cash cow with no literary ambitions. Nicholson discovers he's been not only torpedoed, but replaced by his ambitious young marketing chief (James Spader). Spader's a wonderful actor who does particularly well with vicious, smarmy, yuppie roles.

Prior to all this, while on a trip to transact business with one of his authors, Nicholson is bitten by a wolf he's hit with his car on a wintry nighttime Vermont road. Nicholson figures a clean bandage and a tetanus shot will fix everything up just fine. Naturally he's as wrong as wrong can be.

Then comes the coup at the publishing house, coupled with the twin tragedy of being betrayed by his wife (Kate Nelligan), with James Spader no less. Things are not looking up for Nicholson. Not until he meets Michelle Pfeiffer, the daughter of the rapacious tycoon who's bought the publishing house.

We get to see Nicholson hit emotional bottom and then start to change, subtly at first, then more visibly. His makeover is both psychological and physical. It's that Vermont wolf-bite. . . . One of the archetypal plots is "the biter bitten," wherein some nasty character gets a dose of his own medicine as the audience cheers. *Wolf* is the obverse of that. Here it becomes a matter of the bitten becoming, quite literally, the biter.

Nicholson discovers he's looking younger (and hairier). He's more fit. He's sexier. He learns to mark his territory, lupine style. He's no one's doormat anymore. But no sooner does he accept his new role as a werewolf (after ranging the suburban night and killing a deer with his bare paws and teeth), than his estranged wife is found savagely murdered. Did Jack do it in his wolfish fugue state?

And it accelerates from there.

This is a role tailor-made for Nicholson. And it's a role off which such actors as Pfeiffer, Spader, and Nelligan can play beautifully and to advantage.

One of the things that intrigued me about the film is that the term "werewolf" appears not once anywhere in the script. Reference is made to Nicholson's being taken over by the spirit of the wolf, but that's about as specific as anything gets. I think this was partly done to avoid the stigma of the horror genre and partly because everybody concerned wanted to do a movie that would appeal, without talking down, to the ever-expanding market of literate, "spiritual," yuppie viewers. Well, hey, it works. The movie's got both action and sensuality (though it's never quite so hot as some observers would have you believe), along with a nice metaphysical message about integrating the beast and the human soul.

I also noted that Harrison/Strick/May's script felt perfectly okay about reinventing werewolf mythology. Remember that most of what most of us think we know about lycanthropes comes not from some ancient tradition of folklore, but rather from the somewhat newer mythology fabricated in the 1930s Universal *Wolfman* pictures.

So good for Jim Harrison, Jack Nicholson, Mike Nichols, and the rest. This one's firstrate all the way.

If you wanted a lightweight fantasy for the summer, *The Flintstones* probably sated your lust for heavily buttered popcorn and a giant mound of cotton candy. What with both Amblin Entertainment and Hanna-Barbera behind this one, there was considerable clout in evidence.

Content? Well, forget that. What you did get was a lot of amiable yuks and guffaws courtesy of old favorites Fred (John Goodman), Wilma (Elizabeth Perkins), Barney (Rick Moranis), and Betty (Rosie O'Donnell). The slight plot was helped by good work by Kyle MacLachlan and Halle Berry. It was a treat to see the return of Elizabeth Taylor, as Pearl Slaghoople. Brian Levant directed from a script by Tom Parker & Jim Jennewein and Steven E. de Souza.

You watched this one for jokes, especially in-jokes, and bizarre cultural references. ILM and Jim Henson's Creature Shop created the effects, all properly cartoony. And you listened for the soundtrack music courtesy of the B-52s (billed as the BC-52s), the Thrill Kill Kult, Green Jelly (not your everyday contributing artist to a movie's musical tapestry), and so on.

So is *The Flintstones* a Guilty Pleasure? Naw, it's a profound reflection of our times and recent past.

Truthfully, I really wanted *The Shadow* to be a solid Guilty Pleasure. Australian Russell Mulcahy directed from a David (*Jurassic Park*) Koepp script. Based on the old pulp series by Walter B. Gibson, *The Shadow* gave us Alec Baldwin as ambivalent hero Lamont Cranston ("Who knows what evil lurks in the hearts of men . . . the Shadow knows . . . heh, heh, heh . . .") and Penelope Ann Miller as sidekick Margo Lane. A solid supporting cast included Peter Boyle, Tim Curry, Jonathan Winters, and Sir Ian McKellen. The always impressive John Lone played the villain, Shiwan Khan.

So what went awry? Something went very wrong with this picture. It looked beautiful, set for the most part in a wonderful deco fantasy cityscape. I'm afraid the fault probably can be assigned back to the script. Dumb, dumb, dumb. It did not help that the filmmakers couldn't quite seem to get their collective tongue out of their collective cheek.

The result, sadly, is silly pulp fiction, rather than smart pulp fiction.

While I'm at it, I suppose I ought to mention *Street Fighter*. There really is a proposition more dubious than basing big budget films on pulp novels and comic books (hey, look at *Batman*!)—creating major productions around computer games. Remember *Super Mario Brothers*? Next year, you'll be treated to *Mortal Kombat*. This year saw *Street Fighter*. Actually, this slam-bang adventure film with Jean-Claude Van Damme was based on the game Street Fighter II, but there was the problem with misrepresenting the picture as a sequel. . . . After officials read the script, the United Nations chose not to cooperate with the filming. The reason to see this movie, if you're over twelve, is very simple: Raul Julia. In his final movie role, this fine actor played the villain. In an interview, Julia said he wanted to take on the role for his kids. R.I.P.

Then there's a fantasy picture I expected to hate a lot; or if not hate, at least to feel a profound boredom while watching. Imagine my surprise when I sat through all two hours plus of Bernardo Bertolucci's *Little Buddha* with Keanu Reeves and came way feeling fairly charitable. Bertolucci tells a 1990s-anchored tale of the young Siddhartha, the young guy who 2,500 years ago in India became the Buddha, and intercutting it with the account of a young kid in contemporary Seattle who's told by Buddhist monks that he is likely the reincarnation of a revered lama. The script's by Mark Peploe and Rudy Wurlitzer.

Keanu Reeves plays Siddhartha, looking very brown and suave in eye makeup. So is he as vacuous and Southern Californian as his botched role in *Francis Ford Coppola's Dracula* might forecast? Nope. His role is not incredibly terrific, but neither is it anything like a disaster. The problem with his part of the picture is that he mysteriously starts to fade out of the plot about midway through the film. We get to see Prince Siddhartha, always overprotected by his daddy the King, discover the existence of the poor, the old, the afflicted. The prince goes off to find out what all this means and becomes involved for some years with a rough gang of ascetics. But the movie zips us along like a Disney World panoramic ride, and disappointingly skips over such nifty episodes in Siddhartha's life as when he learned about the uglier side of being a businessman, and when he received considerable instruction in sex and sensuality.

Back in the twentieth century, Chris Isaak (yup, the singer) and Bridget Fonda do well as the rationalist parents who are naturally a little skeptical that their Nordic-looking young son might be the avatar of a Tibetan teacher.

But eventually they go along with the plan to have their kid visit Bhutan. There, father and son meet the young boy and young girl who are the other two possible incarnations of the lama. It's all spectacularly shot on location. Regardless of your spiritual orientation, this is one beautiful picture.

Though I did think the Siddhartha track got shorted, I still found myself going along with the whole idea of the film. In a sense, this is sort of a nicely humanistic version of *The Omen*. You can consider reincarnation either as a flat-out fantasy element—or as a reasonable and realistic alternative to contemporary American urban rationalism.

Because of that last, Bertolucci's film made me think of Michael Tolkin's *The Rapture*, that major feature of several years back with Mimi Rogers. The movie was a perfectly serious and respectful treatment of fundamentalist Christianity's anticipation and reception of the Rapture without ever being a piece of propaganda. It's an intellectual effort I'm delighted to see expended.

And I hope to see more efforts along this line.

The horror of violent movies? Well, shucks, there were a couple of really good ones in 1994, and a bunch more not-so-hot examples. The best were, of course, *Pulp Fiction* and *Natural Born Killers*.

Quentin Tarantino's *Pulp Fiction* couldn't be more different from *Forrest Gump*, its primary competition for the Oscar for Best Picture. Tarantino's cynical, hilarious, inventive, nonstop entertainment offended some people who simply didn't like its values (read attitude). If you didn't take it as the final word on how the world and all the people in it function all the time, then you probably got an enormous kick out of it. Every Guilty Pleasure in the book is here, including seeing John Travolta make yet another successful comeback in company with Uma Thurman. The twist competition is great. A scene in which Travolta attempts to revive Thurman after she snorts the wrong powder is purely astonishing. Bruce Willis does well as a washed-up boxer in this set of plaited plot cords. Tarantino proves with this major critical and crowd-pleasing success that he can treat nasty people and nasty subjects with more panache than virtually any other young director.

Oliver Stone adapted and directed *Natural Born Killers* from an early Quentin Tarantino script. The version as shot is something of a contemporary updating of the Charles Starkweather/Caril Fugate teen murder spree in the fifties. Woody Harrelson drops neatly into his role as Mickey; Juliette Lewis works fine as Mallory. They're two crazed young folks on a surreal, speed-edited search for the real America. Robert Downey, Jr., plays the sleazoid British tabloid reporter hot on their trail to document their presumed contribution to modern mythology. Actually everyone in this film comes across as crazed, including Tommy Lee Jones playing the warden of the prison where Mickey and Mallory end up incarcerated. There are lots of questions set up here, some wit, considerable violence, and, thankfully, not much in the way of lead-footed answers.

It's all too easy to think of *Romeo Is Bleeding* as something of a tourist version of *The Bad Lieutenant*. Gary Oldman is a British actor who can do a wonderful American accent. In this case, he's a corrupt New York City cop named Jack Grimaldi. Poor Jack manages to get himself in all manner of trouble with his colleagues, the Feds, the mob, his wife, his girlfriend, and an eastern European hitwoman played by Lena Olin. It's a good cast with his wife being played by Annabella Sciorra and his girlfriend by Juliette Lewis. With director Peter Medak (*The Ruling Class*), one expects style, and there's a lot of that. The only problem is that Hilary Henkin's script all too frequently abandons reality. It's not so much the glitch that all the dirt that is dug out of a brand-new grave neatly fills it back up, it's more the weirdness of everyone agreeing that a certain event will be celebrated six months apart—on May 1 and December 1. Is this an alternate world where August has vanished? Is it symbolic of Jack's simply being really screwed up? Who knows? Roy Scheider has a great time playing a Mafia boss. The audience frequently enjoys the nice moments, along with the naughty bits. But this is a movie where the aim and accomplishment swing widely. I believe this was meant as a *noir* homage. Too frequently it comes across as noir hash.

Actually one of the best crazed-killer movies of 1994 was John Waters's *Serial Mom*. It's good to see witty, wacked-out psychotic humor, especially when focused through Kathleen Turner, as the suburban mom of the title. She's a nice but obviously troubled lady who discovers that murder can be a useful tool for surviving the vicissitudes of dealing with the kids' schools, obnoxious neighbors, and other topical irritants. This film demonstrates a whole different path that could have been taken by her character in *Body Heat*.

The small screen saw some fine attempts at big-screen ambitions through made-for-TV movies. The biggest and boldest was ABC's eight-hour, $28 million miniseries version of Stephen King's *The Stand*. Mick Garris helmed this mammoth undertaking for Laurel Entertainment. As executive producer and screenwriter, Stephen King was in the catbird seat in terms of keeping this adaptation faithful to the spirit and, often, the letter of the original novel.

From the chilling tour of a bioweapon-slaughtered underground complex to the tune of "Don't Fear the Reaper," to the apocalyptic ending in neon-cooked Las Vegas, the movie captured the feel of the book. The cast did fine: Gary Sinise (Stu Redman), Laura San Giacomo (Nadine Cross), Ray Walston (Glen Bateman), Miguel Ferrer (Lloyd Henreid), Matt Frewer (Trashcan Man), Rob Lowe (Nick Andros). Bill Fagerbakke did fine as retarded Tom Cullen, as did Ruby Dee as Mother Abigail Freemantle. There were nice cameos courtesy of Ed Harris, Kathy Bates, and many others. As the Walkin Dude, evil personified, Jamey Sheridan did well, even if the role was one that every viewer had his or her own specific opinion about who should have filled it. Poor Molly Ringwald could never quite bring Frannie Goldsmith to life.

Lots of location shooting added to the verisimilitude and sweep. Utah stood in for Boulder, Colorado, the abode of the forces of good, but probably only local residents noticed the discrepancies.

The pace held up, even over several evenings. Finally my only real problem with the production was the same one I'd had with the book. It's probably a personal metaphysical thing, but I thought—and still do—that the drama of good versus evil is terribly undercut by a climax in which the hand of God quite literally comes down and saves humankind's bacon. I'd rather see humanity wield the ultimate power of their salvation. Go figure.

But aside from that, *The Stand* was one superb piece of extended storytelling.

On a somewhat less elevated level, the *TekWar* movies in the Universal Adventure SixPack series were pretty cool. Based on William Shatner's SF ideas and starring Greg Evigan as future detective Jake Cardigan, these films function as solid science fiction near-future adventure diversions. Not a lot of brain, but still considerable fun. The look and the effects are firstrate. I can think of no other depiction of cyberspace that's been as effective or convincing.

HBO produced *Witch Hunt*, a dark fantasy detective film set in an alternate history 1950s L.A. where just about everyone but maverick private detective H. Philip Lovecraft practices magic. Paul Schrader directed from the script by Joseph Dougherty. In a previous film in this series, Fred Ward played Lovecraft. This time around, Dennis Hopper fills the role. As much as I like Hopper, I feel Ward was more convincing. The plot concerns McCarthyesque hearings equating magic-wielders with Commies. The cast includes Penelope Ann Miller, Eric Bogosian, and Sheryl Lee Ralph. Good entertainment.

Ditto for HBO's *Fatherland*, adapted by Ron Hutchinson and Stanley Weiser from Robert Harris's novel about a murder investigation in an alternate history track in which the Nazis won World War II. Rutger Hauer plays the SS cop investigator; Miranda Richardson's the visiting U.S. reporter. The plot revolves around political machinations on Der Führer's birthday in 1964, and a terrible secret that, revealed, could bring down the Reich. Christopher Menaul directs. Not bad as political intrigue goes, but none too startling for readers accustomed to alternate world plots.

The Fox Network did a very good thing by reactivating the wonderful series *Alien Nation*, even if only for a two-hour movie, *Alien Nation: Dark Horizon*. A couple years ago, viewers had found the series to be vastly superior to the original feature film. The characters were involving; the plot about alien slave-refugees marooned on Earth made a good reflecting mirror for plots that examine California's role as a multicultural melting pot. Then the series was cancelled abruptly. *Dark Horizon* wraps up some of the loose ends. Eric Pierpoint and Michelle Scarabelli, Tenctonese detective George Francisco and his wife in the show, along with Gary Graham (the human detective Matthew Sikes) and Teri Treas (Sikes's Tenctonese friend, Cathy Frankel) all return to the cast. The previous cliffhanger is resolved as the Newcomers' slaver overlords discover where their missing "possessions" have ended up. The TV film is very good; but it whets the appetite for the return of the series.

The X-Files continues to be one of the coolest series on television. One of the Fox Network's most successful acquisitions, the series garnered a Golden Globe Award for best dramatic series during its second season. The relationship between FBI agents Mulder (David Duchovny) and Scully (Gillian Anderson) continues to deepen in complexity and warm up a bit as the pair investigates bizarre federal cases ranging from clones and alien bounty hungers, to middle-class WASP satanists and invisible elephants (!). At its best, this series created by Chris Carter demonstrates high imagination, clever construction, genuinely affecting moments, and a modicum of wit. It does this often through the method of effectively trying to cram a 90-minute drama into an hour slot. Hardly an episode goes by in which there is not some peculiar plot element that, even in the context of the series, just doesn't make a lick of sense. But the episodes slide by so quickly, the viewer just figuratively shrugs and eagerly anticipates whatever's going to happen next. *The X-Files* is still building; there's no sign yet of peaking, burn-out, or that inevitable downward slide.

The long-awaited J. Michael Straczynski SF series, *Babylon 5*, appeared a bit more than a year after its pilot. This is one of the first offerings of Warner's Prime Time Entertainment Network. At this point, the show's appearing in many parts of the country on Fox stations. I think everyone's known from the git-go that this show would have the advantage of state-of-the-art computerized effects (it's not hard to imagine hordes of eager young FX types hunched over their video toasters in a scene out of *Brazil*). The question in many minds seems to have been, will the show have good characters, decent acting, and something that will set it off from endless comparisons to *Star Trek*s Classic, Crystal, and Lite. The temptation has been, I frankly think, to keep trying to correlate elements of the show with influences from all the zillions of previous SF movies and TV shows. X-wing fighters? Hmm. The commander keeps going out to where the action is instead of hanging around the bridge like a real-world administrative officer? Hmm.

The series was a bit of a slow starter. No big splash at the beginning. But it's become incremental. Creator Straczynski's planned a five-year plot arc for the whole show. What he wants is a hundred-hour novel for television. Now that's ambition. And it could work.

I think *Babylon 5* really hit its stride about the third or fourth week with an episode called "Infection." In this one, David McCallum plays a university academic who comes to the station with some boxes of alien artifacts and a corporate stone-killer sidekick. McCallum wants help from the station doctor (Richard Biggs) since he needs some clandestine help in figuring out how the artifacts apply to biomechanical technology. Naturally everything goes hideously wrong and the killer sidekick gets transformed into a humanoid biomek weapon that ambitiously starts to hunt down and slaughter all the quarter million humans and aliens on Babylon 5. Episode writer Straczynski manages to pull some reasonable surprises out of his hat, ringing changes on both *Alien* and any number of *Star Trek* action scripts. It *does* occur to the crew that maybe they ought to deep-six the alien intruder right out the airlock. And there's a very nicely affecting conversation in which the security chief (Jerry Doyle) and the commander (Michael O'Hare) discuss this matter of the commander constantly going out into the field and putting his life on the line. Then there are two separate morals, well delivered, about going to the stars, and not ignoring the lessons of history. The episode even manages to end on a dark political note. Well done.

By the end of the year, O'Hare had departed the show, and Bruce Boxleitner replaced him as the new commander. The interstellar politics, the buried plot revelations, the character interactions, all continue to evolve into more complex forms. While by no means a paradigm for cutting-edge nineties science fiction, *Babylon 5* has made great strides in showing the kind of on-screen SF the various *Star Trek* series could have been, but never have been able to achieve.

Speaking of the *Star Trek* universe, *The Next Generation* passed on to its greater glory in syndication, and *Deep Space Nine* retooled slightly with a new spaceship and made noises about becoming more exciting. *SeaQuest* DSV also retooled, with a new cephalopod-shaped submarine, but it didn't help a whole lot. But then the show's evidently not intended to be a fully adult series.

June saw the debut of MTV's own half-hour cyberpunk series, something of a clumsy hybrid of *The Fugitive* and *Logan's Run*, with just a dash of *Neuromancer*. Now admittedly this was something like *Masterpiece Theater* as compared to *Beavis and Butthead*, but it was still not everything one could hope for. *Dead at 21* stars Jack Noseworthy as Ed, a young dude who has just turned twenty. At his party, he 1) meets a foxy, bored dudette, but just as things look promising, 2) a guy on the run bursts through Ed's window, closely pursued by a homicidal Federal agent named Winston (Whip Hubley). There's a dismally orchestrated action sequence, and then Ed and Maria take off on a motorcycle, along with a bag that turns out to hold an informative videotape. So Ed breaks into a closed Silo (good product placement there) and watches an account by the now-dead fugitive. He's told that twenty-something years ago, the U.S. government set up a secret experiment to implant microchips in a whole bunch of babies. The idea was to boost everybody's intelligence, turn them into "neurocybernauts." Only problem is, there's a problem. When the kids hit about twenty-one, they mentally melt down. Bummer. All this is a set-up so that Ed and Maria have to flee the government bad guys and seek help from a disappeared adult scientist. The script's by Jon Sherman; Ralph Hemecker directed. The quick-cut dream sequence effects are pretty good, but the melodrama's on the slack side. The writing's perfunctory, and there's not much by way of acting to reclaim it. It's not even good music video production level stuff.

While *Dead at 21* lasted about as long as the *Tammy Grimes Show*, there was plenty of other series tube fodder. Good, bad, and occasionally ugly, you could fill your tapes with *Space Precinct*, *Space Rangers*, *TekWar: The Series*, *RoboCop*, *Forever Knight*, *Highlander*, *Lois and Clark*, *The Simpsons*, *Picket Fences*, *Mantis*, *Tales From the Crypt*, *Earth 2*, the newest incarnation of *Kung Fu*, and on and on.

But just wait. *Star Trek: Voyager* and *VR-5* are on their way.

It's hard to keep up with music that either contains fantastic elements or else complements the more orthodox entries in the field of the fantastic. But, with a little help from my friends, I've got a few suggestions for diverse listening.

Somtow Sucharitkul's second feature film, his contemporary, L.A.-at-night, street-gritty, elf-punk version of *A Midsummer Night's Dream*, *William Shakespeare's Ill Met By Moonlight*, isn't in release yet, but the merchandising's coming right along. Hard on the heels of the satin crew jackets is the audiocassette edition of the soundtrack. It's fascinating, an accomplished piece of film scoring, and is well worth checking out. Now I admit to having something of a conflict of interest here, since I played Peter Quince, the author of the play within the play in the production. But having said that, I'll simply offer several observations about Somtow's music. The first amazing thing is that the performance is nearly all Somtow's. All the approximately 48 minutes of included music is the product of digital sampling. It's a quantum level above the ambition and quality of Somtow's music in his initial feature, *The Laughing Dead*. The only participation by another human being here is the startling soprano of Stacey Tappan on two pieces. The rest . . . well all of it is eclectic as all get-out. This is a magnificent magpie album with hundreds of references, musical allusions, parodies, homages—some blatant, some sly—to film music spanning the century. You'll find parodic gestures here to composers ranging from Nina Rota to Ennio Morricone, and Miklos Rosza to James Horner. It may be that Somtow missed Danny Elfman. I'm not sure. But I did note the five different variations rung on the "Sugar Plum Fairy" theme: horror movie, rap, industrial/metal, cocktail lounge, and rockabilly. Incredible. And hysterical. Other influences? Oh, both Japanese and Bavarian. A little more Wagner. Lions and tigers and bears, oh my! This album's an oddity, but it's a keeper.

On Sunday night, May 29, 1994, booksellers crowded the Hollywood Palladium for the third yearly concert of the Rock Bottom Remainders. The supergroup of writers (their T-shirt says "3 chords and an attitude") this year included such as Stephen King, humorists Roy Blount, Jr., and Dave Barry, novelists Amy Tan and Ridley Pearson, cartoonist Matt Groening, critics Dave Marsh and Joel Selvin, sportswriter (and Elvis impersonator) Mitch Albom, and the originator of the Remainders, Bay Area literary escort, Kathi Kamen Goldmark. Proceeds from the performance benefitted the American Booksellers Foundation for Free Expression and several other charities such as Right to Rock.

The evening launched with a stand-up routine by Roy Blount, Jr., and a set by Damn Right I Got the Blues, a British blues band headlined by thriller writer Ken Follett. Considering it was white British guys playing black American music, it was pretty fine. Especially good were freelance journalist Graham Coster on harmonica and vocals and Curtis Brown literary agent Antony Harwood (onetime guitarist for the punk group The

Vibrators). The quality of music was vastly improved from Follett's group last year (which included Douglas Adams on guitar).

The second act was an irreverent unplugged set by Texas country-and-weirdness rocker and mystery novelist Kinky Friedman. I suspect the audience will never forget his renditions of "Get Your Biscuits in the Oven and Your Buns in the Bed" (signed for the audience by a comely young blond interpreter) and "I'm an Asshole from El Paso."

Then the Rock Bottom Remainders took the stage for a solid set of oldie covers, some very straight, some, well, altered in peculiar ways. . . . Studio musician ringers Josh Kelly on drums and Jerry Peterson on sax are still with the band and add considerable professionalism. Musical director Al Kooper was not on hand for the performance. But time and practice tell. The band's enthusiasm is undiminished, and their musicianship keeps improving. Stephen King's never going to replace Richard Thompson, but what the hell—he's a solid symbol for all us other vicarious rockers out in the sea beyond the stage.

So the musical level was pretty good, and the fun level was *way* up there. Amy Tan did a great recap of her last year's dominatrix version of Nancy Sinatra's "These Boots Are Made for Walking." Even more butch this year, in a leather costume, she convincingly whipped the male band members into line.

Ah, but then came the finale. All the Remainders and Ken Follett's group crowded onto stage for the traditional rendition of "Gloria." And then Dave Barry told the audience that someone wanted to sit in on the finale, but he was a little musically impaired, and so we all should be kind.

And that's when Bruce Springsteen ambled out. The crowd went berserk. About two hundred women who had smuggled cameras past the security guards rushed past me toward the stage. The Boss's jamming with the Remainders was the perfect cap to a great evening.

I must say that Stephen King is not the only writer in the field of the fantastic who takes a turn on stage and jams with the best of 'em. Richard Christian Matheson still occasionally drums. John Mason Skipp, half of the notorious Skipp & Spector collaborative horror-writing team, writes and performs with the L.A. band Mumbo's Brain. Their first album, *The Book of Mumbo*, has just been completed and I look forward to hearing it. And then, of course, there's Joe Stefko, the drummer for the classic rock band The Turtles, who is both a major collector in the horror field and a prominent specialty-press publisher, creating lavish editions under the Charnel House imprint.

Tia Travis is a remarkable young horror writer who also plays bass for Curse of Horseflesh, a most peculiar Calgary band. There's a distinctly surreal quality to the alternating tracks of traditional (well, sort of) country and surf band (Dick Dale would be jealous) on the self-titled mini-album (try writing the Curse of Horseflesh Fan Club, c/o Alan Wayne, PO Box 64252, Calgary, Alberta, Canada T2K 6J1). "Andromeda Stomp" could easily be on the sound track of a remake of *Dark Star*. "Wreck of the Old 97" sounds a little like the Beat Farmers on crank. "Andromeda Stomp," backed with "Old Joe Clark," can also be obtained on an old-fashioned 45 RPM vinyl disc by contacting Roto-flex at the fan club address above.

The concept album *The Last Temptation* (Sony Epic) by 1995 World Horror Convention guest (though he had to bow out at the last minute to film a TV series episode) Alice Cooper is an accomplished dark fantasy treatment of matters Faustian and theological.

The soundtrack album from *The Crow* (Atlantic) is solid basic stuff—good background sounds for standing at your window on a rainy wind-whipped midnight, staring out with a Byronic glower before retreating inside to read another few chapters of *The Fountainhead*. Of course it helps if you're under twenty-three, but the thrill of rebellion's still there if you're older—so long as you've got a good in-dash stereo in your car. High points include tracks by the Rollins Band, Nine Inch Nails, the Violent Femmes, The Jesus and Mary Chain, and Jane Siberry.

Horror writer Gary Jonas, along with recommending Alice Cooper's *The Last Tempta-*

tion, suggested checking out current albums from Queensryche and Soulhat—solid, dark, nasty stuff. Writer and laborer in the vineyards of music retail Trey Barker nominated Soundgarden's *Superunknown*; Cracker's "Movie Star," "Kerosene Hat," and "Take Me Down to the Infirmary"; Rush's "Alien Shore" and "Between Sun and Moon." He also suggested the music from *Weird Romance*, a Broadway show billed as "two one-act musicals of speculative fiction." The music is by Alan Menken (*Beauty and the Beast, Little Mermaid, Aladdin*); the book by familiar novelist and TV writer, Alan Brennert. Barker also recommended some really hip jazz in the Broadway show, *Jelly's Last Jam* with Gregory Hines. The presentation's about a group of musicians bringing Jelly Roll Morton back from the dead to explain how he invented jazz. Amazingly enough, Jelly Roll looks very much like Gregory Hines.

As eclectic as my musical tastes are, one of my biggest kicks is mining country music for songs of the weird and fantastic. This year's World Horror Convention in Atlanta showcased a wonderfully entertaining panel dealing with horror/country crossover, a topic in which writer Randy Fox is marvelously well versed. It's too bad the compilation tape soundtrack for the panel can never be commercially released.

Each year I hope for something of the quality of "Ghost of a Texas Ladies Man" or "Midnight in Montgomery." Well, 1994 provided at least two real goodies. The title tune from Joe Diffie's *Third Rock From the Sun* (Sony Epic) is an inventive and wry demonstration of how chaos theory can be adapted as subject matter for songs. Or, for the more traditional listener better versed in Newtonian physics, the song's plot can be taken as a simple explication of cause-and-effect phenomena. Either way, Diffie entertains with the account of how a small Southern town falls into complete chaos (including an alleged alien landing) after the local police chief decides to pick up a bimbo in a smoky tavern.

The other notable country cut, a bit more startling, is Doug Supernaw's "What'll You Do About Me?" from his album, *Deep Thoughts From a Shallow Mind* (BNA). Hey, it *would* be country that showcased a bouncy, upbeat ballad about a psycho guy stalking an independent woman. And, just like in all the best slasher-movie sequels, the point of view is the stalker's. On the surface, the lyrics are about a good ol' boy picked up by a woman for a one-night stand. But the next day, while she wants to go on her way, he's got different ideas, hence the title. One verse poses the socially relevant question of what'll the woman do if she invites another guy over, but the narrator's lurking on her porch with a 2-by-2? Trust country to come up with a lyric-driven song that could fuel a heated political discussion for hours. But then, that's what I love about this vein of music. It's as often emotionally powerful as it is facile, the word play of the lyrics is superior to most other pop music, and you can dance to it.

Finally, a few words about *Ed Wood*. Tim Burton's production isn't exactly fantasy or science fiction—but it is *about* fantasy. Burton's *Batman* movies, his *Edward Scissorhands* and *The Nightmare Before Christmas* have all demonstrated a strong idiosyncratic bent for dark fantasy with a layer of genuine sweetness. He manages to attain the same effect with his bio-pic of the man often accorded the peculiar status of being called America's worst film director. Ed Wood's heyday was the 1950s when he directed such amazing works as *Glen or Glenda, Bride of the Monster*, and *Plan 9 From Outer Space*. Wood combined a ferocious desire to create movies with an astonishingly tin ear for all forms of cinematic style. Wood was also a Marine veteran and a transvestite who loved angora. But was he truly the worst director ever? By my own definitions, probably not. There's an innocence in Wood's work that imparts a charm not found in many more forgettable works. No one forgets Wood's filmic achievements. . . . Any director who becomes the peculiar legend that Wood has is probably not the worst of a bad lot.

Still, Wood cannot be overestimated as a cultural icon. His general ability to put a movie together makes such comparable talents as director William "One Shot" Beaudine look like Orson Welles. And don't get the idea that Tim Burton is faithfully crafting a true biography. Ed Wood's face-to-face meeting with Orson Welles at a critical moment is not to be taken for documentary truth. This is a freak show with compassion. Burton also never really touches on the alcoholism that ultimately killed Wood.

Burton's created instead an affecting portrait of a man who is both pitiable and lovable, an ambitious yet talent-challenged guy who has encounted the Peter Principle and bludgeoned it into submission. If it falls short of any deep empathy for the title character, maybe that's part of the point.

Ed Wood didn't make a lot of money for Touchstone Pictures. Not only was it about a Hollywood weirdo and included no car chases, it was also in black and white. On the other hand, the movie gave Johnny Depp, as Wood, another opportunity to range very far away from his early image in *21 Jump Street*. In a spectacular role as the aging, dying Bela Lugosi, Martin Landau thoroughly earned an Oscar for best supporting actor.

I can't guess how the general viewing public (i.e. teenagers on a Friday night date) really reacted to *Ed Wood*. But as a writer myself, I can appreciate the film as a primary entry into the catalog of movies such as *All That Jazz* and *Reuben, Reuben* that all young aspiring artists should be obliged to see. Homework.

Ed Wood, charged with Tim Burton's quirky talent, demonstrates just what it is that makes America weirdly great. But then we see some of that weirdness each year, and we'll see more of it through 1995.

Comics 1994
by Will Shetterly and Emma Bull

If this were a "Best of the Year" article for comics fans, we'd save the best for last. Since this is appearing in a book that's intended for all readers of fantasy and horror, we'll start with the comics that we think are worth a look regardless of your opinion of comics as a storytelling medium.

The most interesting work of the year is either *Jar of Fools* (Black Eye Productions) or *The Tale of One Bad Rat* (Dark Horse Comics). Bryan Talbot's *The Tale of One Bad Rat* may win by default, simply because all four of its issues have been released. If its publisher has any sense, a bound album should be available by the time you read this. *The Tale of One Bad Rat* is a meditation on survival through imagination, as experienced by an English runaway whose best friend is a rat and who finds the world of Beatrix Potter far more congenial than the one she inhabits. Like so many of the comics we recommend, the story is not overtly fantastical, but the telling is wonderful. Talbot's art is detailed and exquisite. Beatrix Potter never would have expected someone to use her work this way, but we think she would have approved.

Jason Lutes's *Jar of Fools* is the story of Ernie, a.k.a. The Great Ernesto, an alcoholic stage magician; Esther, his former lover; The Great Flosso, his senile mentor in magic; Nathan and Claire, a homeless con man and his young daughter; and Howard, Ernie's brother, an escape artist who may or may not have drowned during his last performance. This seems to be a story of redemption, but what form that redemption may finally take, only Lutes knows. This is an astonishingly mature work by a previously unknown cartoonist. As a comics artist, Lutes understands design and visual pacing. As a writer, he understands the power of simplicity—that what's shown is only weakened by being explained. Lutes's storytelling is marvelously cinematic. If there are any clever movie producers following the world of comics, this has already been optioned for film.

Jar of Fools was a receipient of the Xeric grant established by one of the creators of the Teenage Mutant Ninja Turtles to support struggling cartoonists. The Xeric track record is excellent. Anything that they fund deserves a look.

That's certainly true of Adrian Tomine's *Optic Nerve* (originally self-published, now published by Drawn and Quarterly), a collection of short stories and vignettes that provoke most reviewers to resort to that easy label, "Generation X." Tomine is better than any easy label suggests. He's young, and he's writing about people who might be contemporaries, but he writes with an honesty and a gentleness that's true to all times.

Jon Lewis also received a Xeric grant. His *True Swamp* (originally self-published, now available from Slave Labor) is brilliant, idiosyncratic work that mixes a love of amphibians, insects, and small mammals with a nineteenth-century understanding of fantasy. There are faeries in this swamp, but they're alien and unsentimental beings. The art is crude, but it improves with every issue. Jon Lewis's *True Swamp* could be an alternate universe offspring of Walt Kelly's *Pogo*. Lewis deserves the same success.

Neil Gaiman is one of the finest writers who has ever worked in comics. *Mr. Punch* (DC Comics) reunites him with Dave McKean, his collaborator on *Violent Cases*, for a book that is a thematic sequel to that work. It's about youth and age and love and betrayal and all the good stuff. Set primarily at an amusement arcade on a British beach, with a mermaid and a Punch and Judy show, it's a meditation on memory and innocence and killing the devil. This is some of Gaiman's best work; no more need be said.

Gaiman's *Sandman* (DC Comics/Vertigo) is in its final story arc. Morpheus, master of dreams, has killed a member of his family, and the Furies are after him. This is the best series to appear from a major comic book publisher since Alan Moore left DC. Many of us will be sad to see it end, but it's nice to see it come to a close in its own time, rather than suffer the usual comic book fate of withering away for as long as the market will support it. DC continues to issue collections of *Sandman* work; the recent *brief lives* is grand.

The Dance of Lifey Death (Dark Horse) by Eddie Campbell is a collection of short pieces about Alec, a comic artist living in Australia who bears a remarkable resemblance to his creator, Eddie Campbell, perhaps the most underappreciated man in comics. Campbell writes and draws brilliantly, and he offers up the oddest and most delightful bits of esoterica in the context of whatever unpredictable tale he tells. His work ranges from the contemplative Alec tales to the almost superheroish exploits of the Eyeball Kid, a descendant of Greek gods who's doing his best to get by after the greatest Olympians have died.

From Hell (Mad Love/Kitchen Sink Press), written by Alan Moore and drawn by Eddie Campbell, is a novel in sixteen parts about Jack the Ripper. Each installment maintains the high standards of its predecessor. We said last year that this may prove to be the best work done in any medium about Jack the Ripper; we haven't changed our minds yet.

Those are our picks for the very best of 1994. We've undoubtedly overlooked something wonderful; the field of comics is too large to be surveyed by any one or two people. Comics fans may prefer some of the following titles to the ones we've mentioned already:

Action Girl Comics (Slave Labor), an anthology of strips by women, edited by Sarah Dyer. Check out the paper dolls, and the Japanese manga-influenced story in issue 2 by Elizabeth Watasin featuring Action Girl and Flying Girl.

Atomic City Tales (Black Eye Productions) by Jay "Sin" Stephens is a guilty pleasure. Hip superheroes done with affection but without reverence, perhaps the best way to deal with the superhero, comicdom's most successful and silliest genre.

Bone (Cartoon Books) by Jeff Smith. If *The Lord of the Rings* had been a collaboration between Tolkien and *Pogo* creator Walt Kelly, it might have been a little like this. Did we say something like that last year? It's still true. Crisp, masterful cartooning and a story that snaps from humor to suspense to the best kind of sweetness.

Boom Boom (Aeon) by David Laskey. The second issue is the story of James Joyce creating *Ulysses*, presented as though Stan Lee and Jack Kirby had decided to do educational comics instead of *The Fantastic Four* in 1962. There is no way to do justice to this comic, other than to say that anyone interested in Joyce or *Ulysses* should take a look. We think it works brilliantly and suspect that Joyce would have adored it—if it were about some other writer.

Dark Horse Presents (Dark Horse Comics) is an anthology series that's always worth a look. In 1993, they published a collaboration by Jane Yolen and Charles Vess that put an interesting spin on King Henry VIII and his wives. You'll have trouble finding that sort of work anywhere else in comics. What's best about *Dark Horse Presents* is that you can't predict what's likely to appear in it next. Eddie Campbell's latest series, "The Picture of Doreen Grey," began with issue #94. It's contemporary fantasy about the last of the Greek gods. That issue also includes Shannon Wheeler's inimitable Too Much Coffee Man and a strip by Terry LaBan, the true heir of the best underground comics of the 1960s. *Dark Horse Presents* is probably the finest anthology series in comics.

Donna Barr's *The Desert Peach* (Aeon) continues to prove that you can do sensitive work about homosexual German military officers during World War II. Funny, moving, sometimes shocking, but always sympathetic.

Colleen Doran's *A Distant Soil* (Aria Press). Arthurian apocrypha, contemporary psi-powers, and distant-future space fantasy combined—can you do that? Doran's taking a good shot at it.

Tim Barela's *Domesticity Isn't Pretty* (Palliard Press) is a collection of stories about two gay men and their lives in San Francisco. Fans of *Tales of the City*, either the novels or the PBS series, will be very glad that this book has been published.

Dan Clowes's *Eight Ball* (Fantagraphics) is the comic book of choice for hip young surrealiests; it's no surprise that Clowes is one of the featured artists for O. K. Cola. Clowes walks the curious line between misogyny and misanthropy. He's observant and intelligent. He can be hilarious and horrific, often simultaneously. If you like the films of David Lynch, try Clowes.

GirlHero by Megan Kelso (High Drive Publications). Deceptively simple art and fierce, comix grrrl stories make this one of the best women-cartoonists-kick-butt titles.

Hands Off! (Benefit Comics) bills itself as "Comics by over 35 artists collected to fight discrimination and homophobia." It's a Who's Who of comicdom's coolest cartoonists, and it's a good cause to boot.

Kane (Dancing Elephant Press) by Paul Grist. Is this hard-boiled police-action mystery? Well, except for the guy in the rabbit suit taking the mayor hostage . . . And the humane rat-catcher with a bad case of post-traumatic stress syndrome . . . Engrossing storytelling and some of the best use of black and white since Orson Welles.

Legionnaires and *Legion of Super-Heroes* (DC Comics). Remember fun, idealistic space opera comics stories? The clubhouse for teen superheroes is open again; check your rocket-pack at the door.

Love and Rockets (Fantagraphics) by the Brothers Hernandez. These are the guys who invented punk comics over ten years ago, but the phrase doesn't do justice to their masterful comics style. They write about mostly Hispanic characters who inhabit a world where anything might happen, but the focus is always on the characters. The Bros are Gilbert and Jaime. Comics fans argue about who's best. We admire them both.

Palooka-ville (Drawn & Quarterly) by Seth is about a Canadian artist who wanders around his city trying to find work by forgotten *New Yorker* cartoonists. It's quiet, perceptive, nostalgic, and very human, and it's charmingly post-postmodern: the story is simple, the setting is the world and time we inhabit, but the style is strongly influenced by those forgotten *New Yorker* cartoonists.

Radioactive Man (Bongo Comics Group) by Steve Vance is a six-issue series that has to be the greatest parody of superhero comics ever published. Each issue pokes fun at a different period; our favorite was number two, which skewers the Marvel Comics of the early 1960s without the slightest malice. If you like superheroes and/or *The Simpsons* TV show, this one's for you.

Rick Veitch's *Rare Bit Friends* (King Hell) is a collection of dreams, mostly Rick Veitch's, sometimes his friends', illustrated by Veitch. The second issue includes one of Neil Gaiman's dreams.

Stinz by Donna Barr (Mu Press) continues to do one of fantasy's best tricks—to tell a down-to-earth story in an extraordinary way—with a grace and style that makes it look easy. Her centaurs face conflicts of family, community, and race in one of the most convincing fantasy settings in comics.

Terry Moore's *Strangers in Paradise* (Abstract Studio) falls into the popular category of comics about two girls in the modern world, but it's a category made richer by Moore's contribution, and each issue is better than the last.

Tales from the Heart (Slave Labor) by Cindy Goff, Rafael Nieves, and Aldin Baroza is the story of a young woman who goes to Africa to serve in the Peace Corps. This comic deserves to be a major success (okay, every comic we mention here deserves to be a major success). Goff is funny and insightful. Her understanding of people and Africa is entirely convincing. Her collaborators are very, very good. Only one issue came out this year, but there's also a collection of the first several issues available from Slave Labor.

Ellen Forney's *Tomato* (Starhead Comix) is a charming series of short pieces about lesbians, love, grandparents, growing up in the seventies, dreaming, and the human condition. Forney has a grand sense of whimsy. Support this comic.

Chester Brown, the creator of *Yummy Fur,* has a new book, *Underwater* (Drawn and Quarterly). So far, *Underwater* is told from the point of view of an infant, which means the word balloons are a mixture of recognizable words and a language that the infants (and, at least in our case, the readers) can't decipher. The second half of *Underwater* is devoted to Brown's ongoing comics version of the book of Matthew. Brown presents the angriest, ugliest Jesus we've encountered, yet it's an interpretation that honest Christians should respect.

XXXenophile (Palliard Press) by Phil Foglio is an ongoing collection of funny hardcore sex comics in science fictional or fantastical settings. Foglio writes and pencils these, and various inkers do the finished art. This is one of the few adults-only comics that we recommend to adults. The first six issues have been collected in a trade paperback.

Addresses for Comics Mentioned in this Article:

For more information about any of the comics in this article, send a self-addressed stamped envelope to its publisher.

Abstract Studio, PO Box 271487, Houston, TX 77277.
Aeon/Mu Press, 5014-D Roosevelt Way NE, Seattle, WA 98105.
Aria Press, 12638-28 Jefferson Avenue Suite 173, Newport News, VA 23602-4316.
Black Eye Productions, 338 Kribs Street, Cambridge, Ontario N3C 3J3 Canada.
Bongo Entertainment, 1999 Avenue of the Stars, Los Angeles, CA 90067.
Caliber Press, 621-B S. Main Street, Plymouth, MI 48170.
Cartoon Books, PO Box 16973, Columbus, OH 43216.
Dancing Elephant Press, 207 Marlcliffe Road, Sheffield S6 4AH England.
Dark Horse Comics, 10956 S.E. Main Street, Milwaukie, OR 97222.
DC Comics, 1325 Avenue of the Americas, New York, NY 10019.
Drawn & Quarterly, 5550 Jeanne Mance St. #16, Montreal, Que. H2V 4K6 Canada.
Fantagraphics Books, 7563 Lake City Way, Seattle, WA 98115.
High Drive Publications, 4505 University Way NE #536, Seattle, WA 98105.
King Hell, c/o Kitchen Sink Press, 320 Riverside Drive, Northampton, MA 01060.
Kitchen Sink Press, 320 Riverside Drive, Northampton, MA 01060.
Palliard Press, c/o Dreamhaven Books, 1309 4th St. SE, Minneapolis, MN 55414-2029.
Slave Labor, 979 S. Bascom Avenue, San Jose, CA 95128 (800-866-8929).
Starhead Comix, PO Box 30044, Seattle, WA 98103.
Ward Sutton Productions, 501 N. 36th Street #350, Seattle, WA 98103.

Obituaries

Part of reporting on the state of the field for the year is noting the passage of those who left this mortal coil during the calendar year. Writers, artists, workers of magic and myth in various media all died in 1994, destined to create no more works for those left behind. But the works they created while they were alive are still available to us, in books, on film, and in other recorded media. If any of the names that follow are unfamiliar, one could do worse than to investigate their creative works.

Robert Bloch, 77, was best known for his novel *Psycho* (1960), which was the basis for the Alfred Hitchcock film that kept people out of showers for several years. But Bloch was far more than the author of a famous film. He wrote a number of successful suspense novels, as well as hundreds of fine fantasy, horror, and science fiction short stories. He won numerous awards, including the Hugo for his story, "That Hellbound Train"—really a fantasy—and the World Fantasy Award for Life Achievement. He was a wonderful raconteur, for years the toastmaster of choice among science fiction conventions. Bloch was that rarest of people: an enormously talented, successful person who is also a genuinely warm, generous person. He was considered a friend by all who knew him; he was given to acts of unexpected and unsolicited kindness; he never failed to thank those who helped him, and he helped or befriended many, many writers who came after him. And Bloch had a wicked sense of humor, perhaps best exemplified by his comment to an interviewer who questioned his character, asking what kind of a person Bloch must be, to write the dark, sometimes gruesome stuff he is famous for. Bloch protested, "But I have the heart of a young boy," and then added, sardonically, "I keep it in a jar on my desk!"

Eugene Ionesco, 84, born in Romania but a French citizen and resident since just before World War II, was one of the best known and most brilliantly iconoclastic playwrights identified with the "Theater of the Absurd." His plays, and what little short fiction he wrote, dealt with the inherent absurdity and randomness of life, in a fantasy idiom part mundane, chaotic life, part surreal vision. His plays were produced worldwide and accorded the major attention their seriousness deserved. The 1961 New York production of *Rhinoceros* became a turning point in the career of its star, comic actor Zero Mostel. Another major work was *The Bald Soprano.*

Frank Belknap Long, 90, was the last surviving member of H. P. Lovecraft's circle. Long wrote supernatural fiction and science fiction, and is probably best remembered for his stories "The Hounds of Tindalos" and "The Space Eaters," early tales he wrote that used Lovecraft's concept of the "Cthulhu Mythos." He was a regular contributor to both the original *Weird Tales* and *Unknown,* and at least one of his *Unknown* stories, "Johnny on the Spot," is considered a real classic of fantasy with a hard-boiled sensibility. He was a fine writer whose poetics informed all of his fiction, to lovely effect. Long also wrote poetry, comic books, and nonfiction, including a memoir of Lovecraft, *Howard Phillips Lovecraft: Dreamer on the Night Side* (1975). Long was a figure who, in the 1970s, when Lovecraft's work saw a great revival of interest, was able to shed light on Lovecraft's life and give a personal slant on the background that produced the seminal works of Lovecraft and other writers in his circle. Toward the end of his life, Long received many kudos, including, in 1978, the World Fantasy Convention's Life Achievement Award. He was not only a great figure in fantasy, he was also a true gentleman who, with his unique presence, bridged generations of writers.

Jack Kirby, 76, was a pioneer in the comics industry. He, along with Joe Simon, created Captain America for DC Comics. In 1958 he moved to Marvel Comics, where he created with Stan Lee a number of their perennial favorite superhero characters, including Mighty Thor and the Incredible Hulk. His drawing style was unmistakable—bold and energetic—and gave Marvel a look that helped make them a major force to rival DC.

Karl Edward Wagner, 49, was a fantasy and horror writer and editor. He edited DAW Books's *The Year's Best Horror* series from 1980 until his death; his fantasy writing included five novels about Kane, a complex, brutal man in a hard world, including *Darkness Weaves* (1970), *Bloodstone* (1975), and *Night Winds* (1976). He also wrote novels based on the work of Robert E. Howard: *The Road of Kings* (1979), featuring Conan, and *Legion of Shadows* (1976), featuring Bran Mak Morn. He wrote a considerable amount of horror, particularly psychological horror, not surprising, considering he was a psychiatrist before he became a writer. His short story, "Sticks," won the British Fantasy Award for short fiction; he also won a World Fantasy Award for his novella "Beyond All Measure." In addition to his writing and editing, he was a pillar of the fantasy and horror community in many other ways, from his copublishing with David Drake of the Carcosa small-press imprint, and his championing of the works of a number of neglected dark fantasy and horror writers, including Manly Wade Wellman, Hugh B. Cave, E. Hoffman Price and others, to his efforts to shine a spotlight on young writers whose work wasn't already well known. The last such set of selflessness was his recommendation to the World Fantasy Award judges for 1994 of the work of Terry Lamsley, whose book, *Under the Crust*, was missed by many in the field until pointed out by Wagner in his *Year's Best*.

Robert Shea, 61, was possibly best known as the co-author, with Robert Anton Wilson, of the *Illuminatus!* trilogy. He and Wilson met when both were editors at *Playboy*; Shea also wrote solo novels of fantasy, including *Shike* (1990), *Shaman* (1991), and in two parts, *The Saracens*: (1) *Land of the Infidel* (1989) and (2) *The Holy War* (1989). **Pierre Boulle,** 81, was the author of *Bridge Over the River Kwai*, and *Planet of the Apes*, among other novels. The French writer also wrote short stories. It's safe to say that his novels and shorter fiction had more wit and insight than could be seen in the film version of *Planet of the Apes*. **James Clavell,** 69, was the author of the extraordinary bestseller, the Japanese epic *Shōgun*, and other novels set in the Far East. He was also a screenwriter.

Russell Kirk, 75, won a 1976 World Fantasy Award for his novella "There's a Long, Long-rail A-Winding." He wrote a number of other stories, tending to the weird and dark fantasy, with the occasional foray into the thriller. Kirk was also known as a Conservative political theorist. He was a syndicated columnist and wrote a number of nonfiction books, including *The Conservative Mind* (1953).

Devendra P. Varma, 71, was a scholar of Gothic literature who particularly favored vampire lore.

Helen Wolff, 88, was a major figure in book publishing. She and her husband, Kurt Wolff, who was Franz Kafka's first publisher, founded Pantheon in 1942; they later had their own imprint at Harcourt. She edited many fine literary writers, with a list international in scope, including Italo Calvino and Stanislaw Lem, among others.

Burt Lancaster, 80, was a star of both stage and screen. In his long and storied career he starred in such fantasies as *Field of Dreams*, *Seven Days in May*, the TV film of *The Phantom of the Opera*, and many other productions.

Raul Julia, 53, was a brilliantly talented and versatile actor of stage, screen, and television. He played the title role in Edward Gorey's stage version of *Dracula*, played in a number of Joseph Papp's productions of Shakespeare in the Park in New York City, was a wonderful Gomez in the surprisingly enterprising box-office hits, *The Addams Family* and *Addams Family Values*. He played many other roles in numerous productions, almost always enhancing the quality of the ensemble playing with his considerable presence and theatrical talent.

Cesar Romero, 86, was an actor in both film and television. Best remembered for his turn as the Joker in the *Batman* TV series, he made a reputation as a Latin leading man in the 1930s and '40s. In the 1950s and '60s he was a guest star on many TV shows and featured in a number of films, including a number of low-budget horror films.

Irwin Kostal, 83, was a conductor and musical director for stage, screen, and television. He worked on a number of Disney films, and received Oscar nominations for his work on *Mary Poppins* (1964), *Bedknobs and Broomsticks* (1971), and *Pete's Dragon* (1977). **Walter Lantz,** 93, was an animator for more than a half-century. Known best for inventing the Woody Woodpecker character, he invented many other characters in a career that spanned several studios. **Noah Beery, Jr.**, 81, was a veteran character actor who appeared in dozens of film and television productions, including *The Seven Faces of Dr. Lao* (1964). He was the son of actor Wallace Beery. **Roy Castle,** 62, was a British actor who starred in various television and screen productions, including *Dr. Terror's House of Horrors* and *The Legend of the Werewolf.*

Lawrence E. Spivak, 93, was best known as a journalist, particularly for the radio and television show, *Meet the Press,* which he created. He was also the cofounder of *The Magazine of Fantasy,* which became *The Magazine of Fantasy and Science Fiction.* He was bought out by his partner, Joseph L. Ferman, in 1954. **Donald Swann,** 70, was a composer, lyricist, and musical performer best known for his longterm collaboration with the late Michael Flanders. Swann collaborated with J. R. R. Tolkien on a song cycle, "The Road Goes Ever On," and even performed it at Tolkien's fiftieth wedding anniversary, in 1966. Both singly and with Flanders, he adapted other fantasy material to music.

Don Thompson, 58, a longtime fan of comics and a pioneer in comics fandom, was the co-editor with Richard A. Lupoff of two books about Golden Age comics, *All in Color for a Dime* and *The Comic-Book Book.* He and his wife, Maggie Thompson, were co-editors of *The Comics Buyers Guide,* which she continues to run. **Sean Spacher,** 51, was an artist and sculptor known for his metal sculpture of fantasy subjects.

John James was a British writer of historical fiction and fantasy. His novels included *Votan* (1966), a Norse tale, *Not for all the Gold in Ireland,* a Roman historical, and *Men Went to Cattraeth* (1969), a nominally Arthurian book. **John Preston,** 48, was an author and anthologist of gay fiction, some of which included fantasy content.

Michael Carreras, 66, was a writer and producer, best known for *One Million Years, B.C.* In 1972 he took control of his father's company, Hammer Films, but was never able to turn it from its downward course into receivership. Director **Alexander Mackendrick,** 81, helmed the Alec Guinness fantasy, *The Man in the White Suit,* as well as many other British comedies. Composer **Hans J. Salter,** 98, began as a conductor of silent-film orchestras, and moved into composition of film scores with the advent of sound films. He scored many films before and after World War II, having moved to California before the war. His credits include *Creature from the Black Lagoon, House of Frankenstein,* and many others. **Carroll Borland,** 79, co-starred with Bela Lugosi in *Mark of the Vampire* (1935), and acted in a number of low-budget films in the thirties. **Heather Sears,** 58, starred in the 1961 remake of *The Phantom of the Opera,* among various film roles. **Lynne Frederick,** 39, was a film actress who was featured in *Vampire Circus* (1971), and other films in the seventies. She was the widow of actor Peter Sellers. **Ashley Boone, Jr.**, 55, was a film marketing executive who contributed to many successful films in the seventies, including *The Omen, Ghostbusters,* and others.

The magic of their work will remain with us always, to keep their memory alive.

—James Frenkel

TRANSMUTATIONS

Patricia A. McKillip

I am already on record as firmly believing that Patricia A. McKillip is one of the most skilled prose stylists gracing the fantasy field today. The following lyrical story, about the transformative properties of alchemy and poetry, is a fine example of McKillip at her best. It is reprinted from the anthology *Xanadu 2*, edited by Jane Yolen.

McKillip is the World Fantasy Award–winning author of *The Forgotten Beasts of Eld*, *Stepping from the Shadows*, *Fool's Run*, *The Sorceress and the Cygnet*, and numerous other works for both adult and young adult readers. She grew up in America, Germany, and England, and currently lives in New York State's Catskill Mountains.

—T. W.

Old Dr. Bezel was amusing himself again; Cerise smelled it outside his door. The shade escaping under the thick, warped oak was blue. A darker shadow crossed it restively: he must have conjured up his apprentice, who had been among the invisible folk for five days. Cerise planted the gold-rimmed spectacles Dr. Bezel had made for her firmly on her nose, and opened the door.

As usual, Aubrey Vaughn, slumping into a chair, looked blankly at her, as if she had fallen through the ceiling. She noted, with a sharp and fascinated eye, the yellow-grey pallor of his skin. She slid her notebook and pens and the leather bag with her lunch in it onto a table, then opened the notebook to a blank page.

"I'm sorry I'm late," she said in her low, quiet voice. She added to the velvet curtains over the windows, for Dr. Bezel beamed at anything she said and rarely listened, and Aubrey simply never listened, "At least I'm not five days late."

But this time Aubrey blinked at her. He could never remember her name. She was a slender, colorless wraith of a woman who appeared and disappeared at odd times; for all he knew she was conjured out of candle smoke and had no life beyond the moments he encountered her. But gold teased him: the gold of her spectacles catching firelight and lamplight among laughter, sweat, curses, music . . . He made an incautious movement; his elbow slid off the chair arm. He jerked to catch his balance and felt the mad, gnarled imp in his brain strike with the pick, mining empty furrows for thought.

"You were there," he breathed. "Last night."

Behind her spectacles, her grey eyes widened. "You can see me," she said, amazed. "I've often wondered."

"Of course I can see you."

"How long has this been going on? Dr. Bezel, he sees me. You will have to dispose of one of us."

"Yes, my dear Cerise," Dr. Bezel agreed benignly, peering at his intricate, bubbling skeleton of glass. "Now we will wait until the solution turns from blue to a most delicate green."

"You were there," Aubrey persisted, holding himself rigid to calm the imp. "At Wells Inn."

"You are beginning to see me outside of this room? This is astonishing. What is my name?"

"Ah—"

"You see, I had a theory that not only am I invisible to you, the sound of my voice never reaches you. As if one of us is under a spell. Apparently even my name disappears into some muffled thickness of air before you hear it."

"I can hear you well enough now," he said drily. He applied one hand to his brow and made an effort. "It's a sound. Like silk ripping. Cerise."

She was silent, amused and half annoyed, for on the whole, if their worlds were to merge, she preferred being invisible to Aubrey Vaughn. He was seeing her clearly now, she realized, as something more than a mass and an arbitrary movement in Dr. Bezel's cluttered study. She watched the expression begin to form in his bleared, wincing eyes, and turned abruptly. His voice pursued.

"But what were you doing there?"

"Now see," Dr. Bezel said delightedly, and Cerise forgot the curious voice in the chair as she watched a green like the first leaves flush through the bones of glass. "That is the exact shade. Look, for it goes quickly."

"The exact shade of what?" Aubrey murmured, and for once was himself unheard and invisible. "Of what?" he asked again, with his stubborn persistence, and, unaccountably, Dr. Bezel answered him.

"Of the leaves there. Translucent, gold-green, they fan into the light."

"What leaves where?"

"No place. A dream." He turned, smiling, sighing a little, as the green faded into clear. "I was only playing. Now we will work."

What leaves? Aubrey thought much later, after he had chased spilled mercury across the floor and nearly scalded himself with molten silver. Dr. Bezel, lecturing absently, let fall the names of references intermittently, like thunderbolts. Cerise noted them in her meticulous script. What dream? she wondered, and made a private note: Green-gold leaves fanning into light.

"Also there is a well," Dr. Bezel said unexpectedly, at the end of the morning. Aubrey blinked at him, looking pained. Dr. Bezel, distracted from his vision by Aubrey's expression, added kindly, "Aubrey, if you tarnish the gold of enlightenment with the fires and sodden flames of endless nights, how will you recognize it?"

Aubrey answered tiredly, "Even dross may be transmuted. So you said."

"So you do listen to me." He turned, chuckling. "Perhaps you are your father's son."

Cerise saw the blood sweep into Aubrey's face. Prudently, she looked down at her notebook and wrote: Well. She had never met Nicholaus Vaughn, who had enlightened himself out of existence; he had not, it seemed, misspent his youth at Wells Inn. Aubrey said nothing; the sudden stab of the pickax blinded him. In the wash of red before his eyes, he saw his bright-haired father, tall, serene, hopelessly good. Passionless, Aubrey thought, and his sight cleared; he found himself gazing into a deep vessel, some liquid matter gleaming faintly at the bottom.

"Analysis," Dr. Bezel instructed.

"Now?" Aubrey said hoarsely, bone-dry. "It's noon."

"Then let us lay to rest the noonday devils," Dr. Bezel said cheerfully. The woman, Cerise, was chewing on the end of her pen, deliberately expressionless. Aubrey asked her crossly.

"Have you no devils to bedevil you?"

"None," she answered in her low, humorous voice, "I would call a devil. I am intimate with those I know."

"So am I," he sighed, letting a drop from the vessel fall upon a tiny round of glass. Unexpectedly, it was red.

"Then they are not devils but reflections."

He grunted, suddenly absorbed in the crimson unknown. Blood? Dye? He reached for fire. "What were you doing at Wells Inn?" he asked. He felt her sudden, sharp glance and answered it without looking up, "In one way, I am like my father. I am tenacious."

"You are not concentrating," Dr. Bezel chided gently. They were all silent then, watching fire touch the unknown substance. It flared black. Aubrey raised his red-gold brows, rubbed his eyes. At his elbow, Cerise made the first note of his analysis: Turns obscure under fire. Aubrey reached for a glass beaker, poured a bead of crimson into a solution of salts. It fell as gracefully as a falling world.

Retains integrity in solution, Cerise wrote, and added: Unlike the experimenter.

The puzzle remained perplexing. Aubrey, sweating and finally curious by the end of the hour, requested texts. Dr. Bezel sent him out for sustenance, Cerise to the library. There she gathered scrolls and great dusty tomes, and, having deposited them in the study, retired beneath a tree to eat plums and farmer's cheese and pumpernickel bread, and to write poetry. She was struggling between two indifferent rhymes when a beery presence intruded itself.

"What were you doing at Wells Inn last night?"

She looked up. Aubrey's tawny, bloodshot eyes regarded her with the clinical interest he gave an unknown substance. She said simply, "Working. My father owns the place."

He stared at her; she had transformed under his nose. "You work there?"

"Five nights a week, until midnight."

"I never saw—"

"Precisely."

He backed against the tree, slid down the trunk slowly to sit among its roots. "And you work for Dr. Bezel." She closed her notebook, did not reply. "Why?"

She shrugged lightly. "I have no one to pay for my apprenticeship. This is as close as I can get to studying with him."

He was silent, eyeing the distance, his expression vague, uncertain. The woman beside him, unseen, seemed to disappear. He looked at her again, saw her candlewax hair, her smoky eyes. It was her calm, he decided, that rendered her invisible to the casual eye. Movement attracted attention: her inner movements did not outwardly express themselves. Except, he amended a trifle sourly, for her humor.

"Why?" he asked again, and remembered her in the hot, dense crush at the inn, hair braided, face obscure behind her spectacles, hoisting a tray of mugs. She wore an apron over a plain black dress; now she wore black with lace at her wrists and throat, and her shoulders were covered. He tried to remember her bare shoulders, could not. "What do you need to transmute? Surely not your soul. It must be as tidy as your handwriting."

She looked mildly annoyed at the charge. "Why do you?" she asked. "You seem quite comfortable in your own untidiness."

He shrugged. "I am following drunkenly in my father's footsteps. He transmuted himself out of this world, giving me such a pure and shining example of goodness that it sends me to Wells Inn most nights to contemplate it."

Her annoyance faded; she sat quite still, wondering at his candor. "Are you afraid of goodness?"

He nodded vigorously, keeping his haggard, shadow-smudged face tilted upward for her inspection. "Oh, yes. I prefer storms, fire, elements in the raw, before they are analyzed and named and ranked."

"And yet you—"

"Cannot keep away from my father's one great passion: to render all things into their final, changeless, unimpassioned state." The corner of his mouth slid up: a kind of smile, she realized, the first she had seen. He met her eyes. "Now," he said, "tell me why you study such things. Do you want what my father wanted? Perfection?"

"Of a kind," she admitted after a moment, her hands sliding, open, across the closed notebook. She was silent another moment, choosing words; he waited, motionless himself, exuding fumes and his father's legendary powers of concentration. "I thought—by immersing myself in the process—that perhaps I could transmute language."

A brow went up. "Into gold?"

Her mouth twitched. "In the basest sense. I try to write poetry. My words seem dull as dishwater, which I am quite familiar with. Some people live by their poetry. They sell it for money. The little I earn from Dr. Bezel turns itself into books. I work mostly for the chance to learn. I thought perhaps writing poetry might be a way to make a living that's not carrying trays and dodging hands and stepping in spilled ale and piss and transmuted suppers."

His eyes flicked away from her; he remembered a few of his own drunken offerings. "Poets," he murmured, "need not be perfect."

"No," she agreed, "but they are always chasing the perfect word."

"Let me see your poetry."

"No," she said again swiftly, rising. She brushed crumbs from her skirt, adjusted her cuffs, the notebook clamped firmly under one elbow. "Anyway, the bell has rung, Dr. Bezel is waiting, and your unknown substance is still unknown." He groaned softly, a boneless wraith in the tree roots, the shadows of leaves gently stroking his father's red-gold hair. She wondered suddenly at the battle in him, tugged as he was between noon and night, between ale and alchemy. "Do you never sleep?" she asked.

"I am now," he said, struggling to his feet, and groaned again as the hot, pure gold dazzled over him, awakening the headache behind his eyes.

Dr. Bezel, bent over an antique alembic and murmuring to himself, remained unaware of their return for some time. "How clear the light," he said once, gazing into the murky, bubbling alembic. "It reveals even the most subtle hues in water, in common stones, in the very clay of earth." Cerise, flipping a poem away from Aubrey's curious eye, made another note of Dr. Bezel's rambles through his dream world: Clarity. Something within the alembic popped; a tarry black smeared the glass. Aubrey winced at the noise and the bleak color. Dr. Bezel, surprised out of his musings, sensed the emanations behind him and turned. "Did you see it?" he asked with joy. "Now, then, to your own mystery, Aubrey. Cerise has brought your texts."

Aubrey, sweating pallidly, like a hothouse lily, bent over the scrolls. While he studied, Cerise ventured a question.

"Is there language, in this lovely place, or are all things mute?"

"They are transmuted," Aubrey murmured.

"Puns," Cerise said gravely, "do not transmute: there are no ambiguities in the perfect world."

"Nor," Dr. Bezel said briskly, "is there language."

"Oh," she said, disconcerted.

"It is unnecessary. All is known, all exists in the same unchanging moment." He poured a drop of the tarry black onto a glass wafer. Aubrey gazed bewilderedly at his back.

"Then why," he wondered, "would anyone choose to go there?"

"You do not choose. You do not go. You are. Study, study to find your father's shining path, and someday you will understand everything." He let fall a tear of liquid onto the black substance. It flared. The smell of roses pervaded the room; they were all dazed a moment, even Dr. Bezel. "It is the scent of childhood," he said wistfully, lost in some private moment. Aubrey, saturated by Wells Inn, forgot the word for what he smelled. Driftwood, his brain decided, it was the smell of driftwood. Or perhaps of caraway. Cerise, trying to imagine a world without a word, thought instantly: roses, and watched them bloom inside her head.

Aubrey, after some reading, requested sulphur. Applying it to his unknown and heating it, he dispersed even the memory of roses. Cerise, noting his test, wrote: Due to extreme contamination of surroundings, does not react to sulphur. Neither does his unknown. She drew the curtains apart, opened a window. Light gilded the experimenter's profile; he winced.

"Must you?"

"It's only air and light."

"I'm not used to either." He shook a drop of mercury into a glass tube, and then a drop of mystery. Nothing happened. He held it over fire, carelessly, his face too near, his hand bare. He shook it impatiently; beads of red and silver spun around the bottom, touched each other without reacting. He sighed, ran his free hand through his hair. "This substance has no name."

"Rest a moment," Dr. Bezel suggested, and Aubrey collapsed into a wing-backed chair patterned with tiny dragons. They looked, Cerise thought with amusement, like a swarm of minute demons around his head. He cast a bleared eye at her.

"Water," he ordered, and in that moment, she wanted to close her notebook and thump his head with poetry.

"We are not," she said coldly, "at Wells Inn."

"Look, look," Dr. Bezel exclaimed, but at what they could not fathom. He was shaking salts into a beaker of water; they took some form, apparently, before they dissolved. "There is light at the bottom of the well. Something shines . . . How exquisite."

"I beg your pardon," Aubrey said. Cerise did not answer. "How can I remember," he pleaded, "which world we are in if you flit constantly between them?"

"You could frequent another inn."

"I've grown accustomed to your father's inn."

"You could learn some manners."

Silent, he considered that curious notion. His eyes slid to her face, as she stood listening to Dr. Bezel's verbal fits and starts, and writing a word now and then. Limpid as a nun, he thought grumpily of her graceful, calm profile, and then saw that face flushed and sweating, still patient under a barrage of noise, heat, the incessant drunken bellowings of orders, with only the faint tension in her mouth as she hoisted a tray high above heedless roisterers, betraying her weariness. He rubbed his own weary face.

"I could," he admitted, and saw her eyes widen. He got to his feet, picked up a carafe of water from a little ebony table. He went to the window, stuck his head out, and poured the water over his hair. Panting a little at the sudden cold, he pulled his dripping head back in and heard Dr. Bezel say with blank wonder,

"But of course, it is the shining of enlightenment."

"Where?" Aubrey demanded, parting plastered hair out of his eyes as if enlightenment might be floating in front of his nose. "Is it my unknown?"

"It is at the bottom of the well," Dr. Bezel answered, beaming at his visions, then blinked at his wet apprentice. "From which you seem to have emerged."

"Perhaps," Aubrey sighed. "I feel I might live after all."

"Good. Then to work again. All we lack now is a path . . ."

Path, Cerise wrote under her private notes for Dr. Bezel's unknown. Or did he speak of a path to Aubrey's unknown? she wondered. Their imponderables were becoming confused. Aubrey buried a drop of his under an avalanche of silvery salts, then added an acid. The acid bubbled the salts into a smoking frenzy, but left the scarlet substance isolated, untouched.

"Sorcery," Aubrey muttered, hauling in his temper. "It's the fire-salamander's tongue, the eye of the risen phoenix." He immersed himself in a frail, moldy book, written in script as scrupulous as Cerise's. Dr. Bezel, silent for the moment, pursued his own visions. Cerise, unneeded, turned surreptitiously to her poem, chewed on the end of her pen. It lacks, she thought, frowning. It lacks . . . It is inert, scribbles on paper, nothing living. I might as well feed it to the salamander. But, patiently, she crossed out a phrase, clicked words together and let them fall like dice, chose one and not the other, then chose the other, and then crossed them both out, and wrote down a third.

"Yes," she heard Dr. Bezel whisper, and looked up. "There." He gazed into a beaker flushed with a pearl-grey tincture, as if he saw in it the map to some unnamed country. Aubrey, his head ringing with elements, turned toward him.

"What?"

"The unknown . . ."

"In there?" He eyed the misty liquid hopefully. "Is that the catalyst? I'd introduce my unknown into a solution of hops at this point." He reached for it heedlessly, dropped a tear of crimson into the mystery in Dr. Bezel's hand.

It seemed, Cerise thought a second later, as if someone had lifted the roof off the room and poured molten gold into their eyes. She rediscovered herself sitting in a chair, her notebook sprawling at her feet. Aubrey was sitting on the floor. The roof had been replaced.

Of Dr. Bezel there was no trace.

She stared at Aubrey, who was blinking at her. Some moment bound them in a silence too profound for language. Then, a moment or an hour later, she found her voice.

"You have transmuted Dr. Bezel."

He got to his feet, feeling strange, heavy, as if his bones had been replaced with gold. "I can't have."

She picked up her notebook, smoothed the pages, then held it close, like a shield, her arms around it, her eyes still stunned. "He is gone," she said irrefutably.

"I couldn't transmute a flea." He stared bemusedly at his unknown. "What on earth is this?" He looked around him a little wildly, searching tabletop, tubes, alembic. "His beaker went with him."

"No, you see, it was transformed, like him, like your father—it is nothing now. No thing. Everything." Her voice sounded peculiar; she stood up, trembling. Her face looked odd, too, Aubrey thought, shaken out of its calm, its patient humor, on the verge of an unfamiliar expression, as if she had caught the barest glimpse of something inexpressible. She began to drift. He asked sharply.

"Where are you going?"

"Home."

"Why?"

"I seem to be out of a job."

He began to put his unknown down, did not. He was silent, struggling. Her mind began to fill with leaves, with silence; she shook her head a little, arms tightening around her notebook. "Stay," he said abruptly. "Stay. I can't leave. Not without knowing. What he found. How he found it. And there are unknowns everywhere. Stay and help me." She gazed at him, still expressionless. He added, "Please."

"No." She shook her head again; leaves whirled away on a sudden wind. "I can't. I'm going back to buckets and beer, mops and dishwater and voices—"

"But why?"

She backed a step closer to the door. "I don't want a silent shining path of gold. I need the imperfect world broken up into words."

He said again, barely listening to her, hearing little more than the mute call of the unknown, "Please. Please stay, Cerise."

She smiled. The smile transformed her face; he saw fire in it, shadow, gold and silver, sun and moon, all possibilities of language. "You are too much like your father," she said. "What if you accidentally succeed?" She tore her notes out and left them with him, and then left him, holding a mystery in his hand and gazing after her while she took the path back into the mutable world.

BOTTOM'S DREAM

Rachel Wetzsteon

Rachel Wetzsteon's first book of poems, *The Other Stars*, won the 1993 National Poetry Series Open Competition and was published by Penguin in 1994. She received an Ingram Merrill award in 1994, and her poems have been published or are forthcoming in *The Kenyon Review, The New Republic, The Paris Review, The Partisan Review, The Yale Review* and other journals. She is a doctoral candidate in English at Columbia.

"Bottom's Dream" comes from Wetzsteon's first collection, *The Other Stars* (with thanks to Lawrence Schimel for bringing it to our attention). "Venus Observed," from the same collection, is also recommended.

—T. W.

Players, are you assembled? Quince is bound and gagged
  and cannot holler "Cut." Two things
are now imperative: that we use our freedom wisely,
  never allowing an upstart ham
to throw the symmetry of our pack seditiously off,
  and that we take advantage of
our newfound liberty, striking the lines we hated—
  the one about the lover's heartache
cutting like glass, for example—and, most fun for us,
  adlibbing where we please. Only
remember the dignity it is incumbent on
  our noble profession to uphold:
beating our breasts, we must have the good sense to know when to stop;
  giving speeches, we cannot abandon
decorum and say what we please, be it ever so moving.
  Are we ready? Then let us leave off learning
our parts and begin our play. Ladies, gentlemen,
  presenting a story of woe, and—so
you know the end right away, the better to grasp the style
  of the piece—lovers and kingdoms restored.
Act One, Scene One. The place: an ancient wall by moonlight,

somewhere in . . . but what is that shape
moving in the trees, above your painted heads?
I never saw such golden ringlets,
thought only a speech could strike so suddenly at the heart!
For God's sake, duck! It disappears,
and I must see where it goes! The show must go on? What show?
This is better than all our weddings,
sadder than all our deaths combined! The spectacle
can wait; there will be time enough
for cheap impersonations when the real thing is gone.
Fair friend, where are you? See what a flawless
jewel it is! Are you real, or a demon sent to haunt me?
Leave my sight and I'll crawl after you;
stay and I'll promise to slay this company of punks.
It goes. Oh what a sudden distaste
I feel for you all! Go on, complete your dreary drama;
it has become impossible
for me to take your hijinks seriously, and
I never liked your kind anyway.
Oh my receding love, oh patron saint of asses,
grant me the wit to get out of the woods!

LA PROMESA

Leroy Quintana

Leroy V. Quintana is a native of New Mexico and currently teaches at San Diego Mesa College. His publications include *Hijo del Pueblo: New Mexico Poems, Sangre, Five Poets of Aztlan, Interrogations,* and *The History of Home.* He is also co-editor of *Paper Dance,* a new anthology of Latino poetry. Quintana is a recipient of the Before Columbus Foundation American Book Award, the Border Regional Library Association Award, an NEA Creative Writing Fellowship, and was recently nominated for the Pushcart Prize.

Quintana's gonzo tale, "La Promesa," walks the line between magical and realist fiction—as so much of the best Latino fiction does. He writes of a place where *milagros* (miracles) are wound so exuberantly into the fabric of daily life that to try to separate fact from fiction becomes quite beside the point. . . .

"La Promesa" is reprinted from the Autumn 1994 issue of *Pleiades,* a literary journal published in Missouri.

—T. W.

At the time of this story, there were rumors flying all over the country about "El Hombre Sin Cabeza," the headless man. He had been seen (it seems he appeared only at night) just this side of Las Animas, then near the dirt road that winds west from Gallinas to Los Lobos. Mosco Zamora (yes, the famous Mosco Zamora who years back was in the newspapers statewide for two weeks, photo after photo of him with that eighteen-foot rattler, well, with the skin of the eighteen-foot rattler he found in Farnsworth Arroyo) had seen him, coincidentally, in Farnsworth Arroyo (in fact, Mosco was the very first to see him) one moonless night, the headless one walking towards him, arms outspread, shouting (?) "Mosco! Mosco! Mosco!" And what about Caruso Zamora (who Saturday night after Saturday night won the demolition derby and who had been issued more traffic citations than anybody else in the entire county), Caruso had seen him as he was flying down the highway in his tow truck somewhere between Gallinas and Los Brasos, and when he saw him he floored the accelerator and zoomed right by Sheriff Sapo Sanchez' speed trap at well over a hundred miles an hour and kept it floored all the way to San Miguel where Sapo wrote out citations for "Espeeding, and violation of Civic Code Two-Twenty-nine point one, for Hazardous Driving, a

Two-Fourteen point three, Failure to Yield the Right of Way, a Two-Twenty Point Ten, for Failure to Stop at a Posted Sign, a Two-Seventeen point eleven, for Running through a Barrier at a Railroad Crossing, a Two-Twelve point three zero, for Driving the Wrong Way on a One-Way Street.

Many had seen "El Hombre Sin Cabeza" in the cemetery outside San Miguel on his hands and knees, desperately clawing at the ground, as if attempting to unearth a coffin. In every story, he had shredded, bleeding fingers, his pants were frayed, tattered, and soaked with blood at the knees.

But enough of "El Hombre Sin Cabeza." For now.

This story really begins the morning Botas Meadas (who had begun seeing moscas divebombing at him a week or so before) broke the window of The Emporium, not even realizing that he (a drunk for at least half of his fifty-five years) had been chosen by God as a vehicle for a milagro (a milagro by far more authentic than that of Pepe, his next-door neighbor, who claimed he had seen a burning rosary on his bedroom wall and gave up drinking, only it turned out it was just one of those new rosaries that glowed in the dark that his wife had bought and hung up hoping that on the last day of her novena to St. Jude, the Saint of the Impossible, that St. Jude would grant Pepe some willpower so he would stop stopping by La Golondrina all day long for one, just one little tragito, absolutely his last, of Thunderbird, absolutamente just one little, tragito, this one absolutely his las absolutamente).

Later that day, when Botas Meadas learned about the miracle, he not only made a promesa to stop drinking ("NO MORE THUNDERBIRD! FOREVER!"), and to prove, yes to prove, that he really meant it, that this time he intended to keep his promesa, he announced he would make a pilgrimage to the old church across more than a mile of llano, no, not walking, but on his knees (if somebody could convince his brothers Jose, Felipe, and Roberto to accompany him).

At about ten that particular morning, Botas Meadas (at first the moscas were only sounds buzz, buzz-mas o menos an arm's length away, buzz buzz) grabbed a tin of buttery macaroons that Maria Martinez had placed on a table outside The Emporium's front door and flung it against the window, (and then before long the sounds were accompanied by moscas, only two or three and then suddenly there were squadrons, huge eyes, furry legs buzzbuzz) the tin hitting the very spot where one of Sheriff Sapo Sanches' stray bullets had hit only an hour or so before (squadrons, so you throw whatever you can find), causing the web-like pattern to expand (and so you break a window and they threaten you first with jail and then with the Mayor's Mafia friends), scattering buttery macaroons all over the sidewalk. Had Maria Martinez known Botas Meadas had just set the workings of a milagro in motion, she wouldn't have run out from behind the counter shrieking "My macaroons! My macaroons!" threatening Botas Meadas with jail (but wait a minute, that meant calling that idiota Sapo Sanchez who had just shot a hole in the window trying to stop Estaban Zamora, who had just held up the bank, thank God, oh gracias a Dios! that Caruso happened to pass by just then on his way for parts, Y gracias a Dios que Caruso had rammed Esteban's Dodge all to hell with his tow truck, putting a quick and sure end to his getaway! No it was useless to call Sapo, that pendejo. Say, maybe Caruso should run for sheriff, as county chairwoman of the Republican Party she could see if . . .) Yes, Maria Martinez threatened to use her husband the mayor's political connections, but if she had known Botas Meadas had set the workings of a milagro in motion she wouldn't have bounced one, two, three tins of buttery macaroons off his thick skull. But how could she have possibly known? After all, it wasn't until around three that afternoon, when the sun's rays hit the window at just the right angle, that Maria Martinez, his honor the mayor's wife, saw the face of Jesus on the wall, right in the very spot where Esteban Zamora's WANTED poster had been before Maria ripped it off immediately after Esteban's capture: right between the WANTED posters of the other two biggest thieves in San Miguel County, the Sanchez brothers, Tranquilino, (who, like Esteban, robbed banks), and Salvador (who worked for the IRS).

Later that day, Father Schmidt (who had already suffered through such milagros as Natalia Sanchez' image of Jesus scorched on one of her tortillas along with Pepe's burning rosary) is praying the rosary after rosary in front of The Emporium and Sapo is going crazy issuing parking tickets ("Running a Red Light, a Two-Twenty-Nine point three four, Failure to Obey a Stop Sign, a Two-Seventeen point nine nine, Failure to Park Properly, that's a Two-Eleven point zero nine, and Driving the Wrong Way on a One Way Street, a Two-Nine-Nine point seven seven"), and Maria Martinez is smiling and offering three boxes of her famous macaroons and the key to the town to Botas Meadas as he walks through the crowd (como el Charlton Heston parting the Red Sea) into The Emporium as the sun is going down, and as he sees the face of Jesus, Jesus speaks to him: "Ven m'hijo, (buzzbuzz), Come to me my son, (buzz)."

As the sun sets he announces his promesa not only to give up drinking (perhaps he has been responsible for other milagros this day throughout San Miguel) (the brick he heaved at the front window of La Golondrina . . . the empty bottle he flung down at Martinez' Car Lot), but also to make a pilgrimage across the wide llano—on his knees.

The pilgrimage began like this: Jose, the oldest brother (who owned a cherry red T-Bird with porthole windows, chrome rims and etc.), said, "What, again? No, no, no, no, no!"

Juanita, his wife, who had been in The Emporium when Maria Martinez saw the face of Jesus, pleaded, "But he's responsible for a milagro. He needs you . . ."

"No, no, no, no, no!"

Then she tried convincing Jose that Botas Meadas was perhaps a saint, and Jose said "Ese pendejo?" and finally Jose gave in when Juanita told Jose, quite forcefully, that the only little favor he had to do for his sainted brother was to pick him up at the church at midnight after Botas Meadas had completed his pilgrimage.

"In my T-Bird? No, no, no, no, no!" shrieked Jose, thinking of the clouds of dust settling on the paint job even if he drove slowly, slowly, and the dirt on the carpet he'd have to vacuum. "No, no, no, no, no!" He'd have to wash and wax it and what about the old bridge sagging so badly in the middle.

"The transmission, Juanita, the transmission. No, no, no, no, no!" and all Juanita said again, quite forcefully, was: "Si, si, si, si, si. En to T-Bird."

Felipe (who was the second oldest and didn't own a vintage cherry-red T-Bird with porthole windows, chrome rims and etc., and was therefore more tolerant, but not so tolerant that "No, no, no, not again!" didn't fail to escape from his lips) drove down to The Emporium immediately (in his Pontiac, after picking up Roberto) and parted the crowd easily (como el Charlton Heston) with Roberto immediately behind him, and when Botas Meadas (buzzbuzz "Chingadas moscas! No more THUNDERBIRD forever!") saw him, he held out both arms like a martyr of old, ready to take the first step of his bloody pilgrimage.

Roberto, who owned a Ford pick-up, and because he was the youngest, had very little say in the matter, said, patiently, "That's the third time this year he's announced in public he's never going to drink again! Last time he swore he was never going to touch another drop of Thunderbird."

Well, you can imagine how the pilgrimage went if by the end of the first block Botas Meadas' khakis were torn to shreds, his knees scraped and bleeding. He tried to swat away horde after horde of moscas, while Felipe and Roberto fought desperately to keep hold of his arms in order to help him along by lifting him with each painful step.

Once they turned the corner of First and Martinez where the large clock on the front of the First National Bank (owned by the Mafia connection Maria Martinez had threatened to sic on Botas Meadas) read eight o'clock, there was nothing but the railroad tracks and a mile or so of llano to the church where Jose would be waiting impatiently at midnight.

By nine o'clock they had covered about a quarter of a mile after pausing time and again for Botas Meadas to swat away moscas, to gather up courage to continue, his knees torn by the rocks, cactus ("Moscas! NO more Thunderbird! Forever!"), Felipe and Roberto struggled to keep him on course.

By ten o'clock Botas Meadas had covered half a mile only because Felipe and Roberto had lifted and carried, lifted and carried him with each step he attempted, across the moonless llano.

Eleven o'clock. One mile (mas o menos).

Eleven thirty. Botas Meadas claimed he saw the church steeple, refused any further help, insisted Felipe and Roberto walk behind him.

Midnight. Botas Meadas stands up, yells he has seen the light. "Never again another drop . . . ," and begins running in the direction of the rays God has sent down especially for him, two golden rays that will guide him directly to the kingdom of Heaven. Truly today has been a day of milagros! Truly a day of milagros! He has been forgiven! All that is necessary now is to cross the bridge that spans Heaven and Earth.

Jose eases the cherry-red T-Bird with porthole windows and chrome rims and etc. down, down the wide V in the middle of the bridge, carefully, slowly, s-l-o-o-o-w-l-y, and it seems to him the bridge has sagged even more since the last time (son of a bitch, easy, s-l-o-w-l-y, s-l-o-o-o-w-l-y, come on, . . .). The bridge is sagging so much the glare of his headlights barely extends to the opposite end.

"MOSCAS! NO MORE THUNDERBIRD!"

Jose looks up, sees a man at the far end of the bridge walking toward him, arms outstretched, and because of the limited range of the Thunderbird's headlights the man has no head. ("¡A la chingada! !El Hombre Sin Cabeza!") And just like

Mosco Zamora reported, the creature was yelling "Mosco! Mosco!" with his hands dripping blood, his knees torn, also dripping blood and swearing he'll destroy the Thunderbird. ("Bullshit!") Jose lurched into action: ("Reverse Chingao! First Chingao! Reverse Chingao!")

"(Buzz) MOSCAS! NO MORE THUNDERBIRD!"

"(Reverse Chingao!)"

Botas Meadas had smelled that smell before. On earth. The smell of tires burning! He couldn't understand . . . perhaps . . . Yes! It was perfectly clear! He had to walk over the burning sinners in hell in order to inherit the kingdom of Heaven!

The cherry-red T-Bird with porthole windows, chrome rims and etc. finally lurched out of the V. First the left rear lights and fender were smashed, then the entire side scraped and crunched against the steel railings, then it ricocheted clear across to the other side of the bridge where first the rear lights and fender were battered, then the entire side crunched and smashed into the railing, and finally came to a stop.

"(Buzz) NO MORE THUNDERBIRD!"

("Reverse chingao!")

The spider gears clanged, whinnied, brayed, shuddered, and then clanged again, metal crunching, crushed by metal.

And then Jose noticed that attached to the cabeza was a body. That not too far behind were two more cabezas coming into his headlights, the only things on his cherry-red T-Bird with porthole windows, chrome rims and etc. that seemed to work. "No, no, no, no, NO!"

At one A.M., Father Schmidt arrived at the old church with Monsignor Chavez, who had driven the sixty miles from Albuquerque in even less time than when he had rocketed down to San Miguel to see the burning rosary, driving Caruso into a bout of depression that he finally overcame at the next demolition derby. He had been unable to cross at the bridge because it was sagging so much it seemed ready to collapse, and had had to circle back by way of Los Brasos where he almost crashed head-on with Caruso, who had been at the church, along with the same faithful who had congregated outside Pepe's house during the time of his milagro, when Botas Meadas and his sons arrived, and had driven them back to the bridge, hooked the Thunderbird and soared through the llano, where "El Hombre Sin Cabeza" roamed on a moonless night such as this, back to San Miguel in a time that would have made Monsignor Chavez shudder with envy. The faithful were kneeling on the scarred earth, holding candles, praying rosary after rosary. The skeptics, of course, were gathered in the rear, arguing about Botas Meadas, placing bets.

AWEARY OF THE SUN

Gregory Feeley

Gregory Feeley's first novel was *The Oxygen Barons*; he is currently at work on his second, *Neptune's Reach*. His short fiction has been published in *Full Spectrum*, *Asimov's*, *Science Fiction Age*, and elsewhere. He has also made a name for himself as an astute literary critic and book reviewer for the *Washington Post*, *Newsday*, *The New York Review of Science Fiction*, and other journals.

The story that follows, "Aweary of the Sun," is an enchanting, entertaining, and skillfully penned tale about witches and playwrights in sixteenth-century England. It comes from a rather quirky anthology called *Weird Tales From Shakespeare* edited by Katharine Kerr and Martin H. Greenberg.

—T.W.

Serviceable John sat not wholly at his ease, before him curling sheets of foolscap held fast by inkpot and cup of claret. Writing in an inn was not his accustomed way—it smacked of vainglory, Tourneur or one of his fellows scribbling amidst a brawl—but he was driven forth that day while his rooms were smoked for lice. Weak sunlight slanted through a dirty window to fall imperfectly upon Fletcher's table. He reached carefully for his cup. It would not do to slosh drink upon the playscript, especially with pages not his own.

Some commotion by the door reached his ears, but Fletcher had returned to his duty, repairing without outward complaint the occasion of his grievance. Chary with his praise, he stood rebuked, and was charged now with expanding Cranmer's prophecies of the young Elizabeth by half again their natural length, lest the coarse-eared multitude miss their import. When *All Is True* was rehearsed for the Princess' wedding, the crack-spined pageant had sped quickly: the Generoso knew well his sovereign's taste for short plays. Now it opened at the Globe, for which Fletcher must needs revise it to fit the greater resources of that house.

"Let not ambition mock thy useful toil," he murmured. Well he understood the sharers' concern; yet might they have voiced it more prudently. Had it been he who had announced his present retirement to the country, the sharers would have turned to Francis with greater confidence, yet less reason.

He examined the speech before him. The pious Cranmer, expatiating upon the infant's glorious future, likened her to "the maiden phoenix," divining that she would secure a good succession without ever marrying. Given such augury, why could he not foresee his own coming death at the stake? No matter; let nothing come before the King's Men's premiere playwright when he is praising his betters. With grim pleasure Fletcher added to the count, letting Cranmer give her long life, and even (let none call him stinting in praise of the late Queen) predict that she shall die "a virgin, A most unspotted lily." Indeed, Fletcher knew better, for the "aged princess," spotted and bilious with age, had blighted his family at a stroke. Again, no matter: Fletcher swallowed his claret and wrote. And may no groundling wonder why Henry does not strike his Archbishop to the ground for such prophecy.

"Needst thou all this patch of sun?"

He had not heard her approach beneath the sounds of commerce. Squinting in the light, Fletcher found a face for the voice: a crone of past sixty, grinning toothlessly at him. I am justly requited, he thought: Sit in taverns of a morning, and you will be addressed familiarly by drabs.

Fletcher smiled. "If you took your bones without, Granny, 'twould be sun aplenty."

The crone cackled. "And if I took my bones to potter's field, 'twould vex one gentleman less." Boldly she surveyed his labors, as though well conversant with the sight of paper. But before he could speak, she dropped her finger upon a loose sheet and pronounced: "This is not thy hand."

Fletcher stared. But the answer, he saw quickly, was plain: one of his own half-finished sheets was before him, and even an unlettered eye could discern a different hand upon the other. Fletcher quirked his lips and began to frame a dismissive reply when the woman amazed him again:

" 'Tis the hand of that cozening blackguard, Will Shakespeare."

At first he thought he had not heard her right. A part of his mind sought to parse the sentence otherwise, *Blackguard will shakes pair*, then stuttered into silence. Fletcher looked at her with frank astonishment. "And pray tell, Granny, how thou camest to know the hand, indeed the name, of Will Shakespeare."

The crone laughed, delighted to be abruptly courted. "Buy me sack," she said, "and let me sit in that pool of sunlight. You may rest opposite, in your nest of papers."

Warily, Fletcher vacated his seat. From across the room he caught the eye of the tapster, who stared as the gentleman gave way to the stinking beldam. "More claret," he called, "and a cup of sack for my old nurse."

In the sunlight the woman looked even worse: balding beneath a greasy cap, so hunched she could not touch her shoulders to the back board, she wriggled with pleasure at the bench's warmth. Fletcher observed her eyes follow the sack as it was brought across the room to her. As her clothes warmed, he thought, she would begin to smell.

She snatched up the cup and drank deeply, smacking her lips at the end like a starving dog. "Stay, hold," he warned. "Th'art not used to such."

She offered a purple grin. "I've supped on sack as 'twere my mother's milk."

"But not lately." Fletcher had been musing and thought he had his answer. "Thou hast dallied with actors and seen their scripts. Imagine'st thou that every play is Will Shakespeare's?"

The crone took his meaning at once. Taking up a sheet, she held it close to her face, then turned it right side up and read in a quavering but unhesitant voice:

> "*Why, this it is: see, see!*
> *I have beene begging sixteene yeares in Court,*
> *(Am yet a Courtier beggarly) nor could*
> *Come pat betwixt too early, and too late*
> *For any suit of pounds: and you, (O fate)*
> *A very fresh Fish heere—fye, fye, fye upon*
> *This compel'd fortune: have your mouth fild up*
> *Before you open it.*"

"Enough." Had she made her point by naming a second playwright Fletcher would have been surprised enough; this left him faintly dizzy. "Thou canst read, and mayhap cipher as well. Art thou a goodwife, reduced in widowhood to vagrancy?"

"I am a witch," she said.

Fletcher blinked. Watching her drink, he thought: Of course, she's mad. The reply answered all, until he remembered that mad crones don't read.

Wiping her chin, she regarded him sharply: a crow eyeing a cat it knows is too far to pounce. " 'Tis not safe to say such things," he said carefully, "not even in London town. Not in the reign of our Scottish majesty."

She cackled. "And Elizabeth loved witches? 'Twas in her father's day," she gestured at the pages, "that the first statutes against us were passed. I was but a child, yet remember."

"Thou art not so old." Elizabeth died at seventy but had Christendom's finest physic to preserve her so long. Fletcher would not believe this drab so old, startled as he was that she had gleaned the play's theme in a glance.

"Old enough to remember witches accused in Chelmsford; confessions forced with the tools of hell and four women hanging like dressed deer." She glared at him like a true witch, red-laced eyes come suddenly alive.

Fletcher found he had no reply to this. He pulled close a loose sheet before she could set her cup on it, then had a thought. "Canst thou write as well as read?" he asked. He turned over a foul sheet, presenting its unblemished backside, and held up his plume.

She reached for it directly. None who'd ever written, even a schoolboy laboring sums, could resist (thought Fletcher) his fine nib and clean foolscap. He watched as the crone grasped the quill, bringing her nose almost to the paper as she arduously scrawled a short line. Fletcher took it as soon as she lifted the nib and studied the crabbed apothecarial hand: *Alizon Wyckliffe her mark*. And below it, *B. 26 Ianuarie 1549*.

Too young to have known Henry even if she wrote true; but the signature spoke much else. The lettering recalled those found on bottles, and it was in no wise impossible that an herbalist or simple-woman should possess some rudiments of writing.

Her cup struck hollowly on the table. "More."

"Thou shalt fall to sleep, thy tale untold."

"Nay, the tongue is dry. Another cup, i'th'name of Jesus."

The last words rose to a whine. Startled, Fletcher looked closer. He had seen sodden players in whom little drink, or none, could bring the tremors, which more drink would allay. He did not want to see this leathern frame of sticks collapse before him foaming.

He pushed his cup toward her. Snatching it, she drained the dregs in a draught.

"Tell thy tale, and I'll buy thee a pie. Should thy story please, thou shalt have another cup."

She looked ready to protest, then fell to mumbling. Fletcher signaled the taverner who, frowning, brought a pie, though not one of his best.

"Speak," he told her.

And she spoke. The tale she told twisted like a byway overgrown with scant use, and at times he had to pull her through brambles or chop rudely at a growth that threatened to beguile her. No milestones marked the turnings of her tale; and Fletcher, who had learned in grammar school to con his dates, grew vexed at her incapacity to set years to her occasions. But only one occasion truly mattered, and he knew its date well enough.

By then she was in Southwark, and past fifty if her birth-date be trusted. Fletcher had brushed aside her maundering on earlier years: her maidenhood in Essex, marriage to an aged grocer, and later to a sailor who gave her the clap and left her penniless. Only a moment's musing did he permit: gathering autumn herbs in the short Sussex afternoons, the list of which simples—henbane, senna, belladonna, camomile—struck him with its artless music. Beyond that, he hastened her onward: the recollections of a country witch (or city witch), however interesting, were not to his purpose.

The heavens themselves blaze forth the death of princes; and the heavens seemed to blaze that night, as though gobbets of flaming firmament had fallen to earth and set fire to houses and men's hearts. Young John, newly come from Cambridge and without a patron's protection, had stared like a fascinated deer as the earth shook about him. That one prince would die was certain; fell rebellion, loosed like a fifth horseman over England, would not be quenched save in the blood of one of its principals. Perhaps both, and more, should die, and civil war break like a thunderplump of gore over the world that Fletcher scarce knew.

On the eve of rebellion rumor raced through town like sparks through straw. The Privy Council had demanded an accounting of Essex, who claimed illness and did not appear. Conspirators were massing at Essex House; the Council's officers would ride. And in Bankside, where Fletcher had taken the meanest lodgings, the boldest intimations of revolt were seen, for the day before, the Chamberlain's Men had performed the *Tragedy of Richard the Second*, specially commissioned (everyone knew) by one of Essex's knights. The populace had cheered to see the idle king deposed and killed, and had taken away—who could say aught otherwise?—the glowing coals of treason in their hearts.

Listening, Fletcher remembered his own story more vividly than he heard hers. A calf cut off from the herd, he had felt terror and exhilaration to see the city erupt about him. Crowds gathered in the streets and were not dispersed. Riders pulling up were beset for news. Terrible Elizabeth, a great oak gone rotten with age, was about to be kicked to flinders by valiant young men.

Little of this touched Alizon, though she followed more than Fletcher would have guessed. She lived in a disused outbuilding among roots and turnips, and ventured into the streets only to the degree necessary to sell the nostrums and charms that sustained her. She might have heard nothing till it was over had not the players spoke in her presence.

—And why was this? Fletcher interrupted. He could think of fewer likely occupations for an aging herb-woman who called herself witch than to comport with Bankside men.

"Why, for my hand," she replied, at once injured and sly. She gestured to the page she had scribbled, and then Fletcher understood. She had written to order, probably taking down the words of disloyal players who would spout their lines to printers or rival sharers eager to steal a play.

She affirmed this. The first time, she had been rousted from sleep by some sharper she had once sold to and set at a table in an inn's back room. A player had declaimed (very foully, she averred) and she had written down his speech. The sharper, peering over her shoulder, had exclaimed and struck her: for she had written the lines as though setting forth a grocer's account. It was then, she said, she learned how to set out the verse of a play-script and did so without spoiling more paper.

And thus she knew players and was suffered sometimes to stay when they filled a tavern. Essex was a great patron of acting companies, as was another, she forgot his name—

"Southampton," said Fletcher.

Yes. His younger ally, beloved of the Chamberlain's Men. Passions ran high on Bankside for the noble rebels, higher than elsewhere as events proved, for the Uprising fizzled in less than a day, failing like damp gunpowder to ignite the populace.

Fletcher remembered. He said nothing but nodded taut-faced that she should continue.

In the aftermath players scattered, bleating. Deputies of the Privy Council were said to be crossing the bridge, asking for the man who played Bolingbroke, and Richard as well. The Globe was closed, assemblies broken up.

And in the rains of February, a poor player appeared at her door: hat-brim running with water and his thin shanks shivering, to beg sanctuary in her hovel. He had silver, and he spoke well.

He was Master William Shakespeare, the Chamberlain's Men shareholder who had penned Richard's words, and a hunted man. His patron was in the Tower, his friends, men of influence, now scattered. Mayhap they would intercede for him, once the tumult was ended and things resettled in their natural order. Mayhap, no surely, the Privy Council would recognize that the play, written five years earlier, cast no reflection of present troubles; had been commanded performed by lord and knights they could ill refuse. All this would come in time; he need only meanwhile survive the Queen's present wrath.

She took him in, took his silver, threw costly faggots on the smoky fire to parch the air. Shaking in the moldering horse-blanket she gave him while his clothes dried, the fugitive sipped scalded tea and sought to justify his plight. More than a player, he was landholder and indeed gentleman—his claim recognized by the College Heraldry—and entitled to be called "generoso." His was a place of established degree; but now the heavens were torn asunder, and even fixed stars rained down flaming.

When his tremors increased uncontrollably, Alizon fetched forth a stoppered bottle of spirits. Not (she told Fletcher plainly) the smoother stuff of taverns, it burned even when poured in tea, and slight-shouldered Shakespeare convulsed sputtering at its first swallow. As the liquor took hold, his ague subsided, but his humor likewise declined, veering between choler and despair. He railed at fortune, spoke of years of labor to redeem his family's dignity, endless toil, and bitter disappointments. Now all was cast down, his every hope a wrack on time's rock shore.

"His son," Fletcher murmured.

The witch did not hear him. She had (she continued) already recognized Master Shake-scene, thinner at the crown but manifestly the same Johannes Factotum she remembered from the years before the plague had closed the theaters, now plainly realized in his ambitions to please lords and rise in the world. Sweet-tempered and agreeable, with good clothes and fine gloves, he had shown no interest in horoscopes or charms, so had not held her notice during those hard years. When the plague blew the players from town like chaff, depriving her of their custom but occasioning much business in cataplasms, she had forgotten him.

And now he lay in her blanket, seeking sanctuary in her hovel as though 'twere St. Savior's. She told him that should the authorities reject his plea that the players had mounted the seditious performance under compulsion, no more would they accept hers, if caught, that she had had no choice but to harbor a wellborn fugitive. He stared at this show of logic, then produced more silver. In fact, no one would think to seek him there.

She went out the next morning, with the gentleman's silver, and bought meats and a better quality of greens than she had known in years. More to the purpose, she had lingered without the grocer's and sat in the alehouse (paying for her malmsey with a bright sixpence that made the tapster stare), head down but ears open for word of the snuffed revolt and its issue.

She heard more questions than answers, for all was still confusion, as in a catastrophe whose dust takes days to settle. Essex was in the Tower, his life surely forefeit, and Southampton, too. (At word of this, Master Shakespeare gave a great groan.) But while the players' performance, and the forty shillings paid them for it by the conspirators, were widely mouthed, there was no word of Augustine Phillips being seized, nor John Heminges, and—Shakespeare fastened upon this—surely it would be the talk of the taverns were the senior Lord Chamberlain's men arrested. Alizon, bringing out cold roast meats, shrugged. She had supper to prepare, and her mouth was watering.

The next day found Bankside subdued, even chastened. No deputies rode the streets, no fresh news either, but the populace seemed chagrined, as though remembering its cheers for the regicide on Friday afternoon. Shakespeare bid her go forth again, and she did, but spent the short afternoon digging tubers for her medicines. When she returned, she found him sitting at her one rude window, looking through the papers spread before him.

"These are spells of witchcraft," he said upon her entrance.

Alizon had her arms full, so could not shrug. She had already told him she was a witch, as one confides secrets to the dying. "Mayhap we shall both be hanged," she said.

He winced. "Such evidence would damn thee, were thy rooms searched. A friend of mine—"

"Recipes and charms, little more." The player was acute, to discern nigromancy and maleficia in the lists of herbs and preparations. He was right, withal: investigators, should ever her hovel serve as the unlikely focus of their interests, would be led by the hounds of their fancy straight where Shakespeare's reason had taken him.

But now he wanted news. As she made her brief recitation, her eyes fell upon a clean sheet before him, now covered with writing not hers. Shakespeare, following her gaze, turned the sheet over and left his hand upon it.

Later he made bold to speak. "I have devised a means for my deliverance," he told her as the coals burnt down, bringing dimness and chill to the shuttered room. He had been scribbling as she prepared supper, and he had called for her single candle. "Thou shalt go forth on a journey, greater than thou hath ever taken."

He spent the night in the root cellar, lest deputies bang on the door, but emerged in the morning, grimy and smelling of earth, to explain. She was to ride from the city, a journey of three days' duration, to a great house, there to deliver a message to a great lady. The gentleman-player was at pains to impress that she not give offense with her rude demeanor, prompting Alizon to draw herself up and, calling upon accents long unused, berate him in the respectable tones of her vanished shopkeeper's days. He sighed and said that this would suffice for a messenger.

He sent her forth with two shillings for a passable cloak, also sending for good paper and wax. Upon her return he took the paper and bade her leave him for two hours. Alizon sat in the noonday sun, heart pounding at the prospect of travel. When she returned, he presented her with a letter and instructions for its delivery. More shillings he gave her, gulping as he counted them out, and instructions for her voyaging.

And thus it was that the hedge witch presented herself to an inn at Newgate, and the next day boarded a wagon headed out Uxbridge Road, west toward Wiltshire. The ostler looked her askance, seeing a widow traveling alone, not unheard of but strange. Her travel companions, servants on their masters' business, gave her not a glance. The wagon was loaded with city goods bound for Salisbury, and Alizon sat two days on the jouncing crates.

The journey was memorable, but Fletcher cut her short. Yes, she had looked at the name on the sealed letter directly she was out of Shakespeare's sight: it was Mary, Countess of Pembroke, Wilton House. (At this, Fletcher started.) The wagon emptied at Salisbury market, whence she walked six miles to the great house. A man in livery stared at her from the servants' entrance, then took the letter and studied its fine hand. She sat forty minutes in the kitchen, warming her feet while cooks' helpers regarded her suspiciously, when the doors opened and the finest lady she had ever seen entered.

Alizon stood, and the two regarded each other a moment, as across worlds.

The countess of Pembroke was perhaps forty, redheaded and comely for her age, dressed in a bright-colored bodice that looked as if it had been slashed by knives and a collar that stood up about her neck like a builder's scaffold surrounding a steeple. Glad for her good cloak, Alizon met her gaze squarely.

"The man that sent thee this," said the countess, "is safe now in thy lodgings?"

Master Shakespeare had evidently not seen fit to disclose that he was hiding in a root cellar. "He is, subject to forced search. But I do doubt that mischance."

"I see." The countess tapped the open letter absently. "Tell him I shall do what I can."

Alizon nodded, then remembering herself, curtsied stiffly. The countess was headed for the door, then paused before the servant who held it open. "Is the market coach returning to London?" she asked him.

"Yes, my Lady."

"Conduct her there tomorrow." And she swept through the door, not looking back.

That night Alizon slept in a bed, better than her own, and was taken in the morning to the inn where she had debarked. In the courtyard of Wilton, however, a young man accosted her, saying, "A moment, an it please thee," as he strode easily up. Dressed in London fashion, he was a guest, not a household member. "Thou art the woman brought a message from Will Shakespeare?"

Chary of speaking to strangers, she could see no evasion here. "Aye," she said guardedly.

"And did he actually sanction a performance of his *Richard* on the rebellion's eve?"

"So he says."

The man shook his plump cheeks, as though amazed at the folly of the world. "Ah, Will," he said.

> "*By discordant tunes are e'en the great o'erthrown,*
> *Thou should have pitch'd thy song to the* middle-tone."

He gave her a coin. "If thou see'st him again, tender him my love."

She didn't know how she was to know this young popinjay's name, and repeated his couplet bemusedly on her ride to the inn. Perhaps his fellow poet in the cellar would understand it.

Alizon's tale was almost finished. She returned to London more than a week after the abortive rebellion, and found the city calm. Dozens of knights and bravos filled the Tower, but she heard no report of players charged with treason.

And when she entered her room, she found it empty, its unsought tenant gone. Worse, half her papers were gone as well. Turning their pages in disbelief, she found her best spells taken, including one tucked into an herbalists' guide, her one book, which she had not seen Shakespeare peruse.

On the floor lay the sheet on which he had drafted his letter, verso (as it proved) of one of her recipes. His grammar-school hand had stared at her this past dozen years, whenever she turned over that leaf as she searched, eyes failing, for a charm that eluded her memory.

She never saw Shakespeare again.

* * *

Fletcher was staring at her. When he spoke, it was of an apparent inconsequentiality. "What did the letter say?"

The witch laughed. "Come and read it, if you like. He begs for noble intercession: '*As you have done me honor in the past, I call, from my disgraced and hunted state—*' " She gestured negligently. "He spoke of his roots being withered and his buds blighted, and that the terrible woodsman was now come to hack at his poor bare trunk. In short, he fell at her feet."

Fletcher was still nibbling at the edges of this story, rather than its heart. "But why would he steal your papers?"

"Because they were fine spells, and he had an eye for quality. Mayhap he wanted to write a play about witches."

"Shakespeare nev—" Fletcher began, then stopped.

The witch picked up her cup. "Sack," she said, thrusting it forth.

Fletcher took the cup to the bar himself. He felt an agitation he could not explain and brought back claret as well. The woman took her cup from his hands before he sat and was drinking deeply ere he sipped. She would return to her hovel, he thought, and pass out. So much grape, at her age, could surely not be good.

"Write me directions to thy lodgings," he said as she wiped her mouth. He found the sheet where she had signed her name and pushed it to her.

Suspicious, she drew back. "What concerns you where I live?"

Uncertain himself, he made light of it. "Mayhap I should hear another story; and if so, thou should have more pie and sack."

Unlike Will, Fletcher had never been a player, and his imposture rang false. "This tale hath stuck in your skin," the witch said, shrewd. "Comes it too close to your own trade?"

Smiling, Fletcher told her, "Know we work by wit, and not by witchcraft." Quoting the man himself.

But she pursued the point. "What is it to you, a gentleman born? Love you so a tale of your master pinching papers?"

Fletcher made to dispute this, but the crone, watching his face, saw something.

"Of course," she said, breaking out in a wizened grin. "He stole something from you, as well."

Bankside stank at low tide, both shores really, so that Fletcher, midway across the Bridge, felt himself suspended between stenches. We live, he thought, with one foot still in our mother's bloody matrix, the other in the grave. How far he'd come across his own life's span no man could say.

Preparations for the afternoon's performance were well under way, and Fletcher slipped through the players' entrance without being remarked. In the corridor the smell of face paint cut the air, and he heard Nicholas Tooley shout at the boy he was daubing (no doubt as Lucinda) to hold still. Having seen his *Cardenio* performed at Court and in Greenwich, Fletcher had no desire to see it yet again. Half the shareholders were taking roles, and Will was at his house at Puddle Dock. Fletcher would be undisturbed.

The library was on the topmost floor, its valuables beyond the reach of burglars looking in windows. Fletcher closed the door behind him. Bound volumes lined the upper shelves, including the English *Quixote* that had finally allowed uncolleged Will to see the story Fletcher had told him of. The Globe might have presented *Cardenio* to England years earlier, but Will had insisted on waiting until Shelton's long-delayed translation saw print, that he might study it himself. Possibly his business sense, ever acute, had served them well: the members of Court had all heard of Sir Quixote by the time the company mounted the play, although of course they had not read him.

Fletcher left off worrying this old sore. He noted a space missing on the same shelf: some fat volume taken, perhaps by Will who was now brooding upon a fall play. This was also no matter, and Fletcher turned to the meaner shelves, where quartos and prompter's-books were stacked, and lower still, to the two shelves stuffed with scripts, rough papers, and unfinished work. He pulled out a fistful, loosening the rest enough to be riffled, and sat down to sort.

Shakespeare's sheets, being better paper than the other playwrights used, were easy to separate. The first loose batch proved to be the botched *Timon*, which Fletcher regarded sourly. The failures of the gorgeous *Coriolanus* and *Antony* should have told Will what his fellows already knew: that antique histories no longer commanded the public's interest. Withal, he began another, tainted with the bitterness of his unaccustomed failure; and so exercised his bile that he made himself sick. His partners, reviewing the rough copy, advised Will to abandon it. Will waved his hand weakly in acquiescence, and there was an end to it.

When Fletcher, not thinking himself overbold, suggested he have a crack at redeeming the script, he was smacked down like a puppy nosing at table. Five years later the memory still burned. And when (he reminded himself) the great man found his way again, it was with the form of *tragi-comedy* that Fletcher had compounded, *Pericles* rising out of *Philaster* as a zephyr gives breath to a winded traveler. And when Shakespeare, still ill, permitted a second hand to span the disordered scenes of his draft, it was the wretched Wilkins, a family friend, to whom he turned. O tiger's heart indeed.

Fletcher pushed on, marching backward in time as he shuffled deeper. He found the play soon enough, but two-thirds the length of *Lear*, even with the witchy scenes added for public performances. Beneath it lay Will's earliest copy, miraculously light in its corrections. Though it was not to his purpose, Fletcher found himself turning pages, and fell quickly into the tale, as down a well.

Was *Macbeth* always so world-weary a play? Fletcher had not known it so before, when rapt he had watched the King's Men race through its paces, each line a cut gem yet swift-moving as a freshet. "Better be with the dead," says the new king, early in the play—indeed while Banquo still lives—"than on the torture of the Minde to lye In restlesse extasie." How could he think so, this soon? And later: "I have liv'd long enough. My way of life Is falne into the Seare, the yellow Leafe." But Macbeth—Fletcher turned back to check—had not yet learned of his lady's death, nor of Birnam on the march. An o'er-tuned lute, he sang high at the briefest plucking.

Fletcher read twice through the mad king's tremendous soliloquy upon hearing his wife dead, its infernal vision of a babbling and meaningless life gaping like a hole burned in the fabric of faith, disclosing darkness beyond. And a page later, apprised at last that Birnam Wood approaches, Macbeth gives voice again to this more-than-despair:

> *I 'ginne to be a-weary of the Sun,*
> *And wish th'estate o'th'world were now undon.*

Magnificent, yet it stood out of proportion with his troubles. Astonishing how swift pace and flashing poetry can blind one to the odd under-tides of a play. Fletcher hesitated, then put the sheets away. Had *Macbeth* been printed, he would take a quarto home with him; but he remembered otherwise. And his purpose yet lay before him.

Behind the loose sheets of *Macbeth* lay other playwrights' work, and the next script of Will's to turn up was a version of *Lear*. Fletcher dug through the pile but found no loose notes. Where, then? Standing and casting about, he abruptly saw it: a black spine on the finest shelf, much the best-bound book in the room. *Daemonologie* by His Majesty himself, although the book had been first published when James was but King of the lowly Scots (the title page did not mention this), and not likely to have caught the interest of Shakespeare, pleaser of nearer sovereigns.

As soon as Fletcher began turning pages, he had it: a packet of folded papers inside the back cover, coarse and heavily scribbled. He opened one carefully and saw writing he thought he knew: smaller and surer than the scrawl of Alizon Wyckliffe, but recognizably the hand of her younger state. He took it to the window and studied it in the afternoon light.

The first sheet seemed to be a list of demons, along with their attributes. One was underscored by a second hand: "Flibbertigibbet," a demon who (as Fletcher read) walked the earth from curfew to cock-crow, where it causes such bodily infirmities as harelip and squint-eye, besides blighting wheat and shriveling cows' teats. This seemed familiar, though Fletcher could not say from whence.

Several other sheets gave instructions for divers nasty potions, calling for ingredients such as the caul of stillborn babe and the sweated grease of a hanged man. At length one caught his eye:

Eye of Newt yt is midnight caughte; toe of young Frog spyed in its pond by moonlighte; tongue of Dog yt hath ate of wommens fleshe; fillet of Snake fed nine dayes on Sausyge made of living Christians bloode and giv'n but Holie Water to drink . . .

That was it. Fingers trembling, Fletcher restored the pages to the book and shut it. He imagined telling the witch that her lost writings lay between the King's own sheets.

And so? as Francis might say after Fletcher had offered some twist of plot for a coming play. What follows? Fletcher puzzled this as he descended the stairs. William Shakespeare, gentleman, once hid in a witch's hovel while he howled to his protectress. Indeed, he employed the witch to deliver his plea in person to the Countess of Pembroke. And salted a play acted before witch-hunter James with scraps of actual witchcraft, which he stole. And so?

Three cups of claret, their effects held back by the day's mystery, now lapped the edges of his consciousness like tides against a child's sand-battlements. Tobacco would have sharpened his wits, but Fletcher might not light his pipe in the building, by firm company rule. Stepping into the street, he could faintly hear the roars of the bear garden two lanes distant. Ever sensitive to fine verse, he felt a stab of pity for the world, and the beasts' cries played hard upon the strings of his melancholia.

The morning was squandered, the afternoon far gone. The hounds of Fletcher's fancy were loosed on a chase not of his choosing, and he could not call them back.

This had not been a good writing day.

His rooms still stank as though Mephistopheles had held court there, and Fletcher was driven within the hour back into the streets. The long June sun would loiter until ten, good working hours for those who could.

Remembering the disdainful cry of "forty shillings" in *Poetaster*, he crossed the Bridge again to call on sturdy Ben, late returned from Europe. His wife, leaning crossly out an upstairs window, called down that he could be found at the Mermaid; but a bellow behind her turned her head, and she withdrew. Evidently the mistress of the house showed too little care for the comings and goings of the master. A minute later Ben, red-faced and with his doublet half-buttoned for his ease, appeared at the door and ushered Fletcher in.

"I have strange intelligences this day," began Fletcher as they mounted the stairs. The fresh-plastered walls bore prints of classical scenes: Diana discovered bathing, Atalanta distracted in her footrace by the golden apples tossed in her path. Fletcher's own lodgings, which he long had shared with Francis, were raffishly hung with illustrations from the title pages of their early plays.

"We will speak over ale," said Ben. "The best!" he roared, that none might claim not to have heard him.

His desk was covered with proof sheets, heavily corrected throughout. "A new play?" Fletcher ventured.

"Poems," said Ben shortly. As of course Fletcher could see upon closer inspection. "To be included in a great folio of my collected Works."

Fletcher picked up a page. "Are you including none of your longer ones?"

"These will constitute the first Book, called *Epigrammes*. The longer poems will follow." Jonson took the page from Fletcher's hand and gazed at it fondly for a second before restoring it to its place. His wife entered, sullen, bearing two flagons on a tray. Jonson took them and handed Fletcher one, dismissing her with a nod. "Good British ale, unknown in France. Raleigh's brat supped wholly on Medoc and was like to become *bacchanamaniac*."

Fletcher smiled as he drank. Marston, he thought—or was it Peele?—had lanced Jonson for his love of big words, and Jonson had not forgot. Shakespeare had done so, too, he remembered. He set down his glass unhappily, foam like Aphrodite's spume unwiped in his beard.

"What news do you bring me, Jack?" asked Ben, setting himself down.

Fletcher began hesitantly. "You remember the business of the Lord Chamberlain's Men, as they were then called, 'broiling themselves with the Lord Essex's late revolt?"

Ben snorted. "Fools, and worse. 'Twas the neighbor of treason, and they might have swung for it."

"I heard some feared that and fled."

"Aye, so 'twas said," replied Ben carelessly, taking another sip. "Rumor had it that Will Shakespeare holed up for days with a whore."

Fletcher took a breath. "Methinks," he said, "I saw her yesternight."

Ben listened impatiently, interrupting Fletcher more frequently than Fletcher had the witch, though his account was more to the point. When Fletcher described the appearance of the sodden player before the witch, Ben asked sharply, did he identify himself as Shakespeare, or was this her later surmise? Why should he give his name, which could not advance his case with her, and might come later to plague him? Fletcher did not know. When he described her journey to Salisbury, Ben snorted: and in an instant the tale seemed a preposterous romance, a bedside story with a hag instead of a princess.

Only the memory of the scribbled spells assured him he wasn't the gull of an elaborate jape. When he began to describe his visit to the script-room, Ben fell suddenly silent: a sound joiner of tales, he knew Fletcher would not include the scene had it yielded no results.

"And did you find them?" he asked at the end.

"Aye, tucked in the pages of His Majesty's *Daemonologie*."

Ben started, then crossed himself with a mutter. Pushing back his chair, he stood and pulled a book from his shelves, then leafed a moment through its well-turned pages. Closing its fine leather covers, he set it with a sigh on his desk. " 'Twere better she were a whore."

Church bells were ringing outside his window; what was the clock? Fletcher may have intruded upon the supper hour, and would incur further displeasure from Mistress Jonson. Before he could speak, Ben had got up abruptly and headed out the door, muttering something about a piss.

Alone in the study, Fletcher examined the library, grander than his own or the Globe's. No book was so exquisitely worked as James's on the desk, but there were many fine volumes, arrayed with an excellent sense of hierarchy: religious, historical, and law books on the upper shelves, plays and pamphlets below. Fletcher saw *The Faithfull Shepheardesse* in the middle range but knew his brief pleasure at so finding his first-born was a fond one; its presence owed to Ben's dedicatory poem in it. Ben did like the sound of his own verses. Fletcher leafed idly through the proof sheets, then stopped as his eye fell upon one. He was still reading when Ben returned.

"To the Mermaid," he was saying. "What's this?"

"Good Ben, art thou mad?" asked Fletcher, holding up the sheet. He remembered vaguely its verses from a tavern declamation, but he had not expected to find them in proof.

"What, what?" asked Ben gruffly. He tugged at Fletcher's hand to see.

" 'On Poet-Ape,' " said Fletcher.

"And what of it? 'Twas written long ago."

Fletcher read:

> "*Poore* Poet-Ape, *that would be thought our chiefe,*
> *Whose workes are eene the fripperie of wit,*
> *From brocage is become so bold a thiefe,*

As we, the rob'd, leave rage, and pittie it.
At first he made low shifts, would picke and gleane,
Buy the reversions of old playes; now growne
To'a little wealth, and credit in the scene,
He takes up all, makes each man's wit his owne."

"And what of it?" asked Ben truculently.

"Ben, thou know'st who this will be taken for."

"It does not say so; it nowhere names." Ben was growing red in the face, and Fletcher looked away to scan the remaining lines. The poet-ape was indeed not identified, nor did he sound like Shakespeare, save in his contempt for the "sluggish gaping auditor"; but the portrait withal would be taken as his.

"What quarrel led to this?" he asked.

" 'Tis a verse writ long ago, after a forgotten matter. Its cause extinct, the reader may still admire its felicities." Ben plucked at the sheet, and Fletcher let him have it.

"Let us drink," he added before Fletcher could speak again. He grasped Fletcher's arm and, dropping the proof sheet on his desk, led him through the door. Sounds of clatter emerged from the kitchen, but Ben did not slow until they were in the street, where the smell of ovens and baking meat wafted with the more common stinks.

"I am forty years old this week," he said, perhaps by way of keeping Fletcher off the late subject. "My father was broken at forty, but I feel I am in my prime. My masques play in court; the King favors me. When my *Works* appear next year, they shall be shelved in Oxford and Cambridge, where no plays later than the Romans' sit."

"I gave my *Shepheardesse* to my Master at Bene't," said Fletcher, wondering where this was going. "But there are some who call it no play."

Ben was in no mood to be sounded for compliments. "Shakespeare holds shares in the Globe," he said. "This lets him own three houses to my one, yet it compels him to fret his time with purse-strings and accounts. I write, by God! and you—" he swung his walking-stick to point at Fletcher—"should hew to the same policy."

"Think you I stand in danger of buying into the King's Men?" asked Fletcher wonderingly.

"Mark my words." They had turned onto Cheapside, and the smells of vendors and cook-stalls assailed them. Fletcher had not had supper. "You shall be their ordinary poet once Will has retired to his country manor with his family banner, and the temptation to buy shares will be strong. Beware."

It was as painful a subject as Ben could light upon. Fletcher and Beaumont, "the *Palamon* and *Arcite* of poesie," might well have succeeded Will, but Francis's marriage and departure from playwork had plunged the shareholders into a gloom too deep for gentleness to mask, and brought Will back from Stratford. Now Fletcher's plays were subject to Will's approval, and Will's plays given him for enlargement. Shareholders looked at him in frank disappointment, as though to tell them they had lief 'twere he had married and Francis stayed. And Will, saying nothing, fit the mold of tragi-comedy to his own plays like a glove.

"Will shall not retire to the country," said Fletcher absently. "He has just bought Gatehouse, not a stone's throw from Blackfriar's."

"Never you mind Gatehouse," replied Ben at once. "That's not to the point, and not for your enquiring."

"And I'm not to be their ordinary poet. They think me yet their prentice." He walked away from Ben, to a baker's stall where pasties were set out.

Ben followed, swishing his stick like the sword he was no longer permitted to keep. "Mark my words," he repeated. "Will is back to Stratford inside the year. Gatehouse is another matter; but Will is for retirement, and you his successor. They wish only to be sure of you; they are prudent men. No," reverting to a previous theme, "Will is back to his country place, his *maison* with the *blazon* and the title of gentleman. Watch you."

Fletcher wondered at the stream running beneath the earth of Ben's words. Without further remarks they turned onto Bread Street, and the sign of the Mermaid was visible on their right: Venus-breasted and haddock-scaled, it overhung the loudest tavern, whose facade seemed made all of oars and pieces of seawrack. Tobacco could be smelled ere they reached the door, and to cross its threshold was to emerge as though underwater: into murkiness and booming sound, where the air before one rippled and the blood pulsed in one's ears.

"Ben!" Several voices called from a corner. It was not the night when Ben's men gathered, but some were here, nonetheless, at their accustomed table. Ben called for hearty ale as he sat, and Fletcher signaled for claret.

"Hey, Jack," cried one wit, a poetaster from some company that thrived not. "Where is Frank Beaumont? I have not seen him these several weeks."

"Married and gone to country," said Fletcher shortly.

"I am sorry to hear't," the man said, pulling a long face.

"Means this your doxy is now thine alone?" jibed another. Laughter greeted this.

"Damn thee!" cried Fletcher, at once on his feet. Rage erupted like a tormented boil. "I'll not have that from a poxy ape like thou!" He lunged across the table, and hands were upon him, pulling him back. His affronter—a scribbler of pamphlets, patronless—was struggling to his feet, his chair caught against another's. *Sit, sit,* Ben was shouting.

Fletcher was forced back into his seat, someone grabbing his belt where his dagger lay. Friends were pulling the scribbler aside, his face moonlike with surprise. Fletcher strained after the retreating figures but was kept pinned. "Watch thy back," he shouted after him.

"Jack, art thou mad?" Ben's breath was hot in his ear.

"Let me free; I am calm." The hands hesitated, then released him. Faces round the table were staring.

" 'Tis not a fit jape for a gentleman." He stared them back. "Keep you such tales for *players*." The word struck home; half the wits here had served once as players. As had, indeed, that gentleman Will Shakespeare.

"Th'art sensitive." Ben spoke low, kindly. "A shelled oyster."

"Look to thine own pride should it be thus outraged," Fletcher replied, a bit sullenly. He raised his cup to demonstrate his good humor restored. Men around him smiled with some effort, and talk slowly resumed.

He had not behaved well; he should have slashed back with his wit. Yet the point rankled. That foul tale of Francis and him sharing rooms and keeping a wench between them would, repeated enough times, someday lodge in a play or verse, there to mock him unto posterity. He would not have it so.

"And when are you to marry?" asked Holland, rather cautiously.

"Come high July," he said. This was a surprise to many, and several offered congratulations.

"And shall *you* leave playwriting?" demanded cheeky Coryat.

"My Joan is no heiress," Fletcher answered. "I shall make plays till I am knighted or dead."

It was a good reply, especially since it was no secret that Ben fancied himself in line for a knighthood from James. Various sallies ensued from this, while Fletcher signaled for another round. It was a proper gesture after having come near to spoiling the mirth.

Conversation returned to the prior topic, absent writers and their fortunes. Marston's *The Insatiate Countesse* had been glimpsed in the bookstalls against St. Paul's, and someone suggested sending a copy to the retired playwright's congregation in Hampshire, that they might ponder their priest's past productions. Middleton's *A Chaste Mayd in Cheapside* was proving a success for the Lady Elizabeth's Men; and had Fletcher noted its low swipe at Blackfriar's? Fletcher, who had pricked up his ears at the mention of Middleton, confessed his ignorance.

"He tells how a gentleman was threatened there, as though 'twere a rougher place than the bear gardens," explained Jackson. " 'Tis a slander upon the King's Men, whose favor he mayhap no longer enjoys."

"I know not who the King's Men favor," said Fletcher carelessly. Why did all suppose he was soon for the King's Men?

"He could do better than offend his benefactors," someone remarked.

This sounded promising. "Was not his patronness the Countess of Pembroke?" asked Fletcher. "I mean, once of a time?"

"Nay, I know not," the other replied. Fletcher would have pursued it, but got a sharp poke in the ribs from Ben.

Some called for food, though not Fletcher, who felt queasy at the mixture of drinks in his stomach. Mermaid sack mixed ill with Jonson's ale, and he regretted having any. A plate of greasy chops was set on the table directly before him, and when a wit shouted for mustard a wave of nausea rose. "*Non, sanz moutard!*" cried another, to knowing laughter; and as Fletcher lurched to his feet he suddenly had it: the answer—or part of one—flashing above the swirling miasma of his guts like *ignis fatuus* over a marsh.

Outside, he bent over a butt and took great draughts of less fetid air. A hooper across the street watched amusedly, waiting for Fletcher to add to the splashes of vomitus under the Mermaid. After a moment Fletcher stood shakily and gave him an ironical salute.

It was Jonson himself, though Fletcher couldn't remember the play, who had given the mustard taunt. *Not without mustard,* the motto of a Falstaff-like clown whose coat of arms had sported a boar's head. Shakespeare, moving up in the world, had applied for and received a coat of arms from the College of Heraldry, with the motto *Non sanz droict,* Not without right.

Fletcher knew little of these quarrels, whose traces he sometimes glimpsed in the plays, as shepherds might stand gaping while the gods overhead hurled thunderbolts at each other. Thus the blazon and the family banner, scorned by tradesman Ben.

Fletcher breathed deeply and went back in, carrying his stomach as carefully as a tapster with a brimming cup. "I must go," he told the assembly. "I did not write this day and must amend."

"He's training for the married state," said one. "Broken to't already," another added. "Frank took away more'n his own baggage." Laughter.

Jonson turned to eye him speculatively. "Keep thou close," he said softly.

Fletcher nodded. He felt like a player who had found himself on stage with his lines unlearned and no knowledge of the scenes to come.

Some light still lingered outside, but the Cheapside shops had closed up, their space given over to another kind of commerce. No old women here, though some looked well traveled down that road. "Thou shalt not live to see forty," Fletcher told one who tried overmuch to engage him.

The sheets of his bed seemed seasoned with a fine grit, which scoured his skin as he tossed. Was his conscience not similarly chaffed?

The hedge-witch infested his dreams.

The company assembled in the business-room, where there was a place for each shareholder, plus one at table's end for the witness under examination. Fletcher had produced a finished *All Is True*, which was being passed about and studied. John Lowin had paged through selectively, concerned that his share of good lines had been suitably augmented; while Condell merely thumbed its girth to confirm that it had been fleshed out to the Globe's standard. Will, at the end, regarded Fletcher mildly, as though sympathetic to the thanklessness of adding brass fittings to his golden carriage.

"It *is* a loose-knit play," Burbage remarked.

Fletcher looked to Will, who seemed disinclined to answer. "I was commissioned to increase its span, not tighten its weave," he said testily. "Perhaps it should be recast 'round some single crisis, say the chopping-off of Anne Bullen?"

Nobody rose to this. "You have stretched most o'th'scenes, adding few yourself," said Heminges.

"Of course," Fletcher replied. "Will already used what events Harry's life affords. I can do little else should you insist on retaining the plan of ending the play with Elizabeth's birth."

It was a sound reply, yet none seemed satisfied. Fletcher seethed inwardly, seeing well the dimensions of his trap. The King's Men worried that he could not craft a sound play on his own: and given one of Shakespeare's to fill out, he did add little but mortar 'round the bricks. But had he altered the work's structure it would have been called overweening.

"The business with the courtiers is not bad," said Burbage judiciously, flipping back to study it. " 'A French song and a fiddle has no fellow' is good."

Fletcher thought so himself, though he had feared its jests regarding foreign courtiers' superior virility over the local crop might be found inappropriate in a Henry play.

"Does it not clash with the melancholy matter of Buckingham's fall?" asked Condell.

"Do the Porter's japes not clash with the melancholy matter of Duncan's murder?" Fletcher replied. At this Will laughed, and Condell, looking surprised, reddened. You fools, thought Fletcher, I know his plays better than any of you.

"Well said," Burbage rumbled. "And the matter with the old strumpet, that's good, too." More brick-mortar, said the expressions of some. If anyone mentions Francis, thought Fletcher, I shall stand and walk out.

"A history play wants action," said Tooley, plainly uneasy in matters of criticism. "Here are no swordfights, no armies—I know," he said quickly, "this Henry saw none; but the stage needs a tumult."

"This Henry is James's grandfather," said Fletcher evenly. "We cannot take the liberties that Bloody Richard stood still for."

"Nay, true, but the play wants a bang." Tooley looked at his fellows. "We—"

"And you shall have one!" cried Fletcher. He snatched at the pages. "Where is the masque scene? Here; where Henry enters, we shall have chambers discharged, as befits the entrance of a king. No matter he is disguised; the groundlings shall have their bang. The drum and trumpets shall remain off stage, but the chambers will be brought on. And the playgoers driven to napping by our want of tumult will be roused." Glaring, he stood, grabbed inkpot and quill from the sideboard, and began to write.

"Nay, hold, gentle Jack," said Condell. "Thou art not asked to make an Agincourt of Westminster."

"Not Henry and Wolsey at swords' points?" Fletcher's rage was still upon him. "Cranmer raving like Hieronimo, using his madness to lull his enemies?"

"None of that." The sharers seemed embarrassed. "The play's design is not thy province, and moreover stands approved. Thy additions only are at issue, and they suit well."

"Don't blame the tailor for the courtier's paunch," said Will unexpectedly. "Jack's ermine trims my play's frame well." Heads nodded in acquiescence; and that (abruptly) was that.

Glowering, Fletcher subsided. He realized that he might have done himself an injury before the sharers, but cared not. Let them think him tetchy if they cared to.

He would have left then, but the meeting broke up on that point. As the sharers stood, filling the room with sudden several discourses, Fletcher looked across the table to meet the gaze of Will, who gestured for him to wait. Slowly he resumed his seat and shuffled awkwardly through the playscript till the room had emptied.

"They worry about the next ordinary poet," Will explained, as though concerned for Fletcher's feelings. "The post would have been Frank's and thine both, and they feel now that their plans have been knocked from under 'em."

"They should have known Francis was not for this trade," said Fletcher. " 'Twas ever but his jape, to be set aside with the fading of youthful vigor."

"They admired his antic mien," said Will as he pulled the script toward him. " 'Twas the yeast that leavened your combined eruditions."

"Which else would have sunk to th'cellerage?" Fletcher forbore to question the sharers' knowledge of Francis's and his respective contributions, though their scripts were oft so crabbed with each others' corrections that a fair copy was required ere anyone saw them. To say this were to sound as though he were claiming a portion at Francis's expense; and in any event his attention was drawn now to Will, who was paging thoughtfully through Fletcher's scenes.

"This is good, 'Men's evil manners live in brass; their virtues We write in water.' That trips well."

Involuntarily Fletcher began to smile; then he froze as though he had bit upon a sweetmeat rotten at its center. Will was baiting him: the line, once uttered, rang baldly of his own verse. Will wasn't baiting him: he didn't remember his old plays as Fletcher did. Carplike, Fletcher gaped, unable to speak.

Will did not look up. "The Wolsey portions are good. Thou revilest the Church well." There, what did that mean? Wolsey's enemies abuse him in his downfall; should they not? Will's play launched few barbs at the Church, even for a tale that stopped short of Henry's great breach. What Fletcher supplied the scenes did need.

Will was reading aloud. " 'This is the state of Man': I like this line. Spring, greatness ripening, yes . . ." Fletcher felt his cheeks flush: Will, remembering his Seven Ages, was going to see Fletcher well grilled before flipping him over.

He read on, while Fletcher waited in silence, then sat back and removed his spectacles. "Taken in the whole, I think thou dost better in single lines than extended fancies. The image of swimming on bladders goes on too long; but the epigrams—'I feel my heart new opened,' and" (he looked down a moment) " 'I feel within me A peace above all earthly dignities'—ring true."

"Perhaps I should have been a poet," said Fletcher evenly.

Shakespeare smiled. "Thou fret'st overmuch. This is good work," he said, tapping the manuscript. "Thou shall not be offended if I work it further o'er before handing to the scribe?"

Fletcher inclined his head.

Will gathered the papers and stood. "Thou hast a new play in progress?"

"Aye, a tragedy of Bonduca, Queen of Britons. For the Globe."

"We'll need a fall play for Blackfriars. Thou art willing to join in another venture?"

This was equivocal news: Fletcher had evidently not completed probation, but neither had he failed it. Of course, Will might prefer simply to share the playwright's burden which seemed to weigh on his stooping shoulders. "Of course," said Fletcher politely. "I have already thought what this play would be."

"And what is that?" asked Will with a sidelong glance.

"Why, the Second Part of Harry the Eighth."

Will coughed suddenly, as though surprise had taken him in mid-breath. Fletcher continued innocently: " 'Twould continue Harry's tale: Anne's sad fate, the fall of Cranmer and Cromwell, a flurry of wives, and the great crack with Rome. Unhappy Harry, disintegrating with age, sees ruin and dissension, and is remembered as the architect of a schism he never sought. I see Dick as the aging Harry, dost not agree?"

Will smiled weakly. "He is James's near kinsman, Jack. Let us leave such later strifes to the chroniclers, and not touch on broils that trouble us yet."

Fletcher let this pass. "And what then shall this play be?"

"I am thinking of Chaucer's *Knight's Tale.*"

Disappointment showed on Fletcher's face ere he could feign. He said, "Back to Athens, then? Fate-crossed lovers, and betrayal, and a contest among lovers?"

"It is a fine tale," said Will mildly. "With a gladsome ending of high romance."

"An ending settled by the intervention of Saturn, as I recall. You skirt Christian quarrels only to give us paganism."

"We shall play down the business of the gods," said Will, ever calm. "Are you in?"

"Oh, aye, count me in't. I will look into the Tale this night." So to let the Generoso know that he, at least, need not rely on the sharers' library for his classics.

They stepped into a colonnade that opened onto the yard, where the sounds of rehearsal echoed oddly against the empty galleries. As though idly, Fletcher said: "Shall you translate further?"

"Eh?"

"Chaucer wrote of ancient Athens, but it was *translated*: tho' he spoke of the gods, his twins enacted the proper knightly virtues of Chaucer's day. Shall you also translate? I recall," he added mischievously, "that your Hector mentioned Aristotle."

A flush touched Will's high pale forehead. "All plays must live in their time," he muttered. "What translations do you propose?"

"As you say, strike off the gods. The twins might petition other several powers—perhaps witches."

"*Witches?*"

"Oh, aye. Surely some live yet; our good King cannot have slaughtered them all. I would bet there is one living in Bankside."

Will looked at him sharply. "I will tell my partners never to doubt your antic mien," he said. And at the next turn, he nodded and was gone.

In fact, Fletcher had no copy of Chaucer in his lodgings, a discovery he acknowledged (had Francis taken it?) with some rue; he was no better in this than Will. It was six days before he rode to Ashby, where the Carl's great library held folios enough that Fletcher had his choice of the most pleasing edition. Reading in the after-hours of his patron's entertainments, Fletcher found the tale woefully underpopulated: a counterplot must be devised, for preference adding a second lady to the story. If Palamon wastes in prison, there the lady must be; and Fletcher jotted notes for the creation of a Jailer's Daughter.

"Do you, my Lady, know aught of the Countess of Pembroke?" he asked at dinner next evening.

The Countess of Huntingdon looked amused. "She hath a vaster coop of poets than I. Dost thou look to nest at Wilton House?"

"Indeed no, my Lady. I wondered at a story I have heard, that a playwright once sought her Ladyship's intervention after getting in trouble with the late Queen's court."

The Countess laughed at the idea. "Did he enjoy Pembroke's patronage?"

"I assume so, my Lady. I know no way to ask."

"Nothing less would avail him 'gainst Her Majesty's wrath, and likely not that." She fixed him with her eye. "Who was this fellow?"

Fletcher had hoped not to be asked. "Master William Shakespeare, my Lady."

"The man o'the Sonnets. I am not surprised to hear he got in trouble."

"It was not that kind of trouble, my Lady." Here Fletcher decided he must speak no further. "Doubtless a tavern lie, grown wild in players' mouths."

"The late Earl kept a company of players, perhaps your Shakespeare among them; and his Lady filled their house with writers. She was said to be friendly to Catholics—her late brother, Sir Philip Sidney, was godson to the Spanish king, knew'st thou that?"

Fletcher was happy to see the talk shifted to the court gossip of an older generation. That night, however, reading "The Knight's Tale" in his room, he remembered the Sonnets. Another tale of two men and a woman, he thought. How many of thy plays have touched on this, Will?

Back in London, Fletcher continued desultorily with Bonduca. Tacitus had too little to say, and Fletcher need must plump out whole scenes from hints. Turning of an evening back to Chaucer, he read carefully, thinking sometimes of play-carpentry but oft merely savoring the style. Coming to Arcite's death, he found the scene oddly gripping; and when Fletcher read how "the coold of deeth" crept from Arcite's feet toward his heart, he found himself blinking tears. What nonsense was this?

This world nys but a thurghfare ful of wo,
And we been pilgrymes, passynge to and fro.

Such lines would not stand in the play, which must be good blank verse in its scenes; but Fletcher yet lingered over their simple loveliness. The couplet's wearied melancholy recalled some other lines to mind, and after a minute Fletcher identified them. "Fear no more the heat o' the sun, Nor the furious winter's rages." Will again; no wonder he liked this Tale.

Fletcher stood, his roiled emotions now souring. Will's *Cymbeline* was finer drama than *Bonduca* could ever be, for all that it was cooked up from Italian romances while Fletcher had gone to the proper sources. He looked moodily out the window (the sun yet shone), and thought of going for a drink. Turning to his desk, he moved to shut the folio when his eye fell on the line describing the wounded Arcite's extremity: how neither bloodletting

Ne drynke of herbes may ben his helpynge.

At once the face of Alizon rose before him. Fletcher's diffuse complaints gathered at once into a boil, which pressed upon his thoughts intolerably. Seizing his hat, he quitted the room at once, as though to be free of Chaucer, *Bonduca*, and Will Shakespeare at a stroke.

The Eastcheap inn where he had met the witch was rowdy, and Fletcher had to shout her description to the tapster whose attention he attracted with a coin. "Balding and toothless, but with a saucy eye, as though too old to fear offending."

The tapster blinked. "The herbal woman?"

"Aye, that's her."

"She's here betimes. Drinks when she has the brass." He turned and bawled to his goodwife, who shouted something back from the kitchen. "Try Foxfire Field in Southwark, past the pike-ponds," he said. "Know you the district?"

"I do." It was back across the Thames, as Fletcher had expected.

"She'll be out late, gathering simples," said the tapster, ingratiating. "Especially this one night."

"What night is this?" asked Fletcher, passing over the coin.

The man showed surprise. "Why, 'tis midsummer's eve. The longest day o'th'year, and best for picking evening shades."

And a propitious night, thought Fletcher as he headed for the river, for an herbalist who is also a witch. He took a wherry across the Thames, which deposited him near the Swan. Striking out past the few houses lying inland of the river, Fletcher found himself quickly among swampy fields, divided not by hedges but rather ditches bridged by swaying planks. A lone woodcutter stared to see the gentleman striding in the slanting light.

Wildflowers dotted the low ground, in greater profusion than city boy Fletcher could identify. There were few trees and no hills, but he worried about finding her in what daylight remained. Calling would only make her flee, especially if she were engaged in dubious practices. Fletcher looked for high ground from which to espy, but there was none.

He found her at last near a streamlet, plucking milkwort from the boggy soil. She started up at her name and cowered as he loomed over her, unremembering.

"Come, Alizon, we drank sack together a fortnight past." Fletcher helped her to her feet with a firm hand round her thin arm. "Hast thou forgot the tale you told me? Hiding my fellow playwright during the troubles?"

"What do you want with me?" she asked in a fretful tone. "I'm but a poor herbal woman."

"And a witch besides," he said, causing her to recoil fearfully. "Nay, I have only questions for thee, and a shilling for thy troubles. And drink, at the nearest tavern. The sun is setting; look thou to get indoors." He picked up her basket. "Lead me, ere thy wet feet grow chill."

She took him to a Southwark inn he had never seen, and sat shivering until a cup of hot sack was set before her. Fletcher reflected that she likely spent her brass on small beer, and had on their first meeting boldly demanded stronger drink than she was accustomed to. 'Twould loosen her tongue the faster, he thought grimly.

"Remember the tale thou told me? It stretched credulity, yet I have tried it, and found that all was true."

Her eyes, bright raisins, were at once upon his. "Master Shakespeare admitted to't?" she asked disbelievingly.

"Nay, he did not. But I found thy papers 'mongst his writings." Instantly, he realized his mistake.

"My lists? My recipes? Give me them!"

"I have them not; they lie where I found them." Of course she would want them back. Fletcher cursed himself. "I have other questions for thee, and good coin to pay for 'em."

"I want my papers." A fierce longing entered her eyes. "Lost to me these years, while the thief prospered. Can you know, writer that you are, what it is to lose one's pages?"

"They were but spells, not poesie," replied Fletcher. "Thou did'st show me thy skills in conning lines."

"What I had writ down I committed not to memory; why should I have felt the need?" she wailed. "Had I known the pages would be ta'en I'd have conned 'em, but as 'twas, they were lost to me whole." A pleading tone entered her voice.

"That which was lost may be found." A good Romantic credo. "Let us speak of my matters, and thy papers will be heeded anon."

She acceded, grumbling. Her eyes, now suspicious, never left Fletcher's face, as though she feared he would bolt from the table. Watching him even as she raised her cup, they took on a demonic red cast, and Fletcher realized with a start that she had been drinking heavily since last he saw her. Had he given her coin enough to drink herself ill?

"Thou told me of thy journey to Wiltshire. Thou slept at his Lordship's house."

"Aye, in a bed with a quilt. The room was the meanest there, yet had it a mattress and a brass pot beneath. And a *hook on the wall!*" She grinned at him meaningfully.

"Eh, woman? What say'st thou?"

"Too small for hanging clothes, or e'en a candle. But not old, neither: the plaster was not so crack'd as that."

"What art thou babbling of? A hook for what?"

"Why, sir, for *this*—" And solemnly she inscribed a cross in the air, like a priest blessing his congregation.

Fletcher started, then looked quickly behind him. "Thou hedge-witch, watch thyself. Th'art not too old to hang."

"Aye, and the days of tolerance under the old queen are gone. Not that she tolerated greatly, but e'en in the days of Scottish Mary she would let quiet worshipers be."

Fletcher's head was spinning. "Art thou mad? Th'art a witch, not a Catholic."

She tittered. "Can ye be one without the other? God will not hear the English-spoke prayers of Henry's church, nor the Devil neither. All witches be Catholic, get they results."

Fletcher shook his head and took a drink. "I wonder if Will knew this," he muttered.

The witch stared. "Are ye blind? Your friend, thief as he was, weren't that."

Fletcher was nettled. "Watch thy tongue, woman. My friend and colleague is a respectable landlord in Southwark. Know'st thou the Gatehouse at Puddle Dock Hill? Master Shakespeare owns that."

She stared again, as though her bloody eyes would start from her head, then burst into wheezing laughter. "He didn't own it when I saw him, I warrant ye that."

"Why say'st thou that?"

"Because it's rotten with priest-holes, that's why! He could have hid there till Elizabeth died. Have ye seen the house?"

"Hast thou?"

"Aye!" Merriment took her, though her red eyes never left him. "Hidey-holes and passageways, and don't think I haven't been in 'em. Care to ask me why?"

"Nay." Fletcher had had enough of her senile maunderings. "Attend me now. Thou has scribbled stolen plays these many years; hast thou never idly told thy tale?"

"Eh?" Drunk or infirm, she could no longer follow swift changes in the conversation's theme.

"Players will attend gossip from even such as thou. Never spoke thou aught of thy loss?"

She actually drew back at his question, like a horse shying at a torch. "Know you what you say? I should be hanged as a witch if believed, and scourged as a liar if not. Think me a gentleman like you, that can call out for redress?" She shoved her cup toward him. "Another!"

Fletcher signaled the tapster without shifting his gaze. "Thou told none, yet spoke to me?" He didn't know what he was driving at; her explanations satisfied. Something of the tale gnawed at him, and Fletcher worried it, as a fox would its trapped leg, only to feel greater distress.

The witch stared at him, eyes blazing, until her cup had been filled, then drank off half of it in one wattle-rippling series of swallows. "You don't doubt me," she said at last. "You doubt all else. I see't in your eyes."

It was true. Fletcher knew the story as fact, had known it, in truth, all along. Jonson knew something of the matter; had recognized its reflection in things he would not tell. Like a stain upon the air, the matter spread to darken all who heard it.

"Heard you enough? Want the story again? There's no more detail to't. You have your tale, and I—" the cup came down on the table—"want my papers. Give me them."

"That I cannot do." And this, as well, was true. Fletcher imagined the act, and knew it as one he could not perform. "Leave thy witcheries, which can only threaten thy remaining days and immortal soul. Those sheets can bring but sorrow."

"*No!*" The witch rose from her seat, eyes wild. A monstrous expression appeared on her face, like a carved mask being pushed through a curtain. Teeth bared, the rivulet of a vein rising on her temple, she glared at Fletcher like a basilisk.

"Think'st me powerless in mine age and infirmity? Think'st me a hag? I *curse* thee and thy fortunes, curse thy enterprises and thy landlord confederate! May your several ventures founder, your hopes be blighted—"

Fletcher had risen in alarm. People were staring from neighboring tables, and voices suddenly dropped.

"My curth upon thy head, falth benefactor, dethiever and cothen—coth—"

Her face seemed to have split in two: one eye rolled terribly while the second drooped; and her mouth, like an allegory of Tragedy and Comedy, snarled at one side yet turned downward at the other. Spittle flew unevenly, and she abruptly pitched sideways, as though a leg had given beneath her. Cups and pitcher slid from the tilting table as she fell.

Drinkers crowded round them. Fletcher, his chair against the wall, had to kick the table forward to free himself. Pushing through the gapers, he found the witch lying on her back, a bubble at her mouth as one eye swept over the crowd like a watchman's beam.

"Elf-shot," said someone. Heads nodded; a ripple of relief ran through the room. The anxiety that gathered when a nearby person suddenly collapses at once dispersed.

"Get her upstairs," said Fletcher unsteadily. The innkeeper hesitated, looked again at Fletcher's gentle attire, then nodded to two others. Hoisting the witch's limp form, they shuffled toward the stairs.

Men began to resume their seats. "She cursed you, like a witch," said one wonderingly. A few raised their heads, and Fletcher whirled on the speaker. "Your pardon, sir," said the man, taking a step back.

The innkeeper looked uncertainly between the two. "She was subject to rages in her late senescence," said Fletcher shortly. The innkeeper nodded, relieved. Fletcher produced a coin and gave it him, then turned and left the inn without a sideways glance.

Shivering in the warm air, he felt his senses yaw, as though the turbid humours of his body were shifting positions. The tang of horse turds and low tide rode on the shore breeze, rotting and alive. Disoriented, Fletcher turned slowly until he spied the ramparts of the Globe thrust above the low roofing. Steering through the unfamiliar streets, he navigated home with the playhouse as polestar.

Gatehouse. Named for that part which was erected over a great gate, the structure stood on a street leading down to Puddle Wharf, right against the King's Majesty's Wardrobe, where (like the Globe's costume-room) the clothes of ancient kings were stored. A fashionable district, despite the smell from the wharf, and Fletcher could see how the shops and tenements might bring a good rent.

He could also see the outlines of the old priory beneath the alterations, and could understand the building's notoriety as a refuge for papists. Did Will, lodging there on his infrequent London stays, dream of old English kings, who slew each other incontinently but doubted not the authority of Rome?

Two acts of *The Two Noble Kinsmen* lay under Fletcher's arm, the first wholly Will's, the next largely his. Reading his partner's confident script, Fletcher found lines fitting effortlessly into memory: "Heavens lende A thousand diffring wayes to one sure ende." And further:

> *The Worlds a Citie fulle of straying streetes,*
> *And Deaths the Market place where each one meets.*

Fletcher strayed the streets no more after he had returned to the inn to learn that Alizon had died—the innkeeper's servant, ignorant of the cause of her collapse, said only that she had been "taken under a planet"—early the following morn. Asked her name, Fletcher had found his mind stuttering without reply; and had had to return to his lodgings to find the scrap bearing her signature. That he had sent back to the inn, with shillings for the woman's burial at St. Savior's. Let the ecclesiastical authorities, who might balk at burying a Catholic, not know they were burying a witch.

Will admitted him with all courtesy, and conducted him up a winding stair (Fletcher could not help looking for hidey-holes) to a front room washed with writing-light. A hospitable bottle stood beside a pitcher on the table. Beside the bed lay (indeed) the company's Chaucer.

"This is well begun," said Will, sitting down and picking up the outline Fletcher had provided of Acts III and IV. "I like the jailer's daughter; also the rustics. 'Twill fit well with the resolution." He passed over three sheets, which proved to be a detailed outline of the remaining scenes.

Fletcher read them carefully—they made admirable shift with the tale's problems, such as the need to dramatize a tournament—but his mind was not upon the matter. The sight of his partner's hand recalled the pages in the Globe script-room, while the notation that the noble kinsmen petition Mars and Venus made him think wincing of "planet."

Shakespeare was pouring wine, watering his own generously. "I am back for Stratford tomorrow," he said. "Matter of a lawsuit. Can you send me your portions by August?"

"Certainly," Fletcher murmured. Was Will being sardonic? No sign of it in his crinkled eyes. Fletcher lifted his own cup and drank: the Generoso would not offer a guest bad wine.

"Your *Bonduca* shall go upon the stage ere I am returned," said Will. "Good luck to't." He lifted his glass.

"Thank you." Fletcher took Will's meaning: his play would not be submitted to Will for approval. Which meant he could expect little trouble from the other sharers. "I do doubt my hand in tragedies. The comedies are sounder built."

"Your romances and tragicomedies are in pitch with the times," said Will. "Antique subjects, and the death of princes, do not please the present Court, which looks for simpler matters."

Fletcher bristled. "Your plays have not suffered at Court of late. A *Henry* play and divers romances won rare acclaim."

Will sighed as though the recollection pained him. "*Lear* did not please, and *Macbeth* won applause only in its geneological obeisances. We live in degenerate times, where the ladies at Court drink and spew in their revels, and the men prey upon them and each other. What tragedies they like are none of mine, sheer riotous excess. My last plays have been romances, following a taste you awoke i'th'Court. But I tire of plays where all's restored; too weary for such fond lies."

"While my stomach for lies seems stronger," said Fletcher in a dead tone. A stone hand seemed to have grasped his heart, which tightened even as it grew chill. Will had acknowledged Fletcher's contribution to his late manner only to scorn it. Take thou the laurel of these times, which I find valueless.

Will's eyes widened slightly at Fletcher's tone. "Nay, you misunderstand me," he began.

"I understand thee well," said Fletcher. "This foul age has fattened thy purse, and thou mayst retire to Stratford a country gentleman on theater gold. For thy witch-hunting King thou smitest hags and calibans, playing the tune of him thou complainst of after. *Hath a witch ever injur'd thee*?" The question surprised Fletcher as much as Will, who frankly stared.

Too late to halt th'enchafed flood. "I attended the funeral of a woman yesterweek—" untrue, though he had paid for it—"who once helped thee, to her cost. Remember'st thou the name of Alizon Wyckliffe?"

Will stared at him in amazed bafflement, and then recognition dawned ruinously upon his face. His expression seemed to crumple, as though light and air had invaded the crypt where an ancient flower, perfectly preserved after years of inviolate stillness, aged suddenly at a touch.

Fletcher watched him rally, a staggered fighter who would not be felled with one blow. A look came into his eye, crafty and hostile (but there was fear there, too), and Shakespeare said: "You speak of a Southwark herbal-woman, known once to players for her willingness to indite scenes dubiously acquired. I have not seen her this decade and am surprised she had not died long since."

Fletcher said, "Mayhap she knew she was dying" (another lie) "for she told all, without fear o'the consequences."

He hadn't expected this blow to finish the bout, but Will seemed visibly to rock, and something like panic entered his eyes. "And what hath so disturbed thee that she said?" he said at last.

From here there was no turning back. Fletcher answered steadily: "That she sheltered thee, when the Privy Council was seeking thy head; and that thou requited her by stealing divers papers from her room."

As he spoke it, the charge sounded ludicrous, easy to deny. Will opened his mouth, and Fletcher added: "And I found those papers, in her hand, 'mongst the drafts and scraps in the library."

"And that is all?" Will seemed bewildered. "I did seek shelter in the rebellion's aftermath, when bailiffs went seizing men at a rumor; and stayed not with friends who might be suspected. Is that a crime? That beldam was paid well for her trouble and had no complaints I know."

"She was a witch and she kept scraps of sundry spells. She said you took 'em, and I found such scraps in the books you used for *Macbeth*."

"And what better use for them? I had to flee her hovel before her return and took such scraps as would get her hanged. Think you she didn't stand to have her room searched? I took away a pile of blasphemous writings, and saved her life. Know you not what befell Tom Kyd?"

The two men glared at each other. Fletcher felt off-balance—something was wrong about this—but Will looked worse: pale and trembling, as though found out in something he had feared for many years.

"She taxed me for the return of her papers," said Fletcher softly. " 'Twas piteous to see."

Shakespeare winced. A great weariness seemed to settle over his shoulders, as though held till now at bay. "She stole *The Contention*," he said simply. "Or rather abetted in't. I noted the hand on the vile script when I complained to the printer; and recognized it later in her room."

Fletcher merely stared at him.

"She took my property, debased my coin. 'Twas my first play published, and that badly. And so took I *her* writing and put it to my use. Would you have done aught else?"

"Such shifts are not for gentlemen," said Fletcher softly. "But you were not one then, were you?"

And Will, not expecting a thrust from this angle, flinched for a last time.

The sounds of the crowd—anxious to see a play that had been performed successfully at Court during the spring nuptials, and boasted (so rumor went) a dazzling display of pageantry—rose to the upper tier like surf bursting upon rocks. Backstage the players were hastening into costumes, the largest cast the Globe had ever mustered: the compositer had counted more than fifty parts, and the changing room was crammed like sausage in its casing.

John Fletcher had retired to an upper gallery, and as the yard below began to fill he retreated further to the back rooms. The pleasures of hearing his modest lines added to Shakespeare's swell held no attraction for him; and as the Prologue began to speak (the sharers had wanted Will for the role, but he was back in

Stratford) Fletcher went to the script-room, the only space where costumed players did not stand waiting their entrances.

Lined on every wall by close-packed paper, the room was quite peaceful. Fletcher sat at the table, awash in a misery he could not sound. *Bonduca* was being copied for rehearsal, and the *Kinsmen* would open Blackfriars in the fall. Beyond lay a proper comedy, a celebration of his own coming nuptuals. Why then this clawing at his soul?

Writing in every stage of realization surrounded him: leather-bound folios, cheap quartos and octavos, finished scripts and the rougher ones, ideas for plays that had died i'the womb. Half a dozen years ago Fletcher, newly admitted to the ranks of writers for the company, had ransacked this room for unread plays by Shakespeare, Jonson, his just-older rivals. Keeping current of his colleagues' work since, he had never had to search its stacks again.

He did not rise as he idly scanned the shelves, so he spied the protruding sheaf only by chance and noted it in but one regard: its pages were shorter, less ragged, than those shoved in on either side. 'Twas a cut of paper Shakespeare lately favored, of a creamy color that went easier on his weakened eyes. Indeed, Fletcher remembered (without much caring), the *Macbeth* pages he had lately studied were on paler sheets, the same style that the company now used. The pages before him—it was on the shelf nearest, where a man writing at this table might carelessly stow them—were recent work.

Only mildly curious, Fletcher pulled them forth. The top page read, in Shakespeare's hand, *The Phoenix Chain'd*. The master's late style, such an elliptical title. Fletcher shuffled through the sheets: far too few for a full play. He turned over the top one and froze: on the next, a short list of dramatis personae (it was plainly an incomplete piece) was headed: *Mary, Queene of Scotland*. What lunacy was this?

Disbelievingly, Fletcher read the pages that followed, disordered scenes from throughout Mary's life. Advisers of the English Queen (prudently identified only as "Reg.") bring word of a papist plot against her in which Mary has been implicated; Scottish Mary is likened to a "ruffled grouse" that must be sent to the chopping block. The young Queen, charming a Court of factious and feuding Scottish nobles, all of them speaking—sweet Christ! What was Will thinking of?—in comic brogues that mimicked James's own. A sketch for a scene in which Mary, her forces defeated at Langside, must flee to England and an uncertain reception from her Protestant cousin.

A *boom!* resounded through the floorboards: the chambers discharged at the entrance of Henry to Wolsey's banquet. Unmindful, Fletcher read on, one part of his soul falling into the verse while another stood at its edge in horror. Mary, learning that her noble kinswoman intends her eternal confinement, laments:

> *For England? Though a countrie garden*
> *To stonie Scotland, yet but Toades and Serpents*
> *Infest its leafie shade.*
> *Sweete France, reliquairie of the Faithe,*
> *Receedes from me, a chopped branch*
> *Swept in th'ocean streame far from the trunk*
> *That sent it forth. Can this greate Queene,*

Treasons bairn, preserve her Faithful cousine,
Or shall she prove a Cocodrile, that bites
Direct its gueste lies downe?

This was madness. No protest that the poet but conveyed villainous sentiments would avail: 'twould be seen as near to treason.

Fletcher shook his head: the business made no sense. Why were these pages here? 'Twas hardly a Globe play (but no more a Blackfriars one, let alone one for Court: had Will lost his senses?), and why should he tuck it here?—Because, of course, none should seek it here. Rooms could be searched (as well Will knew; but why should he worry over such?); but the script-room, this Wardrobe of old plays, held nothing but the past.

And perhaps Fletcher over-refined upon the matter. Will Shakespeare, sitting of an afternoon in this room, might easily sketch some scenes of a projected play; then, thinking it not one he should want found on his person, push it amongst other papers. Why need one look further?

Faint cries rose through the floor, ragged shouts unseemly for a pageant play. Frowning, Fletcher went to the door and opened it. A blast of hot air broke over him, black with smoke and cinders. Shouts of *Fire!* from below barely carried over the roaring before him. He ran into the corridor, to see flames limn the inner wall in both directions. The smell of burnt thatching filled Fletcher's nostrils, too hot almost to discern. The roof, O God, he thought, the roof's ablaze.

Half a dozen steps toward the stairs were all he could manage, then he was driven back as timbers fell inward. Fletcher retreated to the library and swung the door shut. Smoke was curling up between the floorboards; the room was growing dark with it. Throwing open the casement, he gaped outside. Playgoers were streaming through the doorways, trampling each other in their haste. The theater was burning from the top down, and Fletcher would roast while the last groundlings fled in safety.

"Jump!" cried several boys, spying him. Fletcher looked to the ground, twenty feet to a shallow Bankside ditch. He turned back to the door—it was flickering round its frame, as though it opened onto Hell—and saw the books.

Tacitus, Boccaccio, Holinshed, Plutarch, Seneca. Playscripts unpublished, pieces known nowhere outside this room. They could not, like the Library of Alexandria, now burn.

Fletcher pulled four gilt-edged volumes from the shelves, carried them to the window and leaned out. A small crowd had gathered, but when he tossed the first volume, they shied as though 'twere a cannon ball. The thick folio struck the ground and split in two, its spine dividing like a cloven capon. "Catch!" Fletcher cried, eyes streaming. He lofted a second volume, but none made to catch it. It struck the ground at an angle, tearing loose its heavy cover.

Fletcher turned back to the room, which was thick with smoke. His eyes so burned he scarce could hold them open. He rushed at the shelf of scripts and pulled loose a great handful. Staggering to the window—a dim rectangle of light—he flung them hysterically outward. Loose sheets flew apart like startled fowl, but the playscripts, bound with string, fell intact to the ground. Boys from the company, seeing this, rushed to pick them up.

Sobbing, he fell to his knees, then crawled—the air seemed better—back toward the door. The floorboards burned his palms and knees, and a roaring filled his ears. The bottom shelf, yes, was where Shakespeare's scripts lay. *Macbeth,* and *Timon,* never published. Drawing great coughing gasps, Fletcher pulled a mass of them into his lap.

There was a great *whump!* behind him, and the room was bright. A hot hand smote him, and Fletcher turned to see the far wall rippling in flames. Doubled over by his load, he stumbled to the window and shoved it out. No air—the black smoke pouring past him permitted not a single sweet draught. He fell to the floor, crawled a few steps, grabbed papers. As he rose before the window, his hair caught fire.

The papers flew before him, but Fletcher tumbled rather than leaped. He fell through roiling smoke—*Damned already?*—then was in light, and an instant later struck the ground. Mud and water rushed over him, but Fletcher, stunned, could only gasp. A group of boys ran over and began beating on him.

He was being rolled over, like a drunk being searched for coins. Blows pummeled his back, and Fletcher drew at last a great racking breath. Hands plucked at his clothing: he was being dragged. He got one foot beneath him and promptly collapsed.

The Globe was a crown of flames. Eyes swollen half shut, Fletcher sat in the street and dazedly watched the blaze. Timbers groaned and snapped beneath the world-filling roar. A prentice player ran past, muddy sheets clutched to his chest.

"Saved?" he croaked. "All saved?"

A hand patted his shoulder. "The company got out. All are saved."

That much Fletcher could see; he had meant the plays. A lone sheet floated in the ditch; no others could he see. Were his own plays rescued? He could not remember.

Pain began to seep through numbing shock, a foretaste of woes to come. One ragged boy pointed out Fletcher to another: the man who leaped from the topmost floor and (as in good tragicomedy) lived. The sharers would be pleased: 'twould not do for the company to lose three playwrights in a season. The slightest perhaps was saved; but he had done journeyman's work, and borne the rest to safety. Sign enough, he thought as mist clouded his vision, that (as his betters had predicted) John Fletcher—not only a playwright in himself, but the cause that plays remain by other men—was confirmed at last in his vocation, an ordinary poet.

A WHEEL IN THE DESERT, THE MOON ON SOME SWINGS

Jonathan Carroll

Jonathan Carroll is one of the most imaginative, entertaining, and fascinating writers to grace the modern fantasy field. He consistently blurs the lines drawn between mainstream and magical fiction in such unforgettable books as *Sleeping in Flame*, *A Child Across the Sky*, and *Outside the Dog Museum*.

The following story is mysterious, haunting . . . and pure Jonathan Carroll. It comes from the March issue of *Omni* magazine.

—T.W.

He knew nothing about photography other than he liked a good picture as much as the next guy. Once in a while he'd see one so startling, original, or provocative that it would stop him and make him gape or shake his head in wonder at the moment or piece of the world caught there. But beyond that he had given it little thought. That's what was great about life: some people knew how to take pictures, others build chimneys or train poodles. Beizer believed in life. He was always grateful it had allowed him to walk in its parade. At times he was almost dangerously good-natured. Friends and acquaintances were suspicious. Where did he get off being so happy? What secret did he know he wasn't telling? There was a story going around that when Beizer discovered a letter his girlfriend was writing to a new secret lover, he offered to buy her a ticket to this man so she could go visit and find out what was going on there. He said he wanted her to be happy—with or without him.

But now things would change! God or whoever had decided to give Norman Beizer a taste of the whip via this blindness. Friends were all sure he would change for the worse; start ranting and shrinking into self-pity and end up like the rest of them—tight-lipped, expert shruggers, looking for the answer in tomorrow.

Instead he bought this camera. A real beauty too—a Cyclops 12. Since he didn't know anything about the art, he went into the store an admitted idiot. That's what he told the salesman. "Look, I don't know about this stuff, but I want the best camera you have for absolute idiots. Something I can point and shoot and know it's doing all the work." The salesman liked his attitude, so instead of offering a Hiram Quagola or a Vaslov Cyncrometer, the kinds of cameras used by strict Germans to do black-and-white studies of celebrities' noses, he put the Cyclops on the counter and said, "This one. It'll take you an hour to get the hang of it and then you're on your way." Beizer did something strange. He picked the camera up and, holding it against his chest, said, "Are you telling me the truth?"

When was the last time a stranger asked you that question? The salesman was flabbergasted. His job was lies and false zeal, fakes and passes behind his back. He had told the truth, but this customer wanted him to say it out loud, too.

"It's the best for what you want. Try it a couple of days and if you don't like it, bring it back and we'll find you something else."

The problem with the Cyclops was it was exactly what Beizer had asked for. It took an hour to read and understand the instructions. By the next morning, he had shot his first roll of film and had it developed. The pictures were as precisely focused and uninteresting as fastfood hamburgers. Everything was there; he'd gotten what he paid for, but a moment after experiencing the picture he forgot it. The first of many revelations came to him. How many thousands and millions of times had certain things been photographed since the advent of the camera? How many times had people aimed at their pets, the Eiffel Tower, the family at the table?

Walking around the house one day trying to think of interesting and artistic things to photograph, he got down on his knees in the bathroom and took a picture of his toothbrush up through the glass shelf it rested on. That was pretty clever, but when he saw it developed, he frowned and knew at least a few hundred thousand people had probably had the same idea in one way or the other. Out there in the large world were drawers full of photos of toothbrushes shot "artily." Worse, other people had had to take the time to fix their shutters and set the speeds because cameras had never been so sophisticated as they were now. Now they were point, shoot, baf, you've got your toothbrush. But back whenever, one had to think, adjust and figure out how they'd get that shot. There was process and careful thought involved.

While this played across his mind, he heard shouts through the open window and realized kids were having fun in the park across the street. Their calls were wild and screechy and he thought, if I were going deaf, how could I preserve those great sounds so that in my silence I could somehow remember them exactly and know them again? We're all aware that in the end the only thing left is our memories, but how do you preserve them when one part of you decides to die before the rest? He realized he had bought this camera so he could go around seeing the world he knew for the last time and in so doing, perhaps teach his memory to remember. But that wouldn't work if he had a mindless genius machine that did exactly what he told it to but gave him nothing of himself in return. It was like those exercise machines with electrodes you hook up to your body, then lie down and rest while electricity makes you thin and muscular.

He went back to the store. When the salesman saw him again he was almost afraid. Beizer decided to tell the man everything. About the blindness, about his need to find a camera that would not only do what he told it, but teach him how to see and remember as well.

As he walked to the counter, the thought came that whatever machine he left with this time, he would use a week to learn its principles, then allow himself to take only ten pictures before he put it down forever. The doctor said he had about three months before the disease marched across his vision dragging a black curtain behind it and then that would be the end. In the ninety days he had left, he would try to learn and consider and achieve all in one. Ten pictures. Ninety days to take ten pictures which, when his sight was gone, would have to provide his empty eyes with what he had lost.

The salesman heard him out and immediately suggested he go to a store specializing in books of great photography. "First look at books on Stieglitz and Strand. The guys in the Bauhaus School. They were the masters. That's the best way to start. If you wanted to learn how to paint, you'd go to a museum and look at da Vinci." "It won't help. I'll look and maybe see some great stuff, but that won't help me remember. I don't even want to remember what they . . ." Beizer held his hands up to the sides of his head as if showing the other how little space he had to fill there. "I don't want to learn how to paint or take pictures. I want to remember my sights, not theirs. And I don't have much time left."

The salesman shrugged. "Then I don't know what to tell you. There are two directions to take: I can give you a child's camera. The simplest thing in the world, which means you'll have to do all the work. When you want to take a picture, the lighting will have to be perfect, the focus, everything will have to be there because the camera won't do anything for you but click; just the opposite of the Cyclops which does everything. The other way is to buy a Hasselblad or a Leica, which are the tops. But it takes years and thousands of pictures to figure out how to use them. I don't know what to tell you. Can I think about it some more?" Beizer left the store empty-handed. But for the time being perhaps that was best; having the right camera meant he'd have to begin to start deciding. In this interim without one, he could go around looking at the world, trying to choose.

A few blocks from home, a man sat on the street with a hat turned over on his lap and a hand-written sign that said, "I am blind and heartbroken and have no work. Please be kind and help me." There were a few brown coins in the hat. "Are you really blind?"

The beggar raised his head slowly and smiled. He was used to abuse. Some people taunted him. Now and then they'd ask stupid questions but then give him money if they liked or pitied his response. Before he had a chance to answer, whoever stood above said, "Tell me what you miss most about not seeing and I'll give you ten dollars."

"Fried chicken. Can I have my ten dollars, please."

Beizer was stunned but went for his wallet. "I don't understand." He handed over the money.

The blind man brought the bill to his nose and sniffed it. It was money, he was sure of that. Maybe even ten bucks. Why not? The world was full of lunatics. Why not this one? "You know smoking? A cigarette is three things—smell, taste, and sight. You gotta see that gray going out your mouth and up in the air to really enjoy a cig. I stopped smoking about a month after I went blind. I know guys who can't see but keep doing it, but it's a waste of time, you ask me. Same thing's true with fried chicken. Taste it, smell, do all that, but seeing it's most important. The way that gold skin cracks when you pull it apart, the smoke coming up from the pink meat underneath if it's just fresh, then the shiny oil on your fingertips after you're finished. . . . Don't get me wrong, I still eat it, but it isn't the same. You gotta see to really eat it."

Beizer gave him another ten dollars, and went right home to write that line down: "You gotta see to really eat it." A week later, he found another in a book he was reading on photography: "The celebrated painter Gainsborough got as much pleasure from seeing violins as from hearing them."

Somewhere in the land where those two ideas lived was what he sought and Beizer knew it.

The girlfriend called, having returned from the romantic trip he had paid for. "It didn't work. Know what he did, among other things? Sent these incredible love poems I thought he'd written specially for me. Turns out he only copied them out of an anthology he kept from college.

"I'm sorry I haven't called. What have you been doing?"

"Going blind."

"Oh my God!"

They spoke a long while before she said gently, "Honey, you can't do photography when you're blind."

"Actually you can; I heard there's a whole bunch of blind people taking wonderful pictures. But that's not what I'm after. I don't want to do photographs—I want to be sure to remember fried chicken and what violins look like." After hanging up, he thought over what she'd said about this man trying to pass off other people's poetry for his own. Other people's deepest-felt emotions. It was a clever way to trick a heart but what did it say about the man? Beizer turned a few facts here and there and saw himself showing someone a famous picture he had not taken and saying, "This is one of my ten. This will comfort me when I can no longer see."

That night he woke up and padded slowly across the dark to the toilet. Relieving himself, he realized this was what it would be like when he was old. Getting up, probably nightly, to go to the bathroom because one's plumbing begins to weaken as we grow older. A familiar sound from when he went to visit his parents—the toilet next to their bedroom flushing in the wee hours of the morning. The wee hours. That made him smile. A good title for a poem. "Weeing in the Wee Hours." He should give it to the poem stealer. . . . Sleepily finishing his business, Beizer once again had the feeling of some invisible connection here. Finding it would help him overcome the problem of the pictures he wanted to take.

In bed again quickly slipping back into sleep, he thought poems are as personal as fingerprints. Steal one and you instantly give your own identity, as if you were actually giving up the lines on your fingers or the features on you face.

The features on his face! He started, sat up, very much awake. An old man peeing in the night. What would he, Norman Beizer, look like when he was seventy and holding his old cock in his hand? He'd never know. He couldn't look at someone else's pictures of that! Too soon he'd never know how the first deep lines on his face would change him, what white hair would do to his appearance. These are important details.

He had begun to grow used to the idea of how much time would be wasted in his future. The seconds lost spent on useless fumbling for a wall switch or the string to pull a curtain across. To move a curtain was a much larger concern for the blind. First find the strings, figure out which is the correct one, pull it. A matter of seconds for a person with sight, for the blind it would take three, four, five times unfairness of that, all the time he'd soon need to waste on what he did now with no trouble. But how much of Beizer would he lose when he could no longer see him in the mirror. Watch the progress of time and life across that most familiar geography? He sensed in time he would be able to accept the loss and forced limits that were coming, but until now he hadn't realized something so important—he would also lose large parts of himself.

The next morning he called up the offices of *Vogue* magazine and Paramount Pictures. After running the gamut of questioning secretaries, he was finally put through to the proper people who, in both cases, were surprisingly kind and helpful. He asked the woman at the fashion magazine who she thought was the greatest portrait photographer in the city. Without hesitation she said Jeremy Flynn and gave him the name of the photographer's agent. At Paramount, the vice president in charge of something said the greatest makeup person in the world was so-and-so. Beizer carefully noted the names and addresses. He had expected more trouble finding these things out but perhaps since he had figured out his problem, the solution slicked into place like the gears of a car engaging. He called the photographer and the makeup person and made appointments to see both of them. They charged an obscene amount of money, but the best were always worth it, particularly in this case.

When he met them, he explained his situation with almost exactly the same words: He was fast going blind. Before that happened, he wanted to see what he would look like for the rest of his life. He was hiring them to help him get as close to that as possible. The visagist should make him up to look as convincingly sixty, seventy, eighty as possible. Knowing his family history of bad hearts dying somewhere in their seventies, Beizer assumed his would, too. So his face at seventy would be close enough to his final days to satisfy.

The photographer was fascinated by the idea. He recommended pictures done with no tricks—no special lighting or backgrounds. Just Beizer in a dark suit and a white shirt. That way, his face would take up the entire world. The eye would be forced to look at the face and nothing else. Yes! That was exactly what he wanted.

At the end of their meeting, Flynn asked what good would the pictures be when Beizer could no longer see them. "Because I will have seen them. I'll be able to put them in front of someone and say, 'Is that what I'm like now? Tell me the difference between what's on paper and what you see.' "

"Points of reference."

"Exactly! Points of reference."

"Will you remember what's there? Even after years of not having seen?" "I don't know. I have to try."

The big day came and he had the astonishing experience of seeing himself age forty years in one afternoon. Like time-lapse photography, he saw brand-new wrinkles groove his face, making it into something foreign and funnily familiar at the same time. He saw his hair disappear, his eyes turn down, skin like bread dough hang from his chin and neck. If an experience can be funny and terrifying at the same time, this was it. Each time he was eager to see what the next decades would do to him, but when the makeup man said, "Okay have a look," Beizer was hesitant. He kept saying, "You think that's what I'll really look like?" But down deep he knew it was.

So, this was it. Him for the next forty years. When he was a boy, he was a terrible sneak when it came to Christmas presents. Every year he was driven to find where all of his gifts were hidden, so that weeks before the big day, he knew exactly what he was getting. This was the same thing. Now he knew what he would be "getting" as the years passed.

And one would think that seeing himself across the rest of this life like that would have had some kind of large effect on Beizer, but the only real emotion he felt at the end of the session was amusement. When they were finished, he told the other two this and both said the same thing—wait till you see the pictures. In real life a person wearing makeup looks . . . like a person wearing makeup. Especially if it is thick and involved. But wait till Flynn's photographs were ready. Then he'd see a hell of a difference. Any great photographer knows how to cheat light and time. Flynn loved the idea of showing this man the rest of his life in pictures. He planned to use these as the nucleus of his next exhibition and thus would spend even more time than usual making them as perfect as he could.

The call came very late at night. Beizer had been watching television and eating a plum. He didn't know what he enjoyed more—looking at the TV or the fat purple plum with the guts of a sunrise. "Norman? This is Jeremy Flynn. Am I disturbing you?"

"Not at all. Have you finished the pictures?"

Flynn's voice was slow in coming and when it came, it sounded like he was testing every word before he let it walk across his tongue. "Well yes, yes I just tonight started to work on them. But there's a . . . well, I don't know how to put it. This is a crazy question because I know it's really late, but do you think you could come over here now?"

"At eleven at night? I really want to see them, Jeremy, but can't we do it tomorrow?"

"Yes we can. Of course we can, but Norman, I think you'll want to see them now. I think you'll want to see them very much now."

"Why?"

Flynn's voice went up three notches to semihysterical. The other day in his studio he had been very calm and good natured. "Norman, can you please come? I'll pay for your taxi. Just, please."

Concerned, Beizer put his plum down and nodded at the phone. "Okay, Jeremy, I'll come."

Flynn was standing in the doorway of his house when Beizer arrived. He looked bad. He looked at the other like he'd arrived in the nick of time.

"Thank God you're here. Come in. Come in."

The moment they stepped into the house and he'd slammed the door behind them, Flynn started talking. "I was going to work on them the whole night, you see? I was going to give the whole night over to seeing what we'd done the other day. So I set everything up and did the first roll. Do you know anything about developing film?" He had Beizer by the arm and was leading him quickly through the house.

"No, but I'd like to learn. I don't think I told you, but this whole thing started when—"

"It doesn't matter. Listen to this. I did the developing. I always do my own. And then I—here we are, in here. Then I got down to the first prints. Do you want to sit down?"

Flynn was acting and speaking so strangely, so rushed and strangled, like he'd swallowed air and was trying to bring it back up again.

"No, Jeremy, I'm fine."

"Okay. So I put the first ones down, all ready to see you, you know, looking fifty or sixty? I had all these great ideas of how to work with the paper to get this special effect I've been thinking about—but when I saw what was on the film, the film I took of you, I panicked."

Beizer thought he was joking, but also knew instinctively that he wasn't because of the scared seriousness of Flynn's voice. "What do you mean you panicked? Did I look so ugly?"

"No, Norman, you didn't look like anything at all. You weren't in the pictures."

"What do you mean?"

"Look for yourself." Flynn opened a very large manila envelope and slowly slid out a glossy photograph. It was of a large wheel stuck in the sand of a desert landscape.

"That's nice. What is it?"

"It's you, Norman. Look at this one." Flynn slid out another photograph. A half-eerie, half-romantic picture of moonlight slanting across an empty set of swings on a playground. Beizer tried to speak but the photographer wouldn't let him. He took out another picture, then another and another. All of them different, some strange, some beautiful, some nothing special.

When he was finished, he put his hands on his hips and looked at his subject suspiciously. "That is the roll of film I took of you, Norman. There was no mistake because I purposely left the film in the camera after I shot the other day. Those pictures are what the camera took of you."

"I hate to tell you, Jeremy, but I'm not a wheel, or a swing."

"I know that. I didn't ask you over here to play a joke on you. That's what I have, Norman. This is no joke. Those are the pictures I took of you the other day."

"How am I supposed to respond to that?"

"I don't know." Flynn sat down. Then he stood up. "No, I do know. I have to say something else. I have to tell you, whether it helps or not. Maybe it'll even scare you. When I was young and learning to develop pictures, I took a whole roll one time of a girl I knew who I had a crush on. Kelly Collier. That same day I went into the darkroom to do them because I was so eager to have them. While I was in there, she and her mother were killed in a car accident. Naturally I didn't know that, but none of the pictures came out with her image. They came out like these."

"You mean swings and a wheel?"

"No, but things like that. Objects. Things that had nothing to do with her.

I've never told anyone the story, but Norman, this is exactly the same thing that happened with Kelly. Exactly. I took the pictures and she died. Then I took these pictures while you're going blind. There's got to be a connection."

"You think it's your fault?"

"No, I think . . . I think sometimes the camera is able to catch things as they're about to happen. Or as they're happening. Or . . ." Flynn licked his lips. "I don't know. It has something to do with change. Or something to do with—"

Beizer tried to speak when he heard the other's confusion. Because he realized it did have to do with change. As he looked longer at the picture in front of him and listened to the other speak, he began to understand. What had happened was Flynn's camera had photographed their souls—the dead girl's and Beizer's—as they were going through . . . as they lived different things. A soul was able to try on different existences as if they were clothes in a wardrobe. Of course a soul knows what's coming. Beizer believed the human soul knew everything; naturally with the girl, it knew her body was about to die. And in his own case, it knew what it would be like blind. So even while living in them, their souls were going out looking, traveling, window shopping for what they would become next. That was what the camera had somehow managed to capture. This plain metal and plastic, chemicals and glass had all worked together to catch two souls experimenting or playing, or whatever the word was for living a while in their future. Or was it their past? Maybe they'd like to rest in the moonlight and be swung on by day. Or maybe they were only reliving what it was like to be wheels, useless and thus marvelous out in a desert.

How did he know this? How could a plain, nice, dull man like Norman Beizer realize something so secret and profound? Because as Flynn spoke, Beizer began to recognize the photographs laid in front of him. Whatever part of him had been there in them suddenly and distinctly remembered being cold metal out in the moonlight, or the heat of sand all around him. He recognized and remembered the feelings, temperatures, sounds . . . that were in each of the pictures.

What was even better, he knew that that was what he would remember when he went blind. It would be enough, more than enough, for the rest of one life. He didn't need a camera, or ten unforgettable pictures, or portraits of himself as an old man. With this new understanding, he would have the ongoing knowledge and memories of where his soul had been. Until he died, blind or not, he would share the feelings and adventures of the part of him that was universal and curious. The part that was traveling, experiencing, knowing hotel lives of things. Things like wheels, like swings. One more bustling soul out there looking for what to do next.

WHO WILL LOVE THE RIVER GOD?

Emily Newland

Emily Newland lives in the country outside Ozark, Arkansas. Her first story was published in *The Twilight Zone Magazine* and since then her work has appeared in *Thin Ice*. Her story "With Don and Phil at the End of the World" was published in *The Missouri Review* and won second place in the annual Hemingway Story Competition. It was subsequently adapted for the stage and performed at the Southern New Plays Festival in New Orleans. Newland has had plays performed in each of the last four years at the International One-page Play Festival at La Mama in New York.

Newland deftly creates an original folktale that blends the Other with a realistic Southern rural background. The story was originally published in *Grue* magazine.

—E.D.

Miss Lila does not answer the phone when it rings, knowing, as soon as the first faint tremor comes running up the line, who it will be and what he will say. He will say: "We have to talk." He will say: "Can you meet me? In my office? Right away?"

And what could she possibly say then? It's simply intolerable; she feels almost faint, thinking about it. She just won't answer the phone, that's all there is to it. The phone rings again, and Miss Lila leans over the ancient mechanical press and continues setting the type for this week's edition of the Big Bend Observer: Ladies Auxiliary Plans Fish Fry. City Council Members Attend Annual Prayer Breakfast in Little Rock. Heat Wave Continues.

It is late in the day, the last slice of afternoon, and July is falling through the front window of the office, burning down the walls, blazing across her desk. If she would hire some help instead of trying to set all the type herself in bits and pieces of time between taking ads and waiting on the customers who come in to buy office supplies—if she had some help, the work would be finished by now and she would already be home in bed.

She does not answer the phone. She leans over the press and thinks about how it would be to be home in bed, and the drapes drawn and the room dark and the smell of the river in her hair. *Mmmm.* When she says it out loud it sounds like a prayer: "Mmmm."

She ought to hire some part-time help; she is not a young woman, and she is ill. She knows, deep down in the dark rooms of herself, that she is desperately ill, and that she ought to hire someone, but the thought of writing out payroll checks almost frightens her. So much money! And they would expect overtime pay, Christmas bonuses. Like throwing money away, and she can scarcely manage, what with the cost of living so high these days—the cost of incense, and old wine, and black lace, and sheets made of heavy imported silk the color of boiled shrimp—the cost of everything so high these days. *Where is the cut-off?* she wonders. What source can she quote, where can she point and say, *Here is the difference between unnecessary and necessary luxuries, here is the dividing line between want and need.*

Maybe the phone will not ring again. If the phone rings again she will not answer it; she will not speak to him. But what if it isn't him? What if it's a subscriber, or someone calling with a bit of news or an obituary? She can't just not answer the phone. Maybe it won't ring again. She closes her eyes and bows her head over the press, swallowing mouthfuls of thick heat and the smell of dust and newsprint: *Mmmm.*

She is almost asleep when the door slams open. Her head jerks up with an audible click of bone.

Truman Fowler wants her to take his picture. He is a little man, very old and very, very thin, much thinner and older than Miss Lila and he has been out on the river all day and has caught a waterbaby. Nothing like this has ever happened to him before; it really is the damnedest thing. He wants Miss Lila to take a picture of him holding the fishing pole with the baby dangling wetly on the end of the line.

After the first sick wrench of pity she tries not to look at the baby again. "Not now," she says. "You'll have to come back in the morning."

"No," says Truman. "It'll be dead then." The baby's eyes are already beginning to dry out. It has swallowed the hook; it will stiffen on the line and the smell will get so bad he he can't stand it, and then it will be too late to take his picture.

The baby squirms mutely on the line, its white arms held rigidly out from its body, its mouth stiffly open and flecked with blood. Miss Lila can see where the fishing line has lacerated the pink gums, vanishing into the throat. "I'm sorry." *Oh my God, oh my God.* "I'm sorry, I can't, not right now." She takes Truman's arm and steers him toward the door. "You'll have to come back in the morning."

"No," says Truman. "That won't do, that just won't do at all, not at all. Tomorrow will be too late." The words snap shut like scissors, snipping: *Tomorrow will be too late.*

"All right," she says. *All right, all right, all right.* "I tell you what, you just wait right outside here while I . . ." She opens the office door and steps out onto the sidewalk with Truman in tow.

The heavy brown smell of the river and the smell of sweet summer hay dying in the distant fields settle around her and into her. She can't remember what she intended to say to Truman. Doc is waiting there in his rumpled khakis, leaning against the sun-hot bricks of the building.

"Hello, Lila." He doesn't smile. She doesn't reply. What would she have said to him if she had answered the phone? *No, we don't have to talk. No, I won't meet you. Anywhere. Ever.*

Truman holds the fishing pole out, his arm shaking crazily with the weight of the baby. "Look here, Doc—don't that beat all! Never heard of anybody catching a waterbaby with a baited line and pole, ain't that right?" Oh sure, every now and then somebody manages to snag one out by the dam, or far downstream, where the wide flat coil of the Arkansas river slides into the Mississippi, a fisherman seining for minnows or crawfish sometimes finds a waterbaby tangled in the nets. But actually catching one with a line and a pole—well now!

"Gonna put it in the paper," Truman says, launching into a loud and detailed account of where he'd been fishing and what he'd been using for bait. Heat from the sidewalk slides up over Miss Lila's second-hand shoes, up under her slip and over her thighs. A moan rises in her throat, tasting of something slick and brown and she steps back into the office and shuts the door behind her. Her hand trembles, lifting the camera from its case in the corner behind her desk. What a bother, so late in the day, and the big camera—a relic, really, as out of date as the mechanical press—the camera is so heavy these days she can hardly manage it.

She has to sit down to load the film, making room for the camera amid the unpaid bills and unanswered letters that lie scattered in the dust on her desk. She thinks about the waterbaby with its little mouth full of blood, and Truman sitting down to supper that night, saying grace over platefuls of hushpuppies and waterbaby fillets: *For that which we are about to receive.*

She can still hear his voice, droning on and on, and with an effort she steps outside. Truman bares his dentures at the camera. The baby twitches on the line once; it does not blink when the flash goes off.

Everything is so quiet after that. Miss Lila can hear the baby dying with each step Truman takes as he crosses the street and vanishes around the corner of the Methodist church. She can hear Doc's heart beating, and her own heart; she can hear the whole great weight of the sun falling down the sky, and the river falling down the land, sliding down to the Mississippi and the sea below. In the office the big press is waiting; she still hasn't finished setting the type—the paper's going to be late again this week. She lowers the camera into its case and switches the lights off one by one, closing up for the night. She watches her hand turning the key in the lock; she knows what it's like to be stiffening on the line.

"Drive you home," says Doc, falling into step beside her.

"I can walk," she says. "I want to walk."

"No. Not today." He stops at the corner where he has parked his battered Jeep, and opens the door for her without speaking. Rattling down Main Street in the last green-gold light of the day, she can smell the sun-seared lawns of the town, and charcoal being set aflame in barbecue pits, and meat, somewhere, burning.

"Listen," says Doc. She knows, just as soon as the first faint tremor comes running up his voice, what he will say: "We have to talk." Main Street makes a sharp right turn, lifting itself toward the river bridge; the driveway to Miss Lila's house is straight ahead, a mile-long tunnel through the cottonwoods and cane along the river's edge. The Jeep drops with a bone-aching clatter onto the gravel and weeds, raising the brown dust, braking sharply in front of the house.

Doc doesn't look at her. He reaches out without looking at her, and takes her hand. "Your test results came back from the lab today."

She stares out through the open window of the Jeep. The river is low in its bed this time of year, brown and preoccupied, sliding hugely past her garden where, after the spring floods four years ago, she had found a waterbaby of her own, nearly as long as she is tall and almost too heavy for her to carry. He is full-grown now, her own private centerfold, weaned from the tub to her bed long ago. Who will take care of him after she is gone? Who will love him in the hot night?

She looks down at Doc's hand gripping her own. In the examining room the week before, she had thought he was going to cry, drawing the cold steel speculum out of her; something—it looked like river mud but wasn't quite—had dripped out onto the floor. She pulls her hand away.

He wants to send her down to Dallas for treatment—maybe it's not too late, he doesn't know. But she has to stop; she can't do this anymore. Is there—has there ever been—a dividing line between want and need? "You don't know what it's like," she says. "You don't know what it's like with him."

"My God, Lila, it's an *animal.*" Doc's voice breaks with something that sounds to her like anger. He reaches for her hand again, but she pulls it away. "They're *animals,*" he says. "My God, Lila, people catch them and *eat* them."

She gets out of the Jeep, slamming the door behind her. She wades through the tangle of kudzu and honeysuckle she has let grow up around the tall house. By the time she reaches the top step of the porch Doc is gone, the sun and dust sifting down behind the Jeep like the smoke of a great fire.

Maybe it isn't too late.

What if it is? Maybe she should call out to him. But what would she say? *You don't know what it's like.*

Maybe she won't do it anymore. She will put the waterbaby back in the river. She can rig up something, figure out some way to drag him down the steps, back down to the river. But would he remember how to swim? Would he remember—had he ever learned—the difference between what is safe and what is deadly? She thinks about him far out in the white storm of the dam spillway, swallowing bait, tangled in nets, torn by the terrible three-pronged hooks of the big snag poles.

Maybe she should just kill him. *For that which we are about to receive.* Maybe she should have done it long ago.

It's so quiet inside the house. If she climbs the stairs to her bedroom and throws the balcony doors open, the darkening tide of sky will come in. The waterbaby will be waiting for her there, glittering beneath the mirrors. Maybe she will sail him far out into the deep silk; maybe she will scuttle him like a ship on the reef of her bones; maybe she will say to him: "Mmmm."

BROTHERS

Joyce Carol Oates

Joyce Carol Oates is the author of numerous novels, short stories, poems, plays, and essays; she has won the National Book Award and has twice received the O. Henry Award for Continuing Achievement. Although she is best known in the literary mainstream, her work often has overtones of dark fantasy or psychological horror. Her gothic novel *Bellefleur* is particularly recommended to readers of dark fantasy, as is her recent collection *Haunted*.

"Brothers" is a potent work of dark fantasy about dreams, memory, and the shadows of childhood. It comes from the November issue of *Ellery Queen's Mystery Magazine*.

—T.W.

They came for him one windy October dusk when he was walking alone after his final class of the week. He looked up, and he was descending the steep hill behind the old Hubbard Street neighborhood. His eyes were watering in the wind lifting from the river beyond the Erie Central railroad yard a few blocks from the brick row house where his family had lived. The neighborhood had been razed, bulldozed into oblivion and recast as expressway ramps, cloverleafs, and soaring lanes in the years since he'd left, gone away to college, and begun his adult life; his family too had moved, like all the families and all the merchants of Hubbard Street. Yet here he was on the hill he'd sledded on as a child, a smell of snow in the air and his heart beating in anticipation as if it knew what he did not *They are coming for me!* glancing up to see them where a moment before there'd been no one: an empty stretch of field grasses and scrub trees, of that bleak, sere, wind-tormented color of autumn after the first frost.

They greeted him with boyish excitement.

"John Michael!—you're just in time."

"John Michael!—we've been waiting for you."

At first, they seemed to have corduroy faces, sand-colored. Shiny black button eyes. Sleek shiny black hair like painted-on hair. And it was impossible to gauge how old they were, even how tall they were; he hesitated to stare, not wanting to seem rude. Their voices rang warmly in his ears without actual sound. He was allowed to know *This is the truest way of communication*. What surprised him most, as if it were a revelation of a part of himself hidden until now, was his own childlike excitement, even happiness, in greeting them.

Though his words were strange, and oddly formal: "I tried not to be late. I had to come a long distance."

And this was true, for he lived far away now from the city of his boyhood. Far away, and nearly twenty years, from Hubbard Street.

"John Michael!—we must hurry."

"John Michael!—there isn't much time."

They reached out boldly for him. Their faces were brightened by smiles and were almost blinding. This intense light obscured their features; or their features were fluid, not yet coalesced. *Which is so superior to the average.* He seemed to know there was a plan, everything had been agreed upon beforehand, but he could not remember the plan. At the same time, it had already happened. A buoyant sensation began in his chest as if his heart was swelling.

"My name is—"

"*My* name is—"

He understood that they were brothers though he hadn't been able to hear their names. The vibrations reached his ears as if through an element dense as water but scattered in teasing ripples.

One of them seized his left hand, and the other seized his right hand, and both tugged at him. He was standing on a dirt path slightly above the brothers and the effect of their tugging was to pull him off balance so that he had no choice but to join them; at the same time, he was overjoyed to be with them.

The three of them ran down the hill slipping and sliding and shouting with excitement. The hill was the scrubby field above Hubbard Street, where in John Michael Wells's memory windblown litter had marred the striated surface of the tall grasses, like lint in the nap of a carpet, yet it was suddenly an unknown place, steep and treacherous and coated in ice. Or something sly-slippery underfoot as ice. Shiny, blinding. Intense pleasure and the knowledge *This is the truest way of happiness* rose in him from the ground, through his feet and into his legs and so up into his groin, his belly, his chest *There is no other way of happiness* as the brothers yanked him forward, down the hill. Their breaths were steaming. "It's cold! It's so cold!" he cried, laughing. Knowing that they, his brothers, would warm him.

The next night, he learned their names.

"He's Damm—"

"*He's* Vann—"

Each pointed to the other in an identical mirror gesture, as if practiced. Yet they were not twins, exactly—one appeared to be distinctly older, stockier, than the other; one's hair was that curious sleek-shiny black, and the other had thick deep-textured hair, black also, but separated into sections, with measured parts. They were on Hubbard Street, though nothing looked familiar, the background passed in a blur as if the brothers had not yet worked out where they were taking him exactly, in fact they seemed to be quarreling about this even as they spoke nonstop to him, their warm-rippling soundless words washing over him like caresses. The brothers were on either side of him—Damm to his left, Vann to his right—and they were gripping his hands tight so that he understood he was a little boy, a child, despite his height, which he was trying awkwardly to conceal. They were not on Hubbard Street but in the playground of his elementary school which was not as he remembered it but close enough for him to know what it was meant to be and that there was danger here as so frequently there'd been danger for him in that playground when he was a child attending this school, and so suddenly he tried to wrench himself away, his muscles went into a kind of spasm, and Damm and Vann murmured words of comfort and gripped his hands tight to calm, to steady. He wanted to cry *Seeing how your brothers care for you, that is the only truth* but this too he managed to conceal.

"John Michael!—you want to."

"John Michael!—that's *good*."

They were pulling him forward forcing him to go where he didn't but at the same time did want to go—to another child, or children, in a corner of the playground where the school's brick walls formed an L. Here, certain acts occurred. There were no names given to these acts and so there was no memory accruing to these acts except the memory of revulsion and shame.

Yes but you know nothing ever happened there. You know there was nothing.

Damm was tugging at him, and Vann was tugging at him, and the danger was close by but *your brothers will protect you* and so he felt a radiant buoyancy that shifted into quicksilver anger, strange laughing anger. He saw the face, blurred as if glimpsed through water, of one whom he hated, and of whom he had not thought in thirty years; and other jeering child-faces; but he was laughing, and Damm and Vann were laughing, so it was all right. He passed through these figures as if in fact they were water.

Anger grew in him like a flame rising from his groin into his chest, and into his throat. An actual heat, a flamey tingling in his throat. He was trying to speak to that child-face blankly jeering as a mask but there was something wrong with his tongue, his mouth, the sounds that came from him were guttural and staccato, a rattling in his throat. He was choking, he was dying! Was this dying? *Help me! help me!* he begged the brothers. Swallowing compulsively to quench the fire at the back of his mouth but he could not and as Damm and Vann cried *John Michael! John Michael!* he slipped from the grip of their hands helpless as a child falling on the playground's cracked asphalt pavement. *Don't let me go, where are you?—not so soon.* His head jerked on the damp pillow bunched beneath his neck, his eyes flew open for a long moment sightless, his throat was raw as if abraded—he'd been deeply asleep with his head back, mouth agape. Breathing through his mouth so that his throat had become dehydrated and the uncomfortable sensation had waked him.

Snoring, too—he must have been snoring, like a hog. He'd been hearing it, dry-rasping saw-notched sounds coming, it seemed, from a distance.

Awake, he felt such loss. A sensation as of falling. Paralysis. The lineaments of the dream were rapidly fading like a cinematic image on a screen when the lights are switched on but he felt such loss!—the grip of the brothers' hands on his, his fingers in theirs, only a dream, a phantasm. Nothing.

* * *

Awake, and through the day—a day of many hours populated by many individuals, some of them professional colleagues at the university, some of them social acquaintances, friends, and in the evening his lover Crista and her six-year-old son, with whom he did not live but whom he saw almost daily—Jack retained the vivid, disturbing memory of the brothers like the afterglow of erotic consummation, suffused through his entire body. *Where I really am, and who I really am.*

Did anyone notice his uncharacteristic distraction? The vagueness of his replies, his smiles? Jack Wells who was so skeptical by nature, a specialist in differential geometry and an amateur musician-composer, known among his circle of acquaintances for his dry, acerbic humor, his strong political opinions, how was it possible he felt such yearning—such heartsick yearning? To return as quickly as possible to his dreams, these strange unbidden mysterious dreams that had nothing to do with his life; no connection with the present, nor, really, with the past. *To get back to them, my brothers.*

He'd had the first dream only a few nights before. Yet it seemed to him he'd been having such dreams for years. Or, rather, he'd been experiencing this strange, almost unbearable yearning for years.

How was it possible?—it wasn't. "It's absurd."

Who the brothers were, and why Jack should care so much for them, he had no idea. He could not even remember them clearly. They were young, and there was something not quite normal about them—he seemed to know that. But he could not summon back their faces. *To ourselves, we're invisible. The brain has no face.* And what had happened in the dream of Hubbard Street, the playground of Benjamin Franklin Elementary School? *What you must not remember, you won't be able to.*

He'd never had faith that dreams meant much. Considering them in the stark light of day was largely a waste of time. He was not a man who liked to waste time. He was the kind of man who, at the periphery of a meeting or social gathering that is about to break up, jingles his car keys in his pocket.

He was the kind of man who, if someone begins speaking of his dreams, pointedly conceals a yawn.

Yet the brothers had shown him *the truest way of happiness* which he could not comprehend and which frightened him in its intensity.

For knowing how passionately he felt in these dreams he was forced to realize with what little passion he lived his life—even his sexual, erotic life.

And there were mysteries about the dreams that intrigued him: why, for instance, did the brothers call him "John Michael"?—he'd been "Jack" or "Jacky" most of his life. His baptismal name "John Michael Wells" was as remote to him as the long-deceased grandfather for whom he'd been named and whom he had scarcely known. And why a dream of *brothers* at all? Jack had one brother, Steven, five years his senior, an engineering consultant who lived with his wife and children in an upscale Chicago suburb; even as an adolescent Steve had shared few of Jack's interests in math, science, music—they'd gotten along amicably enough, for the most part, but had not been close. Now, they exchanged Christmas cards and ignored each other's birthday and went sometimes for as long as a year without speaking on the phone. A good, dull, decent man, Steve Wells. About whom Jack would have had to rack his brains to say anything interesting.

But what is there to say about most men and women, after all? Jack was in the habit of observing that human beings are no more *mysteries* than a banana is a *mystery*. You could never deduce what's inside a banana by examining the peel and the inside is entirely different from the peel, but so what? Why is it important?

"Jack, you're so cynical!" Crista sometimes exclaimed, as if his random remarks truly shocked her. Jack supposed she meant to flatter him. Sexual flirtation, sexual banter. But he did not consider himself cynical, only matter-of-fact; a man not given to exaggeration.

Which was why he'd been drawn to math, geometry—figures, pure structures—uninhabited by personalities—unaffected by personalities.

At the university Jack was Mr. Wells, or Professor Wells to his students. Since years ago there had ceased to be surprises in his work as in the very textbook adopted for his undergraduate course—to which Jack himself had contributed—he had no need to be deeply engaged. He was thirty-seven years old. With his steel-gray metal-rimmed glasses and his graying brown hair combed in two severe wings behind his ears and his playful habit of anticipating his students' questions even as they raised their hands, he seemed virtually of no age: not young, as his students were young; yet hardly old, smiling and youthful in his affect, with an unlined face, large dark intelligent sympathetic-seeming eyes, the body of a moderately active man—he swam, dutifully if without enthusiasm. At tennis, he was not competitive enough to be a good player. Why is it important?

One day after the dream of the playground while teaching an honors seminar in Riemannian geometry Jack heard his voice echoing from the room's corners and he realized *If these individuals see and hear me I must be here!* The profundity of this insight overwhelmed him.

And so it was, through the hours of wakefulness: meeting with colleagues and friends, deftly scanning student work with that part of his mind that operated like a computer independent of Jack Wells's moods or "self"—even with Crista and the child whom he loved and to whom he'd become family of a kind. *They see me and hear me, am I deceiving them?*

Even making love with Crista, pushing her and himself to the release of orgasm, he felt the tug of that other yearning and wondered if all human beings harbored such secret, inexpressible desires—for the solace of dreams. If solace was what the brothers offered him.

"John Michael!—you're just in time."

"John Michael!—we've been waiting for you."

And eagerly Jack saw his brothers were not angry.

Yanked the covers off him where he was naked.

Except, bicycling, pedaling frantically to keep up with the brothers, he was wearing oversized flannel pajamas. The elastic waistband was too loose and the pants cuffs got in the way of his pedaling and the brothers were laughing at him. He was laughing too, breathing through his mouth and gasping for air. His bicycle was too big for him and seemed to be made of lengths of pipe with large spoked wheels. Damm's and Vann's bicycles were similar but their legs were longer, they were older boys. Hurtling through the street, which was Hubbard Street except not really. And the corner by the tire shop, the intersection with Mohigan where he lived in the brick row house in a block of such row houses distinguishable from one another by painted front doors and shutters, crimped little lawns, flower beds. But there was much that was blurred. Open spaces like the edge of the world, blank like a television screen with no picture. "John Michael!—John Michael!" The brothers' voices were liquidy and caressing, vibrating in his head, "John Michael!—come *on*." Laughing and teasing and just slightly impatient because he was so slow. Jack's house was fourth from the corner and a hot wave of shame washed over him seeing it so shabby, walls of rust-brown brick and the shutters painted creamy-yellow for a cheery look as Jack's mother insisted but something had happened to the house, which was like a deformed face, a face born to a baby genetically doomed to horror, he was ashamed that the brothers saw but of course the brothers knew for they lived in that house themselves. *If it's too soon if I haven't been born yet where can I go?* He dreaded seeing his parents before they were his parents. There was a shame to this prospect he could taste as something tarry at the back of his mouth.

Sobbing gasping for breath pedaling frantically to keep up with Damm, and with Vann, who were shouting instructions to him he could not hear—such a roaring in his ears! He saw a human shape hurtle toward him and there was a sickening *crack!* as the big front wheel of his bicycle which might have been (the details were fluid, shifting) the front wheel of a car too passed over this figure, a child, or an elderly man, and he could not stop pedaling and did not want to stop pedaling following after the brothers who were drawing farther and farther away now scolding, playfully mocking "John Michael!—*what have you done!*"

In terror then Jack woke, heart pounding and naked body which felt large, clumsy *something not myself* covered in sticky sweat. His mouth was aflame with dryness. His eyes oscillated sideways in his head. Crista, who was a light sleeper, a woman given to quick maternal solicitude, was soothing his damp hair back from his forehead asking was something wrong? had he had a bad dream? and in his confusion Jack pushed at her with his elbow, not hard enough to hurt but unmistakably. Then he saw where he was, and with whom. In his woman friend's bed. *I'm safe, it hasn't happened yet*. He assured Crista it had only been a dream, a confused dream of playing tennis—"Sorry! Try to go back to sleep."

He stumbled sleep-dazed into the hall to use the bathroom, hearing Crista's low anxious voice behind him. As if, poor woman, she halfway feared Jack might slip away in one of his moods in the night without a farewell kiss.

Of course, Jack would never do such a thing. Even if he could have grabbed his clothes and dressed in the bathroom without Crista's knowing.

He was shaken, for something terrible had happened. It helped to rinse his guilty heated face in cold water. Avoiding his eyes in the mirror. *But nobody saw. Nobody except my brothers.*

But he was fully awake, and he was all right. Never can you deduce: the banana is *not* the peel.

He used the toilet and flushed it reluctantly and self-consciously hoping he wouldn't wake Lonnie, whose room was across the hall. Small quarters here in Crista's rented house. She was a legal secretary and the firm for which she worked had suffered financial losses through the recession, she'd had no raise for two years but was embarrassed taking money from Jack, though sometimes she had no choice, if not taking money from him then allowing him to pay Lonnie's dentist's bills, or for a new winter jacket, as if, if he married her, if he brought her and Lonnie to his own more spacious living quarters in a high-rise condominium tower on the hilly, leafy side of the enormous university campus, that would make a significant moral difference.

Fantasizing a note he'd leave for her affixed to the refrigerator door by one of those little dinosaur magnets he'd bought in a packet for the boy *Yes I love you I love you both but I have no heart for marrying you, the walls closing in on us. When I'm away from you I'm lonely for you but when I'm with you—I'm lonely for that part of myself that's somewhere else.* But he'd never do such a thing, he wasn't a cruel man except by accident.

The dream of the hurtling bicycle, the mysterious collision, came in early November. The following day Jack canceled a dinner engagement with Crista and another couple, despite Crista's extreme disappointment—she'd been planning this evening for weeks. Jack stayed home to work on a musical composition he'd begun, set aside in frustration, and forgotten a decade ago. It was a strange little piece scored for piano and strings, highly experimental, dissonant and lyric and meditative; neoclassic, but with startling juxtapositions and leaps inspired by Stravinsky and Varèse; an undercurrent of passionate yearning beneath. No one in this phase of his life even knew he'd once had a hope of writing music—"inventing music," he'd called it. It was his secret, or one of them.

Why Jack decided to work on this old, failed composition, he could not have said. So suddenly inspired, excited. *Yearning—for what?* It was almost a physical sensation, a hunger so extreme as to pass over into rapture. Working at the piano, emending his old composition and pushing ahead, he was so absorbed in the strange musical notes springing from his fingertips he glanced up to see with astonishment that it was nearly two A.M.—he'd been working for six hours virtually nonstop.

Outside, a wet-gusty November night. Leaves blown against the windows of his study like a fluttering of fingers.

How happy I am, and am meant to be.

There came back to Jack Wells now, by degrees, as, at night, not every night nor with any reliable regularity but with consoling frequency, he dreamt of the brothers, a memory of how, as a boy, he'd felt a flamelike excitement when working on mathematical problems; playing piano, and for a while the cello, for which he'd had more feeling than aptitude; trying, in secret, to "invent" original music. He'd been embarrassed by his secret vanity, his conviction at certain incandescent moments *You are a born composer, your destiny is music* and somehow this was bound up with his talent for math, geometry. That remarkable ease with which, as a schoolboy, he'd been able to "solve" problems in his head which his teachers had had to work out on paper.

He'd known, and had not wanted to know. He'd known, and had repudiated the knowledge, as one might hide away in a drawer a gift of disturbing mystery.

As a small child Jack had been brightly inquisitive and persistent in his questions put to adults. *How much are all the numbers in the universe added up? Where does the sun go at night? Where are my dreams during the day? If God is in the sky, why can't we see Him with a telescope?* And as a high-school student, with his air of intense skeptical wonderment, *Why is Benedict Arnold a "traitor," and George Washington a "hero"? Why does the liver work the way it does, and not some other way? Why didn't parthenogenesis evolve as the most efficient means of reproduction?* He was far more intellectually curious than his brother Steven, though Steven always got high grades in school, too; he was nothing like his parents, who were sometimes proud of him but more often puzzled and annoyed by him. Mr. Wells was a low-level public schools administrator, Mrs. Wells a substitute junior-high-school teacher—they'd met at State Teachers' College in Albany and seemed to have married as a way of putting youth behind them. Jack resembled neither of them, he was sure. His most vivid memory was his father's counsel on the eve of Jack's high-school graduation, at which he was to deliver the valedictory speech—"Just don't make a fool of yourself, son!"

Jack had started piano lessons in junior high school, though the Wellses owned no piano; in senior high school, inspired by a televised concert of Pablo Casals, he'd started cello lessons, so avid to learn the instrument, or to try, the school music teacher allowed him to use hers. Later, an adult, Jack had acquired a cello of his own, an exquisite instrument he remembered with feeling, like an old, long-lost lover, but at the time he'd never been serious about taking lessons and eventually he'd sold it. Nor had he been serious about "inventing" music. It became a weekend preoccupation, in time a hobby more contemplated than pursued. Jack's academic work intervened, his dutiful if uninspired citizenry as a member of a university community. He was a vain man and did not want to become one of those mathematicians of whom there are altogether too many characterized as *eccentric*.

His music was a candle flame flickering in his cupped hands and one day he happened to notice that the flame had gone out.

So with his mathematics. Highly promising in graduate school, winner of a prestigious fellowship, one of the more energetic younger professors at the first university at which he'd taught; then, by degrees, after a move to a less demanding university that brought with it promotion to associate professor and tenure, he'd let his research projects atrophy. Too much stress. Too much isolation. And always the risk of failure—*Just don't make a fool of yourself!* Jack found the routines of teaching, the superficial camaraderie of the academic life, the clockwork security of weeks, semesters, years sufficiently rewarding. Differential geometry, curves, surfaces, ghost-structures in three-dimensional space, the mind's very play in pursuit of "higher" knowledge—what was it but a hobby, intriguing and respectable as hobbies go; reasonably well-paying; reasonably secure; to be taken up, put down, taken up again like any hobby. Professor Wells was capable of performing in class, or in the company of his colleagues, like an "animated," "passionate" mathematician, which role he played purposefully from time to time. He was an actor playing his own old self, and he wondered, amused, if he wasn't more publicly effective as an actor than he'd been as that old self.

And there were women, a slow succession of women. Romances that shifted to friendships, with the passage of time. The compass direction of sexual feeling—could it be plotted? Jack supposed, in his case, it could. You move through points a, b, c . . . by the time you get to z, you aren't there any longer.

Fantasizing leaving on Crista's refrigerator door a note that had come to him in one of those waking dreams in which consciousness emerges and recedes and emerges again, where the daylight self touches fingertips with the nighttime self, *A family is a four-dimensional structure one plane of which is Time. A vector originating at a finite point but, since it curves into infinity, unchartable. Unknowable. Terrifying.*

December, the week of the first heavy snowfall, he'd been working several nights in succession on his "Trio in C # minor" and dreaming intermittently of the brothers and his relations with Crista were courteous if strained and guarded *She knows there is someone else, something else: she's jealous* and he felt guilty, sorry for her and at the same time resentful and there came to him a dream of Damm suddenly at his left hand! and Vann suddenly at his right hand! as if springing out of the earth, wholly unexpected. "You are always new to me, no one can invent you," Jack said. The brothers laughed loudly, their eyes squinting up in merriment.

"John Michael!—a surprise for you."

"John Michael!—come with us."

Pulling roughly at him, hands gripping his, tight. He felt a moment's panic. As if he'd pushed his hands into a narrow space and now they were stuck.

"John Michael!—we love you so much—"

"—we have made a place to put you inside of us—"

Though he was dreaming and should not have been capable of such lucidity Jack felt such warmth, such joy thinking *It doesn't matter that they aren't real, nothing in the real world is like this.*

They brought Jack to a clearing in the snow in which there was a tunnel like a rabbit hole and on his hands and knees Jack crawled into it and now Damm and Vann were somehow beside him, or in him, or he was in them, the three of them pushing through the snow-tunnel butting with their heads. *If they abandon me I won't be able to find my way back.* But he felt only mild anxiety knowing *this is the truest way of happiness* and his trust in them was not misplaced for now they were in an open space, it seemed to be a room, overheated and airless and strangely lit as in the reflective, oscillating light of fireworks. There'd been a small boy crawling ahead squealing with excitement or alarm and now it was revealed that this boy was a brother, too—his face a vague sweet blur, his hair the color and texture of butterscotch. His name sounded like "Hänne"—"Hänneh"—a high vibrating syllable that rang in Jack's head.

"John Michael!—see who this is?"

"John Michael!—we've brought him here for a reason."

Jack asked, "What is the reason?" eager to know, but his question came out garbled, like snorting, hiccuping. Damm and Vann laughed even louder than before.

"We thought he was the baby, but *you* are."

"John Michael!—why are you so—"

Cold, or *scared*, or *slow*, or—*old?* Jack was listening intensely yet could not hear. Even as, staring at Damm and Vann and now the boy Hänne who was about the size of an eight-year-old he could not seem to see their faces. *That is because they are inside your head, on the wrong side of your eyes.*

There was a fraction of a moment when Jack seemed to know he'd been in this place before. And Hänne was no surprise to him but someone he knew. And what was going to happen though he could not remember it.

It was expected that Jack stoop to kiss the little brother Hänne with whom he was now alone in this warm, airless cavity but he could not do it, his legs were twisted and his backbone stiff to the point of breaking. And his mouth so damned dry, that snorting-rattling in his throat. Damm and Vann were gone yet were watching and grinning lewdly through a kind of half-window, an old-fashioned dutch door. The strobelike lights pulsed weirdly in their eyes. They were—Jack was able to "see" them because he wasn't looking directly at them and they didn't think to disguise themselves—animated wooden figures, with astonishingly detailed, realistic features, liquidy eyes, thick dark eyelashes, glistening mouths—even their clothing was carved of wood, slick and shiny. At the same time they were thick-muscled high-school boys with blunt, handsome faces, about sixteen years old, the kind of boys who, in Jack Wells's high school, might have respected his intelligence but stared coolly through him as if, in his place, *no one at all had stood.* Except in gym class maybe where they'd expressed mild contempt for his tall skinny-puny body, his pigeon-sized muscles and weak eyes and the sullen-superior frown that was his defense.

But now it was, so delicious, "John Michael!—*we love you.*"

The littlest brother too loved Jack and now came giggling and rushing at him flailing his chubby baby arms in imitation of a bird—a hummingbird—aiming a wet kiss at Jack's mouth. But Jack panicked ducking and shielding his head with his arms and in a spasm of coughing woke dazed to find his legs twisted in damp bedclothes, his mouth agape in an enormous O, and his penis too enormous pulsing stiff with an erection that throbbed to the point of pain.

It was 6:20 A.M. A high whining wind outside. Pitch black, but the night's dreaming was over. In horror of touching himself Jack staggered from his bed.

The week before Christmas, Jack's father had an accident driving his car, suffered minor injuries and had to be hospitalized and Jack went to visit him and saw by the look in his father's face, in and about the cringing eyes, that this was no longer the man Jack had known. Here was an aging man, a badly frightened man, forcing a jaunty smile to ashy lips; trading wisecracks with the nurses to whom he introduced his "professor" son; insisting, "One minute the damned steering wheel was in my hand, the next—it wasn't." He blamed the icy pavement but Jack knew from his mother that he'd had a blackout, he'd simply lost consciousness and woke up in the hospital.

Fortunately, Jack's father's car had been moving at only about twenty miles an hour. It had swerved across several lanes of traffic, sideswiping another car and striking the rear of a motorcycle driven by a young man and coming to a jolting stop against a guard rail.

Jack asked, "Was the cyclist injured?"

"Well—" His mother's eyes were veiled. "—not badly."

"He wasn't killed, for God's sake, was he?"

"Why are you so excited?" Jack's mother asked, staring at him. She'd always been a nervous woman, quick to take offense; you risked insulting her by simply asking questions of the kind that must be asked. "No, certainly he was *not.* He was treated in the emergency room same as your father and *he* was released that same night."

Jack shut his eyes, feeling the *crack!* of the front wheel striking an invisible victim. But that was only a dream, and not at all like his father's experience, really.

"Why am I so excited?" he asked his mother quietly. "In matters of life and death, shouldn't we all be excited?"

And there was another incident at about that time, a spilling-over of his dreams of the brothers into real life, or a spilling-over of real life into his dreams of the brothers: in the university swimming pool where he hadn't swum for months, he was doing laps one frigid January morning when he sighted, padding across his line of vision, a stocky-muscled young man covered in darkish ape-fuzz, pink hose of a penis bobbing at his groin—an undergraduate football player who was the model, unmistakably, for Damm and Vann. Jack stared, appalled: *him?* It was a male-only hour at the pool and in this atmosphere of naked men the young football player, shouting to a friend and diving noisily into the pool, was the most truly *naked*.

Jack Wells swam on in his lane, fumbling, so stricken he swallowed a mouthful of water.

John Michael!—now you know.

And he noted too, one evening at Crista's when Lonnie in his pajamas was running in and out of the living room, squealing breathlessly hoping to avoid being put to bed by his mother—for Jack had been coming less frequently lately, there was tension in his presence—that the child's curly hair was the color of butterscotch. *Hänne—Lonnie?* Jack passed a hand over his eyes, laughing weakly. He must have looked as if he was about to get up and walk out, for Crista said sharply, "Lonnie, *stop*." And to Jack, apologetically, "Jack, I'm sorry. It's past his bedtime and he knows better but—I guess—he's been missing you, and—"

"Well, I've been missing him," Jack said. This was true, or true enough. Lonnie approached him and Crista where they were sitting together, wineglasses in hand, and the boy's brown-amber eyes were wide in that way of a shy child's impetuosity and Jack felt his heart contract with an emotion sharp as pain. *Why don't you love me!* Lonnie demanded with those eyes *Why aren't you my daddy!*

Afterward, when they were alone, Crista asked, "Is there someone else?" quickly amending, in that way of hers that touched Jack deeply, it spoke of such instinctive solicitude for the other's position, "—unless you'd rather not talk about it with me." And Jack said, slowly, "No. No one." They were at the dining room table reluctant to shift into the next phase of the evening inevitable as a locomotive bearing down upon them—would they make love as they had not done in some time, would Jack stay the night—or would he, very shortly now, glance at his watch, make a comment about the time and his work waiting for him at home. And there was silence.

A long awkward moment of silence. Crista rested her hand on Jack's in sympathy. *Where I really am, and who I really am.* Almost, she seemed to know. To forgive, and to release. Outside, a light snowfall fine and gritty as sand was being blown against the windows; there was a humming or vibrating in the air, a teasing, nearly inaudible strain of music.

Crista said, "Jack, goodnight."

He was hunched at the piano. His eyes ached, and his hands. He'd lost track of the time *Which is how you know you are where you are meant to be and that no other could be in your place.* Outside his twelfth-floor window the nighttime city was an attenuated cobweb of lights. It was late, and very cold—the temperature hovering at zero degrees Fahrenheit. Good, nobody will interrupt. Even the wind had died down.

The "Trio in C# minor" emerged from his fingertips feverishly, but had to be continuously revised. For every movement forward there was a movement back. Some nights, the labor of the previous night, hours of finger-stretching chords, annotations, and revisions, was totally unraveled. *If I could just press forward, race to the end* but even in this heightened state of consciousness Jack was cautious, conservative. It filled him with a chill, subdued terror to think that he might not ever complete the composition. He would work, like this, night after night, week following week into infinity.

Already it was February. He'd arranged to take an unpaid leave of absence from the university, to the surprise of his colleagues and friends. Why? they asked. What are you working on that's so demanding? Or are you going to travel?—where? He told them nothing, he was alone much of the time.

He'd called Crista not long ago simply to be friendly, for he did miss her and the child, and Crista had been cool and curt saying she was fine and busy and, no, she couldn't put Lonnie on the phone—"He's too angry with you."

Jack wanted to say, "I'm angry with myself—" but the remark would have sounded facetious, insincere.

Damm laid a heavy, meaty hand on Jack's right shoulder, and Vann laid a heavy, meaty hand on Jack's left shoulder. The child Hänne was crouched nearby in his red pajamas, making a design in the snow with his hands. The butterscotch hair lifted in thick, hardened-syrupy tufts. There was something wrong with Hänne's left eye which Jack had never noticed before.

"John Michael!—you're an angry man."

"John Michael!—don't be a coward."

It was the first time the brothers had spoken quite so harshly to him and he recoiled with the hurt even as he wriggled his shoulders in such a way as to make himself smaller.

In recent dreams of the brothers Jack seemed to be full size—an adult man. He stood taller than his father had ever stood before his father had begun his downward shrinking, the farthest point of which was infinity. Yet, strangely, for all their shrewdness the brothers had no apparent knowledge that Jack Wells was a university professor, a mathematician. Nor did they know anything about his musical life *and so I have protected myself—haven't I?* He seemed to know that the brothers would have been bitterly jealous if they'd known of his other life.

"John Michael!—you don't lie to *us.*"

"John Michael!—you can't get away with that *here.*"

The threat they wielded was the threat of taking away their love for him. Even when the love was a warm golden liquid making his heart float he was fearful of its loss.

Hänne was running squealing and giggling in the snow and it was not clear if he was leading his brothers or whether his brothers, panting and lolling their tongues like wolves, were in pursuit. Suddenly there was excitement! danger! skidding descending the snowy-icy hill above Hubbard Street. A freight train was rattling close by, boxcar after boxcar ERIE CENTRAL RAILROAD ERIE CENTRAL RAILROAD and the noise was deafening vibrating inside Jack's head so hard his teeth chattered. They were in a forbidden place PRIVATE PROPERTY DANGER KEEP OUT having scaled the ten-foot chain-link fence and Jack was very frightened. And he understood he could not turn back.

Here has nothing to do with there. Once you climb the fence and jump down it doesn't matter where you came from.

The locomotive's whistle was a high-pitched shriek. Frantic as a hunted rabbit Hänne ran slipping in the snow in danger of falling beneath the train's wheels but when Jack reached out to grab him the older brothers jerked him back. "John Michael!—you have to choose."

"Choose what?" Jack asked. "Choose who?"

They were in the Erie Central Railroad yard but they were also in the L-shaped corner of Benjamin Franklin Elementary School. The noise of the train was also the noise of the wind blowing leaves and dirt into Jack's eyes. Jack saw Hänne's blunder but could not warm him *It's a corner! a trap!* for Damm and Vann gripped his shoulders too hard as running panicked from his enemies Hänne rushed into the corner and could not escape. His enemies who were the size of rabbits too, but large, vicious rabbits, knocked him down deftly and undid his corduroy trousers pulling them to his ankles and pulling down his underwear as well and rubbing dirt and dead leaves on his tender penis which shrank up inside him like a tiny turtle retracting its head. *Why do they hate me* Hänne was sobbing but the answer was *Oh no it's just play, it just happens to be you in the corner.* Damm and Vann knew better, however. They were laughing angrily in shame of their little brother who could not defend himself. Jack wanted to protest that when it had happened to him he'd learned to stay inside at recess and noon with other quiet children doing their homework in the cafeteria and amassing "extra credit" so at Parent's Day in June there was a row of shiny stars ★ ★ ★ ★ ★ ★ ★ ★ ★ ★ ★ ★ ★ ★ ★ ★ beside John Michael Wells's name on the bulletin board so far ahead of the next-nearest name.

Jack wanted to explain to Hänne who was sobbing *You won't remember the origin of those stars—I promise.*

Damm was shaking Jack's shoulder in disgust, "John Michael!—you'd better choose." And Vann shook Jack's shoulder even harder, as if hoping to dislocate it, "John Michael!—make up your mind."

The terrible locomotive was close behind them. Jack understood that he was to sacrifice one of the brothers, push him beneath the wheels, but he could not. "No, no please," he was pleading, "—don't make me, please—" He was paralyzed and his words too were stopped in his throat like great clots of phlegm. Damm and Vann were panting their harsh steamy breaths in his face saying, "Coward!—

choose. Coward!—*choose*." But Jack was whimpering, his bladder threatened to spill, and in the manner of adolescent boys thrusting another from them in physical repugnance the older brothers shoved him so roughly he woke not at the piano (where with part of his delirious dreaming mind he'd believed himself to be) but fallen like a dead man across his bed. He was fully clothed, even his shoes on. Eyes burning in their sockets as if he'd been staring into a fierce light though his bedroom was darkened and absolutely still. *Choose! choose!* the voices were fading *coward, choose!* already the brothers' voices were fading into the wind against the windows, or into a locomotive's whistle miles away across the river, or into a child's nighttime fretting in the apartment above and though Jack sat up quickly, fully awake now and his senses alert as if he had narrowly escaped great danger, he heard nothing, no one.

How rapidly, how helplessly they were fading, the voices. And the luminous human figures. And the names of these figures. Receding to the size of a spark, a pinprick. Infinity. *What you must not remember, you won't be able to*. The brothers were gone and would not return but what that would mean, what Jack's life would be from now on, he had no idea. It had happened already, but he could not remember.

SUBSOIL

Nicholson Baker

Nicholson Baker is the author of *The Mezzanine; Room Temperature, U and I*, *Vox*, and, most recently, *The Fermata*. His short fiction has appeared in *The New Yorker* and *The Atlantic Monthly*.

"Subsoil" is a wonderfully strange and funny story about . . . fear of spuds. Falling somewhere in that shadowy region between fantasy and horror, it succeeded in making us both laugh, while at the same time giving us the chills. The story is reprinted from the June 27/July 4 issue of *The New Yorker*.

—T. W. and E. D.

For his book-length monograph on the early harrow, Nyle T. Milner, the agricultural historian, decided that he had to pay one more visit to the Museum of the Tractor in Harvey, New York, an inconsequential town not far from Geneva. He had already been to the Museum of the Tractor three times; each time, he left feeling that he had learned everything he needed about the rare implements of harrowage and soil pulverization in its collection, sure that his further photos and sketches would suffice. But always there was some tiny question that lured him back.

The manager of the Harvey Motel took an interest in Nyle's research and wanted him to recall his stay with pleasure; whenever he came she used a headier brand of air freshener in his room. Rather than discuss with her his preference for unflavored air, which might make her regret her earlier acts of kindness, Nyle decided that for this visit he would try to stay someplace else and hope she didn't find out.

Bill Fipton, who owned and curated the Museum of the Tractor, was at first cagey about recommending a bed-and-breakfast close by. "There is one that some people go to," he said, thoughtfully eying a 1931 Gilroy & Selvo variable-impact sod-pounder. "I don't want to dump on anyone, but I say stick with the motel." Bill, who had been quite friendly to Nyle on earlier visits, seemed cooler toward him today—he had been evasive, for instance, about which local hobbyist had done the superior restoration work on one of the more fascinating transitional Unterbey harrows. Nyle got the sense that Bill, who had a habit of doing something muscular with his tongue before he said anything, apparently to reseat his dental plate, was perhaps beginning to resent how closely Nyle was scrutinizing the collection.

"Please," Nyle insisted. "I really need to branch out."

"The Taits," said Bill reluctantly. "They'll give you a room." He gave Nyle the address. "It won't be cheap. And keep an eye open there. I've heard some stories. But they're supposed to make an interesting soup."

Mrs. Tait led Nyle up the stairs and down a narrow hall hung with three tiny black-and-white photographs of sliced mushrooms. A cotton runner, striped in purple and black, ran down the middle of the hall. She opened a door.

"This is a surprise," said Nyle, taking it all in. He gestured at a tall tubular brown vase with a single black branch gnarling artily out of it. "It's so . . . spare. I expected cutesy curtains and ruffled bed skirts."

"We are not exactly *of* Harvey," Mrs. Tait said. She was nearly fifty, with an attractive, prematurely ravaged neck and an expensive haircut. A bit of what seemed to be a tattoo, possibly the tail of something, peeped out past the unbuttoned neck of her silvery linen shirt. "But we do love the town."

"Oh, me too," said Nyle. "The tractors drew me here, as usual—where tractors are I must go! But I've grown very fond of Main Street. That sad little Chamber of Commerce."

"And what about dinner?" said Mrs. Tait.

"Do you offer a dinner package?" Nyle asked.

"We could see what we have on hand."

"I've heard high tidings of soup," Nyle said.

"Ah!" said Mrs. Tait, coming alive. "Is that what you would like?"

Nyle said he would, very much, being a soup person—if it wasn't too much trouble. Mrs. Tait left him to settle in. He took off his shoes and scattered his new farm-machinery sketches on the bed. His monograph was taking far too long to finish. Three years was excessive, even for a subject as far-reaching as his. Nyle was disorganized, a trait surprising in a man so short, and he was having exciting insights now about the evolution of rotary-hoe blades and diggers which he later realized were not new to him, ones that he had written down in a state of euphoria and lost in his briefcase and forgotten. So much of what he knew was only in his head, unfortunately, and his head couldn't always be depended on. Driving to Harvey, he had briefly wondered whether, were he to die suddenly, right then, he would have lived his life—not merely as an agricultural historian but even as a human being—entirely in vain. He'd seen it happen recently with the late Raymond Purty, who had known a great deal about early silos—more than anyone else on earth. When Purty was suffocated that muggy April afternoon under three tons of raw soy, everyone in Nyle's circle had expected at least a partial manuscript to come to light. But, sadly, the history of silage had all been in Ray Purty's head.

"This is the last research trip I'll make," said Nyle sternly to himself. "From now on—synthesis, exclusion, and sequential paragraphs." A faint smell of furniture wax and, underneath it, of something earthy and wholesome cheered him. This bed-and-breakfast—in a Greek Revival house with seven thin columns in front—was much better for morale than the well-intentioned instant headache of the Harvey Motel's air freshener. Maybe the town disparaged the Taits just because the Taits had taste.

The room was furnished with extreme, almost oppressive, care. The bureau was an ornamentally incised, Eastlake-style artifact with a large pair of mother-of-pearl wings inlaid in one side. The bed bore puzzling ovoid knobs, about the size of ostrich eggs, on its headboard and footboard. Five tiny safe-deposit-box keys hung next to a tarnished mirror as decoration. Nyle peered closely at the surface of the wall, fascinated by the stippled effect the Taits had achieved. They appeared to have flung or slapped around lengths of thin rope dipped in cinnamon-colored paint. Risky, Nyle felt, but it worked.

Only one pillow was made into the bed, an arrangement that momentarily concerned him, since he always slept with a second between his legs for comfort, having sensitive knees. But in the closet three spares were neatly shelved. Good—no need to bring up matters of ménage with the somewhat intimidating Mrs. Tait. Above the pillows, on the highest closet shelf, Nyle noticed a ziggurat of old children's games. There was a game called Mr. Ree and period Monopoly and Parcheesi boxes. And there was also—the obvious treasure of the collection—an old Mr. Potato Head kit. "Ho!" he cried, gingerly sliding it from its place on the shelf and carrying it to the bed. He had played Mr. Potato Head a few times as a child—back in the days before child safety, when you used a real baking potato and you stabbed the facial features, fitted with sharp points, into it. The joy of the old game came in imposing the stock nose- and ear- and eyepieces on the unique Gothic shape of a real potato. Man and nature in concert; "the encrustation of the mechanical upon the organic," or however it was that Bergson defined laughter. The modern Mr. Potato Head, which included an artificial base potato with holes, was, Nyle felt, a mistake—now you merely joined bought plastic to bought plastic in various fixed permutations. Why continue the affection of a potato at all?

He pulled the lid slowly off the box, feeling the air slip in to fill the increasing volume. And then he had a nasty shock. Fully prepared for a quick, happy *poof* of nostalgia—needing it, in fact, since he was more than a little discouraged by the progress of his research—he was instead confronted by something unpleasant and even, for a moment at least, outright frightening. A real potato, or a former potato, a now dead potato, still rested within the box. The last person who had played with the set had carelessly left the face he had created inside, with its proptotic yellow eyes and enormous, red-lipped, toothy, Milton Berlesque smile still stabbed in place, and over time—how long Nyle didn't want to guess—the potato's flesh had shrunk to a wizened leer of agonized supplication or self-mockery while it had grown seven long unhealthy sprouts that had curved and wandered around their paper chamber, feeling softly for the earth hold they never found. They resembled sparse hair and gastrointestinal parasites and certain weedy, wormy, albino things that live underwater; Nyle looked on them with disgust. Hurriedly he replaced the top and stuffed the box away in the closet again.

He rested for a moment on the bed, blinking regularly. The expression on the Mr. Potato Head intruded itself several times into his imagination—mummified, it had seemed, but conscious, in a state of sentient misery. The really disturbing thing was that, despite its appliqué grin and hefty comic nose, it had, Nyle felt, looked at him with a fixed intent to do him harm. The apparent animosity, though he could discount it as a trick of decomposition, bothered Nyle; he had never been hated by a potato before.

From downstairs came the cheerful eruption of a blender.

Mrs. Tait held a low green bowl over the table, waiting for Nyle to remove his politely clasped hands from the placemat. "There!" she said, giving the bowl a half turn as she positioned it in front of him. She sat down across from her husband. Mr. Tait had a carefully sculpted silver beard and wore a soft formless jacket over a black sweater with three brown buttons. The two of them were the least likely bed-and-breakfast owners Nyle had run into a long time.

He turned his attention to his dinner. The soup had a grainy pallor, with parsley shrapnel distributed equitably throughout. "Mm, boy," he said, sniffing deeply. "Leek?"

Mrs. Tait gave him an eighteenth-century smile. "And potato."

Potato! Nyle flinched. On each of his hosts' plates were three dried apricots. "Aren't you having any?" he asked them. Mr. Tait discreetly slipped an apricot in his mouth, as if he were taking a pill, and began dismantling it with toothy care.

"We seldom eat the soup ourselves," Mrs. Tait explained. She put a light finger on her abdomen. "I would like to, but I can't. Potatoes upset me now."

"Juliette makes the soup for our guests only," said Mr. Tait. "It's labor-intensive. Please start."

"Oh, potatoes are not for everyone, that's for sure," said Nyle, his mind racing. "Especially sweet potatoes. I know five, no, more—six—people who hate sweet potatoes."

Mrs. Tait slipped a disk of apricot in her mouth and sucked on it like a cough drop. "Please start," she quietly hissed.

"Pumpkin pie's stock has plunged, don't ask me why," Nyle nattered. "I do enjoy a good boiled potato, though, especially mashed up nicely."

"Oh—you like them mashed?" said Mrs. Tait, with a distant look, as if recalling early felonies. "*Please*, won't you?"

Why was he hesitating? What reason could he possibly have for his sense of vague unease? Suppressing his doubts, the agricultural historian took a big noisy spoonful, feeling immediately juvenile, as he always did when he ate soup as a guest. "Very nice," he said.

Mrs. Tait was pleased. "We're known for it, at least within Harvey."

"I'll tell my colleagues," said Nyle.

By the time he had accepted his second bowl, Nyle's doubts and suspicions were altogether gone. And the Taits, who had been keyed up at first, seemed to relax completely as well. They drank wine and ate their dried fruits and asked Nyle informed questions about his field. When he determined that the term "rear-power takeoff," as applied to the tractor, was not entirely new to them, he grew animated and confessional. As he described his work, he began to think that it was—though obviously influenced (as whose could not be?) by the insights of Chatternan Gough, Paul Uselding, and M. J. French—something well worth finishing. He found himself describing to the Taits his recent fears: he sketched the story of Purty and the terrible soy suffocation, from which the history of "spouted beds" and other fermentational mechanisms might never fully recover.

"I'm feeling unusually mortal at the moment," Nyle was finally drawn to say, wiping his mouth and sitting back. His hosts were arranged in casual poses. Slightly more of Mrs. Tait's tattoo was visible: it now looked like part of a vine, perhaps, rather than like a lizard's tail. "If I were Keats," Nyle went on, "and thankfully I'm not, cough cough, I would be making every attempt to use the word 'glean' in a sonnet."

"I hope your stay here will help," said Mrs. Tait carefully.

"Oh, yes. Although . . ." Hesitating briefly, Nyle decided that he would probably trust the Taits more if he just went ahead and told them. "An oddly upsetting thing happened in my room just before you called me down. I probably shouldn't have, but I took a quick peek inside the Mr. Potato Head box in the closet."

"You opened the box," said Mr. Tait, leaning forward.

"I'm a Curious George sort of person," Nyle explained. "It's the historian in me. Well—there was a highly unattractive dead potato in there. Ugh! Not good."

Mrs. Tait looked thoughtful. "Douglas Grieb was the one who saw that set last, if I remember right," she said. "He was here visiting the Museum of the Tractor, too, from the University of Somewhere—Illinois, was it, Carl?"

"Oh, Grieb," said Nyle, waving dismissively. "A controversial figure, not universally liked. Well, his potato head has not aged well. It scared the starch out of me, quite frankly."

Mrs. Tait rose and removed the plates. "Come with me," she said, and led Nyle into the green-trimmed kitchen. Two Yixing teapots in the shape of cabbages were arranged to the right of a vintage porcelain sink. Mrs. Tait bent and opened all the beautifully mitred doors to the cabinets under the counter. In the shadows were three rotating storage carrousels. Crowded on their round shelves were dozens of silent potatoes. Some were dark-brown; some were deep-red. Some had eyes that looked like bicuspids; some had sprouted and evidently had their sprouts clipped off. A few were extraordinarily large. A smell of earth and rhizomes and of things below consciousness pervaded the room.

Nyle made a whistle of amazement. Then he said, "One or two of those larger gentlemen do not look particularly . . . recent."

"The secret to a good earth-apple soup," explained Mr. Tait, squeezing his wife's arm, "is to age the ingredients."

Nyle sent his sensibility on a little stomach check and then quickly recalled it. All seemed well. "I had no idea," he said.

Mrs. Tait bent and gave one of the carrousels a turn. She leaned forward and lightly caressed a huge russet. "We eat only the fruit of a plant," she said, "and never its tuber, since its tuber is not something it intended to offer the world."

"But—" Nyle began, indicating the gleaming components of the blender which were upended in the black dish drainer. The blender blade sat drying like a blown rose. "You made the soup."

"It was our pleasure," said Mrs. Tait. "It was for you." She closed all but one of the doors to the potato cabinets and turned off the light. The only illumination in the room now came from a small bulb within the oven.

"At this time of evening, we generally watch 'Nick at Nite,' " said Mr. Tait, escorting Nyle into the front hall.

"Oh, thanks—I think I'll head on up," said Nyle. "I've got some more notes that I should expand."

"While the tractor museum is still fresh in your mind?" said Mrs. Tait.

"Exactly," said Nyle. He waved a cheerful good night to his hosts and ascended the stairs, humming. But as he walked down the narrow hallway, paying no notice to the riven mushrooms, he suddenly thought, Why did Mrs. Tait use that particular word; that "fresh"? And were those—could those be—*potato prints* of some kind on the walls of his room?

Nyle had difficulty getting to sleep that night. The Taits had kindly provided some light reading on a shelf by the bed; Nyle got through a short Wilkie Collins story and half of a longer Sheridan Le Fanu. He liked being mildly frightened by fiction when he was uneasy in fact. When he turned out the light, waiting for sleep to come, he was visited by the memory of the now sinister-seeming black rectangle of the half-open kitchen cabinet downstairs. Why hadn't Mrs. Tait closed the last cabinet door? This was like trying to fall asleep after you remembered that you'd left a radio on in the basement, he thought. And the sheer size of some of the potatoes she had shown him! They were phenomenal, unnatural. *Boulders* of carbohydrate. Finally, he was able to worm his way into a fairly satisfactory half sleep by imagining himself tearing up large damp pieces of corrugated cardboard.

He woke some hours later feeling sorry for a minor engineer named Shelby Hemper Fairchild, whose career had been cut short in the early thirties by the unfortunate inhalation of a cotton ball. (Fairchild—and not Edward Lyrielle, as some wrongly asserted—developed Bleidman & Co.'s famous Guttersnipe, an erratic but groundbreaking turf flail and trencher.) Without moving, Nyle worked his unpillowed eyeball so as to take in as much of his room as he could. Moonlight furbished the brown cylindrical floor vase and its gnarled branch, as well as an aquarium bibelot in the shape of a ruined arch on his bedside table. He felt strange suspicions and recalled the kitchen cabinet. Big hostile pocked things were waiting in there. That cabinet door was open. Wouldn't it be a good idea to nip quickly downstairs and close it himself? Clearly he wasn't going to sleep properly until this state of affairs was resolved.

Pulling the pillow from between his legs, he put on his paper slippers (hospital wear, salvaged from an appendectomy performed several years earlier) and made his way in the half-light toward the door—where he discovered something. A long, glimmering white sprout, with violet accents—a lengthy potato sprout, by all indications—had grown through the keyhole. It curved motionlessly to the floor. Perplexed, on the verge of being horrified, he glanced at his watch, more to steady himself than to check the time. The notion that this sprout had grown its way out of the kitchen cabinet, originating in one of those prodigies of mass storage downstairs, and that it had then worked its way slowly up to him, all while he slept, disturbed Nyle exceedingly. His watch claimed that it was almost three.

"Hello?" he called softly, in case someone or something was on the other side of the door. There was no answer.

Closer up, the feeler appeared harmless. He touched it quickly, testingly. It was cold and didn't move. He grasped it; he wound it around his trembling finger. He pulled.

The soft, unchlorophylled plant flesh gave way against the metal edge of the keyhole, making a tiny rending sound. Carefully Nyle fed the broken mystery frond back out under the doorway. "Out you go," he whispered. He waited for some time, listening. We have scotched the snake, not killed it, he thought to himself, drawing comfort from the scrap of pentameter—and then, reminded that he had some Scotch Tape in his briefcase, he carefully sealed the keyhole. The sensation of the sticky tape on his fingers left him feeling almost brave. It was time to confront the hall.

He turned the knob and peered tentatively out. The long, pale petitioner with the torn end receded kinklessly from his doorway into the shadows along the black-and-purple runner. Nyle tiptoed along it to the head of the stairway and looked down, craning his neck to determine the shoot's route up the stairs. What he then saw, as his gaze penetrated the grainy obscurity of the front hall, made a terror gong go off in his mind.

A dozen or more sinuous emissaries from the kitchen, similar to the first, were just turning the corner from the dining room and beginning the climb toward him.

"Good gravy!" he gasped, hotfooting it back to his room. "They're out to get me!" He slid the bolt and tried to think. The proliferating sprouts, though he suspected that they were up to no good, were none too strong, judging by the one that he had held. They couldn't push their way past the taped-up keyhole. But he had to take reasonable measures to protect himself. If he stuffed something *under* the door, he theorized, these hellish hawsers would never find him.

He took off his pajama bottoms and wedged them into the space between the door and the floor. Immediately he felt much better. No, they were not strong sprouts. They were not robust. They were attenuated and colorless and slow and soft. That was what he didn't like about them, in fact. That and that they seemed, in their blind, tentative way, to want to find him.

Ten minutes went by. Twelve. Nyle craved to know how fast they were growing, if they were growing at all. Maybe they had withdrawn. Were they already at the top of the stairs? Did they grow only while he slept? In that case, he had but to stay awake all night. A watched pot never boils. Or were they already nudging gently against the pajama-bottom buffer—and, if so, would such insistent pushings finally dislodge it entirely? He wheeled around, looking for some backup. A *drawer*. One of the heavy lower drawers from the big ornamental bureau. He seized its two handles and pulled.

Again he heard a soft rending sound, louder this time. The drawer was not empty. Inside was a plastic sack of enormous aging Valley Star potatoes, the biggest Nyle had ever seen. Through the ventilation holes of the plastic had grown a horror whorl of intertwining white shoots and root hairs. Some of the shoots bore new radish-size dark tubers. The upper surface of the conjoined growth was flat, like a Jackson Pollock, having encountered the plane of the drawer above. Freed and slightly injured, the bureau's brood now began to awaken. Nyle stared for an instant at their sullen stirrings. Then he reverse-salaamed, barking once with shock and revulsion. When he moved, his ankle bone made contact with something more yielding than an electrical cord. He glanced down. A gap in the baseboard molding had allowed entrance to more questing feelers from downstairs. There seemed to be some wispy activity at the window. Something was floating up through a loose floorboard. Nyle stamped on the board, severing the fiendish sucker. Grabbing his briefcase, he backed slowly across the room. "Mr. and Mrs. Tait?" he quavered. But there was no answer.

Sensing his movements and his noise, the sallow stolons began a languorous, low creep toward him. He could see them move now. "No! You're disgusting!" he cried, flicking at them with his fingers. His back bumped against the closet door. I'm doomed, he thought. And yet maybe they feared light. If he could get in the closet and turn on the closet light, maybe they would rethink and withdraw.

He bumbled inside and shut the door. He yanked on the light cord, which sprang away from his hand. A coruscation of bulb yellow filled the space. He waited, squinting, wishing he were wearing his pajama bottoms. A minute or two passed, and he began to think he was safe. And then he heard sounds from the room: his overnight bag seemed to be on the move; softnesses were sweeping the walls. He spotted the tips of three or four lissome elongations peeping under the door. With a terrified, saliva-rich curse, he grabbed a dark-green rubber boot and began pounding their growth tips as they emerged. But the light seemed to stimulate them, and many now vied for entrance. Was there no escape? He looked up. Past the light bulb, which was mounted on the wall, he saw a trapdoor. It must lead to an attic space. He could climb up there, kick out an attic window, climb out onto the porch roof, shimmy down one of the front columns, and run.

He grabbed two clothes hooks and started to hoist himself up toward the closet ceiling. His eyes drew even with the top shelf. From inside the Mr. Potato Head box came a leisurely scrabbling. Its top began to lift. The Parcheesi game slid to one side. The Monopoly game tumbled. The fixed orange eyes of the dead and shrunken Mr. Potato Head appeared from under the rising top, and then one or two—four, *seven*—limply questing spud spawn veered into the air toward Nyle's face, root hairs aquiver.

"Help!" Nyle wailed, and he fell. The floor of the closet was asquirm. Whitish-purple growth enveloped him. He waved his arms and plucked at himself hectically, but the soil-starved delvers were persistent. When they touched his face, he began to feel sad that he would never finish his history of the harrow. A sprout grew smoothly into his right knee, seeking his synovial fluid. Several more penetrated his elbows. These hurt quite a lot, though not nearly as much as the one that found its way into his urethra. One wan ganglion discovered his ear canal, and another a tear duct, and Nyle began to hear only the dim, low pulsation of plant hormones and potato ideology. Let it go, he thought. Let it all go. They found the routes his blood took, and they followed these deeper; by dawn they had grown the fresh, lumpy tuber that burst his heart.

What once was Nyle woke in a very dark place. Many Krebs cycles had passed; many more would pass. He felt himself being slowly turned. His fellows were dozing by the dozen near him. A child's voice was saying, "That one! That big one!" He was lifted and cradled in the child's gentle hand. His vision wasn't working properly—he saw several different views of the world. The child, with a cry of happiness, plunged the fake nose into Nyle's crisp body flesh. Nyle screamed, but it was a potato scream, below the hearing of all but tree stumps and extinct volcanoes. The child stabbed in the orange pop eyes, and then the big red smiley mouth, and the little black pipe. Each face piece had points. The child wasn't quite sure what it wanted; it rearranged the Potato Head features several times. Nyle leaked a little from his puncture wounds. The child grew bored and put Nyle back in the box, tossing the unused face parts in after. Then there was a long, dark time.

He felt himself shrinking, and the shrinking was agony. He forgot what he had known, he began to know only what potatoes know. He sensed the changes of geothermic pressure; he heard the earth's slow resentments. He exhausted himself doing the only thing he could do, which was trying to send out underground shoots to form more potatoes like himself—but the shoots were hindered by a dry, smooth plant product that Nyle dimly remembered as cardboard. Nyle's face collapsed and partially liquefied—an uncomfortable process he did not soon wish to repeat. As moon followed moon he felt long-suffering, and then he forgot how to feel long-suffering and began to feel a crude, incurious misanthropy. When his dark chamber moved, and when suddenly, tumbling, he was swarmed with light prickles that reached down to the few places in his starchy interior that still lived, he made out a looming human face and saw it recoil. There was an exclamation of fear, which pleased him. "It's vile!" he heard the face say. *Ah*, soundlessly chuckled the thing that was once Nyle, *it's another historian of agricultural technology*. Emboldened by the fresher air, he readied his pale tentacles for the final gleaning, waiting for nightfall.

ELVIS'S BATHROOM

Pagan Kennedy

Pagan Kennedy is the editor of *Pagan's Head*, a punk 'zine from Allston, Massachusetts. She also produces *Pagan's World*, a show on cable television in the Boston area. Her stories have appeared in *The Quarterly*, *Story Quarterly*, and *The Village Voice Literary Supplement*; her critical writings appear regularly in *The Nation* and *The Village Voice*, and a new book, *'zine*, will be out soon.

"Elvis's Bathroom" comes from Kennedy's engaging first collection of fiction, *Stripping and Other Stories*, about American life and "females who don't fit in." I highly recommend it.

—T. W.

On Elvis TV specials they tell you he "passed away," makes it sound like he died in bed. Truth is, Elvis died on the can, then he fell on the floor and curled up like a bug. Great, huh? The king of rock and roll dead on the floor with his pants around his ankles.

I never would've found out about that, or any of the cool stuff I found out about, if I hadn't got my tattoo. We'd just hitched to New York, my bullet-headed boyfriend and me, out two days of high school to see a band play. Before the concert we were hanging out in the park and I fell asleep—must've been the shit pot we'd bought. I had this dream about an upside-down Jesus hanging on an upside-down cross. Jesus's lips were all covered with spit and blood and I thought he was saying, "You got to stop ignoring me, Spike."

After the concert, me and my boyfriend went down by the docks—where the slaughterhouses are and it smells like fish—and into one of those all-night tattoo places. Underneath the eagles and naked ladies and anchors hung up over the counter is this tall guy with his eyebrows grown together.

I said I wanted that one on the wall, the cross, only upside-down and with no Jesus on it.

He goes, "Look, kid, I only do what you see up there. I ain't no artist." Then he started telling me what a bitch a tattoo is to get off—but actually that's why I wanted one. When I had the dream, I knew this upside-down Jesus was my Jesus, and he wanted me to do the coolest stuff, like stay in New York and be in a band instead of hitching back to New Hampshire the next day.

But I couldn't figure out how to stay in New York, cause I didn't know anyone. So getting the tattoo was like a pact with the upside-down Jesus.

The guy's hand was on the counter, and I put my hand on his and went, "Aw, mister, aw, pretty please?"

So he finally said okay, and let me up on the chair, which looked like a dentist's chair, except that it was all stained with dark brown spots, maybe dried blood. The guy worked slow, one dot at a time and each one felt like a tiny cigarette burn on my arm. The tattoo didn't look like anything at first, but when it was finished it was just like I wanted. And I was thinking that's how my life would be if I followed the upside-down Jesus—one cool thing after the other, and later I'd see how all along it'd fit together.

A year later, when I'd just gotten out of high school, I was thinking I'd try to move to New York. Then this friend of mine who went to my school in New Hampshire, but a year ahead of me—Oona—called. She was living in the seedy part of Boston, where the hard-core and garage scene was. She said they needed someone in her house.

I went down for a day to look and the place was just my style: graffiti with the names of bands like UFO Baby and Reptile Head (Oona said they used to practice in the basement), stolen gravestone leaning against the banister on the staircase, big plastic Santa with a gas mask out on the porch, and in the kitchen, a bunch of chairs they obviously got off the sidewalk on trash day.

When Oona and me got to the bathroom, I saw this upside-down crucifix hanging from the chain you pull to make the toilet flush. Seeing that made me realize I wasn't supposed to go to New York at all.

I went, "Oona, check it out—just like on my arm," and I showed her my tattoo. I wanted her to see this was something amazing, 'cause for me it was a sign that I should live in this house.

She went, "That's all over the place in this neighborhood. It's a witchcraft thing." Oona's never freaked out by anything. She's great—a real curvy girl with long black hair, wears old lace dresses, smells sweet as a graveyard.

She started telling me about the house. What really freaked me out was that Juan Hombre, who used to be with the Benign Tumors, still lived in the living room. They didn't make him pay rent cause he was a celebrity. Even living up in New Hampshire, I'd heard of the Tumors. They'd do covers of songs like "Going to the Chapel," first straight, like they were a '50s lounge band, and then they'd let loose on their own version and everyone watching would tear each other apart. Just when they were starting to get airplay, they broke up.

They put out one record, which I had. I couldn't even believe I owned it, it was so cool. On the back of the jacket was a picture of each Tumor. In Juan Hombre's he was jumping off the stage, twisted up in the air like a wrung-out rag—a skinny guy with heavy cheekbones, dark skin and wild black hair. He was the coolest-looking one of all of them. And when I thought of that picture again, I realized he looked like the upside-down Jesus in my dream.

I met him the day I moved in; there he was, sitting at the kitchen table, eating bread and reading the *New York Post*. He looked like a vampire, skinny as hell with dark circles under his eyes.

I told him I was the new girl moving in and sat down. I go, "I loved that record you guys put out."

"Thanks," he said, but he seemed embarrassed. I go. "So, is your name really Juan Hombre?"

He said, making fun of himself, "No that's my stage name. My real name's Mark Martinez, and I'm not even Spanish, just a Portugee boy."

I go, "What?"

"Portuguese—you know, sausages, sweet bread, cork farmers."

I was spending a lot of time in the kitchen, wailing away on this African drum I had.

Juan would come in there a lot to get things—a beer or something—but then he'd sit down at the table and we'd start talking. Mostly we talked about Elvis. Me and Juan didn't give a shit about the early Elvis; we were into the late Elvis, like what he ate—fried peanut butter, bacon and banana sandwiches—and all the pills he took.

Before I met Juan, I didn't even know anything about Elvis. I thought he was supposed to be like Pat Boone. But we'd sit there at the kitchen table, and Juan would tell me Elvis stories. When Elvis didn't like a TV show, he'd take his cool-looking gun out of his belt and shoot out the TV; he stayed in his hotel room in Vegas where they brought him new TVs all the time. He could swallow 16 pills at once. He'd get all these girls to strip down to their underwear and wrestle on top of the bed, and he'd sit on the floor watching. He called his dick "Little Elvis."

The weirdest shit was about how Elvis died: like, when they did the autopsy on him, they practically found a drug store in his stomach, but the thing is, though, creepy thing is, none of the pills were digested. What I'm saying is, Elvis didn't die from pills like everyone thinks; he died from something else.

Before the end, he did a lot of reading—right there on the can. He got real religious, but in an Elvis way, reading stuff about UFO cults, Voodoo, Atlantis, raising people from the dead, same time as he was reading the Bible and considering himself some kind of big Christian.

Anyways, just after Juan told me about how Elvis died, I had this dream about him sitting in the bathroom reading—this book just like the Bible only it's the other Bible and it tells about Elvis's own Jesus. Elvis says some words out loud from the book and this other Jesus comes in through the door. He's a skeleton, with flames all around his bones and skull. The skeleton-Jesus touches Elvis on the forehead with one flaming finger, and that's when Elvis dies.

I said to Juan, "I want to go to Graceland. I feel like if I could just see his bathroom, I'd have a revelation or something." I was afraid to ask him to come, but then he said, "Yeah, let's do it. When do you want to go?" Our trip to Graceland—we talked about it a lot, but I think it was really just a way of saying we wanted to sleep together.

A couple days later, Juan asked me out on a "Date with Hombre," as he called it. We went to Deli-King—the diner where all the punks and street people hang out—and it was amazing being in there with him. We could barely get to a table, what with at least six people going, "Hey, Juan, where been? We missed you, man," and they all want to talk to him. The only ones who didn't recognize him were the real hard-core street people—only thing they talk to is their coffee.

Meat Hook, crazy fucker and former star of UFO Baby, stood up and clapped Juan on the back. He was tall and skinny with his hair in a greasy ponytail and a skull tattooed on his forehead. "Juan," he said, "we got a room open in our house. You want to live on Ashford?"

"Right now I'm okay," Juan said as we sat down. Juan was so cool I could practically see an aura around him; I couldn't believe it was me there in the booth with him. He was wearing a leather jacket someone had given him, just like that, cause they liked the Tumors. His hands stuck out of the sleeves, brown and bony with scars all over them from his job in this lab hauling boxes of radioactive waste. I thought how his hands would feel like sandpaper sliding over my skin.

He started telling me Deli-King stories, like the time him and Kirk were in there and tried to steal one of the little pictures of the Parthenon off the wall. That was a few years ago.

"You sure've been here a long time—the way everyone knows you and shit," I said.

Then he came as close as I'd ever seen to getting annoyed. He said he was planning to move to New York real soon. He was sick and tired of Boston—he couldn't get any good band going here cause he already knew everybody and he knew he didn't want to play with any of them.

Nothing happened on our date, except that we came up with an idea for a band. I was already just starting as the drummer in a hard-core band called Train Wreck, but I didn't see why I couldn't do a band with Juan, too. It was going to be called Elvis: What Happened? I was going to be the Elvis impersonator and Juan would play guitar. We'd do the music that Elvis would have done if only the Colonel hadn't put him in all those corny movies. Juan was sure that if it weren't for the Colonel, Elvis would've gotten together with Jimi Hendrix, so he was going to play his guitar like Jimi would've.

I said to Juan, "This is a good idea and all, but something about it seems weird. I mean, everybody talks about what Elvis would've been like, but I've been thinking that you couldn't have an Elvis without a Colonel Parker. That's just the way it is, you know?" I was kind of kidding, but in another way, I wasn't. I said, "It's like, see, at the cosmic level there's an Elvis force and a Colonel Parker force, and the Elvis force is everything young and cool and the Colonel force is everything old and mean and money-grubbing. But they're two sides of the same thing; they're the same person."

Juan was laughing at me, which made me kind of mad, but then he said, "That'll be part of Elvis: What Happened? We'll start with a dimmed light, and you'll walk out in your Elvis costume and explain that." Maybe that's why Elvis: What happened? never got off the ground. Right from the beginning it was too conceptual.

Well, actually, the other problem was Juan. He kept playing out of my singing range, so I go, "Come on, you're only playing in B flat. I can't sing that low."

He goes, "I can't help playing in B flat. That's my key. I'm just a one-key Portugee."

And every time I fucked up, Juan seemed to take it like a sign that the whole thing would never work out. He'd hunch up over his guitar more and maybe run up and down the scales once, like he was already thinking about something else.

I kept going, "Juan, I know it sounds bad now, but it'll get good if we practice."

This guy in Train Wreck used to play with Juan and he tells me, "Juan's a nice guy, and an amazing guitarist when he was with the Tumors. But he was so depressed when I tried to play with him that I had to drop him." I was wondering if maybe Juan was too good of a guitarist for all of us.

One day we went to a party at Timmy's. Timmy and her friends are the fashion kind of punk, like with dyed hair that hangs just right over their eyes, antique clothes and pointy English shoes—and always look like they just took a shower.

Me, I'm tall and I was muscular then because I worked at UPS throwing boxes onto the trucks. Plus, I had a crew cut. This particular day, I was wearing what I always wear: combat boots, jeans and a muscle shirt so my tattoo showed.

All the fashion punks were ignoring me. To top it off, Juan was kind of ignoring me too. He was talking to Timmy mostly and I was wondering whether they'd ever slept together. She had on this '60s miniskirt that showed just how toothpicky her legs were. I couldn't take it. I was sick anyways, so I told Juan I was leaving.

I walked home and got in bed—had chills and was lying under all my blankets shivering. I nodded out in that weird way you do when you get a fever, but woke up when I heard Juan come home. I was thinking, "Is he going to come up to my room?" and he did. He stood in the doorway for a minute, looking at me lying there.

"My face is numb," he said. "I can't understand it; I only had two drinks." He walked over to my bed like he was walking in a moving subway car, hands out in front of him. He looked around for a minute like he didn't know what to do, then he sat on my bed, his hip on my stomach through the covers.

I was sure they'd put 'ludes in his punch, the way he could barely stand up a minute ago but could still talk—which is 'ludes, not booze. I didn't want to waste this opportunity of having him wasted, so I go, "Juan, tell me something. How come people are always saying you were different when you were in the Tumors? And how come you guys broke up?"

He said, "I don't know. After a while it wasn't clicking. One day I walked out of practice and didn't come back. When the band broke up, I realized I was just some moron who carts around radioactive waste for a living."

I couldn't understand how he could think he was a failure. I go, "You're the best guitarist in Boston. You could play with any band you wanted. And, besides, what about New York? You're going to move to New York."

"I'll never get there," he said. "I can't even get a band together here."

"What about our band?" I said.

He massaged my shoulder. "Yeah, well, what we're doing is okay, but it's a joke, a joke band."

When he first came into my room, the sun was just setting, and I'd been watching the sky out my window going from reddish to purple. It was getting to be twilight, but I didn't turn on the lamp next to my bed. It looked like the air in my room was turning purple too. I couldn't see Juan's face anymore. He goes, "Spike," and rakes one drunk hand through my crew cut.

Then Juan, just a shadow, lays down next to me.

"Are you crazy?" I said. "I'm sick. You're going to catch my disease."

"I don't care," he says. Then he kisses me. The way he does it is sucks, like he's sucking all the air out of me and my lungs will collapse. But then his hand on my stomach is real gentle, and he's sweet and calls me Priscilla. And soon all the light fades and it's night in my room.

Later that night I woke up and saw Juan was sitting up in bed with his head leaned against the wall. I thought maybe he was watching me sleep. But when I asked him what he was doing, he said, "Just thinking."

I started thinking how when I was fourteen and didn't even know what punk was, he was hanging out with Meat Hook and all those guys.

I sat up beside him. The moon was over the electric plant out my window, and his chest was lit up white, with shadows where his ribs were. I stretched out my arm, twisting it so he could see my tattoo. "Know why I got this?" I said. I told him about the upside-down Jesus. I said, "In my dream he looked like you."

"As handsome as Juan Hombre?" he said.

"I'm serious. Promise me you won't laugh at me?"

"No," he said.

But he didn't really mean it, so I said, "It seems like everybody who's really cool knows this secret. You know it; I can tell you do. I want to know what it is more than anything."

"Spike, that doesn't make any sense. Believe me, if there was a secret I would tell you what it was." But I thought he was just saying that cause I wasn't cool enough to know it: the secret was what Juan knew in that picture where he's screwed up in the air; what Meat Hook knew when they put him in the bin; what Elvis knew, sitting on the can, when his own Jesus touched him on the forehead, right where his third eye would be.

"Look it's now or never," I said, cause I was getting a week off from UPS soon. In a week, I figured, there wasn't time to hitch or even drive. We'd have to fly. I had the money, cause UPS paid good.

"Okay," Juan said. He said okay but I'd have to lend him some cash.

I was fine now—I always get well right away—but Juan was sick as a dog. He was coughing and sneezing and he slept even more than usual. He'd been sick for weeks, but he wouldn't go to the doctor. He wouldn't even take aspirin; all he'd do is pop downers once in a while. It was like he just wanted to lie there and suffer.

But he said he'd go to Graceland anyways. My UPS job was driving me crazy and I felt like if I didn't go somewhere, I'd go insane. Besides, I guess I had some idiot idea that things would be better if we were traveling. We hadn't slept together since that first time, maybe cause Juan was sick. We'd fool around, but then he'd say, "I'm sorry, Spike, I'm tired now."

This might sound stupid, but once we were in the airport, he looked different. I mean, nobody recognized him as Juan Hombre, and when I saw him kind of slumped in his airport chair, coughing, looking older even than thirty, for the first time I saw him like he probably saw himself.

Plus, we were on this crappy, cheap airline probably just set up for punks and people like that who don't really give a fuck if they crash.

And Juan, he hadn't even bothered to take Contac or anything. We take off and suddenly he gets quiet, just sitting there with his head in his hands, going, "My ears, oh shit," cause his ears couldn't pop since they were all clogged.

We got to Graceland by afternoon. They make us line up outside and the fat people with the "It's hard being this sexy, but someone's got to do it" T-shirts are giving me the eye. I tried to tone down my act for Graceland—sneakers instead of combat boots—but I still stick out way more than in Boston.

This perky Graceland tour girl makes us file through the door all in a line. Juan and me were laughing at her accent cause when she told us to stay with the group it sounded like she was saying for us to stay with the grape.

Inside, in front of every room, was another Barbie-doll zombie tour guide who said stuff and when you walked to the next room you could hear them saying exactly the same thing all over to the next people.

The stairs are right there when you walk in, but we didn't see them at first cause we went with the herd over to the dining room. Then Juan grabbed my arm, going, "Spike, look." The stairs were roped off.

I was pissed, fucking pissed. I went up to one of those Barbie dolls and said, "Are we going to get to go upstairs and see the bathroom where he died?"

"No, I'm sorry, Ma'am," she said.

"This sucks. I can't believe this." I started raving about how pissed off I was, right there in Elvis's living room where he probably did a lot of ranting and raving himself. The difference was at least he got to see the bathroom.

We did it all, every last idiotic Graceland thing—toured the Lisa Marie and the Hound Dog, his airplanes; watched a corny movie called *The Dream Lives On*; took pictures in front of the grave.

When Graceland closed, we sat on the sidewalk of Elvis Presley Boulevard waiting for a bus to come and take us somewhere to sleep—a motel, a park, whatever. Even though it was six, the heat was still blowing off the highway, blasting us every time a bunch of cars passed.

Not having seen the bathroom, man, I still felt so burned I had to smoke a joint and mellow out. I told Juan he shouldn't 'cause of his cough but he did anyways.

We were leaning against the wall around Graceland, which had writing all over it. I started walking up and down, reading; each stone had one message to Elvis written on it like "Motor City Hell's Angels Know Elvis Is Still the King," or "Freddie from Alaska came here to see you 3/12/84." I found an empty stone and wrote, "Elvis I came to see the toilet you died on but they wouldn't even let me upstairs."

When I sat down again, I noticed Juan had kind of fainted. His head was leaned up against the wall and his eyes were slits.

I hit him on the shoulder. "Come on, Juan, man, you can't sleep here."

He said, "Spike, I feel like shit," which was weird, because in all the time he'd been sick, he hadn't complained once I don't think. He looked all pale under his dark skin, and when he coughed he sounded like an old man in a bus station. I slid my eyes over his way, wondering what the hell I was doing there with him.

It was starting to get dark and he'd fallen asleep leaned against the wall when this purple Pontiac, with fins and everything, pulls up to the gate in front of Graceland. A black lady gets out and, real businesslike, opens a vial, pouring white powder in a line across the road, right in front of the gate.

I got up and ran over to her. "Excuse me," I said, "do you know when the downtown bus comes by here?"

"Ain't no buses after six o'clock," she said. She had hair all stiff and wavy, like a wig, and was wearing a cotton dress with little flowers on it. She was old, about my mom's age, I guess. She looked at me for a minute, then said, "If you want a ride somewheres, get on in back."

"Wait a sec. Let me get my friend." I went and waked up Juan. He said, "You got us a ride? You're great, Spike," then limped along behind me and we got in the back seat of the car. I was kind of ashamed for her to see me with him, some old sick guy.

She already had the car running, and when we got in, she backed out onto the highway. I said, "If you could just drop us off downtown, like anywhere, that would be great."

"Don't you children want some dinner? Let me fix you some."

I looked at Juan, but he had his eyes closed. I go, "Sure, that would be really nice. Do you live in town?"

She half-turned her face to me, only for a second, but I thought I saw a design of dots on her forehead, darker than her skin. "No, honey. I live way out in the country."

When she said that, it was like one part of me started freaking, imagining all kinds of ax murder scenes in this house of hers. But this other part of me knew it would be okay.

After a while, she turned off the highway. It was dark now, and I could tell we were in the boonies, 'cause all I saw in the light from her headlights was trees and mailboxes—tin boxes on top of sticks along the road.

Finally, she turned onto a dirt road and parked. We got out and followed her up this hill all covered with weeds and frizzy bushes. On top was her house, which looked like a dark, big box blocking out the stars.

"You live alone?" I said. It kind of occurred to me that she could have a son who would beat us up.

"My husband, Henry, he's over at the Night Owl watching the game on TV. That gets him out of my hair once in a while," she said, kind of laughing. The door wasn't even locked. We walked in and it was dark in there and smelled perfumey, like incense. She turned on a lamp and said, "Now you sit here and I'll get us something to eat."

We were in a living room all crammed with weird shit—a big framed picture of JFK with ribbons hanging down from it, baby dolls, Christmas lights, a deer head trophy with designs painted on its fur, a Buddha with a red lightbulb on top of his head, and a hubcap with a crucifix in the middle of it. Juan and me sat down on this couch the color of a tongue. Juan had waked up some and he said, "Looks like home," meaning our house in Boston.

The lady came back with bowls on a tray, and sat down in a chair opposite us. She handed me a bowl and I started eating this hot, spicy stew.

She said, "Now tell me how come you children are down here?"

I told her about Graceland, about how I wanted to see the bathroom where Elvis died 'cause of my dream about him. She laughed. "I shoulda known." Then she went off on a wild story. She looked at me when she told it, like Juan wasn't there.

"This is a secret," she said, leaning forward. "In the few years before she died, my mamma ministered to Elvis's hairdresser. Mamma was a spiritualist, born with a veil over her face. She lived here with us, and when the hairdresser came for love potions and such, I'd hear all kinds of things, 'cause he was so fond of talking about Elvis.

"Towards the end, Elvis, he was studying Voodoo. He goes down to Schwabs, the five-and-dime on Beale Street, and buys all of them fake books on Voodoo. He reads all them books and thinks he knows everything, like he's some kind of swami, even took to wearing a turban, I hear.

"Mamma, she tells the hairdresser to warn him; she just knows something bad is waiting to happen to him if he keeps this up.

"A few days later, that hairdresser comes back and what do you think? He says Elvis told him he had a funny dream. He dreamed Jesus was standing over his bed looking at him. This Jesus got a crown of flames and he's holding keys.

"Mamma says, 'That ain't Jesus, that's Pappa Legba, king of the dead. Tell Elvis not to mess with Voodoo anymore. Tell him to stop taking them pills.' By now Elvis wasn't just reading the five-and-dime stuff; he'd got ahold of the real thing—bought it from some bad Voodoo men for near five hundred dollars. Listen, honey, if you go making money off Voodoo, that's black magic you're doing. Likewise if you make a spell that hurt anybody else. Those men, they stand down by the river with the drunks. They sold Elvis a book, spells on how to kill people, how to make folks do what you say.

"And a week later, Elvis died. He was reading a book, the bad Voodoo book. We found out from the hairdresser. And you know what page it was on?"

The lady leaned forward and I leaned forward, even though I thought she was bullshitting me. "What?" I said.

"It was open to a spell—a few words you say, that's all—for summoning up Pappa Legba. Now anybody with sense knows you can't make Pappa Legba do anything; only reason you call him up normally is so you can ask his advice kind of, 'cause sometimes things here get out of line with the spirit world."

I was playing along, since it was her house and her food. "Don't you wonder what Elvis asked him to do?"

"Yes, I do," she said, real serious. "Elvis must of told him to do something, then Pappa was mad and struck him dead. Or maybe that's what Elvis wanted in the first place—to be dead."

I looked at Juan. He was still eating, his spoon shaking when he held it to his mouth. He smiled at me, even though I don't think he'd been listening to her really. I was hoping the lady didn't notice how out of it he was.

I thought she was trying to fake me out, so I said kind of sarcastically, "How come you're telling us all this? Isn't it a big secret?"

She said, "I thought you should know, since you got the cross of Legba on you."

She was looking at my arm—at my tattoo I realized. "My tattoo is the cross of Legba? Well, then it's just some kind of coincidence, 'cause I didn't know that when I got it," I said.

She goes, "Ain't no coincidences. You're a child of Legba."

She goes into telling me about him. Says he watches over crossroads and thresholds—that's why the keys. When people die he comes to get them and if you want to talk to spirits, you got to go through Pappa Legba. He's like the bouncer of the spirit world, I guess.

And I had the same feeling I did when I saw the upside-down cross in the bathroom in Boston—like everything was falling into place, and would keep on falling into place.

Viv—that was her name—said to Juan, "Here, take this pill." She was standing over him and he took it from her and put it in his mouth, before I could say anything. Juan, that guy never thought twice before taking a pill.

He looked up at her leaning over him and goes, "Do you mind if I lie down?"

"Not at all, sweetie, stretch your legs out," she said, and I stood up so he could put his legs where I was sitting. I took off his shoes for him. They were black lace-ups, the leather all cracked and scratched, with a hole on the bottom of each.

She showed me the extra room where Juan and me could stay after she made the bed. Like the rest of the house, this room was just full of stuff. There was an old wood cabinet with glass shelves and through the glass I could see all these amazing things, like a little mosaic bird made out of colored mirrors and something that looked like someone's cut-off hand.

She goes, "This was to be my baby's room, but she died before she was even out of me."

I was afraid to say something wrong, so I kept my mouth shut.

"It's okay," she said, "it was 19 years ago—I've come to live with it." I was freaking, 'cause I was 19. I wanted real bad to look in that room, but already we were walking down the dark hall to the kitchen, and we ended up sitting in there. She brought us each a glass of lemonade. I started to drink it, but she laughed and said, "Hang on there," and poured something from a flask into each of our glasses.

The kitchen was all dark, and the floor was crooked, which made me kind of seasick. There were plants, herbs I guess, hanging upside-down from the wooden beams in the ceiling.

I ended up telling her practically my whole life story. She listens like she's heard it before. Her dark skin shines blue sometimes and I like that. Every one of her fingers has a ring on it, like Liberace's. While I talked, I heard her breathing in and out the way she breathes.

Sometimes when I say something she goes, "Ummmmm-hmmmmm." When she heard my story, she said, "Most bad children are just bad, but some few are the children of Legba. They're bad 'cause they've got power gummed up inside them. Never happened to me, 'cause my mamma knew what to do, how to keep the power running through me. She used to sprinkle dirt from a graveyard on me when I was asleep."

"Geez," I said. "I wish someone'd done that for me, man. My childhood sucked."

Somehow we started talking about Juan. "He's not always such a mess," I said. I told her what he was like when he was in the Tumors.

She goes, "The more power you got, more can go wrong."

I said, "What about your mom? Didn't it go wrong with her?"

She leaned forward, even closer than before. She said, "She knew how to hang onto it. It ain't a secret, it's a science, something you got to follow at every turn and keep learning every day." She sat up straight again. "We women pass that science down one to the other 'cause you sure can't trust a man with the power. They spend it like money for booze, but we know how to keep it till we're all sucked up and old. Not that I have anything against men. They start out pretty, and when they're past that, they can work and earn you money, like my Henry. But they sure cannot understand about power, honey."

We were still talking an hour or two later when Juan walked in. He said, "I was wondering if you have any Kleenex?"

"There's paper napkins on the shelf there," she said.

"Thanks." He took one and blew his nose until he'd used up the whole napkin. "Thank you for your help. I'm feeling much better." He can be real polite sometimes.

"You ready for bed now?" Viv said.

"Yeah," he said. It was only about ten, and Viv said she was staying up to wait for Henry.

After Viv finished the bed and left the room, I took a look in that glass cabinet. What I thought was a bird made out of colored mirrors turned out to be the edge of a picture frame. I pulled it out: it was a square made of clay with colored mirrors and gold stars and silver moons all stuck in it. Inside the square was a picture of a black girl. It was all old and faded, and the girl was wearing a black dress, which didn't seem like a dress on her cause she was so muscular.

Juan had been sitting on the bed while I looked around. I sat next to him. "The plane leaves tomorrow," I said.

"It's been a great trip, Spike. I'm glad you got us down here." He was always sweet like that, giving me the credit.

"I don't think I'm going to go back right now. Viv said I could stay here."

I expected him to freak out, but he said, "I thought maybe you were going to say something like that." He put his arms around my waist and leaned his head on my shoulder. "I always knew you were too cool for Boston. You're so cool, Spike." I guess that in his own lazy, half-assed way he loved me.

"I'm going back," I said, kind of weirded out. "I'm just staying here for a week or something, not forever."

"Yeah, right," he said. "I don't know about that."

And then, by way of saying good-bye, we did it for a long time, real gentle. Later, middle of the night, I wake up and see he's staring at the floor where the moonlight, coming through the window, makes six squares.

"What are you thinking about?" I say.

"What I always think about. I'm trying to figure out where I fucked up." The hollow of his neck has a few beads of sweat in it, like a cup with only the last few drops of a magic potion inside. I lean over him to lick out each one.

YET ANOTHER POISONED APPLE FOR THE FAIRY PRINCESS

A. R. Morlan

A.R. Morlan has published two horror novels, *The Amulet* and *Dark Journey*. Over the past few years she has been making a name for herself with short stories in *Night Cry, The Horror Show, The Magazine of Fantasy & Science Fiction, Weird Tales, Obsessions, Shock Rock 2, Cold Shocks,* the Hot Blood series: *Deadly After Dark* and in *The Year's Best Fantasy and Horror.*

Morlan is a flexible and talented stylist, as this nasty take on the war between the sexes demonstrates. It originally appeared in the Hot Blood series *Deadly After Dark.*

—E. D.

Before Bob had a chance to say word one to me that afternoon, I knew that the Nutcracker Sweet had been holding back on him; I could tell from his eyes-averted, head-hanging shamble into the club locker room, that non-look my way that clearly said *Warning: Man who hasn't had a piece entering the room.*

Wondering what did you do to her this time to make her clamp those legs together, I decided to let him do all the talking; just nod or grunt or uhm-*hum* sympathetically, while he opened himself wide and let his guts dangle. I'd discovered long before that afternoon that asking Bob what was wrong would only elicit guarded praise for her from him . . . as if those double-pierced ears of hers could somehow hear him utter so much as one negative word about her miles away.

It was too bad that those bitch-keen ears of hers couldn't pick up the jokes the rest of the guys at the club made about Bob *because* of her; the jokes about Bob, the Ball-less Wonder, or Bob, the Amazing Pussy-Man—had to grow his own so he'd get some once in a while—but even if she could've heard them, I doubt that they would've affected her. Not after all the times she'd called him *"stupid"* in front of the entire tennis club during the annual charity matches, or the times she'd told all the other wives how inept and boring his lovemaking was . . . when and if she decided to allow him into her bedroom. Even though Jeanette made a pretense of speaking oh so softly, her brittle little-girl voice tinkling like wind chimes, that tiny voice had a way of carrying across the courts.

Beside me, Bob tossed his racket and balls into the open locker before him; the metal interior rattled dully, making a sound not unlike two cats trying to hump each other in a Dumpster, just before he slammed the door shut. I calmly began stripping off my whites, concentrating on the knots in my laces while he took off each article of clothing he wore with the sort of seething deliberation that is somehow more furious than flinging away one's shirt, shorts, and socks in open anger. And he folded each piece of clothing the way men who have to do their own laundry do it, before stacking it in a neat, corners-aligned pyramid on the bench before him.

"I have Bob trained," I'd heard Jeanette say on more than one occasion. "I made sure of that after I married him. Just like the other one . . . he did everything for himself."

Jeanette's first husband sure did do everything for himself—including that final blow job on the business end of his .38. And he was considerate enough to do *that* out in the woods, where he wouldn't mess up her spotless floors or pristine wallpapered walls.

Bob was putting his jockstrap (likewise neatly folded, in a tiny soft square) on the very top of his cloth pyramid, a white pinnacle of sweaty elastic, as he finally said, "Y'know, I used to think she was nothing but a witch . . . but I finally have it figured out."

I grunted sympathetically while scooping up my towel and soap on a rope (a rounded globe of tit-shaped pinkish soap, a playful gift from my own girlfriend), before padding off for the showers. No need to ask Bob to follow me; within seconds I could hear the slap-slap of his bare feet smacking against the tile floor. His wife sure did have him trained.

He and I were alone in the locker room/showers; I don't think he would've felt able to speak so freely if the others had been there. I wasn't even sure why he'd picked me to unload on those other times; maybe it was because I was a newcomer to the club and hadn't screwed his wife during those frenzied days between the death of Chump Number One (funny, she'd never mentioned his name—I doubted that even Bob knew it . . . unless the poor schmuck's folks *did* christen him The Other One) and Chump Number Two. Oh, I'd heard about Jeanette's kiss-by-suck-by-fuck climb up the rungs of the membership ladder; whenever Bob couldn't come to the club, the tiled shower walls rang with the stories of her suction-cup blow-jobs and her vise-like pussy, not to mention the intricate things she could do with her tongue. But her prowess between the sheets (or on the car seat, or under the stars) was her undoing; sure, taking a *piece* of something that all but sucks you dry once in a while is okay, but a steady diet of it would leave a man hollow in a month.

Or worse than hollow. Like The Other One with his permanent skylight on the top of his bloodied head.

All the members of the tennis club—be they single, married, or anything in between—had had her; every man knew the taste of her juices, the smell of her, too, but no matter how perfect her icy-blond hair was, or how carefully she applied those graduated shades of makeup to her otherwise slightly puffy and colorless face (Terry Collier once took a shower with her after an extended session and claimed that she was "almost faceless . . . just eyes, a lump of nose and a suction hose below that"), eventually the guy would realize that no matter what she looked like, or what she fucked like, he'd have to actually try to *live* with her—a prospect which sent the majority of the club members running once they'd satisfied their urges.

Until Bob came along. Nobody knew if it was because he'd been the next best thing to a virgin before meeting her, or if he'd had one of Those mothers who'd given him a taste of the whip across his psyche from boyhood on . . . but whatever the reason, she hooked him. *Then* she trained him.

Positioning myself under the shower head, I waited until I saw Bob hovering just at the outer reaches of my peripheral vision before turning on the water. As the fine sprinkling of warm water cascaded down my chest, across my belly and block and tackle, Bob's voice started in again, the words barely audible over the splatter of the shower spray hitting my body and the tile floor below:

"It isn't just that witches are supposed to be as ugly as they are powerful . . . although you wouldn't believe what she looks like without the makeup. 'Course, when I was a kid, that's all you ever heard—that witches were so full of power, the power to make people do whatever they want them to do. Witches had command over *themselves* . . . to fool people, and lure them into doing . . . things. The stories never said anything about their sex lives, y'know, as if women that ugly weren't supposed to want any . . . maybe it was their not ever getting any that made them vulnerable to the fairy princesses. Now *they're* the ones with the real power—"

Caressing my globe of nipple-tipped soap with one wet hand, I worked up a lather while nodding empathetically, all the while fighting the building urge to start caressing myself with my other hand. It wasn't a big deal with the other guys around, but it wasn't the thing to do in front of a guy who was only turning the "cold" knob in front of him and letting the stream of water hit him in his already drooping organ.

"—how else could they survive all the things the witches did to 'em, unless they had the power? Fairy princesses could consume poison apples like they were only covered with candy. Oh, sure, they'd play at being overcome, for sympathy . . . only way to lure in the suckers who'd rescue them—"

Smearing frothy lather across my upper body, I grunted in reply while Bob just stood there, wet dick limp, balls retracting like kicked puppies curling themselves into defensive lumps of quivering fear, and continued to speak to the walls which had echoed with recitations of his own "fairy princess's" exploits:

"She claimed that she couldn't find anyone who really loved her. Her first . . . one didn't. That's why he did what he did. Because he didn't love her. Why he didn't just leave her she never explained . . . only now she doesn't *need* to.

"I think she did to him what she's doing to me . . . and after something like *that*, leaving must've seemed impossible. Leaving means needing to explain, needing to answer questions . . . 'How could you give up a body like hers?' 'The way she flirts, she must want it twenty hours at a pop—couldn't keep up, could you?' 'She wear you out, buddy-boy?' Because they all can see what she is, they've all flirted with her . . . and maybe more. Not that any of 'em will come out and say it, but . . . I can read their eyes.

"But they don't know . . . not at all. Sure, she has the legs, and what's between 'em—*if* it suits her. If not . . ."

Hanging the now-glistening orb of pink soap on the "hot" knob before me, I worked the lather over the rest of my body but did manage to look over at Bob and give him a knowing wink—Sure, pal, every girl pulls the locked-legs bit.

Something in my glance must have connected, for Bob grew slightly agitated, his voice climbing a notch in volume, as he shook his head in protest. "No, no, not just refusing me . . . it's—it's much more than that. I mean, if she doesn't want me to get some, I *can't* . . . you can't get what isn't there at all. All I have to do is say something she doesn't like, or fail to do something she asked me to, and"—here he sucked in his lips until his mouth was merely an indented line hovering on the horizontal under his nose—"*nothing*. Gone . . . no way to get your fingers or tongue or anything in . . . not when there's no hole to stick'em *in*to."

My eyes must've registered my disbelief, for at that point Bob shut off his own water, and as he stood there dripping and shivering slightly, he continued, "I'm not kidding . . . she can pull everything *in*, lips, hair, the works. It's more than muscle control . . . no sexercise book for women can teach her *that*. Maybe it's instinctive—maybe it's something she learned on her own. One minute you're curling her hair around your finger, brushing against her wet lips . . . and the next, it's like . . . nothing. Just rubbing a patch of flat flesh on her belly. And the worst part is, how she smiles when she's doing it, just that little tug at the corners of her mouth while her eyes just stare into you. . . .

" 'Course, it's not something you can ask a marriage counselor or sex therapist about. Because she'd never admit it . . . and who wants to look like a nut? And I've looked in the medical books . . . no woman has that many muscles there, to be able to do *that*.

"But a fairy princess . . . now *she*'d be able to do that. *Would* do that. How else could a fairy princess stay alive when someone's trying to poison her? All she'd have to do is close up something inside, and keep the poison away from her insides. If she can do it down there, she can do it anyplace on her body."

As Bob blathered on, his words trickling like drops of water until the individual droplets formed a small yet mighty flood, I remembered what some of the guys had had to say about his "fairy princess":

"I'd of sworn she was going to slurp out every drop from both balls, she was sucking on me like my dong was a straw and my whole body was the cup holding the milkshake—"

"Remember those woven thingies you'd stick your fingers in, and then the more you'd pull to get free, the faster you'd be stuck? Well, stick hair on one end, and you've got her."

"She was *all* mouth, like she'd suck your lungs out if you let 'er—"

But that's just shower-room talk, I assured myself. And Bob's so starved for a little pussy he's starting to think there isn't any to be had . . . if he lets himself think about what he's missing, he'll really go nuts. If the food isn't there, you won't be hungry.

"—after the first few times, when I managed to reach over and turn the lights on before she completely pulled herself in, just so I could *see* it happening, I decided that she couldn't do it everywhere at once, so I'd reposition myself, dangle the bait over her other lips . . . but all she had to do was say very softly, 'No, I don't *think* so,' in that tiny voice of hers, and I'd start to get just as small as her voice down there. Couldn't even prime the pump with my hands afterward. Like . . . just her voice had been enough to keep me from firming up."

I'd heard that "tiny voice" many a time, her matte-finish lipsticked lips barely moving as that terse voice nonetheless blasted the air, sending shattering waves of sound rippling outward:

"Bob, you're so *stupid*—"

"The man can't do *anything* right—"

"The only way to live with a man is to keep him on his own side of the bed as much as possible—"

And that's just supreme-bitch talk, I thought; thousands of other women say the same things, while their men grovel and scrape and put up with it in the hopes of being rewarded with a blow job and a little action afterwards . . . isn't it?

"—'course, what she can do to herself, and to my body, that's temporary, but what happened to my stuff, now that, *that's* another story altogether," Bob was saying, and at that point, as the soap foam dried with small popping and snapping sounds on my damp body, I reached over and shut off my own mix of hot and cold water. With the sound of the rushing water gone, Bob's words echoed sharply on the steamy white tiles:

"She uses her voice . . . only, when she's really angry, it doesn't stay tiny or soft. Y'know how a dental drill seems to get louder and louder as it comes closer to your mouth, until the sound is *everything?* Just that persistent *drone?* She's something like that . . . only more. I can tell when it'll happen now—her voice goes all sharp and flat at once, and she says my name like it's so much longer than it is: 'Baaahh—ob' before she really gets going.

"Once, we were in the car, I was driving, only she didn't like the way I was driving, she always says I drive too slow, 'pokey,' as she puts it, and she goes 'Baaahh—ob, put your *foot* on the pedal, don't play footsies with it, *stomp* it,' only she was speaking too high to get the pedal itself . . . but when my fingers started to sink into the steering wheel, I knew I'd better get the car moving. It took weeks for the plastic to go back to normal. . . . I stayed away from the club for all that time, because I was afraid someone might see what happened to the wheel and ask what happened.

"Maybe it's their voices . . . maybe fairy princesses can shatter anything that might hurt them, neutralize the poisons in the apple, y'know? Those tight little voices, aimed right at a man . . . or anything he cares about. Tiny, brittle voices, like glass knives or crystal daggers . . . hard, tight voices with no softness in them. Like when she pulls herself *in,* and doesn't leave a bit of softness or moisture . . . and she doesn't even have to close herself up to stop me; I can actually be in her, working up a steady rhythm, then it sort of skids to a stop, no lubrication, you see . . . dry and rigid and unmoving, like trying to hump the hole in a bowling ball, only it's *not* something funny"—he'd noticed the slight smirk on my lips—"not at all . . . and she can make her mouth go dry, too, as if she'd never been able to so much as spit in her entire life. Can you imagine sticking your tongue into a parchment envelope? It doesn't even *taste* like anything. Same goes for the other set of lips. One second, she's a mass of petals and honey, the next—like I'm licking envelope flaps without the glue on them. Worse than nothing. Not even an unpleasant taste in my mouth to complain about afterwards."

I dipped my head to one side, frowning slightly in agreement. Even a slightly salty clam has its appeal, even if that appeal is in the complaining about it afterwards. But to experience . . . nothing? Not even the smell—

As if sensing my flow of thought, Bob leaned forward and went on. "And she won't even allow herself to give off so much as the odor of sweat if she feels I don't deserve to smell her. I suspect it's because that's something about her that I could appreciate without her actually offering it to me, or dangling it like a prize—the brass ring she can keep holding just out of reach. Now it's like . . . I'm not worth teasing. . . ."

Momentarily thankful that Bob had stopped speaking, I quickly turned on the "hot" knob and allowed the water to pummel my skin, rinsing away the drying soap film and Bob's strange words, which seemed almost to cling to my body like a coating of scum.

But my sense of release was short-lived; Bob simultaneously grabbed his bar of deodorant soap and raised his voice while resuming his low-key rant as he lathered his body with sharp, jerking motions of his soap-clutching hand:

"I guess this fairy princess has had her lifetime fill of sympathy, or what*ever* it is she needs. . . . I'm not even allowed to enter her bedroom anymore. Not that she doesn't need stimulation anymore—I can hear that vibrator of hers buzzing through the bedroom wall. . . . Apparently, she likes something she can manipulate at will. I've seen that thing, when she's out of the house and doesn't know I'm in her bedroom. She's . . . melted it, compressed it in spots, to conform to her own cunt. . . . From the little I can remember of it now, I'd say she's turned that trusty vibrator into an exact match to her hole, bump by bump, all the way to the hilt. Like fucking herself *with* herself. . . . I wonder, sometimes, if she'd have done that to me by now, if I'd pleased her enough for her to allow me to continue bedding down with her. Reshaped me to suit her needs, like a flesh-and-blood French tickler. No, not a good idea," he said, almost to himself, "she'd be leaving herself open to too much scrutiny. If it's one thing that fairy princesses must do, it's protect their powers, not let people really know what they're capable of . . . not unless the person witnessing them is so beneath contempt that *no* one would believe them. . . ."

No matter how bizarre his excuse for not getting laid was, that part of Bob's story rang true. The Amazing Pussy-Man was the ultimate joke at the tennis club; by that time, all someone had to do was mention his name, and that utterance would be greeted with snorts of derision and hoots of laughter. Bob had become the prince to his wife's Nutcracker; all she had to do was move those hinged, clicking jaws, and presto—instant eunuch. I glanced over and down; sure enough, his nuts were trying to re-enter the shell of his body, while his dick dangled like a defeated worm. I was almost tempted to take a second look, but didn't want Bob thinking I was going strange on him . . . but didn't it used to be a bit *longer* when flaccid?

Once Bob finished soaping himself, and his skin was covered with a mucus-like filmy coating of tiny-bubbled soap, he looked me in the eye and said, "I'm not just blowing steam . . . Jeanette *is* a fairy princess. If she was a witch, like so many women are, I would leave her in a minute. Let her have everything, pay her off for life. But doing that would just free her up, let her start searching and hunting again. Like what happened after the other one . . . y'know. At least he was able to taste something in his mouth before he did it.

"Taste or not, though, I don't want to do that—"

Beside him, I nodded vigorously and gave a snort of affirmation, sort of like the "good boy" noise you'd make when dealing with an obedient dog.

"—but leaving a fairy princess like her isn't easy no matter which way you go about it. Stay with her, and you might as well be alone. Leave her, and you wonder who she'll be trapping next. It's not ethical, y'know, knowingly doing that to another man."

"Uh-uh," I answered, thinking of all the would-be prey that had escaped her clawed clutches before Bob came along.

"Especially after what she did to me yesterday. I was about to pleasure myself in my bedroom, but when I reached over for the bottle of lotion I keep in my headboard bookcase, I knocked over the open bottle, and it was all curdled, like it'd spoiled or gone rotten, which was nuts, because all it *is* is a bunch of oils—safflower, soy, palm, stuff like that, with some vitamin E mixed in. So there I was, looking at the cheesy clumps of the stuff spilled all over my pillow, when *she* walks past my bedroom door and says through it, 'What do you want to use *that* for?' Just like that. Like either she'd been nosing around in my room, or she'd seen me through the wall and the door. . . .

"Her grubbing through my stuff I could take—I do it to her, after all—but for her to go . . . changing everything of mine, especially when she dries *herself* up in the first place"—here Bob slathered the soap around his already withered organ with a vigor born not of self-love, but of self-loathing—"and then won't let *me* have any lubrication for myself!"

I clucked my tongue in condolence as I hurried up and toweled myself off, hoping I could get dry fast enough to get back into my own street clothes, and then out of there before Bob finished his own shower. Yet, even though his words were growing stranger, something in his voice compelled me to stay. I don't know if it was the raw pain, or the first glimmers of regained self-respect in his words, but instead of hurrying out of there, I found myself lingering. And seeing that his audience wasn't about to leave, Bob placed his soap on the small shelf before him and stood under the pulsing stream of water, poking his head under the spray until his dark hair covered his skull in a flat, shiny layer, conforming to the rounded contours of his head like the shiny skin on an apple, as he concluded softly:

"While I was looking at that spilled mess on my pillow, I got to thinking. If she can do something like this to a fluid, what might she do to the fluids inside of *me?* Did she turn the other one's blood to something that poisoned him, *made* him do what he did out there in the woods? Because if she *can* do that, just like she can melt things or suck them in, there's no escaping her—even for a guy like *you*, someone who's been *warned*, once she gets it into her mind to actually *go* for someone—at least not while she's up and moving. But what to do with a fairy princess like her? Give her yet another poisoned apple? She'd just eat it to the core and go looking for more. By the way, have I ever told you that she finds you quite attractive? Claims she likes the 'quiet type.' So . . . I got to thinking, maybe poisoned apples, things like that, aren't the answer . . . not unless you add a little more poison to the apple, whatever. Maybe . . . someone—or a couple of somebodys—might have to do *something* else to her, even be a little less insidious, a little less subtle. Y'know what I mean. Only question is, would you be willing to be the one to help me add a little more poison to the apple—*or* whatever?"

I hugged my towel against my body, unable to answer him, even though I'd understood the question perfectly. And, as if realizing that despite the fact that the question was received, it couldn't *yet* be acknowledged, Bob added, his eyes (for once) level with my own, "I'm not just asking you because you haven't fucked her yet . . . it's because she *has* noticed you already, and, well, being married to The Other One didn't stop her from roaming and looking and *tainting* other men. Given her interest in you, it would be so simple to just let her *go* for you—and no matter what you might think you could do, I doubt you'd have much more luck resisting her than I did. But then again, The Other One never tried to stop her, or even so much as warn the others . . . like I'm warning *you*. Not that I could stop her if she does decide to try for you . . . but a warning is a warning. And maybe the two of us could turn a warning into an end to a need for all future warnings about her. I'm only doing this for *your* sake. Won't you do something for yourself, while you still can? Or, if not for yourself, then for the next chump she'll adhere to after *you?*"

That speech called for more than a grunt or a nod or an "uh-huh" or "uh-uh." With a few sentences, a scattering of casually uttered syllables, Bob had crossed over from speculation to supposition to surety. But warning to me or not, I didn't think I was ready to follow him *that* far into his personal plan for combined revenge and prevention—so I began to slowly shake my head no (after all, I could always find another tennis club, in another town) when the moist echoing stillness of the shower room was shattered by the shrill jangle of the phone in the locker room a few feet away. Since I was basically dried off, I wrapped my towel around my waist and padded, my soles smacking against the damp tiles like dozens of loud kisses, over to the ringing phone.

I heard Jeanette's voice the second I lifted the receiver, even before I'd had a chance to place it against my ear and mouth:

"Baaahh-ob? Is Bob there? I have to speak with him. Baaah—"

Her voice was almost loud enough for him to hear without coming any closer to the phone, but he did so anyway, walking head down and privates bobbing in time with his slow, defeated steps forward. But just as I was about to hand the receiver to him, I happened to glance at the earpiece, in time to see the formerly tiny holes dilate, then close with infinitesimal slowness after her voice had blasted through the tortured, malleable plastic—and before I gave him the still-contracting receiver, I realized that a fairy princess *that* powerful, that . . . *omnipotent*, might very well find a way to do anything to me, to *any* of the men at the tennis club (or *beyond* the confines of this club), *especially* when she found herself free of Bob. And Bob was so close to unleashing her, either intentionally or by accident (yet he did say *she* found *me* appealing . . . *me*, she'd specifically singled *me* out), and if he was subjected to even one more indignity—so, as I handed the receiver to him, I managed to catch his eye before I reluctantly nodded yes to his question about me helping to add more poison—or something less subtle but more foolproof under our combined effort—to that apple. . . .

THE BIG GAME

Nicholas Royle

Nicholas Royle was born in 1963 in South Manchester, England, and now lives in London. Since 1984 he has published stories in *Interzone, Dark Voices, Obsessions, Narrow Houses, Little Deaths, The Year's Best Horror Stories,* and *Best New Horror.* His first novel, *Counterparts* (Penguin, UK) was recently published in the United Kingdom and his second novel, *Saxophone Dreams,* will be out in 1996 from the same publisher. This is Royle's third appearance in *The Year's Best Fantasy and Horror.*

"The Big Game" is in the tradition of vintage J. G. Ballard and M. John Harrison—a futuristic England where ethics and morality are iffy and the breakdown of society is a fact of life. The story is from *The Anthology of Fantasy and the Supernatural,* edited by Stephen Jones and David Sutton.

—E. D.

"Out," shouted Groom as the ball fell off the edge of the roof 140 stories to the street below. Once again Groom had masked the bounce so that Bolton couldn't see if his return had been in or outside the painted lines of the roofcourt. Instead of protesting, which would pleasure Groom too much, he crossed to the dispenser and collected a fresh ball. He bounced it twice on the asphalt.

"What's the score?" he shouted. Bolton's facility for arithmetic was limited and Groom took advantage of it. He would usually win anyway, so there was little point.

"It's clouding over," Groom said, ignoring the question of the score. "We'll finish this set and we might have time for another."

Bolton bounced the ball again and raised his arm to serve, but a cross in the sky distracted him. He blinked against the emerging sun and deciphered the silhouette of a jetliner. It moved slowly and diagonally upward through his field of vision. He lowered his arm and watched the jet. Out of the corner of his eye he could see Groom's twisted shadow waiting impatiently, shaking its head.

Why had the planes started flying lower?

"It's only a fucking jet," Groom complained. "Are you serving that ball or not?"

Bolton served and failed to reach Groom's return, expertly lobbed into the rear left-hand corner of the court.

"Set point."

Bolton hated playing with Groom but he had no choice. Groom, self-styled commercial artist—in truth, sado-pornographer, purveyor of explicit sex and violence to the discerning psychotic—put regular work Bolton's way, which the photographer desperately wanted to turn down but couldn't. His financial situation was dire. Only halfway to paying off his sister's death duties, he was also struggling to keep up with the repayments on his small apartment. If he lost that he'd be on the streets. Groom gave him regular assignments at a rate which allowed Bolton to survive. Barely.

Photography was Bolton's only skill and while he was good at it, he was unable to get work elsewhere. The photographic art had become as popular as roof tennis—from Groom's roof Bolton could see at least a dozen games in play on neighboring courts—and so it was hard now to get work. To mention the stuff he did for Groom in support of any pitch would only prejudice most picture editors against using him.

So Groom had him. If he refused to play, the assignments would dry up. Groom liked it that way because he enjoyed watching humiliation take place.

Although he knew it was pointless, Bolton tried his hardest to postpone defeat, running, bending, stretching. But the pornographer took the set with his favorite shot: a backhander dropped just over the net with enough spin to bounce it out of the court and off the roof. Bolton swore but swallowed the oath when he saw the plane. A jetliner as big as the previous one, it seemed even lower. Maybe only a thousand feet above the roof.

Two flights down in his sumptuous apartment, where framed covers of *Paris Match* and *Stern* lined the walls, Groom wiped his face with a towel and poured Bolton a drink.

"Have a sauna. You know where to go."

Bolton looked out of the room down the wide hallway. The floor was checkered with black and white tiles. That way lay the bathrooms and sauna of which Groom was so proud. But to Bolton the luxury would feel like a trap.

"I'll wait," Bolton said, clinging to the tatters of his pride, "till I get back."

"Did you see this yet?" Groom tossed a glossy magazine on to the raised floor section in the middle of the room. It landed next to Groom's antique ivory chess set. Bolton caught the magazine's masthead flash: *Mindfuck #7.*

"That can wait too," he said, shivering in his film of sweat as he recalled the stench of open skulls, violated brains and semen. At least no one had been maimed or killed during that particular assignment; the girls were two-day-old auto-crash fatalities, hired out from the morgue.

"Good work, Bolton. Fucking good work," Groom said, as he stripped off and collapsed into the tigerskin sofa like an exhausted king reclining on his throne. "Keep that up, you'll be able to retire soon."

Bolton tipped back his glass and swallowed its contents. Through the open window he could hear the muted roar of a jet passing close overhead. Groom had begun to masturbate languidly.

"I have to get back," Bolton said, rising to his feet and avoiding Groom's eyes. "Some film I have to get for tomorrow."

He left the apartment and, slipping his ID Credit into the slot, took the elevator twenty-four floors down to the hanging corridor that joined Thomason to Jefferson. At the entrance to the corridor he needed the IDC again. The computer debited his account; toll charges were never displayed because they changed whenever the operating company was taken over, which seemed to happen once or twice a month. As he allowed the walkway to carry him along the glass corridor between the two towers, he looked down at the black ants in the sun-bleached streets and wished fervently some route would materialize by which he could escape from Groom. Instead, a jet flew over so low the glass walls of the corridor vibrated.

They *were* flying lower. He wondered if the regulations had been changed. And if so, why? It made no kind of sense, with buildings rising higher all the time.

Once in Jefferson he dropped to fifty and caught the monorail. The trains were a health hazard but he hadn't used his car in over a year because of the prohibitive cost of the Suspended Highways.

Needles, pads and belts littered the bench seats. Before sitting down Bolton picked up a magazine that was lying on the floor. He looked at the cover and was shocked to see his own work. The magazine was *4 × 4 Auto-Crash*, published by one of Groom's subsidiaries. Bolton turned the pages and wondered what sort of depraved individuals devoured the images he had slavishly photographed.

He got out at Anderson and walked home through the teeming streets cratered from tennis games. Once a week someone was hit and killed. But anyone either on the streets or beneath them was considered fair game. As Bolton unlocked the door to his apartment building a fight broke out across the street. He didn't look round. He shut the door behind him seconds too late to prevent the echo of automatic gunfire forcing its way into the narrow hallway.

He cursed, checked his trashed mailbox and headed for the concrete stairway.

The assignment was in an abandoned warehouse on the outskirts of the city. Three 16-year-old girls and an older transsexual in bishop's vestments performed a variety of sexual acts on the dirty, oil-slick floor of the warehouse. There appeared to be no script or attempt at role-playing, not at least until the masked gunmen stormed into the cold, resonant chamber, at which the girls feigned surprise. The gunmen wore black balaclavas and hefted ARX-53s, safety catches off.

Bolton used an automatic winder and self-loading cartridges to get through thirty pictures a minute. Because of the poor lighting and conditions—Groom's shoots were illegal and last-minute location changes very common, requiring a minimalistic approach to sets and equipment—thirty percent of these pictures would be rejected for use in the home market and sold on to third-world syndicates.

In the interests of maximizing profit, a second freelance operative was present on this occasion to film the action for the video market. He and Bolton weaved in and out of each other's paths without a word being exchanged. Both were professionals.

The gunmen, understood to be random terrorists, opened fire on the three girls and the transsexual. The intention was only to maim, never to kill, Groom maintained. They aimed at arms and legs but some shots inevitably went wide, for they were not terrorists by profession, but actors. The participants were paid extra for the risk of sustaining fatal injuries.

Bolton watched a volley of bullets tear into skin and shred the muscle of young limbs. Off target, one bullet opened up a crimson wound in one girl's stomach. He gagged and dropped the camera from his eye. The video cameraman, however, did not cease filming and Bolton knew that if he didn't carry on shooting Groom would not pay him. With great effort he ignored the girl's cries and flexed his shutter finger.

The terrorists continued their assault upon the girls and the transsexual. Serious wounds were sustained, fingers crunched, kneecaps shattered. The girl who had been shot in the belly, he noticed, was lying curled up and still. Avoiding the lines of fire he circled the group until he could see the girl from the front. Blood flowed from her abdomen and formed a greasy pool on the floor.

He faced an excruciating choice: avoid intervention and hang on to his job, or try to save the girl's life, thereby risking his own.

Instinct drove him as he dropped the camera and screamed at the gunmen: "Stop it! Stop shooting, for fuck's sake!"

He threw himself in front of the girl. Pulling a lens duster from his pocket he pressed it hard against the wound. She had already lost a lot of blood. He felt her pulse; it was low, and her face was so white it looked overexposed. A shadow fell over them. Bolton glanced up and saw the cameraman filming them. He increased the pressure on the girl's stomach. The gunfire grew sporadic, sputtered and died out. Rubber-soled footsteps faded away toward the exits. The video camera stopped humming and the girl moaned. Bolton bent right over to keep her warm, shrugging off his jacket to wrap around her. She moaned again.

"It's all right," he murmured. "It's all right."

The other two girls and the transsexual had left. A trail of dark spots on the concrete showed the way they had gone. Groom's money would reach their accounts in the morning, and it would be less than Bolton's fee.

When she had come around sufficiently to apply the compress herself he lifted her up and carried her from the warehouse.

"Bolton." Groom sat on the edge of his desk in the office beneath his apartment. "You know the score, Bolton. Don't touch. It's the golden rule. Look but don't touch." Behind him was a bank of monitors and a Steenbeck. The screens multiplied an image of Bolton shielding the girl from the gunmen. "Don't get involved. You're an observer." He jumped down off the desk and paced the room. "You're just there to take pictures. That's what you exist for. And that's how you exist."

"What can I say? They shot her in the stomach. I couldn't watch her bleed to death in front of me."

"They aim," Groom continued, "to avoid killing anyone. Naturally. I mean, what do you think we're doing here? But there's always a risk and the girl was being paid to take it. People sell their own and others' lives to survive. It's all a big game." He glanced at the ivory chess pieces then took a lilac-colored pill from a small tin and swallowed it without offering one to Bolton.

"Obviously," he was saying, "your fee will have to be adjusted. You lost us five or ten minutes of shooting. It's out of my hands," he lied easily, as he perched once more on the edge of the desk, chin jutting toward the mirrored ceiling.

At least you don't know I've still got the girl. In silent defiance Bolton thought of the girl in his bed. Of his night spent alternately watching over her and bent double on the couch trying to snatch a moment's rest. For so long he'd moved forward one step at a time, earning a little money to pay off a little more debt. Now, with the girl, he'd taken a diagonal move right under Groom's nose and Groom didn't know. Wouldn't even suspect. He had been exposed for so long to his own callousness that he could no longer be sensitive to the possibility of compassion.

Groom's windows rattled in their frames as a jet passed overhead. The soundproofing failed to keep out its bass roar and Bolton felt its cruciform shadow cross his heart.

Groom was still pacing, deciding, perhaps, what to do. Bolton knew he was cruel enough to want to punish him. Would he merely drop Bolton back into the street where he had found him a year ago photographing addicts and scavengers? Or did execution seem the more appropriate option? *Why should the fucker have such control over me?*

"I must think about this," Groom declared as he lit a cigarette. "We can play tennis." He inhaled deeply. "It helps me think." Smoke poured out of his nose like dry ice from a machine. "Be available."

Bolton was in the glass-walled elevator going down.

Total bastard, he thought and his ears popped. A dark shadow fell across the engulfed streets seventy stories below. He looked up. A huge jetliner flew so low it appeared to pass between the two towers. Bolton searched at the round windows lining the jet's sleek body and thought he saw faces smeared by speed and panic.

Walking home he plugged into a credit box and found that his fee had already been paid in, sixty per cent of the normal amount. That was still good, though, because it would cover the withdrawal he had authorized the girl to make in the event of her feeling well enough to book an airline ticket. He'd encouraged her to leave the city and found the only reason she hadn't already flown out was money. He had enough to buy her a flight to the coast where she could wait on tables for tourists and live like a human; the price of a flight being roughly equivalent to that of a clean conscience.

She was up and looking better.

"I booked a flight," she said. "I want to thank you." Her hands fell by her side. She appeared at a loss. One hand began to play with the tail of her shirt which had fallen between her legs.

"No thanks needed," he said, realizing with a stab of regret she was offering all she'd ever had to use as currency. "I'm glad." He began to smile and felt tears welling up inside him out of the struggle between self-disgust and happiness.

They spent the evening eating pizza and sitting at the open window that looked out over the slum quarters of the city where no building rose higher than twenty floors and all of them infested with rats, criminals and viruses. The streets and walkways were patrolled by self-styled vigilante knights.

He had to stop himself putting his arm around her at one point in case she misinterpreted his affection.

"Stay here until you go," he said, feeling glad of her company in the unfriendly neighborhood for a few more days.

* * *

Bolton threw the ball, twisted backwards and swung his racket. Straight down the center line, a long bounce, but Groom got to it and scooped it high and deceptively, deep back to Bolton's base line. He ran and reached for the spinning ball, just managing to pull it back. It fell mid-court and high enough to give Groom the optimum position from which to spin it backhand over the net by the sideline.

Ignoring a dark shape in the sky, Bolton lunged for the ball, knowing that if he failed to make contact the momentum would almost certainly carry him over the edge of the roof—the exhilarating risk for which the sport had become so popular. He felt the racket pull his arm out toward the ball as the shape suddenly mushroomed overhead and roared fit to pierce his eardrums. The ball seemed to hang in the air as if controlled by the jet. On the other side of the net Groom had almost ceased to exist.

The jetliner passed over and Bolton smashed the ball across the court to the far corner. Groom had anticipated a long ball knocked down the near side and was badly placed to make a run. It was his first concession in the game.

Bolton served for advantage but Groom's lob tricked him again.

"You're too good to let go, Bolton," Groom shouted, returning his final serve with ease. "Otherwise I would do so."

Bolton ran to the net and struck wildly. There was a lucky bounce but Groom was there.

"There's more work," he grunted as he drove the ball horizontally with topspin across the net. "There's a new game season starting this weekend. Come along."

Bolton's racket was in the way and the ball ricocheted back over the net. Groom swung for a lob, Bolton hung back, but it was a trick: he pulled the racket back a fraction upon impact and the ball lost its energy, falling tiredly on Bolton's side to bounce once and roll off the roof before Bolton could reach it.

"Season of what?" he asked, exasperated.

"Come to the game," Groom ordered, spitting onto his palms. "Bring your camera."

"Turn toward the window. Just a fraction. That's it." He pressed the trigger. "OK, move."

The girl leaned forward slowly so that her hair fell about her face and caught the transverse light. Using the automatic mechanism he shot a dozen pictures. The high-speed film would keep her features sharp and the movement would melt the light into her hair like hot gold.

"That'll do," he said. "Do you want a drink? You must be tired. I'll get you a drink."

"I'm not tired," she said, leaning back again to look out of the window at the slow-burning sunset. Jetliners droned in the distance low over the city's towering structures. Bolton returned with two thick tumblers of Slivovic. She smiled at him, confusing his emotions all over again.

"Maybe I shouldn't go," she said, referring to her flight booked for the following morning.

He looked down into his drink. "You must. It's your only hope. You've got to get out and live your life."

She swung round on the bench seat and stuck her head out of the window. "The planes are so low," she remarked.

"Yes. I read a report which said it had something to do with pollution levels. Though how aircraft can alleviate the pollution problems by flying lower I don't know. Maybe they want to preserve the upper atmosphere and concentrate all the shit down here."

He watched the short shirt ride up her back as she leaned further out. He wanted to touch the delicate hairs lining her spine, but swallowed the remainder of his drink.

"It wouldn't work if you stayed," he said, more to convince himself than persuade her.

"Why not?" She twisted round and found that he was close behind her. Her eyes were very wide. She seemed to think it would be easy. Without repeating the words she asked him again. He raised his hand to his face but outstretched it toward hers. She closed her fingers around his wrist. Over her shoulder he saw the long, low light thicken like honey and with the monotonous buzz of a fat queen bee drunk on the pollen of a lazy afternoon a jet pursued its trajectory across the sky.

Bolton met Groom at his apartment in Thomason and together they set off in Groom's Mazda on SH62. It was the third time that morning Bolton had used the Suspended Highways.

He had risen at 5 A.M. and resuscitated his own car, an old Ford model, to go and get his film developed and then take Anna to the airport. He drove onto SH6 without paying; he'd take the chance on the fine. The lab where he regularly took his films was open 24 hours. A lot of people in Groom's line of business used it because of that convenience.

When he came back an hour later he was completely wiped out. Anna found him sitting in the kitchenette with his head in his hands, sobbing. She tried to comfort him but he was inconsolable and wouldn't talk.

She climbed reluctantly into the passenger seat clutching a small bag he'd bought her the day before. It contained a wallet and some money, a small mirror and a novel. They drove across the city; it was the first time she had seen it from that perspective and maybe now she saw the sense in leaving. The Highways were busy. Jets flew above the car. Bolton tried not to look at her as he selected the right exit to take them out of the city, through the desolate suburbs, in the direction of the airport.

A line of low hills separated the airport from the suburbs. As Bolton negotiated the contours and they watched the scenery, they both noticed incongruous constructions perched like castles on top of some of the hills. More closely they resembled grandstands and stadiums and they seemed hastily erected and temporary. Bolton and Anna exchanged some brief comments but their words sounded brittle in the small car and they fell silent until they reached the airport.

He kissed her good-bye and felt her tremble. Her skin was like a river to his lips. Last night had not been a dream. *She's too young*, he told himself. Once in the car he didn't look back. Just drove. After the hills he pulled off into a burned-out suburban lot and cried until he felt empty.

He drove back home and some time later took the monorail to Thomason. Inside he was just numb.

"What's the game, Groom?" he asked as they sped out of the city.

"Wait and see, huh?"

He raised his pitch: "What's the fucking game?"

"Hey, hey!" Groom pointed a gloved finger at him. "Don't you fucking talk to your employer like that."

Bolton was in turmoil beneath the surface and he barely contained it. He had to hold his left arm down to stop it reaching over and grabbing the wheel to send them careening into the crash barrier and over the edge.

Keeping his voice level: "Where are we going?"

"Why don't you fucking sit tight and see, boy?"

Groom, you're filth. You're slime. You're Hitler. You're the Devil. You aren't even fit to be buried in the earth.

He recognized the route from the earlier trip. They were heading out toward the airport. Once in the hills, though, Groom drifted down an exit road and then eased the Mazda up a narrow unmarked side road. The slope leveled off and Bolton was surprised to see hundreds of parked cars.

"Let's go," Groom barked as he marched away from the car.

Bolton followed, undecided what to do. A jet buzzed overhead, frightening a mixed flock of rooks and crows.

Around the next bluff was another surprise. They had climbed up to one of the strange erections he and Anna had noticed from his car. Constructed out of wood, with speed in mind rather than durability, it looked like a sketch for or the skeleton of a football stadium. Two long grandstands on either side, nothing at either end and just rough ground in the middle where the pitch would be. The stands were packed with thousands of spectators.

Bolton felt the camera by his side and saw again in his mind's eye the horrible pictures he'd seen four hours earlier at the lab. He looked at Groom's back as the sado-pornographer began climbing the wooden steps to find their reserved seats.

When they sat down Bolton put the camera bag on his left-hand side away from Groom. In addition to his camera, film and lenses, it contained a small automatic pistol—the only weapon he had been able to find in the apartment. He was just waiting for an opportunity. Or was he trying to fathom the depths of Groom's evil soul before he extinguished it?

Groom spoke: "Can you hear?"

The crowd had fallen silent as if stricken by pre-match nerves and Bolton could hear nothing except the ever-present distant roar of a heavy jetliner.

Down at the front, men started shouting and signaling. Wads of bills changed hands and pencils scribbled as if in some atavistic rite. A book had been opened. But on what? The jet engines drew closer. Still there was no sign in the clear sky of the jet they propelled. The air between the two grandstands seemed to crackle with electricity. The roar intensified. Bolton pressed his hands over his ears. Suddenly over the top of the hill a massive jetliner appeared, less than a thousand feet above the ground, traveling at speed.

Groom nudged him and pointed to the corners of the stands. Men wearing protective clothing wheeled out medium-sized laser cannons at all four corners. Bolton felt sick in the pit of his stomach. All eyes around him were on the approaching jet, still climbing. Petrified, he knew he could do nothing. If he took out his pistol and shot one of the marksmen the crowd would lynch him. And someone would take the marksman's place. Shooting Groom would achieve nothing either. He had probably set up this whole thing as an entertainment, and he'd invited Bolton along to take pictures for the magazine specials that would follow. Somewhere in the stadium would be the video operator Bolton had encountered in the warehouse. But martyrizing the impresario would be ill-conceived.

"The point of the game is to try and get it down inside the stadium," Groom explained. "That's what they were betting on. That and the number of survivors."

Bolton recalled a spate of air crashes eighteen months previously. Had they been caused by Groom and his sick colleagues and rivals? He remembered the other ad hoc stadiums they'd seen on the way to the airport. This jet was not the only target of the day.

The shadow of the plane fell over the crowd and the laser cannon operators unleashed their fire as one. Struck in four places the jet was instantly crippled. An explosion ripped apart the undercarriage. A gaping hole was torn in the fuselage beneath the nose. The plane toppled from the sky.

Bolton had begun to pray to a God whose name he had mocked since his sister's death. He prayed that this was not Anna's flight. Prayed that hers would not pass over any of the neighboring hilltop stadiums. *Please God, she's already gone, she's half-way to the coast!* He did frenzied calculations in his head to work out how long a delay there might have been after he left her at the airport before her flight was due to leave. All planes for the coast would have to cross the hills. There was no other way.

The jet was falling. Snapped in the middle like a stale cigar it twisted and dropped. Passengers still strapped into their seats fell out of the wrecked fuselage. Baggage showered the grandstand. The crowd cheered, screaming with excitement. Couldn't they see that one of the wings was directly over their heads?

The jet fell between the two stands with an explosion of fire like an exquisite waterfall. One wing crashed onto the ground and ignited upon impact. The other smacked into one of the stands and ignited with a brilliant flash.

Bolton and several others had begun to run before the jet landed. As the wing hit he was five yards from the wooden stand. The explosion rocked him off his feet and he fell, grabbing at his bag. The ground shook again and a tremendous gust of heat like a solar wind shoved into his back, curling him up. A further explosion wrenched free the strap of his bag. Fire showered around him like a rain of lava and quickly faded.

He looked up. The wrecked plane was ablaze, passengers become human torches, some torn from their seats, some still bound down and flung forward from the waist. Arms and legs lay scattered like charred matchsticks.

In one stand the spectators gazed enraptured. Some took snaps with melting cameras, others mouthed expressions of wonderment. Down at the front they queued up for winnings.

The other stand was on fire. The wing had shed its fuel, spreading its blessing of fire beyond the fall of debris.

Bolton's bag had been shredded. He picked up his camera and adjusted the settings. Narrow aperture. Speed compensation.

Many spectators in the stand were already dead, others in flames screamed in agony. One of these was Groom. The sado-pornographer had staged his final atrocity and he wouldn't live long enough to cash in on it. Bolton thought of the thousands Groom would have made from this "game," far more than from *Rape Inferno*, in which the pyrotechnics had gone disastrously wrong, incinerating the featured young "actress." Even covered with third-degree burns, Bolton's sister's body had been clearly recognizable in the photos he'd seen lying about at the lab. ("What are these?" "An old job for Groom. We're clearing out the old stuff.") The photographs were a shock but the realization not surprising. His sister's death had eventually been reported to him as an auto-crash statistic and he'd supposed, since she didn't drive, that her luck had simply run out—most traffic stayed on the SH network, from which pedestrians were excluded. But you didn't ask questions of the police in the city: "protect and serve" was history.

His sister's murderer—for whom he'd worked to pay off her death duties—burned on the stand. Bolton aimed and squeezed. *These* pictures were for himself. *Groom in Pain, Groom Dying, Death of Groom, Groom in Hell.* He itemized the exhibits in his own private gallery.

His tears flowed as he continued shooting and were dried by the fire. Cinders landed in his hair. The terrible stench of cremation crept up his nose and he thought of Anna.

She was safe, airborne beyond reach of the city and its insanities. She looked out of the small window and saw the coastline approaching. In her lap she tightened her grip on the little bag. She was safe.

There was just a *chance* that she was safe.

People sell their own and others' lives to survive. He remembered Groom's glib justification of his work. *It's all a big game.* Bolton now realized that the jets had only begun flying lower when the game season was approaching. How much did Groom and others like him have to pay the airlines to get them to play? How could one put a price on so many lives. He wondered as he surveyed the charred devastation if the airlines even sent people to the games to place bets.

Helping the girl get to the coast was not enough. He had to chance it himself as well. If he made it he would find her and they would work out a way to survive together.

And if he didn't, he would still have the satisfaction of knowing that Groom's game had ended in checkmate and he would not profit from Bolton's move back to pawn.

BUENAVENTURA AND THE FIFTEEN SISTERS

Margarita Engle

Cuban-American Margarita Engle was born and raised in Los Angeles, and is now a botanist and irrigation specialist in Fallbrook, California. She has published short fiction in *The Americas Review*, *Nuestro*, *Chiricu*, and *Revista Interamericana*; her opinion columns have been syndicated in more than two hundred newspapers. *Singing to Cuba*, her recent first novel, is based on her travels to Cuba as a journalist.

"Buenaventura and the Fifteen Sisters" is based on Engle's research into Afro-Cuban history, written in the Cuban tradition of *lo maravilloso*, in which the natural is portrayed in magical terms. The story comes from *In Other Words: Literature by Latinas of the United States*, edited by Roberta Fernandez.

—T. W.

Imagine fifteen sisters shut inside their house for three years.

"Another rebellion is starting," their father told them, "and the tyrant's police are swarming like bees. You must not leave the house for any reason."

The sisters crept to the windows after their father left for work. They gazed beyond the grillwork of iron bars at the hordes of young men running and shouting. They backed away from the windows and listened only to the sounds inside the house. They listened to the whistling island breeze and the distant chants of vendors.

The sisters quarreled at first, but soon they realized that they were all alone and needed each other.

From the streets came the clash of *machetes* and the clamor of riots and rebellion.

Their father went to work every day. Their brothers disappeared. Their mother sat all alone, as far from any window as she could get, embroidering unicorns and castles and maidens with hair the color of wheat.

"Singing is now forbidden," their father announced one day after work. "Do not sing in this house under any circumstances."

So the chants of vendors ended. The dark woman who used to stop at the windows every day still came with her orange mamey, purple *caimitillo*, tiny red bananas, immense *fruta bomba*. But she no longer sang praises for her fruit, no longer danced at the window to make the sisters notice her. She no longer reminded the sisters of sunshine and wilderness. She seemed a different person.

Knowing that they should not sing, the fifteen sisters began to remember the words of old songs.

"Ugly people can't come to my party," they sang.

"I'm going away with you, dark Saint," they sang, "if you'll carry me to eternity. You want to leave me here. I don't want to suffer. With you I'll go my Saint, even though it means I have to die."

Their father heard them one day as he was coming home from work, and he was furious.

"No singing!" he reiterated, but the fifteen sisters soon forgot.

"Mamá, I want to know, where do the singers come from?" they sang. "Mamá, they come from the hills, Mamá, they sing in the flatlands. I find them very gallant, and I want to get to know them."

When their father came home and found all fifteen sisters singing robustly, he warned and pleaded.

"On every block the bodies of troubadours are rotting," he insisted.

Their father worked as a reader in a cigar factory, so the fifteen sisters decided to demand that he entertain them with stories.

"All day," he told them, "I have to read melancholy poems and silly love stories to foolish girls who cannot work without daydreaming at the same time. So much do they care about these stories that they are willing to each pay me a percentage of their wages just to read to them and keep them from being bored. But how difficult they are! If I forget to express with sufficient passion the flowery praises of some dashing hero, they threaten to replace me. So you see, it's not an easy job telling stories to women, and now you expect me to come home and start it all over again, reading to another pack of amazons?

"Ask Buenaventura to tell you her stories. You'll see, she knows much better stories than I do and, what's more, hers are all true."

So the fifteen sisters approached the maid, a very old, very fat, very black woman who had been born a slave and had been named for a ray of hope that good luck might be just around the corner. The maid had been in the sisters' house for thirty years, but she had seldom spoken to anyone.

When they had pestered her for three months, she said, "Well, okay, I'll tell you a story about a pilgrimage I once made to the shrine of the Miraculous Virgin of Copper. The shrine has windows of colored glass, and the floor and walls are carved from thirteen different kinds of marble from thirteen different faraway lands. The Virgin herself is a miracle, only as tall as the length of a man's arm. She is plump and very pretty, with her dress so fancy, all decorated with jewels. On her head is a golden crown, and she wears an enormous diamond in her hair.

"They fished her from the sea. Imagine, an Indian and an African and a Spaniard, very long ago.

"She stands on a silver pillar, and in one hand she holds a cross with an emerald this big, and in the other a little baby Jesus.

"At her feet are all the gifts she has ever received—butterflies, guns, hats, braids from the heads of little girls, ribbons, medals, shoes.

"I had nothing to give at all, so that is when I broke off this tooth, see, and left it there for her glory.

Buenaventura laughed. "Despite my name," she said, "I haven't had much good fortune."

The sisters, who were not satisfied with the story, but had no other hope for entertaining themselves, escorted the old woman out of the kitchen and into the parlor, where they sat her in their father's most comfortable chair and presented her with a silk fan. They gave her a glass of sherry, and one of their father's best cigars.

So she told them about the *ñáñigos* of the wild backlands, voodoo priests who could swallow flaming candles and smokey cigars.

"They used to walk across a bed of fire," she told the fifteen sisters. "They danced like this, with knives twirling over their heads."

She rose from her chair to show them the dance. Kitchen knives went spinning through the air and clattered against the tables and floor.

"They acted so wild, you would never have known they were just ordinary slaves. When they ate fire, they ate up the evil spirits too, and that is how the spirits were destroyed. Later the *ñáñigos* would calm down and receive their payment in beads and feathers, which they traded for coins. Some were able to save enough coins to buy their freedom, and they started to save more, to buy the freedom of their children."

Every day became a journey into the old woman's past. The fifteen sisters asked for dances too, and ceremonies, and rituals, and mysterious beliefs.

"Once," Buenaventura told them, "there was a man who was in love with a monkey. He had been away to sea, and to the North Pole, and Africa, and Spain, and China. Everywhere he went he killed ferocious animals and stuffed them and sent them to museums in great cities. When he returned, all he had was one live monkey and the skin of a snow leopard. He spread the skin on the floor of his room and sat with the monkey in the window, looking out, just looking out, all day. When a fruit vendor came by dancing and singing, he would buy a banana for the monkey, or a mango. One of the vendors was a wild young brown woman who fell in love with him, but he would have nothing to do with her. He seemed very happy just as he was, with his monkey friend and the ghost of that dangerous creature waiting there on his floor.

"There's no explaining men," the old woman told the sisters. "I wouldn't even want to share my room with a gentle ghost, and certainly not with the spirit of something angry.

"And the strange part is," Buenaventura swore, "that when the monkey started to have babies, the babies looked just like the man. That's when they ran him out of town. Drowned him and his evil monkeys in the river."

The sisters gasped, and Buenaventura went on about the river. "It's the same river where some slaves once went swimming, and what do you think they found there? A treasure chest. The chest was only this big, no bigger than a footstool, but so filled with jewels and gold that it was too heavy to lift. It was inside a rotten boat, the wood so old it was practically not there anymore, just the ghost of a boat. But the chest was still perfect, not a scratch. It was still locked, and not a key to be found anywhere.

"Next to the chest they found a sword with the shape of a crown engraved on one side of the handle, and the shape of a cross on the other. And the strange part is, no one has ever opened that chest. Over a hundred years have passed, and there are many of us who know just where to find the chest, but not one who would dare open it, not one who wants the trouble it holds inside."

The fifteen sisters begged the maid to teach them how to carve baseballs from mahogany branches, how to swing a *machete*, how to sacrifice a rooster, how to sneak up on a shark or an alligator.

After they learned these skills, they then got it into their heads to learn every dance the old woman knew, and poor Buenaventura had to show them the same steps over and over.

"We may not be allowed to sing," they repeated every day, "but no one has said that we cannot dance."

So the old woman got up every morning and instead of polishing tables and mopping floors, she showed the sisters how to shuffle three steps forward, then rest.

"This is how the old Africans danced when they were chained together," she told the sisters. "In a long line, one, two, three, clunk, the chain falls. The chain was their drum."

The sisters found an old rope in the courtyard, and chained themselves together. One, two, three, shoosh. The sound of the rope was soft, but with it they were able to imagine dancing in the first *conga* line.

They danced past their mother in her chair, and past the barred windows where men could be spotted running in scattered groups, hurling rocks and bottles, singing defiant anthems.

When their father was home, they did not attempt to dance.

"Between dancing and singing," he said, "there is very little difference."

In the evenings the sisters cooked for Buenaventura and they served her and fanned her and made her tell them more stories.

"One very wealthy family," she told them, "always had a very dark secret. Long ago the patriarch of the family died without having married the mother of his children, a dance hall girl who ran away when she found that babies were too much for her.

"So when the patriarch died, all his grown sons and daughters propped the corpse up in its bed, and they went out and found a young woman who agreed to stand by the bedside and accept the dead man's hand in marriage. The priest who performed the ceremony was nearsighted to start with, and since the old man was obviously sick, the priest made a point of not looking too close, and that way no one ever knew the difference. The church was satisfied, and the sons and daughters became legitimate heirs of a married man, and each collected a share of the old man's fortune."

"That story," said the father of the fifteen sisters, "is better than any I have ever read to the girls at the cigar factory. If I could read them a story that good, they would give me a bonus and a few extra cigars as well."

The next day he left for work precisely at dawn as he always did, his black umbrella poised to defend himself against a whirl of rocks and *machetes*.

As the doors closed behind him, the din and furor of another day's fighting resumed. Through the barred windows all fifteen sisters heard and memorized the words of the new anthem.

"This," said the maid when she received her command, "is how you dance the *rumba*. The man puffs himself up, like this, very proud, and becomes a rooster in the barnyard. The woman is a coy hen. He ruffles his feathers and pursues her, like this. She dances away, dragging her tail, like this."

That morning not a single lace bedspread or embroidered tablecloth survived. Soon the sisters were wrapped in curtains and shawls, ruffles massed along their arms, fabric fluffed in back to make long tails resembling feathers.

It was very hard to dance without singing, but the sisters became masters of a silent *rumba*, no words, no clicking jawbone of a mule, no rattles or polished sticks or ceramic jugs or serrated gourds, no drums at all.

For more than a year they practiced this dance. Sometimes a rebel would pass close to the window, dodging from house to house, hugging the walls and singing about freedom.

If he happened to glance in the window, he would see a very fat, very old black woman swinging her hips, surrounded by fifteen wheat-colored girls all decorated with layers of lace and ruffles.

The rebel would rest his weapons and think how long it had been since he had seen so many smiles, such a shaking of hips and rolling of shoulders.

And he would wonder if he had grown deaf from the shooting and angry shouts, because certainly there was not a sound to be heard, not a trace of music, not a single enticing lyric.

Then the sound of approaching police would send him scurrying like some jungle creature, and soon the girls were dancing without any audience, just dancing for the joy of movement, for the freedom of being like chickens in a barnyard.

Most of the next two years were spent in preparation for the end of the rebellion, which, the girls had decided, must come sooner or later, just as all the previous rebellions against other tyrants had ended sooner or later.

"All year," the maid had explained, "we were slaves. But we always knew that one day out of every year would be Kings' Day, and we knew that every year on Kings' Day we would be released to dance in the carnival. Some of us would return to the *barracoons* after carnival, and some would not. So we spent every spare minute of every year making our costumes and practicing our steps. And when it came time for the *comparsas*, we were something to see! The masks we wore, the headdresses, the flowers and candelabras, the dances! How we could dance when there was only one chance in a year!

"Some of us would dress up as scorpions, others as *majá* snakes, with real snakes looped around our necks! The cane-cutters danced with their *machetes* flailing, and the washerwoman with their wooden tubs, and some of the dancers dressed as runaway *cimarrones*, and others as masters with whips and dogs. There were *Mambises* fighting against Spaniards, and Arabs who sold Africans, and Spanish aristocrats in velvet coats and powdered wigs, ladies with hooped skirts and black faces. There were gardener girls in short skirts, carrying baskets of flowers, and there I was too, the *Sultana*."

"This is how I sang," the old woman whispered. "Good-bye, Mamá, good-bye, Papá, I'm off to the harem, and I'll not be home until morning."

The fifteen sisters giggled so much that the maid was afraid their mother would emerge from her trance to discipline them, or the police would hear and carry them all away to the dungeons which were so many and so deep that surely they could never be filled.

"Shhh," the old woman warned, "the Spaniards are gone, but their prisons are still here."

There seemed no end to the rebellion. Riots one day, ambushes, battles, public executions, military displays, speeches, marches, notices posted on every door, and then the riots all over again, accompanied by the hilarity of forbidden singing.

None of the brothers ever returned.

The father found his way home by a different route every day; this way one day to avoid a barricade, another way the next day to bypass a burning warehouse, still another the third day to escape interrogation at a checkpoint manned by brutes armed with clubs and bayonets.

As abruptly as it had started, it was over. One day the streets were deserted, littered with corpses and the rubble of destruction. By dawn the next day people were emerging from their houses, singing a new anthem openly. They moved in groups of thousands and ten thousands, beating oil-can drums, shaking gourd rattles, old men clicking their canes against the cobblestone streets, women clattering their wooden cooking spoons against pots and pans.

And the sisters came out dancing. They came out wearing lace and feathers, ruffles and masks, headdresses and velvet, flounces and silver, satin and flowers, beads and shells.

Buenaventura danced with them, holding her silk fan in one hand and one of their father's best cigars in the other.

People watched them and said, "They dance as if they have been dreaming of this moment all their lives."

The fifteen sisters danced the way people dance when they know they will never be able to dance again. They matched their steps to the drumbeat of the new anthem, to the clacking of wild parrots in a long-ago jungle, to the rattle of cookware and the chanting of fire-eaters.

The crowd grew to a hundred thousand, then half a million, then a full million. Every soul on the island was in the streets singing, priests, rebels, children, prisoners emerging from the dungeons, police set free from their duties, housewives longing for the freedom to walk to market.

And in the crowd of one million, only Buenaventura could explain why the dance of the fifteen sisters was so enchanting and so wild.

DE NATURA UNICORNI

Jane Yolen

The unicorn has become such a fantasy cliché that it takes a writer and folklorist with the skill of Jane Yolen to bring fresh wonder to a unicorn tale. In her most recent collection, *Here There Be Unicorns,* Yolen does this not once but many times over in eighteen enchanting stories and poems featuring the legendary one-horned beast. This lovely children's picture book is illustrated by David Wilgus and is recommended to readers of all ages.

Jane Yolen is our own modern Hans Christian Andersen, an award-winning creator of magical tales with more than one hundred and forty books in print. Her adult works include *Cards of Grief, White Jenna,* and the powerful Holocaust novel, *Briar Rose.*

Yolen and her husband have homes in western Massachusetts and in St. Andrews, Scotland.

—T.W.

"The unicorn," Brother Bartholomaeus said, "is a right cruel beast. He files his horn against stone. There is the rhinoceros unicorn, big and fat and slow, but deadly nonetheless. And the monoceros, more like a horse in its body. Though in the Indias, there is one more like to an ass, only less bold and fierce. There are seven clear references to the unicorn in Scripture." As he spoke, he pointed to a chart that he had leaned against the wall. A small wind through the narrow window caught the edge of the vellum, riffling it a bit. Young James, the duke's son, stood up and set his hand against the chart, holding it steady. He was that kind of boy.

Richard studied the chart. It was probably not entirely accurate. Brother Bartholomaeus was good in theory but his drawing left much to be desired. Still, he had spent years in the East, where unicorns were plentiful. And as Duke William wanted his people to make this year's Great Hunt for the beast, one having been sighted weeks earlier by a woodcutter, they were all diligently studying the nature of the unicorn. Even Gregory, who found diligence in anything but wagering a bore.

"What about its eyesight?" the duke asked. The men of the Hunt nodded at the question.

"Keen," Brother Bartholomaeus said, his shortest statement so far.

"And hearing?"

"Equal." Brother Bartholomaeus smiled at young James in thanks and rolled up his scroll slowly. The wind now puzzled the good friar's tonsure. "But as for its sense of smell . . ."

"Like a horse's, I'll wager," Gregory whispered to Richard. "Or like an ass's."

". . . it is more a horse's than a deer's," Brother Bartholomaeus continued placidly.

Gregory grinned. "You owe me a copper piece."

"I did not agree to any such," Richard said. "I know better."

Gregory shook his head, but his grin did not fade. "Then I will wager I get a unicorn horn before you do, and sit higher at the table of honor."

"Now, that," Richard said, knowing himself the better archer, "is a wager I *will* take." He licked his thumb and held it up. Gregory did likewise. Then to seal their bet, they touched thumbs. No one seemed to notice, except for the duke, who noticed everything. But he said nothing, so that was all right.

At dinner, Brother Bartholomaeus continued lecturing through every course. He did not stop talking even when flinging the meat bones over his shoulder for the Breton hounds.

"The great Ctesias," he said, "speaks of the powers of the horn. Powdered, it is a known cure-all. And of course, a surety against poison."

The duke nodded. For as powerful a man as he, with many enemies about, such a medicine was worth an entire city.

The boys, however, had stopped listening by the salad service and had taken to playing mumblety-peg with their knives on the wooden benches. Only bits and pieces from the monk's conversation drifted down the table to them.

When the servants had cleared away the crockery and there was nothing left to do but go to bed or listen to even more of Brother Bartholomaeus, they elected for bed, up in the tower. James, being the duke's only son and therefore his heir, had his own apartment one floor below Richard and Gregory's. But frequently he escaped the ministrations of his manservant and his tutor and went up the secret stair to spend the night with his friends. Young lordlings, they were seven years older than he and therefore held a great fascination for him.

"Do you really think there's a unicorn in the New?" James asked, sitting cross-legged on Richard's bed. He meant the New Forest, so named—of course—because it was the oldest forest in the dukedom.

"Your father certainly seems to think so," Richard said carefully.

"I mean a *real* unicorn, one that is silken and white, with an ivory horn right dab in the middle of its head." James said. "And not just some deer a peasant saw sideways in the moonlight. No one's seen one in ages and Mereton thinks they are all dead." James was very keen on the Hunt, this being the first year he was to be let on one, free of his leading strings.

"Mereton is a tutor, not a hunter," Gregory said. "I bet you a copper he wouldn't know the front end of a hinny from the back end of a hind, much less the fabled unicorn."

James threw a pillow at Gregory, who laughed.

"Stranger things have been found in the New," Richard said in his cautious way. He didn't have to add what strange things. Their heads—monstrous shapes—lined the stairs of the hunting hall.

"He's awfully certain . . ." James said. "Brother Bartholomaeus."

"He's awfully pompous," Richard rejoined.

"He's awfully fat!" said Gregory, which was what they had all been thinking and with that they fell over on the beds, laughing so loudly that the manservant, Bertram, came in and cautioned them. "My lords, if the duke . . ."

It should have been enough. Indeed, no one said anything more about the friar, but Gregory got off his bed and stuffed a pillow beneath his tunic and staggered about as though he were too fat to walk properly. He opened and shut his mouth as if talking without cessation, and that set them to laughing again.

Bertram came back to the door, and behind him was the tutor, Mereton. With an almost imperceptible nod, Mereton separated James from the older boys. James may have been the duke's son but, at seven, he was still biddable. He went downstairs to bed.

They studied about the unicorn for two days more, with Brother Bartholomaeus and his charts and a rather large tome by "the great Ctesias," as the fat friar called him.

"Great bloody book at any rate," whispered Gregory, though Richard blanched at his swearing.

At last, even Duke William got tired of it, sending the friar home to the abbey on a slow, fat jennet whose saddlebags were packed with gifts of cheese and wine and embroidered altar cloths. "Let him bother the abbot with his lectures," the duke was overheard saying to his new young wife, Lady Ann. "I think we know enough now for the Hunt."

Then all the castle turned to the real preparations: Arrows were newly fletched, swords freshly honed, spearheads tightened on their shafts. Journeybread was baked in the castle ovens, wine poured into skins. Saddles were oiled, bridles polished. It was a manly time, and young James fairly quivered with excitement till the night before they were to leave on the Hunt, when he had to be put to bed and made to drink a blackberry tisane to quiet him. *Perhaps*, Richard thought, *he isn't as steady as all that.*

Hunt morning, the sky outside was the color of barley.

Pearly skies
Herald a surprise,

warned Old Langton at the gate as they rode out. But as he always forecast disasters, they ignored him.

Though it was early Autumn, it was cold enough for the breath to stream out of the horses' nostrils in gouts.

"Almost as if they were dragons," James cried.

His father smiled at him indulgently. Dragons had been extinct in the land for over one hundred years. Turning to the master of his Hunt, the duke commented,

"Not much wind. So it won't catch us that way." He nodded at the master. "Lead on, then."

The master, Miles Cavendish by name, headed them west, then north, to the edge of the New Forest: the men on their great-footed horses, Richard and Gregory on small geldings, and young James on his pony. The master of hounds, a dour Caledonian named McBrane, and his pack of greys, Bretons, and two mastiffs the color of flame trotted alongside.

They traveled over a final great meadow, the grass still so fresh and tender that all of them—even Duke William—had some trouble with the horses wanting to stop and graze. Then they passed a patch of nettle and elderberry and a stand of ash crowning a gully. Overhead, crows wheeled about in the sky, warning of their coming. Under the horses' heavy feet, sorrel and buttercup and even long, bendy plantains were crushed. At last the Hunt came into the forest proper, where great branches of holm oak closed over their heads, making a canopy of leaves that held out the sun.

It was cold in the New Forest; it smelled of damp and mold. To the right, a pretty little stream stumbled over stones and rocks and even an occasional boulder, but quietly.

The cold and damp and quiet seemed to get into everything. From the moment they entered under the interlacing of oak leaves, not a word was spoken. Even the horses stopped snorting.

"Magic," young James whispered under his breath, clutching his reins tightly.

Magic, Richard thought, and said a quick Te Deum to himself.

"Magic." Gregory heard it just as if someone had spoken it aloud, but of course no one had. He wagered to himself his next three coppers, though what he wanted to wager about wasn't exactly clear; still, it lent him some comfort.

Cavendish raised a hand and they all stopped, duke and son, lordlings, archers, hunters, hounds. He looked about as if judging the timbre of the forest and the weight of it. As if he kenned something more from the leaves and bark and boles of trees than the rest of them did. Then, having made up his mind about something, Cavendish signaled them toward the right-hand path, and down it they went in a tumbling mob, startling wood pigeons who clattered noisily up from the forest floor into the oaks for safety.

They rode on and on, through lunch and well into the afternoon, till Richard wondered whether they were still going *into* the forest or already starting *out* again. They walked, then trotted, then walked again. Richard didn't say a word, of course. To do so would have been to disgrace himself and his father, who had sent him off to Duke William's service, lord to lord.

At last they came to another fork in the forest road, and this time Cavendish got down off his horse. He kicked about in the undergrowth for a while. Twice he bent over and picked up some fewmets, bringing them to his nose to test their freshness. Then he crumpled them in his hand before letting the pieces fall to the ground.

"Old, my lord," he said to the duke. "And roe deer at that."

"Not unicorn, then?" the duke asked.

"Not here. And not back where the peasant reported it either."

"Should we ride on, then?" the duke asked.

Cavendish looked around, then up at the trees and, higher, to a small patch of sky. "Make camp," he said, "my lord."

Richard noticed that everyone relaxed at that. Secretly, he was relieved he was not the only one.

After a spare dinner—journeybread, a brace of rabbits, and a half dozen pigeons brought in by Cavendish and his three helpers—they sat about the fire and the men traded stories of past Hunts. The stories all ended happily, though Richard knew that was not always the case. Still, on the first night, it would have been considered ill luck to tell anything else. So the boys heard of grand Hunts in which bear and boar and stag and grouse were brought back by the hundredweight, tied onto sledges made of silver birch branches and pulled by the horses.

Later, when the fire had burned down to embers and young James was asleep in his father's tent, Cavendish sang a strange song. He had a surprisingly sweet tenor voice and the song was unlike any Richard had ever heard, full of descending notes. It made him both angry and sad at the same time. The chorus was the same throughout, and after the sixth or seventh verse, they all joined in, but quietly, so as not to wake the sleeping James.

The horn, the horn, the spiral horn
As thick as a tree, as sharp as a thorn,
As long as a life, as bloody as morn,
It will pierce the heart of the hunter.

Richard fell asleep dreaming the words, but he could not—in his dream—identify the hunter.

In the morning, they carefully buried all signs of their encampment, mounted, and rode on. This time, though, Cavendish walked before them, patiently sorting through signs: for tracks, wolf scratchings, and the now-multitudinous droppings of stag and hare. They made little headway, however, for the forest was thick and the pathway grown over with brambles.

By the end of the second day, even the Duke was showing his impatience. Only young James seemed oblivious to the growing dark mood of the Hunt. Richard thought it might be because this was his first such outing and James was afraid to say anything to compromise a second.

But Gregory had no such fear. "This is foolery," he said, his voice dripping scorn. "We shoot at nothing, so as not to frighten the unicorn. But how can we? The unicorn is a right cruel beast indeed. Cruel enough to keep out of sight." And when Richard tried to hush him up, Gregory continued even louder. "My back hurts from sitting this bloody horse. And that's not the only part of me that hurts." It was a wonder the duke did not call him down. Richard suspected it was because the duke felt the same way.

As a result, the second night's encampment was less jolly than the first's. There was no singing that evening, and precious few stories, except for tales about life within the castle walls, a life that now seemed sweeter and easier than when they had left.

Richard had the same dream that night: the cruel unicorn horn piercing the heart of the hunter. As in the first dream, though he could see the face of the beast quite well, he could not make out the features of the wounded man.

The third day dawned exceeding grey, the sun the color of old pearl. Richard suddenly recalled Langton's prophecy. The dreams of the last two nights wrapped around him like a shroud; he could not shrug off the feeling of impending disaster. But to say so aloud would mark him in the Hunt's eyes as a feeble creature, fit only for the fireside. He remained silent.

The Hunt rode on. Around them the wood grew strangely still. Richard found himself shivering uncontrollably, as if he had caught a chill. At that very moment, Cavendish held up his right hand.

"Sign," he mouthed.

They dismounted and gathered around him.

"See," he said, pointing to the ground where hoofprints scumbled together in the fresh earth. "Most likely a male. They live in strife with their own kind, except during rut. The females go in herds, but not the males."

Richard could not remember Brother Bartholomaeus remarking on this, and Cavendish, as if he had read Richard's mind, said, "I had it from my dad, who was master afore me. He hunted a licorne once." He used the old country name for the beast. "Didn't get it, though."

"We will have more luck," James cried out.

"From your young mouth to God's old ear," whispered the master of hounds, signing the cross three times over his broad chest.

They made a great half circle then, for a sweep through the tangled woods, to drive ahead of them any beast so the dogs—now eager and straining at their leads—could bring it down. The archers had arrows nocked and ready. Only Duke William, James, Richard, and Gregory, being of the nobility, rode the final quartering. And Cavendish, of course, that he might better direct the Hunt. And the master of hounds.

They started several hares, and the greyhounds tried to give chase, but the Bretons and mastiffs were of sterner stuff. Even when a covey of grouse flew up before them, clappering into the lightening air, they did not startle. But one young greyhound disgraced himself thoroughly by running behind the master and almost bringing him down with the leather lead.

And then, with a full belling cry, one of the Bretons leaped against his tether and the rest of the pack joined in, leader and chorus.

"Something big, my lord," the master of hounds cried.

"It's the licorne!" called Cavendish, who had a glimpse of white haunch. Richard saw it at the same moment and had a sudden taste of something both sharp and sour in his mouth, like death.

Quickly the dogs were unleashed and pack and men surged forward, a tide of terror, crying out after their prey.

"Hallooooooo!" Gregory shouted in a spirited voice.

The duke and Richard and the archers added their voices to his, but Cavendish and James remained silent. Then the Hunt crashed through the brush, heedless of nettles and briars tearing at their clothing and exposed skin. One man lost his boot and raced on regardless, in a kind of rolling gait. Richard's horse stumbled, righted itself, raced on.

The unicorn led them through a gnarl, then through a small copse of trees. Branches smacked at them as they rode; one even threatened to unseat James on his pony, but gamely he stayed on, though he sported a reddened cheek from the contact.

And then they broke through into a meadow that was covered with thousands of flowers, red and purple and yellow and blue, like a tapestry. There, unexpectedly, the unicorn turned to face them, its white face flecked with silvered foam. The afternoon sun shining down caught the gleam of its horn—not ivory, as Richard had expected, but a pure beaten gold.

The beast was so strange and beautiful, Richard drew in a deep and painful breath before reining in his horse. Then he reached for his bow and two arrows.

In that moment, the dogs were on the unicorn. The greyhounds, being fastest, reached it first, harrying it right, then left. Almost disdainfully, the unicorn kept them at bay, lowering its head and parrying them with its horn. It only nicked one of the older greyhounds, but it caught the young, inexperienced dog—the one who had tangled the master—with a full thrust in the belly. Without a sound, the dog rolled over on its back, frantically licking at the blood and spilled intestines, before it died.

At the sight of the blood, the Bretons sprang forward, going for the unicorn's nose. A circling mastiff managed to sink its teeth for a moment into the beast's haunch, but it could not hold. The blood it drew seemed twice as red as that which had spilled from the hound's belly.

James cried out, as if *he* were wounded and not the unicorn. In all the bustle of beast against beast, it was the only sound.

The duke dismounted and unsheathed his sword. These were his woods and his Hunt, and therefore—they all knew without being told—the honor of slaying the unicorn was his as well. But the others kept their bows and pikes ready, just in case.

As the duke drew toward the harried beast, it threw off all the dogs as though they were of no consequence at all. Two greys went down with opened bellies, and one of the Bretons was bleeding from the nose. The mastiff that had sunk its teeth into the unicorn's flank was now missing those teeth and half its jaw as well, from a back kick. Its partner, as if chastened by the sight, had slunk off to the back of the Hunt. No amount of urging by the master of hounds served to send it forward again.

Still the duke did not waver, and Richard and Gregory leaped from their own horses, ready to help, ready to loose their arrows through the blood-scented air.

As if only then noticing the men, the unicorn raised its head and stared at them. Richard was close enough to see that its eyes were the color of amber and seemed to have in them a light of understanding that was neither a beast's nor a man's but something else altogether, though in that hurly moment, he could not think what.

"You are mine," the duke said. His voice, so definite, so possessive, rang out unnaturally in the stilled meadow.

From somewhere far away, a cuckoopint suddenly began singing, and it seemed to Richard as sweet as if it had been singing in Heaven itself. He was transfixed by the song and, for a moment, could not move.

In that same moment, the unicorn lunged forward. With its horn, it knocked away the duke's sword as easily as if he were a boy playing his first game with the master of swords. The duke seemed dazed and stood there, his body now fully exposed to the spiral horn.

None of them moved, all equally ensorcelled by the song, except for young James. With a cry of "Father! I come!" he flung himself from his pony and stepped between the duke and the harrowing horn.

The horn plunged into the boy's breast, shredding the tunic. The sound of the material ripping started time again, like a swiftly flowing river.

Richard gasped, drew his bow, and let one and then a second arrow fly, without even waiting to take aim. They both went truly into the unicorn's broad chest. At the same time, Gregory's arrow sang into the white flank. The remaining mastiff ran from behind its master and flung itself onto the unicorn's neck, never minding the shuddering flesh beneath. And there it hung on grimly until the end.

That end was swift and sure and angry, for while the duke cradled his son in his arms, the rest of the Hunt thrust and hacked and slashed at the unicorn until it was black with its own blood and their fury. Even the Bretons and greys tore at its flesh, savaging it till there was nothing left of the white beauty.

Richard was sick from the savagery. He would have gone back into the woods and vomited till the smell and sight of the carnage were all purged from him, but he knew what the others would think if he did. So he swallowed it back down. Only when he was certain he was right again did he turn and look at the duke, who was still kneeling with his son in his arms.

Richard was not sure what he expected—what terror and what pain. But he was not prepared for the look of ecstasy on the faces of both father and son. When he ran closer, he saw that James was—unbelievably—not harmed in the slightest. Where the tunic lay open and torn, his bare chest manifested no sign of a wound. Rather, over his heart, the skin was incised with the sign of a cross, like an illumination in a Book of Hours.

"I do not understand," Richard whispered, turning to look back at the unicorn.

What lay there, ripped apart, was a great black beast, more like an ox or an Irish elk. Its skin—what he could still see of it—was ebony and ridged. Its legs were massive, like columns in a church. There was a single horn, fat and riddled with wormholes, protruding from its inelegant nose.

"Monoceros," said Cavendish, kicking at the carcass.

Richard glanced at the duke and James once more. They were gazing far beyond the dead beast to the other side of the meadow, and they were both smiling.

When he turned to follow their gaze, he thought he glimpsed something white and gleaming leaping into the trees. For a moment it was dappled with shadows. Then it was gone.

"Do you want the horn, my lord?" asked Cavendish.

The duke didn't answer at first. He set James down as gently as if the boy had been a young maid. Then he stood. "Of course," he said. "It may be proof against poison. Or at least, so my enemies will think. Besides, my good dogs and that great beast should not have died for aught."

* * *

They rode home the whole way, arriving well after midnight. In the morning, when it was announced that James would enter the monastery at Shrewsbury as an infant oblate, Richard was not surprised.

Gregory's eyes, though, widened at the announcement. "And I would have put a whole gold piece on his becoming as great a hunter as his father," he said. "Did you see how steady he held his ground?"

But Richard understood. The duke's new young wife could have many sons. Why would she want another woman's child as heir? And certainly anyone touched by God's own horn was marked forever. Richard knew this with certainty. For when he dreamed, as he did every night thereafter, he dreamed of the unicorn, white and golden and swift, running through the dappled trees of Paradise, with Richard running, frantically, after. And always he was too slow, too unsure, too unsteady to capture it for his own.

BLUE MOTEL

Ian McDonald

Born in Manchester, England, in 1960, Ian McDonald moved to Northern Ireland in 1965. His short fiction brought him a nomination for the John W. Campbell Award for Best New Writer of 1985, and his novel *King of Morning, Queen of Day* won the Philip K. Dick Award in 1992. Others novels include *Desolation Road, Out on Blue Six, The Broken Land* (published in England as *Hearts, Hands and Voices*), and, most recently, *Terminal Café*. His stories have been collected in *Speaking in Tongues*.

Although better known for writing magic realism and science fiction, McDonald has written a few very powerful horror stories, including "Some Strange Desire," which appeared in last year's volume of this series and was a finalist for the World Fantasy Award. And here is "Blue Motel," which first appeared in *Blue Motel: Narrow Houses Volume Three* and is an homage to Bernard Herrmann, the great movie soundtrack composer who scored much of Alfred Hitchcock's work. According to McDonald, "currently fashionable quantum theory teaches us that an infinity of possible universes can collapse out of any quantum event. What I'm concerned with is why does it always happen to be the universe with the jam-side down? Thus I believe in quantum irony: Out of all possible universes, quantum collapse is configured toward poetic justice."

McDonald embodies this idea in a charming fantasy/suspense story using some familiar characters.

—E. D.

FRENZY

White car, black road.

Marianne Marianne, driving driving. Marianne Marianne, driving driving.

Looking in the mirror—glancing, glancing—away from the headlight dazzle of the oncoming cars—*glance*—is he there, do you see him, in the mirror, behind you, that highway cop? Did you fool him at California Charlie's, or is he still behind you, still suspicious, following, following? He was suspicious from the moment he tapped on the window and woke you up out in the desert where you'd pulled over because you couldn't drive another mile along that black highway.

Black shades, white desert.

Marianne Marianne, driving driving.

On the seat beside her, folded into a battered envelope and secured with a rubber band, fifty thousand dollars. Minus the price of a second-hand California-plate Buick.

Imaginings. Voices. California Charlie, sparky and Sanforized in his shirt and dicky bow: *hell officer, that's the first time I ever saw the customer high-pressure the salesman.*

Mr. Lavery, realtor's habitual spruceness wilting in the Phoenix city swelter: *I don't want it in the office over the weekend, Marianne. On your way home, make sure you put it in the night safe.*

Carmody, whiskey-breathed, flirtatious as only wealth can flirt, smelling of the department-store cologne his wife doubtless buys him every Christmas: *You know what I do with unhappiness? I buy it off. Fifty thousand dollars buys off a lot of unhappiness.*

Tom, damp with the post-coital honey-sweat of lunchtime meetings in cheap Phoenix hotels: *A few years more in that hole of a sports store and my father's debts will be paid off and, when the divorce comes through, we'll be together, Marianne.*

Marianne Marianne, driving driving, catches sight of the reflection of her eyes in the rearview as the first fat drops of rain burst on the windshield like crisp, juicy bugs. Hunted eyes. Guilty eyes. Are they there, Marianne, will they always be there, behind you, following, following? Not tonight. Not now, not on this long, black highway. It will be Monday before any of them notice that good, faithful Marianne, ten years' dedicated service Marianne, trustworthy Marianne, is not in for work; later still before they phone her landlady and find she has not been at home all weekend. And Lavery will leave it to the very last moment before he calls the bank to confirm his worst fears. You work for a man for ten years, you get to know him. She imagines dapper Mr. Lavery breaking the news to the Irish bluster and blow of Carmody. Again, she catches a glimpse of her eyes in the mirror. They are smiling.

She will be in another life by then.

The rain is hammering down now, so fast the wipers cannot keep up. Dark night. Black rain. Slashing wipers, squealing on the glass like the cries of black carrion birds. Blinding headlights. Marianne Marianne, can't drive further. Dazzling raindrops, tired and blinded. Driving rain, creaking wipers, rushing headlights, the money in the envelope. She must stop. Where?

There. The flickering blue neon of a motel sign, glimpsed through the slashing diagonals of rain. Tires munch wet gravel. Not much of a motel; thirteen cabins stretched in an L around the parking space. Rain cascades from faulty guttering: it's going to be a noisy night. On a rise behind the cabins looms a hulk of a house, all California Gothic verticals. Two lit upstairs windows are eyes above the devouring mouth of the porch. A silhouetted figure is a black watching pupil.

The office is unmanned. When she sounds the horn one window-eye is extinguished and a figure comes dashing down the steps, jacket pulled over its head.

Strange boy, such a strange boy. Tall, loose-limbed, ducking and smiling, never looking you straight in the eye. Puppyish, in the sense of a puppy that has been beaten, then rewarded, then beaten again for no comprehensible reason and one day turns on the hand that rewards and beats and tears it into five dangling shreds of flesh and bone. Mother's boy.

A stuffed crow watches from the top of the filing cabinet, black glass eyes glinting.

"Have you got a vacancy?"

"Thirteen cabins, thirteen vacancies." He smiles that ducking, beaten smile, indicating the thirteen keys that hang from the "Let Us Watch Your Keys" rack. "Don't get many visitors since they moved the highway away. You must have taken a wrong turn someplace back a-ways—that's about the only way we ever get anyone. Tell you the truth, some days I don't bother turning the sign on." His hand hovers over the keys. The wooden Ma and Pa on the key rack keep their glass bead eyes strictly averted. "I'll give you cabin one; it's next to the office in case you need anything. Now, if you'll just sign the register."

"Janet Leigh. Los Angeles," she says. Long before Tom and his protracted divorce, men had always told her she looked just like the movie star. December 10. 1959. "Say, is there anywhere I can get something to eat?"

"There's a roadhouse about ten miles down the highway," says the strange boy. "But you're not really going to go out in that again, are you?" Through the open office door, rain is sheeting from the overflowing gutters. "You'd be more than welcome to have something with me up at the house; nothing grand, just milk and sandwiches, but good homely fare."

Though the office is warm, Marianne shivers as if the cold edge of a knife has been drawn across her naked thigh. She feels eyes; watching her, looking into her: the eyes of Carmody as he flirted and teased her with his thick wad of notes, the hidden eyes of the highway patrolman, the slitted eyes of California Charlie closed against the California sun, the eyes of the black stuffed crow on the filing cabinet, the bead eyes of head-scarfed Ma and pipe-smoking Pa on the key rack, the watching eyes of that old, dark house on the hill. Despite ten miles of bad road in the pouring rain, the light and warmth and company of the roadhouse seem mighty appealing.

"I think maybe I will go on to the diner after all," she says. "Thank you for your kind offer. I'll be back later, though."

The strange boy shrugs in that puppyish, cringing way of his.

"Whatever you like, Miss Leigh. I'll be up waiting for you when you get back."

Blue neon. Hammering rain.

Marianne Marianne, driving driving.

In the rearview, the blue motel sign recedes into the spatter of drops. The rain falls unrelentingly, the road stretches undeviatingly before her, the speedo needle is glued to the sixty on the dial: nothing is changed, yet Marianne is haunted by a sense of impending, of potential waiting to be realized. It is as if, instead of turning off the byroad on to the main highway, she has instead turned off the major route on to a tangle of minor roads, some of which lead her on in the way she is to go, some of which lead her back to where she has come from, and some of which lead off to unknown destinations. Though the highway goes straight ahead, she feels lost, a lone traveler in the huge dark night.

When the luminous raindrops coalesce into an orange neon farmer spastically doffing and replacing his hat to her, it seems incongruous, out of space and time, something newly invented, isolated. Secondary neons reassure her, winking pink and mauve from the wooden porch: 90 Mile Roadhouse. Eatz/Drinkz/Snax. Grills/ All Day Breakfast from $1.00. Gas. Food. Ice Cold Beer. Open 25 hours. Light pours from the big, uncurtained windows. It looks like a big liner adrift on the ocean of night, far from any land.

The rain seems to be easing. Marianne switches off the frenetic slashing wipers. Ten miles. Exactly as the strange boy said.

A baker's dozen booths arranged in an L beneath the night-mirrored windows tempt her with smart chrome sugar sifters and patched naugahyde. She declines their invitation and takes a stool at the bar. There is something sad about single women in booths, like a painting she once saw, in *Harper*'s, or *Vanity Fair*, or was it one of the *New Yorkers* Mr Lavery left in the waiting area for clients? *Nighthawks at the Diner*, something like that.

At the piano at the north/northwest end of the L-shaped bar a swarthy Middle-European-looking man in ugly horn-rim glasses squeezes odd, disquieting chords and arpeggios from the keys: uncomfortable intervals, thirds, fifths, major sevenths that circle endlessly, never reaching resolution. A jukebox blows bubbles up its neon-lit columns, waiting its invitation to sing. Not tonight: there is strange, bleak beauty in the notes that hurry, hurry but go nowhere.

Serving You Tonite is Mona, a blousy, tired-looking woman who gives no clues to whether she is hired help or owner/proprietrix after a heavy day. Three calendars hang on the back bar: a local hardware supplier's, the gas company whose pumps stand to attention outside, and one from the Fairfax County Orange Grower's Association. Three calendars. About as good as you can reasonably expect. Four is perfection, but Marianne's never seen one. She reckons they exist only in commercial travelers' legends. Mona slides her a cup and pours coffee without a word.

The piano music spirals inward.

Tonite the 90 Mile Roadhouse has one other customer: a small fat man, perched on a stool like a Spalding Number 8 on a tee. Balding, sweating in the heat of the night. Heavy jowls. He has the look of a man for whom night is his natural element. Perhaps a commercial traveler, but for no goods Marianne can think of. Dark, minority things. He eats all the way around his fried egg, leaves it marooned in a sea of grease.

"Of course, I didn't think he'd bleed so much."

Marianne does not know what surprises her more, the words or the voice in which he speaks them. What is a fruity, oily English accent, like cold-pressed olives, doing in a place like the 90 Mile Roadhouse?

"I did that one in a crowded lift once. Fifty-six floors; fifty-five of them all to myself. I like to think I did their cardiovascular systems a service by making them walk." He stubs out the cigar he has been smoking in the yellow eye of the fried egg. Marianne suppresses a gasp. "No one with any dignity should ever have to eat a fried egg. All respect to your culinary skills, Mona." Mona grimaces and turns her attention to the cream pies beneath their transparent plastic fly covers. "It's just my idea of a conversation starter," says the fat man with the English accent. "People in all-night diners should talk. Ought to talk. Have a positive compulsion to talk, in fact. Someone has to talk the world through its limbo hours, Miss . . ."

"Marianne Byrd."

Handshakes are exchanged.

"Agent of chaos. The bird. The feminine principle. Flighty, mobile, untrustworthy. Peck out your eyes. Peck off your pecker. The Harpies of Greek legend had the heads of women and the bodies of birds. Where from, bringer of chaos?"

"Phoenix," she says.

"Another bird. Where to?"

Careful, Marianne, careful, careful.

"Oh, any place. I'm not fussy. Just driving for the sake of driving."

"A bird of passage. A night bird too. No roost to lay your pretty head."

He is flirting with her. This balding, pompous slab of blubber is flirting with her.

"Oh, not really. I'm thinking of staying the night in a motel about ten miles back down the road. Quiet place, just off the highway. Can't sleep with heavy traffic roaring past my window all night."

"Good girls don't sleep in strange, off-highway motels," says the fat man. "Goodness knows what could happen to them. Horribly murdered by crazed psychopaths; knifed to death while they're taking a shower. Blood gurgling away down the plughole. Tell me, was the proprietor a man or a woman."

"A man."

"Oho. Old or young?"

"A young man. Younger than me. Not much more than a boy." Why is she telling this repellent yet strangely fascinating man these things? Compulsions in nighthawk diners.

"They're the worst. The absolute worst. I bet you if you dragged the swamp nearby—because there's always a swamp nearby—you'd find the bodies of half a dozen pretty young women, just like you, who thought they'd stop the night and ended up staying a lot longer than they'd anticipated. It's their mothers. The motel proprietors' mothers, that is. Freud said it all: they want to kill their fathers and fuck their mothers. Don't pretend to get all shocked on me—Mona, coffee and the night-time special for Miss Byrd here—it's the way we're all put together, thee and me both, in here." A pudgy forefinger spirals forward to tap her forehead. "Of course, most of us never do, except for the odd juvenile motel proprietor who then realizes that he can't ever replace his father as Mother's lover, and so in a fit of jealous rage kills her too; with, say, a knife, or a necktie, or maybe a spade that's lying around somewhere. And he feels guilty: he's killed his rival and still can't have the woman he wants most. Well, you can't blame them, really, I say. Along comes this young woman, blonde, pretty, wants a room for the night: of course he's going to feel attracted to her. What red-blooded male wouldn't? But the rub is: our motel proprietor can't allow himself to do that; it'd be betraying that first and greatest love, see? And it goes round and round in his head, the poor bastard, love, betrayal, fear, death; love, betrayal, fear, death. So he fucks them the only way he knows how. With the spade, or the necktie, or, best of all, the knife. Phallic symbol, you see. It's all in Freud, I tell you."

A sudden squall on the trailing edge of the weather front bows the windows, rattles the shingles, finds strange ways into the roadhouse and lifts the transparent lids over Mona's cream pies. The endlessly circling piano chords are suddenly chill, menacing.

"Doesn't he know any other tunes?" Marianne asks, rattled, and as she snaps out the question the music stops abruptly and the big-faced swarthy piano player spins round on his stool and he is grinning and Mona behind the counter is grinning and the strange fat man is grinning.

"You've a bitch of a sense of humour, Hitch," says Mona. "You and your stories. Mean streak wider'n a four-lane blacktop."

The fat man Hitch's jowls quiver with barely suppressed laughter.

"I'm sorry, but I don't see the joke, mister," says Marianne.

"Who says there's a joke?" says the fat man and at that Mona and the piano player explode with laughter: tears-down-your-cheeks laughter, stitch-in-your-side laughter, piss-in-your-pants laughter. The clatter-clack of Marianne's heels on the maple floor as she storms from the bar only sends them into deeper ecstasies of laughing.

"Mind y'all have sweet dreams in your l'il ol' motel room, now," shouts Hitch in namby-pamby Scarlett O'Hara as the door of the 90 Mile Roadhouse slams. From the car Marianne can see the bodies convulsed in agonies of mirth, framed within the big picture windows.

Car starts, first pull.

In the mirror as she draws away, they are still laughing silently.

Marianne Marianne, driving driving.

The moon has sailed out from behind the storm front. The road is a silver band beneath it, gleaming with passing rain. The dashboard clock has stopped at the stroke of midnight; though she knows it is far later than that, Marianne is not tired. The night wind from the air vents is exhilarating, narcotic; each of the few cars she meets on the highway is fellow conspirator, shiftily averting gazes in a dipping of headlight beams.

When next she awakes it will be in Pleasant City with the heavy warmth and man-smell of Tom beside her. The uncertainties she felt, the limbo of countless roads radiating from this silver highway into an infinity of possible futures are fixed now on that surety. She knows where she has come from, she knows where she is going. There is no doubt now, no possibility of turning back. Perhaps she should be thankful to that weird fat limey for putting her on to this road that only leads forward.

She feels as if she has changed destinies. In this new destiny, she drives through the night and comes with the dawn to Pleasant City and the car park behind Lewis's Sport and Leisure Store. Tom comes unwashed, unshaven, blinking to the knocking, knocking on his door wondering what the/why the hell? and she falls into his arms and never leaves them again. The divorce comes through, the debts are paid off, and they live happily ever after in Pleasant City where no one will ever find them. It is written.

Behind the wheel, Marianne smiles to her reflection in the rearview mirror as she drives down the moonlit highway, fifty thousand dollars minus the price of a California-plate Buick spilling out of her purse on the seat beside her. Behind her, the storm passes into the east. Driving, driving.

White car, white road.

SHADOW OF A DOUBT

Pleasant City is. Otherwise they wouldn't have called it that. Its industries are family-run and non-polluting. Its businesses are personal and friendly. Its doctors are amenable to antisocial hours and the vagaries of family finance; its lawyers advertise their names *twice*—in brass on the wall, in gilt on the window; its accountants, though members of the Fairfax County Country Club, are seldom boring. The 78s in the maltshop jukebox have not been changed since Glen Miller went MIA; the music shop sells *music*, by the sheet, but for those who must have plastic, you can try before you buy in any one of half a dozen soundproofed listening booths. Gumball machines stand unmolested on the sidewalks, domed heads shaded from the noonday sun by striped canvas awnings bearing the names and trades of the founding families: the features in the Cosmotheka Movie House change invariably Mondays and Thursdays (save a unique exception for *Gone With the Wind*), last continuous show 6:30 all seats fully bookable. Cinema, Presbyterian Church and porticoed City Hall face each other across the equilateral triangle of shaved turf called Liberty Park. The bandstand has been locked up since that night in 1946 when homecoming hero Rog O. Thornhill saw Japs in the undergrowth and shot out every window on the square, three ladies leaving the Presbyterian Church Whist Drive and Police Officer Gavin Elster, briefly transforming Pleasant City CA, into the hell that was forever Guadalcanal before blowing the rear two thirds of his head into the rafters. Rotting condoms drifted by the wind against the cast iron balustrade are the only commemoration of the day Marine Sergeant Thornhill achieved his highest ever kill rate.

The houses are white painted wood, each set back behind grass and trees, each with its *own* drive and garage. Where there are fences, they are of the Shaker pierced-picket design. These too are painted white. The people cut the grass verges and keep the streets clean.

Pleasant City, California. Population: 37,500. Elevation: 2,250. The Littlest Big City in the West. Oh yes.

The bell jingles on its curved spring as Marianne Byrd closes the front door of Lewis Sports and Leisure Store behind her and steps into the sunlit street. At first she thought it would drive her crazy, ringing and jinging for every customer, going out *and* coming in, but now she no longer notices it.

Tom said she would.

Tom said she would get to know them. It will take time, people are slow in Pleasant City. He is right about that too.

So she nods to Mr. Jeffries with the broken leg in the Electric Company Office and he nods back to her: *Good morning, Marianne*. And the Robies in the Ice Cream Parlor smile and wave, though Rose, as a good Catholic, officially can't approve of the domestic set-up back of the Sports Store. Behind his lathered-up victim Mr. Rusk the barber heliographs good morning with a silver flourish of his cut-throat, and the Balestero Brothers, who have not moved from their chairs in front of the Loomis Hardware store since before the New Deal, grin monodentally and run their eye up and down Marianne's stocking seams. Marianne doesn't mind, she quite likes the feel of the old men's eyeballs rolling all the way up to her fanny and down again. Between the Balestero Brothers sits a bright parakeet in a rusty cage. Every day they let it out to fly around Liberty Park; just as it comes to the conclusion that it is free forever, they whistle it back to its cage.

It always comes.

There is a bell on the door of Shoebridge Realty, a modern electrical one that heralds customers with a rude blast of ringing and hastens their departure with a vulgar rattle. Marianne hates the doorbell of Shoebridge's. Marianne hates most things about Shoebridge's. The arrangement of the desks, the mock-oak plastic paneling, the languishing, slightly over-watered palms—which one of the two receptionists, the tarty one or the escapee from the Carnegie Library is responsible for them?—remind her too much of another realtors, under another sky, another time.

The magazines on the coffee table have cover paintings of melancholy midnight diners and apartments where no one looks at anyone else.

Marianne always dresses up to go to Shoebridge Realty. Best blouse, best skirt, best stockings, best shoes. High heels. Thus attired she can stand over the younger, prettier receptionist and intimidate her.

"Hello, Miss Byrd. The Lewis account, is it?"

She will not be thought a tramp, least of all by a receptionist in Shoebridge Realty.

"Hello Jessie, yes. I'd like to make another payment."

"Certainly, Miss Byrd."

"Can I borrow your pen, please?"

"Of course."

Out back, behind the little veneered half-walls, Shoebridge is rising from his desk.

Amount in words: *one hundred and forty dollars.* In figures: thousand hundreds tens units. Cents as written. *$140:00/00.* Lewis Sports and Leisure: Number Two Account. Authorized signature . . .

"Good morning, Miss Byrd, isn't it a lovely morning? Hot enough for you?"

"Real California summer, Mr. Shoebridge."

Slipping in behind the tarty receptionist Jessie, he opens a gilt-edged ledger.

Heart pounds. Blood thunders. Far far away, birds, screaming screaming.

Shoebridge purses his lips. Eyes roll down the columns.

"Is there a problem, Mr. Shoebridge?"

"Oh, no problem, Marianne. Quite the reverse. In seven months the account has gone from being in serious arrears to five months in advance. If only all our leaseholders were this conscientious. And successful. The sports equipment business must be booming."

"Well, it is summer, Mr. Shoebridge, when young men's fancy turns to healthy pursuits." Jessie commutes a snicker to a discreet cough. "And Tom's outfitting the Pleasant City Little Leaguers this season. Shirts, shoes, masks, gloves, all with 'Sponsored by Lewis Sports and Leisure' stuck wherever we can get it to stick."

Mr. Shoebridge closes the ledger, steps back and mimes a beautiful smackeroonie, right over the bleachers, right over the Countess Cup Cakes billboard and the advertisement for Equivitol Chickfeed showing a squab carrying an enormous codfish strapped to its back, right over the A.T. & S.F. tracks into Little League Legend.

"Ten men out . . ." says Marianne, closing her purse.

Vrrp goes the rude doorbell behind her. Out of the corner of her eye she glimpses Miss Tarty and Miss Carnegie Library lean forward across their desks toward each other. They will be talking about her. They all talk about her, for all their smiles and waves and "good mornings," behind the closed doors and the pulled-down shutters. *Store assistant my foot; when they lock their doors and close their shutters and shut off the lights, it stops being boss and hired hand soon enough, I tell you; in that back room, that's where it all stops.* Vernon *Lowry actually saw into it when he was making a delivery: there's one bed. Two pillows. That's right. And her things are all over the washroom. Ah hah. He left his wife for her, you know. Soon as the D.I.V.O.R.C.E. comes through there'll be a plain gold band third finger left hand P.D.Q. You can be sure of that.* Las Vegas *wedding. Uh huh. Mexican divorce, soon enough, I reckon. And all those airs and graces she puts on; well, if she's so mighty fine what's she doing working in Lewis's? Ah hah, I tell you, no Yankee cracker or Southern belle ever talked like that, that's right, there's three generations of boondock white trash in there or I'm no judge of people. And the way she pushes herself forward, why, I tell you, she was standing there flirting with old Shoebridge.*

Well, let them talk. The flirtations she makes with the men she pays is part of the game; for all the money she has signed over their counters and into their ledgers, there is still more in the Lewis Sports and Leisure Number Two Account than they will make in their entire lives at Shoebridge Realty. Which of them, between the back-seat fumblings and the twenty-cent Tales of Torrid Romance will ever love a man so much that they will think the unthinkable, dare the undareable, do the undoable for him? Which of them will give up everything she owns, go into exile in a menial job among people who look and whisper; all out of love for a man? What do they know of love?

Marianne is smiling to herself as Tom's doorbell jingles unheard behind her.

"You look happy, honey."

"Oh, just anticipating the future, Tom. Sometimes when I think that nothing will ever change, I remind myself that those divorce papers get that little bit closer every day." Look at him, standing behind that counter with the bats and balls and shorts and shoes racked up behind him, smelling slightly of rubber, sweat and exertion. Like he does in that bed with the two pillows in the stockroom. College football muscles have not yet slackened into middle-age fat. She loves to lie back on that bed at the end of the day, light a cigarette, close her eyes and listen to the clank of weights, the small puffs and heaves of exercise, knowing that he does it for her. He wishes more than just a fit body for her, and becomes morose when he cannot deliver it. What woman, given such love, would not help her man realize his dreams? "Is it all right if I'm a couple of minutes late after lunch,Tom? I want to get a couple of things."

"You don't have to ask, Marianne."

Ting goes the bell as she makes her way across the triangle to the Electric Office to put another little payment of the installment plan dream down on Mr. Jeffries' desk. And to establish her *bona fide,* a brief flirtation with the silks and satins in Wendover's Department Store.

"He'll like this," she says, running her fingers sensuously over the fabric purely to give the shop assistant something to gossip about.

Ting.

She waits until the customer has left contented with his junior baseball kit before showing Tom her goods.

"Well, what do you think?" She holds the brassiere up against her body.

Suggestions of ribbed swellings. Dress to undress. "Preview of coming attractions." Forefingers jiggle the straps. Big and bouncy. Oh yes. Like he says he likes them. In his face.

Not a twitch.

Marianne shimmies behind the counter and drapes the bra over his head. Straps looped around ears; Mr. Tit Head. Twice.

Times past, less than that would have been provocation enough for him to pull down the blinds, turn the *Closed* sign outward and carry her, legs locked around his waist, arms around his shoulders, to the bed with the two pillows among the athletic supports. Today, he unhooks the straps, takes the thing off his head and lets it drop to the floor.

"Mighty fine Marianne," he says, looking anywhere, at anything, but at her. "Always enough for something fine, something soft, something satiny and lacey for Miss Marianne Byrd."

"Tom, honey, what do you mean? What's the matter?" she asks as one by one the sounds of Pleasant City going about its business vanish into the red thunder of her bloodstream.

"Since precisely when has Lewis Sports and Leisure had a Number Two Account?"

It lies on the counter top; a paper accusation, seven inches by three. Pacific Trust Bank, Fairfax County Branch.

A paper annihilation. The sound of it is like the sudden, savage dashing of rosined bows across strings.

"Jessie called round from Shoebridge's while you were out, Marianne. Seems in your haste you forgot to sign it. 'Maybe you could, Mr. Lewis,' " He impersonates Jessie's manufactured dumb-blonde squeak. " 'I'm sure the boss can sign his own Number Two Account.' " And do you know what I did, Marianne? I stood there like a damn fool, and told that girl to her face that there must be some mistake, we don't have a Number Two Account. Like a goddamn fool, I called her and Mr. Shoebridge bare-faced liars."

Tom is looking at her now. There is nothing in his eyes she can remember or recognize.

"I called the bank, Marianne. The Pacific Trust. Mr. Pemberton is the manager. But you know that, don't you? Do you know what kind of fool you feel when you have to ask about the existence of your own bank account? Very helpful, was Mr. Pemberton; very helpful people, the Pacific Trust. I should move my main account there.

"Lewis Sports and Leisure: Number Two Account. A/C No. 1034865, opened January 8, 1960, by Mrs. Marianne Byrd-Lewis, resident at 18b Main Street, Pleasant City, California. Opening balance, forty-nine thousand, two hundred and eight dollars; cash. Current balance, forty three thousand six hundred and forty dollars. Discrepancy between opening and current balances, five thousand six hundred and forty dollars."

Mrs. Kominsky from the donut shop leads her bulbous son up to the door, sees the closed sign and the business being transacted behind it. She pulls him away.

"Where?"

"To pay them off."

"I didn't ask why. I know why. I asked where. Where did it come from? Fifty thousand dollars, Marianne . . ." It's a fortune. It's money so much, so big that it goes beyond reality, into Ripley's Believe It Or Not Land. He is looking at her now as if she is something unbelievable, as if she is a stranger he is meeting for the first time. She supposes she is. When you live so long, so close to guilt and secrecy it works its way into you, it finds a warm, nesting space just below your liver and curls and knots and coils into a new organ; an organ of secrecy that is so much a vital part of you that, like your other organs, you no longer think about it, though your continued existence depends on its functioning. Now those tender sweetbreads and tripes have been torn out, slit open, spread on the formica countertop of Lewis Sports and Leisure Store.

Even so, for a moment she considers lying. Rich relatives, prematurely felled; spinster aunts enthroned in California Gothic. In the same moment she rejects them. They could only be defensive lies to confuse him and protect her and in all the deceits and falsehoods she has spun around herself there was never any intent to hurt him, nor serve herself at his expense. Only him, only his good, only love. He deserves truth. He will have truth.

"It comes from a Mr. Carmody of Phoenix, who intended using it to buy his wife a house as an anniversary present. It was left at the office of Lavery Real Estate to be lodged in the bank's safe deposit box. I stole it." And she tells him. She tells him of the stolen lunch-hours, the snatched weekends, the pay-by-the-hour hotels at motels and the back seats of cars rendezvousing at remote Arizona diners and how she had seen them stretching before her in an endless parade of jotted telephone messages and ciphers in diaries, that would never be more than meat on the hoof, taken on the run because he was chained between the clashing rocks of his dead father's debts and his living wife's threats. She tells back to him all those hopes and dreams of freedom, of how he said he would do anything, anything to pay off the debts, rid himself of his wife and be free to live again, with her. In those motel cabins, those hotel rooms, cradled in warm leatherette with radio playing between the seats beneath her head, he had told her he loved her; over and over; he loved her, he loved her, but love is more than words, love is deeds; true love, great love will contemplate anything for the beloved; love like that speaks itself in the unspeakable; love like that is not a whisper among the sweat-damp blonde curls behind the ear, but the sudden clear, cold courage to walk past the bank with the fifty thousand dollars in your purse, walk into your rooms, pack your things and drive out into the darkness.

As she tells Tom all these things the spirit seems to go out of him. He shakes his head, mumbles *no, no.*

"I did it for you, Tom," Marianne says.

"I didn't ask you to!" Tom cries. "When did I ever ask you to lie for me, cheat for me, steal for me? I don't want that from you, I could never want that from you." Suddenly he is pulling bills, checks, IOUs from the cash drawer, pushing them into her hands, her purse, down the front of her dress. "Take it, take it, I don't want it, I can't have it, take it, put it back, put the whole fifty thousand back where it came from. I'll empty out my accounts, cash in an insurance policy, sell the fucking shop, that should be worth a few thousand even with its debts, but then I'm forgetting, aren't I? There are no debts: Mr. Jeffries at the Electric Company and Mr. Shoebridge at the Real Estate and Mr. Thorwald at the gas and Mr. de Winter at the insurance and Mr. Ferguson the supplier, all paid off and up to date with Mr. Fucking Carmody's fifty fucking thousand dollars!"

Weeping with rage and frustration, he sweeps the loose bills and small change off the counter into her arms. *Throws* them at her.

"I can't take it back, Tom," Marianne says. Outside, in a world from which she is insulated by the thunder of gathering inevitability, one sound penetrates: the Balestero Brothers whistling their parakeet down from the top of the bandstand to its cage. "It's been too long. Carmody'll have claimed on his insurance; he won't have it back now. He wouldn't have, anyway, you didn't meet him, Tom; he's the kind of man always has to get something, and it doesn't have to be money. So you see, I couldn't put it back." *Truth* Marianne. You have promised yourself to tell the truth. Whatever he may damn you for, it will not be for a liar. "Even if I wanted to. But I don't want to, Tom. You know something? I said I did it for you, but that's only part of the truth. The whole truth is that I did it for me. I enjoyed stealing it. It felt good taking the money, more money than you or I could dream of Tom. And I took it, just like that, and everyone's carefully arranged little destinies were all upset. By a little blonde real estate clerk. By little me, Tom. I liked stealing it. I liked having it."

"Then have it," he says, but he has lost the high ground. What had been Jehovah-righteousness is now the whining of kicked dogs; petty, petulant. "Keep it. Keep all of it." Turning his back on her, he pulls down boxes of sports shoes, sends left feet right feet, cleat soles spike soles tumbling. "Keep the whole fucking place. You paid for it, didn't you? I'm only the hired hand, the shop boy, the hired dick in the bed in the storeroom. All paid for, all earned. They were debts, yes, but they were my debts, my responsibilities. My work, my achievement, and you took them away from me. You bought me, Marianne—no, you stole me. You stole me, my hopes, my plans, my world, just like you stole that fifty thousand dollars. On a whim. Without a moment's thought or feeling. Without any regard for consequences. Name of Christ, woman, how did you ever expect to get away with it? Opening secret accounts, openly paying off debts; it was only a matter of time before someone would have told me. You might as well have gone around with *thief* tattooed on your forehead."

Because he is right; because, down there beneath her liver with the pride and the notoriety and the secrecy, coiled closer than any two bodies in a storeroom, lies a guilt that needs to name itself, to stand naked in the street so that it may be punished and thus destroy itself. Because she knows, and hates as much as loves this, she turns on him.

"I never had you for a coward, Tom. Yellow. Afraid. Tied. I gave you the chance to be free. But you can't give them up, can you? This shop, your wife, your dead father, this town, your place in it; your comfortable, familiar world. You can come with me any place on earth, live any life you choose, but that kind of freedom terrifies you, doesn't it? You don't want it, it's too much for you. You're a coward in the end."

Ting! goes the bell of Lewis Sports and Leisure Store behind him.

"Tom!"

No answer.

"I loved you, Tom!"

Not even an early afternoon shadow on the sidewalk. One by one, Marianne Byrd picks up the scattered sports shoes, puts them in the correct boxes by model and size and stacks them on the proper shelf.

Ting.

She whirls, heart flying up within her. A small, squat man, like an ambulatory toad, stands on the mat, peering around him as his eyes adjust from street glare to shop gloom.

"It really is, you know." His voice is a sixty-a-day trudge through melting blacktop. "Pleasant City," he adds, answering his own hookline.

"I'm sorry, we're closed."

"That's all right. I wasn't, ah, looking to buy anything." He advances into the store, sniffs deeply. "Ah. Sweat, linament and warm rubber. Actually, I'm looking for someone."

"Mr. Lewis isn't in at the moment."

The squat man runs the tip of his tongue over his lips, doffs his greasy hat.

"It's not Mr. Lewis I'm looking for. I've heard that a Miss Marianne Byrd works here."

"You've found her. I'm Miss Byrd."

"Oh, that's good. My name is Antrobus; my card." A nicotine-edged rectangle of pasteboard. Pocket fluff clings to the creased corners. "I'm a private detective."

ROPE

She no longer resists the ball gag. She struggles, because he likes her to struggle when he buckles the strap hard across the back of her head, when he pulls tight the knots, when he snaps the locks and fits the little saw-toothed clamps, but she knows better than to resist, now. So she moans, and mimics that look of helpless dread he showed her in the magazines as he fastens her hands above her to the ceiling hook and straps her thighs and ankles to the special trestle he has made for her. She pretends to writhe and fight as he straddles her over the bar.

He steps back across the motel room to admire his handiwork before closing for the final refinements. The ritual is that he presses his sweating face—he is always, always sweating—close to hers and holds up the nipple clips. Her part then is to struggle, eyes wide with fear. When your mouth is contorted around a tooth-marked ball of hard rubber, you learn to do the expressive stuff with your eyes.

She hopes he will not go and buy whiskey tonight. Sometimes, when it's been a bad drive up from Phoenix he will leave her and go out to the liquor store at the crossroads. No one need take two hours to buy a bottle of whiskey and come back. Though the pain in whatever part of her he has pulled out of true is cruel, she would rather that he never came back at all. The whiskey mocks the impotence inside him and the impotence will work out its frustration and anger with a studded leather paddle on the soft places of her body.

Thank God, he does not look like he will need the whiskey tonight. But he'll gloat. He must gloat; it is as much part of it as the rope and the gag. He must crow his cleverness and mastery and dominance over a bound, naked, dumb woman.

He pulls the cracked leatherette lounge chair around to face her and settles deeply into it. Rolls of fat spill softly over each other. Sweat glues his body hair into sleek spines. He will sit, just watching, for several minutes without speaking.

In the next cabin a radio is playing loudly against the stud wall. Out on the highway, cars' lights briefly illuminate the thin floral print curtain on its plastic-coated wire and pass by.

When he does begin to speak, his voice is like some long, many-legged insect emerging from the hole in his creases of facial fat.

"Did you think you were clever? Eh? Did you think you'd get clean away, that no one would ever find you, that you'd live happy ever after with that fuck-brained jock of a boyfriend? Did you? Did you?" At this point the script calls for him to slap the paddle on the arm of the chair. FX: smack of studded leather on leatherette. Her part is to frantically shake her head—depending on the degree of freedom he has allowed her, he is not beyond roping her head and tying it to the wall—and mumble into her gag things that sound like *no, no, never Mr. Antrobus.*

"Let me tell you, girlie, no one ever gets clean away. They always leave something behind them; there's always something they forget to do, or do too well—you'd be surprised how often that one trips them up, the things that are just that teeny bit overdone. Things it takes a trained eye and mind to spot. And you were a good one, Missy Marianne; lesser than J. J. Antrobus, well, they might have lost the scent, but there's the blood of the Navajo in these veins—Great-grandpa Antrobus fucked some squaw up on the Indian nation. Greatest trackers on God's earth, the Navajo."

The plot calls here for her to squirm in fear for her soft white flesh in the hands of the savage red man.

"You see, I reckoned straight off you'd headed west. Natural direction for anyone trying to get away. Go west, young man! So I didn't bother checking with friends or family—you might be stupid, but not that stupid. Thing is, I overestimated you. I reckoned you'd gone straight to Los Angeles, so I overshot Pleasant City and wasted a whole heap of time, and that cost a dirty dime or two—on top of what you've already cost Mr. Carmody." He points the paddle, broad as the palms of both hands, at her and as she has so many times before, she tries to cringe away and roll her eyes just like Betty Page. "But something in my Navajo blood told me the trail was cold, so back I went, and with great diligence and skill, and even more expense, I started all over again."

She knows that he knows that she cannot hold herself off the knife-edge of the trestle much longer.

"And J. J. Antrobus surely hates to be shown to be wrong, girlie. But: diligence. Always diligence. And it paid off. Do you know what I found?"

She knows. She knows. God damn it, she knows.

"I found the excellent Mr. California Charlie, Used Car Dealer of Fairdale in this Sunshine State and he had a very vivid memory of a young blonde who seemed to be in a hell of a hurry to buy a car off him. "Hell, Antrobus, first time I ever saw the customer high-pressure the salesman." Well, being a good citizen who knew what should be done to bad girls who take things that aren't theirs, he was only too pleased to give me the details of the car you'd bought off him."

Marianne watches with numb fascination the sweat break from Antrobus's forehead, roll down his face and drop in heavy, oleaginous spheres down the rolls of belly fat to nestle among the chrome studs of his leather shorts.

"America's greatest strength is her citizens. The free man, responsible to himself and his fellow; how can the Reds ever imagine they could beat that? It warms my old heart; so many good citizens out there. That nice boy at the motel just off the main road: "Why yes, Mr. Antrobus, I recognize that photograph; she booked a cabin here for the night, let me see, December 6, it was. There she is, under the name of Janet Leigh. I didn't think it was her real name—in the hospitality business you get to be able to tell when people aren't what they seem. Went up to the 90 Mile Roadhouse to get something to eat. Never came back. Always imagined something terrible had happened to her.'"

Her nipples sting where salt sweat worries at the serrations. Soon now, soon now, it will be over. In a sense it is worse than the physical pain, for Antrobus is always clever at inventing new ways to surprise her, but the tedious, misogynistic drone of his own cleverness never changes. The litany, the responses, the rubrics are as invariable and holy as high mass in St. Patrick's. Now, he will rise from the chair and caress the line of her jaw with the devil's tail tip of the paddle.

"And the woman at the 90 Mile Roadhouse—well normally, I wouldn't trust a woman to remember anything right—but she surprised me, I'll admit it; every detail of the night you came in, clear as day; her, and that fat limey, and the Jewish piano-playing pisher; they all remembered the bad girl from Arizona with the guilty look. 'Ask her if she's still getting up to trouble in strange men's motels,' that fucking limey told me to tell you. Funny man, real funny. Hah fucking hah, Marianne."

According to the ritual, she has to pant and strain for the rod as if she wants it more than anything.

"And so Antrobus comes to this nice little burg called Pleasant City and, what do you know? there, right in the middle of Main Street, is the car he's been looking for, right outside Lewis Sports and Leisure Store. Of course, it's a sign from God, so in goes Antrobus, and well, I do declare! there is the bad little girl who thought that by hiding she could escape what was coming to her; a very bad little girl who got found out by Mr. James Jonah Antrobus, and now has to get punished."

Stepping behind her, he yanks her off the trestle by her aching arms. With a whistle, the paddle goes up. And comes down.

She was a fool to have let him into the shop that day when Tom walked out forever. She was a fool to have let him stand there sniffing the air like it was purest Chanel to him—it was, she supposes—and given him space to make his little proposition. She was a fool to have listened.

"You can have it back, take it back to him. I have lost the only man I ever loved because of it. I'll pay back what I spent; honest, I will."

The sky can only fall once. When the toad-like man had announced himself as a detective hired to find Carmody's money, she had discovered that there is a limit to pain, even a certain dim joy at the heart of it. Now it could end.

She had thought.

"Uh, uh, Missy Marianne. Too late for that. It's in the hands of the law now. And crossing state lines with it; now that was a damn fool stupid thing to do;

that's a Federal offense. You done wrong, you gonna get punished for it. But J. J. Antrobus is a man who can see his way to reason where others can't. Trying to find one runaway in a big country like this, it's like that old haystack needle, lady, and maybe, in return for the right, eh, inducement? I could persuade my clients that it's a wild goose chase trying to find you."

"I can't go to jail. I can't, it would kill me."

"You won't have to go to jail if you're wise."

"How much do you want?" Out of the purse, on to the counter, the old friendly traitor: Lewis Sports and Leisure Number Two Account checkbook.

"Lady lady lady, I thought someone in your position would understand a little more about discretion, nah? Not here, Missy Marianne, not where people can see. Meet me here." He had written the name and location of a motel on the back of his business card with a silver pencil. Down on the state line, equal distances from Phoenix and Pleasant City. "Saturday. About eight? The first cabin. I've booked it, I'll be waiting for you."

He had turned to leave.

"How much? How much do you want?"

Ting, the doorbell had said.

Lewis Sports and Leisure Number Two Account had been closed, stories spread to the chattering classes of Pleasant City about Tom's sick aunt in Wisconsin, and given the state of her health she didn't really know if he'd be back, let alone when. The money had gone into an envelope and the envelope into a purse and the purse into the front seat of California Charlie's '59-plate Buick and the '59 Buick down the long black road, many hours, down to the state line and the place the detective had written on his card where the blue neon announced *rooms to let*.

She had laid the money on the dressing table in Cabin One. The veneer was coming unglued at the corners.

"How much do you want?" she had asked. "It's all there. Name your price."

"Oh, it's not money I want, Missy Marianne," Antrobus had said sunk deep in the only armchair. "No, no, no, no, not money. I've got more money than I know what to do with. It's you, Marianne, that I want. You're my price."

He had opened his overnight case then, and taken out what he called "the library" and shown her what he wanted to do with her, and how, and for how long, and when he had shown her all those women looking into the camera with expressions that all said *understand, I'm only doing this for the money*, he dug down into the bottom of the bag and brought out the things with which he wanted to do it to her.

And that was the first Saturday. Antrobus's bookings of Cabin One—next to the office, should he need anything—are the only regular money the proprietor has ever seen: the motel is isolated, off the main routes. Its small trade is mostly passing; commercial travelers, geologists, vacationers. It is custom-made for blackmail: Antrobus ensures the proprietor's silence by supplying him with photographs of the sessions. When the proprietor has finished with them, he sells them on to truckers down at the Twin Oaks Tavern across the Colorado. He turns a blind eye to Antrobus's improvements to the fixtures and furnishings. The money is still in Marianne's purse. It goes everywhere with her. She never thinks about it, now.

And it is another Saturday and Marianne is behind the wheel again, driving, driving, down to the Blue Motel on the state line.

Why put yourself through it, Marianne? Jail could be no worse. Why not this Saturday afternoon turn the car along one of those myriad different headings you sensed that night at the 90 Mile Roadhouse, take any one of them away from here and drive? The guilt will not let her. Not merely the guilt of being a thief, but the guilt of being herself, of there being something in her nature that makes men want her, need her and in the end judge her. Antrobus, Tom, Mr. Lavery; they have all sat in judgment over her. All the men she has ever known have been judges, sentencing her to give up her freedom to their desires.

She cannot drive away, not while her guilt finds a little expiation in Antrobus's pain and humiliation in the Blue Motel.

He has a new one for her. He has been working hard. It is a kind of double-ended gallows, with cross-pieces about four feet wide, one fixed to the place where the rope hangs, the other to the crosspiece at the foot. Both are fitted with rope loops. He has been thinking about it all the way up from Phoenix. She takes her clothes off and kneels in the way she has been taught as he shows her with photographs from The Library how the apparatus works.

The gag is fitted. Panting, Antrobus hauls her up. Her ankles are tied to the upper beam, her wrists to the lower. Spreadeagled upside down, Marianne Byrd hangs from the wooden gallows. Antrobus fastens a cinch around her middle, pulls it in to tie it to the main upright, arching her into an elegant, swallow-like crescent.

"Look, you're flying!" he says, proudly. Then he goes and does the gloating, looking thing in his chair.

Tonight, she knows, will be a whiskey night.

After the gloating is done he takes the camera from his overnighter. Blue flashbulbs pop in the Blue Motel as she looks despairingly into the camera, just like Betty Page. He shoots off a complete film. Upside down, she watches him masturbate ferociously by the light from the motel neons. When he is done, he sits a long time, watching, staring, half-aroused, half-disgusted.

Definitely, a whiskey night.

"I'm going out," he says after a time, pulling on street clothes over his smeared leather shorts. He locks the door behind him. In the blue light, Marianne swings on her gallows. With the vast mass of the world balanced above her head, or so it seems, she thinks again about that other Blue Motel on its lonely highway, and how differently the world might have turned out had she turned her back on the rain, accepted that strange boy's invitation of milk and sandwiches, showered off the dust and guilt and madness and the next day gone back to well-paid anonymity.

In the car park patrons come and go in a slamming of doors and honking of horns while in Cabin One the wooden tree creaks beneath the weight of its passenger. It is after midnight before Antrobus returns. He sits in his chair drinking from the bottle watching the California night sweat run down Marianne's body and drip from the nipple clamps to the dirty carpet. Any moment, when he is two thirds down the bottle of Wild Turkey, he will start in with the paddle and not know when to stop.

This night, he does not. The leather lies there on the arm of the chair. Antrobus sits slumped. Whiskey tears force themselves from his eyes.

"What are we going to do, Marianne?" he says gently. "It can't go on like this; weekend nights snatched at some motel miles from anywhere. It's not enough for me. I know you're grateful for what I'm helping you realize about yourself, but it has to be more, I know you understand that. I want it to be more, Marianne; and I know you want it too: a place where we can have each other, explore what we have with each other, reach new heights, explore new understandings of what we've found together."

Heart frozen by pure horror, Marianne's struggles are not feigned this time. Antrobus's knots are tight and strong.

"The money would set us up, Marianne. Buy us a little place; quiet, nice, some out of the way place where people wouldn't talk. We both know what that's like, Marianne; people, and the way they talk. We could fit it out nicely; get better stuff than this fucking junk; a place where we could make a lifetime commitment to each other, to love and serve. That's what I want, Marianne, that's what I need."

The ball gag has never let past any of her other screams. It does not fail now.

"You understand, Marianne, that I only punish you because I love you." Unbelievably, he puts the paddle back into his case and takes out a big pair of scissors. Knots pull tight under weight: he cuts the ropes and lets Marianne down. "You understand what I mean," he whispers as he lays the semi-conscious Marianne tenderly on the bed. "We'll talk, you'll see." Slipping off his leather shorts, he goes to shower off the jizz and sweat and whiskey.

Marianne understands what he means. And she understands what she has to do. The only thing she can do. She understands that every turning she had taken that she thought was a road to greater freedom was in fact a turning away from it, on to ways ever more constricting and restricting, leading here. Nowhere else than this Blue Motel. All her freedoms have been imprisonments, a narrowing down of choice to one point. The point of a pair of silver scissors.

Her hands are numb from the rope, her grip uncertain. Her bare feet are silent on the bathroom tiles. Hot water gushes jollily. She reverses her hold on the scissors to the strong, down-slashing grip. Antrobus is an ungainly black silhouette against the translucent curtain.

She pulls back the curtain. She lifts the scissors high above her head. She knows what she must do.

Yet, she hesitates a fatal moment.

Antrobus turns, sensing her shadow. His eyes bulge in disbelief. Water cascades from the hairy triangle of his genitals.

"You should put that down, girlie, you're going to cut your fingers off."

With a cry like a black bird, Marianne strikes. The tip of the scissors buries itself in the side of Antrobus's neck just above the collar bone.

He stares at the silver scissors, at the striking hand, at Marianne, at his blood spiraling down the plughole.

"Why, you."

She wrenches the scissors free and lashes at him with the open blades. Strike strike strike strike. Long bloody gashes open up in his thighs, chest, belly blubber. Antrobus reels backward against the tiled wall. Hot gushing water washes the wounds clean. Strike strike strike. Marianne pants in exertion as she slashes down with the scissors: *die die die, just die you fat fuck, why won't you die*? She had not realized how difficult it is to kill a man. Antrobus shields his face and genitals with his hands. Marianne drives the point of the scissors into the backs of them again and again and again and again. His fingers flap uselessly before her, a blur of blood and water and flesh and terrified eyes.

The only sounds are the hiss of water and the panting of killer and victim.

Antrobus's fat body bleeds from a hundred slashes but still he does not die. It seems to have gone on forever, the dying, but he is weakening. Marianne stabs a blade deep into Antrobus's shoulder. He lurches away, the blade snaps leaving bloody steel embedded in his meat. His feet slip on the water and blood. He falls backwards.

The sound of brass towel hook penetrating human skull is not easily forgotten. Antrobus thrashes, once.

Marianne levers his body off the hook and lets him drop into the shower tray. While he drains, she dresses, helps herself to his cigarettes and the last inch of Wild Turkey. Eight pints of blood in the average human body. Give it half an hour or so, to get it all washed away, and the piss, and the fear-shit. The water will have run cold long before then. Pity he will not be able to appreciate what it was like for her when he would bundle her up with one hundred yards of washing line, tumble her into the shower and turn the cold full on her.

She goes to look at him. His eyes are not staring at her, but at a persistent cobweb next to the extractor fan. She would not care if they were staring. For the first time, she feels free of guilt. She killed a man, she feels set free. Why should she feel guilt? There can be no guilt where there is no choice, no other way, no right road to take. No one can be held morally responsible for doing what they are fated to do. Destiny admits no guilt.

She sits on the toilet and smokes until no more blood oozes from the hundred wounds. When it is all gone down the plughole, she pulls down the shower curtain, spreads it on the floor and with much effort levers Antrobus out of the shower on to it. She wraps him in his polythene shroud, drags him from the bedroom and with soft blue toilet tissue cleans up, flushing the evidence in job lots of five down the john.

Careful Marianne, careful. Would not do to block the plumbing at this stage.

She grimaces at the gobbets of hair and soft grey matter clinging to the towel hook. One wipe and they are gone. Down to the drains with the rest of him.

A sudden urge to giggle takes her by surprise. Inexplicably, she wants to sit on the toilet and laugh and laugh and laugh. She cannot. She dare not. When it is all done, then will be the time for elation. Now would be foolhardy.

Twenty to one on the clock. From past experience she knows the motel won't be quiet until two. She packs Antrobus's clothes and things. The rope. The paddle. The Irving Klaw Library. She smiles at Betty Page, forever bound. The scissors—she almost forgot. The overnighter closes click on them all. Marianne flicks on the radio and listens, and smokes, and watches the play of headlights across the cheap, thin curtains, and waits. She gives it twenty minutes after the click and lock of the office door before moving.

Outside, the desert night is huge and brilliant and generous. Antrobus bumps as he goes down the steps—no helping it. She ruffles the track he makes in the dusty gravel. For a moment she thinks she is not going to be able to get him into the back of his station wagon, but the sound of a truck coming down the Colorado River line lends her desperation.

Up, and in he goes.

The truck blares past, a fast-moving constellation of riding lights.

The case goes in the back with Antrobus in his plastic sheet. Marianne in the front. Keys. Keys. She forgot to get them out of the overnight case. She glances up as she fumbles but the cabin windows stay dark.

The station wagon starts, first pull. Marianne turns out on to the main route. The night is clear. The stars have never looked so bright.

She first noticed the viewpoint back at Session Two and had memorized it in an abstracted way as the kind of place that would be nice for a picnic, if hers were the kind of life that contemplated picnics. Beyond the line of white painted stones that rather ineffectually mark the edge, the land falls sharply toward a deeply incised tributary of the Colorado. She parks the station wagon far back, almost on the highway. She does not want those stupid stones stopping it. The car is aimed clear between the graffitied picnic tables at the setting stars.

The sound of the cigar lighter springing to life is surprisingly loud in this big country. The red coil of wire ignites the glovebox garbage she has distributed on the passenger seat. The upholstery smokes, bubbles, bursts into oily flames. Marianne releases the handbrake, heaves at the door pillar to help the station wagon on its way. Tires crunch gravel.

The white stones do not even slow it up. She sees the tailgate lights flip up against the bright stars and vanish. Seconds later a soft explosion disturbs the desert night.

She does not trouble herself to look over.

Five miles back to the Blue Motel. Under such a sky, on such a night, it will be a positive pleasure. Good to walk the ache out of her muscles. Should take her an hour, an hour and a half; plenty of time to get away before the motel starts to stir.

Good thing she chose a sensible pair of heels.

NORTH BY NORTHWEST

Marianne Marianne, driving driving. Marianne Marianne, driving driving.

Even in the height of summer this land is green; softly watered by ocean fogs and sudden rains; so different, so welcoming after the deserts and drylands that have been her habitation for as long as she can remember. There is salt in the air coming to her through the open window: sea smells; kelp, ozone, iodine. The road is smooth and good driving as it dips and winds between the low, green hills, drawing her toward the ocean. All things are confirmation that this is the place for her to be: why, at the gas station as she ate a Hershey bar, a little bird, quite oblivious of the surly teenager filling the tank, had dropped on to the hood and looked at her long and hard, first with one eye, then with the other.

It is good to have direction, to at last be going where she chooses to go. When she had driven away from the Blue Motel with the first gray light of the dawn behind her, she had not known where she wanted to go, only that it was away from the things and people that had tied her. Given freedom, she had not known what to do with it; only reveled in the gift of mobility for mobility's sake; driving, driving along the straight black highways of California. The sun had risen, and stood over her, and overtaken her, and she still had driven, driven.

Away: in a northerly direction—she could not have said why that way. Up the great central valley through orchards and farms, overtaking lumbering farm trucks and crop-sprayers on the dusty roads; driving driving.

On the seat beside her, fortysomething thousand dollars.

The sun had steered her until she could not drive any further. She had booked into a family hotel in downtown Sacramento where she had slept for fourteen hours and awoken with a feeling of *potential*, of being mistress of her own way, that she had never really known since that December Friday afternoon in Lavery Real Estate.

She breakfasted in a two-calendar diner decorated in high nauticalia—nets, glass floats that had crossed an ocean from Japan, ships in bottles—though the bay was over an hour's drive west. It was that, over her sausage and waffles, that decided her. The sea. Something west of north, to the ocean. In some coastal fishing town she could find a place to stay, a new community, and new life. Maybe buy a little business with the money. The legendary four-calendar roadhouse, perhaps. She'd have to change her name, her clothes, maybe even the color of her hair: so be it. It couldn't matter. She would be safe. She would be invisible, anonymous. Happy.

The road carries her onward. Between green hills she glimpses blue ocean.

Marianne, Marianne, driving driving, thinks about the 90 Mile Roadhouse, its three calendars and its strange freight of lives. The disquieting music of the piano player: notes hurrying hurrying, going nowhere. That strange Englishman, what had the waitress called him, Hitch? Funny she can remember that. His sad, sick stories. Had he been the oracle of free will, or the agent of predestination? Perhaps you never escape; all your running away is only running to; the long way, the way that goes right around the world to bring you back to the place where you are meant to be.

The road crests a hill and she sees it. Behind its crescent of golden sand, nestling against the foot of the hills against the agoraphobia of the ocean: a tidy town of painted board houses and shingle roofs, webbed with telegraph poles and powerlines and other ugly attendants of civilized living. But the fishing boats seem to rest easily enough against the harbor jetty. Marianne stops the car to look longer.

The road sign announces this place to which she comes: Bodega Bay, two miles.

There seem to be a lot—an awful lot—of birds circling overhead.

A FRIEND INDEED

David Garnett

David Garnett lives in West Sussex, England. He is the editor of *New Worlds* and the author of *Stargonauts*. The latter book represents his return to SF novel writing after a twenty-year hiatus. In the interim he has written stories for *Interzone* magazine and pseudonymous fantasy novels.

Garnett's short fiction has veered toward the horrific in recent years. "A Friend Indeed" begins in the real world and somehow takes a wrong turn into the strange. It first appeared in *Interzone*.

—E. D.

As William walked toward the bar, he glanced briefly and disapprovingly around. It wasn't the kind of pub he'd have entered unless he had to.

There were about a dozen customers inside, all men. The only woman was behind the bar. She finished pulling a pint of beer, took the money, then looked at William.

"Gin and tonic, please," he said.

"Ice and lemon?"

"Please."

He'd arranged to meet Helen from work, but after waiting outside her office block for quarter of an hour, he had gone into reception and asked the girl to call her. Helen had apologized, explaining that she was in a meeting. She said she'd be through in a few minutes and would meet him in the pub on the opposite corner.

If it had really only been a matter of a few minutes, William would have preferred to remain where he was; but he knew from his own experience that meetings always tended to last longer than expected.

He paid for his drink and carried it to a table in the corner furthest from the bar, then opened his briefcase and took out his *Daily Telegraph*. He'd been so busy today that he hadn't even had time to start the crossword.

Someone walked across to the cigarette machine next to him. Automatically, William glanced back—and found himself gazing up into the face of Eddie Brown.

He stared in amazement, unable to believe what he saw.

Years had passed, but there was no doubt that it was Eddie: the one person in the whole world he'd hoped never to see again.

His mind was suddenly flooded with the forgotten horrors of his childhood, and he remembered the absolute unfairness of it all.

Now here he was—the person responsible.

William was stunned, unable to look away.

As Eddie fed coins into the machine, he noticed he was being watched. He turned his head, then his eyes widened with recognition.

"Willy!" he said. "Willy Barber!"

William shook his head in denial. He bent down, trying to hide behind his newspaper. But Eddie plucked the newspaper from his hands and leaned forward, grinning.

William didn't look at him. "You've made some mistake," he muttered.

"You can't fool me, Willy. It's me—Eddie Brown!" He put his beer glass down on William's table and unwrapped his cigarette packet.

"No," said William, shaking his head again. "No, you're wrong."

"Fancy meeting up with you again, Willy. I often think of you, you know, and all the good times we used to have." Eddie lit a cigarette, then tucked the pack in his shirt pocket.

What was he talking about? What good times? They'd all been bad, so far as William was concerned. But it was no use pretending, he realized, and he looked up.

"How are you, Eddie?" he managed to say. "What are you doing in London?"

More than a decade had elapsed. William had moved over 200 miles from his home town, but Eddie had still found him.

"I've been living down here a couple of years. Everyone seems to end up in London sooner or later." His eyes took in William's expensive suit. "You're looking well."

"Thanks."

William could hardly say the same about Eddie: he was wearing faded and patched jeans, scuffed shoes, and old shirt. His hair was long and tangled, his face covered in a week's stubble. A grown up version of the way he used to be.

"We've got lots to talk about," Eddie said.

"No," said William, standing up quickly. "I must be going. I'm meeting someone."

He was surprised to find that he was as tall as Eddie, whereas at school he'd always been much smaller.

But everything was different now, he told himself. He could handle Eddie Brown these days. He was an adult; he'd long outgrown his childish fears. He couldn't be intimidated any more.

Then why was he so nervous. . . ?

Eddie sat down. "You've time for a drink with me, Willy," he said.

The years rolled back, and William said: "Yes."

"I'll have a pint of best," Eddie told him.

William walked slowly to the bar, not glancing back at the specter which had returned to haunt him.

He thought of leaving immediately, of heading straight for the door, but he'd forgotten his briefcase. All he could do was buy the drinks then carry them back to the table.

"It's been a long time," said Eddie.

"Twelve years," William told him. He knew exactly how long it was since his torture had ended, since he'd been allowed to live a life of his own.

"I suppose it must be. I left school, but you stayed on. Then university, I suppose? A good job. A good home. A good wife. Yes?"

Almost, thought William. He didn't have a wife, not yet. That would soon change. He'd known Helen for over a year, and soon they'd become officially engaged.

"Something like that," he said. "What about you?"

He was feeling calmer now, and he watched Eddie without really listening to what he was saying, wondering how he could have spent so much of his life in fear of this man. No—not a man, because they'd only been boys at the time.

It had started when they were both five, going to the same school. Eleven years later, another school, and he was still Eddie's perpetual victim. By then, it was no longer William's toys that he took or broke; Eddie's cruelty had become more subtle but even more damaging.

Looking back, William was only too aware of how Eddie had stolen or ruined everything that he'd ever wanted or cared about. At the time, however, it hadn't seemed to matter. He'd thought that Eddie really was his friend. Friends shared things, didn't they? Eddie played jokes, but it was just harmless fun.

Only later, when Eddie wasn't there, would William realize what had happened—what new torment and indignity had been inflicted on him: how Eddie had got him into trouble, or made the whole class laugh at him, or forced him to do something he didn't want to.

For a long time William used to dream about Eddie Brown, and he'd wake up in panic. Only then would he realize that he'd left school long ago, that the years of embarrassment and humiliation were over.

Now Eddie was back.

He'd obviously fallen on hard times, and William felt pleased. Justice had triumphed at last. He was a success, while his old enemy was an absolute nobody.

Originally they'd lived in the same area, which meant that William wasn't safe from Eddie even when he came home. When he was eleven, his family had moved and he believed that his ordeal was over. But on his first day at secondary school, to his absolute horror, he'd heard that feared voice shouting out: "Willy. . . !"

He hated the name. It was Eddie who started calling him that, and the name had caught on—even with the teachers.

It was just bad luck that they'd run into each other again. He'd be polite to Eddie, finish his drink; then go and wait for Helen outside her office.

He tried to analyze why he'd been so intimidated by Eddie all those years ago, but after so much time it didn't make sense. Maybe it never had. It wasn't as though Eddie had been the school bully; William was his only target.

William had skipped school many days, preferring to wander the streets rather than endure Eddie's continual harassment and victimization.

He closed his eyes, trying to shut out the awful memories. That was all they were: memories. Eddie had become a pathetic specimen, rambling on about the past simply because he had no future. William was glad he'd met him, because finally he could rid him from his mind. The tyrant had become a victim.

"Hello, Bill. Sorry I'm late."

He glanced up in surprise.

"Helen!" He smiled at her and rose to his feet. "Goodbye, Eddie. We've got to be going."

Helen was watching Eddie, obviously wondering why William should be sitting with someone who was halfway to being a tramp.

"Ah, so you're Helen," said Eddie. "I've heard all about you—although not how attractive you were. Why don't you sit down?"

As soon as he'd seen Helen, Eddie had begun to lie: he was always good at that. And at flattery.

"We have to go," said William.

"There's no rush, is there?" Helen said. "Get me a drink, Bill. I'm dying of thirst." She took a seat and smiled tentatively at Eddie, who sat opposite her.

William remained standing. "No," he said, "time's getting on. We ought to go."

"Buy the lady a drink," said Eddie, and he pushed his empty glass forward. "I'll have the same again."

William stared at him, then glanced at Helen.

"Cider?" he asked.

She nodded, and he went to the bar. He bought half a pint of dry cider and a beer for Eddie. When he returned, the other two were talking. Helen was smoking, even though she knew William didn't like it. Eddie had given her a cigarette.

"I was just telling Helen how we grew up together," said Eddie, "that we were best friends for years and years."

"And you met here by chance?" Helen said. "That's amazing, isn't it?"

"Yes," agreed William, without much enthusiasm. "Amazing."

"Bill's always been very reticent about his past," said Helen.

"Listen, Helen," said Eddie, lowering his voice and pretending that William couldn't hear, "if there's anything you want to know about Willy, just ask me."

Helen smiled. "Willy?" she said.

And William felt his guts twist.

He'd always made sure he was known as William, but he let his friends call him Bill. That was a strong, tough, no nonsense name. Not that he'd ever had many friends, male or female, to call him Bill.

His miserable existence had ended when Eddie left school, but it wasn't until Helen came along that William had known the true meaning of living. It had taken more than ten years for him to recover, to gain any confidence in himself. The fourteen months with Helen had been the best he had ever known, without a doubt.

But his nightmare had returned. The worst thing in his life had now met the best that had ever happened to him.

"Willy," Eddie said. "Or Little Willy."

William cringed. His intestines knotted even tighter.

"Little Willy," repeated Helen, and she giggled. "I can vouch for that."

William could hardly believe what he was hearing. Helen had only met Eddie a couple of minutes ago, and already she was making reference to sex. Although she and William had been to bed together a few times, they certainly didn't talk about what went on there.

Eddie laughed uproariously, far more than the comment was worth, and took a gulp of his beer. Helen imitated his action, downing half her cider in a single swallow.

"We'd do anything for each other, you know," said Eddie. "I remember once I had to catch a bus for a swimming competition after school, but I didn't have the fare. Willy lent me the money. It was only later I found out that he'd given me all he had on him, and he had to walk home."

That wasn't the way William remembered it. Eddie had forced him to hand over the bus fare. Somehow it had seemed the right thing to do at that moment; he'd wanted to help Eddie. Only later had he realized what had happened, that Eddie had manipulated him again.

"I admit it, Helen," Eddie continued, "I'm not the brightest of guys, not when it comes to academic subjects. My talents lie elsewhere. If it wasn't for Willy, I'd never have been able to keep up at school. He used to let me copy his homework. In exams, he'd pass me the answers."

Eddie didn't reveal how many times they'd been caught—and that it was always William who was accused of cheating. He'd even been blamed for copying Eddie's homework on several occasions, and he never understood why the teachers didn't realize the truth. Eddie wasn't very clever, but he had animal cunning, and he got away with it. Again and again.

As Eddie talked, Helen was captivated by every word, nodding her agreement and smiling. William wondered what she could see in him.

He was her exact opposite, everything she resented and avoided: crude, loud, dirty, badly dressed.

Eddie had always got on very well with girls. They found him fascinating, and he'd had numerous girlfriends at school—all of whom had delighted in the way Eddie picked on and teased William.

. . . Little Willy.

William forced himself to stay calm. It would be all over in a few minutes. They'd leave soon, and Eddie would be gone from their lives forever.

When Helen drained her glass, she asked for another. William looked at Eddie. It was time that he bought a round, but all he did was slide his glass across the table toward William.

William went to the bar again, and this time he also bought himself a drink.

Helen and Eddie were laughing together when he returned, and he had no doubt that they were laughing at him. They were sitting next to each other by now, and it was as though they'd known each other for years, that William was the outsider.

They spoke about him as if he wasn't there. Even Helen referred to him as Willy. She finally noticed William glaring at her, and she stubbed out her cigarette.

"I think we'd better be leaving," she said. "I'll just be a minute." She picked up her bag and made her way to the door marked *Ladies*.

Eddie watched her walk away.

"You're a lucky man, Willy," he said. "But then you always were."

William looked at him in astonishment.

"You've got everything, haven't you?" Eddie added.

William realized that he was right—because for him Helen was everything, all he'd ever wanted. She was good looking, witty, intelligent. What more could any man ask?

"And I've got nothing," Eddie said, and he gazed into his beer glass, not wanting to meet William's eyes. "I don't suppose you could lend me a few quid?"

William slipped his hand into his jacket for his wallet. Whatever he gave Eddie, it was worth it to get rid of him.

"Thanks," said Eddie. He reached over, took the wallet, and put it in his pocket.

They sat in silence, not knowing what to say to each other, until Helen returned.

"Another drink?" Eddie suggested.

Helen shook her head. "No, we must be going," she said. "It was nice meeting you."

"Good-bye," said William.

"Good-bye," said Eddie, then he stood up and went out with Helen.

Watching them leave, William thought what a coincidence it was meeting up with his old friend after so long. He really envied Eddie. Everything always worked out well for him, the lucky sod. What had he done to deserve such a terrific girl as Helen?

William finished his drink and looked around the pub, wondering what had made him come here tonight. There was something in the back of his mind, but it slipped away. He'd remember later, he supposed, if it was important.

He walked toward the bar, counting out the change from his pocket. He might as well have another drink while he was here. There was nothing else to do.

SOMETIMES, IN THE RAIN

Charles Grant

Charles L. Grant started out writing science fiction and has won awards for his short stories in that genre, however he is far better known these days for his horror. He is the author of many novels, including *In a Dark Dream, The Pet, For Fear of the Night,* and *Raven.* His short fiction has been published in *Post Mortem, Psycho-Paths, Monsters in Our Midst, Best New Horror,* and *The Year's Best Fantasy and Horror.* He was also the editor of the original horror anthology series *Shadows,* which defined quiet horror throughout the 1980s.

"Sometimes, in the Rain" is Grant at his best—literate, subtle, and decidedly chilly. It was originally published in *Northern Frights* 2.

—E. D.

There was rain that day in London, in the last month of the year. A soft rain, not much to it, and most of the noise it made came from falling off the leaves, the eaves, from the tips of people's umbrellas and the brims of their hats as they hurried past the house and never saw me in the chair. I didn't mind. I wasn't after company. And I suppose, if they had looked, they wouldn't have seen me anyway. When it rains in December, you don't expect to see someone sitting on a porch.

So they passed me by and let me watch them until the soft rain became hard rain and the tires spit instead of hissed, and the leaves bowed instead of trembled, and the eaves filled with a harsh rushing sound that slammed against thin metal as the water sped down the spouts and gushed onto the grass at all the house's corners.

I shivered a little, pulled my overcoat closer to my throat, and kind of tucked my chin a little closer to my chest.

Though it wasn't really cold, the snow we've had gone and churned to mud, it wasn't exactly spring either, and the tips of my fingers tingled a little, and the lobes of my ears protested by slightly burning until I rubbed them and made them burn for a different reason. Then I huddled again, and watched the rain.

Sometimes, but only sometimes, you can see things out there.

When everything, and everyone, has been washed of color, when edges blur and perspective distorts and light catches a raindrop and makes it flare silver, you can see things.

I waited.

The footstep a few minutes later didn't startle me, nor did the creak of the railing when she sat on it, one foot firm on the floorboard, the other swinging ever so slightly in time to the breeze that had decided to sweep down the tarmac and drag the rain with it. I watched her without moving my head, didn't say anything, finally let my gaze drift back to the sidewalk, the street, the houses across the way that had no lights yet in any of the windows.

"If you catch pneumonia out here," she said at last, not looking at me, "I'm not going to be responsible."

I shrugged.

I didn't much care one way or the other about her feelings of responsibility.

"I mean it, Len. I'm tired of it. I've had enough."

The dangling foot kicked lightly at the rail spindles.

A man walked by, hunched over in a pea coat, baseball cap yanked down to his Clark Gable ears. He had an old pipe in his mouth, the kind whose stem curves down and away, and up again to the bowl. He stopped at the foot of the walk and squinted at the house.

"Oh, swell," she said. The foot stabbed now. "Just what I need."

I sniffed, loudly.

She wore a cardigan over what they used to call a spinster blouse, and she tucked her hands into its pockets, bulging them as she pushed her fists together for warmth. Her profile was half shadow, half rainlight, enough magic there to take away most of the wrinkles and most of the years. With her short hair and the fact that she'd been lean since the first day out of the womb, she could have been any age from thirty to sixty.

In half shadow.

In the rainlight.

It was the voice that gave her away; it had been used for too many years for too many things that seldom made her laugh.

The man with the pipe saw me, nodded a greeting, and trudged up the walk.

She rolled her eyes, stared at the roof to search for the strength to keep her from killing him before he reached the steps. Me, too, probably; me, too.

"Afternoon, Gracie," Youngman Stevens said politely. His right hand made a tipping-his-cap gesture which she acknowledged by nodding, just barely. He grinned. "Len, you trying to kill yourself or what?"

"I like the rain," I said flatly, still watching the street.

"Well," Gracie said, angry that I'd spoken to an old man like Youngman and not to my own sister. But she didn't move except to kick the spindles again.

The breeze finally reached me, fussed with my hair until I slapped at it to keep it down. Youngman grinned again; hell, he was always grinning. He grinned at the funerals of our enemies and our friends; he grinned when we took our table up at the Aberdeen; he grinned when his wife died in his arms three summers ago, down at the river, in Labatt Park.

He leaned against the post and pulled off his cap, slapped the rain off it, and jammed it on again. Then he took the pipe from his mouth and dropped it into his coat pocket. Shadow or no shadow, there was no mistaking his age—he wore it like a mask he intended to take off any day now, to reveal that, by damn, he was only seventeen. His cheeks used to be chipmunk puffed, his nose round instead of a bulb, his eyes deepset instead of sinking into his skull. He had a habit of pulling at the corner of his upper lip, as if he were pulling at the mustache he used to have. He pulled it now. It drove Gracie crazy.

"So listen," he said to me. "You thirsty or what?"

I almost laughed. "It's pouring, you old fart, or hadn't you noticed? How the hell can I be thirsty?"

Youngman stared at the rain from around the post. "You ain't drinking it, are you?"

I shook my head.

"So?" He lifted a hand. "You thirsty?"

Gracie stood, foot stamping hard, sounding loud in spite of the damp. "Why the hell don't you just leave him be?" She stomped to the door, yanked it open, and stood there. "You're going to kill him, and he's too stupid to know it."

The door slammed behind her.

Youngman and I exchanged looks.

The rain eased its roaring; it was back to soft again, back to quiet.

"Y'know," he said, staring at the door, "when we was married, me and that woman, she wasn't nearly this cranky. What the hell'd you do to her?"

"I lived," I answered simply.

He understood and looked away.

And I stood. Slowly. As if, after all these years, I still had to get used to just how tall I was. I had never stooped, and when the years came that suggested gravity take over and give me a rest, I refused the invitation. Some claim it makes me look younger, or that they can tell when I'm not doing so well because I look somehow shorter; and every time I go to the States, they always, dammit, ask if I ever played basketball.

I pushed my coat into place around various places on my body. My left leg was a little stiff, and I sure didn't feel like racing, but all in all, I felt pretty good. I leaned over and plucked my hat from the floor, smoothed the brim, and said, "If we hurry, we can stay just long enough that it'll be too late to come back for supper. Then we'll have to eat there."

He laughed. He and Gracie had been married for just about four years before she got fed up and left him and moved, of all places, out to Vancouver. Four years of Youngman doing most of the cooking; and when she returned to move in with me, if I didn't feel like cooking, we ate out. I never let her in the kitchen, and she didn't mind. There were lots of things she was stubborn about, my younger sister by a dozen years, but she knew she couldn't boil water without burning the bottom out of the pan. Never thought it necessary to learn the culinary arts, and so she hadn't, with a vengeance.

As he turned to lead us down the steps, I took his shoulder and held him. "What?" I asked.

He didn't look back.

"C'mon, what?"

He shook my hand off, lowered his head, and stepped into the rain.

I frowned, called something hasty over my shoulder in case Gracie was eavesdropping from the living room window, and hurried after him.

The rain was cold.

By nightfall, less than an hour or so away, it would freeze on the streets and pavement, and coat the dead grass white. Maybe snow by midnight, though it didn't feel like it yet; but it would make coming home a treacherous trip. I almost changed my mind. I knew what happened when folks like me fell. We look healthy, maybe; we look like we'll live forever. But bones bust too easily and healing isn't ever easy again, if we ever heal at all. The only thing that kept me moving was the thought of Gracie nagging at me to cook. Weather like this, she wouldn't go out on a bet. Then I'd have to listen to her all night.

By the time I caught up to him he was already on Dundas Street, heading west. A few cars on the road, the streetlamps already on, and the rain. Across the street a woman hurried up a walk with grocery bags hugged in her arms, a small dog racing up the steps ahead of her.

Youngman hesitated when he saw her.

Then I knew.

"Thought you saw her, right?" I said softly.

He didn't nod; it didn't matter.

We walked on.

Funny how it was, back when we thought we knew it all even when we suspected we didn't know a damn thing—funny, I guess, how this little old man was once a little young guy with not much going for him but good hands with wood, and how this woman came along to take Gracie's sting away. Funny how it happens, just when you think you've used it all up and there's nothing left but empty, and having drinks with your friends.

Funny.

A drop exploded on the back of my neck, like being stabbed with melting ice, and I shuddered, twisted my shoulders, and knew that when I got back, my sister would give me hell about not taking an umbrella.

"She was at the park," Youngman said as we reached a corner and habit forced us to check for traffic that was seldom there.

I made a sound, neither believing nor disbelieving.

"Not very clear," he went on, taking his time stepping up the next curb. His right hip was bad, but not as bad as his heart. Or mine. I don't know if she saw me.

"You go up to her?"

He looked at me, astonished. "You kidding? Scared the hell out of me, Len."

"You've seen her before."

"Scared the hell out me then, too."

We walked on.

Finally I couldn't stop the asking: "What do you think she wants?"

He didn't know, didn't have a clue, and we debated the possibilities over a couple of drinks, over supper, over a couple of drinks more; we talked about it to Maggie McClure—theoretically, of course and the Aberdeen's owner had no opinion one way or the other except that she was getting tired of hearing Youngman asking everybody in creation about seeing his wife, what the meaning was, or if he was really crazy.

"Christ, Youngman," she said, "don't you ever watch hockey or anything? Give it a rest, for God's sake. Ask me about the weather."

We didn't have to.

The rain did what it was supposed to for the rest of the night, and Youngman left before he was too drunk to walk. I sat alone for a while. I wasn't worried about ice or snow or finding my way back if I went over my limit. And I didn't laugh, as the others did, telling each other a new Youngman story.

Because sometimes, but only sometimes, you can see things in the rain.

I sat there and held the empty glass until Maggie suggested, very gently, it was time to go home.

I sat there, you know. I sat there out at that damn, goddamn hospital, and held Dad's swollen, darkening hand until the nurse told me twice visiting hours were over. But I couldn't let go. He was thin, he was pale, his lips moved and made no sound, his body shook once in a while, his eyelids bulged whenever he saw something in the dark where he lived. I sat there, thinking that I was damn near fifty, for God's sake, and it was right that Dad should be afraid and should need someone, even me, to hold his hand while he left. He wasn't going to last forever.

I had dozed.

I woke up.

Father didn't.

That was that.

"Len?"

I kind of snorted, shook my head, and grinned at Maggie. "Thinking," I said.

"About what? Winning a lottery?"

A shrug, a few bills on the table without counting, and I stepped outside, flipped up my collar, adjusted my hat, and started for home.

Cold; it was cold that night.

Raindrops caught the bare branches and froze into clear hanging flowers glittering in the streetlamp light; cars moved more slowly, a bus sounded huge and warm, and a pickup backfired softly in the distance; no people but me, and I wondered what the hell I thought I was doing when, instead of heading back to the house, I moved down the street, past the museums, the courthouse, and took the long sloping block down to the park.

The Thames is dark in winter daylight, rushing ebony at night, and the city above and behind, the houses across the way, didn't provide much light, only gave birth to shifting shadows. Especially under the trees that line the tarmac path following the river. I shivered a little and called myself too many kinds of fool to count, and decided, with a sigh that puffed a ghost in front of my face, that maybe it was time Youngman saw a doctor.

A moment later I thought maybe I should see one too.

Because she was there.

She wore a camel's hair coat, a small black hat on her auburn hair, and carried a white purse over one arm.

I would have known her anywhere: Edith Stevens, dead three years and looking no different than the last time I saw her when she was alive.

She was across the water, at the base of the concrete wall that kept the Thames from taking the homes above it. Barely seen in mist and shadow, but it was her, no question about it, and as my left hand reached out to grab the nearest bole to keep me standing, the rain came back and washed her away.

Just like that.

I stood there; I waited; I looked around slowly when someone touched my arm, and Gracie took my elbow, tugged a little, and led me away. She didn't say a word until we were nearly home, but I could feel it and it bothered me—my sister was afraid.

She asked me if I was drunk, and I told her I didn't think so, and told her what I'd seen. A little moan, a disgusted sigh, and we were finally inside, coat and hat hung in the closet, shoes off, socks off, me in my living room chair while she fussed in the kitchen.

Tea, a tray of cookies, napkins, sugar, and spoons.

She set them on a coffee table that separated our chairs, sat, and looked at me.

I smiled; I couldn't help it.

When we were young—or at least younger than we were—I was round and she was angles, but age had swapped our features. And for her age, though I'd never told her, she wasn't at all bad looking. It was the bile that made her ugly.

The front window was at my right shoulder, and as I sipped I looked out. Not much to see when the inside lights are on, only my reflection floating beneath black glass, and a faint cloud of white from the streetlamp down the block.

"What do you think she wants?" Gracie asked.

I couldn't believe it. No scolding, no sarcasm, no verbal whipping for the bad boy who walked around in the middle of a January night, courting pneumonia when he ought to damn well know better. It took me a while to find an answer.

"Gracie, I've had a few drinks, you know, and not a hell of a lot to eat. Edith is dead. She wasn't there, it was just the stories, you know how Youngman is."

She glanced out the window.

The rain had turned to sleet and was scraping at the pane.

For a minute there, I didn't think she was breathing.

"Gracie?"

Two breaths; two slow breaths.

"Do you know why I came back?"

I grinned. "Sure. To devil me into my grave."

Still looking out the window: "Because I thought you might need me. I don't know why. It wasn't much fun out there. You had Dad, and I had a couple of husbands after . . . him. But when they were all gone, I thought maybe you'd need me."

It wasn't in her face—that was as expressionless as one could get without wearing a mask; it was in the tone beneath the monotone, and I nearly choked.

I think she hated me.

She put her cup down, brushed some crumbs from her lap, and left the room. I didn't say anything because I couldn't think of anything to say. I suppose I could have protested that I did in fact need her, despite her carping and belligerence, if only because it was nice to have another person in the house to keep away the hours when the hours were all empty. She wouldn't have believed me, though.

I sat there for another hour, staring blindly out the window, and when I tried the tea again, it was cold enough to make me shudder. So I cleaned up, went to bed, and barely slept.

When I did, it was frightening.

Which not surprisingly left me cranky as hell the next morning, especially when I looked out and saw the goddamn rain.

Gracie and I fought over what to have for breakfast, what to wear to go to the market once the rain had let up enough to let us out of the house, what to watch on TV . . . name it, we snapped and bit and snarled about it. At one point, it got so ludicrous I started to laugh, and that only made it worse. By lunchtime, we couldn't stand to be in the same room together; by midafternoon, I had jammed myself into my chair with a book I didn't want to read and pointedly ignored her every time she stomped through; by dinner, I had had it. I grabbed my coat and hat from the hall closet, marched into the kitchen and said, "I'm going to the Aberdeen. There's frozen dinners in the freezer."

She was at the table, doing a crossword puzzle in the paper. She looked at me without raising her head. "We had an affair, you know."

I looked at the ceiling for deliverance. "What the hell are you talking about?"

"Youngman and I," she answered. And she smiled. "You never knew, did you."

"Oh sure," I said, buttoning my coat. "You flew in from Vancouver while I wasn't looking, hit the hay with him, flew back, and never said a word."

She shrugged. "A couple of times he flew out. A business trip, you know?" She touched the pencil point to her tongue, marked a square in the puzzle.

"Sure you did," I said, and walked out.

No; I slammed out.

The rain had eased, the cold had returned, and it took me forever to get to the pub because the sidewalk had turned to thin ice, the kind you can't really see until you're parked on your ass, wondering what the hell had happened. All the time, I fumed. I knew what she was trying to do—she wanted me and Youngman apart so she could have me to herself. It would, she'd be thinking, be fitting. I had had Dad; she would have me.

Jesus.

What I wanted then was a couple of stiff drinks, and Youngman's ear to bend until he slapped me a couple of times to bring me to my senses. But I had no sooner stepped inside, when Maggie grabbed my arm and turned me around.

"What?" I said, not believing I'd be thrown out before I'd even gotten in.

"That idiot," she said, nodding sharply toward the door. "He comes running in, says he's seen his damn wife again, shouts a hail and farewell and scares half my customers to death, and runs out again."

I tried to think, but Maggie wouldn't let me. She opened the door and gently nudged me to the sidewalk.

"Go get him, Len, before he kills himself, eh? He said he was going to Labatt."

I must have looked my age then, standing at the curb, the rain an evening mist. I was confused, I was unnerved, and I was more than a little frightened that Youngman would do something really stupid. And how was I supposed to stop him?

I hurried to the park as fast as my legs and the weather would let me, still half-burning over Gracie, and half-weeping over Stevens. I had seen it before, and kicked myself for not seeing it now—others my age, the age we all reach when we never think we will, finding not much left of the future and so go sneaking off to the past for something to hold on to when it was time for no future at all.

Like Dad had done with me.

Like Gracie wanted me to do with her.

I stumbled and grabbed a fencepost to keep from falling; I tripped over a curb and went down on one knee, crying out and not caring if anyone could hear; I hurried down the slope, under the overpass, and saw him on the wide grassy bank, not a foot from the water.

Rushing out of the night above, and into the night below.

No light on it at all.

"Hey!" I called weakly, out of breath, sagging against a tree, feeling the cold work up my arms. "Hey, you old fart, I need a drink, you coming?"

His cap was over his ears, his pipe in his left hand, his pea coat glittering as if it had been sewn with stars. He grinned at me, waved the pipe over his shoulder.

"Gotta go, Len," he said.

I shook my head. "Youngman, this is crazy. Please. Just get your sorry ass over here and we'll go have something to eat. Gracie's pissed at me, and I could use the company."

He laughed without a sound, and something dark moved behind him. "Sorry, Len."

"Stevens, dammit!"

A car slashed by, somewhere above us.

Youngman tucked his pipe into his pocket. "I finally figured it out," he said as the dark form met the light. "She's going to show me the way." A tilt of his head. "Gonna miss you, old friend."

I couldn't say it; I felt as if I were strangling.

Edith, camel hair coat and white purse, slipped her hand around his arm, and he pressed it lovingly to his side.

He grinned.

He waved quickly, and they turned their backs to me.

God, no, I thought; please, God, no.

Onto the river, then, and down; into the dark.

I stood there for a while, a couple of seconds, a couple of minutes, before I pushed myself away from the tree, too weary to be angry, too saddened to be scared.

I walked.

That's all; I just walked, and wondered about the funeral. No one would believe me, least of all Gracie, and I hoped that someone, and I knew it would be me, would arrange a memorial service for that stupid idiot in that stupid cap.

A siren exploded somewhere, not very far away, and for a moment my heart and lungs stopped because it sounded like Youngman.

And he was screaming.

I even looked back, mouth open, eyes wide, until I saw flashing lights streak around the corner at the top of the tarmac slope.

But the siren kept on screaming, and it sounded just like him, and I did my best to run, not getting very far because the heart, the lungs, and the legs just couldn't take it. I managed to get up to Dundas Street without stopping, managed to get three blocks more before I realized there were no sirens anymore, but the lights were still spinning, up there by the Aberdeen. I squinted, and counted two patrol cars parked nose-in at the curb, and an ambulance swept by me, making me jump away from the curb.

Maggie, I thought, finally shot a deadbeat customer.

I was wrong.

I went up there, and I was wrong.

When I hadn't come back, she had gone looking for me again. Maggie told me later she had been furious, nearly spitting, when I wasn't at my table. So mad she'd stepped off the curb without looking, and the truck hadn't stopped in time, braking and skidding on the rainmist ice-slick street.

I don't know if I actually passed out or just slid into a stupor, but the next thing I knew there was a funeral, there were people, there was Maggie McClure, there was silence. A day, a week, I don't know how long it was, but the rain stopped, and I spent most of my time packing her clothes to give to charity, or a church, I hadn't made up my mind.

That's when I found the letter—she and Youngman, years after their divorce, carrying on, practically coast to coast.

"Son of a bitch," I said in her empty bedroom. "Son of a bitch."

That, more than anything, made me remember the night they had died.

That, more than anything, made me remember the siren, made me wonder if that first wailing really had been Youngman screaming, because Edith knew.

I don't know.

But there's rain now, never snow, almost every day. It slips from the eaves and rushes along the gutters and no one ever looks while I sit on the porch and watch.

Funny how things are; I used to think it would be Dad who would come to show me the way when the way was open for me to take it.

Not now.

Sometimes, in the rain, I can see her across the street, standing beneath a pine tree, waiting for me to leave.

She isn't smiling, my Gracie.

She isn't smiling at all.

RAIN FALLS

Michael Marshall Smith

Michael Marshall Smith was born in Knutsford, Cheshire, England, and grew up in the United States, South Africa, and Australia. He lives in London and is a freelance graphic designer as well as a writer. His first novel, *Only Forward*, was published to critical acclaim in 1994. His short fiction has been published in *Omni*, *Peeping Tom*, *Chills*, *Dark Voices*, *Shadows Over Innsmouth*, *The Anthology of Fantasy and the Supernatural*, both *Darkland* anthologies, *Best New Horror*, and *The Year's Best Fantasy and Horror*. He has won three British Fantasy Awards.

Smith is particularly talented in laying down the details that firmly set the reader in the world he has created. The story first appeared in one of the *Mammoth* series edited by Stephen Jones.

—E. D.

I saw what happened. I don't know if anyone else did. Probably not, which worries me. I just happened to see, to be looking in the right directions at the right times. Or the wrong times. But I saw what happened.

I was sitting at one of the tables in The Porcupine, up on the raised level. The Porcupine is a pub on Camden High Street, right on the corner where the smaller of the three markets hangs its hat. At least, there is a pub there, and that's the one I was sitting in. It's not actually called The Porcupine. I've just always called it that for some reason, and I can never remember what its real name is.

On a Saturday night the pub is always crowded with people who've stopped off on the way to the subway after spending the afternoon trawling round the markets. You have to get there very early to score one of the tables up on the raised level: either that or sit and watch like a hawk for when one becomes free. It's an area about ten feet square, with a wooden rail around it, and the windows look out onto the High Street. It's a good place to sit and watch the passing throng, and the couple of feet of elevation gives an impression of looking out over the interior of the pub too.

I didn't get to the pub until about eight o'clock, and when I arrived there wasn't a seat anywhere, never mind on the upper level. The floor was crowded with the usual disparate strands of local color, talking fast and loud. For some reason I always think of them as beatniks, a word which is past its use-by date by about twenty years. I guess it's because the people who hang out in Camden always seem like throwbacks to me. I can't really believe in counterculture in the '90s: not when you know they'll all end up washing their hair some day, and trading the beaten-up Volkswagen for a nice new Ford Sierra.

I angled my way up to the bar and waited for one of the Australians behind it to see me. As I waved some money diffidently around, hoping to catch someone's eye, I flinched at the sound of a sudden shout from behind me.

"Ere, you! Been putting speed in this then 'ave you?"

I half-turned to see that the man standing behind me was shouting at someone behind the bar, gesticulating with a bottle of beer. He was tall, had very short hair and a large ring in his ear, and spoke—or bawled—with a Newcastle accent of compact brutality.

My face hurriedly bland, I turned back to the bar. A ginger-haired bar person was smiling uncertainly at the man with the earring, unsure of how seriously to take the question. The man laughed violently, nudged his mate hard enough to spill his beer, and then shouted again.

"You 'ave, mate. There's drugs in this."

I assume it was some kind of joke relating to how drunk the man felt, but neither I nor the barman were sure. Then a barmaid saw me waiting, and I concentrated on communicating to her my desire for a Budweiser, finding the right change, that sort of thing. When I'd paid I moved away from the bar, carefully skirting the group where the shouting man stood with three or four other men in their mid-twenties. They were all talking very loudly and grinning with vicious good humor, faces red and glistening in the warmth of the crowded pub.

A quick glance around showed that there was still nowhere to sit, so I shuffled my way through the crowd to stand by the long table which runs down the center of the room. By standing in the middle of the pub, and only a few feet away from the steps to the raised area, I would be in a good position to see when a seat became available.

After ten minutes I was beginning to wonder whether I shouldn't just go home instead. I wasn't due to be meeting anyone: I'd spent the day at home working and just fancied being out of doors. I'd brought my current book and was hoping to sit and read for a while, surrounded by the buzz of a Saturday night. The Porcupine's a good pub for that kind of thing. The clientele are quite interesting to watch, the atmosphere is generally good, and if you care to eavesdrop you can learn more about astrology in one evening than you would have believed there was to know.

That night it was different, and it was different because of the group of men standing by the bar. They weren't alone, it seemed. Next to them stood another three, and another five were spread untidily along one side of the long table. They were completely unlike the kind of people you normally find in there, and they changed the feel of the pub. For a start they were all shouting, all at the same time, so that it was impossible to believe that any of them could actually be having a conversation. If they were all talking at the same time, how could they be? They didn't look especially drunk, but relaxed in a hard and tense way. Most of all they looked dangerous.

There's a lot of talk these days about violence to women, and so there should be. In my book, anyone who lays a hand on a woman is breaking the rules. It's simply not done. On the other hand, anyone who gets to their twenties or thirties before they get thumped has had it pretty easy, violence-wise. It's still wrong, but basically what I'm saying is: try being a man. Being a man involves getting hit quite a lot, from a very early age. If you're a teenage girl the physical contact you get tends to be positive: hugs from friends and parents. No one hugs teenage boys. They hit them, fairly often, and quite hard.

Take me, for example. I'm a nice middle-class bloke, and I grew up in a comfortable suburb and went to a good school. It's not like I grew up on an estate or anything. But I took my fair share of knocks, recreational violence that came and went in a meaningless second. I've got a small kink in my nose, for example, which came from it being broken one night. I was walking back from a pub with a couple of friends and three guys behind us simply decided they'd like to push us around. For them the evening clearly wouldn't be complete without a bit of a fight.

We started walking more quickly, but that didn't work. The guys behind us just walked faster. In the end I turned and tried to talk to them, idiot that I was at that age. I said we'd had a good evening and didn't want any trouble. I pointed out that there was a policewoman on the other side of the street. I advanced the opinion that perhaps we could all go our separate ways without any unnecessary unpleasantness. Given that I was more than a little drunk, I think I was probably quite eloquent.

The nearest of them thumped me. He hit me very hard, right on the side of the nose. Suddenly losing faith in reason and the efficacy of a logical discussion, I turned to my friends, to discover that they were already about fifty yards up the road and gaining speed.

I turned to the guys in front of me again. Two of them were grinning, little tight smiles under sparkling eyes. The other was still standing a little closer to me, restlessly shifting his weight from foot to foot. His eyes were blank. I started to recap my previous argument, and he punched me again. I took a clumsy step backwards, in some pain, and he hit me again, a powerful and accurate belt to the cheekbone.

Then, for no evident reason, they drifted off. I turned to see that a police van was sitting at the corner of the road, but I don't think that had made any difference. It was a good eighty yards away, and wasn't coming any closer. My two friends were standing talking to a policeman who was leaning out of the passenger window. There was no sign that any action was going to be taken. There didn't need to be. That's what violence is like, in its most elemental, unnecessary form. It comes, and it goes, like laughter or a cold draught from under a door.

I trotted slowly up the road, and my friends turned and saw me with some relief. The policeman took one look, reached behind into the cab, and passed out a large roll of cotton wool. It was only then that I realized that the lower half of my face, and all of my sweatshirt, was covered in blood.

My face was a little swollen for a couple of days, and my nose never looked quite the same again. But my point is, it was no big deal. The matter-of-fact way in which the policeman handed me something to mop up with said it all. It wasn't important. If you're a man, that kind of thing is going to happen. You wipe your nose and get on.

And that's why when a man walks into a pub, he takes a quick, unconscious look around. He's looking to see if there's any danger, and if so, where it's likely to be located. Similarly, if a fight breaks out, a woman may want to watch, a little breathless with excitement, or she may want to charge fearlessly in and tell them all to stop being silly. Both reasonable reactions, but most men will want to turn the other way, to make themselves invisible. They know that violence isn't a spectator sport: it has a way of reaching out and pulling you in. It won't matter that you don't know anyone involved, that you're just sitting having a quiet drink. These things just happen. There's generally a reason for violence against women. It'll be a very bad reason, don't get me wrong, but there'll be a reason.

Among men violence may be just like an extreme, cold spasm of high spirits. There may not be any reason for it at all, and that's why you have to be very, very careful.

The string of guys standing and sitting near the bar in The Porcupine were giving off exactly the kind of signals that you learn to watch out for. Something about the set of their faces, their restless glances and rabid good humor, said that unreason was at work. The one by the bar was still hollering incomprehensibly at the barman, who was still smiling uncertainly back. Another of the group was leaning across his mate to harangue a couple of nervous-looking girls sitting at a table up against the bar. One of them was wearing a tight sweater, and that's probably all it had taken to kick-start the man's hormones. The look on his face was probably meant to be endearing. It wasn't.

After a couple of minutes the two girls gathered up their stuff and left, but I didn't swoop over to their table. It was too close to the men. Just by being there, by getting too close to their aura, I could have suddenly found myself in trouble. That may sound paranoid, or cowardly: but I've seen it happen. I had every right to sit there, just as a woman has every right to dress the way she wants without attracting unwelcome attention. Rights are nice ideas, a comforting window through which to view the world. But once the glass is broken, you realize they were never really there.

So I remained standing by the long table, sipping my beer and covertly looking around. I couldn't work out what they were doing here. One of them had a woolly hat, which was doing the rounds and getting more and more grubby and beer-stained. I thought it had the letters "FC" on the front somewhere, which would almost certainly stand for Football Club, but I couldn't understand why or how a group of football supporters could have ended up in The Porcupine when it's not near any of the major grounds. One of the groups linked arms to shout some song together at one point, but I couldn't discern any of the words.

I was glancing across to the bar, to see how long the queues were and decide whether it was worth hanging round for another beer, when I saw the first thing. It was very unexceptional, but it's one of the things I saw.

The door onto the main street had been propped open by the staff, presumably in a vain attempt to drop the temperature in the crowded room to something approaching bearable. As I swept the far end of the bar with my gaze, trying to judge the best place to stand if I wanted to get served that evening, a large grey dog came in through the door, and almost immediately disappeared into the throng. I noticed and remembered it because I was sort of expecting its owner to follow him in, but nobody came. I realized he or she must already be in the pub, and the dog had simply popped out for a while. The owner would have to be a he, I decided: no woman would want a dog like that. I only got a very quick sighting of it, but it was very large and slightly odd-looking, a shaggy hound that moved with a speed that was both surprising and somehow oily.

At that moment I saw a couple who were sitting at a table in the raised area reach for their coats, and I forgot about the dog. The couple had been sitting at the best table in the pub, one which is right in the corner of the room, up against the big windows. I immediately started cutting through the mass of people toward it.

Once I'd staked the table out as my territory I went to the bar and bought another beer. It may have been my imagination but it looked to me as if the staff were very aware of the group of men too: though they were all busy, each glanced out into the body of the pub while I was there, keeping half an eye on the long table. I avoided the area completely and got myself served right at the top of the bar, next to the door.

I settled myself back down at the table, glad that the evening was getting on track. I glanced out of the window, though it was mid-evening by then, too late for much to be going on. A few couples strolled by outside in a desultory fashion, dressed with relentless trendiness. Some kind of altercation was taking place in the Kentucky Fried Chicken opposite, and a derelict with dreadlocks was picking through a bin on the pavement near the window. If I can get the window seat early enough I like to sit and watch, but the strong moonlight made the view look distant somehow, unreal.

A fresh surge of noise made me turn away from the window and look out across the pub. One of the men had knocked over his beer, or had it knocked over. Those nearby were shouting and laughing. It didn't look like much was going to come of it. I'd opened my book and was about to start reading when I noticed something else.

There was one more person in the party than there had been before. Now you're probably going to think that I simply hadn't registered him, but that's not true. I'd looked at them hard and long. If I'd seen this man before, I would have remembered it. He was standing with the group nearest the steps which led up to the area where I was sitting. I say "standing with," because there was something about him that set him apart slightly from the other men, though he was right in the middle of them, and had the cocky pub charisma of someone who's used to respect among his peers. He was wearing jeans and a bulky grey jacket, typical sloppy casual, his dark hair was slightly waved, and his face came to a point in an aquiline nose. He exuded a sort of manic calm, as if it was the result of a bloodstream coursing with equal quantities of heroin and ecstasy, and he was listening to two of the other men with his mouth hanging slackly open, head tilted on one side. When there was another wave of noise from the other part of the group he raised his head slightly, the corners of his mouth creased in a half-smile of anticipation, keen to see what was going on, what new devilry was afoot. He was at home here. This is what he knew, what he was good at. This was where he lived.

He had weird eyes, too. They weren't too big or small, and they weren't a funny color or anything. But they were dead, like two coins pushed into clay. They weren't the kind of eyes you would want to see looking at you across a pub, if you were a woman. If you were a man, they weren't eyes you wanted to see at all. They were not good eyes.

I watched with an odd sort of fascination as the man stood with a loose-limbed solidity, turning from side to side to participate in the various shouting matches going on around him. And all the time he had this half-smile, as if he was enjoying every epic moment. I caught a momentary look on the face of one of his mates, a look of slight puzzlement, but I couldn't interpret it any more closely than that. Not at the time, anyway.

After a while I lost interest and finally started reading my book. The pub was warm, but the window next to me was cool, and I can tune out just about anything when I'm reading. I don't wear a watch, so I don't know how long it was before it all went off.

There was the sudden sound of breaking glass, and the noise level in the pub dipped for a moment, before shooting up into pandemonium. Startled, I looked up, still immersed in my book. Then my head went very clear.

A fight had broken out. That's what they do. They break out, appear like rain from clear April skies. Virtually all of the men around the table seemed to be involved, apart from a pair who were gloatingly watching from the sidelines. The rest of the pub were doing what people always do in these situations. The bar staff were either cowering or gearing themselves up to do something, and the other customers were shifting back in their seats, watching but trying to move out of trouble. I couldn't really see what was going on, but it looked as if the men had taken on another, smaller, group who'd been sitting affably at the bar.

Among the general noise and chaos, I saw that the man with the bulky grey jacket was right in the thick of it. In fact it looked rather as if he'd started the whole thing. Once I'd noticed him again the rest of the action seemed to shade away, and I saw him loop a fist into the mêlée. A couple of the male bar staff emerged into the body of the pub, holding their hands out in a placatory way, trying to look stern. The ginger-haired one in particular looked as if he wished this wasn't his job, that he was a waiter in some nice bistro instead. A couple of men responded by ploughing into them, and the fight immediately leapt up to a new level of intensity. People nearby hurriedly slipped out of their chairs and fled to the sides of the room. A beer bottle was smashed and brandished, and it all looked as if it was going to get very serious indeed.

As everybody was watching the new focus of attention, I happened to glance down toward the other end of the long table. The man in the grey jacket, I was surprised to see, had stopped fighting. He had his arm round the tall man with the earring, who'd been hurt, and was leading him toward the toilets at the back of the pub. I clocked this, and then turned to look back at the other end. The manager, a large man with forearms the size of my thighs, had come out from behind the counter. He was holding a pool cue and looked as if he had every intention of using it.

Luckily, I wasn't the only person who thought so. The man waving the broken bottle faltered, only for a moment, but it was enough. The guy he'd been threatening took a step back, and suddenly the mood dropped. It happened as quickly as that. A gust of wind dispersed the cloud, and sparks stopped arcing through the air. The fight had gone away.

There was a certain amount of jockeying as the two groups of men disentangled and took up their previous positions. The manager kept a firm eye on this, cue still in hand. The other customers gradually relaxed in their seats and slowly, like a fan coming to rest, the evening settled.

When I'd finished my beer I started toward the bar for another, and then elected to go to the toilets first. It was a bit of a struggle getting through the crowd toward the far end of the bar, and my route took me a little closer to the men than I would have liked. When I passed them, however, I relaxed a little. They were still up, still feisty, but the main event of the evening was over. I don't know how, but I could sense that. The mood was different, and something had been satisfied. The funniest joke had been told.

I hesitated for a moment before entering the toilets. As far as I knew, the man with the grey jacket and his wounded colleague were still in there. The Porcupine's toilet is not big, and I'd have to walk quite close to them. But then I thought "fuck it," and pushed the door open. You can be too bloody cautious. Quite apart from anything else, the mood in the aftermath of a fight tends to be one of fierce good humor and comradeship. A nod and a grunt from me would be enough to show I was one of the lads.

I needn't have worried, because it was empty. I took a leak into one of the urinals, and then turned to wash my hands at the minuscule washbasin. There was a certain amount of blood still splattered across the porcelain, the result of a bad nosebleed, by the look of it.

Then I noticed that there were drops of blood on the floor too, leading in the direction of the cubicle. The door was nearly shut, but not actually closed, which was odd. It didn't feel as if anyone was behind the door, and people don't generally pull a cubicle door to when they leave. Not knowing why I was doing so, I carefully pushed it open with my finger.

When it was open a couple of inches I nearly shouted, but stopped myself. When it was open all the way I just stared.

The walls of the cubicle were splattered with blood up to the level of the ceiling, as if someone had loaded dark red paint onto a thick brush and tried to paint the walls as quickly as possible. A couple of lumps of ragged flesh lay behind the bottom of the toilet, and the bowl was full of mottled blood, with a few pale chips of something floating near the top.

My mind balked at what I was seeing, and I simply couldn't understand what might have happened until I saw a large metal ring on the floor, nearly hidden behind one of the lumps.

Moving very quickly, I left the toilet. The pub was still seething with noise and heat, and the way through to the raised area was completely blocked. Suddenly remembering you could do such a thing, I ducked out of the side door. I could walk around the pub and re-enter at the front, much closer to my seat. Or I could just start running. But I didn't think I should. I had to get my book, or people might wonder why it was still there.

The air outside the pub was cool, and I hurried along the wall. After a couple of yards I stopped when I saw a movement on the other side of the road.

The dog was sitting there. Now that it was still, I could see just how large it was. It was much bigger than a normal dog, and bulkier. And it was looking at me, with flat grey eyes.

We stared at each other for a moment. I couldn't move, and just hoped to God it was going to stay where it was. I wanted to sidle along the wall, to get to the bit where the windows started so that people could see me, but I didn't have the courage. If I moved, it might come for me.

It didn't. Still looking directly at me, the dog raised its haunches and then walked slowly away, down toward the dark end of the street where the lamps aren't working. I watched it go, still not trusting. Just before the corner it turned and looked at me again, and then it was gone.

I went back into the pub, grabbed my book and went home. I didn't tell anyone what I'd found. They'd discover it soon enough. As I hurried out of the pub I heard one of the men at the table wonder where Pete was. There was no point me telling him, or showing him what was left. I had to look after myself.

I noticed all of those things. I was looking in those directions, and saw what I saw. I saw the earring on the floor of the cubicle, still attached to the remains of its owner's face. I saw that the man in the grey jacket wasn't there when I left, but that nobody seemed to be asking after him. I saw the look one of the other men had given him, a look of puzzlement, as if he was wondering exactly when he'd met this man with grey eyes, where he knew him from. And I saw the look in the eyes of the dog, and the warning that it held.

I didn't tell anyone anything, but I don't know whether that will be enough. It wasn't my fault I saw things. I wasn't looking for trouble. But I understand enough to realize that makes no difference. Rain will sometimes fall, and I was standing underneath.

I haven't been to The Porcupine in the last month. I've spent a lot of time at home, watching the street. In the last couple of days I've started to wonder if there are as many cats around as usual, and I've heard things outside the window in the night, shufflings. They may not mean anything. It may not be important that the darkness outside my window is becoming paler, as the moon gets fuller every night. All of this may amount to nothing.

But it makes me nervous. It makes me really very nervous.

THAT OLD SCHOOL TIE

Jack Womack

Originally from Lexington, Kentucky, Womack is now happily ensconced in New York City where he has assembled a huge collection of nonfiction esoterica. He is the author of the novels *Ambient, Terraplane, Heathern, Elvissey,* and *Random Acts of Senseless Violence. Elvissey* won a Philip K. Dick Award in 1994. Womack has written only a handful of short fiction pieces, but each has been a gem, imbued with his trademark sly humor and eye for character. Unlike his longer works, which have been occasionally labeled cyberpunk, his short fiction focuses on obsessive relationships, which rarely if ever, come to a good end. "That Old School Tie" is reprinted from the anthology *Little Deaths.*

—E. D.

Charles spun webs of charm and guilt around his friends, entwining them tighter if they tried to wander, loosing them once they drew near. The resulting networks were so complex that it was impossible for onlookers, or even participants, to discern who might be spider and who, fly.

We met at college and grew closer over the years, as people do when they have nothing in common but the length of time they've known one another. He taught English at NYU and wrote several books about lesser figures of the Romantic period, who seemed all the lesser once he was through with them. I'd been in pre-med until discovering how readily I weakened at the sight of real blood, and so I edited medico-legal textbooks instead; forensic pathology was my *métier*. Call it slumming amid the stews of human behavior, if you like; Charles once did. The manuscripts arrived in my office exclusive of their photographs—cake without frosting, as it were.

Charles and his wife Elaine, a divorce lawyer, lived on Riverside Drive, in a long-hall apartment overlooking the shadier side of 99th Street; their six-year-old daughter, Cecily, attended a good school, though one unblessed with alumni of more than moderate renown. I lived alone, on 95th Street.

They rented a house in Springs every other August; he invited me out one weekend, the summer before his final semester. On Saturday we went to the beach, smothering sandfleas beneath our towels as we roasted ourselves; Cecily begged her mother to put away the phone she'd brought along.

"Charles," Elaine said, pressing her palm over the mouthpiece. "Put some sunblock on me, please. I'm burning already." While she consulted with her client, Charles rubbed oil into his wife's shoulders until they shone. His own were as muscular as they'd been in college, when he was on the crew; I was never one for sports, myself. Rubbing his hands dry against his plaid swim trunks, he reached into Elaine's bag, extracted a cigarette and lit it.

"He's got nothing to go on, believe me," she told her client. "Give him enough rope, they always use it—"

"*Mommy—!*" Cecily said; Elaine lifted a finger, shushing her. She shook her father's arm as if to break it off, and whispered into his ear. "You take me swimming."

"Mom's a better swimmer," Charles said, gently pushing her aside. "She was on the team at Vassar. Want to go to Vassar?"

"Take me now."

"Shouldn't complain until you have something to complain about, honey."

"*Now!*"

He looked at his daughter, appearing to love her. Charles's parents held old Yankee notions of appropriate behavior, and drummed into him the belief that revealing one's emotions to a feckless world is a shameful act. While young, he perfected an impenetrable façade—bland half-smile, eyes lowered but alert—that served him in every situation, however pleasant or grotesque. The structure was unimportant to the facing; the person, superfluous to the mask.

"*Cecily!*" She quieted.

"The writ's in order. Don't worry, I said. Call you Monday."

Elaine put away her phone and stood, dropping the towel with which she was swathed. Her bathing suit, a white maillot, sheathed her torso with a condom's snugness. None of Elaine's physical attributes would have been unattractive had they appeared, singly, on other women; the ensemble as presented was sadly disconcerting. Her suit rode up her hips with every step as she led Cecily toward the sea. Charles stared at his wife, evincing no more emotion than when he'd watched her talking on the phone.

"Doesn't she look good in that?" Charles asked, his tone assuring me that he'd served as fashion advisor. He snuffed his cigarette in a tuffet of sand, and as speedily lit another.

"She seems uncomfortable," I said. Elaine left Cecily to play near the shoreline; eased her suit over her buttocks before plunging headlong into a wave.

"First thing she told me was take it back. Said she was too old for it. Got her to reconsider. Told her to give it a spin, she agreed. Never guess she was as insecure as she is, would you?"

Elaine and Charles were married twenty years; they had a competition, rather than a relationship, throughout. I declined to sit as judge, however often he handed me the gavel. "When's class start?"

"Two weeks," he said.

"Anticipating or dreading?"

"Got to look at it as a challenge. How long will it take to find the one who stands out from the crowd? If I find them, they make up for the rest. If not, so be it."

"You've still got freshmen courses?"

He shivered; I gathered that the breeze chilled him. "Only one. Up for tenure in January. No more after that. Rest are juniors and seniors."

"Better informed?"

"School's out even when it's in, these days. Not when we were going." He sighed; eyed Cecily as she dug a hole. "What've you been working on?"

"The Pathology of Trauma."

He frowned; his eyelids crinkled as he confronted the sun. "The usual?"

"Nothing unexpected," I said. "One fascinating case study. Suicide by dynamite."

"What did they do? Blow up the house?"

"Used a stick as a cigar, sort of. Astonishing results."

Charles grimaced. "Don't you think you'd ever want to get into the general field? Don't see how you can keep your head on straight, editing what you do. Not healthy. I know people, I could call around. Never too late."

"Sometimes it is," I said. "I like what I'm doing, Charlie."

"I can help," he said. "Trust me."

"Believe me."

Charles's sense of *noblesse oblige*, also grafted onto him by his parents, was as genuine as it was fulsome; still, little disgruntled him more than to have his proffered altruism declined—save when his help was accepted, and the gratitude resulting struck him as incommensurate with his beneficence. "You don't get out enough," he said. "Haven't I always told you that? You're not getting younger, you know."

Charles was my age. "I'm content."

"Fine, then," he said, his expression unchanged, his words rich with hints of disappointment. For a minute he said nothing, containing unseemly emotion; then he changed the subject, lowering his voice, as if afraid that fellow beachgoers would dash off to enter marks into his permanent record if they cared to overhear. He was accomplished at drawing out the guilt in others for having felt its *frisson* so keenly, so often, himself. "Remember Gail Hamilton?"

"Why?" I asked.

"Ran into her on Lexington. Held up pretty well. Told me I'd held up better."

Had his hair still been brown he would have looked two or even three years younger than he was. "I wasn't aware she lived here."

"Moved back from San Francisco in April. Divorced, lives at Second and 68th. Told her we should get together for lunch one day."

"You going to?"

He shook his head. "Been so long. Too many questions. What's she been doing? Why'd she get divorced? Looks fine, but who's to know?"

"Any reason to think that she's not?" I asked. "Is she all right?"

"Says so. They always seem all right at first. Why do you care?"

"Why'd you suggest lunch, then?"

He slipped on his sunglasses. "Have to be polite."

Elaine, treading water beyond the breakers, called to Cecily, who then ran up to us, sprawling herself in the dunes at our feet. "Mommy wants her towel," she told Charles. "She wants *you* to bring it to her."

"Why me?"

"Mommy says just bring it."

He stood up, hoisting his trunks above his deflating waistline. Retrieving Elaine's towel, he followed his daughter to the water and walked in up to his knees. Elaine swam inland; leapt up and took the towel from him. Her suit's fabric, when wet, became so translucent that she appeared to be naked. Cloaking herself, she emerged from the ocean and strode across the sand as if into court. "Excuse me," she said, picking up her bag with one hand, securing her towel with the other. "I have to put on my sun suit. I'll be right back. Charles, watch Ceese."

Charles called after her as he ascended the dunes, "Could wear it at home."

"Give it to one of your students," she muttered, walking away. His smile flattened; he sat down. Cecily slapped his knees with her plastic bucket; then she wandered a few feet away and started filling it with sand. While waiting for Elaine to return we watched a speedboat roar by, scarring the water. He said something I didn't catch.

"Pardon?"

Charles examined his knees closely, as if fearing his daughter had bruised them. "Beautiful day, don't you think?" I couldn't disagree.

Two or three times a month Charles and I met after work for drinks and dinner. After a point in the evening our conversation revolved, inevitably, around our old college days. If our memories differed, it was expected that I support his version, which he felt suffered less from time's numberless rewrites. Often—more often, of late—we'd read obits of acquaintances from school who'd died of coronaries or cancer, and mourn them as we remembered them, their collegiate portraits blurry with thirty years' distance. Charles grew uncomfortable, considering the oft wayward course of postgraduate lives.

Once I was positive that a remarkable case study I'd proofed was one of our housemates during our sophomore year; I told Charles. "Wasn't him," he insisted, with uninflected voice. "If he was going to die, he wouldn't have died that way." I avoided trifling with my old friend's preferred realities, and so concurred in his opinion, without belief. Change didn't disturb him as did unpredictability; one of many talents on which Charles prided himself was his ability to foresee situations early enough to benefit from their results—in truth, he rarely did.

The first time we got together, that semester, Charles raised an unanticipated subject, and told me he'd already encountered the student who stood out. "A brilliant young woman," he said, intoning his new mantra while his fettucine cooled. "Brilliant. Audited my poetry class on the second day. By the end of the hour she was the only one participating. Class was full, but I pulled some strings and got her in. Simply brilliant."

"How brilliant?" I asked, trying to decipher his face; his expression was as he molded it each morning, though I thought he might be on the verge of allowing his smile to wax gibbous. "What's her name?"

"Valerie," he said. "She's twenty-one. We spoke after class. She's formulating her own critical theory. Nontraditional, perhaps wilfully so, but that's half the pleasure of it. And it works. Only meet students like her once in a lifetime."

"Where's she from?"

"Shaker Heights. Left Swarthmore to come here."

"Why?"

He shook his head and chuckled. "Swarthmore didn't get the concept of chaos philology at all."

"Excuse me?"

"Her critical theory," Charles said. "Takes semiotics one step beyond." As he spoke his smile broke loose of its moorings, curling into an unsettling rictus; his eyes shone as if they'd been moistened.

"How?"

"Ask her," he said, rising. "Valerie, like you to meet—"

"Charmed," she said, taking my hand before I offered it. Charles provided her with a chair expropriated from another group's table. Valerie wore a cashmere turtleneck, striped leggings and yellow running shoes; at first glance she looked slim enough to slip through a mail slot. Her ivory skin possessed the matte finish older women sometimes develop when their features are annually updated. She had a child's smile, a doll's eyes; her hair was black as the wing of a carrion crow. Valerie was beautiful, though her beauty was of a sort often attainable only through compulsion. Taking a roll from his plate, she bit into it with sharp little teeth.

"Charles was starting to tell me about your theory—"

"Which?" Seizing a knife, she smeared butter over the remains of the roll; crammed it into her mouth as if she were starving.

"Chaos philology," Charles said. Valerie grinned, and snatched the fork from his plate, wreathing its tines in chilled fettucine.

"Did he explain it?" She brushed her hair away from her face and sucked the fork clean. "The bottom line is that unraveling always works, even where deconstruction doesn't."

"Unraveling what?"

As Valerie reached for another forkful, she overturned my glass, baptizing the table with barely sipped bourbon. "Whatever's communicated," she said, ignoring the spillage. "Written or verbal narratives. Like this. One, unravel the text as presented. Two, reweave into a turbulent pattern of discourse. Three, examine the new design. Chaos philology allows deepest penetration into auctorial intent."

Charles slid his plate in front of her so that she could reload her fork with less collateral damage. "Could you give me an example?" I asked.

"Sure. Let's stick to Romantics. His favorite." Charles smiled. "Take a typical passage from Shelley's *Adonais* such as, 'Peace, peace, he is not dead, he doth not sleep.' From her backpack Valerie took a pen and notebook and began writing, dripping strands of pasta onto the paper while she ate. "Start simple, finish big," she said, presenting it to me. On the page I read *Sleep doth not peace dead not peace is he he*. Each word was harnessed to its mates by curves, lines and arrows; singly, in pairs and as *ménages à trois*.

"Remarkably subtle patterns," I said, regarding the fetishistic intricacy of the lacings.

"They leap out at you, after a while," said Charles.

"If you desire, you can defer the critical climax indefinitely," Valerie continued. "If not, bang and run. Strip sense from nonsense. See what fantasies the author tried to hide. You understand how it works? It's so obvious that what Shelley is doing in that particular line is laughing at the prospect of his own predictable death."

"I wish I'd taken more lit courses," I said. Charles beamed, and gave her a look that gave me a toothache.

"Wouldn't have helped," she said. As she lay down her fork I thought I glimpsed a tattoo of a green butterfly on her left wrist. "Authors never mean what you think they're saying. You have to find a quick way to get them to confess. Chaos philology may seem violent, assaulting the author from behind as it does, but how else do you get to know what's really there? Nothing wrong with that. Nothing's wrong as long as it doesn't hurt someone you don't know."

Valerie slumped, as if her air had run out; she looked at Charles, seeming hungry to hear not only agreement, but approval.

"Method broadens the range of readings," he said. "Makes what's obvious to me obvious to anyone tying themselves into the network. The Romantics always lied about what they were really up to, for example."

"Downright morbid, most of them. If you hadn't had Romantics, you wouldn't have had Hitler," Valerie said. Charles nodded. "Chaos philology is usable in unraveling any fantasy in any field, the more I think about it."

"I'm completely lost," I admitted.

"You're unraveling," she said, bouncing up and down in her chair as if it were hot. Charles interrupted, keen as ever to assist the unassistable.

"Not everybody gets it," he said; his smile reset itself into a shallow, upturned arc. "Try again some other time." He looked at my emptied glass. "When we're more sober, perhaps."

Valerie's nipples rose, appearing as beads underlying her sweater. She rested her chin in her palms; her sleeves drew up as she moved her arms; seeing her wrist more plainly, I realized that the greenish blotch wasn't a butterfly, but a bruise. "You and Charles went to school together?" she asked, seemingly to confirm what he'd earlier told her. "Nothing like an Ivy League man." She caressed my silk tie with her fingers, oiling it nicely. "*These* aren't the school colors."

"Chaos haberdashery," I said.

Valerie laughed again, and then jumped to her feet as if she'd been pricked. "I've got to pee. Be back." Turning away from us, she bent over double and fumbled through her backpack until she found an unlabeled bottle. Her leggings were split along the inseam; she wore no more underwear below than she did above. Reattaining the vertical, she swallowed a pill with a gulp of my water and bounded off.

"She's a corker, isn't she?" Charles said, tapping the table with his fingers, watching me straighten my tie. "Overexuberant, sometimes. Excuse."

"Genius knows its own etiquette," I offered. "How's the family?"

"Fine," he said, staring at the ladies' room door, appearing ready to lunge for it. "Fine, fine, fine."

I supposed his deeper involvement with Valerie began about a month into the semester; suspected that one evening, they'd forged bonds that were other than intellectual—but he didn't tell, and I didn't ask. He'd had an affair once before while married to Elaine, alluding to it only after he'd broken it off, and only to me. Afterward, having confessed, he was able to pretend it never happened. Years later I asked him her name, but she no longer had one.

Throughout the fall Valerie came with him each time we met. They sat on either side of me at the table, rambling about her unorthodox theories, the elaborate projects they dreamed of shortly undertaking, the officials at Barnard he'd contacted, using such pull as he had to grease her way along her chosen path. At no time would it have appeared to anyone who didn't know Charles that anything was ongoing between him and his new associate but a mutual fondness for the workings of the mind—the interest they seemed most deeply to share, as long as theirs were the minds involved.

One afternoon in late October, he called me at work. "Meet me at my office instead of the restaurant, could you?" he asked. "Something I think I want to talk about." Possibly he intended a fresh confession; a moot concern, as it developed. When I arrived, the secretaries were closing up for the night but allowed me to come in. I strolled down the hall to his office; his door was shut. As I prepared to knock, Valerie's voice came from within, rising over the building's white noise; she gasped as if she were hyperventilating.

"Tight enough?" she asked. "Is it? Is it?"

I returned to the reception area without waiting to discover if it was. Ten minutes later they emerged, donning their coats, appearing no more disheveled than if they'd been unraveling one of the thornier passages of Byron. "Look who's here," Charles exclaimed; his evident surprise could have been no greater had I plunged out of the sky to settle on his shoulders. "Thought you'd be at the restaurant already. Hungry?" I nodded. She shook her hands as if something clung to them. "Let's go."

We went. When, later, Valerie made for the facilities, I asked Charles why he'd wanted to talk to me. He closed his eyes while answering, as if to channel an entity better equipped to respond.

"Why do you say I wanted to talk?"

"You called me this afternoon. You said you had something to talk about. Don't you remember?"

"Misunderstood me," he said, slipping his smile into place. "Meant you should meet us there, have more time to talk. Weren't waiting long, were you?"

"Not long. Why'd you seem so surprised to see me?"

"Thought we'd meet out front. Didn't know the building was still open."

"You didn't want to talk?"

"Talking now, aren't we?" Charles concluded. Valerie returned. She scoured her chin with a tissue, studying it as if fearful she'd drawn blood.

"You haven't said anything about Charles's tie," she said, pitching away the tissue. Hooking his repp, she reeled him in. "School colors."

"Out of the closet," he explained. "Dad made me buy one first day we went up. Told me I should wear it once a week on Sundays. Went right to the Co-op, bought it. Never wore it a time after that."

"Because he told you to," Valerie said, releasing her grip. She shook one of her pills from her bottle. I'd earlier asked Charles what she was on; an assortment of the milder antidepressants, he told me. "I tied it for him. He's all thumbs."

Charles shifted his head, swiveling it a fraction of an inch away from me;

frowned at Valerie, making a moue so understated as to be almost nonexistent. "Bit more conservative than what you usually hang around your neck," I commented; he blanched, as if nauseated by memories of those accoutrements of his he hadn't purchased from Brooks Brothers. The dimple in the tie appeared mathematically centered; the knot, too, was perfect, though no wider than my thumb, and fitting against his Adam's apple so closely it might have been glued there. "Isn't that awfully tight?"

"You'd be surprised," he said, stretching his neck as if to free it from a trap.

"Cocteau used to tie his neckties as tight as he could, to lessen the flow of blood to his brain," Valerie said. "He claimed it helped him think."

"Penny for your thoughts," I said to Charles; they looked at one another and smirked as children would, satisfied to have hoodwinked their parents again.

"Thinking about our work," he said. "Going to do a book explaining her theories. Should turn a few heads. My ideas tally well with Valerie's, as it happens."

"We're two of a kind, in our own ways," she said. "In a lot of ways. We've been testing dozens of new concepts. Just wait. We'll hear what they have to say about us, once the book comes out."

Not long after, tiring of their increasingly exclusive camaraderie, I excused myself and went home. Elaine called, soon after.

"I have to ask you something," she said. "When do you think you'll be finishing up this project you and he are working on?"

"Project?"

"I'm only asking because I'm rarely in before ten during the week and I'm going to advertise for a full-time governess for Ceese if you think it'll be much longer. I've asked Charles but he's so vague about these things. Can you give me an idea?"

"Better place an ad," I said.

"That's what I thought."

By morning I'd almost convinced myself that I hadn't lied to her.

Several evenings later Charles called me, sounding considerably more frantic than had Elaine. "I'm at Valerie's apartment. Get over here, fast."

"What's the matter?"

"We're at Broadway and 86th, southwest corner. Number 5E. Please."

In ten minutes I reached the building and rushed upstairs. Charles opened the door as I rang the bell. A lone ribbon of gauze was wrapped around his right hand; a dab of blood marred its whiteness. "It's okay now," he said, aiming his stare at me, allowing his smile to flicker along his face. "Come on in."

Valerie's studio was the size of my living room. Rain blew in the open windows. Notebooks and papers were stacked upon the kitchenette's table, near two uncleared dinner plates. A pair of wire clippers lay atop an unpacked box of dishes. Six hanging baskets brimming with unwatered ivy dangled from hooks in the ceiling, swaying as if they were pendulums. Clothing and linens blanketed two filing cabinets. In the bathroom was a metal wastepaper can split open along the side seam. Hundreds of books, their titles facing inward, were shoved onto the shelves of three bookcases. The décor could have been called Chaotique Moderne.

"Hi," Valerie said; she lay on her futon. Gilt-framed photographs of Houdini and

Isadora Duncan hung on the wall behind her. "Thanks for coming by." A thin quilt covered her from neck to knees; her bare calves appeared more muscular than they did in the leggings she usually wore. She breathed heavily, as if she'd been running. The room's single lamp shadowed her face, making her eyes appear deep-set within her skull. The tip of her nose and her forehead bore fresh abrasions, as if she'd fallen and scraped them on the sidewalk during her sprint. She'd smeared vaseline or another soothing ointment on her cheeks and beneath her jaw.

"You have an accident?" I asked her. "What happened?"

"Damnedest thing," Charles said. "Valerie asked if I'd take the garbage down the hall to the compactor. Sliced my hand open on the door. Thought I'd need stitches. Closed up fast enough, though. Here, I'll show you," he said, motioning as if to unveil his wound.

"That's okay," I said. "So you're both all right?"

"Sorry to make you run over here like this. Tell you what, I've got to be going. Walk you home?"

"Sure." Recalling the panic in his voice, I wondered why he hadn't phoned 911; then realized he'd surely feared that any higher authority upon whom he might rely would notify his wife as to where he'd been found. I still thought it possible that he and Valerie might have been working; Charles always seemed most guilty when he had the least reason. Valerie watched him as he took his raincoat from the closet.

"You can't stay?" she asked, rolling over. Her quilt fell away as she shifted onto her side. Valerie's body was as toned as her legs; she trimmed her pubic hair into a tufted mohawk; thin bruises resembling calligraphic designs laced her ribcage, above and below her breasts. "Get home safe," she said, covering herself, behaving as if neither of us might have noticed her *déshabillé*.

"Got to go. Lock yourself in," he said as we stepped into the hall. "Call you tomorrow." She nodded, staring at the door until it slammed shut. While walking to the elevator I looked for the trash compactor, but saw neither area nor room marked as such.

"I didn't know she lived in the neighborhood," I said as we descended.

"Close to Barnard," he remarked, though Valerie presently attended NYU.

"Elaine called me the night we went out," I said. "She mentioned something about a project we were working on?"

He wore his school tie; he must have knotted it himself this time, as its four-in-hand seemed tied by one unused to opposable thumbs. "We're busy putting Valerie's ideas into shape for publication. Get together sometimes to work on it."

"Who are you talking about?" I asked, believing the confusion deliberate. "Me and you, or you and Valerie?"

"You know how Elaine gets sometimes. Been worse, lately. Started seeing chimeras. Imagining situations. Getting to be that age, you know."

"She's two years younger than us."

"Came in later one night last week than I expected. Had to improvise." He seemed enormously pleased—as if, having daily told himself that the sky was orange rather than blue, he'd awoken one morning and discovered he was right. "Romance at short notice. Got to admit I'm good at it."

"Too good," I said. "What did you tell her?"

"That you're helping me edit my new book as I'm writing it. Kills two birds with one stone. Improves my text, helps you out. Gives you a real book to edit."

"But I'm not editing it," I reminded him. "What do you mean, real book? Don't patronize me."

"That didn't come out right. Of course you edit real books. Too real, if you ask me, but that's not what I meant. You ought to think about why you get so defensive about your work, if you're really satisfied with what you're doing." He slipped on a new look; the exaltation seen moments before was supplanted by an expression suggestive of unassuageable pain.

"If you'd warned me of what you'd told her before she called, I wouldn't have minded," I said. "Not as much."

"My intention. Didn't have the chance. Of course you were upset when she called you, I don't doubt it."

"Is that what you wanted to talk about when you phoned me?" I asked. "Why didn't you tell me at the time? Or when I asked you, later that night?"

"Couldn't say anything in front of Valerie," he said. "She doesn't need to be involved in this."

"She wasn't there when I asked."

"Valerie's young, and hasn't had an easy life, however it may seem," Charles said. "No need to hurt her unnecessarily."

He veered away, seeming to lose his balance, eyeing the closed stores we passed as if windowshopping. There was no reason to belabor the point; Charles remembered the evening differently than I did, and that was that—once his revisions were made the text remained inviolate, whatever the fact-checkers said.

"You two getting along well?" I asked.

"We mesh. Same channel, great minds."

"I hadn't realized she was so athletic. She looks so petite, clothed."

"Did gymnastics in junior high. First rate, I'm sure. Gave it up. It's a shame."

"What happened?"

"Balance beam accident. Made the best of it." Lifting his arms, he snatched at air with his hands; such intensity, in Charles, made him appear to be having a convulsion. "It's impossible to say where she could go if she gets the opportunities. All I'm trying to do is make sure she gets them."

"If she only had some redeeming faults," I said, wishing to lighten his mood.

"Valerie'll do anything." He spoke so softly that I wouldn't have heard him had I not seen his lips as they let the words slip loose; the intonation, and phrasing of his declaration belied that the fact excited no less than it terrified. "Could do anything."

"It's a shame some people get the wrong idea."

"Who?" he asked, nodding sharply as if expecting me to hand over a list.

"Elaine," I said. He frowned. "At least that's what I'm inferring, from what you're saying."

"Elaine's imagining a rival where there is none," he said. "Reality's got nothing to do with it. Wouldn't think she could be jealous of a dream."

"Much gossip at school?"

"Told there's some, around the department. Nine-tenths of it's intellectual envy. Got no desire to know what anyone's saying."

"Is anything they're saying true?"

He didn't respond at once; for an instant I dreamed that I'd draw out a sort of confession. "Troubles me you feel you have to ask that," he said. "Where's your mind been? You hear anything I've said?"

"What's the matter with you?"

"No need to ask, then."

"Charlie, I only wanted—"

We reached 99th Street "Give you the benefit of the doubt. Don't have to, but I don't think you meant to upset me."

"That's big of you," I said, irritated as much by his professorial condescension as by his manipulation of event.

"Situation should be obvious. Just what I've told you, nothing more."

"I was only saying you've got to expect people will think—"

"Doesn't matter. People'll think what they want to, whatever the truth is," he said. "Let'em."

He glared, as if daring me to acknowledge what I thought, if I still fancied I knew. I tired of his games of trick or treat. "It upset me when Elaine called, Charlie. I'm not as good as lying as some people."

"You're not lying," he said, walking toward Riverside, calling back over his shoulder. "Remember that."

In the third week of November he left a message on my machine, asking if I wanted to get together with him before Thanksgiving. When I phoned his apartment, Elaine answered; I hadn't expected to find her at home so early in the evening. "Charles isn't here at the moment."

"Think he'll be in soon?"

"Depends," she said. "How late are you two working tonight?"

No matter how quickly I could have reacted, it wouldn't have been quick enough. "I hadn't heard from him. Thought I should check." The silence following lasted much longer than I'd have preferred.

"Should I say you were looking for him? I suppose I will," she said, before hanging up.

The next morning Charles called me from his office, asking if I was available to see him later in the day; he thought it would be good if we talked. "Be by myself, Valerie's at class," he said. "Don't worry about Elaine. Everything's under control."

"What did you tell her this time?"

He gave no indication of hearing me; deafness at command was an ability to which he had no objection as long as he was the one so conveniently handicapped. By five that afternoon I was at our chosen rendezvous, a coffee shop on 86th near Columbus, and waited outside until he arrived alone, ten minutes later. Charles carried a small suitcase; he sagged, seeming to melt. His eyes were pouched as if lined with sand; his face had more new wrinkles than a floater's. He'd lost weight, but not where it mattered, and coughed with a junkie's rasp. Though he avoided artificial stimuli—save for the three packs of cigarettes filtered daily through his lungs—his ravaged look warned of a dilatory concern for the more mundane aspects of life, as when what was once thought an idle distraction proves addictive unto death.

"What's in there?" I asked, pointing to his bag.

He flashed his demi-smile. "The cat."

"What'd Elaine say when you got home?"

"Taken care of," he replied, his gaze drifting to the mirror affixed behind the counter, perhaps suspecting his wife of lurking beyond the cereal boxes and coffee urns. "Told her we were supposed to hook up last night. Had to go to an emergency department meeting, wasn't able to call."

"That worked?"

"Why wouldn't it?" he asked, seeming baffled as to why I should be unaware of plans I'd not been told.

"I wish you'd tell me what was going on if you plan on using me as an alibi. I don't like it."

"You're right," he said. The waiter brought our coffee; I had no appetite and declined a menu. Charles ran his fingers through his hair, as if combing it. "You're absolutely right."

"Why are you hiding if you've got nothing to hide?"

"That's what you'd call it?"

"If all you're doing with Valerie is working, why do you tell Elaine and God knows who else that you're out with me?"

"You're assuming I was with Valerie last night."

"Weren't you? Is it so hard just to say?"

Charles lifted his cup to his mouth. His hand shook; he splashed coffee on his sleeve. "No need to be hostile," he said, allowing the stain to soak in. "Your work getting to you? Knew it was only a matter of time. Don't get out enough."

"She knew I was lying. I didn't want to lie to her."

"Your decision."

"I've had it, Charlie." Tossing my napkin on the table, I started to get up; he scanned the restaurant to see if anyone was watching. "You got me involved in this and I don't even know what I'm involved in. Tell me what's going on or I'll go home and call Elaine at work and ask her."

"That's unnecessary," he said, grabbing my arm, gesturing that I should sit down. "Get control of yourself. Hadn't realized you were so angry."

"Give me a straight answer and I won't be."

"I can understand transference," he said. "I'll try to explain."

"Fine. Why all the secrecy?"

"It's a private matter, but I'll share it with you if you insist," he said. "You know Elaine's not the easiest person to get along with. Going through a difficult time in her life right now. The woman thing. Up some days, down the rest. We've had more than our share of disagreements since Cecily was born."

"You've never said."

"Nothing to talk about. Cecily's a beautiful child, we love her dearly, but she was an accident, after all. Didn't expect to have one so late. Bad timing. Knocked Elaine right off the fast track at her old firm. Wasn't in the forefront on parental leave. Now she's got her own office, has to work twice as hard. Not many women want to be new mothers at forty-two." Charles shook his head as if reshuffling its contents to see what settled where. "Elaine didn't."

While speaking he tightened his old tie's knot, aligning it precisely between his shirt's frayed lapels. "Didn't please her. Started transferring. Thank God she takes it out on me, not Cecily. Came to an agreement before it went too far, for Cecily's sake. Had upper and lower bunks in the marriage bed since. Get along, though. You have to get along. You have to."

"Both of you always seemed happy."

"Essential precept of chaos philology, remember. Nothing's as it seems," he said. "Situation like ours doesn't make anyone feel secure. And she's always been a worrywart. Insecure, like I've said. Won't surprise you to hear she's never thought much of my students. Early on, I introduced her to Valerie. It was the right thing to do, and it wasn't."

"They must not have much in common."

"Both need my time." He watched the restaurant's entrance as if expecting them to arrive simultaneously. "That's my excuse, take it or leave it. Something about her just sets Elaine off. If she knew I was working with Valerie and not you, she'd eat us alive. No real person threatening her, but Valerie serves as the best model she's found".

"Does Valerie know how she feels?"

"She's perceptive enough, I haven't seen the need to tell her. Call me overprotective, but I don't want to involve her in our problems."

"How can she not be involved?"

Charles sighed, as if accepting that he'd again have to explain the difference between noun and verb before the class could start in on the syllabus. "Questions like that complicate a simple situation. I try to help her, she helps me." Forcing his fingers underneath his collar, he scratched his throat. The skin on his lower neck was inflamed, as if badly sunburned. "Valerie comes on strong because she's so defensive. She's really very insecure. Thinks I'll stop helping her if they keep saying things. Couldn't do that, you can't abandon people. She'd never polish her theories on her own. Valerie needs a certain discipline. I'm able to provide it."

Between sentences he drifted, at moments appearing unaware of my presence. His explanation had been more straightforward than any he'd given me before; he'd revealed nominal truths shorn of convenient tangents. Nevertheless, I saw no reason to entirely believe him. "Charlie, if you were having another affair, what would you want out of it at this point?"

"Why do you say another affair?"

He tapped his spoon rapidly against his saucer as if testing how many strokes it could sustain before shattering. His eyes could have been glass. I had neither the desire nor energy to hurdle another series of circumlocutions, and so reworded my question. "An affair, I mean. What would you want it to be?"

"What if you ever had a relationship? What would you want out of it?"

"That's not important, Charlie."

"I've known women. Have a good marriage. Few problems, not many. Young women like Valerie want to work with me. Why would I have an affair?"

"Hypothetical question. Forget it."

"Average person has an affair to have sex, I think." he said, peering into his coffee as if cribbing from notes earlier taken; staring at me when he found the answer sought. "Having sex's a given with most people."

"I wasn't asking about most."

"Ever imagine you're in school again?" he asked, his eyes half-shut. "Remember what it was like then? How you'd dream of having sex with a beautiful young woman. One who'd do anything. *Anything.*"

"That was a long time ago, Charlie—"

"Imagine you're twenty, and with her," he said. "She's naked. Squeezes your chest between her thighs till you can't breathe. Drowns you when she sits on your face. Rides you like a horse and whips you to the finish. Rolls on her stomach, spreads her legs. Says do what you want, she can't get away." His voice never rose above a stage whisper. "She screams your name."

"Charlie, stop."

"You'd like that, wouldn't you?" he asked. "Wouldn't you?"

"Stop it," I said, more loudly than I would have wanted; he fell silent, and lit a cigarette. "Please stop."

"Why's that make you uncomfortable?" he asked. "You brought it up."

"Why did you do that?"

"Have to be careful applying chaos philology to anything other than a text," he said. "Finding out what's what can be as hard on the one unraveling as it is on what's being unraveled."

"I don't know what's the matter with you—"

"Why do you distance yourself so fast whenever something takes a sexual turn? Always have. Ever wondered why? People don't live up to your fantasies? Afraid somebody else's doing better than you? Is that it?"

"Leave it at that," I said, picking up my jacket.

"Understandable how people might get the wrong idea about you if they were to only go by your behavior." As I stood I looked at the floor, so he couldn't see my face; I noticed that he wore only one sock. A furrowed black bruise encircled the exposed ankle. "Be realistic. My business is mine, yours is yours."

"I've got to go." I threw a dollar on the table. "If I don't talk to you before Thanksgiving, give my love to your family."

"Just my family? You sure about that?" A semblance of avuncularity reappeared on his features; his smile remained embedded in his face. "Thanks for your help with Elaine," he said. "I mean it. Have a good Thanksgiving."

"Don't tell her you're with me when you're not," I said as I left. He had no further response; he'd probably stopped listening. Some texts defy unraveling. Upon reaching my apartment I discovered that Elaine had left a message on my machine.

"Are you there, Charles?" her voice asked. "Charles? Charles?"

Two weeks before Christmas, they had their annual party. For days I debated whether or not I should go, finally deciding on the afternoon anteceding the event. I worked late, editing manuscripts; by the time I arrived, everyone else was there. Half of those attending were Charles's friends, half Elaine's; there was little commingling of subcultures beyond the initial encounters.

"Good to see you," Elaine said, greeting me by kissing the air in the vicinity of my cheek. Strangers might have imagined we'd only met once before, and not by choice. "Charles is in the kitchen. I told him to bring in more eggnog if he thought he could handle it."

"How are you?" I asked.

She glared, as if offended by my question. "Have the man fix you a drink. You're usually thirsty."

The caterers had the setups in the library; they performed their duties with the enthusiasm of galley slaves. Cecily wore a red velvet party dress and spent the night believing that she entertained the guests. An eight-foot Norwegian pine bedizened with white lights and blue balls was in the living room; the soundtrack from *A Charlie Brown Christmas* played mercilessly over the stereo. The press of the crowd was so great that had it not been for those yuletide touches I should have imagined that a celebration of the Black Hole of Calcutta was underway. I shoehorned myself in near a group that appeared no less lawful than they did academic, and eavesdropped.

"Is she here?" asked a man whose eyebrows resembled caterpillars. "Tell me she's not."

"She is," said an older woman with a forbidding mien. "Arrived with Lit's Derridadas. They got away from her as fast as they could."

"He got her away from them," said a woman wearing red-rimmed glasses. "Shook them off like flies. I just can't see the attraction."

"I'd hope it's other than physical," said the scary woman.

"Or intellectual," said caterpillar eyes. "Ah, there's Columbine and Pantaloon now."

They ploughed separate paths across the room, so intent on ignoring each other as to be unignorable. Charles wore a black pullover with oversized turtleneck. Valerie, perhaps believing the event a masquerade, came as a party favor, enshrouded in green ruffles. She'd wrapped a red silk scarf around her neck and carried a tureen of eggnog. "Match made in heaven, if you ask me," said the scary woman.

With deliberate steps Charles inched into the dining room, schmoozing briefly with those he passed. He reached the breakfast table; commandeering two empty chairs, he sat in one and placed his drink on the other. A sheet draped over the table and the legs of the guests sitting around it was imprinted with the phrase BAH HUMBUG! several thousand times. Valerie materialized so immediately at Charles's side that she might have been teleported from space. Academics from departments other than theirs hovered buzzard-like around them; his cigarettes smouldered in the ashtray while he declaimed opinions.

Charles and I hadn't seen each other since our contretemps; we'd spoken, once or twice, but the memory of his assault remained and I wasn't anxious to talk to him. I squeezed down the hall toward the library, feeling as a clot traveling through a clogged artery. After refreshing my drink I lingered, casting glances in the direction of the momentarily distracting. Lawyers so often approached me that I felt I'd been in an accident. Returning to the dining room, I encountered Elaine. She stood in the doorway, watching her husband and his comely protegé.

"You're not leaving yet, are you?" she asked me.

"Not for awhile." She was smoking; I remembered how much trouble she had quitting while pregnant with Cecily, and I'd not expected her to backslide. Her gown sagged around her waist; I estimated she'd lost twenty pounds, either by accident or design, since August.

"You've said hello to Charles?"

"Hard to get his eye."

"Depends, don't you think?" By her intonation I could tell she expected no answer. "Go talk to him, why not? I'll be over shortly."

Valerie waved briskly as I approached. "You've got a school tie, too," she said, recognizing my cravat, having seen its mate often enough around Charles's neck.

"I didn't know if you were coming or not," he said, smiling. "You know the chairman of the English department? Doctor Buebenhofer?" The doctor, bald and dowdy, lounged in a chair across the table; looking up at me from behind the bowl of eggnog he grunted, as if to be polite.

"Mutual," I said.

"His latest project's a video for the MLA," said Charles.

"Doctor, let me tell you about something." Valerie said. He seemed nominally more interested in her than he had in me. "Charles and I are developing a new critical approach."

"I've heard," said the chairman.

"Like to hear it from people who know what they're talking about?"

"No one works at a party," Charles said, interrupting. "Some other time."

"This isn't work."

"*Valerie!*" He spoke her name as he would have called Cecily's. Tapping me on the arm, he gestured that I should lower my head, to hear something he had to say. Valerie scooted her chair forward, and then she reclined; with movements as obvious as they were subtle, she took his left hand in hers and pulled it off the table.

"Having a good time?" he asked, his mouth at my ear. "You're not still mad at me, are you?"

"I don't understand why you acted as you did."

"There're reasons," he said. "We should talk. We should."

"Well?"

"Not here. Later." His gaze fixed itself upon the ceiling, as if he saw heavenly hosts hung from above. Valerie stared ahead, appearing hypnotized by the candelabra's electric flames. Bringing up her hands, she fondled her scarf; loosening its knot, she retied it tightly, drawing the silk around her throat. "Shame to have trouble over the holidays," he muttered. Elaine smiled, sidling up to her husband.

"Charles," she said. "I need to ask you something."

"Be right with you, dear," he said, not moving.

"It won't take a minute."

"After the party, Elaine."

Bending down, she seized the tablecloth's hem in her hands. With effortless motions she whipped it away; glassware and crockery shattered against the floor. Eggnog drenched the doctor's tweed. Through the glass-topped table all saw Valerie's panties hanging loosely around one knee, resembling a loosened restraint. Her feet were braced against the table legs as the curtain rose; at the instant of exposure she clamped shut her thighs, entrapping Charles's hand within her dark curls. He couldn't immediately free himself; when he did, jerking back his arm, his ring rapped sharply against the glass, concluding the cacophony, calling the company to attention with a resounding chord as if announcing a toast.

"Are you moving in with her before or after Christmas?" Elaine asked, her attitude preternaturally calm. She left the room, pushing Cecily back from the door. Her supporters hastened after her. Charles's associates glanced at one another before filing into the hall, refusing to look behind them. The doctor rushed to the bathroom to see if his suit might be salvaged.

Valerie looked at me as she stood; matching my stare, she lifted her dress and pulled up her underwear with the aplomb of a bather preparing to leave the beach. Charles looked to have had electroshock, if not a lobotomy; he clasped his hands before him as if to say grace.

"Honey?" he called out. "It's not what it seems."

In February I ran into Valerie as she emerged from a drugstore on Columbus. "Got a few minutes?" she asked, entwining her arm with mine. We went to the coffee shop on 86th. Valerie left her muffler on; the fluorescent glare illuminated a dime-sized bruise on her forehead.

"Charles misses you," she said. "He'd never say, but I can tell. Half a dozen times I've tried getting him to call you, but it's like talking to the wall."

"We argued the last time we got together before the party. Right here, in fact."

"I know. He felt bad about it, once I told him he should. Keep in mind he's been himself more than he's not been himself, lately." She dumped seven packs of sugar into her coffee and stirred it into a whirlpool. "You probably just misread each other's texts, though I wonder for how long."

"The longer we were friends, the less I knew him."

"The first time I met you I thought you two were lovers once," she said, slipping off her shoes, lifting her legs onto the booth's seat. Contorting herself into a variorum lotus position, tucking her feet beneath her, she began rocking back and forth, as if hearing music. "Your body language fooled me. But I can't figure out why you've stayed friends so long. Do you know? Would you say, if you do?"

"We went to school together." I hadn't better reasons to offer.

"Do you like me?" Valerie asked. "I mean, you don't dislike me, do you?"

"Why do you ask?"

"Most of his friends think I'm bad for him. Elaine does, certainly."

"You're surprised?"

"We've had an equal relationship," she said. "I was sure you liked me. I'm glad you admit it. Men your age usually don't talk at all. Ones my age never shut up. Are you as close-mouthed about yourself as Charles is?"

"Different reasons."

"He's better, but it's still like pulling teeth. Ask me anything and I'll talk about it, I have neither pride nor shame." Valerie patted her muffler while she bobbed in place; sighed, as if relieved it was there. "He talks about you."

"What's he say?"

"You care? You disappointed him. He thought you'd understand."

"How could I? Wouldn't tell me what was going on—"

"Charles said that's what you should have understood." Valerie swept her hair from her face. "He told me he wanted to be closer to you, but you wouldn't let him. When you think someone's getting too close, you run. That's what he said."

"Distance myself if something's too painful. Sure not alone in that."

"When you kept pressing him that time, he told me he blew up." Her body's rhythm counterpointed that of her speech. "Said he knew how to drive you away. That's what he did, obviously. I don't believe he knew how upset you'd be."

"What'd he expect?" I asked. "Don't know if I'd talked to him, even if he'd called."

"I doubt it," she said. "Otherwise you'd have called him. I gave you my number once, and you could have guessed he was staying with me." She drank her coffee in two swallows and signaled the waiter for more. He served her at once. "What got you so upset?"

"He did something, reminded me of something he did before." Resting her elbows atop the table, moving her body as before, she reached up and wound her muffler once more around her neck. "Doesn't bear repeating," I concluded.

"That's what he'd say. You two are more alike than you'd ever admit."

"How is he?"

"Could be better. NYU might let him return for the summer semester but tenure's a moot point. He's told Elaine she can have everything, but that's not enough. She won't let him see Cecily. His wife's so insecure. I think they stayed together because each reminded the other of their least intimidating parent."

"What's he doing?"

"Hangs around the apartment. Rewrites our notes. My ideas were easy to understand until he improved them. I write a sentence, he rewrites a chapter. He puts masks on, I try to get them off." Her eyes widened; they were bluer than I'd remembered. "Charles thinks nothing's academic if you understand it."

"I know. That causing you trouble?"

"We have our disagreements," she said. "I'm not sure we bring out the best in each other, but we have brought out what's really there. That's as much as you can expect in a relationship. Too much for most people. I don't know if he'll be staying with me after March. Couldn't stand many more rewrites."

"You and Charles have been having an affair, haven't you?" I asked.

"He wouldn't call it that." She rocked more slowly; her muffler slipped away from her throat, which was as red as his had been. "He never expected to have this kind of relationship, so he thinks of it as being something apart. If you asked do we fuck each other, there's no denying. How did we seem when you saw us together?"

"Isolated."

"I asked him why we had to pretend we were Warren Harding and niece around you. He said it would make you uncomfortable if we didn't, and you'd run."

"No," I said. "He's hurt everyone, the way he's acted. Needlessly hurt himself. It's masochistic."

"You think so?" she asked, holding her muffler against her neck with her hands. "It's as much deliberate as needless. Not entirely masochistic."

"Masochists love the sin and hate the sinners. That's Charles."

"Not in every situation," she said. "You can't be happy without pain. Charles does what he can." I nodded. "Do you know anything about his childhood?"

"His parents were old guard. That's all he's said."

"Something happened to him back then that he won't let me unravel. May not have been anything major. You never know what'll affect you most, years later." Valerie returned one of her feet to the floor, resting it alongside mine. "But he won't tell me what happened," she said. "I could tell you a horrible thing that happened to me."

"Some people have no trouble doing that."

"That's what Charles told me," she said, closing her eyes. "It was in junior high. One afternoon I was practicing gymnastics after everyone else had left."

"Valerie, if it's something I don't need to know, don't—"

"Maybe you do," she said, her movements more deliberate. "Two girls jumped me while I was in the shower and dragged me into a practice room that was being redone. They jammed an empty paint can on my head. They bent me over a balance beam and tied me to it. They held my legs apart and then their boyfriends came in. First one, then the other."

Valerie told of what was done to her as if recounting the plot of a movie she'd seen, weaving the narrative with such precision that I would never have attempted an unraveling. The flat manner in which she related her story assured me of its essential truth; the details, almost lovingly expressed, led me to believe that her remembrance had been told not infrequently but many times, if only to herself. Perhaps the act of continual revision enabled her to tell it at all.

"My coach came back to get something and heard me trying to get loose. He untied me but I couldn't get the can off my head. I was suffocating. When I passed out I relaxed, and he was able to work it loose. When I came to he was standing over me, looking. I was still naked."

Letting go of her muffler, she stopped rocking, opening her eyes as if she'd been screamed awake; her body shivered, her face flushed. At first I thought she was going to cry; then realized her tears wouldn't have flowed in sorrow. No one was watching; Valerie moved the foot upon which she'd been sitting down to the floor, where she prodded my shoe with her toes.

"I was fourteen," she said.

"Are you all right? I mean—"

She smiled. "It affected me, but I deal with it."

"The boys and girls who hurt you," I said, convincing myself that I shouldn't find an excuse to leave. "You reported them? Were they arrested?"

"They were on the team. They knew people. Knew my coach. I was suspended. They went to good schools."

"That's—"

"Typical," Valerie said. "I dealt with it. Stare at a wound long enough and it doesn't hurt anymore. You'll see its beauty, eventually." She studied the table's surface, as if becoming aware of something previously unseen. "Has part of your problem been that you're attracted to me, too?"

Caught unaware as I was, I'm uncertain of what I showed; Charles once told me my face was as readable as a cheap novel. Valerie must have inferred much from my hesitation. "You're beautiful," I said. "You have a remarkable mind."

"Charles said that when I asked him what he thought of me. Were you two ever in love with the same woman?"

The nature of his response to Valerie was clear to me that afternoon—it was fascination as well as attraction, as when a deer freezes, seeing oncoming lights. Either of us would have confessed to anything if she said we should. "It's more complicated than that," I said.

"What was her name?"

"Gail," I said. "We were together through our junior year."

"What happened?"

"I don't think about it."

"Except when you do," she said. "Tell me. We'll keep each other's secrets."

"We argued, one night," I said. "About what, I don't remember. Charles saw I was upset. He told me he'd talk to her. Smooth things over. Next night he went to her apartmmet. She lived off campus. Valerie, I don't think—"

"What did he do?"

"He was still asleep when I woke up. I called Gail. She hung up when she heard me. Wouldn't let me in when I went to her apartment. Stood at her door and asked her what happened. She said go ask your friend. When I got back to the house Charles was having breakfast."

"Keep talking. It's all right. What did he say?"

"He told me she was drunk. One thing led to another. When she woke up, he said she got weird and he left."

"You didn't believe him."

"I kept saying tell me what really happened. He started telling me what they'd done. What she did to him. In detail. Smiling the whole time he told me. Finally said if Gail and I ever slept together again he wouldn't be surprised if she called out his name instead of mine."

Valerie stroked my face with her hand, caressing my cheek, pressing her fingertips under my ear. "She was your first girlfriend?" she asked. "Only girlfriend?"

"She thought I sent him over to her. I did. He offered to go, I said yes. It was my fault too."

"It wasn't," Valerie said. "It's all right. It is. What happened to Gail?"

"She didn't report it. No one did, back then. We didn't get back together. Month later she transferred to Berkeley."

"And you stayed friends with Charles after that?" I nodded. She petted my ear; ran her tongue along her lips, as if they were dry. "I guess you do understand masochism."

"Getting late, Valerie," I said. "I better go."

"But you don't have to run, do you?" she asked. "Not this time."

"Give my best to—" She slapped my face, as if in play. "Get home safe."

"He's home, or I'd say walk me there. I keep telling him he doesn't get out enough. I'm glad you live close by." She watched me rise. "We should start hooking up more often."

"I'll call."

"Charles gave me a lot of new material," Valerie said, smiling. "I could use a good editor."

FORWARD TO: Editorial Production
Legault & Van Gelder/Adv Forens Compan/JANUARY

The following account appears to be the only case in the literature involving joint participants in what has been recently (Hazelwood, Dietz, Burgess, 1983) termed Kotzwarraism, [FLAG 32] or hypoxyphilia. The diagnostic criteria for these paraphilia include the acting out

32Correct? Not in Stedman's.
OK.

of masochistic fantasies involving torture, abuse or execution and a desire for sexual arousal through risk-inherent situations, being generally in these cases the employment of a preferred mode of self-induced (or, induced through the agency of others; *op.cit.* Asa and Burroughs, 1978) sexual excitement by means of mechanical or chemical asphyxiation. This case should be considered *sui generis* but the patterns are unmistakable.

129. The victims were a fifty-year-old Caucasian male and a twenty-two-year old Caucasian female. A good state of preservation was observed, the temperature within the female deceased's studio apartment being forty degrees Fahrenheit [FLAG 33].

Both victims were nude, obliquely reclined back to back in arched positions, touching only at the head and heels. An electrical cord was attached at one end to the female deceased's neck by a slip knot, and tied at the other end around the male deceased's ankles. Another cord interconnected her ankles to his neck in like manner. Both victims were also tied together at the neck with a blue and white repp necktie looped and knotted around the throats of the victims [FLAG 34]. Commercial lubrication cream was detected in the rectum of the female deceased. A small pink ribbon was tied in a bow at the base of the male deceased's penis. No signs of struggle were noted. Neither a suicide note nor any writings indicative of depressive states were found.

The positioning of the victims assured that the leg movements of one would exert increasing pressure upon the neck of the other, compressing the carotid baroreceptors, slowing the heart rate, within a short time causing unconsciousness. The male deceased died of asphyxia due to laryngeal ligature. The female deceased died concurrently through vagal inhibition. Examination of the slip knots, in these cases often serving as a self-rescue mechanism, revealed that the female deceased's hair had become entangled in her cord's knot, precluding release. It was not evident that such release was attempted.

Six metal hooks had been installed in the ceiling to facilitate bondage activity. A dented metal wastepaper can showed signs of having been recently worn on the head by the female deceased as an entrapment device. Thirty-nine standard school notebooks kept in file cabinets were found to contain variant texts of a masochistic fantasy written in the hand of the female deceased.

Prescriptions for Stelazine and Tofranil in the name of the female deceased had been recently filled. The male deceased's evident possessions consisted of a travel-size toiletry case. Among the female deceased's

---

33 Dangling.
Not unexpected in these accounts. Fix.

---

34 Hard to picture as described.
Photo en route to Art Department should clarify.

possessions were a braided leather whip of the type known as a cat o'nine tails, lengths of 3/8" diameter hemp rope, three spools of cloth twine, two children's red jump ropes, twenty feet of clothesline, a roll of piano wire, a pair of wire clippers, battery cables, two Polaroid SX-70 cameras and eight boxes of film, seventy-three developed Polaroid photographs depicting the female deceased in earlier asphyxial episodes, battery-operated vibrating devices of assorted sizes including one capable of ejecting warmed fluids, six books on yachtsmanship and sailing, a sculler's oar, two wooden paddles of a model used frequently in fraternity/sorority initiations, scrotum weights, a penis vice, and a leather belt studded along its inner length with carpet tacks [FLAG 35].

Smiles noted on the faces of both deceased were ascribed to rigor mortis until investigators ascertained the estimated time of death [FLAG 36].

---

35 Authors as obsessional as victims. Cut?
List already trimmed by half.

---

36 Necessary?
Stet.

ANIMALS BEHIND BARS!

Scott Bradfield

Scott Bradfield publishes both mainstream fiction and genre fiction and is one of the best writers working today in either form. *Dream of the Wolf*, a collection of his tales, is a tour de force. His novels *The History of Luminous Motion* and *What's Wrong With America* are also highly recommended. Bradfield was born in California. He is currently teaching at the University of Connecticut.

Recently Bradfield has begun to write adult animal fables that are wry, wise, and wonderful. "Animals Behind Bars!," which he calls his version of *Animal Farm*, comes from *Conjunctions*, a literary journal.

—T. W.

I think I could turn and live with animals, they are so placid and self-contained . . .

They do not sweat and whine about their condition,
They do not lie awake in the dark and weep for their sins,
They do not make me sick discussing their duty to God,
Not one is dissatisfied . . .

—Whitman

In London's City Zoo there are turtles, macaws, penguins and rhinoceri. Large ancient gray elephants sunning themselves on lonely islands of concrete. Swinging baboons with extravagant genitalia. Lanky prowling jungle cats emitting heat from their muscles and light from their eyes. Strong noble creatures, witty and cynical creatures, ironic and curmudgeonly and creaturely creatures. But of all the beautiful and widely admired inhabitants of City Zoo, Scaramangus the wildebeest was easily the most vain and self-involved. Standing proudly among the females he was born to service and protect, deep-boned and flatulent from all the fresh greens and tropical fruits presented to him each morning by the deferential zoo staff, Scaramangus basked in the steam and power of his own magnificent presence. He could feel himself being exerted in every direction like an elemental force.

There was the intermittently blue sky. There was the white muted sun. There was the round earth diminishing in every direction, soft and convex. And at the center of everything, wearing a crown of hard keratinous horns, there was Scaramangus. King of the animals. Chief zoological attraction of the planet Earth. Master of laws and idol of men.

"Out of all the countless wildebeest in the entire jungle," Scaramangus exclaimed proudly every morning when the crowds came, "human beings chose *me* to represent my species to the world. I am here for the people. I exist for no other reason than to provide the quivering masses someone to emulate and admire." Every time Scaramangus brayed his self-approval, spectators lining the perimeter of Scaramangus's enclosure cheered and pointed. They held up their babies for Scaramangus to see. And, with a curt formal nod of his mighty head, Scaramangus blessed them. And told them he cared.

Scaramangus gloated shamelessly while dining, bathing, mating, and having his nails trimmed by the vet. During meal times, he hogged all the best berries and compressed protein pellets from the warped aluminum food troughs. And every spring he mounted all the strongest and most attractive females as often as he desired. "Wherever I go and whatever I do," Scaramangus said, picking bits of lint from his coat with his flat, chloryphyll-stained incisors, "I'm constantly being filmed for posterity by home video equipment and high-tech Japanese Nikons. If I belch, those flashes start a-hummin and a-poppin. If I scratch my back in the sand, or take a nice steamy dump in the grass, the human beings hold up their children so they don't miss a minute. Here's a nice hot fart, I pronounce. Here's a veiny blue erection. "Oh boy," they exclaim. "What's *that*, Mummy? What's he doing *now*?" They ooh, they ahh, they purchase exorbitant soda-water, hot dogs and laminated postcards, fifty pence apiece. Postcards with *my* picture on them, like I'm Madonna or something, or even Bruce Springsteen. Only difference is: When Springsteen plays Wembly? What sort of crowd does he draw—forty, fifty thou? I draw that many every day, seven days a week, fifty-two weeks a year. So who's the real Boss, huh, babes? It doesn't take too much figuring. Who's the real Boss *now?*"

"Oh Scaramangus," his latest female conquest moaned compliantly while Scaramangus disengaged himself with a hippy little swagger. Then he snorted disdainfully and pawed the ground for effect. "You're the Boss," she cried, "*you* are. You who are so big. You who are so strong."

"Not to mention terrifically endowed," Scaramangus added. "Don't forget the primary genetic gift, sweetheart. The procreative gift of giving."

"Oh yes," the females cheered in chorus, and scampered around the exercise track with a briefly expiring flare of adrenalin. "*Mister* Scaramangus. *Mister* Stud-of-the-Yard. *Mister* Wonderful."

Ironically enough, it's often in a zoo that animals forget their own community. Intimate sounds and smells recede in their relative imaginations like memories of old seaside holidays; they dully eye one another through the bars, and wonder idly about who they used to eat and why. Dead food arrives in their compartments with a regularity which always fails to astonish, arrayed on slabs of concrete, or stuffed with mineral supplements like vitamin sushi. When it rains, the animals don't get wet; when there is a drought, they don't go thirsty. During recessions and hard times, animals don't notice the attrition of their numbers, or the thinning of their social services. Animals become so used to the routine satisfaction of impulses that they begin to forget themselves altogether. They develop a sly sneaky dissatisfaction with the physical life. They pick at their own sores, just for a stray sensation. They scratch their gums, or bite themselves, or feel disinclined to sport with their mates. They grow complacent, mournful and soporific. They think too much, and resort to a sort of melancholy solipsism. As a result, great thoughts are often thought in zoos, but these thoughts are almost never shared.

"The camels think you're a louse," Charlie, the black crow, told Scaramangus. "The otters think you're perennially all wet. There are white wolves from Borneo who make you the butt of all their jokes, and then laugh like hyenas. How many Scaramanguses does it take to feed fifty wolves for a year? One—so long as it's his mouth." Whenever it was sunny and warm, Charlie liked to drop by and perch on the wire fence. He would nibble and arrange his darkling plumage. He enjoyed the slow abrasive charge in the air as he got Scaramangus all worked up.

"I met this white pelican the other day," Charlie said, "and guess what? He quoted Shakespeare at me. Sound and fury, Scaramangus, that's all you are. And according to the white pelican, how much do you signify? Absolutely nothing, Scary, nothing absolulutely. It quite amazes me, frankly. That a single unexceptional animal such as yourself can arouse such universal contempt from his peers. And I'll bet you didn't even realize you *had* any peers, did you, Scary? You just thought there was you. You and you and you forever."

"Bad faith," Scaramangus muttered, and pawed the ground with a little snort. He refused to grant Charlie even the minor concession of a glance. "Small animals, small minds. Ignoble thoughts are all the ignoble masses deserve." Behind him Scaramangus heard the females growing restless. Scaramangus's anger scented the air like disease or bad weather.

"Small animals, Scary. Medium-sized animals, large-sized animals and really big, *big*-sized animals, too. We're talking about an unprecedented consensus on the part of our incarcerated animal population. From molluscs to pachyderms, from mammals to invertebrates. If you were running for office, Scary, the voting would be bloody unanimous. You stand as an example to all living creatures everywhere. You remind us that whatever our differences, whether we're live-bearing or egg-bearing, whether we're warm-blooded or eat our young, that basically, essentially and perhaps even genetically, there's still a few basic things we all share in common. Us animals don't like pain, Scary. Us animals don't like ringworm, rap music, being pointed at, sinus headaches, pigeon shit or going to the vet. And on top of it all, Scary, us animals don't like you. You remind us of everything we don't want to be. And because you do that, Scary, you remind us of everything we could be and are."

Whenever Charlie got excited, he flapped his wings and tested his grip against the rusty wire mesh.

"Caw caw," Charlie said. "Caw caw, Scary. Caw caw."

The rage ignited Scaramangus's blood like a fulminate, and he experienced sudden visions of bloody and senseless murder, flames rushing across the park, the sky falling, exploded and mutilated bodies, a blizzard of flies consuming everything. Then, with a quick irrepressible beat of his heart, he charged and Charlie leapt. There was nothing Scaramangus could do to control himself. He saw Charlie leap to the perch of another segment of mesh, leaning just beyond the dimensions of Scaramangus's perfection and integrity. Then Scaramangus charged again and again. And Charlie leapt from one segment of fence to another, laughing and taunting.

"Oh Scaramangus. Oh Mister Powerful. Have yourself a big fat tantrum, Mister Wonderful. Caw caw caw caw."

For the entire day after one of Charlie's visits the wildebeest compound was not a very happy place. Scaramangus grew moody and disconsolate, radiating a severe black funk which irritated and discolored everything. On days like this, the food tasted stale and the water sour; the crowds of human beings passed hurriedly, as if this particular exhibit reminded them of other places they would rather be. Every so often a smattering of dark clouds eclipsed the sun. Inconstant winds pushed bits of human debris through the bars: candy wrappers, torn ticket stubs, twisted zoo brochures and Heritage Foundation newsletters.

Sometimes Scaramangus sat down in the cold gray dirt and just glowered. His black scowl and dark ruminations turned the entire world inside out, like a photographic negative or a political decree. The female wildebeests huddled behind the water trough, anxious and deferential. Next door, the spider monkeys scampered up and down their skeletal wooden gymnasium, hurling peanut shells and pebbles at one another. The ducks waddled into the green canal and paddled away, honking at long red and green barges anchored to iron-black moorings. Sometimes, on an impulse, Scaramangus leapt to his feet, charged the nearest convenient female, and mounted her with rude authority. But even after he was spent, he wasn't satisfied. Something had infected his world, reconfiguring its contours and redefining its clarities. This something had not changed things exactly. It did not express its own force, or heat, or angularity. Instead, this something altered the fundamental way Scaramangus looked at things. It reached through the cages of language and identity. It made everything shifting and uncertain.

"Oh Scaramangus," the females whispered with a weird, rustling dissonance. "Oh Mister Powerful. Oh Wildebeest Number One."

On days like this, Scaramangus began to suspect that other intentions existed in the world besides his own. Something teased him like a quality of physics, at once elemental and profound. Scaramangus began to worry that even when things were what they seemed, they might simultaneously represent other things entirely. Things that weren't so obvious. Things that lacked cages to define them. Things that roamed freely in the night.

"We're so lucky to have a big strong he-male to protect us," the females muttered to themselves, nibbling at stray weeds. "Oh how lucky, very lucky we are."

But Scaramangus was strong. Scaramangus endured. There was nothing wrong with Scaramangus that a good night's sleep couldn't cure. Or even a bright dreamy nap in the sun.

"Whenever you've been on top as long as I have, there's always a world full of other animals out there trying to bring you down." Scaramangus stood at the perimeter of his enclosure, watching the inarticulate crowd watch him. "Big fish eat little fish, so the little fish quite naturally resent it—and who'd blame them? It's the second law of nature, coming right after 'Eat what you can before it eats you.' Let them gossip—that's the *real* opiate of the masses. Blab blab blab until they're blue in the face." Scaramangus brayed his wise words at the crowd, wrapped in *lèse majesté* as if in a comfortable old robe. The children were peering up at him in wonder, forgetting about their spongy cotton candy and dripping Ice-lollies. They heard only the words. They heard only the words of Scaramangus.

"But what does he *do?*" one child implored her mother. "Does he just *stand* there, Mum? Doesn't he get bored standing around like that? Maybe we should take him home with us and he could watch the telly. He could sleep in my room—I wouldn't mind."

Scaramangus lifted his gaze above the rapt crowd. A true visionary had to look beyond the mean and the stupid. He had to see the wide world in all its glory, and not just some tiny perimeter of dirt he happened to be stuck in. The day was sunny, and Scaramangus looked down the hill at elevated giraffes and bright concession stands. The tourists trudged about in their day-glo dacron and skintight spandex, their pale pudgy faces gleaming with sunscreen and cholesterol. The world was firm and strong, just like Scaramangus. It was filled with noise and commerce that went on forever. You just have to believe in yourself, Scaramangus thought. Believe in yourself, and the world will believe in you.

And then, out of the corner of his eye, Scaramangus thought he saw him. A darkling flutter, skimming low over the park. Cold and concise, he landed on a glass wall circumscribing a blue, kidney-shaped swimming pool. And all the dim addled penguins came waddling up to greet him.

Across the white noise of the milling crowds, one word carried clearly, one word was always hard and certain. It spoke through everything—smelly tourists, bad music, crying children and flushing toilets.

"Caw caw," the crow declared distantly, to anybody who would listen. "Caw caw caw caw."

Winter came early that year. Many animals retreated into their makeshift wooden dens and plasterboard caverns to resume the long furry dream of themselves. Others fattened their jackets with rich nuts and refined white breads, and slumped formidably in the corners of their cages, bits of food staining their muddled faces. The crowds of human visitors thinned; the voices of the human children grew increasingly irritable and plaintive.

"Why don't they *do* anything, Mum?" the children cried. "Why do they just sit there? And where are the giraffes hiding? Where are all the elephants?"

Exhibit after exhibit was closed, sometimes due to the ticking of intimate hibernal clocks, at other times due to improper funding. The giant pandas caught cold and went to the hospital. The snakes shed their skin and hid underneath rocks and logs in slow, greedy ceremonies of digestion. The solitary okapi, one of the shiest animals in the entire zoo, began weeping uncontrollably at the slightest provocation. "I don't know what it is," he told himself. "I try to be friendly. I really do. But I just feel more comfortable when I'm alone. So why can't I ever forgive myself?"

Wanda the gorilla, pregnant with her fourth child, sat in her cage all day being steadfastly disregarded by her massive, emotionally unsupportive mate, Roy.

"All I ever do anymore is eat," Wanda complained. She was tearing apart celery stalks and devouring them into fibrous bits. Her belly was swollen, distended, and littered with crisp green celery leaves. "I just sit here eating all day, getting fatter and fatter, dropping baby after baby. Tell me—is this any sort of life for a lady?"

The penguins stood poised around their blue pool, or up and down their spiral sliding exercise-platform like dancers in some bizarre Busby Berkeley number. "Somebody's made a terrible mistake!" the penguins cried in unison. "We only *look* like penguins, but we're *not* penguins, really! Let us out of here! Our parents must be worried sick! Take us back to our warm beds in Camberwell Green!" Every afternoon at four the caretaker hosed them down with a spray gun and scrubbed their concrete patios with a wooden push broom.

The tiger paced in his cage, back and forth, back and forth, a feral metronome. On the other side of the plate-glass barrier, children raced him from one end of the cage to the other and then back again. "Just one, and I swear I'll never ask for anything else ever again," the tiger muttered, pacing, pacing, feverishly pacing. "Please God, if you're out there, I'll be good, I'll be grateful. I'll get down on my knees and worship at your feet—I swear on my mother's sharpest incisor. Just a little one without too much hair. That's all I'll ever need to be happy."

The animals began hearing a lot of "R" words they couldn't pronounce. Words like recession, redundancy and rationalization. They heard rumors of leveraged buyouts, corporate takeovers, asset-stripping, privatization, the ECU, Princess Di's mood swings and the planet-wide bio-diversity crisis. The zoo personnel began to look more pale and unraveled than usual. They didn't sweep the grounds as often, or disinfect the living quarters as thoroughly. In fact, the zoo personnel were beginning to develop attitudes as aimlessly belligerent as those of the animals themselves.

"You beasts don't know how lucky you got it," Dave the night watchman told them. "Me and my wife, right? We're graftin', day after day, year after year. And what've we got to show for it? Some crummy two-bedroom flat in Finchley, a lousy conversion job and mortgaged to the hilt. At least in a cage you got your three square meals. You got your crowds of adorin' people like you was big war heroes or something. You ain't got to make your own living with nobody to count on in the entire world but yourself."

Then, with his copy of *The Sun* folded strategically under one arm, and two cans of Tennant's Super Strong lager brown-wrapped under the other, Dave took his briefcase into the Life-Watch Visitors' Center, where he stared bitterly at his portable TV and fell asleep on the convertible sofa.

One night in bleak November, a radical-extremist guerrilla faction of A.R.Y.A.N., the Animal Rights Youth-Action Network, blew the front gate off the zoo with Semtex and dynamite caps. They were wearing black wool ski-masks, black jeans, black turtleneck T-shirts and black leather gloves, like a team of down-market ninjas. Within moments, they had bound and gagged Dave the night watchman in the Visitors' Lounge. They had disconnected the zoo's various overhead video monitors, burglar alarms and telephones. A series of smaller explosions sounded, cages came unsprung, pop pop pop. Then, as casually as if he were flagging a cab, the leader of the guerrilla band raised a triumphant fist to the moon-blond sky.

"We all breathe the air!" he cried. "We all love the earth! Endangered species of the world—unite!"

The black-clad guerrillas leapt back over the turnstiles and disappeared into Regents Park, bobbing and weaving across the green fields as if they were being pursued by enemy sniper-fire. Suddenly, the entire zoo was dark again, silent, preemptive, dense. It was as if the zoo had not suffered an event so much as a lapse of attention. Everybody sat up in their ruptured enclosures, dazed and blinking, as if they were waiting around for something that had already happened.

"Mama mia!" chirped Charlie the crow, perched atop one of the recently embattled ticket kiosks. "Talk about your popular uprisings, your basic *fait accompli*. This is what I'd call a *deus ex machina*, my fellow beasties. Holy bloody cow."

Charlie could hardly contain himself. He performed a little salsa on the kiosk's slate roof, a half-pirouette and a full spin. Something was happening. Something was happening in the zoo, and for once it wasn't something Charlie himself had initiated.

Charlie dove into the shining air. A fine mist sprayed his face, the cool conflux of moonlight hummed. Across the zoo's triangular, compartmentalized map, animals were slowly awakening to themselves. Intact plumes of smoke drifted here and there like helium-filled feather boas. Charlie wheeled, spreading his black wings, pumping cold air deep into his lungs. "Caw caw," Charlie told them. "Caw caw caw caw."

The wolves sniffed the broken gate of their wrought-iron fence. Scorched metal, wide spaces, a dim primal scent of antelope like a memory of fire. The wolves retreated, sniffed again, conferred. It was almost like hysteria. Freedom made you giddy, a little uncertain about who you wanted to be.

For some animals, however, doubt never entered their minds. Wanda the gorilla took one look at Roy and she knew. Roy had already fallen asleep again. He was picking his nose and snoring. Wanda tossed a half-eaten Winesap over one shoulder and swung through the open door. She was pursued by two tumbling children, but she didn't look back. Anywhere, she thought. Except where I already am.

Charlie turned and turned again. Movements, smells, new awarenesses, old routines being casually forgotten. In their hay-strewn domiciles, even the slumbering elephants were beginning to rouse. Tiny kernels of disbelief flared in their muggy brains. I am not asleep, the elephants thought. The world is changing and I am not asleep.

Charlie saw a community of animals beginning to take shape. Ruminants, primates, rodents, carnivores and marsupials. Wild ground-squirrels and golden lion tamarinds, meerkats and mongooses, Fennee foxes and old spotted pigs. The animals were journeying into the strange, neutral territories between their cages where existing systems of animal language failed to operate. They were discovering the same unreality of freedom. They were opening their collective eyes to the same dissonant recognition.

We are all different, they realized. And yet we are all somehow the same.

When Charlie arrived at Scaramangus's enclosure, Scaramangus was sitting in front of his open gate with thick, immovable composure. His haunches were quivering; heat streamed in gusts from his flaring nostrils. He emitted a low, guttural purr from his throat.

"Let them come," Scaramangus was saying, over and over again. "They know where to find me. Let them come and find me here."

"Oh Mighty Scaramangus," Charlie said. "Oh ye of muddled mind and rumpled brow. Leave your delusions of grandeur back in your cage. Come out here with us and you won't need any ego to validate. We're taking *collective* action, bro. We're forging the uncreated conscious of our race and so on. This thing is bigger than you and me, Scary. Much bigger by far."

"I will stand my ground," Scaramangus ceremoniously intoned. He was alone in his enclosure, except for a few deliberately placed logs and stumps. "I will continue to be Scaramangus, no matter how hard they try to diminish me. They want to make me the same as them, but I refuse to be anybody except myself."

"You don't get it, do you, Scary? You've completely missed the boat." Charlie flapped his wings for emphasis. "Don't you get lonely all locked up inside your own head? Don't you want to come out and join the fun?"

But Scaramangus refused to be persuaded. Scaramangus refused to be moved.

The animals were assembled in the amphitheater, where chimps had activated the sound system and microphone. By the time Charlie got there, the amplifiers were wailing with feedback. In response the animals joined their discordant voices into one terrific African clamor.

With a swoop and a flourish, Charlie switched off the superfluous speakers and took the mike from Wanda, who was fruitlessly trying to incite the multiply distracted crowd with tales of her husband Roy's ruthless banana consumption.

Charlie landed on the rim of the podium, spun the mike in his direction and cawed.

"You know what you sound like!" Charlie shouted. The black rhinos were blustering and bullying their way into all the best seats. The giraffes, swatting girlishly at mice, knocked their tender horns against overhead lights, spilling broken bulbs and scratchy mortar everywhere. Butterflies, confused by the harsh illumination, fluttered ungracefully like headlight-stricken moths.

"You sound like a bunch of *animals!*" Charlie roared. Charlie's mimicry of human speech sent a hush over the crowd. The animals looked over their shoulders, feeling abruptly complicit, wary and insecure.

"You want to get pissed off about something?" Charlie shouted. "Then I'll give you something to get pissed off about. If we want to speak to one another, what language do we have to use? The language of our oppressor, that's what! You want to know what *that's* called, my fellow beasties? It's called being co-opted. They haven't just been locking us in cages. They been *co-opting* us. And us too stupid to know otherwise!"

The animals heard a strange, collective voice emerge from their various animal throats. One long, gathering note of disquiet, anguish and terrible remorse.

"Now, for the first time in our far-too-miserable lives, we've got a chance to speak for ourselves!" Charlie told them. "We've got a chance to form our own government, make our own laws, and relearn our own culture. Haven't you guys seen *Spartacus!* Haven't you guys seen *The Battle of Algiers!*"

"Spih, spih, *spih*," hissed the sibilant snakes.

"Al-*geesh*," sneezed the white pelicans. "Al-*geesh*, *geesh!*"

Charlie shrugged off the momentary lapse of momentum. "Okay, maybe not. But you don't need to watch telly to know when you're being robbed of your freedom. You don't need to be a genius to know when you're being fed another line of vulgar bourgeois homo-sap horse-shit! Stay in your little cage, they tell us. This way you won't be *exterminated!* What sort of reasoning is *that?* I'll tell you what sort of reasoning it is. It's malevolent, genocidal, terraphobic, uncompromising right-brain-thinking human aggression—*that's* what it is! And have we had enough? Have we? Have we had *enough?* I'm asking *you* guys! Don't look over your shoulder. No caretaker's coming along to answer this one for you! Have *we* had *enough?*"

It wasn't even a word at first. Just a low, mildly inflected swerve of vowels. Affirmative. Regular. Long.

"I can't *hear* you," Charlie screamed. "What are you—dumb animals or *wild beasts of the jungle?* Let me hear it, beasts! Who's had enough? Who's fed up with being lied to? Who's ready to take control of their lives?"

And then it was a word. Intact. Hard. Anchored to the special reality of their intimate animal-selves.

"Us!" the animals cried. "Us, us, us, us, *us!*"

(Us. Us.)

Scaramangus started to his feet with a gasp, blinking at the bright lights of the distant auditorium. The slow blue dream disassembled like a warm wool blanket being pulled from his shoulders. It was a dream that had arisen from Scaramangus's weary heart like a sort of respiration, a dream of air and aspect his hard blunt mind could not endorse. No, he thought. No way. No way by a long shot.

Scaramangus saw the distant brassy swarm of presumptuous animals spilling from the mouth of the auditorium in every direction. Someone had started a small bonfire in one of the litter-bins. Someone else had overturned the refrigerated cabinets in the Raffles Bar and Restaurant, and animals were riotously sucking on frozen hot dogs and fistfuls of gluey pizza dough.

Not *us*, Scaramangus corrected. Not us, but *them*.

Scaramangus shook the sand from his linty jacket. He stepped hard against the leaning iron gate. The gate swayed on exploded hinges, agonized, and fell with a loud dull clatter. No longer would Scaramangus wait for them. It was time for Scaramangus to make the first move.

Stepping through the broken gate was like slipping into a warm bath. A sort of electrical or cosmic force passed through Scaramangus's body, bristling in his blood and matted black hair. He felt giddy and disoriented. Standing on the pathway previously reserved for human beings, Scaramangus felt deeply confused at the molecular level, as if the tiniest cells of his body were being invaded by foreign enzymes, proteins, germs.

As he stood in the flickering, tribal illumination spreading rapidly across the compound, two stray zebras galloped past. One was saying to the other, "I *love* a party. I mean—at least I always *imagined* I'd love a party, though I've never actually *been*."

The animals were piling picnic tables and broken lumber against the front gates when Scaramangus arrived. The ticket kiosks and fast-food carts were being hammered into pieces by the elephants and horses. Long-limbed ostriches were striding about squawking hasty encouragements. There was the buzz of insects in the air, the slow-lidded bemusement of lizards and opossums. High in the trees, owls blinked and watched.

"Here I am," Scaramangus told them. "I'll take you on one at a time, or I'll take you on all at once. I don't care how much you hate me. I'm everything none of you could ever be."

The animals continued hurrying in every direction. They were reinforcing the front gates with barbed wire transferred from cages. They were turning the idea of the zoo inside out.

Scaramangus stood proudly among them, straining against the tension of his own rage. This was the purest form of malice—deliberate disregard. They were trying to inspire his false confidence. Then, the moment Scaramangus let his guard down—*bam!* Meat for somebody else's stew.

Scaramangus had never been so aware of the depth and intensity of his own anger before. It blazed in the pit of his stomach, lapping at his stone heart. He felt consumed by the fire of himself, this pure force that burned him and made him strong. Slowly, Scaramangus grew aware of a pair of eyes trained on his haunches. No matter how much the hurrying animals pretended to ignore him, Scaramangus knew he was being watched. They want to make me the object, Scaramangus thought. They want to make an object out of me before I make an object out of them.

"Hey there, Mister," the voice said.

Scaramangus turned, pawed the ground, and breathed his immortal contempt into the chill air. This was the challenge. The supreme test was now.

Wanda the gorilla had adorned herself in a torn floppy sunhat, terrycloth leg warmers, and a large green plastic rain poncho liberated from one of the trash bins. The poncho was swung low to reveal an unabashed glimpse of hairy cleavage.

"I say darling—have we met?" Wanda batted her eyelashes and offered him the last bits of Kit Kat bar from her chocolaty fingers. "Are you an antelope or something? I dig those horns."

Scaramangus felt the rage seeping from his lungs as he exhaled. He took another, deeper breath. He wanted to regain the hot integrity of himself. He wanted to be sure he was who he had always pretended to be.

"I," Scaramangus said, "am a wildebeest. The proudest, and mightiest, and most handsome on the face of the planet."

Wanda's eyes widened.

"Oh, *really?*" Wanda said. "So tell me this, then. Where have you *been* all my life, huh?"

The prospect of dawn had never possessed so much thrill and expectation before. The animals, armed with broken bottles, splintery sticks and a shrill, keen charge of adrenalin, were entrenched behind the overturned Information Booth, listening to the occasional rush of cars outside, feeling the moon's cold glare on their shoulders. It was almost like contentment, but without the lassitude. For Charlie, perched atop a rackety aluminum turn stile, the coil and heat of the animals felt claustrophobic, like prison or responsibility. And beyond the circle of corporate warmth loomed the immensely solitary figure of Scaramangus, staring into the red anger of his own heart, terrified by the beat and implication of his own blood.

Some of us just need to be liberated from our cages, Charlie thought. But others of us need to be liberated from ourselves.

Every so often Charlie looked into the glowing sky for portents he might recognize, rare apocrypha or strange weather. Out there, stars flickered but planets never did. It was not the encouragement Charlie wanted, but it was the truth he would accept.

"When we chart our courses according to the stars," Charlie reflected out loud, "we're often yearning for the light of suns long extinguished. We're often aspiring to the achievements of civilizations that didn't last."

"What's the matter, Charlie?" muttered the tigers. "Where are all your big words now? Words like self-determination, animal equity, moral imperative, praxis, historicity, idealism and faith?"

"Faith doesn't mean you know The Way," Charlie said, his chest and face filling with the hiss of a vast, impossible sadness. It reminded him of the time when, purely out of spite, he had punctured a child's zoo-balloon and accidentally inhaled helium. "Faith just means hoping you'll know The Way once you find it."

Dawn didn't approach; it gradually pervaded.

First the helicopters arrived; then a siege of police vans, bomb disposal squads and BBC news minicams. "Please, we know you're upset," Chief Constable Heathcliff declared over his new high-tech lightweight megaphone. "Who wouldn't be? But why can't we talk this over face to face? Open up the gate and let us in. We're only here to *help*." The Chief Constable was wearing a crisp white shortsleeve shirt and pleated navy-blue slacks.

"Lousy bastards," Charlie sighed. "I knew they'd try a little false compassion first, just to loosen us up. Those lying heathen will stoop to just about *any*thing!"

"Look, we realize you big animals can take care of yourselves," Chief Constable Heathcliff continued. "But think about the little ones—the tarsiers, say, or even the cute little penguins. They're pretty far down the old food chain, wouldn't you say? Another night's sleep with the rest of you meat-eaters and, well. Let's face it. An unregulated zoo can get pretty messy."

Charlie could feel the mood of the assembled animals starting to turn. The penguins whined, "But we *aren't* penguins, really—we've been *trying* to *tell* you. But those jungle cats don't listen, either." The cliquish wolves conferred in whispers, glancing over their collective shoulders at a twitching orange huddle of doormice.

"When we need human intervention to settle our quarrels—we'll *ask* for it!" Charlie cried back.

"Give us a chance," the Chief Constable said, oozing a treacly substance he pretended was sympathy. "We *want* to improve your standard of living, but at the same time we've *got* to be fiscally responsible. We're working on a whole lot of new ideas, but we'll need *your* help to implement them. Why don't you let me in and I'll explain a few of these new ideas to you right now?"

"For example," Charlie said.

"Well, market forces. We open up the zoo to what they call Free Enterprise Zones. We farm you out to extracurricular jobs—serving tea for the handicapped, fetching groceries and newspapers, or a little rudimentary shop and construction work. We give you all an individual opportunity to improve your lives through hard work and competitive negotiation. Those who work hard, benefit. Those who don't—well, they've still got their warm cages to go to. They've still got two square meals a day, plenty of highly trained medical supervision, and, when they consent to appear in any of the zoo's afternoon kiddie-shows, as many sweet treats as they can gobble. And between you and me, Mr. Crow, what sort of animals do you think might benefit from such a scheme? Well, those with opposable thumbs are going to clean up, of course. But then a bright bird such as yourself, who has mastered the fundamentals of human speech and grammar—let's just say that such a hypothetical bird won't do too badly either. If you know what I mean."

"Yeah, *right.*" Charlie was pacing irritably back and forth on a strand of rusty barbed wire. Down below, vans and ambulances flashed while complacent news reporters spoke into portable cassette recorders. "You mean you'll put us on overcrowded tubes and trains every morning and night, other people sneezing on us, no air conditioning. You'll tax the bones out of us and instead of investing it in animal services, you'll spend it to subsidize the chemical and weapons industries. You'll give us two different groups of corrupt politicians to choose from every few years or so, all of whom represent the same multinational banking and oil interests. Then you'll profit from our vacancy and despair through exorbitantly taxed sales of tobacco and alcohol, and regulate how much we spend on our homes and families through state control of interest rates and import quotas. Look, buster, do you really think we'll fall for this bogus 'free-market forces' folderol? We may be animals—but that doesn't mean we're *stupid!*"

The animals, startled by their own abrupt consensus, roared. The trees shook. The sky expanded with oxygen and light.

"Well, don't claim I didn't try, friend," said the handsome Chief Constable. "I've done my best to get through to you, but there are other people in my department with different ideas about how to handle public insurrection. I'll do what I can to hold them off, but I'm only one man. If you want to talk this thing over at *any* time, just ask for Chief Constable Heathcliff. And I wish you—and I mean *all* of you—the best of luck. You're going to need it."

From that point it was only a matter ot time. The animals had already gorged themselves on all the best junk food and candy bars, and sprayed graffiti across the walls of the caretaker's offices and public restrooms. FREEDOM OR DEATH! ANIMAL RIGHTS NOW! FREE THE SERENGHETI SEVEN! EAT THE RICH BEFORE THEY EAT YOU! Their exhausted invective settled over the zoo like the thin, ashen fallout from a receptacle bomb. The animals knew they had uttered truth as clearly as their crude tongues allowed. Now they could only drift in the white, resonant spaces of their own anonymity. Just a slight buzz of interference, barely less than an echo. And then only the memory of sound, the flat wide incognizance of liberty, reminding them of what they could never entirely understand.

"If every animal in the entire world could journey into space on an orbital satellite, they would experience the same revelation." Charlie was sucking warm Tetley's out of a pint-sized aluminum can Wanda had opened for him, feeling groggy and sentimental. "They would look out into the blackness. They would not see light, but only light's reflection. A bit of blue-green mold, pear-shaped, slowly spinning, tenderly constrained by primeval forces. Other planets and other suns out there, maybe other life forms, maybe not. The fragile momentary testimony of it. Each animal, alone in its metal capsule, would gaze out at the general amorphous shapes of mountain and cloud, atmosphere and ocean. Forests broken and slashed. Cities stupefied by their own poisonous emissions. The blue waters turning gray and disconsolate in patches. Every animal would feel itself diminish into its own expanding awareness of our planet. Not a sense of responsibility, really. Just a sense of location, a grounding in space and time. No more floating around in the abstract nothingness of self. At this point, the animal would be given a choice. To go spinning off in its tiny immaculate capsule, or to return splashing into the Earth's immensities of ocean. Then, after everyone had made their own decision, we'd finally have a planet of animals who wanted to be here. No more nationalism, disintegrating cities, or competitive incorporate selves. Just countless blundering and hungry animals, trying to help one another out the best we can. This, friends, is my dream. When I fly, this is the dream that carries me."

Charlie carefully inserted his beak into the aluminum can for another long sip. Around him, the animals drowsed in the morning sun. They no longer bothered to look over the fence at what the humans were up to. By this point, everything was out of their hands.

"I mean look at you, Scaramangus," Charlie said, wiping his beak against the aluminum rim. "All wrapped up in the glory of your own fire and blood. Surrounded by a world you want to devour and destroy. You just don't get it, do you, Scary? You just don't see the big picture. A bit of blue-green mold floating in space."

Scaramangus stood with his back to the barricades, watching the crowd of animals not watch him. They were collectively gazing over his head at the inconstant amethyst flash of police vans and emergency vehicles. They were collectively listening for sounds the police hadn't yet started to make.

"You play your game and I'll play mine," Scaramangus said. "You and your friends keep on your side of the line and I'll keep on mine."

They came in the late afternoon, a time usually reserved for the animals' second feeding. The wet plop of tear-gas canisters drew arcs of smoke across the blue sky. Hypo-darts were fired by snipers from elevated cranes and rooftops. An ambuscade of water cannons, smoke grenades, and antiterrorist Green Beret units attired in green khaki military fatigues. The largest animals fell first, feeling the barbiturates bite into their flanks and haunches, then the startled murky descent into solitary darknesses. Panicked, the remaining animals stampeded wildly blinded by the gas, knocking over fences and water fountains, trampling one another into the boiling gray dust. Tanks and armored trucks climbed the barricades. The police wielded billy clubs and mace. Outside in the parking lot, reporters politely observed the top-security news blackout which unnamed government officials had pulled over the entire operation. They obediently scribbled notes into their palms, or videotaped one another videotaping everybody else.

"Oh shit," Charlie moaned from a high telephone line. "Oh why, oh why, oh why can't I keep my big mouth shut."

For Scaramangus, the line between himself and the other animals suddenly vanished, threatening to take him with it. The chaos of bodies, the utterly random brutality and anguish, the feverish incongruous clash of animals and men. A universe of pure aggression, a physics of undifferentiated violence. A billy club glanced off Scaramangus's forehead and he staggered, turned. The Bobby came at him again and Scaramangus, trying to run, toppled over the fallen insensible body of a lion. The lion's mouth was wide open, its paws outstretched in every direction. It resembled a trophy draped beside some tourist's safari fire, drained of vital juices, a memory now for everyone but itself.

Scaramangus tried to cry out. "Stop!" he wanted to tell them. "You don't know who I am!"

The Bobby lifted the billy club again. The Bobby was wearing a hideous off-green gas mask which made him resemble a cross between an aardvark and an elephant.

"You don't even know my name, or whose side I'm on," Scaramangus cried. "I might as well be an ocelot, or a rat, or a parakeet so far as you're concerned." Scaramangus couldn't believe these were his words on his lips. There was something about them—a weight, a contour, a fugitive texture—which carried information Scaramangus had never suspected before. "A big fat alligator," Scaramangus said during that slow attenuate moment while the billy club continued to descend. "A cheetah, a reindeer, a centipede, or a finch." The billy club continued descending. Time, Scaramangus thought. Time, terrible time.

The sky wasn't blue anymore.

The billy club came down.

For the next week to ten days the animals were kept tranquilized in their cages and enclosures. They weren't allowed to frequent the exercise yards or the children's petting zoo. They were fed more cereal and less meat. Every day the wind blew scraps of morning newspapers into their cages, and the animals perused them for articles about their brief fling with liberation. But the newspapers only mentioned interest rates, third world death squads, an Earth summit in Rio, American tobacco exports to Thailand and Hong Kong. The newspapers were filled with politics, finance, sports and diplomacy, but hardly any news about animals whatsoever.

Chief Constable Heathcliff was now interim Head Caretaker, assigned to oversee the zoo's imminent foreclosure.

"Well," the new Head Caretaker announced one day, his voice, as always, eminently reasonable and firm. "I tried to warn you, didn't I? I told you we were facing some pretty severe economic shortfalls around this place—you can't expect the public to continue paying your bills forever, you know. What it comes down to is this—I'm afraid we'll be closing the zoo in September. We're already looking around for new homes for all of you. I think the change of climate can only do you a world of good."

"Divide and conquer," Charlie said. "Turn one animal against the next. Yin from yang, blood from bone, mind from body. Ouch."

Charlie had resumed his regular perch on Scaramangus's gate, but Scaramangus didn't seem to notice. Scaramangus had received unusually large dosages of quaaludes over the past week or so, and felt thick with fatigue and anomie.

"Trick is," Charlie continued, "you can't cage an entire nation. You can only cage individual animals, one or two at a time. Ergo—a competitive economy. Animal versus animal, male versus female, the have-somes versus the have-nones. Don't let them fool you with this bullshit about economic retrenchment, Scary. What's being retrenched is *us*. Us animals. Because we're bigger together than we are apart—and don't you forget it."

Scaramangus was dimly aware of Charlie chattering away on the wire fence. He was dimly aware of both his enclosure and the pall of inactivity that had settled over the entire zoo. Everything seemed smaller, frailer, and more faded than it had before the revolution. Scaramangus's female companions had taken to sleeping at the other end of the enclosure, where they tended to mutter in their sleep, or burst into tears every so often for no apparent reason. Scaramangus felt very distant from the world he used to inhabit. There were times when he mistook his lassitude for sadness, and his abstract anomie for concrete political conditions.

"Maybe the Japs are right," Charlie jabbered, pacing back and forth on the wavering wire. It wasn't Charlie's fault, Scaramangus realized. Of all the animals in the zoo, only Charlie lacked a cage to define the dimensions of his enclosure, and only Charlie possessed mind enough to be baffled by the paradox. "Maybe it really *is* the end of history, and we're witnessing a point in history which has given up on history altogether. The sense that we are shaping a collective future, that we have debts and responsibilities not only to the corporations who pay our salaries, but to the planetary forces which loan us this flesh in which we're wrapped. That history is something we carry with us and inside us, and isn't just more material to be swapped for a lot of 'B' words. Bonds, bucks, Beamers, babes, bricks, bureaucracy, booze and tax-deductible business lunches. We keep exchanging what we are for what we never wanted to be. We're turning into, like, what do you call them? Cyborgs, man, but without the metal. Bits and pieces of what we once were, locked up in mechanical collaboration with a system of government we can't even pretend to understand. I think it's a very difficult time to be living, Scary. No matter what they tell us in the newspapers, I think it's a pretty difficult time, indeed."

Scaramangus lifted himself unsteadily to his feet and shivered the dust from his jacket. He shook his face, trying to pump blood into his brain and loosen his lips. The females were still asleep behind the food trough—or at least the three of them who remained. The fourth female, the one with the best legs, had been taken to the infirmary that morning by two spotty, suspicious-looking men in frayed white uniforms. For the first time in his life, it struck Scaramangus as odd that he didn't even know the fourth female's name. After years of sharing food and sex with her in the same enclosure, Scaramangus only knew her as Best Legs. He felt there was a lesson to be learned in this recognition, but he didn't feel clever enough to figure out what that one lesson was.

"I don't know. I guess I really just don't know." Charlie was starting to moan regretfully to himself again. He was looking across the zoo at large wooden crates being unloaded from a red and green lorry. Ever since the revolution a spark had gone out of Charlie, an edge, an element of vulgarity. As if to disguise what he had lost, Charlie never seemed to stop talking, even when he had nothing to say. "I guess I don't know. Maybe I just like to hear myself talk. Maybe I'm completely wrong about everything, and everything the politicians say is right. Maybe, maybe, maybe, maybe." It was as if Charlie was flying far away from the zoo even when he sat here perched on one of its fences. Scaramangus still hated Charlie, but Charlie was flying so far away that Scaramangus's hate couldn't reach him anymore.

Out in the zoo's central arena, the Head Caretaker was speaking over the microphone to an assembly of local businessmen and community leaders who had come to make bids on the soon-to-be disenfranchised animals.

"And for the first order of the day," the Head Caretaker announced cheerfully, "we have a very, very special young lady. Bring her out here, boys, so the gentlemen can see."

Wanda, stripped down to one forlorn, bruised banana, was resting her forehead against the bars of her portable cage and wheezing softly.

"We're talking about a prime bit of animal real estate here, friends," the Head Caretaker told them. "Almost as smart as a human being—that's our hairy animal-cousin, the mighty black gorilla. Stronger, friendlier, and better coordinated than any child. They make great exhibits—in the mezzanine of your office building, say. Or at that stockholders' meeting you're planning for the Bahamas next spring. Let's start this off right. Do I hear one thousand pounds?"

"Maybe, maybe, maybe, maybe," Charlie moaned, over and over again, trying to drown out the caretaker's magnified voice in his ears.

Suddenly, all the anger Scaramangus had ever felt in his entire life lifted up out of his body and deposited itself on the gate where Charlie was sitting. It was a hard, raw recognition, as approachable as a barrier, as clearly articulable as a word. Scaramangus pawed the gray dust. He looked at Charlie self-consciously moaning on the evil iron gate.

"I hear fifteen hundred," the caretaker declared. "Do I hear seventeen-five?"

Across the zoo, the defeated animals felt the weather start to turn. Bristling, dry, abrasive, charged. They sat up in their cages. They tried to see into the central arena, but it was surrounded by walls and trees.

It was only a word, but Scaramangus knew it. With a sudden roar and a lunge, Scaramangus threw his entire body against the gate and the impact flung Charlie high into the air, wheeling, catching his balance with a staggered flurry of wings, the earth literally knocked out from under him. Scaramangus reared against the gate with his horns. It was the word. The word versus the gate and something had to give.

Scaramangus backed up a few steps and threw himself against the gate again, rearing against the indomitable reality of it, all the hate and rage he had never adequately spoken before.

"Us!" Scaramangus shouted, straining against the bars with his back, his shoulders, his haunches and his brain. "Us! Us! Us! Us!"

Throughout the zoo, the animals felt the voice rising in their throats again. The voice was theirs. The voice was not theirs.

"Us!" Scaramangus cried again.

He backed up. He saw the gate. He saw the world beyond the gate. He saw the overweight men with bad complexions standing in the arena, brushing off their three-piece suits, turning their pale faces toward the word Scaramangus was trying to tell them.

"Us!" Scaramangus cried and charged the gate again.

Across the zoo the word was lifting them in their cages, reminding them of the reality they would not accept. It was time. They would say it now.

The animals began to roar.

MONUMENTS TO THE DEAD

Kristine Kathryn Rusch

Kristine Kathryn Rusch has published numerous SF and fantasy short stories in genre magazines and anthologies, as well as several novels—*Traitors*, her most recent, is recommended. She was a founding member of the Pulphouse Publishing company in the Pacific Northwest, and is currently the editor of *The Magazine of Fantasy & Science Fiction*.

The following story is one of the most mature pieces of work to come from this prolific author to date: a contemporary American fantasy tale about the "disappearance" of Mt. Rushmore. It is reprinted from *Tales from the Great Turtle*, a collection of original fantasy stories drawn from Native American traditions (edited by Richard Gilliam and Piers Anthony). Two other stories from the volume are also recommended reading: "Going After Old Man Alabama," by mystery writer William Sanders, and "Counting Coup," a mainstream story by Jack Dann.

—T. W.

The California Perspective: Reflections on Mt. Rushmore
by L. Emilia Sunlake

> The union of these four presidents carved on the face of the everlasting hills of South Dakota will contribute a distinctly national monument. It will be decidedly American in its conception, in its magnitude, in its meaning, and altogether worthy of our country.
>
> —*Calvin Coolidge at the dedication of Mt. Rushmore, 1927*

Cars crawl along Highway 16. The hot summer sun reflects off shiny bumper stickers, most plastered with the mementos of tourist travel: Sitting Bull Crystal Cave, Wall Drug, and I ♥ anything from terriers to West Virginia. The windows are open, and children lean out, trying to see magic shimmering in the heat visions on the pavement. The locals say the traffic has never been like this, that even at the height of tourist season the cars can go at least thirty miles an hour. I have been sitting in this sticky heat for most of the afternoon with Kenny, my photographer, moving forward a foot at a time, sharing a Diet Coke, and hoping the story will be worth the aggravation.

I have never been to the Black Hills before. Until I started writing regularly for the slick magazines, I had never been out of California, and even then my outside assignments were rare. Usually I wrote about things close to home: the history of Simi Valley, for instance, or the relationships between the Watts riot and the Rodney King riot twenty-five years later. When *American Observer* sent me to South Dakota, they asked me to write from a California perspective. What they will get is a white, middle-class, female California perspective. Despite my articles on the cultural diversity of my home state, *American Observer*—published in New York—continues to think that all Californians share the same opinions, beliefs, and outlooks.

Of course, now, sitting in bumper-to-bumper traffic in the dense heat, I feel right at home.

Kenny has brought a lunch—tuna fish—which, in the oppressive air, has a rancid two-days-dead odor. He eats with apparent gusto, while I sip on soda and try to peer ahead. Kenny says nothing. He is a slender man with long black hair and wide dark eyes. I chose him because he is the best photographer I have ever met, a man who can capture the heart of a moment in a single image. He also rarely speaks, a trait I usually enjoy, but one I have found annoying on this long afternoon as we wait in the trail of cars.

He sees me lean out the window for the fifth time in the last minute. "Why don't you interview some of the tourists?"

I shake my head and he goes back to his sandwich. The tourists aren't the story. The story waits for us at the end of this road, at the end of time.

When I think of Mount Rushmore, I think of Cary Grant clutching the lip of a stone-faced Abraham Lincoln with Eva Marie Saint beside him, looking over her shoulder at the drop below. The movie memory has the soft fake tones of early color or perhaps early colorization—the pale blues that don't exist in the natural world, the red lipstick that is five shades too red. As a child, I wanted to go to the monument and hang off a president myself. As an adult, I disdained tourist traps, and had avoided all of them with amazing ease.

Later I tell my husband of this, and he corrects me: Cary Grant was hanging off George Washington's forehead. Kenny disagrees: he believes Grant crawled around Teddy Roosevelt's eyes. A viewing of *North by Northwest* would settle this disagreement, but I saw the movie later, as an adult, and found the special effects not so special, and the events contrived. If Cary Grant hadn't, stupidly, pulled the knife from a dead man's body, there would have been no movie. The dead man and the knife were an obvious setup, and Grant's character fell right into the trap.

Appropriate, I think, for a Californian to have a cinematic memory of Mount Rushmore. As I study the history, however, I find it much more compelling, and frighteningly complex.

* * *

The Black Hills are as old as any geological formation in North America. They rise out of the flatlands on the Wyoming-Dakota border, mysterious shadowy hills that are cut out of the dust. The dark pine trees made the hills look black from a distance. The Paha Sapa, or the Black Hills, were the center of the world for the surrounding tribes. They used the streams and lakes hidden by the trees; they hunted game in the wooded areas; and in the summer, the young men went to the sacred points on a four-day vision quest that would shape and focus the rest of their lives.

According to Lakota tribal legend, the hills were a reclining female figure from whose breasts flowed life. The Lakota went to the hills as a child went to its mother's arms.

In 1868 the United States government signed a treaty with the Indians, granting them "absolute and undisturbed use of the Great Sioux Reservation," which included the Black Hills. The terms of the treaty included the line "No white person or persons shall be permitted to settle upon or occupy any portion of the territory, or without the consent of the Indians to pass through the same."

White persons have been trespassing ever since.

Finally I can stand the smell of tuna no longer. I push open the door of the rental car and stand. My jeans and T-shirt cling to my body—I am not used to humid heat. I walk along the edge of the highway, peering into cars, seeing pale face after pale face. Most of the tourists ignore me, but a few watch hesitantly, fearing that I am going to pull a gun and leap into their car beside them.

Everyone knows of the troubles in the Black Hills, and most people have brought their families despite the dangers. Miracles only happen once in a lifetime.

I see no one I want to speak to until I pass a red pickup truck. Its paint is chipped, and the frame is pocked with rust. A Native American woman sits inside, a black braid running down her back. She is dressed as I am, except that sweat does not stain her white T-shirt, and she wears heavy turquoise rings on all of her fingers.

"Excuse me," I say. "Are you heading to Mount Rushmore?"

She looks at me, her eyes hooded and dark. Two little boys sleep in the cab, their bodies propped against each other like puppies. A full jug of bottled water sits at her feet, and on the boys' side of the cab, empty pop cans line up like soldiers. "Yes," she says. Her voice is soft.

I introduce myself and explain my assignment. She does not respond, staring at me as if I am speaking in foreign tongue. "May I talk with you for a little while?"

"No." Again she speaks softly, but with a finality that brooks no disagreement.

I thank her for her time, shove my hands in my pockets, and walk back to the car. Kenny is standing outside of it, the passenger door open. His camera is draped around his neck, reflecting sunlight, and he holds a plastic garbage bag in his hand. He is picking up litter from the roadside—smashed Pepsi cups and dirt-covered McDonald's bags.

"Lack of respect," he says, when he sees me watching him, "shows itself in little ways."

* * *

Lack of respect shows itself in larger ways too: in great stone faces carved on a mother's breast; in broken treaties; in broken bodies bleeding on the snow. The indignities continue into our lifetimes—children ripped from their parents and put into schools that force them to renounce old ways; mysterious killings and harassment arrests; and enforced poverty unheard of even in our inner cities. The stories are frightening and hard to comprehend, partly because they are true. I grasp them only through books—from Dee Brown to Peter Matthiessen, from Charles A. Eastman (Ohiyesa) to Vine Deloria, Jr.—and through films—both documentaries (usually produced by PC white men) such as *Incident at Ogala,* and fictional accounts (starring non-Natives, of course) from *Little Big Man* to *Thunderheart.*

Some so-called wise person once wrote that women have the capacity to understand all of American society: we have lived in a society dominated by white men, and so have had to understand their perspective to survive; we were abused and treated as property within our own homes, having no rights and no recourse under the law, so we understand blacks, Chicanos, and Native Americans. But I stand on this road, outside a luxury car that I rented with my gold MasterCard, and I do not understand what it is like to be a defeated people, living among the victors, watching them despoil all that I value and all that I believe in.

Instead of empathy, I have white liberal guilt. When I stared across the road into the darkness of that truck cab, I felt the Native American woman's eyes assessing me. My sons sleep in beds with Ninja Turtles decorating the sheets; they wear Nikes and tear holes in their shirts on purpose. They fight over the Nintendo and the remote controls. I buy dolphin-safe tuna, and pay attention to food boycotts, but I shop in a grocery store filled with light and choices. And while I understand that the fruits of my life were purchased with the lives of people I have never met, I tell myself there is nothing I can do to change that. What is past is past.

But the past determines who we are, and it has led to this startling future.

I remember the moment with the same clarity with which my parents remember the Kennedy assassination, the clarity my generation associates with the destruction of the space shuttle *Challenger.* I was waiting in my husband's Ford Bronco outside the recreation center. The early-June day was hot in a California-desert sort of way—the dry heat of an oven, heat that prickles but does not invade the skin. My youngest son pulled open the door and crawled in beside me, bringing with him dampness and filling the air with the scents of chlorine and institutional soap. He tossed his wet suit and towel on the floor, fastened his seatbelt, and said, "Didja hear? Mount Rushmore disappeared."

I smiled at him, thinking it amazing the way ten-year-old little boys' minds worked—I hadn't even realized he knew what Mount Rushmore was—and he frowned at my response.

"No, really," he said, voice squeaking with sincerity. "It did. Turn on the news."

Without waiting for me, he flicked on the radio and scanned to the all news channel.

". . . not an optical illusion," a female voice was saying. "The site now resembles those early photos, taken around the turn of the century, before the work on the monument began."

Through the hour-long drive home, we heard the story again and again. No evidence of a bomb, no sign of the remains of the great stone faces. No rubble, nothing. Hollywood experts spoke about the possibilities of an illusion this grand, but all agreed that the faces would be there, behind the illusion, at least available to the sense of touch.

My hands were shaking by the time we pulled into the driveway of our modified ranch home. My son, whose assessment had gone from "pretty neat" to "kinda scary" within the space of the drive (probably from my grim and silent reaction), got out of the car without taking his suit and disappeared into the backyard to consult with his older brother. I took the suit and went inside, cleaning up by rote as I made my way to the bedroom we used as a library.

The quote I wanted, the quote that had been running through my mind during the entire drive, was there on page ninety-three of the 1972 Simon and Schuster edition of Richard Erdos's *Lame Deer: Seeker of Visions*:

> One man's shrine is another man's cemetery, except that now a few white folks are also getting tired of having to look at this big paperweight curio. We can't get away from it. You could make a lovely mountain into a great paperweight, but can you make it into a wild, natural mountain again? I don't think you have the know-how for that.

Lame Deer went on to say that white men, who had the ability to fly to the moon, should have the know-how to take the faces off the mountain.

But no one had the ability to take the faces off overnight. No one.

We finally reach the site at around 5:00 P.M. Kenny has snapped three rolls of film on our approach. He began shooting about sixty miles away, the place where, they tell me, the faces were first visible. I try to envision the shots as he sees them: the open mouths, the shocked expressions. I know Kenny will capture the moment, but I also know he will be unable to capture the thing that holds me.

The sound.

The rumble of low conversation over the soft roar of car engines. The shocked tones, rising and falling like a wave on the open sea.

I see nothing ahead of me except the broad expanse of a mountain outlined in the distance. I have not seen the faces up close and personal. I cannot tell the difference. But the others can. Pheromones fill the air, and I can almost taste the excitement. It grows as we pull into the overcrowded parking lot, as we walk to the visitors' center that still shows its 1940s roots.

Kenny disappears into the crowd. I walk to the first view station and stare at a mountain, at a granite surface smooth as water-washed stone. A chill runs along my back. At the base, uniformed people with cameras and surveying equipment check the site. Other uniformed people move along the top of the mount; it appears that they have just pulled someone up on the equivalent of a window-washer's scaffold.

All the faces here are white, black, or Asian—non-Native. We passed the Native woman as we drove into the parking lot. Two men, wearing army fatigues and carrying rifles had stopped the truck. She was leaning out of the cab, speaking wearily to them, and Kenny made me slow as we passed. He eavesdropped in his intense way, and then nodded once.

"She will be all right," he said, and nothing more.

The hair on my arms has prickled. TV crews film from the edge of the parking lot. A middle-aged man, his stomach parting the buttons on his short-sleeved white shirt, aims a video camera at the site. I am not a nature lover. Within minutes I am bored with the changed mountain. Miracle, yes, but now that my eyes have confirmed it, I want to get on with the story.

Inside the visitors' center is an ancient diorama on the creation of Mount Rushmore. The huge sculpted busts of George Washington, Abraham Lincoln, Thomas Jefferson, and Theodore Roosevelt took fourteen years to complete. Gutzon Borglum (Bore-glum, how appropriate) designed the monument, which was established in 1925, during our great heedless prosperity, and finished in 1941, after the Crash and the Depression and at the eve of America's involvement in World War II. The diorama makes only passing mention—in a cheerful, aren't-they-cute 1950s way—to the importance of the mountain to the Native tribes. There is no acknowledgment that when the monument was being designed, the Lakota filed a court claim asking for financial compensation for the theft of the Black Hills. A year after the completion of the monument, the courts denied the claim. No acknowledgment, either, of the split between Native peoples that occurred when the case was revived in the 1950s—the split over financial compensation and return of the land itself.

Nor is there any mention of the bloody history of the surrounding area that continued into the 1970s with the American Indian Movement, the death of two FBI agents and an Indian on the Pine Ridge Reservation, the resulting trials, the violence that marked the decade, and the attempted takeover of the Black Hills themselves.

In the true tradition of a conquering force, of an occupying army, all mention of the ongoing war has been obliterated.

But not forgotten. The army, with its rifles, is out in force. Several young boys, their lean, muscled frames outlined in their camo T-shirts and fatigue pants, sit at the blond wood tables. Others sit outside, rifles leaning against their chairs. We were not stopped as we entered the parking lot—Kenny claims our trunk is too small to hold a human being—but several others were.

One of the soldiers is getting himself a drink from the overworked waitress behind the counter. I stop beside him. He is only a few years older than my oldest son, and the ferocity of the soldier's clothes make him look even younger. His skin is pockmarked by acne, his teeth crooked and yellow from lack of care. Things have not changed from my youth. It is still the children of the poor who receive the orders to die for patriotism, valor, and the American Way.

"A lot of tension here," I say.

He takes his iced tea from the waitress and pours half a cup of sugar into it. "It'd be easier if there weren't no tourists." Then he flushes. "Sorry, lady."

I reassure him that he hasn't offended me, and I explain my purpose.

"We ain't supposed to talk to the press." He shrugs.

"I won't use your name," I say. "And it's for a magazine that won't be published for a month, maybe two months from now."

"Two months, anything can happen."

True enough, which is why I have been asked to capture this moment with the vision of an outsider. I know my editor has already asked a white Dakota correspondent to write as well, and she has received confirmation that at least one Native American author will contribute an essay. In this age of cynicism, a miracle is the most important event of our time.

The boy sits at an empty table and pulls out a chair for me. His arms are thick, tanned, and covered with fine white hairs. His fingers are long, slender, and ringless, his nails clean. He doesn't look at me as he speaks.

"They sent us up here right when the whole thing started," he said, "and we was told not to let no Indians up here. Some of our guys, they been combing the woods for Indians, making sure this ain't some kind of front for some special action. I don't like it. The guys are trigger-happy, and with all these tourists, I'm afraid someone's going to do something, and get shot. We ain't going to mean for it to happen. It'll be an accident, but it'll happen just the same."

He drinks his tea in several noisy slurps, tells me a bit about his family—his father, one of the few casualties of the Gulf War; his mother, remarried, to a foreman of a dying assembly plant in Michigan; his sister, newly married to a career army officer; and himself, with his dreams for a real life without a hand-to-mouth income when he leaves the army. He never expected to be searching cars at the entrance to a national park, and the miracle makes him nervous.

"I think it's some kind of Indian trick," he says. "You know, a decoy to get us all pumped up and focused here while they attack somewhere else."

This boy, who grew up poor hundreds of miles away, and who probably never gave Native Americans a second thought, is now speaking the language of conquerors, conquerors at the end of an empire, who feel the power slipping through their fingers.

He leaves to return to his post. I speak with a few tourists, but learn nothing interesting. It is as if the Virgin Mary has appeared at Lourdes; everyone wants to be one of the first to experience the miracle. I am half-surprised no one has set up a faith-healing station: a bit of granite from the holy mountain, and all ailments will be cured.

The light is turning silver with approaching twilight. My stomach is rumbling, but I do not want one of the hot dogs that has been twirling in the little case all afternoon. The oversized salted pretzels are gone, and the grill is caked with grease. The waitress herself looks faded, her dishwater blond hair slipping from its bun, her uniform covered with sweat stains and ketchup. I go to find Kenny, but cannot see him in the crowds. Finally I see him, on a path just past the parking lot, sitting beneath a scraggly pine tree, talking with an elderly man.

The elderly man's hair is white and short, but his face has a photogenic cragginess that most WASP photographers find appealing in Native Americans. As I approach, he touches Kenny's arm, then slips down the path and disappears into the growing darkness.

"Who was that?" I ask as I stop in front of Kenny. I am standing over him, looming, and the question feels like an interrogation, as if I am asking for information I do not deserve. Kenny grabs his camera and takes a picture of me. When we view it later, we will see different things: he will see the formation of light and shadow into a tired, irritable woman, made more irritable by an occurrence she cannot explain or understand, and I will see the teachers from my childhood enforcing some arbitrary rule on the playground.

When he is finished, he holds out his hand and I pull him to his feet. We walk back to the car in silence, and he never answers my question.

Speculation is rife in Rapid City. The woman at the Super Eight on the Interstate hands out her opinion with the old-fashioned room keys. "They're using some newfangled technology and trying to scare us," she says, her voice roughened by her five-pack-a-day habit. Wisps of smoke curl around the Mount Rushmore mugs and the tourist brochures that fill the dark wood lobby. "They know if that monument goes away, there's really no reason for folks to stop here."

She never explains who she means by "they." In this room filled with white people, surrounded by mementos of the "Old West," the meaning of "they" is immediately clear.

As it is downtown. The stately old Victorian homes and modified farmhouses attest to this city's roots. Some older buildings still stand in the center of town, dwarfed by newer hotels built to swallow the tourist trade. Usually, the locals tell me, the clientele is mixed here. Some businesspeople show for various conventions and must fraternize with the bikers who have a convention of their own in nearby Sturgis every summer. The tourists are the most visible: with their video cameras and towheaded children, they visit every sight available, from the Geology Museum to the Sioux Indian Museum. We all check our maps and make no comment over roads named after Indian fighters like Philip Sheridan.

In a dusky bar whose owner does not want to be named in this "or any" article, a group of elderly men share a drink before they toddle off to their respective homes. They too have theories, and they're willing to talk with a young female reporter from California.

"You don't remember the seventies," says Terry, a loud-voiced, balding man who lives in a nearby retirement home. "Lots of young reporters like you, honey, and them AIM people, stirring up trouble. There was more guards at Rushmore than before or since. We always thought they'd blow up that monument. They hate it, you know. Say we've defaced"—and they all laugh at the pun—"defaced their sacred hills."

"I say they lost the wars fair and square," says Rudy. He and his wife of forty-five years live in a six-bedroom Victorian house on the corner of one of the tree-lined streets. "No sense whining about it. Time they started learning to live like the rest of us."

"Always thought they would bomb that monument." Max, a former lieutenant in the army, fought "the Japs" at Guadalcanal, a year that marked the highlight of his life. "And now they have."

"There was no bomb," says Jack, a former college professor who still wears tweed blazers with patches on the elbows. "Did you hear any explosion? Did you?"

The others don't answer. It becomes clear they have had this conversation every day since the faces disappeared. We speak a bit more, then I leave in search of other opinions. As I reach the door, Jack catches my arm.

"Young lady," he says, ushering me out into the darkness of the quiet street, "we've been living the Indian wars all our lives. It's hard to ignore when you live beside a prison camp. I'm not apologizing for my friends—but it's hard to live here, to see all that poverty, to know that we—our government—have caused that devastation because the Indians—the natives—want to live in their own way. It's a strange prison we've built for them. They can escape if they want to renounce everything they are."

In his voice I hear the thrum of the professor giving a lecture. "What did you teach?" I ask.

He smiles, and in the reflected glare of the bar's neon sign, I see the unlined face of the man he once was. "History," he says. "And I tell you, living here, I have learned that history is not a deep, dusty thing of the past, but part of the air we breathe each and every day."

His words send a shiver through me. I thank him for his time and return to my rented car. As I drive to my hotel, I pass the Rushmore Mall—a flat late-seventies creation that has sprawled to encompass other stores. The mall is closing, and hundreds of cars pull away, oblivious of the strangeness that has happened only a few miles outside the city.

By morning, the police, working in cooperation with the FBI, have captured a suspect. But they will not let any of the reporters talk with him, nor will they release his name, his race, or anything else about him. They don't even specify the charges.

"How can they?" asks the reporter for *The New York Times* over an overpriced breakfast of farm-fresh eggs, thick bacon, and wheat toast at a local diner. "They don't know what happened to the monument. So they charge him with making the faces disappear? Unauthorized use of magic in an un-American fashion?"

"Who says it's magic?" the CNN correspondent asks.

"You explain it," says the man from the *Wall Street Journal.* "I touched the rock face yesterday. Nothing is carved there. It feels like nothing ever was."

The reporters are spooked, and the explanations they share among themselves have the ring of mysticism. That mysticism does not reach the American people, however. On the air, in the pages of the country's respected newspapers and magazines, the talk revolves around possible technical explanations for the disappearance of the faces. Any whisper of the unexplainable, and the show, the interviewee, and the story are whisked off the air.

It is as if we are afraid of things beyond our ken.

In the afternoon I complain to Kenny that, aside from the woman in the truck and the man he talked to near the monument, I have seen no Natives. The local and national Native organizations have been strangely silent. National spokespeople for the organizations have arrived in Rapid City—only to disappear behind some kind of protective walls. Even people who revel in the limelight have avoided it on this occasion.

"They have no explanations either," Kenny says with such surety that I glare at him. He has been talking with the Natives while I have not.

Finally he shrugs. "They have found a place in the Black Hills that is *theirs*. They believe something wonderful is about to happen."

"Take me there," I say.

He shakes his head. "I can't. But I can bring someone to you."

Kenny drives the rental car off the Interstate, down back roads so small they aren't on the map. Old, faded signs for now-defunct cafés and secret routes to the Black Hills Caverns give the area a sense of *Twilight Zone* mystery. Out here, the towns have names that send chills down my back, names like Mystic and Custer. Kenny leaves me at a roadside café that looks as if it closed when Kennedy was president. The windows are boarded up, but the door swings open to reveal a dusty room filled with rat footprints and broken furniture. Someone has removed the grill and the rest of the equipment, leaving gaping holes in the sideboards, but the counter remains, a testament to what might once have been a thriving business.

There are tables near the gravel parking lot outside. They have been wiped clean, and one bears cup rings that look to be fairly recent. The café may be closed, but the tables are still in use. I wipe off a bench and sit down, a little unnerved that Kenny has left me in this desolate place alone—with only a cellular phone for comfort.

The sun is hot as it rises in the sky, and I am thankful for the bit of shade provided by the building's overhang. No cars pass on this road, and I am beginning to feel as if I have reached the edge of nowhere.

I have brought my laptop, and I spend an hour making notes from the day's conversations, trying to place them in a coherent order so that this essay will make sense. It has become clearer and clearer to me that—unless I have the luck of a fictional detective—I will find no answers before my Monday deadline. I will submit only a series of impressions and guesses based on my own observations of a fleeting moment. I suppose that is why the *American Observer* hired me instead of an investigative reporter, so that I can capture this moment of mystery in my white California way.

Finally I hear the moan of a car engine, and relief loosens the tension in my shoulders. I have not, until this moment, realized how tense the quiet has made me. Sunlight glares off the car's new paint job, and the springs squeak as the wheels catch the potholes that fill the road. Kenny's face is obscured by the windshield, but as the car turns in the parking lot, I recognize his passenger as the elderly man I saw the day before.

The car stops, and I stand. Kenny gets out and leads the elderly man to me. I introduce myself and thank the man for joining us. He nods in recognition, but does not give me his name. "I am here as a favor to Little Hawk," he says, nodding at Kenny. "Otherwise I would not speak to you."

Kenny is fiddling with his camera. He looks no different, and yet my vision of him has suddenly changed. We have never discussed his past, or mine for that matter. In California, a person either proclaims his heritage loudly or receives his privacy. I am definitely not an investigator. I did not know that my cameraman had ties in this part of the Dakotas.

I close my laptop as I sit. The old man sits beside me. Silver mixes with the black hair in his braid. I have seen his face before. Later I will look it up and discover what it looked like when it was young, when he was making news in the 1970s for his association with AIM.

I open my mouth to ask a question, and he raises his hand, shaking his head slightly. Behind us, a bird chirps. A drop of sweat runs down my back.

"I know what you will ask," he says. "You want me to give you the answers. You want to know what is happening, and how we caused it."

My questions are not as blunt as that, but he has a point. I have fallen into the same trap as the locals. I am blaming the Natives because I see no other explanation.

"When he gave his farewell address to the Lakota," the old man said in a ringing voice accustomed to stories, "he said, 'As a child I was taught the Supernatural Powers were powerful and could do strange things. . . . This was taught me by the wise men and the shamans. They taught me that I could gain their favor by being kind to my people and brave before my enemies; by telling the truth and living straight; by fighting for my people and their hunting grounds.'

"All my life we have fought, Ms. Sunlake, and we have tried to live the old path. But I was taught as a child that we had been wicked, that we were living in sin, and that we must accept Christ as our Savior, for in Him is the way.

"In Him, my people found death over a hundred years ago, at Wounded Knee. In Him, we have watched our Mother ravaged and our hunting grounds ruined. And I wish I could say that by renouncing Him and His followers, we have begun this change. But I cannot."

The bird has stopped chirping. His voice echoes in the silence. Kenny's camera whirs once, twice, and I think of the old superstition that Crazy Horse and some of the others held, that a camera stole the soul. This old man does not have that fear.

He puts out a hand and touches my arm. His knuckles are large and swollen with age. A twisted white scar runs from his wrist to his elbow. "We have heard that there are many buffalo on the Great Plains, and that the water is receding from Lake Powell. We are together now in the Hills, waiting and following the old traditions. Little Hawk has been asked to join us, but he will not."

I glance at Kenny. He is holding his camera chest-high and staring at the old man, tears in his eyes. I look away.

"In our search for answers, we have forgotten that Red Cloud is right," the old man said. "The *Taku Wakan* are powerful and can do strange things."

He stands and I stand with him. "But why now?" I ask. "Why not a hundred years ago? Two hundred years ago?"

The look he gives me is sad. I am still asking questions, unwilling to accept.

"Perhaps," he said, "the *Taku Wakan* know that if they wait much longer the People will be gone, and the Earth will belong to madmen." Then he nods at Kenny and they walk to the car.

"I will be back soon," Kenny says. I sit back down and try to write this meeting down in my laptop. What I cannot convey is the sense of unease with which it left me, the feeling that I have missed more than I could ever see.

"Why don't you go with them?" I ask Kenny as we drive back to Rapid City.

For a long time he does not answer me. He stares straight ahead at the narrow road, the fading white lines illuminated only by his headlights. He came for me just before dark. The mosquitoes had risen in the twilight, and I felt that the essay and I would die together.

"I can't believe as they do," he says. "And they need purity of belief."

"I don't understand," I say.

He sighs, and pushes a long strand of hair away from his face. "He said we were raised to be ashamed of who we are. I still am. I cringe when they go through the rituals."

"What do you believe is happening at Mount Rushmore?" I keep my voice quiet, so as not to break this, the first thread of confidence he has ever shown in me.

"I'm like you," he says. His hands clutch the top of the wheel, knuckles white. "I don't care what is happening, as long as it provides emotion for my art."

We leave the next morning on a 6:00 A.M. flight. The plane is nearly empty. The reporters and tourists remain, since no one has any answers yet. The first suspect has been released, and another is in custody. Specialists in every area from virtual reality to sculpture have flooded the site. Experts on Native Americans posit everything from a bombing to Coyote paying one last great trick.

I have written everything but this, the final section. My hands shook last night as I typed in my conversation with Kenny. I am paid to observe, to learn, to be detached—but he is right. So few stories tug my own heartstrings. I won't let this one. I refuse to believe in miracles. I too want to see the experts prove that some odd technology has caused the change in the mountainside.

Yet, as I lean back and try to imagine what that moment will feel like—the moment when I learn that some clever person with a hidden camera has caused the entire mess—I feel a sinking in my stomach. I want to believe in the miracle, and since I cannot, I want to have the chance to believe. I don't want anyone to take that small thing away from me.

Yet the old man's words do not fill me with comfort, either. For the future he sees, the future he hopes for, has no place for me or my kind in it. Whatever has happened to the Natives has happened to them, and not to me. Please, God, never to me.

The sunlight has a sharp, early-morning clarity. As the plane lifts off, its shadow moves like a hawk over the earth. My gaze follows the shadow, watching it move over buildings and then over the hills. As we pull up into the clouds, I gasp.

For below me, the hills have transformed into a reclining woman, her head tilted back, her knees bent, her breasts firm and high. She watches us until we disappear.

Until we leave the center of the world.

UNTERSEEBOOT DOKTOR

Ray Bradbury

Ray Bradbury enjoys an almost legendary status as the author of science fiction and fantasy classics such as *The Martian Chronicles*, *Dark Carnival*, and *Something Wicked This Way Comes*. To the delight of fans of Bradbury's short fiction, his work has been appearing in genre magazines again after years in which his creative output was focused on poetry and theater. The hilarious fantasia that follows was not published in an SF/fantasy magazine, however, but in the January 1994 issue of *Playboy*.

—T.W.

The incredible event occurred during my third visit to Gustav Von Seyffertitz, my foreign psychoanalyst. I should have guessed.

After all, my alienist, truly alien, had the coincidental name, Von Seyffertitz, of the tall, aquiline, menacing and therefore beautiful actor who played the high priest in the 1935 film *She*. In *She* the wondrous villain waved his skeleton fingers, hurled insults, summoned sulfurous flames, destroyed slaves and knocked the world into earthquakes. After that, he could be seen riding the Hollywood Boulevard trolley cars as calm as a mummy, as quiet as an unwired telephone pole.

Where was I? Ah, yes.

It was my third visit to my psychiatrist. He had called that day and cried, "Douglas, you stupid son of a bitch, it's time for beddy-bye!"

Beddy-bye was, of course, his couch of pain and humiliation, where I lay writhing in agonies of assumed Jewish guilt and Northern Baptist stress as he from time to time muttered, "A fruitcake remark," or "Dumb," or "If you ever do that again, I'll kill you."

As you can see, Gustav Von Seyffertitz was a most unusual mine specialist. Mine? Yes. Our problems are land mines in our heads. Step on them! Shock-troop therapy, he once called it, searching for words. "Blitzkrieg?" I offered. "*Ja!*" he said, grinning his shark grin. "That's it!"

So, on my third visit to his strange office—a metallic-looking room with a most odd series of locks on a roundish door—suddenly, as I was maundering and treading dark waters, I heard his spine stiffen behind me. He gasped a great death rattle, sucked air and blew it out in a yell that curled and bleached my hair:

"Dive! Dive!"

I dove. Thinking that the room might be struck by a titanic iceberg, I fell to scuttle beneath the claw-footed couch.

"Dive!" cried the old man.

"Dive?" I whispered, and looked up to see a submarine periscope, all polished brass, slide up to vanish into the ceiling.

Gustav Von Seyffertitz stood pretending not to notice me, the sweat-oiled leather couch or the vanished brass machine. Very calmly, in the fashion of Conrad Veidt in *Casablanca*, or Erich Von Stroheim, the manservant in *Sunset Boulevard*, he lit a cigarette and let two calligraphic dragon plumes of smoke write themselves (his initials?) on the air.

"You were saying?" he said.

"No." I stayed on the floor. "You were saying. Dive?"

"I did not say that," he purred.

"Beg pardon, you said, very clearly, 'Dive!' "

"You hallucinate." He exhaled two more scrolled dragon plumes. "Why do you stare at the ceiling?"

"Because," I said, "unless I am further hallucinating, buried in that valve lock up there is a nine-foot length of Leica brass periscope."

"This boy is incredible, listen to him," muttered Von Seyffertitz to his alter ego, always a third person in the room when he analyzed. When he was not busy exhaling his disgust with me, he tossed asides at himself. "How many martinis did you have at lunch?"

"Don't hand me that, Von Seyffertitz. That ceiling, one minute ago, swallowed a long brass pipe, yes?"

Von Seyffertitz glanced at his large, one-pound-size Christmas watch, saw that I still had 30 minutes to go, sighed, threw down his cigarette, squashed it with a polished boot, then clicked his heels.

Have you ever heard the *whack* when a real pro like Jack Nicklaus hits a ball? *Bam.* A hand grenade! That was the sound my Germanic friend's boots made as he knocked them together in a salute.

Crrack!

"Gustav Mannerheim Auschlitz Von Seyffertitz, Baron Waldstein, at your service!" He lowered his voice:

"*Unterseeboot Kapitän*."

I scrambled off the floor.

Another *crrack* and—

The periscope slid calmly down out of the ceiling, the most beautiful Freudian cigar I had ever seen.

"No!" I gasped.

"Have I ever lied to you?"

"Many times!"

"But," he said, shrugging, "little white ones."

He stepped to the periscope, slapped two handles in place, slammed one eye shut and crammed the other angrily against the eyepiece, turning the periscope in a slow roundabout of the room, the couch and me.

"Fire one!" he ordered.

I almost heard the torpedo leave its tube.

"Fire two!" he said.

And a second soundless and invisible bomb motored on its way to infinity.

Struck amidships, I sank into the couch.

"You, you!" I said mindlessly. "It!" I pointed to the brass machine. "This!" I touched the couch. "Why?"

"Sit down," said Von Seyffertitz.

"I am."

"*Lie* down."

"I'd rather not," I said uneasily.

Von Seyffertitz turned the periscope so its topmost eye, raked at an angle, glared at me. It had an uncanny resemblance in its glassy coldness to his own fierce hawk's gaze. His voice, from behind the periscope, echoed.

"So you want to know, eh, how Gustav Von Seyffertitz, Baron Waldstein, was suffered to leave the cold ocean depths, depart his dear North Sea ship, flee his destroyed and beaten fatherland to become this *Unterseeboot Doktor*—"

"Now that you mention—"

"I never mention! I declare. And my declarations are sea-battle commands."

"So I noticed."

"Shut up. Sit back—"

"Not just now," I said uneasily.

His heels knocked as he let his right hand spider to his top coat pocket and slip forth a bright, thin monocle, which he screwed into his stare as if decupping a boiled egg. I winced, for now the monocle was part of his fiery glare and regarded me with cold fire.

"Why the monocle?" I said.

"Idiot! It is to cover my good eye so that neither eye can see and my intuition is free to work."

"Oh," I said.

And he began his monolog. And as he talked on and on, forgetting me, I realized his need had been pent up, capped, for years. During this monolog a strange thing occurred. I rose slowly to my feet as *Herr Doktor* Von Seyffertitz circled, his long, slim cigar printing smoke cumuli on the air, which he read like white Rorschach blots. With each implant of his foot, a word came out, and then another, in a sort of plodding grammar. Sometimes he stopped and stood posed with one leg raised and one word stopped in his mouth, to be turned on his tongue and examined. Then the shoe went down, the noun slid forth and the verb and object in good time.

Until at last, circling, I found myself in a chair, stunned, for I saw *Herr Doktor* Von Seyffertitz stretched on his own couch, his long spider fingers laced on his chest.

"It has been no easy thing to come forth on land," he sibilated. "Some days I was the jellyfish, frozen; others, the shore-strewn octopus, at least with tentacles, or the crayfish sucked back into my skull. But I have built my spine, year on year, and now I walk among the land men and survive."

He paused to take a trembling breath, then continued: "I moved in stages from the depths of a houseboat to a wharf bungalow to a shore tent and then back to a canal in a city and at last to New York, an island surrounded by water, eh? But where, where, in all this would a submarine commander find his place, his work, his love and activity?

"It was one afternoon in a building with the world's longest elevator that it struck me like a hand grenade in the ganglions. Going down, down, down, other people crushed around me, and the numbers descending and the floors whizzing by the glass windows, rushing by flicker-flash, flicker-flash, conscious, subconscious, id, ego, ego-id, life, death, lust, kill, lust, dark, light, plummeting, falling, 90, 80, 50, lower depths, high exhilaration, id, ego, id, until this shout blazed from my raw throat in a great all-accepting, panic-manic shriek: "Dive! Dive!' "

"Ah," I said.

" 'Dive!' I screamed so loudly that my fellow passengers, in shock, urinated. Among stunned faces I stepped out of the lift to find one sixteenth of an inch of pee on the floor. 'Have a nice day!' I said, jubilant with self-discovery, then ran to self-employment, to hang a shingle and nest my periscope, carried from the mutilated, divested, castrated *Unterseeboot* all these years. And I was too stupid to see my psychological future and my final downfall in it, my beautiful artifact, the brass genitalia of psychotic research, the Von Seyffertitz Mark Nine Periscope."

"That's quite a story," I said.

"And more than half of it true," snorted the alienist, eyes shut. "Did you listen? What have you learned?"

"That submarine captains should become psychiatrists."

"So? I have often wondered: Did Captain Nemo really die when his submarine was destroyed? Or did he run off to become my great-grandfather, and were his psychological bacteria passed along until I came into the world, thinking to command the ghostlike mechanisms that haunt the undertides, to wind up with this 50-minute vaudeville routine in this psychotic city?"

I got up and touched the fabulous brass symbol that hung like a scientific stalactite in mid-ceiling.

"May I look?"

"I wouldn't if I were you." He only half heard me, lying in the midst of his depression as in a dark cloud.

"It's only a periscope—"

"But a good cigar is a smoke."

I remembered Sigmund Freud's quote about cigars, laughed and touched the periscope again.

"Don't!" he said.

"Well, you don't actually use this for anything, do you? It's just a remembrance of time past, from your last submarine, yes?"

"You think that?" He sighed. "Look!"

I hesitated, then pasted one eye to the eyepiece, shut the other and cried:

"Oh, Jesus!"

"I warned you," said Von Seyffertitz.

For they were there. Enough nightmares to paper a thousand cinema screens. Enough phantoms to haunt 10,000 castle walls. Enough panics to shake 40 cities into ruin. The first psychological kaleidoscope in history. My God, I thought, he could sell the film rights to this worldwide!

And in the instant another thought came: How much of this stuff in here is me? Are these strange shapes my maundering daymares, sneezed out in the past weeks? When I talked, eyes shut, did my mouth spray invisible founts of small beasts that, caught in the periscope chambers, grew outsized? Like the microscopic photos of those germs that hide in eyebrows and pores, magnified a million times to become elephants on *Scientific American* covers: Are these images leftovers from my eyelashes and psyche?

"It's worth millions!" I cried. "Do you know what this is?"

"Collected spiders, Gila monsters, trips to the moon without gossamer wings, iguanas, toads out of bad sisters' mouths, diamonds out of good fairies' ears, crippled shadow dancers from Bali, obscene finger-pantomimes, cut-string puppets from Gepetto's attic, little boy statues that pee white wine, sexual trapeze performers alley-oop, evil clown faces, gargoyles that talk when it rains and whisper when the wind rises, basement bins full of poisoned honey, dragonflies that sew up 14-year-olds' orifices to keep them neat until they rip the sutures, aged 18. Towers with mad witches, garrets with mummies for lumber. . . ."

He ran out of steam.

"You get the drift."

"Nuts," I said. "You're bored. I could get you a $5 million deal with Amalgamated Fruitcakes Inc. and the Sigmund F. Dreamboats, split three ways!"

"You don't understand," said Von Seyffertitz. "I am keeping myself busy, busy, so I won't remember all the people I torpedoed, sank, drowned mid-Atlantic in 1944. I am not in the Amalgamated Fruitcake Cinema business. If I stop, I will fly apart. That periscope contains all and everything I have seen and known in the past 40 years of observing pecans, cashews and almonds. If I lost my periscope in some shoddy fly-by-night Hollywood strip poker, I would sink three times in my waterbed, never to be seen again. Have I shown you my waterbed? Three times as large as any pool. I do 80 laps asleep each night. Sometimes 40 when I catnap noons. To answer your millionfold offer, no."

And suddenly he shivered all over. His hands clutched at his heart.

"My God!" he shouted.

Too late, he was realizing he had let me step into his mind and life. Now he was on his feet, between me and the periscope, staring at it and me as if we were both terrors.

"You saw nothing in that. Nothing at all."

"I did!"

"You lie! How could you be such a liar? Do you know what would happen if this got out, if you ran around making accusations? My God," he raved on, "if the world knew, if someone said—" His words gummed shut in his mouth as if he were tasting the truth of what he said, as if he saw me for the first time. "I would be laughed out of the city. Such a goddamn ridiculous . . . hey, wait a minute. You!"

It was as if he had slipped a devil mask over his face. His eyes grew wide. His mouth gaped.

I examined his face and saw murder. I sidled toward the door.

"You wouldn't *say* anything to anyone?" he said.

"No."

"How come you suddenly know everything about me?"

"You told me!"

"Yes," he admitted, dazed, looking around for a weapon. "Wait."

"If you don't mind," I said, "I'd rather not."

And I was out the door and down the hall, my knees jumping to knock my jaw.

"Come back!" cried Von Seyffertitz behind me. "I must kill you!"

I reached the elevator and by a miracle it flung wide its doors when I banged the down button. I jumped in.

"Say goodbye!" cried Von Seyffertitz, raising his fist as if it held a bomb.

"Goodbye!" I said. The doors slammed.

I did not see Von Seyffertitz again for a year.

Meanwhile, I dined out often, telling friends and strangers on street corners of my collision with a submarine commander become head doctor.

I shook the tree and the ripe nuts fell—pecans, cashews, almonds. They brimmed the Baron's lap to overload his bank account. His grand slam: appearances with Phil Donahue, Oprah Winfrey and Geraldo in one single cyclonic afternoon. Von Seyffertitz laser games and duplicates of his submarine periscope sold out at the Museum of Modern Art and the Smithsonian. With the inducement of an advance of a half million dollars, he dictated and published a bad best-seller. Duplicates of the animalcules and curious critters trapped in his brass viewer arose in pop-up coloring books, paste-on tattoos and inkpad, rubber-stamp nightmares at Beasts R Us.

I hoped that this bounty would cause him to forgive and forget. No.

One noon a year and a month later, my doorbell rang and there stood Gustav Von Seyffertitz, Baron Waldstein, tears streaming down his cheeks.

"How come I didn't kill you that day?" he mourned.

"You didn't catch me," I said.

"Oh, *ja*. That was it."

I looked into the old man's rain-washed, tear-ravened face and said, "Who died?"

"Me. Or is it I? Ah, to hell with it: me. You see before you," he grieved, "a creature who suffers from the Rumpelstiltskin syndrome."

"Rumpel—?"

"Stiltskin! Two halves with a rip from chin to fly. Yank my forelock, go ahead! Watch me fall apart at the seam. Just like zipping a psychotic zipper. Two *Herr Doktor* admirals for the sick price of one. Which is the *Doktor* who heals and which is the sellout best-seller admiral?"

He stopped and looked around, holding his head together with his hands.

"Can you see the crack? Am I splitting again to become this crazy sailor who desires riches and fame, being sieved through the hands of crazed ladies with ruptured libidos? You should have such a year. Don't laugh."

"I'm not laughing."

"Then cheer up while I finish. Can I lie down? Is that a couch? Too short. What do I do with my legs?"

"Sit sidesaddle."

Von Seyffertitz laid himself out with his legs draped over one side. "Hey, not bad. Sit behind. Don't look over my shoulder. Avert your gaze. Neither smirk nor pull long faces as I get out the Krazy Glue and paste Rumpel to Stiltskin, the name of my next book, God help me. Damn you to hell, you and your damned periscope!"

"Not mine. Yours. You wanted me to discover it that day. I suppose you had been whispering 'Dive, dive' for years to patients, half-asleep. But you couldn't resist the loudest scream ever: 'Dive!' That was your admiral speaking, wanting fame and money enough to choke a school of porpoises."

"God," murmured Von Seyffertitz, "how I hate it when you're honest—I'm feeling better already. How much do I owe you?" He arose.

"Now we go kill the monsters instead of you."

"Monsters?"

"At my office. If we can get in past the lunatics."

"You have lunatics outside as well as in now?"

"Have I ever lied to you?"

"Often. But," I added, "little white ones."

"Come," he said.

We got out of the elevator to be confronted by a long line of worshipers and supplicants. There must have been 70 people strung out between the elevator and the Baron's door, waiting with copies of Madame Blavatsky, Krishnamurti and Shirley MacLaine under their arms. There was a roar like a suddenly opened furnace door when they saw the Baron. We beat it on the double and got inside his office before anyone could surge to follow.

"See what you have done to me!" Von Seyffertitz said, pointing.

The office walls were covered with expensive teak paneling. The desk was an exquisite Empire piece worth at least $50,000. The couch was the best soft leather I had ever seen, and the two pictures on the wall were a Renoir and a Monet. My God, millions! I thought.

"OK," I said. "The beasts, you said. You'll kill them, not me?"

The old man wiped his eyes with the back of one hand, then made a fist.

"Yes!" he cried, stepping up to the fine periscope, which reflected his face, madly distorted, in its elongated shape. "Like this. Thus and so!"

And before I could prevent it, he gave the brass machine a terrific slap with his hand and then a blow and another blow and another, with both fists, cursing. Then he grabbed the periscope as if it were the neck of a spoiled child and throttled and shook it.

I cannot say what I heard in that instant. Perhaps real sounds, perhaps imagined temblors, like a glacier cracking in the spring, or icicles in midnight. Perhaps it was a sound like a great kite breaking its skeleton in the wind and collapsing in folds of tissue. Maybe. I thought I heard a vast breath insucked, a cloud dissolving up inside itself. Or did I sense clock machineries spun so wildly they smoked off their foundations and fell like brass snowflakes?

I put my eye to the periscope.

I looked in upon—

Nothing.

It was just a brass tube with some crystal lenses and a view of an empty couch. No more.

I seized the eyepiece and tried to screw it into some new focus on a far place across an unimaginable horizon.

But the couch remained only a couch, and the wall beyond looked back at me with its great blank face.

Von Seyffertitz leaned forward and a tear ran off the tip of his nose to fall on one rusted fist.

"Are they dead?" he whispered.

"Gone."

"Good, they deserved to die. Now I can return to some kind of normal, sane world."

And with each word his voice fell deeper within his throat, his chest, his soul, until it, like the vaporous haunts within the peri-kaleidoscope, melted into silence.

He clenched his fists together in a fierce clasp of prayer, like one who beseeches God to deliver him from plagues. And whether he was once again praying for my death, eyes shut, or whether he simply wished me gone with the visions within the brass device, I could not say.

I only knew that my gossip had done a terrible and irrevocable thing to this incredible captain from beneath Nemo's tidal seas.

"Gone," murmured Gustav Von Seyffertitz, Baron Waldstein, for the last time.

That was almost the end.

I went around a month later. The landlord reluctantly let me look over the premises, mostly because I hinted that I might be renting.

We stood in the middle of the empty room, where I could see the dent marks where the couch had once stood.

I looked at the ceiling. It was empty.

"What's wrong?" said the landlord. "Didn't they fix it so you can't see? Damn fool Baron made a damn big hole up into the office above. Rented that, too, but never used it for anything I knew of. There was just that big damn hole he left when he went away."

I sighed with relief.

"Nothing left upstairs?"

"Nothing."

I looked up at the blank ceiling.

"Nice job of repair," I said.

"Thank God," said the landlord.

What, I often wonder, ever happened to Gustav Von Seyffertitz? Did he move to Vienna to take up residence, perhaps, in or near dear Sigmund's very own address? Does he live in Rio, treating fellow *Unterseeboot Kapitäns* who can't sleep for seasickness, roiling on their waterbeds under the shadow of the Andes Cross? Or is he in South Pasadena, within striking distance of the fruit-larder nut farms disguised as film studios?

I cannot guess.

All I know is that some nights in the year, oh, once or twice, in a deep sleep I hear his terrible shout, his cry.

"Dive! Dive! Dive!"

And wake to find myself, sweating, far under my bed.

YOUNG WOMAN IN A GARDEN

Delia Sherman

Delia Sherman is one of the brightest new lights in fantasy fiction. She won the 1989 Campbell Award after the publication of her first novel, *Through a Brazen Mirror*, inspired by an old English folk ballad. Her second novel, *The Porcelain Dove*, based on French history and folklore, recently won the Mythopoeic Society Award. Sherman lives near Boston.

The following ghostly tale about the life of an imaginary Impressionist painter comes from Volume 2 of the *Xanadu* anthology series edited by Jane Yolen.

—T. W.

Beauvoisin (1839–1898)

Edouard Beauvoisin was expected to follow in the footsteps of his father, a provincial doctor. However, when he demonstrated a talent for drawing, his mother saw to it that he was provided with formal training. In 1856, Beauvoisin went to Paris, where he worked at the Académie Suisse and associated with the young artists disputing romanticism and classicism at the Brasserie des Martyrs. In 1868, he married the artist Céleste Rohan. He exhibited in the Salon des Refusés in 1863, and was a member of the 1874 Salon of Impressionists. In 1876 he moved to Brittany where he lived and painted until his death in 1898. He is best known for the figure-studies *Young Woman in a Garden* and *Reclining Nude.*

Impressions of the Impressionists
(Oxford University Press, 1970)

M. Henri Tanguy
Director
Musée La Roseraie
Portrieux, Brittany
France

January 6, 1994

Monsieur:

I write to you at the suggestion of M. Rouart of the Musée d'Orsay to request permission to visit the house of M. Edouard Beauvoisin and to consult those of his personal papers that are kept there.

In pursuit of a Ph.D. degree in the History of Art, I am preparing a thesis on the life and work of M. Beauvoisin, who, in my opinion, has been unfairly neglected in the history of Impressionism.

Enclosed is a letter of introduction from my adviser, Professor Boodman of the Department of Art History at the University of Massachusetts. She has advised me to tell you that I also have a personal interest in M. Beauvoisin's life, for his brother was my great-great-grandfather.

I expect to be in France from May 1 of this year, and to stay for at least two months. My visit to La Roseraie may be scheduled according to your convenience. Awaiting your answer, I have the honor to be

Your servant, Theresa Stanton

When Theresa finally found La Roseraie at the end of an unpaved, narrow road, she was tired and dusty and on the verge of being annoyed. Edouard Beauvoisin had been an Impressionist, even if only a minor Impressionist, and his house was a museum, open by appointment to the public. At home in Massachusetts, that would mean signs, postcards in the nearest village, certainly a brochure in the local tourist office with color pictures of the garden and the master's studio and a good clear map showing how to get there.

France wasn't Massachusetts, not by a long shot.

M. Tanguy hadn't met her at the Portrieux station as he had promised, the local tourist office had been sketchy in its directions, and the driver of the local bus had been depressingly uncertain about where to let her off. Her feet were sore, her backpack heavy, and even after asking at the last two farmhouses she'd passed, Theresa still wasn't sure she'd found the right place. The house didn't look like a museum: gray stone, low-browed and secretive, its front door unequivocally barred, its low windows blinded with heavy white lace curtains. The gate was stiff and loud with rust. Still, there was a neat stone path leading around to the back of the house and a white sign with the word "*jardin*" printed on it and a faded black hand pointing down the path. Under the scent of dust and greenery, there was a clean, sharp scent of salt water. Theresa hitched up her backpack, heaved open the gate, and followed the hand's gesture.

"Monet" was her first thought when she saw the garden, and then, more accurately, "Beauvoisin." Impressionist, certainly—an incandescent, carefully balanced dazzle of yellow light, clear green grass, and carmine flowers against a celestial background. Enchanted, Theresa unslung her camera and captured a couple of faintly familiar views of flower beds and sequined water before turning to the house itself.

The back door was marginally more welcoming than the front, for at least it boasted a visible bellpull and an aged, hand-lettered sign directing the visitor to "*sonnez*," which Theresa did, once hopefully, once impatiently, and once again for luck. She was just thinking that she'd have to walk back to Portrieux and call M. Tanguy when the heavy door opened inward, revealing a Goyaesque old woman. Against the flat shadows of a stone passage, she was a study in black and white: long wool skirt and linen blouse, sharp eyes and finely crinkled skin.

The woman looked Theresa up and down, then made as if to shut the door in her face.

"Wait," cried Theresa, putting her hand on the warm planks. "*Arrêtez. S'il vous plait. Un moment.* Please!"

The woman's gaze traveled to Theresa's face. Theresa smiled charmingly.

"*Eh, bien?*" asked the woman impatiently.

Pulling her French around her, Theresa explained that she was making researches into the life and work of the famous M. Beauvoisin, that she had written in the winter for permission to see the museum, that seeing it was of the first importance to completing her work. She had received a letter from M. le Directeur, setting an appointment for today.

The woman raised her chin suspiciously. Her smile growing rigid, Theresa juggled camera and bag, dug out the letter, and handed it over. The woman examined it front and back, then returned it with an eloquent gesture of shoulders, head, and neck that conveyed her utter indifference to Theresa's work, her interest in Edouard Beauvoisin, and her charm.

"*Fermé*," she said, and suited the action to the word.

"*Parent*," said Theresa rather desperately. "*Je suis de la famille de M. Beauvoisin.*"

From the far end of the shadowy passage, a soft, deep voice spoke in accented English. "Of course you are, my dear. A great-grandniece, I believe. Luna," she shifted to French, "surely you remember the letter from M. le Directeur about our little American relative?" And in English again. "Please to come through. I am Mme Beauvoisin."

> In 1874, Céleste's mother died, leaving La Roseraie to her only child. There was some talk of selling the house to satisfy the couple's immediate financial embarrassments, but the elder Mme Beauvoisin came to the rescue once again with a gift of 20,000 francs. After paying off his debts, Beauvoisin decided that Paris was just too expensive, and moved with Céleste to Portrieux in the spring of 1875.
>
> "I have taken some of my mother's gift and put it toward transforming the ancient dairy of La Roseraie into a studio," he wrote Manet. "Ah, solitude! You cannot imagine how I crave it, after the constant sociability of Paris. I realize now that the cafés affected me like absinthe: stimulating and full of visions, but death to the body and damnation to the soul."
>
> In the early years of what his letters to Manet humorously refer to as his "exile," Beauvoisin traveled often to Paris, and begged his old

friends to come and stay with him. After 1879, however, he became something of a recluse, terminating his trips to Paris and discouraging visits, even from the Manets. He spent the last twenty years of his life a virtual hermit, painting the subjects that were dearest to him: the sea, his garden, the fleets of fishing-boats that sailed daily out and back from the harbor of Portrieux.

The argument has been made that Beauvoisin had never been as clannish as others among the Impressionists, Renoir and Monet, for example, who regularly set up their easels and painted the same scene side by side. Certainly Beauvoisin seemed unusually reluctant to paint his friends and family. His single portrait of his wife, executed not long after their marriage, is one of his poorest canvases: stiff, awkwardly posed, and uncharacteristically muddy in color. "Mme Beauvoisin takes exception to my treatment of her dress," he complained in a letter to Manet, "or the shadow of the chair, or the balance of the composition. God save me from the notions of women who think themselves artists!"

In 1877, the Beauvoisins took a holiday in Spain, and there met a young woman named Luz Gascó, who became Edouard's favorite—indeed his only—model. The several nude studies of her, together with the affectionate intimacy of *Young Woman in a Garden*, leave little doubt as to the nature of their relationship, even in the absence of documentary evidence. Luz came to live with the Beauvoisins at La Roseraie in 1878, and remained there even after Beauvoisin's death in 1898. She inherited the house and land from Mme Beauvoisin and died in 1914, just after the outbreak of the First World War.

Lydia Chopin, "*Lives Lived in Shadow: Edouard and Céleste Beauvoisin*,"
Apollo, Winter, 1989

The garden of La Roseraie extended through a series of terraced beds down to the water's edge and up into the house itself by way of a bank of uncurtained French doors in the parlor. When Theresa first followed her hostess into the room, her impression was of blinding light and color and of flowers everywhere—scattered on the chairs and sofas, strewn underfoot, heaped on every flat surface, vining across the walls. The air was somnolent with peonies and roses and bee-song.

"A lovely room."

"It has been kept just as it was in the time of Beauvoisin, though I fear the fabrics have faded sadly. You may recognize the sofa from *Young Woman Reading* and *Reclining Nude*, also the view down the terrace."

The flowers on the sofa were pillows, printed or needlepointed with huge, blowsy, ambiguous blooms. Those pillows had formed a textural contrast to the model's flat-black gown in *Young Woman Reading* and sounded a sensual, almost erotic note in *Reclining Nude*. As Theresa touched one almost reverently—it had supported the model's head—the unquiet colors of the room settled in place around it, and she saw that there were indeed flowers everywhere. Real petals had blown in from the terrace to brighten the faded woven flowers of the carpet, and the walls and chairs were covered in competing chintzes to provide a background for the plain burgundy velvet sofa, the wooden easel, and the portrait over the mantel of a child dressed in white.

"Céleste," said Mme Beauvoisin. "Céleste Yvonne Léna Rohan, painted at the age of six by some Academician—I cannot at the moment recollect his name, although M. Rohan was as proud of securing his services as if he'd been Ingres himself. She hated it."

"How could you possibly . . ." Theresa's question trailed off at the amusement in Mme Beauvoisin's face.

"Family legend. The portrait is certainly very stiff and finished, and Céleste grew to be a disciple of Morisot and Manet. Taste in aesthetic matters develops very young, do you not agree?"

"I do," said Theresa. "At any rate, I've loved the Impressionists since I was a child. I wouldn't blame her for hating the portrait. It's technically accomplished, yes, but it says nothing about its subject except that she was blonde and played the violin."

"That violin!" Mme Beauvoisin shook her head, ruefully amused. "Mme Rohan's castle in Spain. The very sight of it was a torture to Céleste. And her hair darkened as she grew older, so you see the portrait tells you nothing. This, on the other hand, tells all."

She led Theresa to a small painting hung by the door. "Luz Gascó," she said. "Painted in 1879."

Liquid, animal eyes gleamed at Theresa from the canvas, their gaze at once inviting and promising, intimate as a kiss. Theresa glanced aside at Mme Beauvoisin, who was studying the portrait, her head tilted to one side, her wrinkled lips smoothed by a slight smile. Feeling unaccountably embarrassed, Theresa frowned at the painting with self-conscious professionalism. It was, she thought, an oil study of the model's head for Beauvoisin's most famous painting, *Young Woman in a Garden*. The face was tilted up to the observer and partially shadowed. The brushwork was loose and free, the boundaries between the model's hair and the background blurred, the molding of her features suggested rather than represented.

"A remarkable portrait," Theresa said. "She seems very . . . alive."

"Indeed," said Mme Beauvoisin. "And very beautiful." She turned abruptly and, gesturing Theresa to a chair, arranged herself on the sofa opposite. The afternoon light fell across her shoulder, highlighting her white hair, the pale rose pinned in the bosom of her high-necked dress, her hands folded on her lap. Her fingers were knotted and swollen with arthritis. Theresa wondered how old she was and why M. Tanguy had said nothing of a caretaker in his letter to her.

"Your work?" prompted Mme Beauvoisin gently.

Theresa pulled herself up and launched into what she thought of as her dissertation spiel: neglected artist, brilliant technique, relatively small ouvre, social isolation, mysterious ménage. "What I keep coming back to," she said, "is his isolation. He hardly ever went to Paris after 1879, and even before that he didn't go on those group painting trips the other Impressionists loved so much. He never shared a studio even though he was so short of money, or let anyone watch him paint. And yet his letters to Manet suggest that he wasn't a natural recluse—anything but."

"Thus Luz Gascó?" asked Mme Beauvoisin.

"I'm sorry?"

"Luz Gascó. Perhaps you think she was the cause of Beauvoisin's—how shall I say?—Beauvoisin's retreat from society?"

Theresa gave a little bounce in her chair. "That's just it, you see. No one really knows. There are a lot of assumptions, especially by *male* historians, but no one really knows. What I'm looking for is evidence one way or the other. At first I thought she couldn't have been . . ." She hesitated, suddenly self-conscious.

"Yes?" The low voice was blandly polite, yet Theresa felt herself teased, or perhaps tested. It annoyed her, and her answer came a little more sharply than necessary.

"Beauvoisin's mistress." Mme Beauvoisin raised her brows and Theresa shrugged apologetically. "There's not much known about Céleste, but nothing suggests that she was particularly meek or downtrodden. I don't think she'd have allowed Luz to live here all those years, much less left the house to her, if she knew Luz was . . . involved with her husband."

"Perhaps she knew and did not concern herself." Mme Beauvoisin offered this consideringly.

"I hadn't thought of that," said Theresa. "I'd need proof, though. I'm not interested in speculation, theory, or even in a juicy story. I'm interested in the truth."

Mme Beauvoisin's smile said that she found Theresa very young, very charming. "Yes," she said slowly. "I believe you are." Her voice grew brisker. "Beauvoisin's papers are in some disorder, you understand. Your search may take you some weeks, and Portrieux is far to travel twice a day. It would please me if you would accept the hospitality of La Roseraie."

Theresa closed her eyes. It was a graduate student's dream come true, to be invited into her subject's home, to touch and use his things, to live his life. Mme Beauvoisin, misinterpreting the gesture, said, "Please stay. This project—Beauvoisin's papers—it is of great importance to us, to Luna and to me. We feel that you are well suited to the task."

To emphasize her words, she laid her twisted hand on Theresa's arm. The gesture brought her face into the sun, which leached her eyes and skin to transparency and made a glory of her silvered hair. Theresa stared at her, entranced.

"Thank you," she said. "I would be honored."

Young Woman in a Garden (Luz at La Roseraie), 1879

Edouard Beauvoisin's artistic reputation rests on this portrait of his Spanish mistress, Luz Gascó, seated in the garden of La Roseraie. As in *Reclining Nude*, the composition is arranged around a figure that seems to be the painting's source of light as well as its visual focus. Luz sits with her face and body in shade and her feet and hands in bright sunlight. Yet the precision with which her shadowy figure is rendered, the delicate modeling of the face, and the suggestion of light shining down through the leaves onto the dark hair draw the viewer's eye up and away from the brightly-lit foreground. The brushwork of the white blouse is especially masterly, the coarse texture of the linen suggested with a scumble of pale pink, violet, and gray.

"The Unknown Impressionists"
exhibition catalogue
Museum of Fine Arts, Boston, Mass.

"This is the studio."

Mme Beauvoisin laid her hand on the blue-painted door, hesitated, then stepped aside. "Please," she said, and gave Theresa a courteous nod.

Heart tripping over itself with excitement, Theresa pushed open the door and stepped into Beauvoisin's studio. The room was shuttered, black as midnight; she knocked over a chair, which fell with an echoing clatter.

"I fear the trustees have hardly troubled themselves to unlock the door since they came into possession of the property," said Mme Beauvoisin apologetically. "And Luna and I have little occasion to come here." Theresa heard her shoe heels tapping across the flagstone floor. A creak, a bang, and weak sunlight struggled over a clutter of easels, canvases, trunks and boxes, chairs, stools, and small tables disposed around a round stove and a shabby sofa. *The French sure are peculiar*, Theresa thought. *What a way to run a museum*!

Mme Beauvoisin had taken up a brush and was standing before one of the easels in the attitude of a painter interrupted at work. For a moment, Theresa thought she saw a canvas on the easel, an oil sketch of a seated figure. An unknown Beauvoisin? As she stepped forward to look, an ancient swag of cobweb broke and showered her head with flies and powdery dust. She sneezed convulsively.

"God bless you," said Mme Beauvoisin, laying the brush on the empty easel. "Luna brings a broom. Pah! What filth! Beauvoisin must quiver in his tomb, such an orderly man as he was!"

Soon, the old woman arrived with the promised broom, a pail of water, and a settled expression of grim disapproval. She poked at the cobwebs with the broom, glared at Theresa, then began to sweep with concentrated ferocity, raising little puffs of dust as she went and muttering to herself, witch-like.

"So young," she said. "Too young. Too full of ideas. Too much like Edouard, *enfin*."

Theresa bit her lip, caught between curiosity and irritation. Curiosity won. "How am I like him, Luna?" she asked. "And how can you know? He's been dead almost a hundred years."

The old woman straightened and turned, her face creased deep with fury. "Luna!" she snarled. "Who has given you the right to call me Luna? I am not a servant, to be addressed without respect."

"You're not? I mean, of course not. I beg your pardon, Mlle . . .?" And Theresa looked a wild appeal to Mme Beauvoisin, who said, "The fault is entirely mine, Mlle Stanton, for not introducing you sooner. Mlle Gascó is my companion."

Theresa laughed nervously, as at an incomprehensible joke. "You're kidding," she said. "Mlle Gascó? But that was the model's name, Luz's name. I don't understand. Who are you, anyway?"

Mme Beauvoisin shrugged dismissively. "There is nothing to understand. We are Beauvoisin's heirs. And the contents of this studio are our inheritance, which is now yours also. Come and look." With a theatrical flourish, she indicated a cabinet built along the back wall. "Open it," she said. "The doors are beyond my strength."

Theresa looked from Mme Beauvoisin to Mlle Gascó and back again. Every scholar knows that coincidences happen, that people leave things to their relatives, that reality is sometimes unbelievably strange. And this was what she had come for, after all, to open the cabinet, to recover all the mysteries and illuminate the shadows of Beauvoisin's life. Perhaps this Mlle Gascó was his illegitimate granddaughter. Perhaps both women were playing some elaborate and obscure game. In any case, it was none of her business. Her business was with the cabinet and its contents.

The door was warped, and Theresa had to struggle with it for a good while before it creaked stiffly open on a cold stench of mildew and the shadowy forms of dispatch boxes neatly arranged on long shelves. Theresa sighed happily. Here they were, Beauvoisin's papers, a scholar's treasure trove, her ticket to a degree, a career, a profession. And they were all hers. She reached out both hands and gathered in the nearest box. As the damp cardboard yielded to her fingers, she felt a sudden panic that the papers would be mildewed into illegibility. But inside the box the papers were wrapped in oilcloth and perfectly dry.

Reverently, Theresa lifted out a packet of letters, tied with black tape. The top one was folded so that some of the text showed. Having just spent a month working with Beauvoisin's letters to Manet at the Bibliothèque National, she immediately recognized his hand, tiny and angular and blessedly legible. Theresa slipped the letter free from the packet and opened it. *I have met*, she read, *a dozen other young artists in the identical state of fearful ecstasy as I, feeling great things about Art and Beauty which we are half-shy of expressing, yet must express or die.*

"Thérèse." Mme Beauvoisin sounded amused. "First we must clean this place. Then you may read Beauvoisin's words with more comfort and less danger of covering them with smuts."

Theresa became aware that she was holding the precious letter in an unforgivably dirty hand. "Oh," she said, chagrined. "I'm so sorry. I *know* better than this."

"It is the excitement of discovery." Mme Beauvoisin took the letter from her and rubbed lightly at the corner with her apron. "See, it comes clean, all save a little shadow that may easily be overlooked." She folded the letter, slipped it back into the packet, returned it to the box, and tucked the oilcloth over it.

"Today, the preparation of the canvas," she said. "Tomorrow, you may begin the sketch."

Edouard Beauvoisin had indeed been an orderly man. The letters were parceled up by year, in order of receipt, and labeled. Turning over Manet's half of their long correspondence, Theresa briefly regretted her choice of research topic. Manet's was a magic name, a name to conjure up publishers and job offers, fame and what passed for fortune among art historians. She'd certainly get a paper or two out of those letters, maybe petition for permission to edit them, but she didn't want a reputation as a Manet scholar. Manet, documented, described, and analyzed by every art historian worth a pince-nez, could never be hers. Beauvoisin was hers.

Theresa sorted out all the business papers, the bills for paint and canvas, the notes from obscure friends. What was left was the good stuff: a handful of love notes written by Céleste Rohan over the two years Beauvoisin had courted her, three boxes of letters from his mother, and two boxes of his answers, which must have been returned to him at her death.

It took Theresa a week to work through the letters, a week of long hours reading in the studio and short, awkward meals eaten in the kitchen with Mme Beauvoisin and Luna. It was odd. In the house and garden, the two old women were everywhere, present as the sea smell, forever on the way to some domestic task or other, yet never too busy to inquire politely and extensively after her progress. Or at least Mme Beauvoisin was never too busy. Luna mostly glared at her, hoped she wasn't wasting her time, warned her not to go picking the flowers or walking on the grass. It didn't take long for Theresa to decide that she didn't like Luna.

She did, however, discover that she liked Edouard Beauvoisin. In the studio, Theresa could lose herself in Beauvoisin's world of artists and models. The letters to his mother from his early years in Paris painted an intriguing portrait of an intelligent, naïve young man whose most profound desire was to capture and define Beauty in charcoal and oils. He wrote of poses and technical problems and what his teacher M. Couture had said about his life studies, reaffirming in each letter his intention *to draw and draw and draw until every line breathes the essence of the thing itself.* A little over a year later, he was speaking less of line and more of color; the name Couture disappeared from his letters, to be replaced by Manet, Degas, Duranty, and the brothers Goncourt. By 1860, he had quit the Ecole des Beaux Arts and registered to copy the Old Masters at the Louvre. A year later, he met Céleste Rohan at the house of Berthe Morisot's sister Edma Pontillon:

> *She is like a Raphael Madonna, tall and slender and pale, and divinely unconscious of her own beauty. She said very little at dinner, but afterwards in the garden with Morisot conversed with me an hour or more. I learned then that she is thoughtful and full of spirit, loves Art and Nature, and is herself something of an artist, with a number of watercolors and oil sketches to her credit that, according to Morisot, show considerable promise.*

Three months later, he announced to his mother that Mlle Rohan had accepted his offer of hand and heart. Mme Beauvoisin the elder said everything that was proper, although a note of worry did creep through in her final lines:

> *I am a little concerned about her painting. To be sure, painting is an amiable accomplishment in a young girl, but you must be careful, in your joy at finding a soul-mate, not to foster useless ambitions in her breast. I'm sure you both agree that a wife must have no other profession than seeing to the comfort of her husband, particularly when her husband is an artist and entirely unable to see to his own.*

When she read this, Theresa snorted. Perhaps her mother-in-law was why Céleste, like Edma Morisot and dozens of other lady artists, had laid down her brush when she married. Judging from her few surviving canvases, she'd been a talented painter, if too indebted to the style of Berthe Morisot. Now, if Céleste had just written to her future husband about painting or ambition or women's role in marriage, Theresa would have an easy chapter on the repression of women artists in nineteenth-century France.

It was with high hopes, therefore, that Theresa opened the small bundle of Céleste's correspondence. She soon discovered that however full of wit and spirit Céleste may have been in conversation, on paper she was terse and dull. Her letters were limited to a few scrawled lines of family news, expressions of gratitude for books her fiancé had recommended, and a few, shy declarations of maidenly affection. The only signs of her personality were the occasional vivid sketches with which she illustrated her notes: a seal pup sunning itself on the rocks at the mouth of the bay; a cow peering thoughtfully in through the dairy window.

Theresa folded Céleste's letters away, tied the tape neatly around them, and sighed. She was beginning to feel discouraged. No wonder there'd been so little written on Edouard Beauvoisin. No wonder his studio was neglected, his museum unmarked, his only curators an eccentric pair of elderly women. There had been dozens of competent but uninspired followers of the Impressionists who once or twice in the course of their lives had managed to paint great pictures. The only thing that set Edouard Beauvoisin apart from them was the mystery of Luz Gascó, and as Theresa read his dutiful letters to his mother, she found that she just could not believe that the man who had written them could bring his mistress to live with his wife. More importantly, she found herself disbelieving that he could ever have painted *Young Woman in a Garden*. Yet there it incontrovertibly was, hanging in the Museum of Fine Arts, signed "Edouard Beauvoisin, 1879," clear as print and authenticated five ways from Sunday.

A breeze stirred the papers scattered across the worktable. Under the ever-present tang of the sea, Theresa smelled lilies of the valley. She propped her chin on her hands and looked out into the garden. A pretty day, she thought, and a pretty view. It might make a picture, were there anything to balance the window frame and the mass of the linden tree in the left foreground. Oh, there was the rose bed, but it wasn't enough. A figure stepped into the scene, bent to the roses, clipped a bloom, laid it in the basket dangling from her elbow: Gascó, a red shawl tied Spaniard-wise across her white morning gown, her wild black hair escaping from its pins and springing around her face as she stooped. Her presence focused the composition, turned it into an interesting statement of light and tension.

Don't move, Theresa thought. For God's sake, Gascó, don't move. Squinting at the scene, she opened a drawer with a practiced jerk and felt for the sketchbook, which was not on top where it should be, where it always was. Irritated, she tore her eyes from Gascó to look for it. Lying in the back of the drawer was a child's *cahier*, marbled black and white, with a plain white label pasted on its cover and marked "May-June 1898" in a tiny, angular, blessedly legible hand.

"Out of place," she murmured angrily, then, "This is *it*," without any clear idea of what she meant by either statement.

Theresa swallowed, aware that something unimaginably significant had happened, was happening, that she was trembling and sweating with painful excitement. Carefully, she wiped her hands on her jeans, lifted the *cahier* from its wooden tomb, opened it to its last entry: June 5, 1898. The hand was scratchier, more sprawled than in his letters, the effect, perhaps, of the wasting disease that would kill him in July.

> *The Arrangement. A pity my death must void it. How well it has served us over the years, and how happily! At least, C. has seemed happy; for L.'s discontents, there has never been any answer, except to leave and make other arrangements of her own. Twenty years of flying into rages,*

> *sinking into sulks, refusing to stand thus and so or to hold a pose not to her liking, hating Brittany, the cold, the damp, the gray sea. And still she stays. Is it the Arrangement that binds her, or her beloved garden?* Young Woman in a Garden: Luz at La Roseraie. *If I have a fear of dying, it is that I must be remembered for that painting. God's judgment on our Arrangement, Maman would have said, had she known of it. When I come to make my last Confession, soon, oh, very soon now, I will beg forgiveness for deceiving her. It is my only regret.*

By dusk, Theresa had read the notebook through and begun to search for its fellows. That there had to be more notebooks was as clear as Monet's palette: the first entry began in midsentence, for one thing, and no man talks to himself so fluently without years of practice. They wouldn't be hidden, Beauvoisin hadn't been a secretive man. Tidy-minded. Self-contained. Conservative. He stored them somewhere, Theresa thought. Somewhere here. She looked around the darkening studio. Maybe it would be clearer to her in the morning. It would certainly be lighter.

Out in the garden, Theresa felt the depression of the past days release her like a hand opening. A *discovery! A real discovery!* What difference did it make whether Beauvoisin had painted two good paintings or a dozen? There was a mystery about him, and she, Theresa Stanton, was on the verge of uncovering it. She wanted to babble and sing and go out drinking to celebrate. But her friends were three thousand miles away, and all she had was Mme Beauvoisin. And Luna. Always Luna.

Theresa's quick steps slowed. What was her hurry, after all? Her news would keep, and the garden was so lovely in the failing light, with the white pebble path luminous under her feet, the evening air blue and warm and scented with lilies.

In the parlor, an oil lamp laid its golden hand upon the two women sitting companionably on the velvet sofa, their heads bent to their invisible tasks. The soft play of light and shadow varnished their hair and skin with youth. Theresa struggled with a momentary and inexplicable sense of déjà vu, then, suddenly embarrassed, cleared her throat. "I found a notebook today," she announced into the silence. "Beauvoisin's private journal."

Luna's head came up, startled and alert. Theresa caught a liquid flash as she glanced at her, then at Mme Beauvoisin.

"A journal?" asked Mme Beauvoisin blandly. "Ah. I might have guessed he would have kept a journal. You must be very pleased—such documents are important to scholars. Come. Pour yourself a brandy to celebrate—the bottle is on the sideboard—and sit and tell us of your great discovery."

As Theresa obediently crossed the room and unstoppered the decanter, she heard a furious whisper.

"*Mierda!*"

"Hush, Luna." Mme Beauvoisin's tone was happy, almost gleeful. "We agreed. Whatever she finds, she may use. It is her right."

"I withdraw my agreement. I know nothing of these journals. Who can tell what he may have written?"

A deep and affectionate sigh. "Oh, Luna. Still so suspicious?"

"Not suspicious. Wise. The little American, she is of Edouard's blood and also Edouard's soul. I have seen him in her eyes."

Theresa set down the decanter and came back into the lamplight. "Wait a minute. I don't understand. Of course I have the right to use the journals. M. Tanguy promised me full access to all Beauvoisin's papers. And he didn't say anything about you or needing your permission."

Mme Beauvoisin's dark, faded eyes held hers for a moment. "Please, do not discommode yourself," she said. "Sit and tell us what you have found."

Hesitant under Luna's hot and disapproving gaze, Theresa perched herself on the edge of a chair and did as she was told.

"I'd no idea he was so passionate," Theresa said at last. "In his letters, although he speaks of passion, he's always so moderate about expressing it."

"Moderate!" Luna's laugh was a scornful snort. "Hear the girl! *Madre de Dios*!"

"Hush, Luna. Please continue."

"That's all. I didn't really learn much, except that he knew in June that he was dying. One interesting thing was his references to an Arrangement—that's with a capital A—and how he'd never told his *maman* about it." Excitement rose in her again. "I have to find the rest of the journals!"

Mme Beauvoisin smiled at her. "Tomorrow. You will find them, I'm sure of it."

"Céleste," said Luna warningly.

"Hush, my dear."

Theresa retired, as always, before her elderly companions. As polite as Mme Beauvoisin was to her, she always felt uncomfortable in the parlor, as if her presence there were an intrusion, a threat, a necessary evil. Which, she told herself firmly, in a way, it was. The two women had been living here alone for heaven only knew how long. It was only natural that they'd feel put out by her being there. It was silly of her to resent her exclusion from their charmed circle. And yet, tonight especially, she did.

Theresa curled up in a chair by the window, tucked the duvet around her legs, and considered the problem of Edouard's notebooks. A full moon washed the pale roses and the white paths with silver. In her mind, she followed Edouard down one of those luminous paths to the studio, where he sat at his desk, pulled his current notebook from the right-hand drawer, and reread his last entry only to discover that he'd barely one page left. He shook his head, rose, went to the cabinet, opened one of the long drawers where he kept his paints and pigments neatly arranged in shallow wooden trays. Carefully, he lifted one tray, slipped a new marbled *cahier* from under it, returned to his desk, and began to write.

When Theresa opened her eyes, the garden was cool in a pale golden dawn. Her neck was in agony, her legs hopelessly cramped, but she was elated. The notebooks were in the cabinet under the paint trays—they just had to be!

Twenty minutes later, she was in the studio herself, with the paint trays stacked on the floor, gloating over layers of black-and-white-marbled *cahiers*.

There were more than a hundred of them, she discovered, distributed over four drawers and forty-two years, from Beauvoisin's first trip to Paris in 1856 to his death in 1898. Theresa took out five or six of them at random and paged through them as she had paged through books as a child, stopping to read passages that caught her eye. Not entirely professional, perhaps. But thoroughly satisfying.

April 20, 1875

Paris is so full of bad paintings, I can't begin to describe them. I know C.'s would enjoy some modest success, but she will not agree. One of Mlle Morisot's canvases has sold for a thousand francs—a seascape not so half as pretty as the one C. painted at La Roseraie last month. I compliment her often on her work, and am somewhat distressed that she does not return the courtesy, from love of the artist if not from admiration of his work. But then C. has never understood my theory of light and evanescence, and will not agree with my principles of composition.

Theresa closed the notebook with a snap, unreasonably disappointed with Beauvoisin for his blindness to the structures of his society. Surely he must have known, as Céleste obviously knew, that men were professionals and women were amateurs, unless they were honorary men like Berthe Morisot and Mary Cassatt. Poor Céleste, Theresa thought, and poor Edouard. What had they seen in one another?

Over the next few days, Theresa chased the answer to that question through the pages of Edouard's journals, skipping from one capital C. to the next, composing a sketch-portrait of a very strange marriage. That Beauvoisin had loved Céleste was clear. That he had loved her as a wife was less so. He spoke of her as a traveling companion, a hostess, a housekeeper. A sister, Theresa thought suddenly, reading how Céleste had arranged the details of their trip to Spain in the winter of 1877. She's like the maiden sister keeping house for her brilliant brother. And Edouard, he was a man who saved all his passion for his art, at any rate until he went to Spain and met Luz Gascó.

I have made some sketches of a woman we met in the Prado—a respectable woman and tolerably educated, although fallen on evil times. She has quite the most beautiful skin I have seen—white as new cream and so fine that she seems to glow of her own light, like a lamp draped with heavy silk. Such bones! And her hair and eyes, like black marble polished and by some miracle brought to life and made supple. C. saw her first, and effected an introduction. She is a joy to paint, and not expensive. . . .

Eagerly, Theresa skimmed through the next months for further references to the beautiful *señorita*. Had Edouard fallen in love at last? He certainly wrote as if he had—long, poetic descriptions of her skin, her hair, her form, her luminous, living presence. At the same time, he spoke fearfully of her temper, her unaccountable moods, her uncontrollable "gypsy nature." In the end, however, simple painterly covetousness resolved his dilemma and he invited Gascó to spend the summer at La Roseraie.

May 6, 1878

Luz Gascó expected tomorrow. C., having vacated the blue chamber for her, complains of having nowhere to paint. Perhaps I'll build an extension to my studio. Gascó is a great deal to ask of a wife, after all, even though C. knows better than any other how unlikely my admiration is to overstep propriety. As a model, Gascó is perfection. As a woman, she is like a wild cat, ready to hiss and scratch for no reason. Yet that skin! Those eyes! I despair of capturing them and ache to make the attempt.

Fishing Boats *not going well. The boats are wooden and the water also. I shall try Gascó in the foreground to unbalance the composition. . . .*

How violently the presence of Luz Gascó had unbalanced the nicely calculated composition of Edouard Beauvoisin's life became clearer to Theresa the more she read. She hardly felt excluded now from her hostesses' circle, eager as she was to get back to the studio and to Edouard, for whom she was feeling more and more sympathy. Pre-Gascó, his days had unfolded methodically: work, walks with Céleste, drives to the village, letter-writing, notebook-keeping, sketching—each allotted its proper time and space, regular as mealtimes. G. *rises at noon*, he mourned a week into her visit. *She breaks pose because she has seen a bird in the garden or wants to smell a flower. She is utterly impossible. Yet she transforms the world around her.*

Imperceptibly, the summer visit extended into autumn and the autumn into winter as Beauvoisin planned and painted canvas after canvas, experimenting with composition, technique, pigment. By the spring of 1879, there was talk of Gascó's staying. By summer, she was a fixture, and Beauvoisin was beside himself with huge, indefinite emotions and ambitions, all of them arranged, like his canvases, around the dynamic figure of Luz Gascó. Then came July, and a page blank save for one line:

July 6, 1879
Luz in the parlor. Ah, Céleste!

A puzzling entry, marked as if for easy reference with a scrap of cheap paper folded in four. Theresa picked it up and carefully smoothed it open—not carefully enough, however, to keep the brittle paper from tearing along its creases. She saw dark lines—a charcoal sketch—and her heart went cold in panic. What have I done? she thought. What have I destroyed?

With a trembling hand, she arranged the four pieces on the table. The image was a reclining woman, her face turned away under an upflung arm, her bodice unbuttoned to the waist and her chemise loosened and folded open. A scarf of dark curls draped her throat and breast, veiling and exposing her nakedness. The sketch was intimate, more tender than erotic, a lover's mirror.

Theresa put her hands over her eyes. She'd torn the sketch; she didn't need to cry over it too. Spilt milk, she told herself severely. M. Rouart would know how to restore it. And she should be happy she'd found it, overjoyed to have such dramatic proof of Beauvoisin's carnal passion for his Spanish model. So why did she feel regretful, sad, disappointed, and so terribly, overwhelmingly angry?

A shadow fell across the page. A gnarled, nail-bitten forefinger traced the charcoal line of the subject's hair.

"Ah," said Luna softly. "I wondered what had become of this."

Theresa clenched her own hands in her lap, appalled by the emotion that rose in her at the sound of that hoarse, slightly lisping voice. Luna was certainly irritating. But this was not irritation Theresa felt. It was rage.

"A beautiful piece, is it not?" The four torn pieces were not perfectly aligned: the woman seemed broken at the waist; her left arm, lying across her hips, was dismembered at the elbow. Luna coaxed her back together with delicate touches. "A pity that my own beauty may not be so easily repaired."

Surprised, Theresa looked up at Luna's aged turtle face. She'd never imagined Luna young, let alone beautiful. Yet now she saw that her bones were finely turned under her leathery skin and her eyes were unfaded and bright black as a mouse's. A vaguely familiar face, and an interesting one, now that Theresa came to study it. Something might be made of it, against a background of flowers, or the garden wall.

Luna straightened, regarding Theresa with profound disgust. "You're his to the bone," she said. "You see what you need to see, not what is there. I told her a stranger would have been better."

Theresa's fury had subsided, leaving only bewilderment behind. She rubbed her eyes wearily. "I'm sorry," she said. "I don't understand. Do you know something about this sketch?"

The old woman's mouth quirked angrily. "What I know of this sketch," she spat, "is that it was not meant for your eyes." And with a haughty lift of her chin, she turned and left the studio.

Was Mlle Gascó crazy, or senile, or just incredibly mean? Theresa wondered, watching her hobble across the bright prospect of the garden like an arthritic crow. Surely she couldn't actually know anything about that sketch—why, it had been hidden for over a hundred years. For a moment, the garden dimmed, as though a cloud had come over the sun, and then Theresa's eyes strayed to the notebook open before her. A sunbeam dazzled the single sentence to blankness. She moved the notebook out of the glare and turned the page.

The next entry was dated July 14 and spoke of Bastille Day celebrations in Lorient and a family outing with Céleste and Gascó, all very ordinary except that Beauvoisin's prose was less colorful than usual. Something was going on. But Theresa had already known that. Beauvoisin had grown immensely as a painter over the summer of 1879, and had cut himself off from the men who had been his closest friends. She was already familiar with the sharp note he'd written Manet denying that he had grown reclusive, only very hard at work and somewhat distracted, he hinted, by domestic tension: "For two women to reside under one roof is far from restful," he had written, and "Céleste and I have both begun paintings of Gascó—not, alas, the same pose."

Theresa flipped back to July 6. *Luz in the parlor. Ah, Céleste*! Such melodrama was not like Beauvoisin, nor was a week's silence, nor the brief, lifeless chronicles of daily events that occupied him during the month of August. Theresa sighed. Real life is often melodramatic, and extreme emotion mute. Something had happened on July 6, something that had changed Beauvoisin's life and art.

In any case, late in 1879 Beauvoisin had begun to develop a new style, a lighter, more brilliant palette, a more painterly technique that broke definitively from the line-obsessed training of his youth. Reading the entries for the fall of '79 and the winter of '80, Theresa learned that he had developed his prose style as well, in long disquisitions on light and composition, life and art. He gave up all accounts of ordinary events in favor of long essays on the beauty of the ephemeral: a young girl, a budding flower, a spring morning, a perfect understanding between man and woman. He became obsessed with a need to capture even the most abstract of emotions on canvas: betrayal, joy, contentment, estrangement.

> *I have set G. a pose I flatter myself expresses most perfectly that moment of suspension between betrayal and remorse. She is to the left of the central plane, a little higher than is comfortable, crowded into a box defined by the straight back of her chair and the arm of the sofa. Her body twists left, her face is without expression, her eyes are fixed on the viewer. The conceit pleases G. more than C., of course, G. being the greater cynic. But C. agrees that the composition is out of the ordinary way and we all have great hopes of it at the next Impressionist's Show. Our Arrangement will answer very well, I think.*

Reading such entries—which often ran to ten or fifteen closely written pages—Theresa began to wonder when Beauvoisin found time to paint the pictures he had so lovingly and thoughtfully planned. It was no wonder, she thought, that *Interior* and *Woman at a Window* seemed so theoretical, so contrived. She was not surprised to read that they had not brought as much as *Young Woman in a Garden* or *Reclining Nude*, painted two years later and described briefly as *a figure study of G. on the parlor sofa, oddly lighted. Pure whim, and not an idea anywhere in it. C. likes it, though, and so does G.; have allowed myself to be overborne.*

June had laid out its palette in days of Prussian blue, clear green, and yellow. In the early part of the month, when Theresa had been reading the letters, the clouds flooded the sky with a gray and white wash that suppressed shadow and compressed perspective like a Japanese print. After she found the notebooks, however, all the days seemed saturated with light and static as a still life.

Theresa spent her time reading Beauvoisin's journals, leaving the studio only to eat a silent meal alone in the kitchen, to wander through the garden, or, in the evenings, to go down to the seawall where she would watch the sun set in Turneresque glories of carmine and gold. Once, seeing the light, like Danaë's shower, spilling its golden seed into the sea, Theresa felt her hand twitch with the desire to paint the scene, to capture the evanescent moment in oils and make it immortal.

What am I thinking of? she wondered briefly. It must be Edouard rubbing off on me. Or the isolation. I need to get out of here for a couple days, go back to Paris, see M. Rouart about the sketch, maybe let him take me out to dinner, talk to someone real for a change. But the next day found her in the studio and the next evening by the seawall, weeping with the beauty of the light and her own inadequate abilities.

As June shaded into July, Theresa began to see pictures everywhere she looked and gave in at last to her growing desire to sketch them. Insensible of sacrilege, she took up Beauvoisin's pastel chalks and charcoal pencils and applied herself to the problem of reproducing her impressions of the way the flowers shimmered under the noonday sun and how the filtered light reflected from the studio's whitewashed walls.

At first, she'd look at the untrained scrawls and blotches she'd produced and tear them to confetti in an ecstasy of disgust. But as the clear still days unfolded, she paid less and less attention to what she'd done, focusing only on the need of the moment, to balance shape and mass, light and shade. She hardly saw Mme Beauvoisin and Luna, though she was dimly aware that they were about—in the parlor, in the garden, walking arm in arm across her field of vision: figures in the landscape, motifs in the composition. Day bled into day with scarcely a signpost to mark the end of one or the beginning of the next, so that she sketched and read in a timeless, seamless present, without past, without future, without real purpose.

So it was with no clear sense of time or place that Theresa walked into the studio one day and realized that she had left her sketchbook in the parlor. Tiresome, she thought to herself. But there was that study she'd been working on, the one of the stone wall. She'd just have to go back to the house and get it.

The transition from hall to parlor was always blinding, particularly in the afternoon, when the sun slanted through the French doors straight into entering eyes. That is perhaps why Theresa thought at first that the room was empty, and then that someone had left a large canvas propped against the sofa, a painting of two women in an interior.

It was an interesting composition, the details blurred by the bright backlight, the white dress of the figure on the sofa glimmering against the deep burgundy cushions, the full black skirts of the figure curled on the floor beside her like a pool of ink spilled on the flowery carpet. Both figures were intent on a paper the woman on the sofa held on her up-drawn knees. Her companion's torso was turned into the sofa, her arms wreathed loosely around her waist.

What a lovely picture they make together, Theresa thought. I wonder I never thought of posing them so. It's a pity Céleste will not let me paint her.

Céleste laid the paper aside, took Gascó's hand, and carried it to her lips. Her gaze met Theresa's.

"Edouard," she said.

Theresa's cheeks heated; her heart began a slow, deep, painful beating that turned her dizzy. She put her hand on the doorframe to steady herself just as Gascó surged up from the floor and turned, magnificent in her rage and beauty, to confront the intruder. Her face shone from the thundercloud of her hair, its graceful planes sharpened and defined by the contemptuous curve of her red mouth, and the wide, proud defiance of her onyx eyes. Edouard released the door frame and helplessly reached out his hand to her.

"Be a man, Edouard!" Gascó all but spat. "Don't look like that. I knew this must come. It would have come sooner had you been less blind. No," as Edouard winced, "I beg your pardon. It was not necessary to say that. Or the other. But you must not weep."

Céleste had swung her legs to the floor and laid the sketch on the sofa-back on top of the piled cushions. She looked composed, if a little pale, and her voice was even when she said, "Sit down, Luna. He has no intention of weeping. No, get us some brandy. We must talk, and we'd all be the better for something to steady us."

"Talk?" said Edouard. "What is there for us to say to one another?"

Gascó swept to the sideboard, poured brandy into three snifters, and handed them around, meeting Edouard's eyes defiantly when she put his into his hand.

"Drink, Edouard," said Céleste gently. "And why don't you sit down?"

He shook his head, but took a careful sip of his brandy. The liquor burned his throat.

"Doubtless you want us to leave La Roseraie," said Céleste into a long silence.

"Oh, no, my heart," said Gascó. "I'll not run away like some criminal. This house is yours. If anyone is to leave, it must be Beauvoisin."

"In law," said Edouard mildly, "the house is mine. I will not leave it. Nor will you, Céleste. You are my wife." His voice faltered. "I don't want you to leave. I want things as they were before."

"With your model your wife's lover, and you as blind as a mole?"

Edouard set down his half-finished brandy and pinched the bridge of his nose. "That was not kind, Gascó. But then, I have always known that you are not kind."

"No. I am honest. And I see what is there to be seen. It is you who must leave, Edouard."

"And ruin us all?" Céleste sounded both annoyed and amused. "You cannot be thinking, my love. We must find some compromise, some way of saving Edouard's face and our reputations, some way of living together."

"Never!" said Gascó. "I will not. You cannot ask it of me."

"My Claire de Lune. My Luna." Céleste reached for Gascó's hand and pulled her down on the sofa. "You do love me, do you not? Then you will help me. Edouard loves me too: we all love one another, do we not? Edouard. Come sit with us."

Edouard set down his brandy snifter. Céleste was holding her hand to him, smiling affectionately. He stepped forward, took the hand, allowed it and the smile to draw him down beside her. At the edge of his vision, he saw the paper slide behind the cushions and turned to retrieve it. Céleste's grip tightened on his hand.

"Never mind, my dear," she said. "Now. Surely we can come to some agreement, some arrangement that will satisfy us all?"

The taste in Theresa's mouth said she'd been asleep. The tickle in her throat said the sofa was terribly dusty, and her nose said there had been mice in it, perhaps still were. The cushions were threadbare, the needlework pillows moth-eaten into woolen lace.

Without thinking what she was doing, Theresa scattered them broadcast and burrowed her hand down between sofa-back and seat, grimacing a bit as she thought of the mice, grinning triumphantly as she touched a piece of paper. Carefully, she drew it out, creased and mildewed as it was, and smoothed it on her knees.

A few scrawled lines of text with a sketch beneath them. The hand was not Edouard's. Nor was the sketch, though a dozen art historians would have staked their government grants that the style was his. The image was an early version of *Young Woman in a Garden*, a sketch of Gascó sitting against a tree with her hands around her knees, her pointed chin raised to display the long curve of her neck. Her hair was loose on her shoulders. Her blouse was open at the throat. She was laughing.

Trembling, Theresa read the note:

> My Claire de Lune:
>
> How wicked I feel, how abandoned, writing you like this, where anyone could read how I love you, my *maja*. I want to write about your neck and breasts and hair—oh, your hair like black silk across my body. But the only words that come to my mind are stale when they are not comic, and I'd not have you laugh at me. So here is my memory of yesterday afternoon, and your place in it, and in my heart always.
>
> Céleste

Theresa closed her eyes, opened them again. The room she sat in was gloomy, musty, and falling into ruin, very different from the bright, comfortably shabby parlor she remembered. One of the French doors was ajar; afternoon sun spilled through it, reflecting from a thousand swirling dust motes, raising the ghosts of flowers from the faded carpet. Out in the garden, a bird whistled. Theresa went to the door, looked out over a wilderness of weedy paths and rosebushes grown into a thorny, woody tangle.

Céleste's letter to Luz Gascó crackled in her hand, reassuringly solid. There was clearly a lot of work to be done.

THE MAN IN THE BLACK SUIT

Stephen King

Perhaps the most popular writer of our generation, Stephen King is known best for his novels of suspense, both supernatural and psychological. More than two dozen of his novels and shorter works have been filmed, including notable critical triumphs such as *Stand by Me* and *The Shawshank Redemption*.

"The Man in the Black Suit" has all the hallmarks of King's finest short works. Set in the Maine woods he loves so much, it involves a boy's brief but harrowing brush with death . . . and the devil. Infused with warmth and charm, this tale is a perfect, sweet gem. It is reprinted from *The New Yorker*.

—E. D.

I am now a very old man and this is something that happened to me when I was very young—only nine years old. It was 1914, the summer after my brother, Dan, died in the west field and not long before America got into the First World War. I've never told anyone about what happened at the fork in the stream that day, and I never will. I've decided to write it down, though, in this book, which I will leave on the table beside my bed. I can't write long, because my hands shake so these days and I have next to no strength, but I don't think it will take long.

Later, someone may find what I have written. That seems likely to me, as it is pretty much human nature to look in a book marked "Diary" after its owner has passed along. So, yes—my words will probably be read. A better question is whether anyone will believe them. Almost certainly not, but that doesn't matter. It's not belief I'm interested in but freedom. Writing can give that, I've found. For twenty years I wrote a column called "Long Ago and Far Away" for the Castle Rock *Call*, and I know that sometimes it works that way—what you write down sometimes leaves you forever, like old photographs left in the bright sun, fading to nothing but white.

I pray for that sort of release.

A man in his eighties should be well past the terrors of childhood, but as my infirmities slowly creep up on me, like waves licking closer and closer to some indifferently built castle of sand, that terrible face grows clearer and clearer in my mind's eye. It glows like a dark star in the constellations of my childhood. What I might have done yesterday, who I might have seen here in my room at the nursing home, what I might have said to them or they to me—those things are gone, but the face of the man in the black suit grows ever clearer, ever closer, and I remember every word he said. I don't want to think of him but I can't help it, and sometimes at night my old heart beats so hard and so fast I think it will tear itself right clear of my chest. So I uncap my fountain pen and force my trembling old hand to write this pointless anecdote in the diary one of my great-grandchildren—I can't remember her name for sure, at least not right now, but I know it starts with an "S"—gave to me last Christmas, and which I have never written in until now. Now I will write in it. I will write the story of how I met the man in the black suit on the bank of Castle Stream one afternoon in the summer of 1914.

The town of Motton was a different world in those days—more different than I could ever tell you. That was a world without airplanes droning overhead, a world almost without cars and trucks, a world where the skies were not cut into lanes and slices by overhead power lines. There was not a single paved road in the whole town, and the business district consisted of nothing but Corson's General Store, Thut's Livery & Hardware, the Methodist church at Christ's Corner, the school, the town hall, and half a mile down from there, Harry's Restaurant, which my mother called, with unfailing disdain, "the liquor house."

Mostly, though, the difference was in how people lived—how *apart* they were. I'm not sure people born after the middle of the century could quite credit that, although they might say they could, to be polite to old folks like me. There were no phones in western Maine back then, for one thing. The first one wouldn't be installed for another five years, and by the time there was a phone in our house, I was nineteen and going to college at the University of Maine in Orono.

But that is only the roof of the thing. There was no doctor closer than Casco, and there were no more than a dozen houses in what you would call town. There were no neighborhoods (I'm not even sure we knew the word, although we had a verb—"neighboring"—that described church functions and barn dances), and open fields were the exception rather than the rule. Out of town the houses were farms that stood far apart from each other, and from December until the middle of March we mostly hunkered down in the little pockets of stove warmth we called families. We hunkered and listened to the wind in the chimney and hoped no one would get sick or break a leg or get a headful of bad ideas, like the farmer over in Castle Rock who had chopped up his wife and kids three winters before and then said in court that the ghosts made him do it. In those days before the Great War, most of Motton was woods and bog—dark long places full of moose and mosquitoes, snakes and secrets. In those days there were ghosts everywhere.

This thing I'm telling about happened on a Saturday. My father gave me a whole list of chores to do, including some that would have been Dan's, if he'd still been alive. He was my only brother, and he'd died of a bee sting. A year had gone by, and still my mother wouldn't hear that. She said it was something else, *had* to have been, that no one ever died of being stung by a bee. When Mama Sweet, the oldest lady in the Methodist Ladies' Aid, tried to tell her—at the church supper the previous winter, this was—that the same thing had happened to her favorite uncle back in '73, my mother clapped her hands over her ears, got up, and walked out of the church basement. She'd never been back since, and nothing my father could say to her would change her mind. She claimed she was done with church, and that if she ever had to see Helen Robichaud again (that was Mama Sweet's real name) she would slap her eyes out. She wouldn't be able to help herself, she said.

That day Dad wanted me to lug wood for the cookstove, weed the beans and the cukes, pitch hay out of the loft, get two jugs of water to put in the cold pantry, and scrape as much old paint off the cellar bulkhead as I could. Then, he said, I could go fishing, if I didn't mind going by myself—he had to go over and see Bill Eversham about some cows. I said I sure didn't mind going by myself, and my dad smiled as if that didn't surprise him so very much. He'd given me a bamboo pole the week before—not because it was my birthday or anything but just because he liked to give me things sometimes—and I was wild to try it in Castle Stream, which was by far the troutiest brook I'd ever fished.

"But don't you go too far in the woods," he told me. "Not beyond where the water splits."

"No, sir."

"Promise me."

"Yessir, I promise."

"Now promise your mother."

We were standing on the back stoop; I had been bound for the springhouse with the water jugs when my dad stopped me. Now he turned me around to face my mother, who was standing at the marble counter in a flood of strong morning sunshine falling through the double windows over the sink. There was a curl of hair lying across the side of her forehead and touching her eyebrow—you see how well I remember it all? The bright light turned that little curl to filaments of gold and made me want to run to her and put my arms around her. In that instant I saw her as a woman, saw her as my father must have seen her. She was wearing a housedress with little red roses all over it, I remember, and she was kneading bread. Candy Bill, our little black Scottie dog, was standing alertly beside her feet, looking up, waiting for anything that might drop. My mother was looking at me.

"I promise," I said.

She smiled, but it was the worried kind of smile she always seemed to make since my father brought Dan back from the west field in his arms. My father had come sobbing and bare-chested. He had taken off his shirt and draped it over Dan's face, which had swelled and turned color. *My boy!* he had been crying. *Oh, look at my boy! Jesus, look at my boy!* I remember that as if it were yesterday. It was the only time I ever heard my dad take the Saviour's name in vain.

"What do you promise, Gary?" she asked.

"Promise not to go no further than where the stream forks, Ma'am."

"Any further."

"Any."

She gave me a patient look, saying nothing as her hands went on working in the dough, which now had a smooth, silky look.

"I promise not to go any further than where the stream forks, Ma'am."

"Thank you, Gary," she said. "And try to remember that grammar is for the world as well as for school."

"Yes, Ma'am."

Candy Bill followed me as I did my chores, and sat between my feet as I bolted my lunch, looking up at me with the same attentiveness he had shown my mother while she was kneading her bread, but when I got my new bamboo pole and my old, splintery creel and started out of the dooryard, he stopped and only stood in the dust by an old roll of snow fence, watching. I called him but he wouldn't come. He yapped a time or two, as if telling me to come back, but that was all.

"Stay, then," I said, trying to sound as if I didn't care. I did, though, at least a little. Candy Bill *always* went fishing with me.

My mother came to the door and looked out at me with her left hand held up to shade her eyes. I can see her that way still, and it's like looking at a photograph of someone who later became unhappy, or died suddenly. "You mind your dad now, Gary!"

"Yes, Ma'am, I will."

She waved. I waved, too. Then I turned my back on her and walked away.

The sun beat down on my neck, hard and hot, for the first quartermile or so, but then I entered the woods, where double shadow fell over the road and it was cool and fir-smelling and you could hear the wind hissing through the deep, needled groves. I walked with my pole on my shoulder the way boys did back then, holding my creel in my other hand like a valise or a salesman's sample case. About two miles into the woods along a road that was really nothing but a double rut with a grassy strip growing up the center hump, I began to hear the hurried, eager gossip of Castle Stream. I thought of trout with bright speckled backs and pure-white bellies, and my heart went up in my chest.

The stream flowed under a little wooden bridge, and the banks leading down to the water were steep and brushy. I worked my way down carefully, holding on where I could and digging my heels in. I went down out of summer and back into mid-spring, or so it felt. The cool rose gently off the water, and there was a green smell like moss. When I got to the edge of the water I only stood there for a little while, breathing deep of that mossy smell and watching the dragonflies circle and the skitterbugs skate. Then, further down, I saw a trout leap at a butterfly—a good big brookie, maybe fourteen inches long—and remembered I hadn't come here just to sightsee.

I walked along the bank, following the current, and wet my line for the first time, with the bridge still in sight upstream. Something jerked the tip of my pole down once or twice and ate half my worm, but whatever it was was too sly for my nine-year-old hands—or maybe just not hungry enough to be careless—so I quit that place.

I stopped at two or three other places before I got to the place where Castle Stream forks, going southwest into Castle Rock and southeast into Kashwakamak Township, and at one of them I caught the biggest trout I have ever caught in my life, a beauty that measured nineteen inches from tip to tail on the little ruler I kept in my creel. That was a monster of a brook trout, even for those days.

If I had accepted this as gift enough for one day and gone back, I would not be writing now (and this is going to turn out longer than I thought it would, I see that already), but I didn't. Instead I saw to my catch right then and there as my father had shown me—cleaning it, placing it on dry grass at the bottom of the creel, then laying damp grass on top of it—and went on. I did not, at age nine, think that catching a nineteen-inch brook trout was particularly remarkable, although I do remember being amazed that my line had not broken when I, netless as well as artless, had hauled it out and swung it toward me in a clumsy tail-flapping arc.

Ten minutes later, I came to the place where the stream split in those days (it is long gone now; there is a settlement of duplex homes where Castle Stream once went its course, and a district grammar school as well, and if there is a stream it goes in darkness), dividing around a huge gray rock nearly the size of our outhouse. There was a pleasant flat space here, grassy and soft, overlooking what my dad and I called South Branch. I squatted on my heels, dropped my line into the water, and almost immediately snagged a fine rainbow trout. He wasn't the size of my brookie—only a foot or so—but a good fish, just the same. I had it cleaned out before the gills had stopped flexing, stored it in my creel, and dropped my line back into the water.

This time there was no immediate bite, so I leaned back, looking up at the blue stripe of sky I could see along the stream's course. Clouds floated by, west to east, and I tried to think what they looked like. I saw a unicorn, then a rooster, then a dog that looked like Candy Bill. I was looking for the next one when I drowsed off.

Or maybe slept. I don't know for sure. All I know is that a tug on my line so strong it almost pulled the bamboo pole out of my hand was what brought me back into the afternoon. I sat up, clutched the pole, and suddenly became aware that something was sitting on the tip of my nose. I crossed my eyes and saw a bee. My heart seemed to fall dead in my chest, and for a horrible second I was sure I was going to wet my pants.

The tug on my line came again, stronger this time, but although I maintained my grip on the end of the pole so it wouldn't be pulled into the stream and perhaps carried away (I think I even had the presence of mind to snub the line with my forefinger), I made no effort to pull in my catch. All my horrified attention was fixed on the fat black-and-yellow thing that was using my nose as a rest stop.

I slowly poked out my lower lip and blew upward. The bee ruffled a little but kept its place. I blew again and it ruffled again—but this time it also seemed to shift impatiently, and I didn't dare blow anymore, for fear it would lose its temper completely and give me a shot. It was too close for me to focus on what it was doing, but it was easy to imagine it ramming its stinger into one of my nostrils and shooting its poison up toward my eyes. And my brain.

A terrible idea came to me: that this was the very bee that had killed my brother. I knew it wasn't true, and not only because honeybees probably didn't live longer than a single year (except maybe for the queens; about them I was not so sure). It couldn't be true, because honeybees died when they stung, and even at nine I knew it. Their stingers were barbed, and when they tried to fly away after doing the deed, they tore themselves apart. Still, the idea stayed. This was a special bee, a devil-bee, and it had come back to finish the other of Albion and Loretta's two boys.

And here is something else: I had been stung by bees before, and although the stings had swelled more than is perhaps usual (I can't really say for sure), I had never died of them. That was only for my brother, a terrible trap that had been laid for him in his very making—a trap that I had somehow escaped. But as I crossed my eyes until they hurt, in an effort to focus on the bee, logic did not exist. It was the *bee* that existed, only that—the bee that had killed my brother, killed him so cruelly that my father had slipped down the straps of his overalls so he could take off his shirt and cover Dan's swollen, engorged face. Even in the depths of his grief he had done that, because he didn't want his wife to see what had become of her firstborn. Now the bee had returned, and now it would kill me. I would die in convulsions on the bank, flopping just as a brookie flops after you take the hook out of its mouth. As I sat there trembling on the edge of panic—ready to bolt to my feet and then bolt anywhere—there came a report from behind me. It was as sharp and peremptory as a pistol shot, but I knew it wasn't a pistol shot; it was someone clapping his hands. One single clap. At that moment, the bee tumbled off my nose and fell into my lap. It lay there on my pants with its legs sticking up and its stinger a threatless black thread against the old scuffed brown of the corduroy. It was dead as a doornail, I saw that at once. At the same moment, the pole gave another tug—the hardest yet—and I almost lost it again.

I grabbed it with both hands and gave it a big stupid yank that would have made my father clutch his head with both hands, if he had been there to see. A rainbow trout, a good bit larger than either of the ones I had already caught, rose out of the water in a wet flash, spraying fine drops of water from its tail—it looked like one of those fishing pictures they used to put on the covers of men's magazines like *True* and *Man's Adventure* back in the forties and fifties. At that moment hauling in a big one was about the last thing on my mind, however, and when the line snapped and the fish fell back into the stream, I barely noticed. I looked over my shoulder to see who had clapped. A man was standing above me, at the edge of the trees. His face was very long and pale. His black hair was combed tight against his skull and parted with rigorous care on the left side of his narrow head. He was very tall. He was wearing a black three-piece suit, and I knew right away that he was not a human being, because his eyes were the orangey red of flames in a woodstove. I don't mean just the irises, because he *had* no irises, and no pupils, and certainly no whites. His eyes were completely orange—an orange that shifted and flickered. And it's really too late not to say exactly what I mean, isn't it? He was on fire inside, and his eyes were like the little isinglass portholes you sometimes see in stove doors.

My bladder let go, and the scuffed brown the dead bee was lying on went a darker brown. I was hardly aware of what had happened, and I couldn't take my eyes off the man standing on top of the bank and looking down at me—the man who had apparently walked out of thirty miles of trackless western Maine woods in a fine black suit and narrow shoes of gleaming leather. I could see the watch chain looped across his vest glittering in the summer sunshine. There was not so much as a single pine needle on him. And he was smiling at me.

"Why, it's a fisherboy!" he cried in a mellow, pleasing voice. "Imagine that! Are we well met, fisherboy?"

"Hello, sir," I said. The voice that came out of me did not tremble, but it didn't sound like my voice, either. It sounded older. Like Dan's voice, maybe.

Or my father's, even. And all I could think was that maybe he would let me go if I pretended not to see what he was. If I pretended I didn't see there were flames glowing and dancing where his eyes should have been.

"I've saved you a nasty sting, perhaps," he said, and then, to my horror, he came down the bank to where I sat with a dead bee in my wet lap and a bamboo fishing pole in my nerveless hands. His slicksoled city shoes should have slipped on the low, grassy weeds dressing the steep bank, but they didn't; nor did they leave tracks, I saw. Where his feet had touched—or seemed to touch—there was not a single broken twig, crushed leaf, or trampled shoe-shape.

Even before he reached me, I recognized the aroma baking up from the skin under the suit—the smell of burned matches. The smell of sulfur. The man in the black suit was the Devil. He had walked out of the deep woods between Motton and Kashwakamak, and now he was standing here beside me. From the corner of one eye I could see a hand as pale as the hand of a store-window dummy. The fingers were hideously long.

He hunkered beside me on his hams, his knees popping just as the knees of any normal man might, but when he moved his hands so they dangled between his knees, I saw that each of those long fingers ended in not a fingernail but a long yellow claw.

"You didn't answer my question, fisherboy," he said in his mellow voice. It was, now that I think of it, like the voice of one of those radio announcers on the big-band shows years later, the ones that would sell Geritol and Serutan and Ovaltine and Dr. Grabow pipes. "Are we well met?"

"Please don't hurt me," I whispered, in a voice so low I could barely hear it. I was more afraid than I could ever write down, more afraid than I want to remember. But I do. I do. It never crossed my mind to hope I was having a dream, although it might have, I suppose, if I had been older. But I was nine, and I knew the truth when it squatted down beside me. I knew a hawk from a handsaw, as my father would have said. The man who had come out of the woods on that Saturday afternoon in midsummer was the Devil, and inside the empty holes of his eyes his brains were burning.

"Oh, do I smell something?" he asked, as if he hadn't heard me, although I knew he had. "Do I smell something . . . wet?"

He leaned toward me with his nose stuck out, like someone who means to smell a flower. And I noticed an awful thing; as the shadow of his head traveled over the bank, the grass beneath it turned yellow and died. He lowered his head toward my pants and sniffed. His glaring eyes half closed, as if he had inhaled some sublime aroma and wanted to concentrate on nothing but that.

"Oh, bad!" he cried. "Lovely-bad!" And then he chanted: "Opal! Diamond! Sapphire! Jade! I smell Gary's lemonade!" He threw himself on his back in the little flat place and laughed.

I thought about running, but my legs seemed two counties away from my brain. I wasn't crying, though; I had wet my pants, but I wasn't crying. I was too scared to cry. I suddenly knew that I was going to die, and probably painfully, but the worst of it was that that might not be the worst of it. The worst might come later. *After* I was dead.

He sat up suddenly, the smell of burnt matches fluffing out from his suit and making me feel gaggy in my throat. He looked at me solemnly from his narrow white face and burning eyes, but there was a sense of laughter about him, too. There was always that sense of laughter about him.

"Sad news, fisherboy," he said. "I've come with sad news."

I could only look at him—the black suit, the fine black shoes, the long white fingers that ended not in nails but in talons.

"Your mother is dead."

"No!" I cried. I thought of her making bread, of the curl lying across her forehead and just touching her eyebrow, of her standing there in the strong morning sunlight, and the terror swept over me again, but not for myself this time. Then I thought of how she'd looked when I set off with my fishing pole, standing in the kitchen doorway with her hand shading her eyes, and how she had looked to me in that moment like a photograph of someone you expected to see again but never did. "No, you lie!" I screamed.

He smiled—the sadly patient smile of a man who has often been accused falsely. "I'm afraid not," he said. "It was the same thing that happened to your brother, Gary. It was a bee."

"No, that's not true," I said, and now I *did* begin to cry. "She's old, she's thirty-five—if a bee sting could kill her the way it did Danny she would have died a long time ago, and you're a lying bastard!"

I had called the Devil a lying bastard. I was aware of this, but the entire front of my mind was taken up by the enormity of what he'd said. My mother dead? He might as well have told me that the moon had fallen on Vermont. But I believed him. On some level I believed him completely, as we always believe, on some level, the worst thing our hearts can imagine.

"I understand your grief, little fisherboy, but that particular argument just doesn't hold water, I'm afraid." He spoke in a tone of bogus comfort that was horrible, maddening, without remorse or pity. "A man can go his whole life without seeing a mockingbird, you know, but does that mean mocking birds don't exist? Your mother—"

A fish jumped below us. The man in the black suit frowned, then pointed a finger at it. The trout convulsed in the air, its body bending so strenuously that for a split second it appeared to be snapping at its own tail, and when it fell back into Castle Stream it was floating lifelessly. It struck the big gray rock where the waters divided, spun around twice in the whirlpool eddy that formed there, and then floated away in the direction of Castle Rock. Meanwhile, the terrible stranger turned his burning eyes on me again, his thin lips pulled back from tiny rows of sharp teeth in a cannibal smile.

"Your mother simply went through her entire life without being stung by a bee," he said. "But then—less than an hour ago, actually—one flew in through the kitchen window while she was taking the bread out of the oven and putting it on the counter to cool."

I raised my hands and clapped them over my ears. He pursed his lips as if to whistle and blew at me gently. It was only a little breath, but the stench was foul beyond belief—clogged sewers, outhouses that have never known a single sprinkle of lime, dead chickens after a flood.

My hands fell away from the sides of my face.

"Good," he said. "You need to hear this, Gary; you need to hear this, my little fisherboy. It was your mother who passed that fatal weakness on to your brother. You got some of it, but you also got a protection from your father that poor Dan somehow missed." He pursed his lips again, only this time he made a cruelly comic little *tsk-tsk* sound instead of blowing his nasty breath at me. "So although I don't like to speak ill of the dead, it's almost a case of poetic justice, isn't it? After all, she killed your brother Dan as surely as if she had put a gun to his head and pulled the trigger."

"No," I whispered. "No, it isn't true."

"I assure you it is," he said. "The bee flew in the window and lit on her neck. She slapped at it before she even knew what she was doing—*you* were wiser than that, weren't you, Gary?—and the bee stung her. She felt her throat start to close up at once. That's what happens, you know, to people who can't tolerate bee venom. Their throats close and they drown in the open air. That's why Dan's face was so swollen and purple. That's why your father covered it with his shirt."

I stared at him, now incapable of speech. Tears streamed down my cheeks. I didn't want to believe him, and knew from my church schooling that the Devil is the father of lies, but I *did* believe him just the same.

"She made the most wonderfully awful noises," the man in the black suit said reflectively, "and she scratched her face quite badly, I'm afraid. Her eyes bulged out like a frog's eyes. She wept." He paused, then added: "She wept as she died, isn't that sweet? And here's the most beautiful thing of all. After she was dead, after she had been lying on the floor for fifteen minutes or so with no sound but the stove ticking and with that little thread of a bee stinger still poking out of the side of her neck—so small, so small—do you know what Candy Bill did? That little rascal licked away her tears. First on one side, and then on the other."

He looked out at the stream for a moment, his face sad and thoughtful. Then he turned back to me and his expression of bereavement disappeared like a dream. His face was as slack and as avid as the face of a corpse that has died hungry. His eyes blazed. I could see his sharp little teeth between his pale lips.

"I'm starving," he said abruptly. "I'm going to kill you and eat your guts, little fisherboy. What do you think about that?"

No, I tried to say, *please no*, but no sound came out. He meant to do it, I saw. He really meant to do it.

"I'm just so *hungry*," he said, both petulant and teasing. "And you won't want to live without your precious mommy, anyhow, take my word for it. Because your father's the sort of man who'll have to have some warm hole to stick it in, believe me, and if you're the only one available, you're the one who'll have to serve. I'll save you all that discomfort and unpleasantness. Also, you'll go to Heaven, think of that. Murdered souls *always* go to Heaven. So we'll both be serving God this afternoon, Gary. Isn't that nice?"

He reached for me again with his long, pale hands, and without thinking what I was doing, I flipped open the top of my creel, pawed all the way down to the bottom, and brought out the monster brookie I'd caught earlier—the one I should have been satisfied with. I held it out to him blindly, my fingers in the red slit of its belly, from which I had removed its insides as the man in the black suit had threatened to remove mine. The fish's glazed eye stared dreamily at me, the gold ring around the black center reminding me of my mother's wedding ring. And in that moment I saw her lying in her coffin with the sun shining off the wedding band and knew it was true—she had been stung by a bee, she had drowned in the warm, bread-smelling kitchen air, and Candy Bill had licked her dying tears from her swollen cheeks.

"Big fish!" the man in the black suit cried in a guttural, greedy voice. "Oh, *biiig fiiish!*"

He snatched it away from me and crammed it into a mouth that opened wider than any human mouth ever could. Many years later, when I was sixty-five (I know it was sixty-five, because that was the summer I retired from teaching), I went to the aquarium in Boston and finally saw a shark. The mouth of the man in the black suit was like that shark's mouth when it opened, only his gullet was blazing orange, the same color as his eyes, and I felt heat bake out of it and into my face, the way you feel a sudden wave of heat come pushing out of a fireplace when a dry piece of wood catches alight. And I didn't imagine that heat, either—I know I didn't—because just before he slid the head of my nineteen-inch brook trout between his gaping jaws, I saw the scales along the sides of the fish rise up and begin to curl like bits of paper floating over an open incinerator.

He slid the fish in like a man in a traveling show swallowing a sword. He didn't chew, and his blazing eyes bulged out, as if in effort. The fish went in and went in, his throat bulged as it slid down his gullet, and now he began to cry tears of his own—except his tears were blood, scarlet and thick.

I think it was the sight of those bloody tears that gave me my body back. I don't know why that should have been, but I think it was. I bolted to my feet like a Jack released from its box, turned with my bamboo pole still in one hand, and fled up the bank, bending over and tearing tough bunches of weeds out with my free hand in an effort to get up the slope more quickly.

He made a strangled, furious noise—the sound of any man with his mouth too full—and I looked back just as I got to the top. He was coming after me, the back of his suit coat flapping and his thin gold watch chain flashing and winking in the sun. The tail of the fish was still protruding from his mouth and I could smell the rest of it, roasting in the oven of his throat.

He reached for me, groping with his talons, and I fled along the top of the bank. After a hundred yards or so I found my voice and went to screaming—screaming in fear, of course, but also screaming in grief for my beautiful dead mother.

He was coming after me. I could hear snapping branches and whipping bushes, but I didn't look back again. I lowered my head, slitted my eyes against the bushes and low-hanging branches along the stream's bank, and ran as fast as I could. And at every step I expected to feel his hands descending on my shoulders, pulling me back into a final burning hug.

That didn't happen. Some unknown length of time later—it couldn't have been longer than five or ten minutes, I suppose, but it seemed like forever—I saw the bridge through layerings of leaves and firs. Still screaming, but breathlessly now, sounding like a teakettle that has almost boiled dry, I reached this second, steeper bank and charged up.

Halfway to the top, I slipped to my knees, looked over my shoulder, and saw the man in the black suit almost at my heels, his white face pulled into a convulsion of fury and greed. His cheeks were splattered with his bloody tears and his shark's mouth hung open like a hinge.

"*Fisherboy!*" he snarled, and started up the bank after me, grasping at my foot with one long hand. I tore free, turned, and threw my fishing pole at him. He batted it down easily, but it tangled his feet up somehow and he went to his knees. I didn't wait to see any more; I turned and bolted to the top of the slope. I almost slipped at the very top, but managed to grab one of the support struts running beneath the bridge and save myself.

"You can't get away, fisherboy!" he cried from behind me. He sounded furious, but he also sounded as if he were laughing."It takes more than a mouthful of trout to fill *me* up!"

"Leave me alone!" I screamed back at him. I grabbed the bridge's railing and threw myself over it in a clumsy somersault, filling my hands with splinters and bumping my head so hard on the boards when I came down that I saw stars. I rolled over on my belly and began crawling. I lurched to my feet just before I got to the end of the bridge, stumbled once, found my rhythm, and then began to run. I ran as only nine-year-old boys can run, which is like the wind. It felt as if my feet only touched the ground with every third or fourth stride, and, for all I know, that may be true. I ran straight up the right-hand wheel rut in the road, ran until my temples pounded and my eyes pulsed in their sockets, ran until I had a hot stitch in my left side from the bottom of my ribs to my armpit, ran until I could taste blood and something like metal shavings in the back of my throat. When I couldn't run anymore I stumbled to a stop and looked back over my shoulder, puffing and blowing like a wind-broken horse. I was convinced I would see him standing right there behind me in his natty black suit, the watch chain a glittering loop across his vest and not a hair out of place.

But he was gone. The road stretching back toward Castle Stream between the darkly massed pines and spruces was empty. And yet I sensed him somewhere near in those woods, watching me with his grassfire eyes, smelling of burned matches and roasted fish.

I turned and began walking as fast as I could, limping a little—I'd pulled muscles in both legs, and when I got out of bed the next morning I was so sore I could barely walk. I kept looking over my shoulder, needing again and again to verify that the road behind me was still empty. It was each time I looked, but those backward glances seemed to increase my fear rather than lessen it. The firs looked darker, massier, and I kept imagining what lay behind the trees that marched beside the road—long, tangled corridors of forest, leg-breaking deadfalls, ravines where anything might live. Until that Saturday in 1914, I had thought that bears were the worst thing the forest could hold.

A mile or so farther up the road, just beyond the place where it came out of the woods and joined the Geegan Flat Road, I saw my father walking toward me and whistling "The Old Oaken Bucket." He was carrying his own rod, the one with the fancy spinning reel from Monkey Ward. In his other hand he had his creel, the one with the ribbon my mother had woven through the handle back when Dan was still alive. "Dedicated to Jesus" that ribbon said. I had been walking, but when I saw him I started to run again, screaming *Dad! Dad! Dad!* at the top of my lungs and staggering from side to side on my tired, sprung legs like a drunken sailor. The expression of surprise on his face when he recognized me might have been comical under other circumstances. He dropped his rod and creel into the road without so much as a downward glance at them and ran to me. It was the fastest I ever saw my dad run in his life; when we came together it was a wonder the impact didn't knock us both senseless, and I struck my face on his belt buckle hard enough to start a little nosebleed. I didn't notice that until later, though. Right then I only reached out my arms and clutched him as hard as I could. I held on and rubbed my hot face back and forth against his belly, covering his old blue workshirt with blood and tears and snot.

"Gary, what is it? What happened? Are you all right?"

"Ma's dead!" I sobbed. "I met a man in the woods and he told me! Ma's dead! She got stung by a bee and it swelled her all up just like what happened to Dan, and she's dead! She's on the kitchen floor and Candy Bill . . . licked the t-t-tears . . . off her . . . off her . . ."

Face was the last word I had to say, but by then my chest was hitching so bad I couldn't get it out. My own tears were flowing again, and my dad's startled, frightened face had blurred into three overlapping images. I began to howl—not like a little kid who's skinned his knee but like a dog that's seen something bad by moonlight—and my father pressed my head against his hard flat stomach again. I slipped out from under his hand, though, and looked back over my shoulder. I wanted to make sure the man in the black suit wasn't coming. There was no sign of him; the road winding back into the woods was completely empty. I promised myself I would never go back down that road again, not ever, no matter what, and I suppose now that God's greatest blessing to His creatures below is that they can't see the future. It might have broken my mind if I had known I *would* be going back down that road, and not two hours later. For that moment, though, I was only relieved to see we were still alone. Then I thought of my mother—my beautiful dead mother—and laid my face back against my father's stomach and bawled some more.

"Gary, listen to me," he said a moment or two later. I went on bawling. He gave me a little longer to do that, then reached down and lifted my chin so he could look down into my face and I could look up into his. "Your mom's fine," he said.

I could only look at him with tears streaming down my cheeks. I didn't believe him.

"I don't know who told you different, or what kind of dirty dog would want to put a scare like that into a little boy, but I swear to God your mother's fine."

"But . . . but he said . . ."

"I don't care *what* he said. I got back from Eversham's earlier than I expected—he doesn't want to sell any cows, it's all just talk—and decided I had time to catch up with you. I got my pole and my creel and your mother made us a couple of jelly fold-overs. Her new bread. Still warm. So she was fine half an hour ago, Gary, and there's nobody knows any different that's come from this direction, I guarantee you. Not in just half an hour's time." He looked over my shoulder. "Who was this man? And where was he? I'm going to find him and thrash him within an inch of his life."

I thought a thousand things in just two seconds—that's what it seemed like, anyway—but the last thing I thought was the most powerful: if my Dad met up with the man in the black suit, I didn't think my Dad would be the one to do the thrashing. Or the walking away.

I kept remembering those long white fingers, and the talons at the ends of them.

"Gary?"

"I don't know that I remember," I said.

"Were you where the stream splits? The big rock?"

I could never lie to my father when he asked a direct question—not to save his life or mine. "Yes, but don't go down there." I seized his arm with both hands and tugged it hard. "Please don't. He was a scary man." Inspiration struck like an illuminating lightning bolt. "I think he had a gun."

He looked at me thoughtfully. "Maybe there wasn't a man," he said, lifting his voice a little on the last word and turning it into something that was almost but not quite a question. "Maybe you fell asleep while you were fishing, son, and had a bad dream. Like the ones you had about Danny last winter."

I *had* had a lot of bad dreams about Dan last winter, dreams where I would open the door to our closet or to the dark, fruity interior of the cider shed and see him standing there and looking at me out of his purple strangulated face; from many of these dreams I had awakened screaming, and awakened my parents as well. I had fallen asleep on the bank of the stream for a little while, too—dozed off, anyway—but I hadn't dreamed, and I was sure I had awakened just before the man in the black suit clapped the bee dead, sending it tumbling off my nose and into my lap. I hadn't dreamed him the way I had dreamed Dan, I was quite sure of that, although my meeting with him had already attained a dreamlike quality in my mind, as I suppose supernatural occurrences always must. But if my Dad thought that the man had only existed in my own head, that might be better. Better for him.

"It might have been, I guess," I said.

"Well, we ought to go back and find your rod and your creel."

He actually started in that direction, and I had to tug frantically at his arm to stop him again and turn him back toward me.

"Later," I said. "Please, Dad? I want to see Mother. I've got to see her with my own eyes."

He thought that over, then nodded. "Yes, I suppose you do. We'll go home first, and get your rod and creel later."

So we walked back to the farm together, my father with his fish pole propped on his shoulder just like one of my friends, me carrying his creel, both of us eating folded-over slices of my mother's bread smeared with blackcurrant jam.

"Did you catch anything?" he asked as we came in sight of the barn.

"Yes, sir," I said. "A rainbow. Pretty good-sized." *And a brookie that was a lot bigger,* I thought but didn't say.

"That's all? Nothing else?"

"After I caught it I fell asleep." This was not really an answer but not really a lie, either.

"Lucky you didn't lose your pole. You didn't, did you, Gary?"

"No, sir," I said, very reluctantly. Lying about that would do no good even if I'd been able to think up a whopper—not if he was set on going back to get my creel anyway, and I could see by his face that he was.

Up ahead, Candy Bill came racing out of the back door, barking his shrill bark and wagging his whole rear end back and forth the way Scotties do when they're excited. I couldn't wait any longer. I broke away from my father and ran to the house, still lugging his creel and still convinced, in my heart of hearts, that I was going to find my mother dead on the kitchen floor with her face swollen and purple, as Dan's had been when my father carried him in from the west field, crying and calling the name of Jesus.

But she was standing at the counter, just as well and fine as when I had left her, humming a song as she shelled peas into a bowl. She looked around at me, first in surprise and then in fright as she took in my wide eyes and pale cheeks.

"Gary, what is it? What's the matter?"

I didn't answer, only ran to her and covered her with kisses. At some point my father came in and said, "Don't worry, Lo—he's all right. He just had one of his bad dreams, down there by the brook."

"Pray God it's the last of them," she said, and hugged me tighter while Candy Bill danced around our feet, barking his shrill bark.

"You don't have to come with me if you don't want to, Gary," my father said, although he had already made it clear that he thought I should—that I should go back, that I should face my fear, as I suppose folks would say nowadays. That's very well for fearful things that are make-believe, but two hours hadn't done much to change my conviction that the man in the black suit had been real. I wouldn't be able to convince my father of that, though. I don't think there was a nine-year-old who ever lived would have been able to convince his father he'd seen the Devil walking out of the woods in a black suit.

"I'll come," I said. I had come out of the house to join him before he left, mustering all my courage to get my feet moving, and now we were standing by the chopping block in the side yard, not far from the woodpile.

"What you got behind your back?" he asked.

I brought it out slowly. I would go with him, and I would hope the man in the black suit with the arrow-straight part down the left side of his head was gone. But if he wasn't, I wanted to be prepared. As prepared as I could be, anyway. I had the family Bible in the hand I had brought out from behind my back. I'd set out just to bring my New Testament, which I had won for memorizing the most psalms in the Thursday-night Youth Fellowship competition (I managed eight, although most of them except the Twenty-third had floated out of my mind in a week's time), but the little red Testament didn't seem like enough when you were maybe going to face the Devil himself, not even when the words of Jesus were marked out in red ink.

My father looked at the old Bible, swollen with family documents and pictures, and I thought he'd tell me to put it back, but he didn't. A look of mixed grief and sympathy crossed his face, and he nodded. "All right," he said. "Does your mother know you took that?"

"No, sir."

He nodded again. "Then we'll hope she doesn't spot it gone before we get back. Come on. And don't drop it."

Half an hour or so later, the two of us stood on the bank at the place where Castle Stream forked, and at the flat place where I'd had my encounter with the man with the red-orange eyes. I had my bamboo rod in my hand—I'd picked it up below the bridge—and my creel lay down below, on the flat place. Its wicker top was flipped back. We stood looking down, my father and I, for a long time, and neither of us said anything.

Opal! Diamond! Sapphire! Jade! I smell Gary's lemonade! That had been his unpleasant little poem, and once he had recited it, he had thrown himself on his back, laughing like a child who has just discovered he has enough courage to say bathroom words like shit or piss. The flat place down there was as green and lush as any place in Maine that the sun can get to in early July. Except where the stranger had lain. There the grass was dead and yellow in the shape of a man.

I was holding our lumpy old family Bible straight out in front of me with both thumbs pressing so hard on the cover that they were white. It was the way Mama Sweet's husband, Norville, held a willow fork when he was trying to dowse somebody a well.

"Stay here," my father said at last, and skidded sideways down the bank, digging his shoes into the rich soft soil and holding his arms out for balance. I stood where I was, holding the Bible stiffly out at the ends of my arms, my heart thumping. I don't know if I had a sense of being watched that time or not; I was too scared to have a sense of anything, except for a sense of wanting to be far away from that place and those woods.

My dad bent down, sniffed at where the grass was dead, and grimaced. I knew what he was smelling: something like burnt matches. Then he grabbed my creel and came on back up the bank, hurrying. He snagged one fast look over his shoulder to make sure nothing was coming along behind. Nothing was. When he handed me the creel, the lid was still hanging back on its cunning little leather hinges. I looked inside and saw nothing but two handfuls of grass.

"Thought you said you caught a rainbow," my father said, "but maybe you dreamed that, too."

Something in his voice stung me. "No, sir," I said. "I caught one."

"Well, it sure as hell didn't flop out, not if it was gutted and cleaned. And you wouldn't put a catch into your fisherbox without doing that, would you, Gary? I taught you better than that."

"Yes, sir, you did, but—"

"So if you didn't dream catching it and if it was dead in the box, something must have come along and eaten it," my father said, and then he grabbed another quick glance over his shoulder, eyes wide, as if he had heard something move in the woods. I wasn't exactly surprised to see drops of sweat standing out on his forehead like big clear jewels. "Come on," he said. "Let's get the hell out of here."

I was for that, and we went back along the bank to the bridge, walking quick without speaking. When we got there, my dad dropped to one knee and examined the place where we'd found my rod. There was another patch of dead grass there, and the lady's slipper was all brown and curled in on itself, as if a blast of heat had charred it. I looked in my empty creel again. "He must have gone back and eaten my other fish, too," I said.

My father looked up at me. "*Other* fish!"

"Yes, sir. I didn't tell you, but I caught a brookie, too. A big one. He was awful hungry, that fella." I wanted to say more, and the words trembled just behind my lips, but in the end I didn't.

We climbed up to the bridge and helped each other over the railing. My father took my creel, looked into it, then went to the railing and threw it over. I came up beside him in time to see it splash down and float away like a boat, riding lower and lower in the stream as the water poured in between the wicker weavings.

"It smelled bad," my father said, but he didn't look at me when he said it, and his voice sounded oddly defensive. It was the only time I ever heard him speak just that way.

"Yes, sir."

"We'll tell your mother we couldn't find it. If she asks. If she doesn't ask, we won't tell her anything."

"No, sir, we won't."

And she didn't and we didn't, and that's the way it was.

That day in the woods is eighty years gone, and for many of the years in between I have never even thought of it—not awake, at least. Like any other man or woman who ever lived, I can't say about my dreams, not for sure. But now I'm old, and I dream awake, it seems. My infirmities have crept up like waves that will soon take a child's abandoned sand castle, and my memories have also crept up, making me think of some old rhyme that went, in part, "Just leave them alone / And they'll come home / Wagging their tails behind them." I remember meals I ate, games I played, girls I kissed in the school cloakroom when we played post office, boys I chummed with, the first drink I ever took, the first cigarette I ever smoked (cornshuck behind Dicky Hamner's pig shed, and I threw up). Yet of all the memories the one of the man in the black suit is the strongest, and glows with its own spectral, haunted light. He was real, he was the Devil, and that day I was either his errand or his luck. I feel more and more strongly that escaping him was my luck—*just* luck, and not the intercession of the God I have worshiped and sung hymns to all my life.

As I lie here in my nursing-home room, and in the ruined sand castle that is my body, I tell myself that I need not fear the Devil—that I have lived a good, kindly life, and I need not fear the Devil. Sometimes I remind myself that it was I, not my father, who finally coaxed my mother back to church later on that summer. In the dark, however, these thoughts have no power to ease or comfort. In the dark comes a voice that whispers that the nine-year-old fisherboy I was had done nothing for which he might legitimately fear the Devil, either, and yet the Devil came—to him. And in the dark I sometimes hear that voice drop even lower, into ranges that are inhuman. *Big fish!* it whispers in tones of hushed greed, and all the truths of the moral world fall to ruin before its hunger.

"IN THE TRADITION . . ."

Michael Swanwick

Michael Swanwick's work in the speculative fiction field has been published to increasing acclaim since his debut—with *In the Drift*—in Terry Carr's Ace Science Fiction Specials series. He has since been nominated for the Nebula, Hugo, and World Fantasy Awards. His stunning new Dickensian fantasy novel, *The Iron Dragon's Daughter,* is at the cutting edge of the fantasy field, and highly recommended.

In the following nonfiction piece, Swanwick is our tour guide through the modern fantasy genre. Thought provoking and informative, the essay is as beautifully penned as any of the works lauded therein.

Swanwick lives in Philadelphia, Pennsylvania.

—T. W.

And so we set sail.

The green hills and haunted mountains of Middle Earth sink into the sea behind us. They are beauteous and filled with wonder, but already our attention is elsewhere. Our eyes strain ahead, searching for the mysterious islands that have called us away from our hearths and hobbit-holes, away from the comfortable and familiar. A fresh breeze parts the mists like curtains. The keel bites into iron-cold waters. Our ship leaps forward.

We are bound for the Fantasy Archipelago.

There was a time not many decades past when fantasy was not the prosperous marketing category it is today or even a marketing category it is today or even a marketing category at all. Indeed, fantasy of any description was as rare as griffins. Fantasy writers routinely disguised their work as historicals or Arthuriana or (with the addition of a quickly forgotten spaceport or two) science fiction, or else they didn't get published at all.

J. R. R. Tolkien changed all that. The American paperbacks of his *Lord of the Rings* trilogy hit the publishing industry with the force of revelation. They either created or demonstrated the existence of (accounts vary) an enormous audience for fantasy. They made a lot of money. Publishers, many of them perilously close to being entirely without a clue, scrambled to find something, anything, to fill this previously unsuspected appetite.

In the aftermath, there was a blurb often seen bannered above the title of that occasional fantasy hastily resurrected and thrown back into print by a bewildered editor who could think of no way else to describe it: IN THE TRADITION it read OF ROBERT E. HOWARD AND J. R. R. TOLKIEN!

At the time I thought this was the single worst description of a book ever attempted. Howard's and Tolkien's universes are, to understate the obvious, mutually exclusive. The image of that mighty-thewed barbarian, Conan, sometime yclept the Warrior, the Avenger, the Buccaneer, and the Conqueror, striding through the Shire to crush the settees and jeweled umbrella stands of the Sackville-Bagginses under his sandaled feet seemed to me irresistibly comic, the stuff of a Monty Python routine.

But age softens the hasty judgments of youth. A quarter-century later, I've come around to the side of that anonymous editorial drudge and decided he was right after all, that all my favorite works of fantasy are indeed In The Tradition of Robert E. Howard and J. R. R. Tolkien. Which is to say that they are each no more like the other than Gandalf the Grey is akin to Red Sonja. They are chimeras, *sui generis*, unique.

I'm going to write about what Tove Jansson called "the lonely and the rum," the unschoolable and ungroupable, those strange and shaggy literary creatures that have no ilk or kin and that mathematically can be contained in no set smaller than the set of all sets contained in no other sets. For ease of argument, I'm going to call this congeries of works *hard fantasy*, because I honestly believe that it holds a central place in its genre analogous to the place hard science fiction holds in SF.

Our voyage will be treacherous, for the waters are uncharted and by the very nature of our quest many an important work will be ignored entirely. It is possible, too, that we shall occasionally land on what only appears to be an island. These are Faerie isles, after all, and some that seem solid now may turn to whales or mist in the morning. But the danger is justified not only by the beauty and wonder of our destinations, but because these are the works that drive fantasy, the source and justification for the entire genre, the engine that burns at the heart of its star.

Which is not to imply that there is anything wrong with the mighty continents of High Fantasy or of Mannerism or of Celtic Twilight or of Urban Fantasy or even of Mainstream. Shakespeare is a fine fellow in his place. But his place is not here.

White water hisses in our wake. From the crow's nest our elven lookout cries in a voice high and clear as that of a seabird. Everyone not engaged with the ropes or rudder rushes to the starboard rail to follow his pointing finger. Land!

Rising from the water before us are a triplet of isles: E. R. Eddison's Zimiamvian trilogy, *Mistress of Mistresses*, *A Fish Dinner in Memison*, and *The Mezentian Gate*. *The Worm Ouroboros*, often represented as being the first book in the sequence, is seriously flawed, only peripherally related, and is best read last, as a mantissa. The trilogy itself, however, is strong drink for connoisseurs of highly wrought prose. Eddison was a British career civil servant and these books contain the world he would rather have been born into, an alchemical marriage of the Renaissance and Middle Ages as they should have been, compounded of great passions, Elizabethan rhetoric, and genuine erotic feeling. Elizabeth Willey has characterized these books as "Tolkien with sex," but they might equally well be described as "Howard with politesse." They are In The Tradition.

Nor are they alone. More islands lift their heads from the sea, one after the other, misty with distance but rich with strange pleasures: Mervyn Peake's *Gormenghast* trilogy; Lord Dunsany's more-than-lapidarian tales of the Gods of Pegana and the lands Beyond the Fields We Know; Clark Ashton Smith's misanthropic explorations of Zothique, Hyperborea, and Poseidonis; James Branch Cabell's *Jurgen* and select other books; and Hope Mirlees's singular and incomparable *Lud-in-the-Mist*, which Neil Gaiman has noted deals with the central issue of the genre, "the reconciliation of the fantastic and the mundane."

This is a motley and argumentative crew to put into one boat. Tolkien disdained Dunsany, Cabell despised the critics, and Smith loathed the human race at large. Hard fantasy creates its own ancestors and antecedents, and it's doubtful that it would alter one word of any of the above works had the others never existed at all. But they belong with each other for the simple reason that they belong nowhere else.

Again the lookout shouts! We have come upon our first contemporary example of hard fantasy.

It is John Crowley's *Little, Big*.

Like most of the works I am anxious to discuss here, *Little, Big* is difficult to summarize. For an instant our task seems horribly daunting: We stand like children at the edge of the dark Wood and we know there are wolves within, witches mad for our flesh, and stranger things besides that are resistant to being put into words. Somewhere in the night an ogre chuckles.

Like children, we cannot resist going just a little deeper in.

Little, Big is a sort of family chronicle, a swirl of relationships radiating backward and forward in time, but always returning to Smoky Barnable and his son Auberon. Smoky, a quiet cipher of a man, falls in love with Daily Alice of the extensive Drinkwater clan, who cures him of anonymity and gives him a place in what her family calls the Tale. He comes to Edgewood, the Drinkwater folly, to marry her, and in an old volume titled *Upstate Houses and Their Histories*, makes a disquieting discovery:

> And here was a photograph of two people sitting at a stone table, having tea. There was a man who looked like the poet Yeats, in a pale summer suit and spotted tie, his hair full and white, his eyes obscured by the sunlight glinting from his spectacles; and a younger woman in a wide white hat, her dark features shaded by the hat and blurred perhaps by a sudden movement. Behind them was part of this house Smoky sat in, and beside them, reaching up a tiny hand to the woman, who perhaps saw it and moved to take it and then again perhaps not (it was hard to tell), was a figure, personage, a little creature about a foot high in conical hat and pointed shoes. His broad inhuman features seemed blurred too by sudden movement, and he appeared to bear a pair of gauzy insect wings. The caption read "John Drinkwater and Mrs. Drinkwater (Violet Bramble); elf. Edgewood, 1912."

Disquieting, but not exactly proof of anything. The reader is left in a position similar to Smoky's, knowing that there is some family connection to the Little People (early on, Daily Alice goes to a pool to ask advice of Grandfather Trout, who unequivocally speaks to her), but never—until the end—clear as to the nature of that connection.

Though he brushes up against it from time to time, Smoky is forever an outsider to the strangeness. He can never truly be a member of the family, for he simply cannot bring himself to believe in fairies. This alienation he inadvertently passes on to his son.

Little, Big opens with Smoky's pilgrimage into the Tale. Auberon makes his first appearance as an adult, when he goes to the City in a vain attempt to escape it. But for all the coziness of their early manifestations, there are large and dangerous forces astir. A vitality is being leached from the decaying world. The City settles into an endless recession. Eternal winter looms. Almost incidentally, Auberon undergoes a corresponding deterioration. Whatever is going on, Auberon is firmly ensnared in its workings.

It is an extreme set of daring that Crowley has performed here. He has crafted a work of contemporary adult literature from the Matter of fairy tales and nursery rhymes. (His debt is acknowledged with nods to Milne, Lofting, Burgess, Carroll, MacDonald, Lewis, and other authors from that great continent of children's fantasy that lies east of the sun, west of the moon, and beyond this essay's purview entirely.*) That he pulls it off at all is nothing short of miraculous. But the greatest single accomplishment of *Little, Big* is how it manages to be consistently fey and homely both, without ever once falling over that razor-edged precipice into the abyss of the twee.

Crowley's book is backward-turning, nostalgic, and tinted in the hues of a nineteenth-century chromo. But I would not have you believe that hard fantasy never boogies to the intellectual beat of the day.

With the ascendance of the information economy over manufacturing and the ensuing rise of semiotics (for each new ruling elite requires theoretical validation), has come a corresponding need to rewrite intellectual history. Medieval Scholasticism, neglected for centuries, has made a resurgence; Giordano Bruno—conveniently martyred by the Church for sins of intellectual hubris—has been grandfathered in as an ancestral figure; and the protoscience of alchemy is looked at afresh not as the progenitor of chemistry or as a spiritual endeavor, but as an occult mental discipline whose chief purpose is the ordering and describing of the universe.

Thus, Mary Gentle's *Rats and Gargoyles*.

In the alchemical world of *Rats and Gargoyles*, triangles have four sides and

---

*As does the somewhat smaller continent of young adult fantasy, any discussion of which must surely include Michael de Larrabeiti's "Borrible" books, Alan Garner's *The Weirdstone of Brisingamen*, and the collected works of Diana Wynne Jones, as well as border-adult fantasies such as Patricia A. McKillip's *The Forgotten Beasts of Eld*, to say nothing of . . . Oh God, no. No, no, no, no, no. This is too much. This is madness. Somebody else will have to write that neverending essay. Not me.

squares have five. Humans are an underclass, forbidden to carry weapons or money, ruled by an aristocracy of Rats. Who in turn are subject to the whims of winged monstrosities in the service of twenty-four Decans, the creators and maintainers of the universe, incarnate in an immense cathedral. "We have strange masters" is a byword in the city known only as the Heart of the World.

Indeed. Nor does the strangeness stop there. This is a world in which rulers send their heirs to study at the University of Crime. Where a mysterious black Boat carries the dead back to life. Where the Katayan people have long, prehensile tails. Where flash cameras and mechanical computers coexist with swordplay. We're definitely not in Kansas anymore.

The organizing principle for all this is alchemy, and the narrative strategy is confusion. The alchemy, I suspect, is more a source of imagery than a rigidly enforced system. The confusion is deliberate, a result of the decision to show everything and explain nothing, so that the reader is inevitably a step or two behind the characters at all times. But not entirely in the dark—comprehension is arrived at in retrospect, after the fact. The reader is put in the position of that bird which, flying backward, knows not where it's going but only where it's been.

The *events* of the novel concern a snarl of conspiracies, plots, and blind attempts to stave off disaster. There are at least six factions in play, each with its own agenda. Trying to ride the gathering storm are the White Crow (a Soldier-Adept of the Invisible College), the master architect and comic slob Casaubon, a distinctly Delanyesque young woman whose eidetic gift makes her a King's Memory, and a student prince in commoner's guise, among others. There are dozens of distinct and individually motivated characters, all working at cross purposes.

All the old, familiar pleasures of the genre are here in the double-handfuls: High-rhetoricked, sword-carrying lords, a warrior in crimson armor, romantic sexual liaisons, and dark gods in Leiberesque profusion. But the lords are Rats, the warrior and her seducer both women, the gods ultimately not terribly sinister. There is a constant confounding of expectations in big and little ways throughout. As when disgruntled laborers plan their resistance:

> This ziggurat will rise between two pyramidical obelisks that are equal in thickness to the building itself. A mile away an identical pair of obelisks arises, completed two generations ago. Great hieroglyphs are burned into their stone sides. This burning of stone happened during an eclipse of the sun that lasted four days.
>
> "No. We don't wait." This speaker is the most assured. "You're right: they need us to build, because they can't. So—"
>
> "If we stop work, they'll kill enough of us that the rest will go back to work. We've tried that before."
>
> To north and east and aust of the ziggurat, more of the Fane's perpendicular frontages cut the sky. Here, the sky itself is the color of ashes.
>
> "They can force us to work," the first speaker says, "but who can force a man to eat or to sleep?"

Which is not how job actions work in *our* world.

In the end alchemy makes a wonderfully convenient system for what Gentle is doing here: questioning the nature of genre fantasy and challenging the assumptions underlying its appeal while taking full advantage of their power.

William Gibson once remarked that William S. Burroughs, of *Naked Lunch* and *Nova Express* fame, was the first writer to treat science fiction like a rusty egg-beater, something he could pick up and use as a found object in his own art. Gentle here is engaged in a quieter version of the same game, retooled for fantasy. The trademark characteristics of postmodern fiction, it has been much remarked, are pastiche and appropriation. And *Rats and Gargoyles* is—never doubt it—a distinctly postmodern work. Whether anybody deigns to follow or not, it is one of several works that point out a totally new direction for the genre to take.

Running close by the coast of Science Fiction under cover of darkness, we douse the running lights and break out rifles for the crew. We are in disputed waters here, and despite the fact that it won a World Fantasy Award, not everyone would agree that Geoff Ryman's *The Unconquered Country* lies within our territory.

The single most vivid and horrific moment in Ryman's novella (for it is a brief work, though packaged as a stand-alone volume) comes right at the beginning. It's a description of what Third Child, the protagonist, must do to survive. Here's the gist of it:

> Third rented her womb for industrial use. She was cheaper than the glass tanks. She grew parts of living machinery inside her—differentials for trucks, small household appliances. . . . When Third was lucky, she got a contract for weapons. The pay was good because it was dangerous. The weapons would come gushing suddenly out of her with much loss of blood, usually in the middle of the night: an avalanche of glossy, freckled, dark brown guppies with black, soft eyes and bright rodent smiles full of teeth. No matter how ill or exhausted Third felt, she would shovel them, immediately, into buckets and tie down the lids. If she didn't do that, immediately, if she fell asleep, the guppies would eat her.

Nothing that follows rises to such appalling heights (thank goodness), but the tone has been set. *The Unconquered Country* is a fantasy treatment of the recent genocidal history of Cambodia and of what Ryman has termed "the blasting of culture, the homogenization of the world," merged into one grim fable. These are not easy things to read about, and I wonder whether I would have finished the book had it been nonfiction or even "straight" fiction? Some nightmare truths come perilously close to being not only unbearable but untellable.

A land known to Third only as the Neighbors has done the unthinkable and, aided by the Big Country, conquered her homeland, the Unconquered Country. The war as perceived by a back country peasant is sketched out in quick strokes: The houses of a village attacked by flying Sharks panic and stampede. A dead suitor returns in the form of a crow to protect and comfort Third. Delicate life-saving devices, evicted from a hospital, plead with soldiers not to be destroyed.

The ultimate enemy of the People, however, is not the Neighbors or even their (American) sponsors, but something less tangible and harder to fight: the cultural Holocaust of the twentieth century. When the rebels finally win back their country, they are no longer People. The Unconquered Country is an imaginary land with invented customs and a make-believe culture. No reader, however, will mistake its climactic scenes for anything but the forced evacuation of Phnom Penh by the Khmer Rouge. The rebels in victory have become yet another set of aliens.

This work is no mere allegory, however, or facile conceptualization. It is a genuinely moving human-scale story. Ryman's central achievement is that the events are all seen through the eyes of a traditional peasant woman, and that this is done without condescension or false sentiment. He writes of Third as you or I would of a member of our own family, with respect and the occasional touch of exasperation.

I implied earlier that *The Unconquered Country* might easily be read as science fiction. Everything in it could be justified by speculative science—bioengineering, nanotechnology, and the rest of the conceptual tool kit. I've seen less plausible in works proudly labeled "hard SF." But the mere presence of machinery (though viewed with keen suspicion in the provinces) does not invalidate a work as fantasy. And the truth here is that this is not a work concerned with the uses to which human beings put technology. Rather it's an examination of what happens to a culture that has been passed through Hell.

In the end, after the horror, *The Unconquered Country* is not about war, atrocity, genocide, or the destruction of cultures. It is about what comes after: What remains untouched, what is of value, and what endures.

Terry Bisson's *Talking Man* must be the only fantasy in existence which contains a careful description of the workings of a hand-clutch John Deere "A" tractor. It's a good description, too. Bisson has worked as an auto mechanic. He knows machines.

Here's how it starts:

> There are two ways to tell a wizard. One is by the blue light that plays around his tires when he is heading north on wet pavement under the northern lights, his headlights pointed toward the top of the world that so many talk about but so few have actually seen.
>
> The other is by his singing.
>
> Talking Man was a wizard who had a small junkyard on the side of a hill on the Kentucky Tennessee line. He sold parts and cars, swapped guns and cars, fixed farm machinery and cars, dug ginseng and may-apple in season, and had a 1,100-pound allotment of burley tobacco which he let his daughter raise. He kept no chickens, no hogs and no dogs.

The ironically named (he never speaks) Talking Man is a wizard from the end of time. He continually dreams the world into being. He is the sole guardian of existence from the all-negating blight of "the unbeen." He lives in a trailer with his sixteen-year-old daughter Crystal.

Mostly, though, he's a hell of a mechanic. "He could take the knock out of a poured-bearing Chevrolet with a set of ⅜-inch sockets and a wood file in an afternoon; he could free a stuck valve by pouring pond water through a carburetor, set points with cigarette papers, and sharpen a chainsaw without a file by passing the bar through a green-persimmon fire and singing a certain unhearable, to most people, song." (I had a mechanic like that once, and I live to find his equal.)

The unbeen was dreamed up by Talking Man's sister and creation and lover (it's nothing if not lonely at the end of time) Dgene. One day she arrives to unsettle his life and undo all of creation. He steals a car and flees.

The car is stolen from one William Tilden Henricks Williams, a dreamer and dropout who is first seen squandering the limited inheritance that was optimistically supposed to get him through law school on an arcade game called Missile Command. Williams and Crystal hit the road, looking for her father, looking for Williams's cousin's car (it's borrowed), looking for answers. Mostly they hit the road because they're at that age when it seems the reasonable thing to do.

Thus begins a car chase to the North Pole and Edminidine, the city at the top of the world. Along the way Bisson explains how to grow tobacco, the true character of Owensboro, and how to heal a punctured oil pan with blood sacrifice.

The chase is beside the point, really. The very best parts of *Talking Man* are all about cars, country life, and those parts of the continent where most writers never go. Particularly Bisson knows Kentucky and points west, landscapes, saints and yahoos included, and can write about them without hysteria or sentimentality. Even in those transformed passages where Illinois has mountains and the Mississippi lies at the bottom of a canyon six miles wide and a thousand feet deep, the text is radiant with his familiarity with and love for nonurban, non-Coastal America.

In one important way, this novel is precursor to the author's acclaimed "Bears Discover Fire." Here for the first time, Bisson found his voice, a gentle Kentucky diction that is at times as smooth and potent as the finest sipping bourbon.

The mythological underpinning—with its brother-and-sister wizards, a city at one end of time and a tower at the other, and so on—is unquestionably high fantasy. Instead of working with the received set of crofts, castles, and cryptic ruins, however, Bisson has created a world out of Exxon stations, Chryslers, and 7-Elevens. As a result *Talking Man* completely transcends its sources.

It's an amazing demonstration of what power there is to be found by rethinking the basics.

Bisson lives in New York City and his novel is an exemplar of the expatriate's love for lands left behind. Rebecca Ore is a native and current inhabitant of Critz (it rhymes with "heights"), Virginia, who once left for Bohemia and the Big Apple but later returned home to stay. Her love for the South in general and the Blue Ridge foothills region in particular is equally genuine but distinctly qualified. As is amply demonstrated by *Slow Funeral*, her fifth novel and first fantasy.

Maude Fuller is a witch, hiding from her inherited powers in Berkeley, California, faking psychosis to obtain welfare, and living in a commune of witch wannabes for camouflage. Her grandmother, Partridge, is dying, however, and just as she gets involved with an interesting man—an engineer—Maude is called back to Bracken County to watch over Partridge's death. Not coincidentally, she must also face up to the temptation to seize the magic that is her birthright.

The magic is embedded in the county's bedrock micro-plate, the Bracken County allochthon, an anomalous visitor to North America from 600 million years ago, rich in the iron-alumina-silicate crystals that Virginians call "fairystones." It manifests itself as capricious discorporate entities that only select individuals can use and be used by. And it is weakened by logic and rational thought:

> Mid October was the season of the last overflights with National Guardsmen and the sheriff's deputies looking for drug patches. Most older Bracken County people hated having the helicopters overhead because that much unadapted machinery in the air spread logic all over the place and killed magic. Even people who didn't rely on entities allied themselves to people who did, made secondary use of the magic. But the children looked around when the machines flew. Freed of a compulsion to stay in the county and fetch and carry for someone powerful, some local kids from the powerless classes joined the military under the protection of its vast machines, the helicopters, the jets from Norfolk that flew practice bombing runs against the high school, afterburner booms canceling a teacher's drone forever. And left, got educated, and never came back.

Most of us think it would be pretty darned Neat if magic really existed. Maude knows better. Magic is inherently cruel. A world in which some people can make deals with the universe and others can't inevitably leads to a social order in which the elite believe that owning people is an absolute right.

You'll be wondering by now how open magic-working (including compulsions, mutilations, and an entire research institute housed in the back of a pickup truck) is supposed to be kept secret. It isn't. One of the best-reasoned elements of *Slow Funeral* is that everybody in the county knows the score, and nobody pretends otherwise. But it's understood that spilling the beans will do no good whatsoever. After all, what cosmopolitan in his right mind is going to listen to a bunch of hick Southerners?

Maude's engineer, Doug, follows her to Bracken County. But the logic she was counting on bolstering her has completely abandoned him. Disgusted by his own labor because it is used to "empower inferior people," he longs for magic, thinking it just another technology he can learn and master. He doesn't realize that magic cannot be learned. That by surrendering his status as a member of the technological elite he's made himself one of the inferiors. That he's just become a victim.

Maude struggles to protect herself, save her feckless engineer, and help Partridge to an easy death by keeping her Aunt Betty from eating the old woman's soul. In the course of which she pieces a quilt, takes Doug to a "chicken fight" (locals don't say "cock" in public), flirts with a homicidal handgun, engages in family politics, and observes the social mores of her part of the world.

It is here that Ore shines, in her observations of the complex interrelationships between blacks and whites, between fundamentalists and nonbelievers, between those who own and those who are owned. She is particularly good with the ruthless politeness that in the South hides bitter truths, and the blind obligations that bind person to person. Especially within families. As any matriarch will tell you, just because a relative is plotting to kill you and eat your soul doesn't get you out of Sunday dinner at her house.

There are expectations to be upheld.

* * *

A silent shadow slips over our ship. The crew stare upward with wonder and some little fear. For topping the craggy cliffs of the nearest island is that grim and endlessly rising castle named Gormenghast. Here is one of the great eccentricities of English literature, a more-than-Gothic construct builded upon three books. *Titus Groan* and *Gormenghast* are both set in that pocket universe, vast and rambling, ruled by tradition and inertia, a treasure-box of repressed and stunted souls. Within are such vividly warped caricatures of humanity as Charles Dickens might have penned in a sour mood. Even their names—Slagg, Barquentine, Flay, Swelter, Sepulchrave—seem little more than flakes chipped from the great stones of Gormenghast.

Yet, paradoxically, when the gloriously villainous Steerpike threatens the social order, the reader is not on his side. And when the monstrously large Gertrude, Countess of Groan, trailed always by a white froth of cats, heavy and abstracted, the very soul of Gormenghast, awakens to the presence of an enemy in the castle, even the dullest spirit must experience a thrill of excitement.

Titus Alone, the third book, is by contrast a lamed thing, for the action takes place outside of Gormenghast, and for all the charming grotesquerie of its characters, it is the castle itself that is the real star of the series. Peake wrote this book while he was dying, and, alas, it shows.

But Peake was not alone in failing to conclude his sequence satisfactorily. E. R. Eddison did not live to complete the third book of his Memison series—the middle chapters of *The Mezentian Gate* exist only in detailed synopses. Avram Davidson failed to finish several multi-volume works. He wrote *The Island Under the Earth* and stopped. He wrote *Peregrine: Primus* and *Peregrine: Secundus*, two-thirds of the funniest fantasy series ever written, but never arrived at *Terces*. He left *The Phoenix and the Mirror*, with its darkly brilliant vision of Virgil not as the poet history knows but the Magus the Middle Ages thought him, at a cliffhanger, abandoned the project for years, and then went on to write a "non-prequel" to the work. Then he died, a brilliant writer, a tragic figure, and all too typical of what fate awaits even the best fantasists.

There sometimes seems a curse on the entire Archipelago, one that takes the form of broken or flawed trilogies. Tolkien was the grand exception in actually completing *The Lord of the Rings*, and by testimony of the decades he later spent tinkering with and never finishing The *Silmarillion* and related fragments, it was a fluke.

So, despite the fact that it is only the first in a sequence of so far three books that has not yet achieved closure, I have no hesitation in commending to your attention as an important and even core work of hard fantasy, Robert Holdstock's *Mythago Wood*.

The protagonist of *Mythago Wood* is a young WWII vet named Steven Huxley. But the central character is Ryhope Wood, "Three square miles of original, post-Ice Age forestland. . . . Resistant to change." There is a strange power to the wood that makes it a sort of psychic vortex. Movement inward toward the heart-woods grows progressively more difficult and finally impossible. And by interaction with the minds of whoever is daring enough to enter Ryhope, the wood throws off what Steven Huxley's late father George dubbed "mythagos."

As Steven's brother Christian explains:

> "..it's in the unconscious that we carry what he calls the pre-mythago—that's *mythimago,* the image of an idealized form of a myth creature. The image takes on a substance in a natural environment, solid flesh, blood, clothing, and—as you saw—weaponry. The form of the idealized myth, the hero figure, alters with cultural changes, assuming the identity and technology of the time. When one culture invades another—according to father's theory—the heroes are made manifest, and not just in one location! Historians and legend-seekers argue about where Arthur of the Britons, and Robin Hood *really* lived and fought, and don't realize that they lived in *many* sites. And another important fact to remember is that when the mind image of the mythago forms, it forms in the *whole* population . . . and when it is no longer needed, it remains in our collective unconscious, and is transmitted through the generations."

The mythagos are a stunning invention, dark and powerful visitors from the Jungian depths. Nearly but not wholly human, they exude a breath of menace and potential violence. Typical of them is the briefly glimpsed Twigling—"a man in brown, leathery clothes, with a wide, gleaming belt around his waist, and a spiky, orange beard that reached to his chest: on his head he wore twigs, held to his crown by a leather band." These are not the special-effects scarecrow myth-figures of mediocre fantasy, but the raw thing, shaggy and dangerous.

Before the book begins, Christian has married and lost a mythago named Guiwenneth, a Roman-era warrior princess archetype and precursor of the later Guenevere. Shot through the eye by a Jack-in-the-green, she died and was buried by her grieving husband alongside the Huxley chicken-huts. But Christian, convinced he can regenerate her, retreats to the woods. Soon he is so deeply embedded in the matrix of power he cannot escape, translated himself more than halfway to the archetypal. His very nature is profoundly changed.

The ley lines of obsession run like fire through *Mythago Wood.* Huxley *pater*'s life had been spent cataloguing the mythagos, identifying the periods that gave rise to them, and through them trying to understand the minds of the peoples of ancient and prehistoric times. The search destroyed his marriage and alienated his sons. Yet he kept notes only sporadically, and never published. The scientific impulse gave way to more primal drives. In the end, he fixated on a single mythago—Guiwenneth. Only to lose her to his son. Who in turn loses her reincarnation to Steven. The relationship between brothers turns murderous.

Of all the books under discussion in this essay, *Mythago Wood* is hands-down the single most gripping. For surface plot alone, it is compulsive reading. But like the wood itself, there are depths here. As the brothers discover, the mythagos are at least partially shaped by unconscious expectations. Christian's Guiwenneth is gentle and unwarlike because his father—who knew her first—could not imagine a violent woman. When Steven first encounters her, she is changed, fiercer, because she has been formed this time by Christian. The father died seeking the Urscumug, the primary archetypal image from which all other forms derive. But when the Urscumug finally appears, its boar's face has painted over it in white clay the features of George Huxley.

There is an intellectual excitement to this work that rivals the more visceral appeals of blood-lust and fratricide. Holdstock takes the fragmentary and contradictory elements of folklore and twists them into a new shape. His characters act out a convincing demonstration of the power and nature of myth and how it shapes and drives the human animal, however sophisticated we believe we are, refuse to acknowledge it how we will. There's no denying that *Mythago Wood* is entertaining, but it is much more as well.

I can think of only two writers who can rival Holdstock in his bred-in-the-bone comprehension of the workings of myth. M. John Harrison in his Viriconium books and Keith Roberts in such works as *Pavane* and *The Chalk Giants* each in his own very different fashion displays a startingly sure understanding of the stuff and nature of myth and its historic foundations. It can scarce be coincidence that all three of these writers are English. In the British Isles, children grow up with stone circles, Roman roads, and ring forts sometimes literally in their back yards. In my darker moments, I sometimes wonder if Americans should give up on writing fantasy altogether.

If there is one commonality among the hard fantasists, it is that they are not a prolific lot. Tanith Lee, however, is prolific. Which makes it hard to single out one work for examination. A survey of her *oeuvre* would necessitate the exclusion of other writers. Nor can she simply be skipped over. She is a Power, and has earned her place here.

I've chosen Lee's Arkham House collection *Dreams of Dark and Light* not only in the name of ruthless simplification but also because it is a rare thing for a hard fantasist to work much in short fiction (novels being the preferred length of eccentricity, and eccentricity being the name of the game) and rarer still for one individual to excel at both lengths.

Here's a quick sampler of what happens in *Dreams of Dark and Light*: A selkie beds a seal-hunter in trade for the pelt of her murdered son. The dying servant of an aged vampire procures for her a new lover. A writer becomes obsessed with a masked woman who may or may not be a gorgon. A young woman rejects comfort, luxury, and the fulfillment of her childhood dreams, for a demon lover. These are specifically adult fictions.

There is more to these stories than the sexual impulse. But I mention its presence because its treatment is never titillating, smirking, or borderline pornographic, as is so much fiction that purports to be erotic. Rather, it is elegant, langorous, and feverish by turns, and always tinged with danger. Which is to say that it is remarkably like the writing itself.

In "Elle Est Trois (La Mort)" three artists—a poet, a painter, a composer—are visited by avatars of Lady Death. The suicidal allure of *la vie de boheme*, with its confusion of death, sex, poverty and the muse, has rarely been so well conveyed as here. The artists are captured as their essences, each courting death in his own way. The composer France unwittingly acknowledges this when he tells his friend Etiens Saint-Beuve, "One day such sketches will be worth sheafs of francs, boxes full of American dollars. When you are safely dead, Etiens, in a pauper's grave."

After France himself has been taken, the poet Armand Valier muses on Death's avatars (the Butcher, the Thief, the Seducer) in Lee's sorcerous prose:

> . . . And then the third means to destruction, the seductive death who visited poets in her irresistible caressing silence, with the petals of blue flowers or the blue wings of insects pasted on the lids of her eyes, and: See, your flesh also, taken to mine, can never decay. And this will be true, for the flesh of Armand, becoming paper written over by words, will endure as long as men can read.
>
> And so he left the window. He prepared, carefully, the opium that would melt away within him the iron barrier that no longer yielded to thought or solitude or wine. And when the drug began to live within its glass, for an instant he thought he saw a drowned girl floating there, her hair swirling in the smoke. . . . Far away, in another universe, the clock of Notre Dame aux Luminères struck twice.

This is the apotheosis of decadence—sex, drugs, and death mixed into a single potent cocktail. But, lest the reader suspect her of indulging in mere literary nostalgia, Lee notes in passing that "the poet would have presented this history quite differently," by introducing a unifying device, such as a cursed ring. This sly contrasting of the story's sinuous structure with the clanking apparati of its Gothic ancestors does more than just establish that the fiction is an improvement on antique forms. It hints (no more) that the real horror, the real beauty, the real significance of the story, is that death is universal. She is a true democrat, an unselective lover who sooner or later comes for all, aware of her or not, the reader no less than the author.

Once upon a time the Romantics elevated the emotions above reason, sought the sublime in the supernatural and the medieval, and made a cult of the equation of sex and death. Following generations took their machinery and put it to lesser ends, much as the forms of magic were taken over by performers of sleight-of-hand. They could do no better, for they had lost the original vision.

Lee's work is a return to sources and a rejuvenation of that original vision. It is the higher passions that matter. Viktor, the bored aristocrat in "Dark as Ink" is too wise to pursue his obsessions, and for this sin suffers a meaningless life and early death. But the eponymous heroine of "La Reine Blanche" finds redemption despite her singular regicide and unwitting betrayal of her fated love because she has stayed true to her passions. An erotic spirituality shimmers like foxfire from the living surfaces of this book.

By some standards (though not mine) these are works not of fantasy but of horror. There has long been a midnight traffic between the genres, ridge-runners and embargo-breakers smuggling influences across the borders. But ought we care? No one would dare attempt to expel the late Fritz Leiber from the Empire of the Fantastic. Yet he readily admitted that nearly all his work, at heart, was horror. Even the Fafhrd and Mouser stories, though disguised by ambiguously upbeat endings and the wit and charisma of their heroes, exist in an almost Lovecraftian horror-fiction universe. In the end, the only question that matters is whether the work suits our purposes or not.

"As I supposed," says a raven in one of these tales, "your story is sad, sinister, and interesting." Exactly so. There are twenty-three stories in this volume, and I recommend them all.

* * *

The Obsidian sea turns bottle-green and then turquoise. Sand grates under the keel. We are come upon *Bones of the Moon*. Beaching our ship, we lightly set foot on . . . land?

It is a strange fate that has befallen Jonathan Carroll. A man whose first novel, *The Land of Laughs*, was enthusiastically embraced by the genre readership, has with equal ease been acclaimed by the mainstream as one of its own. The wet smooch of genre is normally the kiss of death as far as literary respectability goes. Yet there he stands.

Well, the mainstream is a funny place. It claims for its own Amos Tutuola's "thronged and grisley" (as Dylan Thomas characterized it) *The Palm-Wine Drinkard*, along with the collected works of T. H. White and C. S. Lewis, Michael Ayrton's *The Maze-Maker*, and even such genre superstars as Ray Bradbury and Ursula K. Le Guin, while stoutly excluding R. A. Lafferty, John Myers Myers' *Silverlock*, and (as yet) Samuel R. Delany. It embraced, lionized, and then abandoned James Branch Cabell, whose antic satire *Jurgen* is still alive with fantastic invention long after the salacious qualities that prompted a famous obscenity trial have become invisible to the modern eye. It treasures Virginia Woolf's *Orlando* while decrying those fantastic elements without which it has neither existence nor purpose. There is no use looking to the mainstream for intellectual rigor.

To discover exactly why the outside world would even consider poaching in the genre preserves, one need look no further than to Carroll's wholly enviable prose style:

> Because Greece was the first "Europe" I had ever known, I loved it like you love your first child: you demand everything of it and what you receive swells your heart like a balloon.
>
> When we returned to Italy after those first two weeks, I had the secret fear that nothing could be as good as those first days overseas. Afternoon light couldn't possibly fall on broken walls the same way as it did in Greece. Where else on earth would someone think of using giant rubber bands to hold the tablecloth down at an outdoor restaurant? On beaches of black sand, men walked alongside ancient mules that carried melons for sale. The men cut the melons in half with one swat of a big knife and the red fruit tasted so sweet and cool in the hot afternoon sun.

Nor is it only in the depiction of sensuous detail that Carroll excels. The fantasy world of Rondua, experienced by his heroine, Cullen James, in a series of connected dreams, is as crisp and vivid as so many illustrations torn from so many classic picture-books. Even his throwaways are evocative, as when Cullen reflects on stories told within her dreams, that "Like jokes we hear and then forget until someone begins telling them again, I could have told my son what came next: how the mountains had learned to run, why only rabbits were allowed pencils, when the birds had decided to become all one color."

Dreaming, Cullen accompanies her young son Pepsi—who in the "real" world was aborted—the wolf Felina, Martio the Camel, and Mr. Tracy, a dog in a big felt hat, on a quest for the five Bones of the Moon. In her waking life, she suffers, loves, weds, suffers more, finds new friends, and faces a final horror at the point where dreams and reality collide.

The ending, as in all of Carroll's fiction, is abrupt and alarming, like an unsuspected trap-door opening underfoot. The first several times I encountered this, it seemed an inexplicable loss of control for an otherwise accomplished writer. Eventually it became clear that for whatever unguessable reasons this was a deliberate effect. It is simply part of the price you have to pay, if you want to read the book.

Yet I'll confess to having my doubts whether this island should be on our itinerary at all. The fantasy world of Rondua, brilliant as it is in glimpses and pieces, is a patchwork creation. Were the real-world sections excised and the rest expanded to fill the gaps, it could never be made into a self-consistent system. Nor, as the reader is reminded by a dozen clever devices, is it meant to.

When an author doesn't deep down, on some level, believe in the reality of his invented world, he is not engaged in fantasy but metaphor. *Bones of the Moon* is like unto the sea-monster Jasconius on which Saint Brendan and his mariner monks celebrated a Mass to the glory of God every Easter Sunday for seven years. It is no true island at all but a fabulous beast, and one that owes its allegiance not to our own dear lords but to the masters of cislunar literature.

The less daring members of the crew shift uneasily, ready to bolt for the ship at the least sign that vast Jasconius is preparing to plunge down into those airless and Stygian realms and dominions where such as they cannot thrive. The ground trembles underfoot.

James Blaylock first got the field's attention with *The Digging Leviathan*, which profoundly puzzled science fiction readers by narrating a frenzied round of slapstick activity by a crew of suburban misfits, all centered on the eponymous digging machine, without ever quite getting around to having his characters switch the damned thing *on*. He's written several very good books since, but I've fixed on *Land of Dreams* because it indirectly explains exactly why this was beside the point.

Land of Dreams focuses on Skeezix, Helen, and Jack, three young-teen orphans in a coastal Northern California village. In stark contrast to most genre fiction, it is not immediately clear in which direction the book intends to go. For a time odd events simply accumulate: A midnight train thunders down rusty and incomplete tracks incapable of supporting it. Unwholesome fish are taken from the sea. A man the size of a human thumb is briefly glimpsed, holding a mouse-head mask in his arms. The carnival comes to town. An enormous shoe washes ashore and the three friends resolve to salvage it and take it to their friend, Dr. Jensen:

> Jack set a hooded lantern on a driftwood burl, so that the light was shining down on the shoe, and then all three of them started bailing water out of it with milk buckets . . . They shoved one of the timbers—an immense broken oar, it seemed, from a monumental wrecked row-boat—in under the toe and then wedged the other timber under it, levering away at the first until the heel edged around and down the hill. They inched it along, burying their fulcrum timber in the soft

> beach sand and pulling it out and resetting it and burying it again, until water rushed from the toe to the heel. Then they bailed it clean, shoved it farther, bailed once more, and then pushed the shoe entirely over onto its side, ocean water cascading out past the tongue and the laces and the heel edge along with a school of silvery fish that flopped and wriggled on the wet sand.

Which is as good a description of how to bail out a giant shoe as I've ever encountered. The shoe joins the doctor's collection of big stuff, including "a round, convex sheet of cracked glass, like the crystal of an impossible watch; a brass belt buckle the size of a casement window; and a cuff link that might as easily have been a silver platter." Later, Dr. Jensen caulks the shoe, rigs a mast, fits a tiller across the heel, and takes it out sailing.

It should already be clear that half the novel's population—the good guys—are misfits, cranks, eccentrics, incompetents, or admixtures of all the above. Arrayed against them are an equally motley crew of villains, drawn by Blaylock with great gusto. Miss Flees and her toady Peebles, the choleric MacWilt, the occasionally corviform Dr. Brown, and the rest, are hideous and malignant creatures all, and prey to their own craven, violent, and envious natures.

Luckily, they're even less effective than the heroes. As a kindly ghost explains to Helen, "They're certain *you* hate things too, that the world is made out of dirt. But that's what gives you the edge; they can't understand you." Guided partially by the villains' attempts to stop them, the kids ultimately manage to penetrate the secret of the twelve-yearly Solstice (whatever this phenomenon might be, one observes, it has nothing to do with the sun) and set matters straight.

The significant explanatory moment I promised earlier comes when Helen, Jack, and Skeezix finally put the pieces back together and break through the membrane separating them from a new realm of reality: One where unimaginable trains carry throngs of people backward and forward in time, with stops in all eras. For a brief moment all possibilities are theirs, all times and places open to them. Nothing is forbidden. They are become Illuminati, knowers of great secrets and holders of immense power.

They can't get back to their own world fast enough.

Power and knowledge hold no charm comparable to that of the world they know: A world in which the vibration of unseen machines is a constant whisper underfoot. Where strange events proliferate and disperse. Where revelation is always imminent but never quite arrives.

Skeezix, typically, gets the last word. Reflecting on life, he muses that "it seemed that the precariousness of the business lent a sort of flavor to it; it would be a dreary place all in all if his existence were mapped out too thoroughly."

It is precisely this love of the quotidian, of the homely, of simple pleasures and quirky people and natural oddities, that burns at the heart of Blaylock's art. This is why the digging leviathan was doomed to failure. This is why the subway system of the gods is discovered and abandoned. The world is enough, he suggests. Who could ask for more?

Iain Banks has the pleasant distinction of simultaneously holding down two separate literary careers, one as the mainstream author of such acclaimed works as

The Wasp Factory and *Canal Dreams*, and the other as an equally admired science fiction writer.

I'll confess that I don't know which hat Banks was wearing when he wrote *The Bridge*. It hardly matters. What matters is the remarkable setting he has chosen for the bulk of the book—an enormous and seemingly endless bridge stretching from horizon to horizon across a nameless ocean. An entire society lives upon the bridge, employing bicycles, rickshaws, and motorcycles for short-term transportation and steam trains for longer voyages. Here is the scene from a platform above the main train deck:

> Over the noise of the milling people, the continual hisses and clanks, grindings and gratings, klaxons and whistles of the trains on the deck beneath sound like shrieks from some mechanistic underworld, while every now and again a deep rumble and a still more profound quaking and rattling announces a heavy train passing somewhere below; great pulsing clouds of white steam roll around the street and upwards.
>
> Above, where the sky ought to be, are the distant, hazily seen girders of the high bridge; obscured by the rising fumes and vapors, dimmed by the light intercepted outside them by their carapace of people-infected rooms and offices, they rise above and look down upon the rude profanity of these afterthought constructions with all the majesty and splendor of a great cathedral roof.

The first-person narrator is being treated for amnesia. He finds himself in a mannered society rather like that of Freud's Vienna but riddled with small absurdities, not the least of which is the total lack of curiosity its citizens display toward the bridge itself. What lands does it connect? Who built it? How old is it? Only the protagonist cares, and he cannot find out.

His sporadic search for answers is the chief of three alternating narratives. The second follows the life and difficult romance of a (young, at first) man in contemporary Scotland, and the third . . . well, it can only be characterized as the adventures of Conan the Glaswegian.

At first the farcical adventures of a nearly brainless swordsman with an overintellectualized familiar and a hideous accent ("I luv the ded, this old basturt sez to me when I wiz tryin to get some innfurrmashin out ov him. You fuckin old pervert I sez, gettin a bit fed up by this time enyway, and slit his throate; ah askd you whare the fukin Sleepin Byootie woz, no whit kind of humpin you like. No, no he sez, splutterin sumthin awfy and gettin blud all ovir ma new curiearse, no he sez I sed Isle of the Dead" and so on) seem jarring and even intrusive. There are moments in the main narration when the fabric of reality wears thin and opens a window into the second plot-line. But this barbarian stuff is straight out of left field.

These segments are so engaging, however, so funny in an awful way, that the reader comes to accept them while doubting they'll ever quite make sense.

The Bridge is, underneath all, a novel of psychological revelation. So I am forced to be a little coy about the plot. In broad terms, it is about the protagonist's reluctance to deal with the mystery of his situation. He is a man in serious peril and it is his task to discover its nature. However, life on the bridge is pleasant, and he has met an engaging woman, an engineer's daughter named Abberlaine Arrol.

The sections on the bridge are more vivid and engaging than those set in Scotland. The same could be said of the swaggering, cigar-smoking Abberlaine compared to her real-world counterpart. Small wonder that the protagonist is uneager to rock the boat. But little things start going wrong. Telephones cease to work for him. He loses his social position. Mad events proliferate. He must finally find the resolve to ask tough questions and face their consequences.

Morals are out of fashion these days, even in the retrogressive universes of fantasy. But if there is one message to be taken away from the book, it is this: That sometimes the reason life seems difficult is that we are engaged in difficult and important work.

And our foul-mouthed, sexually deplorable, and bloody-handed barbarian? One of the many delights of *The Bridge* is the marvelously orchestrated revelation by story's end that he is integral to the plot. Central, even.

Do I violate my own definition if I cite Ellen Kushner's *Swordspoint* as a hard fantasy? It's a tough call. The critic and editor Donald G. Keller denies that he took its subtitle, "A Melodrama of Manners" and used it to define a previously undiscerned school of fantasy which he called "fantasy of manners" and others puckishly dubbed "mannerpunk" before settling on the more decorous "mannerism." But there is no getting around the fact that *Swordspoint* has become the figurehead work for that nascent subgenre.

We are in dark waters here, murky with wrack and seaweed. Those clear, pellucid depths through which could be seen, fathoms deep, Grecian triremes with coral-encrusted amphorae holding ancient wine still drinkable, are no more. And whose fault should this be but science fiction's?

With the rise of science fiction as a genre, the currents of influence became tangled and recomplicated.* John Brunner's *The Traveler in Black* was strongly influenced by Lord Dunsany's exquisitely crafted tales of the kingdoms at the Edge of the World; Michael Moorcock's marvelous *Gloriana* was in part a conscious homage to the Gormenghast books, in token of which it is dedicated to Mervyn Peake; and Gene Wolfe's *Book of the New Sun* (a work in which on examination all the fantastic elements have hard science rationales—but what of that?) is a direct descendant of Jack Vance's *The Dying Earth* which in its turn was clearly derived from Clark Ashton Smith's chronicles of the final civilizations of humanity. To name but a few examples.

The temptation to claim that the authors of these works have transformed their influences so thoroughly as to render these books fit for our colonizing banner is strong. But, as a famous out-of-genre fantasist once put it, it would be wrong.

Still . . . water does not run uphill, nor do we inherit our looks from our

---

*For a good example of exactly *how* tangled, consider only Avram Davidson's *The Phoenix and the Mirror* which employs the tools of hard science fiction to describe the creation of virgin speculum (a mirror that has never known a reflection) couched strictly in the technology of the Roman Empire as it was later misunderstood by Dark Ages scholars.

grandchildren. The recognition by Wolfe, Vance, Moorcock, Brunner, that there was much to admire about their predecessors does not invalidate those works they loved so dearly. *On the day it was published*, Kushner's *Swordspoint* was undeniably a hard fantasy.

But—this is a question the author herself has raised in conversation—is *Swordspoint* a fantasy at all? Well . . . if I can say this without challenging every rogue swordsman, masterless samurai and cheap gunsel with a gaudy line of patter to an exchange of definitions, it seems strange that so little has been made of the deep connection between fantasy and fantasies. By "fantasies" I mean of course those pleasant meditations on the world not as it is but as we wish it were and know it cannot be. *Swordspoint* is a demonstration that it is not the furniture—the dragons, ogres, elves, and wizards, the magical swords, cups, and corkscrews—that make a work fantasy but that hopeless yearning vision of life as it cannot be that burns green and eternal as its heart.

But here. On the first page, Kushner sets the scene:

> Let the fairy-tale begin on a winter's morning, then, with one drop of blood new-fallen on the ivory snow: a drop as bright as a clear-cut ruby, red as the single spot of claret on the lace cuff. And it therefore follows that evil lurks behind each broken window, scheming malice and enchantment; while behind the latched shutters the good are sleeping their just sleeps at this early hour in Riverside. Soon they will arise to go about their business; and one, maybe, will be as lovely as the day, armed, as are the good, for a predestined triumph. . . .

This is an elegant stick of prose, but what is more important is what follows upon it. For it is immediately undercut by the next paragraph, which enumerates the lies, evasions, and deliberate misleadings its predecessor employs. Leaving only the grace of the writing and an admirable warning of the unexpected turns of wit that will inform the narration of events.

This high wit is integral to the purpose of the novel. For the fantasy that drives this book and its characters is the vision of a life without regrets or consequences, in which all that matters is making a figure of oneself and winning the admiration of a scorned universe. This is an equipoise that cannot be maintained, although the swordsman Richard St Vier tries hard, as do in their own ways the villainous Ferris, the duchess Tremontaine, and the callow Lord Michael. Even the human engine for the novel's events—Alec, failed student, St Vier's lover, and proverbial Boyfriend from Hell—who knows from hard experience that it cannot be done, tries to hold the world in despite. Secretly, all know they are doomed.

In the face of this knowledge, only wit can keep them going. Posture is forever threatened by reality, for as Lord Ferris aphorises, *Every man lives at swordspoint*. "I mean," he explains, "the things he cares for. Get them in your grasp, and you have the man—or woman—in your power. Threaten what they love, and they are absolutely at your mercy: you have a very sharp blade pressed to their throat."

Can, then, a dissolute failed student find happiness with a swordsman whose self-image requires that he die young? Well . . . it *is*, after all, a fairy tale of sorts. But in a novel that begins with St Vier vaulting a wall and running through lightless streets to escape not retribution for the murder he has just committed but the cloying compliments of the bystanders on his style, nothing is to be taken for granted.

There is a type of young woman we have all either known or been: who worships at the altar of the Romantic; plays old border ballads on pennywhistle, recorder, or hammer dulcimer; tacks a hand-lettered sign reading MAGIC IS AFOOT on her dormitory room door; reads the Tarot for friends and *The White Goddess* for pleasure; and treasures a hundred obscure books by measure of how close they come to an ideal world in which gypsies and scarecrows, old marbles and long skirts, elves, quilts, candles, hot chocolate with cinnamon, feathered caps, rainy days, and snug houses with big fireplaces are part of a single, inexpressibly significant enterprise. There have been attempts to set a novel in this young woman's world view, but those I have seen all (but I have not seen all) fall short of the mark by the same process that mars most stories about writers' friends. The heroine is gifted with such preternatural grace and good will, wit, insight, fighting skills and fashion sense as to make the reader either resolve to lose some weight and take in a few night classes at the university or else hurl the book across the room in disgust. Usually the latter.

This is not a mistake that Greer Ilene Gilman makes in *Moonwise*. Her heroine slouches through the novel submerged and half-lost in language, desperately in love with her invented worlds, faintly ridiculous, totally convincing, and altogether charming. Ariane is the type-specimen for her kind, and it is her absolute unquestioning belief in the immanence of the fantastic that allows the reader to accept it when those fantasies overswell their banks one evening and sweep away her best friend Sylvie in a torrent of words.

Here's a sample of *Moonwise*'s prose in a quieter moment:

> She remembered a game of croquet, played by mothlight on their cant of crooked lawn, amid the gangling bygone lilacs, and the rose-thorns and the currants, in the Lyonesse of dusk. Their set was old, the heavy balls and mallets battered colorless, and the iron wickets grim as Newgate gallows. It was a fierce and freakish game; the air was flawed with wild giggles, pibrochs of ecstatic fury, threats and jeers and ranting taunting triumphs. Ariane was battledrunk, amazed by her own rapacity. The others played elusively, erratically as moths: now belantered in the bushes; now undone by the backlash of a clacking, cleverstick riposte; now flying with uncanny grace through hoops that should have been unassailable as rainbows. Ariane stonewalled. Her floating, fluttering muslin skirt was caught and rent, entangled in the thorns of roses, where she skulked with cunning strategy; the others unpicked her from the brambles.

Now, either you think there is something magnificent about a croquet game rendered thus, or you do not, and if you do not I fail to see how you will get past even the first chapter. Much less the genuinely difficult passage in which Sylvie disappears. This is a book in which dreams, memories, desires, and reality are not distinct, but merely regions on one continuum among whose convolutions one can lose oneself in an absentminded moment. The shift in levels can occur within a single sentence, and honesty compels me to admit that there were times late at night when I felt I had been invited to fling off my shoes and dance through the brambles.

But a difficult style, it has been observed, is its own defense. It scares away the faint of heart. Once the reviewers and critics were done with them, there is nobody who ever finished Frederick Rolfe's *Hadrian the Seventh* or Alexander Theroux's *Three Wogs* or Brian Aldiss's *Barefoot in the Head* with anything less than delight. *Moonwise* is a willfully special book whose partisans will be treasuring its virtues well into the long night of the coming century.

In its influence, *Moonwise* was certainly the most important fantasy work of the past decade for the simple reason that it roused an entire generation of new and unknown fantasy writers to Ambition. For a year after it came out, the conventions and writers' workshops buzzed with a constant mutter of amazement. A total unknown, with her first book, had reinvented not only the substance but also the language of the fantasy novel, all to the satisfaction not of the perceived marketplace but of her own inner demons. It inevitably raised the unspoken but potent question, If she can do it, then why not me? *Why not me?*

And, indeed . . . why not?

The mutinous crew gather on the foredeck, every dwarf and man-jack of them outraged that their favorite works have been passed over. One cries out for Delia Sherman's *The Porcelain Dove*. Another for A.S. Byatt's *Possession*. A third for John M. Ford's *The Dragon in Waiting*, and a fourth for something—anything!—by Tim Powers. Partisans demand Joy Chant, Poul Anderson, Andre Norton, Gregory Frost, Susan Cooper, Leigh Brackett, Fletcher Pratt. Everyone is angry that I have overlooked L. Sprague de Camp.

It is vain to point out that *The Porcelain Dove* is a historical fantasy and that historical fantasy is currently a growth literature, with enough going on in it to support any number of essays the length of this. That Byatt's book is not really a fantasy but, as she subtitled it, "A Romance" and has more in common with the works of the Sisters Brontë than with Ursula K. Le Guin's Earthsea tetralogy. That originality and good writing are not enough—to be included herein requires Blind Luck as well. That the cataloguing of islands is an arduous and—elder gods willing—endless task.

This satisfies nobody. One burly ruffian demands to know where R. A. Lafferty's work fits into this scheme. It doesn't, really, any more than does Neal Barrett, Jr.'s *The Hereafter Gang*. Some fish are so odd as to escape even our all embracing net. Howard Waldrop is a good example. Is he still considered an outlaw fantasist? Does outlaw fantasy even exist anymore? Linnaeus notwithstanding, a comprehensive taxonomy of fantasy is more than simply difficult. The mere thought of it is a nightmare.

The crew will not listen. Their passions are aroused. Eyes flash. Knives glint. Mystic runes on blades and hilts glow with murderous intent.

But a muttered word of power stills them all. Voices fade. The ship recedes, becomes nothing more than a figure on the written page, harmless. I take up the typed sheets of this essay, tamp their edges even, and reach for an envelope.

Beyond the limited horizons of these pages, a hundred fantastic islands appear in the distance like waterspouts, like strange similes, like exotic flowers blossoming from so many gun-barrels. It was never my ambition to chart out the Archipelago and pin its isles down on paper like so many dead butterflies. Rather it was to set out a direction for travel.

It curls like a sleeping dragon, does the Archipelago. No man knows the shape and nature of the submarine geologic forces that brought it into being. We can only conjecture what sea-changing currents wash its divergent shores. Our voyage has brought us to the heart of words, of yearning, to that form of literature in which the nature of each is blended with the other and their essence is revealed to be the transformation from the unbearable What Is to the unreachable If Only.

Algis Budrys once remarked that hard science fiction was not a subgenre but a flavor, the flavor of "toughness." If hard fantasy has a flavor, then surely that flavor must be "regret." And if I have one regret, it is that there is for me neither the time nor the space nor yet the wisdom to lay out for you all the many lands and wonders to be found scattered through the Archipelago. I have failed you. Yet if there be but one book mentioned here you have not yet sampled, I leave you better off than you were when first we met.

Here, good milords and fine ladies, I must leave your presence, for we have arrived at that destination we were fated for since time began, that happy condition that was our object from the very onset of our quest: A most excellent beginning.

And so we set sail.

WORDS LIKE PALE STONES

Nancy Kress

Nancy Kress lives in upstate New York. She is the author of *An Alien Light*, *Brain Rose*, *Beggars in Spain* and other works, for which she has twice won the Nebula Award. While best known for writing science fiction, Kress has also written horror and the delightfully quirky fantasy novel *The Prince of Morning Bells*.

"Words Like Pale Stones" is a powerful dark fantasy, using the bones of old *Rumplestiltskin* tales to build a story about the magic of language, and the power of knowledge. It comes from *Black Thorn, White Rose*, a collection of adult fairy tales.

—T. W.

The greenwood grew less green as we traveled west. Grasses lay flatter against the earth. Brush became skimpy. Trees withered, their bare branches like crippled arms against the sky. There were no flowers. My stolen horse, double-laden but both of us so light that the animal hardly noticed, picked his way more easily through the thinning forest. Once his hooves hit some half-buried stone and sparks struck, strange pale fire slow to die away, the light wavering over the ground as if alive. I shuddered and looked away.

But the baby watched the sparks intently, his fretful body for once still in the saddle. I could feel his sturdy little back pressed against me. He was silent, although he now has a score of words, "go" and "gimme" and "mine!" that ordinarily he uses all day long. I couldn't see his face, but I knew how his eyes would look: wide and blue and demanding, beautiful eyes under thick black lashes. His father's eyes, recognizing his great-great-grandfather's country.

It is terrible for a mother to know she is afraid of her infant son.

I could have stabbed the prince with the spindle from the spinning wheel. Not as sharp as a needle, perhaps, but it would have done. Once I had used just such a spindle on Jack Starling, the miller's son, who thought he could make free with me, the daughter of a village drunkard and a washerwoman whose boasting lies were as much a joke as her husband's nightly stagger. *I have the old blood in me. My father was a lord! My grandmother could fly to the moon!* And, finally, *My daughter Ludie is such a good spinster she can spin straw into gold!*

"Go ahead and spin me," Jack leered when he caught me alone in our hovel. His hands were hot and his breath foul. When he pushed both against my breasts, I stabbed him with the spindle, square in the belly, and he doubled over like scythed hay. The spindle revolved in a stone whorl; I bashed him over the head with that and he went down, crashing into the milk pail with a racket like the end of the world. His head wore a bloody patch, soft as pulp, for a month.

But there was no stone whorl, no milk bucket, no foul breath in the palace. Even the spinning was different. "See," he said to me, elegant in his velvets and silks, his clean teeth gleaming, and the beautiful blue eyes bright with avarice, "it's a spinning wheel. Have you ever seen one before?"

"No," I said, my voice sounding high and squeaky, not at all my own. Straw covered the floor, rose to the ceiling in bales, choked the air with chaff.

"They're new," he said. "From the east." He lounged against the door, and no straw clung to his doublet or knee breeches, slick with embroidery and jewels. "They spin much faster than the hand-held distaff and spindle."

"My spindle rested in a whorl. Not in my hand," I said, and somehow the words gave me courage. I looked at him straight, prince or no prince. "But, my lord, I'm afraid you've been misled. My mother . . . says things sometimes. I cannot spin straw into gold. No mortal could."

He only smiled, for of course he was not mortal. Not completely. The old blood ran somewhere in his veins, mixed but there. *Fevered and tainted*, some said. Only the glimmerings of magic were there, and glimmerings without mastery were what made the cruelty. So I had heard all my life, but I never believed it—people will, after all, say anything—until I stood with him in that windowless room, watching his smile as he lounged against the door, chaff rising like dusty gold around me.

"I think you are completely capable of spinning straw into gold," he said. "In fact, I expect you to have spun all the straw in this room into gold by morning."

"Then you expect the moon to wipe your ass!" I said, and immediately clapped my hand over my mouth. Always, *always* my mouth brings me trouble. But he only went on smiling, and it was then, for the first time, that I was afraid. Of that bright, blue-eyed smile.

"If you don't spin it all into gold," he said silkily, "I will have you killed. But if you do, I will marry you. There—that's a sweet inducement, is it not? A prince for a husband for a girl like you. And for me—a wife with a dowry of endless golden fingers."

I saw then, as if in a vision, his fingers endlessly on *me*, and at the expression on my face his smile broadened.

"A slow death," he said, "and a painful one. But that won't happen, will it, my magical spinster? You won't let it happen?"

"I cannot spin straw into gold!" I shouted, in a perfect frenzy of loathing and fear, but he never heard me. A rat crept out from behind the bales and started across the floor. The prince's face went ashen. In a moment he was gone, whirling through the door and slamming it behind him before the rat could reach him. I heard the heavy iron bar drop into its latch on the other side, and I turned to look at the foreign spinning wheel, backed by bales to the rough beams of the ceiling.

My knees gave way and I sank down upon the straw.

There are so many slow and painful ways to die.

I don't know how long I shrank there, like some mewling and whimpering babe, visioning horrors no babe ever thought of. But when I came back to myself, the rat was still nosing at the door, trying to squeeze underneath. It should have fit; not even our village rats are so thin and mangy. On hands and knees, I scuttled to join the rat. Side by side we poked at the bottom of the door, the sides, the hinges.

It was all fast and tight. Not even a flea could have escaped.

Next I wormed behind the bales of straw, feeling every inch of the walls. They were stone, and there were no chinks, no spaces made rotten by damp or moss. This angered me. Why should the palace be the only sound stone dwelling in the entire damp-eaten village? Even Jack Starling's father's mill had weak stones, damn his crumbling grindstone and his scurrilous soul.

The ceiling beams were strong wood, holding up stronger, without cracks.

There were no windows, only light from candles in stone sconces.

The stone floor held no hidden trapdoors, nor any place to pry up the stone to make a tunnel.

I turned to the spinning wheel. Under other circumstances I might have found it a pretty thing, of polished wood. When I touched the wheel, it spun freely, revolving the spindle much faster than even I, the best spinster in the village, could have done. With such a thing, I could have spun thread seven times as fast. I could have become prosperous, bought a new thatch roof for our leaky cottage, a proper bed for my sodden father . . .

The rat still crouched by the door, watching me.

I fitted straw into the distaff. Who knew—the spinning wheel itself was from some foreign place. "From the east," he'd said. Maybe the magic of the Old Ones dwelt there, too, as well as in the west. Maybe the foreign wheel could spin straw. Maybe it could even spin the stuff into gold. How would I, the daughter of a drunkard and a lying braggart, know any different?

I pushed the polished wheel. It revolved the spindle, and the straw was pulled forward from the distaff, under my twisting fingers, toward the spindle. The straw, straw still, broke and fell to the floor in a powder of chaff.

I tried again. And again. The shining wheel became covered with sticky bits of straw, obscuring its brightness. The straw fell to the stone floor. It would not even wind once around the spindle.

I screamed and kicked the spinning wheel. It fell over, hard. There was the sound of splintering wood. "By God's blood," I shouted at the cursed thing, "damn you for a demon!"

"If it were demonic, it would do you more good," a voice said quietly.

I whirled around. By the door sat the rat. He was a rat no longer but a short, ratty-faced man, thin and starved-looking and very young, dressed in rags. I looked at his eyes, pale brown and filmy, like the floating colors in dreams, and I knew immediately that I was in the presence of one of the Old Ones.

Strangely, I felt no fear. He was so puny, and so pale. I could have broken his arm with one hand. He wasn't even as old as I was, despite the downy stubble on his chin—a boy, who had been a rat.

What danger could there be in magic that could not even free itself from a locked room?

"You're not afraid," he said in that same quiet voice, and if I *had* been, the fear would have left me then. He smiled, the saddest and most humble smile I have ever seen. It curved his skinny mouth, but it never touched the washed-out brown of his eyes. "You're a bold girl."

"Like my mam," I said bitterly, before I knew I was going to. "Bold in misfortune." Except, of course, that it wasn't *her* who would die a slow and painful death, the lying bitch.

"I think we can help each other," he said, and at that I laughed out loud. I shudder now, to remember it. I laughed aloud at one of the Old Ones! What stupidities we commit from ignorance!

He gave me again that pitiful wraith of a smile. "Do you know, Ludie, what happens when art progresses?"

I had no idea what we were talking about. Art? Did he mean magic arts? And how did he know my name? A little cold prickle started in my liver, and I knew I wouldn't laugh at him again.

"Yes, magic arts, too," he said in his quiet voice, "although I was referring to something else. Painting. Sculpture. Poetry. Even tapestry—everything made of words and colors. You don't weave tapestry, do you, Ludie?"

He knew I did not. Only ladies wove tapestries. I flushed, thinking he was mocking me.

"Art starts out simple. Pale. True to what is real. Like stone statues of the human body, or verse chanted by firelight. Pale, pale stone. Pale as straw. Simple words, that name what is true. Designs in natural wool, the color of rams' horns. Then, as time goes on, the design becomes more elaborate. The colors brighter. The story twisted to fit rhyme, or symbol, or somebody else's power. Finally, the designs are so elaborate, so twisted with motion, and the colors so feverish—look at me, Ludie—that the original, the real as it exists in nature, looks puny and withered. The original has lost all power to move us, replaced by a hectic simulacrum that bears only a tainted relation to what is real. The corruption is complete."

He leaned forward. "The magic arts are like that, too, Ludie. The Old Ones, our blood diluted by marriage with men, are like that now. Powerless in our bone-real paleness, our simple-real words."

I didn't have the faintest idea what he was talking about. His skin was so pasty; maybe a brain pox lay upon him. Men didn't talk like that, nor boys either. Nor rats. But I wanted to say something to cheer him. He had made me forget for a few minutes what awaited me in the morning.

"*A slow and painful death*" . . . the rack? The red-hot pincers? The Iron Maiden? Suddenly dizzy, I put my head between my knees.

"All you have to do," the Old One said in his thin voice, "is get me out. Of this room, of the palace, of the courtyard gate."

I didn't answer. *A slow and painful death* . . .

"Just that," he said. "No more. We can no longer do it for ourselves. Not with all this hectic . . . all this bright . . ." I heard him move wearily across the floor, and then the spinning wheel being righted. After a long moment, it whirred.

I raised my head. The wheel was whole, with no break in the shining wood.

The boy sat before it on a bale of straw, his ashen face sad as Good Friday. From under his fingers, winding around the spindle turning in its wheel-driven whorl, wound skein after skein of feverishly bright gold thread.

Toward morning, I slept, stretched out on the hard stone floor. I couldn't help it. Sleep took me like a drug. When I woke, there was not so much as a speck of chaff left in the room. The gold lay in tightly wound skeins, masses and masses of them, brighter than the sun. The boy's face was so ashen I thought he must surely faint. His arms and legs trembled. He crouched as far away from the gold as possible, and kept his eyes averted.

"There will be no place for me to hide," he said, his voice as bone-pale as his face. "The first thing they will do is paw through the gold. And I . . . have not even corrupted power . . . left." With that, he fell over, and a skinny rat lay, insensible, on the stone floor.

I lifted it gingerly and hid it in my apron. On the other side of the door, the bar lifted. The great door swung slowly on its hinges. He stood there, in turquoise silk and garish yellow velvet, his bright blue eyes under their thick lashes wide with disbelief. The disbelief changed to greed, terrible to watch, like flesh that has been merely infected turning dark with gangrene. He looked at me, walked over to finger the gold, looked at me again.

He smiled.

I tried to run away before the wedding. I should have known it would be impossible. Even smuggling out the rat was so hard I first despaired of it. Leaving the room was easy enough, and even leaving the palace to walk in the walled garden set aside for princesses, but getting to the courtyard gate proved impossible. In the end I bribed a page to carry the rat in a cloth-wrapped bundle over the drawbridge and into the woods, and I know he did so, because the child returned with a frightened look and handed me a single stone, pale and simple as bone. There was no other message. There didn't need to be.

But when I tried to escape myself, I couldn't. There were guards, pages, ladies, even when I went to bed or answered the call of nature. God's blood, but the rich were poor in privacy!

Everywhere, everyone wore the brightest of colors in the most luxurious of fabrics. Jade, scarlet, canary, flame, crimson. Silks, velvets, brocades. Diamonds and emeralds and rubies and bloodstones, lying like vivid wounds on necks brilliant with powder and rouge. And all the corridors of the palace twisted, crusted with carving in a thousand grotesque shapes of birds and animals and faces that never were.

I asked to see the prince alone, and I came at him with a bread knife, a ridiculous thing for bread, its hilt tortured with scrollwork and fevered with paint. He was fast for so big a man; I missed him and he easily disarmed me. I waited then for a beating or worse, but all he did was laugh lazily and wind his hands in my tangled hair, which I refused to have dyed or dressed.

"A little demon, are you? I could learn to like that . . ." He forced his lips on mine and I wasn't strong enough to break free. When he released me, I spat in his face.

"Let me leave here! I lied! I can't spin gold into straw—I never could! The Old Ones did it for me!"

"Certainly they did," he said, smiling, "they always help peasants with none of their blood." But a tiny line furrowed his forehead.

That afternoon a procession entered my room. The prince, his chancellor, two men carrying a spinning wheel, one carrying a bale of straw. My heart skittered in my chest.

"Now," he said. "Do it again. Here. Now."

The men thrust me toward the wheel, pushed me onto a footstool slick with canary silk. I looked at the spinning wheel.

There are so many different kinds of deaths. More than I had known just days ago.

I fitted the straw onto the distaff. I pushed the wheel. The spindle revolved in its whorl. Under my twisting fingers, the straw turned to gold.

" 'An Old One,' " mocked my bridegroom. "Yes, most certainly. An Old One spun it for you."

I had dropped the distaff as if it were on fire. "Yes," I gasped, "*yes* . . . I can't do this, I don't know how . . ."

The chancellor had eagerly scooped up the brief skein of gold. He fingered it, and his hot eyes grew hotter.

"Don't you even know," the prince said, still amused, disdaining to notice the actual gold now that he was assured of it, "that the Old Ones will do nothing for you unless you know the words of their true names? Or unless you have something they want. And how could *you*, as stinking when I found you as a pig trough, have anything they wanted? Or ever hope to know their true names?"

"Do you?" I shot back, because I thought it would hurt him, thought it would make him stop smiling. But it didn't, and I saw all at once that he did know their true names, and that it must have been this that gave his great-great-grandfather power over them for the first time. True names.

"I don't like 'Ludie,' " he said. "It's a peasant name. I think I shall call you 'Goldianna.' "

"Do it and I'll shove a poker up your ass!" I yelled. But he only smiled.

The morning of the wedding I refused to get out of bed, refused to put on the crimson-and-gold wedding dress, refused to speak at all. Let him try to marry me bedridden, naked, and dumb!

Three men came to hold me down. A woman forced a liquid, warm and tasting of pungent herbs, down my throat. When I again came to myself, at nightfall, I was standing beside a bed vast as a cottage, crusted with carvings as a barnacled ship. I wore the crimson wedding gown, with bone stays that forced my breasts up, my waist in, my ass out, my neck high. Seventeen yards of jeweled cloth flowed around my feet. On my finger was a ring so heavy I could hardly lift my hand.

The prince smiled and reached for me, and he was still stronger, in his corrupted and feverish power, than I.

The night before my son was born, I had a dream. I lay again on the stone floor, chaff choking the air, and a figure bent over me. Spindly arms, long ratty face . . .

the boy took me in his arms and raised my shift, and I half stirred and opened my legs. Afterward, I slept again to the whirring of the spinning wheel.

I woke to sharp pain in my belly. The pain traveled around to the small of my back, and there it stayed until I thought I should break in two. But I didn't shriek. I bit my tongue to keep from crying out, and when the pain had passed I called to the nearest of my ladies, asleep in my chamber, "Send for the midwife!"

She rose, rubbing her eyes, and her hand felt first for the ornate jewels in which she slept every night, for fear of their being stolen. Only when she found they were safe did she mutter sleepily, "Yes, Your Grace," and yawn hugely. The inside of her mouth was red as a wound.

The next pain struck.

All through that long morning, I was kept from screaming by my dream. It curled inside me, pale and wispy as woodland mist in the morning. If . . . maybe . . . God's blood, let it be true! Let the baby be born small, and thin, and wan as clean milk, let him look at me with eyes filmy as clouds . . .

Near the end, the prince came. He stood only inches inside the door, a handkerchief over his mouth against the stench of blood and sweat. The handkerchief was embroidered with gold and magenta threads. Above it his face gleamed brightly, flushed with hope and disgust.

I bit through my lip, and pushed, and the hairy head slid from between my legs. Another push, and he was out. The midwife lifted him, still attached to his bloody tether, and gave a cry of triumph. The prince nodded and hastily left, clutching his handkerchief. The midwife laid my son, wailing, on my belly.

He had a luxuriant head of thick bright hair, and lush black eyelashes. His fat cheeks were red, his eyes a brilliant, hectic blue.

I felt the dream slide away from me, insubstantial as smoke, and for the first time that morning I screamed—in fury, in despair, in the unwanted love I already felt for the vivid child wriggling on my belly, who had tethered me to the palace with cords as bloody and strong as the one that still held him between my legs.

I walked wearily down the palace corridor to the spinning room. My son toddled beside me. The chancellor met me outside the door, trailing his clerks and pages. "No spinning today, Your Grace."

"No spinning?" There was always spinning. The baby always came with me, playing with skeins of gold, tearing them into tiny bits, while I spun. Always.

The chancellor's eyes wouldn't meet mine. His stiff jeweled headdress towered two feet in the air, a miniature palace. "The Treasury has enough gold."

"Enough gold?" I sounded like a mocking-bird, with no words of my own. The chancellor stiffened and swept away, the train of his gown glittering behind. The others followed, except for one courtier, who seemed careful not to touch me or look at me.

"There . . . is a woman," he whispered.

"A woman? What woman?" I said, and then I recognized him. He had grown taller in three years, broader. But I had still the stone he gave me the day he carried the stricken rat beyond the courtyard gate.

"A peasant woman in the east. Who is said to be able to spin straw into diamonds."

He was gone, his rich velvets trembling. I thought of all the gold stacked in the palace—skeins and skeins of it, filling room after room, sewn into garment after garment, used for curtain pulls and fish nets and finally even to tie up the feet of the chickens for roasting. The gold thread emerged blackened and charred from the ovens, but there was always so much more. And more. And more.

Diamonds were very rare.

Carefully I took the hand of my son. The law was clear—he was the heir. And the raising of him was mine. As long as I lived. Or he did.

My son looked up at me. His name was Dirk, but I thought he had another name as well. A true name, that I had never been allowed to hear. I couldn't prove this.

"Come, Dirk," I said, as steadily as I could. "We'll go play in the garden."

He thrust out his lip. "Mama spin!"

"No, dearest, not today. No spinning today."

He threw himself full length on the floor. "Mama spin!"

One thing my mother, damn her lying soul, had never permitted was tantrums. "No."

The baby sprang up. His intense blue eyes glittered. With a wild yell he rushed at me, and too late I saw that his chubby fist clutched a miniature knife, garish with jewels, twisted with carving. He thrust it at my belly.

I gasped and pulled it free—there was not much blood, the aim of a two-year-old is not good. Dirk screamed and hit me with his little fists. His goldshod feet kicked me. I tried to grab him, but it was like holding a wild thing. No one came—*no one*, although I am usually surrounded by so many bodies I can hardly breathe. Finally I caught his two arms in one hand and his two flailing legs in the other. He stopped screaming and glared at me with such intensity, such hatred in his bright blue eyes, that I staggered against the wall. A carved gargoyle pressed into my back. We stayed like that, both of us pinned.

"Dirk," I whispered, "what is your true name?"

They write things down. All of them, all things. Births, deaths, recipes, letters, battles, buyings and sellings, sizes, stories—none of them can remember anything without writing it down, maybe because all of it is so endlessly complicated. Or maybe because they take pride in their handwriting, which is also complicated: swooping dense curlicues traced in black or gold or scarlet. They write everything down, and sometimes the ladies embroider what has been written down on sleeves or doublets or arras. Then the stonemasons carve what has been embroidered into designs across a lintel or mantel or font. Even the cook pipes stylized letters in marzipan across cakes and candies. They fill their bellies with their frantic writing.

Somewhere in all this was Dirk's true name. I didn't know how much time I had. Around a turn of the privy stairs I had overheard two ladies whisper that the girl who could spin straw into diamonds had already been captured and was imprisoned in a caravan traveling toward the palace.

I couldn't read. But I could remember. Even shapes, even of curlicued letters. But which curlicues were important? There were so many, so much excess corrupting the true.

The day after the privy stairs, the prince came to me. His blue eyes were cold. "You are not raising Dirk properly. The law says you cannot be replaced as his mother . . . unless, of course, you should happen to die."

I kept my voice steady. "In what way have I failed Dirk?"

He didn't mention the screaming, the knives, the cruelty. Last week Dirk cut the finger off a peasant child. Dirk's father merely smiled. Instead, the prince said, "He has been seen playing with rats. Those are filthy animals; they carry disease."

My heart leaped. Rats. Sometimes, in the hour just before dawn, I had the dream again. Even if it wasn't true, I was always glad to have it. The rat-boy bending over me, and the baby with pale, quiet eyes.

The prince said, "Don't let it happen again." He strode away, magnificent in gold-embroidered leather like a gilded cow.

I found Dirk and took him to the walled garden. Nothing. We searched my chambers, Dirk puzzled but not yet angry. Nothing. The nobility have always taken great care to exterminate rats.

But in the stable, where the groom lay drunk on his pallet, were holes in the wall, and droppings, and the thin sour smell of rodent.

For days I caught rats. I brought each to my room hidden in the ugly-rich folds of my gown, barred the door, and let the rat loose. There was no one to see us; since the rumors of the girl who can spin diamonds, I was very often left alone. Each rat sniffed the entire room, searching for a way out. There was none. Hours later, each rat was still a rat.

Dirk watched warily, his bright blue eyes darting and cold.

On the sixth day, I woke to find a pale, long-nosed girl sitting quietly on the floor. She watched me from unsurprised eyes that were the simplest and oldest things I'd ever seen.

I climbed down from my high bed, clutching my nightshift around me. I sat on the floor facing her, nose-to-nose. In his trundle Dirk whimpered.

"Listen to me, Old One. I know what you are, and what you need. I can get you out of the palace." For the first time, I wondered why they came into the palace at all. "No one will see you. But in return you must tell me two things. The true name of my son. And of one other: one like yourself, a boy who was here three years ago, who was carried out by a page because he taught a washerwoman's daughter to spin straw into gold."

"Your mother is dead," the rat-girl said calmly. "She died a fortnight ago, of fire in the belly."

"Good riddance," I said harshly. "Will you do as I ask? In exchange for your freedom?"

The rat-girl didn't change expression. "Your son's true name would do you no good. The blood is so hectic, so tainted"—she twitched her nose in contempt—"that it would give you no power over him. *They* keep the old names just for ritual."

Ritual. One more gaudy emptiness in place of the real thing. One more hope gone. "Then just tell me the name of the Old One who taught me to spin gold!"

"I would sooner die," she said.

And then I said it. Spare me, God, I said it, unthinking of anything but my own need: "Do it or you will die a slow and painful death."

The rat-girl didn't answer. She looked at me with bone-white understanding in her pale eyes.

I staggered to my feet and left the room.

It was as if I couldn't see; I stumbled blindly toward my husband's Council Chamber. This, then, was how it happened. You spun enough straw into gold, and the power to do that did not change you. But when that power was threatened, weakened by circumstance—*that* changed you. You turned cruel, to protect not what you had, but what you might not have.

For the first time, I understood why my mother lied.

The prince was at his desk, surrounded by his councillors. I swept in, the only one in the room whose clothes were not embroidered with threads of gold. He looked up coldly.

"This girl who can spin diamonds," I said. "When does she arrive?"

He scowled. The councillors all became very busy with papers and quills. "Escort the princess from the Council Chamber," my prince said. "She isn't feeling well."

Three guards sprang forward. Their armor cover was woven of gold thread.

I couldn't find the young page of three years ago, who at any rate was a page no longer. But in the stable I found the stablemaster's boy, a slim youth about my height, dressed in plain, warm clothing he probably thought was rags. "In my chamber, there is a rat. If you come with me I will give it to you wrapped in a cloth. You will take it through the courtyard gate and into the forest. I will watch you do this from the highest tower. When you're done, I'll give you doublet and hose and slippers all embroidered with skeins of gold."

His eyes shone with greed, and his color flushed high.

"If you kill the rat, I'll know. I have ways to know," I told him, lying.

"I wouldn't do that," he said, lying.

He didn't. I know because when he came to my chambers from the forest, he was shaken and almost pale. He handed me a stone, clean and smooth and light as a single word. He didn't look at me.

But nonetheless he took the gold-embroidered clothes.

That night, I woke from the old dream. It was just before dawn. The two pale stones lay side by side on my crimson-and-gold coverlet, and on each was writing, the letters not curlicued and ornate but simple straight lines that soothed the mind, eased it, like lying on warm rock in the elemental sunshine.

I couldn't read them. It didn't matter. I knew what they said. The words were in my mind, my breath, my bone, as if they had always been there. As they had: *rampel*, the real; *stillskin*, with quiet skin.

The forest disappeared, copse by copse, tree by tree. The ground rose, and Dirk and I rode over low hills covered with grass. I dismounted and touched some stalks. It was tough-fibered, low, dull green. The kind of grass you can scythe but never kill off, not even by burning.

Beyond the hills the forest resumed, the trees squat but thick-bodied, moss growing at their base, fungus on their sides. They looked as if they had been there forever. Sometimes pale fire moved over the ground, as no-colored as mist but with a dull glow, looking very old. I shuddered; fire should not be old. This was not a place for the daughter of a washerwoman. Dirk squirmed and fretted in front of me on the saddle.

"You're going to learn, Dirk," I said to him. "To be still. To know the power of quiet. To portion your words and your makings to what is real."

As my mother had not. Nor the prince, nor his councillors, nor anyone but the rat-boy and rat-girl, who, I now knew, crept back into the corrupted palace because the Old Ones didn't ever let go of what was theirs. Nor claim what was not. To do either would be to name the real as unreal.

Dirk couldn't have understood me, but he twisted to scowl at me. His dark brows rushed together. His vivid blue eyes under thick dark lashes blinked furiously.

"In the real, first design is the power, Dirk."

And when I finished those words he was there, sitting quietly on a gnarled root, his pale eyes steady. "No," he said. "We don't teach children with fevered and corrupted blood."

For just a second I clutched Dirk to me. I didn't want to give him up, not even to his own good. He was better off with me, I was his mother, I could hide him and teach him, work for him, cheat and steal and lie for him . . .

I couldn't save my son. I had no powers but the tiny, disposable ones, like turning straw into gold.

"This time you will teach such a child," I said.

"I will not." The Old One rose. Pale fire sprang around him, rising from the solid earth. Dirk whimpered.

"Yes, you will," I said, and closed my eyes against what I was about to do: Become less real myself. Less powerful. For Dirk. "I can force you to take him. *Rampel stillskin* is your name."

The Old One looked at me, sadness in his pale eyes. Then Dirk was no longer in my arms. He stood on the ground beside the boy, already quieter, his fidgeting gone. The pale fire moved up from the ground and onto my fingers, charring them to stumps. A vision burned in my head. I screamed, but only from pain: Dirk was saved, and I didn't care that I would never spin again, nor that every gold thread in the kingdom had suddenly become stone, pale, and smooth and ordinary as a true word.

MÄRCHEN

Jane Yolen

Dr. Jane Yolen is a poet, adult novelist, and children's book writer, as well as one of this country's leading authorities on *märchen* (fairy tales). She won the World Fantasy Award for her collected *Favorite Folktales from Around the World*, and is the author of *Touch Magic: Fantasy, Faerie and Folklore in the Literature of Children*.

The following poem is reprinted from *Merveilles*, a folklore periodical from the University of Colorado.

—T. W.

Wilhelm Grimm loved words,
not stories.
they waterfalled from his pen.
He was deaf to the telling,
only the told.

Words like *camphor,*
goblet, ruby, anvil
waxed and waned in him.
He was tidal
with words.

I, on the other hand,
drink in tales,
giving them out again
in mouth-to-ear
resuscitation.

It does not matter
if the matter of the stories
is the coast of Eire
or the Inland Sea,
I swim—ah—ever deeper in them.

GIANTS IN THE EARTH

Dale Bailey

Dale Bailey has had short fiction published in *The Magazine of Fantasy & Science Fiction* and *Amazing Stories*.

According to the author, "Giants in the Earth" was originally suggested by a verse in the Book of Genesis. "Apparently, many of the church fathers believed that the passage referred to angels who had fallen in love with 'the daughters of men' and 'fathered children by them.' I couldn't help but wonder what happened to those beings, and the story was written partly as a response to that question." The story, though, is not really about such creatures but about humans and their reactions to the unknown. It originally appeared in *The Magazine of Fantasy & Science Fiction*.

—E. D.

Burns didn't imagine he could ever bring himself to really *like* Moore, but as he watched the man work the auger in the flickering shaft of his cap light, he had to admit a kind of grudging admiration for the fellow's grace. Down here in the mines, you noticed such things, for a clumsy man could kill you. It was just Moore's piety that bothered Burns; he had a way of preaching at a man.

Now, Moore swung back from the wall, nodding, a thin gaunt-featured man with lips pinched for want of living. The breast auger extended from his chest like a spear; it gleamed dully beyond a glittery haze of coal dust. Burns stepped forward, tamped a charge into the hole, plugged it with a dummy, and turned around to look for Moore, but the other man had already retreated through the blackness into the heading shaft. An empty cart stood on fresh-laid track, waiting to be filled, but otherwise the room was empty. Somewhere a miner hollered musically, and the sound chased itself through the darkness. There was a stink of metal and sweat, and the rattle of dust in his lungs. He could feel that old dread tighten through his chest.

Damn Blankenship for not wetting down the walls, he thought. Tight-fisted sonofabitch.

And then, with a gutteral sigh for the way life had of creeping up on a man—first a wife, and then a baby, and then you were trapped, there was nothing to do but work the coal—Burns turned back to the wall. He struck a match and touched it to the fuse. The fuse sputtered uncertainly, and for a moment Burns thought it might be bad, and then it caught with a hiss that seemed thunderous. It flared a self-devouring cherry, and Burns spun away, squeezing the match between his fingers as he stumbled from the room and flattened himself against the wall in the main shaft.

The charge went up with a muffled thud, and he braced himself for a second, more-powerful explosion that did not come. The dust had not ignited. He heard the wall crumble, tumbling Blankenship's coal out of the seam, and a thick cloud mushroomed into the main shaft. Burns glanced over at Moore. In the glare of the cap light, the other man's face looked pale and washed out, his eyes like glinting sapphire chips set far back in bony hollows.

Moore smiled thinly and lifted the auger over his head. "The Lord's with us."

"Lucky, I reckon," Burns said. He hunkered down, dug through the tool poke, and hefted his shovel and axe. "Reckon we ought to get to it," he said.

Burns stood and ducked back into the room without waiting for Moore to follow. Coughing thick dust, he picked his way through the rubble to the chest-high hole the charge had gouged in the wall. He dropped the shovel and went to his knees to prop the axe against the sloping roof of the undercut and that was when he saw it.

Or, rather, didn't see what he expected to see—what he had seen maybe a thousand times or more in the year since he and Rona had married, the baby had been born, and he had taken to working as a loader in Blankenship Coal's number six hole. What he didn't see was the splash of his cap light against the wall, pitted by the charge he had rigged to loosen the seam. Instead, the beam probed out in a widening cone that dissipated into dust and swirling emptiness.

A black current of stale air swept out at him, and Burns quickly crab-walked backwards. He jarred the prop loose, and the heavy tongue of rock above him groaned deep within itself. Pebbles sifted down, rattling against his hardhat, and then the mountain lapsed into silence. When the callused hands closed about his upper arms, Burns nearly screamed.

"Goddammit," he snapped, "what the hell do you think you're doing?"

He spun around to face Moore, and the other man backed away, flattened palms extended before him. Moore looked like a vaudeville comic in black-face. Coal dust streaked his gaunt features, was tattooed into the very fabric of his flesh, and it would never wash away, not even with years of scrubbing. You could tell the old-timers by the dusky tone of their complexions. Burns knew that if Moore would strip away his shirt, the exposed flesh of his face and hands would meet the pale skin beyond in hard geometric planes.

He knew, too, that someday he also would look as if he wore perpetually a dusky mask and gloves, and he hated it. But there was Rona and the baby. Swirling in the veil of dust that hung between the two men, Burns could almost see them, their features etched with a beauty too real and fragile for life in these mountains. A year ago, he had not known that a man could feel this way, and sometimes still it crept up on him unawares, this love that had led him to this deep place far beneath the earth.

He glanced away before Moore saw his eyes throw back the dazzle of the cap light. "Get that light out of my eyes, you've about half-blinded me," he said, and he turned away to collect himself. The massive tongue of rock that projected over the hole seemed almost to mock him. So close, Burns thought, and then where would Rona and the baby have been?

"You okay?" Moore asked.

Burns looked up. "Hell," he said. "Sorry. I thought the rock was coming down on me."

Moore gave him a curt nod, bent to reset the fallen prop, and then wedged his own axe into the gap. "That ought to hold it," he said, extending a hand to Burns.

Burns took the hand, and lifted himself to his feet. He dusted off his clothes out of habit, not because it would do any good. "There's something else," he said.

"What's that?"

"Something ain't right. That hole don't stop. It just keeps on going."

Moore lifted an eyebrow and studied the undercut for a moment. "Well, let's have a look," he said. "I don't reckon there's anything to be afraid of." He hunkered down, slid into the gap, and vanished.

Examining these last words for some taint of suggested cowardice, Burns followed. The roof slanted down a bit and then disappeared entirely as he emerged into a larger darkness. Though he could not immediately see the space, some quality—the acoustics of a far-away water drip or perhaps the flat, dank taste of the air—told him that it was at least as large as the room he and Moore had been working, that it had been sealed beneath the mountain for long years.

Burns stood. His light stabbed into the dark. "Moore?" Abruptly, he became aware of a sound like muffled sobs. "Moore? What happened to your light?"

"I turned it off."

Burns turned to face the voice. Moore sat just beyond the darker mouth of the opening into the other room, his arms draped over drawn-up knees, his head slumped. When he looked up at Burns, the sapphire chips of his eyes were shiny with a kind of madness. Tears glittered like tiny diamonds on his dusky face, and Burns could see the clean tracks they had carved across his cheeks.

The room seemed to wheel about him for a moment, the gloom to press closer. Uneasiness knotted his guts.

"Why'd you turn off your light?"

"Giants in the earth," Moore whispered. "There were giants in the earth in those days."

"What are you talking about? Why did you turn off your light?"

Moore gestured with one hand toward the darkness farther into the room, and Burns felt ice creep out of his belly and begin the paralyzing ascent into his throat. Almost a year ago, just a month or so after Burns had started to work, a spark from somebody's axe had ignited the dust in the number three hole. The men who survived the explosion came out of the mine with faces smoothed over by experience; the unique lines time and character had carved into their features had all at once been erased. They had no more individuality than babies, fresh from an earthen womb, and it occurred to Burns that Moore looked just that way now.

Burns did not want to look into the darkness at the center of the room. He liked his face. He did not want it to change. And yet he knew that if he did not move or speak, did not take action, the ice that was creeping slowly into his throat would fill up his mouth and paralyze him. He would be forever unable to move beyond this time and place, this moment.

He looked into the room.

In the flickering shaft of his cap light there lay a creature of such simple and inevitable beauty that Burns knew that for him the significance of that concept had been forever altered; it could never again be applied to mere human loveliness. Burns felt as if he had been swept up in a current of swift-running water, and in the grip of that current, he took a step forward, stunned by the apprehension of such beauty, unadulterated by any trace of pettiness, or ugliness, or mere humanity. He thought his heart might burst free of his chest. He had not known such creatures existed in the world.

And then, through that veil of terrible beauty, there penetrated to him the particular details of what he had seen; he came abruptly to a stop as that paralyzing ice of awe and fear at last rose into his mouth.

This is what he saw:

A being, like a man, but different, ten feet long, or twelve feet, curled naked in the heart of the mountain.

Wings, white rapturous wings, that swept up and around it like a cloak of molten feathers.

And in its breast, the rhythmic pulse of life.

Giants in the earth, he thought, and then—because he knew that if he did not look away, the lines of his face would be erased and he would lose forever some essential part of himself—Burns turned to look at Moore, who still sat against the wall. His gaunt face hung slack; tears glistened on his cheeks.

"I couldn't bear it," he said.

"We have to tell someone," Burns said.

"But who?"

"Someone who can do something."

"Who?"

Burns thought furiously. For a moment he thought he heard the rustle of feathers in the darkness behind him, and half-fearful, he turned to face the creature, but it had not moved. They could not be responsible for this, Burns thought—and the word responsible was like a gift, for suddenly he knew.

He crossed the room, crouched by Moore, and peered into his face. The slap sounded like a pistol shot in the enclosed chamber. Burns drew back his stinging palm for another blow, but he saw it wasn't necessary, for the madness in Moore's eyes had retreated a little.

"Get the cashier," he said. "Get Holland." He reached out and snapped Moore's cap alight, saw the man's gaunt features tighten with wonder. "Go on, now," he said. "Not a word to anyone but Holland, hear?"

Moore stood without speaking and ducked through the undercut. Burns was alone. Once again, he remembered the miners, their faces smoothed by experience, as they emerged from the explosion-shattered heading of the number three hole. And as he turned away from the undercut to look yet again at the awful beauty that lay slumberous in the center of the room, a terrible vision fractured his thought: his own face, smooth and featureless as a peeled egg.

In the wavering beam from his cap, Burns caught a single glimpse of the creature—

—the giant, the angel—

—and then he reached up with trembling fingers and shut off the light. In the succeeding blackness, sounds were magnified. The far-away drip of water became an intermittent clash of cymbals punctuated by measureless silences in which the creature's labored respiration sounded clamorous as a great bellows stoking the furnaces of the earth.

Finally, not because he dared to smoke, but because he had to do something with his hands or go mad, Burns fumbled for tobacco and rolling papers and began to make a cigarette. Even in the darkness, his fingers fell without hesitation into the familiar rhythm of the process, and the prosaic nature of the task—here in the midst of wonders—enabled him to envision Moore as he made the long trek through the heading shaft to the surface. He imagined the annoyed glance Jeremiah Holland would direct at Moore when he stepped into the cashier's shack, could almost see the thoughtful look that would replace it when he heard what Moore had to say. Holland, Burns knew, was a thoughtful man, the kind of man who considered the angles of a thing, and could work them to his own advantage.

Burns licked the paper, twisted the cigarette into a cylinder, and slipped it into his mouth. The tobacco tasted sweet against his lips. Holland would be a good friend to have, he thought. Holland could help a man.

And yet . . .

He felt a flicker of doubt. Such beauty . . .

The sound of men crawling through the undercut came to him. A wavering light illuminated the chamber, and Burns's heart broke loose within him as he caught a glimpse of the creature, curled fetal on the stone floor. The light bobbed into the air, and he saw that it was Moore. A second ghostly shaft penetrated the darkness, and Burns heard a metallic rattle of tools. He stood, his fingers fumbling at his cap as he stepped forward to meet Holland.

The cashier emerged from the undercut and pushed himself erect, a thin, wiry man with a battered toolbox clutched in one hand. His lean face looked hollow, even skeletal, in the intersecting beams of the cap lights, and his dark eyes returned Burns's gaze from deeply recessed sockets.

"I hope you're not planning to light that thing," he said.

Burns plucked the cigarette from his mouth with shaking fingers. "I just had to do something with my hands. That thing—" Licking a moist fragment of tobacco from his lips, he slipped the cigarette into his shirt pocket.

Holland lowered the toolbox to the floor with a clatter. "Yes, that thing. Your friend wasn't very articulate about that . . . thing." He glanced ruefully at his clothing, store-bought linen several grades more expensive than the cheap flannel the miners wore, and Burns saw that the cloth was soiled with dark streaks of coal dust. "Where is it?"

Burns glanced at Moore, but the other man had retreated deep into himself.

"It's over there," Burns said. Almost unwillingly, he turned his head and impaled the creature on the flickering shaft of his cap light. Its breast kindled with life; wings stirred in the passing wind of a dream. Burns blinked back tears. It seemed as if each particle of the air had suddenly flared with radiance, and though in fact it did not diminish at all, Burns imagined that the darkness retreated a little.

Jeremiah Holland drew in his breath with a sharp hiss.

"I thought you ought to see it," Burns said. "I wanted to do the right thing. I got a wife and baby and I was hoping—" He stopped abruptly when he realized that Holland wasn't listening.

The cashier's face had gone very white, and as Burns looked on, the tip of his tongue crept out and eased over his lips. He turned to look at Burns through widened eyes. "Have either of you touched it?"

Burns shook his head.

The cashier crouched by the toolbox, threw back the latches with trembling fingers, and withdrew a tamping bar. He stood, clutching the bar in one white-knuckled hand, and looked from Burns to Moore, who stood a few feet away, his face looking new-minted. "Let's see if you can wake it up," he told Burns.

Burns hesitated, and Holland lifted the tamping bar a little. "Go on now."

His heart hammering, Burns began to creep across the room. That paralyzing ice once again edged into his throat. Blood pounded at his temples. He felt as if he had been wrapped in a thick suffocating layer of wool.

And then he was there, standing over the—

—giant, the angel.

The creature, he told himself.

"Careful," Holland whispered, and glancing over his shoulder, Burns saw the flesh beneath the cashier's right eye twitch. "Do you realize—" he said, "—have you any idea what we could *do* with this thing?" He laughed, a quick harsh detonation, abrasive as shattering glass, and brandished the tamping bar. "Go on now."

Burns felt breath catch in his throat. He tried to speak, to protest, but that paralyzing ice had frozen away his voice. Swallowing, he prodded the creature with his boot. Flesh gave, the thing shifted in its age-long sleep: a hush and sigh of wings in the enveloping dark, the rusty flex of ancient muscles, and all at once the creature lay prone, face turned away, arms outstretched, great wings flared across the dusty floor. Conflicting impressions of promethean strength and gentleness swept through Burns, and—like nothing he had felt before—a swift and terrible hunger for such beauty, ethereal and mysterious.

Not until it passed did Burns realize he had been holding his breath. He released it and drew in a great draught of stale air. The ice had retreated a bit. Strangling a gout of hysterical laughter, he turned away.

"Maybe it's hibernating," he said, abruptly reminded of something he had heard at Rona's church—a story of an epoch impossibly distant, when graves would vomit forth the dead. Would angels ascend from the womb of the shattered planet?

Holland had returned to the toolbox. "We can't let it get away."

"Get away?"

Holland stood, his angular features ashen, and extended in his left hand the shining length of a hacksaw. The serrated blade threw off radiant sparks in the shifting luminescence of the cap lights. A sickening abyss opened inside of Burns.

"I don't think that's a good idea," Burns started to say, but he let the last word trail away, for he saw that a kind of lethargic energy had animated Moore's features. With the languor of drifting continents, half-formed expressions passed across the experience-scrubbed surface of his face.

"No," Moore whispered. "Please . . . please don't."

Holland spared him a single dismissive glance, and then he looked back to Burns and shook the hacksaw. The blade rattled against its casing.

Simultaneously, Moore also turned to face him. The twin glare of their cap lights nearly blinded him. He raised a hand to shield his eyes as the chasm that had opened within him yawned wider still. For a single uncertain moment, he felt as if he might plunge into the chaos that churned there.

As though from a great distance, he heard Moore's voice degenerate into sobs of desperation, saw Holland turn and strike him a single blow with the tamping bar. The glare diminished as Moore stumbled away.

Holland stepped up to meet him, the tamping bar upraised, the hacksaw dangling in his left hand; there was no mistaking the threat implicit in his posture.

"Do it," he hissed.

Burns moved closer to the wiry cashier, suddenly aware that he could wrest the tamping bar from the smaller man in less than an instant; in a moment of sudden clarity, he saw that Holland knew this, too. Beyond the mask of his bravado there lay a core of desperate fear. Burns saw that Holland had not perceived the creature's beauty. He could not, for fear drove him; perhaps it always had.

Turning away, he began to move toward Moore, slumped by the dark mouth of the undercut. He hadn't gone more than two steps before Holland spoke. "Did you say you had a wife and child?"

Burns hunkered down by Moore, rested a calloused hand against his shoulder. "That's what I said."

"Sauls Run," Holland said. "Not much work here, unless you're a miner."

"Please," Moore whispered. "Do you know what this means? It's true, all true . . ."

A fleeting image of that church story—the Rapture, Burns suddenly recalled—passed through his mind: angels, erupting by the thousand from beneath the mountains of the dying planet. True? *The Lord's with us*, Moore had said, and he had replied, *Lucky, I reckon*.

The hacksaw clattered to the floor behind him.

"Winter's coming," Holland said. "Hard season for a man without a job. Hard season for his family."

Burns emitted a strangled laugh, lifted his hand, and touched his fingers to Moore's stubbled face. Moore's lips trembled, and tears slid down his cheeks. Burns could smell the sour taint of his breath. "An angel," Moore whispered, and cursing, Burns stood and turned away.

That image—angels erupting from the subterranean dark—returned to haunt him as he stooped to pick up the hacksaw; he dismissed it with an almost physical effort. Not an angel, insisted some fragment of his mind. Some pagan god or demon; a monstrous creature out of myth; an evolutionary freak, caught in the midst of the transformation from beast to man—but not an angel.

A creature, nothing more.

He crossed the room without a word and knelt beside

—the giant, the angel—

—the creature. At the base of the thick-rooted wings, its flesh curled horny and tough, almost pebbled. Its back heaved with the regular cadence of its respiration. He could not bring himself to look it in the face.

Burns closed his eyes and drew in a long breath. He could hear the whispered litany of Moore's prayers, the faraway cymbal clash of the water drip. He thought of the coming winter, harsh in these mountains, and once again, that great love surprised him. For a moment, limned against the dark screens of his eyelids, he could almost see them, Rona and the baby, shining with an all too human beauty. Fragile and ephemeral, that beauty was, but a man could get his mind about it. A man could hold it.

He exhaled and opened his eyes.

Nothing had changed. Winged giants slept in the earth, but nothing had changed. The world was as it had been always.

"Do it, you son of a bitch," Holland said, and despite the fact that less than an hour ago Burns had not known that such creatures existed in the world, despite the fact that even now every molecule of air seemed to flare with a beauty so radiant that it was painful even to behold—despite all this, Burns began the terrible task.

The creature stirred when the hacksaw bit into the root of the near wing; its fingers drew into talons, its breath shuddered into a quicker rhythm, but it did not wake. Burns's muscles tightened into the work; sweat broke out along his hairline. The hide was tough as old hickory, but at last, with a noise like wind through dry leaves, the wing fell away. Burns kicked it aside. In the pale luminescence of his cap light, the wing stump glistened like a bloody mouth. Sighing, he stepped over the creature to start at the second wing. Once again, he leaned into the saw, once again dragged it back through the thick flesh, but this time—for no reason he would ever be able to discern—he looked up, looked directly into the creature's face.

And saw that it was awake.

The sounds of Moore's prayers and Holland's panicked respiration receded as Burns gazed into the creature's eye, so blue it might have been a scrap of April sky.

He felt as if he was falling, down and down into that endless blue, but he felt no fear. A wave of gratitude that he could not contain flooded through him—to have seen such beauty, to have touched it. Once again, the entire room seemed to flare with light, and for the space of a single instant, he perceived, beyond the shabby guise of reality, an inner radiance that permeated all things. Then, as suddenly as if he had shut off his cap light, the radiance was gone, overwhelmed by a tide of wretched exhilaration. No other man had ever mastered such a creature.

Burns flung away the hacksaw in disgust.

The creature's eye had closed. He could not tell that it had ever awakened.

A suffocating knot formed in his throat, and for the first time in the long year he had worked the mines, claustrophobia overcame him. The walls pressed inward. The entire weight of the mountain loomed over him.

Holland stepped up, his face blanched, his eyes reduced to glints far back in shadowy hollows. "Finish it," he said.

Burns wrested the tamping bar away from him and let it clatter to the floor. "Finish it yourself."

With a last glance at Moore, he pushed the cashier aside, ducked through the undercut and the empty room beyond, and emerged into the heading. From far down in the shaft, there echoed the din of a sledgehammer as a work crew snaked new track deeper into the planet.

He wondered what beauty they might eventually lay bare; he wondered what they would do with it.

Turning away, Burns began to walk slowly along the tracks that led to the surface. Men moved by him, nodding as they passed, and sometimes a loaded car muscled through the shaft; in the rooms that opened to either side, he heard the easy talk that came at shift's end. He had no part in that now. Deliberately, he turned his mind to other things, to the surface, where the sky would be fading toward night. He imagined the stench of burning slag riding the high currents; imagined the tin roofs of Sauls Run, faraway in the steep-walled valley, throwing off the last gleam of evening sun.

Presently, he emerged from the earth. He paused by the cashier's shack and fished the cigarette out of his breast pocket. His coal-smeared hands shook a little as he struck the match, and then harsh sweet smoke filled his lungs. He exhaled a gray plume and surveyed the valley below.

Everything—the sky, the smell, the flash of sunlight against the tin roofs of town—was just as he had imagined it. Nothing, nothing had changed. Drawing in another lungful of smoke, Burns started down the mountain to Sauls Run, to Rona and the baby. High above the painted ridges, the day began to blue into darkness, and a breath of autumn wind touched him, chill with the foreboding of winter.

A CONFLAGRATION ARTIST

Bradley Denton

Bradley Denton was born in 1958, grew up in Kansas, and received an M.A. in creative writing from the University of Kansas. He now lives in Austin, Texas. He sold his first story in 1984, and soon became a regular contributor to *The Magazine of Fantasy & Science Fiction*, *Asimov's Science Fiction*, *Pulphouse*, and elsewhere. He was a finalist for the John W. Campbell for Best New Writer in 1985. His first novel, *Wrack and Roll*, was published in 1986, and he won the John W. Campbell Memorial Award in 1992 for *Buddy Holly Is Alive and Well on Ganymede*. His most recent novel is *Blackburn*. His short fiction has recently been collected in two volumes: *The Calvin Coolidge Home for Dead Comedians* and *A Conflagration Artist*, from which this story is reprinted.

Until *Blackburn*, Denton was better known for his science fiction, but that novel's brilliant depiction of a serial killer with a moral code demonstrated the author's ability to write chilling suspense/horror. "A Conflagration Artist" shows further evidence of his talents in its portrayal of a journalist who tries to make sense of a woman's strange and dangerous behavior.

—E. D.

The Amazing Evelyn emerges from the one illuminated door and walks toward the tower at the center of the arena. Her two female assistants, who have been talking with me, fall silent. The other workers who have been milling about fall silent as well. The only sound is the soft crunch of the Amazing Evelyn's slippers on the gritty floor, echoing from the distant, invisible walls.

For her so-called "practice" dive she is wearing a costume similar to the one she will wear tomorrow: a blue swimsuit dotted with silver spangles; white tights; and a silver cape tied at her neck. Her arms are bare. As she approaches I can see the pink ridges and puckers that mar her skin. Or perhaps, in her view, they perfect it. They cause me to look up for a moment at the tower's apex, at the yellow flame burning on the platform there. I am struck again by the incongruity of the television term, *conflagrationary performance art*. Surely this is inappropriate; a "conflagration" is a fire that affects all, wounds all. But here, the Amazing Evelyn will burn alone.

Then I look down from the flame, all the way down, to the surface of the water in the tank beside me. The water is only as deep as my shoulder. I reach over the rim to touch its cool surface with my finger, and the ripples dance across the reflections of the arena lights, splintering them into shards of white.

I look at the Amazing Evelyn again and see that her eyes are focused on me as she comes around the tank. Her hair is amber stubble, a faint shade on her scalp. It is the same color as her eyes. I have seen photographs of her when her hair was long, as have we all. She was one of the most beautiful women in the Midwest then. But today, despite her scars—or because of them?—she is the most beautiful woman in the world.

She stops before me. Her scent is acrid and compelling. I am so surprised that I almost forget to look for a sheen of protective ointment on her skin. I do not forget, though; her beauty and scent are stunning, but I am here as a journalist, and I will do my job. I look her over and see no ointment. Perhaps, then, her costume is impregnated with a flame-retardant chemical. But I do not dare to reach out and touch the fabric. That would be testing a goddess.

Of this, however, I am now certain: Her arms, shoulders, neck, and head are unprotected, as are the tops of her breasts. Her scars bear witness.

"You will not be allowed in the arena tomorrow," she says. These are the first words she has spoken to me. Her voice is like the touch of a feather.

I tell her that I do not understand why she has said this.

"You have been gawking at me all week," she says. "I have allowed it because my management made the agreement, but we are under no obligation to allow you to attend the performance tomorrow."

I point out that anyone with a hundred dollars may attend the performance tomorrow.

"Anyone but you," she says. "I am not a freak to be gawked at."

But the people who will come tomorrow will do so precisely because they do consider her a freak to be gawked at. I do not speak this thought aloud; I do not say anything at all. She knows as well as I do why they are coming. But she needs their money, and so will prostitute herself for them in order to do as she pleases for another year. I am told that she dives at least once a month, sometimes twice a month, for no audience but her assistants and a video camera. But there is no money in that, and she and her assistants must live. So she signed the contract that requires her to dive once a year for a live audience and pay-per-view television. It is clear that she often regrets the arrangement; but she is a woman of honor, and will fulfill her obligations.

She steps around me and walks to the base of the tower. There her assistants attempt to remove her cape, and she stops them.

"We have to give our journalist a good show," she says.

Her voice is bitter, and I am ashamed. She believes I am here to exploit her, and I suppose that I have not given her reason to believe otherwise.

But I know her better than she thinks.

She was married for seven years and gave birth to three children. Her husband's given name was Zachary. The oldest child, a boy, was named Ezekiel; the girl, two years younger, was Emily; the baby, another boy, was Ezra. They lived in a farmhouse in north-central Kansas, where Zachary tended fields of wheat and soybeans.

Their lives seemed neither bleak nor mysterious to their neighbors; nor would they seem so to anyone who could view the Super 8 movies shot by Evelyn. In one of these films, the family has a picnic beside a tree-shaded creek. Zachary eats a chicken leg and winks at the camera; the children's faces become smeared with potato salad. Then the scene shifts to an arched stone bridge that spans the creek, and the children race across it toward the camera. But Ezekiel, who must be six years old, has eaten too much. He holds his distended little belly as he runs, and Emily wins the race. The toddler, Ezra, lags far behind, laughing and flapping his arms. Ezekiel staggers toward the camera, close to tears, and his mouth forms the words, "I lost." Then Zachary comes into view and picks up Ezekiel to comfort him. Emily dances a victory dance, and Ezra spits up on his shirt.

It all appears sweet and normal, and perhaps it was. But Evelyn, serving as camerawoman, appears in none of the films. While the faces of Zachary and the children betray no darkness or despair, hers might have told a different story. We shall never know.

What we do know is that one summer evening during supper, Zachary and Evelyn argued. The argument itself, according to Evelyn's later testimony, was over the fact that Evelyn was serving pork chops too often for Zachary's taste. It seems more likely, however, that the real source of distress was the fact that they were losing the farm. The bank was about to foreclose.

But of human motivations, one can never be sure.

In the midst of the argument, Evelyn ran from the kitchen table and out of the house. (I imagine her wearing an apron over a blue cotton dress, crying as she runs.) She ran across the yard and down the dirt road that passed before their farm. Here there were no trees. The evening was hot and dusty. Evelyn ran almost a mile, and walked a mile farther. Then she started back.

When she drew near the house, she saw black smoke rising from the kitchen windows. She began running again, shouting for Zachary, but Zachary did not answer. Much later, he was found in his soybean field, smeared with dirt, speaking in tongues.

In the kitchen Evelyn discovered the bodies of her children lying on the table, burning. Evelyn beat at the flames with her hands and with a dishrag, and after some minutes, during which her arms blistered and her hair burned, was able to extinguish the fire. But the children were dead, and had been dead before they were set ablaze. Autopsies revealed that Zachary had stabbed each child in the chest before dousing them all with kerosene.

Such events do not bear much commentary. But of the events that followed, more can be said.

After Zachary's trial, conviction, and imprisonment, Evelyn vanished for over a year. No one who knew her, not even her mother or pastor, had any evidence of where she had gone or what she might be doing. Her mother feared that she had disappeared in order to commit suicide. Others, including her pastor, were more inclined to believe that she had left to begin a new life elsewhere under another name, thus wiping out the horror of her children's deaths at the hands of their father.

Then, the following autumn, Evelyn returned. She would not say where she had been or what she had been doing, but moved back into her and Zachary's house as if to resume her former life. By now, though, the bank had taken the fields, and the house would have followed soon had not Evelyn's pastor collected money for her.

It was on the day the pastor delivered the check that Evelyn's new vocation was discovered.

"I was turning into the driveway when I saw her," the pastor told me. "I wouldn't have thought to look up, but the fire caught my eye."

What he saw was Evelyn standing atop the windmill behind the house. As he watched, she dove off, burning, into the water tank at the windmill's base.

"But I couldn't see the tank," the pastor said. "I just saw her disappear behind the house. I thought she was dead. Then I drove back there, and she was coming out of the water . . ."

The pastor's voice softened and fell silent, and I could not persuade him to describe any more of what he had seen.

"Of course we all thought that poor Evvy had gone crazy," her mother said. "Turned out to be crazy like a fox." She said this without any hint of a smile.

I asked more questions, but neither of them said anything else beyond what I had already learned. So the three of us relaxed in lawn chairs in the front yard of the Amazing Evelyn's house, waiting for her to arrive from California for a promised visit. The grass was dry and brown. The vanes of the windmill turned with rasps and squeaks. I sipped lemonade and believed that I had managed to develop a sincere kinship with the Amazing Evelyn's mother and pastor. After all, I had made it clear that I would not paint her as an object of amusement, as television did. It was my hope that their trust would convince Evelyn to trust me as well.

But then the telephone in the house rang, and the Amazing Evelyn's mother went to answer it. When she returned, she told me that Evelyn would not be coming home for a visit after all. She had heard that a journalist was lying in wait for her.

Those were her words: "lying in wait." As if I were a wild animal, hoping to devour her.

And as I watch her ascend, I wonder if she might have been right. My heart is racing, and the sensation in my belly has overtones of both hunger and sex. I do not want to watch her do this thing; I do not want to watch the Amazing Evelyn burn. And yet I watch anyway, as will thirty thousand people here tomorrow, as will millions more via television, as will you all.

She climbs the tower, never looking anywhere but upward, never acknowledging the existence of those of us below. She climbs until she is above the lights and we cannot see her except as a blue shadow in the darkness.

There is a movement beside me, and I am distracted for a moment. I glance to my right and see one of the Amazing Evelyn's assistants training a VHS camcorder upward. The other assistant stands beside her, head tilted back, gazing at the apex of the tower with an expression of beatific awe. She is in love with the Amazing Evelyn.

I look back up just in time. The blue shadow steps onto the platform and stands over the flame.

The flame leaps up, engulfing the shadow, and the Amazing Evelyn burns.

She raises her arms, forming a fiery cross for an instant, and then dives. The sound is a roar; it is the sound of the wind rushing faster and faster, blasting all other sound behind, into the past, into oblivion.

She falls and burns forever. If her clothes are impregnated with anything, it is gasoline. Her head is the amber coma of a comet; her torso a blazing blue spike; her arms and legs orange flames. Halfway through the fall the silver cape explodes, and there is no longer even a hint of head, of torso, of arms, of legs. The Amazing Evelyn is not a woman; she is fire. She is a falling star, a rushing meteor, spearing downward to crush me, to consume me—

I cry out, cringe, and hide my face in my hands.

Then I hear a splash and a sizzle, and drops of water spatter on my neck. The water is hot.

I straighten, uncover my eyes, and stare at the wet ash on my sleeve. Then, slowly, unwillingly, I turn to face the tank. I have a question to ask, the one question that my editor insisted I must ask despite its obvious, pathetic triteness. And ask it I shall; but I have waited until the moment when I know she will be most vulnerable, until the moment when I know that I have some hope of obtaining an answer that is honest, that is true.

The first word leaves my mouth as I turn:

"Why—" I begin, and then I stop.

Her assistants are in the tank, going to her with the robe, just as they will tomorrow. But tonight she waves them away, swims to the ladder, and rises from the water without their help, without the robe. She stands on the top step, at the rim of the tank, and looks down upon me. Her scent is sweet and terrifying.

Her tights and cape are gone, and her swimsuit is a blackened rag over her right shoulder. She is hairless; she is blistered; she is perfect.

Her assistants come up behind her. There is a hush in the arena, as if no one breathes. The Amazing Evelyn looks down upon me, her skin steaming, her eyes glowing.

"Did you get a good tape?" she asks. She is not speaking to me, but to her assistants.

"I think so," the assistant who held the camcorder says.

The Amazing Evelyn nods. "Then you may send it to Zachary."

She descends the outer ladder to the floor, her eyes still on me. She knows that I too am in love with her.

Now she accepts the wet robe, puts it on, and turns to walk back across the arena to the illuminated door. Her assistants remain behind, as do I.

When she is gone, I touch the surface of the water in the tank again. It is warm. My finger comes up with a charred silver spangle, which I press to my lips. The assistants see me do this, but say nothing. They realize that I have finally understood: The Amazing Evelyn is indeed a conflagration artist; for when she burns, all who see her—who do not gawk, but *see*—burn with her.

"Why do you do it?" I was supposed to ask.

But having stood below her tower and watched her fall toward me, blazing through the black air of an empty arena, I know that the answer is as obvious as the question. She does it because it is her art.

She does it because it is her life.

REPORT

Carme Riera

Born in Mallorca, Carme Riera was educated in Barcelona, Spain, and is a lecturer in Spanish literature at the Barcelona Autonomous University. She has written several novels, all in Majorcan—the variation on Catalan spoken in the Balearic island of Majorca. Several have also been translated into Castilian, including *Questio d'armor propi* and *Joc de miralls*, winner of the Ramon Llull Prize.

"Report" is a sensual literary ghost tale set on the north coast of Mallorca. It comes from *Origins of Desire: Modern Spanish Short Stories*, edited by Juan Antonio Masoliver, and is translated by Julie Flanagan.

Deyá,
22 September, 1980

Dear Helen,

I need you to find out for me whether a woman named Maria Evelyn MacDonald, aged about forty, is living in Santa Barbara. For the moment, I can't give you any more details. It's absolutely essential for me to locate her and make contact with her, as you'll see from the story I'm sending you. I'll call you when I can from New York and will keep you informed. Please don't think I've gone crazy. Do everything possible to help me. Ask around, look in the telephone directory . . . whatever you can.

Love,
Stephanie.

This is a small village on the north coast of Mallorca. The stone houses look out over the stream, offering up their tiny mauve gardens. Still-flowering bougainvillea competes with the ivy in its endeavors to scale house and garden walls. Only from the highest windows can you see the sea penetrating the rounded deserted cove

---

This story, like almost all of Carme Riera's work, was originally written in Majorcan. Unfortunately the manuscript was lost and this English translation is, perforce, from a Castilian version the author prepared for the anthology *Doce relatos de mujer* (Alianza, 1982). (Trans.).

in the distance. The last summer visitors, the faithful and the stragglers, left a few weeks ago. They held out until the damp and first autumn rains threatened to vent themselves on rheumatic anatomies addicted to central heating. Apart from the sparse foreign colony established in the village years ago, there are very few of us outsiders still here. I confess right away that I'm leaving soon too. There's no reason for me to delay my departure any longer because yesterday, what I was waiting for, the only thing that kept me here, happened. And yet I'm sorry to go. But I have no other option. I must leave here as soon as I can.

It would never have occurred to me in the early days after my arrival that I'd spend the whole summer here toiling away simply in search of information to write a report. The fact is, I got carried away with the whole affair. Right from the start, I thought the hostility of the local people to the matter seemed abnormal. People living here are used to dealing with foreigners and are by nature helpful and hospitable. Why then did they persist in keeping silent? Even the money I offered them failed to refresh their memories . . . The younger ones made excuses saying they'd never heard anything about the case, while the older people who might have known at close quarters what happened, or who might even have experienced the events, refused to make any statement.

Nobody remembered Anaïs Nin either. "So many artists come through here . . . you will understand . . . we are used to seeing so many people . . . new faces . . ." Thanks to Robert Graves's wife, I found out where she had lived. A cottage in the "Clot"* with a little garden, just like all the rest. Its present owner, a black girl who spends her summers here, was very happy for me to visit her and delighted with the news because she didn't even know that Nin had stayed in Mallorca, let alone in her house. "I could come to some arrangement with the people who own the cells where Chopin and George Sand stayed in Valldemossa and for a bit more money they could round off the tourist trip with a visit to my house. You can't tell me Anaïs Nin isn't someone with international prestige . . ."

Needless to say, the house retained no trace of the writer's stay, but I took photos anyway to illustrate my report which still wasn't making any progress.

I was really very dispirited, realizing that it had begun badly, that I was getting nothing clear; the best thing I could do was to forget about my commitment with Partner and the special number his magazine was putting out in homage to Anaïs Nin, and devote myself to sunbathing. After all, it was my fault. You should never take literally the assertions of any writer who claims she heard the story she's about to tell from other lips . . . But it was difficult for me not to take the case of Nin seriously: "I was spending the summer in Mallorca, in Deya† . . . A strange story was told of the place by the fisherman." These two sentences at the beginning of her story "Mallorca" struck me as being credible enough. Without doubt, the strange story would have unfolded around the forties when Nin was

---

* "The Gully" (Majorcan).

---

† The accent is absent in Nin's English version, *Delta of Venus* (1978, A Star Book, W.H. Allen & Co. Ltd.).

here. If they told her about it then, why didn't they want to mention it now? Did they find it so shameful that a local girl should have a relationship with a foreigner and make love with him on the beach? Was it more outrageous then than now? It was absurd to believe such a thing. But why did they refuse to talk about it? Gisele, my black friend, suggested that maybe they were all telling me the truth . . . they didn't know the story because it had never happened.

I wrote to Partner. Anaïs Nin had only used her imagination. It was a mistake to suppose otherwise. The story "Mallorca" figures among the pages of her book *Delta of Venus*, a collection of stories written on commission. I was very sorry to have got it wrong. As an alternative, I proposed to write a long piece about Graves and his world . . . Partner telegraphed me from New York. He wanted something on Nin, and fast. I re-read her *Diaries*, looking for any item that might orient me . . . How did Nin manipulate reality? What was her concept of truth? I remembered a letter from Henry Miller to her: "All your lines are loaded with meaning, but no matter how much anyone explains their sense, the enigma will persist because you are the only one who can explain it. And in the enigma resides the key to your triumph: you will never reveal it . . ." I underlined several paragraphs of her voluminous confessions, ending up with one succinct affirmation: "What kills life is the absence of mystery." I began to think it all through. Partner had asked me for an article, something light, so I tried sending him a short essay which was too esoteric for the public for whom the magazine was destined. I sent it by urgent mail. He telegrammed me again: "Take time necessary. We delay publication. Get what happened with story. You have key. There's a mystery."

I renewed my enquiries, but changing tactics. I didn't mention Nin at all, nor did I ask if the fisherman's daughter and the young American were still alive, nor whether it were true that in their youth they had made love publicly, in the moonlight. I confined myself to finding out if there were in the village any couples of a foreign man and Mallorcan woman, or the reverse, if this were at all usual, and if it were looked upon favorably. They said no, that there were very few cases, that such relationships always ended dramatically . . . the customs are different, way of life, temperament . . . Not one of these conclusions seemed sufficiently valid to me, nor even explicit. I protested, asked for more details. The little woman who was letting a room to me confessed that every time such a union occurred, some calamity fell on the village . . .

"Such as?"

"Calamities . . . A house collapses, a wall falls down, a rainstorm washes away the vegetable gardens."

"It could be coincidental."

"Don't you believe it. It's a punishment."

"Why?"

"Up there, they don't like people doing such things . . ."

"How long has this been going on?"

"Since they died."

"Who?"

"The ones you're trying to find out about . . . But I'm not telling you any more."

All my efforts were useless. I begged, made offers, promised to keep the secret. Futile. I couldn't get another word out of her. For some days after our conversation she was evasive, and managed not to see me or have the least contact with me. Gisele congratulated me when I told her. "You've got a very strong lead; it's a good starting point." It was her idea: I went down to Palma, and, in the small newspaper archive there, consulted the papers from the summer of '41. Anaïs had been in Deyá during those months. I found nothing of interest. Then '42 . . . In the copy of *Correo** for 21 September 1942, there was a brief item: three bodies had been found floating in the waters of the cove at Deyá. Two of them were women, María Sarrió Companys, daughter of village fishing people, and Evelyn MacDonald, American subject, while the third was a man, George MacDonald, brother of Evelyn. It appeared that heavy seas had swept them from the rocks where they were walking. There were no witnesses to the unfortunate accident and therefore no help was available.

I returned to Deyá with a photocopy of the newspaper item. I discussed it with Gisele. There was no doubt that Anaïs Nin had used part of the story, speaking only of the love between María and Evelyn's brother, without mentioning their tragic deaths . . . Nin wrote before this happened . . . What really occurred? Why was there so much mystery about such a stupid and cruel accident? "There has to be something more to it," Gisele insisted, "for sure."

I had quite a job getting my landlady to read the document. She couldn't see well without her glasses and she'd lost them months before. Nor did she want me to read it to her aloud. Finally, after much persistence, I put it before her myopic eyes. Her chin trembled and she started to cry.

"It's them. Leave them alone. Yes, they're dead, but if you call them, they'll come back again and it will be horrible. They'll come back and they won't let you sleep. None of us will ever sleep again."

"Why? Tell me, please . . . don't cry . . ."

"They died because of their terrible sins. It was a punishment from above, there's no doubt of it. They bewitched her, miss, they bewitched María . . . I can't tell you any more. I can't. If I say anything, they'll come back. At night the sounds of the sea won't let us sleep, the waves will flood this house and with their noise will come the gasping . . . They used to make love on the beach, the three of them, naked, all together. Do you understand? They didn't care if anyone was watching, it was so obscene. Nothing like that had ever happened in the village before . . . It was their fault, those two foreigners. They'd come to Deyá, away from the war,† they said, at the end of thirty-nine. They rented a house outside the village. They used a typewriter, like you. We thought they were married. They used to embrace in public, with no respect for us. The priest gave them a talking to once, but that made it worse. From then on they used to swim naked in the cove, a disgraceful custom which unfortunately became fashionable along this coast more than forty years ago . . . One evening María was walking

* *Post* (Castilian).

† The Spanish Civil War.

on the rocks at the cove—she was my friend, did you know that? The same age as me. Evelyn called out to her from the water. María took off her dress and jumped into the water in her chemise. She swam up to Evelyn. The chemise made it hard for her to move. Evelyn pulled her over to the boat landing and undressed her there. They swam back to the shore and lay on the sand resting in the moonlight with Evelyn's arm around María's waist. They went back there to meet each other every afternoon. María was fascinated by Evelyn's beauty, and the stories she beguiled her with. I was confidante and I knew all too well she'd been bewitched. One day George joined them. He swam out to them and then lay naked on the beach with them. María let them both make love to her . . . That night she got a tremendous beating from her father. She was in bed a week because of it. As soon as she could get up, she disappeared from the village with them. We had no news of her for two years. The Palma police visited us once trying to get information that would help them find out where she was. It was about then that the writer you're working on appeared. I remember her vaguely. Someone told her the story; she was American like them. Later we found out she'd been merciful with María . . . she'd only written about the love affair with George. The next summer, toward the end of September, they came back. They brought a little girl a few months old with them. The father was George, but we didn't know which of the two women was her mother . . . María came to see me but I didn't want to receive her. Nobody in the village did. That evening they went down to the cove, taking the little one in a carry-cot. Everyone in the village was spying on them from behind the bushes. They were making bets about their shamelessness and said we had to teach them a lesson before we called the police. I still marvel at how naturally they took their clothes off. Then, instead of going into the water, they stayed next to the rocks at the right side of the cove. They lay down there and embraced. Their gasps came up to us mixed with the sounds of the waves. It was something disgusting to see the way their bodies moved when they were making love. Some of the men left their hiding places and went across to them with sticks to threaten them. They didn't turn a hair. They had to beat them apart. The three of them were hurt and they ran to the sea. It was their only possible escape. We assumed they'd try to save themselves by swimming to the far end of the cove and climbing up the cliff from there. The sea was coming in furiously, with the waves getting bigger and bigger. We could hardly make out their heads and arm movements. We thought we could hear their voices calling out to each other. The baby started to cry. I took her home with me. Really, it was just an excuse to get away from there. One by one, all the people went back up to their houses. The next day their bodies appeared floating at the mouth of the cove. Dead. The judge from Soller came to take charge of the corpses, but nobody could be surprised by their deaths . . . They took too many risks and everyone had seen them swimming when the sea was rough . . . I took the little girl to the police and it was then that they told me that George and Evelyn were brother and sister. The American consul in Palma contacted their family. Later I found out that María Evelyn went to live with her grandparents in Santa Barbara. To be frank with you, I've done everything possible to forget about it . . . For years I've had terrible problems with insomnia and awful nightmares because of this story, just like everyone in the village, only nobody dares to confess it. Often at night when the sea is rough we've heard them calling out for help from the cove and on other nights when it's calm, their soft voices come up to us and you can hear the panting of their bodies at the moment of pleasure . . . But there's more yet, a lot more. For years after this terrible thing happened, none of the fishermen from here could put down nets anywhere near the cove without putting themselves in grave danger: a tremendous weight dragged them down to the bottom . . .

"It's the first time I've told anyone about it. Maybe you'll think I'm exaggerating, or not right in the head . . . The pity is that these things happened, just as I've told you. If they haven't come back to worry us lately, it's because nobody's mentioned their names, but I fear that without meaning to, you've called them again . . . Ever since you've been trying to find out about it, I've had trouble sleeping and it's the same with some of my neighbors who saw these terrible things . . .

"Do you want proof that I'm not lying? Then go down to the cove on the night of the twenty-first. It will be thirty-eight years since their deaths. Just like every other year, only the boats of the youngest people and the foreigners will go out. They'll come back without catching a thing. The sea is rough and there's usually a storm. Stay by the water's edge and look carefully: at midnight you'll see them come out of the water and lie naked on the beach to make love until morning . . ."

I was totally overwhelmed by the story. I hurried to tell Gisele.

"Your landlady was talking nonsense, sweetheart. They tell me she's crazy. Apparently she was the schoolteacher when she was young but they took her off it because she had bad attacks of depression . . ."

Gisele left at the beginning of September and I stayed on, waiting. Yesterday I went to the cove. It was a full moon. The sea was sparkling. Suddenly I saw them. They were swimming in toward the beach, young, amazingly beautiful as if death and time hadn't been able to touch them. And there near the water's edge, they began their amorous games which lasted until daybreak . . .

When I went back to the house, I couldn't tell my landlady what I'd seen. She wasn't there. She'd left me a farewell note saying she was going, as she did every year, to spend a few months in a sanatorium. She left me instructions for closing up the house and wished me a happy return home. I tried to sleep but couldn't for the murmuring of the sea that came insistently to my ears.

—Barcelona, October 1980.

THE VILLAGE OF THE MERMAIDS

John Bradley

John Bradley's poetry has been published in the *Sonora Review*, *Synaesthetic*, *Poetry East*, *College English*, and other venues. His collection *Love-in-Idleness* won a Washington Prize in 1989. Bradley teaches at Northern Illinois University, and recently edited the anthology *Atomic Ghosts*, of poems about the nuclear age.

The enchanted fantasia that follows was published first by Asylum Arts, a small California publishing house (created by Greg Boyd) committed to publishing books of literary fiction by up-and-coming writers. Bradley's "The Village of the Mermaids" comes from *Asylum 1994*, the publisher's annual journal of fiction and nonfiction.

—T.W.

1

The women said nothing
as I passed, not one objected
to my violating their solitude
on the narrow street littered
with sea shells, though I could hear
a lobster inside an empty room
softly scratch the floor and walls
behind the door of one of the women
who all stared with unblinking eyes.

My report on the promotion
of tourism, the possibility
of a desalinization plant, the necessity
for a nuclear power plant
to attract the future drew me
to the village at the request of the governor
with his twenty-six wives,
fifty eunuchs, six camels,

and thirty-nine children
who each spoke a different dialect
of the language of snails.

This limp
and this cane
and the nature of my illness
brought me there.

Why did each woman look
as if she had been named Genevieve?
Why were their hands so cold
and claw-like?
Where were the men, the children?
What made the mountains appear so indifferent
to any disturbance of air or earth?

On the beach, those other
women who appeared as, forgive me,
I too despise the term, mermaids.
Were they concubines of the sea,
or was the sea their prisoner?

I cling to this
brief entry
in my diary for that day:

> *I have only myself*
> *to blame.*

Perhaps I was referring
to the nature of my illness,
or was it meant as an apology
to the women who I abandoned
to the sexuality of mermaids?
Or was it they preferred to live
in the company of women?

Perhaps I was referring
to the rumor I would later hear
of mermaids washed up on the shores.
Dead from unidentifiable causes.

This limp, this cane,
this report is to blame.
Though if I am guilty
then everyone whose body desires salt

is also guilty, and therefore
no one, finally, is to blame.

If you must
go to the Village of the Mermaids, burn
a white candle, for memory
does not explain anything

except the need of memory
for our flesh.

2

He does not know the body of a mermaid, how it requires the soft lapping of the waves, the tongues of the sea making love constantly to each part of her body, the need to be told without ever saying it, *You are more beautiful than I can ever say.*

He does not know how we sit, day and night, waiting for a message from the sea to tell us that we no longer need sit waiting for a message from the sea.

He does not know what it is to be born in the Village of the Mermaids, to listen to the sea take pleasure in their bodies, while it is all we can do to remain in a chair with hands folded.

He does not know how we despised him, his gloves, his limp, his cane, his cigar, his official report, all the while pleading with our eyes for him to stop, inquire as to the nature of our illness, remove a glove, and touching one of us, any one, on the chin, granting us the strength to relieve him of his illness.

He does not know the weight of the mountains, the taste of salt on a shell found in your bed, the sound of a mountain breathing in your hair those nights when the boots of your absent husband smell like a caged owl a child set aflame.

He does not notice how we all resemble his mother, her tired breasts, the bruises on her neck, hidden behind our high collars. He cannot hear the leeches that feed on our legs beneath our long starched dresses. He never goes to the mariner's hospital, where each Sunday we read to the absent sailors the unsent letters of their wives, the unwritten letters of their children, the lists of injustices done to the mermaids.

He does not know, in short, why he is alive, why he is so dangerous, why the mermaids expired for him on the beaches, their flesh flickering with the light of the half-remembered.

3

Dear Monsieur Paul Delvaux,

Genevieve, my Genevieve, has been missing for three years now. For three years I have been travelling, visiting inns and hostels, train stations and prisons, hospital and mental asylums, bakeries and sailors' bars, looking for the woman whose absence eats at me, the way the whetstone slowly destroys the blade.

A pot of potato soup on the stove. That's how she left me, that's all I know of her disappearance. Even the stray dogs would not touch that soup.

Wherever I go I carry with me a box of her favorite chocolates, a yellow rose, a silver earring of two fish in pursuit of one another, a note in her hand that says, *Potatoes, always more potatoes.*

I'm certain you can help me.

You see I came upon a print of your painting *The village of the Mermaids* and I said to myself, Gabriel, Here is a man you can trust, a man who surely knew my Genevieve as an acquaintance or a model, for how else could her face appear on the women in his painting? How else could he also feel the absence of Genevieve?

Friend, surely you know the woman I speak of, the scar on her left ankle in the shape of the crescent moon, her craving for coconuts, the repentant bruises on her neck, her eyes that will not close even in sleep.

I await your reply. Please write *at once.*

If for some reason you do not reply, I cannot be held responsible for my actions. One night you will dream of your heart placed in a vase, doused with kerosene, and set ablaze. Your chest will burn. The heart, her absence will kill you. But I am sure this will not occur, as you seem such an understanding man, for how else could my Genevieve have befriended you? How else could you have painted *The Village of the Mermaids?*

Your friend and ardent admirer,
Gabriel

—AND THE HORSES HISS AT MIDNIGHT

A. R. Morlan

A. R. Morlan's second story in this anthology, "—And the Horses Hiss at Midnight," takes place at a carnival fairground and uses a primal male fear to create a charming little chiller. The story first appeared in *Love in Vein*.

—E.D.

"Sure you've heard of *that* one," Mona the Tattooed Girl told me as she slipped her vine-covered fingers into my shirtfront. In the busy near-silence of the approaching nightfall, I heard one of the buttons give way and softly roll off into the trampled grass behind the midway, the sound all but lost in the swell of crickets and the distant tire-kisses on the highway far beyond.

Tracing the swell of one halter-trapped breast with my left hand, as my right wound around her bat-and-vine-encircled waist, I whispered once again, "No, I've never heard of snakes hiding in carousel horses. . . ."

Another of my shirt buttons was liberated from the surrounding fabric before Mona replied, "But they do . . . it's only the people who don't believe who say it's untrue. The people who don't dare believe"—another pair of fingers sliding down my chest, another button rolling off to be forever lost in the litter-flecked grass—"and the people who are *afraid* to believe. . . ."

"Why would they hide in wood?" My right hand slid downward, to her needle-embroidered belt with the navel buckle, lingering at that delicate indentation before seeking the softer, far deeper indentation below.

Mona's lips brushed against my chest a moment before she spoke against my skin. "Not in the wood itself . . . they hide in the cracks in the wood, the places hidden by the shadows and contours of the horse's surface . . . places you don't normally look. But just because they aren't seen, doesn't mean they aren't *there*." The last was almost muffled by my own quickly rising chest. My breath was coming in hitches. I let my hand wander across her back to fumble with the knotted ties of her halter as I asked her, "But why be there if no one sees them? What's the point in living just to hide?"

The Tattooed Girl's eyes glittered in the almost-full moonlight; her lipstick shone near-black against her small white teeth as she stared at me in the darkness.

"*What's the point*—That's like saying what's the point in me getting all of these"—she used her button-popping hand to point to her embellished breasts and flatly decorated torso—"if I don't walk around all but naked all the time . . . which I *don't*," she added defensively, and for a moment, I feared I'd lost my chance with her, the chance I'd been all but praying for since I'd first seen her earlier that evening, standing on her small stage in the Fabulous Freaks tent on the midway.

The "Freaks" part may have been something of a misnomer; the best this carnival could come up with was the ubiquitous Headless Woman sitting light bulb–surmounted in her wooden chair, the parabolic mirror which hid her head *almost* flawlessly set up and lit, along with a merely anorexic-looking Thin Man and mediocre sword-swallower (he used no sword thicker than a good-sized shish kebab holder). But "Fabulous" more than applied to the spotlit Mona the Tattooed Girl. I thought, upon seeing her, that the word should've been forever reserved for her alone.

Spread-wing bats flapped with each languid exhalation and inhalation, all but flitting from bloody thorn to moon-kissed leaf. Kudzu vines seemed to grow upon her red-tipped fingers, winding and spreading over and around her knuckles, growing more dense by the second. The arabesques encircling her arms and neck crept up onto the bare sides of her head, touching the roots of her shaggy dyed-blond mohawk before winding upon themselves and snake-trailing down her spine, down to the low-slung waistband of her high-cut shorts. Sylphids and shaggy satyrs chased each other down and around her thighs, around each rose-touched knee, and spiraled down her calves to her flatly braceleted ankles. Below the links of yellow gold sunk into her flesh, branching thinner chains of ink and imagination, leading down to her red-tipped toes. Only her face was free of permanent embellishment; her kohl-lined green eyes and glittering carmine lips had been decorated by her own hand. But the color in her cheeks which bloomed and flushed when she read my silently mouthed *Will you make love to me*? was perhaps the most wonderful, thrilling adornment on her entire ornamented body. . . .

And more wonderful still, she was waiting for average, unadorned *me* after the carny wound down, after the wooden carousel horses did their last prance and canter before resting still and frozen in the moonlight. Taking my sweating, naked-looking fingers in her own cool vine-wound ones, she led me to a place of undisturbed grass and near-silence, her long mythic legs scissoring beside me . . . but before we could undress, before the promised lovemaking could begin, she'd whispered a strange thing about the horses, and the hidden snakes—

Hoping to recapture her ardor, or whatever it was that made an exquisite being like her blush and then mouth "Yes" to my request for sex (was it my use of the word "love" that had swayed her, or did she find my mundane exterior somehow exotic in its ordinariness?), I reached up and caressed the smooth side of her head, then moved my fingers and thumb close to her eyes, her lips, and said, "All right, all right, so they live *to* hide . . . maybe they want to, or like to?"

That brought back her smile, made her dancing eyes glitter. "Yesss," she said in a rush of warm air against my gently probing fingers, "that's what they like best of all . . . the coming out *after* hiding. . . ." Closing her eyes until her lashes cast fluttery crescents across her upper cheeks, she reached behind her and undid her halter ties herself, but allowed me the honor and pleasure of removing the twin triangles of black fabric. Revealed in the moonlight, her nipples and breasts cast small shadows on her flesh; both fleshy protrusions were decorated right up to the very tips of the nipples with petal after layered petal—each breast was a full-blown chrysanthemum surrounded by curling rings of leaves.

Closing my eyes for a moment, I could almost feel the individual petals beneath my delicately tracing fingers, but Mona reached up and thumbed both my eyes open, then let her forefingers linger on my temples. Rubbing them gently, she whispered, "Time for botany later . . . they wait until they're being ridden, before coming out, y'know," she went on dreamily, as she moved her hands down my cheeks and neck, her flesh gliding smoothly, like slick leaves, until she'd reached my chest, and nipples.

Circling my flesh with her thumbs, Mona shifted slightly below me as if trying to squirm out of her cutoffs without touching them with her hands, as she went on in that same lazy yet succinct voice, "It's best when there's a child, or a woman on the horse . . . that's when the snakes slither out of the cracks, one by one, and inch by inch, and when there's a little bit of silence between the notes of the carousel, they start to hiss . . . maybe one at first, then a couple of them, hiss *hiss* . . . and while they're doing that, they undulate, maybe touching the rider's calf, or a kneecap . . . whatever's exposed, whatever's unsus*pecting*—"

Finally taking her nonverbal hint, I reached down and began to undo the buttons under the fly of her cutoffs, wanting to pop the buttons off as she had done to me, but still afraid to be so rough, so obvious. This was her place, her world, and I didn't know who might come running should she cry out or worse.

"—and maybe at first they think it's a bug, or some part of their clothes that's loose and flapping, but then, when the snake's little tongue does that slow flicker and snap-back, *then* the rider knows . . . and *then* the rider hears the hissing for what it is, but the ride is going 'round, y'know? It can't stop . . . there's no emergency brake on a merry-go-round," she added with this little chuckle that never reached her staring eyes. Mona waited until my fingers had freed the last of the buttons before wrapping both arms around my back and whispering in my ear, "So the rider just goes 'round and 'round, while the snakes slither up and around their little knees and feet, hissing and waving, enjoying the ride . . . and all the rider can do is grab hold of the pole and scream against the music . . . and the ride goes so fast, no one else can see the snakes . . . 'specially not the other people on the ride, the ones whose snakes are hiding for now—"

Hitching my fingers into her waistband, I waited until Mona arched her back slightly before tugging down the shorts. Once they were past her hips, her knees, she wiggled until they could be kicked off her body with her lower legs . . . and as she was busy freeing herself of the cutoffs, she relaxed her grip on my body just enough so that I could get a good moonlit look at what was tattooed beneath the place where her shorts had been—

That she was bare down there was a given; hadn't she told me earlier that she was going to get rid of her mohawk, add more snaking swirls and geometric designs on her very skull? But I had to blink my eyes a few times to register what I saw tattooed on and around her gently mounded mons and swollen labia—the second set of carmine lips and sharply outlined, tattoo-crosshatch-shadowed teeth surrounding her lower set of lips, the colored twin curve of the faux carmine-inked lips glistening, as if she'd just licked them moist. I reached down to probe and caress that second waiting mouth, but what I felt only confused me more. The lips seemed to pucker against my flesh, as if to kiss my fingertips, while just beneath them I felt the hardness and rounded smoothness of teeth—some of them sharply pointed. I longed to probe deeper, to touch her hidden depths and moist inner pools, but to do so, I'd have to risk passing those teeth. Something as dangerous as it was unexpected . . . yet something enticing, because it *was* so out of the ordinary.

I started to speak, to question, but Mona shook her head, the thick swath of silvery curls in the middle rippling against the grassy ground under her skull. "Ride's started," she whispered, "No emergency brake, remember?" Wrapping her legs around me, trapping my swelling organ against my undershorts, Mona snaked her right arm down my back and dug her thumb under my waistband until she could pull my jeans and underwear down close to my hips, then lower . . . and she hugged me against her as the snap and zipper let go, and the last of the entrapping, protective fabric pulled free of my lower body. She was hissing in my ear, "I won't bite it *off* . . . but don't be surprised if you feel a tiny pinch down there . . . remember the snakes, how they love to flick their tongues. And the snakes only come out when the ride's going 'round, so be ready to get off once the music's over. . . ."

I could have left her then, before it began, but no other ride at this carnival promised so much, even as it so openly threatened me. Even the horses with their hidden snakes seemed tame in comparison with what Mona was offering me, and me alone—

—and so as she pulled me closer and deeper, I felt a brief, slick hardness as I slid into her. The ridges of the longest, sharpest teeth barely grazed my incoming flesh, but true to her word, those teeth never bore down on me. She began to hum softly, a lilting drone that swelled in my ear . . . and I never got to ask her what the consequences of lingering too long in that tightly warm elastic-walled mouth might be once that melody reached its unexpected end, for the ride had indeed begun, and since there was no stopping, I felt compelled to keep up my own dizzying rhythm while my own lips explored her face and breasts, even as her nether lips explored and sucked deeply on my own imprisoned flesh.

Perhaps she sensed the throbbing in my lower back, a pain barely perceptible through my steadily growing orgasmic haze. Perhaps she sensed the gradual slowing up of the rhythm between us, a union of motion matched to her melodious murmuring. Perhaps . . . she sensed that the snakes longed to be hidden once more. Pushing me up and safely out of her, she abruptly stopped the song, just as I felt a teasing, yet definite nip close to the base of my now slippery organ (accompanied by a deep sucking pull on the pinched flesh). The heretofore melody-masked sound of crickets and highway movement came flooding back against my eardrums. Like a snake shedding its skin, my member shrank and rested as if satisfied against my now-dangling testicles. A glistening black pearl-like drop of blood welled up from the spot where I'd been bitten. *Ride's over, time to get off.* And like the stilled-in-motion carousel horses. Mona's sated set of faux tattooed lips grew flatter and less detailed as they and the teeth below sank back into a pool of inky color and detail against her still moist flesh. Soon only a fine dribble of her own saliva-like juices remained near the natural pucker of her labial lips, as if waiting for a good-bye kiss. . . .

I don't know if she comprehended my last caresses, my last lingering, tongue-probing kisses above and below; only by the slight rise and fall of her nightmare-bloom bedecked rib cage and breasts could I tell she was even alive. Her flushed eyelids were closed, but whether she slept or whether she was merely reliving recent pleasures, recent meals, in the darkened confines of he mind, I could not tell. She was just silent.

But . . . what *was* there to say, or to ask? I doubted she'd answer any of my questions, even if she could. Even if she knew, telling would only spoil her dark, exotic magic for me. Like probing tin cracks and crevices of the carousel horses for hidden snakes before the music and the motion began . . . or like pulling aside her clothing *before* she'd mouthed that magical "Yes" of assent. To have done that would've spoiled the surprise, ruined that pleasure which comes with the gradual revelation *after* hiding and hinting. I could never ask her which came first, the snakes with their teasing tongues, or the tattooed lips and barely grazing teeth, for both were as intertwined as they were unique, one forming the echo to the other's sound, or the shadow to the form. . . . Enough that she'd shared *her* own hidden "snakes" with me . . . and had asked so little in payment for the ride.

I gathered up my clothes and threw them on, alternately peeking at her supine form and quickly looking elsewhere. Beyond, the rest of the carnies were busy taking apart the rides, the booths, and talking softly among themselves. None of them noticed me (or if they did, they knew better than to acknowledge my unoffical presence, perhaps remembering Mona's other rides, and other riders) as I darted, buttonless shirt flapping, through the last remainders of the midway, a rider perhaps *too* ordinary for comment despite what Mona had revealed—and done—to me.

The bite on my now-covered flesh still stung almost pleasantly with each step, even though *I* still seemed to be unchanged. I wondered if one of the carnies would come to fetch Mona from her sated slumber before morning came, provided someone *had* noticed us out there. But as I passed the carousel, its painted mounts air-suspended, hooved legs caught in midarc, I realized that my passing in Mona's domain hadn't gone entirely unnoticed—nor had my small payment for the ride left me unaltered, or *ordinary:*

Emerging from its hiding place for one daring, riderless second, a snake hissed at me from one of the suspended horses. . . .

THE ENTREATY OF THE WIIDEEMA

Barry Lopez

Barry Lopez is perhaps best known as the author of the extraordinary *Of Wolves and Men*, a nonfiction account of the author's journeys through wolf country. His other works include *Winter Count*, *Crossing Open Ground*, *Desert Notes*, and *River Notes*. He has won the National Book Award (for *Arctic Dreams*), and his short stories have received the Pushcart Prize and PEN Award. Lopez is also the author of a delightful children's book titled *Crow and Weasel*.

The following tale comes from *Field Notes*, Lopez's most recent collection of fiction. While most of the beautiful stories therein are in the realist tradition, one other has magical elements: "Lessons from the Wolverine." It is as haunting as the story that follows, and I highly recommend seeking it out.

—T. W.

I should preface my remarks this evening—and I must say that this will not be an entirely hopeful talk, and for that I apologize—with some explanations of how I came to live with—to try to live with, really—the Wiideema.

When I finished my doctoral studies among the Navajo of the American Southwest, I realized, as many students do, that I knew less at the end than I did in the beginning. That is, so much of what I took to be the objective truth when I started—things as self-evident, say, as Copernicus's arrangement of the inner planets—became so diluted by being steeped in another epistemology that simultaneously I came to grasp the poverty of my own ideas and the eternity of paradox within Navajo thought.

Let me put this to you in another way. When I finished my work among the Navajo—or, to be both more precise and more honest, when I gave up among the Navajo—I had as my deepest wish that someone among them would have been studying my way of knowing the world. I might have been more capable then of accepting the Navajo as true intellectual companions, and not, as has happened to so many of us, have ended up feeling disillusionment, even despair, with my own culture. I believe I would have been able to grasp *our* expression of Beauty Way, and in that sense I would have fallen back in love with my own people.

But it did not work this way. My postdoctoral studies brought me here, to Austin, where I declared I wanted to look at something I'd never studied before—among people I'd have to go out and *find*, an undiscovered people. On the strength of my work with the Navajo—and, again, to be candid with you, although I learned to speak that extremely difficult language fluently and though, for example, I memorized the full nine days of Blessing Way prayers, the obsession cost me my marriage, my two children—on the strength of that earlier work, I was granted awards and fellowships by the Wenner-Gren Foundation, the Kellogg Foundation, the University of Texas at Austin, and the Henry Solomon Memorial Trust. This financial support, and the regard with which my own department treated me—my teaching duties here were light to begin with, and I must acknowledge, embarrassing as it is, that I *took* them lightly—with all this underpinning, I set out to find a tribe of people with whom I could explore one idea—hunting.

The conventional wisdom on this, of course, is that there are no intact hunting cultures left in the wilder Southern Hemisphere—not in Africa, not in South America, not in Australia. I'd learned through a friend, however, that it was possible a few, small hunting bands might still exist uncontacted in the Western Desert, in Australia. So I went there immediately. I'll be brief about this part of it. An important question—Why disturb these people if they are, indeed, there?—was one I deliberately ignored. I suppressed it, I will tell you, with a terrible intellectual strength. I importuned every professional acquaintance, until I got myself so well situated in the anthropological community I was able to arrange a small expedition, with the approval of the Central (Aboriginal) Land Council, into a region of Western Australia west of the Tanami Desert, where I was most hopeful of contacting a relict hunting band. It is now safe, though still compromising, to reveal that I lied to arrange this expedition, both to my friends and to the Land Council. I was not interested, as I claimed, in searching out the last refuges of rare marsupial animals and in comparing what I could learn of their biology and ecology with information gathered in conversations with local people and gleaned from scholarly publications on their hunting practices, belief systems, myths. I wanted to find a fresh people, and to pursue with them another idea.

When the Wiideema, in fact, found *us*—in the Northern Territory, technically, not in Western Australia, though the designation of course meant nothing to them—I was ecstatic. As soon as I realized the Wiideema were shadowing us—a fact I was the last to discover, though I believed I was the first—I contrived to abandon my white companions and our aboriginal guides. Under cover of darkness one night I simply walked out of camp. I'd not gone but a mile before I felt the presence, the subtle pressure, of other people. And there they were, standing like so many dark sticks in the sand among tufts of spinifex grass. Truly, it was as though they had materialized.

I made signs that I very much wished to join them and leave my companions. We walked that night until I was delirious with exhaustion. We slept the whole of the next day in the shade of some boulders, walked all the following night, and then did the same again, another two days. My exhaustion turned to impatience, impatience to anger, anger to despair, and despair to acquiescence. In this manner I was bled.

Through it all I took notes, most especially on hunting. My position during those first few weeks, however, could be construed as that of a camp dog. I was given scraps to eat, patted on the shoulder by some of the older women, was yelled at, and served as a source of laughter when performing ordinary tasks—making a double-secure tie in the laces of my boots, for example, or when I examined the binding on a spear shaft with a hand lens.

One day, having had more than my fill of this and being the butt of pranks—the children sniped at me in the same way their parents did, a probing but ultimately indifferent curiosity—I confronted one of the men, Karratumanta, and with a look of defiant exasperation burned a smoking hole in a eucalyptus limb with my hand glass. Karratumanta regarded me blankly. He picked up a stone and threw it with terrific force at a small bird flying by. The stone knocked the bird, a songlark, to the ground, dead. He stripped away and ate its two minute slabs of pectoral flesh and then regarded me as though I were crazy to assume superiority.

You can imagine how this played out, certainly, in those first weeks. On reflection, I realized my plans had probably been transparent to my white companions and to our guides, and that they had no intention at all of searching for me. Instead, they trusted little harm and some good would come from my conceits and lack of integrity. I hope, in the end, you will find that they were correct.

In the early days of my work with the Wiideema—I call it "my work" because it was work, keeping up with them—I was dazzled, predictably, by the startling degree of their intimacy with the places we traveled through. The capacity of every object, from a mountain range to an insect gall, to hold an idea or to abet human life was known to them. I expected this high level of integration with place, a degree of belonging that the modern world envies, perhaps too desperately; but I was not prepared for the day I began to hear English words in their conversations. The first words I heard were "diptych," "quixotic," and "effervesce," words sufficiently obscure to have seemed Wiideema expressions, accented and set off in the run of conversation exactly as they would be in English. But they were not Wiideema words. Over a period of days I began to hear more and more English, not just words but phrases and occasionally entire sentences. What was happening was so strange that I did not want to ask about it. During my years in the field, if I have learned one thing, it is not to ask the obvious question right away. Wait, and you often see the whole event more clearly.

When I could understand almost everything that was being said, though in a way I'd never understood English before, I asked Yumbultjaturra, one of the women, "Where did you learn to speak English?"

"What is that, 'English,' the name of your language?"

"It's what we're speaking."

"No, no," she said smiling. "We are merely speaking. You, *you*, I think, might be speaking that."

"But we can understand each other. How could we understand each other if we both weren't speaking English?"

"We can understand each other because—how should I put this to you?—we do not have a foreign language. You understand what I say, don't you?"

"Yes."

"At first you didn't."

"Right, yes."

"However," she said, "from the beginning we understood you."

"From the start? Then why did you never answer my questions, why didn't you speak to me?"

"We spoke to you all the time," she stated. "And forgive me, but your questions were not compelling. And to be truthful, no one was inclined to speak with you until you put your questions away. You'd have to say this is a strict tenet with us—listening."

Our conversation went on in this manner for five or ten minutes before I understood what she was doing. She wasn't, in fact, speaking English. It was not even correct to say that she was speaking Wiideema. She was just speaking, the way a bird speaks or a creek, as a fish speaks or wind rushes in the grass. If I became anxious listening to her, she got harder to understand. The more I tried to grapple with our circumstances, the less I was able to converse. Eventually, in order to understand and be understood, I simply accepted the fact that we could understand each other.

Now, knowing this, I can imagine what you are perhaps anticipating—but it did not happen. I had no intellectual discussion with the people I traveled with. We did not discuss or compare cosmologies. I did not seek to discover whether the grand metaphors of my own culture—entropy, let us say, or the concept of husbandry—had their counterparts in Wiideema culture. I did not pursue any philosophical issues with them, say Gandhi's ahimsa, or the possibility of universal justice. No Enlightenment notions of universal human dignity. I simply traveled. I drew the country into myself, very much as I drew air into my lungs. Or drank water. I ceased what finally seemed to me my infernal questions and menacing curiosity. And I finally came to see the Wiideema as a version of something of which my own people were a version. What we shared—and it was a source of pleasure as intense as any I had ever known—was not solely food and a common hearth, human touch, small gifts, things I would have expected, but a sense of danger. A sense that it was dangerous to be alive.

I do not mean by such danger poisonous snakes or no water; or solely that you might be bludgeoned in your sleep, all of which occurred. The sense of danger we shared came from accepting consciousness. Human consciousness beckons us all. My Wiideema companions, wary as wild animals, had not accepted it fully. They didn't shun knowledge; and it was not that they were never contemplative or curious about ideas or other abstractions. But their hesitancy had led them off in another direction. All that they knew, all they believed or imagined, they cast in stories. Stories for them were the only safe containers for what consciousness, as we have it, might have elucidated for them about life. Or let me say this another way. When I put my imagination, as distinct from my intellect, together with their stories, having steeped my body in the food, the water, light, wind, and sand of the Wiideema, I found as much in these stories as I could expect to find in the most profound and beautiful Occidental articulation of any idea or event with which I am familiar.

I finally left the Wiideema—a decision awful and hard to arrive at—because I could not exercise the indifference they managed toward violence. On several occasions, the fourteen people I traveled with encountered other groups. Often these encounters were friendly, but three times they were fatally violent. Someone was murdered. And then life started over again. In a troubling way this was like hunting. An animal was killed and eaten, and all were refreshed. The distinction, the emotional and moral separation between human and animal death, was one I could never grasp in my Occidental mind and not perceive in my infant Wiideema mind. They were willing to accept far more suffering in their lives—from heat, from starvation, from thirst, from wounds—than I could abide. And nothing but thoughts of retribution, as far as I knew, were raised for them by incidents of murder.

In the end, I did not consider that the Wiideema lived on some lower plane, or, transcendent in their infinitely clever world of stories, that they lived on a higher plane. I thought of them as companions on the same plane, shielding themselves in a different way from the fatal paradoxes of life.

When I left the Wiideema it was in the same fashion as I had arrived, rising in the night and walking away, though I understood now this was only a ritual, that my departure was not camouflaged. I had learned enough to get on alone in the desert, unless circumstances became truly dire. I walked out at Yinapaka, a perennial lake in the outwash of the Lander River, and eventually met some Warlpiri people who took me to Willowra. From there I came home.

What I hoped to find when I left Austin two and a half years ago was an uncontacted people with whom I could study the hunting of animals. I was curious about how, emotionally and spiritually—if you will allow me that imprecise word—people accustom themselves to daily killing, to the constant taking of life, as I saw it. I was afraid that in my dealings with the Navajo, a people studied nearly to death, all I was learning was a version of what I or others already knew. What I found when I began to travel with the Wiideema was that their emotions, their spiritual nature, was unknowable. When we killed and roasted kangaroo, I could only inquire into my own ethics, question my own emotions. I sought, finally, companionship with the Wiideema, not reason, not explanation.

I have to say, however odd it may sound, that what little true knowledge I returned with is knowledge already known to us—that we and the Wiideema share the same insoluble difficulties, which each day we must abide. And that not "once" but *now* is a time when human beings all speak the same language. (What actually happens, I think, is that people simply speak their own language but it is clearly understood by each listener.)

I wanted, two and a half years ago, to gain another kind of knowledge, the wisdom, so named, of primitive people. One day my friend Karratumanta killed a man called Ketjimidji. He speared him quickly through the lungs without warning. There were six or seven of us standing together when it happened. We had met on a trial, Ketjimidji's people coming from a soak or water hole and our group walking toward it. No voices were raised. No argument broke out. The killing—Karratumanta handled Ketjimidji deftly, coolly, on the spear, until Ketjimidji went down and stopped struggling—was followed by a preternatural silence. Ketjimidji's people went away, carrying the body with them, and we walked ahead to the soak. In the moments right after the killing I was fine but soon I was fighting for air. I felt as if all the bones in my face had exploded.

Ngatijimpa, one of Karratumanta's daughters, came to me that night and told me a story. It had nothing to do, as far as I could see, with what had happened. It was one of a long series of stories about the travels of Pakuru, the golden bandicoot. She was not, I finally understood, offering me allegory or explanation, but only a story, which, as she intended, pulled the sense of horror out of me in some mysterious way. I slept. But I remembered. And my nights afterward were disturbed because I remembered. I couldn't be healed of it, if that is the right word.

Karratumanta, a tutor of mine, had seen me reeling after the spearing and said, "I will not be your martyr."

Many months later I was spattered by blood when another person was killed violently in front of me. Again, Ngatijimpa came to me. She told me another part of the story of Pakuru and his travels and under the soothe of the story I slept deeply. Ngatijimpa was young, only a girl, but she was eloquent and effective with the wisdom she dispensed.

I owe those who have supported me an exact and detailed report of my months with the Wiideema, a scholarly work rigorous in its observations, well researched, cautious in its conclusions. I have begun this paper, and, somewhat to my surprise, I have made progress. In it I'm describing hunting techniques, the ethology of desert animals; but what I am really wondering, night and day, is what I can give the Wiideema. Such questions of allegiance seize upon us all I believe—how can we reciprocate, and how do we honor the unspoken request of our companions to speak the truth? What I wish to do here, the task-in-return I have set myself, is to rewrite the story of Cain. I want to find a language for it that offers hope in place of condemnation, that turns not on aggression and vengeance, but on the mystery of human terror.

I do not know if I will be successful, or—if I am—whether success will mean anything substantial. But having sojourned with the Wiideema, I want to understand now what it means to provide.

WHITE CHAPEL

Douglas Clegg

Douglas Clegg was born in Virginia, but has lived in the Los Angeles area for ten years. He has published the novels *Goat Dance, Breeder, Neverland, You Come When I Call You, The Dark of the Eye,* and most recently, *The Children's Hour.* His short stories have been published in the magazines *Cemetery Dance, Deathrealm, Tekeli-li! Journal of Terror,* and *The Scream Factory* and in the anthologies *Little Deaths* and *Best New Horror.*

"White Chapel" is a tale of a journey, in India, into the heart of darkness. This time, it is a woman who makes the journey, a journalist who seeks the truth about a man called monster and is forced to face her own secrets. It first appeared in the anthology *Love in Vein.* The graphic nature of some of the imagery may be a bit strong for fainthearted readers.

—E. D.

> *"Oh! Ahab," cried Starbuck, "not too late is it, even now, the third day, to desist. See! Moby Dick seeks thee not. It is thou, thou, that madly seekest him!"*
>
> —from *Moby-Dick, or The Whale* by Herman Melville.

I

"You are a saint," the leper said, reaching her hand out to clutch the saffron-dyed robe of the great man of Calcutta, known from his miracle workings in America to his world-fame as a holy man throughout the world. The sick woman said in perfect English, "My name is Jane. I need a miracle. I can't hold it any longer. It is eating away at me. They are." She labored to breathe with each word she spoke.

"Who?" the man asked.

"The lovers. Oh, god, two years keeping them from escaping. Imprisoned inside me."

"You are possessed by demons?"

She smiled, and he saw a glimmer of humanity in the torn skin. "Chose me because I was good at it. At suffering. That is whom the gods choose. I escaped, but had no money, my friends were dead. Where could I go? I became a home for every manner of disease."

"My child," the saint said, leaning forward to draw the rags away from the leper's face. "May God shine His countenance upon you."

"Don't look upon me, then, my life is nearly over," the leper said, but the great man had already brought his face near hers. It was too late. Involuntarily, the leper pressed her face against the saint's, lips bursting with fire-heat. An attendant of the saint's came over and pulled the leper away, swatting her on the shoulder.

The great man drew back, wiping his lips with his sleeve.

The leper grinned, her teeth shiny with droplets of blood. "The taste of purity," she said, her dark hair falling to the side of her face. "Forgive me. I could not resist. The pain. Too much."

The saint continued down the narrow alley, back into the marketplace of what was called the City of Joy, as the smell of fires and dung and decay came up in dry gusts against the yellow sky.

The leper woman leaned against the stone wall, and began to ease out of the cage of her flesh. The memory of this body, like a book written upon the nerves and sinews, the pathways of blood and bone, opened for a moment, and the saint felt it, too, as the leper lay dying.

My name is Jane, *a brief memory of identity, but with no other past to recall, her breath stopped,*

the saint reached up to feel the edge of his lips, his face, and wondered what had touched him.

What could cause the arousal he felt.

II

"He rescued five children from the pit, only to flay them alive, slowly. They said he savored every moment, and kept them breathing for as long as he was able. He initialed them. Kept their faces." This was overheard at a party in London, five years before Jane Boone would ever go to White Chapel, but it aroused her journalist's curiosity for it was not spoken with a sense of dread, but with something approaching awe and wonder, too. The man of whom it was spoken had already become a legend.

Then, a few months before the entire idea sparked in her mind, she saw an item in the *Bangkok Post* about the woman whose face had been scraped off with what appeared to be a sort of makeshift scouring pad. Written upon her back, the name, *Meritt*. This woman also suffered from amnesia concerning everything that had occurred to her prior to losing the outer skin of her face; she was like a blank slate.

Jane had a friend in Thailand, a professor at the University, and she called him to find out if there was anything he could add to the story of the faceless woman. "Not much, I'm afraid," he said, aware of her passion for the bizarre story. "They sold tickets to see her, you know. I assume she's a fraud, playing off the myth of the white devil who traveled to India, collecting skins as he went.

Don't waste your time on this one. Poor bastards are so desperate to eat, they'll do anything to themselves to put something in their stomachs. You know the most unbelievable part of her story?"

Jane was silent.

He continued, "This woman, face scraped off, nothing human left to her features, claimed that she was thankful that it had happened. She not only forgave him, she said, she blessed him. If it had really happened as she said, who would possibly bless this man? How could one find forgiveness for such a cruel act? And the other thing, too. Not in the papers. Her vagina, mutilated, as if he'd taken a machete to open her up. She didn't hold a grudge on that count, either."

In wartime, men will often commit atrocities they would cringe at in their everyday lives. Jane Boone knew about this dark side of the male animal, but she still weathered the journey to White Chapel because she wanted the whole story from the mouth of the very man who had committed what was known in the latter part of the century as the most unconscionable crime, without remorse. If the man did indeed live among the Khou-dali at the furthest point along the great dark river, it was said that perhaps he sought to atone for his past—White Chapel was neither white nor a chapel, but a brutal outpost which had been conquered and destroyed from one century to the next since before recorded history. Always to self-resurrect from its own ashes, only to be destroyed again. The British had anglicized the name at some sober point in their rule, although the original name, *Y-Cha-Pa* when translated, was Monkey God Night, referring to the ancient temple and celebration of the divine possession on certain nights of the dry season when the god needed to inhabit the faithful. The temple had mostly been reduced to ashes and fallen stone, although the ruins of its gates still stood to the southeast.

Jane was thirty-two and had already written a book about the camps to the north, with their starvation and torture, although she had not been well reviewed stateside. Still, she intended to follow the trail of Nathan Meritt, the man who had deserted his men at the height of the famous massacre. He had been a war hero who, by those court-martialed later, was said to have been the most vicious of torturers. The press had labeled him, in mocking Joseph Campbell's study *The Hero With A Thousand Faces*, "The Hero Who Skinned A Thousand Faces." The war had been over for a good twenty years, but Nathan was said to have fled to White Chapel. There were reports that he had taken on a Khou-dali wife and fathered several children over the two decades since his disappearance. Nathan Meritt had been the most decorated hero in the war—children in America had been named for him. And then the massacre, and the stories of his love of torture, of his rituals of skin and bone . . . it was the most fascinating story she had ever come across, and she was shocked that no other writer, other than one who couched the whole tale in a wide swath of fiction, had sought out this living myth. While Jane couldn't get any of her usual magazines to send her gratis, she had convinced a major publishing house to at least foot expenses until she could gather some solid information.

To get to White Chapel, one had to travel by boat down a brown river in intolerable heat. Mosquitoes were as plentiful as air, and the river stank of human waste. Jane kept the netting around her face at all times, and her boatman took to calling her Nettie. There were three other travelers with her: Rex, her photographer, and a British man and wife named Greer and Lucy. Rex was not faring well—he'd left Kathmandu in August, and had lost twenty pounds in just a few weeks. He looked like a balding scarecrow, with skin as pale as the moon, and eyes wise and weary like those of some old man. He was always complaining about how little money he had, which apparently compounded for him his physical miseries. She had known him for seven years, and had only recently come to understand his mood swings and fevers. Greer was fashionably unkempt, always in a tie and jacket, but mottled with sweat stains, and wrinkled; Lucy kept her hair up in a straw hat, and disliked all women. She also expressed a fear of water, which amazed one and all since every trip she took began with a journey across an ocean or down a river. Jane enjoyed talking with Greer as long as she didn't have to second-guess his inordinate interest in children. She found Lucy to be about as interesting as a toothache.

The boatman wanted to be called Jim because of a movie he had once seen, and so after morning coffee bought at a dock, Jane said, "Well, Jim, we're beyond help now, aren't we?"

Jim grinned, his small dark eyes sharp, his face wrinkled from too much sun. "We make White Chapel by night, Nettie. Very nice place to sleep, too. In town."

Greer brought out his book of quotes, and read, " 'Of the things that are man's achievements, the greatest is suffering.' " He glanced to his wife and then to Jane, altogether skipping Rex, who lay against his pillows, moaning softly.

"I know," Lucy said, sipping from the bowl, "it's Churchill."

"No, dear, it's not. Jane, any idea?"

Jane thought a moment. The coffee tasted quite good, which was a constant surprise to her, as she had been told by those who had been through this region before that it was bitter. "I don't know. Maybe—Rousseau?"

Greer shook his head. "It's Hadriman the Third. The Scourge of Y-Cha."

"Who's Y-Cha?" Rex asked.

Jane said, "The Monkey God. The temple is in the jungles ahead. Hadriman the Third skinned every monkey he could get his hand on, and left them hanging around the original city to show his power over the great god. This subdued the locals, who believed their only guardian had been vanquished. The legend is that he took the skin of the god, too, so that it might not interfere in the affairs of men ever again. White Chapel has been the site of many scourges throughout history, but Hadriman was the only one to profane the temple."

Lucy put her hand to her mouth, in a feigned delicacy. "Is it . . . a decent place?" Greer and Lucy spent their lives mainly traveling, and Jane assumed it was because they had internal problems all their own which kept them seeking out the exotic, the foreign, rather than staying with anything too familiar. They were rich, too, the way that only an upper-class Brit of the Old School could be and not have that guilt about it: to have inherited lots of money and to be perfectly content to spend it as it pleased themselves without a care for the rest of mankind.

Greer had a particular problem which Jane recognized without being able to understand: he had a fascination with children, which she knew must be of the sexual variety, although she could've been wrong—it was just something about him, about the way he referred to children in his speech, even the way he looked at her sometimes which made her uncomfortable. She didn't fathom his marriage to Lucy at all, but she fathomed very few marriages. While Greer had witnessed the Bokai Ritual of Circumcision and the Resurrection Hut Fire in Calcutta, Lucy had been reading Joan Didion novels and painting portraits of women weaving baskets. They had money to burn, however, inherited on both sides, and when Greer had spoken by chance to Jane at the hotel, he had found her story of going to White Chapel fascinating; and he, in turn, was paying for the boat and boatman for the two-day trip.

Jane said, in response to Lucy, "White Chapel's decent enough. Remember, British rule, and then a little bit of France. Most of them can speak English, and there'll be a hotel that should meet your standards."

"I didn't tell you this," Greer said, to both Jane and Lucy, "but my grandfather was stationed in White Chapel for half a year. Taxes. Very unpopular job, as you can imagine."

"I'm starved," Lucy said, suddenly, as if there were nothing else to think of. "Do we still have some of those nice sandwiches? Jim?" She turned to the boatman, smiling. She had a way of looking about the boat, eyes partly downcast, which kept her from having to see the water—like a child pretending to be self-contained in her bed, not recognizing anything beyond her own small imagined world.

He nodded, and pointed toward the palm leaf basket.

While Lucy crawled across the boat—she was too unbalanced, Greer often said, to stand without tipping the whole thing and this was, coincidentally, her great terror—Greer leaned over to Jane and whispered, "Lucy doesn't know why you're going. She thinks it's for some kind of *National Geographic* article," but he had to stop himself for fear that his wife would hear.

Jane was thinking about the woman in Thailand who claimed to have forgiven the man who tore her face off. And the children from the massacre, not just murdered, but obliterated. She had seen the pictures in *Life*. *Faceless children. Skinned from ear to ear.*

She closed her eyes and tried to think of less unpleasant images.

All she remembered was her father looking down at her as she slept.

She opened her eyes, glancing about. The heat and smells revived her from dark memories. She said, "Rex, look, don't you think that would be a good one for a photo?" She pointed to one of the characteristic barges that floated about the river selling mostly rotting meat and stuffed lizards, although the twentieth century had intruded, for there were televisions on some of the rafts, and a Hibachi barbecue.

Rex lifted his Nikon up in response, but was overcome by a fit of coughing.

"Rex," Lucy said, leaning over to feel his forehead, "my god, you're burning up." Then, turning to her husband, "He's very sick."

"He's seen a doctor, dear," Greer said, but looked concerned.

"When we get there," Jane said, "we'll find another doctor. Rex? Should we turn around?"

"No, I'm feeling better. I have my pills." He laid his head back down on his pillow, and fanned mosquitoes back from his face with a palm frond.

"He survived malaria and dengue fever, Lucy, he'll survive the flu. He's not one to suffer greatly."

"So many viruses." Lucy shook her head, looking about the river. "Isn't this where AIDS began?"

"I think that may have been Africa," Greer said in such a way that it shut his wife up completely, and she ate her sandwich and watched the barges and the other boatmen as though she were watching a *National Geographic Special*.

"Are you dying on me?" Jane asked, flashing a smile through the mosquito net veil.

"I'm not gonna die," Rex said adamantly. His face took on an aspect of boyishness, and he managed the kind of grin she hadn't seen since they'd first started working together several years back—before he had discovered needles. "Jesus, I'm just down for a couple of days. Don't talk about me like that."

Jim, his scrawny arms turning the rudder as the river ran, said, "This is the River of Gods, no one die here. All live forever. The Great Pig God, he live in Kanaput, and the Snake God live in Jurukat. Protect people. No one die in paradise of Gods." Jim nodded toward points that lay ahead along the river.

"And what about the Monkey God?" Jane asked.

Jim smiled, showing surprisingly perfect teeth which he popped out for just a moment because he was so proud of the newly made dentures. When he had secured them onto his upper gum again, he said, "Monkey God trick all. Monkey God live where river go white. Have necklace of heads of childs. You die only once with Monkey God, and no come back. Jealous god, Monkey God. She not like other gods."

"Monkey God is female," Jane said. "I assumed she was a he. Well, good for her. I wonder what she's jealous of?"

Greer tried for a joke, "Oh, probably because we have skins, and hers got taken away. You know women."

Jane didn't even attempt to acknowledge this comment.

Jim shook his head. "Monkey God give blood at rainy times, then white river go red. But she in chains, no longer so bad, I think. She buried alive in White Chapel by mortal lover. Hear her screams, sometime, when monsoon come, when flood come. See her blood when mating season come."

"You know," Greer looked at the boatman quizzically, "you speak with a bit of an accent. Who did you learn English from?"

Jim said, "Dale Carnegie tapes, Mister Greer. *How To Win Friends And Influence People*."

Jane was more exhilarated than exhausted by the time the boat docked in the little bay at White Chapel. There was the Colonial British influence to the port, with guard booths now mainly taken over by beggars, and an empty customs house. The place had fallen into beloved disrepair, for the great elephant statues given for the god Ganesh were overcome with vines and cracked in places, and the lilies had all but taken over the dock. Old petrol storage cans floated along the pylons, strung together with a net knotted between the cans: someone was out to catch eels or some shade-dwelling scavenger. A nervous man with a straw hat and a bright red cloth tied around his loins ran to the edge of the dock to greet them; he carried a long fat plank, which he swept over the water's edge to the boat, pulling it closer in. A ladder was lowered to them.

The company disembarked carefully. Rex, the weakest, had to be pulled up by Jim and Jane both. Lucy proved the most difficult, however, because of her terror of water—Jim the boatman pushed her from behind to get her up to the dock, which was only four rungs up on the ladder. Then Jane didn't feel like haggling with anyone, and so after she tipped Jim, she left the others to find their ways to the King George Hotel by the one taxicab in White Chapel. She chose instead to walk off her excitement, and perhaps get a feel for the place.

She knew from her previous explorations that there was a serendipity to experience—she might, by pure chance, find what she was looking for. But the walk proved futile, for the village—it was not properly a town—was dark and silent, and except for the lights from the King George, about a mile up the road, the place looked as if no one lived there. Occasionally, she passed the open door to a hut through which she saw the red embers of the fire, and smelled the accompanying stench of the manure that was used to stoke the flame. Birds, too; she imagined them to be crows, gathering around huts, kicking up dirt and waste.

She saw the headlights of a car and stepped back against a stone wall. It was the taxi taking the others to the hotel, and she didn't want them to see her.

The light was on inside the taxi, and she saw Rex up front with the driver, half-asleep. In back, Lucy, too, had her eyes closed; but, Greer, however, was staring out into the night, as if searching for something, perhaps even expecting something. His eyes were wide, not with fear, but with a kind of feverish excitement.

He's here for a reason. He wants what White Chapel has to offer, she thought, *like he's a hunter.* And what did it have to offer? Darkness, superstition, jungle, disease, and a man who could tear the faces off children. A man who had become a legend because of his monstrosity.

After the car passed, and was just two sets of red lights going up the narrow street, she continued her journey up the hill.

When she got to the hotel, she went to the bar. Greer sat at one end; he had changed into a lounging jacket that seemed to be right out of the First World War. "The concierge gave it to me," Greer said, pulling at the sleeves, which were just short of his wrists. "I imagine they've had it since my grandfather's day." Then, looking at Jane, "You look dead to the world. Have a gin tonic."

Jane signaled to the barman. "Coca-Cola?" When she had her glass, she took a sip, and sighed. "I never thought I would cherish a Coke so much. Lucy's asleep?"

Greer nodded. "Like a baby. And I helped with Rex, too. His fever's come down."

"Good. It wasn't flu."

"I know. I can detect the D.T.'s at twenty paces. Was it morphine?"

Jane nodded. "That and other things. I brought him with me mainly because he needed someone to take him away from it. It's too easy to buy where he's from. As skinny as he is, he's actually gained some weight in the past few days. So, what about you?" She didn't mean for the question to be so fraught with unspoken meaning, but there it was: out there.

"You mean, why am I here?"

She could not hold her smile. There was something cold, almost reptilian about him now, as if, in the boat, he had worn a mask, and now had removed it to reveal rough skin and scales.

"Well, there aren't that many places in the world . . . quite so . . ."

"Open? Permissive?"

Greer looked at her, and she knew he understood. "It's been a few months. We all have habits that need to be overcome. You're very intuitive. Most women I know aren't. Lucy spends her hours denying that reality exists."

"If I had known when we started this trip . . ."

"I know. You wouldn't have let me join you, or even fund this expedition. You think I'm sick. I suppose I am—I've never been a man to delude himself. You're very—shall I say—*liberal* to allow me to come even now."

"It's just very hard for me to understand," she said. "I guess this continent caters to men like you more than Europe does. I understand for two pounds sterling you can buy a child at this end of the river. Maybe a few."

"You'd be surprised. Jane. I'm not proud of my interest. It just exists. Men are often entertained by perversity. I'm not saying it's right. It's one of the great mysteries—" He stopped midsentence, reached over, touching the side of her face.

She drew back from his fingers.

In his eyes, a fatherly kindness. "Yes," he said, "I knew. When we met. It's always in the eyes, my dear. I can find them in the streets, pick them out of a group, out of a school yard. Just like yours, those eyes."

Jane felt her face go red, and wished she had never met this man who had seemed so civil earlier.

"Was it a relative?" he asked. "Your father? An uncle?"

She didn't answer, but took another sip of Coke.

"It doesn't matter, though, does it? It's always the same pain," he said, reaching in the pockets of the jacket and coming up with a gold cigarette case. He opened it, offered her one, and then drew one out for himself. Before he lit it, with the match burning near his lips, he said, "I always see it in their faces, that pain, that hurt. And it's what attracts me to them, Jane. As difficult as it must be to understand, for I don't pretend to myself, it's that caged animal in the eyes that—how shall I say—excites me?"

She said, with regret, "You're very sick. I don't think this is a good place for you."

"Oh," he replied, the light flaring in his eyes, "but this is just the place for me. And for you, too. Two halves of the same coin, Jane. Without one, the other could not exist. I'm capable of inflicting pain, and you, you're capable of bearing a great deal of suffering, aren't you?"

"I don't want to stay here," she told Rex in the morning. They had just finished a breakfast of a spicy tea and *shuvai* with poached duck eggs on the side, and were walking in the direction of the village center.

"We have to go back?" Rex asked, combing his hands through what was left of his hair. "I—I don't think I'm ready, Janey, not yet. I'm starting to feel a little stronger. If I go back . . . and what about the book?"

"I mean, I don't want to stay at the hotel. Not with those people. He's a child molester. No, make that child rapist. He as much admitted it to me last night."

"Holy shit." Rex screwed his face up. "You sure?"

Jane looked at him, and he turned away. There was so much boy in Rex that still wasn't used to dealing with the complexities of the adult world—she almost hated to burst his bubble about people. They stopped at a market, and she went to the first stall, which offered up some sort of eely thing. Speaking a pidgin version of Khou-dali, or at least the northern dialect she had learned, Jane asked the vendor, "Is there another hotel? Not the English one, but maybe one run by Khou-dali?"

He directed her to the west, and said a few words. She grabbed Rex's hand, and whispered, "It may be some kind of whorehouse, but I can avoid Greer for at least one night. And that stupid wife of his."

Rex took photos of just about everyone and everything they passed, including the monkey stalls. He was feeling much better, and Jane was thrilled that he was standing tall, with color in his cheeks, no longer dependent on a drug to energize him. He took one of her with a dead monkey. "I thought these people worshiped monkeys."

Jane said, "I think it's the image of the monkey, not the animal itself." She set the dead animal back on the platform with several other carcasses. Without meaning to, she blurted, "Human beings are horrible."

"Smile when you say that." Rex snapped another picture.

"We kill, kill, kill. Flesh, spirit, whatever gets in our way. It's like our whole purpose is to extinguish life. And for those who live, there's memory, like a curse. We're such a mixture of frailty and cruelty."

The stooped-back woman who stood at the stall said, in perfect English, "Who is to say, miss, that our entire purpose here on Earth is not perhaps to perform such tasks? Frailty and cruelty are our gifts to the world. Who is to say that suffering is not the greatest of all gifts from the gods?"

Her Khou-dali name was long and unpronounceable, but her English name was Mary-Rose. Her grandmother had been British; her brothers had gone to London and married, while she, the only daughter, had remained behind to care for an ailing mother until the old woman's death. And then, she told them, she did not have any ambition for leaving her ancestral home. She had the roughened features of a young woman turned old by poverty and excessive labor and no vanity whatsoever about her. Probably from some embarrassment at hygiene, she kept her mouth fairly closed when she spoke. Her skin, rough as it was, possessed a kind of glow similar to the women Jane had seen who had face-lifts—although clearly, this was from living in White Chapel with its humidity. Something in her eyes approached real beauty, like sacred jewels pressed there. She had a vigor in her glance and speech; her face was otherwise expressionless, as if set in stone. She was wrapped in several cloths, each dyed clay red and wrapped from her shoulders down to her ankles; a purple cloth was wrapped about her head like a nun's wimple. It was so hot and steamy that Jane was surprised she didn't go as some of the local women did—with a certain discreet amount of nakedness. "If you are looking for a place, I can give you a room. Very cheap. Clean. Breakfast included." She named a low price, and Jane immediately took her up on it. "You help me with English, and I make coffee, too. None of this tea. We are all dizzy with tea. Good coffee. All the way from America, too. From Maxwell's house."

* * *

Mary-Rose lived beyond the village, just off the place where the river forked. She had a stream running beside her house, which was a two-room shack. It had been patched together from ancient stones from the ruined Y-Cha temple, and tarpaper coupled with hardened clay and straw was used to fill in the gaps. Rex didn't need to be told to get his camera ready: the temple stones had hieroglyphic-like images scrawled into them. He began snapping pictures as soon as he saw them.

"It's a story," Jane said, following stone to stone. "Some of it's missing."

"Yes," Mary-Rose said, "it tells of Y-Cha and her conquests, of her consorts. She fucked many mortals." Jane almost laughed when Rose said "fucked" because her speech seemed so refined up until that point. No doubt, whoever taught Rose to speak English had not bothered to separate out vulgarities. "When she fucks them, very painful, very hurting, but also very much pleasure. No one believes in her much no more. She is in exile. Skin stolen away. They say she could mount a believer and ride him for hours, but in the end, he dies, and she must withdraw. The White Devil, he keeps her locked up. All silly stories, of course, because Y-Cha is just so much lah-dee-dah."

Jane looked at Rex. She said nothing.

Rex turned the camera to take a picture of Mary-Rose, but she quickly hid her features with her shawl. "Please, no," she said.

He lowered the camera.

"Mary-Rose," Jane said, measuring her words, "do you know where the White Devil lives?"

Seeing that she was safe from being photographed, she lowered the cloth. Her hair spilled out from under it—pure white, almost dazzlingly so. Only the very old women in the village had hair even approaching gray. She smiled broadly, and her teeth were rotted and yellow. Tiny holes had been drilled into the front teeth. "White Devil, he cannot be found, I am afraid."

"He's dead, then. Or gone," Rex said.

"No, not that," she said, looking directly into Jane's eyes. "You can't find him. He finds you. And when he finds you, you are no longer who you are. You are no longer who you were. You become."

Jane spent the afternoon writing in her notebooks.

Nathan Meritt may be dead. He would be, what fifty? Could he have really survived here all this time? Wouldn't he self-destruct, given his proclivities? I want him to exist. I want to believe he is what the locals say he is. The White Devil. Destruction and Creation in mortal form. Supplanted the local goddess. Legend beyond what a human is capable of. The woman with the scoured face. The children without skins. The trail of stories that followed him through this wilderness. Settling in White Chapel, his spiritual home. Whitechapel—where Jack the Ripper killed the prostitutes in London. The name of a church. Y-Cha, the Monkey God, with her fury and fertility and her absolute weakness. White—they say the river runs white at times, like milk, it is part of Y-Cha. Whiteness. The white of bones strung along in her necklace. The white of the scoured woman—her featureless face white with infection.

Can any man exist who matches the implications of this?

The Hero Who Skinned A Thousand Faces.

And why?

What does he intend with this madness, if he does still exist, if the stories are true?

And why am I searching for him?

And then, she wrote:

Greer's eyes looking into me. Knowing about my father. Knowing because of a memory of hurt somehow etched into my own eyes.

The excitement when he was looking out from the taxi.

Like a bogeyman on holiday, a bag of sweeties in one hand, and the other, out to grab a child's hand.

Frailty and cruelty. Suffering as a gift.

What he said, Two halves of the same coin. Without one, the other could not exist. Capable of great suffering.

White Chapel and its surrounding wilderness came to life just after midnight. The extremes of its climate—chilly at dawn, steamy from ten in the morning till eight or nine at night, and then hot but less humid as darkness fell—led to a brain-fever siesta between noon and ten o'clock at night. Then families awoke and made the night meal, baths were taken, love was made—all in preparation for the more sociable and bearable hours of 1:00 A.M. to about six or seven when most physical labor, lit by torch and flare, was done, or the hunting of the precious monkey and other creatures more easily caught just before dawn. Jane was not surprised at this. Most of the nearby cultures followed a similar pattern based on climate and not daylight. What did impress her was the silence of the place while work and play began.

Mary-Rose had a small fire going just outside the doorway; the dull orange light of the slow-burning manure cast spinning shadows as Mary-Rose knelt beside it and stirred a pan. "Fried bread," she said, as Jane sat up from her mat. "Are you hungry?"

"How long did I sleep?"

"Five, six hours, maybe."

The frying dough smelled delicious. Mary-Rose had a jar of honey in one hand, which tipped, carefully, across the pan.

Jane glanced through the shadows, trying to see if Rex was in the corner on his mat.

"Your friend," Mary-Rose said, "he left. He said he wanted to catch some local color. That is precisely what he said."

"He left his equipment," Jane said.

"Yes, I can't tell you why. But," the other woman said, flipping the puffed-up circle of bread, and then dropping it onto a thin cloth, "I can tell you something about the village. There are certain entertainments forbidden to women which many men who come here desire. Men are like monkeys, do you not think so? They frolic, and fight, and even destroy, but if you can entertain them with pleasure, they will put other thoughts aside. A woman is different. A woman cannot be entertained by the forbidden."

"I don't believe that. I don't believe that things are forbidden to women, anyway."

Mary-Rose shrugged. "What I meant, Miss Boone, is that a woman is the forbidden. Man is monkey, but woman is Monkey God." She apparently didn't care what Jane thought one way or another. Jane had to suppress an urge to smile, because Mary-Rose seemed so set in her knowledge of life, and had only seen the jungles of Y-Cha. She brought the bread into the shack and set it down in front of Jane.

"Your friend, Rex, he is sick from some fever. But it is fever that drives a man. He went to find what would cool the fever. There is a man skilled with needles and medicines in the jungle. It is to this man that your friend has traveled tonight."

Jane said, "I don't believe you."

Mary-Rose grinned. The small holes in her teeth had been filled with tiny jewels. "What fever drives you, Miss Jane Boone?"

"I want to find him. Meritt. The White Devil."

"What intrigues you about him?"

Jane wasn't sure whether or not she should answer truthfully. "I want to do a book about him. If he really exists. I find the legend fascinating."

"Many legends are fascinating. Would someone travel as far as you have for fascination? I wonder."

"All right. There's more. I believe, if he exists, if he is the legend, that he is either some master sociopath, or something else. What I have found in my research of his travels is that the victims, the ones who have lived, are thankful for their torture and mutilation. It is as if they've been—I'm not sure—baptized or consecrated by the pain. Even the parents of those children—the ones who were skinned—even they forgave him. Why? Why would you forgive a man such unconscionable acts?" Jane tasted the fried bread; it was like a doughnut. The honey that dripped across its surface stung her lips—it wasn't honey at all, but had a bitter taste to it. *Some kind of herb mixed with sap?*

It felt as if fire ants were biting her lips, along her chin where the thick liquid dripped; her tongue felt large, clumsy, as if she'd been shot up with Novocain. She didn't immediately think that she had been drugged, only that she was, perhaps, allergic to this food. She managed to say, "I just want to meet him. Talk with him," before her mouth seemed inoperable, and she felt a stiffness to her throat.

Mary-Rose's eyes squinted, as if assessing this demand. She whispered, "Are you not sure that you do not seek him in order to know what he has known?" She leaned across to where the image of the household god sat on its wooden haunches—not a monkey, but some misshapen imp. Sunken into the head of this imp, something akin to a votive candle. Mary-Rose lit this with a match. The yellow-blue flame came up small, and she cupped the idol in her hand as if it were a delicate bird.

And then she reached up with her free hand, and touched the edges of her lips—it looked as if she were about to laugh.

"Miss Jane Boone. You look for what does not look for you. This is the essence of truth. And so you have found what you should run from; the hunter is become the hunted." She began tearing at the curve of her lip, peeling back the reddened skin, unrolling the flesh that covered her chin like parchment.

Beneath this, another face. Unraveling like skeins of thread through some imperfect tapestry, the sallow cheeks, the aquiline nose, the shriveled bags beneath the eyes, even the white hair came out strand by strand. The air around her grew acrid with the smoke from the candle as bits of ashen skin fluttered across its flame.

A young man of nineteen or twenty emerged from beneath the last of the skin of Mary-Rose. His lips and cheeks were slick with dark blood, as if he'd just pressed his face into wine. "I am the man," he said.

The burning yellow-blue flame wavered and hissed with snowflake-fine motes of flesh.

Jane Boone watched it, unmoving.

Paralyzed.

Her eyes grew heavy. As she closed them, she heard Nathan Meritt clap his hands and say to someone, "She is ready. Take her to *Sedri-Y-Cha-Sampon*. It is time for Y-Cha-Pa."

The last part she could translate: Monkey God Night.

She was passing out, but slowly. She could just feel someone's hands reaching beneath her armpits to lift her. *I am Jane Boone, an American citizen, a journalist, I am Jane Boone, you can't do this to me,* her feeble mind shouted while her lips remained silent.

III

Two years later, the saint lay down in the evening, and tried to put the leper he had met that day out of his mind. The lips, so warm, drawing blood from his own without puncturing the skin.

Or had it been her *blood that he had drunk?*

Beside his simple cot was a basin and a ewer of water. He reached over, dipping his fingers into it, and brought the lukewarm droplets up to his face.

He was, perhaps, developing a fever.

The city was always hot in this season, though, so he could not be certain. He wondered if his fear of the leper woman was creating an illness within his flesh. But the saint did not believe that he could contract anything from these people. He was only in Calcutta to do good. Even Mother Teresa had recognized his purity of heart and soul; the Buddhist and Hindu monks, likewise, saw in him a great teacher.

The saint's forehead broke a sweat.

He reached for the ewer, but it slipped from his sweaty hands and shattered against the floor.

He sat up, and bent down to collect the pieces.

The darkness was growing around him.

He cut his finger on a porcelain shard.

He squeezed the blood, and wiped it across the oversized cotton blouse he wore to bed.

He held the shard in his hand.

There were times when even a saint held too much remembered pain within him.

Desires, once acted upon in days of innocence and childhood, now seemed dark and animal and howling.

He brought the shard up to his lips, his cheek, pressing.

In the reflecting glass of the window, a face he did not recognize, a hand he had not seen, scraping a broken piece of a pitcher up and down and up and down the way he had seen his father shaving himself when the saint was a little boy in Biloxi, the way he himself shaved, the way men could touch themselves with steel, leaning into mirrors to admire how close one could get to skin such as this. Had any ever gone so far beneath his skin?

The saint tasted his own blood.

His skin.

Began slicing clumsily at flesh.

IV

Jane Boone sensed movement.

She even felt the coolness of something upon her head—a damp towel?

She was looking up at a thin, interrupted line of slate gray sky emerging between the leaning trees and vines; she heard the cries of exotic birds; a creaking, as of wood on water.

I'm in a boat, she thought.

Someone came over to her, leaning forward. She saw his face. It was Jim, the boatman who had brought her from upriver. "Hello, Nettie," he said, calling her by the nickname they'd laughed about before, "you are seeing now, yes? Good. It is nearly the morning. Very warm. But very cool in temple. Very cool."

She tried to say something, but her mouth wasn't working; it hurt even to try to move her lips.

Jim said, apparently noticing the distress on her face, "No try to talk now. Later. We on sacred water. Y-Cha carry us in." Then, he moved away. She watched the sky above her grow darker; the farther the boat went on this river, the deeper the jungle.

She closed her eyes, feeling weak.

Ice-cold water splashed across her face.

"You got back to sleep, no," Jim said, standing above her again. "Trip is over." He poled the boat up against the muddy bank. When he had secured it, he returned to her, lifting her beneath her armpits. She felt as if every bone had been removed from her body. She barely felt her feet touch the ground as he dragged her up a narrow path. All she had the energy to do was watch the immense green darkness enfold about her, even while day burst with searing heat and light beyond them.

By the time she felt pins and needles coming into her legs and arms, she had been set down upon a round stone wheel, laid flat upon a smooth floor. Several candles were lit about the large room, all set upon the yellowed skulls of monkeys somehow attached to the walls. Alongside the skulls, small bits of leaf and paper taped or nailed or glued to the wall; scrawled across these, she knew from her experience in other similar temples, were petitions and prayers to the local god.

On one of the walls, written in a dark ink that could only have been blood, were words in the local dialect. Jane was not good at deciphering the language.

A man's voice, strong and pleasant, said, " 'Flesh of my flesh, blood of my blood, I delight in your offering.' It's an incantation to the great one, the Y-Cha."

He emerged from the flickering darkness. Just as he had seemed beneath the skin of Mary-Rose, Nathan Meritt was young, but she recognized his face from his college photographs. He was not merely handsome, but had a radiance that came from beneath his skin, as if something fiery lit him. His eyes, blue and almost transparent, flamed. "She is not native to this land, you know. She was an import from Asia. Did battle in her own way with Kali, and won this small acre before the village came to be. Gods are not as we think in the West, Jane; they are creatures with desires and loves and weaknesses like you or me. They do not come to us, or reveal themselves to us. No, it is we who approach them, we who must entertain them with our lives. You are a woman, as is the Y-Cha. Feelings that you have, natural rhythms, all of these, she is prey to also."

Jane opened her mouth, but barely a sound emerged.

Meritt put his finger to his lips. "In a little while. They used to use it to stun the monkeys—what the bread was dipped in. It's called *hanu*, and does little harm, although you may experience a hangover. The reason for the secrecy? I needed to meet you, Miss Boone, before you met me. You are not the first person to come looking for me. But you are different from the others who have come."

He stepped farther into the light, and she saw that he was naked. His skin glistened with grease, and his body was clean-shaven except for his scalp, from which grew long dark hair.

Jane managed a whisper. "What about me? I don't understand. Different? Others?"

"Oh," he said, a smile growing on his face, "you are capable of much suffering, Miss Boone. That is a rare talent in human beings. Some are weak, and murder their souls and bodies, and some die too soon in pain. Your friend Rex—he suffers much, but his suffering is of the garden variety. I have already played with him—don't be upset. He had his needles and his drugs, and in return, he gave me that rare gift, that"—Meritt's nostrils flared, inhaling, as if recalling some wonderful perfume—"moment of mastery. It's like nothing else, believe me. I used to skin children, you know, but they die too soon, they whine and cry, and they don't understand, and the pleasure they offer . . ."

"Please," Jane said. She felt strength seeping back into her muscles and joints. She knew she could run, but would not know to what exit, or where it would take her. She had heard about the temple having an underground labyrinth, and she didn't wish to lose herself within it.

But more than that, she didn't feel any physical threat from Nathan Meritt.

"You're so young," she said.

"Not really."

"You look like you're twenty. I never would've believed in magic, but . . ."

He laughed, and when he spoke, spoke in the measured cadences of Mary-Rose. "Skin? Flesh? It is our clothing, Miss Jane Boone, it is the tent that shelters us from the reality of life. This is not my skin, see." He reached up and drew back a section of his face from the left side of his nose to his left ear, and it came up like damp leaves, and beneath it, the chalk white of bone. "It may conform to my bones, but it is another's. It's what I learned from her, from the Y-Cha. Neither do I have blood, Miss Boone. When you prick me, I don't spill."

He seemed almost friendly; he came and sat beside her.

She shivered in spite of the familiarity.

"You mustn't be scared of me," he said in a rigid British accent. "We're two halves of the same coin."

Jane Boone looked in his eyes, and saw Greer there, a smiling, gentle Greer. The Greer who had funded her trip to White Chapel, the Greer who had politely revealed his interest in children.

"I met them in Tibet, Greer and Lucy," Meritt said, resuming his American accent. "He wanted children, we had that in common, although his interests, oddly enough, had more to do with mechanics than with intimacy. I got him his children, and the price he paid. Well, a pound or more of flesh. Two days of exquisite suffering, Jane, along the banks of a lovely river. I had some children with me—bought in Bangkok at one hundred dollars each—and I had them do the honors. Layers of skin, peeled back, like some exotic rind. The fruit within was for me. Then, the children, for they had already suffered much at Greer's own hands. I can't bear to watch children suffer more than a few hours. It's not yet an art for them; they're too natural."

"Lucy?"

He grinned. "She's still Lucy. I could crawl into Greer's skin; I was enjoying the game. She could not tell the difference because she didn't give a fuck, literally or figuratively. Our whole trip down the river, only Jim knew, but he's a believer. Sweet Lucy, the most dreadful woman from Manchester, and that's saying a lot. I'll dispose of her soon, though. But she won't be much fun. Her life is her torture—anything else is redundant."

Jane wasn't sure how much of his monologue to believe. She said, "And me? What do you intend to do?"

Unexpectedly, he leaned into her, brushing his lips against hers, but not kissing. His breath was like jasmine flowers floating on cool water. He looked into her eyes as if he needed something that only she could give him. He said, softly, "That will be up to you. You have come to me. I am your servant."

He pulled away, stood, turned his back to her. He went to the wall and lifted a monkey skull candle up. He held the light along the yellow wall. "You think from what I've done that I'm a monster, Miss Boone. You think I thrive on cruelty, but it's not that way. Even Greer, in his last moments, thanked me for what I did. Even the children, their life-force wavering and the stains along their scalps spreading darker juices over their eyes, whispered praise with their final breaths that I had led them to that place."

He held a light up to the papers stuck to the wall. His shadow seemed enormous and twisted as he moved the light in circles; he didn't look back at her, but moved from petition to petition. "Blessings and praises and prayers, all from the locals, the believers in Y-Cha. And I, Miss Boone, I am her sworn consort, and her keeper, too. For it is Nathan Meritt and no other, the Hero Who Skinned A Thousand Faces, who is her most beloved, and to whom she has submitted herself, my prisoner. Come, I will take you to the throne of Y-Cha."

A pool of water, a perfect circle filled with koi and turtles, was at the center of the chamber. Jane had followed Nathan down winding corridors whose walls seemed to be covered with dried animal skins and smelled of animal dung. The chamber itself was poorly lit, but there was a fire in a hearth at its far end; she thought she heard the sound of rushing water just beyond the walls.

"The river," Nathan said. "We're beneath it. She needs the moisture, always. She has not been well for hundreds of years." He went ahead of her, toward a small cot.

Jane followed, stepping around the thin bones which lay scattered across the stones.

There, on the bed, head resting on straw, was Lucy. Fruit had been stuffed into her mouth, and flowers in the empty sockets of her eyes. She was naked, and her skin had been brutally tattooed until the blood had caked around the lines: drawings of monkeys.

Jane opened her mouth to scream, and knew that she had, but could not even hear it. When she stopped, she managed, "You bastard, you said you hadn't hurt her. You said she was still alive."

He touched her arm, almost lovingly. "That's not what I told you. I didn't hurt her, Jane. She did this to herself. Even the flowers. She's not even dead, not yet. She's no longer Lucy." He squatted beside the cot and combed his fingers through her hair. "She's the prison of Y-Cha, at least as long as she breathes. Monkey God is a weak god in the flesh, and she needs it, she needs skin because she's not much different than you or me, Jane. She wants to experience life, feel blood, feel skin and bones and travel and love and kill, all the things animals take for granted, but the gods know, Jane. Oh, my baby," he pressed his face against the flowers, "the beauty, the sanctity of life, Jane, it's not in joy or happiness, it's in suffering in flesh."

He kissed the berry-stained lips, slipping his tongue into Lucy's mouth. With his left hand, he reached back and grasped Jane's hand before she could step away. His grip was tight, and he pulled her toward the cot, to her knees. He kissed from Lucy to her and back, and she tasted the berries and sweet pear. Jane could not resist—it was as if her flesh required her to do this, and she began to know what the others had known, the woman with the scraped face, the children, Greer, even Rex, all the worshipers of Y-Cha. Nathan's penis was erect and dripping, and she touched it with her hand, instinctively. The petals on the flower quivered; Nathan pressed his lips to Lucy's left nipple, and licked it like he was a pup suckling and playing; he turned to Jane, his face smeared with Lucy's blood, and kissed her, slipping a soaked tongue, copper taste, into the back of her throat; she felt the light pressure of his fingers exploring between her legs, and then watched as he brought her juices up to his mouth; he spread Lucy's legs apart, and applied a light pressure to the back of Jane's head.

For an instant, she tried to resist.

But the tattoos of monkeys played there, along the thatch of hair, like some unexplored patch of jungle, and she found herself wanting to lap at the small withered lips that Nathan parted with his fingers.

Beneath her mouth, the body began to move.

Slowly at first.

Then more swiftly, bucking against her lips, against her teeth. The monkey drawings chattered and spun.

She felt Nathan's teeth come down on her shoulder as she licked the woman.

He began shredding her skin, and the pain would have been unbearable except that she felt herself opening up below for him, for the trembling woman beneath her, and the pain slowed as she heard her flesh rip beneath Nathan's teeth. She was part of it, too, eating the dying woman who shook with orgasm, and the blood like a river.

A glimpse of her, not Lucy.

Not Lucy.

But Monkey God.

Y-Cha.

You suffer greatly. You suffer and do not die. Y-Cha may leave her prison.

She could not tell where Nathan left off and where she began, or whether it was her mouth or the dying woman's vagina which opened in a moan that was not pleasure, but was beyond the threshold of any pain she had ever imagined in the whole of creation.

She ripped flesh, devouring, blood coursing across her chin, down her breasts, Nathan inside her now, more than inside her, rocking within her, complete love through the flesh, through the blood, through the wilderness of frenzy, through the small hole between her legs, into the cavern of her body, and Y-Cha, united with her lover through the suffering of a woman whose identity as Jane Boone was quickly dissolving.

Her consciousness: taste, hurt, feel, spit, bite, love.

V

In the morning, the saint slept.

His attendant, Sunil, came through the entrance to the chamber with a plate of steamed vegetables. He set them down on the table, and went to get a broom to sweep up the broken ewer. When he returned, the saint awoke, and saw that the servant stared at his face as if seeing the most horrifying image ever in existence.

The saint took his hand to calm him, and placed his palm against the fresh wounds and newly formed scars.

The saint felt the servant's arousal. Sunil was a beautiful dark man, with piercing eyes, and the great man let his free hand slide down Sunil's back, beneath his shirt, to the curve of his buttocks.

Sunil gasped because he was trying to fight how good it felt, as all men did when they encountered Y-Cha.

The saint found his warmest place and stroked him there, like a pet.

His mouth opened in a small O of pleasure.

He was moist and eager. Already, his body moved, he thrust, gently at first; he wanted to be consort to Y-Cha.

He would beg for what he feared most, he would cry out for pain beyond his imagining, just to spill his more personal pain, the pain of life in the flesh.

It was the greatest gift of humans, their flesh, their blood, their memories. Their suffering. It was all they had, in the end, to give, for all else was mere vanity.

Y-Cha pressed her finger into him, delighted in the sweet gasp of expectation from the beautiful man's mouth.

Words scrawled in human suffering on a yellow wall:

Flesh of my flesh, blood of my blood
I delight in your offering

Make of your heart a lotus of burning
Make of your loins a pleasure dome
I will consecrate the bread of your bones
And make of you a living temple to Monkey God.

The servant opened himself to the god, and the god enjoyed the flesh as she hadn't for many days, the flesh and the blood and the beauty—for it was known among the gods that a man was most beautiful as he lay dying.

The gift of suffering was offered slowly, with equal parts of delight and torment, and as she watched his pain, she could not contain her jealousy for what the man possessed.

THE STONE WOMAN

Linda Weasel Head

Linda Weasel Head, a Salish Native, graduated from the University of Montana in 1989. She lives and teaches fifth grade on the Blood Reserve, and spends much of her time writing, a process that she compares to giving birth: "a lot of love, sweat, and pure energy." The poem that follows, about a young woman and Coyote (the Trickster of Native American myth), is reprinted from *Northern Lights: A Selection of New Writing from the American West*, edited by Deborah Clow and Donald Snow.

—T. W.

A young woman climbed
Into a green and blue stone.
Coyote threw her into the river
  right in the middle
  of winter.
    All she heard
        was clinking ice
    All she saw
        was a brown bottle
    All she felt
        were jagged edges
        that cut her fingers
    All she tasted
        was her own dry lips
        thirsty for water
    All she could smell
        was thick piss
        that clung to her hair
    She remembered
          she had children
          somewhere.
Rolled downstream
By fast melting snows, she tumbled,
Stumbled out an old woman.
Her stone broken.

COYOTE STORIES

Charles de Lint

Canadian author Charles de Lint is both prolific and versatile. His long list of publications includes works of adult fantasy fiction, children's fiction, horror, poetry, and critical nonfiction. He is best known, however, as a pioneer of contemporary urban fantasy, bringing myth and folklore motifs into a modern-day urban context. *Memory and Dream* and *The Ivory and the Horn* are his most recent works in this vein.

Each year at Christmastime de Lint publishes an original story in a limited-edition chapbook form through Triskell Press (Ottowa, Ontario) and sends these small, magical booklets to friends, family, and colleagues. Influenced by Native American legend, "Coyote Stories" is the best of these chapbooks to date.

—T. W.

Four directions blow the sacred winds
We are standing at the center
Every morning wakes another chance
To make our lives a little better
—Kiya Heartwood, from "Wishing Well"

This day Coyote is feeling pretty thirsty, so he goes into Joey's Bar, you know, on the corner of Palm and Grasso, across from the Men's Mission, and he lays a nugget of gold down on the counter, but Joey he won't serve him.

"So you don't serve skins no more?" Coyote he asks him.

"Last time you gave me gold, it turned to shit on me," is what Joey says. He points to the Rolex® on Coyote's wrist. "But I'll take that. Give you change and everything."

Coyote scratches his muzzle and pretends he has to think about it. "Cost me twenty-five dollars," he says. "It looks better than the real thing."

"I'll give you fifteen, cash, and a beer."

"How about a bottle of whiskey?"

So Coyote comes out of Joey's Bar and he's missing his Rolex now, but he's got a bottle of Jack in his hand and that's when he sees Albert, just around the corner, sitting on the ground with his back against the brick wall and his legs stuck out across the sidewalk so you have to step over them, you want to get by.

"Hey, Albert," Coyote says. "What's your problem?"

"Joey won't serve me no more."

"That because you're indigenous?"

"Naw. I got no money."

So Coyote offers him some of his whiskey. "Have yourself a swallow," he says, feeling generous, because he only paid two dollars for the Rolex and it never worked anyway.

"Thanks, but I don't think so," is what Albert tells him. "Seems to me I've been given a sign. Got no money means I should stop drinking."

Coyote shakes his head and takes a sip of his Jack. "You are one crazy skin," he says.

That Coyote he likes his whiskey. It goes down smooth and puts a gleam in his eye. Maybe, he drinks enough, he'll remember some good time and smile, maybe he'll get mean and pick himself a fight with a lamppost like he's done before. But one thing he knows, whether he's got money or not's got nothing to do with omens. Not for him, anyway.

But a lack of money isn't really an omen for Albert either; it's a way of life. Albert, he's like the rest of us skins. Left the reserve, and we don't know why. Come to the city, and we don't know why. Still alive, and we don't know why. But Albert, he remembers it being different. He used to listen to his grandmother's stories, soaked them up like the dirt will rain, thirsty after a long drought. And he tells stories himself, too, or pieces of stories, talk to you all night long if you want to listen to him.

It's always Coyote in Albert's stories, doesn't matter if he's making them up or just passing along gossip. Sometimes Coyote's himself, sometimes he's Albert, sometimes he's somebody else. Like it wasn't Coyote sold his Rolex and ran into him outside Joey's Bar that day, it was Billy Yazhie. Maybe ten years ago now, Billy he's standing under a turquoise sky beside Spider Rock one day, looking up, looking up for a long time, before he turns away and walks to the nearest highway, sticks out his thumb and he doesn't look back till it's too late. Wakes up one morning and everything he knew is gone and he can't find his way back.

Oh that Billy he's a dark skin, he's like leather. You shake his hand and it's like you took hold of a cowboy boot. He knows some of the old songs and he's got himself a good voice, strong, ask anyone. He used to drum for the dancers back home, but his hands shake too much now, he says. He doesn't sing much anymore, either. He's got to be like the rest of us, hanging out in Fitzhenry Park, walking the streets, sleeping in an alleyway because the Men's Mission it's out of beds. We've got the stoic faces down real good, but you look in our eyes, maybe catch us off guard, you'll see we don't forget anything. It's just most times we don't want to remember.

This Coyote he's not too smart sometimes. One day he gets into a fight with a biker, says he going to count coup like his plains brothers, knock that biker all over the street, only the biker's got himself a big hickory-handled hunting knife and he cuts Coyote's head right off. Puts a quick end to that fight, I'll tell you. Coyote he spends the rest of the afternoon running around, trying to find somebody to sew his head back on again.

"That Coyote," Jimmy Coldwater says, "he's always losing his head over one thing or another."

I tell you we laughed.

But Albert he takes that omen seriously. You see him drinking still, but he's drinking coffee now, black as a raven's wing, or some kind of tea he brews for himself in a tin can, makes it from weeds he picks in the empty lots and dries in the sun. He's living in an abandoned factory these days, and he's got this one wall, he's gluing feathers and bones to it, nothing fancy, no eagle's wings, no bear's jaw, wolf skull, just what he can find lying around, pigeon feathers and crow's, rat bones, bird bones, a necklace of mouse skulls strung on a wire. Twigs and bundles of weeds, rattles he makes from tin cans and bottles and jars. He paints figures on the wall, in between all the junk. Thunderbird. Bear. Turtle. Raven.

Everybody's starting to agree, that Albert he's one crazy skin.

Now when he's got money, he buys food with it and shares it out. Sometimes he walks over to Palm Street where the skin girls are working the trade and he gives them money, asks them to take a night off. Sometimes they take the money and just laugh, getting into the next car that pulls up. But sometimes they take the money and they sit in a coffee shop, sit there by the window, drinking their coffee and look out at where they don't have to be for one night.

And he never stops telling stories.

"That's what we are," he tells me one time. Albert he's smiling, his lips are smiling, his eyes are smiling, but I know he's not joking when he tells me that. "Just stories. You and me, everybody, we're a set of stories, and what those stories are is what makes us what we are. Same thing for whites as skins. Same thing for a tribe and a city and a nation and the world. It's all these stories and how they braid together that tells us who and what and where we are.

"We got to stop forgetting and get back to remembering. We got to stop asking for things, stop waiting for people to give us the things we think we need. All we really need is the stories. We have the stories and they'll give us the one thing nobody else can, the thing we can only take for ourselves, because there's nobody can give you back your pride. You've got to take it back yourself.

"You lose your pride and you lose everything. We don't want to know the stories, because we don't want to remember. But we've got to take the good with the bad and make ourselves whole again, be proud again. A proud people can never be defeated. They lose battles, but they'll never lose the war, because for them to lose the war you've got to go out and kill each and every one of them, everybody with even a drop of the blood. And even then, the stories will go on. There just won't be any skins left to hear them."

This Coyote he's always getting in trouble. One day he's sitting at a park bench, reading a newspaper, and this cop starts to talk big to one of the skin girls, starts talking mean, starts pushing her around. Coyote's feeling chivalrous that day, like he's in a white man's movie, and he gets into a fight with the cop. He gets beat up bad and then more cops come and they take him away, put him in jail.

The judge he turns Coyote into a mouse for a year so that there's Coyote, got that same lopsided grin, got that sharp muzzle and those long ears and the big bushy tail, but he's so small now you can hold him in the palm of your hand.

"Doesn't matter how small you make me," Coyote he says to the judge. "I'm still Coyote."

Albert he's so serious now. He gets out of jail and he goes back to living in the factory. Kids've torn down that wall of his, so he gets back to fixing it right, gets back to sharing food and brewing tea and helping the skin girls out when he can, gets back to telling stories. Some people they start thinking of him as a shaman and call him by an old Kickaha name.

Dan Whiteduck he translates the name for Billy Yazhie, but Billy he's not quite sure what he's heard. Know-more-truth, or No-more-truth?

"You spell that with a 'K' or what?" Billy he asks Albert.

"You take your pick how you want to spell it," Albert he says.

Billy he learns how to pronounce that old name and that's what he uses when he's talking about Albert. Lots of people do. But most of us we just keep on calling him Albert.

One day this Coyote decides he wants to have a powwow, so he clears the trash from this empty lot, makes the circle, makes the fire. The people come but no one knows the songs anymore, no one knows the drumming that the dancers need, no one knows the steps. Everybody they're just standing around, looking at each other, feeling sort of stupid, until Coyote he starts singing, *Ya-ha-hey, ya-ha-hey*, and he's stomping around the circle, kicking up dirt and dust.

People they start to laugh, then, seeing Coyote playing the fool.

"You are one crazy skin!" Angie Crow calls to him and people laugh some more, nodding in agreement, pointing at Coyote as he dances round and round the circle.

But Jimmy Coldwater he picks up a stick and he walks over to the drum Coyote made. It's this big metal tub, salvaged from a junkyard, that Coyote's covered with a skin and who knows where he got that skin, nobody's asking. Jimmy he hits the skin of the drum and everybody they stop laughing and look at him, so Jimmy he hits the skin again. Pretty soon he's got the rhythm to Coyote's dance and then Dan Whiteduck he picks up a stick, too, and joins Jimmy at the drum.

Billy Yazhie he starts up to singing then, takes Coyote's song and turns it around so that he's singing about Spider Rock and turquoise skies, except everybody hears it their own way, hears the stories they want to hear in it. There's more people drumming and there's people dancing and before anyone knows it, the night's over and there's the dawn poking over the roof of an abandoned factory, thinking, these are some crazy skins. People they're lying around and sitting around, eating the flatbread and drinking the tea that Coyote provided, and they're all tired, but there's something in their hearts that feels very full.

"This was one fine powwow," Coyote he says.

Angie she nods her head. She's sitting beside Coyote all sweaty and hot and she'd never looked quite so good before.

"Yeah," she says. "We got to do it again."

We start having regular powwows after that night, once, sometimes twice a month. Some of the skins they start to making dancing outfits, going back up to the reserve for visits and asking about steps and songs from the old folks. Gets to be we feel like a community, a small skin nation living here in exile with the ruins of broken-down tenements and abandoned buildings all around us. Gets to be we start remembering some of our stories and sharing them with each other instead of sharing bottles. Gets to be we have something to feel proud about.

Some of us we find jobs. Some of us we try to climb up the side of the wagon but we keep falling off. Some of us we go back to homes we can hardly remember. Some of us we come from homes where we can't live, can't even breathe, and drift here and there until we join this tribe that Albert he helped us find.

And even if Albert he's not here anymore, the stories go on. They have to go on, I know that much. I tell them every chance I get.

See, this Coyote he got in trouble again, this Coyote he's always getting in trouble, you know that by now, same as me. And when he's in jail this time he sees that it's all tribes inside, the same as it is outside. White tribes, black tribes, yellow tribes, skin tribes. He finally understands, finally realizes that maybe there can't ever be just one tribe, but that doesn't mean we should stop trying.

But even in jail this Coyote he can't stay out of trouble and one day he gets into another fight and he gets cut again, but this time he thinks maybe he's going to die.

"Albert," Coyote he says, "I am one crazy skin. I am never going to learn, am I?"

"Maybe not this time," Albert says, and he's holding Coyote's head and he's wiping the dribble of blood that comes out of the side of Coyote's mouth and is trickling down his chin. "But that's why you're Coyote. The wheel goes round and you'll get another chance."

Coyote he's trying to be brave, but he's feeling weaker and it hurts, it hurts, this wound in his chest that cuts to the bone, that cuts the thread that binds him to this story.

"There's a thing I have to remember," Coyote he says, "but I can't find it. I can't find its story. . . ."

"Doesn't matter how small they try to make you," Albert he reminds Coyote. "You're still Coyote."

"*Ya-ha-hey*," Coyote he says. "Now I remember."

Then Coyote he grins and he lets the pain take him away into another story.

THE BOX

Jack Ketchum

New Yorker Jack Ketchum is the author of several novels including *Off Season, She Wakes, Road Kill,* and most recently, *Joyride* and *Only Child*. He has had short fiction published in *Fear Itself,* and in *Vampire Detectives,* with more stories coming in *Stalkers III* and *Book of the Dead III*.

In "The Box," which first appeared in *Cemetery Dance,* Ketchum tells a powerful story with an existential view worthy of Samuel Beckett.

—E. D.

"What's in the box?" my son said.

"Danny," I said, "Leave the man alone."

It was two Sundays before Christmas and the Stamford local was packed—shoppers lined the aisles and we were lucky to have found seats. The man sat facing my daughters Clarissa and Jenny and me, the three of us squeezed together across from him and Danny in the seat beside him.

I could understand my son's curiosity. The man was holding the red square gift box in his lap as though afraid that the Harrison stop, coming up next, might jolt it from his grasp. He'd been clutching it that way for three stops now—since he got on.

He was tall, perhaps six feet or more and maybe twenty pounds overweight and he was perspiring heavily despite the cold dry air rushing over us each time the train's double doors opened behind our backs. He had a black walrus mustache and sparse thinning hair and wore a tan Burbury raincoat that had not been new for many years now over a rumpled gray business suit. I judged the pant-legs to be an inch too short for him. The socks were gray nylon, a much lighter shade than the suit, and the elastic in the left one was shot so that it bunched up over his ankle like the skin of one of those ugly pug-nosed pedigree dogs that are so trendy nowadays. The man smiled at Danny and looked down at the box, shiny red paper over cardboard about two feet square.

"Present," he said. Looking not at Danny but at me.

His voice had the wet phlegmy sound of a heavy smoker. Or maybe he had a cold.

"Can I see?" Danny said.

I knew exactly where all of this was coming from. It's not easy spending a day in New York with two nine-year-old girls and a seven-year-old boy around Christmas time when they know there is such a thing as F.A.O. Schwartz only a few blocks away. Even if you *have* taken them to the matinee at Radio City and then skating at Rockefeller Center. Even if all their presents had been bought weeks ago and were sitting under our bed waiting to be put beneath the tree. There was always something they hadn't thought of yet that Schwartz *had* thought of and they knew that perfectly well. I'd had to fight with them—with Danny in particular—to get them aboard the 3:55 back to Rye in time for dinner.

But presents were still on his mind.

"Danny . . ."

"It's okay," said the man. "No problem." He glanced out the window. We were just pulling in to the Harrison station.

He opened the lid of the box on Danny's side, not all the way open but only about three inches—enough for him to see but not the rest of us, excluding us three—and I watched my son's face brighten at that, smiling, as he looked first at Clarissa and Jenny as if to say *nyah nyah* and then looked down into the box.

The smile was slow to vanish. But it did vanish, fading into a kind of puzzlement. I had the feeling that there was something in there that my son did not understand—not at all. The man let him look a while but his bewildered expression did not change and then he closed the box.

"Gotta go," the man said. "My stop."

He walked past us and his seat was taken immediately by a middle-aged woman carrying a pair of heavy shopping bags which she placed on the floor between her feet—and then I felt the cold December wind at my back as the double-doors slid open and closed again. Presumably the man was gone. Danny looked at the woman's bags and said shyly, "Presents?"

The woman looked at him and nodded, smiling.

He elected to question her no further.

The train rumbled on.

Our own stop was next. We walked out into the wind on the Rye platform and headed clanging down the metal steps.

"What did he have?" asked Clarissa.

"Who?" said Danny.

"The man, dummy," said Jenny. "The man with the box! What was in the *box?*"

"Oh. Nothing."

"Nothing? What? It was *empty?*"

And then they were running along ahead of me toward our car off to the left in the second row of the parking lot.

I couldn't hear his answer. If he answered her at all.

And by the time I unlocked the car I'd forgotten all about the guy.

That night Danny wouldn't eat.

It happened sometimes. It happened with each of the kids. Other things to do or too much snacking during the day. Both my wife Susan and I had been raised in homes where a depression-era mentality still prevailed. If you didn't like or didn't want to finish your dinner that was just too bad. You sat there at the table, your food getting colder and colder, until you pretty much cleaned the plate. We'd agreed that we weren't going to lay that on *our* kids. And most of the experts these days seemed to agree with us that skipping the occasional meal didn't matter. And certainly wasn't worth fighting over.

So we excused him from the table.

The next night—Monday night—same thing.

"What'd you do," my wife asked him, "have six desserts for lunch?" She was probably half serious. Desserts and pizza were pretty much all our kids could stomach on the menu at the school cafeteria.

"Nope. Just not hungry, that's all."

We let it go at that.

I kept an eye on him during the night though—figuring he'd be up in the middle of a commercial break in one of our Monday-night sitcoms, headed for the kitchen and a bag of pretzels or a jar of honey-roasted peanuts or some dry fruit loops out of the box. But it never happened. He went to bed without so much as a glass of water. Not that he looked sick or anything. His color was good and he laughed at the jokes right along with the rest of us.

I figured he was coming down with something. So did Susan. He almost had to be. Our son normally had the appetite of a Sumo wrestler.

I fully expected him to beg off school in the morning, pleading headache or upset stomach.

He didn't.

And he didn't want his breakfast, either.

And the next night, same thing.

Now this was particularly strange because Susan had cooked spaghetti and meat sauce that night and there was nothing in her considerable repertoire that the kids liked better. Even though—or maybe because of the fact—that it was one of the simplest dishes she ever threw together. But Danny just sat there and said he wasn't hungry, contented to watch while everybody else heaped it on. I'd come home late after a particularly grueling day—I work for a brokerage firm in the City—and personally I was famished. And not a little unnerved by my son's repeated refusals to eat.

"Listen," I said. "You've got to have something. We're talking *three days* now."

"Did you eat lunch?" Susan asked.

Danny doesn't lie. "I didn't feel like it," he said.

Even Clarissa and Jenny were looking at him like he had two heads by now.

"But you *love* spaghetti," Susan said.

"Try some garlic bread," said Clarissa.

"No thanks."

"Do you *feel* okay, guy?" I asked him.

"I feel fine. I'm just not hungry's all."

So he sat there.

Wednesday night Susan went all out, making him his personal favorite—roast leg of lemon-spiced lamb with mint sauce, baked potato and red wine gravy, and green snap-peas on the side.

He sat there. Though he seemed to enjoy watching *us* eat.

Thursday night we tried take-out—Chinese food from his favorite Szechuan restaurant. Ginger beef, shrimp fried rice, fried won ton and sweet-and-sour ribs.

He said it smelled good. And sat there.

By Friday night whatever remnants of depression-era mentality lingered in my own personal psyche kicked in with a vengeance and I found myself standing there yelling at him, telling him he wasn't getting up from his chair, *young man*, until he finished at least *one slice* of his favorite pepperoni, meatball and sausage pizza from his favorite Italian restaurant.

The fact is I was worried. I'd have handed him a twenty, gladly, just to see some of that stringy mozzarella hanging off his chin. But I didn't tell him that. Instead I stood there pointing a finger at him and yelling until he started to cry—and then, second-generation depression-brat that I am, I ordered him to bed. Which is exactly what my parents would have done.

Scratch a son, you always get his dad.

But by Sunday you could see his ribs through his teeshirt. We kept him out of school Monday and I stayed home from work so we could both be there for our appointment with Doctor Weller. Weller was one of the last of those wonderful old-fashioned GP's, the kind you just about never see anymore. Over seventy years old, he would still stop by your house after office hours if the need arose. In Rye that was as unheard-of as an honest mechanic. Weller believed in home-care, not hospitals. He'd fallen asleep on my sofa one night after checking in on Jenny's bronchitis and slept for two hours straight over an untouched cup of coffee while we tiptoed around him and listened to him snore.

We sat in his office Monday morning answering questions while he checked Danny's eyes, ears, nose and throat, tapped his knees, his back and chest, checked his breathing, took a vial of blood and sent him into the bathroom for a urine sample.

"He looks perfectly fine to me. He's lost five pounds since the last time he was in for a checkup but beyond that I can't see anything wrong with him. Of course we'll have to wait for the blood work. You say he's eaten *nothing?*"

"Absolutely nothing," Susan said.

He sighed. "Wait outside," he said. "Let me talk with him."

In the waiting room Susan picked up a magazine, looked at the cover and returned it to the pile. "*Why?*" she whispered.

An old man with a walker glanced over at us and then looked away. A mother across from us watched her daughter coloring in a Garfield book.

"I don't know," I said. "I wish I did."

I was aware sitting there of an odd detachment, as though this were happening to the rest of them—to them, not me—not *us*.

I have always felt a fundamental core of loneliness in me. Perhaps it comes from being an only child. Perhaps it's my grandfather's sullen thick German blood. I have been alone with my wife and alone with my children, untouchable, unreachable, and I suspect that most of the time they haven't known. It runs deep, this aloneness. I have accommodated it. It informs all my relationships and all my expectations. It makes me almost impossible to surprise by life's grimmer turns of fate.

I was very aware of it now.

Dr. Weller was smiling when he led Danny through the waiting room and asked him to have a seat for a moment while he motioned us inside. But the smile was for Danny. There was nothing real inside it.

We sat down.

"The most extraordinary thing." The doctor shook his head. "I told him he had to eat. He asked me why. I said, Danny, people die every day of starvation. All over the world. If you don't eat, you'll die—it's that simple. Your son looked me straight in the eye and said, '*so?*' "

"Jesus," Susan said.

"He wasn't being flip, believe me—he was asking me a serious question. I said, well, you want to live, don't you? He said, '*should I?*' Believe me, you could have knocked me right off this chair. '*Should I!*' I said of course you should! *Everybody* wants to live.

" '*Why?*' he said.

"My God. I told him that life was beautiful, that life was sacred, that life was *fun!* Wasn't Christmas just around the corner? What about holidays and birthdays and summer vacations? I told him that it was everybody's duty to try to live life to the absolute fullest, to do everything you could in order to be as strong and healthy and happy as humanly possible. And he listened to me. He listened to me and I knew he understood me. He didn't seem the slightest bit worried about any of what I was saying or the slightest bit concerned or unhappy. And when I was done, all he said was, yes—yes, but *I'm not hungry.*"

The doctor looked amazed, confounded.

"I really don't know what to tell you." He picked up a pad. "I'm writing down the name and phone number of a psychotherapist. Not a psychiatrist, mind—this fellow isn't going to push any pills at Danny. A therapist. The only thing I can come up with pending some—to my way of thinking, practically unimaginable—problem with his blood work is that Danny has some very serious emotional problems that need exploring and need exploring immediately. This man Field is the best I know. And he's very good with children. Tell him I said to fit you in right away, today if at all possible. We go back a long time, he and I—he'll do as I ask. And I think he'll be able to help Danny."

"Help him do what, doctor?" Susan said. I could sense her losing it. "Help him do what?" she said. "*Find a reason for living?*"

Her voice broke on the last word and suddenly she was sobbing into her hands and I reached over and tried to contact that part of me which might be able to contact her and found it not entirely mute inside me, and held her.

In the night I heard them talking. Danny and the two girls.

It was late and we were getting ready for bed and Susan was in the bathroom brushing her teeth. I stepped out into the hall to go downstairs for one last cigarette from my pack in the kitchen and that was when I heard them whispering. The twins had their room and Danny had his. The whispering was coming from their room.

It was against the rules but the rules were rapidly going to hell these days anyway. Homework was being ignored. Breakfast was coffee and packaged donuts. For Danny, of course, not even that much. Bedtime arrived when we felt exhausted.

Dr. Field had told us that that was all right for a while. That we should avoid all areas of tension or confrontation within the family for at least the next week or so.

I was *not* to yell at Danny for not eating.

Field had spoken first to him for half an hour in his office and then, for another twenty minutes, to Susan and me. I found him personable and soft-spoken. As yet he had no idea what Danny's problem could be. The jist of what he was able to tell us was that he would need to see Danny every day until he started eating again and probably once or twice a week thereafter.

If he did start eating.

Anyhow, I'd decided to ignore the whispering. I figured if I'd stuck to my guns about quitting the goddamn cigarettes I'd never have heard it in the first place. But then something Jenny said sailed through the half-open door loud and clear and stopped me.

"I still don't get it," she said. "What's it got to do with that *box?*"

I didn't catch his answer. I walked to the door. A floorboard squeaked. The whispering stopped.

I opened it. They were huddled together on the bed.

"What's what got to do with *what* box?" I said.

They looked at me. My children, I thought, had grown up amazingly free of guilty conscience. Rules or no rules. In that they were not like me. There were times I wondered if they were actually my children at all.

"Nothing," Danny said.

"Nothing," said Clarissa and Jenny.

"Come on," I said. "Give. What were you guys just talking about?"

"Just stuff," said Danny.

"*Secret* stuff?" I was kidding, making it sound like it was no big deal.

He shrugged. "Just, you know, stuff."

"Stuff that maybe has to do with why you're not eating? That kind of stuff?"

"D*aaaa*d."

I knew my son. He was easily as stubborn as I was. It didn't take a genius to know when you were not going to get anything further out of him and this was one of those times. "Okay," I said, "back to bed."

He walked past me. I glanced into the bedroom and saw the two girls sitting motionless, staring at me.

"What," I said.

"Nothing," said Clarissa.

"G'night, daddy," said Jenny.

I said goodnight and went downstairs for my cigarettes. I smoked three of them. I wondered what this whole box business was.

The following morning my girls were not eating.

Things occurred rapidly then. By evening it became apparent that they were taking the same route Danny had taken. They were happy. They were content. And they could not be budged. To me, *we're not hungry* had suddenly become the scariest three words in the English language.

A variation became just as scary when, two nights later, sitting over a steaming baked lasagna she'd worked on all day long, Susan asked me how in the world I expected her to eat while all her children were starving.

And then ate nothing further.

I started getting takeout for one.

McDonald's. Slices of pizza. Buffalo wings from the deli.

By Christmas Day, Danny could not get out of bed unassisted.

The twins were looking gaunt—so was my wife.

There was no Christmas dinner. There wasn't any point to it.

I ate cold fried rice and threw a couple of ribs into the microwave and that was that.

Meantime Field was frankly baffled by the entire thing and told me he was thinking of writing a paper—did I mind? I didn't mind. I didn't care one way or another. Dr. Weller, who normally considered hospitals strictly a last resort, wanted to get Danny on an IV as soon as possible. He was ordering more blood tests. We asked if it could wait till after Christmas. He said it could but not a moment longer. We agreed.

Despite the cold fried rice and the insane circumstances Christmas was actually by far the very best day we'd had in a very long time. Seeing us all together, sitting by the fire, opening packages under the tree—it brought back memories. The cozy warmth of earlier days. It was almost, though certainly not quite, normal. For this day alone I could almost begin to forget my worries about them, forget that Danny would be going into the hospital the next morning—with the twins, no doubt, following pretty close behind. For her part Susan seemed to *have* no worries. It was as though in joining them in their fast she had also somehow partaken of their lack of concern for it. As though the fast were itself a drug.

I remember laughter from that day, plenty of laughter. Nobody's new clothes fit but my own but we tried them on anyway—there were jokes about the Amazing Colossal Woman and the Incredible Shrinking Man. And the toys and games all fit, and the brand-new hand-carved American-primitive angel I'd bought for the tree.

Believe it or not, we were happy.

But that night I lay in bed and thought about Danny in the hospital the next day and then for some reason about the whispered conversation I'd overheard that seemed so long ago and then about the man with the box and the day it had all begun. I felt like a fool, like somebody who was awakened from a long confused and confusing dream.

I suddenly had to know what *Danny* knew.

I got up and went to his room and shook him gently from his sleep.

I asked him if he remembered that day on the train and the man with the box and then looking into the box and he said that yes he did and then I asked him what was in it.

"Nothing," he said.

"Really *nothing*? You mean it was actually empty?"

He nodded.

"But didn't he . . . I remember him telling us it was a *present*."

He nodded again. I still didn't get it. It made no sense to me.

"So you mean it was some kind of joke or something? He was playing some kind of joke on somebody?"

"I don't know. It was just . . . the box was empty."

He looked at me as though it was impossible for him to understand why *I* didn't understand. Empty was empty. That was that.

I let him sleep. For his last night, in his own room.

I told you that things happened rapidly after that and they did, although it hardly seemed so at the time. Three weeks later my son smiled at me sweetly and slipped into a coma and died in just under thirty-two hours. It was unusual, I was told, for the IV not to have sustained a boy his age but sometimes it happened. By then the twins had beds two doors down the hall. Clarissa went on February 3rd and Jenny on February 5th.

My wife, Susan, lingered until the 27th.

And through all of this, through all these weeks now, going back and forth to the hospital each day, working when I was and *am* able and graciously being granted time off whenever I can't, riding into the City from Rye and from the City back to Rye again alone on the train, I look for him. I look through every car. I walk back and forth in case he should get on one stop sooner or one stop later. I don't want to miss him. I'm losing weight.

Oh, I'm eating. Not as well as I should be I suppose but I'm eating.

But I need to find him. To know what my son knew and then passed on to the others. I'm sure that the girls knew, that he passed it on to them that night in the bedroom—some terrible knowledge, some awful peace. And I think somehow, perhaps by being so very much closer to all of my children than I was ever capable of being, that Susan knew too. I'm convinced it's so.

I'm convinced that it was my essential loneliness that set me apart and saved me, and now of course which haunts me, makes me wander through dark corridors of commuter trains waiting for a glimpse of him—him and his damnable present, his gift, his box.

I want to know. It's the only way I can get close to them.

I want to see. I *have* to see.

I'm *hungry*.

For Neal McPheeters

A FEAR OF DEAD THINGS

Andrew Klavan

Andrew Klavan was born in New York City and educated at the University of California at Berkeley. A former newspaper and radio reporter, Klavan is a two-time winner of the Edgar Award. He is the author of *The Animal Hour, Don't Say a Word,* and *Corruption* under his own name, and *The Scarred Man,* as Keith Peterson. He also wrote the screenplay for Michael Caine's *A Shock to the System.* Klavan lives in London and Connecticut with his wife and their two children.

I've been a fan of Klavan's since reading the frighteningly effective *The Scarred Man* and his intricately plotted page-turner *Don't Say a Word.* Klavan is expert at drawing the reader into unpleasant situations with unpleasant (yet spellbinding) characters. In addition to "A Fear of Dead Things" reprinted from the anthology *Phobias,* I highly recommend "The Look on Her Face" from the British anthology *London Noir.*

—E. D.

On Friday evening Dr. Lawrence Rothman found a dead mouse in the bread cupboard and thought of Curtis Zane. The mouse lay curled on its side, the gray fur bristling on its back. There was no sign of what had killed it. Rothman felt a little hitch of disgust in his throat and withdrew his hand—he'd been reaching for the package of wheat bread when he saw it. His first instinct was just to shut the cupboard door again and pretend he'd never found the thing. He could work around it for the rest of the weekend easily enough. On Monday Lily, the cleaning woman, would come in and take care of it for him.

But again he thought of his new patient. He thought of Curtis Zane.

Zane had come into the Manhattan office just that morning, at the end of the morning, the last session before noon. He was a man in his early forties with steady eyes and an iron line of jaw. Good-looking, Rothman thought; dominant-looking; the kind of man women find attractive. Zane said he lived in the Village and owned and operated a trade magazine out of a loft down in SoHo. He managed about seven people, he said, give or take a few steady freelancers. He did not seem nervous as he talked, but crossed his legs at the knee with decision and steepled his fingers quietly under his dimpled chin. And when Dr. Rothman asked him what the problem was he explained it clearly in a firm, deep voice. Some of them liked to play it that way, Rothman thought: as one professional to another.

"I have," Zane said, "a fear of dead things." He waved one hand as if it annoyed him, as if it were flies. "Irrational, terrible," he said. "Even paralyzing sometimes. Bugs—dead bugs—birds, mice. Any kind of . . . *corpse* at all. I can't even take my clothes down to the washers in my building because there are always roaches, dead roaches, in the basement, and . . ." Here, Rothman noticed with some satisfaction, Zane could not pull off an ironic smile. A shudder took him instead across the shoulders. "I can't tolerate the sight of them."

Behind his desk Rothman sat still, his hands in his lap, his face impassive. He let the silence stretch way past the comfort level. But Zane was tough enough for that. He waited it out. At last Rothman said, "Anything else? Are you hypochondriacal? Are you afraid of dying yourself? Of becoming, I mean, one of these dead things?"

Zane appeared to give this some thought. Then he shook his head briskly. "No. No." And he broke into a rakish grin, one side of his mouth going up, one eyebrow lowering. "I guess that sounds kind of funny. But I've often thought that people react more to the symbols of things than to the things themselves. I mean, we react more to things—and people, too—according to what they mean to us instead of what they really are. Don't you think?" He laughed. "Anyway, it would explain why people vote for the politicians they do. And why they fall in love with the people they fall in love with, too."

Rothman hoped his face remained impassive. He was afraid he might have given way to a little pucker of distaste. Already, he found, he disliked this man for some reason. His bush-league insights, maybe, or maybe his take-charge attitude; he wasn't sure. Whatever it was, Zane had set something nervous and unpleasant squirreling around in his stomach. Rothman wanted to move away from him. He wanted to swivel in his chair away from the confidence of Zane's gaze and jaw and gesture. He had to remind himself that he, Rothman, was the doctor, he was in charge. It was Zane who had the problem, who had come to him for help.

Rothman let out a controlled breath. Maybe he could just refer the man to someone else, he thought. He could say he wanted to send him to someone who "specialized in phobias," or some crap like that.

"I guess that's what psychiatry is all about, isn't it?" Zane went on, one guy to another, magazine-guy to psychiatrist-guy. "You show people what things symbolize to them—what other people symbolize to them. You tell them: Your wife represents your mother, your car represents your cock, and all that—and then they can get around their confused reactions, get down to the business of dealing with things as they really are. If things really are anything, that is." He grinned that pirate grin again. Before he could stop himself, Rothman squirmed a little in his chair. "I guess that's the problem right there. What if the symbols are the only reason we react in the first place: Your wife's your mother, your car's your cock. What if things in themselves, people in themselves, don't mean a damn thing to us, don't really exist for us at all?"

"I think for now," Dr. Rothman said, clearing his throat, "we should meet with each other once a week."

* * *

And so he tackled the mouse, the dead mouse, himself. He did not leave it for the cleaning woman. Because he was still the doctor here. He was not the one with the problem. Even if he was thick at the middle where Curtis Zane was trim and taut. Even if he was balding where Zane had wavy salt-and-pepper hair. Even if his shaggy, curly black beard did not entirely hide the face of the high school weakling who, in high school, he had been. . . . Even so, it was Zane who had come to *him* for help, not the other way around. So he swept the dead mouse out of the cupboard and into a dustpan. Then, quick, quick, quick, holding the dustpan as far away from him as he could, he carried the thing to the kitchen garbage can and dumped it in. Turning his face away, he lifted the garbage bag out of the can. Twisted it, tied it shut. Carried it, his face still averted, down the connecting hallway into the garage. And there he dumped it in the can and clamped the lid down tight. And that, he thought, dusting his hands off, was that.

Then he made himself a dinner of eggs and toast. Then he washed the dishes and put them away. And then he went to bed. And then he started to cry.

Actually, he started to sob. Actually, to bawl was probably the best way to describe it. Clutching his pillow, biting, gnawing the corner of it to keep from making those raw, gasping sounds he hated himself for. He cried as he had cried almost every night since Gerry had left him. Not only because she'd left him, although he did believe he loved her, but also, more specifically, because she'd left him for another man.

"I'm sorry, Lawrence, it was just something that happened. I met him through work. . . ." Gerry was a designer for a Guatemalan clothing manufacturer, so Rothman had immediately imagined her tilting limply against the chest of some cocky Latin, some casually smoldering caballero who was quietly amused at how easily the wives of these weak Yanquis . . .

"Don't," he'd said to her quickly. "You don't have to tell me. In fact, really, I don't want to know."

And Gerry fell quiet at once. Her eyes were damp with sympathy. She was genuinely forlorn for him. All in all, in fact, she was excruciatingly kind. Which only made Rothman choke on it the more. Because enough was said, with all her kindness, for him to get the idea. He listened for it. He was trained to catch it. "It wasn't you," she told him. "It was me, it was marriage, I don't know. There was always something *missing* for me. I was just . . . *unsatisfied* somehow. As if some part of me were always *unfulfilled* . . ." Gently she said these things. As if to comfort him. As if she were doing this to him with all the pity in the world. Like the nurse at his castration.

Well, he knew, with his history, it was bound to hit him hard. People under stress tend to crack along their fault lines, after all. But still, this nightly weeping—Jesus, after fifteen years of analysis, it made him doubt—lying there, twisting there, chawing on that pillow corner—made him doubt not only his own mental health, but the value of his entire profession.

And snuff, snuff, snuff, he went, his pillow sopping.

"Now when you experience this fear," he said, "when you see a dead cockroach in the laundry room, for instance, does anything come to mind, does it remind you of anything in particular?"

It was Friday again, and there, again, sat Zane. Aggressively thoughtful in the patient's chair. *Battling* his problem, *wrestling* with it, using strategy, brain power.

"Well, obviously, I've considered this a lot. I mean, my childhood. Right? That's what you're talking about. I've tried to figure out what it has to do with all this. I mean, it sure wasn't a very happy childhood. In fact, I would say it was downright unhappy."

"All right," said Rothman, encouraging him with a nod, with a mild roll of his hand—his practiced gestures. He was going through the motions to hide his dislike of the man.

"Right." And Zane actually began ticking it—his childhood—off on his fingers. "My father. A nobody. Some sort of factotum for the phone company. A gray man. Gray, gray man. Nobody." Finger two. "My mother. She just disdained him. She was merciless about what a failure, what a nobody, he was. A mean, snarling person. She terrified me." Three. "She cheated on him. The milkman, the mailman, the neighbors. Anyone. Everyone in town knew it but Dad. Maybe he knew it, too."

"Did you know it?" Rothman asked.

"Oh, yeah. Oh, yeah. I was downstairs in the playroom half the time it was going on. Mom made me promise not to tell. Said she'd cut my dick off." His pirate grin was quick, but just a little pallid this time. "I hope I'm not making your job too easy for you."

Rothman stroked his beard, hiding a small smile. He had to admit he was gratified by that last stroke, "making your job too easy for you," the hostility in it. For all this brusque display, the finger-ticking, the macho stuff, Zane was ashamed of the sordidness of his early life. He resented the fact that it had to come out like this. But, thought Rothman, stroking away, it always did in the end, didn't it? You got past the shell of people, the shape of them, their defensive loveliness or manliness, their sweetness, their courage, their wit—and there was always just a tarry hell of one kind or another, the shapeless gunk of pain held together by those defenses into something like a human form. There was no hiding it from him, not over the long run. It always spilled out onto his desk eventually. Bubbling, boiling with the anguish of childhood. Sooner or later. He just had to wait for it.

He did wait. And this time the silence worked. Zane pushed ahead bitterly. "She left anyway, my mother, when I was around eleven. My father had a sister I stayed with during the day, and there were baby-sitters. Just housekeepers, really. My mother I never saw again."

Dr. Rothman closed his eyes and shook his head in his usual gesture of uncommitted sympathy. He thought: This guy is going to need the full course, all right, five days a week by the time he's finished. He felt a strange mixture of satisfaction and discomfort at that.

"That's when I began to kill things," Zane said.

Rothman's eyes came open. He looked at the man across his desk, through the frame made by the upright pens in the calendar set Gerry had given him.

"Little things," Zane went on, with merely a rueful shake of his handsome head. "I remember I got an old board once and nailed some earthworms to it. My father liked to go fishing sometimes, and he said they didn't feel any pain, worms, when you put the hook in them. But they do, you know. And . . . what else? I coated a firecracker with sugar once, laid it near an anthill, and waited until it was crawling with ants, then . . ." An embarrassed shrug.

"Any . . ." Rothman cleared his throat. He'd heard this sort of thing before, often—but that didn't help somehow, not this time, not with Zane. "Anything else?"

"A squirrel. Once. Shot it with a BB gun. Stunned it. Then stepped on its head."

"Any . . ." He should have kept at him. He should have asked the question again. But he didn't. He coughed into his fist. "How did this make you feel?" he asked after a while.

"Well . . . not bad or anything, not guilty, at least not that I'm aware of." Zane frowned, considering. "I think it made me feel . . . calm, more than anything. Sort of firmed up inside. I mean, maybe it sounds crazy, but I think it worked as a kind of therapy for me. After it was over I always felt very clearheaded. Strong, directed. And, in most ways, I've been like that ever since." A manly chuckle here. "It's the secret of my success, I think. That attitude. It's always made me very popular, anyway. Especially with women. I always have been very, very popular with women." And the corners of his eyes crinkled handsomely as he gave Rothman a wink. "But I guess you know how that is," he said. "Right?"

Rothman wasn't sure why he kept coming up to the Connecticut house every weekend. The summer was long over, and this humorless, slate October they were having—it seemed to perch on the roof of the place like a great gray crow, with outspread wings the length and width and heaviness of the sky. Gerry was not here now to make a fire for, to pour a brandy for. And all their friends, their laughing houseguests, had turned out to be mostly her friends in the end. And even his happy memories of those old times were ruined for him, knowing that only he'd been happy then, and she . . . "dissatisfied," "unfulfilled." That night, that Friday night, he sat at the dining room table again, alone again, eating his scrambled eggs again, and wondered why he bothered to come here at all anymore. To sit here, mashing his eggs dully, like a toothless old man, a sexless old man. Reading his journals and his Xeroxed articles with distant interest and a muzzy mind. After a while he glanced up and just fell to empty gazing. Not much in the journals that could help him anyway, he thought. Necrophobia—the fear of dead things—was common enough, but it rarely became very intense or crippling. It hadn't inspired any massive amounts of literature, that was for sure. A few up-to-date articles, a couple of case histories, but most of the stuff he found was included in pieces that covered phobias in general. ". . . connected to hypochondria and the fear of death . . ." they said. ". . . associated with sometimes unrelated childhood traumas . . ." Nothing that would guide him in a specific case like this. He gazed out through the picture window at the backyard. He noticed he had neglected to have the swimming pool covered. The water was dark and brackish now, the dead leaves floating in it. A sad sight, a pool in autumn. He sighed, mashing the last of his eggs.

When he was done he carried his plates into the kitchen. He was even walking, shuffling, like an old man now. He'd have to remember to go out and buy himself a pair of baggy pants in the morning, and a flannel shirt. He scraped the plates into the kitchen garbage and rinsed them off. He tied the garbage bag and carried it down the hall to the garage. He flicked on the light and moved to the garbage can. He pried off the lid.

And he cried out. He jumped back.

There was a raccoon in there. Twisted on the bottom of the can. Dead. Its eyes glassy in their mask. Its pink tongue dangling over its bared teeth.

"Jesus," Rothman said. The smell had just now reached him. It was not bad yet. Only a faint, faintly tangy unpleasantness in the air. But it made him think of trash in the summertime gutters. Something that had lived was turning into trash.

Rothman set his garbage bag down hard. He put his hands on his hips and bent over, breathing in and out deeply. He had to fight to keep his disgust from turning into nausea. But he wouldn't even think of shirking this. He would not let it become a problem for him. The thing had crawled in there to get at his garbage, gotten itself trapped, and starved to death; now he had to remove it, that was all.

And in some ways it turned out to be easier than the mouse. All he had to do was get a fresh bag, fit it over the opening of the can, and then upend the can on top of it. The raccoon tumbled right down into the bag, although it did make an unpleasantly soft *phlump* as it hit the garage floor. He carried the bag down to the edge of the woods and squeezed in a little past the trees, brushing away the branches he couldn't make out in the dark. He set the bag down and stepped back from it. Bent over, reached out. Pinched the bottom corner of plastic delicately between thumb and forefinger, careful not to touch anything, any trace of any part of the thing that was inside. And then he lifted the corner, his arm outstretched, and the coon plopped onto the forest floor. Barely even visible, lying there in the night. And the lovable little creatures of the forest could just take care of the rest.

The nauseous jolt of first finding the thing came back to him later, though. That Friday, the session before noon. Even ensconced in his chair with its arms around him and its high wings shielding his head. Even with the stolid bulwark of the desk between him and Zane. The sensation returned, and he felt his muscles go tight and had to lay his finger across his mouth to cover his lips' working. He watched Zane but remembered finding the raccoon. He saw Zane's crags and jawline and flashing eyes, all the tics of his masculinity. . . .

That's when I began to kill things.

And he thought of walking into the garage again, of prying off the lid of the can.

I pried off the lid of the can, he thought.

"Doctor? Are you listening?" Zane said.

Rothman, of course, had been asked this far too often to be caught out. He answered smoothly, "Yes, I'm listening. Just go on," and he forced himself to pay attention.

Zane gave a nod and soldiered ahead. "All right. It happened Wednesday. I was coming home from *Borderlines*—that's the name of my magazine. I was walking home, which is what I usually do. It was around eight o'clock, a little later. I was feeling fine. Striding along. Came around the corner at Fifth Avenue and Twelfth. And there was . . . God, it's ridiculous."

Rothman lowered his hands to his lap, really interested now. *I pried off . . .* he thought. But he forced his mind clear. "There was what?"

"This roach. This cockroach. One of those real New York specials, about the size of Staten Island."

"And it was dead," said Rothman when Zane paused.

"Yeah." Zane rubbed the back of his neck. "It really got me, too. I mean, normally, you know, I might've crossed the street, I might've even turned back and gone around to Sixth to avoid it. I mean, if I'd been with someone, I'm sure I would've just forced myself to look away, just stepped right over it so they wouldn't notice. But this time . . . No. Jesus. I don't know what it was. Maybe because I've been coming here, you know, exposing my feelings, maybe I was more sensitive to it than usual. But I tell you, Doc, it stopped me cold. I felt like the blood was draining right out of my feet, right into the sidewalk, I felt like I was glued to the sidewalk. I couldn't move. Backward or forward. I was that terrified. I just stood there. With the cold sweat all over my face. Staring at the thing. I couldn't even look away. It must've been—I don't know—minutes, three, five minutes before I . . . ran for it. I mean *fled*. Just went scampering back to Fifth, to that café around the corner there. I had to inhale a couple of martinis before I could even bring myself to go around the other way."

Rothman kept his posture relaxed, but he felt the juice going through him. He felt wired and sick, but his patented sympathetic-yet-impassive tone came automatically. "What were your associations? During those three to five minutes when you were confronting the dead roach. Were there any memories, any thoughts that came to you?"

Zane seemed to consider the question. And as Rothman watched, his stomach churning, Zane's attention seemed to drift away, his gaze to drift away to some lower corner of the empty air. "I don't know," he said, and his voice was dreamy, hollow. "I guess . . . I guess I thought . . . that *this* is what we are. You know? That everything else is just . . . bullshit. That it's just, like, some kind of play or something. Walking around, pretending to be somebodies, pretending to . . . sympathize with each other, and love each other, and live. It's like some kind of puppet show, a puppet show done with corpses. People are all just these corpses jerking around according to a pattern of electric pulses in their brains. Smiling and saying things matter, and saying they want cream in their coffee and will vote Democratic and love you, when all the time they're just these . . . things. These animated things. Temporarily animated things."

It was long seconds—silent seconds—before Rothman realized he was staring at the man, just staring at him, all queasy and electrified, his mouth sour and dry. He had to wet his lips before he could speak again. "And you're afraid of that," he said hoarsely, finally. "You're afraid that the people who . . . who love you will soon become . . . inanimate things. Dead things."

"Yes." In that mesmerized voice, that dead voice.

Rothman leaned forward in his chair, leaned far enough to rest one arm upon the table, and yet leaned carefully, as if closing in on something that might turn suddenly, that might strike out. "You know," he said, "in my business, we believe that the thing you fear is also the thing you secretly . . . desire."

It was another moment or so before this reached him, Zane. Then he blinked and came to himself. He raised his eyes to Rothman's. He smiled.

"Yes," he said softly.

* * *

That night—that night was hell. The house was hell that night. Rothman actually searched the place when he came in. He couldn't believe he was doing it. He wouldn't admit he was doing it, but the moment he came in he put his overnight bag down and went through the rooms. Cautiously opening the cupboards in the kitchen, kneeling on the living room floor to peer under the couch and the chairs. He checked the garage and the garbage cans there, the bathrooms and the medicine chest. He did not think, How could it have gotten in, if I pried off the lid? And he didn't think: She met him through work. That's what she told me. She met him through work. But while the night outside was very still, and there was no wind and there were no noises, he sensed a lowering urgency in the ink-blue dark, a sere, severe, almost imperious call to panic. At the windows, at the spaces in the sashes where the cool seeped in, he sensed it, it reached him. He could not keep from moving, moving from room to room, searching room after room until—well, until he just ran out of places. Until, that is, he couldn't put the real thing off any longer. And then he wound up in the bedroom, as he knew he would, seated with slumped shoulders on the edge of the double bed, looking at the phone. Glaring sullenly at the phone.

He had used the phone in his office after Zane left that afternoon. He had done it quickly, before Zane had a chance to get back to his magazine, to *Borderlines*. He had called *Borderlines*. A young woman answered cheerfully. Excuse me, Rothman had said, but just what sort of magazine is this exactly? And cheerfully the young woman had read it off to him: It's the magazine of the fashion and fabric trade between the Americas. Thank you, he had said. And he had hung up.

I met him through work. It was just something that happened. . . .

But there was no shock to it. He didn't go reeling backward, openmouthed, hand to brow. A diffuse instinct simply coalesced, and he had sat then as he was sitting now, sulking over the phone. Sulking and thinking: I'm not actually going to call her, obviously. Thinking: It's ridiculous. Thinking: A neurotic reaction. A sense of inadequacy. Manifestations in fantasy . . . and so on. Which was exactly why the night became hell for him, driving up to the house, reaching the house, standing in front of the house in the imperious ink-blue chill. The house, that night, was hell because there might be . . . *proof* in there. He didn't quite say it to himself. But that pressure of panic from the dark, that's what it was: He knew there might be proof, that there *would* be proof if he was right about it. In the cupboards, in the garbage can, under the chairs. Somewhere. And he couldn't keep from searching.

And afterward, when he had found nothing, nothing anywhere, he felt no relief. He simply sat on the edge of the bed with his options exhausted, and he glared at the phone, without proof, just knowing. He sat by the pillows into which he'd cried, sobbed and cried through the hours night on night until he was humiliated even before himself. He sat and sulked until it began to dawn on him—in one of those cloudy sort of half dawns that you don't even notice coming, that becomes just day after a while all unannounced—that he was not going to call her. That he was damned if he was, he, the more wounded party. He was going to get up and put his pajamas on instead, that's what. He was going to slide under the covers. He was going to lie there without tears. He was going to sleep, all comfy, in this sanctuary of his secret miseries—which was also, he realized now, the temple of his high and terrible rage.

In the morning he made himself a mug of coffee and took it out onto the deck. He sipped it, looking over the backyard, and he saw the deer floating in the pool. He wondered, though only briefly, if he could have the police remove it for him. It must've fallen in and drowned, he would tell them, and he pictured its forelegs thrashing in the water as its sleek, graceful head went down.

The creature's corpse looked bloated and gaping, he noticed, as if it had been in there for days and days.

Curtis Zane did not come to his next appointment, and the last time Dr. Rothman saw him was that evening on Park Avenue as he was walking to his car. The cold was really bitter now. The doctor's ungainly figure was hunched up inside his overcoat. His bulbous nose was red and runny. His chin and beard were pressed down against his chest. He was thinking about Zane, naturally enough, and about the deer in the pool.

It had been easy for him to get rid of the deer, emotionally easy, and he thought that was strange. He had gone to the hardware store for a rope and gloves, but he'd still had to grapple with the creature in the end—and yet he hadn't really cared. He'd grabbed hold of the deer's left foreleg right where it joined the torso, and he'd felt the yield of the flesh through his gloves, felt the flesh bloated drum tight under the sodden fur. The trek down into the woods had been breathless work, but easy, not terrible at all—and that just seemed very strange to him; he had been thinking about it a lot all week. All week, in fact, it had been the same. The thing that was happening, that was going to happen: It was not dreadful to him, not terrible. It was all just very, very strange, and strangely unmoving, as if he had eased without noticing it into an inner state of gray, a state like ashes. It reminded him of that moment by the phone. When he had lapsed so gently into the knowledge that he would not call her. Just as gently, maybe even at the exact same moment, he seemed also to have glided through the borders of something essential, something that had seemed solid but was really only mist. It seemed to him, after long consideration, that he had stepped out of the bubble of his central self, and it had burst, silently, and he had become . . . ashes, walking. . . .

A movement to the side of him made him look up. He stopped, panting. In a doorway, there was Zane.

The man looked robust enough, but dreamy. In a charcoal overcoat, his salt-and-pepper hair stirred by the wind, he cut his usual substantial figure. But just his unexpected presence there, had to believe, and maybe also his distant smile made Rothman blink. He confronted his patient with no knowable emotion. He just sniffled and waited and wiped his nose with his glove.

"Look," said Zane. He held his hand out. "Look."

Rothman didn't look down right away. He would have liked not to have looked down at all, but the man was standing there, holding his hand out, and so he did, finally.

A large cockroach lay in Zane's palm, lay on its back, its six legs pointed upward, shivering, probably with the wind.

Rothman grimaced with distaste and turned away.

"Look," said Zane. "I'm better now."

Rothman hurried on up the avenue.

Small and hunkered in the indifferent dark, the house stood before him when he stepped from his car. Not horrible, not even mysterious. Just a container really, he realized; four walls and a roof built around the empty air. As he came up the walk he could muster only the most miserable sort of suspense: the fear of being startled. And even that much surprise seemed unlikely to him. He let himself in through the front door and headed up the stairs at once.

He turned on the stair light and the upstairs hall light as he went, but the bedroom was still almost completely dark when he came into the doorway. He reached around the sill nervously and snapped the light on in there.

He did start a little when he saw her. And yet she lay in a natural position in the bed, just as she might have lain when they were living together. The covers were pulled up almost to her throat to hide her nakedness. One arm was flung out over her husband's pillow, one rested, a little stiff and clawlike, atop the counterpane. Her head was turned to the side, her black hair trailing out in back. Her eyelids, a little purple in the gray face, were gently closed as if she were sleeping.

For a minute or two Rothman stood there heavily, observing her with a sullen, sidelong look. But even then some unformed energy, not quite excitement or fear or rage, was urging him to move, to move now, move anywhere, so that he seemed to himself at once inanimate and a creature of pure behavior. He felt, that is, like a thing, but like a thing doomed to take action.

He went back downstairs and headed out to the garage to get the shovel.

HE UNWRAPS HIMSELF

Darrell Schweitzer

Darrell Schweitzer is the author of the novels *The Shattered Goddess* and *The White Isle*. His short fiction and poetry has been published in *Pulphouse, The Horror Show, Cemetery Dance, Weirdbook,* and *Grue* magazines, and in the anthology *Masques*. It has been collected in *We Are all Legends, Tom O'Bedlam's Night Out,* and *Transients and Other Disquieting Stories*. He has also written critical nonfiction in the fields of fantasy, dark fantasy, and horror.

"He Unwraps Himself" juxtaposes graceful writing with horrific images. This short poem is reprinted from *Weird Tales*.

—E. D.

He unwraps himself, like a Christmas package,
the ribboned clothing, the greeting-card hair,
nose and ears, nipples, penis, cast aside, off—

He unfolds himself, with silent grace;
the face is next, a delicate mask,
lifted away to reveal
the skull beneath the skin;

Stealing phrases from John Webster—
Or was it Marlowe? One of
those leotarded guys—he unlocks himself,
declaiming "Come Sirrah! Gut me like a fish,
and give these groundlings
their sup of gore!"

Frenzied and fierce, he unbinds himself,
bloody sinews, lungs and heart,
the deeper flesh all steaming
at his feet, the gray-white skeleton
chattering in the dark, "But wait, my Love! There's—more!"

At the very last, he reveals himself,
bones crinkled, heaped like newspaper
the flickering candle's flame of his genuine self,
soul's truth, there, unadorned.
"Dearest, what you see is what you get."

But she hastily escapes through
shattered French windows,
and the night breeze
blows the candle out.

CHANDIRA

Brian Mooney

Brian Mooney's first story was published in *The London Mystery Selection* in 1971. Since then his fiction has appeared in such anthologies as *The 21st Pan Book of Horror Stories, Dark Voices 5, The Anthology of Fantasy & the Supernatural, The Mammoth Book of Werewolves, Shadows Over Innsmouth, Fantasy Tales, Final Shadows, Kadath, Dark Horizons,* and *Fiesta*.

Mooney says, "My thinking on the tale started backwards with the two points that most Frankenstein-type creations are things of pathos rather than horror, and so many horror films I've seen end with fire.

"I then got the idea of suttee, which may be acceptable to Hindu thought but which is anathema to the Western mind. Next I saw the circumstance in which suttee might be acceptable to a Westerner. My narrator had to be a European to see suttee as alien, he had to be in a position of power, and he had to be young and independent enough not to be bound by inflexibility or the imposed rule of a senior. Hence, he would be a young District Officer in the days of the Raj, born in India so that he had a better understanding of the culture." The story is, appropriately, from *The Mammoth Book of Frankenstein*.

—E. D.

I am an old man now and daily I think more and more about death. I think about death and then I recall certain events toward the end of the last century and I start to become frightened.

I am an old man, winter's damp chills gnaw at my bones and rack my joints and I curse the miserable climate of my supposed homeland. Most evenings, even during the more clement months, I sit by a roaring fire and sip from a glass of fine malt whiskey which helps to ease the aches. And sometimes the fire and the whiskey evaporate my terror of death.

But I wasn't always so cold. Most of my life, save for when I was sent away to school, was spent under the torrid Indian sun which leathered my skin and thinned my blood. Nor did I always have a fear of dying. That didn't start until I was all of twenty years of age.

I was born near Poona, where my father was a district officer, and I grew up speaking Marati and Gujarati, dialects to which I was to add in later years. It therefore seemed the proper thing for me to enter the service when I became a man. Certainly India was more home to me than the bleak moors of my ancestors, and my return to the subcontinent as a very junior official was a great joy.

It was much the done thing in those long-ago days of the Raj to send young men like myself to remote stations. It was a way of testing our mettle, to see if we were fit for India and for eventual promotion to the higher grades. I often smirked when I heard the subalterns of the British Army complain of their hard lot. Most of them had only to worry about a suitable mount for the next bout of pig-sticking, or whether they could find a partner for the mess ball, or how to keep their rough and ready subordinates sane. At the age of twenty, I was controller, protector, advisor, tax-collector, administrator, magistrate, mediator, father-figure, all things to all men.

Sometimes now, more and more rarely, I go up to town to spend a day or two at my club. My fellow members like occasionally to hear tales of India from me and some of the younger ones josh me gently, asking about the rope trick and similar myths.

Forget the rope trick, for it is just that, a myth. I have seen fakirs perform strange acts, although these have been feats of physical endurance rather than supernatural demonstrations.

But I did once know a rishi—a holy man—whose powers far transcended such cheap displays. My recollections of that man are what scare me when I think of death. What I discovered of his capabilities impressed and terrified me to such an extent that I have never before told any person of them, mainly because I believed that I would be thought quite mad. However, sixty years and more after the event, I don't much care what anyone thinks of me.

My subdistrict covered perhaps two or three hundred square miles and contained a number of different villages. My supervisor, Barr-Taylor, was an older district officer who would call upon me once every two or three weeks to receive my reports, discuss problems, advise me where necessary, sometimes accompany me on visits around the territory. Most of the time I was left to my own devices, my sole aide being a fiercely dignified old Baluchi Pathan named Mushtaq Khan.

It was during one of Barr-Taylor's visits that I first heard of the rishi. My senior had decided to stay the night, probably to satisfy himself that I was adept at the social graces, district officers at times having to entertain passing dignitaries.

We were sitting on the verandah before dinner, sipping at our gins-and-tonic, listening to a multitude of night-noises and chatting about things in general.

We had been discussing my program of visits and Barr-Taylor said, "Tell me, Rowan, have you been out to Katachari yet?"

Katachari was one of the nearest villages to my HQ but I had not yet visited the place. I had chosen rather to go to the farthest communities first, believing that those nearby would know of me through the local gossip and could attend me more readily if my help was needed.

I explained this to Barr-Taylor who said, "Take my tip, see the place as soon as possible. The local zamindar's name is Gokul. Give him my compliments when you meet, we're old friends. But it's not really Gokul I want you to meet. There's a rishi in the village, fellow called Aditya."

He offered a cheroot and we lit up, blowing clouds of noxious smoke at the ferocious mosquitoes which were just starting their evening forays.

"Very interesting man, Aditya," my senior continued. "He turned up in Katachari a few years ago, told the locals that it was his destiny to die there. As you'd expect, they were deeply honored, welcomed him, built a small home for him and his wife, they've looked after him ever since. Of course, there is an element of quid pro quo, the rishi being expected to pray for the village, intercede with the deities, comfort the sick and the old, that sort of thing.

"You were born in India, Rowan, so I'm not trying to teach you things you don't know. I'd guess you're thinking there's nothing very unusual about this, it's a common enough occurrence. But Aditya is different. He claims to be over two hundred years old, says that his extraordinary willpower has kept him alive. Now I'm not saying that I believe this, but he's assuredly very well on in years and he speaks of certain events as if he was an eyewitness, describes them very convincingly. There does seem to be an inexplicable power about the man. I've been in the service for thirty-odd years now, and Aditya manages to make me feel like a callow youth."

Barr-Taylor pulled a face and drew deeply on his cigar. "There's something else," he admitted, "I have to confess that although he has given me no reason, there is something about Aditya that frightens me."

He stabbed a skinny forefinger at me for emphasis. "Don't delay, Rowan, go to Katachari as soon as you can. This is your district, and if there are likely to be any problems, then you should be aware of them." Barr-Taylor raised his head and sniffed. "Is that korma I can smell? Let's go and see what Mushtaq Khan's got for dinner, shall we?"

I'm not saying that at that time I accepted all of what Barr-Taylor had told me. Hindu holy men, both rishis and saddhus, are commonplace in India, as are Buddhist monks. Some are itinerant, some tend to stay in one place, but all are reliant on the charity of others, and that charity is usually generous. However, the district officer had whetted my curiosity more than a little.

So at the earliest opportunity, I rode out to visit Katachari. As always, Mushtaq Khan accompanied me, alert that I should not come to harm. When first appointed to my district, I had protested to the old warrior that I would be perfectly safe in my travels, that I was sure the people would respect me.

"That may well be, Rowan-sahib," Mushtaq Khan had growled, "I doubt not that your God and mine will watch over you. And yet it will do no harm for you to be seen in my company. The sight of a Pathan is an excellent way of reinforcing respect among these unbelievers."

I had to admit he was right. When he rode high in the saddle, moustaches bristling, vicious curved dagger at his belt, and long Martini-Henry rifle balanced before him, he was fully capable of reinforcing my own respect. I felt that together we could have seen off the worst band of dacoits.

The way to Katachari led through forest, at times quite dense, in other places thinning out so that the path before us was dappled emerald and bronze and saffron by filtered sunlight. It was cooler here beneath the leafy canopy and the air was heady with fragrances of bright flowers and ripening fruits and the mulch of decaying vegetation. Above us flittered jewel-like birds, their cries tolling to their mates, while monkeys squabbled among themselves and scolded us when we passed.

Our conversation tended to be one-sided. Mushtaq Khan talked and I listened. While ostensibly his superior, I had the sense to know that I could learn much from the old man and I'm sure that everything he said to me was intended to impart some lesson. I wasn't his first sprog and I sometimes marveled at his limitless patience.

We were probably about three-quarters of the way to Katachari when I began to catch glimpses of what looked like a stone building further back among the trees.

"What's that?" I asked Mushtaq Khan, pointing toward the structure.

"An ancient Hindu temple, sahib," the Pathan told me. "It was left to the jungle many years ago, long, long before the coming of the sahibs."

"I'd like to take a look," I said. Mushtaq shrugged and tugged at the reins, guiding his horse to follow mine.

At one time, lord knows how many centuries previously, the temple must have stood within a considerable clearing, but now the forest had inexorably reclaimed its own. The gray, weathered stone was gripped by tangles of twisted, verdant branches and crawling vines, and bright blossoms hung from plants which had set themselves and taken life in the crumbling mortar between the gigantic blocks.

As is common with Hindu temples, the edifice was lavishly decorated with row upon row of sculpted figures depicting scenes from their mythology. Gods and warriors struggled, locked in combat until the stones finally crumbled. Nautch girls and courtesans and temple maidens allured, their time-weary enticements frozen and eroding.

Several rows of statuary at the friezes were brazenly erotic and I think I flushed, torn by the conflicting pressures of a young man's lusts and the restrictions of the society in which I was raised.

The focal point, above what probably had been the main entrance to the temple, was a carving much larger than all of the others. I believed it to be of Prithivi, the Hindu earth-goddess, the goddess of fertility. She smiled gently down upon me, her arms extended in welcome. By chance, nature had adorned the goddess with gorgeous hibiscus flowers, lending almost an illusion of fruitfulness.

I think more than anything I was struck by a great sense of peace in this place. And then, almost lost in myself, I was disturbed by a grumpy snort. I turned, to catch a slight frown on the face of the elderly Pathan. I had momentarily overlooked the Moslem disapproval of what they consider idolatry.

I covered by taking out my watch and glancing at the time. "Yes, very interesting, Mushtaq Khan," I said, "but I really think that we'd better hurry on to Katachari."

I still sometimes wonder if the glint in his eye then had been approval or amusement at the transparency of the young Sahib.

We reached the village about half-an-hour later, the forest thinning and clearing as we passed the huts of harijans—the Untouchables—and then those of the poorer farmers. We turned onto a wider road and our route became more busy. Men stooped under the weight of bundles, drivers of ox-carts, women in butterfly colors bearing laundry to the river, elders sitting in the shade, all called out greetings to us as we rode by them. Children began to tag onto us. The closer into the village we came, the longer became our train of frolicking urchins, happily ignoring Mushtaq Khan's admonitions to respect the sahib's dignity.

We guided our horses toward the village square and I was assailed by the odors of dust and frying spices and cattle dung and all those other wonderful smells of India.

A small group of men awaited, their manner respectful. When we had dismounted, one of them came forward, making namaste. "At last, Rowan-Sahib, I am honored to welcome you to Katachari. I am Gokul, the headman and landlord."

I returned Gokul's greetings and conveyed the good wishes of Barr-Taylor. I was quickly introduced to the others, a mixed group of men who comprised the village council. Within minutes all were seated and drinking hot, sweet tea as we discussed matters important to the village and the region. Three men sat slightly apart: two Brahmins whose caste disallowed close contact with non-Hindus, and Mushtaq Khan, guided more by his warrior alertness than by his distaste for infidels.

Then without warning, my hosts fell silent and slowly the councilmen rose to their feet, bowing their heads as they did so. Behind me, I heard an old and dry voice saying, "Enough of such mundane matters, Gokul, I am sure Rowan-sahib hears them daily and to whom is farming of any interest save another farmer? Anyway, I believe the sahib was advised to make this journey to meet me."

I, too, rose and turned to face the speaker. When I looked at him, I felt a breathless shock as if I had suddenly been plunged into an ice-cold bath. Aditya was small in stature and, in common with most holy men, very thin. He was clad in a white robe, and long white hair and beard cascaded down his body. But it was the deeply shadowed, hypnotic eyes and the sense of sheer power emanating in waves from the man which held and enthralled.

Instinctively, I lowered my head, placing my palms together and making namaste to the holy man. I surprised myself in doing this, for protocol was that I should have been greeted first. Even greater was my surprise when I saw, from the corner of my eye, Mushtaq Khan also bowing and making salaam.

The rishi placed his hands over mine. "Come, my son, we will go to my home and talk." He turned and I followed without further bidding. Again I was astounded at the reaction of Mushtaq Khan who, instead of following at his usual discreet distance, resumed his seat and took up his tea.

The rishi's home was small and simple, as would have been expected. I had to stoop to pass through the low portal into the single room, poorly illuminated by lighted wicks floating in dishes of oil. The air was thick with the sweetness of the many smoldering incense sticks balanced in ornate brass holders which were scattered about the floor. And there was another underlying odor that I could not identify. Perhaps it was the smell of old age.

I could see at a glance that the place was sparsely furnished. Two single charpoys were positioned at opposite sides of the room, each furnished with a light blanket. There was a low table and several stools, while at the rear was a small stove and a number of clay cooking pots. There were niches in the mud walls which held statuettes of deities.

As we entered, a woman came silently to her feet and stood with her eyes cast down. Like Aditya, she was clothed entirely in white, but her garb was not the usual sari. Instead, she wore a burkha, the all-enveloping garb worn by most Moslem women. A veil was drawn across her face. Only her eyes, hands and feet were visible.

"Welcome to my home, Rowan-sahib," said the rishi, "this is Chandira, my wife." Turning to the woman, he added, "Bring chai for our guest, Chandira."

As the woman moved to the stove to make her preparations, the rishi gestured me to a stool before taking up the lotus position on one of the charpoys. He closed his eyes, apparently as a signal that until the niceties were observed we should refrain from conversation.

I took the opportunity to study the man. He was certainly unlike other holy men I had experienced. Not counting the Brahmin priests, there are two kinds of Hindu holy men: the rishis, who may marry if they wish, and the saddhus, the celibates.

If most people have a mental picture of Hindu holy men, it will probably be of the saddhus. They are the itinerants, the ones who travel naked or near naked, their bodies covered in ashes and dust. Many of them mortify the flesh as an offering to their pantheon of gods. But even the rishis will often maltreat themselves to demonstrate spirituality.

Aditya was clean, and to the casual glance seemed quite normal other than for his ascetic spareness. He was old, but more than two hundred? I doubted it.

I was startled from reverie by the woman's sudden appearance at my side as she set down tea and a dish of fruit slices. My senses were overwhelmed by the richly musky perfume with which she seemed to have dowsed herself. While not in itself unpleasant, the scent was cloying. I did not look at her too closely as I thanked her, being sensible of how easily I could give offence. I did notice rather beautiful eyes and elegant hands. Then she moved back to a corner and squatted mute on the earthen floor.

Aditya's eyes snapped open and seemed to penetrate my own. Then it was as if they filmed over and he gestured an invitation to the refreshments.

I sipped at the tea, which relaxed me a little and could not restrain my curiosity. "Your wife, Aditya-Sahib, is she a Moslem?" Such mixed marriages were not common, but neither were they unknown.

"A Moslem?" He glanced over at the woman. "No, she is not a Moslem." He smiled. "You have no wife, Rowan-sahib." It was not a question.

"No, sir." The rishi continued to stare at me and I felt somehow that I had to explain. "It's not our custom for a young man making his way in the world to marry. We believe that his career comes first."

"How very strange." Aditya selected a slice of orange and nibbled on it. "Young men of your race are placed in positions of great importance, of great responsibility, so that you may satisfy the urges of the mind, and yet at this time of your possibly greatest potency, you are expected to ignore the more natural urges of flesh. Tell me, Rowan-sahib, do you not find yourself frustrated by the unanswered cry of your loins? Do you not find yourself longing for the soft, naked body of a loving and compliant woman to comfort you in the long hours of the night?"

I thought again of those erotic carvings on the Prithivi temple in the forest and felt my face grow hot. I was thankful for the poor light in the rishi's home, thankful that my embarrassment was not visible to him. "Excuse me, Rishi-sahib, it is not our way to discuss such matters," I prevaricated, wishing that he would let the matter drop.

The holy man laughed, a crackling, raspy noise which was not too pleasant. "Such a young race, such children," he mused. "Now I have been married very many times, for is it not the natural way of life? Certain of my wives were more precious to me than others. Let me tell you of my favorites, let me tell you of the erotic pleasure that each one had to offer a man."

He raised his cup, slurping noisily at his tea. "Kumud had fair looks, great beauty. Her face was a perfect oval, with flesh like that of a fresh peach bearing traces of morning dew. Her eyes held the promise of heaven and her yoni fulfilled that promise.

"Radhika was the daughter of a Kashmiri Brahmin, with light skin, little darker than that of a sahib. Hers was the body which most delighted my senses. From neck to upper thighs she was perfect, with breasts . . . I think your own holy book is most eloquent when it likens the loved one's breasts to young roes feeding among the lilies. Her body hair was plucked, in the fashion of the ancient nobility, so that but a slim arrow showed the way to paradise and such a paradise, sahib, such a paradise."

Quite frankly, I didn't know where to put myself, hearing this talk which seemed to me to be so appallingly candid. I glanced frantically toward the woman, Chandira. The rishi correctly interpreted my hint, but his only reaction was to repeat that arid laugh. "Do not fret that my wife is shocked, Rowan-sahib. Is she not an Indian woman? Talk of sensual pleasures is not anathema to us.

"Now, where was I? Ah, my favorite wives. The loveliest, longest limbs were those of Shamin and Phoolan. Shamin's arms could draw a man close so it was as if being was melting into being. And Phoolan's legs were strong, like pythons, clasping a man to her as he entered, relaxing not until the course was run for both."

The rishi's eyes held me, and his smile seemed to mock my innocence. Selecting another piece of fruit, he continued, "Harpal was blind, and from an early age she had been trained in the art of massage. Her hands and feet were beautiful, well-cared for, strong and delicate. They could coax from a man's well more than he believed himself to contain, so that his essence was as a perpetual fountain.

"These, then, Rowan-sahib, were the most-favored of my many wives." He thrust his head forward, one eyebrow raised sardonically, as if to ask my opinion of his marital history.

Compelled to say something, if only as a necessity to disguise my discomfiture, I asked, "How can a man have had so many wives in one lifetime?"

Yet again, the laugh, which was beginning to make me shiver. "One lifetime? How old do you think I am, young man?"

I hesitated, and Aditya snapped, "The Barr-Taylor has already told you, and yet neither of you believe."

"How did you know what Barr-Taylor-Sahib told me?" I demanded.

"I have powers beyond the extent of your reasoning. As you sat on your verandah, smoking and drinking, he told you that I am more than two hundred years old. This is true, sahib. Indeed, I am very much more than that. I was blessed with an inexorable will, a gift from the gods which has enabled me to defy death."

Aditya changed tack suddenly, his tone becoming less intense, more gentle. "Rowan-sahib, for me the two most powerful forces are those of sex and death, and thus far I have been in total control of both. Despite my great age, I am proud that Chandira and myself still enjoy frequent and vigorous couplings."

He gestured around the room. "Look about you, young sahib, look at the gods I keep in my dwelling. There is Prithivi, and yonder sits Yama, King of the dead. Here is Kama, controller of our desires, and there and there, Shiva and Kali, the Destroyers.

"But even I cannot defer death forever." The rishi smiled ruefully, "Which is why I have settled in this village, for it is my fate to end my days here."

Aditya stood abruptly. "Come with me, Rowan-sahib. I will give you a demonstration of my power over death." He had exited before I realized it.

At the doorway, I turned to thank the rishi's wife for her hospitality. My words were awkward for I was still shaken by Aditya's frankness in front of the woman.

After the inner gloom, the sunlight dazzled and the rishi took my arm to guide me. As we walked, he murmured, "There will be a service you can perform for me, sahib."

"Of course, if I can What is it?"

"You will know when the time comes," he replied, "Ah, I think this will do."

He had led me to the far edge of the village and I became aware of a disgusting stink nearby.

Stepping a few yards into the fringes of the jungle, Aditya kicked aside some heavy grasses to reveal the rotting corpse of a pi-dog. A great cloud of flies arose and with them the smothering stench of death and corruption. The body had an oddly collapsed look about it and I noticed a long trail of ants coming and going from the anal region. Ribs were laid bare and shreds of ripped innards exposed where some small scavenger had been burrowing. The sockets were empty, the eyes no doubt pecked away by crows.

"I think you will agree that this dog is dead, Rowan-sahib?"

"Disgustingly so," I said, holding my handkerchief to my nose and mouth, trying to refrain from gagging.

"Then please, stand back a few yards and observe what happens."

I moved back as requested and carefully watched the rishi. He became motionless and his eyes rolled back until only the whites showed. It was hideously still, for even the normal forest cacophony had quieted. Then I heard a curious grunting noise and my attention was drawn toward the pi-dog.

The dead creature was lurching to its feet, its movements stiff and feeble, like those of a badly-strung puppet. Having gained a precarious standing position, it turned and began to stagger toward me, remnant of tail wagging halfheartedly. A swollen, blackened tongue, partly gnawed by something, lolled from the side of its mouth, and the blind holes gazed into my face. Deep in the sockets, I could see writhing nests of maggots and . . .

. . . And I think it was then that I yelled like a banshee and ran. I was in a blue funk and I'm not ashamed to admit to it.

I ran back through the village square, where Mushtaq Khan still sat with the leaders, dashed to my horse and galloped away. I was to find later that the poor creature was badly marked where I had spurred it so savagely, something I had never done to a horse before.

The Pathan caught up with me about a mile or so down the road, catching at my reins and pulling my horse to a halt. "What is it, sahib, what ails you?"

"The holy man . . . he . . ." I shook my head. "I cannot tell you, Mushtaq Khan. He . . . showed me something. It's enough of a burden for me. I just want to forget, and I never want to see the rishi again."

"Come, sahib, come with me. Let us go to a place of peace." And probably against all of his instincts, the old Pathan led me to that temple in the jungle where I stayed for a long time, staring at the welcoming goddess and trying to find some mental peace.

Life went on. I wrote Barr-Taylor a brief report of my visit to Katachari, mentioning that Aditya had welcomed me into his home. I omitted all reference to the rishi's conversation and nothing would have compelled me to mention the dead dog.

I immersed myself in work, went up country to visit other places, did anything I could to forget that dreadful experience. For a few weeks I had intermittent nightmares, usually involving dead animals, then they faded away. Gradually, as I overcame my horror, I persuaded myself of something that I should have thought of in the first instance. I became convinced that the rishi had somehow drugged or hypnotized me.

I was in my office one evening, smoking a cigar and sipping at a glass of lime juice as I struggled to balance my monthly accounts. It was stiflingly hot and the lazy flapping of the punkah did little to stir the air. I could not be bothered to urge greater efforts from the young lad paid a few annas to perform this menial task. He was probably as jaded by the heat as I was.

I stood up to stretch and to ease the aching muscles around my neck and shoulders, when I became aware of something out of the corner of my eye. I turned and found myself staring at the rishi, although how he had entered the room so quietly I have no notion. His palms were together in namaste, his eyes were closed, and there was a slight smile on his face. Then as I was about to greet him, somewhat irascibly, he faded from sight and I was faced by nothing more than a cornerful of shadows.

"*Sweet Jesus!*" The sweat on my body turned to ice as I lurched across the room to the drinks cabinet. Then came my next shock. As I fumbled with the top of the whiskey bottle, I heard a scratching noise outside, on the other side from the verandah. Almost without thinking, I snatched my Webley pistol from the drawer where I kept it and threw back the shutters.

Staring in at me was the startled face of Yasim, an elderly harijan employed to tend the grounds around my bungalow. I snatched breath in sheer relief.

"Yasim! What are you doing out there? Why lurk about like a sneak thief? You must know that if you wish to see me you need only knock at the door. What is it you want, man?"

My visitor shook his head urgently and raised a finger to his lips. "I should not be here, Rowan-sahib, for there is great danger for me. I am come to tell you of a rumor that is rife in the district. They say that the rishi, Aditya, is very near to death. It may even be that he is gone now."

I cannot say that I was greatly disturbed by this news. The mention of the holy man's name brought back that scene of horror at the forest's edge, and my instinct was that the sooner he died the better.

Then I remembered the rishi's words. "There will be a service you can perform for me . . . you will know what it is when the time comes." The apparition, vision, hallucination, whatever it was that I had just experienced. Had this been some kind of telepathy? Had this been the rishi's way of calling on my services?

"I must go to Katachari, then," I said, "Aditya-sahib will wish me to attend the funeral rites, to represent the Raj."

There was a frightened look in the gardener's eyes. "Sahib, if ever asked, I will deny having told you this, such is the peril. I have to tell you the same rumors whisper that the holy man's wife intends to become suttee."

Suttee. The word chilled me. I knew of it—who born and raised in India did not? Which well-read person or seasoned traveler did not shudder at the hideous and alien concept? Which district officer in the land did not pray that he would never encounter it?

Suttee. A Sanskrit word. Literally, it means a virtuous woman. In practice, it means the self-immolation of a Hindu widow on her husband's funeral pyre for, it is held, why would a virtuous woman wish to survive her husband? And it need not always be *self*-immolation, for it had been known for reluctant widows to be bound and cast into the flames.

The practice had been outlawed some sixty or seventy years previously, but it was tacitly accepted that it continued in remoter places. Now it was to happen in Katachari and it was my duty to stop it.

Early in the morning I arose before anyone else and sneaked out of the bungalow. I saddled my horse and led the beast a good distance away before I mounted and began to ride.

I reached Katachari as the villagers were stirring. Plumes of smoke from early morning fires formed thin columns in the air and I could smell naan-bread baking and tea brewing. I had heard the sounds of chatter among families and neighbors but these fell silent as I rode into the square. I saw a boy running to Gokul's home and moments later the zamindar was scurrying toward me, a small crowd at his heels.

"Rowan-sahib!" His voice sounded anxious. "What are you doing here? And so early in the day?"

"Katachari is part of my district, is it not?" I demanded haughtily, "Surely I have the right to visit when I wish?"

Gokul lowered his eyes and muttered, "Yes, sahib."

"Anyway, I have heard that the rishi is unwell and I have come to pay my respects."

Gokul sighed. "Then I regret that the Rowan-sahib has made a wasted journey, for the holy man died several hours ago. The funeral is to be held at dawn tomorrow. There will be no need for you to stay now, sahib."

"I am sad to hear this," I lied, "I must then, of course, pay my respects to the rishi's widow."

"That would be most unseemly."

I stared hard at the man. "I don't see why," I told him. "In my country, it is an obligation to condole with a widowed person. I am a representative of the

Queen-Empress, and it is her respects which I bear. Surely there is nothing wrong with that, Gokul-sahib?"

Gokul looked around frantically at his cronies, but it seemed that none wished to give him support.

"Anyway," I added, bending the truth somewhat, "it was the rishi's own wish that I do him the service of seeing that all is well with his widow. He told me this himself when we met. You would not wish to go against Aditya's own will."

The zamindar gave in with bad grace and led me to Aditya's hut. Chandira was waiting at the doorway, as if she was expecting me. She was still wearing the burkha and veil. As I neared, she made namaste and said, "You are welcome, Rowan-sahib, please enter our home."

Gokul made as if to wait at the entrance but I stared hard at him until, with obvious bad grace, he made off. Waiting only to ensure that he had truly gone, I accepted Chandira's invitation.

It seemed that even more incense sticks were being burned within the dwelling, and that Chandira had used rather more of her heady perfume than previously. This was understandable, though, for beneath the richness of the scents I caught a faint whiff of death.

I looked around for Chandira and saw that she had taken up position at the far side of the room by the small stove upon which flickered a small fire.

Aditya's white-clad corpse lay on his charpoy, arms resting by the sides, a garland of variegated flowers about the neck. I stepped over and gazed down. The rishi's flesh had assumed a greyish pallor, while the eyelids and cheeks were already beginning to fall in. I studied the lines and folds on that dead face and suddenly I had an inkling that Aditya's claims for greatly advanced age might well be true.

I turned to Chandira, deciding that this was not the time for the customary florid overtures. I was blunt. "I hear gossip that you wish to become suttee."

The woman inclined her covered head a little. "Not gossip but truth, Rowan-sahib," she told me.

I sighed heavily and sat down on one of the stools. "Why do this thing?"

"It is what I wish for, more than anything in the world."

I made a contemptuous gesture at Aditya's still form. "You mean it's what he wished for."

"No, it is *my* wish, my desire even." Chandira shook her head. "*He* died without even having expressed an opinion about it. If it was a matter of *his* wish, and I was able, I might well defy it, for he has used me ill and I have good reason to detest him."

"You know that suttee is outlawed," I said, "And that it is my duty to prevent your death."

"Perhaps I can persuade the sahib that I should be allowed to do this thing." Chandira lowered her veil, showing to me a face of sublime beauty, a face which could have been that of a temple statue given life. Dark and fascinating eyes were lined with kohl and rich, full lips were painted scarlet. I felt breath tightening in my chest.

She took away the covering from her head and then started to loosen her gown.

I found myself torn between a well of longing and a flame of indignation. Chandira was about to offer me the use of her body now in exchange for her right to die tomorrow.

The lonely young man in me wanted to leap up and clasp her in my arms. The well-trained bureaucrat suppressed the young man.

"Stop this now, Chandira!" I snapped. "My duty is clear and I will not let you seduce me from it!"

She paused, and then she laughed. It was a sad, empty noise which made me feel immensely foolish and pompous.

"Be at ease, Rowan-sahib," she told me, "I have no intention of offering you love, or even the sham of love. But I must show you, so that you understand."

Moments later the burkha fell about her feet and she stood there naked. Something in her tone of voice had chilled me, and now I was able to gaze at her without desire.

Chandira's form was graceful, alluring, but in that dim light it seemed somehow to be disproportionate. There also appeared to be some disparity in the flesh tints, and many parts of her body—her neck, for instance, and at the joints—were encircled by weird, bangle-like tattoos. She walked toward me, until just inches separated us.

She offered her right hand and against my will I took it in one of mine. Her palm was silken soft and surprisingly cool. With her free hand she indicated the marking about her wrist.

"Look closely, sahib."

I did so, then I rose quickly to my feet and gripped the woman by the arms. She stood passive as I examined the other tattoos.

But those were no tattoos. They were broad bands of stitches, hundreds of fine, close, delicate sutures layered over faint, long-healed scars.

I heard again Aditya's voice, a mocking remembrance. "Kumud had fair looks . . . Radhika's was the body which most delighted my senses . . . Shamin's arms . . . Phoolan's legs . . . Harpal's hands and feet . . ."

I dropped my hands from Chandira and stepped back, hoping that my sudden horror was ill-founded. "It's not possible . . ." I muttered.

A tear spilled from the corner of an eye, slipping its sad course down the woman's cheek. "No, it is not possible . . . but it is true. Chandira is the name he gave to this . . . creation . . . He could not bring himself to let his favorites rest in peace and so he used the best attributes of each to give life to . . . Chandira."

I slumped back onto the stool. It was either that or perhaps faint. "But how . . ." I floundered.

"He told both of you, you and Barr-Taylor-sahib, of his will-power, of how he could conquer death. Over the years, he told many sahibs. None believed him. He frightened you with a demonstration, but no doubt you thought that he had mesmerized you.

"After the death of each favorite, his will power held the . . . essentials . . . from corruption. He held them over the years until he had sufficient to join as one and breathe life into her. Such was his power that I live now, even beyond his own death. But that will power is slowly waning."

She held out her hand again, this time placing it delicately beneath my nostrils. At first there was only the musk of her perfume, and then I noticed that beneath the exotic fragrance was another aroma, the slightest hint of decay. The suggestion of death in the hut did not come from Aditya's remains alone.

I got up and walked from Chandira's home without another word. Gokul was waiting by my horse. He asked me something but I don't know what it was. I made some sort of noncommittal comment and rode from the village.

When I reached that half-hidden jungle temple, I reined in and clambered down from the horse. I had some thought that perhaps Prithivi could help solve my dilemma. My old school chaplain would have been shocked. Army chaplains in barracks all over India would be shocked. And Mushtaq Khan, if he knew, would throw a blue fit. But, I reasoned, this was a Hindu matter, and a Hindu goddess was better qualified than God or Jesus or Allah to help.

I stepped through the trees and came to where the goddess sat. Something was different here now. The petals woven about Prathivi had faded and withered, like a dotard's skin, and as I gazed a great insect crawled from one of the stony nostrils, weaving about in parody of a blindly feasting grave-worm.

I was up early again the next day. This time, as I stepped from the bungalow, strapping on my Webley in its large holster, Mushtaq Khan was waiting for me.

"Where are you going this time, sahib?"

"I must go to Katachari on urgent business," I told him. "There will be no need for you to come."

"If you hope to stop the suttee singlehanded, Rowan-sahib, then you are a very foolish young man," the Pathan told me. He folded his arms across his chest and glowered at me. "Allah knows that these Hindus are little better than sheep, but when their beliefs are interfered with they are very dangerous sheep.

"And you, Rowan-sahib, are stubborn, as stubborn as any young warrior from my own hills. If I were your father, I would be concerned. Concerned and . . . proud. I will not be able to sway you from your duty, so do not try to sway me from mine. Come, sahib, our horses are saddled and ready."

Katachari was quiet and deserted when we reached it, the only life to be seen or heard; a few pi-dogs, some poultry searching the dust for tidbits, the odd raucous crow.

Mushtaq Khan pointed beyond the village. "The burning ground is about a mile that way," he said. We rode on.

A little way on we began to hear a low, rhythmic drone. Although not yet fully audible, it was a sound filled with foreboding. The further we rode, the louder the drone became, until at last it was clear. It was the chanting of many voices, a repetitious, hypnotic, "*Ram-ram . . . ram-ram . . . ram-ram . . .*"

At length we came upon the thickly clustered chanting crowd. There were many more than belonged to Katachari: people must have traveled from great distances around to attend the cremation. From our vantage point on horseback, we could see clearly over their heads.

The funeral pyre—a platform of interwoven sticks and branches soaked in ghee—was about head height, roughly the same length, and perhaps four feet wide. The corpse, blanketed with great masses of flowers, rested on the top, and Chandira knelt at its head, hands clasped before her. She had discarded the burkha for a plain white sari. The area was filled with the combined stenches of decomposition and ghee.

We dismounted and approached slowly. Some of the mourners at the back of the crowd had seen us and glared threateningly.

I unstrapped my pistol and handed it to Mushtaq Khan. "Wait for me here," I instructed.

"They'll tear you to pieces, sahib!" he protested.

"Wait for me," I repeated. I clasped the old man's shoulders. "It will be all right."

"Very well, sahib." His hawk's eyes glared and his tone was grudging. He laid one hand upon his dagger and brandished my pistol with the other. "But let one of those unbelievers raise a hand against you and they'll find what it means to have the Pathans fall upon them," he growled. "If we die, we die together giving a good account."

I pushed my way into the crowd which parted before me. I think it was bravado that carried me through, that and their astonishment at my foolhardiness. I reached the pyre where the Brahmin priests were chanting their prayers. Gokul stood to one side clutching a burning faggot of wood. As I reached them, the prayers turned to cries of outrage.

I held out a hand. "Give me the torch, Gokul-sahib," I ordered.

"*Go!*" he hissed. "Go now you foolish young man, we have no wish to harm you."

"*Give me the torch!*" I repeated, filling my voice with as much quiet savageness as I could muster.

The zamindar did so, reluctantly. The crowd fell silent, waiting I believe for the command to rend me.

I turned to look at the woman on the pyre. Her face was older, much older, than before and I detected livid streaks of subcutaneous mortification. Her cheek bones had become prominent, the flesh below them concave, and her eyes, now lacklustre, were already sinking back.

"Namaste, Chandira," I greeted her.

She bowed a little. "Namaste, Rowan-sahib." Her voice was but a dry croak.

"Your husband once told me that I was to perform a service for him. I am here to give that service."

Stepping forward, I thrust the torch deep into the tinder of the funeral pyre and leapt back as the mound of wood and ghee ignited with a roar.

I like to believe that I saw a look of gratitude and peace pass over Chandira's withering face before the purifying flames engulfed her.

FEVER

Harlan Ellison

The following exquisite little piece falls somewhere between prose and poetry. It comes from *Mind Fields*, a gorgeous collection of paintings by the extraordinary Polish surrealist Jacek Yerka, accompanied by thirty-three haunting stories by Harlan Ellison.

Ellison is one of the most acclaimed short fiction writers of our day. He has published more than sixty books, in excess of seventeen hundred stories, essays, columns, film and TV scripts, and is the editor of the landmark *Dangerous Visions* anthologies. He has won the World Fantasy Lifetime Achievement Award, the British Fantasy Award, the Mystery Writers of America Edgar Award (twice), the P.E.N. Award for journalism, and more Hugo and Nebula awards than any other writer. His short fiction has been included in *Best American Short Stories*. He lives in Los Angeles, California.

—T. W.

Icarus did not die in the fall.

What his father, Daedalus, never saw was this:

Icarus fell toward the Aegean Sea; fell through clouds; through billows and canopies and flotillas of clouds; and was lost to the sight of his father. The wings melted and fell away. They were carried on the stratospheric currents, miles away from the drop point at which Icarus had vanished through the cloud foam. When Daedalus banked and swooped and did his air-search, he found the pinions floating in the Sea. But he did not find his son, because Icarus had come down miles away.

In a wagon filled with sheep's wool.

But even from that height, even falling that distance, even though he had blacked out with fear and the air wrenched from his throat . . . the impact was enormous. And Icarus broke both legs. And Icarus slipped an intervertebral disk. And Icarus went into total systemic shock. And Icarus had his memory smashed out of him.

When he awoke in the hospital, he could not tell his name, could not relate the facts of his accident, could not offer a clue as to where he had come from, who he was, what he did for a living. He was *tabula rasa*.

He was taken in by a kindly family; and they raised him as their own son. The family was poor, but honest. Traditionally, they were vineyard hands and Certified Public Accountants during the months of October through April.

After many years, Icarus left home and immigrated to Switzerland, where the need for vintners and notaries and young men who never seemed to age was limitless.

He settled in Berne. Where he works to this day. Frugal, fair-haired, unmarried, and neat, he shares his two-room flat with a small gray dog, and gets nine hours sleep every night. And dreams of the sky.

Every morning he washes the fever sweat from his body.

And sees unfamiliar faces in the clouds.

THE BEST THINGS IN LIFE

Lenora Champagne

Lenora Champagne is both a writer and a performer. She has received fellowships from the National Endowment for the Arts and support from the New York State Council on the Arts for her work as a performance artist and theater director. She was the editor and a contributor to *Out from Under: Texts by Women Performance Artists*. Her stories and performance texts have appeared in *Between C & D, Benzene, Blatant Artifice*, and *Heresies*. Play excerpts have been published in *Best Men's Stage Monologues of 1993, Best Stage Scenes of 1993*, and *Best Women's Stage Monologues of 1994*.

Champagne's "fairy tale for adults" uses the themes of old, familiar stories to comment upon modern society and the storytelling process. This wry tale, which Champagne has performed as a solo in New York and Paris, comes from the Spring/Summer issue of *The Iowa Review*.

—T. W.

(FAIRY TALES FOR ADULTS)

I.

Once upon a time there were two children, a brother and a sister. They were advanced for their ages and agreed to leave childhood behind. So they took off down the garden path and soon entered a wood. They were smart and knew how to catch birds and trap squirrels and mice and other small animals. They ate some and built cages for the others. When the sister gathered mushrooms and wild berries, she'd feed them to the animals to see if they were poisonous. Then she and her brother ate what was good. The brother preferred to stay by the stream, where he perfected the fish-catching mechanism he'd conceived while gazing at the sky.

Life was carefree, but it wasn't ideal. For instance, they didn't have any salt or dairy products, and they missed these things. So they decided to journey further into the forest to see what they might find.

Sure enough, they soon smell something strange. Lo and behold, it's a house made entirely of Gruyère!

While this is not the siblings' favorite cheese, it is welcome and will do.

The brother coughs discreetly, careful to avoid getting phlegm on the Gruyère, to let any inhabitants of the Dairy Hut know that visitors have arrived. Just as he and his sister are about to chow down on the cheesy gatepost, the front door peels open to reveal the svelte inhabitant of the hut.

"Welcome," she greets them, with just a touch of a British accent.

"Good day, ma'am," the children say sheepishly. "Please excuse us for disturbing you. We were just walking through the forest when we caught a whiff of your house and . . ."

A jab of his sister's elbow in his chest stops the boy in mid-phrase.

"You are not disturbing me, children. I am happy you have come. I rarely have visitors anymore."

There was an awkward silence.

"You don't recognize me? Perhaps you're too young to remember. Let me introduce myself. I am the Dairy Queen."

"The Dairy Queen! So that is how you are so fortunate as to have a cheese house!" exclaimed the children.

"I am not so fortunate as I may seem," explained the Dairy Queen, "as I have developed lactose intolerance and cannot eat the products I produce. They provide me with no nourishment and make me ill besides. However, you are welcome to eat your fill."

So the children gobbled up as much as they could, until they had stomach aches and constipation. The Dairy Queen invited them to spend the night and finish their digestion.

That night she told them tales of the good old days gone by. The children were enchanted by her tales and her manner of telling. She was a pretty, elegant, thin queen who wore top-of-the-line designer fashions and ate only the leaf of a green plant that grew by her doorstep. Both siblings fell under her spell. The brother tried to think of ways to please her, although he'd never worked by his father's side so didn't have a heroic male role model to know how to be a man, and the sister tried to become thin herself, although the green plant just wasn't enough for her and every now and then she'd have to sneak a chunk of cheese.

Compared to the Dairy Queen, they were imperfect. They only way they'd ever be able to stand themselves was to leave. One day they decided to go.

"Your Highness, we are, as you know, precocious children, and you have taught us much. With you we have come to know love and envy, not to mention self-loathing, which are complicated feelings at so tender an age. We have come to understand that Gruyère is among the best things in life, regardless of its odor, but now we must be on our way."

A single tear marred the perfect complexion of the Dairy Queen. "I understand. You must seek other experiences. But don't forget me. Please remember the Dairy Hut in the forest, and send other children to keep me company. And sign me up for any high-quality mail-order catalogs you find on your way."

The children left with heavy hearts. They turned back once to catch a final glimpse of the Queen, alone in her thin perfection, surrounded by goodness she could not eat.

II.

Once upon a time there was a hard worker. She cleaned and was careful to fluff all the dust from the cracks. The rough surface made this task difficult. There were other obstacles, too, like the long lists that never got crossed off.

Every year her space felt more cramped, but recently she'd been given a wide expense of floorboards to cover.

She was called Cinderella because the powdery black dust that creeps in everywhere in the city resembles cinders. It is the dirt version of sand in Cairo. It shows up under fingernails, coats windowsills, dusts the soap dish.

Her shoes are covered with the grey powder. The leather is cracked in the crevice that forms when she bends down to Pledge the molding. A big hole in the sole of her right shoe lets rain in to wet her sock.

This morning the bedroom is a mess. As she reaches down to lift the pillow from the space between the bed and the wall where it always slips, two mice run out. One large and one small, slick and quick.

The word on the streets is that these little fellows are friends of Cinderella's, and even help get the job done, but this is just another false rumor put out by the authorities—and Disney. The little guys always mean more work, which is what anyone can tell you who knows the difference between ordinary dirt and a mouse turd. She surveys for damage and sees her flowered housecoat lying on the floor. Expecting the worst, she picks it up. No turds, but the mice gnawed big holes in the cloth.

So now they're after the clothes off her back! Her wardrobe was already limited. Her overcoat, for instance, was getting snarly and thin in the seams, and there's a big hole in the pocket. When she holds it up to the light, she sees the mice have eaten it too!

Cinderella sat on the bed and sobbed. For the moment she was overcome. The combination of dirt and despair threatened to drive her out. Without protection! With holes in her shoes and no overcoat! Not even a decent housecoat!

"Damn those *sourcis*! I mean *souris*!" She'd made this mistake before. She always confused the French word for mice, *souris*, with the slang word for pin money or small change. Once when she'd spent all her savings on a trip to France to learn about the best things in life, she'd thought friends talking about "sourcis" were keeping mice in a change purse. She could use that change now.

She blew her nose and shrieked when she spotted the tall, thin, swan-necked woman in a tutu in the corner.

"Hello. Don't you recognize me? I'm. . . . Nevermind. I'm here to give you a tip."

"I'm not permitted to accept tips."

"It's more of an opportunity. I can help you out of the no options you live with. I started off like you—low, dirty, practically a scullery maid, nearly in the gutter—and now look what a great outfit I'm wearing!"

"It's lovely."

"I can help you get a job. I have a friend who's opening a nightclub based on one in Paris, and if you can work with him, you can kiss this gig good-bye."

Cinderella wasn't very big on nightclubs. Her fantasy date was more along the lines of a light supper at a quiet restaurant. But she was eager to try something less dusty.

"What will I do for clothes? Who'll hire me wearing these rags?" She poked at her shabby overcoat.

"Just leave it to me."

The tutu-clad lady zapped Cinderella a few times with a yo-yo she'd hidden in the tulle as she mumbled over her.

"I'll just go to the neighbor's to borrow some thread for this button. For sewing this button back on. For fastening this item of clothing that's come undone. For this ball gown needed for a special occasion. For this organdy soufflé shirred with waffle piqué. For this magenta taffeta with yellow yolk rim. For this watermark silk shot with jet beads gathered into the wasp-waisted bodice of black moire. Tomorrow is not soon enough for inset sleeves to taper into raglan! Grossgrain binding, the zipper teeth want to tear into the silver lining. The merino wool penetrates the needle's eyes. The seam won't say until brocade drapes the light of day."

Cinderella gasped as the breath was pressed out of her. She found herself bound in one of those skin-tight leather numbers topped by a satin bustier.

"Are you sure these clothes are still in?"

"Trust me. I know what he likes."

By now Cinderella expected a limo, but the ballerina look-alike stepped to the curb and whistled for a mere yellow cab. At the nightclub, Cinderella discovered the job was a dancer and clothes really weren't necessary. The management supplied the g-string.

This wasn't what she'd had in mind. It was hardly her idea of the best things in life. But it would be a change—and much less dusty.

She took her place in a long line with other women trying to break in, trying to break out of the no options they were living with. One by one, they entered the manager's office bright and determined, and soon left in a hull or in tears.

When the bored-looking manager came to the door for the hundredth time and said, "Next," Cinderella bunched her overcoat over her arm so the holes wouldn't show and strode into the office, hoping the cracks in her shoes wouldn't detract from her stylish but uncomfortable outfit.

Once she was alone with him, Cinderella noticed the manager was darkly attractive in a scary kind of way. Despite his weariness, he had charm and an alarming yet exciting intensity about him. Regardless of her policy on not mixing work with pleasure, Cinderella felt the tug of desire.

He smiled and she saw herself reflected in his teeth.

He reached under his desk and pulled out a pair of six inch stiletto heels.

"There is only one position, and it will go to the girl who can wear these shoes."

So that was why everyone was so upset. They already had backaches from their waitressing jobs, and now they were going to have to dance on stilts, too.

As he handed her the first shoe, she noticed how small it was. She prepared to try stuffing her foot in, but it slipped on easily. After all, she wore size four.

The manager's breath came more quickly as he leaned over to look. He pressed a button on the tape player on his desk. A lovely melody wafted out. "I know you. I walked with you once upon a dream." "At last," he said. "Dance for me," he said, stroking her ankle.

Now she wanted to get away. She felt smothered and took a big gulp of air.

"Excuse me," she said. "I forgot a big dustball under the bed." She ran off, leaving the stiletto behind in his hand.

And the manager held that shoe and cried. He sent his henchmen out to search for her, but she evaded them and found a safer job. She was never again visited by the tall woman in a tutu, although she sometimes spied her on street corners, hailing the last available yellow cab.

III.

If Snow White and Eve both eat an apple and fall—down, from grace—are they the same woman? If Paradise is over, what does she wake up into?

She and the Prince start wandering, his castle has been repossessed.

At the laundromat, she thinks back on life with the dwarves. Things were simple then. Now the work has to be shared by two instead of seven.

Life with the Prince is far from easy. Sometimes she thinks it would have been better to stay asleep. She had ambitious dreams then. When she woke up, she had gray hair.

The Stepmother was pleased to see that Snow White was no longer the fairest of them all. She'd had plastic surgery while her rival was sleeping off the effects of too much knowledge, and now her taut, angular features graced the cover of all the glossy magazines. Just bones and eyes.

Snow White winced every time she went to the drugstore for tampons, or the newsstand for cigarettes, so for a while she sent the Prince on these errands for her.

She was grateful the Prince had decided to kiss her. Not every man would be so willing to rescue a woman who'd lived with seven men, even if they were dwarves, even if her name was Snow White.

Snow White skimped and saved. When she and the Prince had children, she dressed them all in red. The eldest Princess showed great promise and took dancing lessons from a young age. When the Prince left, he gave her a microscope, and the next year he sent a telescope. Her father wanted her to understand vastness. They'd talk long distance about how difficult it is to understand the ends of things, while Snow White struggled to feed the family.

The eldest Princess showed great progress. No longer did she learn five new five-letter words from her father each night. Now she was studying French.

IV.

Bon. Allons-y.

Il était une fois deux soeurs. L'une était riche, sans enfants. L'autre était pauvre, veuve en plus, avec cinq enfants. Elle n'avait pas assex à manger. Une fois, elle est allée chez sa soeur pour demander un morceau de pain.

"Soeur, mes enfants sont en train de mourrir de faim. Est-çe que je peux avoir un morceau de pain?"

"Non!"

Elle l'a chassé de la porte.

Mais, quand le mari est revenu chez lui, il a eu envie d'un morceau de pain. Mais, quand il a commencé de couper le bout, du sang rouge a coulé.

Did you get that? Okay, I'll explain.

Once upon a time, there were two sisters.

One was rich, with no children.

"Hello. Don't you recognize me? I'm the Dairy. . . ."

The other one was poor—said she was a widow but there was no evidence of a marriage license—with five kids, on public assistance, food stamps running out. Her kids are still hungry, so she goes to her rich sister to ask for a handout.

"Sister, could you spare some leftover bread?"

"No!"

And she shut the door on her poor sister. When the rich sister's husband came home, he was hungry for bread.

"More mergers! More acquisitions! What do we have tonight dear? A little rye, a little pumpernickel, some sourdough with Gruyère?"

But when he cut the bread, blood splattered everywhere.

He was so surprised, he knocked over a candelabra and the house caught on fire. It spread to the neighbor's house and down the block and raged through the entire development. Then the city was in flames, burning down!

And the only survivor was the rich sister. She wandered about amid the ashes, weeping tears of remorse. Wherever a tear fell, a tree sprang up. Soon she was surrounded by a forest. Then her tears turned to cheese, and she fashioned a Diary Hut for shelter.

And the cheese stands alone
the cheese stands alone
Hi ho the derry-o
the cheese stands alone.

V.

Cinderella washes the floors and the windows. She saves the leftovers and makes soup. She enjoys this soup and considers it among the best things in life because it is delicious and cost free. She makes things now, and words, and puts them on display or gives them away.

Everything turns to work in her hands. It's what she knows how to do. Sometimes she meditates on chance. Or on how things happen in time. She often goes back to what she knew first—cleaning. When she cleans, her blood moves, and the blood in turn moves her mind.

Her mind wanders into corners. She follows with her broom and pail. She is grateful for the hard wood and long, smooth planks. She thinks—about sisal matting. Last Spring, in a store filled with elegant imports and tight men in manager suits, she'd seen a mouse eating the sisal matting that was part of the luxurious display of unnecessary things.

"Look, a mouse."

The tight men were unamused, at a loss; they put the security guard in charge.

"What is he doing?" she asked her companion, afraid to look.

"He's beating it with his night stick," was the reply.

She didn't stick around to find out what became of the small rodent with the temerity to wander out among the stuffed bunnies laid out for Easter. (It crosses her mind that on Easter Day the remaining rabbits might rise from their stuffed state and join the mouse in devouring what remained of the matting—if the mouse had the sense to withdraw before the law.)

The law is also elsewhere, busy banning things, like body parts in art and queens in Colorado and fairy tales because of violence. As far as the evil stepmother ordering Snow White's heart torn out, why that had happened to her more than once already, and it wasn't so bad in the long run, you got over it, although it was very painful at the time.

She has to stand up to the law. She and Snow White are sisters under the skin. She likes cleaning, Snow White kept house for the dwarves. They'd both lived like outlaws with various men, and each had an appetite for freedom and apples. If they stopped Snow White's story, might not hers be next?

Her story? Her story about the mouse? Her difficulty with responsibility. She said,

"Look, a mouse"

to remind the men that they were mortal. But she hadn't thought of what the consequences might be for the mouse. She hadn't thought that the men, annoyed by this sign that their mighty fortress of objects could be invaded by the lowest of creatures, might want to snuff out the furry fellow. She'd rather not take responsibility for that.

This is why action and speech are so difficult. All those unforeseen consequences fall down around you. But act now, speak now, she must. Time is changing and she hurries to fill it as it rushes by.

Speech is the body part of thinking, the voice of the mind. Writing is the blood and mind mixing to speak through the fingers, through the hands.

She gives her mind a rest. She cleans more slowly, and looks for apples to assuage her hunger.

MENDING SOULS

Judith Tarr

Judith Tarr, who holds a doctorate in Medieval Studies from Yale, is a prize-winning writer with over ten novels in print, including *The Hound and Falcon Trilogy*, *A Wind in Cairo*, *Arrows of the Sun*, and *His Majesty's Elephant*. She also teaches writing and has been a lecturer at Yale and Wesleyan universities. Tarr currently lives in Tucson, Arizona.

In "Mending Souls," Tarr spins a beautifully crafted, utterly magical Irish yarn, set in the green hills of Kilkenny. The story is reprinted from *Deals with the Devil*, edited by Mike Resnick, Martin H. Greenberg, and Loren D. Estleman.

—T. W.

Tim Ryan was a cobbler in the old country. That was in Ireland, in Kilkenny, where the cats are, and also where, they say, lived a famous witch.

This isn't about the witch, though Widow Kyteler makes a fine tale for a winter evening. No, this is about plain Tim Ryan the cobbler—not even a shoemaker, he didn't aspire to that dignity. He mended soles and put on new heels and took the occasional stitch in time; and being an honest man, if he couldn't mend it he wouldn't, nor charge for it. Which was most of why he was poor, and why his sons and two of his daughters had to go across the water when the Famine came, but this isn't about them, either.

Tim Ryan the cobbler was poor in goods but rich as a good Irish Catholic is, with eight babies in the cottage and a ninth on the way. His wife Mary, being Irish, wasn't what you'd call a long-suffering woman, but being Catholic she knew what her duty was, and if she muttered about Tim sparing the rod on Saturday nights, she was no more eager than he was to stop tempting God to make them another baby when the last one was ready to wean. So they had the six boys and the two girls, and Mary prayed for another girl to give her mother some peace of a morning, which the good Lord knew a pack of boys would never do.

Tim, being duty-bound to earn the children's bread, got his peace in his little cubby of a shop, over behind the cathedral that the bloody English took from the Irish. He didn't think much on that, except to admire the colored glass in the windows, what he could see from the outside, and to tell time by the bell in the round tower. He was as good a Catholic as any man in Ireland, went to church of a Christmas and an Easter and saw Mary off to mass every morning that she could, and made sure the young Ryans went to Father McGowan and the nuns to be brought up in the right and proper faith.

All things considered, Tim Ryan was a contented man. He was poor but not, on this fine day in October, so poor that his children had to go hungry, and he had enough work in front of him to keep them in bread and to pay the landlord his rent, which was all a simple man could ask. He hummed to himself as he set a new heel on a lady's dancing shoe, a brisk tune that made the hammer dance and the nails fall in without a slip or a tumble.

When the bell rang over the door, he looked up with a smile, still humming his tune and setting the heel. As bright as the sun was even so late in the day, and as dim as the shop could be even with the gaslight turned up high, he wasn't perturbed to see a vast cloaked shadow filling the door. It was a gentleman, he knew from the sound of the sole on the step, a sharp clean sound that no working man's brogue had ever made, and from the shape of the shadow against the light, cape and top hat and all.

The gentleman hesitated, as they often did, blind in the dark of the shop. Tim finished putting on the heel, turned the shoe in his deft fingers, just for the pleasure of handling fine silk and dainty workmanship, and set it carefully in the row of mended shoes. "And there," he said affably to the shadow of the gentleman, "goes Lady Ellen to her ball again on Viscount Roderick's arm. They'll wed within the year, or I don't know a lady's mind."

"And how would you know that?" asked the gentleman. His voice was deep and rather hoarse, but cultured enough. He had come inside the shop and no longer loomed so huge, though he was both tall and broad. His face was shadowed under the brim of his hat, which he could have had the courtesy to take off under a roof, but Tim was not the man to chide him for it.

"Ah, now," said Tim, as affable as ever, because he would keep a cheerful face no matter how it rained, "I think I know what a pretty lady's thinking when she hangs on a young man's arm and smiles. And he has land in County Meath and she has land in County Kerry, but they both have lands in County Clare, which would be a fine thing joined together."

"You know a great deal," said the gentleman, coming closer, which was not so difficult in a shop as small as Tim's. Now Tim could see his face, and a hard strong face it was, and white as spume off Aran, which is whiter even than bone. "Do you know how to mend a sole?"

"And it's a cobbler I am," said Tim, "and you're needing to ask me that?"

"No," said the gentleman like the sound of dolmens shifting. "Do you know how to mend a sole?"

Now Tim was a simple man, but he had never been a stupid one, and he knew what it meant when a man with a face whiter than bone looked down at him with eyes that gleamed just faintly in the dimness, as an animal's will. Not being stupid, he shivered, but being a man without over-much on his conscience, he was no more afraid than he should be. So he turned the gentleman's question around in his head, and heard it as the gentleman meant. "Do you know how to mend a soul?"

"That would be Father McGowan, I'm thinking," said Tim, "or the English in the cathedral, if it's the Protestants you're wanting."

"No," said the gentleman, who seemed to be a man of few words, but those repeated at regular intervals, "there's no priest can help the likes of me. I've need of a man who can mend my soul, not preach it into a stupor."

Tim knew better than to smile at that, which was disrespectful in the extreme, although he was inclined to agree with the gentleman. "Sure and the priests will preach, but they have the care of souls. I'm but a mender of shoes."

"Shoes and soles, men and souls," the gentleman said. "What's in the sound of a name that makes it strong enough to conjure with? I've need of a cobbler here, and you're the best I've found."

Tim crossed himself. The gentleman didn't go up in a cloud of smoke, which was just a little disappointing.

"Well done," the gentleman said, and there was no telling if he intended any irony, because the dark was coming fast in the way it has in Ireland at the end of October. "Will you come tonight where our guide brings you?"

The words were a simple question, but Tim heard command not far beneath. It came to his mind that this was no night to be walking abroad: All Hallows' Eve as it surely was, when the dead walked, and the hills opened and strange things came forth to spy on the living.

Still and all, he thought, he was as good a Christian as a man could be, and the gentleman had not flinched even a little when Tim made the sign of the cross. And Tim, it must be said, had always been a little wild. Before Mary led him willing to the altar, he had slept all night on a haunted hill and come back neither a poet nor mad, which would have made a bitter man of one less equable than Tim.

Maybe that night had marked him after all. At the time it had been a disappointment: nothing but stars and moon to keep him company, and a shadow in the grass that turned out to be a fox. Finally he slept, and woke in the gray morning, unharmed and unchanged, and no more to show for it than a crick in his neck.

"Sure it's a strange thing you ask," he said when he had thought the gentleman's question through, or as much as he meant to. "Will you give your word that no harm will touch me?"

"None that you don't wish for yourself," the gentleman said. "My word on it." And he crossed himself as devoutly as any priest.

Tim eyed the gentleman narrowly. There was a twist in the tail of that, he was sure. But he was eager as a man will be who has been respectable for too long to be comfortable, and he was intensely curious. "So then," he said. "And will I be paid for this?"

"Certainly," said the gentleman. "And well, if gold is your pleasure; or if you have another desire . . .?"

"No," Tim said hastily. "Oh, no. Gold would be splendid indeed."

"Then gold it shall be, enough to fill your hands and pour right over, if you succeed. And if you fail . . ." Tim held his breath. "If you fail, a guinea for your trouble, and a half crown now to seal the bargain."

Tim looked down at the coin that had appeared, it seemed, from air, to settle gently on the bench. He didn't pick it up, or insult the gentleman by testing it for soundness. His heart beat hard at the promise of gold, but he wasn't a greedy man, no more than a father of nine had need to be. It wasn't the gold that lured him but the promise of something out of the ordinary.

"You'll send a guide," he said, "and I'll be waiting. It's midnight it will be, I suppose, and I should have my tools in my pocket?"

"Earlier than midnight," the gentleman said. "You have to come where you're needed, after all."

He held out his hand. Tim had half expected bare bones, but it was a man's right enough, and warm, not corpse-cold, though it was as white as the gentleman's face. He had passed a test of sorts, he thought as he clasped that strong white hand.

"Tonight," the gentleman said, bowing slightly; then he turned and left the shop.

Tim didn't tell Mary that he'd made a bargain with a dark man to go out on All Hallows' Eve. Mary would have put her foot down, he knew very well. He kept his tongue behind his teeth, and she didn't notice anything. The baby was fretful, and Mary was tired with the new one growing in her. They all went to bed as soon as their supper was over.

Tim lay wide awake but pretending to sleep. When the last restive child had gone blessedly quiet, he lay for a long count of heartbeats. No one woke, not even the baby.

He got up carefully and dressed in the light of the banked fire. The gentleman's half crown was in his pocket still, cold to the touch and hard, like a promise made solid. He put on his coat and his cap and took his brogues in his hand, and tiptoed for the door.

There he paused. They were all sound asleep: Mary in the bed with little Pegeen in her arms, Eileen curled like a kitten against them; the boys on their pallets, Young Tim and James and John, Paddy and Michael and Frank, not a sound out of them but the soft sea-swell of their breathing. Softly then, with a last glance back, Tim slipped the latch.

The night was cold, edged with frost. Nothing stirred in it but a lone small shadow that came to wind meowing round Tim's legs. From the sound and heft of it, Tim knew Mary's ginger cat. He bent to stroke the beast, and it arched and purred against his hand. Tim found himself leaning forward, then stepping out, to keep from trampling the cat.

One step led to another. The cat wove and purred, then trotted ahead, then trotted back. His white bib was distinct in the starlight, the rest of him gone grey as all cats are at night.

"So then," said Tim. "Is it my guide you are and all?"

"Yow," said the cat, and purred.

And why not? thought Tim. What better guide on such a night than a cat? And king of cats at that, as Mary always said: he was that big and that strong, and that proud of all his battles. There were more ginger cats in Kilkenny these days than there used to be, and most of them with Tam's big coin-yellow eyes.

And so Tim had his guide, right down through Kilkenny town, then out where the houses were few and far apart, and the road wound up and down through hills dark in the starlight. No creature passed them, no man met them. All the wise and the foolish were safe abed, while the dead were not yet up and walking.

* * *

The cat led Tim down one road and up another, and then left into a lane, and at the end of the lane was a house. Dark as it was and looming against the stars, maybe it was no house at all but a hollow hill, and the door opening in it, casting light far into the night.

It was house enough inside, wide and high and old, such as the gentry lived in. And gentry in it, too, with a starched-stiff manservant to meet Tim at the door. Tim pulled off his hat and wished that he'd known where to find the servants' entıance, which this surely was not, but the manservant looked no more disapproving than menservants ever do. He greeted the cat with an inclination of the head, and Tim with one slightly less pronounced, and said, "This way, if you please."

Tim wouldn't have been surprised if the cat had left him to his fate, but the cat stayed, walking just ahead of him, its long tail up at its jauntiest angle. Tim took heart from that, and put on a bit of a jaunty air himself, walking lightly after the servant.

The house seemed ordinary enough, as far as Tim could tell; he hadn't spent overmuch time in the houses of gentry, and then mostly belowstairs. He was led down a passage and round a corner and into a room like a parlor, full of people dressed as gentry dressed. Tim in his well-worn laborer's clothes knew the moment of panic that every man knows when he should have worn his Sunday best, but he had no time to turn and run. The servant had announced the guests: "Tim Ryan the cobbler, and Red Tam of Kilkenny."

Tam the cat walked into the circle of eyes, strolled up to the fire that was burning bright and hot on the hearth, and stretched himself in front of it as if he were a king and the hearth his throne. Tim, who lacked the cat's aplomb, wavered in the doorway till one of the gentlemen separated himself from the rest and came to greet him.

They were all alarmingly alike, men and women both, with their white harsh faces and their narrow height and their bright, bright eyes. But Tim knew the one who had come to his shop; that one was taller than the rest, and broader, and he wore a leaf-green stone in his cravat. The other men had white stones or none, and the women's ornaments were all jet or ivory, set with stones like the moon. All the women were in white and all the men were in black, stark in the warmth of that room, with its fire and its rich hangings and its carpets like jewels poured out on the floor.

"Here," said Tim's gentleman when he had said the words of welcome, "by the fire. Will this do?"

This was a cobbler's bench, and as fine a one as Tim had seen, all shiny and new, with every tool a cobbler could dream of. His own honest tools looked worn and shabby beside them.

Still, thought Tim, they were his, and his hands knew the heft of them. He sat on the splendid new bench, found it not too ill for new, and he said so before he thought. He flushed and would have stammered an apology, but the gentleman forestalled him. "Indeed it's new and lacks a craftsman's character, but you can bring that to it."

So Tim could, he supposed. He arranged his own tools among the strange ones and could think of nothing better to do than wait. The ladies and gentlemen had drawn into a circle about him and his bench and the fire with the cat in front of it, and their eyes made him shiver and look down at the worn and friendly handle of his favorite awl.

Someone was standing over him. He looked up. There was a lady, and she had something in her hand. "My soul," she said. "Can you mend it, good cobbler?"

Her face was white and sharp, but it had its own beauty. Her voice was sweet. In her hand was what looked for all the world like a lady's dancing slipper. It was a little thing, and to be sure the toe that peeped beneath her hem was not so large either; and its sole was worn as thin as a baby's cry.

Tim took it, because if he did not, she would have dropped it on the floor. It felt like a shoe, and one beautifully made, the way they made them for great ladies. He wondered if he was being made sport of, brought in to this rich house to mend shoes for some lording's game.

But there was Red Tam by the fire purring, and the circle staring, and something in the thing that he held that was not—quite—all that it seemed to be.

He took a breath and let it go. There was leather on the bench, or what looked and felt and smelled like leather, and very fine, too; there were nails as good as any he had seen, and thread on spools for any stitching that he might need; and he had his own hammer and his awl and the rest of his tools in their places. He knew nothing of souls, but soles he knew, and this one he could mend.

One by one they came to him. Some brought dancing shoes, some boots such as the gentry rode to hunt in, and one even had a brogue no finer than Tim's own. That was a young gentleman as elegant as the rest, but he was the only one who seemed to know what a smile was. While Tim mended his shoe he knelt to rub Tam's chin. The cat's purr swelled to thunder.

Abruptly it stopped. The young gentleman raised his head. By then, the others had drawn back to leave Tim in peace; those whose shoes were mended were talking softly, or had been till the cat stopped purring.

A new figure stood in the door. Tim heard the servant behind him, crying, "My lord! I could not keep him out."

"Surely," said the gentleman with the leaf-green stone, "and what man could?"

Tim's hammer paused. The cat hissed. So did the young gentleman: "Keep on. Don't stop."

Tim's hand moved of itself, set in another nail, hammered it home. His eyes were on the door.

This was a gentleman like the others, but where they were white, he was ruddily dark, and where they were tall and elegant, he was thickset and burly. But his eyes were as bright as theirs, with the same strange gleam, and its edge, Tim thought, was anger.

When he spoke, his voice was surprisingly soft, smooth like a priest's or a lawyer's, no roughness in it at all. "Ah, then, I feared I'd find you done and gone. Such a pity as that would have been, to come too late on this of all nights in the year."

No one moved, and no one spoke but the stranger. "Well, my friends. Will you not invite me in?"

"No," said someone in the circle.

But the leader of the circle sighed. "I fear we must," he said. "He has as much right to be here as any of us, and more maybe than some."

No one gainsaid that, though faces went harder even than nature had made them.

"Come in," said the gentleman with the leaf-green stone, "and be welcome."

"So shall I be," said the stranger, stepping into the room and the circle. Both seemed to shrink with his coming, to dwindle to tawdriness: colors faded in the carpets, threads worn bare, the white of the ladies' gowns gone faintly yellow and the black of the gentleman's coats turned to rust. But the stranger seemed as vigorous as ever.

"And what have we here?" he asked, as if he had just now seen what Tim was doing. "A cobbler at the gathering? What new game is this?"

Tim kept on with his mending, though his hands were so cold and shaking that they could barely hold the hammer or the nail. He didn't know who this man was, no, not at all. He didn't want to know. He was mending shoes, no more, and if it was a game, then well for the players.

And now the stranger was standing over him, and his presence was hotter than the fire, yet cold, as cold as the breath of the dead. And indeed as Tim sat there, the clock on the mantel chimed the hour: twelve sweet awful notes, like keys in the lock of the Otherworld.

The stranger spoke in the silence that followed the chimes. "What are you doing?" he asked in the most ordinary and harmless of voices.

Tim had no choice but to answer. "Mending soles," he said. He held up the brogue that needed only its last few nails, good strong ones for a good strong shoe.

The stranger's face darkened with anger. "You are *what?*"

"He is a cobbler," said the gentleman with the leaf-green stone. "He entertains us with his craft."

"So?" The stranger stretched out a hand. Tim recoiled, taking the shoe with him. The stranger laughed. "Why, how dull! What happened to the dance you used to dance?"

"We'll dance when all our souls are mended," said the gentleman.

"And what need had you of that? Your souls are quite as sturdy as any. Sturdier, some might say, with the kind of dancing you do."

"Still," said the gentleman, "it wears them down in time. Not even the strongest can walk the roads we walk, or dance the dance at the end of it, without some price to be paid."

"Surely," the stranger said, "and that price I came to take. And here I find you in thrall to a common laborer, a mortal man as ever there was, and the stink of popery on him. Have we all sunk so low as that?"

"We do as needs we must," said the gentleman. "Without us to dance down the year, who knows what would come out of the hills?"

"Why," murmured the young gentleman, still on the floor with the silent, bristling cat, "what but you, old breaker of the dance?"

The stranger went as red as the fire that was sunk now to coals. "So, young breaker of faith, you forget what promises you made? You were born for the dance, but you were born as mortal men are, and like all mortal men, in your time you must die."

"But not now," the young gentleman said, rising in a fine flare of courage.

"We found a way to make ourselves stronger, to give ourselves more years for the dance. We never promised not to do that."

"Only, in your time, to give yourselves to the ones below the hills," said the stranger. "That time was set before the earth was made. You cannot defer it by such shabby expedients as this." He flung out his hand. Tim felt the buffet, though it came nowhere near him. It made him miss his stroke with the hammer and nigh crush his own thumb.

One more nail. One more, and the shoe—the soul—was mended. It was the last. And Tom could not move, could not reach for the nail, could not drive it home.

"We were not all to be taken this night," said the gentleman with the leaf-green stone. "Only the eldest of us, and the youngest were to be granted new partners in the dance. I bid you take us, then, fine new souls or no, and let our children be."

"But you see," the stranger said as if it were the most reasonable thing in the world, "you broke your faith; I'm no longer bound to keep mine. I'll have you all, even the least of you, and swiftly, too."

"We must dance the dance," the gentleman said. "We must shut the doors of the hills. You cannot deny us that."

"Oh," said the stranger with a flash of teeth that had nothing human in them at all, "but I can."

Tim was blind with terror, but somehow he found the nail at last, and firmed his grip on his hammer, and set nail to sole. He didn't know why he did it, or what use it would be. He had to finish it, that was all, as he always finished what he had begun.

Something warm pressed against his leg. Tam the cat looked at him with eyes like golden guineas. Tim cared not a whit for the gold that he was promised—and not likely he would get it, from all that he'd heard. But the cat's eyes had courage in them, enough to go on with at least. Tim drove the nail home.

And nothing happened. The stranger and the gentleman faced one another in simmering silence. The young gentleman looked ready to leap into the fray, if one ever began. The rest of the gentlemen and ladies seemed frozen in shock or bewitchment.

"Young sir," Tim said. His voice wavered, but it was loud enough for that. "Your soul is mended."

The young gentleman spun. The older one jumped like a deer. The stranger's face was as red as blood.

"Dance," said Tim, and where the words were coming from, he never knew. "Dance for your souls' sake."

One of the ladies began it: the one who had come first to have her soul mended, who seemed to be as brave in her own way as the young gentleman who leaped to take her hand. Then another lady stepped out, and another gentleman with her; and the next, and the next. Musicians there were none, but there was music, wailing of pipes and beating of drums that might have been Tim's own heart hammering under his breastbone.

And they danced. It was not the stately swirl of the cotillion, nor quite the lively measure that Tim knew best, but something betwixt and between. And in the middle stood the stranger, as if with his stillness he could drag all the rest to a halt.

Maybe he slowed them a fraction at first, but once they began they took strength from their speed. Tim at his bench was dizzy, watching. He dared not get up or run. The night was outside, and the dark, and the armies of the dead. Not a few of whom, he suspected, served the stranger here. They would not spare the man who had made a mock of their master.

The cat sprang into his lap. Its purring calmed him somewhat. He stroked it as much to give his hands something to do as for any other reason, and watched the dance, and maybe he prayed a little, too, as time went on and on. None of the dancers approached him, though once or twice a lady's skirt brushed past him, sweet with the scent of flowers.

They danced the night into dawn, each step a nail in the door of the Otherworld, each turn a turn of the key. And the stranger stood in their center, stiff as a pillar and as still.

Far away and faint, a cock crowed. The dance swirled to a halt. The last of the fire was gone. The light was gray, and there were no walls but air, no carpet but grass and the mold of years.

Tim blinked and gaped. He sat on a green lawn, and beyond him was a circle of trees, birch and beech, white and silver-gray, and in their center a standing stone. He clutched at the bench on which he sat. It was stone, and his tools were scattered on it, and the cat sitting in the midst of them, blinking at him with coin-gold eyes.

"And that's all the gold I'll be getting," he said wryly. He was not about to call it all a dream. Oh, no, not Tim Ryan, who knew what was real when he saw it.

The cat yawned, curling a long pink tongue, and stretched. His claws caught in a shape of leather. Tim snatched it before it fell to the grass. It was part of the stock of leather that he had worked with in the night, and there were the nails, and in a bag near by them, such tools as cobblers dream of.

He laughed, there in the gray cold morning. "Not gold," he said, "after all, but means to make my own." He turned and swept a bow to the trees. Maybe they bowed back. Maybe it was only the wind coming up with the sun. "And a fair morning to you, and may God hold you in His hand."

They wouldn't take that amiss, he didn't think. He was whistling as he began the long walk home, even knowing what Mary would say when he came in as late and rakish as the cat. He would tell her everything, he knew that very well, and she might even believe him.

And maybe she did, and maybe she didn't, but in the end she let him be. He never did come into the gold that he'd hoped for. He did well enough while he could, and when the Famine came, the children left, all but Maeve, the last. She married a shoemaker in Dublin and had her own tribe of children, and one or two of them inherited their father's skill. And now and then, it's said in the family, one of them will go away for a night and come back whistling in the morning, with new tools in his bag—or her, the last generation or two—and a look of someone who carries a secret. But the rest know where he's been. He's been mending souls again, as his father did before him.

THE OCEAN AND ALL ITS DEVICES

William Browning Spencer

William Browning Spencer lives in Austin, Texas, and is the author of the novels *Maybe I'll Call Anna* and *Résumé with Monsters* and the collection *The Return of Count Electric and Other Stories*. A new novel entitled *Zod Wallop* will be published soon.

Spencer's short stories are strange and eclectic. "The Ocean and All Its Devices" is more overtly horrific than most of Spencer's work—and although it is very much in the tradition of a certain great American master, it is ultimately sui generis. The story is reprinted from *Borderlands 4*, edited by Thomas F. Monteleone.

—E. D

Left to its own enormous devices the sea
in timeless reverie conceives of life,
being itself the world in pantomime.
—Lloyd Frankenberg, *The Sea*

The hotel's owner and manager, George Hume, sat on the edge of his bed and smoked a cigarette. "The Franklins arrived today," he said.

"Regular as clockwork," his wife said.

George nodded. "Eight years now. And why? Why ever do they come?"

George Hume's wife, an ample woman with soft, motherly features, sighed. "They seem to get no pleasure from it, that's for certain. Might as well be a funeral they come for."

The Franklins always arrived in late fall, when the beaches were cold and empty and the ocean, under dark skies, reclaimed its terrible majesty. The hotel was almost deserted at this time of year, and George had suggested closing early for the winter. Mrs. Hume had said. "The Franklins will be coming, dear."

So what? George might have said. Let them find other accommodations this year. But he didn't say that. They were sort of tradition, the Franklins, and in a world so fraught with change, one just naturally protected the rare, enduring pattern.

They were a reserved family who came to this quiet hotel in North Carolina like refugees seeking safe harbor. George couldn't close early and send the Franklins off to some inferior establishment. Lord, they might wind up at The Cove with its garish lagoon pool and gaudy tropical lounge. That wouldn't suit them at all.

The Franklins (husband, younger wife, and pale, delicate-featured daughter) would dress rather formally and sit in the small opened section of the dining room—the rest of the room shrouded in dust covers while Jack, the hotels's aging waiter and handyman, would stand off to one side with a bleak, stoic expression.

Over the years, George had come to know many of his regular guests well. But the Franklins had always remained aloof and enigmatic. Mr. Greg Franklin was a man in his mid or late forties, a handsome man, tall—over six feet—with precise, slow gestures and an oddly uninflected voice, as though he were reading from some internal script that failed to interest him. His much younger wife was stunning, her hair massed in brown ringlets, her eyes large and luminous and containing something like fear in their depths. She spoke rarely, and then in a whisper, preferring to let her husband talk.

Their child, Melissa, was a dark-haired girl—twelve or thirteen now, George guessed—a girl as pale as the moon's reflection in a rain barrel. Always dressed impeccably, she was as quiet as her mother, and George had the distinct impression, although he could not remember being told this by anyone, that she was sickly, that some traumatic infant's illness had almost killed her and so accounted for her methodical, wounded economy of motion.

George ushered the Franklins from his mind. It was late. He extinguished his cigarette and walked over to the window. Rain blew against the glass, and lightning would occasionally illuminate the white-capped waves.

"Is Nancy still coming?" Nancy, their daughter and only child, was a senior at Duke University. She had called the week before saying she might come and hang out for a week or two.

"As far as I know," Mrs. Hume said. "You know how she is. Everything on a whim. That's your side of the family, George."

George turned away from the window and grinned. "Well, I can't accuse your family of ever acting impulsively—although it would do them a world of good. Your family packs a suitcase to go to the grocery store."

"And your side steals a car and goes to California without a toothbrush or a prayer."

This was an old, well-worked routine, of course, and they indulged it as they readied for bed. Then George turned off the light and the darkness brought silence.

It was still raining in the morning when George Hume woke. The violence of last night's thunderstorm had been replaced by a slow, business-like drizzle. Looking out the window, George saw the Franklins walking on the beach under black umbrellas. They were a cheerless sight. All three of them wore dark raincoats, and they might have been fugitives from some old Bergman film, inevitably tragic, moving slowly across a stark landscape.

When most families went to the beach, it was a more lively affair.

George turned away from the window and went into the bathroom to shave.

As he lathered his face, he heard the boom of a radio, rock music blaring from the adjoining room, and he assumed, correctly, that his twenty-one-year-old daughter Nancy had arrived as planned.

Nancy had not come alone. "This is Steve," she said when her father sat down at the breakfast table.

Steve was a very young man—the young were getting younger—with a wide-eyed, waxy expression and a blond mustache that looked like it could be wiped off with a damp cloth.

Steve stood up and said how glad he was to meet Nancy's father. He shook George's hand enthusiastically, as though they had just struck a lucrative deal.

"Steve's in law school," Mrs. Hume said, with a proprietary delight that her husband found grating.

Nancy was complaining. She had, her father thought, always been a querulous girl, at odds with the way the world was.

"I can't believe it," she was saying. "The whole mall is closed. The only—and I mean only—thing around here that is open is that cheesy little drugstore and nobody actually buys anything in there. I now thought, because I recognize stuff from when I was six. Is this some holiday I don't know about or what?"

"Honey, it's the off season. You know everything closes when the tourists leave," her mother said.

"Not the for-Christ-sakes mall!" Nancy said. "I can't believe it." Nancy frowned. "This must be what Russia is like," she said, closing one eye as smoke from her cigarette slid up her cheek.

George Hume watched his daughter gulp coffee. She was not a person who needed stimulants. She wore an ancient gray sweater and sweatpants. Her blond hair was chopped short and ragged and kept in a state of disarray by the constant furrowing of nervous fingers. She was, her father thought, a pretty girl in disguise.

That night, George discovered that he could remember nothing of the spy novel he was reading, had forgotten, in fact, the hero's name. It was as though he had stumbled into a cocktail party in the wrong neighborhood, all strangers to him, the gossip meaningless.

He put the book on the night stand, leaned back on the pillow, and said. "This is her senior year. Doesn't she have classes to attend?"

His wife said nothing.

He sighed. "I suppose they are staying in the same room."

"Dear, I don't know," Mrs. Hume said. "I expect it is none of our business."

"If it is not our business who stays in our hotel, then who in the name of hell's business is it?"

Mrs. Hume rubbed her husband's neck. "Don't excite yourself, dear. You know what I mean. Nancy is a grown-up, you know."

George did not respond to this and Mrs. Hume, changing the subject, said, "I saw Mrs. Franklin and her daughter out walking on the beach again today. I don't know where Mr. Franklin was. It was pouring, and there they were, mother and daughter. You know . . ." Mrs. Hume paused. "It's like they were waiting for something to come out of the sea. Like a vigil they were keeping. I've thought it before, but the notion was particularly strong today. I looked out past them, and there seemed no separation between the sea and the sky, just a black wall of water." Mrs. Hume looked at herself in the dresser's mirror, as though her reflection might clarify matters. "I've lived by the ocean all my life, and I've just taken it for granted, George. Suddenly it gave me the shivers. Just for a moment. I thought, Lord, how big it is, lying there cold and black, like some creature that has slept at your feet so long you never expect it to wake, have forgotten that it might be brutal, even vicious."

"It's all this rain," her husband said, hugging her and drawing her to him. "It can make a person think some black thoughts."

George left off worrying about his daughter and her young man's living arrangements, and in the morning, when Nancy and Steve appeared for breakfast, George didn't broach the subject—not even to himself.

Later that morning, he watched them drive off in Steve's shiny sports car—rich parents, lawyers themselves?—bound for Wilmington and shopping malls that were open.

The rain had stopped, but dark, massed clouds over the ocean suggested that this was a momentary respite. As George studied the beach, the Franklins came into view. They marched directly toward him, up and over the dunes, moving in a soldierly, clipped fashion. Mrs. Franklin was holding her daughter's hand and moving at a brisk pace, almost a run, while her husband faltered behind, his gait hesitant, as though uncertain of the wisdom of catching up.

Mrs. Franklin reached the steps and marched up them, her child tottering in tow, her boot heels sounding hollowly on the wood planks. George nodded, and she passed without speaking, seemed not to see him. In any event, George Hume would have been unable to speak. He was accustomed to the passive, demure countenance of this self-possessed woman, and the expression on her face, a wild distorting emotion, shocked and confounded him. It was an unreadable emotion, but its intensity was extraordinary and unsettling.

George had not recovered from the almost physical assault of Mrs. Franklin's emotional state, when her husband came up the stairs, nodded curtly, muttered something, and hastened after his wife.

George Hume looked after the retreating figures. Mr. Greg Franklin's face had been a mask of cold civility, none of his wife's passion written there, but the man's appearance was disturbing in its own way. Mr. Franklin had been soaking wet, his hair plastered to his skull, his overcoat dripping, the reek of salt water enfolding him like a shroud.

George walked on down the steps and out to the beach. The ocean was always some consolation, a quieting influence, but today it seemed hostile.

The sand was still wet from the recent rains and the footprints of the Franklins were all that marred the smooth expanse. George saw that the Franklins had walked down the beach along the edge of the tide and returned at a greater distance from the water. He set out in the wake of their footprints, soon lost to his own thoughts. He thought about his daughter, his wild Nancy, who had always been boy-crazy. At least this one didn't have a safety-pin through his ear or play in a rock band. *So lighten up*, George advised himself.

He stopped. The tracks had stopped. Here is where the Franklins turned and headed back to the hotel, walking higher up the beach, closer to the weedy, debris-laden dunes.

But it was not the ending of the trail that stopped George's own progress down the beach. In fact, he had forgotten that he was absently following the Franklin's spore.

It was the litter of dead fish that stopped him. They were scattered at his feet in the tide. Small ghost crabs had already found the corpses and were laying their claims.

There might have been a hundred bodies. It was difficult to say, for not one of the bodies was whole. They had been hacked into many pieces, diced by some impossibly sharp blade that severed a head cleanly, flicked off a tail or dorsal fin. Here a scaled torso still danced in the sand, there a pale eye regarded the sky.

Crouching in the sand, George examined the bodies. He stood up, finally, as the first large drops of rain plunged from the sky. No doubt some fishermen had called it a day, tossed their scissored bait and gone home.

That this explanation did not satisfy George Hume was the result of a general sense of unease. *Too much rain.*

It rained sullenly and steadily for two days during which time George saw little of his daughter and her boyfriend. Nancy apparently had the young man on a strict regime of shopping, tourist attractions, and movies, and she was undaunted by the weather.

The Franklins kept inside, appearing briefly in the dining room for bodily sustenance and then retreating again to their rooms. And whatever did they do there? Did they play solitaire? Did they watch old reruns on TV?

On the third day, the sun came out, brazen, acting as though it had never been gone, but the air was colder. The Franklins, silhouetted like black crows on a barren field, resumed their shoreline treks.

Nancy and Steve rose early and were gone from the house before George arrived at the breakfast table.

George spent the day endeavoring to satisfy the IRS's notion of a small businessman's obligations, and he was in a foul mood by dinner time.

After dinner, he tried to read, this time choosing a much-touted novel that proved to be about troubled youth. He was asleep within fifteen minutes of opening the book and awoke in an overstuffed armchair. The room was chilly, and his wife had tucked a quilt around his legs before abandoning him for bed. In the morning she would, he was certain, assure him that she had tried to rouse him before retiring, but he had no recollection of such an attempt.

"Half a bottle of wine might have something to do with that," she would say.

He would deny the charge.

The advantage of being married a long time was that one could argue without the necessity of the other's actual, physical presence.

He smiled at this thought and pushed himself out of the chair, feeling groggy, head full of prickly flannel. He looked out the window. It was raining again—to the accompaniment of thunder and explosive, strobe-like lightening. The sports car was gone. The kids weren't home yet. Fine. Fine. None of my business.

Climbing the stairs, George paused. Something dark lay on the carpeted step, and as he bent over it, leaning forward, his mind sorted and discarded the possibilities: cat, wig, bird's nest, giant dust bunny. Touch and a strong olfactory cue identified the stuff: seaweed. Raising his head, he saw that two more clumps of the wet, rubbery plant lay on ascending steps, and gathering them—with no sense of revulsion for he was used to the ocean's disordered presence—he carried the seaweed up to his room and dumped it in the bathroom's wastebasket.

He scrubbed his hands in the sink, washing away the salty, stagnant reek, left the bathroom and crawled into bed beside his sleeping wife. He fell asleep immediately, and was awakened later in the night with a suffocating sense of dread, a sure knowledge that an intruder had entered the room.

The intruder proved to be an odor, a powerful stench of decomposing fish, rotting vegetation and salt water. He climbed out of bed, coughing.

The source of this odor was instantly apparent and he swept up the wastebasket, preparing to gather the seaweed and flush it down the toilet.

The seaweed had melted into a black liquid, bubbles forming on its surface, a dark, gelatinous muck, simmering like heated tar. As George stared at the mess, a bubble burst, and the noxious gas it unleashed dazed him, sent him reeling backward with an inexplicable vision of some monstrous, shadowy form, silhouetted against green, mottled water.

George pitched himself forward, gathered the wastebasket in his arms, and fled the room. In the hall he wrenched a window and hurled the wastebasket and its contents into the rain.

He stood then, gasping, the rain savage and cold on his face, his undershirt soaked, and he stood that way, clutching the window sill, until he was sure he would not faint.

Returning to bed, he found his wife still sleeping soundly and he knew, immediately, that he would say nothing in the morning, that the sense of suffocation, of fear, would seem unreal, its source irrational. Already the moment of panic was losing its reality, fading into the realm of nightmare.

The next day the rain stopped again and this time the sun was not routed. The police arrived on the third day of clear weather.

Mrs. Hume had opened the door, and she shouted up to her husband, who stood on the landing, "It's about Mr. Franklin."

Mrs. Franklin came out of her room then, and George Hume thought he saw the child behind her, through the open door. The girl, Melissa, was lying on the bed behind her mother and just for a moment it seemed that there was a spreading shadow under her, as though the bedclothes were soaked with dark water. Then the door closed as Mrs. Franklin came into the hall and George identified the expression he had last seen in her eyes for it was there again: fear, a racing engine of fear, gears stripped, the accelerator flat to the floor.

And Mrs. Franklin screamed, screamed and came falling to her knees and screamed again, prescient in her grief, and collapsed as George rushed toward her and two police officers and a paramedic, a woman, came bounding up the stairs.

Mr. Franklin had drowned. A fisherman had discovered the body. Mr. Franklin had been fully dressed, lying on his back with his eyes open. His wallet—and seven hundred dollars in cash and a host of credit cards—was still in his back pocket, and a business card identified him as vice president of marketing for a software firm in Fairfax, Virginia. The police had telephoned Franklin's firm in Virginia and so learned that he was on vacation. The secretary had the hotel's number.

After the ambulance left with Mrs. Franklin, they sat in silence until the police officer cleared his throat and said, "She seemed to be expecting something like this."

The words dropped into a silence.

Nancy and Steve and Mrs. Hume were seated on one of the lobby's sofas. George Hume came out of the office in the wake of the other policeman who paused at the door and spoke. "We'd appreciate it if you could come down and identify the body. Just a formality, but it's not a job for his wife, not in the state she's in." He coughed, shook his head. "Or the state he's in, for that matter. Body got tore up some in the water, and, well, I still find it hard to believe that he was alive just yesterday. I would have guessed he'd been in the water two weeks minimum—the deterioration, you know."

George Hume nodded his head as though he did know and agreed to accompany the officer back into town.

George took a long look, longer than he wanted to, but the body wouldn't let him go, made mute, undeniable demands.

Yes, this was Mr. Greg Franklin. Yes, this would make eight years that he and his wife and his child had come to the hotel. No, no nothing out of the ordinary.

George interrupted himself. "The tattoos . . ." he said.

"Didn't know about the tattoos, I take it?" the officer said.

George shook his head. "No." The etched blue lines that laced the dead man's arms and chest were somehow more frightening than the damage the sea had done. Frightening because . . . because the reserved Mr. Franklin, businessman and stolid husband, did not look like someone who would illuminate his flesh with arcane symbols, pentagrams and ornate fish, their scales numbered according to some runic logic, and spidery, incomprehensible glyphs.

"Guess Franklin wasn't inclined to wear a bathing suit."

"No."

"Well, we are interested in those tattoos. I guess his wife knew about them. Hell, maybe she has some of her own."

"Have you spoken to her?"

"Not yet. Called the hospital. They say she's sleeping. It can wait till morning."

An officer drove George back to the hotel, and his wife greeted him at the door.

"She's sleeping," Mrs. Hume said.

"Who?"

"Melissa."

For a moment, George drew a blank, and then he nodded. "What are we going to do with her?"

"Why, keep her," his wife said. "Until her mother is out of the hospital."

"Maybe there are relatives," George said, but he knew, saying it, that the Franklins were self-contained, a single unit, a closed universe.

His wife confirmed this. No one could be located, in any event.

"Melissa may not be aware that her father is dead," Mrs. Hume said. "The child is, I believe, a stranger girl than we ever realized. Here we were thinking she was just a quiet thing, well behaved. I think there is something wrong with her mind. I can't seem to talk to her, and what she says makes no sense. I've called Dr. Gowers, and he has agreed to see her. You remember Dr. Gowers, don't you? We sent Nancy to him when she was going through that bad time at thirteen."

George remembered child psychiatrist Gowers as a bearded man with a swollen nose and thousands of small wrinkles around his eyes. He had seemed a very kind but somehow sad man, a little like Santa Claus if Santa Claus had suffered some disillusioning experience, an unpleasant divorce or other personal setback, perhaps.

Nancy came into the room as her mother finished speaking. "Steve and I can take Melissa," Nancy said.

"Well, that's very good of you, dear," her mother said. "I've already made an appointment for tomorrow morning at ten. I'm sure Dr. Gowers will be delighted to see you again."

"I'll go to," George said. He couldn't explain it but he was suddenly afraid.

The next morning when George came down to breakfast, Melissa was already seated at the table and Nancy was combing the child's hair.

"She isn't going to church," George said, surprised at the growl in his voice.

"This is what she wanted to wear," Nancy said. "And it looks very nice, I think."

Melissa was dressed in the sort of outfit a young girl might wear on Easter Sunday: a navy blue dress with white trim, white knee socks, black, shiny shoes. She had even donned pale blue gloves. Her black hair had been brushed to a satin sheen and her pale face seemed just-scrubbed, with the scent of soap lingering over her. A shiny black purse sat next to her plate of eggs and toast.

"You look very pretty," George Hume said.

Melissa nodded, a sharp snap of the head, and said, "I am an angel."

Nancy laughed and hugged the child. George raised his eyebrows. "No false modesty here," he said. At least she could talk.

On the drive into town, Steve sat in the passenger seat while George drove. Nancy and Melissa sat in the back seat. Nancy spoke to the child in a slow, reassuring murmur.

Steve said nothing, sitting with his hands in his lap, looking out the window. *Might not be much in a crisis*, George thought. A *rich man's child*.

Steve stayed in the waiting room while the receptionist ushered Melissa and Nancy and George into Dr. Gowers' office. The psychiatrist seemed much as George remembered him, a silver-maned, benign old gent, exuding an air of competence. He asked them to sit on the sofa.

The child perched primly on the sofa, her little black purse cradled in her lap. She was flanked by George and Nancy.

Dr. Gowers knelt down in front of her. "Well, Melissa. Is it all right if I call you Melissa?"

"Yes sir. That's what everyone calls me."

"Well, Melissa, I'm glad you could come and see me today. I'm Dr. Gowers."

"Yes sir."

"I'm sorry about what happened to your father," he said, looking in her eyes.

"Yes sir," Melissa said. She leaned forward and touched her shoe.

"Do you know what happened to your father?" Dr. Gowers asked.

Melissa nodded her head and continued to study her shoes.

"What happened to your father?" Dr. Gowers asked.

"The machines got him," Melissa said. She looked up at the doctor. "The real machines," she added. "The ocean ones."

"Your father drowned," Dr. Gowers said.

Melissa nodded. "Yes sir." Slowly the little girl got up and began wandering around the room. She walked past a large saltwater aquarium next to a teak bookcase.

George thought the child must have bumped against the aquarium stand—although she hardly seemed close enough—because water spilled from the tank as she passed. She was humming. It was a bright, musical little tune, and he had heard it before, a children's song, perhaps? The words? Something like *by the sea, by the sea.*

The girl walked and gestured with a liquid motion that was oddly sophisticated, suggesting the calculated body language of an older and sexually self-assured woman.

"Melissa, would you come and sit down again so we can talk. I want to ask you some questions, and that is hard to do if you are walking around the room."

"Yes sir," Melissa said, returning to the sofa and resettling between George and his daughter. Melissa retrieved her purse and placed it on her lap again.

She looked down at the purse and up again. She smiled with a child's cunning. Then, very slowly, she opened the purse and showed it to Dr. Gowers.

"Yes?" he said, raising an eyebrow.

"There's nothing in it," Melissa said. "It's empty." She giggled.

"Well yes, it is empty," Dr. Gowers said, returning the child's smile. "Why is that?"

Melissa snapped the purse closed. "Because my real purse isn't here, of course. It's in the real place, where I keep my things."

"And where is that, Melissa?"

Melissa smiled and said, "You know, silly."

When the session ended, George phoned his wife.

"I don't know," he said. "I guess it went fine. I don't know. I've had no experience of this sort of thing. What about Mrs. Franklin?"

Mrs. Franklin was still in the hospital. She wanted to leave, but the hospital was reluctant to let her. She was still in shock, very disoriented. She seemed, indeed, to think that it was her daughter who had drowned.

"Did you talk to her?" George asked.

"Well yes, just briefly, but as I say, she made very little sense, got very excited when it became clear I wasn't going to fetch her if her doctor wanted her to remain there."

"Can you remember anything she said?"

"Well, it was very jumbled, really. Something about a bad bargain. Something about, that Greek word, you know 'hubris.' "

"Hewbris?"

"Oh, back in school, you know, George. Hubris. A willful sort of pride that angers the gods. I'm sure you learned it in school yourself."

"You are not making any sense," he said, suddenly exasperated—and frightened.

"Well," his wife said, "you don't have to shout. Of course I don't make any sense. I am trying to repeat what Mrs. Franklin said, and that poor woman made no sense at all. I tried to reassure her that Melissa was fine and she screamed. She said Melissa was not fine at all and that I was a fool. Now you are shouting at me, too."

George apologized, said he had to be going, and hung up.

On the drive back from Dr. Gowers' office, Nancy sat in the back seat with Melissa. The child seemed unusually excited: her pale forehead was beaded with sweat, and she watched the ocean with great intensity.

"Did you like Dr. Gowers?" Nancy asked. "He liked you. He wants to see you again, you know."

Melissa nodded. "He is a nice one." She frowned. "But he doesn't understand the real words either. No one here does."

George glanced over his shoulder at the girl. *You are an odd ducky,* he thought.

A large, midday sun brightened the air and made the ocean glitter as though scaled. They were in a stretch of sand dunes and sea oats and high, wind-driven waves and, except for an occasional lumbering trailer truck, they seemed alone in this world of sleek, eternal forms.

Then Melissa began to cough. The coughing increased in volume, developed a quick, hysterical note.

"Pull over!" Nancy shouted, clutching the child.

George swung the car off the highway and hit the brakes. Gravel pinged against metal, the car fishtailed and lurched to a stop. George was out of the car instantly, in time to catch his daughter and the child in her arms as they came hurtling from the back seat. Melissa's face was red and her small chest heaved. Nancy had her arms around the girl's chest. "Melissa!" Nancy was shouting. "Melissa!"

Nancy jerked the child upwards and back. Melissa's body convulsed. Her breathing was labored, a broken whistle fluttering in her throat.

George enfolded them both in his arms, and Melissa suddenly lurched forward. She shuddered and began to vomit. A hot, green odor, the smell of stagnant tidal pools, assaulted George. Nancy knelt beside Melissa, wiping the child's wet hair from her forehead. "It's gonna be okay, honey," she said. "You got something stuck in your throat. It's all right now. You're all right."

The child jumped up and ran down the beach.

"Melissa!" Nancy screamed, scrambling to her feet and pursuing the girl. George ran after them, fear hissing in him like some power line down in a storm, writhing and spewing sparks.

In her blue dress and knee socks—shoes left behind on the beach now—Melissa splashed into the ocean, arms pumping.

Out of the corner of his eye, George saw Steve come into view. He raced past

George, past Nancy, moving with a frenzied pinwheeling of arms. "I got her, I got her, I got her," he chanted.

Don't, George thought. *Please don't.*

The beach was littered with debris, old, ocean-polished bottles, driftwood, seaweed, shattered conch shells. It was a rough ocean, still reverberating to the recent storm.

Steve had almost reached Melissa. George could see him reach out to clutch her shoulder.

Then something rose up in the water. It towered over man and child, and as the ocean fell away from it, it revealed smooth surfaces that glittered and writhed. The world was bathed with light, and George saw it plain. And yet, he could not later recall much detail. It was as though his mind refused entry to this monstrous thing, substituting other images—maggots winking from the eye sockets of some dead animal, flesh growing on a ruined structure of rusted metal—and while, in memory, those images were horrible enough and would not let him sleep, another part of his mind shrank from the knowledge that he had confronted something more hideous and ancient than his reason could acknowledge.

What happened next, happened in an instant. Steve staggered backwards and Melissa turned and ran sideways to the waves.

A greater wave, detached from the logic of the rolling ocean, sped over Steve, engulfing him, and he was gone, while Melissa continued to splash through the tide, now turning and running shoreward. The beast-thing was gone, and the old pattern of waves reasserted itself. Then Steve resurfaced, and with a lurch of understanding, as though the unnatural wave had struck at George's mind and left him dazed, he watched the head bob in the water, roll sickeningly, bounce on the crest of a second wave, and disappear.

Melissa lay face down on the wet sand, and Nancy raced to her, grabbed her up in her arms, and turned to her father.

"Where's Steve?" she shouted over the crash of the surf.

You didn't see then, George thought. *Thank God.*

"Where's Steve," she shouted again.

George came up to his daughter and embraced her. His touch triggered racking sobs, and he held her tighter, the child Melissa between them.

And what if the boy's head rolls to our feet on the crest of the next wave? George thought, and the thought moved him to action. "Let's get Melissa back to the car," he said, taking the child from his daughter's arms.

It was a painful march back to the car, and George was convinced that at any moment either or both of his charges would bolt. He reached the car and helped his daughter into the back seat. She was shaking violently.

"Hold Melissa," he said, passing the child to her. "Don't let her go, Nancy."

George pulled away from them and closed the car door. He turned then, refusing to look at the ocean as he did so. He looked down, stared for a moment at what was undoubtedly a wet clump of matted seaweed, and knew, with irrational certainty, that Melissa had choked on this same seaweed, had knelt here on the ground and painfully coughed it up.

He told the police that Melissa had run into the waves and that Steve had pursued her and drowned. This was all he could tell them—someday he hoped he would truly believe that it was all there was to tell. Thank god his daughter had not seen. And he realized then, with shame, that it was not even his daughter's feelings that were foremost in his mind but rather the relief, the immense relief, of knowing that what he had seen was not going to be corroborated and that with time and effort, he might really believe it was an illusion, the moment's horror, the tricks light plays with water.

He took the police back to where it had happened. But he would not go down to the tide. He waited in the police car while they walked along the beach.

If they returned with Steve's head, what would he say? *Oh yes, a big wave decapitated Steve. Didn't I mention that? Well, I meant to.*

But they found nothing.

Back at the hotel, George sat at the kitchen table and drank a beer. He was not a drinker, but it seemed to help. "Where's Nancy?" he asked.

"Upstairs," Mrs. Hume said. "She's sleeping with the child. She wouldn't let me take Melissa. I tried to take the child and I thought . . . I thought my own daughter was going to attack me, hit me. Did she think I would hurt Melissa? What did she think?"

George studied his beer, shook his head sadly to indicate the absence of all conjecture.

Mrs. Hume dried her hands on the dish towel and, ducking her head, removed her apron. "Romner Psychiatric called. A doctor Melrose."

George looked up. "Is he releasing Mrs. Franklin?" *Please come and get your daughter*, George thought. *I have a daughter of my own*. Oh how he wanted to see the last of them.

"Not just yet. No. But he wanted to know about the family's visits every year. Dr. Melrose thought there might have been something different about that first year. He feels there is some sort of trauma associated with it."

George Hume shrugged. "Nothing out of the ordinary as I recall."

Mrs. Hume put a hand to her cheek. "Oh, but it was different. Don't you remember, George? They came earlier, with all the crowds, and they left abruptly. They had paid for two weeks, but they were gone on the third day. I remember being surprised when they returned the next year—and I thought then that it must have been the crowds they hated and that's why they came so late from then on."

"Well . . ." Her husband closed his eyes. "I can't say that I actually remember the first time."

His wife shook her head. "What can I expect from a man who can't remember his own wedding anniversary? That Melissa was just a tot back then, a little mite in a red bathing suit. Now that I think of it, she hasn't worn a bathing suit since."

Before going to bed, George stopped at the door to his daughter's room. He pushed the door open carefully and peered in. She slept as she always slept, sprawled on her back, mouth open. She had always fallen asleep abruptly, in disarray, gunned down by the sandman. Tonight she was aided by the doctor's sedatives. The child Melissa snuggled next to her, and for one brief moment the small form seemed sinister and parasitic, as though attached to his daughter, drawing sustenance there.

* * *

"Come to bed," his wife said, and George joined her under the covers.

"It's just that she wants to protect the girl," George said. "All she has, you know. She's just seen her boyfriend drown, and this . . . I think it gives her purpose perhaps."

Mrs. Hume understood that this was in answer to the earlier question and she nodded her head. "Yes, I know dear. But is it healthy? I've a bad feeling about it."

"I know," George said.

The shrill ringing of the phone woke him."Who is it?" his wife was asking as he fumbled in the dark for the receiver.

The night ward clerk was calling from Romner Psychiatric. She apologized for calling at such a late hour, but there might be cause for concern. Better safe than sorry, etc. Mrs. Franklin had apparently—well, had definitely—left the hospital. Should she return to the hotel, the hospital should be notified immediately.

George Hume thanked her, hung up the phone, and got out of bed. He pulled on his trousers, tugged a sweatshirt over his head.

"Where are you going?" his wife called after him.

"I won't be but a minute," he said, closing the door behind him.

The floor was cold, the boards groaning under his bare feet. Slowly, with a certainty born of dread, expecting the empty bed, expecting the worst, he pushed open the door.

Nancy lay sleeping soundly.

The child was gone. Nancy lay as though still sheltering that small, mysterious form.

George pulled his head back and closed the door. He turned and hurried down the hall. He stopped on the stairs, willed his heart to silence, slowed his breathing. "Melissa," he whispered. No answer.

He ran down the stairs. The front doors were wide open. He ran out into the moonlight and down to the beach.

The beach itself was empty and chill; an unrelenting wind blew in from the ocean. The moon shone overhead as though carved from milky ice.

He saw them then, standing far out on the pier, mother and daughter, black shadows against the moon-gray clouds that bloomed on the horizon.

Dear God, George thought. *What does she intend to do?*

"Melissa!" George shouted, and began to run.

He was out of breath when he reached them. Mother and daughter regarded him coolly, having turned to watch his progress down the pier.

"Melissa," George gasped. "Are you all right?"

Melissa was wearing a pink nightgown and holding her mother's hand. It was her mother who spoke: "We are beyond your concern. Mr. Hume. My husband is dead, and without him the contract cannot be renewed."

Mrs. Franklin's eyes were lit with some extraordinary emotion and the wind, rougher and threatening to unbalance them all, made her hair quiver like a dark flame.

"You have your own daughter, Mr. Hume. That is a fine and wonderful thing.

You have never watched your daughter die, watched her fade to utter stillness, lying on her back in the sand, sand on her lips, her eyelids; children are so untidy, even dying. It is an unholy and terrible thing to witness."

The pier groaned and a loud crack heralded a sudden tilting of the world. George fell to his knees. A long sliver of wood entered the palm of his hand, and he tried to keep from pitching forward.

Mrs. Franklin, still standing, shouted over the wind. "We came here every year to renew the bargain. Oh, it is not a good bargain. Our daughter is never with us entirely. But you would know, any parent would know, that love will take whatever it can scavenge, any small compromise. Anything less utter and awful than the grave."

There were tears running down Mrs. Franklin's face now, silver tracks. "This year I was greedy. I wanted Melissa back, all of her. And I thought, I am her mother. I have the first claim to her. So I demanded—demanded—that my husband set it all to rights. 'Tell them we have come here for the last year,' I said. And my husband allowed his love for me to override his reason. He did as I asked."

Melissa, who seemed oblivious to her mother's voice, turned away and spoke into the darkness of the waters. Her words were in no language George Hume had ever heard, and they were greeted with a loud, rasping bellow that thrummed in the wood planks of the pier.

Then came the sound of wood splintering, and the pier abruptly tilted. George's hands gathered more spiky wooden needles as he slid forward. He heard himself scream, but the sound was torn away by the renewed force of the wind and a hideous roaring that accompanied the gale.

Looking up, George saw Melissa kneeling at the edge of the pier. Her mother was gone.

"Melissa!" George screamed, stumbling forward. "Don't move."

But the child was standing up, wobbling, her nightgown flapping behind her.

George leapt forward, caught the child, felt a momentary flare of hope, and then they both were hurtling forward and the pier was gone.

They plummeted toward the ocean, through a blackness defined by an inhuman sound, a sound that must have been the first sound God heard when He woke at the dawn of eternity.

And even as he fell, George felt the child wiggle in his arms. His arms encircled Melissa's waist, felt bare flesh. Had he looked skyward, he would have seen the nightgown, a pink ghost shape, sailing toward the moon.

But George Hume's eyes saw, instead, the waiting ocean and under it, a shape, a moving network of cold, uncanny machinery, and whether it was a living thing of immense size, or a city, or a machine, was irrelevant. He knew only that it was ancient beyond any land-born thing.

Still clutching the child he collided with the hard, cold back of the sea.

George Hume had been raised in close proximity to the ocean. He had learned to swim almost as soon as he had learned to walk. The cold might kill him, would certainly kill him if he did not reach shore quickly—but that he did. During the swim toward shore he lost Melissa and in that moment he understood not to turn back, not to seek the child.

He could not tell anyone how he knew a change had been irretrievably wrought and that there was no returning the girl to land. It was not something you could communicate—any more than you could communicate the dreadful ancient quality of the machinery under the sea.

Nonetheless, George knew the moment Melissa was lost to him. It was a precise and memorable moment. It was the moment the child had wriggled, with strange new, sinewy strength, flicked her tail and slid effortlessly from his grasp.

STRINGS

Kelley Eskridge

Kelley Eskridge lives in Atlanta, Georgia. She has published short fiction in *Pulphouse: The Hardback Magazine*, *Pulphouse*: *A Fiction Magazine*, and *Little Deaths*, and has recently finished her first novel. Eskridge was the 1992 winner of an Astraea Foundation Writer's Award.

"Strings" is a science fiction horror story about the creative process and those who would fetter it—set in a chilling future wherein music is strictly regulated. The story was originally published in *The Magazine of Fantasy & Science Fiction*. Another highly recommended Eskridge story from 1994 is "And Salome Danced" published in *Little Deaths*.

—E. D.

She took the stage, head shaking. Her jaw and the tiny muscles in her neck rippled in sharp adrenaline tremors. She moved her head slowly back and forth while she walked the twenty yards from stage right to the spotlight; it was always the same, this swooping scan, taking in the waiting orchestra, the racks of lights overhead, the audience rumbling and rustling. She moved her head not so much to hide the shaking as to vent it: to hold it until center stage and the white-light circle where she could raise the violin, draw it snug against the pad on her neck; and at the moment of connection she looked at the Conductor and smiled, and by the time he gathered the orchestra into the waiting breath of the upraised baton, she had become the music once again.

After the final bows, she stood behind the narrow curtain at the side of the stage and watched the audience eddy up the aisles to the lobby and the street and home. She could tell by their gentle noise that the current of the music carried them for these moments as it had carried her for most of her life.

Nausea and exhaustion thrust into her like the roll of sticks on the kettledrum. And something else, although she did not want to acknowledge it: the thinnest whine of a string, phantom music high and wild in a distant, deep place within her head.

"Excuse me, Strad?"

She jerked, and turned. The orchestra's First Clarinet stood behind her, a little too close.

"I'm sorry." He reached out and almost touched her. "I didn't mean to startle you."

"No. No, it's O.K." She felt the tension in her smile. "Was there something you wanted?" Her right hand rubbed the muscles of her left in an old and practiced motion.

"Oh. Yes. The party has started; we were all wondering. . . . You are coming to the party, aren't you?"

She smiled again, squared her shoulders. She did not know if she could face it: the percussion of too many people, too much food, the interminable awkward toasts they would make to the Stradivarius and the Conservatory. She had seen a Monitor in the house tonight, and she knew he would be at the party, too, with a voice-activated computer in his hands; they would be soft, not musician's hands. She wondered briefly how big her file was by now. She wanted desperately to go back to the hotel and sleep.

"Of course," she said. "Please go back and tell them I'll be there just as soon as I've changed." Then she found her dressing room and began, unsteadily, to strip the evening from herself.

She was tense and tired the next morning as she packed her music and violin and clothes. Her next guest solo was with an orchestra in a city she had not visited for several years. A Conservatory limo picked her up at the airport along with the current Guarnerius, who handed his cello into the backseat as if it were an aging grande dame rather than hardwood and almost half his weight. He was assigned to the same orchestra, but for only two weeks. She was glad she would have a week alone with the musicians after he left. She did not like him.

He chattered at her all the way to the hotel, mistaking her silence for attention. She tried to listen, to allow him to bore her or anger her, to distract her. But she could not hook her attention onto him: it slid away like the rain down the windshield of the car, dropped into the steady beat of the tires on the wet road, *thud-DUH thud-DUH*, the rhythm so familiar and comforting that she relaxed into it unguardedly and was caught and jerked into the welter of other sound that was also the car and the road and the journey: *thwump thwump* of the wipers, the alto ringing of the engine, the coloratura squeak of the seat springs as Guarnerius leaned forward to make an earnest point, the counterpoint of the wheels of the cars around them, *thudduh thudduh THUMPthump-thump THUD-duh*—and no matter how hard she tried, she could not make it something she recognized; she had no music for it. No Bach, no Paganini, no Mozart or Lalo or Vivaldi would fit around the texture of the throbbing in her bones—and she was suddenly sure that if her heart were not pounding so loud, she would hear that distant wailing music in her head; it would wind around her like a woman dancing: sinuous, sweating, lightly swaying, wrapping her up—

She jerked. The edge of Guarnerius's briefcase pressed against her arm. She remembered G did not like to touch other people or be touched by them. She wondered if he chose to play the cello so he would never have to sit next to another passenger on an airplane. She wondered if he had ever heard phantom music.

". . . *waiting*, Strad." The cold rim of the briefcase pushed at her arm.

She blinked, looked up at him.

"We're here, for God's sake. The whole orchestra is probably on pins and needles, poor idiots, waiting in there for the Strad and Guarnerius to arrive, and here you sit gaping off into the middle distance. Or were you planning to ask them to rehearse in the car?"

She could feel herself flush. "No," she said shortly, definitely, as if it would answer everything, and stepped out.

She never made friends easily. There were a thousand reasons: she was too shy; she was the Strad, and other people were shy of her; she was busy. Sometimes she thought she was too lonely to make friends, as if the solitude and separateness were so much a part of her that she did not know how to replace them with anything else. So it was simply another sign of how upside down things were that she found a heart-friend in the first two days of rehearsals with the new orchestra. They might have been friends the first day, if he had been there.

"I'm very sorry, Stradivarius," the Stage Manager said. She was a thickset woman with a clipboard and a pinch-eyed look. She was also, Strad thought, worried and not hiding it as well as she wished.

"I'm very sorry," the SM began again. "I'm afraid we can't rehearse the Viotti this afternoon as planned."

Strad rubbed her left hand with her right. She wished for one improbable moment that the SM would give her an excuse to fly into a rage so that she could howl out all her fear and tension safely disguised as artist's pique. But she could not: all other considerations aside, it reminded her too much of something G might do.

She sighed. "What seems to be the problem? My schedule requests were quite clear."

"Yes, Stradivarius. But our Piano isn't here."

"Then get someone over to the nearest bar or videohouse or wherever she or he . . . he? . . . wherever he is and bring him along."

"It's not like that. He. . . ." The SM swallowed. "He's at a Conservatory disciplinary hearing. We're not sure if he's coming back or not . . . but we don't want to replace him until we're sure, because it's not *fair*." She stopped, gripped the clipboard tighter against her breasts. "I beg your pardon," she said formally. "I did not intend to question the decisions of the Conservatory. The entire orchestra apologizes for the inconvenience caused by one of our members."

"Oh, put a sock in it," Strad said, surprising them both. "What's he done?"

"He's been accused of improvising."

He was back the next day. Strad knew it the moment she walked into the hall for the morning rehearsal. The room seemed brighter, as if there were more light and air in it than the day before.

She saw him in the midst of a crowd of players, like a young sapling in the sun. From habit, she noticed his hands first. They were thin and strong-looking, with long, square-tipped fingers; expressive hands. *Good*, she thought, and looked next at his face.

He's so young. His eyes and mouth moved with the same emotion as his hands, but none of the control. Someone touched his shoulder, and as he turned, laughing, he saw Strad watching him. His eyes widened, the laugh turned into a beautiful smile; then, quite suddenly, he looked away. It jolted her, as if a string had broken in mid-note.

She felt movement behind her. Guarnerius appeared at her left shoulder, with the Conductor in tow.

"Is that him?"

"Yes, Guarnerius."

"What did the disciplinary committee decide to do about him?"

"He's on probation. He's been warned." The Conductor shrugged. "I couldn't prove anything, you see; it was just a matter of a few notes. They really couldn't do anything except cite him for faulty technique." The Conductor sounded unconcerned; Strad thought committee hearings were probably all in a day's work for her. No wonder the orchestra was tense. No wonder their Piano was playing forbidden notes. She could imagine herself in his place, young and impatient, aching to prove she was better than the music she was given to play, knowing that one note added here or there would support the piece and give it more resonance, wanting to hear how it might sound. . . . And then she did hear.

It started slow and soft, the music in her head. It swirled through her skull like a thread of heavy cream in hot coffee. It seeped down her spine. *I mustn't move,* Strad thought, *if I can just not move, it won't know I'm here, and it will go back wherever it came from.* The almost-audible music bubbled in her bones. *Go find somebody else to play with!* she thought wildly. Then she looked again at the Piano, and knew it had.

"How soon can you find someone else?" Guarnerius's voice grated against the music. For a confused moment, she wondered if he were talking about her, and a huge, voiceless *no* swelled inside her.

"I have no grounds to replace him," the Conductor said.

G shrugged. "Contract privilege. If Strad and I find him unacceptable, you're obligated to provide a substitute."

"There isn't going to be anyone as good. . . ."

"There isn't going to be any substitute," Strad interrupted.

"What are you talking about?" Guarnerius looked sharply into her eyes, but she knew the Conductor was looking at her shaking hands.

"He was warned, G, not expelled."

"He was improvising."

"The Conservatory apparently doesn't have reason to think so. Besides, what's the point of upsetting everyone again? We've already missed a day's rehearsal, and your Strauss is difficult enough without having the orchestra tense and angry and playing badly."

Guarnerius frowned. Strad turned back to the Conductor, who was managing to look attentive and unobtrusive all at once. Strad could feel her hands still trembling slightly. She folded them carefully in front of her, knowing the Conductor saw.

"Perhaps you'll be kind enough to gather the players?"

"Perhaps you'd like a moment to yourself before rehearsal?" The other woman's voice was carefully neutral. Strad wanted to break something over her lowered head.

"No, I would not," she said, very precisely. "What I would like is a few moments with my music and a full orchestra, if that can be arranged sometime before opening night."

The Conductor flushed. "My apologies, Stradivarius."

"Well, let's get on with it," G said crossly.

She did not get to speak with the Piano until the next day. She sat on the loading dock at the back of the hall during the midday break, enjoying the sun and the solitude. She was far enough from the street that no mechanical noises reached her: she heard only the creak of the metal loading door in the breeze, the muffled, brassy warble of trumpet scales, the hissing wind in the tall grass of the empty lot behind the building. The sun was warm and red on her closed eyelids. A cricket began to fiddle close by.

"I thought you might like some tea."

The cricket stopped in mid-phrase. She felt suddenly angry at the endless stream of infuriating and intrusive courtesies that were offered to the Strad. Nevertheless she smiled in the general direction of the voice. "You're very kind," she said. She kept her eyes closed and hoped whoever it was would put down the tea and go away.

"Well, no, I'm not. I just didn't know how else to get to talk to you."

"I'm available to any musician. It's part of being the Strad; everyone knows that. Please don't feel shy."

"I'm not shy. I just thought you might not want to be seen talking to me, considering everything."

Strad opened her eyes and sat up straight. "Oh. It's you. I didn't realize. . . ." He stepped back. "No, please don't go," she said quickly, and put one hand out. "Please. I'd like to talk to you." He came back slowly, tall, dark, close-cropped hair, those beautiful hands. He held two mugs that steamed almost imperceptibly.

"Sit down."

He handed her a cup and sat next to her on the edge of the loading dock, curling into a half-lotus, tea cradled in his lap. She took a sip and tasted hot cinnamon, orange, bright spices.

"Can I talk to you?" he said.

"Of course. I just told you. . . ."

"No," he said quietly. "Can I talk to you?"

The rich yellow taste of the tea seeped through her. She felt transparent and warm, caught between the sun and the tea and the young man who wore his music like skin.

"Yes. You can talk to me."

He let out a long breath. Everything was still for a moment. The cricket began to play again.

"It was awful at the disciplinary committee," he said, as abruptly and comfortably as if they had known each other for years. "They would have dismissed me if they could. There was an old man with long gray hair who made me take the phrase note by note to prove that I knew how to play it. He wanted me to repeat what I had done during the rehearsal that made the Conductor charge me."

"Boethius." Strad nodded. The Piano looked at her. "He's the Master Librarian," she explained. His eyes widened and then closed for a moment.

"I suppose he does all the notation of the scores as well."

"Mmm," Strad agreed. "He doesn't like having his toes stepped on."

"Well, at least now I know why he . . . he really scared me. I'll never be able to play that piece again without freezing up at that movement." He grinned at her. "Don't say it: I know I'm lucky to even be able to think about playing the piece again at all." His smile faded. He took a gulp of tea, swallowed, studied the inside of the cup. Strad stayed still, watching him.

He looked up after a while, up and beyond her into the empty field.

"I never improvised half as much in the music as I did in that room." He was silent for a moment, remembering. His fingers twitched.

"You know I did it, don't you." It was not a question.

She nodded.

"Thought so. Some of my friends in there—" he looked at the hall—"don't believe I could have done it. They wouldn't understand. They just . . . they play what they're told, and they seem happy, but that's not music. It's *not*," he said again, defiantly. His cheeks were red, and his voice shook. "So how can they be happy?" He swallowed, took a deep breath. "Maybe they aren't. Maybe they're just making do the best they can. I can almost understand that now, you know, after the hearing. . . . I wish that cricket would just shut up." He picked up a piece of gravel from the edge of the dock and threw it out into the field. The cricket fiddling stopped.

"What's it like, being an Instrument?"

"It's good." She saw, in a blur, all her Competitions, all her challengers. "It's hard. It can be amazing. The Conservatory orchestra is wonderful." She set down her cup. "You're thinking of the Competition? Of challenging the Steinway?"

He bit his lip. "I've thought about it. Maybe we all do. . . ." He sighed. "I know if I ever want to be the Steinway I'll have to . . . I'll stop improvising. But Strad, I don't know how to stop the music in my head."

She felt herself go very still. She had made no sound, but he looked up and out of himself and saw her. "Oh," he said gently, hopefully, sadly. "You, too?"

She found the muscles that moved her mouth. "I don't know what. . . ." . . . *you're talking about*, she meant to say, and have it finished. But she could not. She had a sudden, clear image of how he must have looked in the disciplinary hearing: a new suit, an old shirt, his breath sour with anxiety, and his mouth suddenly not very good with words. He would have appreciated the piano they had him use, she knew; it was undoubtedly the finest instrument he had ever played. She thought of him carefully wiping the fear-sweat from his hands before he touched it, of him playing it and denying the music he heard lurking within its strings. It broke her heart.

"I don't know what to do," she said, and behind her the cricket began to play again.

That night she dreamed of her first competition. She stood with the other challengers backstage while a crowd of people with no faces settled into the arena seats. She played in her dream as she had in the real moment, with the passion that the music demanded and the precision that the Judges required of a Strad, as if the piece were a new, wondrous discovery, and at the same time as if she had played it a hundred thousand times before. She forgot the audience was there, until they began to clap and then to shout, and she could not see them clearly because she was weeping.

Then the audience disappeared, and the building vanished into a landscape of sand under a sand-colored sky. Directly ahead of her, a door stood slightly ajar in its frame. She heard her violin crying. She stumbled forward into dark. The violin screamed on and on as she searched for it. She found it eventually, high on a shelf over the door. It went silent when she touched it. She pulled it down and hugged it to her, and fell on her knees out onto the sand.

She looked at the violin anxiously, turning it over, running her fingers across the bridge and the strings. She could not see any damage.

Suddenly a voice spoke from the darkness inside the open door. "It only looks the same," the voice hissed, and the door slammed shut inches from her face at the same time that the violin stood itself on end and burst into song. And then she awoke, clutching a pillow to her side and sweating in the cool air of her hotel suite.

She lay still for a few moments, then got up and went into the bathroom, filled the tub full of water so hot that she had to lower herself into it an inch at a time.

She closed her eyes as the water cooled around her neck and knees; she remembered the music that had burst from her violin at the end of her dream. She recognized it: the distant, maddening music that she had heard earlier; the haunting melody that stirred her hands to shape it; the illegal music that she could never play.

When she tried to stand up, her hand slipped on the porcelain rim, and her elbow cracked against it. The pain drove the music from her head, and she was grateful.

"Let's have a picnic," the Piano said a few days later, at the end of an afternoon's rehearsal, the rich, rolling energy of good music still in the air. There was a moment of quiet, as if everyone were trying to work out what picnics had to do with concert performances. Then the SM set down the pile of scores she was carrying with a solid paperish thunk.

"That's a great idea," she said. Behind her, Guarnerius rolled his eyes and went back to packing up his cello.

The SM produced a clipboard and a pen. "Who wants to bring what?" She was surrounded by a crowd of jabbering voices and waving hands. It took a few minutes for the group to thin out enough to let Strad get close.

The SM looked up at her, obviously surprised. "Was there something you wanted, Strad?"

"I'd like to bring something, but you'll have to tell me what we need."

"Oh no, we'll take care of it, Strad. There's no need to trouble yourself."

"I'd like to." But the SM had already turned away. *Damn it.* Strad thought. She gathered up her violin and left the hall, walking alone through the double doors into the sun and smell of the street.

The limo waited alongside the curb. The driver got out and moved around the car to take her things. She gave him her violin and music, but shook her head when he opened the rear door for her.

"I'll walk. Guarnerius is still packing up; I don't know how long he'll be. Wait for me outside the hotel, and I'll pick up my things. Don't give them to anyone but me."

"Yes, Stradivarius," the driver answered. He looked down at the ground while she talked, so she could not tell if he minded being told what to do. *Damn*, she thought again.

She walked fast the first few blocks. Then she realized that no one recognized her, that no one was paying her any more than casual attention, and gradually she felt safe enough to slow down. She was sweating lightly, and she stopped under a canvas awning in front of a shop to catch her breath. She pressed herself against the cool concrete of the building, out of the way of people moving along the sidewalk, and watched the world go by.

A man stood at a bus stop, absorbed in *Wuthering Heights*, humming Brahms. A couple passed her with a transistor radio, Vivaldi trickling fuzzily from the speaker. A pack of little boys on bicycles pedaled down the street, bellowing the *1812 Overture*, booming out the cannon with gleeful satisfaction. *My audience*, Strad realized with wonder. She thought of all the musicians, all the hours and the work for a few minutes of song that lived and died from one note to the next. *But they hear. They hear.*

She stepped out from the shadow and wandered up the sidewalk. It was as though the whole world had opened up since she had talked to the Piano, since she had told someone how it was with her. She saw things she had not seen in a long time: dirt, children's toys, hot food ready to eat out of paper containers, narrow alleyways and the open back doors of restaurants where people in grubby aprons stood fanning themselves and laughing. And everywhere music, the works of the masters, clear and rich and beautiful, the only music; the sounds and feelings that had shaped and contained her life since she was young; as young as the child who stumbled on the pavement in front of her. Strad stopped and offered her hand, but the little girl picked herself up with a snort and ran on down the street.

Strad smiled. As she craned her neck to watch the child run, she saw a smear of bright color beside her. She turned and found herself in front of a window full of lines and whorls and grinning fantastical faces that resolved into dozens of kites, all shapes and sizes and shades of colors. "Oh," she breathed, catching her hands up to her ribs.

"Everybody does that," someone said, and chuckled. She saw a woman standing in the open door of the shop. Bits of dried glue and gold glitter and colored paper were stuck to her arms and clothes.

"They're beautiful," Strad said.

"Come in and have a closer look."

She left the shop with a kite bundled under her arm, light but awkward. She walked slowly; the hotel was only a few minutes away, and she wished she had farther to go so that she could enjoy herself longer.

She passed a woman who smiled and then wrinkled her eyebrows and gave Strad an odd look. It was only then that she realized that, like so many others, she was humming as she walked. But the music that buzzed in her mouth was the alien music that she had thought was safely locked in her head. She knew the other woman had heard it; then she began to wonder who else might have heard, and she spun in a circle on the sidewalk, trying to look in all directions at once for someone with a hand-held recorder or a wallet with a Monitor's badge. She was sweating again. Suddenly the hotel seemed much too far away. She wished for some sunglasses or a hat or the cool of the Conservatory limousine. The music lapped against the back of her tongue all the way back to her room.

The kite was an enormous success. Most of the players wanted a turn, although G and the Conductor made a point of turning up their noses when offered. The kite had a large group that leaped and shouted under it as it bobbed along in the clear sky over the park.

The Piano had brought his wife. "You're someone famous, aren't you?" she said to Strad when they were introduced. The Piano poked her sharply in the ribs. "Stop it, hon," she said calmly, and went on shaking Strad's hand. "Not everybody knows music, as I keep trying to point out to the whiz kid here. Everyone says you're very good. Did you really tell the SM to put a sock in it?" She was a tall, loose-boned woman with deep-set brown eyes. Strad liked her.

They sat on the grass and talked while the Piano joined the group running with the kite. His wife smiled as she watched him. "He was so excited about meeting you. He needs friends who understand his work. I guess you do, too."

"Yes," Strad agreed. "What do you do?" she asked, suddenly very curious.

"I teach literature to fifth graders. They all wanted to come with me today. I told them it was my turn for a field trip."

Words and music, Strad thought. What a household they must have together.

"What are you thinking?"

"I was just envying you," Strad said.

Later, after the others had worn themselves out, the three of them took the kite to the edge of the park green for one last flight.

"I know what it reminds me of," the Piano's wife said. "With those deep colors and the tail swirling. It looks like something the Gypsies would have had, something that I read to my kids about. They loved to sing and dance. I'll bet it was just like that, all dips and swirls and jumping around. They played violins, too—did you know that?" she added, with a grin for Strad. "I wonder what it sounded like."

I think I know, Strad thought.

"Careful, hon," the Piano said warningly. He jerked his chin toward the other side of the park. A man stood on a slight hill overlooking the common, staring down at the players. He carried a hand-held recorder.

"They don't leave you alone at all, do they?" his wife muttered. "At least I only have to worry about them on the job. Although I hear it's worse if you're a history teacher. . . ." She sighed and began to reel in the kite.

They walked back to the group together, but they found separate places to sit. Strad put the kite away.

"Well, I for one will be extremely glad when this particular tour is over," Guarnerius announced, and put his drink down on Strad's table. Strad wished he would just go away. It was the last night of his engagement with the orchestra, and she was heartily sick of him.

"Where do you go from here?"

"Back to the Conservatory. Time to get ready for the Competition. Well, you know that of course." He patted at the wrinkles in his jacket. Alcohol fumes drifted lazily from his mouth. "You should be rehearsing yourself. What's your schedule like?"

"Well, there's next week here, and I've got one more city."

"I don't envy you another week with this miserable orchestra."

"Mmm," she said noncommittally. G's engagement had not gone well, and two clanging wrong notes in his solo that night had not improved his temper.

"Really, Strad. That Conductor is as wooden as her baton, the entire brass section needs a good kick in the rear, and that Piano . . . well, small wonder they had trouble with him, considering the state of the rest of the group." He nodded, took another swallow of his drink, and set the glass down so that it clacked against the wooden table as if helping to make his point.

"I thought the Piano played very well."

"Well, of course he did, Strad, don't be an idiot. He's already screwed up once, and now he's being monitored. Of course he's going to play well."

Monitored. She picked up her glass and leaned back in her chair, let her gaze wander around the room. And there he was, the same Monitor that she had seen at her last orchestra. Had he been the one at the park? Was it normal for the same Monitor to turn up again and again? She had never noticed before. She realized now how much she, like the Piano, had always taken the Monitors for granted. She felt a cramp like someone's fist in her stomach. The sickness brought with it the faint, sweet music inside her skull. The Monitor's head came up like a hunting dog's, as if somehow he had heard it, too. She watched him scan the room, making whispered notes into his recorder, and she saw as if through his eyes: *how scared they all look, how stiff and anxious; see a hand moving too sharply there, a voice raised slightly too high, the smell of hunger for something illegal. . . .* Strad dropped her gaze back down into her glass.

There was something cold and wet against her arm.

". . . your problem lately, Strad?" Guarnerius nudged her again with his glass.

"What?"

"That's exactly what I mean," he said with a smile that was not altogether nice. "You're very preoccupied lately, aren't you, dear?"

She could only stare at him in shock.

"Oh yes, I've noticed. It hasn't shown up in your music yet, but it will. Bound to. One of these fine days, you'll be up onstage, and your hands will slip on the strings, and then we'll see what it's like when the Strad loses that precious control, that fucking *precision* that everyone's always going on about, oh yes. . . ." The words trailed off. Strad realized for the first time how drunk he was. She remembered that he had made bad mistakes that night, and the Monitor had been there.

Guarnerius stared into his glass as if he wanted to climb in and hide among the ice cubes. Strad stood up and grabbed her violin, music case, coat, bag into a loose, awkward bundle.

"I'm sorry, Strad," she heard him mumble, but she was already moving. She smiled and excused her way across the crowded room without seeing or hearing anything properly until she came to a wall and could go no farther. There was an empty chair by the wall. She dropped her things on the floor next to it and sat down.

The chair made her invisible somehow; at least, no one approached her. The party happened in front of her, like a video. She rubbed her hands, left with right, right with left, watching the groups mingle and break apart and spiral into new forms: the currents matched the music that swelled in gentle waves in her head. And it was too much; she could not fight it any longer. Somewhere inside her a door edged open, and the music trickled through.

She did not know how long she sat before she realized that someone was standing in front of her. She looked up. It was the Piano. She could not speak. He took her arm and pulled her to her feet, tugged her out a side door of the restaurant onto an open patio. He sat her hard into a wrought-iron chair at one of the tables. The metal bit cold and sticky through her light dress. She opened her mouth and took in great heaving bites of air, one after the other, until she felt the door inside her push tightly closed, the music safely behind it.

The Piano sat next to her. She held his hand so hard that the ends of his fingers turned bright red.

"Oh, thank you," she whispered. "How did you know to bring me out here?"

He reached over and brushed a finger against her cheek. It came away wet. "You were crying," he said. "You were sitting in that chair, staring at nothing and crying like the loneliest person on earth, and you weren't making a sound. So I brought you outside."

She put her hands up to her face. Her skin felt puffy and hot.

"What is it?" he asked.

"It's so beautiful," she said.

And then: "I'm scared."

The next morning she met some of the players in the hotel to have breakfast and say good-bye. The Piano was there. She kept him in the lobby after the others had left.

"I hate to say good-bye," he said.

"I have something for you," she said. She gave him the kite.

"I'll fly it for you."

She looked at him closely. "You be careful," she said.

"Don't worry."

"I mean it."

"So do I. I'll keep the kite, and every time it flies I'll be thinking of you and the music we both have in us. The trick is to keep it alive somehow. There has to be a way, Strad. There has to be a way to have it and play it and be what we are."

He stood looking at her, and she thought he would say more. But in the end, he only nodded and kissed her gently on the cheek.

She went to her next city, to the rehearsals and dinners and performances and parties, and then back to the Conservatory, to the soundproofed suite of rooms and the tiny private garden that were hers for as long as she was the Stradivarius. She rested, ate, played with the other musicians, all the Instruments gathered together to face their yearly challengers. She rehearsed her Competition piece. One day, Guarnerius asked her, stiltedly, how her last engagement had gone.

"It went fine," she told him. "No problems."

He muttered, "Oh, how nice," and stepped around her, moved stiffly down the hallway toward one of the Conservatory practice rooms. She wondered how he would have reacted if she had told him that she had played as well as ever, and that it had all been empty: hollow, meaningless sound.

It was a relief to put her violin away when she got back to her rooms. There were letters on the desk. There were instructions and announcements from the Conservatory. There was a note from the Conductor of an orchestra she had guested with once before. There was a package from the Piano.

The note was unsigned: he would know that her mail might be monitored. She did not realize it was from him until she opened the package and saw the kite. She put it slowly on the desk and set the note beside it on the polished wood. She read it again without touching it. A little of the silence inside her gave way to the remembered sound of his voice.

> *I am sending you this as an admirer of your work and your talent. The beauty of this kite reminds me of the music that you carry within you, that you as the Strad keep in trust for us all. Do be careful of the kite; it is not as delicate as it looks. I have been told recently, by those who love me best and who watch me closely, that I can no longer risk flying it myself, as it is too strenuous and dangerous to my health. I will miss it. I would not suggest that you fly it, but it is beautiful to look at.*

She folded the note into a small rectangle and tucked it inside her shirt, against her skin. She thought about the Piano running in the park, whooping and pointing at the kite. Then she went out of her rooms into the garden and pushed a chair into the sun, sat and closed her eyes against the light and let the silence fill her up.

She stayed in her rooms for the next four weeks, rehearsing for the Competition. Her practice was painstaking. She wrung the piece dry. Every note, every phrase, every rest was considered and balanced. Every nuance of tone and meaning was polished until the notes seemed to shine as they shot from the strings.

She felt hollow and open, as wide and empty as a summer sky. She slept without dreaming. She spoke only when necessary. She touched everything gently, as if she had never known texture before.

The night of the Competition, she waited calmly in the wings. The challengers stared at her, or tried not to. She smelled their sweat. One of them, a young woman with pale lion-gold hair, was very good. Strad smiled encouragingly at her when she came offstage, and the young woman smiled back with all the joy of accomplishment, and then blushed desperately.

The Assistant Stage Manager came to her. "Five minutes, please, Stradivarius," he said, and gave her a little bow and smile that meant *good luck*. She rose and walked to the place that she would enter from. Through the gap in the curtains, she could see the Judges frowning over their evaluations of the challengers, the audience shifting in their seats.

She waited. The violin and bow hung loosely from her relaxed right hand. She thought of all the entrances, all the stages, all her years of Stradivarius. Her arm began to tingle, like the pinprick feeling of warm blood rushing under cold skin. All her years of Stradivarius. All the music that she had played, always with the correct amount of passion and control. All the music that she had been in those moments suddenly swelled in her; she heard every note, felt every beat, tasted every breath that had ever taken her through a complicated phrase. She felt dizzy. A pulse pounded in her stomach. Her hand, and the violin, began to tremble.

The ASM cued her entrance.

She took the stage, head shaking. The audience shifted and rumbled. She found her place in the hot light, and when she breathed, the audience breathed with her. The Judges nodded. She lifted the violin. It felt warm against her neck. One of the Judges asked, "Are you ready?", and she smiled. "Yes," she said, and white heat shot through her; "yes," she said again, and felt a hum inside her like a cricketsong in her bones; and *yes*, she thought, and the door that had been shut so tight within her burst open, and the music battered through, spinning inside every part of her like a dervish, like a whirlwind, like a storm on the ocean that took the tidewater out and spit it back in giant surges. The music in her exulted and laughed and wept and reached out, farther, farther, until she wondered why everyone in the room did not stop, look, point, dance, run. It poured out sweet and strong through her heart and head and hands into the wood and gut of the violin that was her second voice, and her song was *yes* and *yes* and *yes* in a shout and a whisper and a pure, high cry. She played. She saw Monitors stumbling down the aisles and out from backstage, slowly at first and then fast, faster, toward her with outstretched hands and outraged eyes. She saw men and women in the audience rise to their feet, mouths and eyes and ears open, and *they hear*, she thought as the Monitors brought her down, *they hear* as her violin hit the floor and snapped in two with a wail, *they hear* as her arms were pinned behind her, *they hear*, and she smiled. Her hands were empty. She was full of music.

SUPERMAN'S DIARY

B. Brandon Barker

B. Brandon Barker was born in Cambridge, England, and raised in Little Rock, Arkansas. He recently graduated from Sarah Lawrence College, and now lives in Texas.

"Superman's Diary" is a wonderful, offbeat piece—and Barker's first published work of fiction. It comes from the Spring issue of *Global City Review*, a small journal of fiction and nonfiction, edited by Linsey Abrams and E. M. Broner and published in New York City.

—T. W.

TUESDAY (FIRST ENTRY)

I have paper and pen before me, but I am unable to decide how to begin this journal, or how to inform you of the changes I have recently made in my life. I am, as you probably know, a surviving member of a broken home. My father was a powerful political figure in my hometown, and our relationship was as contrived and regulated as one of his press conferences. We rarely spoke. We rarely laughed. Oh, what am I saying? I was only a year old when we parted. Maybe I should reconsider this diary thing. After our planet exploded, I wound up on Earth, as you know.

Notice how I've been using the phrase, "as you know," frequently. Do you know? Have you heard of me, my dear diary? Have you read the comic books, watched the television shows, or, God forbid, seen any of the films? I know you haven't, and I can trust the foundation of our relationship that you are paper, blank, yellow paper, and your history is the same. You are for me an idea right now; I am not positive who you are yet, but that is the purpose of this. Soon, I hope, we together will discover our selves by filling in the blank spots with formidable truths, and overcome the great misunderstandings around which this world careens.

To begin, I'll describe my new setting. I live now in an apartment on the upper East Side, and in an apartment off Broadway and Fifty-Seventh Street. Why do I have two apartments in Metropolis? This is where the troubles begin. In October of last year, while I was living in my ice palace at the tip of the Northern Territory (and also in Clark's apartment off Broadway during the week), I received a letter from Canadian environmentalists pointing out the potential danger present in the use of my energy source. They had no record in their files of the green generating metal I was using to keep the place up, so they quickly passed an ordinance to have it shut down. I did not protest, on the advice of my lawyer. (Superman doesn't need bad publicity.) So I found an apartment on the upper East Side, a very nice Metropolis neighborhood, and I began to set the place up like home. But what should Superman have in his apartment? To be honest, I was not quite sure. Reporters would drop by occasionally for interviews and comments, and I did not know how they would expect a superhero to decorate. I did not, for any reason, want to threaten my job. So, I went to the Sharper Image and bought a few of those glass balls with lightning inside, and some laser/art things you shine against the ceiling. I thought they helped create a kind of mysterious, outerspaceish atmosphere. And I got a set of nice weights, though I'd never need to use them.

I think it might be helpful now to note that I receive two sources of income. One source is the measly reporter's pay Clark Kent receives from the Daily Planet. The other is a yearly grant I received from the U.S. Government. It is a very nice sum, and I'm proud to receive it, though my lawyer told me it's because they're scared I'm going to move to Japan. Sometimes I wonder why I keep the job at the Planet, and why I continue to masquerade as Clark Kent. My lawyer doesn't know of my identity, Lois doesn't know, so why is it so hard for me to let go of this guy, this nerd, this underachiever? I'm looking for something in life now, a connection to the opposite side of myself. I think this diary is one of the ways I'm trying to reach Clark.

Another new event in my life, other than the housing switch, has been the governmental updating of my responsibilities on earth. One of the conditions of my salary is the promise to obey the "truth, justice, and American way" clause that has recently been adopted by Congress. An ordinance was passed limiting my flying time and public aerial appearances to twice a week, in order to keep havoc from overcoming the people of Metropolis, who seem to stop *everything* they're doing when they see me. It seems that traffic jams and general shifts of public attention hurt business and industry production. As I didn't argue with the environmentalists, I yielded to this measure. Furthermore, *my* benefits from this edict protect me from being hassled by big business here and abroad for product endorsements.

While we're on that note, I'd like to get a few things off my chest. There are many myths about me. I do not leap tall buildings in a single bound: it usually takes me at least three bounds, and lately I've been resting halfway on the flagpoles. I am faster than a speeding bullet, this is true, but not one that's been shot already. If you time a bullet, we might be even, or I might be a little faster, but I won't chase a bullet. I can't bring myself to be so silly. Also, I do not always wear my Superman suit under my business suit. I did that in the beginning, I guess, for the attention. I liked the colors and the "S," but I eventually grew tired of it, especially after people began to expect me to wear it; they couldn't stand seeing a guy fly around in a turtle neck and slacks. And there was the obvious risk that Clark Kent's identity might be revealed. It was this silent restriction placed on me that made me feel even more distant from him. He was supposed to wear a suit, and I was supposed to wear the cape and blue tights; to fly around in a suit that

Clark would wear might give it away. But then again, I am Clark also, I suppose. It is all too complicated a situation. It makes me wonder if Clark has a place in this world.

THURSDAY (SECOND ENTRY)

I have just begun lunch hour here at the Daily Planet, after having worked for three hours on an article about a puppet maker who has a shop next to the construction site of a new skyscraper. The puppet and doll-making community is backing him in his fierce struggle to hold onto his property. It's not a very intriguing story, and it makes me wonder about my credibility at this newspaper. Is there not a more challenging story to report on? Lois is in the middle of an investigation on the Mayor of Metropolis and two legislators, who have been illegally selling city property to Peruvian drug traffickers. She told me that last night, during a stakeout in a tree above the mayor's home in the suburbs, she set off his grounds alarm while taking snapshots of a secret meeting with Wolfgang "the Wolfman" Hirschberg, an undercover Nazi who's been doing deals for the Peruvians. She said the German shepherds came *this* close to biting off her heel when she jumped through the back seat window of Jimmy Olson's car as he sped away.

If only I could get a break here. I get the impression that they don't think I could handle a challenging assignment. And it makes me wonder if I've overdone the Clark Kent act. Have I been so concerned about my superhero identity that I have lowered my standards of regular life? But then again, what is my real identity? I sometimes feel more like Clark. I feel very secure in his clothes. He is calm, courteous, unassuming. He doesn't notice the rudeness of the busy people around him, but introverts his scope to work out his own faults. I enjoy being as him. We spend most of our time together, of course. Sometimes, when I'm walking down the street, I just want to take him flying. I don't care about saving anyone, or being a world-wide hero, I only want to throw off my shoes, fly to the sky and show him the most beautiful view of the earth. But these thoughts make me feel selfish and think about the people, the kids who look up to me, and I realize they don't want to see a stiff nerd flying in a brown suit with his tie flapping in the air like a dog's parched tongue. They want to see the hero, they want what they expect.

You might wonder why I separate my two selves so sharply. I do it for authenticity, and for my own sound mind. If I ever let Clark and Superman eat the same food, watch the same television, or use the same brand of deodorant routinely, I would get myself mixed up, off schedule. I have this paranoia that some day I'm going to walk into the office with a cape around my neck instead of a tie. They need, I need, separation. Inconvenience is not a sacrifice when the nation's security is an issue. Ahh, there I go again with the PR talk. Whoever said that heroes have to speak such jargon?

THURSDAY EVENING (THIRD ENTRY)

Lois came home with me, Superman, and we ordered Chinese food. She talked less with me about her investigation than she did with Clark. And I got the feeling that she was happy to be with me, reverent of me, and considered me to hardly be interested in the petty office jaw exercises she wastes on Clark. Instead of thinking too much about this, I enjoyed myself, as I always do when I'm Superman. We danced a little to Abba, Superman's favorite pop group, kissed a little, removed each other's clothing, Lois admired the glass ball of purple lightning shortly, and we then had sex on the ceiling—her constant, irrational, erotic devotion.

Afterwards, we lifted weights and played a few hands of cards. I wonder why Lois enjoys competing with me so much. I can't remember a time when we finished having sex and had a nice talk. We always finish with an arm wrestle and then a game of gin. And if she doesn't win the first few games, we end up playing all night. I *would* try to lose purposely, but I have the strange feeling that she would lose interest if there weren't so much competition. It's pathetic when we're lifting weights. I don't even want to describe it. However, we have our romantic times. I love comforting her. I love loving her. And I'm ashamed of my jealousies. When I fear she has other men in mind, I feel the need to keep an eye on her, but I don't, because if she really is seeing another man I don't want to know about it. The one thing I do wish about her, though, is that she would respect Clark a little more. It isn't fair that Clark gets the raw end of the deal. He plays the average man, the idiot, and Superman gets to make love to Lois above his halogen lamps.

Lois left about ten minutes ago. She said she had a marvelous time, and would love to spend the night, but has to catch a plane early in the morning to Oregon, where another one of those tankers has sprung a leak. But, as Lois informed me, the press has turned over a new page: As this thing gushed out oil, and the dumbfounded Coast Guard watched, the crude coated bodies of Afghan rebels began to spurt out of the ship's belly. She said it might be the espionage cover-up of the century. And obviously, she'd get the assignment. Definitely not Clark.

I kissed her goodbye, and she looked deep into my eyes and said she loved me, loved me more than any other man in the world. She called me the best man in the world, and said there was not another like me. For all my strength, diary, and all my acrobatics, I cannot summon the will from my soul to feel secure with her.

FRIDAY MORNING (FOURTH ENTRY)

What I have to tell you is the most confusing choice, the most capricious pinch I've ever come across. This morning, as I was typing away and sipping Lemon Tea, Clark's drink, I look up and see Lois standing in the doorway of my office. She was supposed to be on a plane! The questions that flooded my head lifted my insecurities to the surface, making them seem so plenty and out of control. But I held my tongue, held back my sweat, because I was not supposed to know about the trip. I had to remind myself that, when she told Superman about her trip to Oregon, Clark was in bed with the Tonight Show glowing before him as he nodded his head to sleep. I could only hope for a subtle explanation for her change of plans.

She sat down in a chair by the door and crossed her legs. She was wearing purple pantyhose, very out of character for her, and she had a nice dose of perfume on her beautiful neck. She looked scintillating, potently floral, florally potent, and had an unusual look in her eye. The way she looked at Clark made me feel awkward, inexperienced. Who knows how long it's been for Clark? She asked me how I was, and I said fine as I made myself clumsily knock a stack of papers off my desk. She didn't respond to this blunder. Her eyes remained in a frozen, enlivened gaze I had never experienced before. I began to get a sick feeling in my stomach.

She reached into a portfolio she was carrying to pull out an envelope, and I noticed another oddity: her nails were painted. She asked me what I was doing this weekend and I said that I might do a report on the Little League World Series, or possibly come into the office to help them lay out the classifieds. She smiled and her eyes penetrated Clark's thick lenses, despite the numerous times I pushed them up higher on my nose. My gut sunk lower and lower. I had no idea of what would become of this conversation, but I still felt like the turnout would change the way things were, the way I'd been living. There was the definite mix of malice, sex, and curiosity brewing in her eyes as she pulled out the contents of the envelope before me.

And then the full shock was finally delivered, diary. She approached my desk and touched my chin softly. Two plane tickets in her hand made my gut drop as far as it could, thudding rock bottom with the offer to accompany her to the Bahamas for the weekend. I was completely speechless. I thought of the nice things she had told Superman, and our love, our special moments, I didn't know what to think, or what to say. It was an absolutely unbelievable situation. I rose quickly, scanning my mind for a desperate act of clumsiness I could pull, something to remind her, to remind myself even, that she *was* speaking to Clark Kent. I told her I'd think about it and I ran out to the bathroom to brood in front of the mirror; a little reality, a little relief.

FRIDAY EVENING (FIFTH ENTRY)

Harbor Island, Bahamas, is a very bright place. The sun has plenty of water and sand to reflect its rays. The people are always smiling and saying "hello." There are many bicycles, few motor vehicles, and the days seem to be unhinged from time. Why do I have such a difficult time enjoying it? I told myself, when I decided to accompany Lois here on this excursion, paid for by the newspaper (Lois gets all the perks), that I would do this for Clark. The man never gets asked to move out of the way, much less on a date, and I consider this to be my fault because I play him to be such a boring fool. To refuse Clark a sunny vacation with a beautiful woman, one whom he has an office crush on, would be a cruelty. Believe me, I was a bit flattered at the offer once I cooled down and got my cards in place. I thought Lois didn't notice Clark for a hanging plant. I thought the only thing that could attract her attention was a superman, and she turns around and shows interest in me. It's confusing; believe me, I understand. But just hold on, and try not to think about it. I'm trying not to, because i know that if I do try to over-think this situation, I'll find something to be angry about.

(When I'm flying I feel the same way. I'm in control of myself when I'm up there, soaring over skyscrapers far above the maze of busy people. When I'm caught in this moment, I feel so free and high that an embarrassing realization comes that I cannot stay there forever; that I have to eventually return to my prudent, all-American image, the hero's instinctual respect for every meager thing around him. I realize that there is no solid floor below me, and I look up to the infinite sky from where I came, and I feel like I'm falling helplessly back down . . . What a nice pack of selfish thoughts I have! It is the unmistakable indicator of the hero's undoing.)

So, here I am, on Harbor Island, staying in a nice bungalow that looks out over the water. We arrived about an hour ago, and I'm sitting here on the porch in a woven hanging chair, looking out at the rich, blue line of horizon, where the sun is setting. There are some beautifully colored birds perched in the trees around me, and they are sharing the view. The surf is sloshing against the rocks below, creating the only audible sound. The breeze is like soft linen or silk rubbing up against my toes. And here I am, Clark Kent from Smallville, right in the middle of it.

While we were unpacking, she stopped a few times to look at me. It wasn't the kind of look I was expecting, that's for sure. I had been expecting, at any moment, for her to start biting her nails, pacing, burning in the realization that she was doing something deceptive. But that look did not surface, or has not yet. It was a look of supreme satisfaction, a look of success, and pride. And though this look was in her favor, it didn't give me the feeling she could see through me (wouldn't *that* be a switch!). She looked happy and complete. Yes, complete! And wouldn't it make sense? All the competition with Superman, all the acrobatics, the Sharper Image lightning balls? In Clark she finds someone normal, someone down-to-earth, someone *she* can fly around the world.

At the moment, Lois is in town buying fishing equipment because she wants to eat fresh Marlin tomorrow night on the outdoor grill. On the plane ride over, she read a book on how to filet it, which also told where to catch the best ones around Harbor Island. She said she might also snoop around the docks and find out from the fishermen what's the best bait to use. I might withdraw my participation, but I have the feeling she'll want me to drive the boat while she reels the things in. She's also spoken of dancing tonight. Does Clark know how to dance well? Has he ever been dancing before? Oh, Hell. Should I keep playing the role while we're down here? I really don't want to. Clark deserves a fine time, a flawless vacation. No drink spills at the bar, no pulling the push door, or wandering into the kitchen looking for the men's room. I don't want Lois to think I'm always pitiful and silly. I don't want her to regret asking me down here. See, there I go, already trying to ruin the vacation. If I ever acted like Clark before in my whole life, I am acting like him now.

I hear Lois driving here about a mile away. She's listening to the segment of the Nixon tapes that comes right before, and after, the "eighteen and a half-minute gap." In her free time, for about six years now, she has been trying to "crack the code." Until later . . .

SUNDAY AFTERNOON (SIXTH ENTRY)

Whether or not I feign clumsiness, Clark simply doesn't know how to drive a boat. I pulled us out of harbor fine. I got us on a steady roll out to where Lois wanted to fish. I made sure we had plenty of gas, and I did my best to listen to the man explain how to anchor. But the fishing trip was a personal failure. I stalled the boat every time Lois got a bite and needed to pull it, and she consequently lost every Marlin opportunity except the last one she caught with a net and a flare gun. I felt so useless when we got off the boat back at the harbor; all of the equipment she bought, and the reading she did. I'm sure I just about ruined her vacation. But, of course, again, I am overreacting. She laughed at my clumsiness, and made me feel like my problems were as unimportant as her simple chuckle. She said that she felt silly for even thinking she could catch a Marlin, and for me to laugh with her and enjoy the breeze. And she was very right about that breeze.

But despite her easy nature, nothing burned me up more than the fact that I could have ripped off the dumb tee-shirt I had on, flown out to the water, swiped up the biggest fish I saw, and brought it to her faithfully, making up for my ineptness. What a triumphant scene that would have made! Lois would have seen me rising up from my stupid blunders to super heights. However, it would have ruined the vacation, because Lois would realize that we, Clark and Superman, are one, and something, though I'm not exactly quite sure what, would be ruined between us. Remember, this *is* Clark's vacation, not Superman's. No super-stuff. If Lois invited Clark, she must have expected his clumsiness. It's possible she even likes it.

(It's times like these when I wonder whether the ability to perform these wonderful stunts and the knowledge that I have the ability to make everything right for me—that uplifting moment when I am on the verge of super feats—is much better than the actual performance of those feats. It's very hard for me to hold myself back in these situations unless I tell myself that knowing I'm the best is better than showing it off for everyone. By acting on every impulse I feel I have to execute, I am making what is a reality for me, one for everyone else, which is not something I feel like sharing all the time. I used to console myself by saying that I should be happy about my abilities, that being a normal man wouldn't make me happy. But the fact that I can be a normal man also, and that the normal man inside me has the ability to hold back the superman, is a special gift that I'm appreciating more as every day goes by.)

So, later that afternoon, we cooked the fish out on the grill. Lois had already prepared the sauce, and, except for the grilling and some fresh coconut that was imperative to the recipe, which she retrieved by climbing a tree in the front of our bungalow, we were ready. We ate the fish as the sun went down, lit a few candles. I mentioned something about the office and she shushed me, came to me and kissed me. She was sitting on my lap and holding me close when I realized that the moment of truth, the supreme turning point of the vacation was upon us. This moment sealed the evidence that she was formally, definitely, and without question cheating on Superman. Between you and me, diary, Clark never felt better in his whole life. It came to me while we were moving ourselves, undressing, toward the small grassy lawn by our back porch view, that Clark was finally getting his deserved respect, and that it was being recognized by a woman that could spend the night with Superman anytime she wanted. What a wonderful distinction.

Of course, afterwards I expected something like a game of cards, maybe thumb wrestling, something that Lois would be likely to do after sex. But we did not play any games of competition. In fact, I got to do something I've never done before: listen to Lois talk about things. . . . Things! When I'm with her she either talks about her job, her assignments, all of the great people she meets and interviews, or she arm wrestles me and matches me weight for weight on the barbell until she faints. It was such a wonderful experience to just talk with her about simple, incidental things. It's hard to explain these things because they're so simple. They're things that just come naturally in a conversation. Like, "those leaves look pretty," or "I like the shape of your nose." We spent about forty-five minutes saying these things to each other, and it was hardly boring. There were no worries in the words, no concerns, no time. Just the relaxed fluidity of contentment. It was the best talk Superman or Clark has had with anyone.

Around ten we got dressed and drove into the town where we found a Calypso bar already beginning to swing. The place had a huge exotic bird roost behind the bar with an open roof above. Sitting at the bar, you have the exquisite choice of watching the people dance, or the colorful birds landing and taking off from their moon-lit hovel of palm and greenery. I preferred to watch the dancers, for personal reasons (I did not want to think about the act of flying), and soon, to my surprise, Lois was dragging me out to dance.

The music flowed from a group of young men in loose, linen shirts with ruffly cuffs that convulsed like the wavy stems of a coral flower when they shook maracas. There was a vigorous accordion swaying and plenty of horns to keep the melody rippling over the floor. I was enjoying it so much. Lois was smiling. We were both very happy. And thoughts began to enter my mind about the time we'd spent so far on the islands. And I was led to the inevitable conclusion that my love for Lois could no longer be suppressed. This was quite a daring thing for Clark to be thinking—himself . . . up against Superman, faster than a speeding bullet. But did it ever occur to you that she might enjoy the company of Clark more? Maybe he is simply a better mate, a healthier relationship? Lois was so relaxed dancing with me, being my partner, keeping in time with me. We were sharing each other, holding each of our personalities down to earth, level to each other in order to be together.

I have to admit, I was beaming in love, soaring through the clouds in my own individual way, and full of life and truth. I decided at that moment, not twenty minutes into our dancing, that I was no longer going to wear the cape, that Superman was going to have to yield forever to Clark Kent, the man who really did not live until this day; who deserves to live on, loving this woman and respecting himself at his work. I discovered a side of me that really needed me, and all my attention. To hell with all the ordinances, the lawyers, the kids that look up to me—I was not sent from outer-space for them. It was for you, Clark, and all the men around the world like you, that I write to now.

ISOBEL AVENS RETURNS TO STEPNEY IN THE SPRING

M. John Harrison

M. John Harrison's writing career began during his seven-year stint as literary editor on *New Worlds* magazine, when he published his first novel, *The Committed Men*. Since then he has published six novels, three collections, and a graphic novel, the latter in collaboration with artist Ian Miller. In 1989 he won Great Britain's Tasker Memorial Award for his mainstream novel, *Climbers*, the first work of fiction ever to do so. His most recent novel is *The Course of the Heart*.

His writing has been a major influence on some of the newer British writers (including Nicholas Royle and Michael Marshall Smith, both in this book) and he continues to write complex stories that hover just at the edge of fantasy, just at the edge of horror. "Isobel Avens Returns to Stepney in the Spring" was originally published in the British edition of *Little Deaths*. Harrison's work has appeared in our first, second, and sixth annual collections.

—E. D.

The third of September this year I spent the evening watching TV in an upstairs flat in North London. Some story of love and transfiguration, cropped into all the wrong proportions for the small screen. The flat wasn't mine. It belonged to a friend I was staying with. There were French posters on the walls, dusty CDs stacked on the old-fashioned sideboard, piles of newspapers subsiding day by day into yellowing fans on the carpet. Outside, Tottenham stretched away, Greek driving schools, Turkish social clubs. Turn the TV off and you could hear nothing. Turn it back on and the film unrolled, passages of guilt with lost edges, photographed in white and blue light. At about half past eleven the phone rang. I picked it up. "Hello?"

It was Isobel Avens.

"Oh, China," she said. She burst into tears.

I said: "Can you drive?"

"No," she said.

I looked at my watch. "I'll come and fetch you."

"You can't," she said. "I'm here. You can't come here."

I said: "Be outside, love. Just try and get yourself downstairs. Be outside and I'll pick you up on the pavement there."

There was a silence.

"Can you do that?"

"Yes," she said.

Oh, China. The first two days she wouldn't get much further than that.

"Don't try to talk," I advised.

London was as quiet as a nursing home corridor. I turned up the car stereo. Tom Waits, *Downtown Train*. Music stuffed with sentiments you recognize but daren't admit to yourself. I let the BMW slip down Green Lanes, through Camden into the center; then west. I was pushing the odd traffic light at orange, clipping the apex off a safe bend here and there. I told myself I wasn't going to get killed for her. What I meant was that if I did she would have no one left. I took the Embankment at eight thousand revs in fifth gear, nosing down heavily on the brakes at Chelsea Wharf to get round into Gunter Grove. No one was there to see. By half past twelve I was on Queensborough Road, where I found her standing very straight in the mercury light outside Alexander's building, the jacket of a Karl Lagerfeld suit thrown across her shoulders and one piece of expensive leather luggage at her feet. She bent into the car. Her face was white and exhausted and her breath stank. The way Alexander had dumped her was as cruel as everything else he did. She had flown back steerage from the Miami clinic reeling from jet lag, expecting to fall into his arms and be loved and comforted. He told her, "As a doctor I don't think I can do any more for you." The ground hadn't just shifted on her: it was out from under her feet. Suddenly she was only his patient again. In the metallic glare of the street lamps, I noticed a stipple of ulceration across her collarbones. I switched on the courtesy light to look closer. Tiny hectic sores, closely spaced.

I said: "Christ, Isobel."

"It's just a virus," she said. "Just a side effect."

"Is anything worth this?"

She put her arms around me and sobbed.

"Oh, China, China."

It isn't that she wants me; only that she has no one else. Yet every time I smell her body my heart lurches. The years I lived with her I *slept* so soundly. Then Alexander did this irreversible thing to her, the thing she had always wanted, and now everything is fucked up and eerie and it will be that way forever.

I said: "I'll take you home."

"Will you stay?"

"What else?"

My name is Mick Rose, which is why people have always called me "China." From the moment we met, Isobel Avens was fascinated by that. Later, she would hold my face between her hands in the night and whisper dreamily over and over—"Oh, China, China, China, China." But it was something else that attracted her to me. The year we met, she lived in Stratford-on-Avon. I walked into the café at the little toy aerodrome they have there and it was she who served me. She was twenty-five years old: slow, heavy-bodied, easily delighted by the world. Her hair was red. She wore a rusty pink blouse, a black ankle-length skirt with lace at the hem. Her feet were like boats in great brown Dr. Marten's shoes. When she saw me looking down at them in amusement, she said: "Oh, these aren't my real Docs, these are my cheap imitation ones." She showed me how the left one was coming apart at the seams. "Brilliant, eh?" She smelled of vanilla and sex. She radiated heat. I could always feel the heat of her a yard away.

"I'd love to be able to fly," she told me.

She laughed and hugged herself.

"You must feel so free."

She thought I was the pilot of the little private Cessna she could see out of the café window. In fact I had only come to deliver its cargo—an unadmitted load for an unadmitted destination—some commercial research center in Zurich or Budapest. At the time I called myself Rose Medical Services, Plc. My fleet comprised a single Vauxhall Astra van into which I had dropped the engine, brakes, and suspension of a two-liter GTE insurance write-off. I specialized. If it was small, I guaranteed to move it anywhere in Britain within twelve hours; occasionally, if the price was right, to selected points in Europe. Recombinant DNA: viruses at controlled temperatures, sometimes in live hosts: cell cultures in heavily armored flasks. What they were used for I had no idea. I didn't really want an idea until much later; and that turned out to be much too late.

I said: "It can't be so hard to learn."

"Flying?"

"It can't be so hard."

Before a week was out we were inventing one another hand over fist. It was an extraordinary summer. You have to imagine this—

Saturday afternoon. Stratford Waterside. The river has a lively look despite the breathless air and heated sky above it. Waterside is full of jugglers and fire-eaters, entertaining thick crowds of Americans and Japanese. There is hardly room to move. Despite this, on a patch of grass by the water, two lovers, trapped in the great circular argument, are making that futile attempt all lovers make to get inside one another and stay there for good. He can't stop touching her because she wants him so. She wants him so because he can't stop touching her. A feeding swan surfaces, caught up with some strands of very pale green weed. Rippling in the sudden warm breeze which blows across the river from the direction of the theater, these seem for a moment like ribbons tied with a delicate knot—the gentle, deliberate artifice of a conscious world.

"Oh, look! Look!" she says.

He says: "Would you like to be a swan?"

"I'd have to leave the aerodrome."

He says: "Come and live with me and be a swan."

Neither of them has the slightest idea what they are talking about.

Business was good. Within three months I had bought a second van. I persuaded Isobel Avens to leave Stratford and throw in with me. On the morning of her last day at the aerodrome, she woke up early and shook me until I was awake, too.

"China!" she said.

"What?"

"China!"

I said: "What?"

"I flew!"

It was a dream of praxis. It was a hint of what she might have. It was her first step on the escalator up to Alexander's clinic.

"I was in a huge computer room. Everyone's work was displayed on one screen like a wall. I couldn't find my A-prompt!" People laughed at her, but nicely. "It was all good fun, and they were very helpful." Suddenly she had learned what she had to know, and she was floating up and flying into the screen, and through it, "out of the room, into the air above the world." The sky was crowded with other people, she said. "But I just went swooping past and around and between them." She let herself fall just for the fun of it: she soared, her whole body taut and trembling like the fabric of a kite. Her breath went out with a great laugh. Whenever she was tired, she could perch like a bird. "I loved it!" she told me. "Oh, I loved it!"

How can you be so jealous of a dream?

I said: "It sounds as if you won't need me soon."

She clutched at me.

"You help me to fly," she said. "Don't dare go away, China! Don't dare!"

She pulled my face close to hers and gave me little dabbing kisses on the mouth and eyes. I looked at my watch. Half past six. The bed was already damp and hot: I could see that we were going to make it worse. She pulled me on top of her, and at the height of things, sweating and inturned and breathless and on the edge, she whispered, "Oh, lovely, lovely, lovely," as if she had seen something I couldn't. "So lovely, so beautiful!" Her eyes moved as if she was watching something pass. I could only watch her, moving under me, marvelous and wet, solid and real, everything I ever wanted.

The worst thing you can do at the beginning of something fragile is to say what it is. The night I drove her back from Queensborough Road to her little house in the gentrified East End, things were very simple. For forty-eight hours all she would do was wail and sob and throw up on me. She refused to eat, she couldn't bear to sleep. If she dropped off for ten minutes, she would wake silent for the instant it took her to remember what had happened. Then this appalling dull asthmatic noise would come out of her—"zhhh, zhhh, zhhh," somewhere between retching and whining—as she tried to suppress the memory, and wake me up, and sob, all at the same time.

I was always awake anyway.

"Hush now, it will get better. I know."

I knew because she had done the same thing to me.

"China, I'm so sorry."

"Hush. Don't be sorry. Get better."

"I'm so sorry to have made you feel like this."

I wiped her nose.

"Hush."

That part was easy. I could dress her ulcers and take care of what was coming out of them, relieve the other effects of what they had done to her in Miami, and watch for whatever else might happen. I could hold her in my arms all night and tell lies and believe I was only there for her.

But soon she asked me, "Will you live here again, China?"

"You know it's all I want," I said.

She warned: "I'm not promising anything."

"I don't want you to," I said. I said: "I just want you to need me for something."

That whole September we were as awkward as children. We didn't quite know what to say. We didn't quite know what to do with one another. We could see it would take time and patience. We shared the bed rather shyly, and showed one another quite ordinary things as gifts.

"Look!"

Sunshine fell across the breakfast table, onto lilies and pink napery. (I am not making this up.)

"Look!"

A gray cat nosed out of a doorway in London E3.

"Did you have a nice weekend?"

"It was a lovely weekend. Lovely."

"Look."

Canary Wharf, shining in the oblique evening light!

In our earliest days together, while she was still working at the aerodrome, I had watched with almost uncontainable delight as she moved about a room. I had stayed awake while she slept, so that I could prop myself up on one elbow and look at her and shiver with happiness. Now when I watched, it was with fear. For her. For both of us. She had come down off the tightrope for awhile. But things were still so precariously balanced. Her new body was all soft new colors in the bedside lamplight. She was thin now, and shaped quite differently: but as hot as ever, hot as a child with fever. When I fucked her she was like a bundle of hot wires. I was like a boy. I trembled and caught my breath when I felt with my fingertips the damp feathery lips of her cunt, but I was too aware of the dangers to be carried away. I didn't dare let her see how much this meant to me. Neither of us knew what to want of the other anymore. We had forgotten one another's rhythms. In addition she was remembering someone else's: it was Alexander who had constructed for me this bundle of hot, thin, hollow bones, wrapped round me in the night by desires and demands I didn't yet know how to fulfill. Before the Miami treatments she had loved me to watch her as she became aroused. Now she needed to hide, at least for a time. She would pull at my arms and shoulders, shy and desperate at the same time; then, as soon as I understood that she wanted to be fucked, push her face into the side of mine so I couldn't look at her. After awhile she would turn onto her side; encourage me to enter from behind; stare away into some distance implied by us, our failures, the dark room. I told myself I didn't care if she was thinking of him. Just so long as she had got this far, which was far enough to begin to be cured in her sex where he had wounded her as badly as anywhere else. I told myself I couldn't heal her there, only allow her to use me to heal herself.

At the start of something so fragile, the worst mistake you can make is to say what you hope. But inside your heart you can't help speaking, and by that speech you have already blown it.

* * *

After Isobel and I moved down to London from Stratford, business began to take up most of my time. Out of an instinctive caution, I dropped the word "medical" from the company description and called myself simply Rose Services. Rose Services soon became twenty quick vans, some low-cost storage space, and a licence to carry the products of new genetic research to and from Eastern Europe. If I was to take advantage of the expanding markets there, I decided, I would need an office.

"Let's go to Budapest," I said to Isobel.

She hugged my arm.

"Will there be ice on the Danube?" she said.

"There will."

There was.

"China, we came all the way to Hungary!"

She had never been out of Britain. She had never flown in an airplane. She was delighted even by the hotel. I had booked us into a place called the Palace, on Rakoczi Street. Like the city itself, the Palace had once been something: now it was a dump. Bare flex hung out of the light switches on the fourth-floor corridors. The wallpaper had charred in elegant spirals above the corners of the radiators. Every morning in the famous Jugendstil restaurant, they served us watery orange squash. The rooms were too hot. Everything else—coffee, food, water from the cold tap—was lukewarm. It was never quiet, even very late at night. Ambulances and police cars warbled past. Drunks screamed suddenly or made noises like animals. But our room had French windows opening onto a balcony with wrought-iron railings. From there in the freezing air, we could look across a sort of high courtyard with one or two flakes of snow falling into it, at the other balconies and their lighted windows. That first evening, Isobel loved it.

"China, isn't it fantastic? Isn't it?"

Then something happened to her in her sleep. I wouldn't have known, but I woke up unbearably hot at 3:00 A.M., sweating and dry-mouthed beneath the peculiar fawn-fur blanket they give you to sleep under at the Palace. The bathroom was even hotter than the bedroom and smelled faintly of very old piss. When I turned the tap on to splash my face, nothing came out of it. I stood there in the dark for a moment, swaying, while I waited for it to run. I heard Isobel say reasonably: "It's a system fault."

After a moment she said, "Oh no. Oh no," in such a quiet, sad voice that I went back to the bed and touched her gently.

"Isobel. Wake up."

She began to whimper and throw herself about.

"The system's down," she tried to explain to someone.

"Isobel. Isobel."

"The system!"

"Isobel."

She woke up and clutched at me. She pushed her face blindly into my chest. She trembled.

"China!"

It was February, a year or two after we had met. I didn't know it, but things were already going wrong for her. Her dreams had begun to waste her from the inside.

She said indistinctly: "I want to go back home."

"Isobel, it was only a dream."

"I couldn't fly," she said.

She stared up at me in astonishment.

"China, I couldn't *fly*."

At breakfast she hardly spoke. All morning she was thoughtful and withdrawn. But when I suggested that we walk down to the Danube via the Basilica at St. Stephen's, cross over to Buda and eat lunch, she seemed delighted. The air was cold and clear. The trees were distinct and photographic in the bright pale February light. We stared out across the New City from the Disney-white battlements of Fishermen's Bastion. "Those bridges!" Isobel said. "Look at them in the sun!" She had bought a new camera for the trip, a Pentax with a motor-wind and zoom. "I'm going to take a panorama." She eyed the distorted reflection of the Bastion in the mirror-glass windows of the Hilton hotel. "Stand over there, China, I want one of you, too. No, *there*, you idiot!" Snow began to fall, in flakes the size of five-forint pieces.

"China!"

For the rest of the day—for the rest of the holiday—she was as delighted by things as ever. We visited the zoo. ("Look! Owls!") We caught a train to Szentendre. We photographed one another beneath the huge winged woman at the top of the Gellert Hill. We translated the titles of the newsstand paperbacks.

"What does this mean, 'Nagy Secz'?"

"You know very well what it means, Isobel."

I looked at my watch.

I said: "It's time to eat."

"Oh no. Must we?"

Isobel hated Hungarian food.

"China," she would complain, "why has *everything* got *cream* on it?"

But she loved the red and grey buses. She loved the street signs, TOTO LOTTO, HIRLAP, TRAFIK. She loved Old Buda, redeemed by the snow: white, clean, properly picturesque.

And she couldn't get enough of the Danube.

"Look. China, it's fucking huge! Isn't it fucking huge?"

I said: "Look at the speed of it."

At midnight on our last day we stood in the exact center of the Erzsebet bridge, gazing north. Szentendre and Danube Bend were out there somewhere, locked in a Middle European night stretching all the way to Czechoslovakia. Ice floes like huge lily pads raced toward us in the dark. You could hear them turning and dipping under one another, piling up briefly round the huge piers, jostling across the whole vast breadth of the river as they rushed south. No river is ugly after dark. But the Danube doesn't care for anyone: without warning the Medieval cold came up off the water and reached onto the bridge for us. It was as if we had seen something move. We stepped back, straight into the traffic which grinds all night across the bridge from Buda into Pest.

"China!"

"Be careful!"

You have to imagine this—

Two naïve and happy middle-class people embracing on a bridge. Caught between the river and the road, they grin and shiver at one another, unable to distinguish between identity and geography, love and the need to keep warm.

"Look at the *speed* of it."

"Oh, China, the Danube!"

Suddenly she turned away.

She said: "I'm cold now."

She thought for a moment.

"I don't want to go on the airplane," she said. "They're not the real thing after all."

I took her hands between mine.

"It will be okay when you get home," I promised.

But London didn't seem to help. For months I woke in the night to find she was awake, too, staring emptily up at the ceiling in the darkness. Unable to comprehend her despair, I would consult my watch and ask her, "Do you want anything?" She would shake her head and advise patiently, "Go to sleep now, love," as if she was being kept awake by a bad period.

I bought the house in Stepney at about that time. It was in a prettily renovated terrace with reproduction Victorian street lamps. There were wrought-iron security grids over every other front door, and someone had planted the extensive shared gardens at the back with ilex, ornamental rowan, even a fig. Isobel loved it. She decorated the rooms herself, then filled them with the sound of her favorite music—The Blue Aeroplanes' *Yr Own World*; Tom Petty, *Learning to Fly*. For our bedroom she bought two big blanket chests and polished them to a deep buttery color. "Come and look, China! Aren't they beautiful?" Inside, they smelled of new wood. The whole house smelled of new wood for days after we moved in: beeswax, new wood, dried roses.

I said: "I want it to be yours."

It had to be in her name anyway, I admitted: for accounting purposes.

"But also in case anything happens."

She laughed.

"China, what could happen?"

What happened was that one of my local drivers went sick, and I asked her to deliver something for me.

I said: "It's not far. Just across to Brook Green. Some clinic."

I passed her the details.

"A Dr. Alexander. You could make it in an hour, there and back."

She stared at me.

"*You* could make it in an hour," she said.

She read the job sheet.

"What do they do there?" she asked.

I said irritably: "How would I know? Cosmetic medicine. Fantasy factory stuff. Does it matter?"

She put her arms round me.

"China, I was only trying to be interested."

"Never ask them what they do with the stuff," I warned her. "Will you do it?"
She said: "If you kiss me properly."
"How was it?" I asked when she got back.
She laughed.
"At first they thought I was a patient!"
Running upstairs to change, she called down:
"I quite like West London."

Isobel's new body delighted her. But she seemed bemused too, as if it had been given to someone else. How much had Alexander promised her? How much had she expected from the Miami treatments? All I knew was that she had flown out obsessed and returned ill. When she talked, she would talk only about the flight home. "I could see a sunrise over the wing of the airliner, red and gold. I was trying hard to read a book, but I couldn't stop looking out at this cold wintery sunrise above the clouds. It seemed to last for hours." She stared at me as if she had just thought of something. "How could I see a sunrise, China? It was dark when we landed!"

Her dreams had always drawn her away from ordinary things. All that gentle, warm September she was trying to get back.

"Do you like me again?" she would ask shyly.

It was hard for her to say what she meant. Standing in front of the mirror in the morning in the soft gray slanting light from the bedroom window, dazed and sidetracked by her own narcissism, she could only repeat: "Do you like me this way?"

Or at night in bed: "Is it good this way? Is it good? What does it feel like?"

"Isobel—"

In the end it was always easier to let her evade the issue.

"I never stopped liking you," I would lie, and she would reply absently, as if I hadn't spoken:

"Because I want us to like each other again."

And then add, presenting her back to the mirror and looking at herself over one shoulder:

"I wish I'd had more done. My legs are still too fat."

If part of her was still trying to fly back from Miami and all Miami entailed, much of the rest was in Brook Green with Alexander. As September died into October, and then the first few cold days of November, I found that increasingly hard to bear. She cried in the night, but no longer woke me up for comfort. Her gaze would come unfocused in the afternoons. Unable to be near her while, thinking of him, she pretended to leaf through *Vogue* and *Harper's*, I walked out into the rainy unredeemed Whitechapel streets. Suddenly it was an hour later and I was watching the lights come on in a hardware shop window on Roman Road.

Other times, when it seemed to be going well, I couldn't contain my delight. I got up in the night and thrashed the BMW to Sheffield and back; parked outside the house and slept an hour in the rear seat; crossed the river in the morning to queue for croissants at Ayre's Bakery in Peckham, playing *Empire Burlesque* so loud that if I touched the windscreen gently I could feel it tremble, much as she used to do, beneath my fingertips.

I was trying to get back, too.

"I'll take you to the theater," I said: "*Waiting for Godot*. Do you want to see the fireworks?" I said: "I brought you a present—."

A Monsoon dress. Two small stone birds for the garden; anemones; and a cheap Boots nailbrush shaped like a pig.

"Don't try to get so close, China," she said. "Please."

I said: "I just want to be something to you."

She touched my arm. She said: "China, it's too soon. We're here together, after all: isn't that enough for now?"

She said: "And anyway, how could you ever be anything else?"

She said: "I love you."

"But you're not in love with me."

"I told you I couldn't promise you that."

By Christmas we were shouting at one another again, late into the night, every night. I slept on the futon in the spare room. There I dreamed of Isobel and woke sweating.

You have to imagine this—

The Pavilion, quite a good Thai restaurant on Wardour Street. Isobel has just given me the most beautiful jacket, wrapped in birthday paper. She leans across the table. "French Connection, China. Very smart." The waitresses, who believe we are lovers, laugh delightedly as I try it on. But later, when I buy a red rose and offer it to Isobel, she says, "What use would I have for that?" in a voice of such contempt I begin to cry. In the dream, I am fifty years old that day. I wake thinking everything is finished.

Or this—

Budapest. Summer. Rakoczi Street. Each night Isobel waits for me to fall asleep before she leaves the hotel. Once outside, she walks restlessly up and down Rakoczi with all the other women. Beneath her beige linen suit she has on gray silk underwear. She cannot explain what is missing from her life, but will later write in a letter: "When sex fails for you—when it ceases to be central in your life—you enter middle age, a zone of the most unclear exits from which some of us never escape." I wake and follow her. All night it feels like dawn. Next morning, in the half-abandoned Jugendstil dining room, a paper doily drifts to the floor like a leaf, while Isobel whispers urgently in someone else's voice:

"*It was never what you thought it was.*"

Appalled by their directness, astonished to find myself so passive, I would struggle awake from dreams like this thinking: "What am I going to do? What am I going to do?" It was always early. It was always cold. Gray light silhouetted a vase of dried flowers on the dresser in front of the uncurtained window, but the room itself was still dark. I would look at my watch, turn over, and go back to sleep. One morning, in the week before Christmas, I got up and packed a bag instead. I made myself some coffee and drank it by the kitchen window, listening to the inbound city traffic build up half a mile away. When I switched the radio on it was playing Billy Joel's *She's Always a Woman*. I turned it off quickly, and at 8:00 woke Isobel. She smiled up at me.

"Hello," she said. "I'm sorry about last night."

I said: "I'm sick of it all. I can't do it. I thought I could but I can't."

"China, what is this?"

I said: "You were so fucking sure he'd have you. Three months later it was you crying, not me."

"China—"

"It's time you helped," I said.

I said: "I helped *you*. And when you bought me things out of gratitude I never once said 'What use would I have for that?' "

She rubbed her hands over her eyes.

"China, what are you talking about?"

I shouted: "What a fool you made of yourself!" Then I said: "I only want to be something to you again."

"I won't stand for this," Isobel whispered. "I can't stand this."

I said: "Neither can I. That's why I'm going."

"I still love him, China."

I was on my way to the door. I said: "You can have him then."

"China, I don't *want* you to go."

"Make up your mind."

"I won't say what you want me to."

"Fuck off, then."

"It's you who's fucking off, China."

It's easy to see now that when we stood on the Erzsebet Bridge the dream had already failed her. But at the time—and for some time afterward—I was still too close to her to see anything. It was still one long arc of delight for me, Stratford through Budapest, all the way to Stepney. So I could only watch puzzledly as she began to do pointless, increasingly spoiled things to herself. She caught the tube to Camden Lock and had her hair cut into the shape of a pigeon's wing. She had her ankles tattooed with feathers. She starved herself, as if her own body were holding her down. She was going to revenge herself on it. She lost twenty pounds in a month. Out went everything she owned, to be replaced by size 9 jeans, little black spandex skirts, expensively tailored jackets which hung from their own ludicrous shoulder pads like washing.

"You don't look like you anymore," I said.

"Good. I always hated myself anyway."

"I loved your bottom the way it was," I said.

She laughed.

"You'll look haggard if you lose anymore," I said.

"Piss off, China. I won't be a cow just so you can fuck a fat bottom."

I was hurt by that, so I said:

"You'll look old. Anyway, I didn't think we fucked. I thought we made love." Something caused me to add, "I'm losing you." And then, even less reasonably. "Or you're losing me."

"China, don't be such a baby."

Then one afternoon in August she walked into the lounge and said, "China, I want to talk to you." The second I heard this, I knew exactly what she was going to say. I looked away from her quickly and down into the book I was pretending to read, but it was too late. There was a kind of soft thud inside me. It was something broken. It was something not there anymore. I felt it. It was a door closing, and I wanted to be safely on the other side of it before she spoke.

"What?" I said.
She looked at me uncertainly.
"China, I—"
"What?"
"China, I haven't been happy. Not for some time. You must have realized. I've got a chance at an affair with someone and I want to take it."
I stared at her.
"Christ," I said. "Who?"
"Just someone I know."
"Who?" I said. And then, bitterly, "Who do you know, Isobel?" I meant: "Who do you know that isn't me?"
"It's only an affair," she said. And: "You must have realized I wasn't happy."
I said dully: "Who is this fucker?"
"It's David Alexander."
"*Who?*"
"David Alexander. For God's sake, China, you make everything so hard! At the clinic. David Alexander."
I had no idea who she was talking about. Then I remembered.
"Christ," I said. "He's just some fucking *customer.*"
She went out. I heard the bedroom door slam. I stared at the books on the bookshelves, the pictures on the walls, the carpet dusty gold in the pale afternoon light. I couldn't understand why it was all still there. I couldn't understand anything. Twenty minutes later, when Isobel came back in again carrying a soft leather overnight bag, I was standing in the same place, in the middle of the floor. She said: "Do you know what your trouble is, China?"
"What?" I said.
"People are always just some fucking this or that to you."
"Don't go."
She said: "He's going to help me to fly, China."
"*You always said I helped you to fly.*"
She looked away.
"It's not your fault it stopped working," she said. "It's me."
"Christ, you selfish bitch."
"He wants to help me to fly," she repeated dully.
And then: "China, I *am* selfish."
She tried to touch my hand but I moved it away.
"I can't fucking believe this," I said. "You want me to forgive you just because you can admit it?"
"I don't want to lose you, China."
I said: "You already have."
"We don't know what we might want," she said. "Later on. Either of us."
I remembered how we had been at the beginning: Stratford Waterside, whispers and moans, *You help me to fly, China.* "If you could hear yourself," I said. "If you could just fucking hear yourself, Isobel." She shrugged miserably and picked up her bag. I didn't see her after that. I did have one letter from her. It was sad without being conciliatory, and ended: "You were the most amazing person I ever knew, China, and the fastest driver."
I tore it up.

"Were!" I said. "Fucking *were*!"

By that time she had moved in with him, somewhere along the Network South East line from Waterloo: Chiswick, Kew, one of those old-fashioned suburbs on a bladder of land inflated into the picturesque curve of the river, with genteel deteriorating houseboats, an arts center, and a wine bar on every corner. West London is full of places like that—" shabby," "comfortable," until you smell the money. Isobel kept the Stepney house. I would visit it once a month to collect my things, cry in the lounge, and take away some single pointless item—a compact disc I had bought her, a picture she had bought me. Every time I went back, the bedroom, with its wooden chests and paper birds, seemed to have filled up further with dust. Despite that, I could never quite tell if anything had changed. Had they been in there, the two of them? I stayed in the doorway, so as not to know. I had sold Rose Services and was living out in Tottenham, drinking Michelob beer and watching Channel 4 movies while I waited for my capital to run out. Some movies I liked better than others. I cried all the way through *Alice in the Cities*. I wasn't sure why. But I knew why I was cheering Anthony Hopkins as *The Good Father*.

"You were the most amazing person I ever knew, China, and the fastest driver. I'll always remember you."

What did I care? Two days after I got the letter I drove over to Queensborough Road at about 7:00 in the evening. I had just bought the BMW. I parked it at the kerb outside Alexander's clinic, which was in a large postmodern block not far down from Hammersmith Gyratory. Some light rain was falling. I sat there watching the front entrance. After about twenty minutes Alexander's receptionist came out, put her umbrella up, and went off toward the tube station. A bit later Alexander himself appeared at the security gate. I was disappointed by him. He turned out to be a tall thin man, middle-aged, gray-haired, dressed in a light wool suit. He looked less like a doctor than a poet. He had that kind of fragile elegance some people maintain on the edge of panic, the energy of tensions unresolved, glassy, never very far from the surface. He would always seem worried. He looked along the street toward Shepherd's Bush, then down at his watch.

I opened the nearside passenger window.

"David Alexander?" I called.

I called: "Waiting for someone?"

He bent down puzzledly and looked into the BMW.

"Need a lift?" I offered.

"Do I know you?" he asked.

I thought: Say the wrong thing, you fucker. You're that close.

I said: "Not exactly."

"Then—"

"Forget it."

He stood back from the car suddenly, and I drove off.

Christmas. Central London. Traffic locked solid every late afternoon. Light in the shop windows in the rain. Light in the puddles. Light splashing up round your feet. I couldn't keep still. Once I'd walked away from Isobel, I couldn't stop walking. Everywhere I went, *She's Always a Woman* was on the radio. Harrods, Habitat, Hamleys: Billy Joel drove me out onto the wet pavement with another armful of children's toys. I even wrapped some of them—a wooden penguin with rubber feet, two packs of cards, a miniature jigsaw puzzle in the shape of her name. Every time I saw something I liked, it went home with me.

"I bought you a present," I imagined myself saying, "this fucking little spider that really jumps—

"Look!"

Quite suddenly I was exhausted. Christmas Day I spent with the things I'd bought. Boxing Day, and the day after that, I lay in a chair staring at the television. Between shows I picked up the phone and put it down again, picked it up and put it down. I was going to call Isobel, then I wasn't. I was going to call her, but I closed the connection carefully every time the phone began to ring at her end. Then I decided to go back to Stepney for my clothes.

Imagine this—

Two A.M. The house was quiet.

Or this—

I stood on the pavement. When I looked in through the uncurtained ground-floor window I could see the little display of lights on the front of Isobel's CD player.

Or this—

For a moment my key didn't seem to fit the door.

Imagine this—

Late at night you enter a house in which you've been as happy as anywhere in your life: probably happier. You go into the front room, where streetlight falls unevenly across the rugs, the furniture, the mantelpiece and mirrors. On the sofa are strewn a dozen colorful, expensive shirts, blue and red and gold like macaws and money. Two or three of them have been slipped out of their cellophane, carefully refolded and partly wrapped in Christmas paper. "Dear China—" say the tags. "Dearest China." There are signs of a struggle but not necessarily with someone else. A curious stale smell fills the room, and a chair has been knocked over. It's really too dark to see.

Switch on the lights. Glasses and bottles. Food trodden into the best kilim. Half-empty plates, two days old.

"Isobel? Isobel!"

The bathroom was damp with condensation, the bath itself full of cold water smelling strongly of rose oil. Wet towels were underfoot, there and in the draughty bedroom, where the light was already on and Isobel's pink velvet curtains, half-drawn, let a faint yellow triangle of light into the garden below. The lower sash was open. When I pulled it down, a cat looked up from the empty flowerbed: ran off. I shivered. Isobel had pulled all her favorite underclothes out onto the floor and trodden mascara into them. She had written in lipstick on the dressing table mirror, in perfect mirror writing: "Leave me alone."

I found her in one of the big blanket boxes.

When I opened the lid a strange smell—beeswax, dried roses, vomit, whiskey—filled the room. In there with her she had an empty bottle of Jameson's: an old safety razor of mine and two or three blades. She had slit her wrists. But first she had tried to shave all the downy, half-grown feathers from her upper arms and breasts. When I reached into the box they whirled up round us both, soft blue and gray, the palest rose-pink. Miami! In some confused attempt to placate me, she had tried to get out of the dream the way you get out of a coat.

She was still alive.

"China," she said. Sleepily, she held her arms up to me. She whispered: "China."

Alexander had made her look like a bird. But underneath the cosmetic trick she was still Isobel Avens. Whatever he had promised her, she could never have flown. I picked her up and carried her carefully down the stairs. Then I was crossing the pavement toward the BMW, throwing the nearside front door open and trying to get her into the passenger seat. Her arms and legs were everywhere, pivoting loose and awkward from the hips and elbows. "Christ, Isobel, you'll have to help!" I didn't panic until then.

"China," whispered Isobel.

Blood ran into my shirt where she had put her arms round my neck.

I slammed the door.

"China."

"What, love? What?"

"China."

She could talk but she couldn't hear.

"Hold on," I said. I switched on the radio. Some station I didn't know was playing the first few bars of a Joe Satriani track, *Always with You, Always with Me*. I felt as if I was outside myself. I thought: "Now's the time to drive, China, you fucker." The BMW seemed to fishtail out of the parking space of its own accord, into the empty arcade-game of Whitechapel. The city loomed up then fell back from us at odd angles, as if it had achieved the topological values of a Vorticist painting. I could hear the engine distantly, making a curious harsh overdriven whine as I held the revs up against the red line. Revs and brakes, revs and brakes: if you want to go fast in the city you hold it all the time between the engine and the brakes. Taxis, hoardings, white faces of pedestrians on traffic islands splashed with halogen pink, rushed up and were snatched away.

"Isobel?"

I had too much to do to look directly at her. I kept catching glimpses of her in weird, neon shop-light from Wallis or Next or What She Wants, lolling against the seat belt with her mouth half open. She knew how bad she was. She kept trying to smile across at me. Then she would drift off, or cornering forces would roll her head to one side as if she had no control of the muscles in her neck and she would end up staring and smiling out of the side window whispering: "China. China China China."

"Isobel."

She passed out again and didn't wake up.

"Shit, Isobel," I said.

We were on Hammersmith Gyratory, deep in the shadow of the flyover. It was twenty minutes since I had found her. We were nearly there. I could almost see the clinic.

I said: "Shit, Isobel, I've lost it."

The piers of the flyover loomed above us, stained gray concrete plastered with anarchist graffiti and torn posters. Free and ballistic, the car waltzed sideways toward them, glad to be out of China Rose's hands at last.

"Fuck," I said. "Fuck fuck fuck."

We touched the kerb, tripped over our own feet, and began a long slow roll, like an airliner banking to starboard. We hit a postbox. The BMW jumped in a startled way and righted itself. Its offside rear suspension had collapsed. Uncomfortable with the new layout, still trying to get away from me, it spun twice and banged itself repeatedly into the opposite curb with a sound exactly like some housewife's Metro running over the cat's-eyes on a cold Friday morning. Something snapped the window post on that side and broken glass blew in all over Isobel Avens' peaceful face. She opened her mouth. Thin vomit came out, the color of tea: but I don't think she was conscious. Hammersmith Broadway, ninety-five miles an hour. I dropped a gear, picked the car up between steering and accelerator, shot out into Queensborough Road on the wrong side of the road. The boot lid popped open and fell off. It was dragged along behind us for a moment, then it went backward quickly and disappeared.

"China."

Draped across my arms, Isobel was nothing but a lot of bones and heat. I carried her up the steps to Alexander's building and pressed for entry. The entry-phone crackled but no one spoke. "Hello?" I said. After a moment the locks went back.

Look into the atrium of a West London building at night and everything is the same as it is in the day. Only the reception staff are missing, and that makes less difference than you would think. The contract furniture keeps working. The PX keeps working. The fax comes alive suddenly as you watch, with a query from Zurich, Singapore, LA. The air conditioning keeps on working. Someone has watered the plants, and they keep working too, making chlorophyll from the overhead lights. Paper curls out of the fax and stops. You can watch for as long as you like: nothing else will happen and no one will come. The air will be cool and warm at the same time, and you will be able to see your own reflection, very faintly in the treated glass.

"China."

Upstairs it was a floor of open-plan offices—health finance—and then a floor of consulting rooms. Up here the lights were off, and you could no longer hear the light traffic on Queensborough Road. It was 2:50 in the morning. I got into the consulting rooms and then Alexander's office, and walked up and down with Isobel in my arms, calling:

"Alexander?"

No one came.

"Alexander?"

Someone had let us in.

"Alexander!"

Among the stuff on his desk was a brochure for the clinic. ". . . modern 'magic wand,' " I read. "Brand new proteins." I swept everything off onto the floor and tried to make Isobel comfortable by folding my coat under her head. "I'm sorry," she said quietly, but not to me. It was part of some conversation I couldn't hear. She kept rolling onto her side and retching over the edge of the desk, then laughing. I had picked up the phone and was working on an outside line when Alexander came in from the corridor. He had lost weight. He looked vague and empty, as if we had woken him out of a deep sleep. You can tear people like him apart like a piece of paper, but it doesn't change anything.

"Press 9," he advised me. "Then call an ambulance."

He glanced down at Isobel. He said: "It would have been better to take her straight to a hospital."

I put the phone down.

"I fucked up a perfectly good car to get here," I said.

He kept looking puzzledly at me and then out of the window at the BMW, half up on the pavement with smoke coming out of it.

I said: "That's a Hartge H27-24."

I said: "I could have afforded something in better taste, but I just haven't got any."

"I know you," he said. "You've done work for me."

I stared at him. He was right.

I had been moving things about for him since the old Astravan days; since before Stratford. And if I was just a contract to him, he was just some writing on a job sheet to me. He was the price of a Hartge BMW with racing suspension and 17-inch wheels.

"But you did this," I reminded him.

I got him by the back of the neck and made him look closely at Isobel. Then I pushed him against the wall and stood away from him. I told him evenly: "I'm fucking glad I didn't kill you when I wanted to." I said: "Put her back together."

He lifted his hands. "I can't," he said.

"Put her back together."

"This is only an office," he said. "She would have to go to Miami."

I pointed to the telephone. I said: "Arrange it. Get her there."

He examined her briefly.

"She was dying anyway," he said. "The immune system work alone would have killed her. We did far more than we would normally do on a client. Most of it was illegal. *It would be illegal to do most of it to a laboratory rat*. Didn't she tell you that?"

I said: "Get her there and put her back together again."

"I can make her human again," he offered. "I can cure her."

I said: "She didn't fucking want to be human."

"I know," he said.

He looked down at his desk; his hands. He whispered: " 'Help me to fly. Help me to fly!' "

"Fuck off," I said.

"I loved her, too, you know. But I couldn't make her understand that she could *never* have what she wanted. In the end she was just too demanding: effectively, she asked us to kill her."

I didn't want to know why he had let me have her back. I didn't want to compare inadequacies with him. I said: "I don't want to hear this."

He shrugged. "She'll die if we try it again," he said emptily. "You've got no idea how these things work."

"Put her back together."

You tell me what else I could have said.

* * *

Here at the Alexander Clinic, we use the modern "magic wand" of molecular biology to insert avian chromosomes into human skin-cells. Nurtured in the clinic's vats, the follicles of this new skin produce feathers instead of hair. It grafts beautifully. Brand new proteins speed acceptance. But in case of difficulties, we remake the immune system: aim it at infections of opportunity: fire it like a laser.

Our client chooses any kind of feather, from pinion to down, in any combination. She is as free to look at the sparrow as the bower bird or macaw. Feathers of any size or color! But the real triumph is elsewhere—

Designer hormones trigger the 'brown fat' mechanism. Our client becomes as light and as hot to the touch as a female hawk. Then metabolically induced calcium shortages hollow the bones. She can be handled only with great care. And the dreams of flight! Engineered endorphins released during sexual arousal simulate the sidesweep, swoop, and mad fall of mating flight, the frantically beating heart, long sight. Sometimes the touch of her own feathers will be enough.

I lived in a hotel on the beach while it was done. Miami! TV prophecy, humidity like a wet sheet, an airport where they won't rent you a baggage trolley. You wouldn't think this listening to Bob Seger. Unless you are constantly approaching it from the sea, Miami is less a dream—less even a nightmare—than a place. All I remember is what British people always remember about Florida: the light in the afternoon storm, the extraordinary size and perfection of the food in the supermarkets. I never went near the clinic, though I telephoned Alexander's team every morning and evening. I was too scared. One day they were optimistic, the next they weren't. In the end I knew they had got involved again, they were excited by the possibilities. She was going to have what she wanted. They were going to do the best they could for her, if only because of the technical challenge.

She slipped in and out of the world until the next spring. But she didn't die, and in the end I was able to bring her home to the blackened, gentle East End in May, driving all the way from Heathrow down the inside lane of the motorway, as slowly and carefully as I knew how in my new off-the-peg 850i. I had adjusted the driving mirror so I could look into the back of the car. Isobel lay awkwardly across one corner of the rear seat. Her hands and face seemed tiny. In the soft wet English light, their adjusted bone structures looked more rather than less human. Lapped in her singular successes and failures, the sum of her life to that point, she was more rested than I had ever seen her.

About a mile away from the house, outside Whitechapel tube station, I let the car drift up to the curb and stop. I switched the engine off and got out of the driving seat.

"It isn't far from here," I said.

I put the keys in her hand.

"I know you're tired," I said, "but I want you to drive yourself the rest of the way."

She said: "China, don't go. Get back in the car."

"It's not far from here," I said.

"China, please don't go."

"Drive yourself from now on."

If you're so clever, you tell me what else I could have done. All that time in Miami she had never let go, never once vacated the dream. The moment she closed her eyes, feathers were floating down past them. She knew what she wanted. Don't mistake me: I wanted her to have it. But imagining myself stretched out next to her on the bed night after night, I could hear the sound those feathers made, and I knew I would never sleep again for the touch of them on my face.

THE SISTERHOOD OF NIGHT

Steven Millhauser

Steven Millhauser, who teaches at Skidmore College, is the author of six wonderful works of mainstream and magical realist fiction, including *The Barnum Museum, Edwin Mullhouse,* and *Little Kingdoms.* His story "The Illusionist" was reprinted in *The Year's Best Fantasy & Horror: Third Annual Collection* and won the World Fantasy Award.

The following mysterious, extraordinary short piece comes from the July issue of *Harper's Magazine.*

—T. W.

WHAT WE KNOW

In an atmosphere of furious accusation and hysterical rumor, an atmosphere in which hearsay and gossip have so thoroughly replaced the careful assessment of evidence that impartiality itself seems of the devil's party, it may be useful to adopt a calmer tone and to state what it is that we actually know. We know that the girls are between twelve and fifteen years old. We know that they travel in bands of five or six, although smaller and larger bands, ranging from two to nine, have occasionally been sighted. We know that they leave and return only at night. We know that they seek dark and secret places, such as abandoned houses, church cellars, graveyards, and the woods at the north end of town. We know, or believe we know, that they have taken a vow of silence.

WHAT WE SAY

It is said that the girls remove their shirts and dance wild dances under the summer moon. It is said that the girls paint their breasts with snakes and strange symbols. They excite themselves by brushing their breasts against the breasts of other girls, it is said. We hear that the girls drink the warm blood of murdered animals. People say that the girls engage in witchcraft, in unnatural sexual acts, in torture, in black magic, in disgusting acts of desecration. Older girls, it is said, lure younger girls into the sisterhood and corrupt them. Rumor has it that the girls are instructed to carry weapons: pins, scissors, jackknives, needles, kitchen knives. It is said that the girls have vowed to kill any member who attempts to leave the sisterhood. We have heard that the girls drink a whitish liquid that makes them fall into an erotic frenzy.

THE CONFESSION OF EMILY GEHRING

Rumors of a secret society had reached us from time to time, but we paid little attention to them until the confession of thirteen-year-old Emily Gehring, who on June 2 released to the *Town Reporter* a disturbing letter. In it she stated that on May 14, at 4:00 P.M., she had been contacted on the playground of David Johnson Junior High by Mary Warren, a high-school sophomore who sometimes played basketball with the younger girls. Mary Warren slipped into her hand a small piece of white paper, folded in half. When Emily Gehring opened it, she saw that one of the inner sides was entirely black. Emily felt excited and frightened, for this was the sign of the Sisterhood of Night, an obscure, impenetrable secret society much discussed on the playgrounds, at the lockers, and in the bathrooms of David Johnson Junior High. She was told to speak to no one and to appear alone at midnight in the parking lot behind the Presbyterian church. Emily Gehring stated that when she appeared at the parking lot she at first saw no one but was then met by three girls, who had slipped out of hiding places: Mary Warren, Isabel Robbins, and Laura Lindberg. The girls led her through the church parking lot, along quiet roads, and through backyards to the woods at the north end of town, where three other girls met them: Catherine Anderson, Hilda Meyer, and Lavinia Hall. Mary Warren then asked her whether she liked boys. When she said yes, the girls mocked her and laughed at her, as if she had said something stupid. Mary Warren then asked her to remove her shirt. When she refused, the girls threatened to tie her to a tree and stick pins in her. She removed her shirt and the girls all fondled her breasts, touching them and kissing them. She then was invited to touch the breasts of the other girls; when she refused, they seized her hands and forced her to touch them. Some of the girls also touched her "in another place." Mary Warren warned her that if she spoke of this to anyone, she would be punished; at this point Mary Warren displayed a bone-handled kitchen knife. Emily Gehring stated that the girls met every night, at different times and places, in groups of five or six or seven; and she further stated that members of the group were continually changing, and that she was told about other groups meeting in other places. The girls always removed their shirts, fondled and kissed one another, sometimes painted their breasts with snakes and strange symbols, and initiated others into their secret practices. Emily Gehring remembered, and listed, the names of sixteen girls. By the end of May, according to her statement, she could no longer live with herself, and two days later she delivered to the *Town Reporter* her written confession and urged the town authorities to stop the sisterhood, which was spreading among the girls of David Johnson Junior High like a disease.

THE DEFENSE OF MARY WARREN

In response to these charges, which shocked our community, Mary Warren issued a detailed rebuttal that appeared in the *Town Reporter* on June 4. She began by saying that absolute silence was the rule of the sisterhood and that any statement whatever about the group by one of its members was punished by instant expulsion. Nevertheless, the attack by Emily Gehring had convinced her that she must speak out in defense of the sisterhood even at the expense of banishment. She acknowledged that she had contacted Emily Gehring, who had been selected for initiation by a group of "searchers," whom she refused to name; that she had passed Emily Gehring the blackened piece of paper, and had met her, in the presence of two other members, whom she also refused to name, at the back of the Presbyterian church at midnight and led her into the woods. From this point on, Mary Warren stated, Emily Gehring's report was utterly false, a vicious, hurtful attack the motive for which was all too clear. For Emily Gehring had failed to report that on May 30 she had been expelled from the sisterhood for *violating the vow of silence*. It is not clear from Mary Warren's defense precisely what the vow of silence demanded of a member or how Emily Gehring violated it, but it is clear, according to her statement, that Emily Gehring was deeply upset by the order of expulsion and threatened to take revenge. Mary Warren then repeated that Emily Gehring's confession was nothing but vicious lies, and she stated that she refused, by reason of her vow, to discuss the sisterhood in any way, except to say that it was a noble, pure society dedicated to silence. She feared that the slander of Emily Gehring had caused harm, and she ended with a passionate plea to the parents of our town to disregard the lies of Emily Gehring and trust their daughters.

NIGHT WORRIES

We were of two minds concerning Mary Warren's denial, for if on the one hand we were impressed by her intelligence and grateful to her for giving us grounds for doubting the confession of Emily Gehring, on the other hand her silence about the sisterhood raised doubts of a different kind and tended to undermine the case she was attempting to make. We noted with concern the existence of the group of "searchers," the ritual of the blackened paper, the secret meeting in the woods, the rigorous vow; we wondered, if the girls were innocent, what it was they vowed not to reveal. It was at this time that we began to wake in the night and to ask ourselves how we had failed our daughters. Now reports first began to circulate of bands of girls roaming the night, crossing backyards, moving in the dark; and we began to hear rumors of strange cries, of painted breasts, of wild dances under the summer moon.

THE DEATH OF LAVINIA HALL

The daughters of our town, many of whom we suspected of being secret members of the sisterhood, now began to seem moody, restless, and irritable. They refused to speak to us, shut themselves in their rooms, demanded that we leave them alone. These moody silences we took as proof of their membership; we hovered, we spied, we breathed down their necks. It was in this tense and oppressive atmosphere that on June 12, ten days after the confession of Emily Gehring, fourteen-year-old Lavinia Hall climbed the two flights of stairs to the guest room in her parents' attic and there, lying down on a puffy comforter sewn by her grandmother, swallowed twenty of her father's sleeping pills. She left no note, but we knew that Lavinia Hall had been named by Emily Gehring as a member of the sisterhood and a participant in their erotic rites. Later it was learned from her parents that the Gehring confession had devastated Lavinia, a quiet, scholarly girl who practiced Czerny exercises and Mozart sonatas on the piano two hours every day after school, kept a diary, and stayed up late at night reading fantasy trilogies with twisting vines on the covers. After Emily Gehring's confession, Lavinia had refused to answer any questions about the sisterhood and had begun to act strangely, shutting herself up in her room for hours at a time and moving around the house restlessly at night. One night at two in the morning her parents heard footsteps in the attic above their bedroom. They climbed the creaking wooden stairs and found Lavinia sitting in her pale blue pajamas on the moon-striped floor in front of her old dollhouse, which had been moved into the attic at the end of the sixth grade and still contained eight roomfuls of miniature furniture. Lavinia sat with her arms hugging her raised knees. Her feet were bare. She was strangely still. Her mother remembered one detail the long forearm, revealed by the pulled-back pajama sleeve. In the dollhouse three little dolls, thick with dust, sat stiffly in the moonlit living room: the child on the cobwebbed couch, the mother on the rocker, the father on the armchair with tiny lace doilies. The parents blamed themselves for not recognizing the seriousness of their daughter's condition, and they condemned the sisterhood as a band of murderers.

THE SECOND CONFESSION OF EMILY GEHRING

Scarcely had we begun to suffer the news of the death of Lavinia Hall when Emily Gehring released to the *Town Reporter* a second confession, which angered us and filled us with confusion. For in it she repudiated her earlier confession and, siding with Mary Warren against herself, accused herself of having fabricated the first confession in a spirit of revenge for her expulsion from the sisterhood. Emily Gehring now confessed that on the night of May 14 she had been led into the woods by Mary Warren and two other girls, as she had truthfully reported on June 2, but that "nothing at all" had happened there. Of her initiation she said only that it "consisted of silence"; for the next two weeks she had met nightly with small groups of the sisterhood, during which "not a single word" was uttered by anyone and "nothing at all" took place. On May 30 she was expelled from the sisterhood for violating her vow: she had spoken of the secret society to her friend Susannah Mason, who in turn had spoken to Bernice Thurman, not knowing that Bernice was a secret member of the sisterhood. Emily Gehring now claimed that she had regretted her false confession from the moment she had given it to the *Town Reporter*, but had been ashamed to admit that she had lied. The death of Lavinia Hall had shocked her into confessing the truth. She took upon herself the blame for Lavinia Hall's death, apologized to the grieving parents, and spoke fervently of the sisterhood as a pure, noble association that had given meaning to her life; and she looked forward to the day when the glorious sisterhood would spread from town to town and take over the world.

RESPONSE TO THE SECOND CONFESSION

As might be expected, the second confession thoroughly damaged the credibility of Emily Gehring as a witness, but our doubts, which at first were directed at the confession of June 2, soon turned upon the second confession itself. We noted that Emily Gehring used the very words of Mary Warren to describe the sisterhood; and this coincidence led some of us to argue that Emily Gehring had been persuaded by Mary Warren to retract her confession and take upon herself all blame, in return for reinstatement in the sisterhood or for some other reward we could only guess at. Others noted with distaste the fervent turn at the end of the confession, and argued that if an Emily Gehring was now telling the truth, then the truth was both incomplete and disturbing. For if in fact the girls were innocent of the original charges, then the nature of the sisterhood remained carefully hidden, while at the same time its troubling power was revealed by the passion of Emily Gehring, who couldn't tear herself away. In this view the second confession, while seeming to absolve the sisterhood, to reveal its innocence, in fact demonstrated an even more frightening truth about the secret society: its tenacious grip on the girls, the terrible loyalty it exacted from them.

THE TESTIMONY OF DR. ROBERT MEYER

It was during this time of uncertainty and anxiety that new information appeared from an unexpected quarter. Dr. Robert Meyer, a dermatologist with an office on Broad Street, had been deeply disturbed when his daughter, Hilda, was named by Emily Gehring in her confession of June 2. His daughter, he said, had called Emily Gehring a liar but had refused to speak of the sisterhood; after the first confession she became moody and irritable, and he could hear her pacing about at night. After three nights of terrible insomnia Robert Meyer made a fateful decision: he determined to follow his daughter and disrupt her lesbian experiments. At midnight on the fourth night he heard her footsteps creaking in the hall. He threw off his covers, slipped into sweatpants, sweatshirt, and running shoes, and followed her into the cool summer night. A block from the house she was met by two other girls, whom Meyer did not know. The three girls, wearing jeans, T-shirts, and nylon windbreakers tied around their waists, set off for the woods at the north end of town. Meyer, a deeply moral man, felt immense distaste and self-disgust as he pursued the three girls through the night, ducking behind trees like a spy in a late-night TV movie and creeping through backyards past swing sets, badminton nets, and fat plastic baseball bats. It struck him that he was doing something at once unsavory and absurd. He did not know what he planned to do when he arrived at the woods, but of one thing he was certain: he would bring his daughter home. Once in the woods he was forced to advance with fanatical caution, since the snap of a single twig might give him away; he was reminded of boyhood walks on pine-needle trails, which became confused with childhood daydreams about Indians in hushed forests. The girls crossed a stream and emerged in a small moonlit clearing well protected by pines. Four other girls were already present in the clearing. Standing behind a thick oak at a distance of some twenty feet from the group, Meyer experienced, in addition to his self-revulsion, an intense fear of what he was about to witness. The seven girls did not speak, although they greeted one another with nods. Following what appeared to be a prearranged plan, the girls formed a small close circle and raised their arms in such a way that all their forearms crossed. After this silent sign the girls separated and took up isolated positions, sitting against separate trees or lying with arms clasped behind their heads. Not a single word was uttered. Nothing happened. After thirty-five minutes by his watch, Meyer turned and crept away.

RESPONSE TO MEYER'S TESTIMONY

Meyer's testimony, far from resolving the problem of the sisterhood, plunged us into deeper controversy. Enemies of the sisterhood heaped scorn on Meyer's report, although they disagreed about the nature of its untrustworthiness. Some insisted that Meyer had invented the whole thing in a crude effort to protect his daughter; others argued that clever Hilda Meyer had plotted the entire episode, cunningly leading her father to the woods in order to have him witness a staged scene: The Innocent Maidens in Repose. Others pointed out that even if no deception had been practiced, by either Robert Meyer or his daughter, the testimony was in no sense decisive: Meyer, by his own admission, did not remain during the entire meeting, he observed the girls only a single time, and he observed only a single group of girls out of many groups. Was it not unlikely, people asked, was it not highly unlikely, that girls between the ages of twelve and fifteen would sneak out of their houses night after night, risking parental disapproval and even punishment, in order to meet with other girls in secluded and possibly dangerous places, solely for the purpose of doing nothing? This was not necessarily to say that the girls were engaging in forbidden deeds, although such deeds could never be ruled out, but merely to suggest that what they did do remained exasperatingly unknown. It was even possible that the girls, at the very time they were being observed by Meyer, had engaged in secret practices that he had failed to recognize; perhaps they had developed a system of signs and signals that Meyer had not been able to read.

THE TOWN

Night after night the members of the secret sisterhood set forth from their snug and restful rooms, the rooms of their childhood, to seek out dark and hidden places. Sometimes we see, or think we see, a group of them vanishing into the shadows of backyards lit by kitchen windows, or gliding out of sight along a dark front lawn. Disdainful of our wishes, indifferent to our unhappiness, they seem a race apart, wild creatures of the night with streaming hair and eyes of fire, until we recall with a start that they are our daughters. What shall we do with our daughters? Uneasily we keep watch over them, fearful of provoking them to open defiance. Some say that we should lock our daughters in their rooms at night, that we should place bars on their windows, that we should punish them harshly, over and over again, until they bow their heads in obedience. One father is said to tie his thirteen-year-old daughter to her bed at night with clothesline rope and to reward her cries with blows from a leather belt. Most deplore such measures but remain uncertain what to do. Meanwhile our daughters are restless; night after night bands of girls are seen disappearing into dark places beyond the reach of streetlights. The sisterhood is growing. There are reports of girls moving across the parking lot behind the lumberyard, meeting in the small wood behind the high-school tennis courts, climbing from the cellars of half-built houses, emerging from the boat shed by South Pond. Always they move at night, as if searching for something, something they cannot find in sunlight; and we who remain at home, awake in the dark, seem to hear, like the distant hum of trucks on the thruway, a continual faint sound of footfalls moving lightly across dark lawns and dimly lit roads, over pebbled driveways and curbside sand, through black leaves on forest paths, a ceaseless rustle of lines of footfalls weaving and unweaving in the night.

EXPLANATIONS

Some say that the girls gather together in covens to practice the art of witchcraft under the guidance of older girls; there is talk of spells, potions, a goat-haired figure, wild seizures and abandons. Others say that the girls are a sisterhood of the moon: they dance to the ancient moon goddess, dedicating themselves to her cold and passionate mysteries. Some say that the sisterhood, made restless by the boredom and emptiness of middle-class life, exists solely for the sake of erotic exploration. Others see in this explanation a desire to denigrate women, and insist that the sisterhood is an intellectual and political association dedicated to the ideal of freedom. Still others reject these explanations and argue that the sisterhood betrays all the marks of a religious cult: the initiation, the vow, the secret meetings, the fanatical loyalty, the refusal to break silence. The many explanations, far from casting rays of sharp and separate light on the hidden places of the sisterhood, have gradually interpenetrated and thickened to form a cloudy darkness, within which the girls move unseen.

THE UNKNOWN

Like other concerned citizens, I have brooded nightly over the sisterhood and the proliferating explanations, until the darkness outside my window becomes streaked with gray. I have asked myself why we seem unable to pierce their secret, why we can't catch them in the act. If I believe that I have at last discovered the true explanation, the one we should have seen from the beginning, it isn't because I know something that others do not know. Rather it's that my explanation honors the unknown and unseen, takes them into account as part of what is actually known. For it's precisely the element of the unknown, which looms so large in the case, that must be part of any solution. The girls, as we try to imagine them, keep vanishing into the unknown. They are penetrated by the unknown as by some black fluid. Is it possible that our search for the secret is misguided because we fail to include the unknown as a crucial element in that secret? Is it possible that our loathing of the unknown, our need to dispel it, to destroy it, to violate it through sharp glittering acts of understanding, makes the unknown swell with dark power, as if it were some beast feeding on our swords? Are we perhaps searching for the wrong secret, the secret we ourselves long for? Or, to put it another way, is it possible that the secret lies open before us, that we already know what it is?

THE SECRET OF THE SISTERHOOD

I submit that we know everything that needs to be known in order to penetrate the mystery of the Sisterhood of Night. Dr. Robert Meyer, sole witness to a gathering, reported that nothing whatever took place during the thirty-five minutes he observed the girls. In her second confession Emily Gehring insisted that nothing happened, that nothing ever happened, there in the dark. I suggest that these are scrupulously accurate descriptions. I submit that the girls band together at night not for the sake of some banal and titillating rite, some easily exposed hidden act, but solely for the sake of withdrawal and silence. The members of the sisterhood wish to be inaccessible. They wish to elude our gaze, to withdraw from investigation—they wish, above all, *not to be known*. In a world dense with understanding, oppressive with explanation and insight and love, the members of the silent sisterhood long to evade definition, to remain mysterious and ungraspable. Tell us! we cry, our voices shrill with love. Tell us everything! Then we will forgive you. But the girls do not wish to tell us anything, they don't wish to be heard at all. They wish, in effect, to become invisible. Precisely for this reason they cannot engage in any act that might reveal them. Hence their silence, their love of night solitude, their ritual celebration of the dark. They plunge into secrecy as into black smoke: in order to disappear.

IN THE NIGHT

I maintain that the Sisterhood of Night is an association of adolescent girls dedicated to the mysteries of solitude and silence. It is a high wall, a locked door, a face turning away. The sisterhood is a secret society that can never be disrupted, for even if we were to prevent the girls from meeting at night, even if we were to tie them to their beds for their entire lives, the dark purposes of the association would remain untouched. We cannot stop the sisterhood. Fearful of mystery, suspicious of silence, we accuse the members of dark crimes that secretly soothe us—for then will we not know them? For we prefer witchcraft to silence, naked orgies to night stillness. But the girls long to be closed in silence, to become pale statues with blank eyes and breasts of stone. What shall we do with our daughters? Nightly the secret sisterhood moves through our town. There is talk of the sisterhood spreading to younger girls, to older girls; even the wives of our town seem to us restless, evasive. We long to confront our silent daughters with arguments, with violence; we wake in the night from dreams of bleeding animals. Some say the sisterhood must be exposed and punished, for once such ideas take root, who will be able to stop them? Those of us who counsel patience are accused of cowardice. Already there is talk of bands of youths who roam the town at night armed with pointed sticks. What shall we do with our daughters? In the night we wake uneasily and tiptoe to their doors, pausing with our hands outstretched, unable to advance or retreat. We think of the long years of childhood, the party frocks and lollipops, the shimmer of trembling bubbles in blue summer air. We dream of better times.

WINTER BODIES

Noy Holland

Noy Holland lives in Florida with her husband and dog. Some of her short stories have appeared in *The Quarterly*.

In less than two pages Holland sharply describes the downward arc of a relationship, and possibly a life. "Winter Bodies" is from her first collection, *The Spectacle of the Body*.

—E. D.

There is a poisoned mouse in the corner, under the TV stand. There are scarves on the bureau, implements, needles, salve. She is growing thinner. Even her slippers she cannot keep on. There is the TV, the lamp in the room, the things they can see by the light in the room, one another—otherwise, they see nothing. They keep the passing days in mind, inasmuch as they keep the days in mind, by the curtains, drawn, by the door, pulled to—the inevitable flaws, the incisions of light. At night, if they wake, as they often do, the light pales to a humming fluorescence.

She looks up at him from the bed. He has combed his hair back. He carries a picture of her in his wallet.

"What else do you love?" she asks him.

"Nothing."

"Not the wind?" she says.

"Nothing."

He carries a bowl of water to her, a razor, folds the sheet away from her, puts the lamp at the foot of their bed. He begins with the few hairs he has seen on the tops of her toes, the tops of her feet, the hollows she has always missed by the knob of the bone of her ankle. She falls to sleep. He works up her—her shin, nicked, dented, the darker skin of her knee. He slips his hand behind her knee, lifts to bend her leg up, then kneels on the bed between her legs. He shaves swaths in the hair on the backs of her legs. The TV is on. The fine coat of her belly, he shaves. There are tiny hairs on her breasts he shaves, on her shoulders. He goes over her elbows, the backs of her hands, stands up, straightens her legs. He picks the lamp up from the foot of the bed, props it against the pillow.

Then he moves off. He unscrews the handle of the razor, lifts the used blade away from the head. He runs water, holds the razor's head under the water—his hands pale, healed, this boy's. The hair of her hands and her shoulders, some few caught hairs of each place he has shaved, catch against the scoop of the sink or wash off into the pipe of the sink in the running water. There are no surprises. There is a used-blade slot. Probably you cannot hear it—the sound the blade makes in the wall when it drops. Still, you might listens for it. He listens for it. He picks up a pair of scissors that rust in the steady leak of the faucet. He carries these back to the bed.

Oh, the body—the tracks, the lesions, the pumiced knees.

Her lips, her throat, her eyebrows, he shaves. His cock gets hard as he shaves her. He straddles her, leaning over her body. He cuts away her hair with the scissors he has found, close against her skull. His hands are aching. Her hair is heaped on the carpet. He leaves it for the mice on the carpet. He thinks of Tucumcari, of the room they slept in there. Streets, he remembers, and weather. He snips her eyelashes—slowly now, quietly—as though she will never know.

THE SLOAN MEN

David Nickle

David Nickle lives in Toronto, Canada, and works as a political reporter for a metropolitan Toronto weekly newspaper. His story "The Toy Mill," co-authored with Karl Schroeder, for *Tesseracts 4*, won Canada's 1992 Aurora Award for Best Short Story in English. He has had other stories in *Transversions*, *On Spec*, *Pulphouse*, and the anthologies *Christmas Ghosts* and *Northern Frights*.

"The Sloan Men" was originally set to be published in *Northern Frights* 2 in 1993, but that anthology was delayed until 1994. I was impressed the first time I read the story, thinking it terribly romantic for all its horror. After reading "The Sloan Men" several times I'm even more impressed by the story's effectiveness.

—E. D.

Mrs. Sloan had only three fingers on her left hand, but when she drummed them against the countertop, the tiny polished bones at the end of the fourth and fifth stumps clattered like fingernails. If Judith hadn't been looking, she wouldn't have noticed anything strange about Mrs. Sloan's hand.

"Tell me how you met Herman," said Mrs. Sloan. She turned away from Judith as she spoke, to look out the kitchen window where Herman and his father were getting into Mr. Sloan's black pickup truck. Seeing Herman and Mr. Sloan together was a welcome distraction for Judith. She was afraid Herman's stepmother would catch her staring at the hand. Judith didn't know how she would explain that with any grace: *Things are off to a bad enough start as it is.*

Outside, Herman wiped his sleeve across his pale, hairless scalp and, seeing Judith watching from the window, turned the gesture into an exaggerated wave. He grinned wetly through the late afternoon sun. Judith felt a little grin of her own growing and waved back, fingers waggling an infantile bye-bye. *Hurry home* she mouthed through the glass. Herman stared back blandly, not understanding.

"Did you meet him at school?"

Judith flinched. The drumming had stopped, and when she looked, Mrs. Sloan was leaning against the counter with her mutilated hand hidden in the crook of crossed arms. Judith hadn't even seen the woman move.

"No," Judith finally answered. "Herman doesn't go to school. Neither do I."

Mrs. Sloan smiled ironically. She had obviously been a beautiful woman in her youth—in most ways she still was. Mrs. Sloan's hair was auburn and it played over her eyes mysteriously, like a movie star's. She had cheekbones that Judith's ex-boss Talia would have called sculpted, and the only signs of her age were the tiny crow's feet at her eyes and harsh little lines at the corners of her mouth.

"I didn't mean to imply anything," said Mrs. Sloan. "Sometimes he goes to school, sometimes museums, sometimes just shopping plazas. That's Herman."

Judith expected Mrs. Sloan's smile to turn into a laugh, underscoring the low mockery she had directed toward Herman since he and Judith had arrived that morning. But the woman kept quiet, and the smile dissolved over her straight white teeth. She regarded Judith thoughtfully.

"I'd thought it might be school because you don't seem that old," said Mrs. Sloan. "Of course I don't usually have an opportunity to meet Herman's lady friends, so I suppose I really can't say."

"I met Herman on a tour. I was on vacation in Portugal, I went there with a girl I used to work with, and when we were in Lisbon—"

"—Herman appeared on the same tour as you. Did your girlfriend join you on that outing, or were you alone?"

"Stacey got food poisoning." *As I was about to say.* "It was a rotten day, humid and muggy." Judith wanted to tell the story the way she'd told it to her own family and friends, countless times. It had its own rhythm; her fateful meeting with Herman Sloan in the roped-off scriptorium of the monastery outside Lisbon, dinner that night in a vast, empty restaurant deserted in the off-season. In the face of Mrs. Sloan, though, the rhythm of that telling was somehow lost. Judith told it as best she could.

"So we kept in touch," she finished lamely.

Mrs. Sloan nodded slowly and didn't say anything for a moment. Try as she might, Judith couldn't read the woman, and she had always prided herself on being able to see through most people at least half way. That she couldn't see into this person at all was particularly irksome, because of who she was—a potential *in-law*, for God's sake. Judith's mother had advised her, "Look at the parents if you want to see what kind of man the love of your life will be in thirty years. See if you can love them with all their faults, all their habits. Because that's how things'll be . . ."

Judith realized again that she wanted very much for things to be just fine with Herman thirty years down the line. But if this afternoon were any indication . . .

Herman had been uneasy about the two of them going to Fenlan to meet his parents at all. But, as Judith explained, it was a necessary step. She knew it, even if Herman didn't—as soon as they turned off the highway he shut his eyes and wouldn't open them until Judith pulled into the driveway.

Mr. Sloan met them and Herman seemed to relax then, opening his eyes and blinking in the sunlight. Judith relaxed too, seeing the two of them together. They were definitely father and son, sharing features and mannerisms like images in a mirror. Mr. Sloan took Judith up in a big, damp hug the moment she stepped out of the car. The gesture surprised her at first and she tried to pull away, but Mr. Sloan's unstoppable grin had finally put her at ease.

"You *are* very lovely," said Mrs. Sloan finally. "That's to be expected, though. Tell me what you do for a living. Are you still working now that you've met Herman?"

Judith wanted to snap something clever at the presumption, but she stopped herself. "I'm working. Not at the same job, but in another salon. I do people's hair, and I'm learning manicure."

Mrs. Sloan seemed surprised. "Really? I'm impressed."

Now Judith was sure Mrs. Sloan was making fun, and a sluice of anger passed too close to the surface. "I work hard," she said hotly. "It may not seem—"

Mrs. Sloan silenced her with shushing motions. "Don't take it the wrong way," she said. "It's only that when I met Herman's father, I think I stopped working the very next day."

"Those must have been different times."

"They weren't *that* different." Mrs. Sloan's smile was narrow and ugly. "Perhaps Herman's father just needed different things."

"Well, I'm still working."

"So you say." Mrs. Sloan got up from the kitchen stool. "Come to the living room, dear. I've something to show you."

The shift in tone was too sudden, and it took Judith a second to realize she'd even been bidden. Mrs. Sloan half-turned at the kitchen door, and beckoned with her five-fingered hand.

"Judith," she said, "you've come this far already. You might as well finish the journey."

The living room was distastefully bare. The walls needed paint and there was a large brown stain on the carpet that Mrs. Sloan hadn't even bothered to cover up. She sat down on the sofa and Judith joined her.

"I wanted you to see the family album. I think—" Mrs. Sloan reached under the coffee table and lifted out a heavy black-bound volume "—I don't know, but I hope . . . you'll find this interesting."

Mrs. Sloan's face lost some of its hardness as she spoke. She finished with a faltering smile.

"I'm sure I will," said Judith. This was a good development, more like what she had hoped the visit would become. Family albums and welcoming hugs and funny stories about what Herman was like when he was two. She snuggled back against the tattered cushions and looked down at the album. "This must go back generations."

Mrs. Sloan still hadn't opened it. "Not really," she said. "As far as I know, the Sloans never mastered photography on their own. All of the pictures in here are mine."

"May I . . .?" Judith put out her hands, and with a shrug Mrs. Sloan handed the album over.

"I should warn you—" began Mrs. Sloan.

Judith barely listened. She opened the album to the first page.

And shut it, almost as quickly. She felt her face flush, with shock and anger. She looked at Mrs. Sloan, expecting to see that cruel, nasty smile back again. But Mrs. Sloan wasn't smiling.

"I was about to say," said Mrs. Sloan, reaching over and taking the album back, "that I should warn you, this isn't an ordinary family album."

"I—" Judith couldn't form a sentence, she was so angry. No wonder Herman hadn't wanted her to meet his family.

"I took that photograph almost a year after I cut off my fingers," said Mrs. Sloan. "Photography became a small rebellion for me, not nearly so visible as the mutilation. Herman's father still doesn't know about it, even though I keep the book out here in full view. Sloan men don't open books much.

"But we do, don't we Judith?"

Mrs. Sloan opened the album again, and pointed at the polaroid on the first page. Judith wanted to look away, but found that she couldn't.

"Herman's father brought the three of them home early, before I'd woken up—I don't know where he found them. Maybe he just called, and they were the ones who answered."

"They" were three women. The oldest couldn't have been more than twenty-five. Mrs. Sloan had caught them naked and asleep, along with what looked like Herman's father. One woman had her head cradled near Mr. Sloan's groin; another was cuddled in the white folds of his armpit, her wet hair fanning like seaweed across his shoulder; the third lay curled in a foetal position off his wide flank. Something dark was smeared across her face.

"And no, they weren't prostitutes," said Mrs. Sloan. "I had occasion to talk to one of them on her way out; she was a newlywed, she and her husband had come up for a weekend at the family cottage. She was, she supposed, going back to him."

"That's sick," gasped Judith, and meant it. She truly felt ill. "Why would you take something like that?"

"Because," replied Mrs. Sloan, her voice growing sharp again, "I found that I could. Mr. Sloan was distracted, as you can see, and at that instant I found some of the will that he had kept from me since we met."

"Sick," Judith whispered. "Herman was right. We shouldn't have come."

When Mrs. Sloan closed the album this time, she put it back underneath the coffee table. She patted Judith's arm with her mutilated hand and smiled. "No, no, dear. I'm happy you're here—happier than you can know."

Judith wanted nothing more at that moment than to get up, grab her suitcase, throw it in the car and leave. But of course she couldn't. Herman wasn't back yet, and she couldn't think of leaving without him.

"If Herman's father was doing all these things, why didn't you just divorce him?"

"If that photograph offends you, why don't you just get up and leave, right now?"

"Herman—"

"Herman wouldn't like it," Mrs. Sloan finished for her. "That's it, isn't it?" Judith nodded. "He's got you too," continued Mrs. Sloan, "just like his father got me. But maybe it's not too late for you."

"I love Herman. He never did anything like . . . like that."

"Of course you love him. And I love Mr. Sloan—desperately, passionately, over all reason." The corner of Mrs. Sloan's mouth perked up in a small, bitter grin.

"Would you like to hear how we met?"

Judith wasn't sure she would, but she nodded anyway. "Sure."

"I was living in Toronto with a friend at the time, had been for several years. As I recall, she was more than a friend—we were lovers." Mrs. Sloan paused, obviously waiting for a reaction. Judith sat mute, her expression purposefully blank.

Mrs. Sloan went on: "In our circle of friends, such relationships were quite fragile. Usually they would last no longer than a few weeks. It was, so far as we knew anyway, a minor miracle that we'd managed to stay together for as long as we had." Mrs. Sloan gave a bitter laugh. "We were very proud."

"How did you meet Herman's father?"

"On a train," she said quickly. "A subway train. He didn't even speak to me. I just felt his touch. I began packing my things that night. I can't even remember what I told her. My friend."

"It can't have been like that."

Judith started to get up, but Mrs. Sloan grabbed her, two fingers and a thumb closing like a trap around her forearm. Judith fell back down on the sofa. "Let go!"

Mrs. Sloan held tight. With her other hand she took hold of Judith's face and pulled it around to face her.

"Don't argue with me," she hissed, her eyes desperately intent. "You're wasting time. They'll be back soon, and when they are, we won't be able to do anything.

"*We'll be under their spell again!*"

Something in her tone caught Judith, and instead of breaking away, of running to the car and waiting inside with the doors locked until Herman got back—instead of slapping Mrs. Sloan, as she was half-inclined to do—Judith sat still.

"Then tell me what you mean." she said, slowly and deliberately.

Mrs. Sloan let go, and Judith watched as the relief flooded across her features. "We'll have to open the album again," she said. "That's the only way I can tell it."

The pictures were placed in the order they'd been taken. The first few were close-ups of different parts of Mr. Sloan's anatomy, always taken while he slept. They could have been pictures of Herman, and Judith saw nothing strange about them until Mrs. Sloan began pointing out the discrepancies: "Those ridges around his nipples are made of something like fingernails," she said of one, and "the whole ear isn't any bigger than a nickel," she said, pointing to another grainy polaroid. "His teeth are barely nubs on his gums, and his navel . . . look, it's a *slit*. I measured it after I took this, and it was nearly eight inches long. Sometimes it grows longer, and I've seen it shrink to less than an inch on cold days."

"I'd never noticed before," murmured Judith, although as Mrs. Sloan pointed to more features she began to remember other things about Herman: the thick black hairs that only grew between his fingers, his black triangular toenails that never needed cutting . . . and where were his fingernails? Judith shivered with the realization.

Mrs. Sloan turned the page.

"Did you ever once stop to wonder what you saw in such a creature?" she asked Judith.

"Never," Judith replied, wonderingly.

"Look," said Mrs. Sloan, pointing at the next spread. "I took these pictures in June of 1982."

At first they looked like nature pictures, blue-tinged photographs of some of the land around the Sloans' house. But as Judith squinted she could make out a small figure wearing a heavy green overcoat. Its head was a little white pinprick in the middle of a farmer's field. "Mr. Sloan," she said, pointing.

Mrs. Sloan nodded. "He walks off in that direction every weekend. I followed him that day."

"Followed him where?"

"About a mile and a half to the north of here," said Mrs. Sloan, "there is an old farm property. The Sloans must own the land—that's the only explanation I can think of—although I've never been able to find the deed. Here—" she pointed at a photograph of an ancient set of fieldstone foundations, choked with weeds "—that's where he stopped."

The next photograph in the series showed a tiny black rectangle in the middle of the ruins. Looking more closely, Judith could tell that it was an opening into the dark of a root cellar. Mr. Sloan was bent over it, peering inside. Judith turned the page, but there were no photographs after that.

"When he went inside, I found I couldn't take any more pictures," said Mrs. Sloan. "I can't explain why, but I felt a compelling terror, unlike anything I've ever felt in Mr. Sloan's presence. I ran back to the house, all the way. It was as though I were being pushed."

That's weird. Judith was about to say it aloud, but stopped herself—in the face of Mrs. Sloan's photo album, everything was weird. To comment on the fact seemed redundant.

"I can't explain why I fled, but I have a theory." Mrs. Sloan set the volume aside and stood. She walked over to the window, spread the blinds an inch, and checked the driveway as she spoke. "Herman and his father aren't human. That much we can say for certain—they are monsters, deformed in ways that even radiation, even Thalidomide couldn't account for. They are physically repulsive; their intellects are no more developed than that of a child of four. They are weak and amoral."

Mrs. Sloan turned, leaning against the glass. "Yet here we are, you and I. Without objective evidence—" she gestured with her good hand toward the open photo album "—we can't even see them for what they are. If they were any nearer, or perhaps simply not distracted, we wouldn't even be able to have this conversation. Tonight, we'll go willingly to their beds." At that, Mrs. Sloan visibly shuddered. "If that's where they want us."

Judith felt the urge to go to the car again, and again she suppressed it. Mrs. Sloan held her gaze like a cobra.

"It all suggests a power. I think it suggests talismanic power." Here Mrs. Sloan paused, looking expectantly at Judith.

Judith wasn't sure what "talismanic" meant, but she thought she knew what Mrs. Sloan was driving at. "You think the source of their power is in that cellar?"

"Good." Mrs. Sloan nodded slowly. "Yes, Judith, that's what I think. I've tried over and over to get close to that place, but I've never been able to even step inside those foundations. It's a place of power, and it protects itself."

Judith looked down at the photographs. She felt cold in the pit of her stomach. "So you want me to go there with you, is that it?"

Mrs. Sloan took one last look out the window then came back and sat down.

She smiled with an awkward warmth. "Only once since I came here have I felt as strong as I do today. That day, I chopped these off with the wood-axe—" she held up her three-fingered hand and waggled the stumps "—thinking that, seeing me mutilated, Herman's father would lose interest and let me go. I was stupid; it only made him angry, and I was . . . punished. But I didn't know then what I know today. And," she added after a brief pause, "today you are here."

The Sloan men had not said where they were going when they left in the pickup truck, so it was impossible to tell how much time the two women had. Mrs. Sloan found a flashlight, an axe and a shovel in the garage, and they set out immediately along a narrow path that snaked through the trees at the back of the yard. There were at least two hours of daylight left, and Judith was glad. She wouldn't want to be trekking back through these woods after dark.

In point of fact, she was barely sure she wanted to be in these woods in daylight. Mrs. Sloan moved through the underbrush like a crazy woman, not even bothering to move branches out of her way. But Judith was slower, perhaps more doubtful.

Why was she doing this? Because of some grainy photographs in a family album? Because of what might as well have been a ghost story, told by a woman who had by her own admission chopped off two of her own fingers? Truth be told, Judith couldn't be sure she was going anywhere but crazy following Mrs. Sloan through the wilderness.

Finally, it was the memories that kept her moving. As Judith walked, they manifested with all the vividness of new experience.

The scriptorium near Lisbon was deserted—the tour group had moved on, maybe up the big wooden staircase behind the podium, maybe down the black wrought-iron spiral staircase. Judith couldn't tell; the touch on the back of her neck seemed to be interfering. It penetrated, through skin and muscle and bone, to the juicy center of her spine. She turned around and the wet thing behind pulled her to the floor. She did not resist.

"Hurry up!" Mrs. Sloan was well ahead, near the top of a ridge of rock in the center of a large clearing. Blinking, Judith apologized and moved on.

Judith was fired from her job at Joseph's only a week after she returned from Portugal. It seemed she had been late every morning, and when she explained to her boss that she was in love, it only made things worse. Talia flew into a rage, and Judith was afraid that she would hit her. Herman waited outside in the mall.

Mrs. Sloan helped Judith clamber up the smooth rock face. When she got to the top, Mrs. Sloan took her in her arms. Only then did Judith realize how badly she was shaking.

"What is it?" Mrs. Sloan pulled back and studied Judith's face with real concern.

"I'm . . . remembering," said Judith.

"What do you remember?"

Judith felt ill again, and she almost didn't say.

"Judith!" Mrs. Sloan shook her. "This could be important!"

"All right!" Judith shook her off. She didn't want to be touched, not by anyone.

"The night before last, I brought Herman home to meet my parents. I thought it had gone well . . . until now."

"What do you remember?" Mrs. Sloan emphasized every syllable.

"My father wouldn't shake Herman's hand when he came in the door. My mother . . . she turned white as a ghost. She backed up into the kitchen, and I think she knocked over some pots or something, because I heard clanging. My father asked my mother if she was all right. All she said was no. Over and over again."

"What did your father do?"

"He excused himself, went to check on my mother. He left us alone in the vestibule, it must have been for less than a minute. And I . . ." Judith paused, then willed herself to finish. "I started . . . rubbing myself against Herman. All over. He didn't even make a move. But I couldn't stop myself. I don't even remember wanting to stop. My parents had to pull me away, both of them." Judith felt like crying.

"My father actually hit me. He said I made him sick. Then he called me . . . a little whore."

Mrs. Sloan made a sympathetic noise. "It's not far to the ruins," she said softly. "We'd better go, before they get back."

It felt like an hour had passed before they emerged from the forest and looked down on the ruins that Judith had seen in the Polaroids. In the setting sun, they seemed almost mythic—like Stonehenge, or the Aztec temples Judith had toured once on a trip to Cancun. The stones here had obviously once been the foundation of a farmhouse. Judith could make out the outline of what would have been a woodshed extending off the nearest side, and another tumble of stonework in the distance was surely the remains of a barn—but now they were something else entirely. Judith didn't want to go any closer. If she turned back now, she might make it home before dark.

"Do you feel it?" Mrs. Sloan gripped the axe-handle with white knuckles. Judith must have been holding the shovel almost as tightly. Although it was quite warm outside, her teeth began to chatter.

"If either of us had come alone, we wouldn't be able to stand it," said Mrs. Sloan, her voice trembling. "We'd better keep moving."

Judith followed Herman's stepmother down the rocky slope to the ruins. Her breaths grew shorter the closer they got. She used the shovel as a walking stick until they reached level ground, then held it up in both hands, like a weapon.

They stopped again at the edge of the foundation. The door to the root cellar lay maybe thirty feet beyond. It was made of sturdy, fresh-painted wood, in sharp contrast to the overgrown wreckage around it, and it was embedded in the ground at an angle. Tall, thick weeds sprouting galaxies of tiny white flowers grew in a dense cluster on top of the mound. They waved rhythmically back and forth, as though in a breeze.

But it was wrong, thought Judith. There was no breeze, the air was still. She looked back on their trail and confirmed it—the tree branches weren't even rustling.

"I know," said Mrs. Sloan, her voice flat. "I see it too. They're moving on their own."

Without another word, Mrs. Sloan stepped across the stone boundary. Judith followed, and together they approached the shifting mound.

As they drew closer, Judith half-expected the weeds to attack, to shoot forward and grapple their legs, or to lash across their eyes and throats with prickly venom.

In fact, the stalks didn't even register the two women's presence as they stepped up to the mound. Still, Judith held the shovel ready as Mrs. Sloan smashed the padlock on the root cellar door. She pried it away with a painful-sounding rending.

"Help me lift this," said Mrs. Sloan.

The door was heavy, and earth had clotted along its top, but with only a little difficulty they managed to heave it open. A thick, milky smell wafted up from the darkness.

Mrs. Sloan switched on the flashlight and aimed it down. Judith peered along its beam—it caught nothing but dust motes, and the uncertain-looking steps of a wooden ladder.

"Don't worry, Judith," breathed Mrs. Sloan, "I'll go first." Setting the flashlight on the ground for a moment, she turned around and set a foot on one of the upper rungs. She climbed down a few steps, then picked up the flashlight and gave Judith a little smile.

"You can pass down the axe and shovel when I get to the bottom," she said, and then her head was below the ground. Judith swallowed with a dry click and shut her eyes.

"All right," Mrs. Sloan finally called, her voice improbably small. "It's too far down here for you to pass the tools to me by hand. I'll stand back—drop them both through the hole then come down yourself."

Judith did as she was told. At the bottom of the darkness she could make out a flickering of light, just bright enough for her to see where the axe and shovel fell. They were very tiny at the bottom of the hole. Holding her breath, Judith mounted the top rung of the ladder and began her own descent.

Despite its depth, the root cellar was warm. And the smell was overpowering. Judith took only a moment to identify it. It was Herman's smell, but magnified a thousandfold—and exuding from the very walls of this place.

Mrs. Sloan had thoroughly explored the area at the base of the ladder by the time Judith reached her.

"The walls are earthen, shorn up with bare timber," she said, shining the light along the nearest wall to illustrate. "The ceiling here tapers up along the length of the ladder—I'd guess we're nearly forty feet underground."

Judith picked up the shovel, trying not to imagine the weight of the earth above them.

"There's another chamber, through that tunnel." Mrs. Sloan swung the flashlight beam down to their right. The light extended into a dark hole in the wall, not more than five feet in diameter and rimmed with fieldstone. "That's where the smell is strongest."

Mrs. Sloan stooped and grabbed the axe in her good hand. Still bent over, she approached the hole and shone the light inside.

"The end's still farther than the flashlight beam will carry," she called over her shoulder. "I think that's where we'll have to go."

Judith noticed then that the tremor was gone from Mrs. Sloan's voice. Far from sounding frightened, Herman's stepmother actually seemed excited. It wasn't hard to see why—this day might finish with the spell broken, with their freedom assured. Why wouldn't she be excited?

But Judith couldn't shake her own sense of foreboding so easily. She wondered where Herman was now, what he would be thinking. And what was Judith thinking, on the verge of her freedom? Judith couldn't put it to words, but the thought twisted through her stomach and made her stop in the dark chamber behind Mrs. Sloan. A *little whore*, her father had called her. Then he'd hit her, hard enough to bring up a swelling. Right in front of Herman, like he wasn't even there! Judith clenched her jaw, around a rage that was maddeningly faceless.

"I'm not a whore," she whispered through her teeth.

Mrs. Sloan disappeared into the hole, and it was only when the chamber was dark that Judith followed.

The tunnel widened as they went, its walls changing from wood-shorn earth to fieldstone and finally to actual rock. Within sixty feet the tunnel ended, and Mrs. Sloan began to laugh. Judith felt ill—the smell was so strong she could barely breathe. Even as she stepped into the second chamber of the root cellar, the last thing she wanted to do was laugh.

"Roots!" gasped Mrs. Sloan, her voice shrill and echoing in the dark. "Of course there would be—" she broke into another fit of giggles "—roots, here in the root cellar!" The light jagged across the cellar's surfaces as Mrs. Sloan slipped to the floor and fell into another fit of laughter.

Judith bent down and pried the flashlight from Mrs. Sloan's hand—she made a face as she brushed the scratchy tips of the two bare finger bones. She swept the beam slowly across the ceiling.

It was a living thing. Pulsing intestinal ropes drooped from huge bulbs and broad orange phalluses clotted with earth and juices thick as semen. Between them, fingerlike tree roots bent and groped in knotted black lines. One actually penetrated a bulb, as though to feed on the sticky yellow water inside. Silvery droplets formed like beading mercury on the surface of an ample, purple sac directly above the chamber's center.

Mrs. Sloan's laughter began to slow. "Oh my," she finally chuckled, sniffing loudly, "I don't know what came over me."

"This is the place." Judith had intended it as a question, but it came out as a statement of fact. This *was* the place. She could feel Herman, his father, God knew how many others like them—all of them here, an indisputable presence.

Mrs. Sloan stood, using the axe-handle as a support. "It is," she agreed. "We'd better get to work on it."

Mrs. Sloan hefted the axe in both hands and swung it around her shoulders. Judith stood back and watched as the blade bit into one of the drooping ropes, not quite severing it but sending a spray of green sap down on Mrs. Sloan's shoulders. She pulled the axe out and swung again. This time the tube broke. Its two ends twitched like live electrical wires; its sap spewed like bile. Droplets struck Judith, and where they touched skin they burned like vinegar.

"Doesn't it feel better?" shouted Mrs. Sloan, grinning fiercely at Judith through the wash of slime on her face. "Don't you feel *free?* Put down the flashlight, girl, pick up the shovel! There's work to be done!"

Judith set the flashlight down on its end, so that it illuminated the roots in a wide yellow circle. She hefted the shovel and, picking the nearest bulb, swung it up with all her strength. The yellow juices sprayed out in an umbrella over Judith, soaking her. She began to laugh.

It does feel better, she thought. A lot *better*. Judith swung the shovel up again and again. The blade cut through tubes, burst bulbs, lodged in the thick round carrot-roots deep enough so Judith could pry them apart with only a savage little twist of her shoulders. The mess of her destruction was *everywhere*. She could taste it every time she grinned.

After a time, she noticed that Mrs. Sloan had stopped and was leaning on the axe-handle, watching her. Judith yanked the shovel from a root. Brown milk splattered across her back.

"What are you stopping for?" she asked. "There's still more to cut!"

Mrs. Sloan smiled in the dimming light—the flashlight, miraculously enough, was still working, but its light now had to fight its way through several layers of ooze.

"I was just watching you, dear," she said softly.

Judith turned her ankle impatiently. The chamber was suddenly very quiet. "Come on," said Judith. "We can't stop until we're finished."

"Of course." Mrs. Sloan stood straight and swung the axe up again. It crunched into a wooden root very near the ceiling, and Mrs. Sloan pried it loose. "I think that we're very nearly done, though. At least, that's the feeling I get."

Judith didn't smile—she suddenly felt very cold inside.

"No, we're not," she said in a low voice, "we're not done for a long time yet. Keep working."

Mrs. Sloan had been right, though. There were only a half-dozen intact roots on the cellar ceiling, and it took less than a minute for the two women to cut them down. When they stopped, the mess was up to their ankles and neither felt like laughing. Judith shivered, the juices at once burning and chilling against her skin.

"Let's get out of this place," said Mrs. Sloan. "There's dry clothes back at the house."

The flashlight died at the base of the ladder, its beam flickering out like a dampened candle flame. It didn't matter, though. The sky was a square of deepening purple above them, and while they might finish the walk back in the dark they came out of the root cellar in time to bask in at least a sliver of the remaining daylight. The weeds atop the mound were still as the first evening stars emerged and the line of orange to the west sucked itself back over the treetops.

Mrs. Sloan talked all the way back, her continual chatter almost but not quite drowning out Judith's recollections. She mostly talked about what she would do with her new freedom: first, she'd take the pickup and drive it back to the city where she would sell it. She would take the money, get a place to live and start looking for a job. As they crested the ridge of bedrock, Mrs. Sloan asked Judith if there was much call for three-fingered manicurists in the finer Toronto salons, then laughed in such a girlish way that Judith wondered if she weren't walking with someone other than Mrs. Sloan.

"What are you going to do, now that you're free?" asked Mrs. Sloan.

"I don't know," Judith replied honestly.

* * *

The black pickup was parked near the end of the driveway. Its headlights were on, but when they checked, the cab was empty.

"They may be inside," she whispered. "You were right, Judith. We're not done yet."

Mrs. Sloan led Judith to the kitchen door around the side of the house. It wasn't locked, and together they stepped into the kitchen. The only light came from the half-open refrigerator door. Judith wrinkled her nose. A carton of milk lay on its side, and milk dripped from the countertop to a huge puddle on the floor. Cutlery was strewn everywhere.

Coming from somewhere in the house, Judith thought she recognized Herman's voice. It was soft, barely a whimper. It sounded as though it were coming from the living room.

Mrs. Sloan heard it too. She hefted the axe in her good hand and motioned to Judith to follow as she stepped silently around the spilled milk. She clutched the doorknob to the living room in a three-fingered grip, and stepped out of the kitchen.

Herman and his father were on the couch, and they were in bad shape. Both were bathed in a viscous sweat, and they had bloated so much that several of the buttons on Herman's shirt had popped and Mr. Sloan's eyes were swollen shut.

And where were their noses?

Judith shuddered. Their noses had apparently receded into their skulls. Halting breaths passed through chaffed-red slits with a wet buzzing sound.

Herman looked at Judith. She rested the shovel's blade against the carpet. His eyes were moist, as though he'd been crying.

"You bastard," whispered Mrs. Sloan. "You took away my life. Nobody can do that, but you did. You took away everything."

Mr. Sloan quivered, like gelatin dropped from a mold.

"You made me touch you . . ." Mrs. Sloan stepped closer ". . . *worship* you . . . you made me lick up after you, swallow your filthy, inhuman taste . . . And you made me *like* it!"

She was shaking almost as much as Mr. Sloan, and her voice grew into a shrill, angry shout. Mr. Sloan's arms came up to his face, and a high, keening whistle rose up. Beside him, Herman sobbed. He did not stop looking at Judith.

Oh, Herman, Judith thought, her stomach turning. Herman was sick, sicker than Judith had imagined. Had he always been this bad? Judith couldn't believe that. Air whistled like a plea through Herman's reddened nostrils.

"*Well, no more!*" Mrs. Sloan raised the axe over her head so that it jangled against the lighting fixture in the ceiling. "*No more!*"

Judith lifted up the shovel then, and swung with all her strength. The flat of the blade smashed against the back of Mrs. Sloan's skull.

Herman's sobbing stretched into a wail, and Judith swung the shovel once more. Mrs. Sloan dropped the axe beside her and crumpled to the carpeted floor.

The telephone in Judith's parents' home rang three times before the answering machine Judith had bought them for Christmas switched on. Judith's mother began to speak, in a timed, halting monotone: "Allan . . . and . . . I are . . . not . . ."

Judith smoothed her hair behind her ears, fingers tapping impatiently at her elbow until the message finished. She nearly hung up when the tone sounded, but she shut her eyes and forced herself to go through with it.

"Hi Mom, hi Dad." Her voice was small, and it trembled. "It's me. I know you're pretty mad at me, and I just wanted to call and say I was sorry. I know that what we did—what Herman and I did, mostly me—I know it was wrong. I know it was sick, okay? Dad, you were right about that. But I'm not going to do that stuff anymore. I've got control of my life, and . . . of my body. God, that sounds like some kind of feminist garbage, doesn't it? *Control of my body*. But it's true." With her foot, Judith swung the kitchen door shut. The gurgling from upstairs grew quieter.

"Oh, by the way, I'm up at Herman's parents' place now. It's about three hours north of you guys, outside a town called Fenlan. You should see it up here, it's beautiful. I'm going to stay here for awhile, but don't worry, Herman and I will have separate bedrooms." She smiled. "We're going to save ourselves."

Judith turned around so that the telephone cord wrapped her body, and she leaned against the stove.

"Mom," she continued, "do you remember what you told me about love? I do. You told me there were two stages. There was the in-love feeling, the one that you get when you meet a guy, he's really cute and everything, and you just don't want to be away from him. And then that goes away, and remember what you said? 'You'd better still love him after that,' you told me. 'Even though he's not so cute, even though maybe he's getting a little pot belly, even though he stops sending you flowers, you'd better still love him like there's no tomorrow.' Well Mom, guess what?"

The answering machine beeped again and the line disconnected.

"I do," finished Judith.

IS THAT THEM?

Kevin Roice

Kevin Roice and his wife, Janna, run Hungry Jack's General Store, a non-hokey old-fashioned general store in Wilson, Wyoming, a small town outside of overbuilt, tourist-ridden Jackson, Wyoming. He has had stories published in the literary magazine *Young Wyoming Writes*, in *Cthulhu Call*, a local semiprofessional magazine, and in *Jam To/Day*.

"Is That Them?," told from a child's point of view, is based solidly and frighteningly in reality. It is reprinted from *Grue magazine*.

—E. D.

"It should be painfully obvious," his mother told his father, her face twisting and wrinkling the way it did sometimes when Walter's room wasn't "picked up and put away."

He shifted in the backseat, watching his father's face as he turned from his driving and stared at her. There were bad things on his skin, too, but what was there was somewhat less disconcerting because he did not care to display anger, to waste it within his face. He would use his hands. They were strong, and they could pinch. How they could pinch!

Come *on*, Dad, he thought, say something. When his father spoke, no matter how badly the situation was churning within him, things calmed a bit. The hands would lose their bone-piercing, knuckle-whiteness and settle back to their driving, or whatever his father had them doing. Things would be okay then, for a while. The hands would not strike his mother's cheek, or her bumpy nose. The hands would not pinch.

Walter looked at Joe, who was looking out of his own window. Joe, who'd chosen the old Thundercats costume this year. Joe, who did not look, at all, like Lion-O, even with the mask and its red, flaming hair, and the plastic sword with the Eye of Thundera centered at its handle. Joe, whose feet did not tremble when Mom and Dad started arguing. Joe was two years younger, but he was older somehow, and somehow already gone from this family, though both of them were only in fourth and sixth grades. It would be a long time catching up to Joe.

"It's only tonight," said Father, turning back to stare directly ahead. "They only just had them last week, you know. They get tired of us bringing them over all the time."

"They don't like Joe *or* Walter. They only watch them when they *have* to. It's not like *they're* going anywhere tonight, for Christ's sake! You think they might like to help us out once in a while." His mother's voice was loud, and growing louder, penetrating Walter's ears and pushing him, making him wish he could slip outside of himself and run in the opposite direction of the one the car was following, out where the cool air, the darkness and most of all, the quiet, could fill him up again.

"I think you'd better shut your mouth about my parents, or I'll shut it for you! You wouldn't be in such a damned fever if Bill Williams wasn't going to that dance, and I know it!" Dad's voice exploded inside the car, and having no place to go, the sound threatened to puncture Walter's eardrums.

"What's *that* supposed to mean?" his mom said, sounding as though she already knew.

Walter didn't know this Bill Williams, but he'd heard talk about him before. Bad talk; this kind of talk. It made Walter feel as if he were in some strange house with rules of order that were unexplained and unknowable.

"If I ever find out that these kids were—" Dad started to say, gesturing toward the back seat.

"Think what you want! It doesn't matter! Go get a blood test if you're so fucking—"

Dad's hand came up from the steering wheel and flew toward her, then froze, index finger jabbing toward her left cheek. It hovered two inches or so away. She shrunk back from it. "Shut up. Now." Even tones, quiet, dangerous.

She moved closer to the passenger door and stared at him, her twisted mask softened, her mouth open, her eyes large. Walter felt this was how he must appear to their father just before the hands did their hurting to *him*. He was afraid and ashamed of that look, and he discovered that his face was burning pink in the cool darkness of the October air.

Joe, never once turning, continued to peer out at the houses and whatever else he found in his silence.

The hand went back to the steering wheel a few seconds later. Walter was surprised, but relieved. It was not often his father held the hands at bay. Usually, if he did restrain them, they would break free later, at a far more unexpected moment. And the hitting or the pinching would be very severe then. Walter still thought that was how his mother's arm had been broken a year ago. She would never say anything more than that she had fallen on some ice, but Walter saw the holes in her eyes, the black place that had grown larger over the years. This was a place, a thing he understood. Her hate-thing lived there, as it did in Dad's eyes, as it did even in Joe's.

It hadn't been so long ago, maybe a few months, that he'd seen it in Joe. He supposed Joe could probably see it in him, too, though he tried to keep it out, make it stay in its awful cave or wherever it was that hate-things lived, when not preying on good people.

Walter moved a sweating hand over the large orange pumpkin he held in his lap. There was barely enough candy to cover its plastic bottom. They'd only been to six houses when his mother insisted they go to Grandma and Grandpa's.

Joe had looked at him then, and he'd looked right back. As they'd approached the car, their feet crunching on the bed of leaves in their friend Sam Wolver's yard, he'd picked a piece of candy, a Tootsie Roll, out of his pumpkin, unwrapped it, and put it between his lips like a cigarette. He looked just like their mother, before she had supposedly quit.

"If we have to go to Grandma and Grandpa Marshfield's house, we'll be there all night. You *know* they won't take us trick or treating," Joe had said, the hate-thing pressing behind the dark in his eyes. Then he bit the Tootsie Roll in half and offered part to Walter, but it was all slobbery, and Walter refused, knowing Joe wasn't really offering anything. It was all the hate-thing, and tonight it was roaming freely among the members of his family.

"We can go some other time. I told you you should have tried to get that Melissa to baby sit. You should have done what I said," Dad told Mom. His voice was the voice of moldy lemons.

"I'm not paying someone three dollars an hour to use our telephone for panting practice when your parents live so close. *We* need a break, too."

Walter rubbed his forehead beneath the upraised mask. He was sweating, and his hair seemed to have sagged down toward his eyebrows. It was plastered there, moist and uncomfortable. He felt as though he were wearing a wig.

The car windows were closed and fogging over with the hot moisture from their breath. He'd always wanted to write his name on the film, as he'd done on the school bus, but such things weren't allowed in his father's car.

"Nothing, when we get there. If they offer, then fine. If not, the kids get their candy and we go away. Understand me?" Dad was looking at her again. She did not answer in words.

Walter wondered suddenly if the creature who made them hate could occupy them all at once, or if it had to skip back and forth, like he did when he spoke to make-believe friends. Walter believed it probably could, and did.

If that were true, how would any of them ever break away from it?

The car slammed to a stop near the drive that held Grandpa Marshfield's purple car. Its own Halloween costume was a ghost—without the eye holes. Every year, Grandpa covered his favorite car with an old sheet. He seemed overly worried about eggs. The idea amused Walter, since few kids ever came to this part of the city for trick-or-treat. This house, and all the other houses on Carver Street, were filled with older folks who did not participate in Halloween and did not give candy to children.

Walter thought he saw one of the pale, white curtains move, exposing a male-looking nose, but before his eyes could catch the face and hold it, the face slipped away and the curtain fell back, closing off the triangle and stopping the yellow light that shone from inside. Behind that window was the television room, where Grandpa watched any and all news programs, his wrinkled lips moving with each word broadcasted from the face on the screen. Walter did not care for this room when Grandpa was there, because Grandpa did not politely surrender the set when he was entertaining guests, which was something mandatory at Walter's house when Grandpa came over. And Walter hated the news. It always made him feel depressed or bored, and he had no room left for more slices of those pies.

"Can't believe I let you talk me into coming here. They aren't going to care, in the least, you know." Dad got out of the car, not turning when she answered him:

"So why don't you *shut up* about it before they hear you?"

"Can we go inside now?" Walter spoke up, hoping to interrupt Dad's concentration.

"I'm talking to your father, Walt! Have you completely forgotten your manners?" his mother shouted, then went on without his answer, which was fine with him because he had none to give.

As she got out of the car and walked toward the house, he heard her muttering something about how she was always being challenged, and that "we never should have had any kids, to begin with."

Walter got out of the car behind Joe, pulling his Spider Man mask down over his moist face. He wondered what things would be like if he just wasn't around anymore. Would he be someone else then, someone with other parents and maybe, someone with at least one other brother or sister? Or would he be nothing, no one at all? That seemed more likely.

One thing he knew for sure, though: he hadn't been surprised that his Mom had finally vocalized her truth to the world. Walter had lived with its consequences for a long time. He thought he should feel bad about that, as he knew Joe did, but somehow that wasn't what lay inside him. He was, in fact, happy about this lack of feeling, because he did not like to hurt. He knew that he could take it all, and spit it back out, and perhaps this would be the weapon with which to fight the hate-thing's presence within him.

Mom was first to the door, then Joe, then Walter, and last came Dad, who walked the same way he did when he was taking Joe and Walter to one of the various city parks within distance of their home—slowly, with long steps, face drawn down at the mouth. Sometimes his mouth would move, or hang open, revealing upper and lower teeth ground together in rapid, side-to-side motions. He had spared Mom a second time tonight, and Walter could see there would be no third time. Anyone who crossed him now was, as Charlie Brown would say, *doomed*.

Joe knocked on the front door, and Walter knocked as well, trying to match Joe, but his action was rough, and their sound together was like old Ichabod's horse, racing over the wooden bridge toward freedom. Was there freedom here? Walter pictured Grandpa's eyes, then Grandma's. He measured their frowns and the urging of palms pressed to his back. Walter thought that there was not freedom, but that behind those walls, there *could* be change.

A sound of rattling metal came to Walter's ears, and in the picture land of his mind, he could see one of them, probably Grandma, sliding back the safety bolt she always kept closed, daylight or dark. The door would open and there she would be, expectant, smiling her grandma-smile, which was not the same as her Christmas-smile, or the smile of roses she wore when talking to Felicita Peterson on the telephone.

The door angled away from its frame to reveal the cautious but shifting expression on her face, as Grandma made her inspection of the entryway. Her features were lined and grooved, like the clay masks in those books about vanished Indians that Grandpa had in his den.

Grandma's eyes were yellow-brown, protected closely by her eyelids. As usual, her brown-framed glasses sat in the strange, sweating groove on her nose.

She peered at Joe, and then at Walter, her mouth shifting into that grandmotherly smile. At the same time, Walter could see the hate-thing focus on them, its burning, shadow-pupils somehow darker and full of great hollows—hollows that gave off the consistency of smoke and the aftertaste of charcoal.

"Trick-or-treat!" Joe whooped, holding forth his bright pumpkin. The head, full and brilliant, laughing with its awful black teeth, swung gently from the handle clutched in Joe's fingers. " *'Eye of Thundera*, give me sight beyond sight!' " Joe added, performing, thrusting his thick, silver-painted sword high, almost into Grandma's nose.

"Watch where you're pointing that!" Dad grasped Joe's shoulder and jerked him backward a step.

"Trick-or-treat," said Walter, desperately hoping to retain some semblance of Halloween. He didn't want to see Joe get his ears pinched, here, on the steps of Grandma's house.

"You . . . *know better than that!*" Dad hissed through his teeth. There was something, frighteningly, almost like *pleasure* in his tone. With one hand, he took the back of Joe's mask and shoved it forward. Then he wrenched hold of Joe's left ear and squeezed as he twisted it, jerking Joe's head backward and sideways.

Joe screamed, but he did not resist. He even dropped his pumpkin on the cement steps. Walter heard paper-wrapped candies bouncing, and one of them, probably one of several judging by the sound, rolled across the toe of his tennis shoe, having escaped the sanctuary of Joe's pumpkin.

"Now tell your grandmother you're sorry," Dad said, twisting that ear even further, pulling Joe's mask off with his other hand and throwing it to the ground.

One of these days, thought Walter, he's going to tear one of them right off, and it'll probably be mine.

Walter moved back, giving his father plenty of room, as Mom watched, and Grandma watched, and Grandpa didn't even bother coming to the door.

"Turn and run," came the voice that was not the hate-thing, for the hate-thing never spoke. "Get away, to the tall shadows behind the trees. Something has to get better. Just take those first steps, and get away from all of this."

But he couldn't quite do that. He didn't believe he could outrun his father, and that would mean more physical pain than anything Joe was getting. Maybe if he waited until Monday, when he was supposed to be going to school, and Dad was supposed to go to work, maybe he could do it then. Maybe then, but not tonight.

"I'm sorry, Grandma," Joe stuttered, his chest heaving, tears rolling down silently without the moaning that Walter would have let loose.

Dad jerked the ear and Joe squealed, then fastened his upper teeth over his bottom lip and closed his eyes.

"What are you sorry for? Tell your grandmother. Do it correctly." With each loud word that Dad spoke, Joe's head was jerked, ear first.

In the light of the doorway, Walter could see blood beginning to well at the tear forming in the top of Joe's ear. His stomach balked, and he could feel thick, burning acidity surge upward inside his chest.

"I—I'm—sorry, Grandma, for poking my sword at you," Joe said, his voice cracking.

Walter's stomach was curdling now. He could feel the beginning of a dull, low ache that would turn heavy and painful later. There was a sour taste in his mouth. He could feel chocolate, and Sugarbabies, and Sweettarts ready to come out the same way they'd come in. But God oh God if he let loose here on the steps, Dad would kill him. He *had* to keep it down, *had* to.

"Yeah, that's right. Now let's start over without all the show-off business." And Dad let go of Joe's bleeding ear, wiping his hand on his pants. Left behind was a small, dark smear.

Joe bent slowly, so slowly that Walter was reminded of Grandpa stooping over his belly to tie those black shoes. He picked up his mask, but didn't draw it over his head. He picked up loose pieces of candy and dropped them into his pumpkin. Then he stood up, and Walter joined him, removing his Spider-Man mask.

They both said, "Trick-or-treat."

"Why *sure*! We can have treats for *nice* boys. Can't we, Grandpa?" Grandma said loudly, triumphantly.

There was the muffled sound of a voice that came from deeper inside the house. It sounded rough and irritated; it was Grandpa, saying "Whaaa—aaat?"

"I *said*," said Grandma, closed hands rising to rest on the plump shelf that made up her hips, "we have Halloween treats for Joe and Walter, don't we?"

"Of course; of course we do. Is that them?" came Grandpa's voice.

"You know it is," Grandma said, smiling her mask-smile at Joe and Walter. "Oh, but I'm forgetting, leaving you all out on the steps. Do come in. Be welcome."

Mom turned, her face not a smile, and she looked at Dad. He was not seeing her. They moved past Joe and Walter, entering first, Dad stopping to hug Grandma and kiss her cheek. "Joe didn't poke you with that sword, did he?"

"No, of course not. I'd have tanned his hide myself." Grandma's head turned toward Mom, who did not respond.

Once inside, Walter could smell something warm, sweet and freshly cooked. Grandma's house always smelled like a bakery. It was a welcome difference for Walter, who was used to the fragrance of Lysol, which Mom seemed to find reason to spray every day. He looked through the entryway into the flowery yellow of the kitchen and saw a large ceramic bowl fill with cellophane-wrapped chocolates—usually nuts and caramels, but also fudge and brittles, puffs of powdered-sugar cookies. Grandma had said once that these things were ordered "overseas" to arrive for the holidays, beginning right before Halloween.

Next to the bowl of sparkling wrappers, Walter could see two metal trays, one lined with white wax-paper. The bakery smell came from those rich chocolate brownies sprinkled with powdered sugar. Next to them was Walter's personal favorite, a tray of thick and shiny caramel apples on sticks. He could taste the apple and the buttery-sweet caramel.

"*My*," said Grandma, looking into Walter's pumpkin, "you're just *beginning* trick-or-treat, aren't you?"

"Yeah," said Walter, looking into his bucket and noticing that he'd eaten all the Hershey's kisses out of his take. "We've only been to six houses in our neighborhood."

"Have you been *eating* your *candy?*" his Mom demanded.

Walter tried not to look at Joe, thought of the wrappers in his coat pocket, and thought that they hadn't been to very many houses at all. And probably weren't likely to go to any more, if Mom had her way.

"No, Mom," he told her, flashing a look at Dad to see if he might attack. But Dad was looking down the hallway to the left, through which Grandpa could be seen, getting up from a red padded chair, pulling his infamous belt up. Sounds of a male newscaster rolled down the hall. The volume Grandpa liked was the same as shouting, to Walter's ears.

"We just don't know that many people in our neighborhood," Mom offered to Grandma.

Oh no? thought Walter. There were at least three others whose houses they hadn't visited. His friend Peter Kaiser's house, the Morrisey's, Mrs. DeVanden. It might be too late to go back to these places later.

"Well, I can recommend several houses around us," Grandma said, gesturing to the left with her thumb. "Bill and Maggie Climber, right next to us." Then to her right: "Walter and Linda Saulk. After them, there's Mr. Oriole, the Watercrests, Miltons. Most of the houses here would be okay to try. None of us seem to get many trick-or-treaters out here. So we have to eat most of that candy ourselves." She looked at Joe, who was shuffling toward the goodies in the kitchen. She frowned.

"We'll help you eat them, Grandma," said Walter. But he wondered about those other houses. He'd heard from Sam Wolver, also a sixth-grader, that coming out here was a waste of time: half of the people would be in bed, and the other half would just snarl at you and tell you to get the hell off of their property. And something about the tone in Grandma's voice made him think she didn't believe in what she was saying.

Heavy footfalls came from the hallway. Grandpa was slightly behind Dad as they approached the kitchen from the TV room. As they got further from the blast of the squalling television, Walter could hear what they were saying to each other.

"I don't know," said Grandpa, looking at the floor. "I've been thinking for a week now about what you said. It doesn't at all surprise me, you know."

"Yeah, Dad, I know," Dad grumbled.

"Well, I'm damn tired of it! What kind of a man are you, anyway? I didn't raise you poorly. Have you forgotten yourself *that* quickly? Do I still need to take care of *everything* for you, wipe your snotty nose?" Grandpa stopped near the end of the hall and looked Dad in the eye.

"I told you I don't know for sure," Dad said quietly, his lips stretched tightly.

"Well, *I* knew enough to take care of it. And I shouldn't have to say it, but I told you so." Grandpa started walking again, taking the lead. This time Dad walked behind. "*Bill Williams*. Christ!" Grandpa shook his head.

Mom stared at Grandpa, her mouth open for a moment. Then she turned back to Grandma.

"Since . . . since you know most of those people," she said to Grandma, doing exactly what Walter and Joe had feared she'd do, "why don't you take the boys trick-or-treating for a while? Maybe an hour or so?" His mother's eyes seemed like searchlights, shifting about, seeking an agreeable wrinkle in the other woman's face.

Grandma's smile fell away, and her face smoothed into a much more natural, if not very pretty, state. It was all true Grandma now, and no coating of any kind fell over the hate-thing that squinted greedily through her eyes.

"I told you, no about that. They're your responsibility." The voice was gray, dark, like the one she'd used when Walter broke one of her best pieces of china, and she had cried and spanked him.

"It's not for very long, I told you that! I want a little time to myself, that's all. Can't you help us out?"

"We *have*, Mary. Wilford and I have helped you both *so* many times. One day you'll leave the boys on our doorstep, and you'll be gone. We haven't got the time, not to mention patience. So let's have tricks-or-treats, and then you take your children where I told you to." And Grandma wiped her hands against each other, the way she did when they were coated with flour. She called Joe's name and went to him, telling him to keep his fingers out of the brownies. Mom looked at a countertop.

Now Grandpa approached, and Dad. Dad was moving closer to Mom, his arms folded, a warning on his face. His lips were closed. There was no gnashing of teeth. He looked at her, and it seemed there was no Dad in his eyes anymore. The hate-thing had swallowed him and come back out, pushing its face into the gray behind Dad's shell. He was holding back from striking her now, but not because of the urge to put those hands to work.

Grandpa, it seemed, had taken care of that.

Grandpa's eyes moved over Mom, first her face, then lower. She did not look at anyone. Her eyes were tracing out something among Grandma's spice bottles and canisters of flour that were strewn along the counter, near the white enamel sink.

Grandpa Wilford came closer to Walter, as the room filled with Grandma's speech to Joe about what was cooked up in her brownies.

Walter looked up at the yellow lightbulb on the ceiling. There was a moth there, flittering crazily in circles, thrashing its body against the bulb. Again and again, it never tired, never seemed to feel the heat of the bulb, never noticed that its efforts were useless.

"Boy," said Grandpa. Walter didn't think Grandpa liked the name, "Walter." He'd certainly never used it.

"Yes sir?" Walter asked, looking at that yellowish, graying beard. Grandpa's fairly thick eyeglasses made the hate-image in his eyes seem more alive, more vocal somehow.

"You have something to say, boy?" Grandpa put out a thick, cracked fingernail on the end of a crooked, knotted finger. It touched Walter's chest ever so lightly.

Walter looked at his Mom and Dad. Dad was gesturing toward the front door, his eyes only for Mom. She moved close to him, eyes meeting his, mouth pulled tight enough to have been sewn on. She moved outside, ahead of him, and Dad followed. Once they were off the steps, Walter could hear his Dad's voice rise to almost a yell.

"*Boy* . . ." Grandpa said, his voice quietly reminding Walter of the belt around his large waist. The belt was very painful. Only a week ago, Walter had been subjected to its bite. Grandpa had caught him sitting in his red chair—or rather, had felt the warmth left by Walter's body. Grandma had been taking one of her naps, and Grandpa had gone downtown on some mysterious errand, as was his way. Walter had parked himself in Grandpa's chair and watched *The Munsters* on cable. He'd kept a sharp eye out for Grandpa, but had forgotten about the warmth that his body left in the chair. Nor was this his first experience with Grandpa's belt. Grandpa used it freely, heavily.

"Sorry sir. I *do* have something to say. I—" And he stopped, because he didn't think Grandpa would understand, and he certainly wasn't sure he wanted to tell him even if he *could* understand.

But then he thought about the weather-cover over Grandpa's car, and he realized that Grandpa also knew about worrying over things that hadn't materialized yet. And evil. Grandpa, he was sure, knew all about evil.

"Damn it, boy," Grandpa said, his right hand moving to his belt. He propped his thumb inside and began undoing the buckle.

"Do you see something, sometimes, in my eyes?" Walter said quickly, glad to be out with it, hopeful that he hadn't stalled too long.

Walter did not ask the other question in his mind: Grandpa, what do you see when you look at your eyes in a mirror?

"See *what*," Grandpa stated, not asking.

"It's like . . . something like *hate*. When I look in the mirror. When I look at Joe. When Mom and Dad get mad. The eyes," and he reached up, touching a fingertip to his own lower eye, below the lashes. The skin there was soft, cool, oily. He took his hand away, watched Grandpa, and wiped thumb and finger on the seat of his costume. "The eyes get darker, and there's something there that's *not* them, or *too much* them; I don't know which."

"*Really*?" said Grandpa. "And do you see it in *my* eyes?"

Walter looked up into the older man's face and searched each eye as if he'd never checked before. He wondered if he dare lie now.

"I think I do," he told Grandpa, then lowered his eyes, fully expecting to see the hands finish unstrapping the belt.

"Young child like you shouldn't be thinking about things like that," Grandpa said, turning his head toward the doorway. Outside, his Mom was yelling, though Walter could not make out her words.

Grandpa took up the slack in his belt and fastened it. "It's there, isn't it? Can you see it in me?"

Walter looked back up at the old face.

Grandpa slipped his glasses off, pulled a dark blue handkerchief from his back pocket and rubbed at both lenses. He lifted them back up to his face. Walter saw nothing but smudge on them as Grandpa replaced the glasses, yet the film did not hide what lay in his old eyes.

"I see it," Grandpa said.

Walter sighed heavily. "Do you know how I can get rid of it?" he asked.

"Don't worry about it. It will go away. Nothing lasts forever, boy. Things like that, especially. Why, I wouldn't be surprised if it's gone by tonight. So don't trouble yourself with it. Those kinds of thoughts are not for a young feller like yourself. You know?" And then Grandpa reached out with a huge hand and squeezed his shoulder, something Walter had not experienced from him before.

"Thanks, Grandpa," Walter said, breath coming and filling him up, replacing the bulk of pain in his stomach.

Mom and Dad continued to argue, but Walter found that for once he didn't need to listen to their words.

Grandpa guided him over to where Joe stood, watching the big tray of brownies and licking his bottom lip.

"Well, Grandma," said Grandpa, his theatrical voice full and deep, loud enough to drown the sounds of Mom and Dad that came in through the still-open doorway, "what have we to treat these little goblins?"

"I'm not a goblin!" Joe hollered, frowning at Grandpa. "I'm Lion-O, the Thundercat. Can't you see?"

Grandma frowned again, squinting at Joe. She looked at Grandpa. He shook his head, but only, it seemed, for her. He said nothing to Joe.

"Well, Lion-O, for you, an old favorite. Brownie with powdered sugar." Grandma pushed a metal spatula underneath one of the brownies, lifted it and placed it on a napkin.

Grandpa nodded at her. She gave the napkin to Joe. He took the brownie, his eyes hungry.

"What do you say?" Grandma asked, setting down the spatula.

"Thank you," Joe mumbled. He held the brownie with both hands, and then almost put his nose onto its white surface.

"You're welcome. Remember, you're not to be eating those things in your father's car."

"Yes, ma'am," said Joe.

"And you?" asked Grandpa, looking at Walter with stone eyes.

"I think a nice caramel apple would fit him just right. Don't you, Walter?"

"Yes *please*," Walter told her.

"Okay!" she hooted. She picked one of the twelve apples off of the tray.

"No, no. The one with the extra caramel, there by itself," Grandpa said, his voice impatient. He pointed at one that looked bigger than all the rest.

"Oh," said Grandma.

She picked up the biggest apple, caramel thick and luscious, waxed paper on one end, and handed it to Walter who took it gingerly.

"Thanks, ma'am," Walter said.

"You're welcome. Now you two go finish that trick-or-treating."

Grandma guided both boys to the door just in time to see Dad slap Mom across the face with the back of his hand. She rolled backward and smacked the outside passenger mirror on their car. She grunted, tears starting to spill out of her eyes. She looked up, saw Grandpa, Walter and Joe, and Grandma watching her.

As Dad, whose back was to the house, came toward her, hand raised again, she said: "It's time to go," with a voice that was barely there, and she pointed toward the house.

Dad turned to look. His arm came down. "Well, come on! Let's go!" He motioned at the two boys, then looked at their mother.

Walter and Joe said goodbye to Grandma and Grandpa, both of whom merely stared at them and kept silent, their faces reminding Walter of the way the moon looked when full: pale, ghostly, with secrets swamped in shadow.

Walter and Joe slid into the back of the car, as Dad spoke some sort of abrupt farewell to Grandma and Grandpa. This time, both of the old folks waved.

As the car pulled away from the curb, Mom sniffling, curled into the passenger door as if she would leap out at any second, Dad turned to glare at Joe and Walter for a moment.

"Don't be eating that sticky stuff in this car, either." Then he, and the hate in his eyes, turned to driving, and silence.

Walter looked at Joe, who still explored his brownie with his nose. Joe looked right back at him, grinning. He stuck his tongue out and licked the edge of the brownie. In the darkness of the car, Walter could see a smudge in the pale, almost glowing powdered sugar.

Walter shook his head. Joe threw back his own head in mock, silent laughter. Then he took a big bite out of the brownie and began chewing. He watched their father as he ate, first that bite, then another.

Joe elbowed Walter, and nodded toward the caramel apple. He took another bite of brownie as Walter shook his head, no.

Walter thought about taking a bite. He was worried about what might happen if Dad heard him or saw the evidence. He could stick the leftovers in his pumpkin under a thin shelf of candy, or maybe in his coat pocket. The way things were looking, their trick-or-treating seemed to be over. And Walter was afraid to ask Dad if they would be stopping at any more houses.

Joe elbowed him again, grinning, thick clumps of darkness that must have been brownie clotting his teeth.

Walter looked at the apple, shiny even in this gray light. The caramel would be homemade, with cream, delicious. He opened his mouth wide and sunk his teeth in, then pulled the bite away, using a finger to gather stray strings of caramel. Then he put his hand over his mouth and looked at Dad, hoping the biting of the apple hadn't stirred him. Dad did not turn. Walter began to munch, savoring the sweet, crisp moisture of the apple mixed with the buttery-smooth taste of caramel. His stomach was smiling, he was sure.

Joe reached down with a finger and plunged it into the brownie. He pulled the finger free, looked at it; it was covered with brownie innards. He stuck the finger in his mouth and licked it, then pulled it out. There was still some brownie left there.

As Walter fastened his front, upper teeth into the caramel apple again, Joe said aloud, "This brownie tastes funny."

Walter bit down all the way, and he was suddenly accosted by a sharp, almost electric pain in his mouth. He grunted, "Ouch!" and pulled back, but something held fast to his mouth. The skin began to throb. He pulled harder, and a piece of apple came away from the whole. Part of the apple bit separated from the caramel. The other part was stuck to him as the stinging pain increased. He put his fingers to his mouth and pulled at the apple and caramel. There was something hard and smooth and—"Aaagh!" he yelped, pulling his sliced fingers away. A picture formed in his mind, and he could see the razor blade that had sunk into his lips and upper gums. He looked at his fingers; they were dark and wet.

Walter screamed.

Dad put the brakes to the car, then turned in his seat.

Joe screamed now too. Walter looked at him; Joe was looking at Walter's mouth. He held a pale, terrified pose there. Then he looked at his brownie. He began to shriek in earnest, then. Long, piercing howls of fright.

Dad said, "Oh, *Jesus!*"

Mom turned to look, her mouth opening when she saw. No sound escaped.

There was an awful, coppery taste in Walter's mouth as it filled with liquid.

But as Joe screamed, and Mom stared, and Dad jumped out of the car and threw open the back door, Walter found himself drawn to all their eyes. Dad's, Mom's, Joe's.

There was no sign of the hate-thing in any of them. It had gone, maybe for good. Walter knew it must be gone from his own eyes as well.

Just as Grandpa Wilford had said.

THE KINGDOM OF CATS AND BIRDS

Geoffrey A. Landis

Geoffrey A. Landis is a scientist and science fiction writer by trade. It thus comes as a delightful surprise to discover he also has a taste for fairy tales. The charming, whimsical story that follows is reprinted from *SF Age* magazine.

Landis has made a name for himself as the author of a number of fine science fiction stories published over the last several years, including "Ripples in the Dirac Sea," which earned him a Nebula Award, and "A Walk in the Sun," which won a Hugo Award. As a former member of the Cambridge SF writers group (which includes Steven Popkes, David Alexander Smith, and Alexander Jablokov), Landis is a contributor to the group's collective SF anthology, *Future Boston*. He currently lives in Brook Park, Ohio.

—T. W.

Once there was a poor widow who had three daughters.

The oldest daughter, Anne, was very beautiful. She loved to sing and play her harp, and it was said that her singing was more beautiful than the song of any turtledove.

The youngest, Celia, was lithe and slender. She loved to run and hunt and scamper to the top of all the hills in the neighborhood, and it was said that there was no mountain she could not climb, and no boy she could not best at any game he would care to name.

But the middle daughter, Beth, was neither beautiful like her older sister, nor athletic like her younger sister, but had only her wit, common sense and good humor.

One day the poor widow called her daughters to her. "Times have been hard," she said, "and I have nothing to give you. You will have to go out into the world and make your own way. Anne, you are fair and have a good heart, but you are too easily fooled by the world. Celia, you are agile and have a strong spirit, but you are too straightforward, while the world is crooked. You both must promise to listen to your sister Beth, and do what she says. Beth, you must use your cleverness to take care of your sisters, and see that no harm comes to them." And so the two sisters promised to obey their wise middle sister, and they set out into the world.

After traveling for a very long time, they found themselves in a deep forest. The night got darker and darker, and soon they saw that they were surrounded by hundreds of glowing yellow eyes. The oldest sister tried to hide, and the youngest sister prepared to fight, but the middle sister looked calmly back into the night, and said, "We are three sisters alone in the world and mean you no harm."

Out of the darkness stepped an uncommonly large red cat. He rubbed up against a tall tree, and spoke in a low, meowy voice. "You may mean us no harm, but you may not stay here, for I am the king of the cats, and this is the country of the cats, and none but cats may stay here." And as he spoke, cats of all sizes and colors came out of the woods by twos and threes and dozens, until the clearing was full of cats, all of them looking at the sisters with glowing yellow eyes.

But Beth, the middle sister, boldly replied, "Then all is well, for we too are cats."

The red cat laughed in a purring sort of voice and said, "I think you are no cats, but for the moment I will let you live, and we shall see. Night has fallen, and it is time for us to hunt. I shall see what you bring back."

The red cat stretched, then in a single bound disappeared into the woods. By twos and threes and dozens, the other cats likewise disappeared into the night.

"What shall we do?" asked Anne, "for we are surely lost now." But Beth only nodded to Celia, who disappeared into the woods.

After a while the cats began to return, by twos and threes and dozens. One had a mouse, and another a mole. This one had a chipmunk, and that one a squirrel, and yet another brought a rabbit. At last the king of the cats came back, bringing a woodchuck that was quite larger than he was. They all looked at the two sisters.

Just then Celia burst into the clearing, bringing with her a doe she had chased down and caught. She put the doe down in the middle of the glade, and it stood there for a moment, dazed, then turned and bounded off into the woods.

"It seems you can hunt," said the king of the cats, "but yet and still, I think you are no cats. We shall see. It now approaches midnight, and time for the cats to serenade." With that, all the cats commenced to yowling, in high voices and low, with growls and hisses and meows of every pitch and timbre. Celia put her hands over her ears to block out the awful din, but Beth only nodded to Anne.

Anne began to sing, a song with no words that blended in and harmonized with the wailing of all the cats. So pure and lovely was her voice, that it made the caterwauling of the cats seem like a choir backing up a singer. After a while the cats began to stop their yowling to listen, until at last only three continued, a small white cat with a contralto meow, a huge old tom with scarred ears yowling in baritone, and the king of the cats singing along in a perfect tenor.

When they finally stopped, and the last note hung on the night air like a dandelion seed, the king of the cats spoke again. "It seems you can sing," said the king of the cats, "but yet and still I think you are no cats. We shall see."

The king of the cats commenced to sit down and wash his paws and then his ears, and then he curled around and began to wash the length of his tail. All around, the cats began to wash each other, holding each other down with their paws and, with great seriousness, washing each others' whiskers, ears, and necks.

Beth pulled out her hairbrush and began to brush the cat king behind his ears and down his back.

"I still think you are no cats," said the king of the cats, but he purred as he spoke. "But yet and still, you may stay with us if you will."

And so the three sisters stayed snug and warm in the kingdom of the cats, even over the winter, surrounded by cats of all descriptions.

After many months the king of the cats said to the middle daughter, "Spring has arrived, and it is the tradition of cats to go our separate ways, meeting only on the dark side of the moon. But you have been very good to us, and if there is ever any favor you need of us, you need only to clap twice and call me, and I will be there."

With a bound the king of the cats disappeared into the forest, and by twos and threes and dozens the other cats followed, each stopping briefly by the daughters to be stroked one final time. But soon the three daughters were again alone.

"What shall we do?" said Anne.

"We shall go forth into the world and seek our fortunes," Beth replied firmly, "for that is what our mother has told us to do."

And so they went forth.

After they had walked a long long way, evening came, and the sky began to grow dark. They were walking through a wide meadow filled with bushes and plants, and all around them they could hear rustlings and low noises, though they could see no one following.

At last Beth called for the other two sisters to stop. She peered into the evening darkness and called out in a clear, strong voice, "Who are you? Why are you following us? We are three sisters alone in the world and mean you no harm."

Out of the darkness spoke a high, trilling voice. "You may mean us no harm, but you may not stay here." Into the clearing stepped an enormous bird, with magnificent plumage of every color and a wickedly pointed beak. "For this is the country of the birds, and I am the queen of the birds. Only birds may stay here, and here you may not stay."

And in truth, as the sisters' eyes began to see into the gloom, they saw that birds were fluttering and flitting all around them, and that they were surrounded by birds' nests, so that it was a wonder that they had not trampled through nests in their walking. Before them was the largest nest of all.

"So then all is well," said the intrepid sister, "for indeed we are birds ourselves."

"If you are birds, you are most peculiar birds indeed," said the queen of the birds, turning her head to look at them first with one eye, then with the other. "If birds you are, they you can do whatever it is we birds can do?"

"Of course," said the dauntless sister.

"Of course," said the queen bird. "In the distance, then, look on yonder crag. It is a haven against the four-legged and two-legged creatures that steal eggs, for its sides are so steep that none might climb there. On the summit is the nest of the rare misander bird. Perhaps you would fly there and bring me back a feather, of which there are many discarded in the nest?"

"Certainly," said Beth. "My sister Celia will gladly fetch a feather for you." And Celia disappeared into the night, while Beth and Anne told stories of their travels to keep the queen bird amused.

In a while, Celia returned. And since there was no crag so steep that Celia could not scamper to the top, she carried in her hands a lovely feather of a deep purple hue, the feather of the rare and beautiful misander bird.

The queen bird looked at the feather in silence and then looked at the sisters. After a while she spoke again. "Night has fallen," she said, "and it is time for the birds of the evening to sing the sun to rest. Since you have not yet tucked your heads under your wings like the birds of the daytime, perhaps you would care to join our serenade?" Without waiting for a reply, the queen bird began to trill, and with her a thousand bird voices sang out of the darkness.

Beth nodded to her sister Anne, and Anne joined her voice to the chorus. Her voice was so pure and sweet that after a while the birds fell silent to listen, saving only for a nightingale singing alto, who swept down out of the trees to sing on Anne's right shoulder; a turtledove tweeting harmony in soprano, who fluttered down out of the trees to perch on Anne's left shoulder; and the queen of the birds leading the melody in a treble warble.

At the rising of the moon the birds fell silent, and Anne sang the last chorus alone.

"You sing as sweetly as any bird," said the bird queen, "but in one thing you are sadly remiss. It is nesting season, and all of us treasure our eggs above everything else and keep them warm. But it has now grown quite cool, and even I, myself, must return to my eggs, which are certainly growing chill." But when the bird queen looked into her nest, she discovered that while they were singing Beth had covered up the eggs with a shawl to keep them warm against the night air.

"You are most peculiar birds," said the bird queen, "if indeed birds you truly are. But I do declare that you are welcome to stay here with us, if so you desire."

And so they stayed in the country of the birds.

After many months all the eggs were hatched, all the birds were restless and all the fledglings were flitting and fluttering in longer and longer flights. "Autumn has come," said the queen of the birds, "and it is time again for us to fly away to the south. Will you not be flying with us?"

Beth shook her head.

"Then we must part, and you must make your way as you can. But, if ever you need a favor from the birds, you have only to clap three times and call, and I shall help you, if it is within my powers. Farewell."

And so the queen of the birds flapped her huge wings once and flew away into the sky, followed by her children, each one chirping, "Goodbye! Goodbye! Goodbye!" until they were so distant that all that could be heard was the plaintive sound of the wind. And flock by flock, the other birds trilled and chirped their farewells to the three sisters, the ducks and the herons and the geese, leaving only the birds of winter, who scattered to the winds to scratch out their livings one by one until spring came.

"Be of good cheer, my sisters," said Beth, dauntless. "We must continue on to seek our fortunes in the wide world."

The sisters walked on, and after much traveling they came again to a land of fields and farms. Beth grew fearful for their safety as they were three defenseless girls traveling alone, and so told her sisters that perhaps it would be prudent if they were to change their garb.

Beth and Celia cut off their tresses and donned the trousers and jerkins of young men. Anne, though, had filled out in their travels to become quite a comely young woman, and they agreed that no amount of disguise could make her appear to be a man. So they journeyed onward in the guise of two brothers traveling as guardians and protectors of their beautiful sister.

In time they came to a great castle. Judging that in such a castle none would offer them harm, Beth strode forthright to the thick wooden door and knocked on the huge brass knocker for admittance.

Beth was surprised when the gate was opened and they were welcomed in by none other than the king himself. The hour was late, and with her most humble manner she explained to him that they were weary travelers who asked only for the most meager of shelter in the stables and whatever scraps of food might be considered too poor to be eaten at his table.

The king, though, would not be persuaded but to feed them from his dining room, summoning the chief cook out from his quarters to prepare a lavish repast for the weary travelers. After they had eaten, he had them shown to a sumptuous suite of rooms.

In the morning they found that for the two boys (for such he took them to be) the king had laid out rich clothing to replace their worn cloaks, and for their sister nothing would do but that she replace her simple frock with the best dress in the royal wardrobe. After they were well rested he invited them to break their fast at the royal table.

The king was a melancholy young man, and after Beth had treated him to a much abbreviated account of their travels, he sighed. "Though I would invite you to stay as my guests for as long as you would," he said, and sighed again, "mine is a sorely troubled kingdom, and it would not be right for me to ask you to share my problems. To the north are only the mountains, but to the south is the kingdom of Banting, a rich and prosperous place. I expect that there you could indeed find yourselves a home."

"I thank you for your kind wishes and your advice," said Beth. "The responsibilities of kingship, I am sure, are a difficult burden. It is to your credit that you have concern for your people, but perhaps excessive worry may make your troubles appear worse than they truly are."

"I would that it were so," said the king, "but my troubles are several, and any of them alone would be enough to unmake my kingdom. Long ago my father quarreled with the king of Banting, and since my father has died, he covets my kingdom, and has promised his kingdom and mine to whichever of his sons can conquer my land. Prince Fobbish is a dutiful son and has promised his father that he will conquer my country before the spring. And his other son, Prince Bantingroy, is a brave and hearty warrior, and he, too, has promised his father that he will conquer my lands by spring. What army I have could not even fight off one prince, and certainly not two.

"Were that not enough, my country has been beset with troubles. Every spring a swarm of locusts comes to eat the seedlings as fast as my farmers can plant, and a plague of mice comes to eat all of my stores of grain, and so I have emptied the royal treasury just to feed my people, and there is no money left to pay soldiers. When spring comes, the land will belong to Prince Bantingroy," he shrugged, "or perhaps Prince Fobbish. I only hope that the prince—whoever it will be—will bring grain to feed my people. If he does, he will be a better ruler to the people than I have been."

Beth's heart went out to the young king, and she resolved to help him in any way she could. "Your troubles are indeed great," she said. "But appoint me your chief counselor, and perhaps we can find a way to reverse your fortunes."

The king was surprised that a penniless stranger should make so brash an offer, but after a moment of reflection he accepted the offer. "After all," he said, "your advice could not make the situation any worse than it already is."

"Then tell me more about this Prince Fobbish, and also of Prince Bantingroy," she said.

And so the king and Beth spoke together well into the afternoon, and indeed on into the early night. After hearing all, Beth said, "Make my si—ah, brother here general of all your army against Prince Bantingroy, and with your leave I will have a look at the army of Prince Fobbish. And, with God's grace, all will yet turn out well."

Although the king's soldiers were not many, Celia was quite pleased to have command of them and drilled them with enthusiasm. Soon her example inspired all the soldiers, and they were eager to face the armies of Prince Bantingroy, for they considered this to be an easier task than that of pleasing their new general, who could—and frequently did—best any one of them at any form of combat you could name.

In the meanwhile, Beth looked over the armies of Prince Fobbish and came back to the castle asking for a pail full of black walnut dye, and another pail of red berry dye. These the king provided.

Following Beth's instructions, Anne trained the women and girls of the castle to play the fife, blow the bugle, and beat the heavy war drums that army commanders use to communicate maneuvers to their flanks.

As Celia led her small squad out to meet Prince Bantingroy's army, the women drummers went out by a different path, to make a cacophony of sound like that of a very large army.

And so the armies of Prince Bantingroy were led around and around in large circles and small, first by catching a glimpse of the squadron of General Celia, and then hearing the drums and bugles of an army across the nearby hill, but never catching up to the army they could quite well hear but never see.

At last Prince Bantingroy grew disgusted with such tactics. Ignoring the temptation to chase after the phantom army, he marched his army straight for the castle. Camping just half a day's march from the castle, he sent his seneschal to issue a challenge: "Enough of this skirmishing and pointless marching. Let the battle be decided man to man. If this mysterious general has courage to equal his skill at skirmishing, let him show it. Prince Bantingroy challenges him. Let each promise that if the other should win, he shall surrender his forces immediately."

Celia sent a messenger back to accept his offer, and a date was set for the combat.

When the day of the combat dawned, Prince Bantingroy arrived in full armor upon a huge and restless steed of midnight black. He was a tall and muscular young man, with a beard of darkest black and piercing black eyes. He saluted the castle with his lance, then threw the lance down into the ground and issued his challenge again.

From the castle rode out a single armored rider on a chalk white filly. The rider drew up to the line, dismounted, and removed his visor, and Prince Bantingroy was surprised to see a slender and graceful youth meet his curious gaze with steadfast gray eyes.

"I accept your challenge," said the youth. "I am the general you seek."

The prince was surprised that such a beardless youth could be the general of such an army, but his heart went out to the boy, who was brave enough to stake his life to certain defeat for the sake of his men and his king. And so he resolved to spare the life of the boy if he could. "I propose, then, that the first trial of the day be archery," said the prince, "three arrows each at a maple leaf set to a bale of straw at a furlong's distance, the winner to be the closest shot."

"Three shots to hit a maple leaf a mere furlong away?" The youth shrugged carelessly. "Very well, then, I accept. Give me leave to send my page back for my bow."

While the target was being set, the page returned with the bow. Prince Bantingroy shot first. His first arrow hit the straw halfway between the edge of the bale and the leaf. His second shot was a mere finger's span from the leaf, and the third shot grazed the edge of the leaf.

The prince smiled and put down his bow. "Match that, if you can."

The youth carefully strung his bow and selected arrows fletched in green, silver, and white. He paused for a moment, eyeing the target and feeling the air, then drew and fired.

Before the first arrow had struck the target the bow twanged twice more, and its two brothers were on the wing as well. One, two, three, the arrows struck the target, and all three pierced the leaf within the span of a silver crown from the center. A great cheer went out from the crowd.

"Your aim was true," the youth said calmly, "but you must pay more heed to the breeze caressing your cheek."

Prince Bantingroy, who had thought himself the best archer in the countryside, nodded in silence.

"For the second contest," said the youth, "I propose a footrace, three times around the castle."

"I accept," said the prince. "We shall race at sunset."

At sunset the two challengers were ready, the prince stripped down to barely more than a loincloth, the youthful general still wearing his white tunic. The prince thought this slightly odd, but forbore to comment. The seneschal banged his starting drum, and the race began.

Once around the castle, and the runners appeared from behind the castle, the prince first and the young general far behind. A groan came from the castle, but the prince's men cheered loudly.

A second time around and the prince was still ahead, although perhaps not so much. The crowd was silent.

The third time the runners appeared, though, the two were abreast. Prince Bantingroy was panting, his face purple and sweat pouring across his chest. The youth, though, was calm, his legs moving with an even rhythm. As they approached the finish line, the prince was unable to keep his pace and fell behind. The crowd from the castle cheered anew. "Hurrah! Hurrah! Hurrah for the boy general!"

The prince collapsed on the ground. "Enough of games," he said, gritting his teeth and gasping. "The last and final contest shall be wrestling, winner take all, the contest to continue until one of the contestants concedes the match and with it his army. I shall meet you three days hence, at dawn."

The crowd groaned aloud, for Prince Bantingroy was a burly man, for outmuscling the slender youth. The youth, however, was undaunted. "Very well, then," he said. "A wrestling contest for the final challenge, winner take all."

In the meanwhile, Beth and Anne had slipped out to meet the armies of Prince Fobbish, who was even at that very moment on the march toward the kingdom.

Prince Fobbish rode in a silver carriage decorated with golden braid, and his army held long lances carried high, each with a gold and silver pennant flying from the end, for the prince believed that an army that looked its best would fight all the harder for its prince.

As the prince traveled, he grew perplexed. At last he ordered his carriage stopped. "Do you hear a maiden singing?" he asked his general, who was riding a war horse along side the carriage. "It seems to me that the voice is uncommonly sweet. Find out from where it is coming."

"Yes, my prince," said the general, who rode off into the forest. In a minute he was back. "In a clearing in the forest, there is a forest maid, of brown hair and apple-blossom complexion," he said. "She sings as she combs her hair."

"Ask her if she would come here," commanded Prince Fobbish, "that she may sing to us for luck." The general rode again off into the forest.

In a moment he returned. "She is gone."

"Find her. I hear her singing yet; she cannot be far," said the prince, although in truth the voice did seem fainter, at times almost indistinguishable from the noises of the forest. "Send your men to find her. Today I shall not ride farther until I see her face and listen to her sweet voice."

The general saluted and sent his army out to search the woods. Often they caught a glimpse of brown hair, or heard a voice singing, but as they turned to look closer, it would turn out to be no more than a little brown bird perched in the low branches of a tree, singing. And, chasing after the singing of little birds all the morning and afternoon, they wandered in circles through the forest.

"It seems to me that there are an uncommon number of birds in this woods," said the general, "but then, as I do not usually walk through the woods seeking a brown-haired maid, perhaps it is only that I have never before noticed. Still, it would not seem that a single maid would be so hard to find."

When the evening came the soldiers returned one by one to their prince, admitting defeat. The prince took it in good humor. But as his men raised the silver- and gold-trimmed tent for Prince Fobbish, the prince could not help but think of the distant song, and he slept dreaming of a brown-haired maiden.

The next day they broke camp at dawn and returned to the march, the silver and gold pennants of the army making a glorious sight in the morning sun. They had not traveled many miles, though, before again the prince heard singing, and indeed a melody even sweeter than before. Again he ordered his carriage stopped, and the prince walked out himself with his general into the woods.

They came to a clearing where sat a maiden with hair of autumn-leaf red, playing a lap harp and singing softly. The prince made a soft noise of wonder at her beauty, and she looked up. For a moment she smiled, and it seemed to the prince that the sun then shined, and that it had been a long time since he had seen the sun. He was too far from the maiden to talk to her, and between them was a stand of thorn bushes.

By the time he had found the path through the bushes and reached the clearing, she was gone.

"Find her," commanded the prince. "Tell her I only wish to listen to her singing and gaze upon her face. Only that and no more."

As the men searched the forest, they would often see a flash of red hair and hear a snatch of song, only to find looking back at them nothing but an orange tomcat, sitting on a branch mewing.

"It does seem to me," said the general, "that I have never before seen so many cats in the forest. But doubtless, since neither have I ever searched a forest for a red-haired maiden, it is only that I have never noticed." And again the men returned at sunset to report their failure.

That night, when the prince finally fell asleep, it was of a red-haired maid that he dreamed.

On the next day the prince resolved to ride directly to the battle. But again he heard singing, and this time the singing was so clear and so strong that he thought the singer could be no more than a few feet away from the road.

The prince motioned his men to stay back and went alone into the woods.

The maid sat in a clearing, and her hair was the color of the honey made by bees that have fed only on spring clover. Again she looked up at him, and it seemed to the prince that she said something, but he was just far enough away that he could not quite catch her words before she slipped off into the woods. "Wait," shouted the prince. "I mean you no harm! I just want to. . . ." But the maid was gone.

He called his men. "A hundred crowns of silver to the man who finds her," he said. "And heed me well, she is not to be harmed or coerced."

While the men searched the forest, chasing after birds and cats, the prince sat in melancholy by the road. But his mood could not be dark for long, for the singing lifted his spirits. He looked up, and there was the maid. "Wait," he shouted, but she again slipped away.

He followed her into the woods, but whenever he caught a glimpse of her, she was just ahead of him, slipping out of sight.

In the meanwhile, prince Bantingroy arrived at the field for the wrestling match. He stripped to the waist, but the mysterious youth again declined to strip down, preferring to wrestle in his tunic. They bowed to each other, and the match began.

While the prince was much the stronger, the mysterious youth was agile, and every time the prince nearly made a hold, the youth would twist out of it and slip to the other side. But neither could the youth gain any advantage over Prince Bantingroy.

The match went on for an hour, and yet another, and while both sides were panting and covered in sweat, neither would yield.

But in wrestling some secrets cannot be kept, and after a while the prince had a most peculiar suspicion about his mysterious young opponent. Finally he sprang back and stared at the youth. With his tunic wet down with sweat and clinging to his body, there was no way to conceal the truth. "You are no lad, but a maid," said the prince in surprise.

"Indeed, and so I have always been," said the girl. "Do you yield?"

"I will yield on the day you marry me," said Prince Bantingroy.

"Very well, then," said Celia. "Let us go find the king, and his counselor, whose sister I am, to tell them of our decision."

When they reached the castle, camped in the fields all around were armies flying the pennants of Prince Fobbish. "It is my foolish brother!" exclaimed Prince Bantingroy. "I cannot allow him to conquer. Let me go to fetch my army, and you yours, and we shall drive my brave but foolhardy brother back home crying to my father."

"The army does not seem arrayed for fighting," said Celia, looking at the soldiers with a practiced eye. "I think we should first talk to the king and see what is occurring."

And, indeed, when they got to the castle, Prince Fobbish was already there in company with the king, as well as Anne and the still-disguised Beth.

"I have negotiated peace with Prince Fobbish, who has just asked me for the hand of my counselor's sister in marriage," said the king. "So I therefore declare this a day of celebration and feasting, even though—as I assume—you have come to demand that I surrender my kingdom."

"Not at all," said Prince Bantingroy. "I have come to ask for peace between our kingdoms, and, with your permission and the leave of your counselor here, to ask for the hand of your general in marriage."

The king was surprised to find that his general was in fact a girl, but made haste to give his permission, as, with a smile, did his counselor. And so the two sisters went back to make wedding preparations.

"Alas," said the king to Beth, "though all your work has prevented the war, still my kingdom is sorely troubled. The granaries of the kingdom are full of seed, but every spring, mice and rats come and eat it all before we can plant. And as for what seed we plant, as fast as the seedlings sprout, a horde of locusts comes and devours them."

"Then with your leave I shall make a visit to the farms and fields," said Beth. And so she did.

When she reached the royal granary she proceeded to clap her hands twice and call for the king of the cats.

From seemingly nowhere came the large red tomcat. He sat down in front of Beth and began to wash his paws. "And what do you want?" he said querulously. "You have already asked your favor of me, to mislead soldiers in the woods, and I do not think I feel like granting another favor to you today."

"I did not call you to ask a favor," Beth replied, "but to thank you. In gratitude, I would like you to take note of the granaries and farms of this kingdom, which are full of plump and lazy field mice."

"Is that so?" said the king of the cats in a purring voice. "That is most interesting news indeed. I thank you." The cat king got up, stretched once, and bounded off.

Next she visited the fields, and when she was again alone she clapped three times and called for the queen of the birds.

In a few moments the enormous bird swooped out of the sky and landed before her. "I am glad to see you again," said the bird queen, looking at her first with one eye and then with the other, "but we birds are quite busy now preparing for our migration, and in any case, I think that we no longer owe you any favors. So if you don't mind, I shall continue on my way."

"I did not call you to ask a favor," said Beth, "but to make a gift to you. Every spring a swarm of locusts settles onto these fields. It would be quite a fat repast, should any birds wish to stop by."

"Indeed?" said the queen of the birds. "Then this is most welcome news, for we are most hungry from migration. I shall tell my flock." And the bird queen flapped once and vanished into the sky.

So when the spring came, again the winter-hungry mice returned to invade the seed stores, but there were cats everywhere to catch them, and so this time the farmers had plenty of seed to sow. When the seedlings began to sprout, again swarms of locust descended to dine on their accustomed feast of tender young plants, but as fast as they could arrive, flocks of birds swooped down to eat them, and the plants were saved.

And so when the day of the royal weddings came, there was much to celebrate indeed. The king of Banting was far too pleased over the marriage of his sons to be disappointed that the princes had not conquered the kingdom. And after the feasting, he came over and privately promised the full support of his armies should anyone else ever think to invade.

Her sisters now seen to safety and their wanderings finished, the king's counselor finally decided to end her deception as well and revealed to the king that she was no lad at all.

After getting over his surprise, he declared that since her sisters had wedded royalty, nothing less would suit than that she should marry royalty as well, and so he asked for her to be his queen. Since the king was himself still a young man, she readily agreed, and he promised her that he would accept her wise advice just as intently when she was his queen as he did when she was his counselor.

And so it was that three sisters became queens of three kingdoms.

It was often remarked upon by the people that wherever the queens were, there were always birds of every description singing in the trees, even in winter, and also that there were always friendly cats that the three queens would invariably pet and pamper with milk and tidbits of meat. Since the three queens had brought prosperity and peace with them, birds and cats came to be considered signs of luck throughout the kingdoms, and so it happened that no one in the kingdoms would shoot a bird, and that stray cats were welcomed to a warm hearth and the choicest assortment of scraps at even the poorest household.

And perhaps there is some truth to the stories of luck, since the lands remain prosperous and peaceful, even to this very day.

ANGEL COMBS

Steve Rasnic Tem

Steve Rasnic Tem grew up in the Appalachian Mountains of Virginia and now lives in Colorado. His novel *Excavations* was published in 1987, but he is better known for his fantasy and horror short stories and poetry. He won the British Fantasy Award in 1988 for his story "Leaks." His short work has been widely published in such magazines as *Fantasy Tales*, *Fear*, *Weirdbook*, and *Deathrealm*, and anthologies such as *The Mammoth Book of Vampires*, *Borderlands*, *MetaHorror*, *Love in Vein*, *Snow White, Blood Red*, *The Year's Best Fantasy and Horror*, and *Best New Horror*. Collections of his work can be found in the chapbooks *Fairytales*, *Celestial Inventory*, *Decoded Mirrors*, and *Absences: Charlie Goode's Ghosts*.

Tem consistently writes literate yet disquieting stories. This one begins in a very real world of poverty and deprivation and only gradually goes elsewhere. "Angel Combs" was originally published in Great Britain in *The Anthology of Fantasy and the Supernatural*.

—E. D.

The morning had sharp edges. Annie could see them.

Her mother had gotten her up an hour before dawn—the earliest she could remember ever getting up, except for that Christmas Uncle Willy had stayed with them, and she knew she was getting something nice that Christmas because she had seen a half-moon sliver of the doll's face with the long blonde hair in the big brown sack Uncle Willy had carried in. That night she hadn't slept at all. She had dreamed of the doll's hair, how it might be arranged, how long it might grow. Maybe the doll was a little magical and the hair might grow forever. She dreamed of it stretching around her little room, catching her other toys up in its waves, carrying them along like colorful boats in a river. She dreamed of drowning pleasantly in the flood it made. Most Christmases it didn't much matter. Most Christmases Momma couldn't afford much of anything.

Her bedroom window looked out on the back yard. In the brownish streetlight: the rough darkness of her dead father's old car, wheelless, drowning in weeds. The occasional razor-sharp gleam of a discarded tin can.

Annie kept thinking maybe they should clean up the backyard a little. Maybe turn it into a garden or something. They could have fresh vegetables, their own peas and lettuce and corn. But Annie was too scared to be in the backyard very long: the weeds were too tall, and sharp, and things were always moving there. And her mother kept saying she just didn't have the heart.

There was usually a little bit of a fog in the backyard. A mist. This morning was no different. This morning the fog looked torn, like some ferocious beast had ripped into the middle of it, pulled it to shreds. Great long pieces of it hung from tree branches, eaves, and junked machinery like fingers, or teeth. It fascinated Annie, but it also made her nervous to look at. Eventually she turned away and started getting dressed.

She could hear Momma getting dressed in the next room. Humming, happy. Only now and then snapping at one of the twins to get a move on. "Tommy! You don't want me to dress you! Nossir. You *don't* want *me* to squeeze your scrawny little butt into them tight jeans!" Then she'd go back to humming, singing, as if nothing had happened. It had been a long time since they'd made, as Momma put it, "a major purchase." She always said that with a soft, serious voice, like she was talking about somebody that'd died. Her mother was almost funny when she talked like that.

Momma had found this ad in the paper. "Bedroom Sets. REDUCED! $40!" And they had just a little over forty dollars saved. The little over would go for the tax, Momma said. And if the tax didn't take all of that, they could use the left over for an ice cream treat. The twins were excited by that, all right. They didn't care much for the idea of bedroom sets, but the prospect of a special ice cream, a separate one for each of them without having to share, that had kept them talking most of the past evening.

Her mother said it was like a miracle, the way they'd just gotten that very amount saved, and for sure a hard saving it had been, too, and here this furniture store comes out with this nice sale. And them needing the bedroom furniture so bad. Like a dream, Momma said. A fantasy come true. She'd shown Annie the picture in the paper. It was a drawing so you really couldn't tell that much. That's what Annie had told Momma, but her momma had said, "No. They couldn't do it up in the paper like that if it wasn't true." And of course that wasn't what Annie had meant at all, but she just nodded and let her mother point out each piece and tell her how fine it must all be.

There was a bed with four posts (the sketch in the paper showed wood grain so Momma said it must be oak and "oak is about the best there is"), a bedside table with two drawers (not just one like most bedside tables had), a set of drawers, and a little dresser with an oval mirror ("they call that *fine detail*").

"Now maybe I can buy my children something that will *last*," Momma said.

Maybe it was because Annie hadn't shown enough enthusiasm about the "major purchase" to satisfy Momma, or maybe it was the way Annie had looked at that dresser. But last night, after she'd gotten the twins into bed, her Momma had said, "You know I've been thinking. I think maybe you should have the dresser. I've got that dresser Grandma Smythe willed me, and it's special enough. Why, it's an antique. And you need a private place to comb your hair. Every woman, or about-to-be-a-woman, needs a private place to comb her hair."

Unconsciously, Annie began stroking her long, brownish-blonde hair with her palm, then opening the fingers slightly—as if they were the teeth of a huge, heavenly comb—and catching her hair now and then with those finger-teeth, using them to melt away the day's filth, making the tangles and snarls vanish one by one into the cool night air.

Annie had looked up at her mother, seen her mother's satisfaction, then realized what it was she'd been doing. And stopped it immediately. She'd seen herself in that dreamed-of oval mirror, seen herself combing the hair that was so much like her mother's, hair that was the only thing even remotely special about her. Hair even the rich girls in her class envied. She'd seen herself combing herself in that fine and private place that once was her bedroom, that special place because the dreamed-of dresser was there.

And at that moment Annie was almost angry with her mother because of the dream.

They arrived at the furniture store only a few minutes after it opened. There were a few other customers already inside: two well-dressed women, an older man in a ragged overcoat with dark spots on its sleeves, and a tall young man casually dressed, but Annie thought his clothes might be expensive since she'd seen some just like that on one of her favorite detective shows.

Her mother looked a little panicky when she saw those other customers. She'd wanted to be at the store *before* it opened, but the twins had gotten in a fight at the last minute—Momma tried to slap at least one of them but they got away from her—and then their old car had stalled three times on the way over. Annie had been wondering the whole time how they were supposed to get the new bedroom set back to the house. Surely they just couldn't tie it to the top of the car. She'd heard about having things delivered but she didn't know if the furniture store would do that, especially for something on sale like that, or even how that sort of thing was done. She doubted Momma knew how that sort of thing was done either. It would be just awful if they couldn't get the bedroom set after all because they didn't have a truck and somebody who had a truck got there first, or because they didn't have enough money to pay for the delivery.

Again, Annie found herself absently stroking her hair, seeing her reflection in each display case they passed, something glinting between hand and hair, and almost hating her mother. Suddenly she just wanted to get out of there. She just wanted to go home where no one could see her.

Her mother made her way quickly to the back of the store, clutching the newspaper ad, looking around to see if any of the other customers were looking at the bedroom set.

As they stood there waiting for someone to notice them, Annie looked around the store. Nobody seemed to be paying them any attention. A man in a blue suit and tie was talking to the casually dressed young man, who was looking at sofas. Two other men in suits were talking to the well-dressed older women, showing them something in a huge book on one of the counters. The man in the dirty overcoat was going from chair to chair, sitting in each one, occasionally saying something aloud to no one. Nobody seemed to be paying any attention to him, either.

All the bedroom furniture had been shoved into a far corner of the store. From that distance Annie didn't see anything that resembled the picture, but she reminded herself that you really couldn't tell anything from those sketches. One of the well-dressed women was making her way toward the bedroom furniture, and Annie's mother was watching the woman, licking her lips nervously, her back rigid, hands fisted tight. But still she didn't try to get the attention of one of the sales clerks. It was all crazy. Annie's face was growing warm with anxiety and unfocused embarrassment. The man in the filthy overcoat looked at her and grinned with broken, brown teeth. Annie closed her eyes and imagined herself combing her hair with a beautiful curved, silver comb. Gazing into a mirror that made her look far better than she thought possible. Combing away all her nervousness, all her fear. Combing peacefulness and beauty back into her.

"May I help you?" a practiced male voice asked.

Annie opened her eyes. A tall man in a suit leaned over them. Annie's mother bobbed her head spastically, as if she had just awakened from a trance. "This ad," she said, shoving it into the salesman's hands. "We'd like to buy . . . to *purchase* that bedroom set." Then, anxiously, "You still got it, don't you?"

"Oh, yes. Several, in fact. Right over here." The salesman started toward the bedroom furniture. Annie's mother breathed deeply, relieved, and hurried after him. For all her hurrying, Momma was trying to look queenly.

"Here we are. A *fine* set. And a very good price."

"Oh yes, a very good price," her mother said. "We're not against paying the money for quality, mind you," she said hurriedly. "But why pass up a bargain, I always say." Momma laughed off-key.

"Hmmm. Yes. Of course. Anything I can tell you about this particular set?"

Annie could see that her Momma could hardly look at the set, she was so nervous. She just kind of moved her eyes around the furniture, going "Hmmm, hmmmm, yes, oh yes," all the time. Not really seeing anything. Annie, on the other hand, looked at every piece. It wasn't much like the newspaper sketch. A slightly different style, and of lighter color than she had imagined. Certainly not oak. The color, in fact, was unlike any wood she had ever seen. She went around to the back of the headboard and the set of drawers and discovered some other kind of board with little chips pressed into it, and plastic. But still it was nice enough looking. Certainly better than anything else they had.

And the oval mirror was real nice. Not expensive and elegant like they'd imagined, but clear and shiny. Her hair looked good in it. It caught the highlights. At a certain angle her hair seemed to grow dozens of brilliant sparkling places, as if she had filled it with all these tiny silver combs.

Someone touched her hair, softly. But she didn't see anyone in the mirror, and when she turned there was no one there.

Her mother was crying. Louder and louder, until she was almost wailing. People were turning around. The two elegantly dressed women were whispering to each other. Annie saw all this, looking all over the store before she could bring herself to look at her mother.

"But the ad says *forty dollars!*" her mother cried.

The salesman looked embarrassed and a little angry. He was looking around too, as if he were trying to find someone to come help him, to help him shut up this bawling, embarrassing lady. For a panicky moment Annie imagined him calling the police. "That's forty dollars reduced, ma'am. The price has been *cut* by forty dollars. Four sixty down from five hundred. It's . . ." He looked ready to plead with her. "It's still really a very good price." He looked around, maybe to see if his boss had shown up yet. "Maybe you could finance?"

Annie's mother looked thunderstruck. The casually dressed young man was looking their way, smiling. The raggedy old man was smiling, too. Annie wanted to kick them both in their smiling mouths. Annie wanted to kick them all. Something cool and metallic was in her hair, stroking it. She turned to the salesman. Her mother was like a doll, a dowdy mannequin. "We can't . . . *finance*," Annie told the salesman. "We don't have the money."

The salesman nodded, and for a moment it looked like he was going to reach out and touch her hair. But her mother had moved behind her, and now was breathing cold and sour into her hair. "How *dare* you," her mother whispered harshly. "We're going," her mother told the twins.

"What about our *ice cream?*" one of the twins cried. Annie didn't know which one.

Her mother turned around and grabbed both the twins by the arm and started dragging them toward the door. They both screamed, and her mother had to threaten them with slaps and worse before they faded into sniffles and whimpers.

Annie took one last look at the mirror. In her reflection, sharp-edged glints of silver seemed to be attacking her hair. She broke away and followed her family out to the car.

That night Annie had been sitting in the kitchen, just staring out the window, absently stroking her hair. Her mother came into the room, looking drawn and pale, but at least she had calmed down. She pulled an old purple brush out of her robe and began brushing Annie's hair. "I just wanted to get you something *nice*," her mother said.

Annie squirmed away from her mother and walked quickly to her bedroom. Her hair felt warm, uncomfortable.

The next morning Annie found the first comb under her pillow. She had had bad dreams all night, of sick smiles and dirty poor people and of teeth, mostly teeth. Biting and ripping, or sometimes just pressing up against her soft skin and resting there, as if in anticipation.

When she woke up she'd still felt the teeth, working their way into her skull like the worst kind of headache. Then she'd lifted her thin pillow and discovered the comb. Long, curved metal. Not silver, she didn't think, but something like it. The teeth long and tapered, spaced just the right amount apart, it seemed, so that they wouldn't snag the hair, but pass through softly, like a breeze through the woods.

Tentatively she pressed the beautiful comb into her hair. It was as if all her nerves untangled and flowed as softly as her hair. She could hear a soft buzzing in her ears. Her skull went soft as moss. She hated to take the comb out of her hair. Her hair clung to the comb, making it hard to take away. She could feel her skull pull toward the comb.

Annie took the comb, holding it like a baby to her chest, into the kitchen where her mother was drinking coffee. "Oh, Momma. *Thank you*," Annie said.

Her mother looked up at her out of ugly, red-rimmed eyes. "What's that supposed to mean?"

Annie was suddenly confused. "The comb. You put it there, didn't you?"

Her mother pursed her lips, put her coffee down. "Let me see that thing."

Anxiously, Annie handed her mother the comb, already thinking about what she would do if her mother refused to hand it back.

Her mother dropped the comb onto the kitchen table. It made a musical sound, like a triangle or a very small cymbal. "You steal this at that store yesterday?"

"Momma! That was a *furniture* store! Besides, I don't *steal*. I found it under my pillow this morning; I thought you had given it to me for a *present*." Annie felt on the verge of tears.

Her mother grunted and stood up, took her coffee and started back to her own bedroom. Much to Annie's relief, the beautiful metal comb was still on the kitchen table. "Well, I don't care if you stole it or not," her mother said as she was going out the door.

When Annie got back to her bedroom, moving her beautiful new comb through her hair rhythmically, in time with her steps, she thought she saw two silver wings resting on the edge of her bed. When she got a closer look, however, she could see that they were two small, metal combs, only a couple of inches long.

Something unseen whispered through her hair. Insects buzzed at her ears. The comb moved rapidly through her hair, dragging her hand.

Annie thought she could see bits and pieces of her reflection in the air around her. Slivers of face, crescents of shoulder. Long flowing strands of hair, floating through the air like rays of silver dust.

Row upon row of long silver teeth dropping through the morning air.

"You dream too much. You eating junk before bed?" her mother said, when Annie told her about the eight metal combs she had found around her bedroom.

"Just a glass of milk." Her mother looked at her skeptically. "But see," Annie said, reaching into a worn paper bag and dropping the musical assortment of combs onto the table. "This isn't a dream."

It gave Annie satisfaction to see the dumbstruck look on her mother's face. Her mother stared at the assortment of combs for a very long time before actually touching one of them. "This one's cool," she said, running her finger along the spine of the longest comb. "Like ice." She picked up the smallest comb, one so curved and delicate it resembled the skeleton of a tiny sunfish. "And I swear this one's warm as a kitten." She stared at them a while longer, then looked up at Annie. "But what good are they goin' to do us?"

Over the next few days Annie discovered combs everywhere. In the silverware drawer, nestled cosily among the forks and knives. Arranged in a circle under the front door mat. Hanging from the ivy that grew up the back wall of the house. Flowering from otherwise dusty mason jars in the cellar. Planted in rows in her mother's flower boxes. Jammed into the house foundation's cracks along with leaves and twigs. Raked into the weeds that had swallowed the back yard. The combs' positions changed a bit each day, so that Annie imagined a steady drift of combs, grooming the weeds into ornate stylings.

Annie felt blessed, richer than she could ever have imagined. Who needed a fancy mirror when the combs seemed able to make each window, each shiny surface the clearest of mirrors? She tried out each comb she found, at least once, spending hours sitting, humming to herself, the combs harvesting all the tension from her head.

And still it was the original comb, the one she had first found under her pillow, nibbling at her head, that was her favorite. She let it mouth her long hair every chance she could.

But her mother was not as enamored with the things. "They scare me," she'd say, "all these shiny, sharp, toothy combs. Where'd they all come from? Can you tell me that?"

Annie just smiled a lazy smile, the only kind of smile she could manage these days. Broad smiles, grins, they all seemed just a little angry to her now. "I don't know. Does it matter? Maybe the angels left them," Annie said.

"That's crap," her mother said, trying to remove a particular sharp-toothed comb that had gotten snagged on her sweater. She got it out finally, but in the process lost a small swatch of material.

Annie just smiled.

Like their mother, the twins grew to dislike and distrust the combs. They'd sit down in front of the TV to watch cartoons and a wayward comb would work its way out from under the living room rug, snag their socks and scrape their ankles. They'd reach into their toy boxes for a truck or gun and one or several combs would bite them. And early one morning Tommy found his pet kitten stiff and matted in the front yard, a long shiny rattailed comb protruding from one ear.

More and more the family found combs soiled with the occasional fleck of red.

At dinner a spoon might arise from the soup with a small comb nestled in its hollow. The hamburger grew crunchy with their discarded teeth. They collected in boxes, in bags, in suitcases and every unused pocket. They gathered in the cold dark beneath the steps. They held meetings in the mailbox.

"I'm gonna sell some," Annie's mother announced one day. "You can keep that first one you found; you seem to like it best anyway. But we need the money. I'm sellin' the rest." She waited for Annie to say something. The twins were cranky, complaining about going with their mother, afraid to help her pick up the combs. They didn't want to touch them. Annie said nothing, just continued stroking her hair with her favorite comb. Her mother looked almost disappointed that she didn't get an argument.

Not bothering to repackage them, her mother carried them away in the vessels in which they'd naturally gathered. She filled their old car with suitcases, jars, bags, and boxes, cans and glasses and pots and pans full of combs. The car jangled musically as she and the twins sped off for town.

While they were gone Annie dreamed of unseen presences, riches by the bagful, and a quiet place where the combs could make love to her hair. For hours she waited for her family's return.

"They wouldn't take 'em, *none* of 'em!" her mother shouted, slamming through the door. "The recycle man said they weren't any metal he'd ever seen, and all the other stores said they weren't good as combs anyway. Too sharp. Might hurt somebody, they all said."

"Where are the combs now?" Annie asked quietly, stroking her hair.

"At the *dump*, that's where! That's where they *belong*—bunch of junk! Lord knows I wasn't going to haul 'em all the way back here!"

If her mother expected an argument, she wasn't going to get one from Annie this time, either. Annie held her last remaining comb to her ear, then looked up at the ceiling. Her mother looked up, too. "What the hell?" she began.

"You wanted things. That was your dream," Annie said, as the metallic rain began. "You gave me the dream, Momma. And now we're rich. Just *listen* to all we have."

The sound on the roof was unmistakable. Metal against metal. Metal against gutter, against shingle. Comb against comb, a steady downpour.

Her mother ran to the front window. Annie could see past her, through the window and into the front yard. Where thousands of combs fell in a shimmering, silver-toothed deluge.

Her mother turned from the window. "Annie!" she screamed. Her mother dashed across the room. The twins were bawling.

"Annie!" Her mother reached for her, angry and scared. "Annie, give me that comb!"

The comb flew from Annie's hand like an escaping bird. It landed in her mother's hand, pulled her mother's fingers around it like the individual bits of a fancy-dress ensemble. Then it pulled her hand to her head and began to comb.

Annie smiled her lazy smile. The floor grew soft with the thick pile of her mother's harvested, blood-clotted hair, her mother's discarded pain.

SNOW, GLASS, APPLES.

Neil Gaiman

Neil Gaiman is a transplanted Briton who now lives in the American Midwest. He is the author of the award-winning *Sandman* series of graphic novels and coauthor (with Terry Pratchett) of the novel *Good Omens*. His short fiction has been collected in *Angels and Visitations*. His work has been published in the two previous volumes of this series.

"Snow, Glass, Apples." was published as an original chapbook by DreamHaven to benefit the Comic Book Legal Defense Fund. This is one of two stories in our anthology that looks at fairy princesses from an unusual point of view.

—E. D.

I do not know what manner of thing she is. None of us do. She killed her mother in the birthing, but that's never enough to account for it.

They call me wise, but I am far from wise, for all that I foresaw fragments of it, frozen moments caught in pools of water or in the cold glass of my mirror. If I were wise I would not have tried to change what I saw. If I were wise I would have killed myself before ever I encountered her, before ever I caught him.

Wise, and a witch, or so they said, and I'd seen his face in my dreams and in reflections for all my life: sixteen years of dreaming of him before he reined his horse by the bridge that day, and asked my name. He helped me onto his high horse and we rode together to my little cottage, my face buried in the gold of his hair. He asked for the best of what I had; a king's right, it was.

His beard was red-bronze in the morning light, and I knew him, not as a king, for I knew nothing of kings then, but as my love. He took all he wanted from me, the right of kings, but he returned to me on the following day, and on the night after that: his beard so red, his hair so gold, his eyes the blue of a summer sky, his skin tanned the gentle brown of ripe wheat.

His daughter was only a child: no more than five years of age when I came to the palace. A portrait of her dead mother hung in the princess's tower room; a tall woman, hair the color of dark wood, eyes nut-brown. She was of a different blood to her pale daughter.

The girl would not eat with us.

I do not know where in the palace she ate.

I had my own chambers. My husband the king, he had his own rooms also. When he wanted me he would send for me, and I would go to him, and pleasure him, and take my pleasure with him.

One night, several months after I was brought to the palace, she came to my rooms. She was six. I was embroidering by lamplight, squinting my eyes against the lamp's smoke and fitful illumination. When I looked up, she was there.

"Princess?"

She said nothing. Her eyes were black as coal, black as her hair; her lips were redder than blood. She looked up at me and smiled. Her teeth seemed sharp, even then, in the lamplight.

"What are you doing away from your room?"

"I'm hungry," she said, like any child.

It was winter, when fresh food is a dream of warmth and sunlight; but I had strings of whole apples, cored and dried, hanging from the beams of my chamber, and I pulled an apple down for her.

"Here."

Autumn is the time of drying, of preserving, a time of picking apples, of rendering the goose fat. Winter is the time of hunger, of snow, and of death; and it is the time of the midwinter feast, when we rub the goose-fat into the skin of a whole pig, stuffed with that autumn's apples, then we roast it or spit it, and we prepare to feast upon the crackling.

She took the dried apple from me and began to chew it with her sharp yellow teeth.

"Is it good?"

She nodded. I had always been scared of the little princess, but at that moment I warmed to her and, with my fingers, gently, I stroked her cheek. She looked at me and smiled—she smiled but rarely—then she sank her teeth into the base of my thumb, the Mound of Venus, and she drew blood.

I began to shriek, from pain and from surprise; but she looked at me and I fell silent.

The little Princess fastened her mouth to my hand and licked and sucked and drank. When she was finished, she left my chamber. Beneath my gaze the cut that she had made began to close, to scab, and to heal. The next day it was an old scar: I might have cut my hand with a pocket-knife in my childhood.

I had been frozen by her, owned and dominated. That scared me, more than the blood she had fed on. After that night I locked my chamber door at dusk, barring it with an oaken pole, and I had the smith forge iron bars, which he placed across my windows.

My husband, my love, my king, sent for me less and less, and when I came to him he was dizzy, listless, confused. He could no longer make love as a man makes love; and he would not permit me to pleasure him with my mouth: the one time I tried, he started, violently, and began to weep. I pulled my mouth away and held him tightly, until the sobbing had stopped, and he slept, like a child.

I ran my fingers across his skin as he slept. It was covered in a multitude of ancient scars. But I could recall no scars from the days of our courtship, save one, on his side, where a boar had gored him when he was a youth.

Soon he was a shadow of the man I had met and loved by the bridge. His bones showed, blue and white, beneath his skin. I was with him at the last: his hands were cold as stone, his eyes milky-blue, his hair and beard faded and lusterless and limp. He died unshriven, his skin nipped and pocked from head to toe with tiny, old scars.

He weighed near to nothing. The ground was frozen hard, and we could dig no grave for him, so we made a cairn of rocks and stones above his body, as a memorial only, for there was little enough of him left enough of him left to protect from the hunger of the beasts and the birds.

So I was queen.

And I was foolish, and young—eighteen summers had come and gone since first I saw daylight—and I did not do what I would do, now.

If it were today, I would have her heart cut out, true. But then I would have her head and arms and legs cut off. I would have them disembowel her. And then I would watch, in the town square, as the hangman heated the fire to white-heat with bellows, watch unblinking as he consigned each part of her to the fire. I would have archers around the square, who would shoot any bird or animal who came close to the flames, any raven or dog or hawk or rat. And I would not close my eyes until the princess was ash, and a gentle wind could scatter her like snow.

I did not do this thing, and we pay for our mistakes.

They say I was fooled; that it was not her heart. That it was the heart of an animal—a stag, perhaps, or a boar. They say that, and they are wrong.

And some say (but it is *her* lie, not mine) that I was given the heart, and that I ate it. Lies and half-truths fall like snow, covering the things that I remember, the things I saw. A landscape, unrecognizable after a snowfall; that is what she has made of my life.

There were scars on my love, her father's thighs, and on his ballock-pouch, and on his male member, when he died.

I did not go with them. They took her in the day, while she slept, and was at her weakest. They took her to the heart of the forest, and there they opened her blouse, and they cut out her heart, and they left her dead, in a gully, for the forest to swallow.

The forest is a dark place, the border to many kingdoms; no-one would be foolish enough to claim jurisdiction over it. Outlaws live in the forest. Robbers live in the forest, and so do wolves. You can ride through the forest for a dozen days and never see a soul; but there are eyes upon you the entire time.

They brought me her heart. I know it was hers—no sow's heart or doe's would have continued to beat and pulse after it had been cut out, as that one did.

I took it to my chamber.

I did *not* eat it: I hung it from the beams above my bed, placed it on a length of twine that I strung with rowan-berries, orange-red as a robin's breast; and with bulbs of garlic.

Outside, the snow fell, covering the footprints of my huntsmen, covering her tiny body in the forest where it lay.

I had the smith remove the iron bars from my windows, and I would spend some time in my room each afternoon through the short winter days, gazing out over the forest, until darkness fell.

There were, as I have already stated, people in the forest. They would come out, some of them, for the Spring Fair: a greedy, feral, dangerous people; some were stunted—dwarfs and midgets and hunchbacks; others had the huge teeth and vacant gazes of idiots; some had fingers like flippers or crab-claws. They would creep out of the forest each year for the Spring Fair, held when the snows had melted.

As a young lass I had worked at the Fair, and they had scared me then, the forest folk. I told fortunes for the Fairgoers, scrying in a pool of still water; and, later, when I was older, in a disc of polished glass, its back all silvered—a gift from a merchant whose straying horse I had seen in a pool of ink.

The stallholders at the fair were afraid of the forest folk; they would nail their wares to the bare boards of their stalls—slabs of gingerbread or leather belts were nailed with great iron nails to the wood. If their wares were not nailed, they said, the forest folk would take them, and run away, chewing on the stolen gingerbread, flailing about them with the belts.

The forest folk had money, though: a coin here, another there, sometimes stained green by time or the earth, the face on the coin unknown to even the oldest of us. Also they had things to trade, and thus the fair continued, serving the outcasts and the dwarfs, serving the robbers (if they were circumspect) who preyed on the rare travellers from lands beyond the forest, or on gypsies, or on the deer. (This was robbery in the eyes of the law. The deer were the queen's.)

The years passed by slowly, and my people claimed that I ruled them with wisdom. The heart still hung above by bed, pulsing gently in the night. If there were any who mourned the child, I saw no evidence: she was a thing of terror, back then, and they believed themselves well rid of her.

Spring Fair followed Spring Fair: five of them, each sadder, poorer, shoddier than the one before. Fewer of the forest folk came out of the forest to buy. Those who did seemed subdued and listless. The stallholders stopped nailing their wares to the boards of their stalls. And by the fifth year but a handful of folk came from the forest—a fearful huddle of little hairy men, and no-one else.

The Lord of the Fair, and his page, came to me when the fair was done. I had known him slightly, before I was queen.

"I do not come to you as my queen," he said.

I said nothing. I listened.

"I come to you because you are wise," he continued. "When you were a child you found a strayed foal by staring into a pool of ink; when you were a maiden you found a lost infant who had wandered far from her mother, by staring into that mirror of yours. You know secrets and you can seek out things hidden. My queen," he asked, "what is taking the forest folk? Next year there will be no Spring Fair. The travellers from other kingdoms have grown scarce and few, the folk of the forest are almost gone. Another year like the last, and we shall all starve."

I commanded my maidservant to bring me my looking-glass. It was a simple thing, a silver-backed glass disk, which I kept wrapped in a doe-skin, in a chest, in my chamber.

They brought it to me, then, and I gazed into it:

She was twelve and she was no longer a little child. Her skin was still pale, her eyes and hair coal-black, her lips as red as blood. She wore the clothes she had worn when she left the castle for the last time—the blouse, the skirt—although they were much let-out, much mended. Over them she wore a leather cloak, and instead of boots she had leather bags, tied with thongs, over her tiny feet.

She was standing in the forest, beside a tree.

As I watched, in the eye of my mind, I saw her edge and step and flitter and pad from tree to tree, like an animal: a bat or a wolf. She was following someone.

He was a monk. He wore sackcloth, and his feet were bare, and scabbed and hard. His beard and tonsure were of a length, overgrown, unshaven.

She watched him from behind the trees. Eventually he paused for the night, and began to make a fire, laying twigs down, breaking up a robin's nest as kindling. He had a tinder-box in his robe, and he knocked the flint against the steel until the sparks caught the tinder and the fire flamed. There had been two eggs in the nest he had found, and these he ate, raw. They cannot have been much of a meal for so big a man.

He sat there in the firelight, and she came out from her hiding place. She crouched down on the other side of the fire, and stared at him. He grinned, as if it were a long time since he had seen another human, and beckoned her over to him.

She stood up and walked around the fire, and waited, an arms-length away. He pulled in his robe until he found a coin—a tiny, copper penny—and tossed it to her. She caught it, and nodded, and went to him. He pulled at the rope around his waist, and his robe swung open. His body was as hairy as a bear's. She pushed him back onto the moss. One hand crept, spider-like, through the tangle of hair, until it closed on his manhood; the other hand traced a circle on his left nipple. He closed his eyes, and fumbled one huge hand under her skirt. She lowered her mouth to the nipple she had been teasing, her smooth skin white on the furry brown body of him.

She sank her teeth deep into his breast. His eyes opened, then they closed again, and she drank.

She straddled him, and she fed. As she did so a thin blackish liquid began to dribble from between her legs. . . .

"Do you know what is keeping the travelers from our town? What is happening to the forest people?" asked the Head of the Fair.

I covered the mirror in doe-skin, and told him that I would personally take it upon myself to make the forest safe once more.

I had to, although she terrified me. I was the queen.

A foolish woman would have gone then into the forest and tried to capture the creature; but I had been foolish once and had no wish to be so a second time.

I spent time with old books, for I could read a little. I spent time with the gypsy women (who passed through our country across the mountains to the south, rather than cross the forest to the north and the west).

I prepared myself, and obtained those things I would need, and when the first snows began to fall, then I was ready.

Naked, I was, and alone in the highest tower of the palace, a place open to the sky. The winds chilled my body; goose-pimples crept across my arms and thighs and breasts. I carried a silver basin, and a basket in which I had placed a silver knife, a silver pin, some tongs, a grey robe and three green apples.

I put them down and stood there, unclothed, on the tower, humble before the night sky and the wind. Had any man seen me standing there, I would have had his eyes; but there was no-one to spy. Clouds scudded across the sky, hiding and uncovering the waning moon.

I took the silver knife, and slashed my left arm—once, twice, three times. The blood dripped into the basin, scarlet seeming black in the moonlight.

I added the powder from the vial that hung around my neck. It was a brown dust, made of dried herbs and the skin of a particular toad, and from certain other things. It thickened the blood, while preventing it from clotting.

I took the three apples, one by one, and pricked their skins gently with my silver pin. Then I placed the apples in the silver bowl, and let them sit there while the first tiny flakes of snow of the year fell slowly onto my skin, and onto the apples, and onto the blood.

When dawn began to brighten the sky I covered myself with the grey cloak, and took the red apples from the silver bowl, one by one, lifting each into my basket with silver tongs, taking care not to touch it. There was nothing left of my blood or of the brown powder in the silver bowl, nothing save a black residue, like a verdigris, on the inside.

I buried the bowl in the earth. Then I cast a glamour on the apples (as once, years before, by a bridge, I had cast a glamour on myself), that they were, beyond any doubt, the most wonderful apples in the world; and the crimson blush of their skins was the warm color of fresh blood.

I pulled the hood of my cloak low over my face, and I took ribbons and pretty hair ornaments with me, placed them above the apples in the reed basket, and I walked alone into the forest, until I came to her dwelling: a high, sandstone cliff, laced with deep caves going back a way into the rock wall.

There were trees and boulders around the cliff-face, and I walked quietly and gently from tree to tree, without disturbing a twig or a fallen leaf. Eventually I found my place to hide, and I waited, and I watched.

After some hours a clutch of dwarfs crawled out of the hole in the cave-front—ugly, misshapen, hairy little men—the old inhabitants of this country. You saw them seldom now.

They vanished into the wood, and none of them saw me, though one of them stopped to piss against the rock I hid behind.

I waited. No more came out.

I went to the cave entrance and hallooed into it, in a cracked old voice.

The scar on my Mound of Venus throbbed and pulsed as she came toward me, out of the darkness, naked and alone.

She was thirteen years of age, my stepdaughter, and nothing marred the perfect whiteness of her skin save for the livid scar on her left breast, where her heart had been cut from her long since.

The insides of her thighs were stained with wet black filth.

She peered at me, hidden, as I was, in my cloak. She looked at me hungrily. "Ribbons, goodwife," I croaked. "Pretty ribbons for your hair . . ."

She smiled and beckoned to me. A tug; the scar on my hand was pulling me toward her. I did what I had planned to do, but I did it more readily than I had planned: I dropped my basket, and screeched like the bloodless old pedlar woman I was pretending to be, and I ran.

My gray cloak was the color of the forest, and I was fast; she did not catch me.

I made my way back to the palace.

I did not see it. Let us imagine though, the girl returning, frustrated and hungry, to her cave, and finding my fallen basket on the ground.

What did she do?

I like to think she played first with the ribbons, twined them into her raven hair, looped them around her pale neck or her tiny waist.

And then, curious, she moved the cloth to see what else was in the basket; and she saw the red, red apples.

They smelled like fresh apples, of course; and they also smelled of blood. And she was hungry. I imagine her picking up an apple, pressing it against her cheek, feeling the cold smoothness of it against her skin.

And she opened her mouth and bit deep into it. . . .

By the time I reached my chambers, the heart that hung from the roof-beam, with the apples and hams and the dried sausages, had ceased to beat. It hung there, quietly, without motion or life, and I felt safe once more.

That winter the snows were high and deep, and were late melting. We were all hungry come the spring.

The Spring Fair was slightly improved that year. The forest folk were few, but they were there, and there were travelers from the lands beyond the forest.

I saw the little hairy men of the forest cave buying and bargaining for pieces of glass, and lumps of crystal and of quartz-rock. They paid for the glass with silver coins—the spoils of my stepdaughter's depredations, I had no doubt. When it got about what they were buying, townsfolk rushed back to their homes, came back with their lucky crystals, and, in a few cases, with whole sheets of glass.

I thought, briefly, about having them killed, but I did not. As long as the heart hung, silent and immobile and cold, from the beam of my chamber, I was safe, and so were the folk of the forest, and, thus, eventually, the folk of the town.

My twenty-fifth year came, and my stepdaughter had eaten the poisoned fruit two winters' back, when the Prince came to my Palace. He was tall, very tall, with cold green eyes and the swarthy skin of those from beyond the mountains.

He rode with a small retinue: large enough to defend him, small enough that another monarch—myself, for instance—would not view him as a potential threat.

I was practical: I thought of the alliance of our lands, thought of the Kingdom running from the forests all the way south to the sea; I thought of my golden-haired bearded love, dead these eight years; and, in the night, I went to the Prince's room.

I am no innocent, although my late husband, who was once my king, was truly my first lover, no matter what they say.

At first the prince seemed excited. He bade me remove my shift, and made me stand in front of the opened window, far from the fire, until my skin was chilled stone-cold. Then he asked me to lie upon my back, with my hands folded across my breasts, my eyes wide open—but staring only at the beams above. He told me not to move, and to breathe as little as possible. He implored me to say nothing. He spread my legs apart.

It was then that he entered me.

As he began to thrust inside me, I felt my hips raise, felt myself begin to match him, grind for grind, push for push. I moaned. I could not help myself.

His manhood slid out of me. I reached out and touched it, a tiny, slippery thing.

"Please," he said softly. "You must neither move, nor speak. Just lie there on the stones, so cold and so fair."

I tried, but he had lost whatever force it was that had made him virile; and, some short while later, I left the Prince's room, his curses and tears still resounding in my ears.

He left early the next morning, with all his men, and they rode off into the forest.

I imagine his loins, now, as he rode, a knot of frustration at the base of his manhood. I imagine his pale lips pressed so tightly together. Then I imagine his little troupe riding through the forest, finally coming upon the glass-and-crystal cairn of my stepdaughter. So pale. So cold. Naked, beneath the glass, and little more than a girl, and dead.

In my fancy, I can almost feel the sudden hardness of his manhood inside his britches, envision the lust that took him then, the prayers he muttered beneath his breath in thanks for his good fortune. I imagine him negotiating with the little hairy men—offering them gold and spices for the lovely corpse under the crystal mound.

Did they take his gold willingly? Or did they look up to see his men on their horses, with their sharp swords and their spears, and realize they had no alternative?

I do not know. I was not there; I was not scrying. I can only imagine. . . .

Hands, pulling off the lumps of glass and quartz from her cold body. Hands, gently caressing her cold cheek, moving her cold arm, rejoicing to find the corpse still fresh and pliable.

Did he take her there, in front of them all? Or did he have her carried to a secluded nook before he mounted her?

I cannot say.

Did he shake the apple from her throat? Or did her eyes slowly open as he pounded into her cold body; did her mouth open, those red lips part, those sharp yellow teeth close on his swarthy neck, as the blood, which is the life, trickled down her throat, washing down and away the lump of apple, my own, my poison?

I imagine; I do not know.

This I do know: I was woken in the night by her heart pulsing and beating once more. Salt blood dripped onto my face from above. I sat up. My hand burned and pounded as if I had hit the base of my thumb with a rock.

There was a hammering on the door. I felt afraid, but I am a queen, and I would not show fear. I opened the door.

First his men walked into my chamber, and stood around me, with their sharp swords, and their long spears.

Then he came in; and he spat in my face.

Finally, she walked into my chamber, as she had when I was first a queen, and she was a child of six. She had not changed. Not really.

She pulled down the twine on which her heart was hanging. She pulled off the dried rowan berries, one by one; pulled off the garlic bulb—now a dried thing, after all these years; then she took up her own, her pumping heart—a small thing, no larger than that of a nanny-goat or a she-bear—as it brimmed and pumped its blood into her hand.

Her fingernails must have been as sharp as glass: she opened her breast with them, running them over the purple scar. Her chest gaped, suddenly, open and bloodless. She licked her heart, once, as the blood ran over her hands, and she pushed the heart deep into her breast.

I saw her do it. I saw her close the flesh of her breast once more. I saw the purple scar begin to fade.

Her prince looked briefly concerned, but he put his arm around her nonetheless, and they stood, side by side, and they waited.

And she stayed cold, and the bloom of death remained on her lips, and his lust was not diminished in any way.

They told me they would marry, and the kingdoms would indeed be joined. They told me that I would be with them on their wedding day.

It is starting to get hot in here.

They have told the people bad things about me; a little truth to add savor to the dish, but mixed with many lies.

I was bound and kept in a tiny stone cell beneath the palace, and I remained there through the autumn. Today they fetched me out of the cell; they stripped the rags from me and washed the filth from me, and then they shaved my head and my loins, and they rubbed my skin with goose grease.

The snow was falling as they carried me—two men at each hand, two men at each leg—utterly exposed, and spread-eagled and cold, through the midwinter crowds; and brought me to this kiln.

My stepdaughter stood there with her prince. She watched me, in my indignity, but she said nothing.

As they thrust me inside, jeering and chaffing as they did so, I saw one snowflake land upon her white cheek, and remain there without melting.

They closed the kiln-door behind me. It is getting hotter in here, and outside they are singing and cheering and banging on the sides of the kiln.

She was not laughing, or jeering, or talking. She did not sneer at me or turn away. She looked at me, though; and for a moment I saw myself reflected in her eyes.

I will not scream. I will not give them that satisfaction. They will have my body, but my soul and my story are my own, and will die with me.

The goose-grease begins to melt and glisten upon my skin. I shall make no sound at all. I shall think no more on this.

I shall think instead of the snowflake on her cheek.

I think of her hair as black as coal, her lips as red as blood, her skin, snow-white.

Honorable Mentions 1994

Adams, Harold, "Retribution," *Murder For Father.*
Adley, Rupert, "Meet Murder, My Angel," *High Risk* 2.
Ahern, Jerry and Ahern, Sharon, "Silent Pace," *Phobias.*
Aldiss, Brian W., "The Dream of Antigone," *Blue Motel: Narrow Houses Volume Three.*
———, "The God Who Slept With Women," *Asimov's Science Fiction,* May.
Alishan, Leonardo, "Three Tales," *Ararat,* Autumn.
Ames, John Edward, "Love Drips and Gathers," *Bizarre Bazaar,* Volume 3.
Amies, Christopher, "Down to the Sunless Sea,"*Dreams From the Strangers' Cafe #4.*
Andersen, Anastasia, "All the Sea Wives," (poem) *Dreams & Nightmares* 42.
Anderson, Jessica, "Journey's End," *Grotesque #4.*
Anderson, Kevin J. and Peart, Neil, "Drumbeats," *Shock Rock II.*
Anonymous, "The Painted Skin," (Chinese) *Daughters of the Moon.*
———, "Vikram and the Dakini," (Indian) Ibid.
Antieau, Kim, "The Girl With No Hair," *Trudging to Eden.*
———, "The Involuted Man," Ibid.
Ash, Constance, "Made by Hand," *South from Midnight.*
Aycliffe, Jonathan, "The Reiver's Lament," *Blue Motel.*
Bailey, Dale, "Home Burial," *The Magazine of Fantasy & Science Fiction,* Dec.
———, "Notes Toward a Proof of the Theorem: Love Is Hunger," *Amazing,* Spring.
Bair, Bruce, "Wouldn't it Be Wonderful," *After Hours #24.*
Bannister, Ivy, "The Chiropodist," *Panurge New Fiction: Debatable Lands.*
Barker, Clive, "Animal Life," *The New York Daily News-Special Summer Fiction Issue.*
Barlow, Vivienne, "Indians," *Microstories.*
Barrett, Neal, Jr., "Donna Rae," *The King Is Dead.*
Bayliss, Peter, "The Stone Dog," *Chills #8.*
Beal, John, "Beyond Reflection," *The Starry Wisdom: A Tribute to H. P. Lovecraft.*
Becquer, Gustavo Aldolfo, "The Gold Bracelet," *Connecticut Review,* Spring.
Beechcroft, William, "Paperwork," *Voices from the Night.*
Belbin, David, "Home For Christmas," *Mysterious Christmas Tales.*
Benchley, Chaz, "Scouting For Boys," *London Noir.*
Bennett, Jill, "Squatters," *Mysterious Christmas Tales.*
Bennett, Nancy, "China Dolls," (poem) *Transversion #1.*
Bergstrom, Elaine, "The Weaver's Pride," *Tales of Ravenloft.*
Bjorkquist, Elena Diaz, "The Hershey Bar Queen," *The Americas Review.*
Black, Terry, "Bob, From Out of Town," *Skull* issue 1.
———, "Lucky Lyles' Big Surprise," *Grails: Visitations of the Night.*
Blackcrow, Lee, "Black Rock Woman," *Side Show.*
Blevins, Tippi N., "Steel My Soul," (poem) *Diaries of the Damned.*
Bloch, Robert, "The Scent of Vinegar," *Dark Destiny.*
Boshinski, Blanche, "The Imprints," *Ellery Queen's Mystery Magazine,* Sept.
Boston, Bruce, "Anathesia Man," *The Third Alternative,* Autumn.
———, "Tale of the Crone Goddess," (poem) *Xanadu* 2.
Bowes, Richard, "I Died, Sir, in Flames, Sir," *F & SF,* June.
———, "The Shadow and the Gunman," *F & SF,* Feb.
Bradbury, Ray, "From the Dust Returned," *F & SF,* Sept.

———, "The Very Gentle Murders," *EQMM*, May.
Bradfield, Scott, "Heaven Sent," *The Printer's Devil*, Issue D.
Brand, Ken, "Swagger," (poem) *Prairie Fire*, vol. 15 No. 2, Summer.
Brandner, Gary, "Mr. Pants," *Shock Rock II*.
Brendan-Brown, Sean, "Nowhere When it Burns," *The Silver Web*, Issue 11.
Brèque, Jean-Daniel, "Sight Unseen," *The Anthology of Fantasy & the Supernatural*.
———, "The Fat Lady," *Cold Cuts* 2.
Bretnor, Reginald, "Rokuro-Kubi," *Worlds of Fantasy & Horror #1*.
Brock, James, "To the Coroner Who Didn't Have to Draw My Blood," (poem) *Northwest Review* vol. 32 #2.
Brunner, John, "Tantamount to Murder," *The Mammoth Book of Frankenstein*.
Bryant, Taerie, "Slate," *Prisoners of the Night*, Issue 8.
Buggé, Carol, "A Day in the Life of Comrade Lenin," *Masterpieces of Terror and the Unknown*.
Bunce, William, "Jitterbug Season," *A Theater of Blood, #5*.
Burch, Milbre, "Metamorphosis," *Xanadu* 2.
Burleson, Donald R., "The Wind at the Top of the Tree," *Four Shadowings*.
Byers, Richard Lee, "Kingsfire," *Elric: Tales of the White Wolf*.
Cabeen, R. Payne, "Doctor Volmer," (poem) *Tainted Treats*.
Cacek, P. D., "Mid-Wife Crisis," chapbook.
———, "Recession," *The Urbanite, #4*.
———, "Salt," *Return to the Twilight Zone*.
Cadger, Rick, "Clarity," *The Science of Sadness*.
Cadigan, Pat, "Not Just Another Deal," *Deals With the Devil*.
———, "Paris in June," *Omni*, Sept.
———, "Serial Monogamist," *Little Deaths*.
Cady, Jack, "The Butterfly Archive," *Glimmer Train*, Summer.
Cahoon, Brad, "BloodStrip," *Phantasm #1*.
Callahan, Barbara "The Mists of Ballyclough," *EQMM*, Sept.
Cammuso, Frank and Seely, Hart, "And to Think That They Landed on Mulberry Street," *The New Yorker*, Nov. 14.
Campbell, Ramsey, "A Side of the Sea," *Borderlands* 4.
———, "Where They Lived," *Phantasm #1*.
Campbell, Terry, "Armadillo Village," *Young Blood*.
———, "Monkeyspeak," *Space & Time #84*.
Canavan, Neil, "Tight Puppet," *Bizarre Bazaar Volume* 3.
Cannell, Dorothy, "One Night at a Time," *Murder For Halloween*.
Canty, Kevin, "Blue Boy," *A Stranger in This World*.
———, "Dogs," Ibid.
———, "Junk," Ibid.
Carper, Steve, "The Taste of Worms," *Tales of the Unanticipated #13*.
Carter, Lin, "Visions From Yaddith," (poem) *The Shub Niggurath Cycle*.
Castle, Lara, "My Eternal," *Fresh Blood #2*.
Castle, Mort, "The Call," *Voices from the Night*.
Castro, Adam-Troy, "Messenger," *Return to the Twilight Zone*.
———, "The Slow Hit," *South from Midnight*.
Cave, Hugh B., "Chernick," *Phantasm #1*.
———, "Gordie's Pets," *Return to the Twilight Zone*.
———, "Puss Puss," *The Urbanite* No. 4.
Cawood, Anthony, "Candles of the Soul," *Dreams From the Strangers' Cafe #4*.
Cedar, D., "Cat," *Psychotrope* 2.

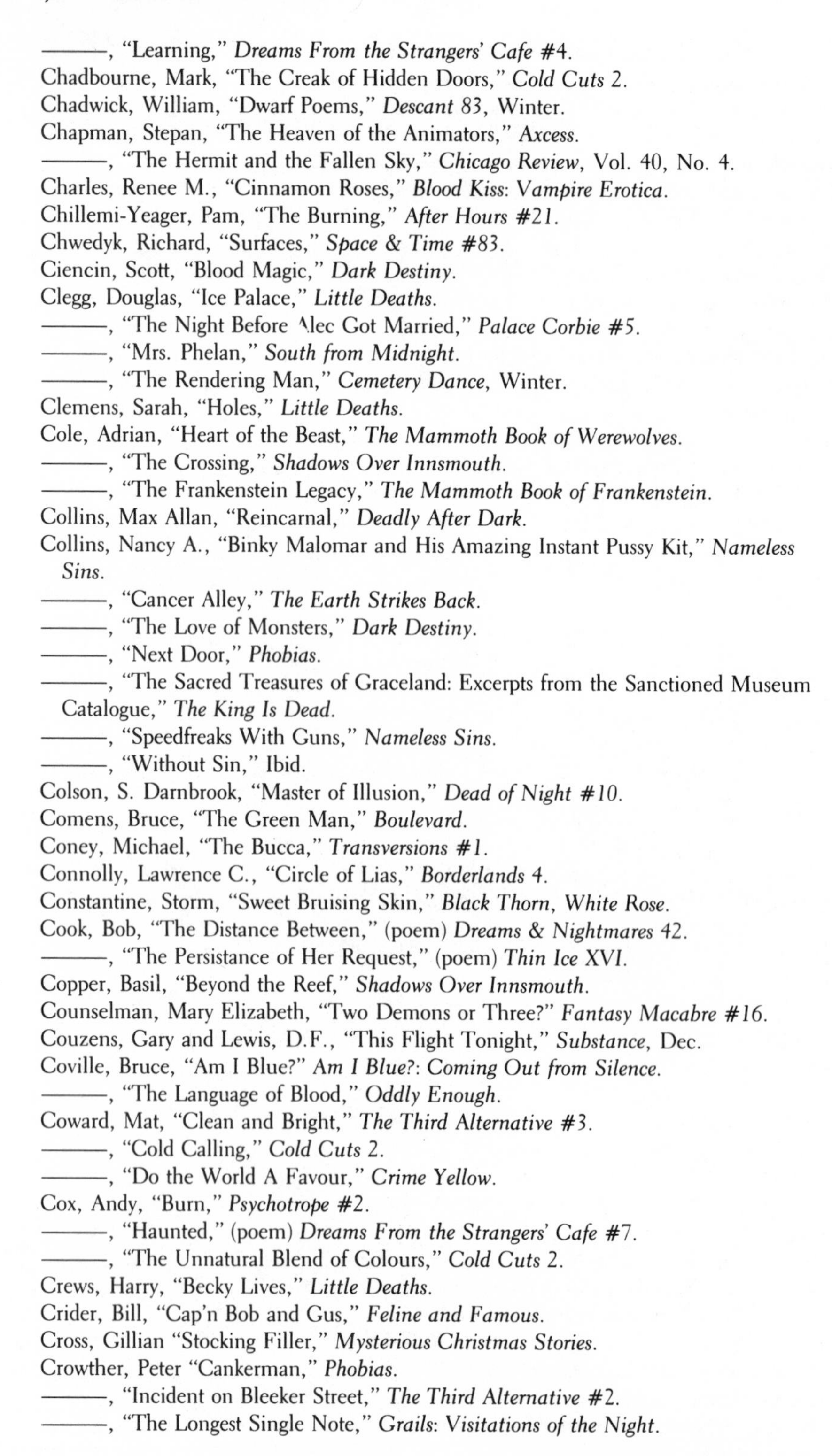

———, "Learning," *Dreams From the Strangers' Cafe #4.*
Chadbourne, Mark, "The Creak of Hidden Doors," *Cold Cuts 2.*
Chadwick, William, "Dwarf Poems," *Descant 83,* Winter.
Chapman, Stepan, "The Heaven of the Animators," *Axcess.*
———, "The Hermit and the Fallen Sky," *Chicago Review,* Vol. 40, No. 4.
Charles, Renee M., "Cinnamon Roses," *Blood Kiss: Vampire Erotica.*
Chillemi-Yeager, Pam, "The Burning," *After Hours #21.*
Chwedyk, Richard, "Surfaces," *Space & Time #83.*
Ciencin, Scott, "Blood Magic," *Dark Destiny.*
Clegg, Douglas, "Ice Palace," *Little Deaths.*
———, "The Night Before Alec Got Married," *Palace Corbie #5.*
———, "Mrs. Phelan," *South from Midnight.*
———, "The Rendering Man," *Cemetery Dance,* Winter.
Clemens, Sarah, "Holes," *Little Deaths.*
Cole, Adrian, "Heart of the Beast," *The Mammoth Book of Werewolves.*
———, "The Crossing," *Shadows Over Innsmouth.*
———, "The Frankenstein Legacy," *The Mammoth Book of Frankenstein.*
Collins, Max Allan, "Reincarnal," *Deadly After Dark.*
Collins, Nancy A., "Binky Malomar and His Amazing Instant Pussy Kit," *Nameless Sins.*
———, "Cancer Alley," *The Earth Strikes Back.*
———, "The Love of Monsters," *Dark Destiny.*
———, "Next Door," *Phobias.*
———, "The Sacred Treasures of Graceland: Excerpts from the Sanctioned Museum Catalogue," *The King Is Dead.*
———, "Speedfreaks With Guns," *Nameless Sins.*
———, "Without Sin," Ibid.
Colson, S. Darnbrook, "Master of Illusion," *Dead of Night #10.*
Comens, Bruce, "The Green Man," *Boulevard.*
Coney, Michael, "The Bucca," *Transversions #1.*
Connolly, Lawrence C., "Circle of Lias," *Borderlands 4.*
Constantine, Storm, "Sweet Bruising Skin," *Black Thorn, White Rose.*
Cook, Bob, "The Distance Between," (poem) *Dreams & Nightmares 42.*
———, "The Persistance of Her Request," (poem) *Thin Ice XVI.*
Copper, Basil, "Beyond the Reef," *Shadows Over Innsmouth.*
Counselman, Mary Elizabeth, "Two Demons or Three?" *Fantasy Macabre #16.*
Couzens, Gary and Lewis, D.F., "This Flight Tonight," *Substance,* Dec.
Coville, Bruce, "Am I Blue?" *Am I Blue?: Coming Out from Silence.*
———, "The Language of Blood," *Oddly Enough.*
Coward, Mat, "Clean and Bright," *The Third Alternative #3.*
———, "Cold Calling," *Cold Cuts 2.*
———, "Do the World A Favour," *Crime Yellow.*
Cox, Andy, "Burn," *Psychotrope #2.*
———, "Haunted," (poem) *Dreams From the Strangers' Cafe #7.*
———, "The Unnatural Blend of Colours," *Cold Cuts 2.*
Crews, Harry, "Becky Lives," *Little Deaths.*
Crider, Bill, "Cap'n Bob and Gus," *Feline and Famous.*
Cross, Gillian "Stocking Filler," *Mysterious Christmas Stories.*
Crowther, Peter "Cankerman," *Phobias.*
———, "Incident on Bleeker Street," *The Third Alternative #2.*
———, "The Longest Single Note," *Grails: Visitations of the Night.*

———, "Other Trains," (poem) *The Third Alternative* #1.
Csernica, Lillian, "The Family Spirit," *Dark Infinity*, June.
Cullen, Tom, "The Longest Kiss," *Dark Voices 6*.
Dann, Jack and Zebrowski, George, "Afternoon Ghost," *Return to the Twilight Zone*.
Darnell, Cooper, "26–52–78–104," *The Silver Web*, Issue 11.
Daron, Wendy, "Body and Soul," *Fiction Furnace* Vol. 1 #6.
Daum, G. L., "Seven Images From the Gallery of a Photographer," *Terminal Fright* #5.
Davies, Barbara, "Companion to Owls," *Grotesque* #5.
Davison, Liam, "Burning Off," *Microstories*.
Dawson, Laura, "Nixon Thieves," *Asylum Annual*, 1994.
Dedman, Stephen, "The Lady of Situations," *Little Deaths*.
Delany, Samuel R., "The Mad Man," *Meltdown*.
Delillo, Don, "The Angel Esmeralda," *Esquire*, May.
———, "Videotape," *Harper's*, Dec.
de Lint, Charles, "The Forest Is Crying," *The Earth Strikes Back*.
———, "Heartfires," Triskell Press chapbook.
———, "In This Soul of a Woman," *Love in Vein*.
———, "Saxophone Joe and the Woman in Black," *Catfantastic III*.
De Noux, Debra Gray and De Noux, O'Neil "A Few Pieces," *Over My Dead Body*, Winter.
Dharmarajan, Geeta, "Nuts," *The New Renaissance*, Vol. IX, No. 1.
Dionne, Ron, "Ichneumon," *Palace Corbie* #5.
Dobles, James, "Dead Leaves," *Borderlands 4*.
Dooling, Richard, "Bush Pigs," *The New Yorker*, October 10.
Dorr, James S., "Deaming Saturn," (poem) *Dark Destiny*.
———, "Mist at Evening," (poem) *Wicked Mystic*, Summer.
———, "The Snow Wraith," *After Hours* #22.
———, "The Winning," *Over My Dead Body*, Spring.
Dozois, Gardner, "A Cat Horror Story," *F & SF*, Oct./Nov.
DuBois, Brendan, "The Necessary Brother," *EQMM*, May.
Duchamp, L. Timmel, "Things of the Flesh," *Asimov's SF* Jan.
Ducornet, Rikki, "Bedtime Story," *The Complete Butcher's Tales*.
Duffield, John, "Our House," *Grotesque* #4.
Duke, Madelaine, "The Image of Innocence," *2nd Culprit*.
Dumars, Denise, "In These Hills," (poem) *Star * Line* Sept./Oct.
Dunford, Caroline, "The Shadow-Pane," *The Science of Sadness*.
Dyer, S.N., "Paging Dr. Death," *The Best of Whispers*.
Dyers, Lawrence, "Jack Limer's Monsters," *The Third Alternative* #4.
Dyson, Jeremy, "All in the Telling," *Blue Motel*.
Edward, Bryan, "They're Back, Jack" *Terminal Fright* #5.
Edwards, Martin, "A House is Not a Home," *Crime Yellow*.
Edwards, Wayne, "Blind of Hand," *Not One of Us* #12.
———, "Lip Sync," *Crossroads 10*.
Eikamp, Rhonda, "Peepshow," *The Urbanite*, No. 4.
Eipper, Chris, "The Fix," *Microstories*.
Eisenstein, Phyllis, "No Refunds," *Asimov's SF* Feb.
Elliott, Tom, "Forty Miles of Bad Road," *Skull* issue 1.
Ellison, Harlan, "Base," *Mind Fields*.
———, "Sensible City," *F & SF*, Oct./Nov.

Emshwiller, Carol, "Modillion," *Green Mountain Review: Women, Community and Narrative Voice.*
Engstrom, Elizabeth, "Elixir," *Love in Vein.*
Epperson, S. K., "The Lady of the House," *Phantasm #1.*
Eskridge, Kelley, "And Salome Danced," *Little Deaths.*
Etchemendy, Nancy, "Jasper's Ghost," *Bruce Coville's Book of Ghosts.*
Etchison, Dennis," A Wind From the South," *Borderlands 4.*
Evenson, Brian, "Bodies of Light," *Altmann's Tongue.*
———, "The Boly Stories," Ibid.
———, "The Evanescence of Marion Goff," Ibid.
———, "Eye," Ibid.
———, "Her Other Bodies: A Travelogue," Ibid.
———, "Job Eats Them Raw, With the Dogs," Ibid.
———, "Killing Cats," Ibid.
———, "Stung," Ibid.
———, "The Munich Window: A Persecution," Ibid.
———, "Xavier's Luck," *A Theater of Blood #5.*
Falconer, Stuart, "Fugue and Variation," *Interzone, #85.*
Files, Gemma, "Flare," *Vampire's Crypt.*
———, "Mouthful of Pins," *Northern Frights 2.*
———, "Skeleton Bitch," *Palace Corbie #5.*
———, "Skin City," *Grue #16.*
Findlay, Timothy, "The Dead Can Dance: A Gothic Tale," *Bizarre Dreams.*
Fitch, Marina, "Sarah at the Tide Pool," *F & SF*, April.
Fitzpatrick, Mark, "Neighbors," *Asylum Annual, 1994.*
Fletcher, Jo, "Bright of Moon," (poem) *The Mammoth Book of Werewolves.*
Flinn, Maggie, "On Dreams: A Love Story," *Asimov's SF*, June.
Foster, Alan Dean, "Fitting Time," *The King Is Dead.*
Fowler, Christopher, "Perfect Casting," *London Noir.*
Fox, Daniel, "El Sueño de la Razón," *The Mammoth Book of Frankenstein.*
———, "Where it Roots, How it Fruits," *Dark Voices 6.*
Freireich, Valerie J., "Soft Rain," *Asimov's SF*, Aug.
Freixas, Laura, "The Clyptoderm," *The Origins of Desire: Modern Spanish Short Stories.*
Friesner, Esther M., "Death and the Librarian," *Asimov's SF*, Dec.
———, "In the Garden," *Dark Destiny.*
———, "Lovers," (poem) *South from Midnight.*
Gaiman, Neil, "Only the End of the World Again," *Shadows Over Innsmouth.*
Garafolo, Charles, "The Sending," *Crypt of Cthulhu #88.*
Gertler, Nat, "Rockin' On Home," *Shock Rock II.*
Glass, Jesse, Jr., "Cloth of Dreams," (poem) *Grue #16.*
———, "Mister Six," (poem) *Asylum Annual, 1994.*
Gluckman, Janet Berliner, "Wooden Heart," *The King Is Dead.*
Gluckman, Janet and Guthridge, George, "Son of the Shofar," *Bizarre Bazaar*, Vol. 3.
Goingback, Owl, "Fang of the Wolf," *When Will You Rage?*
Goldfine, John, "Wild Anise," *Aberrations 22.*
Goldstein, Lisa, "A Game of Cards," *Travellers in Magic.*
———, "Split Light," Ibid.
Gordon, Alan, "Death and Transfiguration in Oz," *AHMM*, May.
Goring, Anne, "The Shadow Queen," *The Anthology of Fantasy & the Supernatural.*
Gorman, Ed, "Hunk," *EQMM*, March.

———, "Inside Job," *Voices from the Night*.
———, "Kinship," *South from Midnight*.
———, "The Old Ways," *Tales from the Great Turtle*.
Grabinski, Stefan, "The White Wyrak," *100 Creepy Little Creatures Stories*.
Grady, James, "Omjagod," *Murder For Halloween*.
Grant, Charles, "Always, in the Dark," *Return to the Twilight Zone*.
Graves, Gordon A., "Mr. Grey and Mrs. Peal," *Aberrations* 20.
Greco, Ralph, Jr., "The Turning Too Far," *Eulogy*, Issue 8.
Greenland, Colin, "The Station With No Name," *13 More Tales of Horror*.
Grey, John, "The Runner," (poem) *The Thirteenth Moon*, March.
Grice, Gordon, "Rattlesnakes," *Asylum Annual, 1994*.
Griffith, Nicola, "Yaguara," (novella) *Little Deaths*.
Hall, Christopher A., "On the Boulevard," *Aberrations* 15.
———, "Paper Animals," *Young Blood*.
Halsted, Robert, "Up the Hill," *AHMM*, Dec.
Hambly, Barbara, "The Horsemen and the Morning Star," *South from Midnight*.
———, "The Little Tailor and the Elves," *Xanadu* 2.
Hamilton, Pete, "The Guardian," *After Hours* #23.
Hand, Elizabeth, "Last Summer at Mars Hill," (novella) *F & SF*, Aug.
Harland, Richard, "The Bath," *Bloodsongs*, Issue 2.
Harman, Christopher, "Passengers," *All Hallows* 6.
Hauch, Christine, "The Sarum Twins," *Panurge* 20.
Hawkes-Moore, Julia, "The Chocolate Ghost," *The Young Oxford Book of Ghost Stories*.
Heald, D. Lopes, "Snowfire," *Sword and Sorceresses XI*.
Hempel, Amy, "Government," *Epoch*, Vol. 43, No. 1.
Hendee, Barb, "Bringing Home a Stranger," *Young Blood*.
Hendershot, Cynthia, from "Loving the Corpse," *Asylum Annual, 1994*.
———, "Black Leather Room," *Urbanus Raizirr*, No. 5.
Henderson, Samantha, "My Big Fish Story," *A Theater of Blood*, #5.
Hendrickson, Robert, "The Blue Pig," *Sonora Review*, Spring.
Herter, David, "The Late Mr. Haval's Apartment," *Borderlands* 4.
Higginson, Ella, "The Footfall on the Stair (c. 1898)," (poem) *Fantasy Macabre* #16.
Higham, Prunella, "Factors Unknown," *Prairie Fire*, Summer.
Highsmith, Patricia, "Summer Doldrums," *EQMM*, April.
Hill, David W., "The Whispering of Flies," *Terminal Fright* #5.
Hivner, Christopher, "Morning Hours," *Shadowdance* #11, Feb.
Hodge, Brian, "The Alchemy of the Throat," *Love in Vein*.
Hoffman, Barry, "Double-Edged Sword," *The Earth Strikes Back*.
Hoffman, Nina Kiriki, "Haunted Humans," *F & SF*, July.
Hoffman, Theodore H., "Something Black," *AHMM*, Feb.
Holder, Nancy, "Bird on a Ledge," *Phobias*.
———, "Cafe Endless: Spring Rain," *Love in Vein*.
———, "Fatal Age," *The Anthology of Fantasy & Supernatural*.
———, "Leaders of the Pack," *Dark Destiny*.
Holland, Noy, "The Change in Union City," *The Spectacle of the Body*.
Hood, Robert, "Rough Trade," *Aurealis* issue 13.
Hook, Andrew, "Pussycat," *The Science of Sadness*.
Hopkins, Brian, "And Though a Million Stars Were Shining," *After Hours* 22.
Houarner, Gerald Daniel, "Dead Man's Park," *Into the Darkness* # 2.
———, "Nests," *Aberrations* 15.

———, "Painfreak," *Into the Darkness #1.*
Howell, Brian, "In," *The Third Alternative # 4.*
———, "She Stands in Flames," *The Science of Sadness.*
Hua, Yu, "One Kind of Reality," *Running Wild: New Chinese Writers.*
Hughes, Pamela, "Chicken Little Was Right," (poem) *Magic Realism,* Spring.
Humphrey, Kate, "Love, Pain & Self-Will," *Bloodsongs #1.*
Hunter, C. Bruce, "The Salesman and the Travelling Farmer's Daughter," *The Anthology of Fantasy & Supernatural.*
Huyck, Ed, "Darkness," *Shadowdance #11,* Feb.
Isle, Sue, "Kill Me Once," *Alien Shores.*
Jackson, Geoff, "Dogging," *Not One of Us #12.*
Jacob, Charlee, "The Bloom," *Bizarre Dreams.*
———, "Salt," *Palace Corbie #5.*
Jennings, Philip Sidney, "The Widow's Legacy," *Panurge New Fiction.*
Jens, Tina L., "The Gargoyle Sacrifice," *100 Creepy . . . Stories.*
———, "Red Whiskey," *South from Midnight.*
Jensen, Jan Lars, "The Nosferatu Contagion," *Grue #16.*
Jeter, K.W., "Black Nightgown," *Little Deaths.*
Johnson, Kij, "Myths," *Under Ground 4.*
Johnson, Roger, "The Souvenir," *All Hallows 6.*
Joyce, Frances, "The Wheel," *EQMM,* mid-Dec.
Kandel, Michael, "Ogre," *Black Thorn,* White Rose.
Karásek ze Lvovic, Jiri, "The Death of Salome," *Fantasy Macabre #16.*
Kaufman, David, "Grossie," *Shub Niggurath Cycle.*
Kearns, Richard, "Raven, Jade and Light," *Xanadu 2.*
Keating, H.R.F., "Mr Idd," *3rd Culprit.*
Kenan, Randall, "Hobbits and Hobgoblins," *Writer's Harvest.*
Kelly, Brigit Pegeen, "Song," *Song: Poems by Brigit Pegeen Kelly.*
Kelly, Ronald, "Tyrophex-Fourteen," *The Earth Strikes Back.*
Keltia, Thomas, "The Diner," *Black Tears* issue 5.
Kennedy, Pagan, "The Monument," *Stripping and other stories.*
———, "The Underwear Man," Ibid.
———, "Single Track Road," *Grotesque #4.*
Ketchum, Jack, "The Rose," *Deadly After Dark.*
Kharms, Daniil, "The Old Woman," *Incidences.*
Kidd, A. F., "The Witch's Room, "*All Hallow's 7.*
Kijewski, Karen, "Tule Fog," *The Mysterious West.*
Kilpatrick, Nancy, "An Eye For an Eye," *Cold Blood V.*
———, "Punkins," *Northern Frights 2.*
Kilworth, Garry, "The House That Jack Built," *13 More Tales of Horror.*
———, "The Tallow Tree," *Cold Cuts 2.*
———, "Wayang Kulit," *Interzone #90.*
Kinkade, Russell T., "Dogged," *Thin Ice XV.*
Kisner, James, "Ground Water," *The Earth Strikes Back.*
Klavan, Andrew, "The Look on Her Face," *London Noir.*
Knight, Tracy, "Mothercloud, Fatherdust," *Murder For Father.*
Koja, Kathe, "The Disquieting Muse," *Little Deaths.*
———, "Jubilee," *Ghosts.*
———, "Queen of Angels," *Omni,* July.
Koja, Kathe and Malzberg, Barry N., "The Careful Geometry of Love," *Little Deaths.*
———, "Modern Romance," *Dark Voices 6.*

Kopecky, William, "Within Our Garden," (poem) *Dreams From the Strangers' Cafe* # 4.
Kraus, Stephen, "White Walls," *F & SF*, Oct./Nov.
Kremers, Rose, "The Executioner," *Xanadu* 2.
Krist, Gary, "Ever Alice," *Bone By Bone*.
———, "Medicated," Ibid.
Kyota, Izumi, "Chimera," *The East*, Sept./Oct.
Laidlaw, Marc, "The Black Bus," *F & SF*, June.
Lamsley, Terry, "Living Waters," *Under the Crust*.
———, "Something Worse," Ibid.
———, "The Two Returns," Ibid.
———, "Under the Crust," Ibid.
Landis, Geoffrey A., "The Singular Habits of Wasps," *Analog*, April.
Lane, Joel, "An Angry Voice," *The Earth Wire*.
———, "And Make Me Whole," *The Anthology of Fantasy & Supernatural*.
———, "Branded," *The Earth Wire*.
———, "Every Scrapbook Stuck With Glue," *Ambit* #137 Aug.
———, "Like Shattered Stone," *The Science of Sadness*.
———, "The Outer Districts," (poem) *Chills* #8.
———, "Pieces of Silence," Ibid.
———, "Playing Dead," *The Earth Wire*.
———, "The Pain Barrier," *Little Deaths*.
———, "Real Drowners," *Cold Cuts* 2.
———, "Take Me When You Go," *The Third Alternative* #1.
Langford, David, "Deepnet," *Irrational Numbers*.
Lannes, Roberta, "A Complete Woman," *The Mammoth Book of Frankenstein*.
———, "Essence of the Beast," *The Mammoth Book of Werewolves*.
———, "Lithium Nights," *Skull* issue 1.
Lansdale, Joe R., "Bubba Ho-tep," *The King Is Dead*.
———, "Godzilla's Twelve-Step Program," *Writer of the Purple Rage*.
Le Guin, Ursula K., "The Hands of Torturers," (poem) *Going Out With Peacocks*.
Lea, Christina, "Denial," *Microstories*.
Lee, Edward, "Mr. Torso," *Deadly After Dark*.
Lee, Tanith, "Mirror, Mirror," *Weird Tales* #308.
———, "One For Sorrow," Ibid.
———, "The Persecution Machine," Ibid.
Leech, Ben, "The Gift," *Cold Cuts* 2.
Lees-Milne, James, "Ruthenshaw: A Ghost Story," chapbook.
Lepovetsky, Lisa, "Finding the Wind," *EQMM*, Sept.
———, "House of Mirrors," (poem) *Skeletal Remains* #4.
———, "The Frog's Place," *EQMM*, April.
Lesperance, Katherine, "Shape Shift," *Heliocentric Net* 28.
Lessing, Doris, "The Thoughts of a Near-Human," *Partisan Review*, No. 1.
Lethem, Jonathan, "Mood Bender." *Crank*, Spring.
Levesque, Richard L., "Like a Kiss of Wormwood," (poem) *Palace Corbie* #5.
Levine, Judith, "The Girl and the Sparrow," *Asylum Annual*, 1994.
Lewin, Michael Z., "Cormorants," *London Noir*.
Lewis, D. F., "The Absence," *The Third Alternative*, # 3.
———, "Apple Turnover," *Dead of Night* # 9.
———, "Aspen," *Bloodsongs* #2.
———, "Cigarettes and Dandelions," *Fantasy Macabre* #16.

———, "Living in the Corner," *Grotesque #4.*
———, "Watch the Whiskers Sprout," *Cthulhu's Heirs.*
———, "Scaredy & Whitemouth," *Chills # 8.*
Lewis, Paul, "Dirt," *Cold Cuts* 2.
Light, John, "Delivery Man," *Black Tears #3.*
Ligotti, Thomas, "Notebook of the Night," (novella) *Noctuary.*
Limón, Martin, "The Mists of the Southern Seas," *AHMM,* June.
Linzner, Gordon, "Pickman's Legacy," *Cthulhu's Heirs.*
Little, Bentley, The Numbers Game," *Deadly After Dark.*
———, "The Pond," *Blue Motel.*
Llywelyn, Morgan, "The Earth Is Made of Stardust, and So Is the Life Thereon," *Worlds of Fantasy & Horror # 1.*
LoBrutto, Patrick, "Vision Quest," *Masterpieces of Terror and the Unknown.*
Loeber, Jon, "Game Face," *Aberrations #20.*
Lopez, Barry, "Lessons from the Wolverine," *Field Notes.*
Logan, David, "Liars," *The Science of Sadness.*
Long, Nathan, "Skin Crawl," *Skull* issue 1.
Lovegrove, James, "Rosemary for Remembrance," *Blue Motel.*
Lovesey, Peter, "Pass the Parcel," *EQMM,* mid-Dec.
Loydell, Rupert M., "Only Shadows," *The Third Alternative #1.*
Luce, Carol Davis, "Shattered Crystal," *AHMM,* March.
Lurie, Alison, "Double Poet," *Women and Ghosts.*
———, "In the Shadow," Ibid.
Luvaas, William, "Yesterday After the Storm," *Glimmer Train,* Fall.
Lutz, John, "The Chess Players," *EQMM,* May.
Lynch, H. Andrew, "C awlspace," *Young Blood.*
Lyon, Hillary, "The Kiss," (poem) *Dreams and Nightmares #43.*
Macdonald, Caroline, "The Dam," *Hostilities: Nine Bizarre Stories.*
———, "Dandelion Creek," Ibid.
———, "Hostilities," Ibid.
———, "I Saw My Name in a Book," Ibid.
———, "The Thief in the Rocks," Ibid.
MacLeod, Ian, "The Dead Orchards," *Weird Tales #308.*
Maitland, Sara, "Siren Song," *By the Light of the Silvery Moon.*
Malenky, Barbara, "Elvis's Secret," *Heliocentric Net* 28.
Malzberg, Barry N., "Allegro Marcato," *By Any Other Fame.*
———, "The Only Thing You Learn," *Universe* 3.
———, "Sinfonia Expansiva," *Little Deaths.*
———, "Understanding Entropy," *Science Fiction Age,* July.
Marcinko, Thomas, "Whiter Teeth, Fresher Breath," *Interzone* 80.
Marcus, Daniel, "Angel from Budapest," *Àsimov's SF,* March.
———, "Heart of Molten Stone," *SF Age,* Sept.
Marner, Robert, "At Times, An Island," *Tomorrow,* Dec.
Martin, Mark O., and Benford, Gregory, "Strong Instinct," *South from Midnight.*
Marunyez, Jack, "Bates Motel," (poem) *Grue #16.*
Mason, Todd, "Bedtime," *Tomorrow,* April.
Massie, Elizabeth, "I am Not My Smell," *Expressions of Dread,* Spring.
———, "Snow Day" *Not One of Us # 12.*
———, "What Happened When Mosley Paulson . . .," *Voices From the Night.*
Masterton, Graham, "J.R.E. Ponsford," *13 More Tales of Terror.*
———, "Mother of Invention," *The Mammoth Book of Frankenstein.*

———, "Suffer Kate," *Deadly After Dark*.
Mater, Barbara, "Delving in the Dark," *Asimov's SF*, mid-Dec.
Matera, Lia, "The River Mouth," *The Mysterious West*.
Matheson, Richard Christian, "Ménage à Trois," *Little Deaths*.
Matthews, Christine, "Gentle Insanities," *Deadly Allies* 2.
McAuley, Paul J., "The Temptation of Dr Stein," *The Mammoth Book of Frankenstein*.
McBain, Ed, "Monsters," *Murder For Halloween*.
McCarthy, Wil, "The Blackery Dark," *Asimov's SF*, Oct.
McDowell, Ian, "Geraldine," *Love in Vein*.
McGonegal, Richard F., "The Devil's Chair," *Not One of Us #12*.
McGowin, Kevin, "Lines Spoken by the World's Oldest Witch on Halloween," *Rosebud*, Autumn/Winter.
McKimmey, James, "Manhattan Chops," *AHMM*, Nov.
McLoughlin, Mark, "The Last Poetry Night at the Saturnalia Coffeehouse," *Dreams from the Strangers' Cafe #4*.
Meacham, Beth, "A Dream Can Make a Difference," *By Any Other Fame*.
Meikle, William, "Aboard the Vordlak," *Dreams From the Strangers' Cafe #4*.
Melville, James, "Night Flight," *3rd Culprit*.
Merino, José Maria, "Cousin Rosa," *New Mystery*, Vol. III, #1.
Michaels, Samantha, "The Keeper," *EQMM*, Sept.
Middleton, Scott, "Where the Snowmen Go," *The Best of Whispers*.
Milán, Victor, "Mr. Skin," *Cthulhu's Heirs*.
Miller, Rex "Mouthtrap," *Bizarre Bazaar*, Vol. 3.
———, "Shock Rock Jock," *Shock Rock II*.
Misha, "Angel of Hearth and Home," *Ke-qua-hawk-as*.
Mitchell, D. M., "Ward 23," *The Starry Wisdom*.
Moix, Ana Maria, "That Red-headed Boy I See Every Day," *The Origins of Desire*.
Molina, Antonio Muñoz, "The Ghost's Bedroom," Ibid.
Moody, Susan, "Better to Forget," *2nd Culprit*.
Mooney, Brian, "The Tomb of Priscus," *Shadows Over Innsmouth*.
———, "The Waldteufel Affair," *The Anthology of Fantasy & Supernatural*.
Moore, Alan, "The Courtyard," *The Starry Wisdom*.
Moorcock, Michael, "The White Pirate," *Blue Motel*.
Morales, Rosario, "I Didn't Hear Anything," *Callaloo Journal of African-American Arts*, Sept.
Morlan, A. R., "Cinnamon Roses," *Blood Kiss: Vampire Erotica*.
———, "He's Hot, He's Sexy, He's . . ." *Shock Rock II*.
———, "Powder," *Heliocentric Net #9*.
Morlan, A. R., and Postovit, John S., "Norm Littman's 15 Minutes," *Worlds of Fantasy & Horror #1*.
Morrell, David, "Presley 45," *The King Is Dead*.
Morris, Mark, "Green," *Blue Motel*.
———, "Immortal," *The Mammoth Book of Werewolves*.
———, "Scuzz," *Cold Cuts* 2.
Morrison, Grant, "Lovecraft in Heaven," *The Starry Wisdom*.
Morrow, James, "Bible Stories for Adults No. 20: The Tower," *F & SF*, June.
Morton, Lisa, "Poppi's Monster," *The Mammoth Book of Frankenstein*.
Mosiman, Billie Sue, "The Shape of Its Absence," *Phobias*.
Murillo, Enrique, "Happy Birthday," *The Origins of Desire*.
Murphy, Joe, "1968 RPI," *Cthulhu's Heirs*.
Murphy, Pat, "Games of Deception," *Asimov's SF*, April.

Murray, Stephen, "The Train," *3rd Culprit*.
Murray, Will, "To Clear the Earth," *Shub Niggurath Cycle*.
Nagle, Pati, "Coyote Ugly," *F & SF*, April.
Nasrin, Taslima, "Happy Marriage," (poem) *The New Yorker*, Sept. 12.
Natsuki, Shizuko, "Solitary Journey," *New Mystery*, Winter/*EQMM*, June.
Nelson, Dale J., "Lady Stanhope's Manuscript," *Lady Stanhope's Manuscript*.
Newman, Kim, "Completist Heaven," *The Mammoth Book of Frankenstein*.
———, "Out of the Night, When the Full Moon is Bright . . .," (novella) *The Mammoth Book of Werewolves*.
———, "Where the Bodies are Buried: Sequel Hook," (novella) *Dark Voices 6*.
Nickels, Tim, "The Science of Sadness," *The Science of Sadness*.
———, "Tooley's Root," *Back Brain Recluse #22*.
Nickle, David, "The Dummy Ward," *Transversions #1*.
Nicoll, Gregory, "Just Say No," *Cthulhu's Heirs*.
Nolan, William F., "The Francis File," *The Best of Whispers*.
———, "The Giant Man," *Voices from the Night*.
Nunn, Randy, "Teaching the Devil to Dance," *Bizarre Dreams*.
Nutman, Philip, "Showdown at the Hong Kong Bar-B-Que and Grill," *Expressions of Dread: Third Annual*.
Nyman, Gregory G., "To Sweeten the Kitty," *Aberrations #16*.
Oates, Joyce Carol, "Blind," *Worlds of Fantasy & Horror #1/Haunted*.
———, "Elvis Is Dead: Why Are *You* Alive?" *The King Is Dead*.
———, "Fever Blisters," *Little Deaths*.
———, "Posthumous," *EQMM*, June.
———, "Zombie," *The New Yorker*, Oct. 24.
Oe, Kenzaburo, "Aghwee the Sky Monster," *Teach Us to Outgrow Our Madness*.
O'Driscoll, Mike, "The Lie That Once I Dreamt," *The Third Alternative #1*.
O'Driscoll, M. M., "Daring Night," *Cold Cuts 2*.
O'Keefe, Claudia, "Heretical Visions," *Deadly After Dark*.
O'Rourke, Michael, "The Old Master," *Skull #2*.
Ortese, Anna Maria, "The House in the Woods," *A Music Behind the Wall*.
Oyerly, Karen, "Wolf," (poem) *Dreams and Nightmares # 43*.
Padgett-Clarke, Kimberley, "Cut Flowers," *The Third Alternative #4*.
Pallamary, Matthew J., "The Small Dark Room of the Soul," *The Small Dark Room of the Soul*.
Palmer, Jessica, "Full Moon Rising," *London Noir*.
Panek, Nathaniel, "The Lean Winter," *Fantasy Macabre #16*.
Park, Paul, "A Man on Crutches," *Omni*, Jan.
Parks, K. D., "Temple," *Aberrations #16*.
Partridge, Norman, "Do Not Hasten to Bid Me Adieu," *Love in Vein*.
———, "The Entourage," *Thunder's Shadow*, Feb.
———, "Minutes," *Phantasm #1*.
———, "Tooth & Nail," *Palace Corbie #5*.
———, "Tyrannosaurus," *Cemetery Dance*, Summer.
Paul, J. A., "The Mirror," *AHMM*, June.
Pautz, Peter Dennis, "And the Spirit that Stands by the Naked Man," *The Anthology of Fantasy & Supernatural*.
Pavey, Jack, "The Rabbit," *Peeping Tom #16*.
Peifu, Li, "The Adulterers," *Running Wild: New Chinese Writers*.
Perez, Dan, "The Likeness," *Cthulhu's Heirs*.
Perez, Dennis L., "Neatly, Now" *Eulogy Magazine #6*.

Perry, Clark, "Little Black Bags," *Young Blood.*
Peters, Ellis, "The Frustration Dream," *2nd Culprit.*
Phoenix, Adrian Nikolas, "Dark Closets Silent Mirrors," *Pulphouse #17.*
Piccirilli, Tom, "Neverdead," *Terminal Fright #6.*
———, "Rave," *Dead of Night#10.*
Pierce, J. Calvin, "Sahib," *Little Deaths.*
Ping, Wang, "A Flash of Thought from the River," *Chicago Review*, Vol. 40, No. 1.
Pinn, Paul, "The Burn Zone," *Black Tears #6.*
———, "The Cleanser of the Land," *Black Tears #5.*
———, "Fat Man in Cafe," *Psychotrope 1.*
———, "Scattered Remains," *Grotesque #6.*
———, "Third & Shift," *The Third Alternative #4.*
Pond, Whitt, "The Trail Down," *Terminal Fright #6.*
Powell, James, "Grist for the Mills of Christmas," *EQMM*, Dec.
Price, Robert M., "A Thousand Young," *The Shub Niggurath Cycle.*
Price, Susan, "Christmas Game," *Mysterious Christmas Tales.*
———, "The Cat-Dogs," *14 More Christmas Tales.*
Prout, Will, "Jenny's Playmate," *Aberrations #19.*
Ptacek, Kathryn, "Hair," *Phobias.*
Pugmire, W. H., "Beyond the Realm of Dream," *Carnage Hall #5.*
Purcell, J.Q., "The Village Alchemist (1620)," *The Carolina Quarterly*, Vol. 46, No. 3.
Quinn, Daniel, "The Frog King, or Iron Henry," *Black Thorn, White Rose.*
Ragan, Jacie, "Ecstasy," (poem) *The Silver Web #11.*
———, "Sweet Maze of Dreams," (poem) Ibid.
Rainey, Stephen Mark, "Circus Bizarre," *Bizarre Bazaar*, Vol. 3.
———, "The Devils of Tuckahoe Gorge," *Midnight Zoo*, vol. 3 #10.
———, "Sabbath of the Black Goat," *The Shub Niggurath Cycle.*
Raisor, Gary, "The Right Thing," *Cemetery Dance*, Winter.
Randal, John W., "Suburbia," *Year 2000*, No. 1.
Ranieri, Roman A., "Night in the Red City," *Dead of Night #10.*
Rathbone, Wendy, "Ink and the Moon Goddess," *Rites of Passage.*
———, "The Saint," *Prisoners of the Night #8.*
Read, II William, "The Montague Fragment," *All Hallows #6.*
Recktenwalt, D. M., "The Gingerbread Man," *The Magic Within.*
Reed, Rick R., "Tool of Enslavement," *Dark Destiny.*
Reeves-Stevens, Garfield, "The Eddies," *Northern Frights 2.*
Remick, Jack, "Crocodile," *Terminal Weird.*
———, "Lizard," Ibid.
———, "Ravens," Ibid.
Reveley, Peter, "Nowhere," *Peeping Tom #13.*
Reynolds, William J., "The Lost Boys," *The Mysterious West.*
Rich, Mark, "The Gift," *Dead of the Night #10.*
Richards, J. V., "Blood Ties," *After Hours #23.*
Richerson, Carrie, "Sous la Mer," *F & SF*, March.
Richman, Elliot, "The Breakout," (poem) *Asylum Annual, 1994.*
Ricker, Kat, "Everlasting Grace," *Terminal Fright #2.*
Ritchie, James A., "Wild Strawberries," *EQMM*, Oct.
Roberts, Charles, "The Saint of St. Andrew," *The Silver Web #11.*
Robertson, R. Garcia y, "Wendy Darling, RFC," *F & SF*, April.
Robins, Madeleine E., "Somewhere in Dreamland Tonight," *F & SF*, July.

Roden, Barbara, "Dead Man's Pears," *All Hallows* 7.
Rodgers, Alan, "Diana's Lover," *Voices from the Night*.
———, "The Judgment of Robert Johnson," *South from Midnight*.
Roessner, Michaela, "Welcome to the Dog Show," *Strange Plasma #8*.
Rogers, Bruce Holland, "Chambers Like a Hive," *Year 2000*, No. 1.
———, "Something Like the Sound of Wind in the Trees," *Quarterly West*, Winter/Spring.
Rogers, Lenore K., "Invitation to the Dance," *Skull #2*.
Rosen, Barbara, "Experiment," *Split*.
Rosenblum, Mary, "California Dreamer," *F & SF*, May.
Rosenman, John B., "Feather Kisses," *Terminal Fright #5*.
Rowand, Richard, "A Rush of Wings," *Realms of Fantasy*, Dec.
Royle, Nicholas, "Anything But Your Kind," *The Mammoth Book of Werewolves*.
———, "Buxton, Texas," *ABeSea*, Spring.
———, "Coming and Going Like the Sea," *The Third Alternative #1*.
———, "The Homecoming," *Shadows Over Innsmouth*.
———, "The Mad Woman," *The Science of Sadness*.
———, "Off," *Interzone #79*.
———, "The Swing," *Little Deaths*.
———, "The Trees," *Dark Voices 6*.
———, "Trust Me," *Cold Cuts 2*.
Rozan, S. J., "Film at Eleven," *Deadly Allies 2*.
Rusch, Kristine Kathryn, "Without End," *F & SF*, April.
Rushdie, Salman, "The Prophet's Hair," *East West*.
Russ, J. J., "Listening at Graves," *Weird Tales #308*.
Russell, J. S., "Limited Additions," *The King Is Dead*.
Russell, Ray, "The Little Snakes of Tara," *Voices from the Night*.
Russo, Gianna, "The Klansman in My Blood," (poem) *South from Midnight*.
Ryan, Kyle, "Mr. Rogers of the Future," *The Louisville Review*, Spring.
Sagara, Michelle, "What She Won't Remember," *Alternate Outlaws*.
———, "Winter," *Deals With the Devil*.
Saladrigas, Robert, "Child Rodolfo," *The Origins of Desire*.
Salazar, Dixie, "The Chameleon," *Black Warrior Review*, Spring/Summer.
Sallee, Wayne Allen, "The Dead Weight of Copper Tears," *Murder for Father*.
———, "Elviscera," *The King Is Dead*.
———, "The Girl With the Concrete Hands," *Bizarre Bazarre*, Volume 3.
———, "Go Hungry," *Dark Destiny*.
———, "Lover Doll," *Little Deaths*.
———, "We Crawl Stylish: The American Dream vs. the Derby Geeks," *Palace Corbie 5*.
Salmonson, Jessica Amanda, "Bearskin Woman and Grizzly Woman," *Daughters of Nyx #2*.
———, "House of Omens," (poem) *Blue Motel*.
———, "Lilacs at a Windy Wall," (poem) *Deathrealm #21*.
———, "Princess of Shades," (poem) *Weird Tales #308*.
———, "The Remembering Soul," (poem) *Deathrealm #21*.
Sampson, Robert, "Matters of Substance," *Phobias*.
Sánchez, Javier García, "The Fourth Floor," *The Origins of Desire*.
Sanders, William, "Going After Old Man Alabama," *Tales from the Great Turtle*.
Sands, Marella, "Star Bright, Star Byte," *Cthulhu's Heirs*.
Saplak, Charles M., "The Scourge," *Cthulhu's Heirs*.

———, "Celebrated Skeleton," *Proud Flesh #1*.
Savage, David, "Grim," *Threads*.
Savage, Felicity, "Ash Minette," *F & SF*, May.
———, "Brixtow White Lady," *F & SF*, March.
———, "The Earth's Erogenous Zones," *F & SF*, Aug.
Scarborough, Elizabeth Ann, "Jean-Pierre and the Gator-Maid," *South from Midnight*.
Schimel, Lawrence, "Journeybread Recipe," *Black Thorn, White Rose*.
———, "The Shoemaker and the Elves," *Lan's Lantern*.
Schindler, David, "Rites of Passage," *Palace Corbie #5*.
Schow, David J., "Sand Sculpture," *Black Leather Required*.
Schweitzer, Darrell, "The Adventure of the Death-Fetch," *The Game Is Afoot*.
———, "On the Last Night of the Festival of the Dead," *Interzone #90*.
———, "One of the Secret Masters," *Dark Destiny*.
Schweitzer, Darrell and Van Hollander, Jason, "Those of the Air," *Cthulhu's Heirs*.
Segriff, Larry, "Unkindest Cut," *Murder for Mother*.
Shannon, Lorelei, "Anything for You," *Young Blood*.
Sharp, Damian, "A Native Son," *When a Monkey Speaks*.
———, "The Reign of Frogs," Ibid.
Shepard, Lucius, "The Last Time," (novella) *Little Deaths*.
Sherman, C. H., "In the Valley of the Shades," *Masterpieces of Terror and the Unknown*
Shiner, Lewis, "The Shoemaker's Tale," *The King Is Dead*.
Shubin, Seymour, "Perfect in Every Way," *EQMM*, Oct.
Shwartz, Susan, "The Carpetbagger," *South from Midnight*.
Silverman, Leah, "Lenses," *On Spec*, Spring.
Simpson, Martin, "Last Rites and Resurrections," *The Silver Web*, Spring/Summer.
Singer, Glen, "Harold's Blues," *The Shub Niggurath Cycle*.
Skinner, Brian, "A Beast of One's Own," *The Thirteenth Moon*, March.
Smeds, Dave, "Short Timer," *F& SF*, Dec.
Smith, Barbara A., "The Sylvan," *AHMM*, July.
Smith, Guy N., "Hollow Eyes," *Black Tears #5*.
Smith, Margaret, "Huracan," (poem) *The End* Vol. II
———, "Kites," *Into the Darkness #2*.
Smith, Michael Marshall, "To Receive is Better," *The Mammoth Book of Frankenstein*.
———, "To See the Sea," *Shadows Over Innsmouth*.
———, "The View," *The Anthology of Fantasy & the Supernatural*.
Sobezak, A. J., "Central Park," *Aberrations #16*.
Somtow, S. P., "Mr. Death's Blue-Eyed Boy," *Phobias*.
———, "The Voice of the Hummingbird," *The Beast Within*.
Soukup, Martha, "The Spinner," *Xanadu 2*.
Springer, Nancy, "The Blind God is Watching," (novella) chapbook.
Stableford, Brian, "The Bad Seed," *Interzone #82*.
———, "Les Fleurs du Mal," *Asimov's SF*, Oct.
———, "Nephthys," *Peeping Tom #13*.
———, "The Scream," *Asimov's SF*, July.
———, "The Storyteller's Tale," *The Anthology of Fantasy & the Supernatural*.
———, "Reconstruction," *Cold Cuts 2*.
———, "The Unkindness of Ravens," *Interzone #90*.
Stack, Eddie, "Angel," *Fiction*, No. 12, Vol. 1.
Stansfield, Frederick, "The Exile," (poem) Ibid.
———, "His Lordship's Viola," *Deathrealm #22*.

———, "The Thousand Burning Questions," (poem) *Crypt of Cthulhu* #88.
Steel, Jim, "Apple for Teecha," *The Third Alternative* #2.
Steer, John, "Candles," (poem) Ibid.
Stewart, Alex, "The Cat in the Wall," *The Anthology of Fantasy and the Supernatural.*
Stone, Del, Jr., "Do You Come Here Often?" *Argonaut* #19.
Stone, Roger, "Four Miles to the Hotel California," *The Third Alternative* #3.
Storm, Sue, "The Bone Woman and the Owl Baby," *Sirius Visions* #3.
Strasser, Dirk, "At Rain's Grey Remembering," *Alien Shores.*
———, "Watching the Soldiers," *Borderland* 4.
Straub, Peter, "Ashputtle," *Black Thorn, White Rose.*
———, "Pork Pie Hat," (novella) *Murder for Halloween.*
Strickland, Brad, "The Hungry Sky," *Phobias.*
Strieber, Whitley, "I Walk the Night," *The Best of Whispers.*
Sucksmith, Harvey Peter, "Any More Ghost Stories For Me?" *Those Whom the Old Gods Love.*
———, "Ape Island," Ibid.
———, "The Boat of the Dead," Ibid.
———, "The Man Who Translated an Unknown Language," Ibid.
———, "A Silver Horn," Ibid.
———, "That Infernal Machine," Ibid.
———, "Those Whom the Old Gods Love," Ibid.
Sullivan, Thomas, "To Walk the Earth," *Deals with the Devil.*
Swannick, Frank I., "Toyworld," *Threads.*
Swanwick, Michael, "The Changeling's Tale," *Asimov's SF*, Jan.
Swindells, Robert, "Cloud Cover," *Mysterious Christmas Tales.*
Tamsi, Tchicaya U., "Wedding," *Callaloo: Journal of African-American Arts*, Jan.
Tarr, Judith, "Elvis Invictus," *By Any Other Fame.*
Tassone, G. L., "The Volkswagen Heart," *AHMM*, Sept.
Tawada, Yoko, "The Talisman," *Fiction International.*
Taylor, Lucy, "Baubo's Kiss," *Unnatural Acts.*
———, "Child of Mine," *Eldritch Tales* #29.
———, "The Flesh Artist," *The Flesh Artist.*
———, "Hungry Ghosts," Ibid.
———, "Hungry Skin," *Little Deaths.*
———, "Idol," *Unnatural Acts, Bizarre Dreams.*
———, "Knockouts," *Unnatural Acts.*
———, "The Safety of Unknown Cities," (novella) *Unnatural Acts.*
———, "Things of Which We Do Not Speak," *Deadly After Dark.*
———, "Wall of Words," *Cemetery Dance*, Winter.
———, "Windowsitting," *The Flesh Artist.*
Tem, Melanie, "Fingers," *The Best of Whispers.*
———, "The Rock," *Little Deaths.*
Tem, Steve Rasnic, "Lost Cherokee," *Tales from the Great Turtle.*
———, "The Garden in Autumn," *Deathrealm* #22.
———, "Release of Flesh," *Deadly After Dark.*
———, "Time and the Exile," *Conadian Souvenir Book.*
Tem, Steve Rasnic and Tem, Melanie, "The Marriage," *Love in Vein.*
Tessier, Thomas, "I Remember Me (But I'm Not Sure About You)," *The Earth Strikes Back.*
Thomas, Jeffrey, "Fallen," *Terminal Fright* #4.
Tiedemann, Mark W., "Drink," *Asimov's SF*, July.

Tilton, Lois, "Expendable," *The Beast Within.*
Timlett, Peter Valentine, "Flies," *Dark Voices 6.*
Trambley, Estela Portillo, "The Burning," *In Other Words: Literature of the Latinas of the United States.*
Travis, Tia, "The Sad Story of Billy Psych-Out and the Psyched-Out Encyclopedia of Rock 'n' Roll," *Shock Rock II.*
Tuttle, Lisa, "Manskin, Womanskin," *By the Light of the Silvery Moon.*
Tyson, Noëlle, "Cat in an Armchair," *Threads.*
Tz'it, Tziak Tza'pat, "X'anton and the Fox," *TriQuarterly*, Fall.
Urban, Scott H., "Chitin," *The Urbanite* No. 4.
Urwin, Steve, "Tightrope Walker," (poem) *The Third Alternative* #4.
Vachss, Andrew, "Into the Light," *Under Ground.*
Valdron, Dennis, "The Viruses of Quiet Desperation," *Transversions* #1.
Valdron, D.G., "Tell Me," *After Hours* #24.
VanderMeer, Jeff, "London Burning," *Worlds of Fantasy & Horror* #1
———, "Death by Drowning," (poem) *Heliocentric Net*, Autumn.
Van Gelder, Gordon, "Something More," *Young Blood.*
Verba, Karen, "Weeding the Garden," (poem) *Transversions* #1.
Villaseñor, Victor, "Bullfighting the Train," *Walking Stars: Stories of Magic and Power.*
Vukcevich, Ray, "Quite Contrary," *Pulphouse* #17.
Wade, Holly, "La Pucelle," *Asimov's SF*, Sept.
Wade, Susan, "The Black Swan," *Black Thorn, White Rose.*
———, "The Convertible Coven," *F & SF*, March.
Waggoner, Tim, "Mr. Punch," *Young Blood.*
Wagner, Karl Edward, "Passages," *Phobias.*
Wakefield, Paula, "A Gift of Love," *Interzone* #84.
Waldrop, Howard, "Why Did?," *Omni*, April.
Ward, Kyla, "Mary," (poem) *Bloodsongs* #3.
Watkins, William John, "The Mist of Avalon Nine," *Argonaut* #19.
Watts, Peter, "Nimbus," *On Spec*, Summer.
———, "Flesh Made Word," *Prairie Fire.*
Wayman, Tom, "The Call," *Ontario Review*, Fall/Winter.
Webb, Don, "The Evil Miracle," *F & SF*, Aug.
———, "The Haunting of the Hashknife," *Fiction International.*
———, "Other: Please Explain," *The Third Alternative* #4.
———, "The Sound of a Door Opening," *The Starry Wisdom.*
———, "The Way Out," *Back Brain Recluse* #22.
Weinberg, Robert, "The Midnight El," *Return to the Twilight Zone.*
Weinstein, Debra, "The Dead," *Global City Review*, Spring.
Weissman, Benjamin, "Accessory," *Dear Dead Person.*
———, "Flesh is for Hacking," Ibid.
———, "Real Me," Ibid.
———, "The Present," Ibid.
———, "The Why-I-Love-Violence Speech," Ibid.
Welsh, D. E., "The Bait," *Aberrations* #20.
Werner, Irving, "Pictures," *Masterpieces of Terror and the Unknown.*
Westall, Robert, "The Cats," *Shades of Darkness.*
Wetzsteon, Rachel, "Venus Observed," *The Other Stars.*
What, Leslie, "Clinging to a Thread," *F & SF*, April.
Wheeler, Milton E., "Juiced and Done," *Heliocentric Net*, Autumn.
Whitbourn, John, "Walk This Way," *All Hallows* 7.

White Plume, Debra, "Mother Called It Daddy's Junkyard," *Tales from the Great Turtle.*
Whitechapel, Simon, "Walpurgisnachtmusik," *The Starry Wisdom.*
Wilber, Rick, "Bridging," *Phobias.*
———, "The Murderer Explains," (poem) *South from Midnight.*
Wilder, Cherry, "Willow Cottage," *Interzone* #81.
Wilhelm, Kate, "I Know What You're Thinking," *Asimov's SF*, Nov.
Wilkerson, Cherie, "Through the Eyes of a Child," *After Hours #21.*
Williams, Conrad, "Bitter Land," *Cold Cuts* 2.
———, "The Burn," *Blue Motel.*
———, "The Lady of Situations," *Chills* #8.
———, "Other Skins," *Panurge #20.*
———, "Supple Bodies," *The Third Alternative #1.*
Williams, Sean, "New Flames For an Old Love," *Doorway to Eternity.*
———, "Reluctant Misty and the House on Burden Street," Ibid.
Williamson, Chet, "Double Trouble," *The King Is Dead.*
———, "The Last Belsnickel," *Christmas Magic.*
———, "The Vanished Ones," *Tales of Ravenloft.*
Williamson, J. N., "The Autonomic Nervous System . . ." *Voices from the Night.*
———, "Child of the Sea," *Pulphouse #17.*
———, "Indecent Proponent," *Bizarre Bazaar*, Vol. 3.
Willis, Connie, "A Little Moonshine," *Realms of Fantasy*, Dec.
Wilson, David Niall, "The Level of the Flame," *Cemetery Dance*, Winter.
Winter-Damon, t., "Chaunt of the Gray Man," (poem) *Worlds of Fantasy & Horror #1.*
Winter, Douglas E., "Black Sun," chapbook.
Winter, Kelly, "The Alphabet of Birds," *Daughters of Nyx*, Spring.
Wisman, Ken, "Grandma Babka's Christmas Ginger and the Good Luck/Bad Luck Leshy," *Blue Motel.*
Wolfe, Gene, "Queen of the Night," *Love in Vein.*
Womesley, Steve, "The Union Buries its Dead," *Microstories.*
Wright, Eric, "The Duke," *2nd Culprit.*
Wu, William F., "House of Cool Air," *Borderlands* 4.
Wynne, John, "The Other World," *The Other World.*
Wynne-Jones, Tim, "The Goose Girl," *Black Thorn, White Rose.*
Yarbro, Chelsea Quinn, "Do Not Pass Go Do Not Collect $200," *The Earth Strikes Back.*
———, "A Question of Patronage," *The Vampire Stories of Chelsea Quinn Yarbro.*
Yolen, Jane, "Blood Sister," *Am I Blue?*
———, "The Death of the Unicorn," (poem) *Here There Be Unicorns.*
———, "Granny Rumple," *Black Thorn, White Rose.*
———, "The Lady's Garden," *Here There Be Unicorns.*
———, "Orkney Lament," (poem) *Xanadu* 2.
———, "Mrs Ambroseworthy," *Bruce Coville's Book of Ghosts.*
———, "A Southern Story," (poem) *South from Midnight.*
———, "The Woman Who Loved a Bear," *Tales from the Great Turtle.*
Young, Elizabeth, "Short Eyes and the Green Dice," *Seduction.*
Zambreno, Mary Frances, "The Ghost in the Summer Kitchen," *Bruce Coville's Book of Ghosts.*
Zelazny, Roger, "Godson," *Black Thorn, White Rose.*
Zepeda, Eraclio, "Don Chico Who Flies," *TriQuarterly*, Fall.

The People Behind the Book

Horror Editor ELLEN DATLOW has been fiction editor of *OMNI* magazine for over a decade. She has edited a number of outstanding anthologies, including *Blood Is Not Enough*, *A Whisper of Blood*, *Alien Sex*, *The OMNI Books of Science Fiction*, *Little Deaths*, and (with Terri Windling) *Snow White, Blood Red* and *Black Thorn, White Rose*. She lives in New York City.

Fantasy Editor TERRI WINDLING, five-time winner of the World Fantasy Award, developed the innovative Ace Fantasy line in the 1980s. She currently is a consulting editor for Tor Books' fantasy line and runs The Endicott Studio, a transatlantic company specializing in book publishing projects and art for exhibition. She created and packaged the ongoing *Adult Fairy Tales* series of novels (Tor), the *Borderland* "punk urban fantasy" series for teenagers (Tor & HB), and co-created the *Brian Froud's Faerielands* series (Bantam). She has published over a dozen fine anthologies, including the recent book, *The Armless Maiden* (Tor), has a novel forthcoming this year from Tor Books, and a TV film in development at Columbia pictures for NBC. She lives in Devon, England, and Tucson, Arizona.

Packager JAMES FRENKEL & ASSOCIATES is JAMES FRENKEL and JAMES MINZ. James Frenkel edited Dell's SF line in the 1970s, was the publisher of Bluejay Books and was consulting editor for the Collier-Nucleus SF/Fantasy reprint series. A consulting editor for Tor Books since 1986, he edits and packages a variety of science fiction, fantasy, horror, and mystery books from his base in Madison, Wisconsin. Mr. Minz presides over a legion of interns from the University of Wisconsin, who help create various projects.

Comics Critics EMMA BULL and WILL SHETTERLY are the publishers of SteelDragon Press, and the co-editors of the *Liavek* series. Bull is the author of the acclaimed urban fantasy *War for the Oaks*; her fourth novel, *Finder*, was published last year by Tor Books. Shetterly is a popular fantasy author and has recently written two *Borderlands* novels, *Elsewhere* and *Nevernever*. They live, along with several cats, in Minneapolis, Minnesota, where Shetterly is currently recovering from his recent run for the Governorship.

Media Critic EDWARD BRYANT is a major author of horror and science fiction, having won Hugo awards for his work. He reviews books for a number of major newspapers and magazines, and is also a radio personality. He lives with his rubber sharks in the Port of Denver, Colorado.

Artist THOMAS CANTY is one of the most distinguished artists working in fantasy. He has won World Fantasy awards for his distinctive book jacket and cover illustrations, and is a noted book designer working in diverse fields of book publishing; he has active projects with a number of publishers, including some with various small presses. He also created children's picturebook series for St. Martin's Press and Ariel Books. He lives in Massachusetts.